EMPTY WIGS

Jonathan Meades

unbound

First published in 2025

Unbound
c/o TC Group, 6th Floor King's House, 9–10 Haymarket,
London SW1Y 4BP
www.unbound.com

Empty Wigs is a work of fiction. The people and the animals are not to be
confused with real recidivists. The loci and the incidents are equally inventions
whose only existence is in a compact between the reader and the writer.

Text design by Jouve (UK), Milton Keynes

A CIP record for this book is available from the British Library

ISBN 978-1-80018-324-7 (hardback)
ISBN 978-1-80018-325-4 (ebook)

Printed and bound in Great Britain by Clays Ltd, Elcograf S.p.A.

1 3 5 7 9 8 6 4 2

For C, again

With special thanks to John Pritchard for his generous
support as a patron of this book

'Face down in a sump of Grosz'
JAMES JESUS ANGLETON

'Eugenics eucharist exhumation euthanasia
endogamy – but not necessarily in that order'
TAMARA COOLMANS

'To cure the sickness of others god gave us weapons.
To cure our sickness god gave us empty wigs'
ERSKINE GARN

'Saints are friends to nobody. They love nothing but their altars and
themselves. They make debauches in piety as sinners do in wine'
JOHN VANBRUGH

Contents

Yoni Alfasi.
Là-Bas – The Lost Idyll

The scents of my early teens were barbecued lamb and burning buildings. We listened to yé-yé and explosions, doo-wop and gunfire. We smoked Royale Gout Maryland. We picnicked at rocks under stone pines. The sea lapped our feet while a war raged around us. We danced the Madison by a battlefield's edge. We couldn't admit that paradise was provisional, that our heaven on earth was turning into hell. A hell we would have to flee. Lime sorbet tastes of immeasurable loss.

I can still see it as though it were yesterday. Dewachter's window on rue Hoche. Chocolate brown corduroy, rope thick, Cardin style, collarless. It was the day before my fourteenth birthday when my father refused to buy me that jacket. I had set my heart on it. In his opinion it looked Bavarian, it was Bavarian – the collarlessness. That was it then, nothing more to say. I didn't know where at Germany Bavaria was. But, because he had spoken of it so often, I did know that it was the fount of the greatest evil. The waisted jacket he bought me instead had a collar and narrow rounded lapels, three buttons, raised stitching, a flap over the breast pocket, a single vent. I liked it good enough. He was bemused by my sartorial preoccupations. His uncle and two cousins had died in Buchenwald.

Was I even then, all those years ago, a Jew?
My mother was not Jewish so I was not a Jew according to the dictates of Judaism. My father was non-observant, it might be said

anti-observant. A Crémieux[1] intégriste. He could not reconcile modern science with the ancient faith of his and my ancestors. Even though one of them, a rabbi, had given his life for being a Jew, beheaded on the orders of the Bey, the Ottoman Military Governor, a decade before the French arrived. We French . . .

Nonetheless, so far as he himself was concerned, my father was not a Jew. Or only on his own terms. He considered himself above tribalism, above cults and sectarianism. *Ahavath Israel* was divisive. He insisted for example – mistakenly, with wearisome obstinacy – that Eichmann's crimes had been committed against all humanity. In his version it was *humans*, not Jews, whom Eichmann had put on trucks to oblivion. This does not accord with Eichmann's own statements to Höss, the Auschwitz commandant. My father believed that being Jewish didn't mean belonging to a religion, obeying what he called its archaic foibles and murky prescriptions. He even claimed to despise dietary regulation, he pretended to take pleasure in eating pork. But in truth he never touched it. I doubt that he ever tasted for example *sobrasada* or *blanquicos* or *longanisses* – what he might, had he lived so long, have learnt to call 'king rabbit'. He joked that pigs must be anti-Semitic because Jews objected to the purpose for which they were bred.

Being Jewish on his own terms meant having a Hippocratic duty to the sick, whoever they were, irrespective of faith, and having a humanistic duty to succour the oppressed, *idem*. We who have been oppressed throughout all history must side with anyone else who is oppressed. We must care for them because only we have shared their fathomless suffering. Only we have both the competence and the charity to alleviate it. We are chosen because we own extreme empathy. It is a duty and a curse. It implies no divine favouritism. We must side with justice. We must not think of ourselves. We must above all not allow ourselves to be defined as victims for that strengthens the tormentors. (I had observed at the avenue Jonnart baths that many Catholics were circumcised. I was not. My father,

---

1 Adolphe Crémieux, sometime Minister of Justice, was the author of the decree (1870) that granted French citizenship to Algeria's Jews.

who was, decreed it was mutilation by folk tale. He did not want me to have a religious penis.)

I learnt from him the paramountcy of justice. There are many forms of justice. Mine differed from his. The figure of Judex that I have incarnated throughout my life derives from the god whose justice is vengeful, stern, pre-Christian: Jesus was not much of a Jew. He was the first appeaser, a wet dupe with faith in rehabilitation and redemption.

I saw the films of Belsen. If they can do that to us, why cannot we do it to them? A Jew must believe in an eye for an eye, a tooth for a tooth, a pyre for a pyre. Death follows me, scavenging. I never wear a kippa. I do not identify myself. Besides, it would play havoc with my hair, an object of congratulation.

His parents and, especially, his sister considered my father's exalted compassion to be mere vanity. For them his humanitarianism was an expression of guilt, a form of masochism. They thought his work at the hospital was show-off self-denial. That's what I thought too. His work and his library frightened me.

He was a proctologist – you see what I mean about masochism. He was an expert in venereal infections of the anus, in malignant anal melanomas, in anal fistulas, suppurations and abscesses. He was the author of *A Haemorrhoid Atlas*. His bookshelves were no incitement to sexual congress.

He cured filthy incestuous kebas of their filthy incestuous diseases. Diseases I wished never to suffer.

(What sort of gratitude do you get from such people? This sort of gratitude: a bomb in a bar, a van packed with plastic explosives, a Jewish baby's throat slit by a keba marbia.)

His family wanted to bind him to his race. They mocked his enthusiasm for sailing. Jews don't sail. Why sail when you could have a motor boat? His small yacht, which they called his goy-toy, was his only luxury. He was always trying to slip away from the ancestral burden. But in the end you can't. He was too good a man to understand the frailty of goodness.

Was I, all those years ago, French?

My passport said I was. My mother was French, *française de souche*, *frangaouie*, as they say. She came from Talence, was brought up in the Reformed Church. A Protestant, and, I have to say, worthy of that name. Many people admired her.

She protested at the least injustice provided it was an injustice done to someone other than herself. She believed, as my father did, that she should work for the good of others. The poorer, the more backward, the more downtrodden, the more wretched these others the better. The more resistant to her efforts the better. My mother was a paragon of republicanism. Imparting the values of the Republic was an act of necessary charity. And of virtuous mental flagellation. Training ingrate barbarians to be French was the finest of callings and the most trying. They were 80 per cent illiterate and would remain so. They wished to remain so. She had reservoirs of energy to spend on making excuses for the thieving behaviour of her charges at youth camps.

She strove for equality. She could never see that those whom she treated as equal were not her equal. She demeaned herself. She offered friendship, knowledge, sympathy, succour to people whose only reaction was to consider that she must be weak to do so. They despised her enduring attempts at brotherhood. She was blind to the chasm that divided her from them. She saw the good in everyone even when they spent half the day kneeling and keening to Ramalama and beating their wives and stealing and never getting their rotting teeth fixed because they were too superstitious to go to the dentist. She did not rail against our fate. She accepted the wrong that had been done to us, that was being done to us, that would go on being done to us as though it were inevitable and deserved. She believed for example that no wrong that was done to us could match the iniquity of the wrong done to the 'indigenous people' who shared our country. My mother did not consider us indigenous.

★

4

What does indigenous mean? How is indigenousness measured?

How long does it take to become indigenous? How long have your ancestors' ancestors to live somewhere? How many generations? Are we not indigenous? Will half a millennium do? Five and a half centuries ago, that's when my mother's husband's people, my father's people, my grandmother's people arrived on this blessed shore to till and worship and procreate and cook and build. How are we connected to the earth? Familiarity. Use. We frequent the place, we attach ourselves to it. It responds with fruit and plenty. That is its side of the affectionate bargain.

My mother wrapped herself in penitence. She made herself bear the burden of illusory crimes, invented crimes, crimes that had not been committed by people dead before she was born – in short, crimes created by our enemies to promote her penitence and the penitence of all who thought like her: that penitence about our being in someone else's land, of our being là-bas, there – which was, then, *here*.

She did not hate our enemies. She did not castigate them. She did not even regard them as enemies, rather as victims. Victims! Victims to be pitied.

In the last days she went about tidying the house, cleaning whatever would be left, as though it were guests who were expected rather than bled squatters. Word had spread fast. Thousands had left the brousse for the city and the promise of a house. They had already for example taken over Jani's parents' house. They awaited our house. These *mendiches* lingered across the street all along a crumbling wall sheltering in the shade of plane trees. They walked to and from the fountain in the tiny public garden at the end of the street. They watched our every move. An entire extended family, several of them cripples with vicious stumps like wooden boxing gloves, waited apathetically. They were surrounded by sacks, kitbags, chickens, bantams, caged songbirds, wheelbarrows, buckling pram frames, handcarts – all piled high with the scraps and rags that are the destitute's riches. Soon these lurking thieves would add to their wealth. They would appropriate what was ours. My mother says it's what is due to them.

★

It is not due to them. There wouldn't be 'them' had there not been French medical science in Algeria. There would have been no Algerians to give birth to the generations who killed in the pursuit of 'independence'. They'd have died from malaria, cholera, typhus, smallpox. They could not cure themselves. They were hardly more than animals, obedient, superstitious, racialist animals who despised animals of a different caste and would never help them.

Independent, they would soon contaminate our home with smoke and spit and the shit-smeared hands who touch the food they eat. Left hand exclusively, oh yes?

My father was French, his passport said so. His family had been French since the Crémieux decrees, since my great-great-grandfather's time. My father had studied medicine at the faculty in Bordeaux, which is unquestionably in France. He had even met my mother, a fellow tyro sailor, at le Cercle de la Voile d'Arcachon where they were well taught, as I would be, in turn.[2]

But France was now our enemy. French barbouzes, some of them collaborationist criminals who had worked for the Gestapo, tried to pick us off with sniper fire. They hurled grenades at us. They shot us with automatic weapons. French soldiers drove armoured vehicles at us. French policemen besieged us. French judges imprisoned us. The French state had made an alliance with our enemy, with the terrorists who had been *its* enemy only months before. Its army stood proudly side by side with the murdering kebas who were now known as freedom fighters. It attacked its fellow citizens. It remained callously passive while we were prey to the psychopathy of independence.

The state, a traitor to itself, made truce with its habitual opponents, the self-righteous germanopratin traitors of the Marxist imperium,

2 According to *L'Esprit Mensuel* March 1954 the 'uniform' for spring was: Navy blue windcheater. Blue and white banded Breton sweater. White jeans. Blue, white-laced canvas deck shoes. Black-framed sunglasses worn on top of head 'like a split kippa'.

Jeanson's swine, the bag carriers like Pouillon, the big-hearted fifth columnists, the ones who financed terrorism, the unthinking thinkers who cheered the FLN from the grandstand of their ivory tower, the fellow travellers in their cafés on the Boul'Mich who filled their precious journals and reviews with calumnies about us. These smug grotesques with their complaisant manifestos had no idea of our life save through the misinformation they fed each other. They lied to themselves. They claimed we were fascists.

What did they know of our history? What did they know of our silent suffering? Why did they so hate us?

We were French. That is what we believed, naively.

I had yet to realise that when the French have no one else to turn against they turn against themselves. It was a lesson quickly learnt. France was a nation mutilating itself. It was chewing off a limb that it reckoned gangrenous but which would haunt it. The amputee is forever revisited by the leg that was long since hurled in a hospital incinerator and turned to agri-fertiliser.

I remember a letter from Jani, remember it for several reasons: he did not date it 5 February 1962, but the Feast of Saint Blaise 1962; he signed himself Massimiljanu Brockdorff; he addressed me as Yonatan. He had never called me that. Never. I was always Yoni. We were always Jani and Yoni. Now we had become Massimiljanu and Yonatan. We were different now. Even his handwriting was different. Hurried, jagged, Bic blobs. He was by then in Lyon. He confirmed everything with his own experience. We'd all heard it. Pieds-noirs were pariahs over there. Treated with contempt. His sister was spat at in the street. *Rapatriés* were *repliés*. We were never really going to be *rapatriés*. We were *expatriés*. That's how la Grande Zohra saw us. That's how Judas Joxe saw us. Joxe claimed we were bringing fascism to France. But did he not know that some of us, we were Jewish? Even Catholics, for example Jani, were Jews. The Harkis were Jews. We Jews were always on hand, always *are*, to be Jews, to be cast out and beaten and purged from the face of the earth. What did Sal Missica's father say? 'The *very* oldest profession is scapegoat.'

★

7

Graffito: *Les sartans aux chateaux, les babtous aux bateaux, les youpins aux poteaux.*

Yet the government laughed at us, called us 'holidaymakers'. Yes, the people who don't count, who have lost everything, are going on holiday! In fact we were the greatest enforced displacement of people anywhere in the world since the Second World War. And we were going on holiday. Zohra the Judas wanted us to go and live somewhere else. So far as his government was concerned, we weren't French. We thought we lived in the Metropole.

Jani's letter said his mother is almost suicidal. The dockers in Marseille had stolen the suitcase with all her photos in it. Two doctors refused to treat her for an infection. It was later diagnosed as pleurisy. The five of them were sharing two rooms. When you think of their house on rue de Progrès! Beside the mansions higher up in El Biar it might not have seemed much. But it was a fine home. Now he had to bed down with his father. Anna and Pietra with their mother.

He said their flat stank because the old couple downstairs cooked filthy stews. They were fat, they were as white as *pork* fat. This was one of his jokes. He was always trying to trick me into eating pork. Telling me chorizo was merguez. This couple could hardly read or write. But they still treated Jani like shit. They told him that the last tenants had been nice people, *proper* French people, *franchouillard*. He said something like, 'If we're as filthy rich as these venomous slugs, our so-called compatriots, believe we are, then why are we living in a slum? If we had been filthy rich landowners and slave-drivers making kebas sweat in their burnous and chomping cigars and driving big racialist cars, then Judas would have thought twice about abandoning us.'

But we were little people. It was our fate that this country had been our cradle. We were insignificant. We were nothing. We didn't count. We had no voice. We had no power over our own fate. So the traitorous bastards thought.

We shall take the fight to the mainland.

There is a further reason I remember that letter. He has met up

8

with David Jérome, now a groom at a stud at Chazey-sur-Ain, and Marcel Calafato who spends so much time hanging around clubs in La Croix Rousse that Jani suspects he is a *chouard*. They were thinking about 'doing something'. Thinking about it.

Me, I had already *done something*. I had gone beyond thinking about it. I had acted. I had resolved to devote my life to The Problem.

Before we fled there was work to do. There were selective tasks to be undertaken. There was a legacy to be created. I was almost sixteen years old. There is no such thing as a gratuitous action.

Parc Guerland – they've changed the name. Of course they've changed the name. Parc de la Liberté! The dusty public garden off rue Michelet – also changed: now named Didouche Mourad, one of their sacred fucking murderers. Everyone knew about this park. A roofless house of assignation, which I had never previously wished to visit. Now I needed to.

Late afternoon. I sat on a stone bench beneath contorted dragon trees, argans, planes. The hard, fissured ground was littered with leathery seed pods and sloughed bark that was holed and pocked.

Twenty minutes. There were occasional footfalls and indeterminate figures on the terrace above. I wondered if that was where I should be. Was this the right part of the gardens? Anticipation is a stimulus. My body was taut with excitement.

A further twenty minutes. There was a breath in the stiff leaves. A shadow cast against the sheer wall, veering and bending against the terrace's balustrade. There was a gust of fairground scent – Maderas de Oriente, say, and sweet kif smoke, assassin smoke. A keba whore stood before me. In those days I used to believe that they were all whores. If they looked good enough. The others were failed whores, masked to conceal their faces. I waved a deck of banknotes then held it away from her. She stood over me and raised her skirt to reveal a deep forest of glistening hair in the midst of which was discernible a red sunset. She stroked it raspingly. A liquid, coloured version of the monochrome studies in my father's library of venereal shame. She

9

moved towards me and put her hand on the part of my jeans that enveloped M'sieu Zob.[3] I realised, to my bemusement, that he was erect. She blew smoke at me, showed me a full horsemouth of blue-green teeth stopped with gold. She asked me what I wanted. I gestured her onto the ground in front of me. She knelt, her tongue pushed out of her foul mouth. She was swift with my zip. My worry was getting blood and tissue on my ice blue jeans, on my punched toecap chisel toes. That was the last thing I wanted. Almost the last: more than anything I did not want any part of her to penetrate my clothes and touch my flesh.

The pistol was in the inside pocket of my cobalt chamois blouson. A Beretta M1951 that, when he had passed it to me with his indecently leathery, almost woody pelota-hardened hands, Bébé called 'one of our little Egyptian friends'.

I shot her through the head just as he had instructed me. Diagonally: entry above the left eye, exit behind the right ear. A clean, neat strike. A selective task expertly prosecuted. She looked surprised. The last thing she did was to implore me with her eyes to undo what I had done. Too late. Yooyooyoo. An urgent sensation of warmth surged through my very core.

Even silenced, the report was cracking loud. Maybe my fear accentuated it. No, it *was* loud. The suppressor was not worthy of the name. Yet if anyone heard, there was no reaction. Such was the frequency of shots in the city.

I realised that I had ejaculated.

It was quite interesting in a way to watch her go from life to death. An experience to learn from, no doubt. Hot semen trickled pleasurably down my left thigh. Keba blood nourished keba soil, the soil to which they claimed exclusive right. I wouldn't say I felt elated. Satisfied, yes. I did up my zip and stamped out her drugged cigarette with my foot. I checked thoroughly that there was no embarrassing old person's damp patch visible.

---

3 The word *zob* derives from *zeb* and *zubb*. It is a borrowing, by way of the Zouaves, from Arabic. The ecumenical chose it over the more usual French *zizi* as an egalitarian gesture.

A special occasion merits the best. Ennio Conti was open. I celebrated the loss of my virginity with a lime sorbet.

Madame Ortéga-Nagy was a superstitious woman.

Every morning she walked to the church of Saint Joseph. At the van by the west front she drank thick chocolate and ate churros. She pitied the owner, a sorrowful man who seemed to bear a backbreaking burden and whose arms were constantly blistered by hot oil. She made her communion and prayed to god that la Grande Zohra might meet a violent death. On the way home she stopped at Pâtisserie Azzopardi for more churros and a café crème. When she had finished she bought some churros to take with her just in case she got hungry.

Every evening she draped a greasy tasselled shawl over her thinning pate and pulled it down over her face to gaze into the future. Munching and spraying poppyseed cake she talked of 'the infinite path before us'. She knew the formulae for eternal life. Immortality recipe: her herb garden was divided into plots according to the organs the plants affected. Liver and bile, digestive system, nervous system etc. etc. Immortality was attainable by the application of faith, and nutritional science. By purges, elixirs, tonics. Daily doses of a punishing bouillon derived from a shamanic recipe: fungi, bark, insects beneath the bark, musk, udder, stramonium, spotted cowbane and species of wild fungi the means of whose cultivation had now been achieved. Daily injections of anti-cancer remedies from the laboratory. Eternal life was a tangible, material entity: she didn't elaborate.

The shawl's repetitive pattern was of a sled hauled by prancing, rearing stags. The garment was so obviously a charlatan's prop that no self-respecting charlatan would have dared use it. Nor would have dared coo and mumble inside it. This was just bluff, according to Bébé, just an act. She was a mystic or medium, a soothsayer or seer. Something in that field anyway. A 'sleepwalker', so called because she appeared to be in a trance. Her predictions were persuasive for the very reason that they were hesitantly expressed, diffident, mined from deep. Her futures were conditional. Another bluff?

★

Bébé Biskarret was fearful about who he shared his opinion with. He had been at the workbench showing me how to assemble a *strounga*'s components when Denis Renucci, loudmouth heir to a chain of gela-terie and restaurants, had suggested that selective tasks' targets ought not to be determined by *reading tea leaves* and that *deciphering entrails* was no way to conduct a military campaign. Doctor Ortéga-Nagy broke Renucci's jaw with a claw hammer. It left him screaming in a puddle of two-stroke on the garage floor. Doctor Ortéga-Nagy threw his car keys to Bébé and told him to drive Renucci to hospital.

His mouth was crammed with calentita. He spluttered: 'Without industrial accidents like that surgeons would be out of work.' We all shared the obese quack's joke. His wife had been the most senior woman in the Organisation. Doctor Ortéga-Nagy was a loyal hus-band. He encouraged her capricious strategies. He was himself an advocate of medical procedures that were rare in those less gullible days: acupuncture (which he had learnt, approximately, from a former military doctor who had himself learnt it, approximately, in Saigon), homeopathy, herbalism. He was fond of saying that the circumstances will dictate the method; we must not be inhibited by convention.

The Villa Eucalyptus was behind a three-metre-tall black iron wall. A cedar's boughs stretched over the chevaux de frise along its top. To ring the doorbell you pushed an enamelled button, the bullseye at the centre of a glazed brick target. After some minutes there were footsteps then the grind of an unoiled mortice violated by a key. The door, as high as the wall and equally topped by chevaux de frise, shrieked as it was effortfully hauled open by a featureless sullen domestic, the sort of person who is never noticed so has cause for resentment, so believes she has reason to turn on her employers des-pite their having given her a good wage for two decades: that's how it was with *them*. She relocked it – a further expression of pain – then led me into the house and thence to the garden.

In the last of the light (*between dog and wolf*) Madame Ortéga-Nagy was scrabbling around in a flowerless flowerbed. Her posture was simian. She had the habit of picking leaf matter and twig fragments from her sparse hair like a chimpanzee picks nits and crunches them. She started when she heard me, trod down an earth clod with a heavy foot.

The lime sorbet had been delicious but too cold. Ennio Conti's ices were matchless but you needed to wait till they had lost their numbing edge. My molar throbbed. I asked her if she had any clove oil. She nodded irritably. She would fetch some when she had finished. Her shapeless cardigan was turning to felt, its pockets were weighed down by shelled hard-boiled eggs, woolly and hairy, which she ate whole, in a single assault on herself, pushing the blunt end into her mouth and blocked tracts. She blindly thrust her hands into the powdery soil. Even though I had not seen her do this before, I had heard of her obsessional quest for coins, crockery shards, parts of toys, lumps of coal, birds' bones, stones and whatever else might be unearthed with her hands, exclusively with her hands.

Never use a trowel or fork. Such tools might diminish her bond with the essence of these archaeological vestiges of French Algeria, the only Algeria that had ever been: this country was *our* invention. She at last sighed a sigh of satisfied relief and straightened up grasping an indiscernible trove in her hands. The objects she exhumed were more than keepsakes that she would take into her inevitable exile (which we all knew now was simply a question of when). She aspired to capture or preserve the soul and soil of her country, a soul that was contained in the soil. The soil that it was our duty to destroy before we abandoned it to the terror.

She asked me if Bébé – *ce gougnafier*, she called him – had told me to throw away the gun; she said *flingue*. They sounded strange, almost indecent, these gutter words spoken by her. She was bossy about vocabulary. She fussed over grammar. She thought your accent shouldn't give you away. She mocked Ortiz and his garrulous gang for their *pataouète*. She snorted *chachchahim!* – the very word Dudu would use so rashly many years later and make me fear for him.

Bébé had indeed warned me to get rid of the gun. Madame Ortéga-Nagy rolled her eyes. When I told her that I had ignored Bébé she told me what a brave boy I was: 'You dandy wraith.' She stroked my cheek with a dirty callused knuckle. I winced and remembered that Bébé called her *the old witch*. Can witches be fat? They have a reputation as scraggies. She hurried me inside to a plug of cotton wool doused in clove oil. I bit hard on that memory of early infancy.

She went to tell the doctor I had arrived. I waited in the long overlit hall. The house was savoury scented from cooking. Faces in the damask wallpaper grimaced. Heavy curtains, ebony candelabra, claw-footed consoles – all Second Empire style. They proclaimed that this *pompier* villa was on French soil, was part of le Métropole. An ornately framed painting showed poplars, soggy meadows, watery grey skies, a thatched cottage, a river barge and plump cattle. This was the riverside life of a temperate country, our country, where a boy might fish in peace seated on a willow stump with his stout wicker basket beside him.

I reflected on my achievement. I was considering how to build on it when the old-fashioned doorbell rang. Madame Ortéga-Nagy came from the doctor's office.

'That'll be The Mycologist,' she said as she passed me. She went out through the front door to unlock (and relock) the street door. She returned with an exceptionally tall man, sallow, wearing dark glasses and a grubby neck brace. He was clutching a blue Sabena bag. When he saw me he started. He made to turn away in alarm. She took his arm and muttered something. The man appeared reluctantly placated. As Madame Ortéga-Nagy hurried him past me he averted his eyes as though to make himself invisible. (Despite our subsequent contact I was never to discover his name so I shall refer to him as The Mycologist.)

Some minutes later he and the doctor emerged from the office. The doctor stretched up to rest his hand on his shoulder – the man was so much taller that he breathed different air. They went through the front door to the street door. The doctor was now in insistent mode. He pointed the forefingers of both hands at the blameless prosthesis round his neck. He pointed at his watch. They shook hands meaninglessly. The doctor urged swiftness, hands like a frantic accordionist now. Then he double-locked the street door. He beckoned me to follow him.

★

One end of his office was dominated by a black and gold marble mantelpiece. Obese alabaster cherubs clambered over it. It was absurdly grandiose. Base metal water polo trophies littered it. The walls were hung with photographs of a younger, slender Doctor Ortéga-Nagy in a one-piece swimming costume, here with his arms linked to a rangy young man, here alone in a pool beside a netted water polo goal, here strangely dressed in baggy trousers and a lace-up shirt holding one handle of a sporting trophy, the other held by the rangy young man. There were, too, embossed copperplate certificates and quasi-heraldic diplomas printed on paper treated to resemble parchment.

His face was high gloss sweat – bladderwrack glistening with blood-flecked sperm. His suit was an anthology of slobbered meals. Food crumbs were everywhere, rotting empanada, half-eaten gougères, slivers of saucisson, a bowl of desiccating mechoui with a spoon in it, liberally scattered olive pips, an empty packet of tortas cenceñas. What precisely was he a doctor of? No one knew. A winter garden accessed through glass doors from his office was a laboratory – a long metal table, a microscope, scales, clamps, retorts, Erlenmeyer flasks, funnels, pipettes, test tubes, more nutritious kitchen scraps. What institutes or universities had awarded him his many important degrees and doctorates? Where was he originally from? I knew better than to ask.

He claimed to speak several languages. A priori, French was his native language. But he spoke like a schoolmaster scared to make a mistake. It sounded as if it were a second language, though one he had mastered. I spoke already enough good English for me to suspect that his was laboured, stilted. His idioms were a joke: *he ties his boots too tight* etc. His Italian was apparently not so much better.

It was his Spanish that decided his fate within the Organisation. Despite half of his family name, despite his boasts of fluency, despite his bombast, he was incomprehensible, his vocabulary was limited. These are the facts or the misinformations, perhaps. This, anyway, is what I learnt from Sal Missica:

In mid-November Doctor Ortéga-Nagy has been sent to a clandestine meeting in Alicante with three of the Organisation's Falangist contacts, for example Isidoro Sarabia. They were to plan the collection by boat of ordnance taken from captured and often despatched FLN fighters: much of it of Soviet origin, some of it American (we were fighting everyone). It was to be delivered to the Organisation in the Metropole. Several raids on army and police arsenals had been thwarted. There was still only one firearm for each three or four activists. When the ordnance is in Spain its conveyance across the Pyrenees in French Catalonia will be facilitated by a high-ranking Guardia officer name of Gomez-Benet.

Twelve crates – submachine guns, ammunition, explosives – were taken in a drycleaner's van by Doctor Ortéga-Nagy, Denis Renucci, Bébé and Sal Missica to an unfrequented cove near Gouraya. To be picked up during the night of Sunday 3/Monday 4 December. The vessel despatched from Cartagena was a speedboat. It was capable of carrying two crates. The pilot was surprised when he discovered he was expected to take twelve crates. He made it clear that his instructions were there would be two crates. Even to Doctor Ortéga-Nagy it is obvious that more than two crates will sink the speedboat. The pilot would return in a larger vessel the night after next if he gets a sufficient reward. Doctor Ortéga-Nagy accused him of being an extortionist. It takes one to know one. Doctor Ortéga-Nagy managed to restrain himself. The left-over crates were reloaded into the van. They went and hid out in the safety of Bébé's uncle's fruit farm in the bled.

The second vessel, a fishing boat, arrived the night after next. It was three hours late. It couldn't gain access to the cove because its draft was too large. It anchored some fifty metres offshore. It had no tender and one could not be found. Renucci, Bébé and Sal Missica had to carry the crates on their shoulders to the boat while Doctor Ortéga-Nagy paddled about on the shore yelling to them to hurry. By the time they reached the fishing boat the cold water was high up their chest. Some of the arms were damaged, some of the ammunition and explosives were ruined, one crate was lost. The unwilling porters were bruised, chilled, exhausted. A crowd of a dozen had gathered soon after dawn to watch the end of this far from clandestine spectacle.

★

The Organisation puts blame for these blunders exclusively on Doctor Ortéga-Nagy. They were said to have been caused by this great polyglot's inability to pronounce *doce* (twelve) so that it was not sounding the same as *dos* (two). *Infantile* inability. Furthermore he has kept no record of the meeting in Alicante.

Micheli and Valensi berated him for not having done so.

Our meetings are minuted. We are not a terrorist rabble. We belong to an army. We are soldiers.

Micheli and Valensi were martial. But they were not soldiers. They were not belligerent. No stomach for the fight.

For sure, they had the military obsession with carbon paper, files, rubber stamps, staplers, paper hole punches, different colour inks, maps. This banal kit fed their self-regard. Jean-Jacques (I would never in that epoch have called him Jean to his face) had been a junior anaesthetist. The joke was 'Doctor Micheli puts people to sleep'. David Valensi was a dancer sometime and physical training teacher. He indulged me because he too was a Jew. He called me his little Saint-Just, complimented me on my skin, which he wanted to touch. He knew my father by reputation and spoke well of him. I ran errands for the Organisation's high command. I was proud to be trusted. With the exception of leaflets I seldom knew what I was carrying or the identity of the person I was delivering to. I kept my inquisitiveness to myself, made deductions, asked no questions, obeyed without demur.

The more we are taken for terrorists the less we appeal to the mass of pieds-noirs who crave that we, who act wholly on their behalf, are legitimate. It is in contrast to the Fifth Republic's illegitimacy that we must present ourselves.

If only we had been terrorists.

Even after it was so obvious that la Grande Zohra had not only betrayed us but was ready to side with the FLN, the Organisation deluded itself that provided we did not abandon our houses and farms and little businesses there was still hope for us. One of its strategies for gaining the masses' support and persuading them not to flee was to portray the Organisation as an army of one hundred thousand soldiers that would fight on, that would protect them, that could overcome the State on behalf of the Nation. In fact it never numbered much more than five thousand. The masses were, in this instance, not fooled.

My parents listened with increasing disbelief to the broadcasts made whenever the Ouled Fayet transmitter was working or the Organisation had commandeered a television studio. They shook their heads at its out-of-touch newspaper polemics. The leaflets I distributed without my parents' knowledge went unread. They littered foetid stairwells, formed drifts in abandoned office lobbies.

For some months the printing press was installed in la Villa des Arcades on the heights at El Madania. Oh how I long for the leaning breeze-twisted pines, for their baked resin scent! The very earth là-bas touches olfactory receptors the way no other earth ever has.

The villa was occupied by Micheli and Degueldre, mutually distrustful going on hateful: a would-be politician and a true soldier. Its owner, the narcissistic architect M. Fernand Pouillon, was in prison in Paris. A fraudulent property development. He was widely reputed as the most useful of the FLN's many idiots, a bag carrier, a signatory of open letters and manifestos militating for independence. A traitor.

The villa of such a man could hardly have been a surer refuge.

Nor could it have been a better place from where to fail to sense the mood of the masses. My rucksack and my Moby's paniers were loaded with leaflets from the press that I would distribute in Bab-el-Oued when I was meant to be at school. Distribute increasingly pointlessly, for Bab-el-Oued had ceased to believe. Throughout much of the previous year it had believed, blindly, that the Organisation would be its salvation. It had wanted to believe. It had had too much faith.

Now in the cafés and on the street corners the talk was of a division in the Organisation. Everyone claimed to be in the know. The idea of that division became banalised. The rank and file were fighting for the pieds-noirs because the rank and file were pieds-noirs. But – according to the rumours spread by the Ramalama telephone – the army officers who comprised the Organisation's top echelons nurtured a far-fetched fantasy of a further coup d'état. A further attempt doomed to stillbirth.

Our country was the platform from which that coup would never be launched. It was becoming a playground for former résistants and nostalgic dissenters. They garrulously yarned the dangers of their vaunted youth, they longed to turn back the clock to the Vercors in 1944, to the perfectly timed demolition of a railway bridge at Decazeville in '43, to the camaraderie of the cave and the maquis. Yet Godard, Argoud, Sergent, Henriot etc. were unwilling to relinquish the camaraderie of Algiers. They congregated and they talked and talked and talked. They knew that their coup was a pipe dream. Older now, their audacity withered, they wouldn't take the battle to the Metropole where the risks were mortal.

It was under their influence Micheli devised a further ineffective strategy: to stigmatise those who did attempt to flee, to shame them as deserters – to treat them as though they were soldiers! And to threaten them with summary justice. Six months previously – when there was still hope – among the earliest leaflets I had conveyed as a proud tyro messenger were those that warned that the Organisation knew who was aiming to flee under cover of vacations: it had the lists of passengers on every form of transport. Bluff? Probably not.

Even though it was militarily exhausted and deprived of arms, the FLN's propaganda was credible. Menaces of terror and death were more persuasive than Micheli's needling harassment. The man was no Goebbels: would Goebbels have disguised himself as a fireman as Micheli did? He was crazy about dressing up. But no theatrical costume could mask that gap-toothed smile of self-esteem. Its flicker across his face made him momentarily oriental, a sly mandarin.

He was correct in one regard: the Organisation was *not* a terrorist group. It attempted, then, to forbid random bombings, *terrorist* bombings. It held that the prosecution of selective tasks by *casuals* was undisciplined, counter-productive, unworthy of an army. It was jealous of its monopoly in sudden death. 'Freelance' actions undertaken without headquarters' sanction were deemed detrimental to the cause. What they were actually detrimental to was the Organisation's authority, especially Micheli's. And what was the cause they claimed?

A million people facing death or exodus grew restless at the high command's detachment, at the Organisation's idealism and its caution. Its grip on realpolitik was flimsy. I can't believe now how I was taken in by it, I wasn't a child. Its preposterous ambition was to create a secular republic. Such a republic had for decades existed *in theory* – but it had never been an actuality. Yet they kidded themselves and a swiftly diminishing audience that a secular republic, independent of France, could be magically pulled out of the hat . . .

Our homeland would experience a utopian métissage. Sephardi, Mizrahi, Ramalamas, Christians, Berbers, kebas, Lals, Caucasians, black Africans, blue Tuaregs – all would link hands as one happy band of francophone brotherhood and exemplary desegregation.

The notion was laughable. It was 130 years too late to re-educate the majority as enlightened citizens. The majority comprised superstitious illiterates, vectors of barbarism, resistants to any indoctrination other than that of the taber. It was 130 years too late to counsel tolerance in the despised minority. Things had gone far too far.

Besides, as we have learnt, within Ramalama there is no self-seeded germ of secularisation. No possibility of evolution. No separation of the secular and the sacred. Within Ramalama there is:
    No *Render unto Caesar the things that be Caesar's and unto God the things that be God's.*
    No *Song of Solomon.*
    No *My Kingdom is not of this world.*

It was common practice among the Organisation's higher ranks to adopt Ramalaman orphans as it once had been to adopt Indo-Chinese orphans – in order to rescue them, to civilise them, to rear them in their image, to proclaim the fellowship of races and the iniquities of segregation. This was kidnapping with a supposedly ethical face. No doubt some consciences were salved.

Now, after all these years, it is not so hard to see that the split in the Organisation foretold its collapse. At the time we didn't see where that split was leading. Or we didn't admit to ourselves that the split was irremediable.

In one camp, the former legionnaires and regular soldiers who had deserted on pain of death at the time of the putsch.

In the other, the little people they claimed to protect, the shop-keepers and clerks, the agriculturalists, the rank and file who kept the Organisation floating with its 'taxes'. To start with they had been paid gratefully. There was relief. The Organisation had promised hope. But the willingness to pay evaporated when it became apparent that its interests were not the people's. Money was subsequently extorted by menace, moral blackmail, something along those lines.

This split was almost as great as the split between the majority of pieds-noirs and the majority of Ramas. For most people military or paramilitary mores are alien: mutual dependence, unquestioning obedience, sacrifice, control, order etc. Most people live without them.

The Organisation failed to understand that it could have won round the rank and file with the straightforward ploy of inciting indiscriminate violence against kebas. That would also have made Paris think again. Would have boosted morale. Go on the attack! It was too obvious a tactic for Micheli. He was manipulative. He was more a politician than a soldier, let alone a terrorist. He was, till the end-game was played, more preoccupied with the possibilities of compromise, with the hierarchy of command rather than with battle, with internecine reprisal rather than the enemy.

His vanity was dangerous.

The television journalist Louis Ghislain repeatedly pronounced Micheli with a hard 'c' as though the name were Italian (of course it was, almost – his origins were Corsican) and not 'sh', in the French way. Micheli was infuriated. He took it as an insult designed to challenge his Frenchness. Louis Ghislain was selected. This creature of habit was eating lunch at his usual table on Chez Maître Didier's terrace near the RTF in rue Cognacq-Jay, Paris 7ème. A Lambretta drew up beside him.

A waiter said that most of the blood had been absorbed by bread and that there was little mess to clear up. He was a valued customer who would be missed although gluttony would have taken him soon. The stolen Lambretta was found four days later in a courtyard off rue Eugène-Süe in Menilmontant. It yielded no information. The task had been expertly accomplished. The weapon was correctly identified as a Skorpion machine pistol. No arrest was made.

Observation of Micheli's and the Organisation's flaws taught me valuable lessons in future tradecraft.

Some of those flaws were beyond repair. The very structure, for example. Because it adopted a conventional military structure rather than employing semi-autonomous and independent cells it was a denial of its name.

L'Organisation Armée Secrète was many things, but only seldom secret.

Too many people knew too much that they didn't need to know. Certain of the people who rallied to the Organisation were not so discreet. When a drunken braggart, for example Nico Migliorini, is familiar with the innermost workings of a cadre it surely follows that he must be told shush by that cadre to prevent him blabbing incontinently to the smiling enemy: *have another glass Nico – tell us again that story of . . . remind me who was there . . . Bruno Berg! . . . ah that's interesting . . . and Bruno's catamite?*

Squealers can only squeal if they have the information. No matter how many amps a gégène sends through his testicles, an ignorant man cannot yield useful intelligence.

Betrayals became commonplace. Those of Degueldre and Dovecar caused especial anger but, worse than that, despondency, despair.

★

The ordnance destined for the Metropole – a quarter of it lost because of Doctor Ortéga-Nagy's incompetence – had not been intended for *bandits'* selective tasks but for the ghost squadrons who would stage the famous armed coup in Paris. Wishful thinking! Micheli was a different sort of fantasist from Doctor Ortéga-Nagy.

Two days before Christmas 1961, as his wife had been before him, Doctor Ortéga-Nagy was 'transferred' from operational duties in the Organisation. Henceforth he was restricted to administrative tasks. Maintenance of the treasury, maintenance of light arms arsenal. He was warned not to attempt to make 'social capital' by hinting that he was an important figure in the Organisation in the way that Alain Marty had done.

It goes without saying, Doctor Ortéga-Nagy told me nothing of this. His bluster was predictable: how important he was to the Organisation; certain parties' fear of him; those (or perhaps other) parties' jealousy of his success – it was plain to see, was it not?

Nor did he mention the blunder at Gouraya – did he really assume that I was ignorant of it? He poured two glasses of wheat-coloured distillate. From far off came the rolling rumble of a distant explosion. He listened as though to a favourite passage of music, checked his watch, smiled a proprietary smile and raised his glass in apparent self-celebration. The smell of alcohol repulsed me. He indicated that I should sit. I sunk into a squeaky leather canapé. He congratulated himself as much as he congratulated me. He thought he was being good natured not tiresome when he patted me. He ruffled my carefully managed Caesar cut: 'You have the hair of a raven, Yoni. An opportunist predator.'

Then he wheezingly sunk himself into his absurdly ornate, quilted velvet chair, all gilded claws and distraught eagles. He might have been sexually united with it. He might have thought of it as a throne. It was more like the catafalque of a tinpot absolutist.

He was a preposterously ugly figure: the complexion betokens the man. Fat hung from him like dropsical fruit. He used the coercive first-person plural.

We had carried out the selective task successfully.

We must decide on which of the quarries revealed to Madame Ortéga-Nagy must be disqualified next.

He went on, the number of people who were *warriors* with the nerve and the courage to do what had to be done was declining. They all talk. Few act. They swear their fidelity to the Organisation. But they look to someone else to do their duty for them. Why? Because the Organisation is turning against its own people. It doesn't value its best. (He meant himself.) It has turned into a clique. (He meant it excluded him.) Such valiant men as the late Alain Marty were also excluded. He, too, had been warned, in all seriousness, against *putting himself above the law* by continuing to assign selective tasks to what Micheli called *a troop of ruffians and mechanicals.* (Bébé had been among them.) Alain Marty ignored the warning. Revolutionaries kill their kin. They fight among themselves about what they are fighting for. This in-fighting takes precedence, it is a diversion. The movement is debilitated.

Alain Marty fell from the window of a fourth-floor apartment on boulevard Général Farre.

Do you realise, Doctor Ortéga-Nagy asked me, what Meursault's problem was?

I would have replied that his problem is being a character in a boring book, but to many people at that epoch *L'Étranger* was a sacred text. And to thousands at Bab-el-Oued who had never read him Camus was an idol. I didn't want to provoke Doctor Ortéga-Nagy's anger. I shook my head.

Meursault's problem, in his opinion, was that he expires only one keba. 'Only one!' He said that he'd like to see me do much better than Meursault.

'Only one!' He belched smug laughter, rose from his desk and handed me a tie. Knitted silk, horizontal stripes, charcoal and lemon, squared end. This was my prize. He told me such ties were the latest fashion. Hardly: they had been around for at least four years. It had probably been a gift, unwanted and unwearable because its narrowness – 4.5

centimetres – would have emphasised his adolescent girl's breasts and his taut glutton-tummy, so immense it might have been a primitive weapon.

It could be teamed with my mid-grey tab collar shirt. I wished my tooth would respond to the swab that stung my gums.

'Only one! You know, Yoni, I have a feeling that you have what it takes to be a pale horse.'

Maybe the eau-de-nil stripes with the penny round collar and the steel-grey Tonik jacket: would that be too much?

Pale horse: I didn't understand then what it meant.

He could not, as it happens, have been more right. Nor could Madame Ortéga-Nagy: 'My wife is a remarkable woman. She shares my opinion.' He spoke as though there could be no greater compliment, as though I should be grateful.

I hadn't noticed earlier that the blue Sabena bag was on the floor in front of the overwrought fireplace. A scruffy canvas satchel and a webbing bag lay beside it. He was standing over me, menacing me with that belly, boasting about Madame Ortéga-Nagy's psychic abilities. She was a seer. She could divine special qualities, exceptional qualities, qualities people didn't suspect they possessed. She was a virtuoso in dowsing potential. Seeing was a form of involuntary anticipation. Or maybe it was time travel. It was knowing what was to happen before there was any exterior sign. She had foreseen my future. He gripped my shoulder: his idea of a gesture of comradeship. Something prevented me from asking him what she had foreseen there – modesty or embarrassment; it wasn't incuriosity.

And then he was talking about her next gift: the recipe for immortality that had been bestowed on her. According to Doctor and Madame Ortéga-Nagy, immortality of the soul had no scientific basis. Soul was a matter of the theological bragging (*fanfaronades théologiques*) privileged by credulous naïfs. The very idea of soul itself is an infantile creation of those credulous naïfs. We are chemical entities. The only immortality possible is that of the mutually dependent body and brain. He pointed to the laboratory: 'That, then, is what we're working towards. The project of a lifetime . . . a lifetime without end.'

Of course he was a quack, of course he was a fake, of course her talents were bogus and if not bogus then delusory. But it is the massive lies that get the better of us, that debilitate reason. What was the elixir? Where did the recipe come from? I didn't ask. When we are young myths are potent. We don't yet realise that their roots are in ignorance and wishfulness. We are drawn to fantasy and extravagance. Probability doesn't trouble us. At the age of fifteen I believed myself immortal – no need of magical draughts. It was more than likely that by the time I came to need magical draughts they would be available all about. That is how the future would be – wherever it was, wherever I was, whoever I was.

Among much else, I had yet to learn that immortality was a cosmic punishment. A punishment, then, to be relished.

Doctor Ortéga-Nagy ducked beneath the horizon of his desk, rummaging, wheezing, searching for breath. He popped up with a cardboard box, placed it next to his typewriter, opened it to reveal a long-barrelled revolver. Then he crossed the knotted room and returned with a forest-green doeskin bag of the kind that I believed English gentlemen kept their snooker balls in. It contained four hand grenades. From shelves and cupboards and plan chests he gathered a *strounga* in a saddle bag, a *strounga* in a tiffin box, a Skorpion machine pistol with a thick gauge wire stock, a metre-long anti-tank rifle that he stroked lasciviously, murmuring 'Carl Gustav'. He disgusted me, the weapons intrigued me. He beamed at his arsenal, a porcine chef posing with his specialities. He invited me to select weapons as I might select specialities.

As though it had been rehearsed, Madame Ortéga-Nagy was suddenly in the room, transported to her husband's side, an apparition borne on a gust. Her speech was uninflected, expressionless, brisk – that of a simultaneous translator. Maybe that was what she intended it to be. It didn't *seem* it might be an act. Obviously convincing acts don't seem to be acts. That is their point. All illusionism is hidden.

★

26

The detective novelist Tanguy Varesano wrote: 'The greatest artifice is the artifice that leaves no trace, like the perfect crime, the crime that no one knows has been committed.' (Varesano was guillotined in 1936 for the murder of his mistress at her house in the Chevreuse valley.)

The voice that inhabited Madame Ortéga-Nagy spoke of:
A chain-smoking, heavy-lashed, peroxided, back-combed former prostitute whose Mordhund's cropped ears were like horns – the dog was called Mac or Maxi . . .
The junction of place Carnot and boulevard Doumer . . .
An apartment building with twisted columns at its entrance . . .
A courtyard containing a makeshift workshop or garage . . .
The giant Joris Wymeersch, the giant Joris Wymeersch . . .
The wind shrieked in the garden. Shrubs juddered.

She stopped. Less than a minute had exhausted her. The voice was replaced by asthma's faint rattle, another interior colonisation of the body. Doctor Ortéga-Nagy held his tranced messenger-animal with a shocking tenderness. She smiled weakly at me, she lay her head against her husband's chest. I thought of a failed mollusc. He stroked her. Her breath was a bellows'. She left the room punch-drunk. The doorbell rang. It was impossible to assess whether she had heard it.

Joris Wymeersch, he told me, was a sometime Carlingue,[4] an amnestied milice, a turned traitor, a war criminal who had done the Germans' bidding with enthusiasm, who had hunted starving Jews and ammunitionless résistants in the southern Auvergne, Livradois-Forez, all about that sector. He and his squad tracked their prey to pitiable sanctuaries in the harsh hills – typically, hermitages and shepherds' *burons*. Naked save for a pair of turned-up shorts and heavy boots, with an MP40 slung over his shoulder with Flocon, his albino Mordhund, beside him, Wymeersch – a tall athletic 'Viking

---

4 A phalanx of collaborators employed to undertake operations the Gestapo was too squeamish to undertake. It included the sometime captain of the French national football team Alexandre Villaplane, executed in 1944.

type', 1.98 metres – would pose for a photo, beaming, blond-haired, blond-bearded, an immense studded boot on the back or neck of one of his prone captives. He delivered them for deportation and death. Some were murdered in their rude shelters. Others were given a minute's start before the Mordhund was released. Of the many who were subjected to this sport only two survived. They would be witnesses at his trial. He was also a member of the commando that pursued those maquisards, including Colonel Yves Godard, who had survived the massacre on the plateau des Glières. Sometime in the early autumn of 1944 Wymeersch vanished.

Twelve years later, the proprietor of the Rio Mambo Fun Club in Antwerp was among five people arraigned for proxénétisme. His identity papers and passport were discovered to be forged. After prolonged examination Kenith Stove admitted that he was actually Bart ten Heuvel: these names they are so so memorable . . .

The proxénétisme trial was already under way when one of his co-defendants, former policewoman Anke Postma, knowing how hopeless her case was, did a deal with the prosecution. All charges (kidnapping, demanding money with the threat of a gale viper, people trafficking *avant la lettre*) were dropped in exchange for the information that Bart ten Heuvel had died at the age of three months in December 1920. The man hiding behind two false names and countless bottles of hair dye was Joris Wymeersch, the fugitive Lillois war criminal.

He served a short sentence in Oudenaarde Prison for pandering. On his release Wymeersch was rearrested, extradited to France, tried at Lyon in June 1959 for treason and murder and sentenced to twenty-four years' hard labour.

Twenty-four years!
He was, hissed Doctor Ortéga-Nagy, released after less than two years!
Judas Zohra admired him for being even taller than he was. The order for his release came from the very highest office. His release was effected by the bastard Foccart so that he could resume hunting.

★

Colonel Godard had escaped him once. Now he was quarry again. Once again Wymeersch would be hunting Jews, hunting French patriots on behalf of a usurper president whose only legitimacy was that the coup d'état by which he had achieved power was bloodless. This murderer was now employed, on the black, by a treacherous French government. His existence would never be acknowledged by the puppet-masters of the shadow world, themselves phantoms. He was the Devil's quartermaster, the coordinator of the FLN's clandestine rearmament by la Grande Zohra's criminal cabal.

Over and over Doctor and Madame Ortéga-Nagy repeated that Wymeersch was a lucky man – but it was time his luck ran out. Shall we agree that this is our next selective task, Yoni . . . Now you have shown you are up to it . . . We have to see to it that his luck runs out . . . We have to prevent the arms being distributed.

Where was the apartment building with the twisted columns? Doctor Ortéga-Nagy shrugged. And the courtyard? And the peroxided woman with the dog that was a weapon?

He insisted his wife, now busily plumping paisley pattern cushions, knows no more than is revealed to her, which she has revealed to us. She is a seer not a guide. She furnishes us with clues not answers. There are reliable reports from the Organisation in the Metropole that Wymeersch is here, in the city. He is not using any of the barbouzes' safe houses. He must realise that they are compromised by that criminal rabble's indiscipline. They're easy meat, Degueldre's Delta commando is taking care of them – drunkards, pimps, thieves, murderers, collaborators, fascists. And all of them off-guard, mere target practice. More than twenty of them were successfully released into the atmosphere in a bespoke action at Brasserie Romano at the bottom of the Marcel Morand stairway. The explosion could be heard six kilometres out to sea.

Wymeersch, on the contrary, is shrewd, cautious, *pathologically* cautious. Risk is not in his make-up. There was no proof that the former policewoman Anke Postma was murdered. She was living in Sweden under an assumed name. Her car left the road near Kungälv and sunk in the Göta Canal.

Were Madame Ortéga-Nagy's revelations actually hallucinations based in rumours called *reliable reports*? I thought of how we reach into half-remembered dreams, fumble blindly, never quite grasping who or where.

How was I to find this man who had disappeared, avoided arrest, travelled on false papers, changed his appearance? How was I to find him with nothing but cryptic, partial clues to follow?

That is what I was wondering when Doctor Ortéga-Nagy accompanied me through the echoing Villa Eucalyptus, his key ring clanking. He led me through the front door, closed it behind him and unlocked the door in the metal wall. He clasped my arms in further unspoken congratulation, instructed me to return in the next couple of days to inform him of the progress of my pursuit, of Wymeersch's whereabouts, or, even, of his successful selection . . .

I summoned the nerve to ask him: *How? How am I to find him? This magical chameleon of a man? A seborrhoea-collared clerk one moment, a rampant minotaur the next. And where . . .*

Doctor Ortéga-Nagy giggled. He shook his head as though there were something obvious that I had failed to grasp which he would gently explain to me. But just then the phone in the house rang. He grunted his exasperation, wished me good luck and hurried to answer it, flapped a bloated farewell hand at me as he waddled-at-the-double, blubber-all-a-wobble (Dudu's expression, I love it!).

My toothache had gone. It had taught me a lesson: not to celebrate the accomplishment of future tasks so unthinkingly, so greedily.
Let the act be its own reward.

Even though it was only intermittently lit and deserved its ill reputation I took a chance on the long flight of stairs down to avenue Père de Foucauld. I was armed, confident. The metal banisters attached to the rubble-stone walls were polished to a shine by a century of hands, a century of germs: I didn't touch them. The steps were smoothed to slippery hazard. I trod with care; my two-eye, punched toecap, almost weltless chisel toes had a composite sole that lacked grip.

It was not until I was three-quarters of the way down that I realised that I had forgotten my reward, the horizontally striped tie. A mental grimace moved from my head to the yoke of my back. My sigh of frustration broke the night's tranquillity. I suppressed a curse. Ought I to leave it till next time? Doctor Ortéga-Nagy might by then have forgotten about it, so my asking for it might appear presumptuous.

I turned and briskly ascended the mountain. You're less likely to lose your footing going up. That made me worry about the prospect of redescending a few minutes later.

The Villa Eucalyptus's door to the narrow road had been left ajar. This was surprising, troubling even. Had Doctor Ortéga-Nagy forgotten to lock it after he had finished his phone conversation? Or maybe he was still on that call? Either way it was a lapse in security that, committed by someone else, would have provoked his boiling ire. Rather than go straight in, it occurred to me that I should warn them of my reappearance. My behaviour towards these people was at odds with my contempt for them. I again feared being considered presumptuous even though I was now a Reckoning Executant. I pressed the bell and heard it ring within the house. When there was no response I peered through the stained glass into the hall and the corridor beyond. There was no one to be seen. I pushed the heavy door to the road so it at least appeared shut. It made my hand stink of metal; there was nowhere to wash. The old-fashioned key was still in the lock. The ring of equally long keys hung from it. They summoned dungeon gaolers' glistening torsos and shaven heads. I was wondering how long I should wait when I heard Doctor Ortéga-Nagy's voice coming from the side of the house near the winter garden. The wind gusted and rushed and muffled him. But his squeaky tone of exasperation was evident enough. I walked to the corner of the house – hesitantly, for my invitation had, so to speak, expired. I was trespassing. It felt awkward.

I was about to rectify my presence by hailing Doctor Ortéga-Nagy when I saw that he was not alone. Another figure loomed over him. I told myself: Squint!

The figure resolved itself into The Mycologist. This, then, was whom Doctor Ortéga-Nagy had been berating. Despite his immense height his posture was servile. He still wore dark glasses even though the winter garden's terrace was illumined only by a pale wedge from within the house. What I saw as I stood in the shadows, hidden between a tamarisk and flaking quoins, was a scene that was not meant to be witnessed by snooping eyes. The touchy urgency and panicky gestures betokened secrecy. The terrace was not overlooked, nonetheless their behaviour was furtive, darting – so far as a man the doctor's size could be darting. Madame Ortéga-Nagy scampered (ditto) in and out carrying ill-balanced shoe boxes, box files, a carpet bag, bulging envelopes, reams of paper tied with string, tightly clasped carrier bags with shops' logos.

The Mycologist and the doctor had lifted some of the terrace's floor tiles to reveal the entrance to a semi-basement. The former, thin as he was tall, disappeared down a ladder. Every few seconds his disembodied hands reached up to be fed by Doctor Ortéga-Nagy. There was evidently some sort of subterranean cache into which they were putting whatever she brought from the house. I thought of the secret passages in Sebastian Cormier's tales and priest-holes in the Worcestershire from the Aubrey Quested adventures we read in English classes. What were these papers? The Organisation's records? Memoranda of meetings? Lists of personnel, selective tasks, Discretional Events? The whereabouts of funds? Directions to safe houses? Inventories of ordnance? Or personal material? Confidential medical records? Legal papers? Deeds?

She handed her husband the Sabena bag. He listened to something that his hidden colleague said. He flapped at the air in consternation.

Instead of handing The Mycologist the bag he reluctantly removed its contents and passed them down in lavish handfuls. Its contents were money. If all the parcels had contained banknotes, many millions of francs – nouveaux francs, as we still called them – were being stowed away. It was money that was being buried. Money. It scared me. This was the Organisation at its most opaque, most factional, most deadly. Here was a rare occasion when the Organisation really was secret, secretive. Were my presence to be detected I would be in grave danger. Quite by chance – but that's no excuse. I knew what I was not supposed to know.

When the wind abated the silence was leaden. I dared not move. The horizontal striped tie had slipped out of my mind. I watched instead as The Mycologist relaid and made good the tiled floor: bucket, cement, grout, trowel, float, rags. He did this with such precise rapidity that he must have been a builder or – a worrying thought – well practised at disappearing bodies in infrastructure. His work met with Doctor Ortéga-Nagy's approval; a tepid pat on the back together with, thankfully, a gestural invitation to take a glass. As soon as they had gone into the house by way of the winter garden I tiptoed to the still unlocked door to the road and sidled silently into the night.

I am Judex. I was Judex. I shall forever be Judex until the foul scaley faces of wrath are turned against me – which they will be, long hence, over the hills, over time's far distant horizon where terrible chancres of the skin are as common as thistles and henbane.

It is not because I was heartless, criminal, psychopathic, misanthropic or 'troubled' that I enhanced a number of lives before I was sixteen.

Nor had I what Anglo-Saxons now call 'issues'. I was not mindless.

My motive was rational, straightforward, both worldly and sanctioned by the scriptures.

They took my country from me. I took their breath from them. Fair exchange.

My actions did not make me repine. Far from it, the righteousness of the just brought me the intense satisfaction of knowing that I had punctiliously and professionally discharged moral tasks. Witnesses, should any remain, will invariably be unable to remember anything other than the dark glasses. Many people wear dark glasses. Few people have eyes as memorably, as startlingly, as instantly recognisable as mine: liquid zircon.

For a boy in search of his quarry, they were exhilarating days, those days that followed that strange, unforgettable evening in the Villa Eucalyptus and its shadowy gardens.

A boy? I was a man. A man in search of his quarry, quarries. I had to remember that. A man. These definitive interventions made me a man. My pursuit was single-minded. I rode my hand-me-down Moby. I walked with intent, took trams when they were running. I stared, I wondered, I gaped, I gazed . . . I followed tall men, any woman with sluttish fake blonde hair (a sign of a plagued labia most likely). A crop-eared Mordhund – *the* Mordhund? – swaggered as though it knew I was trailing it. It led me down lanes whose existence I was previously ignorant of. Its ears were a torturer's. I feared it might trap me in an impasse.

I searched our city far from my habitual itineraries. So far distant it was no longer our city but a vague terrain without name. Squalid health-hazard shacks made of scrounged, found, stolen components, holed fencing and tarpaulin, corrugated iron and broken doors. Here a wall of car batteries. Here another of damp cement sacks sprouting weeds. Beside these straggling bidonvilles stood randomly sited blocks. Newly built HLM apartments and the half-built skeletons of more: freshly anti-colonial France's contrite gift to its dependent enemies who were now its friends by the decree of a negligent signature a thousand kilometres away. There were sand piles, builders' rubble, stinking tips of rubbish and rags where feral cats and rats played cache-cache to the death. Although nothing was finished it was already worn out, trashed by the ungrateful inhabitants suffering the usual collective Lalism that incapacitates hope on this earth, that prevents them doing anything that might obviate their succumbing to the fate ordained for them.

★

The ignorant gullibility of the credulous: if their Qu'tel tells them neon is god's lightning they believe him. When Luftwaffe planes had dropped leaflets in the bled encouraging Ramalama to join their foul cause they would have gathered thousands of recruits had the Ramas not been illiterate. Ramalamism is a disease. Like many forms of psychosis it is curable. It responds to electroconvulsive therapy and to neuroleptics. But the cure depends on the will of medical authorities to administer it. That will was absent because of the political pretence that every inhabitant of our country was French and that the French were not to be forcibly treated.

They stared vacantly. Hollow eyed, expressionless, scrawny – no feast for a cannibal save in extremis. They revelled in their own filth – they were less evolved than the greedy, mischievous macaques who gave their name to le Ruisseau des Singes at Chiffa: a childhood weekend treat. Broken buses with screaming, flag-waving[5] fellagha on their roofs would appear from nowhere. They jolted along the unmade roads parping their horns to get donkeys out of the way. The apartments' brise-soleils provided cover for snipers. I didn't hang around.

When I was aching or saddle-sore I would while away time with an Orangina and a patisserie at the Café Rstakian on the corner of boulevard Doumer and place Sadi Carnot. The tables I favoured were those that gave a view of the immense outdoors stairway to avenue Domrémy. Three hundred and eighty-four steps, every child knew that number. Madame Ortéga-Nagy had had a vision of this place. She believed that the chocolate and blood orange confection called a P'tit Clamart was to be eaten in anticipatory celebration of a major operation's success. I thought this presumptuous but remained silent.

The life of the flesh is in the blood, and I have given it to you on the altar to make an atonement for your souls . . . I would count the number of people on the stairway then compute the volume of blood their bodies contained.

---

5 The Algerian flag was designed by the French traitor Emilie Busquant, wife of the terrorist Messali Hadj. Leader of the Mouvement National Algérien, which was extinguished by the even more murderously terrorist Front de Libération National.

And without any willed effort I would see the stairs as a cascade of blood, red and ordered and frothing. Every child once knew the stairway climbed to paradise. No longer. La Boulangerie Frangolacci near the bottom of the staircase was a charred carcass. It had been firebombed. All that remained of its window was diagrammatic mountain peaks. The carbonised skeleton of a Renault Dauphine rested on the pavement outside it. Its melted tyres were granular. Some of the shattered letters that had spelled the shop's name on the fascia hung by the wires that had lit them. It had been our city's most modern bakery. The Frangolacci family had left for Siracusa. M. Frangolacci referred to it as 'home': he knew it was a lie, he knew that we knew it was a lie. But in such sore times we are comforted by desperate delusions.

It was my duty to avenge the enforced fates of such decent people, my moral duty, my duty to my people, to us the fugitive people stripped by the state of everything – our identity, self-esteem, nationality, home, possessions, livelihood . . . everything save our memories. We were the people who were *not* . . . From the country that was no longer . . . that was about to end its existence. We were the abandoned, the inconvenient beings who ought never to have been. We got in the way.

I never lost heart, never lost faith in Madame Ortéga-Nagy. Her prophecies and goals touched me. They were more effective than Micheli's strategies: his politician-posing-as-a-soldier's martial logic had no place in our war, which was improvised, opportunist – and lost. But there were revanchist battles to be won. Madame Ortéga-Nagy's divinations were absurd, crazy, *badjok* as they say in Bab-el-Oued. Of course they were crazy. She was touched. Her claim to be in contact with the Organisation's martyrs 'on the other side' (among them Sacha Gil, Valentin Durbach, the Mendes brothers etc.) was *frappadingue*. Reincarnation, she asserted, begins with people literally rising from the grave . . . What, I wondered, happens to those who have rotted, were cremated, were coated in concrete beneath autoroutes? I didn't ask. But it was incontrovertible – her hunches were all I had to go on. They were the threads that would guide me. She could *feel* the whereabouts of our enemies.

★

They were everywhere. There were more of them each day. For example: my father's medical receptionist, Nabila Dib, had worked for him since 1952. She was paid well above the average let alone the minimum salary for such a job. They exchanged birthday gifts. He had saved her second son's life by diagnosing oesophageal cancer that had gone unidentified by what he called 'the tribal witchdoctor'.

The day after the predictable details of the Evian Betrayal were published she shocked my mother. She spat at her, said we were just *kafir roumis*, called her a 'colonial slave madame' and warned her to leave 'my country'. It was obviously rehearsed behaviour, prepared speech (in French, for she had no other language). A decade's bonds of amity and respect were brutally cut in a few seconds. Needless to say, my mother saw her point of view, put herself in Nabila's place. Such incidents were widely repeated, often verbatim.

The Organisation torpidly woke up to the actuality of the situation. That's to say it realised that it was too late. Micheli's beginner's posturing as a statesman was at an end. Henceforth tasks were no longer obliged to be selective. The net might be cast wider. Decisive action could be indiscriminately directed. All djellabas and veils could be volunteered for absence. Mercy was not an option. The Organisation rolled up its sleeves, so to speak. Which is to say that it was, *de facto*, no longer the Organisation but a web of clandestine cells unanswerable to old soldiers. At last we got down to business.

For as long as I could recall I had visited my paternal grandparents' grave at Saint-Eugène cemetery in Bologhine. Initially, dutifully, in the company of my father. Then, as I grew older, alone, in a different register of duty. I visited when I needed their presence. They had both died before we were betrayed. They could never have foreseen so much of a disaster. They could never even have foreseen la Grande Zohra, repeatedly defeated at the ballots, posturing as president. A traitor to France like Bazaine at Metz. Lately I would lie supine on the stony ground beside the slab, incised with Roman alphabet not Hebrew. I stared at the sky pierced by a cypress. I'd talk to them in whispers, in moderated language, telling them what was happening to their ancient homeland, putting a brave face on it even though brave, in this instance, means softly mendacious, maybe delusional. I promised them that as a good Jew and good Frenchman I would, despite my belonging to these superior civilisations, steel myself to exact barbaric revenge wherever the opportunity presented itself . . . an eye for an eye, a tooth for a tooth, a pyre . . . I promised them in the knowledge that they would be appalled. They would despair at my atavism. I put my ear to the warm baked earth to hear them turning. Oh the horror . . . then they smiled for sure. I laughed at myself. I respectfully pushed my Moby so its screeching motor did not wake the dead. I felt good.

Two comatosed bleds were lazing at the entrance, slumped against a bulbous gate pier. They stunk of hashish, which is the stink of the killer, the assassin. One held a carved pipe. The other looked at me through a suppurating eye. I eased them along their way. They hardly noticed, the gap between the two shots was perhaps a second. Neat, quick, precise. And effected without thought, without doubt, without reservation, without hesitation, without consideration of these creatures' claims on our air and land.

Over the next few weeks while I hunted Wymeersch I would make several random interventions, led by instinct and duty:

Middle-aged man with filthy crumbling teeth and laundry bag in a doorway at Saint Agathe. The display of bell pushes and exposed wires might be a danger for the residents.

My father put his head round the door of his surgery, asked my mother to check a telephone number in his appointments diary. My mother was upstairs. I found the book. The person due to see him at 11.10 was an Yves Kerbellec. Phone 206.18. No address. I transmitted the name and number to him. I recalled the late Alain Marty's observation that barbouzes had a habit of adopting Breton pseudonyms. When M. Kerbellec left the surgery after treatment I followed him. He was oblivious. He walked swiftly, he marched. The noise of his studded boots shut out the soft tread of my moss suede moccasins.

Two youths fly-tipping, one wearing swimming trunks, the other in the back of a van hauling out sheets of corroded metal. Their crimes were environmental as well as religious.

Boy of about ten years old. Spared from growing up a warrior for Ramalama. He fell awkwardly into a floral display at Parc Combes. Graceless.

These actions brought grandeur of purpose to bleak days that accelerated towards the day *when* . . . for *if* was now no longer a possibility.

Doctor Ortéga-Nagy encouraged my access to his armoury, much of it seized ordnance that had been smuggled by former SS in Egypt and Syria to the FLN, many of whom had fought alongside them in the death's head corps. I was a quick learner and nimble: I could make a rudimentary explosive device.

The donkey was all that ever scored my conscience. Being a donkey it was incapable of free will, of renouncing faith and culture. It was an innocent afflicted with moral stasis, with the impossibility of evolution. It would not climb the ladder of species. It was not like a foal, not a horse in waiting, a quadruped pupa. It was donkey for ever. The donkey that gave me the opportunity was broken-backed, all but. Callously weighed down, sagging swollen bags that nearly touched ground both sides. It was parked in a sunless narrow alley. A cave between decrepit, high, crumbling deuxième empire buildings draped in clothes and bedsheets. On the ground floor of one hole-in-the-wall café where in days of justice I could get a fine shoeshine. No longer. Now the baby *bicots* were so grand, jumped up, too full of pride in their new nation to pursue their calling. Pride! They would learn soon enough. They no longer waited at their post. They were the masters.

So they didn't bother to keep watch. Heedless.

From within came the wail of the usual music, Ramalama's music of whining self-pity, complaint, resentment.

There would be more to resent in a moment. I was as swift as I was dextrous. Doctor Ortéga-Nagy had called the device Cain the

Firstborn. I wound the clock to three minutes then placed it in the drooping bag further from the café's wall. I rode 150 metres to the two-stroke pump at the Depasquale filling station. I sat astride, watching.

Old M'sieu La Misère was grudgingly getting round to attending to me, limping from the office, when it went up. A noise to make ears bleed. Then the silence of a muted world. Then the whistling whoooosh of Gargantua's exhalation.

I resolved never to explode another donkey so long as I lived. I have been loyal to that bond. A part of the creature described a parabola leaving in its trail red spray. One of the few regrets life has delivered me. I thought of Modestine salted for figatelli. Otherwise . . . I was proud. The tremor burst the blocks. Bodies were spun through windows by the force of relief blasts. Djellaba'd Nazis' limbs flew like hooked crosses. Laundry caught fire. Trousers twisted, possessed, whirling, spreading the flames, setting alight rubbish heaps, landing on cars that had no choice but to join the conflagration. Fleeing men scraping their hair like they had fleas. Rashie discovers flames are contagious. They danced here and they skipped there, mapping gas pipes and stroking curtains. What busy bees they are! The groans of the guilty were indistinguishable from those of the collapsing beams. The café door's lintel collapsed on the men beneath it. A wall evaporated into rubble. An arm without an owner thrust itself forward baroquely from a smog of particulates. A flaming veil trembled Saint Vitus' dance. I had brought neurological mayhem to the street. I had turned smug morning into screaming night. M'sieu La Misère did something I didn't know he knew how to do. He smiled. He nodded his head in approval at the display of improvised pyrotechnics. What a grand day it was turning out to be. I was accessing heaven.

'*Ça fait comme un mascaret.*'

Rolls of black smoke were filling the street. I didn't know what he was talking about.

He explained: a tidal bore. I'd never heard the word. Nor had I seen one. He described it.

It made me feel more than ever like a force of nature . . . *the* force of nature. With fortune on his side.

Anarchy is as ugly as it is necessary. I was strife. I was the smiler with the knife. Destruction whets the appetite for destruction, chaos for chaos, harm for harm, confusion for confusion. Bombs, bullets, *stroungas*, Semtex, Pentex, plastiques . . . these were my faithful friends.

The receptionist Nabila Dib's loutish chain-smoking husband Samir and his loutish chain-smoking strabismic brother Houcine visited without warning in the early evening two days after the massacre in rue d'Isly. They were initially more courteous than she had been. They announced that they had come to see my parents, a discreet matter. My father was with a patient. My mother was due home soon. I offered to make them tea. They feigned surprise. Samir sort of winked. Houcine didn't, couldn't. Samir said he'd have a Suze. And Houcine? He'll have the same. The smell, gentian and chemicals, repulsed me. They sat down, awaited my parents, talked urgently to each other in their crude, stupidly accented French. I fetched an ashtray.

They wanted to buy the house and surgery. My parents looked at each other with astonishment. They proposed a sum of 1,500 nouveaux francs. My parents burst out laughing. Samir and Houcine were affronted. It was a buyers' market: did we not know? Such a sum was better than nothing. They threatened that the ever more numerous *pecnauds* slouching against the wall across the street brazenly coveting the house were sure to grow impatient. If the house was legally the Dibs' they could guarantee our safety till we went back to our own country. My mother suggested they leave. Houcine removed his cigarette from his mouth and hawked copiously. Because of his wall-eyed aim it wasn't clear which of us was the intended recipient: a glistening pat of the Ramalama's lung butter landed on the floor.

The next day the surgery's reinforced gate to the street was painted with the words SAL JUIF. My father had saved Samir's son's life.

The 'French' army was being strengthened. Squads of last week's, last decade's, terrorists, *militarily vanquished terrorists*, were now Judas's allies. They were provided with uniforms and arms: most of their arms had been captured, hence the farrago at Gouraya. They demanded titles: senior FLN murderers insisted on being accorded the rank of at least colonel. Their impertinence was rewarded. Their fraudulent 'legitimacy' did not make them any less brutal. Now, today, if your genitals were sliced off and put in your mouth they were sliced off and put in your mouth by a French officer.

With so much extra manpower at its disposal a new tactic was being used. Barriers were erected to stop every vehicle on certain clusters of roads. Everyone mistrusted everyone else. So even police and military vehicles were checked, to the fury of their passengers. Changing sides had become a collective pathology. Identity papers had to be shown to illiterates who laboriously pored over them. The clusters of roads were changed daily. Sometimes a trap was set by not changing them. It caused traffic jams and uncertainty.

It was late afternoon when Bébé Biskarret and I left the fronton court at Parc d'Hydra. We had recently played every couple of weeks. We were sitting on a bench sweating and breathless, aching a bit, replaying points, pretending to kid with each other. Pretending . . . it was self-aggrandising bullying on his part. He was the better player and knew it. But then I was a novice. And he wasn't that good. He had been playing since he could walk. That's the Basque way, jai alai in mother's milk. He had to boast because he had no aptitude for anything else. He boasted about the number of exams he had passed, the girls seduced, the operations prosecuted. He was difficult to believe. Did he believe that he was believed?

There was a roadblock at the rond-point. We were about to leave when an AML-90 armoured car arrived. The man standing in the turret was bearded, blond, dressed in combat fatigues and wearing a helmet at an angle that invited a shot to the forehead. He was immensely tall, over 1.98 metres. He could not disguise his height. Was this Joris Wymeersch? We each knew what the other was thinking. He sprung down like an athlete. We looked at each other. He was followed by his Indo-Chinese driver. Then after a brief moment a rangy albino Mordhund emerged from the turret to leap like a lion. That settled it. Bébé and I looked at each other. This, we told ourselves, is it.

He was soon issuing orders, strutting among the queuing vehicles. He scrutinised every driver, every passenger with suspicion, hoping to identify us – us, the enemies of the state. He was notoriously an adept of forged documents. Even if our forged documents are in order he might have a hunch, a flash of recognition. His base talents had not left him. The weapons-grade Mordhund was all sullen eagerness and aggressive sniffing, just waiting for the command. Wymeersch randomly ordered people out of their cars. He instructed soldiers to search vans. Once a milice . . .

After twenty minutes throwing his weight about he spoke intensely to the troop commander – evidently his junior – signalled to the driver, leapt back in the armoured car and departed in the direction he had come from. We ran to Bébé's old Panhard Dyna van a hundred metres away on the far side of the park from the roadblock. The long traffic queue was in the opposite direction, making for the centre of the city. The road north was unusually clear. We duly caught up with the armoured car, easily distinguishable by a hastily applied patch of khaki paint intended to erase a graffito. We followed from a judicious distance descending Birmandreis's zigzag roads, down the ravine past the old entrance to the mad Irishman's grotto, through the (still) fine affluent quarters and beside the hippodrome. Then the decor changes: abruptly we were in a lost land of swarf, tar hills, crumbling silos, dump trucks with crawlers, windowless factories and sullen stevedores making their way home.

Wymeersch was heading out of the city. I was worried Bébé wouldn't have enough petrol. Aucun souci. Wymeersch took the sandy coast road that Bébé claimed to know by heart. Over the girder bridge at l'Harrach, Fort-de-l'Eau, cabins, cars on wooden blocks, blinds, honeycombed brise-soleils, makeshift fences, marram grass, half-built houses, houses with absurd crenelations, listing bungalows with basketball nets attached to their facades, fishing boats pulled up on the beach, stretched nets between them, cracked concrete slipways. Then as the dog began to melt into the wolf we were thankful for the single tail light.

From the cliff road the outline of the city across the bay was exhilarating. It was as though we could touch it. For the moment . . . The lights were going on. They were as thrilling as fireworks. When Wymeersch reached Jean Bart he took boulevard Charles X then turned into the park of the former École Jules-Emile Jacquet, now requisitioned as a barracks. He waved to the sentries who saluted him. There were tricolours everywhere. Rolls of barbed wire everywhere. A dormered roof signalled the Heavy Hand of Hausmann's Epigone as Tamara would teach me to say many years later. The building's facade was long, symmetrical, austere but for the pairs of twisted columns that flanked the central doorway . . .

'Where better to hide a leaf?' said Bébé.

He had stopped across the road from the gate, twenty-five metres from the sentries.

'Move . . . we do not hang about here. Bébé! Let's get out of here. Just get going!'

Bébé looked hurt. He had the metabolism of the dead.

We – our crumbling Organisation – had no one on the inside at the makeshift barracks. The 'soldiers' there were not from here. With the exception of some former *goumiers* they were dupes, cannon fodder. Criminals, delinquents, given the choice between a military adventure or refusal of remission in their *maisons de correction*. Of course they chose the former. They were straight off the boat, with no local contacts, no idea of where they were, no conception of loyalty to the ideal of France rather than to the Usurper and his 'certain idea of France', which was that He Was France. An obviously vainglorious man then but also very stupid. The example of dead barbouzes had been instructive. This brigade was denied contact with the outside world. Its letters, received and sent, were read. It was confined to barracks when not on duty. The less they were seen the more powerful the rumours that would inevitably attach to them. Whatever neighbours thought, they didn't complain. They didn't ask questions. They were reluctant to talk despite their dislike of this second wave of barbouzes, despite their disgust at the loud fraternisation with syphilitic keba prostitutes who were bussed in to squeal, to scream with pained delight at the love of their new liberators. Unmarked lorries came and went by night. Mobile houses of dolls.

The brigade's name, Schlagergesselschaft, was Wymeersch's coinage. No longer employed to smuggle arms to the FLN, which could now obtain them legitimately, he had found a new role for himself sanctioned, as ever, by the bastard Foccart, the man who slaveringly licks Judas Zohra's turds from the Élysée floor. And creates phantom armies – which never existed.

That the FLN could help themselves to a French arsenal *after the ceasefire* shows just how profoundly committed it was to that treaty. Not only did French troops fire on us. So too, with impunity, did the castrating, throat-slitting rapists equipped with French ordnance and kit including condoms issued by the Service de Santé des Armées.

Bébé drove from the Schlagergesselschaft barracks to the cove where we had dived from the rocks when we were children in paradise.

For old times' sake we walked along the shore, our shore, clambering over rocks, our rocks.

For half an hour we were two old men remembering, reminiscing. We were already nostalgic for là-bas even though we were still là-bas and the sea was rotting. We were longing for our lost home before we had lost it. We were anticipating the dispossession we soon would suffer. It seemed that for Bébé there would be nothing after loss. He couldn't understand that he would have to remake himself or perish.

A blind shepherd had brought his frail flock to graze on a patch of sandy mud and beachgrass. The expiring creatures' ribs were visible.

We went back to the van. We had driven for no more than half a minute when, to our astonishment, we saw Wymeersch.

He was now in mufti, walking briskly along the haphazardly illumined road in the direction we had come from. There he was, in plain sight with the albino Mordhund on its leash. I cursed myself for not being armed. Bébé cursed himself too but not so much as me. Cowardly avoidance of risk was his rule. Hence his instruction to dispose of the little Egyptian friend from Parc Guerland. Hence no weapons in the car save when operational.

He slowed. Where the road widened in front of Café Beau Rivage he attempted to turn the Panhard Dyna through 180 degrees, as unobtrusively as he might manage, difficult given the vehicle's unwieldy lock and the reverse gear's stiffness. We had attracted the attention of a fat man clearing cups from the café's terrace. I urged Bébé to hurry. But his metabolism! So sluggish. He wins at pelota not because he is quick but because he is crafty. I was staring over this shoulder then that shoulder to see where Wymeersch went. But by the time Bébé had completed what proved to be a five-point turn Wymeersch was nowhere to be seen.

We sat in silence. We had been so close to having him in our grasp. Bébé banged his head on the steering wheel.

'Well,' I said at last, after reflection, 'we didn't have the tools anyway. I'm thirsty.'

Apart from the fat man, the proprietor, the café was deserted. Like every PMU café it was all brimming ashtrays and ripped-up betting slips, crumpled hopes. He twitched when we entered. Our presence made him nervous. His face was tripe colour. I asked for a menthe à l'eau. He reacted as though he had never heard of it. The back of his head was visible in the mirror behind the bar. There was a crimson volcano of subcutaneous cyst on his neck. It disgusted me. He overfilled Bébé's pression glass. He spilled a little bowl of peanuts on the bar. He looked at us as though we were a visitation he didn't know how to deal with. Who did he think we were? I think we *were* a visitation.

He seemed to gather himself from the bits . . . He leaned across the bar. So close I could see *longanisse* crumbs and cheese filaments between his yellow teeth with brown piping, so close I could smell the fat of his breasts melting into his nylon shirt. The gap between his eyes was so insufficient that he was near monocular, an apprentice cyclops.

His accent was *pataouète*: 'You have the wrong car for the job . . . Five, avenue des Albizias. *Now get out! Out* . . . And do not come back.'

I reached for my wallet.

He held up his palms and shook his head slowly: 'On the house . . . I won't be coming to your funeral.'

I felt so much like a man who stands firm against his race's oppressor.

If this long chapter of my life should end in heaven, so be it.

We were not Delta. We were hidden. We were fighting for our lives along with Degueldre, but not beside him. We had little support in the field. But we were silent, swift, sly. Men in the crowd. We struck when we wanted where we wanted . . . Where – there was no question of definitive intervention against Wymeersch anywhere but 5 avenue des Albizias or the 400 metres between there and the former École Jules-Emile Jacquet building. Did he live there? Was he visiting? How often?

We had the house's address. That was enough. That was the gen. That was the griff. That was all that was needed. It was not hard to remember. The rest was fieldcraft, cunning and a couple of sleeping bags.

In those days all Lambrettas looked the same, two-tone, burgundy and cream. Do you know how easy it is to hotwire one? Easier even than a Vespa. And I needed a vehicle that was quicker than my chugging Moby. I requisitioned one from rue du Hamma opposite the Opera. We struggled to lift it into the back of the van. Our arms were hidden beneath the front seats. Two machine pistols and a mortar, not the tool for this job, an absurd weapon for Bébé to have chosen. I said nothing. We guessed that if we were stopped it would be the back of the van that would be searched.

We got to Jean Bart without encountering a roadblock.

Avenue des Albizias was an unmetalled road of flat roof houses.

The abundant trees in the gardens were twisted in agony. There were no streetlights. Number five was the third on the right, at least seventy-five metres from the corner. There was a high wall to the road, a pedestrian door and a garage door. The sandy 'pavements' were separated from the sandy roadway by lines of scrubby grass. The parallel road, avenue des Hortensias, was less developed. Wymeersch's house backed onto a plot where foundations had been laid, trenches dug, pipes stacked up – and construction abandoned *sine die* so that sugar canes could take root. There were by now throughout the suburbs thousands of such sites of flourishing vegetation and gloomy premonitions. There were, too, thousands of white, cubistic houses such as Wymeersch's. His was unusual only in that it was three storeys rather than two. There was a roof terrace with a sunshade. Much of the house lower down was, like the front, obscured by trees lopsided as amputees, shrubs and a purposeful-looking wall.

Across the Cap Matifou road from the junction with avenue des Albizias there was a scrapland place where insensate, purposeless, oblivious kids skipped school, smoked hashish, drank beer, wasted their lives talking about film stars and yé-yé. They skidded their Solexes and Vespas and pushbikes between oil drums, oil puddles, piles of tyres, makeshift chicanes. We were invisible among them.

A bob-haired girl of my age asked me if I was a fan of Les Rafales. I said I wasn't sure but would reflect on it. She twisted her hair. Would I like one of her cigarettes? I declined. When I smoked I smoked Royale Gout Maryland. Brown tobacco made me cough: I didn't want to be an old man with phlegm in its whiskers. Her name was Marie-Yvonne. She was, I suppose, pretty and downy-skinned but unwashed. What about Bobby Fitoussi's 'Chemin du Rock?' Great tune don't you think? Where do you make your communion? I was non-committal but I kept talking about this and that like any other wastrel not taking responsibility to shape the future, not creating his and his people's destiny, just whiling away the time till it was time to go. I wanted them to get used to my presence. They were my camouflage. There was nowhere else to loiter. Boredom and resultant lack of alertness was our enemy. Bébé's concentration was partial. He kept changing radio stations. He made several visits on foot to a mobile friterie where they must have fried in engine oil. He wanted to move the van. I repeatedly told him this was the only place whose shadows and shrubs provided the watcher with cover. I tried to make friends with the bloody-eyed feral cats.

At just the same time as the previous evening Wymeersch strode breezily from boulevard Charles X with the albino Mordhund on a long leash threatening plants, fences, roots, stones, fallen telephone wires. His proud master might even have been humming to himself. Not a care in the world. Yet.

It was not part of my plan that my requisitioned Lambretta's ignition should fail.

By the time I'd rewired it and reached the corner of avenue des Albizias, Wymeersch, without bothering to look about him, was confidently unlocking the pedestrian gate. Bougainvillea boas spilled over the high wall on either side of it. He was too distant for me to attempt a shot. And the Lambretta's motor uttered a yelp of pain, quit this life. I pushed it back across the road and abandoned the wretched thing. I had requisitioned without diligence. Yoni culpa.

What I had learnt was that Wymeersch's avoidance of risk seemed to have deserted him in the illusory safety of this suburb.

Not perhaps, then, as smart as Bébé had assumed. But then Bébé believed everyone was as inertly cautious as he was.

He was sitting in the driver's seat despondently pushing slices of salted calentica into his mouth.

He sprayed me with batter shrapnel as I got in beside him. He pointed a greasy finger at me. He reckoned this was a mission for Delta. He was going back to where he might be useful . . . He offered me the van if I really wanted to stay. I could keep it for the moment. It might get picked up. It was stolen. Did he think that I didn't know? *Le gougnafier* . . .

★

He had three times more chins than I had. He was three years my senior and old enough then to underestimate me, to feel he had the right to patronise me. He advised me to 'face facts'. Wymeersch was a big cheese, too big for us (he meant too big for him, for Bébé). When I wasn't facing facts I should be considering that he was such a big big cheese that . . . only one of Degueldre's Delta commando squads could achieve constructive perfection. I was, he accused, insulting Degueldre (whom I had never met. I looked up to him – but he was a soldier and this did not demand a martial resolution. It demanded quiet cunning.).

Bébé couldn't see that we had every advantage over the quarry who doesn't know he is quarry, who has let his guard down, who takes the same route every night, who is comfortable, complacent, careless, a sitting duck . . .

Bébé insisted that two nights is not a pattern. He held up two even greasier fingers as an insulting aid to my numeracy. Two, in his opinion, proved nothing.

This occurred to me: when he had told me with such certainty how to help my first love over the line – fire diagonally, entry above the left eye, exit behind the right ear – he had, maybe, not based his advice on first-hand field experience but on something he had read in the manuals he self-importantly quoted, *Theory and Practice of Counter-Insurgency, Intelligence Resources: A User's Guide*, that sort of thing.

Les Cars Chausson ran a reliable service no matter what terror they had to navigate. We were near the start of route 23. The reluctant assassin handed me his pistol. He was looking forward to his mother's mechoui. He leeringly, conspiratorially, wished me good luck with *la p'tite nana*. He told me in lubricious detail what he would do with her if he had the chance. He was grosser than ever. He set off across another abandoned building site towards the bus stop.

He was beside two high piles of wooden scaffolding planks when he turned abruptly. He was evidently puzzled that I should be following him. Alea jacta est. Maybe he understood. My already bruised hand stung. I never saw him again.

Did you ever laze on a quayside watching boats at work, breathing in the grating scent of their outboards' fuel, listening to screaming gulls and strumming halyards, eating churros and drinking chocolate then setting out to exact vengeance on behalf of your people, your land, your history? On behalf of probity and of all that is ethically beyond doubt. The sugar, heat, crispness, oil, dense unctuousness give you strength. They are weapons.

I knew this was going to be my day. I knew because of probability, because of discerning a behaviour pattern, because you get hunches when patterns are repeated till they are the rule and they take control. It's like when riding a bicycle or swimming becomes first nature, no longer something that had to be learnt. From the van I observed 5 avenue des Albizias throughout the day.

My concentration and high purpose watchfulness were not hampered by Marie-Yvonne twisting her hair, asking questions: why do you sleep in a van . . . do you have a home . . . where do you make your communion (again) . . . have you had a girl yet . . . can you sail . . . do you play canasta . . . are you an orphan . . . why is your hand so bruised . . . what are you doing here . . . do you know what an alpaca is . . . have you been to Paris . . . ?

She did not insist on answers. She might have been talking to herself.
What was *she* doing here? Her 'friends' seemed hardly to know her. They didn't look out for her. They came and went. Fine. Most people would consider two teenagers in a van natural. The way of the adolescent world. Just enough privacy. Second nature, though not *my* second nature.
I was working on the disposition of the house to the road, and a vehicle on the road's relationship to the house.

There was activity in the target zone. I held up an important arm to mute her. A Jeep camouflaged for operations in another climate, say the lush green Ardennes on geography classroom posters, turned into avenue des Albizias and stopped outside no. 5. The vehicle was a boast. A token of hubris and ostentation. Wymeersch and the Mordhund jumped out. The driver handed him a tan and navy couturier's bag wrapped with a tan and navy striped ribbon. He appeared to joke with the driver, tapped him on the shoulder in a jocular male way then went through the pedestrian gate.

I replayed the couturier's bag over and over. I read the situation. I depth-focused it the way Madame Ortéga-Nagy would. I imaged it. The bag might as well have been a semaphore.

I asked Marie-Yvonne whether she could drive. I turned from the driver's seat to where, to my disgust, she sat on my sleeping bag painting her toenails.

She was indignant that I should ask. *Of course* she could drive. Her brother let her drive their father's car when she was nine years old. She offered to show me.

She needed a cushion to lift her high enough to see through the windshield. I told her to take whatever route she wished. We went towards Ain-Taya. She drove well enough for what was needed.

I shouted instructions to test her responses. Then put her at her ease, encouraging her to relax, lulling. Which she didn't. When I suddenly screamed at her to turn round as quick as she could she reacted smartly. A straight stretch of road past the lizard-infested ruins, palms on one side, the sugar refinery's towering silos on the other. She did a handbrake turn. The van tilted perilously. A lorry driver, forced to brake, yelled at her. The smell of burning rubber excited my nose. The scene alarmed two idle kerbside bleds selling gourds. They wore the newly common expression that said we are in control now. Ha! What seeds of delusion are sown by Ramalama and his prophet son the kiddy-fiddling warrior rapist.

★

She asked me if I was an orphan. She said that she was – probably. She spoke calmly. She slowed the car. Pulled off the highway. She twisted her hair. She pointed to a sprawling building just visible among cypresses and cedars high up a slope the other side of a crumbling wall. It was, she said, her family's house. She was scared to return to it. She was staying with a neighbour whom she disliked. It was almost as bad as being alone with ghosts who had only silhouettes. Their faces disappeared when they turned in unison towards her screaming.

Her brother was a probationary teacher in Ghardaïa. The Ligne de Hoggar bus that he was travelling home on had disappeared. Her parents had set out to find him. There had been no word from any of them. It was ten and a half days since her parents went. She was holding back tears.

I realised I should be feeling sorry for her, making a demonstrative show of sympathy. I thought about holding her hand but on practical reflection decided against it because I would have nowhere to wash after. Furthermore it is a drably conventional gesture that means nothing. Which I believed she would understand.

Did I want to see the house? To see her room? She would be OK in the house with me there. I feared her dependence. She had work to do for me. I was determined that we should get back as soon as possible now she had proved her driving to my satisfaction. I told her my job demanded it. She was taken aback by my professionalism. She drove the van like she was driving a sports car. She told me that I was the only person who had been kind to her for ten and a half days. We returned to the scrapland to wait and wait and wait. And talk. The more she talked the less likely she was to lose concentration.

She said: I like what boys want to do with me . . . it's wonderful feeling for me . . . I don't care that for them it's only so they can go boast . . . go tell their friends what they did like it's a competitive arena . . . officially I only meet ten or twelve boys but there are always the others just hanging around the bushes watching or snooping in the house – I used to find this activity area troubling . . . but I'm OK now with it . . . I make my confession . . . you know Yoni you're different . . . I see you don't want to be with me . . . I ask myself is that because you are you are Jew . . . I can tell . . . no worries, I'm not minding Jew. Enrico Macias is Jew.

That was generous, that *not minding*, that was gracious. I should have been indignant, racially slurred. Instead I had to hold back laughter. Besides, I didn't want to carelessly reproach her so that she'd be antagonised and uncooperative. She was essential to my strategy now Bébé was no more.

She said: I want to get married so I can have all the time in the world with a boy being with me with god's blessing . . . all the time in the world. I am unblessed till then. My wedding dress will be white for purity. You could marry me if you want . . . I will be a virgin for you . . . I'll be a virgin again when I marry. My hymen will be reconstructed for you by the famous Doctor Spencer Prestige – my father was in medical school with him . . .

Remember! We were in an airless van surrounded by broken plasterboard, glass daggers, ripped mattresses and splintered window frames watching for the man I was going to help along the way . . . and an increasingly infantile adolescent was suggesting I marry her . . . She must have been mad with distress, a common fate in the country that has just been forced to commit assisted suicide, that has just been visited by the League of Endless Sleep.

My parents, she went on, my parents . . . also I want to get married . . . *because* . . . my parents and brother are missing . . . what if the worst . . . they could be murdered . . . they could be . . . I need someone to live in the house with me . . . I'll observe your thing – shabbat. I promise. Her eyes pleaded with me.

I lied. I told her that we shall see, that I needed time to reflect, that first she must accompany me, must drive me to my task. I lied on behalf of my people. I lied because I lacked what we are taught is a natural instinct – to pair, to bond, to physically exhibit generative disparities, to relish their union – was not natural instinct to me. It was alien to me. I was sensitive to the ubiquity of the products of that exhibition and union: humans, millions of 'fellow' humans. Though fellowship is frailty based on the delusion that two are twice as strong as one. They are not, they are both diminished by a half. Teams are where the weak hide. Humans are animals, everywhere begot by animal behaviour, everywhere vectoring animal diseases. Incontinent and savage brutes. See how kebas reproduce, see how they obey without question, obey without thought because obedience is the enemy of thought, it replaces thought with dogma before thought's germ can assert itself. These are examples of natural behaviour, programmed habits, authentic mores that can be suppressed only by education, learning and definitive intervention.

I was right. I knew it. Visualisation had told me Wymeersch would appear with a woman dressed in her birthday present. I didn't know that it would be a pencil skirt and matching bolero with raglan sleeves that didn't reach the wrists. The fabric appeared in the distance in the fading light to be blue-green shantung, petrol in a puddle. Chic. Not to be despoiled. She waited beside the pedestrian door while he went to the garage. The Mordhund's tongue drooped.

Wymeersch reversed an open-top pink Caravelle from the garage. Where you're going your past will be there to greet you when you arrive.

Go go go, I said to Marie-Yvonne. Foot down, screaming tyres – then two sugar tankers lumbered ponderously in front of us. They precluded our advance, they hid the target. She braked so hard I was thrown forward against the dash. The sense of opportunity lost urged me on. I told her to follow them. That sports car was quicker than a van aspiring to be a sports car. It headed towards La Pérouse, two human silhouettes with the dog between them. When we arrived they were nowhere to be seen but the Caravelle was parked across the street from Les Ondines, the blowsiest of our city's streamlined venues. *Partout on mange, mais aux Ondines on dîne.* A place where the oblivious whiled away what they failed to realise were their last days. Oysters and cha cha cha – that's how civilisation ends.

We drove past slowly but not too slowly, turned and drove back. As I expected I couldn't see them from the van. It was an inappropriate vehicle, a giveaway, so shabby it might have been designed to be noticed at such a place. I told Marie-Yvonne to keep the engine running. The Skorpion machine pistol was too large to fully fit in a pocket. That's where I put the extra magazine. I had to get out of the van holding the pistol. Only then could I snag it in my belt inside my charcoal and white houndstooth jacket. I wore heavy wrap-round dark glasses, a black scarf and what my mother called my Apache cap. I was embarrassed by how young I was. I felt I would stand out, this was not a place for people of my age. They were still dancing the cha cha cha after all. That was my only fear . . . no, not fear, worry. Worry that I and the van would attract attention before I had time to terminate disinfection. Aproned waiters abounded. True to their calling, they failed to observe anyone trying to catch their eye let alone a figure of justice who sought invisibility. I walked past the bar, past a band of etiolated porkers in tight tuxedos setting up its instruments beside the small dance floor. The main restaurant. An all-glass wall overlooking the beach and bay. On the other side a mural of a gruesomely bloated female sea monster, a sort of Madame Ortéga-Nagy with mother of pearl scales, conjunctivitis and scores of tentacles, each ending in a mouthful of pointed teeth, wrapped about a youth clutching a trident. Circular blue neon strip lights shone down on blue leatherette banquettes and a blue and gold tessellated floor. Money had been spent to make it look cheap.

Three-quarters of the tables were occupied yet it was quiet. A particular heavy hush as if it were forbidden to raise your voice. The tension of those days was palpable. People drank in search of oblivion. Hoping to shut out the nightmare that could never end. Whispering, vinegary faces, everyone on the qui vive, waiting for the unknown, in limbo. Without letting on to themselves, not knowing what was going to be, trying to believe that despite years of attrition and the great betrayal and the sudden jolt of the massacre in rue d'Isly they still had a future in our land. I was going to feign searching for someone, some group. I realised I need not bother given the self-preoccupation of the diners. Of course I was looking for someone. It didn't need to be advertised. The end of the room was open to a terrace, wedge-shaped because of a flight of stairs cut in the rocks down to the beach.

I strolled towards it.

My quarry, from close to, two metres away, was the very picture – a caricature even – of the leathery blond Nordic type that believes it should rule the world, that is so entitled to gas and garotte due to its proud mythical heredity. From the corner of my eye as I gaped about me I saw him glance at me. Nothing about me alerted him, he continued talking. He felt no frisson. Nor did the dog, slumped beside him, panting. The woman was elegant. The corners of her mouth were severely downturned. Her face proclaimed her unworthiness. The three creatures were posed on a banquette, staring out to sea. They were side by side by side, their left side to me, lit by blue light. They had not even ordered an apero. They would not have the chance to.

He was obscured. The woman and the dog between him and me. I glanced at my watch, I was feigning now, shaking my head at my imaginary friend's lateness. I turned towards the muralled wall to pull the pistol from my belt unobserved. I held it under my jacket. As I raised it and fired she leaned forward to pick a snack from a bowl on the table. I shot her. Brain and bone and blood and toasted chickpeas struck his astonished face. I had time to take in the frozen tableau before I fired again. The pink-eyed dog was sniffing the air. The woman was sprawled across the dog's flank. Wymeersch was in the act of reaching in his jacket. I fired again. I was shooting him on behalf of all his victims. The shot's blow hurled him from the banquette. Up, up, high – then down. He fell trying to clutch his throat but not finding it. New decor: the woman was no longer on the dog but on Wymeersch's hip. His head was somewhere beyond the far end of the banquette. I didn't know where he was struck. His army-booted foot was on the table – how? I fired again. I fired again. He

57

fired his pistol. Anywhere: he had already lost his mental discipline. Now his motor functions were fleeing. The world was tipped from under him. The spinning chaos of a shoot. The speed of it. Vortex angles when you are under fire and the space denounces gravity. A large pane of glass made an elegant bow as it tipped and turned into violently erupting shards. The albino Mordhund came arcing through the air to open up my left cheek. It took away part of my face. Its last memory of violence towards my people was making a window in my left cheek. The wound whose deathly white scar I still bear was inflicted by gleaming enhanced canines polished by its doting master, companion in murder. Its claws merely drew furrowed weals across my chest. I believe that is what happened. But I don't know. Never will. I have often replayed it. The cascade of glycerine-thick slaver from its gums. The scar still stings, still prompts second glances. It is also a barometer. It tells me when rain is coming. My blood smeared the foul creature when I shot its chest. And it still attacked. And again I shot. This time the tautness abated. The table took its terrible weight. Here's another metal gift for M. Joris Wymeersch. A gun had appeared in his left hand. Waving weakly beyond the woman's body. His head would appear again from the floor beyond the banquette. It did appear, bemused and insulted at his nemesis's impudence.

Nothing like this had ever happened to him before. Nothing like this would ever happen to him again. My aim was good. I made a hole in his face where his left eye had been all his life till that moment. His tongue rushed out of his mouth, curling, foaming pink spittle, wanting to call for help, failing. He disappeared behind his dead woman.

I was made of ice. I changed the magazine. I turned to regard the restaurant. These people's fate was my choice. Faces of fear. With coordinated collectivity they fell to the floor, heads in hands.

It was Judex that sauntered through that silenced room. Judex, invincible harbinger of right. Protected by his aura. I was outside him . . .

He let off shots. Gentle warnings. Struck neon exploded in a storm. A nerveless walk, the longest walk – and he could not be touched.

He had the power of life and death over these people. The clickclack of spent rounds bouncing like deadly hail in the aftermath of a report. That's music. And he walked tall so no one would dare impede him. Walked forwards, walked backwards, the pistol's wire stock now against his shoulder, now at arm's length. The threat of threat. They sheltered on the floor, clutching, clinging together, hugging. They were five-backed beasts evacuating shit and humiliation. The room stank of unprocessed seafood. Treyf. Some, believing themselves invisible beneath tables and cowering, held up napkins, waved them as white flags. A defeatist puppet show. They knew the score – it's what they had done for years. Did they deserve the country they were not prepared to fight for? Which Judex was prepared to fight for? They couldn't see.

Poor barman, bold barman. He was scrabbling for a weapon in a freezer cupboard behind the bar. Foolish barman. An exception in cowardice's domain. He ought not to have risked it. A bevelled peach mirror turned into bloody shrapnel. He didn't have what it takes to play at this level. Collateral . . . as no one said in those days. The smell of war was invigorating. It scrapes the nostrils. It's a delicious rushing balm. Scorched blood and scalded bone. An intact pane of mirror told me my face was falling apart. I tore the telephone cord from the wall.

Marie-Yvonne drove calmly. Not recklessly. Not wanting to attract attention. I bled profusely. My grey giraffe collar shirt and black jeans were stained. Thankfully my jacket was untouched because I had worn a scarf. There was little pain but I needed a bandage, a suture, something. Maybe a rabies injection. Certainly a place to hide. I had to go to the mattresses.

There would soon be roadblocks everywhere. There was no question of getting back to the city unimpeded. I told her to go to her parents' house. Past the scrapland, past the corner of avenue des Albizias, past the no. 23 bus stop, past the building site where a kettle of black sea-vultures (*Coragyps tracheliotus*) was gathering, circling, darkening the sky above the piles of scaffolding planks, awaiting their turn after the first sitting below had had its fill between fighting off the packs of pi-dogs. Once we were past Le Beau Rivage we were off the route between the Schlagergesselschaft's barracks, where the multiple sirens were coming from, and La Pérouse, where they were speeding to. The less they shrieked the safer I was, for the moment. How long would that moment last?

She asked me who the man was that I had shot.

Off the main road, a sandy lane led through a tunnel of skewbald eucalypti picked out one by one by the headlights. The house was flash sprawl. Twenties Castanets-and-Mantilla style. Pantiles, palms, tall sculpted chimneys, galleries – make that romantic galleries. It recalled something I had never seen. A folly that belonged to an era of security and servants. I told her he wasn't a man but an animal. An animal whose tribe would attempt to avenge its leader.

She drove the van into what looked like a carriage house. The roof was partly glazed. Birds nesting in the eaves scattered in panic. Their shit was everywhere. It was disgusting. There were old chairs on their sides, wardrobes, teetering columns of magazines, rusty harrows and hoes, rodents scurrying in crumbling blankets shitting their venom pellets. From the centre of a broken pane spread a web of cracks like scrambled runes. The wreck of a holed-hull motor boat rested on a towing trailer. She told me later: the building was originally a studio, designed for himself by the Australian artist Linsel Murly when he was paid unprecedentedly high fees for designing and making stained glass for the new churches programme initiated by Archbishop Combes and expanded by Archbishop Leynaud: Saint Francis Xavier, Sacré-Coeur d'Alger, Notre-Dame de l'Océan and Saint Augustin at Annaba. They resembled tabers and were intended to attract the barbarians, to persuade them to convert. Small chance. The age of *moriscos* was long past. It would not come by again. The well-meaning idiocy of these people!

While she dressed my wound I told her about Leynaud's successor, the traitorous Archbishop, soon to be Cardinal, Léon-Etienne

Mohammed Ben Duval, an ecumenicist fellow traveller of the FLN. He enjoyed his own god's protection and Ramalama's too. This Judas shit-slime escapes four attempts to hurry him up to heaven. His luckiest escape would be in Rome when a nicely prepared commando led by Jean de Brem is thwarted by a hailstorm. Ice golf balls were hurled from the sky. Maybe it was merely unprecedented weather. If it was divine intervention god was showing that he is biased in favour of his fellow paedophiles. With their visibility reduced, the shooters mistake police horses for cardinals.

Marie-Yvonne, concentrating on ministering me, misunderstood or misheard. She was impressed that I had been a member in de Brem's commando. (I hadn't.) She called me a hero. After she wiped my cheek with alcohol she applied the largest plaster she could find, she cut gauze exactly, she attempted to suture the wound with an adhesive bandage. The suture was crude. It wouldn't last long.

I slumped on a chaise longue dizzy from fatigue, exhilarated by my affirmation of my vocation, itching, struggling to keep my head still, alive, all alive. I repeatedly told her that I must see a doctor. I was familiar from my father's library with the effects of rabies. She went to another room to telephone a doctor who lived not far away. He could be trusted. He would come in thirty minutes. 'When he has finished his puzzle.'

The once luxurious house was now run-down and unkempt. I feared the chaise longue harboured fleas or bedbugs. I swatted randomly. The floor was strewn with mangey pale pelts. The decoration was sleek, not as Hispanic as the exterior. Cracked Vitrolite, desiccated 'classical' marquetry curlingly unglued from its base, black marble. Foxed mirrors floor to ceiling doubled the room. It can hardly have changed since Linsel Murly transformed the harmless villa that had stood on the site. That was now indiscernible, buried beneath all the fol de rol extensions and bizarre caprices. There was a repetitive frieze of the horned piper Pan, a leering hunter chasing, catching, violating nymphs and well-fattened cherubs. The usual penetrative force and submissive reception. Bodies risking disease, dislocations and sciatica for momentary pleasure and the proliferation of this benighted species.

★

On a shelf of framed family photos I was surprised to see a familiar one of Doctor Ortéga-Nagy memorably dressed in baggy trousers and a lace-up shirt holding one handle of a sporting trophy, the other held by a rangy young man.

'He's a good friend of my father,' she replied. 'That's my father. When he was young . . . I love going to his house . . . Madame always tells my fortune.'

There was a framed illustration on an easel, incomplete. Found abandoned and gnawed in Murly's studio. Dazzling bright colours despite the conditions it had been kept in. A haggard, sweating, bad-tempered Jesus, crowned with barbed wire, suffering under the weight of the cross, was vindictively passing down a sentence on a handsome sleek raven-black-haired youth in a half-drawn tunic who has just jabbed him on his way with a richly ornamented stick.

In the top right corner a decorative lozenge in English, an exaggerated italic script, letters wrapped in ivy:

> *I shalt here remain —*
> *Thou diest not till I come again.*
> Percy Bysshe Shelley

Her parents must be rich to own a house like this, I thought. She screwed up her face. They weren't rich. They were desperate to show off with an unusual house. Competing with the Ortéga-Nagys. They had bought it because no one else wanted it. The price was absurdly low. It had remained empty for many years. It was infamous. People were scared. She hated it. It was haunted by its future inhabitants. Buildings' histories are invitations to irreason. Linsel Murly and his complicated 'family' had absconded before they were detained. Algeria even then had been a place to flee.

The 'doctor' was not a doctor. He was a drunken veterinary surgeon, a foetid octogenarian. Alphonse-Blaise Roumieu reeked of brandy. His suit was sordid, shiny, sticky. He wore several matted cardigans and pyjamas beneath them. Marie-Yvonne kissed him fondly. His

abnormally long fingers and ridged nails stroked her cheeks. He scrutinised me. His smile was a henge of scorched stumps.

He warned knowingly that I could be in grave trouble. Had I heard
the news? he lisped insinuatingly. Had I heard the news?

He demanded 150 NF: he had come out at night, he was banned
from driving.

I had heard the news. Marie-Yvonne, keen, went to search for
money in her father's study.

He smiled: he recognised me. I was the already notorious Alfasi,
the baby of the Organisation.

He had heard all about me, how I was recruiting children even
younger than me as messengers. (I resented being called a child.)

He told me that I armed them, bullied eight-year-olds to throw
grenades indiscriminately in markets and on buses.

Yes . . . I was proud of my achievements – I had wanted to be a child
soldier, I was too old. I was proud to give my juniors a chance, a life
start in retaliation and fieldcraft. Kids like Jean-Pax. But I was
alarmed that he knew anything about me.

Maybe he had guessed I was responsible for what Radio Alger, still in
the hands of the Organisation, had just described as 'a moral settling
of scores and a warning that we strike where we want when we want'.
I found a bottle of fig eau-de-vie. Placed it enticingly on a grand
piano whose white paint had flaked. He began work when he had
counted and pocketed the notes Marie-Yvonne handed him.

He stitched my cheek, ineptly, painfully, while telling me of his
adventures as a yachtsman. I winced hard on a handkerchief. The scar
is a souvenir of là-bas. It has greeted me, every me, every day of my
life. I have lost count of the number of people who assume that I am
an alumnus of Heidelberg University or a duellist. Let them believe
what they will. I seldom explain that I am a lifetime pariah from là-
bas, down there, which is where heaven was before it became hell and
truly figuratively là-bas: I prefer to invent my provenance. A Jew moves.

★

He was equally clumsy administering the injection in my upper arm. The syringe was old worn electroplate. Ideal for sheep, goats, camels. He snapped a vial neck and poured its contents into it. The needle hurt. Sheep, goats, camels don't know how to complain. He warned that I might be delirious for a while, dazed. I was. I was dizzy. My balance was not true. I felt I was stumbling even though I was standing still. I felt I was pushing through night, a dark dense liquid that left no trace of damp.

He asked Marie-Yvonne to entertain him as she used to. In those days oh in those days he took her on his little dinghy round bays and coves, past headlands. She did what he asked. She adored the sea, his beard, his oiled pullover. When it was done he drank and she sunbathed.

He reached for the eau-de-vie. He watched greedily as she danced to Gillian Hills's lovely silly giggly '*En Dansant Le Twist*'. He turned to me with a lubricious grin, a proprietorial smirk. He claimed that she danced even better than this when she was little. Watch her dance on the boat, the *Glasspar Del Mar*. '*Chien dans la Vitrine*' had been her favourite song. He had provided the barking sounds that echoed across the mute water. She had been like a performing bitch from the Cirque Fernando. That was the highest accolade he could grant.

She had been so trusting, so grateful for his applause, so comforted by his extra cuddles, so ready to help with his countless jigsaw puzzles showing scenes of the riverside life of a temperate country, his country, our country, where a boy might fish in peace seated on a willow stump with his stout wicker basket beside him.

Invented scenes that returned to me, that I dreamed of . . . with the Cirque Fernando's tents parked beside a thick green river bridged by medieval arches. The opaque reedy still cool water where sly pike lurked, ambushing their offspring and eating them. Then there was already a pall of sticky haze. The raggedy troupers had set camp between the river and a drowsy orchard. The meadow was bright with cowslips and buttercups. There were tents with fringes and oriflammes, caravans and gaudy coaches.

★

When I woke I was hearing accordions, fiddles and harmonicas. I was no longer on the chaise longue. I was on a cold surface. Marie-Yvonne stood over me. She was naked. I found that problematic. I realised I had never knowingly seen a cowslip or a buttercup.

I looked around the room. I lifted my head from the tiled floor I was supine on. Laid out in dreamstate. Post-anaesthesia anyway. Doctor Roumieu was on the chaise longue. He seemed to be in a bit of trouble with his head. Hair matted with lots of blood . . . blood on the bolster, blood on a cushion, blood on a throw, blood on the rug. He was motionless, half over the side of the sofa. The disgusting decrepit creature had evacuated himself. His trousers were soaked, discolouring. His head was stoved in, not wholly holed but near.

'Bonce blight' as the English are wont to put it. Did I know that then? I did not.
    I was still hallucinating? Was I?
    'What happened?' I asked.
    She looked at me like I was loufoque.
    '*What happened?*' I asked again.
    'What happened . . .' She shook her head disbelieving. Then, as to a child: 'What do you mean what happened? You hit him. Don't you remember . . . with the statue . . . you hit him with the statue.'
    'Statue. Statue?' I felt I was missing something.

Where does time go when you are anaesthetised? It doesn't *go*. Anaesthesia tells us that time isn't, never was. It is to time what atheism is to theolatry. Time's an invention: there is no definitive division of the indivisible – Lenin had a calendar, Stalin had another; the English rioted when eleven days were 'stolen'; we French had ten decimal hours of a hundred decimal minutes and months whose names spell tyranny. Then there were the Aztecs, the Eskimos, the Parsis – each with their own time. The invention is meaningless. Time's ineluctable progress is a delusion. Time doesn't flow, water does – or is meant to. The order of clocktime collapses. Anaesthesia is a premonition of death, a free sample – please place your spoon in the bin provided after use. When you die the world itself dies with you.

Look at it that way – it may be selfish but it's comforting. No interior world, no exterior.

'Statue, statue.' Echoes from somewhere.

She pointed. On the floor lay a hefty metal figurine of what I learnt to call the If-It's-African-Inspired-It-Must-Be-Good school of European self-hatred. There was blood on the face and body armour. Brass? Bronze? What? The material was concerning me more than the blood. When it all breaks down, when it all caves in around us we are strangers to ourselves, preoccupied by farfelus we never knew we carried within us.

I heard myself ask: 'What's it made of?'

When it all breaks down we are strangers to others too. She suddenly seemed much older. I think that was because she stood over me. She was accusatory in a way only the naked can be:

'I liked being touched by him . . . he always touches me. That's how we were. Ever since I was a kid he touches me – he was my special uncle type friend. You couldn't understand. You wanted to protect me from him but I didn't want to be protected from him, I just wanted to dance for him . . . he's an old man, he's got a mad screaming wife in Blida . . . she's in a straitjacket half the time . . . I'm his treat. Not much of a life, is it . . . jigsaw after jigsaw . . . it's good to have compassion . . . good to let him touch me if he wants . . . his little sister of charity, that's what he called me.'

He had besmirched my night of triumph. I was a victor. I should have been celebrating. Joris Wymeersch was dead. Doctor Roumieu had contaminated a Satisfactory Outcome with sly intimations of blackmail, of informing on me, even though I was acting for him too. How did he expect to be treated by the conquering *bougnous*? His ingratitude was offensive. I congratulated my unconscious self on the judgement it had made. I hadn't even been operational.

★

66

'What are we going to do with him?' she asked. 'You can be a ruthless person, I can tell from your eyes – they don't look real.'

My eyes are for sure startlingly liquid zircon. They startle even me.

'What are *you* going to do? Do you want to touch me?'

I was astonished. Nothing could have been further from my mind. My face evidently showed that.

'I helped you. You could . . .'

I thought of my father's library, of Prynne Owen Prynne's forbidden classic *Milady Gleet's Greeting to Pokey Jiggy-Boum*. I considered her urchin friends. I feared that her generative organs were a hostel for pubic lice, burrowing, laying eggs, searching for fresh territories to invade. I recalled a hand-coloured photo of one malevolent beast so huge magnified it might have been found as a centrepiece at Pierrot Prince des Coquillages and equally in the pages of *Malédictions*. I imagined worse lay within.

She whined: 'I'm so frightened . . . I'm alone . . . I can't believe they will ever come back. I miss them so much . . . I miss their love. I want affection, love.'

She looked at me pleadingly.

Love – a meaningless word, I thought then, I think now. Showing affection by mixing salivas. Touching and hugging are means of vectoring rashes and buboes. Sharing . . . Why? These are things lower grades – subs, people from housing projects, unters, *beurs* – apparently experience in their sentimental incontinence. But for us higher humans it's a learnt experience, a social rite, a programmed state that is expected of us at a certain stage of life. But conditioning can be resisted, unlearnt, ignored.

Then she began to cry. She was vulnerable. Her being was an open wound. She knelt beside me. I didn't dislike her. Indeed she was kind, obedient, moderately attractive, not entirely stupid. She smelled warm and comforting. But I did not want to touch her. Nor did I want her to touch me. I summoned up a crisp asperity to tell her so. She didn't challenge me. I made one concession.

The young women, not much older than Marie-Yvonne, who pout and strut and gaze – wantonly! insolently! – at the camera in *Crevasse, Abricot Mousse, Cocotte, Hypoclito, Les Pipes d'Antan* were undeniably arousing because they were unknowable, anonymous, impersonal, masked by a false name, never to be encountered. They inhabited a separate monochrome world where no touching was possible. No one ever leapt off a page: not from *Atala* and *René* nor, a long way distant, from *Baby Fesses*. I've kept sex that way, forever monochrome, forever anonymous. The only admissible touching was self-celebration.

I did not explain that I feared infection or infestation. Nor that kissing was as fraught with germ-threat as vaginal or anal sojourns. It would have been discourteous, ungentlemanly, to raise the matter of disease's versatility.

We would lie together like the doting siblings Petr and Petra beneath the quilt of kindly doves' feathers in the fairy tale. She was bemused but considered this acceptable. I also feared the possibility of Marie-Yvonne buffing up her button (the expression is from *La Moustache Écossaise de Madame Gouine*). Doctor Roumieu's dead eyes watched us. They were the sort of eyes that tiresomely follow you round the room. Firing a small arm is more thrilling than contact. It sends a charge through you. I thought of exploding lorries, walls tumbling, death coming to greet the whore in Parc Guerland, fire's dragon whoosh, the back of Bébé's head, destruction's eager crackle, the Sabena bag, Wymeersch's surprise, la Grande Zohra swinging from a buckling gibbet.

It was a pleasing result after the jolt of my oblivioned engagement with Doctor Roumieu. I reprimanded myself for causing the old quack terminal offence without intending to. But he can't have had much life left in him anyway. And I was exhilarated that he noseyparkered from the other side, though without coitus there is no sadness to share, only mild desolation. We had crammed him into a cupboard with a vacuum cleaner, dusters, sponges, mop, bucket, brushes, bleach.

Tuesday, 3 April 1962

That was the day Zohra le Dégueulasse spoke of the Harkis as a 'magma of good for nothing auxiliaries to be got rid of forthwith', so condemning them, 150,000 soldiers of France, to certain death at the hands of his new friends of the FLN. Their families and even their villages would be murdered too.

It is not, however, for that act of presidential cowardice or statesmanlike cruelty that I remember that day. Black Tuesday.

'*Whatever* are you wearing, Yoni?' my mother laughed at Marie-Yvonne's father's suit, baggily cut for an apparently colour-blind man taller and bulkier than me. It embarrassed me to wear such clothes. It embarrassed me to wear his homburg hat. But wearing those clothes and dark glasses got us through the roadblocks in Doctor Roumieu's reeking old Peugeot, now parked outside, an object of curiosity with the *pecnauds*.

'And whatever have you done to your face?'

My mother had never seen me with a girl before. She was more curious about Marie-Yvonne than she was about my wound. She wasn't sure what to do so I offered her a tisane. Then suggested she might like a dash of rum in it. Marie-Yvonne declined.

My mother asked rather flirtatiously: 'Ah . . . has he been lecturing you then?'

This presumption of intimacy was embarrassing. I went to change into clean clothes. The house smelled different. It was full of packed boxes, tea chests, suitcases, trunks, bursting sacks you had to squeeze between. My bed was piled high with my clothes. My books and records were in boxes. The walls were mute maps of what had been pasted on them. The furniture, carpet, mirror and curtains would stay. No room for the bulk. The past was the past. Gone. This was no longer home. This was someone else's house, a stranger's. It would soon belong to the valiant thieves, the burnoosed parasites, the self-styled victims who are doomed to succeed. They transmute into victors. Hermit crabs squat in other species' shells. They cannot change their preordained behaviour.

We can. We are lifetime pariahs. Forever the little people from là-bas, down there, deep down there, the people from the hell that once was heaven. Whatever we have, we have nothing to compare with what we lost. Lost! It was taken from us.

Caste exists in France. We were outcaste.

But we can change. We have changed.

Our possessions were too many for the car. My father had part-exchanged it for a Renault 1,000kg van. (I could have saved him the money and stolen it.) He had a ferry ticket, which he persistently inspected as though he couldn't believe his eyes that he had won a lottery. He hadn't. Towards the end of the two sweaty hours it took to finish loading it he asked me about Marie-Yvonne. I replied that her parents and brother were missing, that I would take her to some people who would look after her till her family returned, that I now needed to change clothes again.

He was on the point of making a man-to-man gesture to indicate that his smooth-skinned, newly scarred son was now a man but he looked into my deathly eyes and reconsidered. Instead he clapped me on the shoulder and reminded me of what my mother had said several times, that I must be ready to leave that evening at 21.00.

I went to my room, my former room, to change. My mother asked me to sort out my clothes. She couldn't figure my delight in clothes, in the clothes that she had once worn. She didn't understand my devoted appreciation of them nor that my pride in her depended on what she wore. To her they were no more than things to be worn then discarded. For me throwing away clothes is throwing away my skin's memories. Divesting a part of myself. A denial of who I am, who I was. I wanted to keep everything I had ever worn. Here's a grey and tan cotton jersey zip-front shirt from when I was six. Here's a pair of black jeans with green stitching, a belt with a plastic buckle in the form of a Colt 45, chipped but still charged with tales. I dallied.

There was animation across the usually mute street. Doctor Roumieu's twenty-five-year-old condemned slum on wheels was parked in front of the house. The Dib brothers had arrived to inspect it with disdain. They were granting themselves status. They were becoming discriminate. From now on only the best will do, only the most up to date. Two-tone paintwork and whitewall tyres.

The apparent elders of this ragged group from the bled were otherwise preoccupied. I watched as they capitulated at a rancorous discussion with the Dib brothers. Apart from when their voices were high-raised I couldn't hear them. I didn't need to. They were arguing over our house, our house, in public, without shame – they are absolved from shame by their submissive faith, obedience, precious destiny, bogus free will, lifelong mental imprisonment. They have evolving to do. Had Ramalama taken Europe, France would not have been enlightened. Nor would Scotland too. We'd still have been scraping our shit from our arses with our hands as these barbarians do during the festival of falnadath.

Bled gesticulates to town. Ragged peasant *pecnauds* outwitted by sly *voyous* trying to dress like *babtous* in market stall clothes and leatherette pickers. There was anxiety and mystification among the group. A reluctance, though, to join the squabble. The Dibs' aggression was for sure not matched by the majority of the bemused group. The Dibs were braggart know-alls. They pointed at the house proprietorially. They pointed repeatedly. Bami stared at me, tried to frighten me. I laughed at him. He explained my insolence to Houchi who tried to stare: Ramalama the divine oculist had blessed the loutish creature with such wall eyes that he gaped anywhere but at me.

★

71

They shook their heads in disbelief with the *pecnauds'* incomprehension, they feigned their own incomprehension at the *pecnauds'* failure to understand this: you do not bring the ways of the bled to the town. There's a different form in town, different rules apply. The Dibs were making up the drill as they went along. Houchi jabbed his cigarette in a wooden-legged cripple's face. He incited no response. He was winning. He stroked Doctor Roumieu's car.

'I shall see you later.'

My mother advanced towards me arms spread wide. I blew a kiss at her rather than get involved in all that stuff.

I called to my father: 'I won't be late. Promise!'

He was in his surgery. He didn't look up. He was preoccupied sorting through the drawer where he kept our passports, identity cards, insurance policies, bank details etc. He was putting files into his capacious leather medical bag.

A framed colour photograph of his yacht *Le Wassermann* lay on the floor beside it. I knew how much he would miss it. The ticket was in the back pocket of his trousers. He waved a hand in acknowledgement.

'OK!'

Something fast and tiny sped by my eyes. I turned: nothing.

Because of the unprecedented febrility in the street we left the house by the back. I struggled with her big suitcase, Marie-Yvonne carried the smaller and her duffel bag. In those days everyone, infamously, had a suitcase.

'Yoni, I knew you were coming! Marie-Yvonne . . .' caressed Madame Ortéga-Nagy after she had opened the shrieking door, just, but before she saw us. Her little ruse was to pretend to have foreseen our unannounced arrival.

I had telephoned her to explain Marie-Yvonne's predicament. Why, when she did have genuine predictive powers, did she undermine them by such triteness? She embraced Marie-Yvonne, wiping floury doughy hands on her. She repeated with me; I sort of ducked away. We went into the house.

Doctor Ortéga-Nagy speed-waddled down the corridor in flapping fur babouches like giant insects, thirty-centimetre-long jambon beurre in hand. He gripped it with his teeth, an aboriginal with a horizontal lip plate, so he could shake my hand vigorously, clasping my wrist too, then ruffling my hair no matter of my loathing for his fat maggot fingers wriggling and the bread crust scratching my scar. He took a bite. He put his arm about my shoulders, pulled me to him with comradely gripping vigour so I could feel the mighty firmness of the belly that hung to his knees too, a dilated third waltzer. He belched roaringly.

'You showed him the door, you showed Wymeersch the door. You guided him to the exit. He volunteered for early retirement eh!'

He laughed and attempted a whirl, he danced a little jig. Not for long – breath shortage. Not high either – his body weight prevented him getting his feet more than two centimetres off the floor. Parquet squeaked.
        'You know where Biskarret is, by the way? Biskarret!'

Bébé's surname was a source of amusement to him.
        It was less than twenty-four hours ago, an active twenty-four hours.

'He . . . ah . . . how to put it . . . he didn't want to be part of it . . . took a bus home . . . too risky he thought . . .'

He barked: 'What!! . . . ay ay ay . . . yellow streak? I knew it. Yes. Yellow streak.'
        'I wouldn't say that.'
        'You are a generous comrade, Yoni. A loyal soldier . . . I'm going to have to speak to him.'

Madame Ortéga-Nagy beamed. It might have been a prize-giving. And I was cast to behave as the winning pony of the gymkhana? I felt

73

I was treated that way. My suspicion was, again, that for Doctor Ortéga-Nagy the struggle for our country was a game, maybe an entrepreneurial opening, for sure a money-making scheme. Some moments I compared him in my mind to la Grande Zohra. Look at me – valiantly leading the resistance to the German invasion, to rape and desecration of our country from the cosy comforts of London. Not front line. No. No going anywhere near *there*.

I went with him into his office. The doors to the laboratory were open. The immortality factory. The Mycologist was perched on a stool at a bench releasing colourless drops from a pipette onto a dissected mauve fungus. His neck brace was filthier than ever. He glanced at me, vaguely hostile. He found the mushroom's stipe more interesting.

Doctor Ortéga-Nagy grinned: 'So Yoni – you got the girl. The good guy gets the girl. Like in the Wild West movie.'
 I ignored him: 'She needs somewhere to stay.'
 He leered: 'She's a versatile little thing . . . I used to dandle her on my knee . . .'

That was an improbability of mechanics. And when did he last see his knees?
 'Be nice to have her around the house . . .'

Something suddenly gripped my right thigh, tightly, momentarily. Not from within. Not cramp. I stared at my thigh as though it might explain.

Madame Ortéga-Nagy repeated what she had done so many times before. She draped her greasy tassel shawl over her thinning pate and pulled it down over her face to gaze into the future: 'the infinite path before us'. Her predictions were usually persuasive for the very reason that they were hesitantly expressed, diffident, mined from deep.

That day was an exception. She did not hesitate. Her voice was parade-ground harsh, unspeculative. She gripped a Paris-Brest so firmly that the cream squeezed onto her hands without her noticing.

The walls closed in. The dark shelves threatened to hurl down leather books, the top-heavy armoires to collapse on us from their great
height. She had turned a spritely afternoon into ominous evening
with shutters, blinds, curtains, a burgundy arras, incense.

She spat words: 'Ghosts cast no shadows . . . that is how . . . how
we recognise ghosts . . . walking among us . . . ghosts . . . I am
immersed in the quiddity of existence . . . in prescience of the
immediate . . . of now . . . of this minute. What is this dob . . .
dob? You must go, Yoni . . . you must go to your parents' side! You
must protect them. Go!'

I didn't stop to consider she might be wrongly interpreting whatever
it was she read or heard or felt down her fubsy backbone or saw fleeting by. She was speaking the words in a melodrama. Pure corn. But
her horror was manifest. It was unprecedented. It was not imagined,
it was actual.

'Go! *Flingue!* Right now!'
    Doctor Ortéga-Nagy stumbled about, catching his feet under a
rug, spilling roast chickpeas from a bowl. He returned with a machine
pistol and a brace of grenades.
    'If you could wait,' he began, 'I shall fetch—'
    'Go, Yoni. Just go!' She was calm.

I *dashed*, as a rescuing hero in an Aubrey Quested tale would dash.
Hopskipping two at a time down the long exterior staircase to avenue
Père de Foucauld.
    I had descended all but the last few when I realised that Marie-
Yvonne had followed me.
    'Please fuck off.'
    'I will not,' she said. She did not add 'Whither thou goest I will
go' but might as well have done.
    Where was I going? I was turning a dream (of freedom, democ-
racy, our independence, our rights) into actuality. Over me beat
invisible wings. I was giving myth roots.

★

She bounded, bounced along in tennis shoes. We ran. We stumbled. We sweated. I fell. My feet pummelled. My brain beat in time with them. My city. Which was being taken from me. Where I was born. Why was I destined to have been born *here*? My city by chance . . . City of hills that I loved. City of cypresses and hatred. City of shame. City of bad faith. City of broken promises, broken paving stones: I tripped and slipped and stubbed my feet and turned my ankles and grazed my palms.

I knew what I was going to find. I knew I would be too late to save them. Why, then, rush towards a disaster already done?

Marie-Yvonne stood beside me convulsed with sobs. She pulled at her hair, twisted it sharply. I sensed she was going to touch me out of sympathy or consolation – I turned to look sharply at her.

Ramalamaleth 56.60: We have ordained death among you and we are not to be overcome.
    Ramalamaleth 18.100: We will bring forth hell, exposed to view, we shall present Gehenna before the unbelievers.

The superstitious barbarians from the dark ages had indeed brought forth hell. They had mutilated my parents' bodies so they wouldn't be haunted by them. There are some things a son ought never to see. My mother's right breast was so deeply hacked the lobules were apparent. The malign abstraction of a death dauber. My father's throat had been cut, his eyes stabbed. These hatefully inflicted wounds and the incisions to their face and forehead were tokenistic, symbolic. The actual cause of death was obviously being shot several times from several ranges. I wonder why my father had changed into a navy gingham shirt that really hadn't suited him.

There's no disguising an amateur execution. Unforgivably chaotic. Crude murderous *grinchards* taking a mallet to delicate machinery. It was a relief the mutilations were posthumous. Both my parents had derided the afterlife as a preposterous hope of ignorant ages. There was no excuse for believing that sort of nonsense now. They took pity on believers in supernatural frivolity with their bearded bigots in the sky and mass catering miracle workers (Ramalama and Jesus were both at it).

Once dead they would not have known what was happening to them. My mother's left arm was reaching out for my sprawled father, failing pathetically to reach him. The house I had lived in all my life was transformed into an abattoir. It was reduced to a stage for death. Charnel decor. The walls of the empty rooms were blood spattered. Golgotha-red and sticky. Drying to ancient rust. Bloodied parquet. Bloodied ceiling. The blood that made me, the blood I share. I had only been away for three hours. Here were no ghosts to cast no shadows. I would have said a prayer had I known how. I had never said a prayer. The lifelong non-smoker's last wish before the gallows is a cigarette.

Our god – our good fortune whoever, wherever it was – had deserted us. While Ramalama – the genocide of genocides, he puts Hitler to shame, he bests Stalin – is thriving. And my parents won't rise from the grave to exact revenge, to destroy the djellaba'd bastard with a beard. That was for me to do. That was their legacy to me. That was already my calling. To hasten *bougnous* off the cliff at the edge of the world. (Which is flat according to that almanac of ignorance the Ramalamaleth.) My throat clenched. I was frozen. I might have been skinned by an eskimo. I might have tumbled in frozen cacti. My skin was stung by tiny iced barbs. Unearthly cold. My revenge would not be cold. I was seeing with utmost clarity.

My parents' decision had been that we should take only things that could not be replaced. Impersonal matter, as my mother had put it.

Yet nothing now seemed impersonal: the notepad attached to a cracked china chicken she wrote shopping lists on, the stub of pencil she wrote them with, a white phone that I ripped from the wall, the simple plates we had eaten from, the table we had eaten at, the ugly veneered television whose transmissions they had derided, the bedding they slept under, their old clothes and tired shoes (but not mine), a gaudy bedside lamp shaped like a conch by whose light she read me tales in a voice that suggested she didn't quite believe them (Perrault, La Fontaine). I did believe them. I still do.

These valueless gewgaws suddenly took value. Bits and pieces got cohered themselves. I was surrounded by memento mori. It was not just my too trusting parents who incarnated death, it was every object, every grain of dust, every worn kitchen tool and scrap of fabric drawing-pinned to a wall – why? For some distant forgotten domestic purpose. Marie-Yvonne quit trying to comfort me bodily. She got the message. The last thing I needed in such circumstances was physical proximity, corporeal contact, that stuff.

The loaded van, parked in the surgery's back yard, had been rifled through. Not surprising that little had been taken. The leather medical bag was where I had put it earlier between the front seats. My parents had been frugal intellectual people whose books did not appeal to hardly literate murderers. It was the house that was the prize.

The *pecnaud* tribe had disappeared to prey on safer pickings. There was nothing to indicate they had ever been there. No rubbish, no junk. For sure, gunfire so close to them in the house will have alarmed them. But gunfire was the sound of the city that they must have got used to over the past few weeks. Patience had not been rewarded.

They will obviously have been sent on their way by my home's new 'owners'. The Dibs had scored a victory. Their victory would be short-lived. It was an easy victory: my parents did not have small arms. They had no weapons at all.

Marie-Yvonne's sobbing distracted me. I was not ready to mourn yet. Mourning does not undo the finality of its muted object. It is not reciprocated. So it can be postponed. It was postponed while I figured out what to do, how to respond – the scent of revenge is as beguiling as that of mechoui turning on a spit. The horror, the bafflement, the loss, the newfound state of orphanhood must be assuaged by justice, by the implementation of righteous hatred.

★

Sooner rather than later the Dibs would return, revelling in their theft, unlocking the front door, turning proudly to usher in their happy laughing burbling clucking brood of future killers who were going on holiday forever at someone else's expense. The brothers would show off their victims, their trophy. In that way the next generation learns to obey its parents: it is instructed in slitting throats for Ramalama – that is part of theocratic education.

Ramalama is immutable, generation upon murderous generation pitifully clings to the absolute of the past, resisting change, beheading and button cutting. It doesn't include the ideal of progress: it inhabits a polar world. It wants to be backward, it yearns for the age before yesterday. I know this – I have lived within it.

It's built on obedience and paranoia. It's always seeking the limelight. It's fearful of *kafirs* because *kafirs*, far from opposing it, are indifferent to it. They don't bother to take any notice of it. Here lies these ugly show-offs' problem. They would be ignored (and tolerated) were it not for their attention-craving villainy down the ages, down the centuries.

Me, I learnt from my parents' passivity, which they considered a form of honour. I learnt by not learning. I did not follow their example. I fail to appease. And I am alive. They were both forty-one years old when they were murdered. I am older. I am living much longer. I practise crafts they were oblivious to.

At that epoch, however, I was a mere tyro. I could only guess at what to do. To booby-trap a house requires time, knowledge and tools. I scurried about looking for kit. Marie-Yvonne did as she was told. She placed needles in mattresses. She poured pellets of rat poison, brand name La Cène, into the water tank. I switched off the electricity. I exposed as many wires as I could find, removed the remaining light bulbs. I switched it on again. I connected my two grenades to bedroom doors so that when they were opened the pin would be pulled – if the magpies were on my side. It was obviously not possible to test this improvisation's effectiveness.

★

Kitchen: we excluded all draughts, taped the windows shut, several layers of gaffer. Marie-Yvonne cut the gaffer with a carpenter's knife. I turned on the gas cooker full blast, every ring, the grill, the oven, without lighting it. Then we taped the kitchen's only door, the one into the hall. We had to tape it from the hall side. Otherwise we would have not been able to get out of the house, there was no exit through the kitchen. I hoped that by the time the Dibs returned it would be dark. The door's thick surrounding border of gaffer would not be visible. We left the house by the back entrance. The smell of gas was discernible if you were alert to it; if not, it was, so far, that faint it might not arouse suspicion in a proudly over-excited first-time homeowner.

I tried to hotwire the Renault van. It wouldn't ignite. Incapacitated. The spark plugs had been removed. Who by? One of my father's last actions? The Dibs? They would value the vehicle while dumping the incomprehensible contents.

I had only seen it for the first time earlier that day. I had no attachment to it. Nor to the majority of the books and papers piled up in it. I picked up the leather medical bag, which now contained just one life. As we walked away I realised that abandoning this van was more an ensign of finality than finding my parents dead. I didn't wish it to be so. It was involuntary. Beyond my control – for which I despised myself. I didn't want to disrespect them. But even without their murder the house and all it had contained were used up, worn out, redundant. It had been their bespoke carapace. Now it was a void.

By this oblique means I understood that the door was closed not just on their entire life but on the first act of mine too. Henceforth I was alone. Save for the limpet and millstone by my side.

We walked circuitously through the thickening dusk to the public garden at the end of the street. Things seem fresh in such circumstances. Bushes looked different. I bathed my head in the fountain. I realised how sloping the street was. I heard crickets' din louder than I had ever heard it before. Medicinal trees' odour attained a new pungency. What I had taken for granted was admitted to me anew. My parents were. Now they weren't. The ultimate physical change had been forced on them. I prayed, sort of, at last. For myself. I remembered Jeremiah. Where from? Certainly not from atheistic home or secular school. I had never set foot in a synagogue. I did not read accumulations of Middle Eastern folklore from long ago. Nonetheless I heard in my head:

Weep not for the dead. Weep sore for him that goeth away. For he shall return no more, not seeth his native country.

I would never again pass this way.

When the Dibs arrived it was with noise and clamour, laughter and shrieks. They piled out of two cars. Doctor Roumieu's and a right-hand-drive Fiat. It was uplifting to see both brothers lighting cigarettes as soon as they had stepped from their vehicle.

The wait was tense. I got to thinking that my hurried work in the house was come to nothing.

Then suddenly. Take-off. What exhilarating joy to hear a muffled explosion, to watch a woman with a fiery hijab throwing herself to the pavement wriggling to death, to see a boy feeling blindly about him to find the remains of his face, to hear the screams before they were drowned by another explosion that made the front of the house bulge like a bladder before inner forces transformed it again into the quarry rubble it once had been. Was that Nabila's remnants flung across the bonnet of the Fiat? Was there ever a more sumptuous flame than the tongue of dragon's breath that lit the street? A more stirring boum?

I regretted that revenge's imperatives denied my parents a fit burial. Remorse was something I was going to have to figure out.

Action was taken too late for the next day's newspapers and would not appear till Thursday when it would be overshadowed by the extensive programme of Constructive Arguments to be prosecuted Wednesday afternoon.

Saturday, 7 April 1962

Roger Degueldre who had planned that widescope operation was arrested early afternoon at 91 boulevard du Télemly.

He tried to escape down a service staircase. Half a dozen 'French' soldiers awaited him at the bottom. (Among them a former FLN and a former *malgré-nous*.[6]) He had been betrayed. Most probably by Micheli. Of course Micheli covered himself. Nothing, as usual, could be pinned on him. But it all pointed that way. His personal ambitions were jeopardised by Degueldre's Deltas.

He considered himself a Grande Zohra in the making. He would use us given the chance. He was preparing to treat with the FLN! He wanted to compromise, *to be seen* to compromise, for that would lend him political legitimacy. So he hoped. He was proud that *les bénis oui oui* who formed his court referred to him as *notre führer* and *notre pétit césar*. He did not take into account that the shift from terrorist to freedom fighter to politician is not within one's own gift. It has to be sanctioned by former enemies. The new status has to be acknowledged. Like being elected to a club: you cannot just apply. It was Micheli's fate, which he shared with many other members of the Organisation, that he could not absent himself from his past. He could not launder himself. That takes the guile ideologues lack. They are too principled to dissemble. Too stuck with their preciously authentic selves and their hallowed 'convictions'.

Many years later at Clermont-Ferrand, we watch David Valensi instruct a tango lesson up the steps of the black cathedral and I say to

---

6 Epithet, usually self-exculpatory, for Alsaciens in the Werhmacht and the SS. Some of them responsible for massacres, most notoriously at Oradour-sur-Glane.

Micheli: 'You know, Jean' – by then I had no fear to address him like this – 'you know you should have studied Talleyrand.'

He was for a moment gaping incredulous. He was not used to people talking to him this way. (Or addressing him *tu* not *vous*.)

'How, how, how could someone like me, how could I, me, with my . . . my unswerving . . . my force of character, how could I have been capable of emulating that despicable turncoat? He believed nothing.'

He tries to stare me down.

He asks: 'Are you trying to impugn my integrity, Yonatan . . . Are you deliberately making an insult at me . . . or are you careless about what you say to me?'

I couldn't prevent my momentary laugh. I tried. He looked more hurt than angry, injured pride. He was confronted with the actuality. There was nothing he could do. Our roles were, by then, if not reversed then blurred. No, they *were* reversed. He knew who had the power. And the money. He was now the former *pétit césar*, best days long past, an accumulation of wrong choices and, to be candid, a has-been.

He no longer counted. I was Judex.

I was at the head of a bullying mob in rough ragged clothes. Sacking, burlap, untreated furs, sheepskin. They were jeering a man hauling a piece of wood larger than he was, a coarsely lopped tree trunk that he sometimes tried to carry, mostly dragged. It seemed like a Basque sport, a show of pointless strength. Those near to him spat gingivitis, prodded and goaded. They pushed each other out of the way to get close by him. He stopped to draw breath, crouched and weary, hardly able to stand. I tapped him firmly with an ornamented stick, barked an order to move on. He swung sharply round to me. His expression was contemptuous. There was hatred in him. His minatory eyes bore into me, his liquid zircon eyes that were also blue voids. He stared mercilessly at me. It was a terrible moment.

He was me.

★

And me, *me*, I was looking at my own face, at the man who dared to herd me, intrude on my flank, with a pokestick, the man whose eyes were mine.

The moment stretched agonisingly. I woke screaming. *We* woke – to a sun composed of swirling oscillations. Outstaring me into submission, glaring and winning. The sun was surrounded by suns. All colours of sun, blinding, pulsing, dazing eyes. The sun was in rapture on high. The spectral discs were dependent apostles. I put my hands over my face. Every hue of red swam in my fingers. A squadron of aerobatic motes double-axled in this thick injurious light. How long did their display last? Time without end.

Three days out we were.

Three days was my estimate. Marie-Yvonne nodded as much as she could to confirm my estimate. She was sick again, vomiting, complaining of dizziness. I kept telling her to keep out of the sun until I needed her but she had a horror of being alone even though she could see my feet. She was very susceptible to the dryness. She was selfish about where she vomited. The smell was acrid. Surfaces get slippery.

A southern wind set in all lively, likely to overblow. The vessel wore bravely. It was a very fierce storm. The sea broke strange and dangerous. It was a mottled marbled tomb. Liquid went solid, then it was smoke, then spindrift. Waves attacked, renewing themselves as bucking sea horses, as the old sea gods in fury, hordes of them from every direction, clasping each other to build baroque-topped walls of water that collapsed with a roar. Waves consumed each other. We listed and we sloped, we pitched and we plunged, we were a shaken baby in a Mordhund's maw. During the storm, which was followed by a strong wind west-southwest, we were carried east. I think. Confirmed.

Our provisions held out but we lay in the utmost distress for water. Rationing drops from the can even as she cried croaking and pleading with her eyes, capturing tears before they ran down her cheeks.

Even at its calmest seawater is cruel. Dehydration makes it torture. Dehydration is its speciality. We were Tantalus's undeserving avatars. Birds circled above the boat, black silhouettes, scrambled ideograms, waiting their chance. That meant waiting for us, anticipating our weakness so we could not fight them off when they came for us, for their live feed. And they would come.

I had already seen their kin.

Windless, so becalmed, with lolling tongue and lips blanched by salt and really not quite all there, we moved as the tide drove us. It was driving us to madness. Like harts that find no pasture. Far in the distance on the horizon a tight black cloud appeared, murmurating unvaryingly, joylessly. Flies, like filings obeying a briny magnet.

Out of this solid cloud, not losing sight of their target (as we came to see), not losing their place in the queue to the feast, swooped Prynne's eagles, sea vultures, buteos, gyro-buzzards wheeling and twisting. Vast wings expanded then folded as liturgical garments. Impotent to alter course we crept up on the birds' prey whose stench assaulted us before its sight made us wish it was a hallucination. Which it was not. Here was a rotten carcass of a boat. Not rigged, nor tackle, sail, nor mast; the very rats instinctively had quit it. A ketch that would set forth with a crew of eight at the very most was now an open coffin carrying thirty bodies, our compatriots, escapees, trying like us to reach the 'home' that was an alien shore, that would reject us if it could. That was the only humiliation they were spared. They were meat. Dead, foetid, discolouring, bubbling, condemned meat for raptors with pirate-hook bills and deep delving talons, meat unfit for human consumption, fit for the flies that comprised the black cloud, courteously taking their turn in the puddles of blood and islets of organ meat, brain and nerve, teeth and bone, gristle and rib, shit and mesentery, sac and vein, muscle and mucous membrane (the last much prized in those waters: avian caviar).

It was not like the famous painting; no posed models expiring; no histrionic gestures and stage heroism in the face of ultimate indignity. Nor was it like the painting's parodies. It was a floating dog food factory being repeatedly raided by opportunists tugging and stamping. Their persistence! They fought among themselves, combat troops and guerrillas in the marine jungle. If only the Organisation had shown such resolve.

We know that death is a master from Germany, a god of destruction with eyes like the sun. We know now that he is also a master from France. France was infected by its visitors. Death is a German expertise, a French one too. Bodies piled high. This was a floating death camp. In lieu of Heydrich and Eichmann we give you the FLN and la Grande Zohra. And Belsen sur Mer.

That day, or maybe another, a clipper ship from the past sailed blackly beside us. There was no one on board. I swear it wasn't a hallucination, a dreamed silhouette. It cast a shadow . . . I didn't ask Marie-Yvonne if she had seen it too. We no longer had the energy to speak to each other. And the late Madame Ortéga-Nagy may have been wrong about ghosts' shadows. How did she know? I know I saw it. Just as I saw the sea and the sky conjoin so there was no longer a horizon but infinity, composed of blues without name.

One afternoon Marie-Yvonne died. It was not a sudden death. She had been dragging her frail body about the boat, searching, claiming I had hidden the water from her.

Apart from tennis shoes and turquoise and white striped ankle socks she lay near naked on the cabintop. That's where she took her last breath, supine, staring uncomprehendingly at the killing blue. Death follows me scavenging. No scythe, always in civvies, bespoke and swart.

As though choreographed, a passing tanker's disrespectful crew made in unison the clenched fist and bent arm gesture of coarse licentiousness: *bras d'honneur*. My reciprocal gesture imploring them to rescue me was ignored or misunderstood. The tars (*les loups de mer*) must have believed I was in seventh heaven. The dead and the sleeping, how they resemble one another.

I ate her, not hacking but carving considerately with full respect for her former human status. My Laguiole blade was sharp and strong. The flesh was chewy but so is any uncooked meat. It stuck between my teeth the way tartare always will. I drank her sticky blood diluted with the precious prepenultimate litre of ferrous Mouzaïa water. What if she could speak? What would she say? Would she encourage me to eat her? I won't pretend that this was fieldcraft expertise rather than cannibalism. I had no choice. Besides, a sentence from some-where rang in my head:

'I think you'll find that most modern anthropologists have eaten long pig.'[7]

Pig. Is human flesh kosher? Is Jewish flesh super-kosher while Chris-tian flesh and Rama flesh are treyf?

Would she reprimand me? She couldn't say. And I had to eat. And what was the necessity of her existence? Was she a necessary person? Was she essential? I had to have my second anti-rabies injection.

The birds' plunging attacks were ceaseless. The speed shook me. Kamikaze with the will to live. They grunted as if rutting. They drew asthmatic baby breaths. They too wanted her flesh. Their wings beat my body in synchronised blows. They sought to claw out my eyes. Their breath was sharp as high garbage. They hijacked the boat, strutting amidships. I scurried into the cabin. They tried to break in. They tried to claw through the ceiling. The scraping noise was horrible, the grinding of bone. Their wicked faces stared through the portholes at me. They were used to nesting on floating debris, ripped sails, seaweed, oil drums. An entire vessel was an unprecedented luxury. I put a rug over my head. It smelled of my mother's scent. I cursed myself for having placed my weapons aft.

★

---

7 Long pig is more genteel than *bidoche*.

87

At last I resolved to fetch a gun. No sooner had I opened the cabin door to the deck than a Prynne's eagle landed on my back, ploughing my scalp, ripping my ears, wings punching my face like jokari racquets. I squirmed. I flailed. I feared for my eyes. A buzzard attacked my chest. Its high-pitched mewing mixed with the squeak of its electronic tag to make a gruesome sound. When feathers are shockingly soft they threaten asphyxiation. When they are compressed they are hard, like fasces, strength in numbers. Bodies, wings and quills are an arsenal furnished by violent genes. I flailed long enough to get my hands on the lid of the stern locker, open it and grab an automatic pistol before a razor beak cut into my jaw. I fell on my back and fired. The report scared them. They had gorged themselves.

I was alone with the remnants of their feast. Alone on a sea contaminated by sea nettles, millennia-old nameless reptiles with needle teeth and tufa skin, mycomorphic medusas, nomuras whose venomous tentacles are a giantess's uncoiffed pudenda. All of them feeding, always feeding, always endangering species smaller and slower than they were: who'd be a brine shrimp?

These creatures slunk aboard behind my back. They hid when I turned like in a child's game. I knew that however long my torment lasted I would not die. How old would I be when it ended? I drifted down the days and nights, wiping time, forgetting whether the thin whey of sky was dusk or daybreak. I saw a pale horse, mistreated, all ribs and gums tortured by sticks and usage, unfit to effect Permanent Interruption. My fingernails grew pink. I watched helpless while the pocks on the aluminium mast seethed and expanded. The boom's varnish contracted melanoma. The cabintop succumbed to psoriasis. The mainsail and spinnaker were dry, browning, crisp. The welcoming cliffs I made out in the far distance turned into malignant low clouds. I heard the gurgle of clear water rushing over rocks at Bouamara, pure water, life-giving water. I could smell pine resin, lemons, eucalyptus. I looked in vain for their sources.

The galley gimbals were oxidised, there was nothing to cook, no gas. I looked for one of those symbols that the luckless long for. An affectionate small bird, a trinket dropped by a big bird, a chunk of jetsam maybe, a guardian whale. Nothing doing. My pee was liquid barley sugar. My hair was matt and brittle. My skin was coarsened by salt and sun.

There was no correspondence with the unscarred 'babyface smiler' wanted for 'terrorist crimes' whose photo had begun to appear in newspapers and television news broadcasts. I felt unpresentable to myself. I had become the sort of person I wouldn't want to be seen with. The sort I warned myself against. I did not want to see my reflection again for I saw the figure and visage of madness seeking for a home. Hoping I'd suffer no long-term damage I threw the looking glass with my face in it overboard. Marie-Yvonne was soon to follow. The climate was unsparing, unpropitious. Bad luck with crampons on K2 and you may be preserved in an ice block. Garrotted felons and jewelled usurpers buried in turbaries do not die but become leather (and so frighten humble peat cutters). No such extension of bodily life is granted to those who fester under the sun.

Long smooth milky worms were late to the feast, sliming, sliding, multiplying in her copious wounds and gulleys, exploring eye sockets, nostrils, every aperture death could furnish. What remained of her was putrid and swollen. She had been inflated. Flesh sloughed skin. Mucous membrane's stench recalled crude tanneries. Soft tissue hardened. Rot's many colours darkened by the hour, by the minute, by the day . . .

The vessel was getting frequently buffeted by sharks. Their blades cut through the water. I decided to bury her at sea, with dignity, in the hope that the beasts might be distracted and so desist. Her remnants went in with a plop. Success. The sea turned choppy red for a while.

I really could have done with a change of clothes, my sage-green jeans were stained from this hoboboat sublife. Not that I really cared: the black contrast stitching was offensive. I was conscious of my own smell. I had no eau de cologne and dared not bathe in the marine jungle. I had estimated four or five days at sea. I had perhaps not taken the sea's caprices into account. Nor Marie-Yvonne's incompetence, her wilful obstinacy. It was easier for me to do every task rather than to repeatedly explain to her what was needed. She was a passenger, not crew.

She cried for her parents and her brother, missing presumed dead.

She cried for Doctor and Madame Ortéga-Nagy, dead.

When the motor gave out with a splutter we floated nowhere. Accusingly she whined: 'Five days,' she jeered: 'Five days.'

The malfunction had begun when she ignored my precise, clear, practical, user's manual, child-could-follow-them instructions about how to use the choke. She flooded it, irrecoverably. I passed a day vainly trying to fix it, getting my hands daubed in oil and greasy diesel, breathing vapours that wouldn't ignite.

A merman? Poseidon? Davy Jones's spokesman? An ancient voice, growling, warned me that now I had no choice other than to sail but sail better.

Give me the wind, I screeched, howling like a loon, bellowing at the sea whose responding ripples were Hebrew orthography, or were they Braille? Ghibli, scirocco, samoon. Any wind would do. A wind that kisses, a wind that chides with a blow, a wind that stings like a bully's wet towel. Please, a wind that propulses me. I saw the lights of distant ships, invisible by day, I waved Marie-Yvonne's T-shirt at them. I knew they couldn't see me. Nor could passenger aircraft and military fighters. That knowledge doesn't inhibit the action. Beneath me shoals of pelagic warriors gathered for an assault, a mighty heave. A further zoological offensive by other species in resenting human superiority, resenting their inability to reprogramme themselves. I was feverish hot, I was sorbet cold. Cramp in feet, cramp in calves. Cramp I wanted to kill: I called it Rachid. I vomited nothing, then I vomited it again. There was dangerously little water left to quash the burning acidity. Its meniscus was a trembling skein of tiny insects. They gave it a matt finish.

★

Beating upwind I outsailed a gang of apprentice pirates who had stolen Degueldre's yacht *La Fierté*. They could neither exploit the gusts nor shoot accurately.

I scudded away from them wishing that they should capsize and drown. I left them far behind. I sailed well. I sailed on the lee at the first intimation of land, long low clouds signalling an escarpment, a peak, a cliff. They were not deceivers.

My exhilaration overcame my fatigue, my thirst, my hunger. As I tacked closer I stared up at mighty blanched limestone cliffs, the fortress of giants made of all the creatures that had inhabited this hellish sea millions of years ago. The cliffs descended sheer, striated, stained – the giants had peed on them. Scrub lived a half-life on ledges. Saplings sprouted from vertical clefts.

The second sign of land was olfactory. A pungent assault that bit my nostrils, that made me retch. Sewage. Faecal effluent. The Isle of Cloaca welcomes you to the issue of many thousand bowels. To the spectacle of The Great Evacuation.

Then it was there to be seen. A mephitic browning of the grey sea and, soon, a gross diameter outfall pipe, half-submerged, greenish and slimy. Rats the size of beavers clambered over it, up and down, in and out. They slithered, they slipped off. What a fine old time of it they were having, larking in clover, their clover, shit-furred and squeaking. They had a playground for life and for the life of their litters and their litters' litters. Whoops, another rat skidded and fell. They were unchallenged by birds, discriminating vultures kept away. Shit returns eternally. It is not eradicable. It doesn't just go away. Once deposited it is ever present. It just mutates. Here it was faecal bacteria in seafoam. I thought of the gift of death these rats would bring to users of showerheads and drinking fountains (if there were any in this land I was about to land on). I followed the coast keeping wary of tides and currents, yearning for somewhere to put in. The hostile cliffs were unrelenting. They stretched for hours.

★

It came with a sudden change of wind. That announced a headland. I knew that from yachtcraft. The cliffs now stretched for seconds. They raced past. What had taken aeons to form dissolved in a tick, sped into my past. The wind struck hot and swift. The boat was buffeted. The sky was soot-black sacks filled to bursting. Waves swept over me. My lungs were submerged. Lightning lit the sea, showed its horrors. White sheep swelled so large they were rearing white horses. I clung to lines. I knotted myself to the tiller extension. I knotted my fate to it. For the first time the boat was close to the limit of my control. Thunder claps came from an asylum's orchestra. This storm was so hideous that I wondered if I was going to survive. A reservoir was poured over me. The boom swung. I saw it coming, peripheral sixth sense. But eye's message to brain and brain's to neck were hampered by fatigue. It struck me hard. I heard a crunch, a biscuit splintering crisply, I felt nothing.

A new element surrounded me, greeted me as one of its own, cosseted me. Bathed me in ancient sunlight.

Beyond the headland, beyond the extremity of the cliffs, the coast changed with climatic abruptness. Pine woods lolloped over sunny rocks to the shore. It felt familiar. It felt like home. I forgot for an instant that I had no home. It felt like paradise. The keel sunk into sand. I waded ashore carrying my father's bag and the two Sabena bags I had exhumed from their hiding place at the Villa Eucalyptus. That was so long ago it might have been in a different life.

The water was shallow. The horseshoe-shaped cove was dominated by a long low mas among flat top cedars and umbrella pines.

On the beach in front of it there sat, in black wheelchairs, in an ordered row, in the midday sun, twenty men, some late middle-aged, some ancient. They wore respirator masks like muzzles. Each with tubes in his nose, with a cylindrical silver oxygen tank and regulator dials in a holster attached to his chair. They wore a uniform of white bedshirts and dark glasses. They stared blankly at the sea and the sky. They wheezed. They turned as one to inspect me. And, as one, turned swiftly away.

★

It was clear to me that they recognised me as Judex, feared me. The sun was reflected in their spectacles' lenses. It glinted off the frames. It shone from so high that it provoked no shadows. It was as though it were lit by a cosmic high key light hung perpendicular to this earth.

I approached one of the men. The hair of his big toe was plaited.

'Where can I get my second rabies injection?'

He said nothing. There was a bowl on his lap. The biscuits in it were covered in furry mould. I repeated my question. He again failed to respond. I realised he couldn't understand me.

His neighbour gaped at the sky as though he were watching a film. He held a hand grenade that turned into a cherimoya.

I carried my possessions, my only possessions, across the cropped garrigue (asphodels, euphorbia, juniper, rosemary) towards the mas.

A smiling, gap-toothed, ochre-toothed man with a waxed moustache limped hurriedly towards me down a rocky path from the mas. He was dressed in a white overall with a stethoscope on his chest and a head mirror attached to a beaded band round his pudding basin hairdo.

'I need to get my second rabies injection.'

'Of course you do, My Old Son.'

'Well, where?'

'Good question, Mush.'

'It's urgent.'

'Indeed. Rabies is a nasty business. Not to be underestimated. The foaming . . . No one wants to foam. Unsightly, isn't it. Follow me.'

'You've got immunoglobin?' I asked incredulously.

'Of course.'

'Is this a hospital then?'

'Not as such . . . Perhaps more in the old sense — but without denomination . . . we're extra ecumenical, that's what the Reverend Ursula called us . . . though I think we are all conjoined in believing that Satan clouds men's minds. Wouldn't you agree?'

We walked between the mas and hothouses where women in white habits, baroque scrub caps like wimples designed by the blind and anti-inhalation masks were tending bright flowers – chenilles, hibiscus, African violets. I knew names that I didn't know I knew. More names: wolfsbane, hemlock, datura, foxgloves. I recognised them all. The women were so absorbed in their work that they didn't notice us pass.

When I paused to watch them through streaked panes of condensation the smiling man told me: 'In Asmara they believe the miserable slothful monkeys don't talk because if they did talk they would be made to work. Unlikely . . . maybe the mute monkeys aren't quite as clever as they think they are. You see, work would bring the monkeys a happiness agenda fulfilment.

'They couldn't find the right man so they opted to become brides of Christ, our Lord's harem of hope. Work brings them happiness till he returns – when he'll cover each and every one of them. Everyone is happy here. Happy in the shining sun that causes us to cast no shadows. This is a happy ship. The men staring at the sky are happy in their work.

'Some have been here since they were found. The sainted Ursula Bonbernard rescued living abortions . . . no one else would . . . she gave them a home . . . as full a life as is possible in those terrible circumstances . . . She is no longer with us . . . her immortality was provisional . . . she walked into the sea . . . Phimister rescued some from the caves and forests of the north . . . from bogs. Suckled by wolverines, wild cats . . . bears, some of them. Of course Phimister was accused of kidnapping. What if they wanted to stay in the wild?

'He believed he had a duty to civilise them. Really they were guinea pigs . . . they've all forgotten it now . . . they don't know where they came from. He was a choosy kidnapper . . . he only stole boy children. No time for feral girls.

'They're illiterate, literally illiterate, all of them. But not innumerate. They get a morning dose of odessa then they are ready for their work. Some are like Sicilians . . . they are spending so long perfecting their plan for revenge that they get ill, too weak to carry out their revenge so they come here . . . they compare revenge plots with each other . . . boastfully.

'They pretend to be former dictators . . . or future dictators . . . supreme and duce . . . Genocidal kleptocrats to come. Boasting . . . never stop boasting . . . how many millions they'll cull . . . the serfs they'll work to death according to the folwark principle . . . the size of their palaces . . . their harems . . . their basilicas . . . their tabers. Illiteracy is no handicap to political advancement . . . it helps. Some of them have mated. Their children dream of one day being dictators themselves . . . some of them come and visit . . . The ones who are not so obese that they can't make the journey here.'

My mind contorted, as though faced by an impossible object. Did I hear right? I believe I did.

'They are counting the number of birds in a murmuration. Exacting work . . . it is work without end. More work than can be done in an unenhanced lifetime. Can make you mad. Can make you blind. Some of them have gone blind from staring too long. When that happens we bring them in to work in sausages or moral hygiene. This is the Abode of Happiness. The Land of Recovered Content. What's your name?'

'Luc Shapitra,' I heard myself say.

'Luc Shapitra?' He closed his eyes, nodded his head gently. 'Luc Shapitra – *of course*. Interesting . . . interesting *choice*. Yes. Guileful. Used to be a popular choice . . . don't hear it so much nowadays. You've got the hang of it . . . You know the griff all right.'

We walked through swaying tamarisks mimicking a stand-off between coxcombed roosters. In a distant orchard more women in white habits gathered fruit from ranks of gleaming leaf trees. Each had a basket on her back whose weight she had to struggle against to stretch up for the mauve fruit. White calves grazed among them.

'You know why the fruit's so abundant . . . why the grass is so lush? Phosphates. All the bodies buried there after the insurrection was quashed . . . top quality massacre. Giving their goodness to the earth.'

★

Beyond the mas were more buildings – former vineries, presses, stables, byres, cloches. Polished and buffed, the far side of perfection, it appeared to be a full-scale model of itself. An open door revealed an immaculately neat dormitory. Rows of beds stretched into the far distance, seemed to stretch far beyond the confines of the building.

The shuttered room in what had been a peasant's cottage was equipped as a consulting room. He loaded a syringe from a glass capsule in a fridge full of capsules and vials.

'If you'll take your shirt off . . .'
My shirt was stuck to me like a second skin. He dabbed my shoulder with rubbing alcohol. Then injected me. Ow. Wow . . .
'Thank you . . . ah . . . doctor . . . ?'
'I'm not a doctor.'
'But . . .' I indicated his garb, his head mirror. 'What's your stethoscope for then?'
'It is a reassuring tool. It calms adepts . . . communards . . . paradisians . . . whatever you like to call them – we have no nomenclatural prescriptions. Free and easy, that's the way, Mush. And I do have a particular tendresse for the Hippocratic mien. It becomes me. The apparel oft proclaims the man. Do you not agree?'
'Of course . . . yes . . . What are you if you're not a doctor . . . ?'

The injection had made me feel I was floating. That was not what I expected. I seemed to be ascending. Yet when I looked at my companion I was not above him. Shake it off, I told myself. Myself did not respond.

His smile widened: 'My vocation is less banal. I intend no disrespect to the medical profession . . . but I plough a rare furrow. You might say a unique furrow. Perhaps you have heard of Dream Topping™? What about Smotherland? . . . In a way I hope not. That is my endeavour – nuanced, discreet . . . utterly oysters . . . among other things I lead an Eschatology Enquiry Adaptation . . . I'm a coach . . . By the way my name is—'

'Lamb . . .' I said. To my astonishment, I finished his sentence for him.

I had never seen him before in my entire life, never pronounced that name, those words, never heard them spoken, never read them.

'Of course it is, good man, good man,' he grinned. 'I stand on both sides of the line, Luc . . . I am the afterlife coach.'

At Tolly Dene

DATE RAPE DELL by JASON RENUCCI

Old plastic bags get snagged
on thorns. Bulk gusts stretch them
then they're bladders. Shredded
polythene flutters in boughs: matt
bunting exults the new day's drizzle,
the off-milk sky over Tolly Dene.

Dogs take shivering litter
for fledglings on flight's brink, they
scratch up trees pursuing quarry.
They howl. They scrape the trunks.
They chase billowing brand-names
across this common's soggy squelch.

Yesterday's carrier is today's balloon.
It distends, soars, deflates then crumples
where grass meets bracken's corpse.
It comes to rest with Tetra Paks
and gaudy cans immune to rust.
Junked cartons are slow to bleed their colour.

Here's a seagull, obese with rum'n'raisin
from a nipper's cone. It's buffeted like
a plastic bag. Flattened, contorted,
so jolted a severed finger drops

from its beak to branches shaking with
DTs, to trunks twisted by the Spithead Bite.

Flotillas of wrapping are doldrummed
in year-round puddles. Lout weeds sprout
through webs of moist torn tights.
The old courtesy, knotting a condom after use,
has disappeared. Did he walk home trouserless,
the fellow whose XL jeans are turned to sodden rag?

They say the rats have multiplied because
of lovers' fries. Popcorn doesn't degrade
any more than polystyrene. Burger buns grow fur
with age. Every black leaf has its secret,
its cache of spores, its lining of grubs,
its trousseau of unhatched ill.

There's grit in the slime up Tolly Dene.
There's no soft landing when you take
a tumble: abrasion at best. Or an ugly cut
from flint's rind, a muscle punctured by
something forgotten in the deep dark humus.
Something jagged and long-time buried.

There's hardly a week passes when they
don't find a body, all maggots and fractures,
mouth stuffed with cinders, togs, pages of
porn. It wasn't meant to be a grave, that
wasn't the plan — but this ground is inviting
when your love is quartered in a burlap sack.

Here's Old Carn Vanier. She gamely follows Hector and Arthur.
They bound into copses, they leap through clearings. She whoops
and laughs and pants, scurrying along. Her crinkly cone of steel hair
goes this way, her rainbow scarf goes widdershins, how many cardies
can an OAP bulk-wear at once?

She gimps through the thick coarse clumps: 'Wait for me, boys, wait for Mother!'

She drags herself across thickets as fast as gumboots and her leg will let her. Born with the left four inches shorter than the right in a family of eugenicists, she had to dissemble her disability as best she could. She scurries along little creatures' trails.

The autumnal atmos is dense with fungal particulates. She can feel them invading her lungs, constricting her bronchioles, working up a hearty wheeze. She stops to frisk her multiple pockets, draws hard on her inhaler. She calls their names and trudges on.

Hector and Arthur are up to here in muddy fun! They have scampered and they have rolled and they have hurtled all the way down the steep slope to Tolly Bunny.[8] No one ever goes down there . . .

The springs that dribble into the brook make the ravine a greasy rink. You can slide down but you can't slide up. Mud is on gravity's side. There are steps in the chalk. The wooden risers have mostly disappeared.

The steps were cut in 1888 by varsity men under the direction of Daniel Luke Luttrell Tolly, philanthropist, Ruskinian, ethnographer and archaeologist. He would later endow the city with these sixty or so acres, subject to covenants proscribing flowerbeds, metalled roads, railings and all buildings save those essential to the common's maintenance and its users' wellbeing (i.e. lavatories, a bandstand and wooden shelters in several exotic styles).

He was Old Carn Vanier's grandfather. She takes pride in her sepia forebear, in his generosity, in his kind, craggy face, which she recalls from when he walked beside her holding in one hand her tiny hand and in the other his ash stick, telling her the vernacular and Latin names of flowers, telling her that the word for this excrement is spraints because it is an otter's, telling her that this skull is a jackdaw's and this print a badger's. He is always with her in spirit. She remembers, she pictures him. She sees him every day.

---

8 A bunny is a ravine, typically in soft terrain. The word, synonymous with chine, is particular to the southern English counties of Hampshire, Dorset and Devon.

Father Linsel Murly's sculpture (c. 1905) at Tolly Dene's south-eastern corner may be stiff and grandiloquent but the human who begat her begetter is recognisable – in the prognathous, resolute jaw, in the pedagogically gesturing right hand, in the deltas of kindly smiles beside his eyes. It *is* him, somehow, despite the darkening of the years, despite the corrosive stain of bird droppings. The likeness is sufficient to exacerbate the notion of Daniel Tolly's everpresence a century after his death.

Oh, he'd still be with her even had he not sat for Murly whose worldly, undissembled, Royal Academic and social ambitions he mocked: 'The placeman of all placemen, he changed the placement.' This often repeated sentence stuck even before she understood its meaning.

She incites her adored grandfather's visits as much as she yearns for those of her poor valiant Roddie who died on his twenty-ninth birthday, thrown from his mount beside an icy canal at Armentières, condemning her to a widowhood that her vows demanded never be exchanged for a further marriage.

She had no choice, for he lived beside her. Yet she has spent more than half a lifetime learning that such fidelity and a life without love create their own prison.

She is not proprietorial about what was once her family's land, she doesn't rue the day it passed to the people – even if the people abuse it, and abuse each other in it . . .

If only The Tolly Settlement ('Labor Ipse Voluptas') had been rebuilt after it was bombed and had continued to instruct urchins in anthropology and Mozart. Then, surely, the police would be spared having to place crouched, double-jointed, long-suffering constables in the eaves of the lavatories to witness the emissive encounters below.

Yet she loves this land and believes that she possesses a bodily tie to it. She knows that Daniel Tolly's beneficent shade lingers in the trees he loved. One day this green lung will again be a good place, where industrious folk can recreate themselves without harbingers of fear lurking in the bushes and drilling glory-holes in cubicle walls.

★

In Tolly Bunny smooth roots protrude from the impacted ground like undulating snakes, gleaming in the perpetual dusk. And only last summer a little nipper was bitten by an adder here. The city prayed for him and he survived, but then death from such a cause is rare in victims who are fit. He was still a hero, though, a plucky soldier whose post-traumatic stress may last a lifetime. There are the faces of hellhags and lycanthropes in the broken trunks and severed boughs. She is inside one of the terrifying picture puzzles of long ago. Above, the boughs of the trees have stretched out to intertwine and knit a cathedral roof for the ravine.

'Where are you, boys?'

She stumbles. She winces. The steps are worn, they elide with each other. Old Carn Vanier gingerly broaches the flight and wishes the old shock-absorbers in her old back worked better.

'Oh botherage!' she cries and stops to massage her coccyx through layers of felted wool. That's more like it. She's a vimmish brightsider not given to down-in-the-mouth but the sheer difficulty of the descent and the omnipresent dank and her boys' awol causes her to tut. For which she immediately reproaches herself: she tells herself she's lucky to have her legs and her marbles when her few surviving contemporaries are dribbling liquids from plastic straws in sunset homes.

She does wish, though, that Hector and Arthur weren't quite such exuberant little fellows. She'll never give them up of course, they're all the family she has, the last of the Tollys. But how she wishes they'd quell their curiosity. If only they'd slow down. They have raced far ahead of her, there's nothing to be heard of them. It's so sheltered down Tolly Bunny that the wind and the distant traffic are hardly audible. Drizzle is rain without the pitter-pat soundtrack, mute even when an accretion drops stealthily from one leaf to another. The dense, oppressive silence envelops her. It's intermittently relieved by birds' petulant shrills and ill-tempered croaks – whoever called those mere noises song can never have heard lieder. She takes solace in humming some bars of Weisseite's setting of Lothar Stech-Pelz's 'Es leben immer die Toten', which she has known all her long life since she stood beside Daniel Tolly's piano. She sniffs the air and shrugs in resignation. Oh, drizzle is such *second-rate* rain. There's never a scent of thunder's brimstone when it's drizzling, never an intimation of terror and electric majesty, never a promise of climatic opera, never a chance of routine's rupture. That's what she craves, the unexpected. The older she gets the more she rues unseized opportunities to have discomfited her steadiness, decency, responsibility, selflessness. How many years has she left to her in which to become someone else?

A traveller, say, or even an adventurer. A Carn Vanier who escapes Carn Vanier, who returns to the state of being carefree Caroline Tolly. Anything, anyway, other than the parish saint. Anything other than the bountiful worthy trammelled by familial obligation to the deserving poor who are no longer poor, no longer deserving. They are, rather, violent, sexually incontinent, drugged, self-pitying, impervious to improvement, ceaselessly masticating, obese. When they were thin they possessed a hunger for betterment and aspirates. Now they curse and fight through the endlessly extended happy hour at The Nod's As Good As A Wink: when it was The Skittles it was teetotal and jolly. As a firm but fair magistrate she isn't empowered to hand down the sentences the recidivists deserve.

Today the tenants of Tollygarth Garden Village – the handmade former heaven of smiling mellow tiles and warm bricks north of Tolly Dene – are perpetually in rent-arrears. Despite their uncouth, monosyllabic, opaque-eyed ignorance, they know how to instruct a 'community' solicitor whenever a) eviction beckons, b) they trip on a paving stone that they have themselves broken, c) it is observed that they have contravened the terms of their lease by replacing the mullioned windows or the bucolic front doors or the jolly wicket fences, d) they face charges of living off immoral earnings/keeping a disorderly house/receiving stolen goods.

How she longs for a life devoid of duty and sullen ingrates.

How she longs to be free of unjust accusations of feudalism. A Tolly: feudal! She is so set in her ways she might as well be cast in bronze. She needs a trigger to effect the change that she is powerless to make.

How she longs for a thunderous bolt, a god from a vehicle.

And here, at last, it is. Not that she immediately recognises its providential potential.

Hector comes scurrying towards her through ground elder as fast as his little legs will carry him, which isn't that fast because he has a big surprise for Mother clutched in his jaw and so perfectly balanced that it protrudes equally on either side of his lovable shaggy face. He's wagging his tail with possessive pride. Old Carn is so delighted to have her boy back that she stoops creakily to give him a cuddle:

'Oo's a hunter-gatherer then! Oo's a clever boysywoy! Oo's brought Mother a nice juicy boneyo den!'

Hector skittishly drops his bone, which is neither nice nor juicy but impasted with mud.

A canine gerontophile, he rolls over so his belly can be vigorously stroked. He submits eagerly, he's enjoying it like a lubberly bow-wow should when Old Carn shrieks and his massage stops, precipitously.

'Oh my my . . . Hector, where did you find this? Where did you find it?'

Her delusion of communicative empathy with the dog is exposed by his heartless reaction to her pitiful, lachrymose cry that:

'This is human, Hector. This is a human hip, Hector. Where's it from?'

Hector is indifferent. He wants to go on having his tummy rubbed.

'Where's Arthur, boy?'

Hector growls. Hector wants his bone back.

Old Carn is staring at it with aghast incredulity. She knows a femoral neck and a greater trochanter when she sees them. She has lost count of the number of trophy x-rays of their crippled hips that her coevals have shown her. And she took her years as a Patron of the Royal Infirmary seriously. She knows what she's holding, circumspectly.

And so does Hector, it's his bone. She knows what she's gaping at: part of a dead person. The paralysis of recognition deafens her to his barking.

Then she shakes herself out of it and says: 'Come on, boy – let's find Arthur.'

She stumbles in the direction Hector had approached her from. He yaps around her surgically bound calves. Damp boughs gang up on her. There are thorns and nettles and knots of goose grass sticky as candyfloss. Tolly Bunny's a magnet for bad plants. She fears the horrors she may find in its depths. She fears presciently. When they reach Arthur, as vigorous a digger as Hector, he is excavating a bank with quadrupedal zeal. A furious spume of mud and leafmeal and compost rises behind him.

There are already three more partially exposed bones beside a rivulet. It is a parody of an archaeological site. Hector's appetite is so whetted that a viscous web of saliva has formed around his mouth. He is excited now by Arthur's further troves: shreds of fabric, a wedge of plastic, matted fibres. Old Carn struggles to put on the dogs' leash and drag them from this charnel hollow.

The Central Police Station eventually logged a call from a Mrs Roderick Vanier at 09.56. It was the third she made on a mobile owned by Jason of Charley's Chow Cabin. The initial reaction of the emergency counsellor is to accuse Old Carn of being 'an institutionalised hoaxer'. When she says that she was a magistrate for thirty-two years the reaction is: 'Oh yeh.' The unapologetic sergeant to whom she had at last spoken asked her to wait there. He told her a car would be with her in just a tick.

Charley's Chow Cabin is a gaudy van that reeks of charred onions, burnt abattoir scrape and reused oil even before the day's frying has started. So it is said.

Jason Renucci is a graduate in the Social Psychology of Leisure and is reading for a Master's in Creative Life Writing at Solent Warsash Vespasian Campus. 'Date Rape Dell' (see above) is the most recent work hatched in his Reality Laboratory.

I am Jason Renucci. I am experimenting writing about myself/ himself in third person for reasons of objectivity and distance.

He is the fourth generation Renucci to operate this van, parked as ever on Dene Drive South near the Daniel Tolly sculpture. Specialities include yogurt ice cream, P'tit Clamart ice cream, malted milk ice cream, ginger sorbet, blackberry sorbet.

As a result of a childhood attack by a dog he suffers anosmia so does not know whether the common estimate of the van's noxious smell is accurate or not. Maybe it is a rumour spread by fellow traders with a less favourable pitch. He does concede that 'it's probably not fine dining'.

Old Mrs Vanier sheltered under the ragged candy striped canopy, fed frankfurters to Hector and Arthur, drank a can of Sprite with a shaking hand, repeatedly expressed her shock to the otherwise customerless Jason Renucci who was working on the Insertion of Symbols module.

'It's oh . . . you see so many terrible things . . . but I don't know. It's a park. For public enjoyment . . . and now it's sullied. A body! You can be sure it's not natural causes . . . What poor person ends up . . . I'm sorry to keep going on. Silly old biddy . . . you must be thinking . . . silly old—'

'No! All respect to senior citizens. I help out at Copse Garth, my aunty's care home: I know the value seniors bring societally with their wisdom. Course I wasn't thinking silly old . . . What I was thinking . . .'

Jason Renucci explains that he is a graduate in the Social Psychology of Leisure and reading for a Master's in Creative Life Writing at Solent Warsash Vespasian Campus.

'I'm not into lollies and hot-dogs as a lifestyle choice. Just putting in a shift . . . family business.'

Jason remembers his Alternative Tourism module.

Floods, acts of god etc., earth-slips, fatal derailments, terrorist attacks, aeroplane (though seldom motor traffic) accidents, wars, genocidal massacres, concentration camps, gibbets, mass graves, scaffolds, torture chambers, murders, especially murders, are drivers of putting a place on the map, of creating a tourist magnet destination. A notorious crime or well-publicised accident is a potential instrument of commercial regeneration due to humans' ghoulishness.

Never underestimate the appetite for others' misfortune, nor the willingness to travel to satisfy that appetite. Tourism reflects society;

it doesn't direct it. That would be elitist, them-and-us deterministic, trying to improve humankind by encouraging it to gape at ancestor portraits, to understand the past, to appreciate the pargeter's craft.

It is in the retailer's interest to discourage squeamishness. The purchase common to all sites is cut flowers and soft drinks. They are likely to perform better than comestibles that are deemed site-specific: at kiddy murder sites it's burgers for nutrition, at derailments it's ice cream for the thank-god-it-wasn't-me factor.

Module case study: Bury St Edmunds.

Before Ricky Hughes, no one, in Jason's opinion, had heard of the place. He certainly hadn't.

'Oh no. There's the abbey,' Old Carn corrected him, 'and that wonderful sloping street . . .'

The abbey and that wonderful sloping street were not national news. The missing girls, the murders, the exhumations, the revelations and the trial were.

'Look,' he insisted, 'they molished his house but they *still* got people coming to see it, where it was, yeh? High-profile murder impacts on the micro-economy. Lot of places would murder for a murder on their doorstep. Instant rebrand. You got fantastic through-flow of grockle voyeurs, emotion trekkers . . . One of the coursework learnings I made in my first degree is small traders have got the flexibility to exploit the ignorance-based culture. So he's goin' to move the van up Tolly Bunny: it'll be heaving by lunchtime . . . Scene of crime . . .'

She listens with astonishment. She was speechless. His opportunism was heartlessly callow. Yet she was complicit, she was the catalyst. She was part of this. She was overcome by a realisation that she could not suppress. She was, yes, hoping that the body was indeed that of a murder victim. She was ashamed of this novel frisson, of her flirtation with what seemed like danger, of her contamination by squalor of the ultimate crime.

But she couldn't deny the excitement that this violent rending of routine's fabric had caused her. Her lower spine tingled thrillingly.

'You're such clever detectives, boys,' she told Hector and Arthur.

It wasn't until 11.22 that a police car arrived.

PC Phelp and WPC Duanes explained that the delay was due to their having undergone Prospective Stress Counselling before they left the station.

'Ticked that box – just in case it really is a human body,' says PC Phelp.

'It is,' Old Carn is emphatic.

She pushes Hector and Arthur into the back of the car.

'If you could keep their feet off of the seat.'

'This is a treat isn't it, boys. This is a squad car.'

PC Phelp drives half a mile to the forest-green bridge that spans Tolly Bunny. Its wrought-iron railings are inset with lozenges containing the Tolly crest. He pulls off the metalled surface and parks beneath the beeches beside the start of Dene Drive North.

'Haven't been issued the right boots for this. Going to get my feet all . . .' He steps from the car onto the glistening, grassless rink of chalk and mud. They set off into the ravine down the slope constellated with twigs and beechnuts. Hector and Arthur lead the way. Old Carn slides and whoops in exhilaration. PC Phelp and WPC Duanes tread warily, grab at branches and teeter backwards to keep their balance.

A swollen red rubber thimble protruding from dead leaves catches WPC Duanes's eye. Its pimples have been worn down over many years since it first arrived here (in circumstances not worth recounting). She immediately recognises what it is: she used one at school in Year 7 Comparative Quilting. And yet its visual affinity to a severed nipple – which she knows it is not – appals her, fixes her to the spot. It is by this harmless perishing object of inchoate obscenity that she will recall the horror of that afternoon rather than by bones, hair, teeth, amalgam, non-degradable fibres.

I am getting deteriorations.

I am thinking at last, at last, they are coming to get me. All because

Chair of Beaks Beak Cow's dog is digging. Not like him. He was digging through night with legend goalkeeper big soft hands not used to digging. Grim purpose. I owe him for my different existing and its travel opportunities to everywhere like trees, sand, set under car park, nine-hole bunker. Where am I watching from? How am I listening? These are questions.

Why is Ice Cream Boy Jason talking talking . . . what does he mean when he says empty wigs . . . talking like he is one who is knowing true story of roots and worms and mycelium and bastard larval weevil and hunting ants when I am one knowing true story? I am knowing it because I have been there (or here) since. I am attending it, I am attending my existing – like you are living your life. Almost like. I want to shout putting him right. I am yearning that he is hearing but he isn't.

He is almost telling true story when he is saying at Newspapers' Local Colour Operatives and Regional Telly's Crime Hinterland Quest with scaley eczema camera operator:

'Full on dogging. And how! Dogging by night, naturally. In the headlights. You'll have twenty or thirty up here. Passive doggers, active doggers. On the bonnet doggers. Car roofs some of them. And you got day dogging too. That's what Tolly Dene's come to. Exhibitionist circus, right? Surprising bunch, doggers. It's not victims of society, the unwaged – not what you'd expect. It's mostly professionals, middle managers, nurses, schoolteachers letting off steam, accountants, the undisadvantaged. 5 series BMWs, 7 series even, Mercs. Nice clothes – when they got any on. You'd never take them for crotch sordids if you pass them in the street. I suppose it's like they're guilty about their champagne lifestyle, so they go slumming in public – it's sort of expiation, and how! Pleasurable penance.

'Then there's old folk coming to watch. Some is so old it's like they got out of the grave specially for a guilty shufti. Loads of them. Five up in a rusty Coruna. Six to a Valencia. You'd think they'd have seen enough by the time they got the bus pass – but it's there forever, the sex urge is. That's what working up here has lessoned Jason. Good luck to them. Even if it does come on a bit yuck. Quite a few of the old folk even walk up here, they're that keen. Doesn't do their asthma any favours. You find used puffers everywhere. There's any amount of inhalers in Hodges Wood – like there's been a wheezers' convention. The behaviours get them all excited.'

He is telling selfsame at former schoolchum Detective Constable Nix. Plus:

'Sure. Yeh. You got a considerable through-put of more legit . . . goes without saying. Not everyone's suss. You got multiple puppy-dog exercisers, joggers, sportspeople, outdoor-activities persons, kids playing football, loafers without a decisive leisure agenda, cyclists, kite flyers. Et cetera. But you never know what they're wearing underneath the tracksuit. If you get my meaning.

'What I'm saying is doggers look normal when they're not dogging. Like murderers look normal. Murderers got hobbies too: they're not murdering fulltime.

'Look: I don't keep a diary of all the weird stuff that's going down up here. Never make any sales if I did! There is quite a few troubled loners walking off their heartbreak. You can be sure they got Toni Lo Reno on their earphones. I don't count them. I count the magpies mind, my nan always said you should: you remember my nan. Fifteen for a rollover jackpot.

'There's a lot of whiteflights creeping back all nostalgic. You can tell them by the way they're twitchy about keeping the car doors locked. Like they reckon Tolly Dene is a danger zone now. Maybe they're right. Never see any of your lot up here on patrol, have to say.

'I phoned the police twice last week to report an incident. They just told me I was a nuisance caller and if I did it again I'd be prosecuted.

'You know the Tollygarth Allotments? That footpath like a causeway along the bottom, the side away from the ridge? I sometimes go that way now. I was cycling down there Wednesday afternoon and there's this group of geezers, blokes – right? A chapter of The Smiths and Tinkers of The Shining Beztine. Standing round in a huddle? Some of them's got spades. They're digging next to this sort of half fallen-down shed. There's a big box, cardboard. Like you see in garment trade wholesalers yeh? It's just sitting there in a potato patch or whatever. One of them stops me, he takes this long tunic out the box – like religious clobber – asks me if I want to buy it. In an allotment! And then he pulls out this pair of matching trousers – with elasticated waistband. They're all soaked in . . . well, I'm sure it was blood, half dried, congealed. All the while the others are burying something. In the plot. It . . . it sounds far-fetched – but, well, I could swear it looked like a head. There was meat . . . you know, flesh. There was definitely hair, dark hair. All matted with blood . . . I mean I couldn't quite see exactly. Because they're about five metres away and they were stood round the hole filling it in. I kept thinking *stoned adulteress* – but I wasn't going to ask was I? What d'you make of that then?'

Detective Constable Nix is saying:

'If you was one of us, Jason, you'd get packed straight off to Diversity Awareness Training. You, mate, have got unresolved Diversityphobia issues. Them Smiths and Tinkers lads was just enjoying a good-natured bant. The bloke-folk have high spirits too. That's what it's all about: different cultures expressing theirselves through different customs and practices. That's what makes us a top country multifaithwise. Vibrant with culture and differences.'

Old Carn Vanier seconded Detective Constable Nix, scolding Jason: 'We must not only love one another and tolerate one another, we must respect one another. In Smiths and Tinkers culture burying a head is not the same as burying a head in our culture.'

Shaun Memory: My Wit and Wisdom

When my old chum Henry comes on the dog he goes to me can I help him look for his parents? Is he coming over all post-traumatic or what? They're still there mate I tell him – 'in the cemetery mate, six feet under where you put them mate . . . a couple of months back. Unlikely to have moved mate. It's the soul that goes up isn't it – not the body. But you know that Henry.'

'Dogg on the dog.' Office cry. Like a street cry of old. Everyone is like oh no not *again*. He's always meant to be put through to the Every Trick In The Book ringtone. It's like a warning.

Watching the snoutcasts and vapers drawing on their poison in the designated doorway with the ashtray. Company regs says they have to be cleared and cleaned. Vee-pee-ell – that's my only message for the fat-arsed mouthy one from The Human Flotsam Hub. Got a face like a charity shop. Legs like tree trunks when the bark has all fallen off and you got pasty white wood. Who the fuck hired her?

From Gene Solutions and Family Logistics we've moved double-big-time into security. We did a leveraged reverse buyout of the Sentinelitude Praetorian (Alderley Edge) Group. We have taken it national, grown it way beyond footballers and CEOs to embassies, the City, visiting major heads of state (Burkina Faso, Moldova, North Macedonia).

Someone Else's Baby gives the group our core values.
   Sentinelitude Praetorian was the first to pinpoint footballers. They needed safety and security. It's not just Hale, Knutsford, Eccleston.

It's Solihull, Totteridge, Formby, Jesmond, little Rutland . . . Every Saturday afternoon is Thieves Paradise. *Was* Thieves Paradise. Because one of our new core values is owning some of the most psychotic Marcher Hounds money can buy. Specialists in separating limbs from trunk. The heavily tooled up, totally blocked and stupidly reckless will still chance their arm (and it could be a literal arm). The rest have gone back to less demanding fields – working over sub-post offices and so on.

I outlined my philosophy when I was interviewed on *It's A New Day* after I reunited an octogenarian daughter in her eighties with her nonagenarian mother in her nineties. Only fifteen years between them. Salt of the earth. Hated each other at first sight. The mother had been put in a home. The daughter had been adopted by abusers in the days when there was no word for abuser.

Me: My philosophy is . . . you got to get yourself a philosophy.

Charlotte (Interviewer – I think that was the slapper's name): I think we'd all go along with that. So what's yours Shaun?

Me: What's my what?

C: Philosophy.

Me: I just said . . . my philosophy is you got to get yourself a philosophy.

C: Ah . . . but that's not a philosophy.

Me: What you mean?

C: Saying you've got to get a philosophy isn't a philosophy.

Me: It is. It's my philosophy.

C: So . . . getting a philosophy . . . is your philosophy.

Me: You got there in the end luv.

I'm known as larger than life. I totally refute it means I'm a relentless bully who throws his not inconsiderable weight around whenever I fancy it.

But – I do call a spade a spade. Example: I call Anwar at The Magic Biryani 'My Celebrity Suicide Bomber'. That's fair enough social comment because one of his cousins Masud is a Repeat Offender Suicide Bomber – yes, it is possible. Both times the devices were so badly bodged they didn't explode. If he'd spent a bit more time in technical lessons and less grovelling in the taber he wouldn't be doing twenty years as a Class A in Long Lartin.

He'd be shagging virgins with Lal Lal, winner of a deathtime achievement award at the BBC's Martyrdom Personality of the Year Awards. Lal, like his predecessor, was sadly unable to be physically present. His bruv Horeb collected it on his behalf: 'He did it for all of us. Them tracking shots around the bits that used to be him say it all.'

Who needs a mistress? How many heads can you get in your lap at any one time? OK one or two maybe – but no more than three, watch out for empty wigs and overcrowding!

Informality is key to a top environment. My game plan is all about open necks, anti-hierarchy, awaydays, bonding (paintballing and mudbaths are musts), sharing and family values. I can hear what you're saying: in the final analysis Someone Else's Baby's success and its status as the UK's numero uno trace agency is down to the breakdown of the nuclear family.

Everyone here has an official nickname for extra affirmation of individuality in a caring pastoral environment.

Example: Ray Downs in Predictive Planning we call him 'Syndrome' or Syndy. It took a bit of creativity to come up with that one. He reacted maturely when I told him it was down to choosing between the company ethic and a P45. He doesn't mind now he's used to it.

Example: Roger Dean is 'Triple R'. He's gay as a boat. With him everything's fabulosa or grotterama. His last bumchum emigrated to Anustralia. So he got a new husband/wife off Leather Jocker. He's also called Roger. So Roger rogers Roger. RrR. Simple really. He knows not to be too touchy. Especially cos I know about their little secret dressing up in SS uniform for their privates-on-parade parties and The Stout As Oak Moot.

Example: Landry Nordtveit is 'Chastity'. The girl won't put out for anyone. Mad as a hatter. She's got a virgin Mary thing going. When I told her the way she's going she's going to give birth to the Little Baby Jesus she's going like: I just might, I just might . . . She was on the biscuit with that one. Sadly the world wasn't ready for her kind of Little Baby Jesus.

Example: Ex-Detective Inspector Desmond Hubback (semi-attached freelance) is 'Quasimodo'.

Example: Peter Harbottle is 'Early Onset' – always forgetting his keys, where he parked, his grandkids' birthdays etc. Sadly has to be reminded that he played on Mrs Mills's Party Seven, had top thirty hits as the organist in The Karisma Set and The Barry Island Five way back when. Never forgot his keys then!

Example: Sam Davis in Procurement. Indolent bastard – so fucking lazy he can't give himself a half-decent wrist shandy. He wasn't overjoyed to be called 'The Red Sea Pedestrian', shortened to The Pedestrian. He suffered in silence. But the fucker took offence when I called him an oven-dodging yid cunt. He had just cost the company GBP 140,000 in incompatible anti-malware anti-ransomeware kit. What's all the fuss – it's just joshing isn't it, robust joshing . . . high spirited, ought to be taken in the spirit it's intended. It's what I call 'being up your sandwich'. Glad to report that the employment tribunal decided there is still a place for free speech. The fucker moved on to fresh challenges.

I got a five cabin two stateroom six figure Hatteras motor yacht: *Snow Leopard of the Seas*. I renamed it. *Meisterfelcher* said a bit too much about the previous owner that I didn't want to be associated with. The envy of all my mates Dogg included. Great for tanning, cocktails, entertainment.

What I say to the ladies who come aboard is: 'We all got a little bit of the sailor in us and the lucky ones get a large bit of the sailor!'

Alertness. You're driving around honing your observational powers, you're going 'VPL, VPL, VPL, thong, VPL, thong, commando, undisclosed . . .' Observing and deducing. What I call 'a short one in the tent'.

Sense of belonging is a top sense. So I help people belong. Sense of community. Always a cup of sugar ready to hand over the fence, so to speak. Pride in a well-polished doorstep. Not letting down the street with grimy tiles cos the next thing you know you'll have half of Malawi living next door roasting rats in the garden.

A vocation more than a business. It's more even than a people business. It's all about being a part of a greater something.

Someone Else's Baby is proud to find advantaged parents for disadvantaged orphans. And proud to find disadvantaged orphans for advantaged parents. From the Vietnamese Jungle to Islington, causes and cassoulet is a big step but it's one that can be safely made with the support of Someone Else's Baby. Fees On Demand.

It's our job to provide. You got to think of this enterprise – and it's a business, remember, as well as a vocation, a people business – as being in the dreamsphere. We're making dreams come true. It's what I call leathering the omelette. No square pegs in round holes. The right bolt for the right nut gives me a hard-on.

But when you get the wrong bolt . . . There was this gay couple wanting to adopt. Got no problem with that. All going smoothly till Wendy Whatshername comes into my meeting without so much as a by your leave going you know who these people are . . . They told us they was music industry. Turns out what that means is they got a stable of white power groups Pavement Rape, Nigger's Slum, Sink The Windrush etc. The last thing I need is to be associated with that branch of light entertainment . . . Historic reasons. I've got a reputation to protect. If you could get reputation condoms I'd buy them wholesale. Breach of contract. They had me over a legal barrel. Out of court settlement. They got their fuckbaby from some disreputable source.

A Thai toy was giving me a massage. She finishes: she says you want masturbation? Well you're not going to turn that one down are you. So you say yes. And she says – OK I go fetch you dirty magazine. I felt a real loser. I been done. What a scam! Like a pub with no beer.

Chastity had words of wit and wisdom for me: 'Look at it this way Shaun. Jesus had to heft his own cross and wear a barbed wire crown, he got mocked, he got lapidated, he got roofing nails through his hands and feet – and he got over it. You get over it.'

★

Ornithology. It's good to get to know ladies of different nations and cultures. The Japanese have some tasty tricks up their sleeves. Latinas – cracking. In fact they're all cracking. Though I do draw a line at goubiebabes. They are not oil paintings. No way. Not even B&Q own brand emulsion. I'm all for the mask.

I'm not allowed to have my own memories. I'm meant to have other people's. And to find the people those people have memories of. *Think* they have memories of . . . Can be persuaded they have memories of. Half of them are Alzheimer's anyway. They always leave it too late before they go searching for the kiddies they gave away because of the disgrace they'd have faced.

Mass communications and the digital revolution enable terrorism and porn, the two evils of our epoch: I know which I'd sooner have. A well-rewarded nympho being porked up every orifice by tattooed body fascists. Or thousands of people blown to pieces by a beardy goubiebro in a public concourse without warning. No contest.

We had to let Denzil Space go. Rogue behaviours. One day he's proudly showing off his cock in front of the interns, the next day he won't even show his cuffed hands and his face when he's led into court with a tartan blanket over his head. I'd say there's moral progress there, without a doubt. You can tell he's well on the way to redemption.

I was texting Ginny (telling her I was going to be late at Andrea's Peperoncino). Verity was giving me my pre-lunchtime hundred to eight. Them buttocks – ooh! Tender as filet mignon. Syndrome says she's known around the office as my Penile Assistant not Personal Assistant. One and the same I'd say. Employer/employee relations are improved if I pump up their tyres.

Phone no. 4 with the Lou Christie ringtone. Every trick in the book. Warning: Dogg!

'How do you spell Peperoncino doll?' I asked Verity. And immediately regretted it.

'P. E. P. E. R . . .'

'OK. That's enough. Keep concentrated on the job.'

I texted 'Running late see you Andrea's 1.30'.

'Yes?' I said to Dogg.

'What's the average height and weight of a psychopath?' I heard Syndrome asking someone in the corridor.

Verity was doing that thing she does with the bottom of the shaft. It was swelling nicely, that's to say well painfully going on agonisingly. She pushed her nails into a thick vein. I winced. She grinned up at me.

'I've got,' said Dogg, 'this problem.'

Never!

Sir Geoffrey Shadoxhurst Bt

I feel dead.

A chap sits there in a state of serenity. Or something damned close. Filial gratitude too. And quiet anticipation. Push the seat back so there's no chance of a cuff getting itself snagged by the steering wheel. There's nothing quite like that moment before they begin their great seething journey. Journey? No. Invasion, that's more the ticket. So much sex is invasion. Some, admittedly, not totally welcome. I'd maintain, however, that most is met with greedy thank-yous like the Anschluss or the march into France. (Mention it not to Johnny Frog but his is a nation that cries rape only after it has enjoyed multiple orgasms! This bit fits here, Mademoiselle. Ah . . . you knew it! And why don't you . . . you're such a corker. Und so weiter. Of course there are some ingrates and cowards – some French popsies are such silly-jillies, just like those blighters the Czechs.)

As I was saying: it's that moment when the invasion is in motion but has yet to breach the border so to speak, it's that moment when the stirring begins, when the tension tautens. The spring is wound tighter and tighter. Sort of psychological ligature as the shrinks might put it if you please. You can feel it. Feel free to feel it, darling, says I! But no . . . No, that would be to put the old damper on it.

It is precisely the absence of a second party that's so special about this procedure. Then there's the fact that a space you can normally be seen in, the sitting room on wheels as I call it, gets foaming curtains for a crucial moment. A crucial moment of privacy. That's what does the trick. You have that window of opportunity – a soapy window! – in which to act. This is not one for exhibitionists. Nothing so vulgar. Cripes no! Rather the opposite. For a minute – or longer if you cheat with a so-called deluxe programme of Supashyne Professional &

Wheel Valet Gloss – you are alone in the world, cocooned in stiff brushes, creamy suds and lovely squelch. It's like being swallowed by a dripping cunt. When I used to fetch Justine I'd always keep her waiting so I could hear her say: 'I just had to wipe myself down.' Oh she was a wet one, drowning in her juice, which would soon be sluicing around Tiger. Had to be careful what I drove her in. Much as I loved her and her humid ways I had to respect the upholstery. Connolly leather is super-dependable, it can take just about the lot, but a noggin of minge-ale and the old cockfroth isn't what the doctor ordered. The Facel Vega had been reupholstered in Kydex or Naugahyde or some such which proved sturdily resistant to juicy immersion. Trevor Gammack, whose car wash empire would one day stretch from Waterlooville to Canford Cliffs, was a vulgar little fellow, but on the plus side he had no time for kikes and was happy to have his operatives reprogramme his Supashyne machines to my liking in return for my plaudits on what he calls his 'literature'.

Justine had soap in her blood, shampoo in her heart. Late afternoon during the perineum of the year more than a decade and a half ago the looking glass told me I was a trifle négligé – but not in the right way if you follow my drift, not elegantly négligé; more benefits-and-B&B négligé. The Lagonda, the leather base of its gearshift like a baggy scrotum, sped into town. High wind, trees waving, madly greeting me as though I was their ruler, a benevolent tyrant feeding on the insanity of leaves and loving every minute of it.

She had started at Hair Conditioning only a couple of weeks previously. There was an immediate stirring in Tiger's pen. What fesses! My enquiring mind tried to surmise what she was wearing beneath her overall. She was quite unlike any other junger friseur I had encountered. Such a popsy, such fun, such a sexpot. And bright. While she was massaging my bonce with a deliciously fragrant bay rum she remarked that she was going to see in the New Year at somewhere called Matty's Le Malibu Lounge. She wasn't keen on the idea, 'empty wigs basically'. But her 'possee' was insistent and she didn't want to let them down. They could get the ferry there. But the ferry stopped at 11 p.m. No question of driving themselves back at 3 a.m. with johnny bluebottle lurking in the bushes with his breathalyser. So they'd have to take a taxi. £75 if you please. New Year's Eve tariff.

The darling thing said to me: 'It must be great being so old you don't have to go to clubs.'

Old! Old? I looked at the man in the mirror. There were many qualities on show. Handsome, dashing, suave, gently amused . . . but old? Maybe . . . One realises it. I've spent millions on ladies of the night – though at my stage in life they're more likely to be ladies of the afternoon given that I like to be tucked up by nine o'clock with a mug of Horlicks and a fat joint.

To be on the safe side I reached in my pocket and popped down a couple of Ods.

I was slightly bruised. Nonetheless, noblesse oblige. I gave her a £100 tip.

'No strings attached?'

I replied: 'Entirely up to you.'

She whispered: 'You could be my sugar daddy.'

What a superb artiste she is! £100 tips mount up. More when she stages a little divertissement with the Ice Maiden and Staff's 'road crew'.

The fashion for shaven genitalia has had a splendid impact on us dedicated *collectionneurs*. Let us raise a glass to Brazil and its people, fine samba warriors. First they get rid of the rainforest then they get rid of pubic bushes. It's got to be a psychological quirk. We used to have to hire girls to grow hair or sift through beauticians' waste or, in extremis, rely on the powder in electric razors. Justine has been a boon in this department.

Sixteen years on she has seven salons of her own. I have had the privilege of cutting the ribbon at four, Justine de Montmartre, Justine de Montfaucon, Justine de Montveneris and Justine de Montparnasse. The latter two the former premises of vertical tanning studios bankrupted by the negligence actions of injuriously over-roasted customers, one of whom is said to have appeared to have changed race. She has always resisted, perhaps wisely, my humorous suggestion that a salon should be named Chopchop!

'Where's the class in that?' she asks as I melt with her taunting and wiggles. She allows me glimpses of her over-shoulder-boulder-holder then laughingly cries: 'Down, boy. You really are such a fruity old perv.'

To which I can't help but slobberingly reply: 'I could not possibly agree more.'

I often shave her. I have a steady hand. Est honor meus sollertia.[9]

Then meat meets meat.

I'd be the first to own up to it. The love of lather isn't up everyone's strasse. Obviously there are members of the queer fraternity – community! – who can conceive of nothing chummier than a lusty soap dip in a shower. Queers are schoolboys at heart. Forever yearning for the changing room, the reek of the gusset and all that. Suds away! Pretty unlikely that they can all have shared the same formative experience as I did, though you never know. Justine has kept me young. She's kept Tiger hyperactive. My contemporaries are astonished, aghast (and probably jealous). For example, I saw Constance M in the street. What a doddery old thing she's turned into. She said what about coming over for dindins with her and Billy and whatever he's called the drooling alcoholic son next Friday. Consulted the diary on my phone and had to tell her: 'No can do. I'm going to be fucking.'

I loved Sundays when I was a little chap. Waking up, sitting in bed impatiently gnawing at Raggedy Reggy Fitzroy till I heard the distant bell for matins. It rang out across the misty meadows and the deer park, never quite drowning out the racket of the rooks in the elms. Those bells were my signal. Time to get up and creep past Nanny Shadox's room. Then I walk stealthy as a ghost down the backstairs to my parents' part of the house. The corridor dado was tan Lincrusta with a thistle pattern. All along it on the walls were those ancient framed photos of the family, the house, the lodges, the Redoubt, Home Marsh, Friary Field, the heady hothouses (peaches, figs, apricots, custard apples, persimmons), the staff. While the park church (Henry Woodyer 1861) is extant, the village churchyard was desecrated in the name of progress: the word bypass signifies rotting coffins exhumed and waiting to be removed and corpses too dead to make their escape. So much has gone. People, whatever their station, have their term. All but one of the Shadoxhursts who

---

9 My dexterity is my honour.

came and went and who, in their brief span, got, one after the other, the photography bug, have gone. Astonishing how much places change too.

All the elms, of course, killed off by a fungus, the only successful invasion our friends from the flatlands ever pulled off! And the post and rail fence round Friary Field. Seized by the government to be melted down for the 'war effort' – so it was probably unceremoniously buried in a top secret slag heap, most likely on the Mendips, what the oggies thereabouts call batches. But it's more the accumulation of minuscule, almost invisible nips and cuts, which strikes one after so long. The entire surrounds of Faineant have been remade, over and over. Everything is different. The posture of men back from harvest, their tools, the weft of sheared grass, raked gravel's patterns, the gamut of specimens in a parterre.

That was England. There went England.

'Daaarleenk Boy,' Mama's voice was husky (everyone said so. It was how they avoided mentioning her accent. Husky. It was some years before I sorted out the confusion with the dog breed, and by then it was too late.). Her bedroom smelled of Jicky and toasty laundry.

I didn't have the foggiest at the time – I had nothing to compare it with – but I was born to the best. That's all I knew. I took the exquisite for granted. Menton. Les Baux. The Villa Bleu. The Villa Jana. Molinard. Worth. Petrossian. Fauchard. Cotton from Egypt, native land of the damned traitor Hess. A squash court of one's own. White gold. Books bound in white buckskin to match the library shelves and walls. Petrus. Shad roe for the Shadoxhursts. Jujurieux. Randersacker. The Hispano Suiza. The only Phantom Corsair ever produced. The cobalt blue Stutz Bearcat. Above all the unique Mercedes (Neubauer, Dick Seaman, the Führer). With tastes like mine I should have been as queer as Dada but I was not so blessed.

Mama would pat the bed. I'd snuggle up beside her. A putto beside a voluptuous goddess. I'd tell her my dreams and invent adventures for Raggedy Reggy Fitzroy. He always escaped the werewolves whose howls were as bloodcurdling as I could muster. 'My Daaarleenk Verecub. One day you'll be my Verewolf.' For her there could be nothing better than a lycanthropic son. 'Howl, my leettle Verecub!'

One such morning when I was twelve – old habits! – I was cosy beside her eating warm bread, soft butter and honey from her break-fast tray when Dada marched into her bedroom. He was drying his golden hair.

'Darlink Freddie, you 'ave shave soap like you are Fuzza Chrissmas.'

He repeated what he had said a few minutes earlier when we were listening to the wireless.

'What – what! – has ruddy Poland ever done for us? Poland! All I know of the damned place is that it's so flat it's an invitation to take your tanks for a whirl . . . an invitation it would be discourteous to decline.'

His astrakhan-collared pewter and navy dressing gown lent him the air of the swell boxer he once had been – Public Schools bantam-weight champion 1917 and 1918, quite an achievement notwithstanders that the older chaps had already gone off to war.

'Just let the Führer get on with it. He knows what he's doing. Which is more than can be said of that man Chamberlain. God what a drivelling sniveller the man is. What is he?'

'A drivelling sniveller and a yellow streak down his spine to boot, Dada.'

'That's it. Ruddy pact with Poland . . . Poland! . . . it's just spite towards the Führer, all out of spite. You can be sure that our friends in International Finance are at the helm. And the ineffable Horeb El Isha. God almighty – where does it leave one? It's so . . . compromising.'

Why was our government itching to fight another war? Had not the last one been enough? The tragic mistake to end all tragic mis-takes? The English may be bellicose. The Germans may be martial. But we are brothers.

'Kin folk kin tongued even as we are.' Dada often quoted Hardy, 'the hetero Housman'. What he wrote in 1915 was still spot-on twenty-four years later. I knew 'The Pity of It' by heart. Only a few weeks before, Dada had even read out, with a grudging hear-hear, what Rolf Gardiner,[10] another Dorset man, had rued in *New Pioneer*: 'Those who should be friends and kinsmen are in open enmity.' Grudging

---

10 He wrote that the *Ostjuden* 'have the smell of Asia fresh in their beards'.

because, although Dada was on speakers with Gardiner and considered him basically sound (on sylviculture, agriculture, race, breeding), he was browned off by his twittish scoutmaster tendency. All that airy-fairy, arty-farty, singing-while-we-whittle-round-the-campfire was just so much kidney pee. Required: less hey-nonny-no, more iron will. Dada's work camps for The Offspring of the Urban Misfortunate were more like it. They were foundries of discipline and bodies hard as flint. Harry Umberson-Dogg wrote a splendid paean to the camps in *The Nordic*.

Dada announced, as he did every Sunday: 'I'm going to canter over to Roddie's. Luncheon one thirty? Who've we got coming?'

A few minutes later we could hear the jolly pizzicato clipclip-clopclipclipclop of gaited hooves on the cobbles this side of the tack room.

I went to the window. Marengo was being led by Davy Skitch.

Oh, the splendour of that massive Stralsunder stallion! What delicacy, what barbarous strength! Black body and head, black so black it was almost blue, silver mane and tail. A creature of the finest breeding. And what is breeding if not willed reincarnation, the determination that the genes of the parents should be repeated, visited on generation after generation. It was never my wish to breed for posterity. Seed-release for my pleasure and their profit is a different matter. Should one fertilise the eggs of a mare of inferior caste the progeny must be admitted to a furlough of abrogation.

Dada wore chamois breeches. His black boots, gloves and crop were as glossy as Marengo's coat. He was shirtless, his torso was tanned, lean, muscular, his abundant pelt caught the sun. He was, then, still a blond god to me. But there was something amiss. That day Marengo did not canter. They walked as one, tiptoeing elegantly, across the park towards the cedars of Lebanon and the slope beyond. They took the sandy track that climbed through the bracken to Botanical Wood, The Hermitage and up Slope Hide where the vase and swags and viewing platform railings at the top of the Doric monument rise mightily over the wooded brow. Out of sight of the house he would, as he did every Sunday, dismount and stand by the monument in contemplation and remembrance of a day he couldn't remember, a day he couldn't let go of.

Loyal Pippin was beside them, snuffling about the grass. Davy's little boy The Pathetic Mite Ned limped behind them with a trowel and trug peering through his immensely thick specs to gather Marengo's precious manure, a task he prosecuted with eager gratitude. You never see staunch leg braces like The Pathetic Mite Ned's today. Callipers and leather are so *alter hut. Altmodischen.* More's the pity. A question of the poor just not getting the right diseases any more. I dare say diet plays its part too. Had Germany invaded, under NSDAP rule The Pathetic Mite Ned would unquestionably have been culled. No one went so far as to say so but it was the silent consensus. The admonition to cultivate our garden includes the duty of weeding it. Had it fallen to me to carry out the sentence in the name of racial hygiene I'd have done my duty without, I hope, any animosity on either of our parts.

A plume of smoke rose from beyond the wood. The two Berts, Lugsden and Twibill, would be burning a scarecrow every day for a week to give thanks for the harvest. Like the rest of the mentally enfeebled they'd have been culled too, no matter how fierce their loyalty to their master.

How many more such scenes would I see?

The beginning of war was the end of something else that was not going to be recuperable. The end of the possibility of England conjoined with Germany on equal terms.

The day itself wasn't all doom and gloom. It wasn't chucking it down or anything. It was muggy, slightly hazy. No breeze, High Lake was still. No ominous clouds, indeed hardly a cloud in the milky blue sky. Beyond the lake and the gunnera the splendid southdowns grazed on, happily ignorant of the affairs of man. Now, they actually were like clouds, plump as cumuli and as English as fladge. How English it all was. How green it all was.

The slowness of Dada's progress was disquieting. It was saddening because unprecedented. Ponderous, no joie de vivre or derring-do. That wasn't his way. He was solemnly drinking in all that he could see as though he knew that this great domain would soon no longer be his. Impossible to believe then that sixty years later a kindredly black-booted, black-gloved Stafford Prance would one day grace Faineant Park.

That tense summer. Rollo Gammans:

a term pregnant with foreboding
no draught of tansy shall make an angel of.

In early May Davy had hurried into Dada's den to tell him that two men had driven to the end of the avenue, left their car there, and were now sauntering about the park. One seemed to be photographing the park and jotting down notes. The other had 'this seeing machine thing' over by Friary Field. When challenged they had the impudence to appear affronted. They introduced themselves as Southern Command land agents compiling an inventory of properties that might be requisitioned for military purposes. Without so much as a by your leave they were assessing the potential of the Faineant estate, and of the park. With a theodolite, they were working out whether parts of the park were level enough for prefabricated buildings, Nissen huts and kindred blots; the naked eye would have resoundingly told them yes, without all the fuss of the theodolite. When Dada observed that they were trespassing they insolently told him that a 'new disposal' had been sanctioned. He said he felt like wiping the smug smiles from their chops. One of them had Judath-red hair and a lithp.

Now, on the third of September, that malign future they presaged four months before, which had been subsequently emphasised by further visits and some menacing manila, had very nearly arrived.

Mama was in tears. That beautiful face was contorted, flushed. 'Vhat eez going to happen? Vhat eez going to happen? My sveetingpie.' Her breath was hot and lovely. I cuddled her. Sobbing jerkily, heaving with grief, she repetitively chanted 'Zeese Aimergency Powus Act'. I didn't really have the foggiest about it, I was in the dark about what effect it would have on us, how a government's cruel whims could barge into private lives.

'You get me leettle dreenk and breenk me een bath.'

Mama was not immune to the pleasures of the grape, nor of grain for that matter. I went to her dressing room, took the ingredients from the refrigerator. The Formula – which I had by heart and shall never forget: sugar cube, big splash angosturas, two fingers Asbach brandy, two fingers Jägermeister ('Göring Schnapps'), half bottle Anheuser blanc de noir Spätburgunder. The enamel and silver stein was hardly a lady's vessel. But then she often wore Pour Un Homme and a man's watch, and had always refused to leave the table after dinner.

She lay in the dolphin-flanked, shell-shaped bath sipping, then swigging, smoking New Epochs listening to Ruth Etting on the gramophone, her solution to being down in the mouth. Sandalwood oil marbled the surface. I never got in before she uttered the invitation: 'Soaptime, Darleenk!' She rarely used anything other than Amalfitano's Bois de Cèdre, an ivory cake inset with a delicious cedilla of minge hair. Its unmistakable scent summons her to this day. We'd lather each other, her smooth body, and mine ever more masculine, newly hirsute: how proud I was of the changes that were occurring, and with speed. We were joyful cherubs, pretending we were in a rock pool or a pond in a woodland glade. This was the closest to heaven I ever came. For years I hoped to replicate that soapy bliss. Spent a fortune, hundreds of thousands, yearning to recreate that maternal love. Not that I regret it; the foothills of bliss are pleasurable too. But, well . . . the way her body tautened in response to my sudsy hands was unique, never to be found elsewhere and my god I've searched high and low. Lifelong quest. You can lather an aperture till the proverbial cows come home but you cannot conjure up that sensation of the exquisite and the forbidden. No matter how many lovers we may have, we have only one mother. Only one mother whispering and nuzzling and teaching my hand to touch her crimson bud. Only one mother buffing my now mature Tiger till the big cat explodes in pain and pleasure and my bodily spasms displaced a wave of water from the bath (again! Call the builders!). Motherly love was never so motherly.

'Naughty Mama,' she giggled, 'naughty.' Maybe her self-reproach was more real than she pretended.

The gramophone needle repetitively scraped the centre of the last record on the autochanger; water that won't go down the plughole. A dutiful son, I turned it off.

She took a draught from the stein. As ever she warned: 'Not a word to Dada. Special secrets – not for Dada.'

I didn't let on that I didn't buy the idea that Dada was ignorant. Indifferent was more like it. He wasn't fooled for a moment. Nor was I.

A thing of beauty is a boy forever. Most Englishmen are queers. Maybe more than most. I regret that I am an exception to our proud tradition. Our island tradition. Our unique ancestral mix determines our sexual complexion. Viking, Saxon, Celt, Norman. Quite unlike that of other European countries. It does not preclude procreation, obviously. A woman is for duty. She bears the queers of the future who keep the name alive, who will in their turn spawn heirs born bent as a nine-bob note with genetic bias acquired in the womb. Custom and practice are pre-programmed. Atavism's irresistible pull. There's no escape. Why should anyone want to escape? It comes from the top. The kings – show me a straight king and I'll show you a usurper. That's the nature taken care of.

Here's the nurture. What does it tell us?

The Anglican communion, single sex 'education', Boy Scouts, the armed forces, police section houses, the Masters of the Determinant, theatre and ballet 'communities', masonic lodges, communal toilets without doors, communal showers, prison, ordinands' dormitories, 'Turkish' baths, flight crews' overnighters, the fire service, inns of court, the Idyllic Brotherhood, wrestling, 'gentlemen's' clubs, The Garrick, The Travellers, White's and so on.

What it tells us is this. Even when sodomitical high jinks were punished by spiteful laws the whole caboodle in The Green and Pleasant was, if you cared to take a shufti, a prod to Attic companionship, the lavender life, love of comrades. Newbolt was a sly one. Fais ce que voudras – so long as you don't get nabbed doing it, whatever it is. Rough stubble will speak to rough stubble. Bachelor to bachelor. Sod, sod, sod anyone who tries to stop you. The pleasure of the moment is the only possible motive for action. I'm all for action. Have even been known to enjoy an occasional ride on the mount that comes from behind – but it's never been my natural berth. I suppose that makes me not much of an Englishman.

Masochism was standard issue. The more vindictive the attack on inversion the more inverted the attacker, the greater the depths of his self-loathing. The victim of 'justice' is a proxy for the hypocrite dispensing 'justice' while longing for chastisement, the stroke of the bullwhip, the glans nailed to a plank, the back garden crucifixion. The risk of being caught boosted the thrill. So did punishment. Many queers would just adore to retrofit the rite of coming-up-before-the-bench, getting a talking to from the stipe who, as soon as he has delivered the savage sentence (more in sorrow than anger, of course), is off to a nearby cottage bent on meeting a good sport. Here's hoping there isn't a very special constable in the rafters.

It was all swept under the carpet, wasn't it. But not very far under and anyway the carpet was so threadbare it could be seen through, which doesn't necessarily make it valuable – but don't throw it out. Little Dominic Rose advises that: 'Shabby chic comes round every few years. Shabby chic will be so now before you've even fetched it back from the dedicated drycleaner (the carpet, that is).'

As a young man my Dada Freddie Shadoxhurst may possibly have shopped on both sides of the street. Well why not? Why restrict yourself? But he pretty soon opted for the lavender side. Even before I was ten or so it was pretty damn obvious to me that he was as queer as a carp in a surplice: as if to confirm it, in his dressing room hung a large canvas by the notorious Linsel Murly, a blond rapacious-looking fellow, evil extra-wide lipless crocodile mouth. *Youth* depicted naked boys in a sandy pool splashing each other and fondling each other's Tiger Cubs. Notably less coy than the Roseland School of Everard Bunce, Tingay and Petherick (who, nonetheless, got five years' hard labour and theosophy). I kept my eyes open, I had a taste for eavesdropping, I had an unerring gift for barging into rooms at what I can only call the precise moment. He had that predatory underbite that is a sure sign. I lacked that, just as I lacked the queer gene. It had somehow passed me by. Not, as I say, that I was averse to cottage cruising when I was young – but not for the abundant offal quivering in the half light with a droplet of preseminal magic at the tip. No, it was the thrill of it all, the danger, the promise of Bobby The Plod's clumsy arrival, the panic, the besmirching of the family name. Dada knew it all. He had lived it.

Most of my muckers at preppers had dadas who were just as queer as Dada, even queerer, some of them, real Daddy Queffs. No names, no pack-drill. The poor sods didn't have gorgeous mamas as a solace, though. So I didn't get picked on. At least not because of Dada. My precociously early pubescence – I could projectile ejaculate a massive load by the time I was eleven and four months – and lustrous pelt of bodily hair were a different k of f.

They were jealous!

So, strangely, was Dada who was hardly smooth all over but not nearly so abundantly fleeced as I am. He used to slyly glance at my shiny coat.

In those days, even when the mechanics of reproduction were off-putting, continuing the line was a gentleman's duty to the future of the race.

It was a chap's obligation to the shades of the ancestors who had caused him to exist. Good stock should breed, has to breed. Had I been of that generation my reluctance to spawn an heir would have marked me as a traitor to my kin, my clan, my class. As it is, no one gives a bumper that the baronetcy dies with me. Should I die . . .

One has to face up to it. The world has changed. The war changed it. Seems only yesterday. Prigs, class traitors like Cripps changed it. I'd have served. I was brought up to the idea that I must serve. It is, however, well over half a century since there was, virtually by right, a public post for a Shadoxhurst. We are no longer invested with responsibilities. Should we seek them we are denied them because of the ancestral millstone of our name, because of Faineant, our park, our education, our accent, our very tradition of service, our ancient title and, very likely, our cars, livestock and clubs. We belong to a class that is envied, mocked, derided. The one minority that is fair game. No point in denying it. No point in regretting it.

We enjoy the consolation of being able to revert – as I many years ago had no hesitation in doing – to private vices and irresponsibility, to the unqualified hedonism of bewigged libertines and yoretime Cyrenaics. What the aristocracy was before it became a Christian militia piously charging itself with holy-rolling and spraying moralistic continence hither and thither.

I can't pretend that the mild insult of not being invited to serve has been injurious. Being relieved of all forms of noblesse oblige has not been the least hardship, being spared committees of dullards and the burdens of leadership has hardly impaired the quality of my long life. I've adapted with ease. Despite never having found another Mama, I've never met anyone happier than I am. I have pursued happiness through uninhibited, egotistical immersion in my dominant appetites. No one is spared, not Valentina, not Clara: they enjoy it, they were brought up to enjoy it. They have been tutored in a new kind of normal. I have denied myself nothing. Satiety is bliss. It takes will, concentration, dedication to achieve it. And buckets of dosh.

In a fit of inverse snobbery England turned its back on us. Us – whose ancestors had evolved earlier than the rest. No wonder, for we were first down from the trees to rule the earth. By the time your hoi polloi had tardily stumbled out of its nit-infested ape costume we had fixed things to our own liking.

It's all envy of course. The proletarianisation of everything, absolutely everything, in the name of egalitarianism has given poor stock free rein to multiply, to flourish. It has opened the floodgates to the feeble-minded, the lowbrowed, the neckless, the chronically dependent: all those whom a more enlightened society would have culled. The eugenic urge towards improvement has been destroyed, deliberately discredited by the very same promoters of proletarianisation. The race will resultantly degrade. And I don't give a bumper. I leave it to future generations to discover that egalitarianism is a chimera.

For the present generation, here's a cracking example.

Take kerb crawling. It is, as they say, a lifestyle choice. I'll be the first to admit that it doesn't have a good image. It's badly in need of what Young Peter Wallis calls rebranding, a jolly thorough makeover. Let us call it 'sourcing companionship'.

But before we go that far consider this: if you source company (fka kerb crawl) in a perfectly maintained 1950 Park Ward Bentley with grey and black livery (not unlike a jackdaw!), you have, I'd argue, rather more chance of both enhancing the activity's reputation and making new friends than if you're putt-puttering along the streets where every gaunt villa is a language school in some common little Vauxhall Astra ghetto-blasting aural toxins into the environment and discouraging the leggy cosmo-popsies from mulling over one's offer.

Not fair, not fair, you squeal. Of course it isn't – some company-sourcers are manifestly more equal than others and all that. There is hierarchy everywhere. So ist das Leben, chum. Brace up!

Luncheon that day was a lunch to remember.

Roddie was the first to arrive. Once they'd had their strenuous wrestle on the bank and their larky, grappling, ducking swim in the pool beneath Vetch Weir, he had, as usual, raced on his Matchless through Pope's Gutter and the village (4.5 miles) while Dada had ridden Marengo back the way he'd gone through the park, again at funereal pace (1.75 miles).

Considering that he was resigned to being called up within days, Roddie was full of beans, astonishingly chipper. He knew his hash was settled. Not yet thirty, excellent health, Cadet Regimental Sergeant Major in the JTC at Charterhouse, house captain of Gown-boys, represented the school at Bisley, fluent German learnt in Berlin in the early Thirties.

Which was where and when he also learnt self-loathing. The Machtergreifung could not have come a moment too soon. A mere two years of cocaine, rampant sodomy and concomitant injuries turned Roddie into a prim virgin, at ease with himself only when a celluloid collar was digging into his neck so tightly that beads of blood appeared. He had become a hard-striding cold-bather, a god-bothering Anglican communicant (hence his Sunday suit), a Biff Boy and, god help us, a feebly aspirant heterosexual with a stoutly shod wife and un mariage blanc. He was an enthusiast for the NSDAP's programme of moral regeneration. Purge the nation, scourge deviance, cleanse the people, eviscerate the Reds, eradicate the dysgenic miasma.

We can all go along with that, aye aye. In principle.

But, as they say, it's a damn sight easier to turn over a new leaf if you've got a perforated rectum and a ripped sphincter. Prodigal son and all that, repenting of the reckless use of strangers' violent cocks, light bulbs and loofahs.

Dada fancied him like billy-o but I am as sure as can be that nothing came of it. Roddie had become just too fastidious. Too old-maidish. Though that day he was, by his standards, almost flighty. He scented a new adventure, an escape from the grind of the ever-expanding family corporation whose ever-expanding legal department was his wearisome responsibility. He was a preposterously square peg. He longed for release from month upon month scrutinising the small print of garagists' wills and pig farmers' conveyances as the corporation swallowed up land for 'development'. He despised greedy landowners who sold their birthright. He despised the corporation's voracious appetite for that birthright: 'Makes us look like Izzy Yid.'

Hard as it may be to entertain, there was a jolly odd condition abroad that might be dubbed 'conscript happy', a lightheadedness that occurs when the waiting is over, when the only certainty, other than being called up, is uncertainty, when the map of the future is rent asunder. Roddie's undisguised excitement was not shared by the rest of the table that lunchtime. The only exception being his 'wife' Carn (née Caroline or Plain Jane), last of the holier-than-thou Tolly dynasty of Christian warriors. She was near mute, dowdy, steak and kidney pious, blushing and literally immaculate, so nicknamed 'the eternal virgin'. Her stout calves, the left some inches shorter than the right, were a particular affront to Mama who referred to her as 'zee Inglisch oak'. She had a greater rapport with dogs than humans: her pack of lethal Marcher Hounds was banned from Faineant. The slavering monsters had to remain in her lumbering Lea-Francis shooting brake in case they should scare the horses or attack the Fenant Terriers that Dada had bred by crossing a Wallabarrow with a Norfolk.

The Vair-Vairs were on sparkling form. It went something like this.

Tom Mungoson: 'Thing about world war, yer know, is that yer wait many millennia for one then two come along within twenty-five years of each other. Vair vair uncanny!'

The table was puzzled: no one took public transport in those days apart from Tom who had a 'thing' about bus conductors: their uniform, celluloid cap peak, tarnished ticket machine, harness, badge.

He continued: 'It's not all plain sailing after. Doesn't just revert to business as usual. It leaves a hangover. Funny business. A lot of chaps felt vair vair guilty that they survived – like Xander. Felt they didn't deserve to.'

Pammy Mungoson: 'Yes absolutely. Poor Xander still feels vair vair guilty. It's tairbly sad.'

Xander was a painter who never painted, a writer who never

wrote. He was a self-pitying braggart. He stank of low denomination coins. When he wasn't in the bin he lived like a vagrant in a cottage on his brother's paltry estate. He was rightly banned from every respectable hostelry for miles around. You didn't have to be a medical man to see that his so-called shell shock was just feeble-mindedness and osteo-inertia.

Dada, scornfully, not that his tone was noted by the Mungosons: 'Really? I was vair vair relieved to have been too young, just. I count meself vair vair lucky.'

Mama giggled. Tom and Pammy's house at Menton was known as Vairsailles. We had such fun in those days.

It was a deuced strange luncheon. In that distant era no one ever mentioned what was being eaten. However, Bunny Dyde, quite a celebrated grease monkey in the days when motor racing was motor racing, confessed to 'not understanding' rösti. Mavis Bailhache – a todger-dodger if ever there was one and already a teensy bit woozled though nowhere near so snootered as Mama – was more explicit. She proposed that what Bunny meant was that it was the Jew-food called latke. The entire table turned on Mavis. She was shouted down.

Courtesy to the core, I observed that we always, always, had rösti with Mein Opa in Zurich.

The din ceased as though it might have been switched off. There was an awkward silence. I sensed I was speaking out of turn. The jovially mocking candour permissible in an adult was denied me. Roddie cleared his throat. He proceeded to gallantly defend Mama's insistence on having Gerda cook Swiss and Bavarian dishes that Jews happened to have plundered. And have corrupted, added Mama: rösti, kartoffelpuffer and pommes paillasson comprised nothing other than potato while Jew-greed made them add flour and sometimes egg. Not correct. Latkes were obviously inferior. We all raised a glass to Gerda. Mama had fought a battle of kitchen attrition for years to get rid of the likes of Mrs Cheddy, Staines, 'Boy' Bourne and so on. Dada, being the kind of sweet-toothed gastronomic igno who could happily exist on ice cream and eclairs, had been stubbornly resistant to upsetting the applecart. But even he was beguiled by her cooking. And she was such fun!

Oh! Here's to Gerda's rösti! Her caraway dumplings! Her

speckkartoffeln! Her steinpilzen stewed in butter! Her tafelspitz! Her meerrettichsosse sauce! Her juicy cunt! The second to welcome Tiger, grateful Tiger. 'Not a word to Mama.' She pushed a forefinger deep in my arse. What unexpected delight! Expanding my vocabulary of love. She never removed the cigarette from her mouth even when she came. Then there was her apfelstrudel! Her chocolate cake with toasted walnuts and apricot purée!

No one is willing to go to war for a race that puts flour in potato pancakes . . . Or for the sake of the Poles . . . Mark my words – Horeb El Isha is calling the shots . . . The craven folly of appointing such a man as War Minister . . . It's clear as daylight whose interests he represents . . . You're damn well right, Freddie, more's the pity . . . Versailles . . . Damned French taking it out on Germany for twenty years . . . Reprisals? Revenge! . . . Blum . . . Stavisky – a Jew and a Mason . . . What Germany does with its Jews is Germany's business . . . Bolshevism is vair vair Jewish . . . the Usurocracy is vair vair Jewish . . . We all know who profits from war . . . The only winners will be international communism and Jewry . . . Are the Welsh Jewish? Welsh mountain sheep, the ones with the fleeceless faces, look vair vair Jewish . . .

All this was familiar. I knew it well. My litany, you might say. From Mama's milk. I didn't question it. I haven't questioned it. Three-quarters of a century later I don't question it even though it is somewhat out of fashion – but the sacrifice of truth to fashion's shifting dictates is weak and unprincipled. Call not on me to repent.

Make no mistake about it. Large-scale liquidation is a jolly tough thing to condone. It takes backbone. It takes mental fortitude. It takes pluck to fly in the face of uninformed popular opinion. My considered opinion used to be that the Führer was a bit of a silly sausage – ein blöd wurst! – to have devoted lavish resources to racial cleansing while fighting on several fronts. It caused a diminution of manpower. That particular wash and brush-up could have waited.

But I have, in the fullness of time, come to realise that it was a nasty job well done. He really was such a clever clogs when it came to our cosmopolitan friends! Excelled himself. Won the war that really mattered. Sacrificed himself. For us. That's the mark of a really sound, world-beating Messiah. Top of the form! You have to hand it to him. Chapeau! And you have to hand it to Germany. It was not just one man, one superman, who made that selfless sacrifice. The nation that gave its life. It achieved what other nations merely whispered about then shied away from. It was big enough to take all the opprobrium, all the stinking obloquy heaped on it.

There can be no sympathy or place for so-called Holocaust deniers. Well intentioned no doubt, but what's the matter with these chaps? They're strategically all at sea.[11] They should be celebrating, they should be congratulating the shades of Hitler, Himmler, Heydrich, Höss and so on for having taken the plunge, so to speak.

But not a bit of it. Their claims are tantamount to accusing those sacred inhabitants of Walhalla of not doing their duty and of only divesting the planet of a fraction of the number that is generally and rightly reckoned. It is treacherous to diminish an achievement by lessening its magnitude.

Not that I've got anything against the Jew. Nor Jewesses for that matter, though they're often found wanting in the intense passion department. No matter how vigorously you bang their mouths and their arses and their cunts the lazy Becks can't be bothered to moan at the multiple pleasures I have afforded them, no doubt having weightier matters on their mind, the fate of their race and so on. Perhaps that's the reason why they've put everyone's back up down the ages.

The mood of luncheon lurched. It began with Mama bemoaning the likely unavailability of Jägermeister, Asbach, Rostocker Kümmel, Hamburger Kümmel, Danziger Goldwasser, Killepitsch, Ratzeputz etc.

This list of essential staples without which life at Faineant would be unimaginable prompted Velma Broodbank to stand up, raise her glass and bellow: 'It could never happen. It'll all be over in a matter of weeks. Just you see. Everyone will come to their senses. To peace!'

---

11 The paradoxical practice of deniers invariably lessening the death toll is investigated in *The Denial of Denial* by Wendy Deflorin, Reader in Denial Studies at Rutgers University and co-author of *Mark Aarvold's The Faintest of All Human Passions: A Concordance*.

There was a consensual murmur of assent.

Velma put an arm round Mama. 'In all your days you will never want for Rostocker Kümmel, Viola my darling! Rostocker Kümmel – forever!'

And everyone around the table repeated Velma's toast. They may have believed her. They wanted to believe her.

A freckle-faced man, a lopsided sort of fellow who only looked like a pig in certain lights from certain angles but was always referred to as The Swine and always addressed as Swiney or Swine My Pet because his surname was, unforgettably, Hogworthingham, grinned with relief as though that was the whole matter settled and he could get back under the bonnet of Mama's latest bolide, *tweaking*.

I noticed that Dada raised his eyebrows. His nostrils dilated, his chin tautened to knobbiness, he inhaled as if to inhibit himself from saying something that might spoil the party's collective delusion.

While everyone else stayed at table drinking coffee and kirschwasser and himbeergeist, Dada and I strolled with bounding Pippin towards High Lake.

I asked him if he could recall where we had been on this very day the year previously.

'Nuremberg,' he replied without hesitation.

'Almost!' I corrected him: 'Deggendorf. We were still at Maria and Maxi's. I checked my diary.'

He muttered somewhat half-heartedly that he regretted the cancellation of this year's rally. He shruggingly regretted not knowing when he would see Maria and Maxi again, not knowing when he would see the towers and turrets of their 'toy' schloss above the Danube. Not knowing for that matter when we'd see Florian and Bärbel, the Kluges, the von Otts. Then he paused a while. He said, matter of fact, that he regretted that Maxi or Dieter Kluge might kill their English brothers and that he might kill his German brothers.

I started.

'You're not going to be a soldier, are you?' I asked, incredulous.

'It looks like it, Old Thing. You know, I can see myself ascending pretty damned rapidly . . . if I can make half-colonel within eighteen months I should be on my way. Have me own brigade in two years.'

A sort of nausea struck me. Dada, my blond idol, had turned to a man of straw. What weakness I detected in him! I felt ashamed of him, of his slippery conscience that allowed him to be a traitor to his ideals, of his lily-livered willingness to defect. I was repulsed.

Was this the man whose face had glowed with pride at the magical consecration of the blood flag? Was this the man who had exulted in the Führer's oratorical marathon? Was this the man who had marvelled at the mechanical might of the death's head army, the merciless hyperborean berserkers from the frozen North? Was this the man who talked of having been swept up by the blinding bliss of revelation at the first rally he had attended, back in 1935?

Standing beside me at my first rally, last year, he had once again been so transfixed that he had forgotten my presence! He had again become part of that throng which the Führer moulded with the 'theocratic force of destiny', a throng which felt, thought and moved as one. It was so exciting. So colourful. So relentless. So uplifting. So ecstatic. Like being at the fair. The choreography, the uniforms, the banners, the music. It was in truth the most lavish show Busby Berkeley had ever devised. Art and might met: stormtroopers were the corps de ballet. Hitler and mein Heini Himmler the soloists. What strapping fun! The sun filled Himmler's glasses. His eyes shone golden like a god's. He was unmoving as though carved from the blackest of black stones. This was a man who was more than a man.

Dada talked of duty, of *our* country, of *our* link to all this – expansive wave of arms, of a terrible decision that had to be made, an impossible choice between on the one hand the Führer he admired to 'the far side of idolatry', the Führer who had lifted his people from their degradation, the Führer who blazed like the sun, the Führer who would chart his people's fulfilment and, on the other, the nation the Führer threatened. He felt he had lost a friend. His felt his hero and inspiration had betrayed him.

It escaped him that he owed his newly found fierce love of England to the Führer, to following the example of the Führer's fierce love of Germany.

By jove, it really did escape him. Here, he said, was where he belonged. The language of Shakespeare was the language we spoke. We? I was fluent in German, its complications and curtnesses and poetry were there, too, in Mama's milk. Despite fifteen years of marriage Dada could manage only tourist's German. He listed the myriad customs and quirks that spelled out Englishness. Here around us were immemorial green acres, the patrimonial loam that Shadoxhursts had trodden and tended for centuries, the roots that descended to the very core, the tumuli of our forebears' forebears, the hill forts and holloways . . .

So that is what he had been rustling up in his grey matter as he walked Marengo in the morning. That was what he was hatching with Roddie very likely. I wondered if I could ever trust him again. How could he dare to speak of duty? He had made a choice, *the* choice.

He took in my silence.

He said dryly: 'I'll be gone. You'll be the one who has to look after Mama now.'

Then he strode swiftly towards the bridge, clicking impatient fingers to summon Pippin.

A German child was provided the means to inform the Secret State Police of parental aberration. That the English lacked the machinery of denunciation suggested laxity and spineless sentimentality. It should be obvious that children are a valuable source of intelligence. Even the Red Menace was alert to this truism. The making of the martyr Little Pavlik bore witness to it.

When I returned to luncheon there was laughter and shouting, jazz and desperation. It was not up my street. I went to my room.

My burgeoning collection was my honour.

At Nuremberg I had been treated to two copies of *Der Stürmer* – no half measures there; a pennant – red, white circle with a hooked cross; postcards of the Führer, of Göring, a funny one of hooked-nosed Jews fleeing with their money bags from hooked-cross flags; a pewter eagle; a metal whistle stamped with a death's head; an Allach porcelain figurine of an SS officer mounted on a white steed. These had been presented to me in person by Julius Streicher, in person, Julius Streicher in person. The monumentality of that moment will never leave me. Of course he was a thug and a bully. But he was a thug and a bully who bullied for the Cause, who knotted the throttling kerchief for the Cause.

On the walls were framed photochromes showing the Externsteine, the Bastei, beautiful scenes of autobahnen sweeping through pristine unsullied countryside (no roadside hoardings, no squalid bungalows). On a table with claw feet rested my fawn hat with its red feather in its knitted leather band.

In the wardrobe hung a child-sized SS uniform that even when it still fitted I stopped wearing because I was mocked at a fellow pupil's ninth birthday party. They called me 'the stormtoddler', they called Dada 'goosestepfather'. I protested that he was my real father. There were also Bavarian clothes. Early childhood lederhosen, like those that would be worn by the young Helmut Goebbels in the last noble photograph. I'd outgrown them. They were now tight as a jocker. A loden joppe that brought me much joy. It was collarless, yet had lapels. It was charcoal apart from a green neck band, green facings and piping. The buttons were horn, the pockets and lapels were embroidered with green oak leaves. It was the essence of Bavaria, sartorial essence, from Ingolstadt, the most Bavarian of cities, the spirit and civic conscience of Bavaria.

Twenty-five miles south of it was the Schloss Kaltenborn – four onion domes and forty bedrooms, ballrooms and galleries, hothouses and stables. Its vast estate was where Mama spent her childhood idyll, a lost domain of catkins and ponies, lakes and follies, and best friends Maria and Effie whose nearby estates were not that nearby because hers extended so far. It was taken from her by Weimar tomfoolery and French revanchism (they were always at it).

Mama fled with her father to Switzerland in August 1914 to avoid internment at Holzminden or Ruhleben, which – as is so often the case – turned out to have been very decent billets, really quite a jolly for all concerned. They weren't to have known that.

Zurich held greater appeal though they missed the estate, they missed owning everything. Her father pined for the woods, the follies, the secret paths trodden by animals who were now just skulls on a wall.

The magnificent villa on the Zürichsee, the Truscott steam launch for puttering about in, the lawns, the floral displays, the fountains that recalled Bad Harzburg . . . it couldn't begin to compensate for the loss of thousands of hectares.

Everything about her – appearance, mien, tastes, Weltanschauung, German being her first language, her accent – suggested Mama was German. Not strictly so. She was English, half English, she held an English passport as well as a German one.

She was sired by an English adventurer who got his cock in the till. She was sired out of a Bavarian dam on perpetual heat, a multi-millionairess as plain as she was vast.

Mama always said: 'Ees a miracle I have looks . . . such looks . . . my muzzair – none. Minus looks! Zero from ten for radiant.'

And what a father her father was! My adored and adoring grand-father, Mein Opa. To me he was so wonderful! He dandled me with a grandpaternal pride and fondness that was almost paternal tout court. He told me tales of the forest, of sleeping under the stars, of animals whose languages he could understand, animals who were his friends.

It's a rum business 'scandal'. Certain 'scandals' have legs: Tranby Croft, Cleveland Street, Wilde, Dilke, Henry Prince, Maundy Gregory, the Tichborne Claimant. Others more or less evaporate, wiped from the memory of the public that was not so long ago all-a-prattle about them.

Who today has heard of Valentine Baker? Or Mrs Baxter Monk-Mullinger and 'her French ways' . . . the Druid's Lodge Confederacy . . . Marrack's Patent Resin? As for Spargo Pengelly – totally forgotten!

When I was a little chap mention of any of them prompted a def-inite frisson, that rush of excitement that comes with matters children know they are not meant to know about. Not exactly for-bidden, but spoken of behind closed doors and, if referred to, seldom explained to us innocent angels. How I loved to eavesdrop on stories of salacious transgressions, card cheats, duels, kinky indiscriminacy, audacious frauds, bolters, nobbled horses, phantom mines (anyone taken in by Petroc Spargo Pengelly deserved to be fleeced, says I).

At preppers we'd swap our gen on these and countless other cases just as we swapped latest bulletins on female anatomy, indecent assaults, syphilis and smoking. All four of us Thuggees were, as it happens, that afternoon smoking Capstans in the Jungle Hut where the rollers, mowers and corner flags, pitch markers, nets and things were kept.

A chit called Bottom (can you imagine the sport we had?) was trying to suck up to us. 'Suck': what a delicious word. Bottom was Weasel Woolacott's little boy. What a pretty blond tart!

He said: 'Bet you chaps never heard about Jervoise Vanier and Marcus Phimister?'

I gasped with astonishment. I choked on my cigarette. I coughed and coughed so convulsively that my head throbbed. It was filled with crashing things, guns, drumming. My air pipes revolted. Sinuses too. My chest imploded. My muckers patted my back furiously, rained blows on it. Aarvold was perhaps unnecessarily strenuous, but that was the code of the Thuggees. My lungs heaved. My ears rang with that name, Marcus Phimister, Marcus Phimister.

Marcus Phimister was my big bear of a grandfather. Mein Opa. Whatever was there to hear about him? He was generous, booming, bearded, twinkling as whatever it is that twinkles. He wore fur collars, watch-chains, homburgs. He was full of laughter and conjuring tricks.

And Vanier. Who was Jervoise Vanier? Roddie Vanier had been Dada's closest friend. Dada had wept. Jervoise . . . a relation or a coincidence? Unusual name.

I bided my time, kept mum. I didn't want him blurting whatever it was in front of my fellow Thuggees. 'Scandals' happened to other people, not to one's own sort, who were one's own flesh and blood. After high tea I went to find the tasty young dish. What he told me made me want to biff him but I held back. (It hadn't escaped my notice that Weasel was leaving at the end of term. Not that we were supposed to know, but his people hadn't paid the fees for a year. His dada had a head full of shrapnel from the previous show and was a few volumes short of a library. Something of a malingerer in the employment stakes, 'twas said. Weasel was going to have to be a grammar bug.)

Bottom lived on the Welsh Marches where his dada was a 'country doctor'. It was my opinion, all those many moons ago, that 'country doctor' was an infra-dig occupation with the derisory compensation of being held in awe by inbred oggies. I haven't altered my opinion. About ten miles from his village there was a great house over the hills and far away in a remote valley beyond the Long Mynd and beyond even the Stiperstones. These places, whose splendour I would soon become acquainted with, meant nothing to me then. They were names only, odd names. On which subject: it still rankles that those hills – among England's greatest glories and not vulgar, like mountains – should have attached to them the word Welsh, with its distressing connotation of furtive, racially impoverished, short-arsed Celts. Offa knew a thing or two. Very sound chap, damned fine military strategist.

Although Bottom had never seen the house itself, he had seen an old postcard of it. He described it as a fairy tale castle, all towers and pointed turrets. It sounded as though the fairy tale in question was one of those X-rated jobs that are said to do untold harm to the little 'uns. The place was deserted, ruined, hidden away beyond 'the thickest thorny thickets, woodbine webbed woods' (Rollo Gammans, again). Its great park was overgrown. Its drives were impassable. I imagined heraldic beasts with the wind-gnawed features of congenital idiots, ornate gate piers crumbling, rusted gates, rusted chains, rusted padlocks, tarmac split by shrubs pushing up, scurrying rats, rampant ivy, ground elder. Everyone talked of it in whispers. Everyone denied talking about it, like everyone denied talking about spunky cunts. Everyone was covertly fascinated by it. It was a dirty secret. To speak its name was to soil yourself. You entered the park at your peril. Few dared. It was haunted. Monsters lurking in the undergrowth. Abominable creatures burrowed there. Unnatural beings howled because they were born into pain and were in pain forever. It was called Malpasfang Lodge. Its reputation was due to two men who had lived there long ago, Jervoise Vanier and Marcus Phimister, and to the scandal that surrounded them.

'What scandal?'

'My father wouldn't tell me.' Bottom looked sheepish. I considered giving him a Chinese burn but decided against jeopardising a long-term investment.

Nor, it turned out, would Dada tell me. Perhaps he couldn't tell me. He was discombobulated by my inquisitiveness, or made a show of being so.

I had gingerly mentioned it on my next exeat. It was not a subject he warmed to.

He was on the evasive side: 'Never got to the nitty gritty . . . There was a fuss about . . . He got himself into a bit of a pickle over a business scheme – all a bit dicey . . . Just a storm in a teacup . . . Blown up out of all proportion. Not least by him . . . Always liable to stomp off like a toddler in a bate. Which is just what he did . . . He believes to this day that England didn't deserve him.'

It had not till then occurred to me that I had never seen Dada and Mein Opa together. Mein Opa never visited Faineant, nor England so far as I knew. Dada never came with us to Zurich. Mutual dislike? That's overdoing it. Mutual indifference is more on the button. Just how well or badly they got on was not something Dada was prepared to discuss.

Further bluster: 'Not much of a delver, what? Wouldn't make much of a sleuth, would I?'

'I expect Mama can remember. I'll ask her.'

'Oh I shouldn't do that, Old Boy. No, I'd rather you didn't. Understand? You know how sensitive she is. It was before she was born. Fifty years ago . . . longer perhaps. I doubt that she'd be able to fill you in any more than I can.'

He was unusually testy. Not without reason. The only job he could get in the army was as a civilian auxiliary: 'basically a foreman on a building site'. Strictly speaking he ought not to have been wearing any uniform, let alone one bearing three pips. Further, it was no longer a question of whether the house and part of the immediate estate would be requisitioned but of when. Furniture, paintings, muniments and so on were already being stored, uncatalogued, in Home Farmhouse.

And there was greater ignominy lurking just around the corner.

Mama had gone up to town and wouldn't be home before Davy Skitch drove me back to school. I left a note in what was supposedly the hidden compartment of her elaborate secretaire.

What did she know of Malpasfang Lodge where Mein Opa had lived long ago? I asked her to write to me at school. She did so. She sent me, in an envelope, a turn of the century postcard, a hand-coloured photograph (Trythall & Co., Wrexham) of Malpasfang Lodge. The house was indeed what was then often known as 'blue cheese'. Liable to give you nightmares. Just as I'd imagined it. One of those spikey monstrosities whose parts looked as if they'd never been introduced to each other. There was a bit of everything. Eclectic, that's the word I'm looking for. I still have the card. She wrote: 'My darling boy. I knew that I could not keep from you for ever. What a clever darling you are to have exumed [sic] this skelton [sic, again] from a different time yourself. I would have told. Some day I will tell. I promise.'

A lot of water passed under the bridge before she kept that promise. That last year at preppers was a rum affair.

'It'll all be over in a matter of weeks. Just you see. Everyone will come to their senses.' Velma Broodbank could not have been more wrong.

Weeks dragged into months. Lieutenant Roddie Vanier was on the staff at the British Expeditionary Force HQ at Arras. He would ride whatever horse was available to him from one makeshift brothel to the next. Every woman had a price – of course, that's the way I like them – and many men too. (Not so keen.) He distributed condoms from his saddlebags. Like an apprentice Gladstone, he offered moralistic Anglican advice. Ignored, no doubt.

He arranged appointments at improvised clinics. He had to cajole sexual contacts' names from infected troops who quite properly had no idea whom they had jolly rogered. For heaven's sake, one treats with the cunt, the mouth, the arse – not with the person. Do you have hobbies, my darling my poppet?

What then about addresses? He was well nicknamed: The Bishop. He became a familiar sight trotting down the rainy streets of mining towns. *Au nord c'était les corons*: back-to-back brick terraces were improbable houses of love. They smelled of gas and poverty. Mountains of black slag loomed over them, shut out the sun. He was happy in his work.

His preferred mount was a Laïla de Quiffeu whom he nicknamed Carn. One winter's day Brigadier Esmond 'Dogmeat' Pogson MC[12] who, as well as his spanking bright cobalt and fawn Daimler, had imported a pack of Marcher Hounds, was off with some fellow pongos to hunt anything that moved. He pulled rank and bagged Carn. Roddie could hardly object since it was Dogmeat, a friend of his feckless father-in-law, who had got him his sinecure. He had to settle for a Belgian Black whose fragile temperament he had been warned of. As they cantered along a street beside the frozen Deûle Canal at Armentières his mount was startled by the still seldom heard crackle of gunfire. Its muscles tightened. It reared madly, hurling him to the cobbles bonce first. He got up, shook himself down, patted the horse. Six hours later in the BEFHQ mess he was jawing at the bar with Dogmeat, recounting his happily uninjurious fall, which he ascribed to his thick skull. They were drinking madeirised champagne the colour of barley sugar.

Roddie asked him: 'Can I top you up, Sir?'

Dogmeat schnutted a puddle of snuff from the back of his hand.

'You may indeed, Roddie – schnutt schnutt – just to the brim if you will . . . I like to see a hearty meniscus on mine. Schnutt—'

The bottle fell from Roddie's hand. As Dogmeat had it: 'The dear boy clawed at the air and crumpled up.'

He never regained consciousness.

According to Mama, when Carn was told of his death by Roddie's father she looked puzzled then seemed relieved.

She said: 'Thank you for letting me know. Gosh I'm so sorry for your loss . . . so sorry . . . I hope the horse is all right . . . You know, I'd better take the dogs for a walk.'

He was the first World War II soldier to be buried in the World War I cemetery at Vis-en-Artois.

---

12 He owed his nickname, of which he was proud, to an incident when he was an officer cadet at RMA Woolwich. A keen huntsman with the Old Surrey and Burstow, he was offended by Wilde's 'the unspeakable in pursuit of the uneatable'. He had his batman roast a fox, which he tucked into while his cadre was eating beef. He declared it to be 'delicious – every bit as good as dogmeat'. His Marcher Hounds were abandoned on a Dunkirk beach. They were recruited by the SS and re-educated to sniff out gypsies and acrobats.

Dogmeat had the horse butchered as a security measure rather than as a punishment. He introduced over a dozen officers to a meat that they had thitherto regarded with squeamish reticence but now, initially enjoined by their commander, supped on with gusto, persuaded.

Nearly all the younger beaks at school disappeared into the forces. They were replaced by an ever-changing troupe of over-the-hill jabberers too senile both to defend their country and, mercifully, to inflict their sadistic will on us. You got the impression that most had been dismissed from their last positions at about the time of Ladysmith. They were all too eager to continue where they'd left off. Pigs in clover hoping to make up for lost time. Not up to scratch, I'm afraid. We outwitted them, mentally and physically. Not just for the sport. It was one thing to rub up a golden-locked young English master who called himself a poet. But these dotards equipped with pathetic excuses for their smeggy flaccidity were unstimulating.

Not so Bottom. My god, Weasel had taught him a thing or two! Spunkorama! Never to be forgotten. My wankerchief was permanently encrusted!

Strange to relate, in the early Seventies I was enjoying a somewhat liquid dinner at The Garrick. I was there as Willy Cattle's guest. Not one of my usual haunts, I hasten to add. A jot pinko for my taste. (In those days The Alibi in King's Road was more my pasture – scrumptious totty. E.g. Cressida Neville and her WASP chum Betsy, said to be a bestselling writer. Woozled and willing, yum.) Now, who should I see on the other side of the splendid dining room but His Honour Judge Woolacott QC. His rodent features were little changed, though of course I also knew them from the popular prints. He was supping with a misery-mouthed alice-band, presumably his ladywife, and a somewhat older couple. The chap's puce beamer was familiar. Lord Chancellor? Attorney General? Some such here-today-gone-tomorrow political shyster. I toddled across and congratulated Weasel in no uncertain terms on what a splendid job he'd done with Bottom all those years ago, particularly in teaching him how the perineum responds to sharp fingernails. I have to say that I've rarely come across a chap who took effusive praise so gracelessly. The way he declined my invitation to join me post-prandially in another bottle of Reims's finest without consulting the rest of his table was simply bloody rude. Lawyers!

The one snag with Bottom was that he had some dangerous commie ideas learnt by rote from his dada. Health clinics for everybody. Everybody! Gorblimies included! He totally failed to grasp that by picking on the frail and halt M'sieu Peste and Madame Chancre cleverly strengthen the race in the same way as lack of sanitation, inadequate heating and pauper's diet. It's nature's form of racial hygiene, it weeds out the weak. When he banged on too long about sterile delivery units for the deserving poor I was obliged to stop his lovely gob with Tiger.

No one could become a Thuggee without an initiation test. No exceptions, not even for one's little boy. Bottom had not only to prove himself but to prove himself worthier than another contender, a slutty shag called Halfhead. We, the three Thuggees left after Woolacott had gone, discussed anointing both Bottom and Halfhead. But that would not only have been a break with tradition, it would have been in defiance of the Constitution. There was no place for a fifth Silent Strangler. 'Four for one and one for four, The Foreskin Cavaliers.' Whoever heard of The Fiveskin Cavaliers?

Halfhead was a swot. He took Greek, the swot's option. He swanked that the Greek for all-in, no-holds-barred wrestling was pankration. That is about as much as the poor chap brought to his bout with Bottom; knowing the name didn't make him any good at it.

No togs. We insisted on nakedness. Endows the struggle with a classical nobility, just like an urn. More real for all concerned. More agreeable to watch. To all our regret, as a spectacle it was droppings. Bottom was smaller than Halfhead. He was also quicker, stronger, wirier – and wilier! The ground behind Jungle Hut was hard. Thorns and nettles and grimy tree roots. Halfhead was out of his depth. He was thrown down time after time, flung about like a broken doll. You really had to feel pity for him. He took his punishment like a man. He didn't blub. He shook Bottom's hand. He was a plucky warrior who had learnt, as he put it later, that there's no palm without dust. We soothed his angry skin with dock leaves. He bled where thorns had torn him. He didn't go to the San to get his wounds dressed. Questions would have been asked. Not that he'd have squitted. So impressively stoical was his demeanour in adversity that we unanimously agreed to appoint him a Brevet Thuggee provided he carried out an allotted task.

There was a Jewboy in the school. He had crept in unmentioned – and unnoticed, save by those blessed with a heightened sense of Jewsmell. To me, being so blessed, the newbug's race was clear. There were obvious clues for those adept at recognition.

1) His name was Green. That would have been Grunowski or Grunovitch where they had come from. The Lviv shtetl reeking of lamb fat, the Moldovan steppe, the yurts on the Zalesye.

2) He had joined in the sixth form for just a year because he had had 'trouble' at his last school. Without question 'trouble' meant that he had been rumbled by a stout English oak and quite properly pogromed.

3) He was going to go on to Clifton College, which notoriously boasted (!) of being the only public school with a house exclusively for Jews, Polack's – note the name.

The evidence was overwhelming.

Halfhead's job was to show Green that The Foreskin Cavaliers were the masters. Give his big hooter a bit of a bloodying, a nosender. Something of that sort. Being a swot Halfhead came up with what we all agreed was a more sophisticated wheeze.

With great stealth and no mean courage he crept into Ramillies House's dorm hours after lights out, pinched Green's grey blazer and took it to Remove Scob, little more than a windowless walk-in cupboard in what once had been a staircase tower. A priest-hole. Haunted. Blood seeped from the mortar. On the back of the blazer Halfhead painted a yellow Star of David with black outlines in thick poster colour, waited for it to dry, then tiptoed back to the dorm and replaced it beside the bed where Green whistled and snuffled – Jewboys snore differently from us. That's because they have enormous snozzles designed to steal our air from us.

We got up round dawn. We were as usual shagged from the night's exertions. You don't see much in that half-light when you're dressing as quickly as you can to fight off the arctic chill. It wasn't till during breakfast that someone noticed what had happened to Green's back.

Ramillies's table was at the further end of the refectory from the serving hatch where the foulest of foul grub was doled out. Green was on bread duty. He walked the entire length of the refectory in ignorance. The room grew gaspingly silent, deafeningly silent as the eyes of the whole school settled on his back. What a triumph for the Thuggees and the audacious Halfhead! There was something ceremonial about Green's blind progress towards the hatch. It was as though he was entering an ambush that everyone but he could see. He was to be stoned, used for archery practice like that hapless sod Sebastian. He was a sacrificial animal with not a clue about why he was suddenly the centre of attention. Those animals don't realise till it's too late. The primitive excitement of the moment didn't register with him.

There was a contingent of goody-goody, big-hearted Arthurs who piously expressed their shock. Then merry hell broke loose! Cheers and whistles and someone bellowing: 'We don't want our dadas to die for your sort!' Matron and a couple of nonagenarian beaks faffed about. Someone took advantage of the situation and threw prunes. Cook screamed. Cork's mob started singing 'Hava Nagila', beating their table as they did so.

Later, at assembly in Big School, Vermin Vipond, the acting head, addressed us with all the sanctimony he could muster. He was an evangelical hunchbacked groper with buggers' grips and award-winning halitosis. Only down from varsity for a couple of years, he'd developed a hearty appetite for flogging. Before he flogged he put on a leather armguard like a falconer or archer. Then he flogged till he was exhausted with great gouts of sweat pouring off him. He inspected the bloody welts with a surgeon's gourmandise, apologising profusely for having so enthusiastically carried out his duty. He had found himself elevated to his great role because unlike the rest of the staff he was unfit for military service due to his being a cripple, the product of bad breeding. Another one to cull.

'The war . . . the yoke of tyranny . . . persecution . . . the Christian values we must uphold . . . respect for fellow men . . . the wickedness that confronts us . . . justice . . . moral probity must and will vanquish moral degradation . . . we must trust in god who has charged us with a duty to protect Jewry . . . to succour victims . . . to shelter the helpless . . . bring light where there is darkness . . .'

He flutingly drooled and drooled ad vomitum.

Then the malevolent prick dropped a bombshell. All exeats cancelled till the perpetrator gave himself up. A form of blackmail I'd say.

Once again Halfhead took it like a man. Twelve strokes on his naked buttocks from Vermin who congratulated him on his honesty in owning up. He then asked him why he had done it. Halfhead kept mum about his initiation. He replied that it was because Green was a Jewboy who wouldn't own up to being so. Vermin was apparently taken aback.

He murmured: 'In that case he's unique among Jews in not being circumcised. Let me see your John Thomas, Halfhead.'

A gust of Vermin's breath struck.

'Are you sure, Sir?'

'Quite sure.'

Halfhead bemusedly unbuttoned himself again.

Vermin stroked it. 'Keep this fellow clean and he'll grow to be a mighty handsome one. Do not allow it to provoke unchaste thoughts. Pure of prepuce, pure of heart. Yours is more austere than Green's. His tends to frilliness. I think you'll find that is often the case with Scottish lads. It's in their genes.'

Scottish!

Well, we all make mistakes. This was an honest mistake. My intentions were honourable. I admit to it: I got it wrong. But not that wrong. The Scots and the Jews have much in common. Green turned out to be so oily he might as well have been a Jew.

Lieutenant Hugh Halfhead of the Glosters died at the battle of Kapyong, Korea, April 1951. His grave is in the UN Cemetery in Pusan. He was awarded a posthumous George Cross.

To give one's life in the struggle against the Red Satan is a noble thing. I am jolly proud to reflect that the Thuggees and I set him on course for that destiny.

I would learn most of what follows from Horrocks (oh, the shame!), and bit by bit, over many years, from the days I spent with la

Vicomtesse Riquetti de Besançon and from the years I spent with Mama. It was for me to piece together the titbits and random gen: I ought not to swank but I am no mean sleuth when it comes to deducing griff from photographs; I have discovered a certain aptitude.

Francis Galton. *Hereditary Genius*:

> Let us do what we can to encourage the multiplication of the races best fitted to invent, and conform to, a high and generous civilisation, and not, out of mistaken instinct of giving support to the weak, prevent the incoming of strong and hearty individuals.

Charles Darwin. *The Descent of Man*:

> There is reason to believe that vaccination has preserved thousands, who from a weak constitution would formerly have succumbed to smallpox. Thus the weak members of civilised societies propagate their kind. No one who has attended to the breeding of domestic animals will doubt that this must be highly injurious to the race of man.
>
> It is surprising how soon a want of care, or care wrongly directed, leads to the degeneration of a domestic race; but excepting in the case of man himself, hardly any one is so ignorant as to allow his worst animals to breed . . .
>
> The very poor and reckless, often degraded by vice, almost invariably marry early, while the careful and frugal, who are generally otherwise virtuous, marry late in life.

Who has the temerity to disagree with such giants as Galton and Darwin?

The sorry answer is all too many fools, the bleeding hearts of the do-goodery, the soup kitchen pietists. They are traitors to their own race, which they decline to acknowledge as superior. Blindly, they are committing a slow collective suicide. Meek, meek, meek. Weak, weak. Weak. The ruddy monotheisms are too keen by half on standing up for the underdogs. Who speaks for the overdogs?

Marcus Phimister told Mama that he read *Hereditary Genius* and *The Descent of Man* when he was thirteen. According to her he claimed that they were 'epiphanies'. He had discovered his vocation. He resolved to devote his life to the improvement of the race.

His father, my great-grandfather, the Reverend Clement Phimister had given him the books shortly after he was prosecuted by the Bishop of Lincoln, then deprived of benefices when his appeal against that prosecution was dismissed by the Privy Council. Clement Phimister's heresies were described as manifold. You can say that again!

In his essays and pamphlets collected as *Thou That Dwellest in the Gardens* (Spalding, 1866) he denied or questioned the doctrines of atonement and original sin, the second coming, revelation through scripture.

'Christ,' he wrote, 'was no more god-begotten than any other man or woman.' He maintained that Christ's physical presence in the eucharist is all wishfulness; part cannibalistic gluttony, part homo-erotic sadism.

Nonetheless, even after he had lost his living he continued to believe in god. Simply couldn't get along without the old wrath-monger's blustering. His broad contention was that man does not require the church's intercession to find god in his heart. Fair enough. He insisted to the end on the impossibility of reconciling Genesis with geology. But for him that did not invalidate the book's religious value. There was much he could dump; but justification by faith in whatever he chose to believe was in his very marrow. He enjoyed a good yarn. His public meetings were such a hit that he founded the Mansion of Indivisibility where he preached a sort of humanitarian-ism with a dash of animistic reverence. God was all around. He was to be found in all things including artichokes and beets, which were, then, used to celebrate a form of eucharist. Clement Phimister was shocked by his son's atheism and his libertine behaviour.

Mein Opa, Marcus Phimister, the Heretic's Boy, was sacked from Eton after two terms. It seems unlikely that this expulsion had any-thing to do with the school's embarrassment at his father's scandalous, widely reported apostasy.

More likely Marcus's offence of gross unnatural misconduct was sufficient in itself: no one remembers the dog's name.

A private tutor, a Mr Bull-Devine, was hired. Mama claimed that Marcus refused to talk to this party who was a mere servant – and as for taking instruction from him . . . He insisted that he should continue his education at Shrewsbury School for that was where Charles Darwin had been a pupil fifty years before. The Reverend Clement Phimister relented.

It was on the Severn's right bank, upstream of the school, beside a rotting boathouse, one misty autumn dusk in 1874, that he first talked to the fellow pupil with whose name his would be forever entwined. They already knew each other by sight. It had been love at first sight. They both smiled the sly smile of mutual acknowledgement, they recognised their sameness. This was mere confirmation.

Jervoise Vanier was leaning against a poplar's trunk, shirt-tail wagging, post-coitally shagged, languidly smoking a cheroot. (I'm imagining all this, more or less making it up, hoping I'm getting it right, getting the feel of the thing and so on.) The boathouse was certainly known in some circles within the school as The Dollymopshop. It was still recalled seventy years later, when I was there, even though it had long since sagged into the river to be washed out to sea (or to Bewdley). This is where dollymops, irregulars with names like Buildwas Winnie, came to top up their miserable incomes as shopgirls, seamstresses, domestic servants etc. For a florin they gratefully fucked rich young gentlemen from the grand school up the hill. None was richer than Jervoise Vanier. For a shilling they gobbled rich young gentlemen: gamahuche was the word then, it's got a nice feel to it. Vanier will have said something to Mein Opa along the lines of, 'You're going to be batting on a very sticky wicket.'

Edie Blood, then an apprentice milliner, will have gripped the coins Mein Opa paid her. He pressed her against oars and scorching coils of rope. He grinned at Vanier, who was watching this ne plus ultra of a knee-trembler through a glassless aperture where a window had been. The floorboards were papery from flood after flood. The report of a too-heaving cock-thrust might puncture them. The girl's cunt was deliciously snug. It was doubly welcoming for it was full of Vanier's warm sperm. Mein Opa was fucking his new brother too, staring into his intensely turquoise eyes over Edie's shoulder. The bond they forged was all but instantaneous. 'We became one person,' said Vanier many years later. They would cut each other, gouts of their blood would mix. But not before Mein Opa ejaculated so that their sperm combined in a rich emulsion of fraternal loyalty and dependence. What jolly blancmange methinks! Edie was an intermediary as well as a receptacle.

From that evening on, Jervoise Vanier and Marcus Phimister would be inseparable for more than a quarter of a century. And for much of that time Edie Blood, a nonpareil among counter-jumpers with her freshly acquired accent and airs and graces, was their blowsy toy. She rose from tyro whoredom to become an amply rewarded courtesan whose speciality was accommodating both of them at the same time in all the apertures the good lord had blessed her with. Who said that nothing but ill could come of being on the street or, in this instance, the towpath? Furthermore, her prowess as a proxenetist − lovely word! − proved to be remarkable. At Malpasfang, no matter what other entertainments might be in residence, the three of them shared a vast bed for many years.

I first saw the remnants of that very bed in the early spring of 1944. I found a breach in the wall where roots had triumphed over bricks. Chill with fear I ventured through the jungly park of thorns and roots and barkless boughs where unseen creatures scuttled and groaned. The long neglected, partly roofless, rook racked ruin was surrounded by the swaying high grass of lawns that had long ago gone to seed. The house had been pillaged by oggies: doors, floor tiles, roof tiles, leaded lights, dressers, rainwater heads all disappeared long ago. Everything was long long ago. From the centre of a broken window pane spread a web of cracks like a skeleton's hands. Mother Nature, a malevolent old hag, had done the rest. Trees grew in once stately rooms, ivy invaded mullions and newels. Ceilings had collapsed. A rotten floor had given way sending that huge bed to the room beneath. A brass plate told that its frame had been built by Heale of Aymestrey. It was honeycombed with worm. Powdery, deflated in that palace of dust and bones. Apart from that detail, I have to admit that my account of the house's sleeping arrangements is guesswork for no stairs remained. Believe it as you will. It is based on hearsay, familial lore, Chinese whispers. Mama, however, seldom mentioned the matter. For a person who boasted of being candid she was extraordinarily evasive.

More's the pity; faute de mieux I have to rely on my distant memory of the distant and fractured memories of la Vicomtesse Riquetti de Besançon (dementia was closing in on her, poor old thing) and, regrettably, on the 'historian' – telly 'historian', and vulgarian! – Inigo Horrocks.

Oh the horror of Horrocks! If you can stomach his occasional massacre of our noble language, *Breast Milk Cheese and Placenta Fritters* (London, 2008) certainly makes for a hair-raising read. Salacious to say the least. But he was a sententious so-and-so the way he lays into Vanier and Mein Opa.

'Monsters living in the park . . . the notorious Malpasfang Lodge . . . abominable . . . foul . . . unspeakable . . . disgusting . . . haunted . . .'

His gutter press appetite had been whetted when, researching an earlier hackwork, he had come across a reference to Malpasfang Lodge in the noisome poet-geologist McHarg Bultitude's *A Blister in My Head* and had then found in an issue of *The Paracelsian* devoted to eugenics a short article about a series of experiments carried out there in the last decade and a half of the nineteenth century by Jervoise Vanier and Marcus Phimister.

He wrote:

The experimental farm where Vanier, heir to a Liverpool shipping fortune, and Phimister, son of a heretical Anglican cleric, attempted to breed new species crossing humans with horses, pigs and assorted other animals is now, thankfully, no more than a grubby group of ruined roofless brick sheds sprouting buddleia and strangled by ivy. It is a place that belongs in the same circle of hell as Cold Spring Harbor, Tuskegee and Tiffauges.

Mama didn't live to read him, lucky thing. He has little sympathy for his subjects. At one point he calls what is obviously an enjoyable and, as they say, 'consensual' group romp, actually a rompette (a mere six participants), 'a serial violation of barbaric savagery'. Of course, he describes it in graphic detail before expressing his condemnation. Then there's the old canard of likening them to 'the camp doctors', without pausing to consider that those doctors, highly qualified and dedicated professionals, have been tarnished by black propaganda, victor's lies and Blighty's proud gutter press (to which Horrocks was a contributor). Admittedly one or two of them may, as young doctors will, have overstepped the mark in their enthusiasm for breaking new ground, but our American brethren are all too well aware that Man would not have stepped on the Moon without the information gleaned from those experiments.

As a companiable fellow wordsmith I tried to put Horrocks on the right track on the several occasions he sought my advice about his 'project'. I have to own up – I failed.

Problem Eins with Horrocks and the Horrockses of this world is that they simply don't understand what fair play is all about. His attitude is what I call 'twisted prurience'. He wants to have his cake and eat it. He licks his lips over what he claims to revile. He's a tabloidoid (!) with a thesaurus. My confidence was betrayed. Wrist-slap: silly old me to have trusted him.

Problem Zwei is that I failed to heed the warning. His togs positively shrieked bogusness. Ultra-hirsute tweed jacket; a paisley handkerchief sprawling from a breast pocket is a certain giveaway of thwarted social aspiration; gooseshit-green cords; bristly moustache; galumphing veldtschoen (he lived in Peckham for god's sake! No, no: according to him it was 'Camberwell Borders'). Then there's the extraordinarily strangulated accent obviously covering up some below-stairs whine: it was as though he spoke English as a second language. He assumed he could prove he was a genuine historian by piling on the footnotes and references. You have to take the slant he puts on it all with a pinch of salt. As I say, thank god Mama did not live to read his pusillanimous calumnies.

He refused to be quizzed on his so-called motivation for writing the wretched tome and it's too late now. The blighter popped his clogs in a coach crash outside Ghent. In his capacity as a renowned military historian (!) he was the man with the colourful umbrella held high leading a Poppy Tours party to First World War battlefields, monuments and a few anomalous sites like Roddie Vanier's grave.

Yes, you heard right. A coach crash! There's no getting away from it: it's a common-as-cruet way to go.

Still, at least we no longer have to wince at his Tourette grimaces and bizarre vowels and that involuntary tic-tac malarkey on the box. Mind you, that's probably the clue to his fratchiness. He must have known that with a condition like his he too would have been culled in the Eugenotopia that Vanier and Mein Opa foresaw, the world they promised for me.

Horrocks's alarmingly florid 'widow' Dominic Rose, very likely a former rent-boy who had lost his looks, is a soft furnishings editor (really!) for some vulgar weekend magazine. He has the rectal renegade's giveaway arse, widened and wobbly from being relentlessly porked. He claims to have no knowledge of Mein Opa's later correspondence that, through my interventions, Horrocks was able to locate in Zurich – on condition he passed them to me when he had finished with them. I don't know why I believe Rose is lying, but I am sure of it. It's a particularly frustrating loss because Horrocks appears hardly to have quoted from them.

There is something furtive about young(ish) Mr Rose. It's beyond the furtiveness of the alcoholic who hopes that he hasn't been rumbled. He knows that I know that he's concealing the whereabouts of that correspondence. A private detective may be required. Or un poign americain – so much more elegant a term than knuckleduster. Some of Stafford Prance's 'roadie' employees are proud to be primates!

Here are some facts gleaned from Horrocks:

Octave Mirbeau made two visits in the spring of 1896 in the company of that admirable swordsman Harry Cust whom he had met in Paris. Cust had invited Mirbeau in the hope of employing him as an art critic for *The Pall Mall Gazette*. Arnaud Melchior records in his diary (27.07.1903) Mirbeau's admission that the origin, 'la germe', of Clara in *Le Jardin des Supplices* was an 'unusual young Englishwoman called Eden Blood' whom he described as 'la maîtresse perverse et sadique du Château de Malpasfang dans le comté de Shropshire (surnommé Salop(e)!)'. Was Mirbeau touched? In love? Obsessed? Shocked? Disgusted? They did meet subsequently.

★

Yes, he might have been a gullible pinko. Yes, he might have been a sucker for Uncle Joe. But H. G. Wells was very definitely on the money when it came to the future of the race. The first step being 'the elimination of detrimental types and characteristics' and the 'fostering of desirable types instead'. Aye-aye, Sir.

In 1892 he visited The Malpasfang Experiment in the company of a fellow called Ray Lankester (spelling!), a zoologist who'd been his teacher. Writing to a chap with the deuced silly name of Edward Clodd, Lankester remarked: 'possibly good intentions, palpably bad science, cattle-breeders' science'. Wells, however, kept his counsel. He stayed schtum. Which was unlike Wells, usually a garrulous fellow. There's nothing in his correspondence about it. More than likely he was anxious to conceal that Malpasfang was a source of material for him, indeed the very inspiration for a yarn.

Another distinguished guest was the septuagenarian G. F. Watts. He arrived in the company of his sometime patron Reginald Cholmondeley with whom he was staying at Condover Hall. This was not his first visit. Many years earlier, in 1854, he had made a portrait of Thomas Vanier, now in the Walker Art Gallery in Liverpool. Unlike Wells he did record that day he spent at Malpasfang.

Art historical orthodoxy has it that he was inspired to create his greatest work, painted in just the course of one morning (a likely story!), in response to a series of articles by the over-pious W. T. Stead, Harry Cust's predecessor as editor of *The Pall Mall Gazette*, which addressed the so-called iniquities of the traffic in child prostitutes. A letter to Briton Riviere dated 14 April 1885 – three months before Stead's articles were published – appears, in Horrocks's opinion, to give the lie to that orthodoxy. He quotes Watts:

Towards dusk at Malpasfang I saw a sight I yearn never to see again. A cart with a high wooden crate upon it drew out of the larger farmyard at unusual speed. Its progress was suddenly halted by a ploughing engine. The carter gestured with an impatience out of all proportion to the inconvenience. A movement within the crate caught my eye. I glanced through the slats of the crate. It was a form of cage. Within there lurked a monstrous creature of wonder and terror and infinite pity. Is it absurd to talk of a myth made flesh? Of a satanic atrocity come to life? An atrocity one thought slain many millenia gone [*sic*]? It was as if Frankenstein's monster was a creature by Bosch. I hope and pray never to pass this way again. But what is seen cannot be unseen. However much I try I cannot exorcise the frightful vision of its milky eyes, nor the all-pervading stench of the beast, no, nor the unearthly bellows which might have issued from the caverns of hell itself. When I mentioned this apparition to Young Vanier and his fellow sorcerer they smiled with the satisfaction of youth and they affected puzzlement. They blithely turned the conversation to sick cattle. I fear they believe themselves mightier than the Almighty. They have unleashed a power which they will realise by and by they are unable to control. And Babylon shall become heaps . . . Tom Vanier must be turning in his grave.

On the other hand Edward Carpenter, an inveterate optimist – those sandals! Those sandals the whole year round! – called it 'a Walden with science'. That's an opinion of course.

But it's jolly well a fact that such an opinion was ventured. Horrocks must have taken pleasure in being able to counter that it was, equally, 'a Walden with manure'.

You can't argue with that. That part of the Vanier fortune which was not founded on slavery was indeed founded on manure. Guano. Fossilised bird turd. In Liverpool, where the Vaniers had their companies' headquarters, their fleet, their palatial townhouses and grand suburban villas, they were known by the canaille as The First Family of Shite. (Needless to say, 'palatial' and 'grand' are understatements. The Vaniers were new money through and through. Almost Jewy with their gaudy flaunting.) According to the booklet about the estate, Thomas Vanier, Jervoise's grandfather, bought Malpasfang in the mid-1840s. He was anointed with superlatives. The richest man in England. Didn't have a title, of course.

It goes without saying that the seven-mile brick wall around the estate was the longest in Britain and was predictably known in the locality as the Great Wall of China. It goes without saying, again, that the model farm was the largest in Europe. An agrarian-industrial complex the size of a village with terraced houses for sixty labourers and their families, a park for their recreation and generous allotments where they could grow vegetables and keep fowl.

These were laid out in strips and adorned with quaint hay stooks that resembled long-haired puli dogs. When hunting bison, Thomas Vanier had apparently taken a fancy to Pomeranian field systems. He had then discovered that they were akin to the burgage plots once common in Marches villages and measured by the perch. That settled it; he was surprisingly anxious to embrace tradition in order to ingratiate himself with the yeomanry, stuck-in-the-mud chaps who were suspicious of vast wealth.

'The Town' comprised semi-detached houses and two detached houses for the superintendents, all positively des res compared with the usual tied cottages.

The construction, half a mile distant and a decade later, of a satellite known as Nether Farm was curtailed after only one and a half terraces of houses had been built. They stood in often waterlogged fields unserved by roads or paths, a sorry site in comparison with the church whose spire rose 160 feet.

Close by it stood a school and an 'institute' for the betterment and cultural succour of the workforce.

The Vanier Arms had its own hopyards, pyramidal oast houses,[13] cooperage and brewery.

Malpasfang Halt was on the New Invention, Bishop's Castle and Fron Light Railway whose majority shareholder was Thomas Vanier. He travelled from Liverpool in his private train whose livery was black and navy blue. Each door bore the Vanier coat of arms, an allegory of triumph in which a youth with a trident stood over a dead sea monster.

Streams were diverted and dammed to form reservoirs. Water

---

13 *A Toast to the Oast: Hop Kilns of Kent & East Sussex* by Sir Geoffrey Shadoxhurst Bt and *A Further Toast to the Oast: Hop Kilns of England West of the Severn* by Sir Geoffrey Shadoxhurst Bt are available from all good Asdas, houseofshadox.co.uk and Amazon UK: 'Lazily written in boorish clubman's English', Jonathan Glancey, *Architectural Review*, 12.12.75.

turbines powered a corn mill and a saw mill. Liquid fertiliser – guano, potassium and recycled manure – flowed by force of gravity through subterranean pipes into fields. The source of this malodorous tonic, a hilltop 'tank' known as Fort Shoosmith, was fed by a funicular railway.

There was a separate narrow-gauge railway for fodder transport, a half-timbered poultry house, a dovecote with a conically roofed belvedere, a gasworks, a fire station and tender, a smithy, a hillside of four dozen hives based on the Extremaduran model. They were brightly painted to make the bees contented and productive. The sties, byres, hunt kennels, stables and sheep pens were constructed around eight courtyards.

Certain of the shelters were circular: there was, apparently, a dotty belief at the time that animals were happier if thus housed. Quite how the beasts communicated this preference is not recorded!

It might well be getting on for a century early, but I'd say it has more than a whiff of the collective farms that Wells's chum Uncle Joe inflicted on the truly unfortunate – the ones who had not been starved or shot.

Malpasfang Lodge itself was a very different k of f from the farm. A couple of miles or so distant and surrounded by all the usual gubbins, albeit in unusual profusion: lavish planting of specimen trees and dago shrubs from countries no one had heard of, the greatest show of cedars in England, vast beasts bred in Lebanon, including the Tree of Tyre, transported at vast expense, monkey puzzles from the guano continent, wellingtonias, rock gardens, grottoes, cascades, formal parterres. Like the farm, the school and the church, the house was designed by one Milford Sanders, a Liverpudlian who specialised – and how it showed! – in hospitals for imbecilic children, lunatics and the incurable.

Even then, all those years ago, money was being pointlessly thrown away prolonging useless lives!

The card Mama had sent me showed one of those vast spikey monstrosities. There was a bit of everything, a lot of everything. As I say, eclectic is one word for it. Hodge-podge is more like it.

One knights-of-olde tower had so many apertures, irregular

windows, loopholes, random niches and the like that it might have been gnawed by feasting rodents. Another tower was a ringer for the Villa Jana at Leghorn where we had stayed with the Vair-Vairs. A third had a fourth growing out of it, like a freak with an extra limb.

Odds on that Milford Sanders was a laudanum-addicted, Camelot-obsessed, tertiary-syphilitic god-botherer. You know the type. Keen appreciation of Victorian noovs' taste. A very keen appreciation. Give them more: more crenelations, more machicolations, more turrets, more drawbridges, more strapwork, more Good Queen Bess, more Quasimodo, more Black Death. More, that was always the ticket, more. Sanders was one of those aberrational johnnies whose idea of a single vast monstrosity was a pile-up of several not much less vast monstrosities that looked as though they hadn't been introduced to each other.

With a backdrop as rum as this and a seven-mile-long wall to shelter them is it any wonder that Jervoise Vanier and Mein Opa got up to such larks? My hunch is that it egged them on to further japes. They must have felt encouraged to behave in keeping with the stage. The stage makes the actors, and so forth.

Throughout their time at Shrewsbury they played fives, rowed, hunted with the North Shropshire. While their contemporaries were in prayer or in drink or in both they whored at The Dollymopshop and in Grope Lane. Most of all they talked optimistically of creating humans fit for the next century, humans who might build on the achievements of the most powerful nation on earth without the embuggerance of a dependent imbecile caste. They were nicknamed The Evangelists, which must have been a tad tiresome.

There were countless routes to the genetic perfection of the race. They positively steeped themselves in bloodlines and what-have-you, selective breeding, artificial selection, the lore and practice thereof.

Most mares come on heat every three weeks.

They pee pond-size puddles, respond flirtatiously to the sight of a stallion, lose tautness in their genital muscles.

Not on! Tautness and tightness are very much what the stallion ordered! Sooner penis captivus than waving it about in the Albert Hall.

★

They visited ethnological exhibitions in Manchester and Liverpool.

The summer holidays of 1876 and '77 were spent touring freak shows, fairs and penny gaffs.

They saw: Ronald and Donald, the Siamese Twins from Anstruther, billed as Fife's Authentic Chang and Eng; The Electric Woman; The Gorilla Woman; The Skeleton Woman; The Human Tripod; The Dog-Faced Man; The Bladder-Headed Baby; The Girl With a Tail.[14]

In a marquee beside the Trent they saw The Bearded Woman of Castille (her only English engagement, she came from Sligo).

They revelled in these anomalies whom they believed to be touched by sublimity, they marvelled at them. They admired their exceptionality. They considered them blessed. They wanted to recreate them.

Following a rumour they heard in Gainsborough they rode south to Kesteven, to the village of Eagle where there was a folly, The Jungle, designed by a gentleman called Mr Lovely for Mr Samuel Russell Collett, evidently something of a card, for, in the grounds, he maintained a menagerie of buffalos, kangaroos and crossbred deer. Unhappily, Collett had died a quarter of a century previously and his menagerie had been dispersed. News travels slowly in those parts.

'There's time and then there's Lincoln time,' Nanny Shadox used to say. The folly was now squatted by a family of hostile oggies.

They had no more luck a few miles distant at Stubton where Sir Robert Heron's collection of llamas, alpacas, lemurs, porcupines, armadillos and kangaroos had been eaten by a gathering of his friends during a fourteen-hour celebratory feast after he, too, had died, long ago.

They read stud books, pored over genealogies. They noted that both Charles Darwin and Thomas Malthus had got spliced to ladies with trustworthy genes, their first cousins.

On the other hand, so had Mohammed, Queen Victoria and King Billy whose cousin-wife Mary produced nothing but a single

14 Ten days after they had seen the latter they read that she had been mauled to death by a lion at Buxton. *Derby Telegraph*, 28.07.1877.

miscarriage. The on dit has it that Billy was not as other kings. And just look at Victoria and Albert's progeny! Incapable of anything but marrying their cousins, an inherited trait most likely, doubly inherited.

Ovulation rate is a criterion for the improvement of litter size in merino sheep – if you say so . . .

Genetic improvement causes economic improvement – yup.

A bull's mating behaviour is linked to his testicular size – there's sound logic in that by jove! If Mr Bovril's got a bulky packet in the gentleman area he's going to be aching to express it.

In 1876, at the age of sixteen, Mein Opa, who hunted with a bamboo yumi and arrows almost two feet long, translated Xenophon's great treatises as *An Essay on Hunting* and *An Essay on Riding*. Inigo Horrocks flails about deriding this feat of precocious scholarship. He rubbishes it as morally flawed exhibitionism. Methinks that in his bile he linked it to the yellow press's vindictive fabrications about Malpasfang of more than twenty years later. Mounted Devils In Bee-skeps, Night Terror Wrought By Phantom Riders, that sort of baloney.

'Oxford for classics, Cambridge for science.' 'Twas bandied about when I was young. Whether it was still the case when I was up at Balliol I haven't the foggiest: most of the time I was, thankfully, in no shape to notice, and even had I been, who gives a spayed dog! But there's no doubt that back in 1878 there was a good deal of truth in it.

Nonetheless it was Oxford Mein Opa went up to in that year to read natural sciences, Balliol of course. The long and the short of it was that his mind was made up by Jervoise Vanier who, to his father's delighted incredulity, had elected to study at the Royal College of Agriculture in Cirencester and so prepare himself to take over the running of Malpasfang, to make it pay its way, to recreate his grandfather's vision. Cambridge is over a hundred miles from Cirencester. Oxford is less than forty.

Thomas Vanier had died in 1871. Neither Jervoise's father, who had seldom visited the estate, nor his three elder brothers, all of them partners in the ever-expanding shipping line and assorted unrelated businesses (mines, quarries, steel foundries, boiled sweets), were interested in the management of what they considered to be a caprice, their revered forebear's prodigal plaything. Yet to dispose of it was unthinkable. It would have been to dishonour his shade. Besides, in those years of agrarian depression they were unlikely to find a buyer.

Jervoise bought Macaroni Farm at Eastleach, midway (approx.) between Cirencester and Oxford. Its barn was vast.

The skies were vaster: starlings swirled across them.

McHarg Bultitude was a regrettable fellow but I love these lines:

> *Anthracite black murmurations,*
> *A chorus line in three dimensions.*

Bruiser clouds busied themselves.

The two of them rode to hounds with the Vale of the White Horse, the Heythrop and the Old Berks. They vaulted over drystone walls. They felled hedges. Mein Opa brought down partridge and pheasant with bow and arrows. Crows were shot and nailed to gateposts as an example to other crows. Jervoise took up photography. They grew hothouse peaches.

They installed Edie Blood as chatelaine. She learnt to ride side-saddle on a velvet-covered Champion & Wilton with a jewelled crupper. (I have to intrude to admit that Tiger responds to a crupper as perkily as he does to a string thong cutting tightly between buxom buttocks tanned to tawny perfection.) She relished stiff winds, leather crops, hatpins.

Soon she was called Eden Blood. The stuck-up little thing returned to Shrewsbury in her brougham to recruit several chambermaids and under-chambermaids. A couple of others, plump pieces, sisters, came from further distant Wrexham, or maybe Wem, somewhere round about there. At more than half a century's distance Horrocks had difficulty identifying them. They were called Evans, the most common moniker in those parts.

The Old Berks's nonagenarian stud groom Young Burdis was a fount of practical advice on the mechanics of breeding: 'You 'ave to goide tha' stiff horrn delica' loike, loike you's a poilot on riverr

Severrn.' (Long ago he had worked at Sharpness Docks where the tide rises thirty feet.) It was on his recommendation that they employed a stable lad, his neighbour's great-grandson Jezzard Dogg, a cheerful young shaver who had been unlucky with his previous, unsympathetic employers but was, avowed Young Burdis, a good learner. He had already learnt how to guide that stiff horn. He had a way with animals.

Jezzard Dogg would come to have quite an influence on their future, more than could possibly have been expected of a menial dreg.

Horrocks asserts that Jervoise and Mein Opa could both ride to their places of learning in little more than an hour and a half. I should cocoa! Given the state of the lanes in those days you'd be lucky to do it in under three hours: the places where you might get up a canter were few and far between. They encountered many an amiable vagabond on those journeys, and some not so amiable – hedgesetters with sharpened stakes pointed at a mount's throat, ragged tree monkeys, ditch skippers and crasslemen (whoever they were! Horrocks doesn't explain).

It was on one of these rides that Mein Opa first crossed paths with Mortimer Glyde, The Devil's Crocus, The Autolycus of The Open Road. In his youth he had been a communicant of the Mansion of Indivisibility. He remained a proselytising vegan who never washed lest he be stripped of what he called 'the aura of authenticity'. This skilamalink would become a frequent visitor to Macaroni Farm whose inhabitants fascinated him; and he them.

He was a dandy quack, un faiseur des anges sanctioned by Mary having aborted the son of god (though how one aborts a foetus whose only existence is mythical is both a theological and a medical conundrum). Glyde was skeletal, sibilant, greenish-skinned, garbed in checked broadcloth and an inverness. Strapped to the saddle of his black Kippax stallion Nigredo were a sabre, bought from a veteran of the battle of Reichenfels, two peters, one of them filled with potions, lead plaster, botanical remedies, opiates, distillations and helpful herbs (tansy, pennyroyal, mugwort, hemlock) that he called 'a lady's friends'. In many parts back then he was an infamous figure. He was feared and revered for his powers. He is alluded to, often pseudonymously, in a number of memoirs and diaries. He is mentioned in several court reports. He too would later come to play an important, you might say decisive, role in their life.

> My flock wandered through all the mountains and on every high hill; my flock was scattered over all the surface of the earth, and there was no one to search or seek for them.

Mein Opa's mounts were stabled in Oxford at The Golden Cross. The landlady Mrs Franklin baked what he called 'the finest veal pies in heaven let alone on earth'. The old dear would be prosecuted in 1886 for using squirrel and rat meat in pies. Not guilty. The beak had never tasted anything more delicious. Makes you wonder: would Jew flesh and Lal flesh taste like pig, long pig, as us normal coves do?

Macaroni Farm had been a try-out. It was a rehearsal that whipped up their curiosity no end. They learnt to stretch themselves, to question everything, most of all the gospel according to the chaps they revered. No more unstinting adulation then for Messrs Galton and Darwin, neither of whom could ever have conceived such programmes as those achieved at Malpasfang by 'the gemini visionaries of abandon' (Rollo Gammans: *Dancing Shegog*. Dear Rollo! The epithet, like so many, was not his. A big smack for those light fingers! Though it must be said that he was a choosey klepto. He only stole the best. And as a choosey satyr only fucked the best.).

They at last established themselves at Malpasfang in the early summer of 1882. The caravan from the Cotswolds to the Marches must have been a thing to see: black stallions, liveried coaches, wolfhounds twelve hands tall, carts loaded with ewes and cattle, gypsy vans. There were flags and gaudy. They processed through Cheltenham, Ledbury and Ludlow. The twin princelings of the carnival at its head, clean shaven and long haired. It was a harlequinade. The field of the cloth of gold unfolded. Horrocks includes photographs of the parade taken at Tewkesbury. Black and white of course. Some of the crew dressed in costume: a jolly jester, whom Horrocks takes to be Jezzard Dogg, in a motley, sleeves with bells at the cuff and a hood with donkey's ears; Eden Blood, side-saddle, wears a picture hat by Romney or one of his contemporaries – ribbons, plumes, bows and a swooping brim hiding her face; a grinning monkey in jockey's silks and cap sat behind her astride a rolled mantle. The adult townsfolk look on in bemusement, as well they might. The children are enchanted.

One night they pitched camp between an inn and a hopyard on the right bank of the Teme. Their presence attracted mystified attention, then, after dark, a display of rustic greeting. A mob of taproom oggies and glocks threw sticks and rotten fruit, lobbed clods of earth, roared heavily accented insults and threatened to put out horses' eyes. They taunted Jezzard Dogg: 'What yew bin up to in Roden's paddock then? Backslidin' was it?'

Mein Opa fired shots into the dark heavens. It was a taste of the years to come.

Throughout the 1850s and '60s Malpasfang Lodge Model Farm had been what might be called the apple of agronomy's eye. It's not over-doing it to call it a place of pilgrimage. A veritable cynosure! High Farming's mecca. The curious and plain nosey arrived from Europe and the New World as well as from Britain.

Politicians: William Ewart Gladstone, then Chancellor of the Exchequer (his father had been a Liverpudlian neighbour and busi-ness associate of the Vaniers); Digby Bosher; Selwyn Marrack; the reformer and temperance campaigner James Silk Buckingham deplored the public house as 'a pockmark on the face of paradise' and 'somewhat intemperately' lectured Vanier on the high incidence of alcoholism among Cornish tin miners; 'le Vice Empereur', the French minister of agriculture and public works Eugène Rouher.

Future politicians: Joseph Chamberlain and Jesse Collings.

Land economists, among them Jean-Baptiste Borély.

The hydraulic engineer William Vivary who, the week after his visit, would have the singularly bad luck to be among the 214 people killed when his newly built Gilderthwaite Reservoir burst – he was showing it off to a party of Danish engineers.

Social investigators and journalists: G. A. Sala, Clough Rosser.

The insatiably randy French ambassador the Comte de Flahaut.

The self-styled brother to all humanity Daniel Tolly.

Octavia Hill.

Many noble landowners: e.g. the Margraves of Fulda and Baden-Durlach.

The disturbed Jew-loving Laurence Oliphant. George Eliot and Herbert Spencer.

The Eton schoolboy Henry Salt. The Harrow schoolboy Robert Cunninghame Graham. John Ruskin.

They all beat a path to its door.

By 1882, however, it was in a very sorry state looking decidedly shack. It had been neglected for most of the decade since Thomas Vanier's death. His heirs had taken their eye off the ball. Their indifference was tantamount to slovenliness. Thomas Vanier's private railway had been sold. They had appointed a succession of nincompoop stewards and superintendents who weren't up to the job. These were followed by a plausible fellow, the crafty ginger Mr Vendy Nangle who, ever on the qui vive, took advantage of his employers' slovenliness. The long and the short of it: a reluctance to invest a single penny and a consequent lack of maintenance was compounded by mismanagement and peculation. Open day for jiggery-pokery.

For instance: only a fraction of the income generated by Ambrose Wrockwardine, reputed to be 'the most champion grain-seed-raiser twixt Chester and the Bristol Channel', was declared to the Vaniers. There were countless instances of false accounting, fingers in the till, phantom invoices, fictitious employees, the whole caboodle. That's the way it goes. Butter churners and poultry fatteners operated a thriving black market. Workers who had been dismissed several years previously still occupied their tied houses. Rents were not collected. Other houses had been squatted by moochers. Pigs' weights were falsified. Litters were wilfully miscounted. Receipts from Welshpool and Newtown markets were blatantly inaccurate. There were ringer cattle and sheep: Gower Browns were listed as Herefords; Scaristas as Shropshires, the very breed that Thomas Vanier had been instrumental in developing in the 1840s and which he eventually persuaded or bribed the Royal Agricultural Society to recognise a decade later.

A certifier dispatched from a Liverpool shipping office or a registrar deputed by a north Walian quarry to scrutinise the inventories would have lacked the expertise to distinguish between the breeds. One of the world's greatest business empires — founded on slavery, sharp practice, brutality, threats, mistrust and suspicion – was being quietly taken to the cleaners by muddied oggies who were all low cunning and Welsh slime (or charm). Not as oafish as you might think, these silver-tongued boyos.

In the great scheme of things the sums stolen and embezzled were a drop in the ocean to the Vaniers. 'The Mersey Mammons' (Horrocks's coinages were so facile!) remained ignorant of the multiple frauds perpetrated against them until Jervoise commissioned an audit a few months after they had taken over Malpasfang.

They installed a telephone: Malpasfang 1.

Those were difficult months. Jervoise and Mein Opa struggled to gain control of the estate.

The majority of the farm's labourers had been given the chop long since.

They had left to seek work in the Black Country and the Potteries.

The model village's social structure had collapsed. To Mein Opa's eye the church's ragged unfinished interior suggested some Piranesi of the north. Eden remarked that he saw Piranesi everywhere. Most of the houses were empty. But nature abhors a vacuum! The bush telegraph was all-abuzz. Bothy dwellers stumbled down from the mountains, their shoeless feet were lacerated. They wore burlap and untreated fleeces.

Practised horse thieves, rustlers, sly peasants, spongers, gyppos, dids, moochers, tatterdemalion mendicants and poachers, many of them Welsh monoglots from as far away as Bala and Blaenau Ffestiniog, squatted the abandoned houses. They were the distant descendants of recusants who had taken to the hills to evade persecution long long ago. Mostly illiterate, they practised superstitious sacrifices and celebrated a form of communion. They carried Mariolatrous idols. They annually relived the crucifixion. Because of the ready availability of slate they were versed in frolicsome lapidation, some suffered consequent disabilities. A flockless shepherd dragged behind him a sack containing the remnants of his companion who had fallen to his death. Eating the body and brains maddened him. He howled till his throat would take no more.

The Vaniers' managerial timeservers colluded with them or were too inert or too frit to resist them. Mr Vendy Nangle had disappeared the previous autumn. For several years these hayseed criminals, exemplary capitalists, had ruled the roost. Malpasfang became a byword for lawlessness.

To their bewilderment the rough diamond rustics, good eggs if less than couth, had recently been joined by a second, very different, group of trespassers. A sinister battalion of back-to-the-landers.

The Lord thy God is bringeth ye into a good land, a land of brooks of water, of fountains and depths that spring out of valleys and hills; a land of wheat, and barley, and vines, and fig trees, and pomegranates; a land of oil olive, and honey; a land wherein thou shalt eat bread without scarceness, thou shalt not lack any thing in it; a land whose stones are iron, and out of whose hills thou mayest dig brass.

Mystic militants swathed in shoddy and mungo looking for the promised land, Lancastrian mill town agitators claiming to be victims of the Long Depression. They were in fact nothing but scrimshankers, workshy autodidacts, lucubrators in public libraries – those sumps of unhealthy agitation. Small tradesmen, brick makers, printers, weavers and stockingers with ideas above their station. Hobbies: composition of unreadable pamphlets; soap box oratory; proselytising for vegetarianism and teetotalism:

Water is best for the trees of the forest,
Water is best for the flowers of the field.

Among their number were Pugh Stovin and Albert Jenny, both of them founder members of the Fellowship of the New Life, an airy-fairy soviet of cooperative insurrectionaries. Jenny would enter the House of Commons in the 1906 election as Labour member for Burnley, marking the Common Man's arrival on a stage for which he was demonstrably unfit.

Not exactly the great unwashed, then.

Rather, unwashed by choice, not out of lack of soap! They

belonged to the whining class of so-called idealist that is invariably to be found stirring up revolution, hurling cobbles and cohabiting with manly sexual liberationists, ugly so-and-sos no proud fellow would want to roughly roger – what I call The Monstrous Reggies, the plainest of plain Janes but fecund sows, oh how fecund!

Fired up with their righteous luddite vigour, they smashed industrial plant including a prototype steam combine-harvester. They damaged The Vanier Arms's brewery. The incumbent trespassers went into no end of a strop about that. There was nothing they liked more than being woozled day and night.

These townie loogans were comprehensively chiselled at market. They were dupes. They were flogged sheep infected with frothy bloat, calves suffering grass tetany and goats with Esmond's Prion – their swollen udders scraped the ground. Healthy horses were left to starve in fields; so many flies congregated on their eyes they might have been wearing blinkers. They collapsed, their bellies exploded. Barking rooks darkened the sky. What a sumptuous feast of carrion! The bones were picked clean. Their diseased sheep spun madly and ran round in circles till they died. Their fruit rotted. Their cereal crops failed.

They were nothing but chippy bolsheviks avant la lettre, thick as lard when it came to the seasons and to farming's disciplines, but they held no end of fancypants ideas about redistribution of wealth (better known as theft) and land reform (bka theft). The entire package was a farrago of Chartist blarney,[15] Captain Swing, all manner of Froggy communards and those bearded brutes Marx and Kropotkin – just what is it about rancid face-fungus and subversion? According to Horrocks this rabble was not really a rabble. It was an organised crew, a fact that most previous historians had been reluctant to acknowledge, so he claimed. These pinkos – organised or otherwise – railed against enclosures and the supposedly punitive legacy of the Speenhamland system.[16] (One of Horrocks's lame

15 The Duke of York advises that 'The best that can be said of these Chartist johnnies is that in order to finance their tedious harangues they produced some cracking smut. Works wonders on the noble quarters.'

16 A means-tested form of poor relief devised at a meeting of philanthropic magistrates in the Berkshire village of Speenhamland in 1795. It proved unpopular with both landowners and agricultural workers. It provoked riots.

attempts at humour is the title of a brief chapter on the Poor Laws: 'Serf Without Turf'.)

Surprise! Surprise! The two bands of disparate intruders didn't rub along. They soon got each other's measure and up each other's nose. Mutual mistrust, mutual despisal. They kept their distance, occupied different parts of the village. The bucolics lived in and around one of the original terraces in The Town. The Lancastrian pinkos, who took to wearing white robes, occupied terraced gothic cottages built to house an increasing workforce several years after The Town, half a mile away at Nether Farm. Yet they came, warily, to rely on each other. Hardly bilaterally!

The beastly revolutionaries, every one of them a silk at the bar of natural justice, set about trying to legitimise their own occupancy. They knew all there was to know about the laws of trespass and adverse possession, the 'rights' of squatters, reclaiming enclosures as common land etc. They intimidated Mr Vendy Nangle's ineffectual replacement, another dolt of the nincompoop tendency. They even had the neck to threaten the local rozzers with civil action should they intervene. Disgracefully, the torpid blighters in blue were scared off. They did nothing.

They threatened the illiterate oggies in no uncertain terms.

You teach us the practices we need to survive – animal husbandry, milking, horticulture, crop rotation, hedging and ditching, tending orchards and the enormous greenhouses, slaughtering pigs. In return we will secure your occupancy too through our knowledge of the law, which is a labyrinth you will never master. If you fail to teach us you will be homeless.

The frit panicking oggies had no choice but to succumb to Accringtonian sophistry and casuists from Bacup! Quid pro reluctant quo, as they say.

The second group was rapidly increasing in number. Typical of their type, they proved to be fast breeders who strove, with marked success, to flood the world with their noxious spawn. Every day brought forth a further mewling scrounger. You might have thought that in that era a couple of discreet warning shots to the back of the head would have been all the persuasion required to make them move on. After which life would be tickety-boo. But the foul tide of democracy – suffrage for imbeciles and class warriors – was already sweeping away sensible measures.

It was this group of know-all agitators that was the problem. Utopian parasites! How were they to be got rid of?

The Lancastrians were contemptuous of offers of bribery. Jervoise and Mein Opa talked it over endlessly. Natter, bunnybuns, chat, another B&S – but no action. They were agreed that they should steer clear of the law. The Vaniers were mistrusted. Their bountiful generosity had been taken for boastfulness by the mud-clagged local squirearchy that sat on the bench. They resolved then to involve neither the pusillanimous local constabulary nor The Vanier Primates, the infamous private army of Scouse strike-breakers, debt collectors and punch-drunk barefist-fighters whose approach to their work and unorthodox leisure pursuits would not necessarily be much appreciated outside Liverpool. But further than that . . .

They had taken to a despairing slumber of laudanum. Godfrey's Elixir of Strength: let all who suffer from weakness whatever the cause may be just make one trial of this wonderful remedy. Opium, treacle, alcohol. They had washed it down with iced Kümmel and were twined in each other's arms.

Eden must have listed their targets. The solar plexus, the jugular, the carotid, the femoral, the tibial. But who would administer the blows? Then she thought of drought, of lions. She had loved to snuggle beside them to listen to the ever more elaborately gruesome story of the girl mauled to death by a circus lion at Buxton and her Malmesbury predecessor Hannah Twynnoy. It took the place of the fairy tales she had been denied for she was the despised child of illiterates. (The laughably named oral tradition depends – pretty paradox! – on being written down. Otherwise everything, instead of being passed from one generation to the next, gets buried, and we live in ignorance of our ancestors' quaint lives and befuddling mores. What were oasts? Were they crematoria? Were dog carts really hauled by dogs?)

She thought of divide and rule.

The bucolic wastrels, the oggies, were actually industrious. They had no wish to overthrow the status quo. They knew which side their bread was buttered. Like all dyed-in-the-wool criminals they would have voted Conservative had, god forbid, they had the vote. Conservatism is, after all, nothing more than criminality sanctioned by well-placed criminals. This unbeautiful bevy acknowledged the laws that they broke. Good luck to the buggers. So long as they could get away with it . . . Everyone knows that poacher and gamekeeper come from the same mould. They were the exploited who craved the chance to join the exploiters. The enemies of the establishment who, like satirists (whisper it not), wanted to join that establishment in no matter how lowly a role. And they weren't breeders.

'Feeble-mindedness is largely handed on by heredity. The feeble-minded are merely carriers of their own germ. The proliferation of the mentally diseased is a grave danger to the race. The obliteration of feeble-mindedness is not enough. It is a defensive stratagem. What society demands is a strengthening of the strong.'

Mercifully this band had only one woman of childbearing age to share between them, the raggedy draggle-tail Ronwyn, a pretty imbecile who could not spell her name and did not know where she came from. They presented little danger. They grew fat from over-eating till it hurt, till they swelled like pigs, till they were bloated and immobile. They preferred to slyly suffer because they did not want to leave what they grew for the beastly revolutionaries, they did not even want to sell roots and fruit to them.

Their gradual loss of fitness made bending to pick in the fields a chore. Their patches might have become like the townee tyros' had not at dusk that summer's day Eden Blood, all in Lincoln green, ridden to The Vanier Arms where she knew she would encounter no teetotal vegetarian faction. She wore a high-crowned, narrow-brimmed, lav-ishly feathered hat. She was emboldened by Dutch courage. She carried a Remington 95 in her scarlet velvet diamanté-clasped bag. Nonetheless she must have been quaking with fear as she entered.

The lugubrious room shuddered to a halt. Sudden silence – only the rapacious meat flies failed to obey. Indistinguishable boozer faces, menacing faces, salivating maws like dogs' slime, bared buck-teeth, gap-teethed, brown-teethed, piggy eyes, mocking moues at her finery. Oh, the lot! You've seen the films, you've seen the stock cast of leering, sneering plukes mumbling among themselves, you've seen the foaming ale. Films don't transmit the whiff of raw gusset and oxter and dog breath. Blackened hams and animal corpses hung in the chimney. She held up a warning finger to a wall-eye who made to frot against her bustled buttocks in the snug. Loudly she asked the landlord to point out the leader of the malodorous mob. Which one? she insisted he tell her. She slapped down coins on the bar. Beer for every man – and lots of it. In those days beer was doctored with bitter foxglove. Taken in quantity it makes you nauseous and giddy. It was further adulterated with green copperas to give it the foaming head short-measure landlords favour. She was the youngest person in the room. She turned her back to the bar and addressed the leather-faced rodent the landlord had reluctantly indicated.

She found that she was addressing them all. She discovered a voice to address a multitude. She was electrified by confidence. The sudden realisation of her power made her spine sing. Timings, emphases, ellipses fell into place as though rehearsed. She heard herself as she had never heard herself before, steely and seductive. She began:

'I am going to make you a proposition. I'm going to make you several propositions . . .'

The propositions seemed to flow into her, fed to her by a fearsome power that was nameless yet familiar. She felt she spoke not about the propositions but on their behalf. Queer sensation, no question. Possessed?

'These people. These people with their dreams – which to us are nightmares . . . which to you are nightmares. Nightmares . . . Their intention is to break society. Nothing less. To upset the applecart so it can never, never be put together again . . . To break the structure in which each of us knows our place. In which each of us has a role – which is ours alone. These people, these people want to do away with the bonds that link all of us, the great and the small, the mighty and the humble, the responsible and the dependent . . .

'Now . . . if you assist us in ridding this precious domain of the chancre these people have visited upon it . . . if you labour to excise it we shall reward you.

'When we – we! – are rid of us these people . . . then you will join the commonwealth of Malpasfang's acres.

'Then . . .

'You will till the soil and you will reap all that the soil in its bounty can provide . . .

'You shall maintain your houses in good order, at your cost.

'We will exact no rent . . .

'We shall pay you a living wage . . .

'You shall pay us tithes . . . crops, flowers, fruit, nuts, berries, mushrooms. And game – the deer you stalk and stab. The boar you axe. The fish you stun with your ammonium bombs. The partridge you net . . . But – no more than we need.

'Now . . . you may not breed. Any woman laden with bastard will be expelled. Or have the bastard cut from her or dissolved by potions. Do you understand? You are forbidden to breed. Your bodily pleasures must be . . . must be taken elsewhere. The body is a versatile instrument . . .

'We shall be merciless in the enforcement of this contract . . .

'We shall equally be munificent and generous to those who respect it.'

Well spoken, that woman! She had spoken for twenty minutes.

The landlord uttered an oath, amazement rather than damnation. Her audience parted to allow her to process from the bar. They had heard about visits from the posh, the quality, swells, lords and the like. They had never before been privileged to witness one.

As she returned to Malpasfang Lodge her head echoed with the lilting voice of the Wenlock Evangelist Watkin Bredward who, when she was ten years old, had taken her virginity on the altar of the Shiloh Temple House of God in order to allay her damnation.

She bathed for half an hour then fell into bed between her two lovers. She dreamed of a lion that obeyed her every command.

When, a couple of days later, the communard chummies discovered that there was no longer a running water supply in their houses, a few of them set out for the village fountain. The brass inscription on it read: 'Take the water of life freely.'

Revelations 22.17 had, as so often, got it wrong. There was no water to take. The tilted amphora it usually flowed from was dry as a nun's minge. (My simile! Not Horrocks's – a novice's groin quarters

were not his area of expertise. Nor mine, but you get my drift . . .)
The vessel was held by the coyly draped figure of Belisama, a frankly
third-class Welsh deity, rather proley as goddesses go.

They were further puzzled. It didn't occur to them that they were
being invited to remove themselves from Malpasfang. The penny
took some time to drop. These were unimaginatively obedient
people who wanted to change laws rather than break them: definitive proof that they were out of touch with the real world! They
were unwilling to believe that the Marches were a jungle. Sauve qui
peut, mateys! They couldn't countenance the idea that Nether Farm
had been deliberately deprived of the water of life. They harboured
the hope that it would be miraculously restored. So for the next
week or so they all trooped off in hope to the river, a mile distant,
to wash.

They walked in Indian file across fields gone to seed, white-robed
ghosts in swaying grass, tent-like symbols of purity and perfection.
Until, that is, the first splash of cowpat did for them! Whereupon
they became brown symbols of impurity and imperfection. Not to
mention bad tailoring. If my long life has taught me anything, it is
that perfection is not to be found through the quest for perfection.
Rather the opposite.

Because they were ignorant of nature they believed that the wolfhounds were as fierce as their bark. Their self-pitying petitions to
Malpasfang Lodge were, then, easily shooed away. What did they
expect?

But the buggers dug their heels in. The Town, where The Rustics
squatted, drew its water from the original system that also fed the
Lodge. They could cut off the Lancastrians' water with impunity, it
was supplied by newer pipes. They took to firing catapults at their
houses. Siege. Quietism. And a lack of the desired response. These
people were pacifists. Again, out of touch with reality. No fight.

Hundreds of gelatin prints record life at Malpasfang Lodge, somewhat haphazardly. Few are dated. Here's Mein Opa with his bamboo
yumi bow taller than he is, arrow nocked, posing as though to aim at
prey on the wing, posing with it naked on horseback. Here, oftentimes, is Eden sucking a cock while being double fucked by a brace of

maharajahs. A number show the former snooker room. There are sketches and diagrams pinned to the gothic-trellised walls, chaotically. Two snooker tables are covered with sheets of bumf tracing genealogical lines of persons and primates, races and types. Races were defined by jaws, ears, noses of course, phrenological arcana. A third table is strewn with Guillaume Duchenne's studies of his experiments in applying electricity to gurning loonies. In one of the prints Jervoise and Mein Opa stand beside this table smiling at the camera with imperious scorn – the twin rulers of the world! Eden, seated, strokes the pelt of a silver-necklaced ocelot cub who returns her affection with a fine display of teeth.

This little chap was called Toppity. A nursery name for a decidedly non-nursery creature: you can say that again! He was bought as a house-warming present for Eden from Toft and Bootsma's once celebrated emporium in Fishponds. He pissed liberally, staking out his domain against non-existent all-comers. He soaked Moghul prayer rugs, carpets that showed his brawny feline cousins hunting, carpets that showed Mohammed's ascent to heaven and Akbar's entry into Surat, priceless tapestries from Gobelins and Aubusson. He bit and scratched for the hell of it.

Even after his milk was generously dosed with laudanum the plucky little warrior would still pick on Jezzard Dogg with malign relish: he could scent out fear with the best of them.

It was Dogg, now a privileged factotum as well as top lad and no doubt wincing from a further clawing, who proposed that the Lancastrians might be driven out by animals such as Toppity. He had the knack of making himself useful.

The following is one of Horrocks's more convincing passages of reported speech, though of course it's entirely made up:

'Nat Gedge is back at Tenbury, y'know . . . Indefinitely it appears. Bookings dried up since the monkey died,' offered Jervoise.

Dogg was puzzled. 'Monkey? Don't twig . . . Nat?'

'Gedge. The one and only, my dear Jezzard . . . the inimitable, the nonpareil, the sans pair – Zeus . . .'

'You got me there . . . Nat. Nope . . . And this Zeus lad eh? . . . Who's he when he's at home then?'

'Rather down on his luck I hear . . . Poor Nat. Dame Fortune is scowling at him . . . You could scoot over to Tenbury and see what specimens he might lend us. Well – hire us.'

'What do that mean – specimens?'

'Ooh I don't know – big cats, maybe. Hideous dogs bred for ripping other dogs apart, monsters from Hell's graveyards . . . Things that howl . . . Creatures even Hagenbeck can't tame . . . That bad. Beasts that'll put the fear of god into our white-robed chums. That'll tear out their throats and guzzle their entrails . . .'

'That sounds rumble choice . . . I'll be on me way to Tenbury then.'

'A day's ride . . . if that.'

'I'll get Peterkin to reshod 'im then.'

In *Teratologies: The Normality of Abnormality in the Victorian Freak Show* (London, 1998) Camilla Mangin writes:

Notwithstanding Dusty The Brown Bear, whose celebrity belonged anyway to the mid-Seventies, the major attraction of Zany Zeus's Zodiac Zoo at the end of that decade and the beginning of the Eighties was Mr Swell whose fame was so widespread that his image was used in advertisements for Venko's Macassar Oil and Badenwasser Balm which claimed to cure 'Nausea, Dread, Lumbago, Irritability and Neuralgia'.

Rather than being displayed as a mere entertainment this chimpanzee was held up as a sure vindication of Darwinian theory. It was maintained by Zeus (né Nathaniel Roy Gedge, Stapenhill, Staffs, 17 July 1835) that Mr Swell was 'a gentleman who lived like a gentleman'. That meant he changed from his lilac silk pyjamas in time for lunch, bathed twice a day and doused himself with ample drafts of Gaetano Sbarra's eau de cologne. He dressed and undressed himself. He ate fastidiously though his diet was not exclusively vegetarian. He had a particular fondness for the white meat of chicken and for eel. He favoured double-breasted waistcoats, a middle parting and a nightcap of malted milk with acacia honey. His approximation to human frailty was revealed by his appreciation of stimulants, particularly his fondness for Cuban cigars; his favourite brand

was Lorenzo Ventura. It is estimated that he smoked three packets of cigarettes a day. There are few things he enjoyed more
than Cognac. Just the sight of a Jézéquel-Laloy & Cie label with
its overweight, garlanded, presumably inebriated, plump-arsed,
paedophile-pleasing putti sprawled across a barrel is said 'to
have caused him to beam with beatific content'.

Rambunctious public masturbation and lithe auto-fellation
apart, Mr Swell's daily routine did not substantially differ from
that of other 'gentlemen', the human 'gentlemen' of his era. It
was a catalogue of duties undertaken and pleasures enjoyed. An
entirely prosaic catalogue – which is the salient point.

For what the audience of these spectacles most craved was
simple, even simplistic, role reversal. That is, beasts whose
demeanour, behaviour and appearance were close to those of
'normal' humans and, on the other hand, humans who, by
dint of their emotional nakedness, bedlamite tics and aberrant
grunts, were supposed to resemble caged animals. Thus Mr
Swell slept in a bed, lounged on a sofa, ate with a knife and
fork. He brushed his teeth. He played football and cricket,
boxed like Jurgen Bauer, danced the cakewalk and could carry
the coffins of three children while walking erect. He rode a
bicycle and taught several bears to ride, although he failed
with Dusty who, to the audience's delight, always fell off and
so became an unwitting clown, ever more morose, ever more
resentful. Mr Swell could, further, drive a landau, type on a
Remington No. 2 and fry eggs. His memory was prodigious,
his mentation supple.

He was found dead in his caravan at a halt on the road from
Market Harborough to Stamford on the morning of 3 February
1882. The cause was thought to be cancer of the oesophagus.

With him, near as dammit, died Zany Zeus's Zodiac Zoo.

The enterprise had relied on Mr Swell's drawing power for more
than five years. Nat Gedge, the least prospective and most miserly of
entrepreneurs, had not invested in a replacement. Poor fellow appears
to have been stupidly mean, self-defeatingly mean, cut-off-his-nose
mean. Not quite sixteen annas to the rupee. He had already been

obliged to sell the Black Comic Parade and the Hottentot Venus to a Durdham Downs sherry merchant as domestic servants.

It took Jezzard Dogg two and a half days to reach Tenbury. He wore a bowler hat, with goggles and a silk scarf across his mouth against the furious churn of dirt road dust. The salt-of-the-earth oggies of whom he asked the way recognised his accent was from foreign parts so misdirected him with reassuring smiles. Even had he been provided with a map he could not have read it. Indeed the peasanty little fellow could hardly read at all. But, one wonders, did he need to? Was there really any use in burdening him with reading, let alone writing, when there was so much other evolving that had to be done? 'Literacy for all' was a tiresome cri de coeur, a once fashionable fad that, even then, had had its time. Lesser breeds without the law and, Kipling forgot to add, without letters. The masses do not deserve to have their already overstretched brainboxes cluttered up with gubbins that don't concern them. Just look at the Lancastrians whose fate Dogg was charged with deciding.

Early morning. At last he was there. Dogg sat high astride his splendid Gallanders mare in front of Tenbury's pump rooms, two delinquently angular metal sheds and a jolly[17] panto-oriental tower like layered skirts. It might have been the temple of one of the gimcrack cults that flourished in those years, the Karfarna Bund or some such. He surveyed the scene across the opaque reedy river. There was already a pall of sticky haze.

The raggedy troupers of Zany Zeus's Zodiac Zoo had set camp between the river and a drowsy orchard. The meadow was bright with cowslips and buttercups. There were tents with fringes and oriflammes, caravans and gaudy coaches.

There were Stanislaus Mincedorf The Strongest Man in Europe, Daphne Jump The Contortionist Who Turns Herself Inside Out, Lucia Gammeltoft The Queen of Trapeze and Somersets, the clowns PooPoo and DooDoo, and the one-armed Leo Thor (the accident, at

---

17 Horrocks quotes Nikolaus Pevsner's disparaging 'Gothicky or Chinesey fair stuff, i.e., without seriousness or taste'. *The Buildings of England: Worcestershire* (Harmondsworth, 1968).

Tamworth, could have befallen any lion tamer). He was strapping on his gleaming prosthesis, 'leather and silver, a vampiric tentacle'. Ajax The Lion watched him. The contemptuous creature slouched about a rusting cage on wheels.

Panthers greedily eyed breakfast in its shorts and clogs.

An elephant squatted to dump a lavish knoll of droppings that we now know to be sustainable. Doing its bit for the planet, our Georgie! Never mind the pong!

Even though there was no sign that he intended to escape Nat's employ – whoever heard of a bear running away from a circus? – Dusty The Brown Bear was chained to a plum tree's trunk. His tarnished tricycle was close by him. A martyr to pubic lice, he wearily scratched his groin.

A dwarf on a log ate a toffee apple.

The twin funambulists Molly and Polly played kick the can with tumescent, pop-eyed village oggies who'd not seen their like before.

Bedraggled breeches and threadbare finery swelled on washing lines stretched between the trees. The biggest dog he had ever seen, a dog as big as a pony, slept on a raucous Napoléon III canapé. He too was chained.

The two-headed ram chomped doubly on fallen fruit.

The Human Tripod stumbled and flapped fighting off an early rising wasp.

Lesser freaks shivered despite the heat.

Nat Gedge, barrel-chested, bare-chested, was repainting a carriage with the three-dimensional legend Mighty Mars's Mammalian Menagerie in coarse imitation of Fred Fowle's Fancy or some such font. A change of name would surely herald a change of luck. He halted Dogg with a wave of his maulstick then tried to execute a curlicue; his dexterity did not match his vision. He cursed. Then he greeted the cocky stranger in his barker's purr.

An hour later, haggling done, Nat and Dogg sat down to a fine outdoors breakfast prepared by merry Mrs Gedge; her tipple was Dalby's Carminative and lots of it. Eggs fresh from Ma Griffin's hens in the huts behind the pump rooms; green bacon; fried haslet; bubble and squeak. Washed it down with pokey cloudy perry.

Three hours later Jezzard Dogg set off. He rode a camel. His mount walked alongside the two-horse cart. It was laden with two cages. One contained a pair of scarred and bleeding Carinthian Mastiffs, the other a pair of Canary Dogs. All of them weapons with a record long as your arm, with doormat pelts, power jaws and sharpened claws. Fighting dogs. Nat had staged many a dog fight in his time: Gornal, Rowley Regis, Lye, Brierley Hill. Black Countrymen – the backbone of England, they know their place – were particularly appreciative.

I like to think of these quadruped weapons just as dear sweet Rollo did:

> *. . . rapt amateurs of terrible throes,*
> *last rattle connoisseurs; whose eyes*
> *relish the thoracic demise*
> *their specialist maws propose.*

They were likely even nastier. Very scary customers indeed. Evil bastards. The way I like them!

And Leo Thor followed. He drove the cage on wheels that was, too, a shambles on wheels. Within it Ajax The Lion gnawed a stag's carcass. He made impressively swift work of it. Bone shards, ripped ligament, intestinal tubes, tine shrapnel, bloody rotting organs and sheafs of mesentery littered the floor and clung to the bars. Grown-ups put their hands over children's eyes as the abominable sight lumbered past on powdery roads. This was no longer the circus that had delighted them. This was a hellish visitation. Here was a caravan merrily charged with annihilation, chaos, death.

Hammer to crack a nut? No! Absolutely not, Sir! For while there was no will to see the nut come through the process unscathed, the hope was that the nutshell, so to speak, should not be damaged. Capiche?

The Vanier–Phimister plan was to set the Lancastrian Whiterobes all-a-flit in fear for their wretched lives while causing no material damage to the properties they had stolen, so no expenditure on repairs. They had plans for these houses. No pocking the brickwork with shot, then, no breaking windows, no forcing doors, no flaming faggots. Softly does it. Softly should have done it.

The lion did tear in pieces enough for his whelps, and strangled for his lionesses, and filled his holes with prey, and his dens with ravin. Almost . . . almost.

There is an inconsistency between Horrocks's account of The Eviction and the Vicomtesse's.

He says it was by day.

She said night.

Both adamant.

It reminds me of dear darling Rollo's fellow versifier, McHarg Bultitude, a pongy, passive/aggressive brute whose hygiene was on a par with The Noor Jahan Under New Ownership. Halitotic, greasy, reeking of crusted handkerchiefs, his every pore exuded noxious slime, and the deadweight of cockcheese must have added to his already considerable bulk. His practice of gargling bleach to get rid of the smell of cheap liquor was ineffective.

I am the first to concede, however, that as a poet — albeit a really very minorish minor one — he has, in what he dignified as his oeuvre, every right to change stoat to bread, thief to mayonnaise, door to pain, nimbus to circus.

Whining threateningly, he'd insist: 'It's my reality. Mine. I make it. My vision. I can do what I like with my reality.'

Horrocks hadn't been around to witness an event some sixty years before his birth. He is merely making what appears to be a rational deduction. (Quite how our false friend reason raises his head here is anyone's guess!) In his 'reality', The Eviction, which was intended to be visually threatening, could only have been effective if carried out in daylight hours. That is plausible.

Ever a gentleman, seldom inclined to discourtesy, I'm loath to suggest that the Vicomtesse's memory was literally demented. But, by February 1952 this grandest of grandes horizontales was teetering towards ninety. At which age no title, no thousand-hectare Berrichonne estate, no overheated pompier *hôtel particulier* on boulevard Lannes, no Coppedè villa in Albaro can exempt us from the peasouper in the bonce. I myself am now heading in the same direction; the face that faces me in the mirror is increasingly the face of a crone-age todger-dodger. I can't deny it! My inner Sappho is coming out!

I still haven't the foggiest whether she was in earnest when she said that despite her age she wanted a lover but all she ever got was a walker. Her time marched on; to the chimes of an ormolu and ebony mantelpiece extravaganza; to wafts of la Violette Pourpre, a creation by François Coty she was said to have inspired; to sips of tea from a samovar sweetened with blackcurrant jam.

Undeniably, however, her 'reality' was on the money, sharp as a jab in the old waltzers. Her smile was deliciously malicious though constrained in its expression by the tendency of her impasto facepaint to craze and crackle. I've never in my life met anyone who so furiously applied lipgloss at thirty-second intervals. She was sly and generous. No trouble seeing what it was they had all seen in her. I was bewitched: I was twenty-one, she was seventy years my senior. Had she suggested it . . . The age gap would have vanished. Just a man and a woman . . .

The sad truth is that with dames that old I was still too reticent to casually offer myself as I would routinely, even daily, to any ingé-nue, shopgirl, deb, Waaf, Wrac, Wren, typist, dancer, hostess, landgirl, barmaid, receptionist, chambermaid, manicurist, bus conductress, librarian, hairdresser or soubrette of my own generation. All these years on I wish I had, of course I do. I had yet to learn that it's the importunate who inherit: l'homme propose . . . carpe diem . . . nothing ventured . . . etc. I know now that great age does not curtail the distaff appreciation of Tiger. Oh, they're all up for it. They're all little goers at heart even if they do have to lubricate with udder cream and remove their store-bought clackers the better to show their affection. How I love them for it.

Almost ecstatically, she spoke of torches flaming horizontally in the shrieking wind, screaming chaos in the dark, the most terrible screams she had ever heard, the faces that were astonished before they were scared, a woman jumping from an upstairs room with a child in her arms. How could she have seen what she claimed to have seen if it had been after nightfall? What she saw excited her, repulsed her. She was flabbergasted to be excited but delight properly got the better of shame. Shame is so prissy, so self-righteous, so grapefruit-toilet-freshener, so petit-bourgeois. It's hedonism's enemy. It invites us to consider the consequences before we've strayed. Within her an appetite for cruelty was uncorked. Or was that appetite thrust upon her by the night's hurly-burly?

Night! It was unquestionably night. *The Shrewsbury Chronicle* has been consulted. Oh, the wonders of microfiche! Remember microfiche? There had been a full moon on Wednesday, 27 September 1882. It was cloudless. The newspaper also reported 'rumours of a kerfuffle in the vicinity of Bishop's Castle' but gave no further details.

It may have referred to a different incident. It is, after all, when they come out to howl! They're not called loonies for nothing. Bishop's Castle is five miles distant.

Eden, Mein Opa and Jervoise watched through opera glasses from the shelter of a chalky beech clump high on the remnants of a ring. A Pfostenschlitzmauer. It looked down to Nether Farm, to the unfinished terraces of spikey gabled houses. The boughs creaked, the sky roared, the cosmos groaned. The Lancastrian Whiterobes can have had no warning.

Here they came, the ragamuffin rabble of drunken oggies, all whoops and eldritch ululations. They galloped like the horse thieves they were; they might have been fleeing. Jezzard Dogg was at the fore of the flaming torches up in the sky on a bounding camel, leather hijabed and spitting. The nightriders wore straw bee-skeps with eye holes cut in them. Primitive totem masks, a whiff of the dark continent. This was high theatre, spectacle, sport. Fair play plays no part. All sport, without exception, is taunting, baiting, humiliation. (I give you the dead bull, the bowled batsman, the vanquished athlete, the stag writhing because there's a bolt through his brain.)

The blinkered black horses wore satan's nosegays. The glory of their nostrils was terrible. They glistened in a tourney of malevolent splendour. They whinnied their fury. Their wicked grinning teeth were weapons, each one jutting from foul gum, each one a blunt instrument. Oh, that's where the madness of nags is to be found, in those jaw-smashing ivories! It's an LKF that a horse's bite is as crushing as a crocodile's! The earth beneath the cropped turf shook with hooves a-thumping. The dogs, taller than their handlers, were on leashes, still on leashes: let's not think about their teeth, mein Kinder!

Ajax The Lion was in his cage, pacing in his cage, awaiting his cue from Leo Thor. There were fires, cymbals, keening fifes, numbing drums, the unearthly howls of beasts thirsting for quarry.

Looking down at the stage below them they congratulated each other on the magnificence of their choreography. Choreography with a martial purpose: a premonition of the Zeppelinfeld! Mein Opa fired burning arrows into the night sky. Their mounts fidgeted, snorted batons of air, crushed beechnuts for want of participation. Restless buggers, horses. The rabble they had rehearsed were gesture-perfect, so to speak. As bidden, they swarmed. Vernichtungsgedanke! The Whiterobes were ignorant of their role. They didn't even know they had a role. Till it was thrust upon them! The sods were meant to scaddle in a blind panic, double quick time.

The best laid plans . . .

They did not flee. Would you believe it? They did not flee. They did not do what they were meant to do. They failed to cooperate. They didn't get. They dillydallied. They bolted themselves inside what they claimed were their homes. They sat tight. They had no weapons so could not defend themselves. Even had they had weapons – highly improbable! – they'd have been unwilling to use them. Wouldn't lift a hoe in anger.

Man is warrior. That is our fundament.

Pacifists and conchies and unilateralists are not like us: they might as well belong to a different species which will eventually extinguish itself. The Bible may be chocker with prize-winning landfill, but an eye for an eye is the exception. Well spoken, that man! Sound counsel! There's no dolt like a well-intentioned dolt. Had they got their way we'd all be fellow-travelling barefooted to a spiffing future in the salt mines while joyfully whistling the Internationale.

Spineless! How else can they be described? No one had counted on them barricading themselves in. Their pie-in-the-sky utopian credulousness convinced them that if they all huddled up together and buried their brainless heads in the sand everything would be tickety-boo come the dawn. Idealists who fail to acknowledge that the milk of human kindness is already sour when it comes out of the teat are really not for this world.

Compensation for death of a child at New Farm. What was the

child worth given that the parents had no income and no home? One can have no sympathy for the blighters. Sympathy in general is common as cruet. A steaming midden of self-congratulatory muffa-roo and baloney which condones, even encourages, feebleness. In this circumstance it is, methinks, far worse.

The coyness of the creature! Horrocks giggled in his silly-jilly way and pretended to give himself a little rap on the knuckles followed by an exaggerated moue of pain: 'Perhaps I was a teensy bit naughty . . .' Naughty? The evasion made me wince. His condemnations were mean-spirited and wicked. How dare this turd-burglar apply the prissy moral standards of our own base age to a past age when they didn't beat about the bush, when they did things more resolutely, when they spoke from the heart: a poof is a bender is a nance, and they're all as queer as a nine-bob note. It is not the historian's job to castigate what he considers to be the sins of my grandfather, for when these pranks were played they were not sins but sound housekeeping.

Oh, of course Horrocks said: 'Sighy, so so sighy.'

There's no word that comes more readily to my compatriots' lips. But the damage is done.

The approximately 1,250 'readers' who bought *Breast Milk Cheese and Placenta Fritters* in hardback and trade paperback must wonder – should they have succeeded in wading that far into the book – why there was no criminal prosecution given the weight of evidence Horrocks hurls their way. Murder? Manslaughter? Aggravated whatsit? The case he presents is spurious. His bias is laughable. He does not even entertain the possibility that it was a regrettable accident, that it was just one of those things. His account is based on the hand-me-down folklore of nearby villages, on snug and hearth calumnies. There was no case to answer.

From the beech ring they saw smoke churning above one of the houses. They glanced at each other. Eden's mount, Madame Life, stepped delicately over tentacular roots, then trotted at leisure towards what was not yet an affray.

How swiftly that changed! Who? How? What happened?

There were as many versions as there were witnesses. More indeed: add the sworn testimonies of the absent, of the eavesdroppers, of those who told themselves they had been there. Such is man's capacity for delusion.

Did Ajax The Lion break through the bars of his cage? They were as crumbly and ginger as the speculoos which freckled Mein Opa's beard. The bars were six inches apart, enough space for what today's yellow press calls a Tragic Toddler to squeeze through. Ajax had not an ounce of malice in him. He was a playful old thing. Leo, in his cups, often forgot to feed him. He was, then, very likely so peckish he could have eaten a horse let alone a brace of tragic toddlers. According to one story the children's mother was so panicky that when the scarred, howling, bleeding, slavering dogs stormed the house and lolloped up the stairs she leapt from an upstairs window. She clutched the toddlers who may have been twins. She lay moaning and splayed (no wonder: bad diet plays lulu with ligaments). This was when the toddlers' future began to get tragic, and brief. From now on they were two appetisers of tender meat toddling to their singular destiny. Their mother abjured responsibility by passing out from pain. So much for maternal solicitude, Mummy's bosom and such pieties.

You might say that this was natural selection doing its stuff, weeding out the dependent, the undeserving poor, who breed back to their degenerate ancestors. The very betterment (at the expense of the public purse or whoever's property they have squatted) of their living conditions affords them the opportunity to propagate their unfit kind. The feebler the mind the greater the reproductive capacity. For such people sex is reproduction. Can there be anything more common than vaginal penetration? Strictly for beginners. It's so very common, common as cruet and, dare I say it, an act of aggression – not against the weak-minded woman, no, but against society itself. The sinew is weakened by the enfeebled breeding incontinently, as though it's their damned right. (I must own up to a sneaking regard for Uncle Joe's 'persecution' of blind hurdy-gurdy players who were liable to bump into all and sundry, pass on their affliction and make the most frightful din.)

The hungry lion's irritation must have been exacerbated by the children's mewling. So he playfully attempted to shut them up. A little over-strenuously perhaps, but with the best intentions. The dear chump didn't know his own strength. News spread like ague. It took that mishap for the Whiterobes to savvy – at last (slow on the uptake) – that unless they quit by yesterday further misfortunes might befall them. Ajax digested his snack. He wasn't greedy, he didn't eat it all; a well-bred lion, he left some on the plate, so to speak, for Mr Manners! Jezzard gave echoing orders through a speaking trumpet. He wielded a long whip, he was proud of his knack of making its report crisp as a handgun's. It drew beads of blood from a woman's thigh as she scuttled past, naked and barefoot, clutching coarse blankets. She stumbled: later he is said to have quipped jocularly that the way she fell gave him as long as he needed to glimpse the scraggy folds of her all but posthumous flaps and to decide that this wasn't a cavern of vitality which merited dismounting his steed to pleasure. He might have been a peasanty illiterate but he had taste.

Corinnas such as hers are grimy playgrounds for society's dregs, as the street is for mucous-moustached urchins who don't have gardens let alone countless acres. Not all members of Jezzard's troop were as fastidious as he was. High-spirited chaps without inhibitions, their appetites whetted by alcohol, they splashed their seed and flourished their piss with lusty glee. They hollered in excitement at the shrieks of humans and the roars of animals and the choking smoke and the din of bricks bursting and glass cracking in the fire which skipped languorously through Number One New Farm. It paused here to turn fabric to flame, it strolled up the stairs eating them as it went, it blistered the banisters with bubbling buboes! Now it was leaping across the landing to turn a cupboard to char and, with a spring in its step, to roast a hurrying cripple who just didn't have it in her to hurry more, that's the problem with cripples. Leo Thor was transfixed by the entertainment.

Eden's orders to fetch the fire tender from The Town were met with paralytic incomprehension. By the time it arrived the damage was done. One house was a smouldering wreck, its neighbour was impasted with greasy soot. All but two of the Whiterobes had dispersed. Only a couple of sobbing women remained. They claimed to have been raped – a likely story! We've all heard moaning minnies telling tales out of school! Self-pitying grudge bearers!

They were locked in a shivering embrace of mutual succour in a scullery corner, squatting, keening, failing to engage Eden's sympathy, soaked by puddles of the water which had eventually quashed the fire. They cowered when a wooden scaffold groaned and fell. Eden, dressed in skintight breeches, a hacking jacket and oil-black boots, flourished her whip above them. She was on the point of drawing blood with it. But when she looked at them she was overcome with contempt and pity that they could not hire out their bodies, their saggy imperfect bodies, to their advantage.

The Eviction was the first of the minor incidents that alerted The World, a nosey parker at the best of times, to take a prurient interest in Malpasfang.

Can men be fishwives? Yes, they jolly well can.

These tunbellied bumpkins proved it. The Fones, the Brunts, the Prices, the Preeces, the Breeces, the Prossers, the Ralphs. Such common names! They thought of themselves as plain-dealing yeomen. They were 'landed' squires. But they lacked land. Their beeswaxed houses lacked all modernity. Grim discomfort was regarded as a Christian virtue. Even Horrocks was capable of seeing them for what they were – hypocrites.

Their old money, coin that stained fingers like aloes, was puny, the smallest of small change to a Vanier (or, indeed, a Shadoxhurst). What lumbering provincials! Untouched by vision.

The highlight of their year was the Ludlow Season when they clodhopped injuriously through polkas and mazurkas. Each of these tutting dullards had a bevy of plain-as-cake, horse-toothed, thick-ankled virgin daughters who, they secretly hoped, might marry into the Vanier millions. When it dawned on them that such unions would never happen, to a man they bore seething grudges. No chance Ryvan ap Lewis!

They were the heirs to blustering coves like Sir Wilfull Witwoud, 'brother Wilfull of Salop'. But they weren't funny. Far from it. They were poxed with spite. Resentment is a disease of mean minds. It would eventually cause them to treat Malpasfang Lodge's puzzlingly extended household as an invasive force, occupiers to be got rid of. Disgraceful; all the inhabitants were after was cordial detachment. The Clun & Llewellyn Lloyd-Lewis's meets were often held in front of the house. The hunt was permitted to gallop across a distant part of the estate as it always had. Part of it. Vanier, Mein Opa and Eden Blood rode with it. Tradition was maintained. That was, apparently, not enough.

The tunbellies coveted invitations to the great house as they had in the days of Thomas Vanier. Not that his generosity had for a moment prevented them despising him and his ostentation. Now such invitations were sparse. No more croquet since the moles had enjoyed an untroubled decade turning that lawn to mud: molestation! No more rackets since the court's roofbeams were turned to powder by worm. An occasional tea party. An elaborate banquet now and then, greedily supped but damned as too showy by half and foreign to boot; Escoffier and animal-form moulds, ancient vintages and sentimental toasts. A grand ball on New Year's Eve with an orchestra under sumptuous chandeliers.

They noted the host's charming offhandedness, the amused condescension of his close friend Phimister, this pair's tendency to absent themselves for long periods at parties, their hardly disguised incuriosity about their guests. And their strange entourage.

Who were these froggy exquisites and jewelled maharajahs, these effeminate men with languid wrists? These black-skinned bucks? That aesthete named Linsel Murly striving and failing to bury his accent (Australian? South African? Cockney?), wearing a wide-brimmed hat and a green carnation, hand in chamois-gloved hand with a girlchild who can have been no older than twelve? He was the author of a stained-glass representation of a three-foot-high ejaculating phallus in the chapel. Where did the painted women of unknown pedigree come from? Why were there camels in the park? What was the purpose of the fabulous menagerie which ran free throughout the parts of the house which were not locked or chained? What happened in those other parts of the house which were locked or chained, bolted shut and guarded by men who might have been stone-breaking convicts? They failed to grasp the import of the chasm in wealth. They couldn't see, or wouldn't admit, that it was, too, a chasm in social class.

Their clogged memories stretched back two generations to Thomas Vanier's acquisition of the estate around the dull Georgian house. He bought it from the legatee of the Prynnes, who were of their kind, a family with long roots in this very soil, soil which the Vaniers had usurped.

Colonel Prynne Owen Prynne was an ornithologist and lexicographer. Parts of Foucauld's dictionary of the Berber language were indebted to his scholarship. He was also a cashiered soldier, prolific pornographer, boyo adventurer, disgrace to the name of his family and of his regiment, all round black sheep, blond god (to some) and the last of his line.

He was up to his neck in some wheeze with Johnny Tuareg, inviting caravans of chained sub-Saharans, who would otherwise have been enslaved, to come to recently colonised Algeria, there to be sold as indentured labourers. Give the black chappies an exciting job opportunity and a better life! The humane plan was that out of gratitude the blighters would do work that the indolent native kebas were unwilling to. Some of the more forward-thinking Johnny Frogs were up for Categorical Amelioration of the indolent native kebas but sadly lacked the means that the Third Reich would have so happily vouchsafed.

The colonists got no further than inducing localised famines, burning ricks, inviting the very few potable bints to ornament their jiggity houses. They razed toxic townships and sent the inhabitants scooting off with their plague and buboes to subsist in what's known as le bled.

A certain Doctor Gavrik Skou,[18] a pretty sagacious sort of chap, stated most forthrightly that 'medical imperialism' was an invention of ahistoric apologist guilt-tasters who are wilfully blind to the facts. He advanced the theory that without Johnny Frog's Hippocratic je ne sais quoi the indolent natives with their tussie-mussies of endemic diseases (yaws, bejel etc.) would have expired no matter how fast they bred. Needless to say, he was set upon by the battalions of the bleeding-hearted who inhabit academe's bigoted groves. He was accused, it goes without saying, of 'flirting with fascism'. All the

---

18 Gavrik Morten Skou, *Colonial Pathologies, Imperial Identities* (New Haven, 1998), Winner of the Cold Springs Prize 2000.

more reason, I'd say, to lend credence to Doctor Skou and his wicked revisionism.

Prynne disappeared in 1842. His last known letter, dated 14 April of that year, was sent from Tamanrasset to his friend and patron the thirteenth Earl of Derby, sometime president of the Linnaean Society and a founder of the London Zoological Society. He announced that he had, at last, captured a wholly black Ahaggar or Hoggar eagle, which, according to the indigo people he was living among, is also a hyena and a sand snake when it wills. The massif's twisted black rocks and cliffs are its fortress. Given that it has no natural predator, its concealment mechanisms seem superfluous. Despite their coloration's affinity with the ambient geological formations, they rely on stillness in the nest rather than camouflage, an indication that once upon a time life wasn't so cushy and they did have predators. The wingspan, talons and teeth are greater than those of any other bird. Humans weakened by the desert are occasional prey, though its staples are the northern hyrax and the antelope. It can spot the entrance to a jerboa's burrow from great distances, but the little creatures provide no more than an aperitif snack.

The bird's subsequent classification would be *Taferma anthropaphaga prynnei*, popularly Prynne's Eagle, posthumous proprietorial rights! The letter detailed the arrangements for its shipping to Knowsley Hall where the earl's aviary already included over a thousand species, many of them recorded by Edward Lear. Prynne was worried about how the bird would be nourished en route to Liverpool. He feared that a sufficient number of hyraxes and antelopes to last the journey could not be found and that alternative food sources might be required. He did not specify what these sources might be. The vessel which would transport the bird from Oran was jocularly nicknamed The Ark.

Prynne was said to have harboured a royal flush in the gentleman zone but whether it was that which finished him off is moot. It might equally have been cholera that did for the poor sod. Vomiting till he could vomit no more. Again, it was rumoured that a white man had been involved in sacrificial malarkey at a village in the red lands beyond Djanet where the sentinel rocks were petrified gods.

Regimental tales of his by-blows were rife. His appreciation of tarbrushed beazles was legendary. He cut a swathe through the dark continent and left a proud trail of straw-haired, congenitally syphilitic, flat-nosed piccaninnies. Even had any of the said piccaninnies by some fluke known of his estate they'd have had no claim on it. Whatever, if any, conjugal arrangements Prynne might have made with his desert concubines, he had, in the eyes of our English god, the god of gods, never got spliced. So according to The Law there was no issue.

The squires never forgave him that dereliction. Nor did they forgive the distant cousin whom Malpasfang passed to. He sold it, without having visited the place, to Thomas Vanier who was alerted to its availability by the Earl of Derby, a fellow member of the Liverpool Athenaeum.

Now, had it been a one-off The Eviction would have soon been dumped in what one might call The Collective Oblivion Bin and duly incinerated. But it panned out differently.

During the decade of the estate's desuetude parts of it became cross-hatched with paths and tracks. Trails were ridden, trodden, etched into the land, which was worn down to the topsoil and beyond. Carts' parallel stripes erased grass, fern and heather. These informal droves were reddish dust in summer, midwinter's rutted puddles. They mapped the short cuts taken, the liberties taken by all and sundry. Not to beat about the bush: Rhys Rhys, Evan Evan, Lloyd Lloyd, Dafyd Dafyd and many more enjoyed a field day.

Anyone with a few thousand acres in his stewardship is all too familiar with tomdicks who carelessly treat our land as theirs. The unwashed and their hairy, treetrunk-legged women (unshaven on 'ethical' grounds) gallivant across our land, my land, claiming a 'right to roam', put up to it by the acolytes of that beardy leftist dauber Augustus John who wrote that hedges are proclamations of theft, of exclusive domains. Too right, Gus, too right. They are. No one has a right to another man's domain any more than he has a right to another man's air.

But in those years there was no will to keep them out, no muscle. Many didn't even realise they were abusing private property. Their affront when accused of trespass was all the greater because they felt they had done no wrong. For oggies it's ignorance that is nine-tenths of the law.

'No one ever said nothin bout tha . . . didnt know bout tha' is a refrain the oggie is taught in the cradle.

The tunbellies, most of them justices of the peace sprouting vieux jeu dundrearies, what were called weepers, could not plead ignorance, they knew the lie of the land. Their attitude was simple bloodymindedness: they were damned if they were going to forego a 'right of way' which had been theirs for a decade. Their fubsy rumps had squatted it, so to speak, left their mark.

Mein Opa was trotting Incitatus back to the stable after a prebreakfast persp when, quarter of a mile away, he saw the unmistakable figure of doublesquat Griffith Preece cantering bold as brass past the west front of the Lodge. He was heading towards the gentle slope up to Stants Wood. This was the most frequented of the extemporised paths and the first that they were determined to close. He brisked up his mount. By the time he caught further sight of him, Preece was trotting along the section of path which ran beside the ragged edge of the wood. A flat-backed wagon and a blinkered carthorse blocked the path. Mein Opa noted that the two sawsmen and a carter who were clearing the brambles, undergrowth and bindweed removed their heavy leather gloves to salute Preece. Mein Opa was astonished that he was not afforded the same courtesy. These people failed to acknowledge their employer. Their rude country manners were those of an inferior race. Their ingrained loyalty was to the superiors they had known all their life; they lacked protean self-interest. Preece nodded a greeting. He had a reputation for civility, brusque civility perhaps, but nonetheless civility – by the standards of the tunbellies. He belied it when Mein Opa told him that this trail was not a right of way. He play-acted disbelief, looking to the clouds, to the boughs in spasm, rolling his eyes, pretending to whisper into his mount's ear. He responded to the effect that it looks like a trail – doesn't it? It looks like one. Unmistakably. He beckoned the workmen to agree that this here was a trail. The three oggies dutifully nodded, synchronised puppets. Mein Opa could not contain his laughter. He said later that the swervily patterned rings in the stub of an elm they had recently felled recalled a swooning woman ravaged by an octopus in a Japanese print.

Preece said that he couldn't hang about any longer wasting time or he'd miss his train.

Mein Opa stated very calmly, had it not been for Thomas Vanier's largesse, the New Invention, Bishop's Castle and Fron Light Railway would not exist. He added that the more people who rode this unsanctioned path to Malpasfang Halt the greater the damage that would be inflicted by weight of hoof and bulk on the maze of sub-terranean ceramic fertiliser pipes which descended from Fort Shoosmith and fanned out into a delta. By an unhappy chance this feat of hydraulic and gravitational engineering was situated beneath a point that the path passed over in The Dell. Which wasn't really a dell, more a fecund but boggy valley, a failed gully. (Today, getting on for more than a century and a half later, it is drained dry.) The reason why there had never been a formal path here was that the pipes were inadequately buried so unprotected. The mechanicals and drowners who controlled the 'sluices' were obliged to approach them on foot. Preece harrumphed. Just before he protracted his trespass he said something along the lines of, 'Aha! So shit comes first eh!' And added: 'Old Vanier's sons sold the railway years ago. Don't think that I don't know it, Sir . . .'

Mein Opa watched Preece jog away, buttocks flopping over the flanks of his mount like saddlebags. He suggested to the loggers that if they knew which side their bread was buttered they should report to the Estate Office in an hour's time. Mein Opa pointed to where the sun would be relative to a warped tree on a sandstone hillock when it occurred to him that they thought they were going to be rewarded with bread and butter. He sighed.

When they arrived at the Estate Office, tails between their legs, late, they were greeted by Mein Opa and Jezzard Dogg, self-appointed reeve, a title he had craved, poring over a table covered in sheets of paper on which diagrams had been sketched.

Hardly surprising, they had never heard of chevaux de frise. Fries-ian horses, Jezzard told them, were like cows but with a whinny and a bite. No matter how bemused they were, by four o'clock they had fashioned a dour ugly defence from sturdy spiked stakes and a pine trunk about eight feet long. It was transported to The Dell where it unconvincingly blocked the path.

Over the following weeks they attempted to obstruct several other paths with similar devices. We know for certain that Eden inspected them with growing dismay. Coarse, primitive, rough, easily negotiated, so more for show than exclusion, and, worst of all, a dead cert to get backs up. She said so, repeatedly. And correctly: within a matter of days two of the chevaux de frise had been hacked by axes.

Boudoir colour! Oh what fun! She lay in bed one morning idly eating crisp warm rolls with butter and honeycomb, idly sipping lapsang souchong with an egg yolk poached in it, idly watching Jervoise saunter in and out of his dressing room, idly masturbating (I hope, how I hope . . .) for his sake as much as hers, idly leafing through *The English Agriculturalist*.

Yes, yes . . . These may, I admit, not be the precise circumstances in which she ran her eye over advertisements for innovations displayed at that year's Bath and West Show: thrashing machines from Andover, potato planters, harvester binders, cheap hopyard poles and twine from Inger & Co. of Rolvenden (noted), metal troughs und so weiter. She turned over the page distractedly before her brain had processed the signal. A slice of a second: she turned the page back.

That's what a double-take is, a classic double-take . . . though none can match those performed for my delight, my delight alone I believed, by the peerless stalwart of Quota Quickies, Nugent Boumphrey. (I would watch such films in our cinema at home where there was no risk of contamination by the lusty expectorations of flea-pit urchins.)

Eden investigated, suddenly absorbed.

Blowing its own trumpet the loudest was Billbob Steels, a form of fencing material manufactured in Broken Arrow, Oklahoma, whose British agents, based in Cardiff, claimed that it was 'to repel Red Indians, Cattle Thieves, Bisons, Steppe Wolves, Steers, Coyotes and Prairie Dogs – pretty little "critters" to be sure but heathens with a blackguard's respect for those whom the Good Lord blessed with the fortitude and industry to raise His crops . . .'

Her eyes hurt. They hadn't heard of sans serif in those days. The bragwords' capital letters were wrapped in woodbine. It went on:

It lasts twice as long as any other kind of fence known to
    mankind . . .
The Mighty Missouri's floods do not sweep it away . . .
It is not corroded by the snows of Manitoba . . .
It does not wither in the Dakotan Badlands' summer
    furnace . . .
It withstands the tornadoes which, in His wrath, He visits
    upon Omaha and Wichita, the cities of the plains . . .
Sparks do not set it on fire.
This is His fence.

Guaranteed also, she must have murmured to herself, to repel tun-bellies and plooks. The name barbed wire was not yet current.

The Bath and West Show was held that year at Durdham Down on the heights of Clifton.

Mr and Mrs W. Ashbee and Mr P. A. Fraxi put up in adjacent rooms at Bristol's finest hotel, The Royal. A maid noticed that Mr Fraxi's bed had not been slept in. The hotel's facade amused them no end: so corpulent, so dated. The hamfaced Hansom cab driver was all that we expect of Bristolians, maritime entrepreneurs cruelly forbidden to engage in the only two trades in which they excel, piracy and slavery. They are denied what they consider the entitlements of their heritage. He heard her haughty observations about the really very vulgar wedding-cake mansions beside the Downs. Oh, he could pigsniff a fancy stuck-up toffee-nose Milady Bountiful. He deposited them with the scowl of counterjumping recognition – we all know that scowl, we all know the resentment in the blubbery lips' sudden tautness, the rictal snarl of unacknow-ledged superiority.

'Some polish is gained with one's ruin,' she told him with a prim arctic smile as she stepped down.

It was overcast, the sky was grubby smudges, thin drizzle lustred the gorge. From the heights of Sea Walls they gaped down at the river, hundreds of feet below, the colour of poorhouse gravy. They watched whiskered constables demonstrating their cutlass drill beneath soggy limes. The grass bore the anticipatory tyre prints of a Sabrina Mk1. Crowds dressed in their bowlered west of England best, their south Walian best, thronged and swarmed, gaiters and boots in the mud. Their black umbrellas were carapaces beaded with cocktail onions. Those who held them, hands about bamboo, were faceless. The stalls and booths were half hidden. The wrestling tent announced itself with the reeks of stale sweat, stale man, stale beer. There were coconut shies and aunt sallies.

David fought Goliath in a sawdust ring. David was a dwarfish groom. Goliath – a teratological anomaly with an all-over black pelt – stood seven feet tall, a bit over four cubits. This dribbling ogre was an inmate of the Lunatic Asylum at Fishponds and – would you know – was unfamiliar with the Book of Samuel. He had an imperfect understanding of his role in the entertainment. Despite his size and his ankles being trammelled by manacles he moved lithely. He grinned, jumped repeatedly to stamp on David's ribs and trample his femora. When he attempted to gouge out his eyes he was hauled off by some viders, a couple of mutton-shunters swinging Mangotsfield Correctives and a shivering retiarius from a neighbouring tableau vivant with a wooden trident and a net. To the crowd's wonderment Goliath, in his anguish at being pinned down to the sawdust, mewed squeakily. Like a buzzard, someone said.

They wandered past models of drainage systems and life-size refrigerated wagons. A military band's fifes shrilled in competition with steam ploughs, steam engines, traction engines. Glossy machinery, clean oil, steam as white as fleece, mechanicals in spotless dungarees and apple-cheeked wenches in starched smocks – all perfect, all perfectly pure, all telling the store-bought lie of agrarian life. Rather like dear dear Toby Trinnick's soppy illustrations for the *Little Gay Tractor* series, but garbed in period clobber.

Still, you can't expect the oggies and tunbellies who know the truth of that life – the mire, the blood, the non-optional death – to pitch up at a country show wanting to see the real thing. Even though they may mock the falsity, their longing for reassuring fantasy is understandable.

The entrance to Parry, Son and Nephew's marquee was flanked by two vertical columns of barbed wire formed around thick stakes.

A pleasing reek of sacking and paraffin. They were greeted by a young shaver: Sunday best, first moustache, cupid lips, let us call him Dilwyn. The poor fellow had no sooner opened his mouth to utter Welsh prattle than Eden put a gloved finger to hers to tell him sssh! He didn't know whether to put his hands behind his back or stand with his thumbs in his waistcoat pockets. He curtailed his brief experiment with the latter. He feared that it might appear disrespectfully familiar or too presumptuously swagger. He watched, puzzled, as this trio, who looked nothing like farmers, painted and perfumed and done up to the nines (the nineties, more like, he congratulated himself on thinking), inspected untreated barbed wire, galvanised wire, BWGs 12 and 14 – the only gauges so far imported, information he dared not vouchsafe lest he speak out of turn. The knotted wire bales sparkled. Both men tenderly bent strips of both gauges. Fourteen was the more pliable.

He watched them laughing, caught a few words: stan's . . . country cousins . . . crown of thorns . . . damn their nags . . . relics studio.

The woman beckoned him, handed him a card: 'Deliver us four hundred yards, the thinner one – by the end of the week. C.O.D. Got that?'

'Four hundred . . .' He inhaled profusely. 'Most certainly. Yes. I shall consult with Mr Ryvan junior to expedite on – where are we? – yes, on the sixteenth inst.'

'The sixteenth inst would be ideal,' she smiled, hardly failing to conceal her amusement.

Why was she amused?

He bowed to the dark-eyed beauty. Once she and her carnationed escorts had left the marquee he will have kissed the card. It was scented with her scent! Fougère Royale. The name was wreathed in fern leaves. Blood. How on earth were they to deliver by the sixteenth inst? Why on earth had he committed the company of which he was a junior employee to so soon a date? To please her. To please her. Her very presence had an effect on men. So did her name. What on earth would Mr Ryvan junior say? I dare say our young Dilwyn felt the old collywobbles coming on.

'My my my. My stars and garters! The gemini visionaries of 'bandon. And! And Milady Blood – the object of you mashers' 'bandon or should I say subject of your 'bandon. Grammar grammar. Subject object of my devotion . . . M' dears . . . How are you?'

Reedy, mocking, oily Mortimer Glyde stood proud beside a muddied scraped rococo whatnot whose three shelves displayed bottles of elixirs and balms and potions. Every bottle contained the same unusually potent laudanum. Glyde's Syrup relieved neurasthenia and gout, hepatic miseries and renal encumbrances. Glyde's Family Formulation, 'stronger than thunder, gentler than Mother Nature herself', was a remedy for gout, 'women's problems', pleurisy, catarrh, the niels, diarrhoea, colic, headache, asthma, April chorea. Glyde's Quieting Solution soothed babies to sleep and on occasion steered them to god's domain. Glyde's Female Pennyroyal Pills did much the same. Glyde's Drops were brightly coloured pills that cured 'exotic' diseases The Devil's Crocus has himself invented.

There's an old saw from my childhood when they were still common enough: A crocus is seldom an advertisement for his wares. Mortimer Glyde was no exception. He might have been in an early stage of decomposition. Since they had last seen him, his skeletal face had gone from mould green to death wax. Fungus had brittled his nails. He scratched his neck till it bled. His appetite for opiates caused constipation. So halitotic gusts whistled through his crenelated caramel teeth. The matt black dye on his long lank hair served to draw attention to its grey selvedges.

He told them indignantly about an impromptu visit, made in passing, to Macaroni Farm. He didn't know they had sold it. The new proprietors had been most unwelcoming, discourteously inhospitable as though he were trying to scrounge a bed for the night when he was actually heading for Stroud. Eden wished she had paid more attention to his self-pitying sense of injustice.

They told him about their cosmic schemes for Malpasfang. He squawked with delight. 'I take a keen interest in the young. Full of promise and adventure. Full of promise and adventure.'

'We are indeed,' agreed Eden, stroking Nigredo's flank. The black stallion was hitched to a tree. Drizzle and beads dappled its flanks.

He giggled shrilly, as he often did, when they talked of the Prices, the Preeces, the Breeces. He relished their very names: 'The orderly surface of society is but a mantel which covers up chancres, gangrenes and putrefaction.'

'If only . . .' murmured Eden, 'if only . . . Their mantel covers up pomposity and envy. Nothing so interesting as putrefaction. The woods decay, the woods decay and fall . . . Will you dine with us tonight?'

'You are generous. Alas. Alas . . . A poor surgeon must attend a patient at Hag Hill.'

She found herself saying: 'Do us then the honour of your company at Malpasfang Lodge.'

That would echo down the years.

The walls of the wide corridors are quilted with glimmering burgundy silk velvet. Attached to the walls of this room, a deeply silent, deeply hidden room in the labyrinth of succeeding rooms, are candles in writhingly wrought sconces. (Somewhat chuffed at that sentence!) It was by flickering candlelight that a room deep in the labyrinth was approached. She lay dreamily on a plumply upholstered borne settee, burgundy, again, and maple. She lay dreamily, fortified by opium and brandy. Was she dreaming? The sudden shifts of temperature, the mutations, the immediate forgetfulness. She first heard the muffled snorting, the soft shuffle, the grinding bagpipe, harness's clank, winches squealing. Smell: the primal smell, the metallic smell, the alluring smell, the byre smell. She felt the lowing exhalations stiff as a high wind on her breast, the coarse grating pelt as the weight was lowered, the weight oh the weight, squashed by the weight of a vice, the doughty meat dropping a hooked anchor in its safe berth. There were low urgent voices. There were frightened eyes, what big brown eyes, understanding nothing. The other eyes are different, not comforting, these small eyes are scrutiny eyes. The pain in the madge, the puffledum madge. The body's shriek of incompatibility. The visceral fear of being converted to mince from within. What sort of greed yearns for further pain?

There once was a world before this labyrinth where the tack piano jangled and the air was blue smoke and the brass gleamed from her elbow grease and folks hawked Tunstall oysters and Ernie the potman's nine-month belly was a weapon to force his passage through the lurching throng and prices are complained of and you had to repeat Old Enoch Sprowston's landlord refrain 'loick it or lump it, mih duck' – so mean he'd skin a turd for a farthing. (I think I've got that splendid expression right.) You want away from this to any-where. Anywhere where they pay, where they don't leer and grope and prod like you're free hodge and free haslet at the end of Bull Week. Bull Week . . .

Bovril. The letters a yard high on the upper storey of the passing Dresden to Alsager tram were illumined by gaslight. A soggy dusk, slippery black leaves and droplets. A mighty advertisement. Beside it, diminutive, Nestlé's Milk – oggie pron: nestles, no accent. She was standing on the cinder pavement by the park railings where an ivy-embowered trunk pushed through them, bent the metal, pene-tratively. She watched the tram wheeze and peal up the bank then diminish, a silhouette in the rheumy west.

She was a randy little mystery. But choosey. Picky as a pikestaff, they used to say when I was a little chap. Not a real pro she'd insist, though happy to receive gifts. But, mark, no amateur of a thick lea-ther belt's kiss and the weals it brings, even if the gift is extra generous. No amateur either of her degraded father slumping onto her, not so far gone in his cups that his old fella won't stand to full attention and demand a daughter's ministrations. Pity her. But that was about to change.

The noise of the whip and the noise of the rattling of the wheels and of the prancing horses and of the jumping chariots.

With a whinny a brougham passed slowly by her. It was hauled by a pair of Brabançon stallions of many hands: pewter with ginger tail, mane and feathered feet. The gleaming carriage was black and navy blue, a gilded coat of arms on the door included a youth with a tri-dent stood over a dead sea monster. The carriage was full of quizzing eyes. (Kerb crawling is in the Shadoxhurst blood.) It pained her to see it go. Her teeth chattered. She rubbed her hands. Lace gloves were no protection against the cold. A few minutes later she was exhilarated to watch it clip-clop back towards her. It drew up beside her. The driver looked straight ahead, dead as a mummy.

You don't see many of those vehicles hereabouts. She told her-self she wasn't dreaming. A haw-haw swell descended. Mein Opa, probably: she never could distinguish between the two beautiful men, the dark-eyed scented men of science. Being looked over like kine for the slaughter. He scrutinised the product. This was normal practice – she knew it well, part of the job. The client sizes up the goods.

Abnormally he was followed by a young woman, a dame not much older than she was, fine in finery, feathers and fur, the black pelt of aborted lambs and a russet collar of skinned beaver. Yum. You can be sure that bustled Eden came the lardy-dardy all over, scrutinising with her proxenetist's authoritative eye, beckoning her to spin round for a fuller gleg, commenting as though the cattle couldn't understand. The cattle could understand but didn't mind.

The pretty popsy bobtail must have agreed without much hesitation to their offer, whatever it was, however they couched it. She'd have gone along with anything that this couple proposed. Their courteous voices, their lovely clothes (his abundant moiré), their ease, their brougham, they all signalled wealth. Wealth and ease, sated in leisure. She wanted these people to touch her. They were the quality. They must be sybarites, yes, sybarites!

They were the first people she'd even seen close up who fitted that exciting word which she had learnt from *The Margrave's Ambergris*, a fast novel by Contessa Pavesi.[19] The hero – dashing, sabred, Heidelberg-scarred Sebastian von Lahnstein – dies in a cavalry charge at Reichenfels. Cradled in the arms of his closest comrade, his last utterance is 'Hasu-No-Hana', the name of the scent he had intended to buy for his betrothed after the battle. That scene had made her weep, had made her yearn to belong to that unattainable milieu where noble sacrifice and sensuality were entwined in bloody bandages and eviscerated horses; a hitherto unattainable milieu.

She knew these strangely bewitching people were going to exploit her. That was the fate of her sort. No point in fussing about it: cosi fan tutte and what have you. She could never have guessed how they would use her. But they were her passport. She was proud

---

19 'She was accepted as an artist of genius by a credulous public to whose crass religiosity, gullible mysticism and metempsychotic obsessions she gave a cloying glamour.' McHarg Bultitude in *Silver Fork and After*.

of herself: from street menial to over the hills and far away where there was the promise of sunlight, dapple, magic and the finest Egyptian cotton sheets. They were granting her entry to the secret domain of Malpasfang.

Where? Where was it? It was somewhere distant, far from pregnant kilns' dense grey breath you could hardly see your way through, far from the coal measures' bitumen-stained dependants. Far from her people, her kind whom she could at last disown.

She had never ridden in a brougham. She talked and she talked. She excused herself for being such a flibbertigibbet then apologised for her common accent.

Eden touched her hand: 'No matter, my honeysuckle. I spoke like you once. We can all change . . . can't we? If we are resolved to. We make our own futures. What's your name?'

Eden didn't wait for a reply. In the accent she had long since sloughed Severnsoide in Shorsburye she added: 'Mike owerselfs. Rowbust. Strifin' fer pullish. No sootch word as cunna – eh Pasipheyer me shug!'

'Paz – what?'

Mein Opa murmured: 'Pasiphaë came from Burslem.'

She giggled inquisitively. She was flattered to be renamed. She was carefree on the high road to adventure.

Bestiality, like kerb crawling, is a jolly companionable sport that really doesn't merit the obloquy that's nowadays heaped on it. Why does it provoke such shuddery disgust in the squeamish? I'll tell you why: it's because the mob has lost touch with its rural roots (and farmyard mores)! It's been losing touch since The Green and Pleasant was trounced by smuts, factory chimneys and common as cruet back-to-backs. We're all town mice now, or so we are endlessly instructed. And it is, regrettably, largely true (though not of me). Atavistic links to the agrarian past are down the plughole. We are constantly reminded that 150 per cent of the global population – however many unculled billions it currently is – forms a predominantly urban society. (Academic 'studies' and newspapers passim.)

The mob's sympathy with the old country ways is non-existent, evaporated in ignorance and incuriosity. Turn back the clock – if only! – to a golden era when we, as a race, were at one with our four-legged familiars. They were our equals, our friends, servants, sometimes masters! Mates, muckers, pieces of pelted homework, congenial hearthsiders! As what we are now impelled to call the agrarian sector has diminished so have the everyday habits that were its joyous norm been opprobriated. By the time the Malpasfang Experiment was en marche churchy teaching had reasserted itself. Flings with quadrupeds were decreed nefast, even flingettes were. Wickedness is relative. In the days before priggish tractarian piety colonised minds and consciences, a vigorous workout with a bitch or ewe was a gentleman's prerogative. Jezzard Dogg, enterprising cove, had one bedpost for scrumptious-popsy notches and another bedpost for animals-and-birds notches. Let us not forget that many were the ladies of the quality who quite adored to be tupped by a tapir or Old Nick The Goat or a baudet de Poitou (Froggie flair, you know).

A splendid consequence of the resurgent church's bigoted baloney on the subject of chastity was that zoophilia came to be practised by observant Christians anxious not to surrender their virginity before marriage.

That wasn't the motive of Old Uncle Tom Cobley's coarse crew. Sabine Baring-Gould was a god-bothering Christian militant as well as a folksong collector. He bowdlerised 'Widecombe Fair'. It is well known that Tom Pearce's grey mare died from internal bleeding after being overbanged by lusty woozled oggies. They all had their turn. Bill Brewer, Jan Stewer, Peter Gurney, Peter Davy, Daniel Whiddon, Harry Hawke.[20] The poor chumps are haunted eternally by their victim, in death as in life. They forgot to say 'please'. That's oggie discourtesy for you. Baring-Gould's squeamish distaste for carnal unorthodoxy did not of course stretch to admonishing god for disguising himself as a dove to rape a virgin and threaten her with very bad buboes indeed if she aborted the child who grew up to be famously troubled and delusional. Small wonder that a civilisation

---

20 Hawke was transported for rustling sheep near Tavistock in 1836 approximately half a century before Baring-Gould recorded the song that commemorates him. His great-great-grandson Bob Hawke became twenty-third prime minister of Australia, 1983–91.

founded on his flaky dicta and unlikely deeds is famously troubled and delusional. Enough from the pulpit!

There isn't, regrettably, a great deal of supportive literature on the subject of cross-species intercourse. This is at least partly due to the Malpasfang experiments being blown up out of all hippo. Speak not of . . . They prompted the gutter press's usual expressions of abhorrence and moral outrage, which in turn fomented public vituperation, legal censure and over a quarter of a century's mob hatred.

Ah! the trusty mob, immutable backbone of the nation, the salt of the earth with its hypocritical wisdom of repugnance, which is no wisdom but the common as cruet doxa. Every one of them a Mrs Grundy. There is no pleasing puritans: they can detect impurity in a pristine icicle.

During intercourse the bigger beasts – horses, bulls, cows – are often rather indifferent, unimpressed, even a bit browned off at having to be there. There's no pleasing these blighters. Some of them even seem unaware of what is going on. Stoicism in the face of yet another wicked human intrusion into their habitual sloth? Or simply je m'en foutisme? So much for gratitude. So much for chivalry. So much for manners.

Can an animal consent? In the understanding of Vanier and Mein Opa, yes. What is an erection if not a sign of consent? What is the smile of spring in a mare's eyes and a cow's frisky wink? Only the most mild trauma is suffered by animals. It's in direct proportion to the difference in size between them and their mate. The greater the disparity the greater the pleasurable pain, for one or other party. Not, and this comes as something of a surprise, always the larger party. This applies to human animals too. The doxies who lived and loved at Malpasfang were happy to be roughrogered by Mamble Cobs, former pit ponies not much larger than a large dog but impressive in the noble quarters. The poor chaps were instantly blinded by the sun when ascended from deep beneath the earth where they had been born and where they had spent their entire life of drudgery. One little doxy, rescued bleeding and bruised from Birkenhead Park by Jezzard Dogg, remarked that sex with mere men-proles, 'reeking jakes with stinky fucksticks', was perfunctory and injurious in comparison with the experience of a Mamble Cob, who hardly came up to her waist but was potent and kind. She'd never encountered such kindness in all her life. She multiplied her whoredoms, in calling to remembrance the days of her youth, wherein she had played the harlot in the land of Egypt. For she doted upon their paramours, whose flesh is as the flesh of asses, and whose issue is like the issue of horses.

For several seasons the mothers-to-be of super-hybrids were treated as poules de luxe rather than as any old fowl. Their diet from childhood had consisted of stirabout, broxy, both of them causes of ringworm, Q fever, tetanus, scabby mouth lesions which stretched to the ears as though the face was smeared with scarlet jam containing white pips. And tripe: seagull white tripe, bleached blanket tripe, honeycomb tripe, bible tripe or raggy tripe mostly eaten cold with vinegar, slink,[21] root vegetables. Their diet changed.

They had never previously tasted foie gras, brochet Saint Just, boiled elvers, Gewurztraminer, gelatinous pettitoes, asparagus, baked corncrake, roast swan, roast peahen, plover's eggs, cockscombs, sherbets, syllabubs, vanilla junket, glacé angelica, prunes stuffed with marzipan, prunes steeped in plum brandy.

They had never seen rooks and crows nailed to fenceposts harbouring maggots in their dulled feathers.

Nor had they smelled fields of mauve poppies, fields of lull billowing like laundry, yielding fifteen pounds of opium per acre.

They marvelled at the abundance around them: springy lawns where albino peacocks – much much more stylish than their frankly common iridescent cousins from Las Vegas! – strutted their fracs and screamed their terror that they might be eaten like their plain hens; plants with needles fine as hair; albino cacti – *Euphorbia lactea* ; blue barked trees whose boughs were coiled rouflaquettes; concrete rocks; concrete grottoes; concrete cascades; concrete log fences and bridges; a red sandstone aviary all broken pediments, metal gauze domes and

---

21 'Stirabout is porridge – of a sort. Broxy is carrion, the meat of ewes which have died on hillsides or during transhumance. Slink is the meat of calves stillborn prematurely.' F. Coventry in *The North British Omnivore* (Stirling, 1996).

terrifyingly shrill raptors in fancy dress; a fuggy hothouse where avocados, peaches, peppers, bananas and pineapples flourished no end brightly.

The cages were high as houses. 'Cavey', as we used to say in dorm. Bored albino tigers padded on ramps, albino leopards feasted on the shanks of kine and albino lions snoozed. Albinos are white, pure like marble sculptures, as Hegel noted. They are, then, living sculptures. The estate wall was the wall without end till they found the end at dusk in the woods (mind the mantraps, Jezzard Dogg's corking little jokes). The soil here was so sandy it would not support a wall. In its place lay rolls of vicious thorny wire like a tall metal hedge with lumps of rotting meat attached to the thorns. No horse could jump them to enter this domain – or leave it. Rich brown conical anthills seethed. They thought of themselves as the queens. Formica rufa.

Our distant barrow-building forebears had evidently observed anthills. Clever clogs, they learnt from observing Mother Nature, a source of knowledge which Judaeo-Christianity, civilisation's bane, brutishly quashed. Pagans were more enlightened. They were rooted in their land. So too of course was the NSDAP. Our autobahnen were built in concert with the gifts of landscape Mother Nature had bestowed on us. Our forests and longhouses paid tribute to Her. The volk did not exploit the earth as a resource. To till soil is to respect soil, to form an eternal bond, even to cosset it.

There was never a greater ecologist than Walther Darré. When, as a young man, I plucked up the courage to tell him so tears filled his bloodshot eyes. He wept with gratitude into his himbeergeist and reached out a hand to me but in doing so succeeded only in knocking the bottle off the table onto the café terrace.

At Malpasfang stock which showed potential was succoured. That which showed none was not. There was no room for sentiment. Horrocks simply no capiche. To be sentimental about weakness is itself a weakness. The overdog is the overdog because he has no pity for the underdog who wishes only to drag us down to his level.

G. B. Shaw was wrong about more than he was right about. However, his contention, made after his stay at Malpasfang, that 'the only fundamental and possible socialism is the socialisation of the selective breeding of man' is unexceptionable, so far as it goes. Which is only part of the way. A stroppy ginge who cut a swathe through the theatre and left a trail of virgins could hardly be counted upon to understand that such an ideal could not be achieved without getting under the bonnet, so to speak, creating some unavoidable collateral, as they didn't say in those days. Creating a new species can be a deuced messy business. It takes not only visionaries but grease monkeys (and sometimes monkeys tout court!). They didn't just say bob's your uncle, touch wood, hope for the best and watch it go through its paces, egg to butterfly. They were re-creating the race, inventing new forms, which required new processes of making life.

I don't want to bang on about this but they went beyond Darwin. They went to places he dared not go. He had identified the problem all right but was hamstrung by Christian scruples. Thou shalt not kill. God's ordinance. God of course ignored it. Not one for practising what he preaches! However, his dicta are heeded by his worryingly unquestioning flock, including Darwin who recognised that the society he adorned was the one place where the fittest would not survive because natural selection did not apply. The seething, persistently pupping lower orders were pig ignorant about contraception. It was these unters who, volens nolens, renewed the population while the sexually continent, priggish middle class reproduced at an increasingly sparse rate. The upper class bred both sides of the sheet – but there just weren't enough of us, proportionately.

Generation upon generation of les paumés spurned condoms, made no attempt to avail themselves of the anal tunnel, failed to get off at Fratton and so spawned increasingly weak-minded dolts who, generation upon generation, regress towards the freak show, the banana, the jungle. There were too many of them. Generation upon generation begat further retards who are vectors of their own inadequacy. They pass on the baton of bad genes. Their inexorable spread threatens the very race. Their obliteration is not enough. It is merely a defensive stratagem. Society requires compensation for their swarming ubiquity. They have literally seeped into its bloodstream. A strengthening of the strong is de rigueur. This is what the NSDAP set out to achieve, bless it!

Can you imagine how thrilling it must have been to watch a threesome composed of a handsomely buttocked former mill girl humped by twin albino gibbons swinging from the cage's roof bars to generate penetrative velocity? Ah, such strange beauty in the cause of building a new race, a new breed, a new beginning, a new world. Watch the beasts fight over her! Fight elegantly rather than fiercely, it must be presumed, for all parties were dosed with laudanum. It should have drowsed them as it should have drowsed the great luminaries of that age. But, no, it didn't. It energised them, fed their minds, incited them to higher things.

Without the gift of the poppy we would have no ghostly Flemish novels of forged identities, revenge and dusk, no poems of Florentine passion and daggers, no buildings as fantastical as Malpasfang, no PRB dreams of cupid lips and velvet vixens who decay with the blooms about them. The milk of paradise was the very key to England's greatness. The height of our imperium coincided with the height of our gluttonous appetite for opium. Our happy mania. But by jingo there was no coincidence. It was the cause. It unlocked the probability of the unthinkable, of ruling the globe and making free with its riches and wenches, plundering it like a nation of buccaneers. We, the overdogs, lorded it. We were the victors.

And, twerps that we be, we threw it all away.

Dog nose we didn't have to throw it all away. In the days of the maharajas – Deo, Banjy, Nandy, Saij, Prass – there was no question of us throwing it all away. They didn't want to relinquish what they had gained from the Raj. They led lives of plenty between Orissa and Mount Street, Baroda and Eaton Square, Jaipur and Melton Mowbray. They whored in Paris, gambled in Biarritz, weekended at Malpasfang. Fortified by brandy and poppy, they played cricket in summer: ochre and cobalt striped blazers. They hunted in winter: their pinks were royal blue, a nod to Chambord. On 30 August 1889 there was a joust in commemoration of the Eglinton Tournament that had taken place exactly fifty years previously. The weather obliged. Once again it rained. And once again several riders and their mounts were severely injured. The horses were shot: a crisp bullet to the head. Meat for the zoo.

Having befriended Nandy at Oxford, Mein Opa provided ever more succulent entertainments for him and his fellow princes, diversions that were intended to mimic the temple iconography of their athletic ancestors. He mixed mythologies and belief systems with indiscriminate glee. Horrocks compared the spectators of these exhibitions to Bedlam's Sunday voyeurs who delighted in the cackling and contortions. They prodded their prey. They giggled awkwardly, relieved that there but for the grace . . .

Nandy, the Maharajah of Miscegenation, repaid the hospitality shown him by having a tiger sent from Ujjain. It died of asphyxiation in transit. Its taxidermised ghost can be found in the Horniman Museum, Forest Hill, SE23 3PQ (first floor).

At night braziers burnt groaning spitting wood and incense. The flames lit up cages of animals and humans entwined in vigorous harmony: magnificent equine specimens, big cats, donkeys, goats and long-haired Mangalitsa pigs with eyebrows as rich as baroque pediments and their fleece dyed blue. They threw dervish shadows that scaled trees, hurled themselves up Malpasfang's walls, warping and dancing. Phaedra, once a prim drabbie milliner in Buxton, owned such presence of mind and profound concentration that, while being toughrogered by Cardinal Newman The Albino Ape, she could gobble however much Indian sweetmeat was offered her through the cage's bars. Hotsy totsy! What a poppet! I'd say a poppet is a woman with a man's appetites and morals.

The princely lack of inhibition was startling only to those who had seen neither those ancient temples nor the rooms of multiple lavatories in their modern palaces, extensions of smoking rooms where fifteen noble fellows squatting would cover the smell of their peppered shit with ribaldry and dark tobacco.

The purpose of the exchange between species was a matter of mild dispute. Jervoise Vanier considered his researches purely scholarly. Mein Opa was more like it. He was drawn to making the race stronger, to perfecting man, hence liquidating all imperfect life forms. But who would do the Black Death's work, pandemic cholera's, Spanish flu's? He dreamed of nature's genocide, of famine, plagues, boils. Where were locusts when they were needed? How could he know then that in Linz, Cairo, Buenos Aires, Revel, they were in their earliest infancy, gazing into a common future when they would swarm as black legions, cleansing the continent?

He despaired, don't we all, of Christianity's being champagne socialism in a mask, la gauche caviar in stagey rags. It's the fons et origo of the sort of socialism that claims to elevate the meek though keeps the meek at arm's length. I think we all know that this is hypocritical baloney. Give me la droite tête de veau, give me the steak and kidney right. The far far far right. Just give me . . . With a suet crust that's borderline crisp but not resistant.

Jesus turned out to have lied, a family trait. A priori god has made a noisy pledge about willing the earth to the meek. But have they read the small print? No. The meek are erks. Definitely not going to inherit. Precisely because they are the meek.[22] Got that? But they linger nonetheless, rarely washing themselves, menacingly smearing filth on windscreens, demanding ever more exorbitant stipends to remove it. (Doctor Johnson, crippled by compassion like so many other enlightenment blighters, was utterly wrong about this unter class.)

Vanier would come to the bed they shared with Eden shortly before dawn having spent the night in his taxonomical and anthropometric laboratory, which she called The Shambles. He measured skulls with callipers; took vaginal smears from sterile rats injected with the urine of mares in foal; dissected the reproductive organs of moths; gave rabbits blood transfusions; vivisected with zeal; aborted lamb foetuses to ascertain at what stage they could become viable.

This last project was conducted with the collaboration of the insidious mountebank Mortimer Glyde, whom Eden came to rue having invited to Malpasfang. Like many before her she had been taken by his huckster's charm.

Seventy years on she would still rage against him: 'A walking mould. A chancre. A crum.'[23]

To her swelling indignation he abused the invitation she had casually offered him at Clifton. He took more. He greedily helped himself to seconds, then thirds . . . He was an all too frequent house guest,

---

22 Anthypophora.

23 'Crum' in this instance signifies a body louse. The usage died with the speaker's generation or the previous generation, perhaps. *Pediculus humanus humanus* is a vector of, inter alia, trench fever and typhus. The female can lay as many as three hundred eggs in its lifetime.

'just passing by'. To her even greater annoyance he would become resident. Jervoise – drunk? besotted? spiteful? – had told him he could stay as long as he wished. Mein Opa gently cautioned Jervoise. He somewhat petulantly reminded Mein Opa that it was he who was the owner of Malpasfang Lodge. Was that the first fissure?

You don't have to look too far to see where Glyde's unflattering nicknames came from. As Eden feared he got to work poking his head into places it had no business to be in. He was as energetic a quack as he was pryer. The Devil's Crocus, a quack physician, turned Jervoise into a quack scholar. He transformed him with slow magic and flattery.

There was no form of husbandry or animal welfare practised at Malpasfang he didn't find fault with. He mocked, he sneered, he bullied. He dismissed several years' research. He spoke the fluent bluster of the ignorant. That ignorance was not immediately evident. It didn't sound like bluster. It didn't sound like ignorance. He was smilingly persuasive, the confidence man's sine qua non.

He boasted: 'Improvements will depend on my formidable knowledge of curative regimes, tonic balms, and civilising diets being implemented – yes? – in order to conquer the 'nomalies here present . . . They resist the crude panaceas of sawboned orthodoxy . . . My remedies are based in the practices of Greek and Sumerian sages who studied nature and hooves, the sun and the claw. In those far distant better times no distinction was made between the physician who treats animals and he who treats 'umans.'

He didn't dissemble his contempt for the human flesh he used and abused.

'When I were werking in Toxteth we had a werd for the likes of him . . . An' we got paid.'

At his imperious behest oggies gathered *Datura stramonium*. Spikey pods were emptied of seeds. Flowers were shredded. They were pounded, dried, infused in boiling water and given to unwilling guinea pigs who consequently suffered vomiting, double vision, aural and ocular hallucinations, impaired coordination and motor skills, shortness of breath, a foreboding of imminent death. It failed to kindle sexual desire.

He preyed on orphanages and punitive laundries. For a few pence a superintendent or mother superior in a distant institution reeking of bleach and creed would sell him a half dozen newborns whom he'd slip into Nigredo's rope paniers. He rides through night and wind. A child thief with a pinchbeck crown, marauding teeth, trailing a matted, ratty brush. He believes himself Saint Christopher on his black charger. When he reaches Malpasfang at dawn he walks his mount through a dolorous haze biding awhile listening to the zoo's chorus portending Civilisation's New Epoch of higher miscegenation and cross-species harmony.

Violins – if you'd be so generous!

Only one babe failed to survive the journey, apparently. Too puny to be offered to Ajax as a snack, he or she joined the ranks of the small fallen in the churchyard. Grave: on no account a coffin, for a coffin inhibits the despatch of potassium and vital salts to the earth. A cotton sheet suffices.

The newborns' role was to be blindfolded. His ambition was to starve them of light for many years. His strategy was to play the long game. It indicated how well established he believed he was. The first mask to be removed would be from a five-year-old child. The next, an eight-year-old. And so on. How would they react to seeing? More importantly would the other senses – hearing, touch, smell – have shown greater development than in other, non-sight-deprived children?

His experiment was inspired by the ocular fate of Mamble Cobs and by Mein Opa who had denied two children all contact with spoken language from birth. Each lived on its own in different distant wings of the house. They were bathed daily. They were surrounded by plentiful objects and pictures. They were wet nursed. Later they were well fed. He aimed to replicate the sensory conditions of wild children – deep-forest foundlings, animals' familiars and the like – without the privations they have habitually suffered (starvation, cold, physical danger).

Fred Carrodus – Young Fred, so called to distinguish him from the loyal manual oggies Fred My Man and Fred Over There – had been invited to Malpasfang by Mein Opa, who had read an article he had published in *Prothero's Hebdomary* on the accentuation of inherited characteristics through 'back breeding', endogamous breeding, the very opposite of Glyde's method – which was part of the point.

Young Fred was ever in the throes of religious crises. There was a background of recidivist god-bothering. He was eager to meet Mein Opa for in his early teens he had frequented my great-grandfather Clement Phimister's Mansion of Indivisibility in the south-east London suburbs. He was enthralled by the Hatcham Heretic's (local press's coinage) determination that Christian society could make itself fit to emulate god's fiery beauty on high, his clarity, righteous-ness, omnipotence – qualities whose germ we have within us, that exist in everything, whether natural or configured by humankind.

To make a dovetail joint better than any we have made before brings us closer to that god within. To make a dog more loyal and more vicious than any we have made before brings us closer to the god within. Equally it is our duty to correct, in the name of god, god's rare mistakes. God may be the greatest of craftsmen but like all craftsmen he is inclined to occasional clumsiness, lapses of taste, questionable innovations.

These may be rectified by elimination of: most reptiles, all venom-ous snakes, friable cliff edges, crop failures, fruit trees, dandruff, climatic mayhem (volcanic eruptions, tidal waves etc.), venereal warts, cactus spines that burrow invisibly beneath the skin, the root causes of feeble-mindedness, iconography that is a pageant to keep us in false gaze, plagues, cripples. For example, The Pathetic Mite Ned.

High summer. Figs ripening in the walled garden outside Jervoise's shuttered laboratory. Leo Thor spends all day drinking there, ham-mered by noon, slumped in a ruinous baroque armchair (chipped gilding, caryatid legs), drowsy beside Ajax The Lion's cage. Ajax spends all day in the cage gnawing. They were the very picture of a loving couple in the autumn of their years. Content, indolent, sated, drowsy, dazed, balsamed by opium. Neither was in the best of health. Ajax was in permanent pain. He had moved with discom-fort since being fired at by a trespasser while roaming the woods. Some shot remains, too close to a tendon to have been safely removed. Culprit undiscovered. Who? There were many to choose from. The

impregnable wall was systematically breached. Nettles are comple-
mented by dock leaves, barbed wire by wire cutters. The victim was
crippled. The poor chap can no longer run. He drags his left hind leg,
heavily bandaged as if he's wearing a buskin.

Leo drinks IPA corrected by coarse cider brandy. A still was his
only inheritance. He calls it his 'trousseau'. It makes up for his missing arm. He murmurs and mutters, reciting to Ajax the names of the
towns where the circus pitched. Tewkesbury, Malmesbury, Here-
ford, Tiverton, Yeovil, Weymouth, Fareham, Wootton Bassett,
Banbury, Bicester . . .

'Do you re'e'ber,' he asks Ajax, 'the' girls in Mo'mouth . . .'

He dozes, half wakes and leans close by the crisply rusted cage
bars: 'Did I tell you wha' Jervoise said . . . ?'

As usual Ajax pays no attention, doesn't even look up from his
swiftly diminishing hillock of ox innards.

'He say in fifty year we been able t' 'ave a new liver. Well, no'
exac'ly new. Secon' han'. Bee' used like. Fifty year. No' me meself,
understan'. Too much to expec' me ol china, lon' lon' time, distan'
distance . . . In fifty year I'll have bee' pushin' up daisies . . . for I don'
know how lon' . . . Think about it . . . cullin' for organs . . . What a
miracle age it goin' to be . . . edge of paradise . . . That's how it'll
be . . . Like Jervoise says . . . all this scie'ce . . . golde' age.'

He smiled in satisfaction, swigged another draft, turned when he
heard Squit The Scran's buckboard's clipclop to a halt with a whoa.
The puny lad bid Leo good morning, struggled to lift a hay bale as
big as himself from the cart's flat bed, trembled under its weight, gingerly opened the keeper's slip-door to dump it in the cage.

Ajax barely gave it a glance. Squit The Scran fetched another bale
from the wagon. Again, no response.

'Good bye then, Mr Thor.'

'Righ' y'are, Squi'.' He leaned back in his chair, cosy. He started,
alert. He strained his neck to eye the cage. 'Hey hey – hol' on my la'.
Where's his carcass?'

'Oh – no, he's not having carcass no more. No. Just vegetable
matter.'

'Wha? Jus' . . . Wha y'on ab . . . Wha' yo impartin'?'

'I only doing what I's told, Mr Thor. No meat. Just veget—'

'No mea'? No mea'. E's a lio'. Ajax is. An' what do lios ea'? They ea' mea'. Mea'. They's car'ivals, lios is. So where's my Aja's' mea'? Wha' the' fuck's goi' o'?'

'I bin told just vegetable matter.'

'You bi' tol' wha'? . . .Who tol' yo'?'

'Sir. He come round last night.'

'Sir? Whi' Sir whe' he's a' ho'?'

'Doctor Glyde, Mr Thor. Just vegetable matter he said, Mr Thor.'

'Tha' crocus thinks he's an orchi'.' (Eden's epithet.) 'Dam' 'im. Whas' 'e know? Quack twa'. Murd'rer if yo' as' me.'

He remembers the raggedy vengeful bawlers mafficking outside Winchester Gaol, years back, years back, that dawn when Glyde was released. Deserved to swing. Should have swung. Strangled an upstart with her stockings, an apprentice abortionist in the Southampton suburb of Sholing who was undercutting his prices, stealing his clients. No case to answer, my gonads! Lucky crocus. Stood there like an emperor surrounded by peelers while the mob hurled dung and vegetable matter.

He slips a plaited leather leash round Ajax's neck, ruffles his mane – just the way a lion loves it – clicks tongue and gums, double clipclop, leads him from the cage across the courtyard. He knows where to find Glyde at this hour of day: a fixed abode has prompted a fixed routine, morning ends beneath the glowing-barked cedar called the Tree of Tyre whose boughs dapple Nigredo's pelt. The horse is washed down by a group of stable lads. Each is equipped with three or four buckets. One lad sits on a low bough and as the buckets are passed up to him pours them into a bucket whose bottom is multiply-holed. When the horse is dry and saddled after the crude shower Glyde mounts him for a smoke.

The horse froze at the sight of the limping, dizzy, aged lion dragging his limping, dizzy, aged keeper across the cropped lawn that turned to powder beneath the tree.[24] When Ajax cleared his throat Glyde struggled to prevent the horse bolting.

---

24 Cedars' fallen needles acidify soil. Furthermore, their boughs starve the ground around them of sufficient sunlight to create photosynthesis.

'Where's 'is meat? What's this poppyco' 'bou' veg'able matter?'
Leo was worked up.

Ajax eyed the horse's glistening flank. Meat.

'Dietary science. Mr Vanier has had the wisdom to 'ssent to my counsel. Specialist counsel.'

Ajax pulled at his leash. He could burst a belly with a flick of a paw.

'Look,' sighed Glyde, pointing his greasy nose, 'plain for all to see n'est ce pas – 'ndows them with the wrong stripe of 'ggression. We don't want them pendulous in the groin cantonment . . . I fear I must skidoodle before your cat becomes too hungry. Erotic potency, that's the ticket, not wounding for greed.'

'Yo' was al' for meat a week or two back.'

'It is, you must understand, the prerogative of a gentleman to change his mind. Good day.' He waved dismissively.

'Go!' He cracked the whip, stung the charger, spurred to a gallop. Ajax was crestfallen. Leo led him to a field of sheep. Ajax behaved with comparative restraint. As ever, he left some for Mr Manners. But that was the first day he had been denied meat.

It was Mortimer Glyde's opinion that the newborn can be trained to diverge from parental mores and shun the atavism we all are heir to, irrespective of species. 'It is the prerogative of a gentleman to change his mind' was his mantra, until he decided that it was not the prerogative of a gentleman and changed his mind to the effect that a gentleman did not change his mind. He invented dicta so often, shared them so often with others that they believed the latest bromide and so did he, astonishingly. One of his more persistent aphorisms was 'true leaders are never full bearded'.

Another prerogative: to hold opposing positions simultaneously. Our first civil war is with ourself, he said. According to Glyde, were animals to satisfactorily perform their sexual role whether as seed provider or recipient they must be forbidden meat – meat foments belligerence, gratuitous attacks, boastful displays of violence for its own sake. It suppresses sexual performance while encouraging sexual display, invites sloth and vanity. It further inhibits fertility, stalls dreams of the future, stifles the maternal programme. He himself has shunned meat, milk, eggs for many decades.

Among Glyde's arguments was that the sacred duty of the breeder of a new race is to break inherited habits, bad habits acquired through infinite repetition without thought, to dismantle the atavistic pattern. Snakes must be protected, vipers' rights campaigned for. They understand the land better than we do. Animals are our equals. They must be respected. As our equals they can face courts of law when they transgress: pigs shall be tried by pigs, birds by birds. They can be taught: to talk, to reason, to perform elementary arithmetical sums. Knowledge of the names of trees and shrubs can only benefit them.

That means not eating them. We ought not to eat those we couple with. Animals, our familiars and friends, must follow our vegetarian diet. Carnivores are made not born. A cub or pup or baby gestating in a carnivore mother evidently shares her diet. That diet is, for the foetus, its only alimentary nurture. The foetus has no choice. It does not yet know that choice exists. The parents will, in time, oppose the former foetus's exercise of choice if that choice does not accord with theirs. We are no more born Catholics or Hindus than we are born colliers or podologists. Our parents observe these faiths, profess these trades (god help them). Their hope that we too will follow them is a matter of wishfulness and coercion: their hope that we'll take after them is inscribed in vanity. They seek replicas of themselves.

And I obliged my parents, to a degree. But then there is something of a difference between following one's people into, say, a laundrette franchise or long-distance haulage and undertaking the grave responsibility of stewardship of one of southern England's finest estates.

A qualification. While I have accepted my burden with uncomplaining grace I feel compelled to remind you that I have also struck out alone. I have done what no forebear ever did. No previous Shadoxhurst had ever written a work such as *A Toast to the Oast* (lavishly praised as 'an addition to the literature on this subject' by J. Hanly-Pritchard in *Wealden Life*). No Shadoxhurst had written much at all. And of course they had a sound reason. Writing is a vulgar trade. Borderline prole. And the tradesmen and women are mostly petit-bourgeois toilers out to 'better' themselves: I give you Inigo Horrocks. Still, with my appetite for historical enquiry and my restlessly creative streak, needs must. I bucked the familial trend.

Now, the question posed at Malpasfang Lodge was not whether a newborn cub or pup could survive and flourish on a diet alien to that of its mother and its species. The question was could a mature animal with a lifetime's blood on its breath be weaned from meat, converted to vegetarianism, even veganism, be persuaded by its stomach that sex beats sloth, gluttony and injurious exhibitionism. I should cocoa! The beasts could not or would not adapt. Lions eat big cats. Big cats eat domestic cats. Domestic cats eat birds. Birds eat insects (even though Glyde told them not to).

Cock in hand the sinister halitotic gal-sneaker Glyde prowled the indigo orchard where beds were ranked beneath branches and stars. He treated their occupants as his flock and harem. He exercised droit du seigneur even though he was, all too obviously, no seigneur. His cavernous laugh: 'Nature has no place for celibacy.'

He mistreated Clytie, Antinea (a mulatto fugitive from the Hawarden Asylum for Girls who wore dazzling white pancake make-up like minstrels in negative), Calypso, Antheia, Penelope, Gaia, Terpsichore, Psyche, Circe (who posed with a tiger for the Hon. John Collier), Melissa et al. Many of them recruited by each other with the promise of a fine life and the rumour of equal rights for albinos, often cast off by their families for their very albinism but not before amputated body parts (fingers, ears, an entire hand in one instance) had been sold to itinerant witches and crocuses as vaccines against demons.

Glyde jumped them, he thumped them. No rights there, then.

They lay weeping on pristine sheets rouged with the blood let by his Exemplary Trials.

His drawling lisp released miasmic toxins. He spoke as though having learnt his list by heart: 'Venereal infections of the anus, malignant anal melanomas, anal fistulas, suppurations and abscesses. I am expert in these . . . these retributions, these just punishments . . . The price of concupiscence. High price . . .'

The naked girls clasped each other hugger-mugger.

'Bleed! Plead!' he hissed as he dragged them to pose open-legged in front of his Flat Folding Kodak. 'Beg my thanks.'

A concertinaed Paragon Focuser was attached to his face, held with ribbons knotted tight to the occiput. Proboscis? Ocular ecto-plasm? Certainly a device to scare the living daylights out of the poor mites.

'Beg my thanks, I say . . . beg my thanks for relieving you of sin's unformed face. This camera is expiatory, d'you understand? A tool of expiation.'

The young women shrieked, they whined, they complained, they accused Glyde of injurious cruelty. They went too far. Eden had little sympathy for their self-pity. She told them to bone up. Nor, though, did she take the part of The Devil's Crocus whom she had nightmares about – a revenant from a plague pit, the walking dead beneath a yellow sky full of puss and grudge. His appearance bore her out. He was two tone, waxy etiolation relieved by ruddy eczema highlights.

Rime on lichen. The breath of limber things. Bees calling reveille. Spores in the soft breeze: let's call it a douce zephyr eh! Plump rain-drops vault leaf to leaf. Gossamer domes and paraboloids stretch across the grass. Midges swarming and warping.

No matter what the season, no matter what the weather, fecundity was obviously to be increased by the balm of fresh air. You didn't, according to The Devil's Crocus, need to be a medical man to work that one out. Between the walled orchard's ordered ranks of apple trees and ordered ranks of crab apple pollenisers he had stipulated that there should be ordered ranks of beds. They were cages or pens.

The orchard's northernmost wall was higher than the other walls to protect the trees from the north wind (it didn't) and to reflect sun from the south (it didn't). Skeletal, unflourishing trees were espal-iered against it. Irrigation was poor everywhere. The ground was damp. Manured water pooled year round. Roots rotted. Mildew blossomed. The hives at the far end of the orchard, seldom dry, suf-fered chalkbrood. It really was a pretty pickle. Not quite the site for a plein air dormitory.

He loomed. With his fraying stovepipe he ascended to six feet six inches. He stood with the setting sun behind him and about him. His silhouette was an intimation of shining hell. He was luminescent majesty. They would wake to find him making manual enquiries beneath the bedclothes. Or ejaculating on them. His sperm was said to be the colour of Cheshire Oysters, the baccy phlegm saltworkers hawked onto sawdust floors in Tarporley and neighbourhood. He boasted that it was god's seed. It was just his way of showing affection, sensu stricto hardly different from mine. I think, you know, that, like me, he must have loved women. The marginal difference was that he found it difficult to express that love by the ordained means. Marginal yet crucial. What a fate! I have loved them all my long life in all shapes and forms and positions and have never felt inhibited, never felt embarrassed to say so. Show you're pleased to see me, Honeycracker! I won't smother you.

When he learnt that the spoilsports were complaining of his importunacy he concentrated his attentions on Demeter, so named because her parents were said to be siblings. At Malpasfang Lodge she, like so many, was a refugee without certain identity. Thought to have been born May Brasier. Had fled the tannery at the Colony for Industrious Incurables in Crewe where she had been placed after several convictions for soliciting. She had a fixed smile of benign happiness. Her laudanum consumption was high. She did not speak. Or could not speak. Certainly unequipped to complain. Never said a word. Dumb? Probably. Deaf? No – receptive to song, bird song, neighs, Mamble Cobs' whinnies and the gargling bleats of the lambs that cropped the grass and grew fat on fallers. But she was unresponsive to the human voice. Traumatised? Her disability was a padlock on her mind. What horrors had she witnessed or heard? She was a life form unfit for life of course, likely to pass on her afflictions, but was spared Definitive Intervention because her cheerful willingness to mate with any beast made her a popular attraction. Tickety-boo.

Glyde treated few women with kindness. He treated the majority with varying degrees of disdain. More than thirty years a quack, yet he had not had partiality drummed out of him as would have a real doctor such as Sievers or Hoven. Witches are not scientists. Nor should there have been favouritism in a world where pride of place went to objectivity: knowledge, research, precision, taxonomy, chromatology, measurement, bio-psychic racial identification, crani-ometry, phrenology. Watch out for Mongolian eye. What role had limp 'humanity' in an enterprise devoted to the improvement of the human race? Yet Demeter incited him to tenderness. He sang trilling rhymes to her beneath trees. He showed her what leaf, what bark went with this tree name or that. He fed her fruit. He taught her how to play noughts and crosses with twigs in the dry earth. He did not ejaculate on her without letting her know he was going to do so. She did not reciprocate such tokens of respect. She loathed his terrible skin and skeletal frame and his resemblance to those resurrecting creatures who are surely too frail to lift the stone slab marking their grave yet manage it, just so.

A burgeoning mythology attached itself to Malpasfang Lodge. Chin-ese whispers amplified to a roar and were believed in by the whisperers. It should have been seen as the enemy of reason. It did not take long for a folklore to establish itself both within and without the vast estate (even greater than The Park, my humble patch). That folklore continues to this day passed down from gossip to nosey parker to curtain twitcher to inventive embellisher.

Malpasfang Lodge remains the subject of contaminated fairy tales.

The barbed wire was the barrier of deadly thorns, the briar rose around an ogre's castle. The orchard was poisonous. In a widely shared dream a wraith called Autolycus poured putrid liquid from a fiasco into sleepers' ears. The still night was alive with the cacoph-onic music of caged animals, howling, bellowing, lowing. They could be heard for miles around. The malodour of the animals was visible: the insects that fed on its particulates mapped its trail. It gusted far beyond the walls of what the neighbouring bumpkins increasingly talked of as a fortress or prison. Others called it a Turk-ish brothel, a graver insult than a Parisian brothel, not that the prissy namecaller would have experienced either. Reports of unnatural acts . . . oh, dog nose, there are always unnatural acts, life is not nat-ural, one boar's unnatural act is nought but a doxy's pleasure. Why, the bumpkins wondered, are there guards with shotguns wandering the heaths and fields?

No getting away from it: The Eviction was not forgotten. It left a messy stain. Some of the evicted, loquacious so-and-sos, remained in the locality doing menial work in return for a byre and a crust, spreading rumours.

The Potteries trollops and Black Country putas heard stories of their ill-fated predecessors giving birth to litters of sooterkins, black rodents with needle teeth who hunted in packs of dozens and tore the flesh from lambs and calves.

The doxies were visited by their abortions, skinless transparent foetuses, noiseless as mists and vapours, which grew at the same rate as babies, children, adolescents . . . They came by night to pinch their mothers' throats and scratch their eyes and ask: why? Incubi transformed themselves into succubi. They moved stealthily and silently. They moved clumsily to the piping of fifes with ringing cymbals on their legs. They changed their skin colour. They possessed the ferocious appetites of conquering soldiers, the greedy sexuality of women freed from prison. They harboured arctic chill and infernal heat. Now shrill, now guttural. They flew, they burrowed. They brought exquisite pleasure and eternal malediction.

Horrocks was not necessarily sold a pup – or a kennel of pups! The hand-me-down folklore of nearby villages, the snug and hearth calumnies of old wives, the rumours maturing decade by decade may well have been believed by his informants, the great- and great-great-grandchildren of the people who remembered the Great Wall of China, The Eviction, the albinism and passed it on in good faith. Not all of Cecil Sharp's bucolic ditties were fabricated for a pint of porter.

It was said that:

Four women had absconded from Malpasfang Lodge and were found living naked in a cave on Kinver Edge, daubed red by sandstone dust. They killed sheep with rocks to the head. They ate them raw, jabbering ceaselessly about the life they had led in Hell's Dormitory where they enacted rites with zoo animals. They robbed two cartographers. They felt there were fishhooks in their flesh being pulled in every direction.

★

Some years later one of them, now leading the life in the west at her own domain, Reichenfels Court, a blowsy house of assignation in Alma Square, Maida Vale, suffered abdominal pains. She presented with lithopedion, an extra-uterine pregnancy where the foetus has become calcified. The gynaecologist, a loyal client – 'I play where I work' – was foxed by the form of the foetus. Unprecedented. Who had impregnated her? When she replied that it might be any one of several animals of varying species, he resolved to become an ex-client. Most likely it was his chappish clubland gossip that did for Malpasfang Lodge, brought it to national attention, a term that means no more than the gutter press's prying swiftly pursued by the mob's contumely.

Fugitives, desperate and wounded by barbed wire, had been hunted down by Jezzard Dogg. He called this pursuit 'agrarian reform'. He had long trained gerfalcons and peregrines. Now, armed with brass-framed goggles and a gauntlet, his weapon was the only specimen of Prynne's Eagle in captivity, a demonic black bat that shut out the sun, cast an abominable shadow that turned day to night, plucked out eyes (hence Dogg's goggles) and could lift a disobedient ingrate to a fine height then drop it to certain death on the hard terrain beneath.

In contrast, a group of four had been paid to leave Malpasfang so that it might, unknowingly, provide prey for Marcher Hounds that, let us say, lived up to the name Das Schwarze Korps would give the beasts – and has stuck. You know where you are with these chaps. They scrape the bones clean.

Lost walkers who strayed into the park were turned into albino goats.

A troop of moustachioed, unmarried wet nurses who lived in a tent expressed their milk on roses whose petals curdled.

Exogamy Farm in *The Little Gay Tractor Is Impacted By Biodynamic Issues*, *The Little Gay Tractor Meets Farmer Geddon*, *The Little Gay Tractor's Unusual Discovery* and *The Little Gay Tractor Confronts Tractorphobia* is modelled on Malpasfang Lodge.

★

The notorious paedophile Linsel Murly, the paedophile's paedophile, was inspired to set sail from Brisbane after he had read about Malpasfang. He founded the Idyllic Brotherhood after he had visited the estate.

A grey-skinned woman and her ever-haemorrhaging, primate-like, adult son lived under a pile of blankets and sacks in a railway carriage at Albrighton. They were never apart because the son was attached to his mother by the umbilical cord, described as 'thick as a hawser, pink as a saveloy'. They refused all offers of work in circuses and freak shows, swearing and spitting in approximate unison at the agents who came to their door with promises of untold riches.

Lampreymen who frequent the river at night have down the years seen creatures with a calf's body and the face and canines of a monstrous dog on the beaches of the Severn's left bank south of Gloucester between Epney and The Noose. It eats human flesh and is called Saint Christopher.

The children of the children of the children of Malpasfang have tails and claws. They vault onto horses' necks screeching, tearing at the mane. They attack sleeping foxes, hurl boulders at swimmers, squat in sets from which they have driven the occupants, eat mud and live forever.

The issue of a gorilla and a weaver was born ten feet tall and weighed thirty-five stone. It shrank through childhood and adolescence to achieve approximately normal human proportions by the age of majority.

A weary man the colour of sand wearing glasses that reflected the sun and ragged, bloodied clothes, whose like no one had seen before, who could hardly clutch his bundle of possessions tied with string. His hands, his bare feet, his face were deeply wounded. The abundant sites of encrusted brown blood scared the people of the Marches whom he approached. They turned, some ran. But those who heard his voice . . . his voice was like milk, they said, like balsam, like the purest water. They were captivated, drawn to him. They offered him alms but he refused them.

All he wished for was to find the Tree of Tyre whose seeds he had seen planted many years before. They wanted to help him but no one knew what he was speaking of. After many nights sleeping in ditches and refusing all food he was told by an old blacksmith that there was a cedar of that name at Malpasfang Lodge. The trail of blood led to its western gates.

Everything has been. Everything will come by again. This man was Jesus Christ, searching for the place he had visited eighteen centuries ago. He found the tree that had grown from the seed. He sat beneath it for many days. He beckoned wild beasts to join him. When the devout oggies learnt his identity they held him to the ground, lapidated him, then ate his flesh and drank his blood warm from the vein in the holiest of communions. He knew it would happen. It happened every time he returned, no matter where he returned. The oggies felt fulfilled, blessed, guilty. Their guilt dissipated when the next day they found him sitting beneath the tree whittling. Then he polished his barbed wire crown. He smiled beatifically at his murderers as he had done at his many murderers down almost two millennia. The immortal's afterlife is a state of radiant grace.

And every time he returned, Cartaphilus was supposed to die. He was released from the punishment of eternal life. But he didn't die. Jesus revealed his human side. Like many another chap, he had got it wrong. The errant fellow didn't want to die. He enjoyed eternal life, anagrams, multiple identities: Claus Phirat, Paul Christa, Pilat Rausch, Curtis Alpha, Curt Liphaas, Curt Pailhas and many others. Such a life was a pleasure rather than a punishment for having goaded Jesus with his ornamented stick on the way to Golgotha.

He went on goading him, eternally of course, encouraging others to mock him. The tubercular peasant doubled-up to pick fungus in a pagan wood near Druskininkai was Jesus, out for revenge against the faithless who denied him, who deigned to eat him, to eucharist him. The false morels he distributed free in the town's marketplace are deadly poison if they are not boiled in many changes of water for four hours.

★

The communicants of Saint Joseph d'Alger knew that the sorrowful man, blistered by hot fat, who sold churros and chocolate from a van outside the church was really Jesus, and no more appetising than the greasy snacks he sold.

Over many years Cartaphilus's avatars – and he was sometimes a she, Trish Upalac, for instance – had worked to develop an elixir against death which might allow others – rigorously selected others – to sample eternal life, to tramp the earth with impunity and return at will no matter how many times they were executed for crimes against the pudding mass of humanity, mere undeserving humanity. (Eternists are a bad lot by and large.)

Malpasfang Lodge thronged with noble adulteresses, fallen women of gentle birth, ladies of the quality who had given birth to bastards, sexual adventuresses, and coal-black beauties with pearls in their hair, knee-skirts trimmed with the jassamine sweet. These women suffered hysteria and nymphomania, which are relieved by the removal of the ovaries and the uterus. Some hid the source of their shame by eating or burying the newborn.

A satyr who loved too many, too much, a victim of carnal exhaustion, was embalmed in honey in a glass case in the entrance hall of Malpasfang Lodge. He was a centenarian when he died but had the teeth, shining hair and skin of an adolescent.

Wasps attracted by the honey eventually ate the taxidermised body leaving only hooves, horns, grimacing teeth, tufty clumps of hair, stained bones, flaps of now bark-like skin. Feel! Rough. They nested in the skull.

Black-skinned men in finery came and went from Malpasfang under cover of night when they are invisible. According to the *Magazine of the Movement* the black man is seldom content with sexual intercourse with the white woman, but culminates his sexual furore by killing the woman, sometimes taking out her womb and eating it.

It was said. It was said. It was said . . .

Some of this may be true, as Horrocks evidently believed (or hoped). But come on — most is surely the product of the fearful bucolic imagination, adapted, exaggerated, coloured in.

Glyde had become increasingly fratchy. He blamed the animals' refusal to eat vegetable matter on the excessive quantities of meat they had been 'force fed'. He blamed the overfamiliar guardians for indulging the animals. He blamed the lack of gypsum in the water. The programme, his programme, was 'ambitious, radical, necessary — and visionary'. It was met initially with sniggers. His persistence provoked resentment. Then came the day when the animals, famished for more than a week, broke out of their cages — or were they let out of them? They went in search of meat. The great estate became an abattoir, a shambles. Failing to find deer, foxes, martens, hares, boars in the forest larder, the beasts attacked each other. Those too weak to defend themselves perished. They attacked workers in the fields, cowmen, goatherds. A carter was trampled by a stampede of Mangalitsa pigs — the ones with fancy hairdos who look as though they might be the bride at a Carpathian wedding.

Many of the carnivores were so enfeebled that they could hardly hunt. Normally vulnerable herbivores were able to flee them because their fitness was full. Their bodies had not been impaired by a dotty change of diet.

Glyde watched in despair. Even he recognised it was catastrophe. He had horns coming out of his hands. Before him went the pestilence. A multitude of slain and a great number of carcasses; there is no end of their corpses.

He was high on the crenelated south tower of Malpasfang Lodge. Oh how he got the morbs! He felt no shame. He felt immense self-pity. He had been let down by . . . by everyone. The distant haze on heathery hills was no consolation. He descended stair flight after stair flight. He walked along service corridors till he reached Demeter's dormitory. She had let him down.

What happened next is unclear. She was sucking a boiled sweet[25]

---

25 The women were provided with mouth-cleansing acid drops and bullseyes from the factory of a Vanier subsidiary in Warrington.

and weaving a sampler. He snatched it from her, spat incredulously at the motto My Home Is My Heart, screwed it up, dropped it on the floor, slapped her face. To cheer himself up he attempted to fuck her: age-old solution to many a problem. Vide cave paintings etc. The ancestral poke, eh! He was thwarted and angered by her refusal. He was incensed by her pointing to the site of his erectile failure (nerves, no doubt). In his fury he beat her unconscious.

Voices swam in him . . . I have seen thine adulteries and thy neighings, the lewdness of thy whoredom, and thine abominations . . . wilt thou not be made clean?

He said he didn't hear her muffled grunts because the Lord's presence and the 'zoological symphony' in the park claimed his ears. He said she was willing: a doctor's word against hers! A doctor who, with Jervoise, was carrying out mental capacity trials to determine whether the women were intelligent enough to mate with animals. They devised means of assessing deductive power, reasoning, recognition and, on the other hand, feeble-mindedness. They correlated results against the measurements of the subjects' head. An early achievement was the establishment of indisputable links between prognathism and mental defectiveness, between a widow's peak and innumeracy.

Jervoise envied Glyde's capacity for cruelty. He needed no second bidding to keep Glyde's rather bad manners quiet. He bribed the victim.

'She's used up here anyway. Strange little whore. Not too old to revert to her street back wherever it was – where was it?'

A strategic rather than a moral dereliction, I'd say. It encouraged Glyde to believe that he was authorised to violate as he wished. But why not? For heaven's sake, Man is the Master. It also made him realise that he would miss her. Dare we say he was in love?

'Crewe.'

'Never had the pleasure,' laughed Jervoise.

One of the women found at Kinver Edge (clearly, then, not an invention), ragged, starving, screeching and abandoned by her fellow escapees, was taken to Stourbridge police station where she made a statement: 'Satan's zoo park it were . . . a bad imagining gone real evil . . . the animals out of control . . . going back to the wild . . . like being on the dark continent with dark forces . . . like one of them Bible stories when the animals are attacking the chosen people . . . like god wasn't there to help . . . like he was allowing badness to be visited on the people . . .'

The constable who interviewed her believed she was with the fairies. He noted that she insisted that a man called Gloyd had taught her he was god so could take of her body when he wished.

She was admitted to the Kidderminster Poor Law Union Workhouse. Her protestations were met with shakes of the head, with smiles to acknowledge she was simple: the influence of the Lunacy Commissioners was powerful in those years. When she began to suffer leucous vaginal discharges she was taken to Mason College in Birmingham. Her insistence that they were caused by having sexual intercourse – 'it's like fuckin' like' – with animals was met with scepticism and muted laughter.

However, a venereologist who had worked at the Sir J. J. Hospital & Sanitary Institute in Bombay recognised the complaint as a variant of Petit's Chancre (aka Kamathipura Milk) which was certainly zoonotically transmitted. But there was nothing in the nosology to say it was vectored by going jiggy jig jig (as they have it in those parts). The evidence was reckoned circumstantial rather than absolute. The venereologist in question was Doctor Rustam Barrister. His opinion was not valued by his British superiors. I won't hear it that it was a skin colour matter: no, Doctor Sawbones Ramalama simply won't have had the top training and top acumen that our chaps have.

Still, it was because such diagnoses were overlooked that Glyde was able to wield influence for so long. If it had been a white man's diagnosis, he wouldn't have got away with it. Scarlet tracings and all.

That marvellous day at Pallanza in the early summer of 1951, that elusive golden day, lit by Maxfield Parrish, engraved forever in the memory . . .

I had been to see Mama in the clinic. She was in more of a tizz than ever. She asked about Valentina. I reminded her it was a matter

that was hush hush and not to be mentioned because it discombobulated her.

I needed cheering. I was late. The Vicomtesse's car was untidily
parked. She and Mein Opa had presumably arrived at midday. The
house was surrounded by stone pines. The 1800-ish facade was
symmetrical, austere, ochreish stucco. The front door was open.
In the hall there stood a bust of Mussolini. On one wall were
framed photographs: Mussolini with Hitler, with von Ribben-
trop, in mufti with Skorzeny after the rescue; SS Brigadeführer
Walter Schellenberg and Julius Evola; Schellenberg with the Duke
and Duchess of Windsor at Sintra; the film star Doris Duranti and
the handsome man who turned out to be the owner of the Villa
Scirea – he, lucky fellow, was also pictured with Assia Noris and
Isa Miranda.

It took me all of ten seconds to work out who these friends of the
Vicomtesse were: the frighteningly haggard, withered German with
a mildewed blanket round him was evidently Schellenberg, though
his resemblance to the photographs in the hall and all previous photographs I'd seen was slight. You might say his resemblance to a living
person was also slight. His wife busybodied herself over him. The
Vicomtesse kept brushing her aside so she might fulsomely kiss her
once dashing gallant. He clutched his wracked trachea.

Time had worked equally cruelly on our host. He too bore little
resemblance to the photographs. He was dressed like an ageing chorus
boy in a nautical musical. Hooped matelot T-shirt, a starched neckerchief which stuck out horizontally like the hilt of a dagger plunged in
the thorax, cream flannel bell bottoms and co-respondent shoes.
Tonio Veltri was a name-dropping Torinese lawyer: Agnelli, Bogl-
iolo, Borghese, Borromeo, Borzino, Cicutto, De Masi, Ematrùdo . . .
He let it be known that he knew absolutely everyone, that he had
defended absolutely everyone charged with war crimes, collaboration, currency offences, art thefts, arms smuggling. Presumably he
enjoyed Schellenberg's notoriety. There's a certain JNSQ about so-
called war criminals, a wicked frisson at being in their presence.
There was some intense conversation. I must admit my eavesdropping was less than diligent. They were talking about Odessa. Why? I
wondered. Black Sea port, stairs, film, a light pogrom now and then

conducted by Russian bastards. That's all I knew of it. The meaning was lost on me. It didn't seem v important then.

As for the rest. There was a formerly handsome blond junker, now going to seed as an impressively porcine overeater whose inbred-looking Habsburg jaw struggled to assert itself through banks of suet. There was a sexpot in her thirties who took little notice of us, so far, redheaded with a peek-a-boo hairdo and a clingy bias-cut dress. A luscious piece of homework whom Tiger responded to like a firm young cub.

Lunch was beneath a pergola, shaded by a vulgar superfluity of wisteria. There were broad steps down to the lake's sheer blue water. We were watched over by a squad of baroque figures on plinths, winged babies and mermaids, unicorns and amputee body builders morphing out of walls.

Usual Italian do: delightful food (crunchy small birds, fried lake fish, pike blanquette, goose salmi sartu), wine which no one even pretended was drinkable, super-duper cheese, oversweet desserts, a veritable bottle-bank of post-prandial amari, grappa, fruit brandies etc.

The waxen fatty was not much older than me. Former Haupt-sturmführer Ernst Stech-Pelz. When not trying to join the Odessa conversation he would grant me a few seconds of his precious time mentioning twice that my name 'resonated' with him. But he was damned if he knew where from. He was charming enough in a prickish sort of way. V pleased with himself despite his lobeless ears. The son of an orchestral conductor whom he claimed had been among the most famous in the Reich. He boasted that he had been the youngest member of Himmler's personal staff. Presum-ably, then, a gofor – as we didn't say then. Currently a stenographer. Though he called himself an 'amanuensis', working 'with' SS Bri-gadeführer Schellenberg on the final revision of his memoirs. It was his duty. 'Meine Ehre heisst Treue.' It had been his duty too to contribute to the Lebensborn project. He had covered eight maid-ens in a day and a half. I congratulated him. Jolly surprising the exertion hadn't killed him. Perhaps he had been less porky then. He spoke about the love of his life, a midwife in the project whose hard duty was to slit the throats of damaged babies for the sake of the future Reich. He was taken into custody at a roadblock when they were trying to reach Flensburg in the last days of the war. She had escaped into oblivion.

He said: 'Hitler was married to Germany and the German people. It was only when they deserted him in his hour of need that he was free to marry Eva Braun.'

I could not have agreed with him more. I told him I concurred. But no matter how much I protested that the Führer's death and Germany's defeat were unmatched tragedies and that the march westward of the red beast was an unparalleled threat which promised the end of the world, this vain porker, who wouldn't let me forget the rank he had once held, refused to listen or temper his fat finger-poking Anglophobia. Why had we waged war on our brothers? Why had we criminalised what were merely policy differences? 'We had hardly started . . . that's what I regret. In fifty years' time the unusual measures we had taken would be forgotten . . . the new order would be established for all time.'

He had met many sympathetic English in the years before the war. He stopped suddenly. He stood. He beckoned me stand. He clasped my hand vigorously. 'Shadoxhurst of course . . . I recall . . . Shadoxhurst . . . nineteen thirty-five. Year Three. Fenant, is that right way to say it . . . magnificent house. Magnificent hospitality. I led a party of Jugend on bicycles visiting castles, trying to identify new airfields. Forgive me . . . We were treated as young princes by . . . who . . . your parents I suppose . . . your delightful parents . . . yes yes, must have been your mother . . . delicious Bavarian accent . . . your father's splendid cars . . . jalopies . . . I recall a terrible faux pas for which they forgave me: I thought the name . . . your name . . . was Saxonhurst . . . You must give them my regards . . . how are they?'

The Vicomtesse sipped a tisane. She pecked at miascia. She fed Buboe XIV candied greengages and angelica. She muttered into Mein Opa's ear then asked bold as brass whether the elegant waiter – long-haired for those days – might be a Chosen Person. Tonio assured her that Tarek was purebred 100 per cent Lal from Tripolitania.

All was still. The cypresses were taut at attention. Now and then there was just the faintest of ripples on the lake. A man cast a spinner from an old motor boat. A sculler feathered his oars with powerful grace. We bathed in warm content. Is there anywhere outside England or Germany more beautiful?

It had, she said, been left to her, Eden Blood (the Vicomtesse was, then, in the far future), to deal with the victims of Glyde's self-tutored gynaecological explorations and his splendid collection of fascina.

'Fascina?'

Once the terminally sick Walter Schellenberg – only forty-two but with the dead pallor of an octogenarian – had had the word explained to him he uttered a sort of grunt (amusement? disapproval? ennui?) then resumed his normal level of coughing.

Irene Schellenberg rolled her eyes and made a fake gasp. The other woman, la chienne en chaleur, growled her interest. (I do not, to this day, know her name. I did ask her when, later, she was attending to Tiger in the boathouse but her reply was necessarily muffled. I simply adored the delicacy with which she wiped a glistening goatee of white beluga from her chin.)

Fascina. Ivory incised with cross-hatching. Steel. An Eros-patterned Meissen ceramic phallus which Glyde claimed had been owned by Randy Unmack. Marbled glass ticklers. The Vicomtesse shook her head tutting in remembrance of them. Polished beech monsters. Winged, biped, smooth as mucous membrane, rough as pebble grain. Some had an auxiliary limb designed to stimulate the clitoris while the rambunctious shaft explores the cave.

She agreed that the idea of such an addition was splendid. But the design was inept. She was giggling like a gal.

'No conception of a woman's dimensions.'

Quite confident that everyone was fascinated by a minor incident half a century and two world wars ago, she recounted what she had whispered at Mortimer Glyde.

(The Villa Scirea's gardener, a man with the filthiest fingernails – each one a blueblack quarter-moon – listened as though he was our equal. No one troubled to correct him.)

She had promised condign revenge should Glyde continue to injure his fellow guests. He of all people should recognise that they are laboratory specimens, to be treated with care, to be treated equally.

'Why,' she wondered, 'are you so reliant on your dillydos? Could it be what they tell me – that, my dear Mister Glyde, your cock's a lobcock? No, no – please don't show it me. I've already laughed too much this morning.'

His face had trembled in search of a complementary insult.

'Sssh . . . Now, now . . . Don't be rash,' she said.

She smiled slyly at his worn canvas wilson. He twitched, puzzled. How was he to know that she had nicknamed it 'his summer abortionist kit'? He bowed and processed away, sleek across the carpet, leaving her at the breakfast table spooning posset and pain perdu to her cuddly lap dog Buboe III.

The Vicomtesse had moved on to Amaro di Udine and a new topic. She addressed the table:

'On the occasions when I required the service that fraud claimed to provide I availed miself of a superior class of backstreet abortionist. A boulevard abortionist on dit. A genuine doctor. Genuinely struck off, served his time in tronk – unlike our Mister Glyde. He had never had a single letter after his name. He merely pretended to have been given his marching orders. He had never been struck orf. His very dizgrace was a sham. A sham. He was a never-was . . . Ha! It only came to that a few times. God! Whoever would want children without the assurance that they are perfect . . . the death of a child is never really to be regretted, when one reflects on what the child has escaped. No one has a good word for infanticide nowadays. Quite out of fashion. Who's that in the Goya? We yearned . . . we ought to have created a race without beggars. Without beggar stock . . . the weakened stock these people come from.'

She recalled Jervoise's approbation of Doctor Johnson's silly-billy dictum that we must give to beggars so that they have the wherewithal to continue to practise their profession, which is begging.

Schellenberg, who had been dropping off wrapped further in an unseasonal greatcoat, brisked up bushy-tailed, wet his lips and asked: 'Doktor Johnson, ist das der neue Hepatologe im amerikanischen Militärkrankenhaus?'

The Vicomtesse affected not to have heard.

'A race beggars are not born into . . . That is what we worked for.

Is that not what we strove towards, my darling Marcus? Perfection . . .
We failed. Of course The Cause[26] itself failed.'

She stared pointedly at Schellenberg as though that failure was his
alone. He wore the perpetual half smile of the intellectually boastful.
His inner organs might have been close to shut-down but charm had
not been erased.

He excused himself like this: 'Why did I join the SS? I joined the
SS because the uniform pleased me.' And not just him. Adolf Eichmann in his death's head cap works wonders on the gentleman zone
of many a chap in leather chaps.

'And the fabric was utter bliss – so pleasant not to be itching all
the time.'

There's a bit of the old irony thing here. While we the English
aristocracy, or part thereof, were enthusiastically recognising the
natural aristocracy of the Führer's new order, new look, and its uniforms fit for hunting, the old German aristocracy – hardly famed for
its sartorial nous – was happy to benefit from it all while snobbishly
mocking the petit bourgeois who were the rulers now. This was one
of Walter Schellenberg's discontents. Here was a chap with a superb
mind even when terminally ill. I was just a young buck but even had
I been more versed in the ways of the world I'd still have been mightily impressed by the incisiveness of his thoughts, some of which were
decidedly rum. He claimed an enthusiasm for the queer rogue Baron
Corvo because they were both the sons of financially incompetent
piano makers.

The Vicomtesse was fighting sure that Heaven on The Marches
would have been realised had Jervoise not so pandered to The Devil's
Crocus whose efforts to alter the diet of dedicated carnivores were in
vain. Predictably in vain, wouldn't you say.

She believed those gals had never enjoyed such a fine life till he
smirched the idyll.

'He took it from them . . . Glyde's behaviour . . . so uncouth.
Loubard . . . gougnafier . . . You'd have thought it impossible, no? They
had freedom in those dormitories . . . they had freedom in all their
life at Malpasfang . . . Impossible, what a feat . . . only a bastard like

---

26 The NSDAP. An atypical evasion. Euphemism was not required in such company.

him could make them long for the slums . . . y'know the noisome alleys they came from . . . Liverpool . . . Birkenhead, terrible places . . . Sixpence a nod – there but for the grace . . . young men – Jervoise and Marcus for instance – are susceptible . . . they look up to their elders no matter what they may say, no matter how insidious the elders' influence.'

Mein Opa looked as sheepish as it is possible for a bearded, ursine, near-nonagenarian to look. There were tears in his eyes. No tears, mark, in her eyes. Till ten days previously in Genoa they had not met for many years. Since then she had seemed unable to desist from tearing him off a strip, castigating him for what he once should have been. She was still embittered, though she had little to be embittered about.

He was too courteous to recall Edie Blood on the towpath beside the Severn, sixpence a nod.

Edie Blood wouldn't have had the nerve or knowledge to say what the woman she had become said: 'Specially if that elder is M'sieu Tartuffe.'

Schellenberg perked up again and declaimed: 'Molière starb auf der Bühne.' How he too himself wished to do so – to die on stage to acclaim.

How he too himself wished to do so – to acclaim. But no. Loath as he was to admit it to himself he knew he was no longer in the limelight. It would not be his lot to die on stage like that playwright.

Irene shook a pill box onto the table, handed him a cluster.

Everything has been. Everything will come by again. But when? The Vicomtesse spoke of recurrent inevitabilities: the woods decay and fall; utopia fails. It fails in different ways but it always fails. Utopia is just dystopia putting on its happy face. We all know that utopian actuality never matches utopian aspiration.

I know it now. When you are very old your nails grow quicker in step with the swift passing of the days. You have seen the cycles of the years, you have seen the glasses' prints on the table. They overlap, they almost match those already there, almost. It all comes round again – but approximately, never quite the same as the last time and the time before that.

Mein Opa would not concur. He defended himself as best he could against the most viperish of opponents (whom he had part created). He shook with pride as he recalled having, with Young Fred Carrodus, bred from wolf, Rottweiler, Vizla, Staffordshire, Ridgeback and pinch of Dobermann, a gratifyingly delinquent albino control dog, the Marcher Hound.

'Ah! Yes . . . the bow wow . . . of course, I'd forgotten,' murmured the Vicomtesse.

'Carrodus? Carrodus . . .' Schellenberg mused. 'Merkwürdiger Name. Schottisch? Ich kenne diesen Namen irgendwo.'

The Marcher Hound's most splendid attribute was the ability to identify the inferior races by their stench. (Like Rolf Gardiner!) Its reputation grew due initially to the distress it caused to opponents of Freikorps Oberland and Freikorps Maercker. It would become the favoured breed of the SS Totenkopfverbände, which, understandably eager to bury its English provenance, named it the Mordhund. It pre-dated von Stephanitz's German Shepherd/Alsatian by more than a decade. And despite the experiments in breeding undertaken at the SS's own dog and carrier pigeon school in Sperenberg and the Dienshundwesen Oranienburg (where the neighbouring camp generously supplied sample quarry), the Mordhund's characteristics of absolute viciousness and absolute loyalty were never emulated.[27]

They did sterling duty preventing the inert from escaping from the Experimental Agrarian Colonies. Himmler's compassion for these dogs was limitless; he understood the terrible duties they had to perform in the Colonies.

Schellenberg, mumbling the name Carrodus to himself, suddenly recalled that he spoke English.

He snapped: 'I know nothing, I knew nothing, nothing of what in these farms, these farms they claim was happening. Of twenty thousand people – of more than twenty thousand people from these places the transportation to Sweden I personally organised. Twenty thousand Jews. I earned my redemption. I stopped the reprocessing,

---

27 At the 'liberation' of Nevers two dogs used by the proud patriots of the Milice were captured, subjected to a show trial in a specially convened canine court and sentenced to death by firing squad. Another instance of victor's cowardly 'justice'.

the alleged reprocessing. I ordered that the Jews be fed and given medicine. They were useless eaters, a burden on the Reich's food resources, but I gave them food . . .

'My honour was named fidelity. It was painful, difficult to betray the Führer and the Reichsführer in this way . . . but what if another god is there who shall judge me differently from Hitler? Hitler's reign, his dizzying spell as a god, was coming to an end . . . How long can a man be a god for? How long can a god be a man for? All deities are temporary deities . . . To every deity the moment comes when Thanatos is there sidling alongside, ready to welcome with a smile . . .

'And you know, despite my work to counter them I really knew nothing of the conditions in these farms – as I say, I knew nothing, nothing. My autobiography will confirm that . . . Is that not correct, Ernst?'

'Utterly correct, Brigadeführer,' his voice stood to attention. 'Pages seventeen to twenty-three.'

'There you are,' smiled Schellenberg.

Former Hauptsturmführer Ernst Stech-Pelz proposed that even if these lagers/camps had existed it was not for the British and the Yankees and the savage Reds to condemn them. They had no right to sit in judgement on Germany's internal affairs. They had no right to interfere in the domestic policies of a sovereign state. You know, methinks I concur. Spot on.

Siegerjustiz. They were spitefully dispensing victor's justice. Rather, no justice. Not even a show trial . . . He lambasted the British army for having buried Reichsführer Heinrich Himmler in an unmarked grave on Luneburg Heath. A particularly contemptuous, inglorious, reprehensible act which reflects badly on the British army. And buried by conscripts! Other ranks, impertinent cackling troops . . . The ignominy, the dishonour . . . He was the Reichsführer! The Reichsführer! How can one compare the base morality of the British tommy with Himmler's noble warrior's death? A grave in nowhere. A hole in the soil dug without respect and with the foul-mouthed jokes and songs of coarse cockneys. Without respect . . . Who are these animals? What sort of animals insult a great Germanic warrior? Where is the fair play? The fair play in Ernst's opinion was what the perfidious English always preached but never practised.

How right he was. If they did practise it, they would have granted Himmler the memorial or monument he warranted.

In comparison, Hermann Löns is commemorated more than a hundred times across Germany. The poet of Luneburg Heath and Heimatkunst and a vital inspiration to Himmler and Darré died in battle near Reims in 1914. Various NSDAP agencies exhumed his body – or what is claimed to be his body – on several occasions while a suitable site on the heath could be identified for his final resting place. Walsrode, close by but not on the heath, was chosen. The monument to him there may be puny. It may not be indicative of his transcendent vision. But it is better than no monument.

It was Ernst Stech-Pelz's ambition to give Himmler the funeral he deserved. To celebrate a great hero, a god. To erect a 400-metre-tall memorial to him. Or perhaps a Valhalla like von Klenze's. Or something in the manner of the Kyffhäuserdenkmal or the Befreiungshalle upstream from the Valhalla. No matter what form it took, it had to be large, it had to be on a hilltop, it had to dominate the surrounding country. He imagined a magnificent service at Quedlinburg Cathedral. Full ceremony. Night, dignity, flaming torches, martial drums, men in antlers, horses in heraldic chanfrons and cruppers.

The mise-en-scène got him worked up. He was going to track down the tommies who had carried out this most graceless of burials, track them down and go to whatever lengths were needed to get them to yield up the resting place where no man should rest. He was attempting to raise funds to accomplish this sacred mission. Had he not been such a boor I'd have stumped up what those coarse cockneys call 'a grilla' on the spot. As it was I made him wait, and wait. Why should he enjoy the kudos of effecting the exhumation of the century?

It was obvious that Schellenberg had heard it all before. He held the liver spots at the end of his arms to the sky as though imploring a god of silence to descend and gaffer tape Ernst's mouth. He was browned off with Ernst's posthumous hero worship. It was just the sort of tosh that Himmler himself had gone in for – he had fancied that he was a reincarnation of some chap known as Heinrich the Fowler.

There was, Schellenberg said scornfully, no end to Himmler's superstitious gullibility: the man was a mystically besotted filing clerk who'd believe in any gobbledygook provided it was far-fetched and an insult to reason. He ridiculed the Ahnenerbe's risible preoccupations. You don't win wars with crazed folklore, astrology, bogus history and reflective glasses. You don't found the future on a fake past. Ernst was tolerated because the poor booby was willing to work for a groat or two. Ernst's predecessor Klaus Harpprecht, out of loyalty to Walter Schellenberg, turned up every so often from Munich where he worked for the *Süddeutsche Zeitung*. He tactfully corrected Ernst's excesses. Which of course included constantly egging on Schellenberg to emphasise the regime's magical fount and the inevitability of its return. All that foraging for myths back in the dark forest where Teutonic knights mutate into the gods of the north, creatures of ice and flame . . . It was going to recur. Hollow earth theory, a race of giant Aryan ancestors, the German equivalent of hey-nonny-no, the occult meaning of Etonians' top hats . . .

Schellenberg's resistance to the Ahnenerbe's tomfoolery was not due to anything so scrupulous as an attachment to reason. He had served four years' imprisonment for crimes against peace. Yet to his chagrin he was not considered important enough to warrant a whitewash and so be employed by either of Germany's intelligence agencies. He had a hunch that were he to be suspected of having even a hobbyist's interest in mumbo-jumbo he would make himself even more unemployable. The intelligence agencies which were popping up like mushrooms as the world reconfigured itself were not interested in fantasists. (So he thought.)

These agencies, he claimed, knew how dangerous, how influential he could be. They also knew that just as Reinhard Heydrich had done Himmler's thinking so had Walter Schellenberg done Heydrich's thinking. Schellenberg did not want to be tarred by the brush of cultish religiosity.

He was, he said, monitored day and night. He was living in captivity in a police state.

Mein Opa said: 'I shall send you a Mordhund. There is a superlative breeder in Fulda. He would be honoured . . .'

Schellenberg was slyly grateful. Having a dangerous dog about the house would, he said, be most useful.

He hoped it would be a strong swimmer. He turned and pointed to the lake. That man 'fishing' from a bobbing motor boat and that man sculling were keeping an eye on him and on whoever visited him. Had we, he asked the table, noticed the battered Fiat Topolino, all rust and dents, parked a hundred metres from the villa's gates? People who live round here don't drive cars like that. They most certainly don't sit in them for hours on end. You will glimpse an occasional flash when the sun hits the naval binoculars trained on him from the spur of pine trees and peasanty little houses 500 metres away. Post is tampered with: they don't even cover their clumsy handywork. The phone is tapped: hear the breath.

He boasted of being sounded out by the DDR's Ministerium für Staatssicherheit, MfS (soon to be known as Stasi), and the FDR's Gehlen Org. He had turned down the former because of his visceral contempt for communism and the latter because of his visceral contempt for Reinhard Gehlen, not to mention his jealousy of this ambitious plodder promoted beyond his capabilities.

A man called Angleton, a comer from this new American outfit called the CIA, is arriving this evening: Gehlen's not being up to it is obvious. He has to be replaced. A higher calibre of spy master is needed to take on East Germany and the Soviet Union.

He knew he ought not to be talking about it but he was also expecting an emissary from Lavrenti Beria, sometime.

Did he expect us to believe this slurry? Was he taunting us to challenge him? The poor fellow was sick as a dog. Was he delusional too? His cooked-up amnesia about the camps was unconvincing, and indeed quite unnecessary given the company that day. We were right behind him on that ticklish matter. Presumably he was trying to erase the memory for the sake of his memoir!

Irene Schellenberg, repeatedly, vaguely threateningly: 'Du tust es für die Nachwelt, meine Liebe.' ('You must do it for posterity.') Sanitise! Sanitise! She reminded her husband that, like the SS-WVHA, he had always privately opposed processing enemies of the Reich, fit men and women, when they could be employed under special terms to dig peat in Dorohucza, say.

Last week Schellenberg had, he claimed, met his old colleague

Otto Skorzeny in Madrid. (It was well known that they loathed each other.) But – together they were planning an international commando of strategic assault personnel, paramilitary freedom fighters trained in guerrilla operations against red insurgents. They would use deep-bed espionage and, where necessary, information extraction. Really?

He had a bottle of Glückliche Traüme pills, the formula of a Swiss chemist. A gift from Skorzeny, he said. A validation of his meeting? Proof it had happened?

When, after taking one of the pills, he looked at the lake he saw Böcklin's *Isle of the Dead* surrounded by drowning babies. He had calculated that by the time it would take him to swim to their rescue they would have expired so he remained in his chair and counted the number of needles on a stone pine until the tree turned into a wild boar on stilts.

Those illusions you could put down to a chemical barney in the bonce rather than the desperately craven vanity that none of us wanted to witness.

'Carrodus, ja ja ja!'

He'd cracked it, he'd remembered: 'Sonderfahndungsliste GB . . . ja.'

He clapped his hands and grinned at the memory. The list of dangerous Britons to be immediately taken into custody after the invasion. This was in distant anticipation of the invasion eventually codenamed Operation Sealion. But whatever the codename, whatever the timing, it was imperative that the forces of liberation knew who to detain before they could damage the march of freedom. There had to exist an inventory which would be added to daily – that was impressive – by a team of anglophone researchers. Reading, listening, eavesdropping. He had been appointed by Heydrich to gather this team, lead it, report its findings but above all keep the list growing.

A pretty rum list it was too. Commies, the Labour Party, the warmongering journalist Churchill and his yes-men, Sigmund Freud, Bertrand Russell, H. G. Wells, R. G. Collingwood, Masons, Jews. Yes: better err on the side of caution, better that one Christian mistaken for a Jew die than a single Jew escape. The big-hearted Arthurs in the Protestant clergy – they'd have been bothersome, no question.

But would Boy Scouts really have proved a threat to the liberators?

The Order of Woodcraft Chivalry? The Produce Guild Day Schools? Methinks not. And why should an elderly science teacher have been included? Young Fred Carrodus, now Doctor Frederick Carrodus, was shortly to retire.

As a substantial landowner – Faineant Park, a grand house, a palace really, parkland, miles of surrounding wall (approx. two million bricks), miles of post and rail, follies, farms, stud farm, a popular entertainment heath, woods, river, feeders, weirs, three churches, a brace of villages, two pubs and an hotel, have I forgotten any-thing? – I admired Walther Darré. The stud was organised according to his principles; a tribute, yes, but more pertinently because there was no better route to take to equine perfection. He had been on the ball about racial purity, the fairness of enslaving of the lesser breeds to save them from themselves, mankind's insol-uble bond with place or soil ('a citizen of the world is a citizen of nowhere'), the porker's importance as the indication of a settled peasantry, the superiority of Nordic blood, which has different chromosomes from inferior blood and is a more majestic shade of red hinting at blue, the necessity of respecting our earth which blesses us with fruit and cereal, and above all the primacy of super-lative stock, good breeding.

For reasons which are to be found in the miz-maze of NSDAP internal factionalism, Walter Schellenberg had it in for Darré. Per-sonal slight? Theoretical divergence? No, though he did consider (wrongly in my view) much of Darré's writing to be so much uto-pian kidney pee. Disparaging Darré by association was a means by which Schellenberg ingratiated himself with Heydrich and so with Himmler, who was always keen to have his dim view of Darré's administrative abilities and judgement confirmed. Darré would even-tually be relieved of the Ministry of Agriculture in 1942.

Schellenberg's inclusion of Carrodus in Sonderfahndungsliste GB was merely a tiny nail in the coffin of Darré's career.

I kept my counsel. Who was I to criticise a dying man's joyous memory of vindictiveness, of a back well-stabbed, of the quiet treachery he specialised in? That won't have been the way he saw it.

★

It must be recalled that Schellenberg was a spy of the highest order. Knowing about people, knowing more about people than they know themselves, their foibles, their secrets, their covert mores, was his vocation.

He knew a great deal about Darré. He was rootless and his writing was an extreme reaction to that rootlessness: Argentinian childhood, worldly decadent parents, didn't set foot in Germany till he was twelve. Spoke several languages in tortured accents. As cosmopolitan as a Jew. Even his name was unsettled. Walther, Walter, Richard, Ricardo. A difficult pupil who moved from one school to another. Sent at the age of sixteen, from the Hölderlin Gymnasium in Heidelberg, as an exchange pupil to King's College School, Wimbledon, where he spent the academic year 1911–12.

The school was a common as cruet establishment whose subsequent pupils included that vulgar little spieler William Joyce: unlike Darré, very much the wrong sort of National Socialist. It had been founded a good two and a half centuries after Shrewsbury. It had one boarding house. The housemaster was the science teacher Frederick Carrodus, by then in his forties, a keen eugenicist with rare practical experience of that science, its practices and its ethics. He enthused the lonely, idealistic, taciturn boy in the principles of creating a better world by better breeding. The pupil was hooked. The discipline was a revelation.

Like Mein Opa forty years previously he had found his vocation. He would probably not have found it in Germany where, in the years before the First World War, eugenics was widely regarded as potting-shed science.

He bookwormed in Carrodus's library: Francis Galton, Alfred Ploetz, Austin Freeman, Montague Crackanthorpe, A. F. Tredgold, Charles Davenport. Carrodus was an occasional contributor to *The Eugenics Review*. He took Darré to Eugenics Society meetings at Essex Hall off the blowsy sinful Strand which would be purged by the new discipline.

Darré questioned incessantly. Carrodus was relieved, for Ricardo (as he was then called) had no other interests. He considered his fellow pupils to be frivolous, intellectually incurious and morally supine. He hated team games . . . he politely informed his masters that their teaching of history and geography was chauvinistic and boastfully imperialistic . . . he complained that the food was disgusting.

At the age of thirteen he had renounced Christianity in favour of paganism yet was compelled to attend chapel every day. He did not kneel or sing or join in responses. Carrodus, a lifelong dabbler in many confessions, many denominations (Theosophy, Anthroposophy, Sufism, the Ark of the Redemption in Splendour, Karaism, the Old Catholic Church, the altar of Revived Dominion), had at that time returned to Chemical Transubstantivism and was trying to realise an accommodation between his faith and science.

What he believed back then was that Christianity sanctioned eugenic intervention. No conflict. Those who were sterilised were denied the sacrament of communion because they had deserved to be sterilised. 'He that is wounded in the stones, or hath his privy member cut off, shall not enter the congregation of the Lord.'[28] And while man could never make heaven on earth – to contemplate it was a sin of presumption – he could bring earth closer to heaven by shaping and controlling those who trod it and tilled it. Darré was impressed by Carrodus's recollections of agrarian Malpasfang's devices: the small, low-geared tractors for sloping paths and steep fields; the methane gas plants; the roto-tillers; the use of dwarf rooting stock.

Darré's only friend among his contemporaries was the similarly withdrawn, equally high-minded Gervase Fardell. They distinguished themselves by being ill at ease among their contemporaries and walking for hours along Wimbledon Common's frosty rides, through the bosky copses and around the ponds to the windmill. He wore a thick loden coat, a heavy scarf, gauntlets and a military cap. (Horrocks's encyclopaedic knowledge of the Common was presumably due to his having met some excitingly rough chums there.) Darré announced to Carrodus's wife Betty that he was the steward of perfect germ plasm. He presented Frederick Carrodus with a long list of cacogenic fellow pupils who should be sterilised before they could transmit their impairment. He was astonished that Carrodus should think this was a joke.

---

28 Deuteronomy 23:1. Stones are testicles. The French *valseuses* is more graphic but the authors of the King James Bible were either not apprised of the word or loath to use it.

A small girl skating on an apparently frozen pond fell through thin ice. He declined, despite the imploring screams of her mother, to help rescue her on the grounds that only the feeble-minded would skate without having checked the thickness of the ice.

Spurred on by Tredgold's proposal for a Law for the Prevention of Progeny with Hereditary Diseases, he said: 'Let this incident be a warning to you against irresponsible breeding.' That is not the conventional observation to make to a soaked, freezing, sobbing mother who has just hauled her shocked child from death's maw, but Darré put truth before tact. Chapeau!

In the summer of 1919, having learnt from Frederick Carrodus of his friend's death near Cambrai six weeks before the end of the war, Darré wrote to the parents of Captain Gervase Fardell of the King's Royal Rifles. A letter of condolence turned into a sermon. He rightly blamed the war which had cost the life of Gervase (and his two brothers) on a dispute between racial inferiors unworthy of life. The Slav problem is soluble: it demands a firm hand on the tiller and the toughness to shun compassion.

Never again must our two nations pit themselves against each other in so deadly a manner.

Again: chapeau! (This one with a mischievous feather in it!)

A tiny nail in the coffin of Darré's career . . . but, let us say, the nail that split the plank.

In time-honoured, haven't-I-done-well manner Darré sent his old teacher a signed copy of *Das Bauerntum als Lebensquell der nordischen Rasse* when it was published in 1928. It worried Carrodus. Its sequel in 1930 was *Neuadel aus Blut und Boden*.[29] It too distressed him. And it positively alarmed him when less than three years later Darré ascended from mere ideologue of discrimination to Minister of Food and Agriculture and Head of the SS's Race and Resettlement Office. By then he was already initiating his plans, his people clearances. Compulsory sterilisation was effected according to heredity and race and on medical grounds.

---

29 *The Peasantry as Life Source of the Nordic Race* (Berlin, 1928) and *A New Nobility of Blood and Soil* (Berlin, 1930).

Well, that all sounds tickety-boo to me. Don't let the blighters spread.

But Carrodus was obviously a bit of an old woman. He felt responsible. Darré's sudden ubiquity grated: 'blood and soil' [*sic*] and 'lebensquell' (not translated) were welcome additions to the English language. It all exhumed the guilt of his association with Malpasfang which he had buried years before. It leapt out of the grave with blood-red eyes and dental caries! It gnawed at him no end. He had transmitted his contaminated past to his former pupil who was, by the most extreme chance, now able to initiate the particularly bad dreams which he had disowned in shame (unwarranted, I'd say).

He couldn't bear to think about it. So he did what anyone else would do in such circumstances.

He prayed.

Then he wrote an article. An old man's mea culpa disowning his foolish preoccupation with eugenics even though the eugenics he had toyed with expounded schemes of universal benefit. Shades of Jervoise Vanier: he was, for example, so confident in the advances of medical research that he was sure the day would come where a diseased brain or injured limb or exhausted organ, any body part, would be replaced by a new artificial one or by a transgenic transplant.

He regretted what he called his 'initiatory tutelage' of Darré. But his pupil – of more than two decades previously, he insisted – had taken a wrong turning, had perverted his lessons.

The Eugenics Review, internally riven and far from unanimous in its approach to the NSDAP's Law for the Suppression of Offspring Diseased by Inheritance, refused to publish the article. But *Reynold's News* did publish it.

In Berlin the Sicherheitsdienst was monitoring British reaction to that law. What the eagle-eyed young Schellenberg (thinking cap on!) noted was not this pernickety (kleinbürgerlich) old schoolteacher's indignant misgivings, nor his equation of Darré's theory with an incitement to genocide, but the brute fact that Darré had besmirched the NSDAP by making policy with foundations in, of all places, a London suburb associated with the frivolities of lawn tennis, a game played exclusively by lavenders such as Gottfried von Cramm, a loser. He lost three successive Wimbledon finals: a betrayal of the Reich.

Darré's grand plan for strengthening the race by firm but fair weeding and deadheading (as one might a potentially gorgeous flower-bed gone to seed) was simply an exaggeration of Carrodus's fantasies: with the feeble-minded there really isn't much difference between compulsory and voluntary.

Essentially a plagiarism, then. His self-aggrandising schemes turned out not to be magical virgin births — partheno what's it — but, Schellenberg suspected, stolen. Worse still, he hadn't stolen cunningly. Schellenberg instructed an Ahnenerbe scholar, a specialist in ancient history, to investigate. Darré's texts were littered with thefts from English common law and mythology: entailment of property, propagation of native trees, the Danelaw. Discredited early nineteenth-century, 'romantic' accounts of Cimbrian agriculture in Lindsey, the northern trithing of Lincolnshire, provided the model for Nordic settlements which would endure a millennium. Their godlike inhabitants would routinely live to the age of two hundred years on a diet tied to the earth of their particular soil: estuarial grasses, seaweed, samphire, fermented mare's milk, honey, barley, berries, roots, pork fat, salted pork, salted marsh fish, salted beached whales. Me, I've made jolly near a hundred without all this do this do that.

Misfortune is randomly dispensed. Roll of the dice, a divot, a wonky cobble, the viper in a hollow stump. And so on. My lack of progeny is not, I repeat, a misfortune. No. It is a matter of choice — though, as I am often tiresomely reminded, it's never too late. It is: I have smelled Milton steriliser. Did I fear that my produce, if that's the word, could not live up to its forebears? No.

The very opposite indeed. I feared it might outdo them, might be a creature whom the regressive shades of Shadoxhursts would not smile upon because they had been bettered. It might have matched the matchless. It might have cast a shadow that quashed theirs — and my own.

Then again, it might not.

My genetic legacy, non-legacy, failing to pass on the seed baton, is a paltry matter, unworthy of airing beside the grander baton of idealism, of militating for our race's rights, of hymning loud and clear the immaculacy of monoculturalism, of proclaiming without favour the hierarchy of civilisations and nations, sleuthing out the polyester and the back to front caps (both signs of the workshy), the bad blood and the stench of the cannibal cauldron.

We should not be disheartened by the present. How long is the present the present for?

There – it's gone.

Did the NSDAP fail? Far from it. The Vicomtesse was wrong. It had a death wish that was granted. It will rise again. It will die again. The cycle is written. The eternal returns. While it is waiting to return it sharpens up. Must do better next time – for its efforts are eclipsed in numbers by the Black Death, Spanish flu, countless pandemics. It will spread plague again. But not so selectively. It will purify with greater vigour and less discrimination: the obese – how about them? – the myopic, the left-handed, the loincloths, the narcolepts. There is any number of non-contributors, freeloaders gulping the air of the deserving, eating the planet barren. Apocalypse renews itself, it gatecrashes complacency like a satyr in a convent. (Whoops! That simile doesn't hit the spot. We all know that Carmelites just long for one draggin' on the floor!)

Did the Malpasfang Experiment fail? Again only in the short term, in the years that are a few seconds in our old planet's life. And even then . . .

This progress is no failure: the torch that illumines is lit by Jervoise Vanier and Mein Opa, passed flaming to Fred Carrodus, thence to the student Ricardo Darré and on to Reichsminister Richard Walther Darré who forged the central tenets of the regime without end. This is not failure. This is exoneration of Malpasfang, a justification, as though one were needed, of its brave existence and revolutionary ambition.

Nor is the Marcher Hound which became the Mordhund a failure of canine breeding. It is, throughout Europe, prized by persons of discernment – Patek Philippe wearers, collectors of vintage Bugattis, Mallet-Stevens houses, Ledesma glass and Max Roof's early collages.

Vogue's notorious Animal Issue (October 1981), otherwise devoted to starved models swathed in dead furs, dead leather and dead meat, touted the Mordhund as 'a vibey New Romantic, the must-have poochypoo of the now moment'. Its proud genealogy includes parents, grandparents and great-grandparents who worked at the Experimental Agrarian Research Colonies established throughout the Reich by the Reichsführer SS Heinrich Himmler and Reichsminister für Ernährung und Landwirtschaft Walther Darré. The lie of victor's truth that tells us all what we have heard a thousand times is just that, a lie.

Jervoise Vanier's hunch was correct. May Brasier, Mortimer Glyde's Demeter, went back to work in Crewe.

'My great-gramp used to talk about her. Folks weren't so judgemental in them days:

'Quiet as a mouse, no choice I suppose you'd say, lovely mite, loved her Malmsey and her scratchings, her tots of laudanum from a flask what a geneleman admirer give her. Never no trouble. Sat by the fireplace, helpful with the tender and the fireguard. Got every last stone out of the scuttle. We knew her game but we pretended not to. You'd hardly notice: it was just gestures like, a raised eyebrow, a finger on the lips. Some chap at the bar. Discreet. Of course always did her business elsewhere. Albeit in cold weather in the tun room for the quick stuff. Not sure where she went for the other. We was sorry for her. All the plagues of Egypt had been visited on her. She were saint-like. But, but, but . . . there's no saint in god's dominion can resist a plague like Axel Vernensen. There is bad lots and then there is real bad lots and then there's Axel Vernensen. Protector! Protector . . . Lord High Protector of My May he called himself – Lor High, that's from history isn't it? He were a rodent. Never trust a man who's always ready with a smile. After he took her away we never saw her again. When the tall fella come looking for her she were long gone.'

The 'tall fella' was Glyde. Glyde in love. Glyde on black Nigredo clopping ill-lit streets of infamy where in every sulphurous doorway half-hid a shadow shivering in the drizzle hoping and not hoping to sell her love; to sell it so many times day and night she could never count the times, never count the ways. However many they were, they were never enough for Axel Vernensen.

Mortimer Glyde had ridden from Malpasfang to Crewe. The Autolycus of the Open Road was on the open road again. After three barren nights in Crewe he decided to move on. A gingerbearded man with a monkey in velvet advised him that Axel Vernensen was rumoured to have come from New York, from Galveston, from Antwerp, from Bremen, from Leith, from Hull, from Gothenburg, from every port that ever there was.

By day Doctor Glyde sold potions door to door. At Manchester he took cheap lodgings in Ancoats. Woe to the bloody city! It is all full of lies and robbery. He loathed the stench of industry, of coke burning, of tripe blanching and glue bones boiling, of cotton's particulates, of slimy gennels, of cholera seeping from the cracks in the mortar . . . He was a nomad, independent of population statistics.

By night he prayed he might find her, then he set out to explore the streets nearby, a black silk scarf tied around his face against the swirling vapours that would rot his lungs. He trod and retrod Cupid's Alley. The joyless filles de joie got used to him. They trusted him to the point of answering his question, his one question. But none of them knew May Brasier and Axel Vernensen. Even had this couple (that configuration infuriated him) been using different names it is unlikely that they'd have been forgotten. They tend to stand out: a deaf and dumb woman accompanied by a toothy dandy Apache in checked finery, bearing scars and a lordly knuckleduster.

Nigredo's profile on a former whaler from Birkenhead to Liverpool was noted by so many people it became a powerful part of those cities' collective memory. So powerful that, quarter of a century later, Tolisso Wolf made a painting of it. The horse looked proud. Glyde was never to know that it would be so commemorated.

In Liverpool's dark stews the mounted Glyde, ready with his sabre, frightened the brazen lewd shadows in the jiggers around Nelson Street. They all shook their head. He did not doubt their honesty and Irish ignorance any more than he doubted their true faith in whatever superstitions might be drawn from peat and poteen along with inner and outer fuel and leathery ghosts. He kept on seeing her. But it never was her. In the corner of his eye a figure darted across Epworth Street to The Derby Arms. He hurried. He strode into the bad air of that bevelled-glass gin palace. He frantically looked around him. Oh! What rotten luck. This time she had turned into a specimen crone, cackling in a booth, half her jaw eaten away.

He feared he would never find her. What if she and Axel Vernensen had got on a boat? To who knows where. To Nova Scotia, to La Coruña, to Shanghai! Shanghai . . . China. He tried to hurry but Nigredo did not want to be ridden. The horse's head bobbed up alarmingly. So they walked together to the blocks he had heard of near Pitt Street where an appetite weaned on laudanum could adapt to kicking the gong in rooms frequented by the yellow peril – pigtails, tars, moochers, gamblers playing go. Ah Sing, Low Chung, Kwong Shanglung: groceries, barbers, laundries, cafés. Despite their coarseness, despite their smelling like mutton fat, white people were welcome in the houses of assignation, even fawned on for they pay nice wad for pipe and bounce. The buildings were terraced, shabby. Their windows had blinds rather than curtains. The more girls the owners controlled, the more pipes they sold, the more gold teeth they greeted the world with.

Their smiles were generous. They generously offered Doctor Glyde opium and women and children at what they claimed was a competitive rate. Did they really not understand what he was asking them for? Zhang Jike spoke to Chen Longcan who spoke to Buster Wang and Liqin Rao. It wasn't a matter of language. They spoke Scouse as well as they spoke Cantonese – but they didn't understand, couldn't understand, that he wanted a particular woman not just any woman (or child). All European whores look the same. It was a problem of custom and mores. They all sat at a table covered in American cloth decorated with good luck ideograms. From San Francisco, Buster Wang said proudly. They toasted each other in Green Chartreuse.

And there his quest might have ended had it not been for Nigredo's lameness. The horse had in the past suffered Lugg's Burn, an inflammation of the hoof which in its early stages could be relieved by ice baths, local anaesthetic (cocaine) and reshoeing. He asked, not expecting an answer, if they knew of a horse doctor.

May Brasier, no. A good horse doctor, yes. Their immediacy and unanimity were startling!

Doctor Seamus Penpraze at Grassendale Dreary End, he's your man, tiptop man. All restaurants here buy lots of meat from him, loads, all sorts of meat. Very good meat – the best, tiptop. They patted Nigredo's flank covetously.

They walked to Grassendale Dreary End in thin rain. The squawking Punch and Judy beside a park's gates had an audience of three hatless young men. They passed by aldermanic mansions with multiple hipped gables, the homes no doubt of the Vaniers' junior partners, a jerky coughing car, dog carts and dobbin carts, the vestiges of old villages with lychgates and greens swallowed by the march of bricks and enamel signs, half-built terraces of houses in fields where stooped starving figures gouged the mud for root crops with callused hands. He recalled a painting he couldn't name. A group of dame-school children gaped in awe at the sight of Nigredo. They were dressed in brown smocks and linked to each other by a cord wound around each of them whose end was held by the crippled dame herself. They walked in Indian file singing 'Baa Baa Black Sheep' with the dame attempting an arthritic jump on 'one for the dame' in memory of the days when she could dance like her charges. It almost brought a smile to Glyde's face. Almost. There was a long road with a tram track in its middle, a group of poplars turned into the pinnacles of a church tower, another church was an inflated toy castle with a clock surrounded by petals, a barrel-scraping rose window. A lavish unseasonal cricket pavilion (more hipped gables) was deserted, the pitch in front of it succulent as a water meadow.

As I've said, there's an old saw from my childhood when they were still common enough: A crocus is seldom an advertisement for his wares. Doctor Seamus Penpraze was no exception. He and Glyde recognised their professional sodality. When Penpraze winked, his left eye disappeared into his skull. He was monstrously fat. His leather apron was a bulging mortuary.

No, no, not Lugg's Burn. He diagnosed nothing graver than a displaced nail caused by poor workmanship. Not a farrier of quality, clear for all to see, not a skilled artisan. Shoddily shod you might say. Pains me to see such lack of craft by a so-called farrier.

Words would be had with Peterkin The Smith.

Penpraze directed Glyde to his near neighbour the farrier Swifty Natterjack, so named because he could shoe a horse in less than twenty minutes – hot shoe in thirty-five – and because he never stopped talking: any audience would do. His long low smithy stood on an unmetalled puddled road beside a farmhouse with plants growing from the holed roof and from the opaque broken windows. The winter before last's compressed liver-brown leaves buttressed it. Across the road was a newish villa, all Accrington bloods and black paint, fancy balconies and steep crested roofs. Glyde watched him prattle without cease; he was evidently saying something about the villa but whatever it was was inaudible. The anvil shut out his voice and nearby railway engines roaring, clanking, whistling shut out the anvil.

It was during a brief noiseless interlude that he paid Swifty. He heard a man's shrill laughter and the teeth-grind shriek of an ill-oiled gate. He turned out of curiosity and looked across the road. He saw a couple of lovers hugging as they hurried between the villa's gate piers and down the road. Recognition came slowly. They resolved themselves before his astonished eyes. He could not believe it. There was May Brasier. The man whose hand she was holding must be Axel Vernensen. Her expression was doting, glowing. He told Swifty to keep the change, a lifetime first. He resaddled Nigredo with clumsy haste and set off in pursuit. He was obstructed by two carts unloading bricks. A hod-carrier shrugged at him. A tranter reluctantly moved his vehicle, staring at Glyde malevolently. Glyde could see them approaching a girder bridge across the railway.

Tally-ho! The great stallion responded with a bellow and galloped up. As he drew close by them Glyde shouted at them to stop. Ordered them. Axel Vernensen turned first. He had no idea who this man was addressing them. May Brasier followed his gaze. As soon as she saw the unmistakable figure of Glyde she grasped her man's dove-grey sleeve and ran with the speed of panic. As Glyde eased alongside them Vernensen shook off May Brasier's hand. He lunged at Glyde high above him with his souvenir of the Bowery, a spiked knuckle-duster. The horse teetered, Glyde could not remove his boot from the stirrup to kick out. Vernensen's next blow was to the horse's breast. The spikes broke the skin, drew beads of blood. The horse started and near slipped on the rain-smeared setts.

Glyde drew his sabre. Although off balance he swung it mighty powerful. It proved to be a perfect angled slice, a sheer horizontal slice, extending from the forehead back beyond the ears at which point it gets jolly messy and the more squeamish among you should look away while the white labyrinth that held Vernensen's deductive powers, sorrow, reasoning, imaginings, hurt, shame, dream of legitimacy and much else besides uncoils into a state of eternal forgetfulness: bonce intestines spill out.

Silently keening in the drizzle and smoke, May Brasier half lay, half knelt on the gleaming setts, holding Axel Vernensen in her arms, oscillating rhythmically as though that movement might put a pulse in him. Her hands were smeared with blood and grit, bone shards and warm brain tissue. Steam from a heavy belching train below stung Nigredo's eyes. He reared and circled and screeched a whinny. His shoes shrieked on the stones. A group of rickety toothless guttersnipes gaped: such excitement! Glyde controlled his mount, he was impassive. Feral cats – tigers who haven't made the grade – fought to drink from the puddle of blood. They ripped notches out of each other's ears, tore each other's fur. Glyde sheathed his sabre, dismounted and marched clackingly towards this mockery of a pietà. He stood over her. She looked up at him in her pain and fury as if to say how could you, do you see what you've done, what you've done to him, what you've done to me, what you have done to my life as well as his? All this inferred, for in his contempt for his victim he misread her contempt for him.

He stretched out a hand to her. It was obvious to him that she would follow him, be with him wherever he would go, for evermore. She looked at the proffered hand incredulously. Her face crumpled. She turned away from Glyde and hugged the limp body in her lap. She scrambled with it to put herself beyond Glyde's reach. He was not deterred. He marched with her, his very proximity was a threat. She dragged what had been Axel Vernensen towards anywhere, she didn't know where, towards somewhere the other side of the bridge, towards the relentlessly repetitive streets of brick and cardinal red doorsteps, terracotta and shining slate. She jerked with sobs. She struck out at Glyde. Masked like death by his black silk scarf, he tried to grasp the maiden, greedily, lasciviously. He tried to calm her. He wanted to lock her in dependence. She shrugged him off, contorted with tears, snuffling, wincing at his touch.

A further blast of steam enveloped them. She stood up – and before Glyde could impede her, she 'blundered but nimbly' (that's what they said) to the bridge's parapetal flange and with a gay spring leapt onto it, balancing just so. She stood for . . . how long? Immeasurable. The scene freezes here.

For the first and last time in her life she spoke. Her words were: 'I go.'

Then – slowly, slowly, the victor smiling – she released herself into the chasm of the railway beneath, into eternal anaesthesia. Glyde's head veins stung. The pack of children dwindled. The cats who'd had their fill of blood and brains went in search of further prey.

Alone on the bridge with Vernensen's body he stared at where she had been and no longer was.

Whither thou goest I will go, and where thou lodgest I will lodge.

The Devil's Crocus, the Autolycus of the Open Road died by his own hand. He would look as dead in death as he had in life.

Two weeks after Glyde had murdered Axel Vernensen, Jezzard Dogg reported to him that a posse of rozzers was in the district searching for him, asking how to get to Malpasfang.

'I know. A goose walked on my grave. Should you see them I shall be below the Tree of Tyre,' said Glyde.

He sat on his leaf-dappled mount beneath the tree.

Where is the life that late I led? Oh where has all my past life gone to?

He yelled: 'Go!'

On that word Nigredo sprinted his best as he always did. He sprinted now without his master up. His master dropped into the void where the horse had been. Before you can say Jack Robinson death came crisp and snappy to embrace him. That's what happens when you string yourself up. Glyde was suspended from a stout bough, neatly noosed, cracked boots floating twelve hands above the dusty needles around the Tree of Tyre. A rope well measured.

Where thou diest I will die, and there will I be buried.

Weep ye not for the dead, neither bemoan him.

But weep sore for him that goeth away: for he shall return no more, not seeth his native country.

Nigredo was gone; he galloped through dark forest naves of oaks and birches and bracken so high that he was the wind. He disappeared into a further life of infinite possibilities: he might be transformed into the most lustrous twinkling star, he might father a quack dentist or a vagabond woodcarver, he might map uncharted fells and valleys. His mane might be dyed and his eyes put out. He might be butchered for chop suey.

May Brasier's body was found five days later beside the railway track that serves Maenofferen quarry at Blaenau. It was black with slate dust, decomposing.

May Brasier's body was exhumed sixty years later by peat cutters at Risley Moss beside the Warrington to Manchester line. It was brown, leathery, largely intact.

The posse of peelers had been mustered far away in Liverpool. They had only vaguely heard of the Vanier family's Malpasfang Lodge, had not really believed the tales about it woven with an ever more slanderous stitch. They were, then, flabbergasted by what they found. They were shocked and repulsed. These poor innocent peelers were sensitive peelers. Although deprived of their quarry they consoled themselves investigating the rummest of houses, the strangest of inhabitants and most sinister of parks to puzzle over. They found a shambles, Offa's abattoir, the zoo at Golgotha. Ponies were all bone and eyes of terror. They stood in gore, shit, grease to their fetlocks. An unidentifiable trampled beast's intestines spilled from its belly and split. Oh pestilence, oh putrefaction. Liquid manure seeped from cracked pipes to form merrily bubbling puddles. Carcasses sprawled in condemned parterres. The miasmic stench scraped mucous membrane. All smell is disease. Surprise, surprise: oggie diggers hadn't done their job properly: ribcages of beasts rose out of insufficiently deep graves, poked through the turf. It looked like self-exhumation in an attempt to recapture life. They had never seen vultures at work before, daintily plunging their heads into viscera and bowel. Nor had they seen bustards strutting through crops. Wasps nested in a panther's skull. Raptors and rodents had a high old time! Pale women wandered drugged and expressionless in collapsed greenhouses scavenging for rotting fruit under myco-fogged cloches. Their stalled brains received no message of pain from their shoeless bleeding feet. The Vanier Arms opened during proscribed hours. Had it a magistrate's licence?

They pondered the charges that might be brought. Harbouring a man charged with homicide? Cruelty to animals? Proxenetism? Jervoise Vanier was described in the initial police report as disrespectful. The gentleman 'pulled rank'. Supercilious, uncooperative, almost threatening. He said that he would arrange Glyde's burial. The rozzers were incredulous having seen the botched burials that littered the park. Fair sickening. Jervoise scorned their insistence that there had to be a post-mortem: what did they think had happened?

Was the horse guilty of hanging its master? Arrest Nigredo?

When instructed that his proposal to arrange the funeral was out of the question Jervoise asked whether the Liverpool constabulary was going to petition the Treasury Solicitor to bring Glyde to posthumous trial. He told them to leave. They had no warrant to explore his estate at will. They were trespassing. Nonetheless they bivouacked nearby on Throstle Common while awaiting orders from Liverpool. Jervoise appeared to them to consider himself above the law. Damned right, he was. Not least because the rozzers and, subsequently, several officers of the RSPCA were, as they say, not insensitive, at a sub-rational level, to the penumbra of an historic name.

A name, moreover, attached to what was still one of the greatest fortunes in the land. (It's a cross we superior types must bear.) And a name that could drop other names, indeed hurl them, the names of the Lancastrian judiciary, of past and present Lords Lieutenant, of magnates and tycoons, of statesmen and ministers, of dukes and princes, the heir to the throne, the crowned heads of Europe . . . A name.

Vanier is a great name.

Shorthand for unimaginable wealth, great power, the pinnacle of society, virtuous charity, opposition to slavery, child labour and support of the ten-hour movement, funding workers' housing, roads, bridges, locks, patronage of churches (Anglican, Methodist, Unitarian), of schools, mechanics institutes and galleries. A portfolio of Christian righteousness not to be undone by one bearer of that name.

Ah! Jervoise and his youthful exuberance! His high spirits, his odd peccadillos. It was a long-extended youth. He was, though he was loath to admit it to himself, a remittance man, a dependant.

Unlike Mein Opa's vision his was tainted with dilettantism, an amateur levity, improvised scholarship and a cradle taste for religious mystery. That somehow made it just about excusable to his family, who feared their great name would become tarnished. Tarnish endures through generations. That was their concern, not the extravagant sums spent on chimerical wheezes. They had had enough of Mein Opa's alleged depravity, of the horizontale Eden's perverse influence, of quack doctors, of press reports, of police investigations, of paying detectives to listen to local nosey parkers, of rumour rolling like a black cloud that will swart the name forevermore.

They were not aristocrats. Their mores and ethics were plum borgy. Jervoise soon readopted them. He joined the family business.

He married into what I've heard called, in all seriousness, 'Birkenhead's mercantile quality' – can you imagine! He sired four sons, lived in Hamilton Square grandeur, built a house in the arts and crafts style near Tarporley: both the Isle of Man and Snowdon were distantly visible. Still devoted to photography, he abandoned monochrome tintype teratological studies in favour of landscape. He would be the first user in Britain of the Lumière Company's Autochrome process. He remained an enthusiastic motorist who owned a Rolls-Royce Silver Cloud, a Mercedes Simplex, a Lanchester Thirty-Eight and a Chadbon Mallows Landau. He would drive with his Gandolfi camera in every direction save south where Malpasfang lay, a rotting monument to his former self which, from his pulpit, he now reckoned to have been rotting too.

Nonetheless he didn't make a clean break with that impetuous youthfulness which had extended into middle age. He clung to his interest in the betterment of the race. Purely intellectual, no experiments. His theoretical position was not impaired by his newfound Christian faith. Like slavery it was indeed compatible with that faith. He believed that the Bible explicitly condoned the eugenic urge.

'Be ye therefore perfect, even as your Father which is in heaven is perfect.'

It is regrettable but necessary to prohibit the imperfect and the feeble-brained from taking communion. Those who have been sterilised in order to prevent them passing on their infirmity are excommunicated because they are unable to fulfil their duty to reproduce: something of a double-bind for our soft in the bonce brethren. It's pudding common to believe that Christian ethics teach the duty of preserving and multiplying life at all hazards.

He instructed his sons in the new tradition of nobility. The youngest was Roddie. Like his father he escaped the clutches of family for a life of sexual and psychotropic abandon. Like his father, but more swiftly, he returned. He came to accept that it was his fate and duty to desiccate himself as a paragon of modest Englishness and decent imperialism. He did not wish to find himself disinherited. His death in the service of king and country was his redemption, always a messy business.

Unlike Vanier, unlike Shadoxhurst, Phimister is not a great name save among apostasy watchers, devotees of minor ecclesiastical scandals, scholars of Anglican heresy, readers of the yellow press's lies.

And not having a name like Jervoise's, Mein Opa was 'cast out to the eye of obloquy's red storm' (Erskine Garn). Infamy searched for him. His curiosity, research and experiments had drawn prying attention, then moralistic indignation, then puritanical vilification. He was lambasted. Inhuman! Sacrilegious! Perverted! Satanic! Diabolic! Crimes against nature! The Mephitic Monster of Malpasfang! Perpetually expressing himself through his heavy gonads, humping the entire ark. Und so weiter.

He was smeared as scandalous. Press prigs and priest prigs prigged against him. He came to be regarded as a demonic figure. Friends who had enjoyed his risky hospitality cut him. He had a thin time of it. He might have been made of margarine. His notoriety caused him to be treated as a pariah. It became social suicide to frequent him. He learnt at first hand that neither nature nor history has had the desired effect of creating the brotherhood of man. Disgrace is a powerful force. He was forced to lead the life of a fugitive. Although he had committed no crime he fled this ingrate nation which he loved, whose stock he had worked tirelessly to improve with the seed of panthers and horses possessed of Go! He had pride in his race although it was wretched. His compatriots had no pride. That mob was like all mobs. It descended from the mob that called for Barabas to be freed.

Mein Opa was among the greatest men of his age. This not just family swank. His attempts to transplant the kidneys of a hare to a doxy's sprog suffering renal failure preceded those of Maurice Princeteau.

He wrote:

Let a woman be covered by a negro and give birth. Let her then be covered by a blond Nordic and give birth. The child of the second fertilisation will exhibit characteristic of the negro, to the point where the child may be indistinguishable from a wholly negro child. A pure blond Nordic child cannot be born to a mother who has been previously impregnated (or perhaps even penetrated) by a negro. Here then is a trithing of mongrelism. The child of each transcends the borders of race. It will, despite the social disadvantages and racialist prejudices it must face, be stronger and more intellectually capable than the mono-racial child. Thus the issue of human and stag cannot be but mighty in biomass and fertility.

A woman given shelter from city slums in Malpasfang's holy groves will fain acquire fresh characteristics of behaviour and mien. Natural selection proposes that organisms well adapted to their surroundings survive and reproduce, passing down those successful traits.

Yet our travails and field observations throughout fifteen years demonstrate conclusively that animals are wont to acquire adaptive traits according to their circumstance. They pass down those traits to their offspring who, transported to different surroundings, may lose those traits (because they are not needed) and acquire a fresh gamut of traits which they in turn will pass on. Thus each generation has the capacity to be a new version provided its habitat and climate are different from its predecessor. A generation will then have pronounced differences from its forebears and yet more from its forebears' forebears. It will not perhaps recognise the latter as forebears. That lack of recognition may be mutual. One generation's gods will be unacknowledged by the next. Mongrelism and miscegenation will make *métèques* of us all. Free of atavism, free of ancestral obfuscation, free of the burden which disguises itself as tradition. Blast purity! Damn immaculacy!

Nor was Blood a great name. Despite the ruffian Thomas Blood's derring-do, despite Bindon Blood's martial acumen, it was no support, it didn't spell entitlement, it's not a name like Shadoxhurst to which the etiquette of privilege and favour attaches, to which hats are doffed and curtsies made. Outside the corral of Malpasfang and its exclusive mores it possessed no cachet. Eden recalled the distant past when she was mere Edie in Shorsburye. Folks (as they were called) would remark on her surname. She wanted an upgrade to blue blood, or blueish; a ski, a van, a von or a de would be tickety-boo too.

Methinks she got what she wanted.

This is what I recall of my various chinwags with the Vicomtesse in the spring of 1952. I always addressed her thus. Never Eden.

I made a few notes in the small hours. Most turn out to have been complaints about the unbearable stuffiness of 122 boulevard Lannes and observations, pretty damned acute some of them, about the peculiarity of the household.

There was a perpetually smiling cleaner Georgie whose work was never done. Tonio the chef's contorted face was reflected in the contorting foxed mirrors Georgie spread her hands against while he was buggering her. The handsome Serge, the Majordomo, wore a tailcoat, knee-length underpants, socks with garters, buckled shoes, a waxed moustache. No trousers, shirt or waistcoat. The Vicomtesse appeared not to notice. To escape the airlessness I usually persuaded her to lunch at La Fontaine de Mars, l'Auberge Bressane beside Les Invalides, Comme à Mutzig (for old times' sake) or the terrace at Chez Maître Didier where, years later, the meddlesome Louis Ghislain would be despatched.

Now, nowadays it's my old memory box that isn't quite what it was . . . but let's not plead incapability. She certainly didn't.

La Vicomtesse Riquetti de Besançon

I left them. They had made me what I am . . . ah . . . what I was. I admit it. Without them – no me. They educated me. There would have been no Eden Blood no Eden Blood . . . I was their creation. But I left them. I had to leave them.

J'ai du faire lâcher prise . . . They were going mad . . . We had all acted mad for years but we were not mad. Then they became mad. Why did they become mad? We had created our own world, our order, an ethical system . . . And then – there was nothing there was nothing . . . It slipped away . . . crumbled before our very eyes . . . like . . . oh it all fades . . . a landslip, that's it – irreversible. They fell out of love with each other. I fell out of love with them . . .

It used to be amusing to wonder what animal I was going to wake up beside . . . a lemur . . . a Connemara marten . . . tiger cub . . . they grow up so quickly tiger cubs . . .

I wonder: is this a genuine memory? Were big cats with poor hygiene really in our bed?

Marcus grew a lush pelt, his tusks were coming along, and the germ of tines . . . love makes you do such things . . . then one day . . . pshaw . . . it feels like it's old hat . . . you grow out of it . . . this life's not going to last forever . . . and you know my dear . . . a girl has to eat . . .

I remember walking with Marcus one afternoon . . . up to . . . we walked up to . . . nominal aphasia it's called . . . a rite of dotage . . . oh my dear . . . infuriating that *that* comes so readily . . . nominal bloody aphasia . . . my incapacity mocking me while I forget so much . . . yes yes it was Stants Wood . . . Stants Wood! I shouldn't dare say that word *remember* should I . . .

I told him how much I thought it had gone to pieces . . . we were nothing more than Jervoise's courtiers . . . employees, to be bald about it . . . that's what it had come to . . . it hurt him . . . he wouldn't admit it to himself . . . it was Jervoise who paid for everything . . . ah . . . Jervoise's trust rather . . . Jervoise's family . . . he was secretive about the trips he kept making . . . it was obvious to me . . . he was going to Liverpool . . . reaching some rapprochement with the family . . . powwows powwows . . . negotiating a way back to them . . . Marcus was . . . puh . . . dismissive when I told him . . . we didn't have 'in denial' two world wars ago . . . but that's what he was . . . in denial . . . he didn't grasp the situation . . . he didn't want to.

I left. Under cover of night . . . under cover of black cloud . . . that sounds right, yes? Yes . . . I rode on Madame Life The Third. I rode my mare into a new future . . . I inspire books . . . the film with the Lockwood woman . . . that could have been me . . . I had no idea where I was going . . . I have a taste for adventure . . . also I have a talent for adventure a talent for adventure . . . There is no fate decreed . . . No great plan. No map. There's only what you devise.

My rules my three rules:

One. Carpe diem. Two. Carry a firearm. Three. Subtract ten years from your age.

Destiny is what you will for yourself ness par.

I willed for myself.

The jewellery I carried with me was worth £20,000.[30] That's many gifts . . . I had many admirers among the visitors to Malpasfang . . . many admirers . . . I had lived by my charms. I never saw Jervoise Vanier again.

And Marcus . . . the next time I heard of Marcus was . . . you know I can't quite recall the year . . . I was drinking a lot . . . my darling Petit Loup was dying before my eyes . . . life was seeping from him . . . It was a long time since I had fled Malpasfang . . . I was dining in ooh ooh what was it called . . . that monk the monk . . . oh . . .

(*Le Jeune Pantagruel, I suggested. I had read about it in Mérand's Journal d'un Fainéant, which I was of course drawn to.*)

---

30 A century later it was worth 120 times that sum.

Of course . . . Le Jeune Pantagruel was delightfully vulgar . . . of an era . . . of an era . . . long since disappeared . . . erotic tableaux in marquetry . . . à la Japonais . . .

Our host was Matthias Schafer . . . the archaeologist . . . eminent racial typologist . . . a friend of my darling Petit Loup, indeed a recipient of his beneficent patronage . . . *our* beneficent patronage . . . excavations . . . they're costly enterprises . . . the measurement of heads has to be undertaken scientifically . . . as for exhumation . . . y'know why not just leave them there . . . why force them to tell tales from the grave?

Among the guests was Gertraud Dumpberg . . . immensely desirable despite her quite mountainous body because immensely rich . . . a Bavarian railway heiress . . . *the* Bavarian railway heiress . . . voracious, valetudinary, neurasthenic, cunning . . . she was known as 'the big top' . . . 'the bladder of lard' . . . 'the adipose dirigible' . . . she crammed food into her mouth with her hands . . . she belched . . . she slobbered . . . her reputation preceded her . . . this was the first of the two occasions on which I met her . . .

Matthias was one of her many suitors . . . her great fortune's suitors . . . he had been swooshing his liver clean at Bad Harzburg – y'know those fountains . . . mythological grotesques vomiting rusty water. Matthias could babble . . . but that evening he was fascinating.

His doctors prescribed hikes . . . he twice encountered a man who had been living wild in the caves of the Harz. He sprung through the bracken on all fours. He had long hair, a thorny crown en brosse . . . like he was suffering an electric shock. He was alarmingly furry . . . hardly clothed torso . . . appearance belied him: he turned out to be loquacious and charming. Polyglot . . . curious. He had immersed himself in the forest . . . taught himself quadrupedalism . . . his hands were gnarled . . . cross-hatched with grazes and abrasions like a carver's bench.

Matthias believed he was Welsh. Superstitious Harzburgers feared that he was an incarnation of The Savage Elk With Crown of Infinity Tines who had haunted Hooknose Mountain and had returned every time he was hunted down and feasted upon.

He claimed to enjoy 'sympathetic resonance' . . . he communed with the leathery bodies buried in the high peat bogs . . . millennia old . . . He said he could not hope for a happier fate after death than to be preserved like that. It was those bogs which coloured the spring water. He claimed to enjoy sympa . . .

Ah yes . . . he described the caves he inhabited . . . Piranesian geology: carceral caverns . . . places of punishment by starvation and darkness . . . the tombs of women and children. Cairns of shells of Ushant turtles . . . the bones of black eagles and aurochs . . . petrified claws of extinct amphibians . . . desiccated hair . . . Some of the caves were as big as exhibition halls . . . water sliding down every wall. Sculpting every wall over aeons . . . pleating rock . . . colouring it. I liked that 'pleating'.

Matthias Schafer believed The Welshman must have suffered some form of profound trauma . . .

He said little about himself . . . muttered about an experiment devoted to human perfection . . . he knew or knew of the Idyllic Brotherhood but wasn't interested in talk about it . . . Now he inhabited a world apart . . . he didn't know how long he'd been there for . . . he feared often that he was followed by a Hidebehind who whenever he turned to confront it would vanish or adapt its camouflage to make itself invisible . . . sometimes he was contemplative and unmoving . . . then he'd howl to the skies . . . he'd spend nights quizzing the stars, he'd spend nights watching badgers bury a cow carcass . . . he'd spend days in the mosses and bogs burrowing with his leathery hands . . . his sense of where to exhume was an extra sense. He hoped to exhume bodies: always tomorrow . . . always tomorrow.

He ate birds, bird's eggs, leaves, bark, berries, small rodents, acorns, larch, beechnuts, fungi, roots. He rode a mighty Brandenburger, unsaddled . . . a phrase by Schubert, a wild boneman. He bathed under cavernous waterfalls . . . he befriended lynxes and fought boars: a wound from a tusk would not heal . . . he was halt . . . he hunted with a bow taller than he was . . . a quiver of long arrows and a retiarius's net . . . his quarry was feral boys living in labyrinthine setts, leaving them only in hours of darkness.

There but for the grace of god went your unfortunate . . . The one who might be sacrificed . . . yes that's it, The Pathetic Mite Ned.

These diluters of the race were avatars of the feral famous: 'Victor' found in the Aveyron forests, Kaspar Hauser, the cupid-lipped wild boy 'Peter' hunted down – what sport! – only a hundred miles from the Harz in woods near Hamelin. Lucky fellow became a v tiresome pet at the first Georgian monarch's court (*in the days when a Shadoxhurst was Comptroller of Peculations or Physician-Surveyor of the Royal Gleet . . . something along those lines*).

The Welshman wanted mute quadruped boys to join him in the continuation of the experiment he had made 'at home' . . . the wrong sort wrong sort of feral boys, unsuitable or redundant, could pursue a career in a circus . . . or entertaining more privileged children . . . jumping out of cakes wearing Pierrot costumes and false ears . . . the criterion of suitability was not clear.

Jolly lucky to have such rewarding jobs in any case.

His quarry was feral boys who lived in labyrinthine setts, leaving them only in hours of darkness. He taught them about the great experiment in which he had participated. He told them tales round the campfire while they feasted on berries and leaves. More and more came to him as disciples, acolytes, anchorites, novices.

A rumour spread in Bad Harzburg and Goslar that back in Wales he had forced the children he captured to mate with sheep and blond-maned ponies.

He was himself hunted, to no avail. He disappeared with how did he put it . . . with a squadra, can that be right . . . with a squadra of boys rescued from their setts in the dark dark forest, from bogs and holes. Suckled by wolverines, suckled by wild cats and bears, some of them. He was accused of kidnapping. Preposterous. A sort of pied piper. Nonsense. Nonsense. Perhaps they had wanted to leave the wild? He believed in his duty to investigate them.

They were really guinea pigs . . .

My darling Petit Loup learnt later that the surviving boys have all forgotten their past . . . they don't know where they came from. Memory has to be learnt. Drink young from the waters of Lethe – and you'll remember nothing . . . Memory has to be developed by experience of separateness. It cannot be imparted by the other boys in the sett who themselves have no memory they have no memory . . . no memory . . . memory's a faculty passed from one generation to the next. If you haven't learnt to remember by the age of four or five

you never will. They never will. They never will, they live in a perpetual now . . .

(*You see: it's a question of memory . . . everything is memory . . . remember
knots in the corner of your handkerchief? . . . very sound if you can remember
why you made the knot . . . what it's meant to recall . . . more often than not
you can't . . . If I keep taking the pills . . . if I remember to take them . . .
then I can keep remembering word for word — more or less — some things the
Vicomtesse said that Matthias Schafer had said:*)

He led them to somewhere in the south — the land of cockayne . . .
where all was silk and money, milk and honey, milk and honey . . .
woad-blue seas lapping the shore, stone pines . . . They are mute,
illiterate. They live in an eternal present of crickets and eucalypti . . .
eternal present . . . the present is gone as soon as you utter the
word. Look at it. Then look left at the word which precedes it . . .
you are not looking back . . . you have left that present behind
you . . . nor are you in the future . . . you are in the latest
present . . .

A chill down my spine. My head was all over the place . . . spinning.
My once and past lover . . . my soldier. I could feel him — his spirit,
his sweat, his pelt. Marcus Phimister!

I was about to say I'm certain that I know this man.

Before I could, Gertraud shrieked: 'I want to buy him!'

She slapped the table with food-smothered hands. She grinned
loufoque as a looncoot:

'I'm going to buy this man.'

She looked around her . . . for affirmation of her whim . . . for
congratulation.

Talk withered on the vine. The table fell silent. The score of
chubby putti scrambling along the cornice cupped their hands to
their ears . . . what bizarrerie would come next?

She ignored the obvious astonishment, the napkins stuffed into
mouths to strangle the guffaws and titters . . . the splurts and giggles . . .
the rude corpsing . . . she didn't take a blind bit of notice.

'I need a noble savage. I have a vacancy . . . Where, Matthias, do I
find him? What' — and here she looked around the table as though

someone would know the answer – 'what does a noble savage cost . . . Can I . . . can I . . . afford one!' She could not stop laughing.

'Three grottoes but not a single hermit – what kind of woman am I?'

I resolved to say nothing . . . I had no independent what's the word . . . empirical . . . yes empirical proof that it was Marcus. And what was to be gained from admitting to knowledge of this man in front of my darling Petit Loup . . . shut your trap . . . as I often heard the girls at Malpasfang say . . . shut your trap and keep it trappist . . .

'Where is he . . . There hasn't been a real Kaltenborn Hermit since Timmy died . . . poor fellow was browned off with the strain of his calling . . . he dug a grave beneath a rusty old hopper . . . he filled the hopper with the earth . . . he lay in the grave . . . he had attached a rope to the hopper's funnel . . . he opened it . . . all the earth and stones he had dug poured over him . . . he probably choked before he was asphyxiated . . . a hermit's proud death . . . the correct death . . . an anchorite's initiation . . . courageous . . . Papa had him exhumed so that he could be buried in the cemetery but Father Lothar put his foot down . . . by no stretch of the imagination could it be called an accident . . . divine rules are divine rules . . . no suicides in conse-crated ground . . . so Timmy had to be reburied where he had died . . .

'Papa eventually gave up looking for a replacement . . . Noble sav-ages, primitives, living ornaments . . . he advertised everywhere . . . the only applicants were lunatics . . . amateurs . . . tyros . . . they were not prepared . . . it's a rigorous life . . . they had no vocation no previous experience . . . incapable of demonstrating their contem-plative soul. They simply weren't hermity enough.

'None of them lasted for more than a few days . . . one left after a single morning complaining of cold . . . If Papa gave them Horace to read they took him to heart . . . they learnt to be dissatisfied with their lot. If he gave them Juvenal they misunderstood . . . longed for the fleshpots . . .'

She realised that some sort of opportunity more than an oppor-tunity had presented itself . . . a revelation a coup de foudre . . . by proxy – can one say that? Coup de foudre by proxy . . . She became obsessed with finding The Welshman.

At the reluctant recommendation of the lawyer Röhrenbeck she hired a private detective agency, Enquêtes Thésée (Grumbach and Costello). Their motto was 'effective and discreet'. One can't really argue with that . . . True enough. They might have added outrageously expensive . . . But that was no deterrent to Gertraud . . . She fantasised repetitively fantasised repetitively . . . she would crush her hermit with her mighty weight . . . for weight is might and might is weight. She often described her adventures with the sturdier sort of artisan – woodcutters, tranters, farriers . . . in far distant cities where she was unknown . . . it was all gravy for the soul gravy for the soul . . . surely an indication of imbalance.

Enquêtes Thésée's wiles were taxed . . . peripatetic errancy peripatetic errancy . . . The Welshman who was Marcus Phimister who was the future Hermit of Kaltenborn (*aka distant future Mein Opa*) had been seen by many people . . . Month after month of false leads . . . they eventually got their man . . . south of Salamanca in the Sierra de la Peña de Francia . . . once again he subsisted in a cave.

He tended gaudily painted hives, collected chestnuts, stripped cork from oaks, ate hallucinogenic fungi, killed vipers to sell to smallholders for pig-feed: the ham is said to be the most succulent in Spain.

He was suspicious of Enquêtes Thésée's agents. They over-aspired to be gentlemen. They were tiresomely incorrect in their ambition: such short hair is a sign of deprivation . . . it should be worn only by the poor hauling sacks of stolen slag in le Borinage. All the more reason to refuse to accompany them until they arranged a transfer of 500 pesetas. This took two days to arrange, perhaps longer . . . Mein Opa spent the time lurching about Salamanca from tailor to bar to brothel and back. The agents forbade him getting a shave and a haircut . . . hermits do not have neat beards and partings. He demanded that the transfer be immediately cashed. All the way to unknown Ingolstadt he clutched to his chest the canvas bag containing the banknotes . . .

The carriages – so stuffy in those days . . . so itchy. Airless. So silly to complain when all around were guttersnipes succumbing to cold. If you opened the windows gusts of smuts rushed in. So silly . . .

The private detectives were banal. Their hackneyed conversation just too hackneyed . . . it made him wonder: had he made a big big booboo, allowing himself to be bribed back into the society of humans or whatever it was that he was approaching through recurrent landscapes, prairie, hill, mountain, prairies, hills, mountains. He yearned for the cave . . . in a way that he had never yearned for it when it was his home. Then he would recall the discomforts, the dangers . . .

There were changes, connections in places whose names he recalled through oblivion's fog, many dusty platforms, many smoky hours in frosted-windowed waiting rooms, many meals so rich that he suffered dyspepsia, a condition whose existence reminded him of dinners at Malpasfang in a distant life. He looked forward to reacquainting himself with surfeit. As the train groaned out of Bordeaux Saint Jean he vomited Armagnac and a Paris-Brest from a window: it was caught on the wind, a gift for a shivering donkey. In a trackside hangar outside Reims ragged children drove a treadmill which powered the saw which cut the stone which formed the base of a winged messenger ten metres tall: they breathed dust, he wanted to rescue them.

He watched enviously as a blond boy wearing a neck brace galloped a black stallion across the swaying Lorraine steppe, racing the train, waving, leaving a wake through the high grass and the pools that here and again flattened it. The train crossed the border near Conflans. He was home, again. The dark gothic bulk pitched precariously upon its hill brought back the lines:

> *At Metz cathedral I saw a murder*
> *A flash of blade, an eclipse of life.*

Where were they from? Verlaine? He had not read a book for years. On the other side of the Rhine was Karlsruhe. The river was definitive and blue.

12 April 1952

Dinner at Comme à Mutzig. Splendid Alsacien brasserie near place de la République. Hadn't then quite recovered from having been frequented during the occupation by higher echelons of the SS: tiptop chaps with tiptop taste: presskopf, such a fittingly named dish for patriots in their arduous business. Gestapo not welcome: most of them common as cruet jobbing plods. Not true believers. I had dined here with Hermann and Peter, Helmut and Hans: they knew the names of all the kings of France. I gave them little gifts in return for their attentions. More often I had dined with Walter Schellenberg. He had died a few days previously. It was me – not, as popular gossip has it, Coco Chanel – who paid for the funeral.

My condescension was magnificent to behold – so I am told.

What kind of woman marries her hermit?

Really! I ask you . . . A desperate woman . . . can't see a gold digger even when that gold digger is bucking astride her and she has been brought up to repel all gold diggers . . . even when the gold digger is near suffocated by – oh the relish with which I spoke! – near suffocated by her cascading terraces of limitless lard . . . lard . . . the hanging gardens of human suet.

'*She can't have been that fat.*'

She can . . . she was . . . Marcus was an insouciant gold digger . . . a gold digger despite himself . . . by rights should have been NBG at gold digging. Such passivity . . . he always had that germ within him. Too infected too infected by je m'en foutisme. Gold digging demands conviction . . . determination . . . the dissemblance of determination of course . . . qualities he quite lacked . . . y'know I sometimes wonder if he took into account his actions . . . perhaps the best way . . . to stumble blindly into the future with no expectations . . . Me, I always planned . . . it was easy for me when I was young and beautiful . . . I hooked the catch I sought . . . played it . . . netted it!

My darling Petit Loup never realised . . . never realised I had him in my sights . . . He never knew my age . . . would it have made any difference if he had?

The ambassador was such a sweetie. He sought little in return for a favourably dated passport. Abracadabra – a new me . . . just by turning the clock forward. I felt a tinge of shame . . . it was so banal after Malpasfang . . . that grandiosity . . . our sheer ambition. When one has spent years . . . years . . . trying to remake humanity that sort of ruse seemed tawdry, unholy.

I fear Marcus had lived as he did out of necessity . . . a common tramp a common tramp nothing more than a common tramp . . . he made the best of it dressing it up as noble savagery . . . he may even have deluded himself . . . Jervoise broke him . . . he didn't mean to . . . but he was careless . . . indifferent . . . and he had his own skin to save . . . god save Jervoise . . . probably not probably not . . . god didn't save the king even though he's daily implored to . . . that b awful anthem has no magic . . . it's no Marseillaise . . .

Marcus had no Jervoise to support him . . . nor had I . . . no Vanier gelt . . . no option . . . other than finding someone else to fund his debauchery . . . frightening position to be in for a man of his stature . . . and age his age . . . I used to mock him . . . what are you going to do when you lose your looks . . .

You know his father ended up in an almshouse for pauper heretics . . . an unholy rabble of competing blasphemers . . . your great-grandfather my dear . . . can you believe . . . an almshouse for pauper heretics . . . what rubbed salt in was the nuns. Nuns! It was administered by the Sisters of Saint Blaise . . . patron saint of the throat . . . and gamming of course. Gamming is such a blessing ness par . . . nature's contraceptive . . . sanctioned by the Vatican . . . by the emissions of cardinals down the ages . . . Nuns . . . they are *against* nature . . . absolutely against nature.

It was a terrible fate . . . one that Marcus would have never succumbed to . . . throwing himself at the mercy of thin-lipped wimples . . . hennins . . . he'd sooner have killed himself . . . it would have been demeaning for him to have to seek employment . . . beneath him . . . once a kept man . . . it has to be admitted – fifteen years of Malpasfang Lodge . . . no preparation for . . . the *pieties* of life . . . for mere existence . . . curtailed existence on the vulgo's terms . . . and believe me – the vulgo's day is upon us, the vulgo's day . . .

Gertraud expected a creature of nature . . . all aphorisms . . . all aphorisms and bardic wisdom . . . a creature so close to the origin of the world that he could only be an invention . . . a fantasy . . . Herder . . . Diderot . . .

The man the detectives delivered to Kaltenborn was a man worn down . . . by the life he had led . . . by life itself . . . a defeated man . . . a man starved of succour . . . a patient that craved dependence . . . he'd given up the fight . . . he wanted to seize the chance to be soft and scented . . . dowsed in Atkinson's, dressed in astrakhan and barathea . . . intoxicated by old sweet wines . . . sated with breast milk cheese and placenta fritters . . .

She had prepared for him as one might prepare for a baby . . . the least ruinous of the grottoes had been cleaned, given a brush-up . . . shipshape and Bristol fashion . . . bones . . . ram's bones and tusks . . . swine bones had been incorporated in the plaster . . . the walls had been oh what d'you call it . . . druidical runes . . . sgraffito . . . sgraffito'd . . . Hermit habit had been bought – camlet cloaks and the like . . . subfusc robes . . . a Bible . . . hourglasses . . . a tame deer tethered outside . . . an orrery . . .

I've been meaning to find out what an orrery is for well over half a century. I shall go to the other side wondering.

When he arrived there was a confusion. The Schlossherrin was unavailable. The detectives, presumably sick of Marcus's cafards, had a train to catch. The Gutsverwalter was expecting them a day later. He was a sour man . . . Sebastian Höldrich . . . fiftieth no no hundredth generation retainer so old he could recall seeing the funeral cortège of Grossherzog Frederick II von Reichenfels . . . so his skivvie forelock extended half a metre from his abject forehead . . .

He regarded his employer's whims with hardly disguised contempt, but his honour was his loyalty. So long as no one interfered with his obsessional forest pursuit of an elusive stag known as der Schlager whose vast twenty-two-prong antlers were described by one of the few people to have seen it as 'our Lord's crown of thorns built with logs' then the estate ran smoothly.

He told Marcus that he would be inspected by the Schlossherrin . . . probably from a distance through binoculars . . . that would be in the next few days . . . she was currently indisposed . . . a mild fever . . . radiant flushes . . . he instructed Marcus in his conduct towards his employer should she wish to converse . . . he would be courteous towards tourists . . . he outlined the rules of Hermetical behaviour . . . he must not forget that he was an ornament . . . a living decoration not a being . . . he must not stray further than a hundred metres from the Hermitage . . . Marcus was disappointed that the Hermetical diet was little different to that which he had eaten in the wild . . . He was hoping for quenelles and woodcock.

These rules affronted him . . . one would be . . . but he was patient and passive . . . he could tolerate boredom . . . being gaped at by distant riders and passengers of horse-drawn charabancs, automobilists in goggles . . . he felt like an exhibit . . . which was of course what he was . . . he slept much of the day . . . at night he wandered the estate . . . swam in the gurgling streams that fed the lakes . . . convened with otters and foxes . . .

Then, as they will, the seasons changed . . . the black poplars' seeds appeared . . . cottonwood . . . the flammable fuzz that the Ruskies call *puk* . . . delinquents set fire to it . . . within a couple of days he was suffering asthma and gasping . . . hardly breathing . . . a skeletal rattling in his chest . . . an invader stealing his breath . . . Höldrich had grudgingly brought him into the great schloss . . . he was directed to a bare white room . . . part of the servants' sanatorium . . . three rudimentary metal beds and a water jug – no drapes no curtains . . . a doctor was summoned . . . because the patient was a hermit by trade he was prescribed rabbit lungs, fox fat and owl's blood . . . infusion of coltsfoot leaves . . . hyssop oil . . .

Through the high windows he could see his Hermitage far away on the edge of the trees . . . far away beyond the lake and the ruined temple . . . he did not want to return to it . . . this room might be austere but it was warm and clean . . . it's only when you have shelter you appreciate the hardship of no shelter . . . like money ness par? . . . once you have got it by hook or by crook you recall the absolute beastliness of poverty . . . however did one put up with it . . . the absolute beastliness . . . same applies to sex ness par . . . the act in its harrowing beauty and exquisite pain – if I remember rightly . . . yes I remember oh yes . . .

He was still wheezing still desperate for air . . . he persuaded the doctor he needed morphine . . . it relieved him . . . he had the greatest stroke of luck . . . when Gertraud first saw him he was not in character . . . not playing his role . . . he was wearing what a maid had brought him . . . Jaipur slippers . . . and a nightshirt and a

dressing gown reeking of mothballs . . . he was a man not a hermit . . .
a man.

She was still feverish . . . a neurasthenic prone to high tempera-
tures and lethargy . . . she came . . . she processed into the room . . .
the elegance of the obese ness par . . . she cried out when she saw her
dead father in his favourite dressing gown and those ridiculous slippers which he called his grand vizier slippers . . . embroidered . . . she
called them his jester's buskins . . . she felt faint . . . stumbled . . .
Marcus was alarmed . . . he moved towards her . . . proffered his
hand as she crumpled . . . a barrage balloon deflating . . . he held her
so she didn't fall to the floor . . . helped her to a bed . . . she gripped
his wrist . . . gazed at him in puzzled wonderment . . . finding him in
this haunted mufti this haunted mufti . . . she could never believe in
him as a hermit . . . the illusion was . . . was *vitiated* before it began . . .

Marcus didn't realise this was his patron . . . he thought she was a
housekeeper . . . so he didn't bother to ingratiate himself . . . he was
as much a snob as we all are . . . he was just his amiable dreamy self . . .
Gertraud was delighted to be treated so straightforwardly . . .
not because she would for a moment waive the grades of class
distinction . . . no no . . . not Gertraud . . . never . . . but because it
was such a novelty not to be obliged to respond with due decorum to
bowing and scraping . . . the woman was a sloth . . . too lazy to assert
her superiority . . . a traitor to her class.

It was not till some days later that Gertraud was given away as
Gertraud . . . he observed a young servant bowing to her . . . bowing
and scraping . . . he had never understood that scraping meant writhing on the floor in supplication and abasement. That same day he told
her that he would have to relinquish his position as Kaltenborn's
Hermit . . . he expected every morning no matter what cave he was
living in to wake up and find he had died in the night . . . or, worse,
that a limb had been gnawed by famished rodents . . . he exhaled her
father's Buccal Gym mouthwash and Irex toothpowder . . . she
laughed wildly when he insisted that the slippers were nothing like
buskins . . . they were buskins if she said so for she made the laws in
the schloss . . . whose Ludwig II decoration Marcus considered
unspeakable . . . the rococo delirium of a heavily drugged vizier
achieved with the heaviest of touches, overgilded chairs, polished

stones, mosaics, tiles, cowhorn console tables, anything that could be made with antlers, glittering Moorish columns, horseshoe arches, heraldic hangings, goblin encrusted friezes, onyx menageries, marmoreal bestiaries, bogus ancestor portraits . . . all to her father's taste, and so beyond reproach . . .

It wasn't only her hermit she married . . . it was her father. So many women do . . . so many women do. They celebrated the end of Marcus being a hermit . . . they ate the tethered hind. Gertraud gorged on the liver . . . raw . . . still warm and quivering in its death throes . . . her face and forehead were smeared with blood . . . it glued strands of hair . . . it crazed as it dried . . . filaments of gleaming organ hung from her maw . . . Marcus was shocked . . . Marcus shocked!! . . . shocked at the savage heiress's tooth and claw . . . she called a servant to bring a mirror so she could admire herself . . .

'I am the ogress of Kaltenborn!' she cackled at herself. 'The ogress.'

The on dit is she tormented him . . . her hefty humour . . . all back slapping . . . practical jokes . . . she insisted he run about the schloss on all fours grunting the grunts of the forest . . . making the calls of bears screeching like wolves . . . the servants were instructed not to notice . . . she would make him eat from a plate on the floor . . . screamed at him if he demurred . . . he came to rue his new life . . . but not so much that he'd return to his old life . . . never . . . he gritted his teeth . . . he was obsessed by his teeth . . . was said to clean them six times a day . . . enjoyed being a spoiled pet . . . even though he despised the man he was turning into . . . an increasingly corpulent man . . . waited on hand and foot . . . cosseted and swaddled . . . oh he could cope with the surfeit . . . the surfeit of surfeit . . . that was no hardship . . . but the jocularity . . . hearty good cheer is such a bore ness par . . . don't you run a mile when you hear that gigglemugs has a sunny disposition . . . what a disappointment life is for meliorists . . . never learning not to hope . . . they're the ones who kill themselves . . . they kill themselves . . . thwarted expectations mount up . . . they see themselves as picked upon . . . conspired against . . .

She was desperate for a child . . . she loathed children . . . she was no more maternally inclined than I was . . . but craved an heir . . . to spite her Dumpberg cousins . . . the only way to prevent them getting their hands on the estate . . . that's hearsay of course . . . from Matthias . . . not altogether reliable then . . . he took a massive draught of umbrage when she began walking out with the Hermit . . . waddling out . . . the nincompoop had somehow convinced himself he owned the rights to Marcus . . . as a sort of cupid I suppose . . . he was livid not to be invited to the wedding . . . she had a tendency to edit her address book in a fit of pique . . . minor slights got back to her . . . she was keen as mustard to take offence . . . and even keener to give it . . . cosi fan tutte . . .

Sole occasion I saw them together was Bayreuth . . . summer nineteen oh two . . . the summer of the Schönburg hat . . . I think it was *Holländer* . . . she could be mistaken for that vessel with wind in the poop . . . a four-masted schooner with mink sails . . . she was even vaster even vaster . . . she affected not to recognise us . . . then announced . . . imperiously announced . . . that she was pregnant . . . as though it had never happened to anyone else . . . look around you I thought . . . look around you . . . all these people had one thing in common . . . they had slimed from a mother's cervix . . . apart from the Caesars . . . she was due to give birth in six weeks . . . she took offence when I said that she was just as she had been when I had met her in Paris . . . no one could possibly tell . . .

She turned on her heel pulling her pet husband with her . . . he was looking over his shoulder at me . . . poor Marcus . . . such a baffled lamb . . . he had been astonished to encounter me . . . as though he'd seen a ghost . . . he couldn't put the pieces together . . . and she . . . she had no idea that I knew him . . . which by then I didn't, so far had he diverged from the Marcus of old . . . all our pasts were occluded . . . or were inventions . . . lavishly riddled with omissions . . . omissions . . .

I did jot him a brief note when I heard . . . I was shocked. I think I was surprised . . . but of course one wasn't in possession of the facts . . . the circumstances . . .

Of course he was in hospital when it happened . . . when she did it . . .

One couldn't decently ask why ness par . . . why . . . Indecently one could speculate . . . speculation was all the rage . . . post-partum anomie perhaps? . . . the pain of motherhood? . . . the prospect of all the years to come . . . Then there was the fur . . . the fur . . . the shock of it . . . every inch of your Mama's body was covered in fur . . . one would never know of course . . . she was a sedulous shaver . . . a skilled shaver . . . Marcus was coated in rough hair . . . spontaneous growth . . . out of sympathy with his mounts . . . but a baby with outlaw stubble and a coat like a dog! No no no . . .

There was endless whispering about his infidelities . . . that . . . that drove her to it . . . there were rumours . . . there were certainties . . . he had a cinq à sept he'd visit when they were in Munich . . . he was with her . . . supposedly with her when Gertraud was giving birth . . . that would have deranged her . . . she was eminently derangable . . . eminently . . . He was such a gal sneaker . . . he so loved to pull his rhubarb out . . . encourage the gels to help it swell . . . before Malpasfang went for a burton as you young people put it . . . went for a burton . . . he used to jug-a-jug-jug with so many different creatures . . . the congress of the species . . . oh he was such an irrepressible animal lover . . . it's difficult for a devoted zoophile to adjust to humans . . . for a time the only creatures of his own species he could bear to rub offal with were those horse-faced county gels with enormous teeth . . . it didn't matter to him that they were plain-as-cake and thick-ankled . . . so long as they were horse-faced it was fantoosh . . .

He used to so look forward to the grand balls at Malpasfang . . . nothing gave him greater pleasure than seducing the dreary daughters of the Marcher descendancy . . . the more equine the better . . . his capricious perversity amused him . . . I thought it banal . . .

He didn't reply . . . silence . . . does one reply to letters of condolence . . . what is the form? It was strange to think of him as a widower . . . silent widower . . . yet another role . . . a widower with a small child . . . he lived for her and her alone . . . she was the richest infant in Germany your Mama . . . he feared kidnapping . . . ransom . . . much less wealthy children were routinely abducted . . . he differentiated between abductors who were driven by money – most of them Jews – and the visionaries of nature as he had been . . .

Your Mama was surrounded by a troop of guards . . . Marcus fretted . . . who guards the guards . . . who guards the guards'

guards . . . ad infinitum . . . a kind of militia was employed to look after the Munich house . . . the monstrous Villa Dumpberg . . . which anyone else with Gertraud's fortune would have replaced . . . von Seidl was hopelessly vieux jeu . . . it was often mistaken for the embassy of some arriviste Balkan state no one can pronounce . . .

Marcus was thought to be an eccentric show-off . . . not a quality that impresses Bavarians . . . they're very staid . . . most unusual to see a man in a top hat pushing a pram . . . indeed unheard of . . . when they were in Munich he walked her in the English garden and the botanic gardens . . . guards in front and behind . . . she ran on all fours grunting . . . shrieking . . . imitating him . . . that's how he was in her earliest memories . . . she made such a pretty primate . . . such a pretty primate . . . she loved to please him . . .

He was occasionally joined briefly on his walks by a young woman . . . obviously English . . . touch of the geegees you know . . . splendid blonde mane . . . he made an unpersuasive show of being surprised to see her . . . they spoke with a certain urgency . . .

Sometimes she was arm in arm with a handsome young man . . . they stopped to greet Marcus . . . dutifully smile at the baby . . . stiff courtesies . . . smiles and bows . . . gesturing to the clouds . . . a different . . . a lesser degree of acquaintanceship than when it was just Marcus and her alone . . . small talk . . . no indication of anything more . . . when the handsome young man was striding by himself he was delighted to see Marcus . . . accorded him a jocular bow . . . then a less formal slap on the shoulder . . . a winning grin . . .

The handsome young man and the equine woman – though I must say she doesn't look it in the photographs I've seen – were your paternal grandparents Valentine Shadoxhurst . . . archaeologist . . . ethnologist . . . anthropologist . . . it varied according to which way the wind blew . . . he was attached . . . semi-attached . . . to the university in some capacity . . . he was Matthias Schaffer's pupil and assistant . . .

He was miserably married . . . a vodka-for-breakfast drunk . . . a queer's duty . . . the bugger's burden . . . the heir! where is the heir? She . . . Alexandra . . . was a Shorto-Mexter-Mant-Brook of course . . . that was the attraction – the name . . . the name . . . not her by a long chalk . . . by marrying a Mant-Brook Valentine was marrying archaeology itself . . . he was marrying shrunken heads and shrieking horror masks and flint arrowheads . . . two museums . . .

He was also marrying the neighbouring estate, eight thousand acres of archaeologically fecund downland . . . more farms, more houses, more copses, more employees . . . Consolidation.

I believe Marcus first met Valentine at a lecture by Magnus Hirschfeld . . . height of his notoriety . . . militating for the repeal of whatever act it was that drove homos to alcoholism and suicide . . .

He and Valentine went to talks and congresses together . . . Social Hygiene . . . Bio-typology . . . Prehistoric Archaeology . . . Radical Dermatology . . . the Society of Child Enthusiasts.

Marcus had more money than he knew what to do with . . . more money than sense . . . donations to set up the Library of Human Amelioration and Sexology . . . most of the donations found their way into the pockets of crocuses . . . the von Glydes . . . racial improvement does attract charlatans . . . you'd have thought that he'd have learnt from Doctor Mortimer Glyde . . .

Then there were plans for a permanent ethnogenic exhibition . . . a human zoo . . . like Hagenbeck's . . . the same story . . . no one had stopped to consider that what's on in Hamburg isn't on in Munich. He lost a substantial sum . . .

He became browned off with the city . . . it lost its appeal to him . . . It was no place for a primitive . . . he'd been in the wild too long . . . every society he joined was preoccupied with its protocols . . . reading its minutes . . . but that's the same the world over ness par . . . He inherited Gertraud's friends but that was the rub . . . they were *her* friends . . . they regarded him with compassion . . . his loss . . . they were also suspicious . . . unsurprisingly . . . Apart from Valentine and Alexandra he had few friends of his own . . . few intimates . . .

They returned to Dorset somewhat precipitously somewhat precipitously it must be said . . . without warning . . . no farewells . . . Marcus was left with just a few casual acquaintances . . . and the poor sweet had no gift for acquaintanceship . . . he lacked that ease . . . no doubt what drew him to animals . . .

As your Mama grew up their life changed . . . the pattern . . . it was by all accounts an idyllic childhood . . . the lost domain of cat-kins and ponies, lakes and follies, gymkhanas and governesses of course and a succession of tutors . . . Marcus encouraged her to treat them as servants . . . after all he had been at Eton . . . briefly . . . too many scions of international capital he used to say . . . you didn't get those at Shrewsbury at Shrewsbury . . . no! Shrewsbury . . . heavens! I've prospered ness par . . . me . . . how I've prospered . . .

Marcus gradually came to be regarded as a saintly eccentric . . . apparently denying himself any amorous life apparently . . . devoting himself to his motherless daughter . . . apparently sacrificing himself . . . succumbing to her every whim . . . there was nothing he wouldn't do for her . . . your Mama was a very sporty little girl . . . badminton . . . skiing . . . curling of all things . . . she learnt to sail on the Bodensee . . . Marcus bought her countless pets . . . the more arcane the species the better . . . she loved motoring . . . they would go to Fulda . . . Vierzehnheiligen . . . Salzburg . . . Ottobeuren . . . she had a precocious taste for the boldest baroque and fiddliest rococo . . . Regensburg . . . the monks were astonished . . . her knowledge . . . the drawings she did . . . they drove in convoy with guards aft and fore . . . aft and fore.

They left in the same convoy to Zurich that summer of 1914 . . . they had to . . . he was a British subject . . . he could never have gone back to The Pudding . . . his word our word for all England that lay outside the blessed bounds of Malpasfang . . . he'd anticipated well . . . all liquid assets had been transferred to Switzerland . . . he had thought it through shrewdly enough . . .

When they left there was a void . . . an absolute emptiness . . . it was the end of her childhood . . . the end of everything . . . the end of Kaltenborn . . . a full stop . . . It was requisitioned by the Bavarian government . . . they housed deportees from Alsace . . . the germanophones . . . the accidents of language . . . later it was virtu-ally squatted by unofficial Freikorps Oberland . . . sort of barracks . . . they trained Mordhunds to recognise communists . . . bite out their throats . . . a small parcel of the agricultural estate was sublet to a member of that militia – Heinrich Himmler . . . what a hopeless little man with his silly glasses . . . failing to make his way in chicken farming . . . no great loss to that trade . . . but he already knew his vocation . . . he was practising homeopathic pest control . . . not that the foxes noticed . . . their sense of smell led them to dig up the decomposed corpse of Timmy the Hermit . . . he had to be reburied yet again . . .

Eventually it became a hostel for young women and their Mischlingskinder . . . by-blows . . . the fathers were French colonial troops . . . Zouaves, les frères domtoms, Harkis . . . the crossbreeds that Bavaria must bear . . . the shame . . . of course compulsory sterilisation put an end to that trail of coffee-coloured miscegenation . . .

Of course creating métèques had been an ambition at Malpasfang . . . Marcus would have appreciated the . . . amorous zeal amorous zeal of these warriors . . . he used to insist . . . to preach indeed . . . that the only means by which the race can be strengthened is by broaching the distant shores of exogamy . . . hence his zoophilia . . .

But there is a certain irony . . . a stentorian irony that his greatest achievements in tupping were endogamous . . . the mark of true aristocracy . . . how otherwise does the aristocracy maintain the level it has attained . . . it is a club . . . entry is by blood . . . or cunning . . . no nonsense about the statutory age of consent . . . the age of consent is announced to us by our bodies . . . by blood and semoule . . . the moment we so longed for you say . . . oh wouldn't but I'm such a flighty blabbermouth my dear . . . just too too bavarde . . .

(She passed her sly grin around the table and settled it on me.)

He never went back to Kaltenborn . . . nor did your Mama . . . never. Never go back . . . the world is divided . . . those who go back . . . in an utterly futile search for . . . what? What? Whatever it is it won't be found because the you that inhabited it is a you that no longer exists . . .

Wiser perhaps to live in eternal regret at not having gone back . . . not having tried to recapture whatever it is . . . a page of the past . . . ? You can't will déjà vu . . . you can't click your fingers . . . no . . . preposterous to believe otherwise . . . stick with what's in your loaf . . . picture it . . . its only existence as it was just the way it was is in your loaf. That's where the past is to be found. Where perfection's to be found.

Virtuoso: Ricky van Brabant
(Né Howard Dogg)

The party was smart and cool. We were attracting a more sophisticated after-gig crowd. Maturer strumps who knew just how to play. Sanso just loved us. He was the guy who owned Club Foot in West Hollywood. He asked: What sort of meat turns you on? He was attentive to our needs. Guaranteed supply of exceptional flesh.

Amazing! One week it's conquering in a car seat (a Sabrina Mk1, a rusty old Cosmos), transit-van fucks with borderline-STI boilers, you know them: they're all over you like clingfilm on a buffet. Slaggy bottom of the bill empty wigs from South Wales ('Entertainment's in the family like, Mum was in The Barry Island Five. My Dada they called him Bridgend's Own Mario Lanza'), mouthy receptionists in Cleethorpes, Minehead beauty queens etc. The type you'd happily screw up like a piece of sullied tissue and dump in the bin when you'd finished with them.

Then – fanfare with trumpets – next week you're getting blown by Playboy Bunnies and *Hustler* centrefolds not to mention top socialites from Chicago and Miami. All you needed was stamina. The clip-clop of your feet on the stairs – again! Those dames were goers. Blocked out of their heads. And they always have friends, *farouche* friends up for anything and everything. Quick recovery was all that was required to enjoy max feed. We struggled to keep up with Jimmy Gliss. His recovery time was triple amazing especially with his animal lust for rye Manhattans, not forgetting a tasteful array of powders. Blown by three greedies in twenty minutes in Omaha, Nebraska. Not Bunnies or socialites. They don't have those in Omaha, Nebraska.

Near children frankly. Borderline paedo. Lewis Carroll waifs. Dodgy Dodgson. Jimmy was a little bit naughty selling on his teenies to support bands. But if there's grass on the wicket – Game On!

We were big. So fucking big. We were brash. We were barnstorming. We partied. Really really partied. We were animals. The jungle's top manimals! Apart from Staff. He just likes watching – and pigging out, scraping the buffet clean, gulping down four dozen oysters, a hefty jar of beluga, several lobsters, enough short ribs to feed an army, entire croquembouches.

After our first LaVey Arena gig there was a *Zeitgeist* cover article: 'Legends of the Near Future': what not to believe? We knew how good we were. It didn't need *Zeitgeist* to tell us. I didn't give a toss when *Backbeat* did a thing about me (and the band) called 'The Poser and the Glory'. My guitar was described as 'a wand of venom and honey'. Bully for them. I was on the cover. That's all that counts. 'Tractors of the Revolution' was at no. 1 in *Billboard*. We were grossing mansions with pools. Country estates. Owning as far as you could see. Titled gardeners. Garages full of Stutz Bearcats, Gran Turismo Ferraris, Bugattis. Make that hangars full of Cords and streamline Tatras. Private jets. Yachts with saunas. I'm going to be twenty-seven forever. What!

The third LaVey gig. By special demand. Added at the end of the tour. One of those nights when you just soar. All the pieces fit. Perfectly. You are at one. No clams. The band is more than just four crushed velvet dudes from round Hemel and Radlett (and Adam from Baptist End in the Black Country who genuinely was working class, sort of. His dad got out of Poland. Fought in Italy in the 5th Wilno Infantry. Rewarded for his services to king and country with a bed in a Nissen hut. Adam lived in a DP camp till he was six. His dad was a hoddie. Worked his way up. Now builds entire towns, walkways in the sky, poems in asbestos. Takes cabinet ministers on holiday. Buys them gold Rolexes. Social mobility, what!). The band is a whole that's more than the sum of the individuals. There's this magic when egos are laid aside. Or when they are equally huge but exactly the same size as each other so no one ego is bigger than the other and no one showboats or we all showboat and I showboat most of all. See what I mean?

There was a lot going down at the party after. The ultimate party. Not that there weren't other ultimate parties. So many ultimate parties! I got there late. It was in full swing – pun intended! Low lights. Heady scents. Sex. Hot testosterone. Eucalyptus smouldering. Perfume. What's that smell of shit, babe? Must be hashish. Sweat. Leopardskin walls. Leopardskin banquettes. Leopardskin stockings. Pussy on tap. It looked like a brothel. It was a brothel. A brothel where you didn't have to pay. It was champagne from the bottle. Heavy burgundy velvet. Heavy velvet burgundy. The road crew were all standing round clapping in time while one of Sanso's chicks was getting multi-fucked by three of the guys from The Audiocrats, the soul combo who had opened for us. Opened at no notice. You can imagine how in demand they were. Nice guys but so yesterday. Those sharkskin suits . . . We called them The Over The Hills. Berny, Mr Bass Man aka The Chocolate Gonad, was charvering that arse going in deep, really burying that monster beast. Nature abhors celibacy. He was naked apart from gilded cowboy boots, a ten-gallon hat and aviator shades. Nice touches.

Unfortunately Staff was trying to choreograph this little tableau while stuffing a lobster burger that was dripping mayo all over the heaving flesh. Prat.

Those were the nights of licence and canapés. Guacamole. Pacific salmon mayo. Pacific oysters. Sushi and sashimi. You never saw those in Blighty back then. Raw fish – ugh! Eggs stuffed with caviar. Little Spanish pies. Little birds you ate whole. This and that in aspic. Killer lobsters. Monterey Jack. Pineapple in rum. Staff was cramming his face. There was a six-course meal stuck in his stubble. So many lines of powder laid out it was like art. Mondrian. Amazing wine just amazing from some place the sneery garcon-guy at the bar wanted to put me down for not having heard of. But his just-as-sneery friend knew who I was and gave him the nod so he didn't. The friend! He was like some blond-streak faggoty tennis hustler from *The Sweet Ride*. White Levi's, baby-blue Harrington, taupe suede soft moccasins. So Troy Donahue. So yesterday it was almost tomorrow. So pre-Us. When the garcon-guy started to pour a glass holding it like it was some ritual I just grabbed a bottle and went potato. There were some strange sounds. Very spooky sounds like sounds from the grave. You know skeletons jamming in hell whistling and drumming, shrieking. The living dead making their presence felt from inside the hollow walls where they like to hang. The lights were down. It was a night of promise. The girls in the cuterarium were touching themselves as they danced. In those days pussies weren't shaved. Mauve shone through thickets.

As usual I resisted the lines of ice. I never felt the temptation any more. I was in second balm. Warm in the womb. Applause alone did it for me. I was so applaused I didn't need a line. A line's just empty wigs. Adulation is a gas. A total high. Let no one tell you otherwise. Anyroad, opiates really fuck your bowels. Smackheads never let on. Destroys the mystique. Talk about blockage. It's like one of those epic bank holiday tailbacks. And when you get rid of it, it's a lump of baked clay the size of a Coke can you've had stalled in your rectum, rough clay that doesn't half tear when it's exhumed.

It was obvious the way she was clocking me that the *jolie laide* with a Brunette Bob didn't want to spend any longer pinned against the wall listening to The Toot's rabbit. More *laide* than *jolie* to be frank. Built for comfort rather than speed. But just brimming over with androstenol, just brimming.

I was slowly getting up from the sofa to go help her out when there was this arm. Came from out of nowhere. It was firmly guiding me back into the cushions. Determined I should stay.

'Mister Ricky my friend.' A geezer in a tux knelt down beside me. Shalimar?

'What a privilege to meet you. What a maestro you are! No? Virtuoso I'd say. I say to myself this man is the master of his instrument.'

I guessed this highly perfumed geezer with a weird accent undoing his bow tie was referring to my seventeen-minute solo in 'Antlers Wane'. French? Montreal? Martinique? Where else do they speak French? Mali. He wasn't black.

I wondered to myself: 'Do I Know This Geezer?'

Maybe. Maybe, but then again . . . When you're a Legend (of the future) everyone is your friend. Everyone wants a part of Ricky van Brabant. That's one way of putting it.

The smiley animals with him were super-delicious. Nourishment for a bluevein. Sisters? Triumphs of West Coast dentistry. Not to mention the West Coast craft implant industry. The haircare industry. The fitness industry. They oozed class and refinement. One of them smoked a cheroot. They were the real deal. High gloss. Pheromones poured into slinky dresses.

There were always a few like him around. Come on from dinner in El Zaragozano or The Platinum Lounge. Straight. Smooth. Tanned. Expensive. Groomed. Jet Set. Fifties heart-throb style. Hair so shiny you could see yourself in it. Wanted to be Laurence Harvey back then. Now just longing to be young and hip. Trying hard. But they knew they didn't call the shots any more. Jet travel is for everyone now inc. dudes like us. Democratic travel – we get the upper storey. Big burns and light entertainment flaps of hair over the ears don't cut it. Just don't make the grade. We are the rulers now. Doesn't stop them talking down to us. But they know – they know in their heart of hearts that it's us. We are the overdogs.

One of Argon's PR honchos? Could be a Sanso buddy. His buddies came in all shapes and sizes.

What was that smell? Could have been Habit Rouge? Or Violation? Or Bitch On Heat? Telling one scent from another was my new thing. Expensive meat wears expensive French sauce. Meat's mates too.

'The way your fingers – they dance across the strings. Like, oh, Randersacker. Have you listened to his Goldberg Variations . . . Pure poetry. Truly impressioning.'

He put his hand on the back of my hand laid on the arm of the sofa. I was sat in so deep I couldn't escape. I sort of flinched. I never liked men touching me especially men I didn't know. Maybe it was a sex thing. Homophobia wasn't a crime in those days. It was cool to shout from the stage to twenty thousand screaming teenies that I didn't want some guy's schlong up my arse. It was allowed. Then again maybe it was just I didn't go for strangers being too matey. He might be super-suave but he was blokeish too. Taking liberties. It was distasteful. I moved my hand. Brusque. Like I was telling him off. He didn't notice or pretended he didn't notice.

'Timing – would you say that was your . . . secret Ricky My Friend?'

Acqua di Parma. That was the one.

'Secret? You're joking man. There's no secret. It's down to getting good enough so you don't end up working in a foundry or something. A factory. Day in day out. Going down the pit like your dad.[31] I didn't want to drive a truck. Sorry. Simple as that. Practise then practise more. Old-fashioned work ethic yeh? Survival of the fittest. Sorry – not very rock and roll is it? Who do I have the pleasure of addressing? Who are you? We met before have we? . . . Are you—'

'Oh how discourteous. I'm *so* sorree. I'm Roman . . . Roman Marcato – and here are: my Dolly and my Molly. I know. Confusion.' Laughs.

More smiles. One of them sat down beside me. Cheroot. I felt a stirring. It wasn't till later I came to know this one was Molly. How could I ever forget?

'The girls are as much in awe of your genius as I am. Isn't that so?'

'That thertainly ith so!' agreed Dolly or Molly. I didn't yet know which was which. In fact I never saw Dolly after that night. I heard her though. I heard her. She had the higher voice and the fainter lisp.

'Genius is down to brain and hands – wouldn't you say so ladies? Delicate hands. Virtuosity needs delicate hands. We each find our way in life according to our hands, don't you agree? Hey look at my hands – no chance I could have been a cosmetic surgeon eh?'

His fingers were iffy items in a seafood buffet. I almost pissed myself laughing. He took my left hand to compare. It was a charming gesture.

'You got other talents – yeh?'

'People are kind enough to say so. If you haven't the hands you have to use your brain. And if you haven't a brain there's always being a farmer. A simple peasant farmer.'

'Cool. Now if you'll excuse me . . .'

---

31 There are no mines in Hertfordshire. Van Brabant's father was a GP. His hobby was compiling and editing *The Paracelsian*, a twice-yearly compendium of papers about medical mishaps, model trains used as sex toys, household goods gone missing in people's rectums, the lure of the Hoover Dustette etc. He never grew out of being a prankster medical student.

I was getting up out of that sciatica style sofa when Molly reached out for my thigh. Nice and friendly. I changed my mind. If she wants to play, let it be. Yes! She was a peach. I gave her a widescreen smile. Having a high-volume-jet-detartarisation gives you a lot of confidence about smiling when you've had brown teeth from chain smoking the adolescent poseur's snout of choice, Gitanes.

'Don't go . . .'

'Stick around, Mister Ricky.'

I looked across the room. The Brunette Bob was being felt up by The Toot. Better I guess than having to listen to him spout about tarot and leylines. How everything's connected or inevitable or destined or something. Still looking at me she was, glad to say – and grinning. She winked over his shoulder, the raunchy little cutie. No, not so little.

'Lee-oohhh!' Roman greeted Bamberg. He and his micro-hairweave were sidling by not wanting to be noticed. He pretended to be surprised.

'Oh didn't see you there, Roman – hidin' away. Good to see you.' Bamberg didn't mean a word of it. 'How you doing? Stackin' the crust I trust.'

'Certainly am, Leo . . . of course you know our friend here.'

'*Know* him! You bet I do. To know him is to love him!'

Bamberg was wearing a red-brown velvet jacket that made him look like he was wrapped in raw liver. He had this ever so iffy habit of ruffling my hair like I was a pet. Like he owned me. That's what I didn't like. Because, well, it was true he did sort of own me. Nonetheless I stood up and gave him a hug. I could forgive this man anything. He had made us. And I was his golden goose: me. Not The Toot, not Jimmy Gliss, not Adam, totally not Staff. Staff a) had a foreskin and b) was just too fucking endomorph for whitey rock and roll. He couldn't stop snacking. He had a thirty-four-inch waist for god's sake. You can only get away with a body that shape if you're black. He thought he compensated with his ultra-preposterous hairdo – like a wig straight out of a Restoration comedy. Stab me vitals. What!

I wrote all the music. All the lyrics. I sang at least three-quarters of 'our' repertoire. I played lead. I produced. I designed the album covers.

I was the devil's cherub ('il cherubino del diavolo' according to *Raro!*). I was 'the deep enigma in midnight blue' who never gave interviews – not to Mark Vanier, not even to softly spoken Richard Williams: imagine how thrilled he'd be to get ten in-depth minutes of my precious time. I let my music speak for me. Staff did the interviews. He was jealous of me. He had reason to be: he was a few billion neurons light of acknowledged genius. He made it sound like he was The Man. He wasn't. He came out with lines like 'I'm not so much into the sounds themselves as the texture of the sounds.' The journos teased him for having a swollen head. Typically he didn't notice. What the journos didn't notice was that he had a 'social' anti-Semitic streak. Whenever we discussed replacing Cornelius someone like Eliot Anthony's name would come up.

Staff would grunt: 'He'd have us playing bar mitzvahs and . . . what do you call them . . . purim parties.' (He meant but dared not say 'your people'.)

Tosser. I ignored his little digs. Turned the other cheek. There was class resentment too: Chiswell Green isn't Radlett. One day he'd burst.

I knew I'd made it when bands still wet behind the ears started calling themselves after my songs and lyrics: Bulge In Her Cheek, Serial Offender, Flash and The Plastic Hardware, Beasts, Farmyard, Nun Up The Duff, Epaulettes – 'the hoi polloi got chips, the quality wear epaulettes'. If I'd given Leo Bamberg the nod he'd have aimed the rest of the guys and got together a new band around me. Showcasing me. We'd see. Trouble was we'd been together since before college, apart from Adam. Thinking about the treachery thing was a bit of a downer. But treachery was part of the business. What!

'Ricky is a very great musician. We are honoured to have him under . . . We are proud that he is with us. The jewel in Argon's crown . . .' He started to move away then turned and murmured just audible above the keening sounds: '. . . just so long as he can keep himself buoyant. Yeh, Ricky? Hey ciao, Roman. Check you soon, buddy.'

'What did he mean by that, Mister Ricky? Keep . . . yourself . . . *buoyant* . . . buoyant?'

'Pwhh . . .' I played dumbo. I shook my head. 'Who knows . . . That's Leo.'

'Yeh. Our Hebrew cousins have their ways . . . Schleo . . . Schleo . . . Schleo . . .' Noddy noddy noddy like it was a mantra. I stayed schtum. I did not want an incident. No way José. I did not want an incident. If you went that route life would be all incidents. Nothing but incidents.

Then he laughed and raised his glass. 'To the maestro . . . Tell me – what do you think of this? The same wine you've been . . . drinking. I can see you've been tasting.' My bottle on the low oriental style table was half drunk.

'It's amazing, just amazing. That faggot at the bar came on, well, all faggy when I didn't know where it came from. Should I know?'

'Really? Did he? Came on all *faggy*? Hermm . . . No – you shouldn't know where it came from. But I can promise you, my friend, that in just a few years maybe three maybe five years the whole world will know where that wine came from.'

Scent. Wine. Getting to know the finer things. Becoming a connoisseur. All those years of chords in the bedroom and Mum screaming up the stairs paying off.

'Wine . . .' he came on all dreamy and philosophical with his obscene obese fingers making cat's cradles in the air '. . . it is place. It is earth. It is sun. It is grape. It is risk. It is craft. Most, above everything – to create a great wine – it is *alchemy*. I appreciate your appreciation of my wine.'

'*Your* wine?'

'Yes. My wine. *My wine*. I told you. I am a farmer. A mere peasant farmer. Logwood Estate Winery 1967 cabernet sauvignon, grenache, barbera and – a touch of what you say? counterintuitive, yeh, counterintuitive mastery – zin-fan-del.'

He whispered the last word with reverence. Like it was occult. Three distinct syllables. An increase-your-word-power word, a new one on me. I guess I should have felt bad about necking it from the bottle.

'And you know something – I tell you this in total confidence – it hasn't reached its full potential. Two three four more years and . . . oh, it will be . . . I cannot put it into words . . . I am not a poet like you, Mister Ricky.'

'How about . . . No. How about nectar's heavenly kiss?'

'That is so beautiful . . . so true, too. You know what I'm thinking? I'm thinking it would be a privilege to host you at our humble farm. We have a small gathering of folks tomorrow, very open neck.'

'You know, I'd really like that.' I meant it.

Ricky van Brabant was already thinking of his own winery. The south-facing slope. Quality time to patronise my cruelly exploited loyal pickers. The traditional yet modern labels. The prestige. The kudos – now there's a name. The Kudos Collection. Kudos Kollection would be naff.

'But I got to go back to London tomorrow.'

'Not till late. Quarter to midnight. Your flight.'

It was our flight. The last commercial flight we'd ever take before we had our very own mammoth of the skies with our very own livery (my design).

'That's right. What? Are you . . . How come—'

He giggled: 'I must come on like a stalker. Many apologies. I was just now talking to Marty Gammack.'

'As in our tour manager Marty? How come?' Not exactly a catch, Marty.

'His father is an old friend. Trevor and I go way back. Valued business colleague.'

'Come again – Marty's dad owns car washes . . . down on the south coast. Havant. Fareham . . . Not exactly big business.'

'Trade is very international nowadays.'

'*Havant?!!*'

'I have colleagues and friends in many countries. Including Her Majesty's realm. Which reminds me – we have a good friend in common.'

'Oh right . . . who would that be?'

He was making frantic hand waves at someone across the room with a greasy twinkle. He turned back to me.

'He seems a nice boy, Marty.'

'Nice! Marty? Well, that's one way of looking at it. He's . . . Let's just say he's one of nature's sergeant majors . . .'

A spiteful bully. Devious. Disloyal. Borderline socio. Would have made a good collaborator. The sort of psycho-bastard who can sense your weakness at a thousand paces. Refined his trade working for a strays' sanctuary, threatening old dears. If they didn't make a juicy bequest to Dog's Life Cottage & Barn, 'when the time came' they would not be going to the right place hereafter. Not the kind of guy you want to be in daily contact with for two minutes let alone two months. But he had insinuated himself with Cornelius our manager, convinced him that he was essential. Sure, he kept the show on the road. But so could any number of more pleasant dudes, people you'd enjoy to hang with. The band had already discussed offloading the fucker, ASAP. Cornelius wouldn't be best pleased but, frankly, who gave a toss what he thought.

'Needs to be. Keeps us in order.' Oh my tact.

'Hey, Mister Ricky. How about: we get you to the airport tomorrow night at nine o'clock just to be on the safe side. And you will have passed a beautiful day among vines and orchards. Better than hanging about the hotel.'

Molly stroked my knee. She was such a purry kittycat, Molly.

'Sounds bliss.'

'Bliss's heavenly kiss . . . I'll send a car for you at midday. We shall have a late lunch, a leisurely lunch. Fine wine. Great repartee. Hotel Palisades International. Right?'

I laughed: 'Ha! A stalker misses nothing.'

'Mister Ricky – it has been a great pleasure.'

We stood and shook hands.

'Till tomorrow.' We spoke in unison.

He left with a piece on each arm. A faint swagger. The man who rules.

Molly looked at me over her shoulder. Voraciously. Like I was prey. I've seen vultures watching lost lambs frailing towards death. Waiting for them to be carrion. Sometimes not waiting.

The Brunette Bob had found a way to stop The Toot rabbiting. She was giving him a hundred to eight. He was sprawled prone on a chaise longue kind of thing. Or should that be supine? On his back anyway. Her arse was in the air. No complaints when I hoisted up her dress. I gave myself a clean run at that very cutely puckered aperture. The bull's eye. I wished it had been Molly's. But go with what's there. Love the one you're with. I was gentle. Very gentle. I'm into feminism. She wiggled her willingness.

Well-stretched by previous tour parties, no question. 'Tighten that ass!' I shouted 'Tighten that ass!' I was glad to be on this end of the transaction.

Toot finished before me with a dry croak like he was asthmatic. Which he was.

Then it was just me and her plus a dozen pervy voyeurs who had come to watch a Legend in action. The slap of those buttocks. It was the inspiration not just for the chorus of 'Greasy Quiff, Manual Gear Shift' but for 'Pumping Up Her Tyres' too.

I zipped up. The snot had caked against my pants. Tush. I threw some ludes into my mouth. I got a taxi to the hotel. I played Scarlatti's K391 in Ziegler's transcription. I played it again. More reflective. Not so jolly this time. Play down that bumptiousness! Add in ecstatic mourning. All great art goes many directions at once. Meaningless is our goal. Then the downers kicked in.

Sunday

10.45

Already, a violent sun in the sky. Feels like coming on eye bleed. Everything is out to blind. Gusts off the ocean lifting the lobby curtains like a see-through dress. There's no one else around. No surprise. The day is for sleeping it off. From the concierge desk I called Glen. Not so ape-like as most of Marty's apes. Some of them even out-ape Marty. I'd promised to promote Glen to guitar valet once we'd archered Marty. I slipped him a $750 tip to look after my gear personally till we met at the airport. When he'd get another $750. No one, but no one, was to have access to it. It was even going to go to the john with him.

11.05

Believing your own publicity can seriously damage your mental health. Ricky van Brabant is a star. I tried to stop myself thinking that but the truth will out when you got a pile of newspapers in front of you telling you you are the Pegg, the Desmarais, the Randersacker, the Kerimoğlu of the guitar. You got people your dad's age on a foreign continent giving you compliments (which you accept graciously). They look approvingly at your health-kick diet. Fresh squeezed orange, milkless tea, crispbread – hold the butter. They think what an unspoiled kid. Hasn't let it go to his head. My mask is me.

12.00

Blazing noon. On the dot the low hum murmur in the lobby got fragged. The whole atrium echoed. A cocksure ginger rodent click-clacked across the pink marble floor. Made sure everyone looked up. Some sort of attention seeker. Smile that might have been a scowl or vice versa. Then he barked my name. He made Ricky . . . van . . . Brab . . . ant sound like a disease to be ashamed of. It was embarrassing to be associated with this ding. How did I get the distinct impression this flat-top scrote wasn't a fan! His skin was so tight on his face he was like a yegg with a stocking on his head. He had a tattoo on his neck like a diseased creeper trying to throttle him. He picked up my satchel. I grabbed it back from him. Definitely a scowl. I did my ciaos and adioses and au revoirs and so longs to the manager, duty manager, desk staff, concierges. Courtesy pays. A lesson the ginger rodent had yet to learn. Probably wouldn't learn. Too late. He was thirty-five if he was a day. I followed him out to the car. He was smaller than a jockey. He had a limp. He moved so fast it was a power-limp. He was almost goose-stepping. A miniature soldier making up for his size. The car was a Lincoln Continental. Metallic peppermint. Smoked glass windows. He opened the rear door. Deliberately not enough for me to get in without me having to pull it further. What was with this rodent?

The open road. The closed windows. The switch in the armrest console didn't respond. I told him it was broken.

'It's not broken.'

'It doesn't work.'

'It works. It's disabled.'

'Oh . . . Let's have it *enabled*?'

'Aircon,' he said. As if he was addressing some retard. As if aircon was better than air. In central LA sure. But beside the ocean?

All the fast-food banners and car lot buntings blew horizontal.

You caught a glimpse of the churning ocean now and again between the beach houses. Most of the time you wouldn't have known you were only 150 yards from the Pacific – next stop Japan. Mostly it was just like the rest of America. Billboards, crash barriers, camper cars, car washes, chicken and burgers, fries and donuts – and the victims of chicken and burgers, fries and donuts, waddling, modelling integral lifebelts. (I wrote down that line.)

'Ah . . . I'd like to open the window. Yeh?'

'The windows stay shut. Mr Marcato likes it that way. Particulates damage the burr walnut.' He had high-relief sinews in his neck.

The car turned off Pacific Ocean Highway. The walnut was everywhere. Just tacky veneer. Pretence. Nothing was what it seemed. The flying horse Pegasus high above the ocean was a cloud. Cumulus. So were the racing pigs and leaping deer clouds. A whole menagerie had escaped into the sky. Rare breed poodles. Heraldic lions. The tall thin palms were giraffes. The tall thin telegraph poles were wannabe giraffes. The eroded rocks were faces and limbs. Remember looking for that old biddy in a tree in a comic when you were seven? The macrocarpa (?) were wind-contorted in agony. Pine trees shivered with DTs like Lenny Bernstein conducting. You know those pictures of the Bedlam. The loonies all twisted on the other side of their cell bars. Never learning they couldn't bend the bars. Screeching mouths peeled back. Seeping gums and tooth stubs. Nostrils like cave entrances. Eyes full of pus. Putting on a show for their audience in the bad old days. I wouldn't have wanted to be one of the performers. No way José.

But I'd have joined the spectators at the drop of a hat. I'd have got off on it. Anyone who claims they're not turned on by freak shows is a hypocrite. What the fuck is the crucifixion if it's not an S&M freak show? Other people's pain is our pleasure. *Our* pain is our pleasure. The Hampstead Crucifixion was a gas. I was proud of *The Magician From Thanet* even though it didn't chart. That was down to rock operas just going out of fashion. Then the BBC banning the single 'Nail It to a Plank'.

The road climbed through endless chaparral. Aloe vera and wild citrus, oaks and sycamores, bunny's ears cacti, jasmine. Happy trails to the horizon. Hope beyond the horizon. Scrub and more scrub. Bluewater irrigation channels all of six feet wide slithering through rocks like model canals. Then either side of the road it was all tumble-down shacks and tree houses. The American Dream. Dust and a lean-to. Oil drum braziers and polythene. Health hazard water-butts. Not a straight line in sight. Held together with string. This was hippy central literally built on sand. The pioneer spirit all evaporated leaving just the dregs. The dregs were the pioneer reality. Rusting hippy pick-ups. Hippy wood carvings: Native American head-dresses, bears, elks, what have you. Crude carvings, chisel marks everywhere. Why can't these people go to fucking night school, learn technique? Hippy totem poles high as a house. The Eight Trigrams Café. Hippy fairy lights strung tree to tree. Hippy flower tubs – canna lilies and birds of paradise. Hippy craft shops. Vicious hippy mongrel dogs shitting everywhere. Hippies . . . rural hippies . . . bearded hippies . . . dirty engine oil in their hair hippies . . . emaciated bad-diet hippies with caved-in faces. And the women! In their terrible clothes. No make-up. Flat sandals. And the naked children with snot crust moustaches. (That's where the famous line *cicatrice of mucus* must have started. Not that I knew it.)

You'd have thought the kind of life they led here would have all just vanished. It belonged to a different time. It was like after the end of the world when soap and water have run out. This can't be what Love Street looked like.

Ginger woke from his muteness. He muttered: 'Douche bags. All amnestied now. Douche bags. Lousy customers. Grow their own weed. Inferior product.'

For a moment I was almost sorry for these unmutton losers. The unmutton way they gaped at the flash gas guzzler boasting past them. *Almost* sorry. I shamefully felt the same sneery contempt he did. Well, no, not really all that shamefully. No. I struggled with my inner bastard for all of a nanosecond then threw in the towel. These losers repulsed me.

'I ride these hills. You see them praying for their inferior product. Pathetic. Holding their arms to the sky. Imploring. I died so these bellycrawlers could live like *this*?'

Such sudden verbosity.

Then: 'What's that song of yours? The miserly earth . . . gnarled roots . . . famine.'

'"The Angelus".'

'Puhh. Don't like it. "The Angelus". No, I abhor it, boy. The power of prayer! As if! You need more than prayer when Citizen Gook is pushing a bamboo stiletto into your pee hole. I tell you, boy, only horticultural know-how and hydro savvy gets you a fine crop. Shape up! Prayer gets you nowhere!'

What? He had totally misunderstood the song.

That was the last thing he said before we descended a steep snaking road. The plants and trees changed. The shades of green changed. They lightened. The air was hazier. Soon we were at the gates. The Gates, that should be. They were uber-ornate. As Spanish as an olive oil tin. Twisty and gilded. Baroque? Rococo? Which is which? They opened with a remote control. Brass plates on the gate piers said Logwood Estate Wine Farm. A long avenue of pollarded trees like amputee thieves in Qatar. The house shimmered in the dazzling distance. White and Elvis-pink.

Ranks of vines stretched away on both sides towards the blue hills. What order! What clinical neatness! What riches in trimmed rows! The lawns between the rows were crisply manicured. Like a golf course. Mere peasant farmer, my anus!

Far away beyond the vines a windsock swelled to bursting.

The car halted in front of the house. A flash sprawl. A vast sprawl. Twenties Warner Bros Castanets and Toreador style.[32] Pantiles, palms, tall sculpted chimneys, galleries – make that romantic galleries, so romantic it was easy to imagine Jean Harlow romancing there with a brace of big bad body explorers.

'Here you are, boy. You take care now.'

13.15

It was the man's pride and joy. Cravatted Roman Marcato beamed with pride and joy every time he leapt off the buggy to cradle some

---

32 It was a wedding present for Clover Sevit from her first husband Wade Stopher. The architect was Pelly Duncanson who in 1922 greatly extended a flashy house and studio by Linsel Murly, some of whose homoerotic murals were destroyed.

tiny grapes. He stroked them like family men stroke their bulging unborn kids with pride and joy. Like he was a grape-fiddler. He sniffed them. He hailed me to sniff them. The convoy of buggies proceeded at his say-so along the cropped lawns. I sat beside him on the first one leading through a grid labyrinth.

I learnt: different varietals require different spaces, different soils, different nursing. Look at this vine — older than your great-grandfather.

Look at this chalk — imported: there's no natural chalk in these hills. He crumbled a lump.

Every time he had a thought to share he stopped the buggy. The dangers of over-ripeness; the importance, super-importance, of balance; homeopathic insect control; the wickedness of adulterating big name chateaux wines using 'doctor's wines'.

'Never trust us French. Us Californians are coming.'

'You French? American?'

'Perffhehh . . . Citizen of the world. Citizen of the world. Let us say, my friend.'

He grinned. Then turned to the buggies behind us: 'Will someone please bury the dead coyote? Somewhere. Somewhere, say, where he can share potassium to the soil. Not like certain chosen people, eh? Let's build a new world without their potassium!'

I stayed schtum. I would come to regret my cowardice.

Two flunkies with spades were magicked onto the scene. Most of the varmint's head had been blown off. There was blood, brain tissue, bone. Fur on the fairway.

'Mac, I regret,' he confided in my ear, 'neglects to wash up his victims. No way can you persuade him. How did you find his driving?'

'Mac?? . . .' Penny dropped. That would be Ginger. 'Ah yeh yeh *Mac* . . . fine? Yeh, fine . . . fine driving.'

'Good. He's an esteemed man Mac. He saved my son's life . . . Did he let you open the windows?'

'Neh . . .'

'He will . . . He will. At a price. It will cost you . . . Hey!' With a javelin thrower thrust of his arm he beckoned the convoy on.

'Let's go taste, people!'

I told him I recognised the javelin thrower thrust was copied from Boyd Power in *Yukon The Final Frontier*.

'Mister Ricky – is there no end to your smarts?'

We went down a slope towards a very long low building with a twirly Spanish gable. The winery name was painted on the roof. Strange crinkly paint.

Outside the full-height double doors at one end was a vast table precisely set with bottles and glasses. Inside were barrels on racks as far as you could see.

This was the first time I'd got a proper look at the fifteen or so 'folks' who'd ridden in the other buggies. How do you do, folks! Hullo! So glad to meet you . . . I immediately forgot which were Adnan and Loujain, Rafael and Sana, Vartan and Hadley, Walid and Stephanie . . .

Money – no question. Three bags full. Lawyers, realtors, moguls? Groomed – yes. Tanned – the biscuits were left in too long. One of them was an overdone roast. Straight – and how. Borgy (as we said when we had no respect for money. That was down to not having any). No taste. The men dressed like golf-pros. That's why they watch golf 24/7 – to get fashion tips. His and hers cosmetic adjustments. His and hers slacks: supernaff word, slax. Caramel slax: supernaff garment. Beige slax. Blazers.

Roman worked his way among them. He addressed some in French. Some in DIY Spanish. Some of them had these weird unplaceable accents. He looked pained at a fag end on the cropped grass. Signalled the flunkies to pick it up. Smiles. Not the warmest. It was obvious there were two distinct groups.

His friends, all men, a tight bunch of four of them, heads down, intense.

Second, their wives and these other 'folks'. They were acquaintances, no more. They might have been upscale tourists on a wineries tour. He wasn't interested in them. It was all false informal greetings. He didn't bother them with anything beyond off-the-peg charm. He had that salesman amiability-veneer. Slick professional schmoozing. Everyone knows it's bogus. Everyone goes along with it. Insincerity: the common currency.

There was an oldster he was shaking hands with. The sheer

chutzpah. He didn't even pretend not to be looking over this venerable party's shoulder. He was watching a helicopter landing just this side of the windsock. Watching anxiously I reckoned. Grimaces and so on. He tensely waved at a couple of flunkies: to go there. Now!

One of his chummies had a bulge in his jacket. Familiar sight that, in the music industry. You get used to it. A piece in a shoulder holster. But – an armed Rotarian? At a Sunday barbecue? He realised that I had clocked him. His eyebrows joined in the middle. He was dressed in what he thought was English style: paisley breast pocket handkerchief, paisley cravat, lightweight tweed suit, shoes like mirrors. He honoured me with a military salute, long way up, short way down. None of the guests made any effort to conceal their wonder about me. A lot of amazement going down. They were puzzled by Roman's trophy. What was I? I was an unknown quantity. Belonged not to just a different tribe but a different species. Not a family entertainer. Not a lounge-music monger. They eyed me nervously. Or was it distaste? They didn't know how to behave in the presence of a Legend.

Ricky van Brabant was looking what had been called double-godlike. Exquisitely conditioned hair: and so it should be . . . the hours I put in. Glossy, glossy, not matt and matted. Gleaming perfection. (Coverdale should be so lucky.) Midnight blue silk-corduroy strides. Silk-corduroy is iridescent. Not fucking dull like cotton corduroy. The nap catches the light. It shines like a raven dunked in petrol before you've set it alight. You can only get away with them if you're a wraith. Purple suede biker jacket with gold zips. Nudie shirt: pewter with a mustard yoke, gold stitch embroidery and square gold snap buttons. $2,800 hand-tooled cobalt capybara and cinnamon brown hippopotamus hide rodeo boots with a gold ivy leaf inset that was repeated in miniature on the heel. Well heeled! Once upon a time only the rich wore high heels. Here we are again, people! My belt buckle was a gold longhorn on a jet background. Medium-heft gold necklace and bracelets.

There were troughs to spit the wines into. What a waste when half the world's gagging for a tasty bev! But I didn't want to look like a

novice. Being frugal had gone out the window way back in somewhere like Toledo, Ohio, or Raleigh, whatever state that was. Saving
for a rainy day? No way. Fuck the people! I spat. I swirled and twirled,
glugged and swigged and spat. Like it was second nature. I plunged
my hooter into glasses the size of footballs. Sniffing like a heroic
drugs-squad mutt blessed with millions of receptors. Shifting sensa-
tions from palate to nostril. I murmured and gargled. I copied their
discreet foreplay noises. Ooh . . . ahhh . . . mmmmm . . . ernnn . . .
That seemed to be the way. Their approval of my connoisseurship
was indicated by their amiable smiles, supernaturally dazzling smiles.
Adds bright bright brightness.

Roman spoke loudly: 'Must shut those doors now. To control
temperature it is vital. A crucial part in refining process. In the
alchemy of grape becoming wine.'

A hand stroked the small of my back. Heady musky scent and
cigar smoke. I knew what that meant. I turned. Molly was smiling at
me. I was the cream. She was the cat. Such a pussycat.

'Good golly Miss Molly,' I laughed.

'Sure like to ball,' she laughed back.

15.50

A mocking echo.

'A late lunch, a leisurely lunch. Fine wine. Great repartee.'

You can aim the last one. Stamp on it. Repartee? Jesus! Talk about
yawnzville! No, not yawnzville. Toxicville. That's the one. There's
no escape from a table. Or from the two ugly bints with ugly minds
on either side of you talking across you. Yap yap in English, yap yap
in French. Difficult to suss what was being said in English because of
the accents. The French was nearly all fucking parlayvoo to me. But
I got the gist. If you spend what are called your formative years in
Radlett you get the gist. You can sense it.

Little nudges, little hints. *Chosen. Our friends. How many fridges?*
How many? My mother-in-law lost everything . . . Le Beau Sacha. Arna-
queurs génétiques (I think that's the correctly spelt insult). *Youpin.*
Already. Already. Brought it on themselves. And so on. Repetitively.

It didn't dawn on them that I was one of their best friends, their overfridged friends. Or did it? Were they just mocking me? I might have asked them: Shares in Siemens? In I. G. Farben? Look, I just stayed schtum. I aimed a curse with hitman accuracy at the mouthier one. They wore so much hairspray their big hair was matt finish. Like it was frosted with icing sugar. One was bootblack black. The other sort of marmalade. They smelt like jungle gas stations. I could have incinerated them on the spot. Up in a single whoosh. But me, I prefer the slow game.

We were eating *al fresco*. Five or six shaded tables in an arcaded courtyard. Eyeball white and sex pink. Broad arches. Very picture postcard. Apart from the bints. Bougainvillea. Ornamental cacti. Creepers. Twisted trunks wrapped around themselves like snakes. Very pretty. Apart from the people.

Molly and me, we made eye-lust contact across the yard through the stone pit fire's pale sunlit flames. The pit was beneath a weighted chain barbecue. Every few minutes a flunky wound up the clockwork. Like some torture instrument from the Middle Ages or the Spanish Inquisition. (I knew I'd made it when Eric Idle came backstage in Atlanta and only wanted to talk to me.) Short ribs and baby lambs rotated above the pale sunlit flames. The meat was charred. Delicious. But I wasn't hungry for that sort of meat. I needed to have that woman. I was getting groin hunger. I looked at my watch. Time was running out. Wrist tap gesture. When you make that gesture your lips tauten. Kind of reflex. She shrugged her shoulders. Open palms. All to say she was helplessly captive at that table for the minute. And be patient. Me, be patient. I ate another cherimoya. Another guava. I took a sip of wine. Wine tastes better at night. This example of Logwood Estate Winery's production was just the ticket for a cold winter's evening. Crackling log fire, romantic candlelight, brace of tasties spread and ready on fur rugs. But not under 'California's sun lazing in the sky in July'.

17.00

Lunch sort of evaporated. The bints shifted without a goodbye. Chummy with the piece and the single eyebrow sauntered over to me.

'Roman tells me you're the new big thing with the kids. That's good. I hope it may continue. But look over your shoulder . . . Watch out for the next new big thing. And remember where you came from – if you don't you may find yourself back there.'

Arsehole.

'That sure is quality counsel, Sir.' He took that as a compliment, couldn't read a sneer. 'I'm not into being the new big thing . . . I'm creating an art form.'

'You know Timmy-Boy Niel?'

Pure corn country and western crooner. Saccharine sincerity seeping out of every pore. The Man With The Velvet Thorax. An embarrassing human being.

'Know of him, of course . . .'

'A very good friend. He has a trailer park in the grounds of his mansion – just so he remembers where he came from—'

'So they have trailer parks at Yale?'

He looked puzzled. He smiled, jutted his chin and was on his way. He put his arm round one of the other guys and followed the gang through a flowery arch. I could tell they were talking about me.

It turned out that they had gone to play croquet on a lawn like a golf green. Croquet! So terminally English. English pre-us, pre-rock and roll, pre-libertine. The old island. Delusions of empire. Those fucking straw hats. Those fucking Pimm's. It was like the enforced leisure at Butlin's. (Too common according to my parents.) Or trying to imitate the old stiff upper lip. (Too posh . . . The hazards of being in the middle.) Boston brahmins might play croquet – yes. But not West Coast – what? People . . . people. Some of the women were stuck into canasta on a terrace. Things were turning weird.

Molly said matter of fact: 'We'll go to the studio. Now.'

'What's with this guy?'

I showed her the card Chummy had handed me. *Spencer Prestige*. Followed by so many letters it was like a Scrabble hand that won't form a word.

'What d'you mean – *what's with him?*'

'Why does he carry a shooter?'

'Ah! Hah . . . Yeh. What we thay about Spencer ith that he grew extra limbs – y'know . . . so he had more fingers . . . to get into more pies. He's a real thweetheart. But . . . he has just tho many entreprenurial interests. There's always the possibility of dissatisfied customers . . . Who knows?'

'What sort of customers?'

'Spencer is primarily a gynaecologist. He has an, uh, unusual speciality. Hymenal reconstruction. Rethtoring virginity. He's restored some virginities more than once.'

'That's cheating . . .'

'Depends whether they can get away with it. Some of these keba girls are real hot. They're ath hungry for dick as normal people.'

'So he's armed so he can fight them off . . .'

She pitied me with her smile.

'There have been . . . some incidents, what you might call incidents . . . not often . . . but when you're dealing with kebas . . . they can get funny . . . they want their women to be more virgin than virgin. Matter of family honour.'

'Aren't some of these people here kebas?'

'Be careful who you call keba . . . There are kebas – and then there are kebas . . . Yeh? One of the ladies you were sitting next to is Palestinian. But Mona, she's from Lebanon, originally. Bekaa Valley. Not keba. They're not on a religious trip. They're western.'

We walked a wide grass road beside a white-fenced paddock. Half a dozen horses slouched in it, lazy grazers. On the far side of it Mac stood shaking a feed bucket.

'Criollos,' she said, 'Argentinian: we import them . . . As polo ponies. Horthes . . . Not ponies. Never figured why they're called ponies. D'you play?'

'Do I play . . . ? Play what?'

'Polo.'

'Polo!!'

'Yeh, play polo . . . I thought it was big in England, polo.'

'I've never even seen a polo match . . . chukka whatever it's called . . .' (This was yonks before musicians and their managers started brown-nosing royalty by funding polo teams.)

'He's my chouchou.' She whistled at a beige horse, which took no notice. 'He's such a thweetie. He's my Carlos Babington. What are you into: leather, latex, lathe? You want me to dreth up. I know that much. My crystal ball tells me you're not into the purity of nakedness.'

'Purity . . . Certainly not.'

'Fine and dandy, Babe. I shall entertain you.'

17.20

She was as good as her word. What!

She put on The Meknes Tarab Andaloussi. She left me listening to their slaughterhouse wailing. Like they had sciatic pain not ecstasy at whatever it was – seeing Ramalama or whirling with Glissashab. Impossible to tell when the band stops tuning and actually plays a number. She walked through a wall. Well, she went through a door without a frame that looked just like the wall on either side of it. Candy-striped wallpaper, dado and all. The handle was hardly visible. I think I'd seen them in France, certainly in French movies. They always seemed magical.

I looked around me. The studio appeared to be an extension to the house. A corner of it was a DIY gym. Exercise bike. Wall bars. Weights. It was tall. The roof was half glass. One of the walls too. There were stairs to a mezzanine/gallery. Beneath it a big mirror attached to the wall. And beside that a wall clock with spikey numerals. Plaster decorations – sort of art nouveau nymphs and cherubs. Did they do art nouveau in America? They did: the huge daybed was also art nouveau. It was oval and hefty. Upholstered bolsters, quilted velvet. Not really a bed for sleeping. Ottoman? Is that right? Heavy brocade curtains looking forward to their pension if you know what I mean. There were things you'd get in any art or photography studio. Storm and Po's or Dudley's, say. A Hasselblad on a tripod. 35mm SLRs. Tins of paint everywhere. Tubes of paint. Spray cannisters. An airbrush compressor. No chaos. All very shipshape. Neatly arranged yogurt pots. Rags. Sponges. Buckets. Yard brushes and washing-up brushes, paintbrushes of all refrains. Dozens of Polaroids stuck to a board. I sat on an old polished cabin trunk. A faint odour of beeswax. She was taking her time. The Meknes guys microtoniced. There was nothing to do but look and hope. That's a pretty phone on the floor: touch tone, turquoise. Large canvasses on the floor. Another canvas was about ten feet long. It leaned against a wall. It consisted of the words DISJECTA MEMBRA. Each letter was formed of photos cut into countless tiny fragments and collaged. From very close to it you could see that the photos were from S&M books.

Then it got weird. There was a long table. On it: oh what a joyous surprise! Maquettes? Models? They were realistic life-size versions of horses' dongs. Very precise sketches of horses' dongs on thick paper pinned to stage flats. Kind of scientific? Really freaky. There were sweetshop jars of body parts in formalin. Horses' bodies? I guessed so. Big bones bleached by the sun. The starving nag dies in the hills. It gets to become part of some artsy experiment. What do we call this? Horsing about? Whinny The Dobbin? Stubbs on DMT? (The ideas for lyrics came spurting.) Now to the skulls – dogs? Mountain lions? Wolves?

What was going down here? What dimly lit alley was I heading down? Note: the sun was still strong.

Anticipation was high. Grate Expectations. (Band catchphrase: The Toot never managed to light a fire the winter we had the cold water cottage at Gutch Common. I was different.)

Ricky van Brabant wasn't used to being kept waiting. It made me nervy.

I was looking at all this queer gear with such concentration I didn't hear her. But my nose . . . her scent was potent. Cravache? (Me, I'd come a long way from that fucking primitive cottage beneath Beckford's fiefdom. I knew the word means whip.) She had returned.

She murmured behind me: 'Me voilà – az zay say.'

Ooh I trembled.

I turned. I gasped. I really gasped. I thought I'd seen it all. I hadn't.

It was like she had stepped right out of one of those heavy-duty books – *Rogue* or *Swordsman*, *Submissionary Position* or *Tongue Imperious*. The shiny pornowhore of my dreams. I'd never seen anything like this outside Les Chandelles and Overside. Shiny, shiny . . . whiplash girlchild. A vision all harnessed in black latex. Latex straps. Big taut plum-coloured nipples lifted by a latex waspie. Latex and rubber necklace. Latex gloves almost to her armpits. Latex garter belt and latex stockings. Chains and clasps. Buckles and buckle holes. Terry de Havilland style shoes with six-inch heels and a transparent platform. Nicely coiffed bush. Black latex

Mr Whippy bag. Whip. Never had petrochemical by-products been put to such noble use.

There was just something or other about her that made me love her. It's easy to be sceptical about love. But maybe, maybe, just maybe this was true love, young love, we share . . . at last. I felt myself coming over all Tab Hunter. Rewrite that sentence!

That knowing smile! 'Do whatever you want with me.' She took a lungful of cheroot and put it down. It looked like a dog's drenched cock.

She meant business. She might have been a professional. It's not the sort of thing a Legend enquires about. Between pushing her tongue into my meatus and punishing my balls with her razor red fingernails she told me that the studio and the first part of the house had been designed by Linsel Murly of the Idyllic Brotherhood.

I screamed 'Lindsay who' when she sunk her teeth into my shaft, viciously – like that porky slapper in a rented Allegro up by Clifton Suspension Bridge, said she'd been a beauty queen in Weston-super-Mare. Congruence of teeth: there can only be so many mouth shapes. That's not what I wanted to be reminded of. I ended up in Bristol A&E.

Spot of luck: we were still The Small Town Delons. (The name was too knowing, too arty, meant nothing to the ooh-aahs in Crewk-erne on our world tour of Somerset and the West.) We hadn't evolved, I wasn't even on the cusp of becoming a Legend so the sniggering hospital staff didn't recognise me.

Hey – but come what may I pushed Xenophon hard, as far down her throat as I could. I liked getting his glans wrapped in her straps. She's busy sucking on my dingdong. Stopping now and again to toke her cheroot.

And talk me through the Idyllic Brotherhood: tempera, bestiality, gouache, polygamy, golden hour, paedophilia, carving as fine as that of the netsuke masters, multiple glazes, suicides. They borrowed the morals of Eric Gill and the techniques of Walter Someone and Maxfield Parrish. I was going to say Maxfield Parrish are the guys off the King's Road who make my leather strides (with bespoke gentleman holster) when she fisted my arse without warning. I slapped the cheeky slut. She laughed and stuck out her tongue. I fucked her throat even deeper so, so, so deep it would have daunted a lesser whore. It daunted me.

'What's your safety word?' I whispered.

'One safety word ith *harder*, darling . . . the other ith *more*.'

Then her mouth was so crammed full she wouldn't have been able to say either.

She blew smoke so my glans was wreathed in mystery. I fucked every fuckable aperture. I moved from one to the next. My cruiser, her fiord. She came once with Magister in her cunt. Once with Frere Mandrin in her arse. Her arse was bliss – it was like swimming in a tarn of sweet molasses. She squeezed my balls like they'd never been squeezed before – well, not for some days anyway. Still I couldn't come. But then I often don't on a first date with fucktoys I respect – as people. Fucktoys I'm not using just as a friction vessel but might have a deep chat with – which of my songs she is most into etc.

The phone rang. She leaned across the ottoman and across me to reach it. She invited me to lick. She held my head down while she listened.

'Yethsss. Of courthse. Got it.'

She bent over backwards to look up at the clock: 'Yeth. That would be fine, just fine. Yeh.'

My tongue strummed her clitoris. Like plucking strings. It tasted just the way a young girl should, it tasted of, well, of life-giving oyster. Clitoris extra! Yeh! What!

'*Good* boy!' she yelpy squealed.

She magicked from somewhere a double cock ring, shaft and balls. She pulled it tight. I was so fucking proud of myself. This is how a million fans wanted to see their Legend.

'Bad girl,' she reproached herself an octave lower with a suave smile. 'Such a bold demirep – whatever that means.'

She made me love her.

18.30

Her hand was up my arse again. This time snarking down my prostate. The agony and the ecstasy.

'Let's play. Shall we play. Leth play a game,' she said.

I was up for anything.

She was soon strapping on a strap-on-dick-to-me with an Uber-schlong as gleaming black as everything else. Like polished jet. Modelled on some San Fernando donkey like Jason 'Love Muscle' Barrie or Donald Fuck.

There was a scratching, scraping noise from somewhere. And a croaked whisper? Seemed to come from high in the walls but sounded like the crypt. I kind of jumped: 'What's that?'

'Ah nothing – nothing. It's . . . yeh . . . ith's only the osk martens.'

'The *whats*?'

'The osk martens . . . No? They come out . . . scrounge about round thith time of day. Dustbins. I tell you, when Mac gets them in his sights – hey, no mercy. Pow! He was at My Lai, Mac. Cowering gooks cower ye no more! Meet your Mac. Sure shot. He's into Remorth One Therapeutic Candour. Never fails to make a meeting. Makes no difference – he just loves a gun . . . And he still exchanges Thanksgiving cards with Rusty Calley. Now – let's put this on.'

She was exhuming something else from the Mr Whippy's darkest depths. A latex mask. Or did this one qualify as a helmet? Just one aperture, a zip for the mouth. Before I could react – how should Ricky van Brabant react to the greatest fuck he's ever had, for weeks, wanting to gag him? – she slid it over my head. She tightened the collar. I felt the purring and clicks as she rolled its combination lock. She was trying to make it all-but-constricting but I had to stick in a finger between my neck and the fabric to stop her.

So, no cigar, wild slut! Still, no getting out of it either! In other situations I might have been warier. I couldn't see. Sensory deprivation totalled out. I could hardly hear. The padding was surprising over my ears. But I could trust. How I could trust! And I could anticipate. Wrongly. I couldn't anticipate that she would twirl me round. All part of Wagner's cock ring cycle – we, the chosen with our telltale slice, cannot apply, goyim only.

She spun me on my axis like Peggles the Pegleg. It was dark. It was frightening. It was exhilarating. Like being wound up to whizz through black space. It took me back. Junior school tortures where the other kids got out of control. They picked on me. They put bags over my head. They locked me in cupboards and wardrobes. I didn't let on what a gas it was. Their cruelty was a gift to me. They'd pinch me, they'd punch me, they'd reckon the squeals of joy from my frozen spine were fright not delight.

And here I was again . . . giddy . . . something was making me try to recite the squares of prime numbers . . . checking out my inner cheek with my tongue . . . some slapper had had worries about what she called mouth ulsters.

Hanged for a sheep, hanged for a lamb
Hung like a tup, hung like a ram . . .

I'd forgotten those lines I never found a tune for. By the time I was released from my sweet captivity I'd have forgotten about them all over again. But it would have been real bad form to have asked for a pencil and paper at that juncture. When would I be released?

There was more captivity to come.

'Give me your writhsts.'

'Of course . . .'

She handcuffed me to the corners of the ottoman.

Apocalypse begins with a grin . . . mouthful of protruding teeth captioned 'new pariah priest of Saint Botolph, Shenley' – give him a chance . . . cacti whirred like shrieking tops . . . I flinched to avoid the spines I couldn't see . . . the . . . the . . . *glochids* – got it. The darkness darkened. I felt floaty. I felt leaden. I felt floaty. What speed was I at? I couldn't measure me against anything. Me? A kind of me. A zombie dervish. They're sufis, right?

It rushed, how it rushed, I hurried through her, a man with an urgent delivery, I danced inside her, a waltz, a watusi, sensational increments of blood pumping, of words depositing themselves: the adze in the cart, the horse in the coffin, the stuffing in the well, the bees in the throat, the cream in the jacket, the fox in the cab, the badger in the gable, the hand in the tunnel, the bulb in the lung, the vanilla in the mirror, the cartridge in the dock, the letter in the feather, the cork in the collar, the dove in the sump, the dove in the sump . . . slump, yes, shouldn't it be slump?

Aaaaah! Ow! Sheee-it! That hurt. Different sort of hurt. Aural. That's aural: A-U. Screeching din earpain. Cymbals from the electric crypt, pipes from the garden of tortures. Noise to perforate the inner ear. To put teeth on edge. Grinding squeaking like a metal door scraping on stone. Those osk martens again? How strong were these creatures?

Then, even creepier, I heard them giggling – like humans? Suppressing laughter like they were hiding. I was whirling – right? She busy sucking on my dingdong . . . I thought. I was beginning not to go with the flow . . . The scent changed: lavender and lemon. Also, I detected an unfamiliar set of teeth. I felt a canine. Shaft getting bitten turns me on. Glans no no no. A lack of delicacy. This was pain equals pain. No pleasure. Stop stop stop!!! We had no safety word. Were we we? The hand that grasped my balls felt different, bigger, tougher, leathery. I had the feeling I had been outsourced. The darkness darkened.

I screamed: 'Molly! Molly!'

No answer save a couple of fingers exploring my arse. Followed by a cock. A flesh and blood cock. Not a fascinum, not a non-doctor, not a strap-a-dick-to-me, not a probe. No. A male appendage. Easily distinguished. It wasn't uncomfortably large . . . but there was the thorny question of ownership. Whose meat was I host to? I had issued no invitations. Recall: I was blindfolded and handcuffed. The advantage was not with me.

Whose voice was it said: 'Tighten that ass boy, tighten that ass'?

I clenched. Who?

Who said: 'Let's crunch that butt boy'?

Who stepped on the gas? Who turned up the volume? This was gatecrashing.

I didn't know the voice, generic West Coast reamer I guess. I didn't know where Molly was. I felt insecure sightless helpless. Even with this rectal renegade working hard and breathing hard it was lonely being me. I could feel the dagger tensing. He got off at Fratton. Something to be thankful for. And as he did so there was applause and laughter and my helmet was being removed and I was blinky from light deprivation. The face I saw was Molly, the next face I saw was Roman, then, then . . . that faggy faggot from the bar last night.

This was weird. The guy was smiling. I was beginning to suss. This guy had just fucked me. Roman kissed him on the cheek.

He turned to me, naked me, with a spiteful smile: 'Here's the little faggot who came on all *faggy*. Yes he is a little faggot but he's my little faggot, my Little Dion.'

This was a new one on naked me, naked me with a hard-on . . . I was trying to get it straight. Had he been watching Little Dion fuck me? He had, evidently. So had two of the big-haired bints and Spencer Prestige with the piece, the man proud to know Timmy-Boy Niel. He waved at me from the mezzanine. A little DTs of the hand, the Queen Mother and her sceptred mop. This was a bizarro tableau. Straight out of a Pol Berg painting – bourgeois lounge where everything is ordinary, cocktail party banal, beige, apart from a figure whose guts are falling out to the carpet through a rent in his stomach or a woman pulling the trigger of a pistol in her mouth. I was an exhibit. On show. A turn. Well, it's my vocation. Not the least bit bashful, me.

Had they really been watching Molly and me?

My face was asking the question. Before I could speak Molly ran her hands over Magister.

The sweet honey purred at me: 'He's always here to lend support. Aren't you, Daddy.'

Daddy!

'Why do you call him Daddy?'

'Because he is my Daddy.'

I gasped. I gaped. 'Daddy?! – I thought you were—'

'My concubine?' suggested Roman.

I was just about speechless. I managed: 'Something like that yeh.'

'He watches me because he loves me so he loves to watch me. But he never touches me, not once,' she said. 'He protects me, don't you, Daddy. Ever since I was thirteen.'

'And I never lay a finger on her . . . my gorgeous daughter.'

'That wouldn't be natural would it, Daddy. Not natural at all.'

'It would not. It's theatre . . . Entertainment for my friends. With the added attraction of Ricky van Brabant . . . It's like serving them the finest wine. I just like them to watch my little girl bringing pleasure to my friends.'

'Like this, Daddy . . .'

And she started jerking me then squatted to suck me again. Highway to paradise. It hurt like bliss. I was getting close.

Roman said: 'Remember I said we had a mutual friend in common.'

I couldn't speak. I was fucking her mouth with full force tsunami. I was coming. I came. She was greedy. Magister trembled. The audience clapped.

'Yeh . . . mutual friend in common, Mister Ricky.'

I nodded my head doltish not quite able to speak yet. Bleary.

'Andrija Prodanović.'

I shook my head. Molly was rubbing nature's moisturiser into her tits. Oh her smile! She'd never been in trouble not even in town and never would be with that skin care regime.

I didn't lose my hard-on.

'Doesn't,' I gasped, 'mean anything to me. Sorry, no.'

'Maybe if I call him by name of Croat Andy?'

I lost my hard-on. Whoosh. Instant floppo. Instant panic. Instant blood drought: where does it all go?

Croat Andy – there's a name to make flesh creep. Cornelius Henniker's personal primate, muscle and on-off gofor (off because there are a number of countries, too long to list, which he can't visit) . . .

Nonetheless this grudge-bearing snout, this self-pitying, barely human, multiply-tattooed piece of treachery and shit is a mechanic employed by various government agencies on the black. If The Mother of All Democracies wants to put to bed Fairplay-Nathan Okeke, the laughably titled Justice Minister of Mboki-Bambessa, Croat Andy is the man it turns to. When it was learnt that the Provisionals suspected 'Phil Mathers' and 'Johnny Divney' were plants Croat Andy was the man who silenced them before they could talk. It's rumoured that the Foreign Office (motto: Fair Play Is For Export Only) hires him out to various unsavoury, all-lapidating, all-chanting, anti-Semitic regimes, strictly cash. He's a lucked-out winner who's convinced he's a stitched-up loser. Walking-talking proof of the cock-up theory of paranoid human life. Subject to arrest warrants issued by most of this planet's more civilised countries. Oh, and he's also a blackmailer: goes with the territory.

A weird unprecedented situation went bad, got threatening. I suspected I was in danger. I was naked. I clutched my balls like a footballer in the wall.

Roman looked and laughed: 'Don't worry. We're not going to

castrate you – we don't make steers here at Logwood . . . Nice ziz by the way – good action. No, no . . . that's not our way, Mister Ricky. Though I have to say I do enjoy *les joyeuses* as the French call them . . . *les joyeuses* . . . No, what we want you to do is take Andrija a gift, tribute if you like . . . to make up to him, to say sorry for all the hassle you brought him . . . that's a lot of hassle – he feels you let him down . . . you know he served almost a year as Her Majesty's guest . . . on remand . . . an innocent man . . . long time . . . just you and the bucket you shit in . . .'

'What sort of gift? *Tribute* . . .' Where the fuck did he get that word from?

'You will see. Fullness of time.'

'I've got a plane to catch.'

'Of course you have. Don't worry, Mister Ricky. Calm.'

Everything about Croat Andy being busted for dealing just reeked of corruption, of proxy wars between different police forces trying to show muscle, at least two intelligence services lording it. I kept telling Cornelius to aim him, buy him a remote island without a boat, but Cornelius didn't have the guts. Labyrinth of double crosses, half-truths, strings pulled from on high, men in the shadows (literally). It all screamed of dirty tricks in the Establishment's rotten heart, aka The Travellers Club. And no one got to hear about it because the government issued a D-notice. My role was strictly peripheral. I was a hapless pawn who'd tried to smooth things for the paranoid ape.

'Look: I don't know what Andy's told you . . . No . . . No, actually I can imagine what he's told you. It's what he told everyone . . . He says I grassed him. I didn't. What he means is that I refused to perjure myself. Mind if I put on my threads?'

Can I remind you: Purple suede biker jacket with gold zips. Nudie shirt: pewter with a mustard yoke, gold stitch embroidery and square gold snap buttons. $2,800 hand-tooled cobalt capybara and cinnamon brown hippopotamus hide rodeo boots . . .

I strolled as nonchalant as I could manage, picking up an item here, a boot there, trying to slip into them casual as a naz.

'*I* am not a grass . . . However – your friend Marty is. Right? Marty . . . he fingered Andy. He knew he was scoring a big big bump of carlos. He fingered Andy in exchange for charges against him being dropped . . . The point is Marty is a retard. The filth knew they'd never make the charges stick . . . Course they didn't let on to Marty. They told him he was going down. They conned him. Easily done . . . and he's such a fucking chatty prat . . .'

'Andrija said the detective leading the investigation is a friend of yours . . .'

'Friend! Detective Fucking Inspector Desmond "Quasi" Hubback *friend*?! Strictly a business acquaintance . . . It's useful to have people you can call on . . . on your side. I fixed the meet . . . the drive-in McDonald's up by The Welsh Harp. The idea was Andy hands over six grand so Quasi'll disappear the evidence . . . There were no witnesses apart from Marty, just the physical . . . the gear . . . bury it and the prosecution has no case . . .'

'So he gives this detective six thousand pounds and still ends up in cell?' Roman shrugged and sneered. 'Sounds like a bad bargain to me.'

'It was down to Quasi getting taken off the case. Internal . . . whatever it is – Internal Protocols? Investigated him over some totally unrelated . . . like minor . . . it was an expenses claim or something. They put him on gardening leave.' I sat on the floor to get my boots on.

'They put him *on what*?'

'Gardening leave.'

I was almost fully dressed. Molly was smoking a cheroot like it was a cock.

'A detective? Gardening? What . . . like trimming verges, planting flowers?'

Oh dear. The common language.

'You don't actually do any mowing. Manner of speaking isn't it. It meant he couldn't access his office. Up till then he was the most reliably bent bluebottle you could hope to meet. Not an honest bone in his body. Look – it was all just terrible timing . . . but otherwise Andy was . . . well, let us say he was well looked after. His – what do you call them – his patrons, clients? – saw to it for him.'

'Bluebottle?'

Leave it out.

★

The Hon. Mrs Justice Haskard-Levack's only daughter Demelza had died five years earlier from a cocaine overdose. She was in her fourth term at Newnham College, Cambridge. The tabs had a field day. 'Hooray and Out'. 'Sniffed It, Snuffed It'. 'The Honourable Nostrils of the Entitled'. 'Charlie's Not Her Darling'. 'Sniffy Snob Nob Toots Too Much Toff Snuff'. No surprise then that the judge, bit of a tab herself, was ill disposed towards a man she described on the first day of the trial as 'a dealer in death' and 'a harbinger of lasting misery'. His claim that the 250 grams of cocaine found in his Transit van's glove compartment had been planted there was deemed 'risible'. Her overt bias was obvious. That evening she was telephoned by a senior officer in the MoD and invited to a meeting 'on a matter of national security'. The meeting took place in a car on Barnes Common. She was told that she was going to have an attack of pleurisy that would prevent her working the next day.

At the start of the second day of the trial it was announced that The Hon. Mrs Justice Haskard-Levack was unable to continue. Illness. New trial date, new jury sworn in, new judge appointed: Mr Justice Crompton.

Much of the trial was in camera. No explanation. No reporting due to the D-notice. Cornelius, our manager, said there was some 'unusual activity'. Different sort of people showing up, hurrying through the back entrance. Military maybe, not wearing uniform . . . but that *bearing* gives them away. After less than two days Mr Justice Crompton instructed that all charges were to be withdrawn, the prosecution discontinued, the jury dismissed.

'That's not the way Andrija tells it. Innocent man . . . spent twelve months in custody.'

'Innocent? You're joking.'

'You know better than wise judge, Mister Ricky?'

'Wise judge . . . Do you really buy that . . . independence of the judiciary bollocks? Total fucking C. O. Jones . . . Ha! Your *wise judge* was following orders from the security services – or their freelances . . . all strictly off the record . . . arms' length. There was some weird stuff going down.'

Roman performed a stage yawn exposing his throat to the assembled like a widely split beaver.

I kept going: 'They didn't want Andy to talk. They weren't going to let him have his day in court . . . he could have said exactly what he liked. Name names . . . point the finger. He was one resentful bunny.'

Roman's face went all bony, all pointed and skull. He wasn't listening. He was working up his anger: 'It wasn't just that cell with cockroaches . . . vermin type filth creatures . . . It was loss of income – only so much business you can do from a cell . . . I don't think you make good excuses for how you behaved, Mister Ricky. You're talking made-for-TV movie . . . It's time to pack Andrija's present.'

'Sure.'

'I'm afraid you'll have to take your pants off again . . .'

Little Dion chipped in: 'We need your ass, big boy. We need you to open wide.'

'What?'

Fuck *pants* for trousers, fuck *ass* for arse.

What follows is what I left out of *Ballad of a Legend*. I didn't even mention it to my so-called ghost Dominic Rose. Indolent piece of work, not to be trusted, gossipy. Back then the last thing I wanted was letting on I'd been taken for a patsy. Made into a mule like some starving Yoruba. Bad experiences come in many shapes and sizes. There was nothing I didn't know about objects marooned in the lower gastro-intestinal tract. I was a faithful reader of *The Paracelsian*. Beyond filial duty. Nothing I liked more than tales of stray light bulbs, cutlery, avocados, medicine balls, boxing gloves, an entire internal gymnasium . . . But it was always other people, poor saddos, who got romantically involved with that electric jezebel the Hoover Dustette when cleaning the stairs. I was an outsider to the experience. A distant witness. Empathetically, imaginatively, I knew what having a package the size of a pack of butter in your arse felt like, but bugger empathy for a game of soldiers – I had never felt it myself. I had no muscular point of reference, no muscular memory. Little Dion had already raped me. I do believe I heard the faggy nance whisper 'once is never enough with a man like you'.

'For your scrutiny,' sneered Roman. He held out what looked like two pale aubergines, lilac not purple, torpedo dimensions. 'Not too bulky eh!'

'You really think I'm going to pack those?' I was insulted. Worse, I was frightened.

'I have no doubt you will.'

'Let's quit this fucking charade.'

Roman turned to Spencer Prestige, the big-haired slappers, dressing-gowned Molly, Little Dion. He stretched his arms to signal incredulity: 'A charade, my friends. A charade . . . Mister Ricky has so many talents . . . but, you know, humility is not among them, no . . . as for gratitude . . . I go to all the lengths of professional wrapping, skilled artisans, two layers of latex, wax outer coating . . . and what does he say . . . charade . . .'

He turned to me: 'You know, my friend, Andrija is going to be one big hot collar if he doesn't receive his personal tribute . . . personally handed to him . . . And we have Spencer here . . . leading man in his field . . . knows every inch of the rectal and recreation areas . . . You won't feel a thing . . .

'Of course you could just slip the gifts in your pocket and hope and pray to good lord – or whoever you people pray to – you don't get searched . . . I'd say you've got a one in a hundred chance.'

You people . . . so that's where he's coming from.

'One in a thousand,' advised Little Dion, effortfully moving the decimal point.

'At best,' laughed Roman, 'at best . . . and I tell you Andrija would not go big on appreciation if he learns you just put it in your baggage hold luggage . . . they'll go through your luggage with fine teeth . . . I tell you, Mister Ricky, you are rock star in a hard place . . . how d'you like that . . . rock star and hard place! (Applause) Yes . . . But I tell you – I'm going to make things just hunky-dory for you, tiptop utopia. Hour . . . maybe ninety before plane lands you take Hyper-Lax-Extra plus bomb of chilli-glycerine suppositories . . . Spencer's specials . . . wham bam . . . it'll all come tumbling out. You'll be the new face of Pampers.'

'New face of Pampers . . . oh that's good . . . mmmm, very good,' growled Spencer.

I stoked up my courage. Where was I going? No idea. Nowhere to run to. Nowhere to hide. I spoke as assured as I could: 'Time I was off. I'll leave you to your fantasies. Thank you for the entertainment, Honeybunch.' I felt up her wet butt crack as I moved between the ottoman and some unfinished maquettes towards the door. No one tried to stop me.

Roman merely smiled: 'Don't be a silly boy . . . You know that song "It All Comes Round" . . . ?'

What was it this time? I had heard the song enough to know I didn't want to know it. A crock of maudlin million-selling shit by the former Greg Towell, a duff 'multi-instrumentalist' (and master of none). We once auditioned him way back when we needed a glissando virtuoso as temporary replacement for Jimmy Gliss after he broke his wrist during a weekend at a sex farm. We couldn't afford Nicky Hopkins. Greg was the very pic of the no-hoper. All ambition and no talent. He disappeared without trace for three, maybe four years.

Then – jus' like tha' – his silly pixie face was fucking everywhere, stained with turmeric it looked like. He'd aimed his educationally subnormal hairdo. Now he was six inches taller with a mixed marriage of late Elvis and Louis The Coiffeur. Was that XIV, XV, XVI? So baroque it was rococo – or is it the other way round? He was now Toni Lo Reno, Cavalier on the Highway of Song. His daft name was written in a one-off typeface. (Clever touch that, I thought of nicking it.) He thought he was reinventing as a parody crooner, a comedy act.

But no one laughed. Goes without saying it's usually the other way round: an artiste who takes himself seriously is laughed at, mocked, scorned, dead at the Glasgow Empire. He was so unfunny no one noticed the parody bit. People took him for a crooner, just a crooner. Tout court. They took him seriously for god's sake, a big new crooner, *the* big new crooner. Middle America's Rotarian housewives wet themselves. They never wanted rock and roll. He quietly binned the parody. Not that anyone noticed. If you're going to do parody you need to do more than just imitate. You've got to exaggerate the gap between the genuine article and your take on it.

'. . . you know how that song came about.' Roman added hypocrisy to the charge sheet: he was almost pleading.

'I don't give a toss . . . it's smegma . . . Like I said – it's time I left.'

'You'll feel different when I tell you. I guarantee.' He took me by the hand and sat me down with a glass of water.

Along with many losers down the years Greg Towell dick-whittington'd to the West Coast to seek fame and fortune as a by-the-hour session singer. As far down the hierarchy as it gets. So far down it's like it belongs to a different geological era. For every Merry Clayton there are ten thousand Greg Towells. Each is sitting in your lap taking your order in the latest place on Ventura or Fairfax telling you the Peruvian ribs are gorgeous and he is *really* an actor, a musician, a dancer, a director . . . but not desperate, no no . . . oh no.

Greg Towell came on lucky when he met a fat blonde actress, over the hill, looking for love. She was the sometime starlet, almost star, just about, Dinah Lincoln (née June Doody): the one you'd get if you couldn't get the one who was like the one who was like Shelley Winters, a bit. He congratulated her on that choice: avocado waikiki bedded with brundled pacific cheeks. He was rewarded. He quit waiting restaurants to wait on her. She was the beneficiary of multiple alimonies. Her Googie house in the Hills had ocean views, an infinity edge pool, a spa tub, a sauna, a snacketeria kitchen, waterfalls, five hundred bottle bottom skylights, a freeform log fire in the middle of the Big Feature, a sloping conversation pit. The house was 'magically cantilevered, a triumph of teetering steel, a triumph of will over deflection' (*Coast Homes and Interiors*). He was glad not to be living in a rodents' motel in West Adams, so glad he'd do anything for her. Anything . . .

He was happy to let her shit on him now and again. That was her thing. If it turns you on . . . It turned her on all right . . . it got to be every day, then twice, soon three times daily and counting. An addiction. She ate like a pig and swallowed super-strength laxatives to keep up the flow. She paid him extra pocket money to turn down the few gigs he was offered. The sight of her big big tree trunk thighs impaling his chest . . . it worried him. Had he made a bad life-choice?

Brown coils of gut-processed silt stuck in his chest hair, clogged the chunky ingot necklaces she had gifted him. But without her . . .

330

it was unthinkable . . . And, hey, life wasn't so bad. He used to be an alcoholic sluicing down two or more litres of Cisco, Mad Dog, Thunderbird every day. No more – now he was a connoisseur sluicing down two or more litres of fine old Cognac, Armagnac, Kirsch every day. If he added a bottle of Jack before she dumped on him he didn't really notice . . . and no way did she scrimp on the Wipettes. Yeh. Scrape it all up. And then an ultra-generous chaser after. Not a bad life . . . he was kept in style. The downside of course was the more the shit kept coming the more he drank. And the more he drank the more he stumbled about the place.

One afternoon after she had dropped a super-duper steaming hot lunch he slipped on the sloping floor. He fell into the freeform log fire. It took him a while to figure where he was, what was going down. By the time he oriented himself his right ear was burnt off. The pain was bad. The smell was worse. And his career, as he called it, was gone. Even if he hadn't sung in months it was gone. Whoever heard of a session singer without an ear to cup? The ear is the essential prop.

Reconstructive surgery – porous polyethylene and local advancement flaps to disguise the implants – was cosmetically successful. But the facsimile ear lacked flexibility. It was unpliable. It wouldn't shift in time with the lines being sung. After careful consideration of his future options he gave up being a resting session singer and became a resting musical parodist. He grew big hair and big burns, bought the tackiest tux he could find, smeared his face with Antibes Bronze Oak Mousse and made his debut at Dinah Lincoln's annual fiftieth birthday party singing 'It All Comes Round'.

'This boy has got something,' announced the music mogul Irving 'Porky' Berger, observing the audience moved to cheap tears by the greetings-card tale of a guitarist whose jealous rival beats him up and takes away his most precious gift. Proxy autobiog.

'So husky he's a pack of sled dogs. Hahaha. That's what the ladies like. This boy can be major. Very major.'

'You don't know the last line?' asked Roman, surprised.

'Life's too short to listen to pap. I'm sure you're going to tell me it.'

'The last line, Mister Ricky, goes like this . . . the last two lines is better:

In the stars, it was to be. It was written!
They searched, his fingertips were in the mitten.'

I thought what shit. It doesn't make sense. But it echoed, how it rang in my head. Then I thought, though, how he had scrutinised my hands the night before. Fetishised them. And I'd gone along with it. Fallen for a carnal trap. Molly was bait. What the fuck would I do without my fingers? My fingers are my life, my fortune, my reason for being.

'So you see – it's your fingers or your ass.'

'Get on with it,' I said to him.

'Absolution. That's what you'll get. Absolution. Let's pack, Mister Ricky . . . Molly . . . Spencer – are you ready? Dion . . . Hey, Dion . . .'

The cubic capacity of the human arse is astonishing. Well, maybe not that astonishing if you're into films like *Anal Treacle* and *Backdoor Jack*. But for those with normal tastes definitely astonishing. Spencer Prestige shot me up with a local anaesthetic then buried two packs of 100 per cent pure carlos in mine. He got a laugh for saying that there was room for plenty more. What merry jollity! They all assured me there was no risk of it breaking out of its thick coat. Because they were reading from the same page it set alarm bells ringing. Unanimity is always phoney, not to be trusted. The danger of seepage was physical. Provided I could get through the flight I'd be OK . . . eleven hours with my life in my digestive tract. Eat nothing. Drink as little as possible.

The humiliation was different. Having my legs spatchcocked behind my ears like an Australian backup singer saying she's pleased to see you was a physical slight all right. But more than that it was a psychological blow. It might have broken a lesser maestro, sent him damaged and weeping to a shrink. It was a reverse medical intervention. Impregnation. Having a foetus put up me. Is this what it feels like when you're in the club? Or was I confusing having a stranger aboard, pregnancy, with constipation?

As the insertion was taking place I was yelping to make them feel bad, ashamed, sub-human. I failed.

Roman suggested: 'Don't think of yourself as a smuggler. Such a skid row word. I prefer courier. Amateur courier. You're doing it for love. This is for you. To make amends. To satisfy Andrija that you are seeking redemption. Like I say . . . to be absolved . . . It's a token of thanks from us. It's a tribute from you. And you get it to him, you pay it to him the day after you land. He expects it. Understood? Mister Ricky? Capiche?'

No false cheer this time. I accepted my little sick-joke of a gift-wrapped box of laxatives as gracelessly as I could. Without a word, without eye contact with my aggressors, without even laying a hand on Molly.

I walked out to where Mac was waiting in the limo. I was already planning my revenge. I had rarely given a thought to my fingers. Now I felt obsessively protective towards them. I was so angry that a confederacy of arseholes would dare impair them and me. I only spoke to Mac to ask him why he wouldn't let anyone open the car windows.

'Ghosts. The winders keeps the ghosts out,' he said, as though it were obvious and only a berk would ask. 'Ghosts from the Tet Offensive. Hell on earth, boy. You too young to have gone down the Nam?'

'No – but Wilson kept us out. Played LBJ like a fisherman plays a salmon.' (I forget where I got that comparison.)

'No appetite for the fight . . . real men shoot gooks. Real men don't take it up the shitter . . . did you pray, boy, when you was taking it . . . like your Angelus folk is it? Those Angelus folk praying.'

'The point is—'

'The point is – while you may have a packet in your anus, boy, I cannot begin to approve your sentiments.'

'Irony . . . Lost on Americans.'

'You're better than that, boy. How many times have I heard Americans *don't do irony*? It's like written in your Europeans' script . . . your sacred English irony. Irony? Dramatic irony? Never take nothing at face value.'

Otherwise he stayed mute till we got to the airport when he said: 'Shoulders back. Stand upright or lie flat. Oh and Mr Marcato says only silly boys go blabbing to the cops. We got you, boy. And you got your fingers – provisional. Let's make it permanent . . . why not, boy?' To my amazement he hugged me.

I did sort of pray . . . that I could just get through the next few hours without threats or anal rape. What I needed was Lady Luck to smile on me. Fickle bitch.

Cornelius had booked the upper deck of a 747. A feast of carpeted walls, all ochres and burnt orange. He wasn't with us. He was in Dallas to see some band of hicks with a fiddler that he had a hunch about. Ha!

I gave Glen the rest of his tip and then some. I measured my sleepers so that I'd wake in good time to take the laxatives. Belt and braces: I asked Glen to make sure I was awake three hours before we were due to land.

I made a note to talk to Cornelius about insuring my hands.

The ambient was desperado. Everyone apart from me had a head-ripping hangover and a mouth like a keba's armpit. Glen's eyes looked like one of those cute animals on a greetings card. They were all trying to drink it off so they could get 'sober' and then repeat the cycle before they got to Blighty – when they could start drinking it off again.

I made a second note to talk to Cornelius about discipline. Every freeloader had his own freeloaders. Every hanger-on had his hangers-on. Who was picking up a dozen groupies' fares? How were they getting back to LA? Or were they going on the payroll like anyone else who smiles sweetly at Cornelius? No one would go down on him if he wasn't connected to us. They're his fucktoys littering the office. They aren't even decorative. They genuflect gratefully when they glimpse one of us.

I made a third note to talk to Cornelius about realigning Marty. He's got to go. He had been sort of useful when we were using. But we didn't need a dealer on the staff now we were clean (mostly). Me, I'd given up everything apart from wine and cocktails – Negroni, Manhattan, White Lady, Sidecar, Gin Martini, Old Fashioned, Bullshot (exclusively breakfast). Only tradition will do.

Marty sloped past. He asked me how my day had been. Knowingly.

Dull, I said. He winked grossly: I wondered what he knew. I

wondered what he was up to. His creepoid father's connection to Roman Marcato was total soil-pipe.

I made a fourth note. I reminded Cornelius that a) we employed him, not the other way round and b) his contract was just about up – and if he didn't act on notes 1, 2 and 3 we'd have to reconsider.

And then I slept. How I slept. I slept the dreamless sleep of a minstrel knight of yore with Class A fun in his bowels. And woke with a start remembering the Class A fun in the minstrel's bowels, thinking oh fuck there is a very good reason to be a scaredy cat.

I washed down the Hyper-Lax-Extra powder with fizzy water. I went to the john. It had been a long while back since I got butt bumped (by a super-lunged milf) but there was little I didn't know about open buttocks. You could say I was rebonding with an old friend. The two aubergines and Faggy Dion's dong had made my arse feel like the road taken, a scorched path well trodden. The chilli-glycerine suppositories slid down nice'n'easy.

Then it was waiting. Another bad bit. Staring, all clammy hands, at Blighty down below with the plane at a standstill in the holding stack over some godforsaken place like Reading, same problem as a bike at a standstill, apart from bikes not stalling and plummeting out of the sky. I was a dehydrated bag of nerves. Jimmy Gliss was doing a chess problem with his unique arts and crafts jet and marble set: aaah – of course, that is where I had heard of the Idyllic Brotherhood. He asked if I'd decided to go over to Roger Dubreuil's party next weekend. I had a total blank. I didn't know what he was talking about. I didn't know who Roger Dubreuil was. What party? Jimmy gave me the once over, puzzled: Sainte Maxime – as usual, like last year, and the year before.

This year's different, we'll be the biggest thing there. He asked if I was OK, what had I taken, why was I limping? Was I limping? I didn't know I was limping. I had limped back from the john apparently. I told him it must be cramp. I didn't elaborate. Still having no idea what was going down, I said I'd think about Sainte Maxime.

The relief of a smooth landing. The applause from the downstairs clutzes who clap was audible . . . I'd like to join them if it wasn't just so naff. That's one of the things about holding status like mine. You have to think image, image, image. Also my intestines were so provoked by the laxatives that any unnecessary movement, even of the clapping hands, might niagara them.

In the eyes of Her Majesty's Customs, any country's Customs for that matter, rock bands and our entourages are easy meat. We're there to be frisked at length because we are corrupting the nation's youth. Of course we are. That's our fucking job description. We are role-super-models. As such we are abusively frisked. Those resentful greys would take many lifetimes to earn what we earn in a night. Even their dogs earn more than they do. So you don't want some prick of a hanger-on – e.g. a low-waged music journo on a freebie or an assistant publicist – burying his stash of Tijuana Brass or Cortez Log in your frilly nylon panties. It does happen.

Bands are obvious targets. So no one carries. Customs know that. They know that we know. That didn't stop them hassling us, trying to make us late for ongoing connections etc. Usually we strolled through Nothing To Declare then got searched, sniffed by crotch-crazy bow-wows probing (oh that word!): the King Charles spaniels were pretty enough. The Marcher Hounds froze my blood. I stood head held high. I looked down to see if I was limping . . . My intestines were on a protest march. I'd made sure I was last off the plane, last through passports. I wanted a free run.

A gangly, tall, freckly, smiling, dogless Customs pig with epaulettes like squashed songbirds beckoned me to a metal table. Thin, gingery baby hair. His wire frame spectacles had lenses for the blind. He 'asked' if he could see my satchel.

'No problem.'

He slipped on a pair of surgical gloves a whiter shade of pale than his freckly arms. He gave it a perfunctory frisk. (Peremptory? Dom pls check.)

'Lovely . . . clean as the proverbial eh? . . . I got to say it's a privilege to search . . . well, rifle through!! . . . your bag . . . an artiste of your stature . . . a real privilege . . . makes the job worthwhile . . . I've got all your albums . . . heard everything you done . . .'

'Well . . . thank you . . . thank you very much . . . See you at some gig someday.' I picked up the satchel.

'When is *The Side I Dress On* released? Tell you . . . I'm really really looking forward to it.'

'In about four months.'

'Fantastic preview in *Riff Raff*.'

'Haven't seen it.' (A lie. Short on adulation and respect.)

'And it's got a new version of "Tractors of the Revolution" right?'

'Yeh . . .'

'I love that song. "This is the field this is the plough. This is the boar this is the sow" . . . Fantastic . . .'

He feebly attempted to sing that line, twirled his arms, embarrassingly, sort of dancing on the spot – is it a knitting move, does it have something to do with spinning pasta?

'I must be go—'

'So it's . . . what? More rockier?'

'Well, it's not that simple. Look I really gotta—'

'And you're using strings?'

'Ha! If *Riff Raff* says so . . . You'll have to wait and see . . .' (Nice touch there – conspiratorial and inclusive.) 'I need to push on.'

'Oh, sorry to have taken your time . . . But it's not every day . . . Look how you go now. I'll bet you're exhausted eh?'

'Nice to meet you.'

'I'm Paul by the way.'

'Paul . . . right. Be seeing you, Paul.'

'You bet . . . Ricky – you don't mind if I call you Ricky.'

'Course not.'

I tried to smile my special sincere smile of genuine mateyness and equality among men. I reckon what came out was more like a grimace of pain at trying to contain my tripes. It wasn't just pain. It was unfamiliar. It was humiliating. Me, I was an absolute beginner in faecal sludge management. I was hobbling by now. I shuffled away.

There are times in airports when they are weirdly deserted. The carousels are empty apart from one forgotten taped-up box no one wants because it's a likely very dead lump of endangered species. The teeming corridors aren't teeming. They are gleaming white. There's no one to scoff at the posters advertising Little England's olde attractions. Travelators disappear into the distant void. Not a soul on them. And the toilets, the restrooms, the caballeros, the depositories of tonnes of shit and reservoirs of piss are spotlessly bleached, hospital-wiped like no one ever had a bladder to unload.

I salute the cleaners: every one of us in the band had big Bog Operative Fear, those primordial jitters that if things didn't go our way . . . well . . . that might just be *us* with the slimy mop and toxic bucket, *us* getting treated as invisible, *us* getting silently avoided by the chief-greeting, darky-choking public who naturally share the same terror. I salute them. They are people too. The west's untouchables: if Jesus returned he'd show solidarity . . . he'd be an aggressively meek Bog Operative. Unless his head had been turned by cuties and leavened bread.

I feel a cur if I don't slip them a Nelson or a Nightingale. Noblesse oblige. What!

But there was no one to accept my bounty. It was silent as a morgue. There was no flight info, no MoR drooling, no tap dripping. It was a relief to be alone in a good-size handicrapper with nappy-changing facility, emergency cord, capacious Belfast sink, generous bottle of handscrub. It was a relief to get my strides off, to let go and listen to the laxatives making bubbling music, gurgling like a clear mountain stream. I aborted one arse foetus. Not entirely painless. No sir. I put it in the sink under a powerful tap to say goodbye to the film of rectal caul, shit and blood flecks it had picked up. It was threatening to dry web-like. The second was more stubborn. But out it came, eventually. Thank god you didn't need to go to Eton to get buggered enough to widen the tradesman's entrance. A comprehensive will do just as well. You never know when several times a week from the age of fourteen is going to come in handy. Some of those ruffian hod-carriers of tomorrow had healthy appetites.

Neither blind mullet was damaged. I sat on the can reflecting that the rest of this ordeal, getting the gear to Croat Andy, was a cinch, freewheeling downhill. I smiled at my fingers, at the gift in them, at their perfect liaison with my brain. I felt blessed.

There were footsteps without. They stopped, presumably at a urinal. Then they went up and down the line of cubicles including this one. And again. There was the faintest humming of a tune. More steps. Then the door of the adjacent cubicle was opened. Time, I thought, to go. I dried the packages and was putting the first in my satchel when—

'Oo's a funky junky then? Oo's a funky junky?'

It took longer than it should have to suss where the voice was coming from. Then I looked up. Peering over the dividing wall with his thick spectacles and ginger grin was Paul. Head disjointed from body like a kid's drawing. Must be standing on the can.

'Naughty boy. You could get your bottom smacked. Your BTM-ee-kins could get smacky-wackied.'

I buried my face in my hands.

'Be a good smuggler and open up – you know it's an offence to use the disabled when you're fully fit.'

I stood and opened the door. He shut it behind him.

He near whispered: 'Seven to ten years, Ricky. How much you got there? You might find everyone had forgotten about you by the time you're out . . . Who knows what we'll be grooving to then?'

I was sort of frozen to the spot.

'Bit of a sticky one isn't it.'

I nodded. Sheepishly.

'Very sticky . . . I could tell from the way you were walking . . .'

'Ah.'

'You've got a bit of a problem on your hands I'd say. Long-term problem . . . Me, all I've got is a short-term dilemma. If I bust you . . . I'll get a pat on my back, fast-track promotion . . . the powers-that-be love a celebrity scalp . . . I'll be the coming man for a week or so. But I'll still be a fucking Customs officer . . . very ordinary salary . . . very ordinary flat. Greenford. You can hear the M40.'

He was sweating too. Droplets all over his forehead. He was as nervous as I was.

'Or . . . I don't bust you . . . And we can come to a gentleman's agreement.'

'Tell me more . . . the ball's in your court, Paul.'

'It is isn't it, Ricky. Indeed it is. Yeh, I hold the cards . . . Well – how's about we start with you giving me half your stash.'

I thought of Croat Andy not receiving his full tribute, I thought of Roman and his ubiquitous tentacles . . . But at least I'd be free to work out a scheme . . .

'That's a lot of gear.'

'It is, hmmmm. Yes. I could be greedy. But I don't want to be. Because I admire you. So . . . let's say half that stash plus a with-thanks-to mention on *The Side I Dress On* album cover . . .'

I nodded: 'That can be arranged . . . yes . . . no problem.'

'Make it to Paul Klemens Dobney-Macherzynski.' He pointed to the identity tag on his lanyard.

'You'd better write it down.'

'There are lots of negatives from having a name like mine.'

He took a small notebook from his shirt pocket, tore out a page, he rested on the nappy changer, he stuck out his tongue to write, he handed it me.

'And then a little gesture of gratitude . . . how about you giving me a nice smooth blow job.'

'What the . . .'

He undid his trousers, rummaged like he was searching for a coin in the depths of a pocket. He eventually pulled out a shrivelled lump-ette of flesh. An award-winning micropenis. I'd seen thicker Biros. And it wasn't long. It was very short indeed, shrivelled and straggly. Not in the least bit appetising.

'Suck that meat, Ricky.'

I looked at it. Meat? One of those so-thin-it's-hardly-there wafer slices for Japanese fondue or whatever it's called.

'Suck and swallow! This is the side *I* dress on,' he giggled.

'Oh Christ.'

'Look, Sunshine . . . Ricky . . . you either swallow me or you spend the next seven years of your life swallowing gents with no pride in personal hygiene . . . think thick crusts of smeg.'

So I sucked. And swallowed for the one and only time in my life . . . well, that's not strictly accurate. But since school. Or maybe college. I didn't mind that much. Sexual morality is Abrahamic bullying. Who said that? Me.

My new friend continued his informed critical commentary on my work as I licked his puny glans.

'I've got six bootlegs . . . hold my balls mate, there's a dear . . .

even got that one from the football stadium . . . very sought after . . . come on – stronger grip if you please . . . you know what a soldier likes . . . Aarhus, was it? . . . Malmö? . . . where they shut you down . . .'

I dismissed the idea of biting hard because it might land me further up jissom creek. He pushed my head up and down without animosity. At least with his dong in my mouth I couldn't really clock it. I was sight deprived as they say. So I only had to taste, feel and listen – from within and without, simultaneously: blobglogplopblobglog . . .

'Uppsala . . . Uppsala, that's it . . . security issues, was it – ooh ooh oh yessss yesss!'

He happy-finished. The flavour was neutral. Bit like high-end white chocolate.

He said: 'I've got quick turn-around . . . give me five minutes . . . I'll soap up your arse nice and smooth . . . fuck it tough-rough-gruff. What say you?'

'It's sore.'

'I'll bet it is, me old darling.'

I spent one-third of the journey looking out of the window of the limo. Stan The Tache had almost given up on me. When I showed he whinged it was a hard life for drivers because the airport gave them nowhere to sit. 'The rest of them came through an hour ago.' Meaning: I was an inconsiderate brat who had kept him waiting.

I didn't reply. The low westering sun flushed the blocks beside the flyover pink and gold. Stan drooled on. I heard sounds, noises, couldn't be bothered to unscramble them.

I was working on how to keep Croat Andy happy when half his tribute was missing.

Cut the stuff by 50 per cent? I didn't have the means without involving some loose-tongued dealer or other. Anyway, first taste would tell him.

Claim I'd lost it. Claim it had been stolen. True, of course, but where did the truth ever get anyone especially when dealing with a dealer like Croat Andy, fully paid-up animal. He'd never believe me. I looked at my fingers.

Then I realised where we were. At the traffic lights between the

Natural History Museum and the V&A. Five minutes from home. All of a sudden it came to me, luminously . . .

Stan cooed: 'Come in number one. Come in number . . . Ricky . . . I said Ricky – where we going? Your gaff? You mutt and jeff is it?'

'Here.'

'What d'you mean here?'

I got out. I tapped on the roof. The last thing I wanted was for him to know where I was heading.

I crossed the Cromwell Road, strolled as unhurriedly as I could manage to Daquise.

I ordered a beer and a plate of cabbage pierogi then nipped down the narrow stairs to the phone booth. I flipped through the A–D directory. No listing for Dobney-Macherzynski. I found the number Marcato had given me for Croat Andy and rang it. He took a couple of minutes to answer. He told me I was meant to have called as soon as the plane landed. He told me not to be later than 11.00. He was on edge. He had a buyer. Very reliable buyer. He again warned me not to be late.

'He's famous for getting impatient. Doesn't like to be kept waiting. Hates to be kept waiting. Extra impatient. He's going to be here just before midnight. Important international businessman.'

I thought of car washes.

I called through the pass into the kitchen.

'Hey Ricky, how you doing?'

'OK . . . Tell me, Edek . . . This name. Does it mean anything to you? Dobney-Mach . . . mack? . . . er . . . zynski—' I handed him the piece of paper.

'Us Poles can be a bit of a mouthful.'

My paranoia made me wonder what he was talking about.

'No . . . doesn't ring no bells.'

Not so luminously then.

I ate slowly. I reflected on my fate as a Legend Under Threat. Does this shit happen to normal people? No. Only to Legends. We're the ones who pull the sword from the stone, tame the eagles, turn somersets on water. We're the ones who make the little people heed us. And for that we must face trials, obloquies, calumnies, shit and more shit. It's the price we pay. Status through strength. Sometimes it's not enough. Sid James, Molière, Tommy Cooper – they died on stage, giving themselves to the people. Performance is sacrifice.

I spent the next part of the journey in a black cab. The driver was silent. Dusk was slipping fast.

Then I found myself on a night bus, upstairs at the front. Movement brings tunes, words, melodies, lyrics. Even whole arrangements. It brings inspiration. It was dark now. Familiar streets passed by that I'd never seen before. The marvels of electricity. Brake lights. Shop windows full of oblong fridges. Eerie filling stations. Ice rinks. Poor people's hostels, the poorer the more the sad sign flickered. I was blanked out. I wanted not to take the miracles of everyday, everynight for granted. Look at them afresh, Ricky. I felt I was in the most private place in the world. My arse stung. My scarf was round my face. No one recognised me. I was unaccountably happy. I told myself that Legends have luck. We can overcome the natural order, the unities, the programmation of mankind.

I didn't know the address of Croat Andy's gaff. The road's name was anyone's guess. But I knew how to get there. I wouldn't learn its name till the day after tomorrow. No problem finding my way, though. I skipped down the bus's stairs, jumped off round the corner from Bookseller Crow On The Hill: the board outside announced, 'Jason Renucci reading from *Tolly Dene and Further Jests*. Q&A follows.' The neighbourhood booksters were on folding chairs, listening hard. I got myself across the road to avoid the pub bunch lurched out onto the pavement: I was less confident of my invisibility than Cecil King's psychic wife. This daft witch believed that Cecil – press baron, failed putschist – could make himself invisible. (My inspiration for 'Now You Don't' on *Chihuahua Moods*.) I sauntered down dark suburban roads, abrupt slopes. Cedars, wellingtonias, monkey puzzles rose above the walled gardens of Victorian villas that might have been churches. Then there was the actual church. As soon as you turned the corner you were hit by the bulk of the house The Croat bought, a warren of sitting tenants to be gradually removed by the traditional means (dead fish under floorboards, live snakes, nonfunctioning heating etc.). It stood on a slope above a long-abandoned railway tunnel, sidings, goods yards. The silhouette was clear against the crisp night sky. Towers, cones, weirdly angled roofs, chaos. It squatted sootily. A malevolent animal waiting to pounce, an escapee from the neighbourhood dinosaur pen. Did they build it to frighten the kids, scare off the guttersnipes? The road cut along the escarpment. The slope determined that the house's front door was on a middle floor. Four floors above it, two beneath. Such arrangements are mildly disorientating.

Not so disorientating as the possibility that Croat Andy might not go along with my plan to recover the gear from Senior Preventive Officer Paul Klemens Dobney-Macherzynski. I'd dropped him off with Cornelius several times but had never entered the building, never taken it in from close to. The drive was overgrown. An adjunct former stables was a wreck, bald from lack of tiles. The house was up the junction too. Flaking paint, cracked stained glass in the front door, twisted leading. The bell pushes were dodgily wired. Some had names attached with perishing tape. No indication which was Croat Andy's. The gothic arched windows next to it had grot-rich makeshift curtains in the form of ripped sheets, bobbly counterpanes etc. The windows beyond them were broken and where they weren't broken were impasted with grime. The only light was from the very lowest floor, from what must have been a winter garden and was now jungly, overgrown. Was that his domain? There was movement. At least one person. I pressed bells randomly. It was impossible to know if they sounded inside. I walked to the side of the building. There was an iron stairway like a New York fire escape down to the former kitchens and service quarters presumably. No point in even trying. Its lower half had collapsed. It was more rust than metal.

I was at the front of the house further from the front door figuring what to do when a dark figure filed singly from it, from the deep dark shadows . . . the figure from the shadows who had inhabited the shadows – how can Ricky van Brabant write clichés like those? But the figure really did step from the dark. One moment he was not there, next moment . . . it was theatre. I froze, it felt like a magician's tour de passepasse. Then I tripped. The figure heard me curse. Was this the buyer? The international businessman showing off his famous impatience? We could hardly see each other.

'Aaah . . . *there* you are.' Man's voice. Amused. As though it were the most natural thing in the world to greet a stranger in the dark with amiable familiarity. As though it were hide and seek or kick the can. 'I'm wondering where you gotten to . . . We should leave. Now!'

I felt stranded in the narrow front garden. All broken bottles, broken toys, broken sycamores, broken sundial, broken hopes.

'Hang about,' I said, very deliberately not moving. 'What's going on? Who are you?'

No reply.

'I'm here to see a friend who lives here . . . Andy?'

'Friend!' He laughed rather winningly. 'Ah that fabulous English sense of humour. Friend Andy's down there. I have to insist you come now.'

'Who are you?'

'My name wouldn't mean anything to you. Your name . . . it means much to millions. That's a fact. Not flattery . . . flattery is not my way. We have to go.'

From the light of a distant streetlight I could see a man of indeterminate age. Dark clothes. Dark glasses in the dark. He took me by the upper arm, walked me.

'Where's Andy?'

'Do you care? He's not with us.'

'What d'you mean?'

'He's dead.'

'Dead . . . no . . . come on.' I half laughed. 'What do you mean by dead?'

'How about . . . not breathing any more – that type of dead.'

'What . . . was he ill?'

'No more than usual. Sick in the head . . . otherwise good health so far as I know. I processed him.'

'You *what*?'

'Very neat. Clean. One shot behind left ear diagonally up. Failsafe. No pain. Don't worry. Trusted M.O. Instantaneous. He felt nothing. Your *friend* felt nothing.'

I realised – not for the first time in the last hours, days – I was far out of my depth. Me who struts before tens of thousands in stadia. But that's different. This was the sharp end. Realpolitik's grubby gutter. Something's grubby gutter anyway. Hitmen in bedsits. I wanted to run.

'You *shot* him . . . Why?'

'I'm expert. Good aim. I wouldn't be so . . . *deft* with, say, a cheesewire or clawhammer.'

'No . . . no . . . I mean why did you shoot him?'

'I'll tell you . . . Follow me.'

In the light of a streetlight his blueblack hair appeared *polished*. He was sleek as a panther. Probably as deadly. He let go of my arm.

'Do not turn your head. Keep your head down. Hands in your pockets – it's raining.'

'It isn't raining.'

'If you keep your hands in your pockets, head down . . . it alters how you walk . . . you shuffle . . . makes you less identifiable . . . feel you're facing rain from a Karcher . . . simple fieldcraft.'

'*What* craft?'

'Fieldcraft. What I am using to get you off the hook . . . You need me.'

We walked a deserted couple of hundred yards uphill, the road curved away. Houses hiding in the dark and bosky gardens. He nodded towards an Alfa Giulia Super parked on a pavement beside a phone box. Nice jamjar: possibly the sort I'd have if I was an ordinary person.

'What d'you mean need me – who are you? Sorry, *we* – who are *we*? And where are you taking me? He was a shit but if we shot all shits . . .'

'I got your retaliation in first as they say.'

'They do?' I'd never heard that Irish witticism.

'They do . . . He was more than a shit. He was an enemy of my country . . . enemy of my people . . . active enemy . . . was, I should say, was an enemy. He murdered for money. I silence out of love, out of duty, for the survival of our people . . . does there have to be a reason beyond that . . . Our people are your people too, Mister van Brabant. Get in. My name is Rui Päschlat . . .'

I didn't believe him. But he had saved me from something . . . so he claimed.

I said: 'Heritage, acquired characteristics . . . culty tribal stuff . . . the most Jewish traits I've got are not being tattooed and not coming south of the river unless I have to . . . tonight I had to. I don't make a thing of my ancestry . . .'

He adjusted the rear-view mirror, began to rearrange his alluring hair. Even when it was styled to his satisfaction he continued to glance at the mirror. He counted a few coins, rolled them niftily between his fingers . . . an actor's business.

'Might be an idea if you *did* make a thing . . . others do . . . the Nazis for instance . . . they made a thing of it all right . . . very successful at it . . . and they haven't disappeared . . . just hibernating behind beards and niqabs . . . if you want to avoid annihilation think of your race . . . join your people . . . make a thing of it . . .'

I was spinning.

'Ah – here we are. On time.'

He swiftly got out, took his coins to the phone box. I turned round to see what he had clocked in the mirror. A Mercedes had drawn up outside The Croat's house . . . The Croat's tomb. A vast man was hauling himself from the car. He waddled towards the front door, swaying delicately, waving away his anxious-to-help chauffeur. A Marcher Hound with clipped ears walked beside him.

Rui Päschlat was making a second call. He jumped back in the Alfa. We drove off quietly.

'Not worth risking staying to watch.'

For some minutes he was silent.

Then: 'Other people – Nazis, fascists, intégristes of all colours . . . other people are other, they really are. Agents of immobile history. Afraid of everything apart from stagnation. Their mentalities are other. Their morals are other. They have so little humanity they don't even want to recycle our dead bodies usefully. No potassium. Nothing to exhume. Anti-archaeology . . . anti-digging . . . anti-truth . . . truth is beneath us ready to be exhumed . . . did you know they created their own, they manufactured prehistoric artefacts, the SS . . . not very well but they fooled the volk. The Allach factory outside Munich . . . not to be confused . . . Maybe you don't care. But it'd be sad if there was no more music from you.'

'That bastard said he'd have my fingers done.'

'Marcato . . . Don't worry . . . He'll think the police have boosted the drugs . . . whisked them away. Don't worry . . .'

'Don't worry! Don't worry! How d'you *know what* he'll think?'

'We shall let him know. The Arab telephone is a marvellous instrument.'

'What am I meant to worry about if I don't worry about losing my fingers? Not getting top spot on Russell Harty? And what the fuck's the Arab telephone?'

'Bush telegraph, old boy!' His foreigner's take on nob's English was touching. 'You are famous. You are a Jew. So what do you expect? This world's not a place to be a Jew. A friend's father used to say scapegoat is the oldest profession.'

He finished doing his hair.

'Haven't you found that out . . . what a sheltered life you must lead . . . Why do they smuggle drugs up your arse – as the poet put it – when they have aircraft . . . helicopters . . . they've got boats . . . It was revenge . . . on you . . . on all Jews – you stand for all Jews. It was a helping hand for The Croat . . . a big drink as your cockneys say. Very big drink. After it's cut you're looking at four, maybe five hundred thousand.'

He listened and laughed.

'Ah the amorous Dobney-Macherzynski. A Customs and Excise legend.'

'They have legends in the Revenue?' I felt well shortchanged.

'Yes, of course . . . Haven't you got? You were set up. Dobney was tipped off by Marcato's people.

'So: primo – you have to succumb to his famously strenuous advances . . . secondo – he takes half the drugs . . . terzo – you show up here with what remains of the stuff so you'd feel The Croat's wraths: he might even have killed you. He wouldn't have known he was arnacked by Marcato . . . he'd have retaliated against you. Marcato is sly.

'I didn't want to take a chance. Half a kilo means nothing to them. A few sous. But it means everything to dealers like The Croat. It's a lottery win . . . It ends up at dinner parties, Hamilton Terrace, Bryanston Square, West Eleven . . . people with more money than sense.'

'More money than septum . . .'

'That's a very good line . . . If I can say line.'

I hadn't heard anyone call The Grove 'West Eleven' for years. Strange . . . but not that strange in the scheme of things.

'*I was set up?*'

'You were. We knew this morning . . . intercepts . . . we're always on the qui vive. That number you phoned . . . it was on our radar. The Croat would go for weeks without using it. Then today – twice. You, and before you a certain Rudi Memetov . . . who you saw back there struggling with his bulk – with luck he should by now be under arrest for murder . . . not equipped to make a quick getaway . . . he's a pimp . . . psychopimp . . . set fire to one of his judies' hair . . . she had so much Iron Grip Spray holding it she went up like a torch . . .'

That pressed some bell in my frazzled brain . . .

'He has a charmingly sentimental trait . . . he has a couple of robbers who exhume children's graves . . . steals the toys they were buried with, dolls, jewels, christening cups going back centuries . . . Slick operation. Works with a Crimean fence Timofei Lopatin who's going to die from his gross appetites: regals, enormous meals, alcohol, hookers—'

'Zurich, right? I read about grave robberies when we were playing Zurich.'

Once upon a time the only place we were big was Switzerland. I felt nostalgic for rösti, goyim's latkes.

'Lower echelons are easy . . . our late friend Andrija Prodanović for sample . . . a footsoldier . . . *following orders* . . . they're soft spots . . . they have to put their head out of the set . . . the people further up the ladder – not so easy . . .'

'You heard of this Doctor Prestige guy . . . ?'

'Spencer Prestige. For sure. Genital mutilator by appointment to the countless sultanates and emirates . . . end of story. Except he's a trafficker. Controls a fleet of superyachts . . . may even have tankers . . . uses them for shifting arms. Not strictly criminal. Like Roman Marcato . . . on public display but sort of hidden . . . The players, the real players, are the Mifsud brothers and Gajardo Melik . . . like high command . . . they're ideologues . . . their ideology is to murder Jews . . . the money from drugs, the fortunes, goes into weapons . . . big weapons . . . world-changing weapons – ICBMs. 80 per cent aimed at Israel. The rest funds militias and freelances like our Croat friend. With these people nothing can ever be proven in court so we sing our own roundel as they used to say. We make our own laws.'

He leaned towards me, he mouthed a phrase I could not figure out. I AM JUDEX. Maybe I wasn't meant to figure it. He smiled the most beautiful smile. Cold determination. Such certainty that I, Ricky van Brabant, wanted to be him . . . Me, wanting to be someone else! Me!

Wrong way round. The world upside-down. It's others who want to be me. That's how it should be, how it's always been . . . *Always* meaning ever since I saw the wasted remnants of Brian Jones lurching about The Speak badered and lisping. I didn't want to be him any more. Put that behind me. Didn't want to be the Pageboy From Hell any more. Didn't want to be face down in a pool.

Like I said, I don't know south London. I do know few Jews live there. It's the other side of the valley, the side where bad things happen . . . and they talk different . . . the accent. Like Rui said, other people are other. They live other lives. He drove carefully through this foreign land of undernourished streetlights, cemeteries, windy commons. We crossed the river. It still wasn't familiar till we got to that run of Holloway Road where I'd taken dates to get kitted out at the rubber, latex and tranny shops. (Made to measure is essential with those materials.) He cut through Stock Orchard Crescent, a lovely rural name that reminded me of before we were famous, i.e. poor with no pulling power; we used to hang loose in the Transit outside Holloway Prison waiting for sex-starved slags to be released: they'd be up for anything.

He parked up in a doleful street in Kentish Town or Tufnell Park, somewhere, anyway, downhill from the old Cally Market (four symmetrical pubs where ghosts of cattle moo their last). The street was greasy, low rent. The parked motors weren't: 1954 Bentley Continental, AC Ace, an E-type with a Clarence House parking sticker. He rang a bell at what looked like a closed-down shop. Its window was hung with translucent biscuit-colour curtains that when rucked turned opaque and marmalade colour. It was as super-grimed as The Croat's tenant's.

A man in bloodied chef clothes opened the door, furtively, a suspicious animal. He was pleased to see Rui. He beckoned us in. I was introduced to him, Mr Koritsas, and Mrs Koritsas who was mother to all her customers, homely, smiling – was there really that much to be cheerful about?

The place looked like every other Cypriot taverna in those seedy streets. Paper tablecloths. Refrigerated display of meat and fish. But it didn't feel like them. It felt expensive. It smelled of money and secrecy. Thick cigar smoke. Savoury grill scents. Cognac fumes not Keo or Metaxas, no way. Serge Lutens. A few poules de luxe. Opulent men, the kind that pay to be shaved daily, expensively suited, dressed too English style to be English. Laughter and raillery among the men who ruled the seas. Some smiled at me, acknowledged me – they knew who I was. This is what speakeasies must have been like. Not like The Speakeasy packed with okay-yah teen meat from Queen's College in Harley Street who'll tell you 'I've had clap *so* often it's like applause'. This was grown up. I behaved appropriately.

Less than a couple of years back they'd have asked, all patronising and jocular: 'Are you Moist or are you Groin?' No longer. I'm the sort of rock deity who's known outside Che Guevara teenage bedrooms. They were even dare I say – I dare – impressed to see me. Rui greeted several of them, all seated round taking port after dinner, or baie de houx – the more obscure the better with such hedonists.

We had only been seated for half a minute when a soon-to-be-former pretty boy sashayed – or is it shimmied? – across the room to us, like he was performing for the clientele, charming them, making sure he was noticed. A masterclass in self-adoration. The effect was marred by his shortness. He was only a few steps up from a porg. I knew him from . . . where?

Rui twitched his face, his version of a smile. 'Dudu!'

The nursery name didn't help place him.

Dudu sat and gave me an insolent lingering once-over like I was a lower form of cattle.

Gesturing to me he slurred at Rui: 'Who are you tonight . . . Luis? Luc? Or are you answering to Patric? Answering to Patric.'

I was out of the loop.

Rui took no notice of what sounded like an obscure wind-up. He was civil. He spoke quietly, coldly: 'Rui. OK? Right . . . Dudu – this is Ricky van Brabant. Ricky. Dudu Topaz.'

Dudu giggled again and spluttered. It was suddenly evident he was plegic from drink.

He gestured at my threads, addressed me with a cosmetic dental sneer.

'You some sort of exquisite?'

I shrugged.

'That schmutter . . . that's exquisite's clobber . . . no question . . . tell me man, when you jerk off can you fill up the palm of your hand?'

What on earth?

'I hardly ever need to jerk off. Very seldom.' How off-puttingly prim I sounded.

'Very seldom . . . very *seldom* . . . hmmm. That's not a word you hear a lot of, *seldom*. Anyway – *lucky* boy . . . D'you write longhand or typewriter?'

'Longhand.'

'Really . . . how quaint. Do you have a photocopier?'

'Not at home.'

He shrugged: 'Ah well . . . moon june . . . licks chicks . . . blues dues – you don't have to fill up the page do you . . . *lyrics* . . . little strip down the middle . . . big big borders like the rest of the page got a brazilian . . . everyone has a song inside him!'

'And that is *precisely* where it should stay.'

'Ooh. We're doing repartee are we! . . . I'm getting an *industrial strength* copier next week. Xerox. Nought to sixty in three seconds.'

'Impressive. Terrific . . . so you're a writer – what do you write?'

He looked at Rui with fury like Rui was to blame for my ignorance – which he took to be feigned, to be a calculated insult.

Ought I to have known that he was on the point of metamorphosing into something small – while I was very much going the other way? Not that he'd ever been as big as me. Top of a short ladder shall we say. What! He wasn't exactly going to cross borders.

'Rui will give you my CV.' He scowled: 'Won't you, *Rui*. Full oeuvre. My shows, my sketches, my sitcoms. My forthcoming film which has not, I repeat not, been cancelled. That was just some fuck-wit journalist from *Variety* getting the wrong shoulder.'

What sensitivity! Quick to take offence and even quicker to give it. A skin short of the full onion. Eleven out of ten on the narcissus scale.

An expensive woman in a fedora who must have just arrived half-raised her chin and trembled her fingers to greet Dudu. I knew her – from where? A ramrod-back man stood beside her, a mummified matinée idol fighting back the years, Canute with hair dye and a lifeless leathery face: his eyes stared out of two apertures in an ill-fitting mask apparently a few mm proud of the skin beneath.

'My guests.' He aped the old Queen Mother's wave in response.

'It was a rare delight to meet you,' he told me, meaning the very opposite. He stood up.

Rui took him by the wrist: 'They . . . *those people* are your *guests* . . . you're dining with *them*? You know who they are?'

'If I didn't know who they were why would I have arranged to meet them? Yeh? Lehitraot.'

'Dudu—' But he was sashaying back the way he came. The Fedora was immensely tall. She had to bend to kiss him. The Mummy shook his hand like it was an unnatural act.

Mrs Koritsas demanded we enjoyed. She was disappointed by Rui's lack of appetite. She knew him well enough to desist from a jovial ticking off. Me, I high-hogged it on Ch. Haut Marbuzet 1961 and shipowner dishes from the island of Plutocratia, not Cyprus. Dates stuffed with foie gras, veal tartare and white truffles, lamb with olives (maybe Cypriot). There was still more. Baked Vacherin with caraway and tiny potatoes, rum baba, old Armagnac and granular coffee (definitely Cypriot). It was like she was fattening me up to Staff size.

Dudu was showing off to his guests, expansive gestures, sly smiles. Rui was staring at him. Staring isn't right: it was a glare. Angry, yet pitying and incredulous at what seemed like a betrayal. He displayed a seam of profound disappointment. He had been posed a puzzle that silenced him in meditation. He distractedly picked at the food. A line of men processed across the restaurant to sniff the Fedora's neck and receive a chill gust of condescension in response.

When, atypically, she curled a smile of rapacious complicity I got it. I'd seen that gesture of camouflaged willing before. Incredibly I'd glimpsed her with Staff of all people. Backstage at one party or another. Lyon? Turin? Essen? Rotterdam. That was it. Rotterdam. I'd wondered at the time what he was doing with a dame who was way out of his league. Now I saw her in this milieu, this habitat, with these players I wondered even more.

That was my first encounter with Dudu Topaz whom I wouldn't see again for some while, and with Rui Päschlat whom I would.

He was a man with the knack of appearing from the deep dark shadows when least expected, who might in a blink slip back into them and then down the hidden tunnel to oblivion. He came from nowhere, went back there, wherever there was.

I envied him. Though I wasn't sure what for. He enchanted me. He made me admire him. Maybe adore him. Or should that be hero-worship? I didn't know him or where he was from. He gave away little. He talked of knowing people who wandered in perpetuity. Was he talking of himself? Had he scavenged for food? Had he been sheltered in a forest by robbers who passed their days delousing each other and their nights slitting throats? Had he raided chicken coops for eggs, milked cows in Alpine pastures, dressed in clothes stolen from the boughs where they were hung to dry? Had he stolen horses from the fields where they grazed and coloured their mane so they would be unrecognisable when he sold them? Who did he work for, where did his money come from? What team was he on? He didn't smell gay.

I was thrilled by the icy void at his centre. The joyous callousness. He was otherworldly, like he'd been composed by Schubert. He looked my age though he seemed, in demeanour, old beyond his years, infinitely old, tired as used earth. Like he was impersonating a young man. He wore the weight of the years and all that he had gleaned from wells, people, field systems, ancient erratics scattered from on high. He had travelled not like a troupe of minstrels or mountebanks travels, gig to gig, but wandering endlessly according to some internal compass when he was young, long long ago, orphaned, treading over his beginnings, inventing new ones, inventing a destiny, destinies, making a meaning of chaos and catastrophe knowing all the while there is no meaning. It just is. There is no reason for what is. It just is.

He lived by his own code. An outlaw code. Of course I was an outlaw too, don't forget, a rock outlaw. He had quite likely saved my life: that made him a murderer.

★

The minicab my plump new friend and mama Mrs Koritsas called for me was the usual ashtray. Like cider and Holloway Gaol, it was a memory of poverty times. Vassia the driver had a cat-litter complexion, popped French blues or bombers, ground his teeth, drove jerkily, ignored red lights in the empty city – amber gambler! He played shit music. Europop. I told him I preferred rebetika. He turned round, sniggered it was for old people. He wasn't exactly in the first flush himself. He was a babbling bubble and then some. This was his last job for the night. He had to be home before it was light.

Being out during the day wasn't for him. I wanted to nod off but his warren of rabbit got in the way. In-ter-min-ab-le. I began to listen for want of.

Being out during the day could be dangerous, he said. I sympathised about sensitive skin. He didn't get what I was talking about.

Then I thought of a scenario where he shares his home with a wife he can't stomach and she can't be doing with him so she works days and he works nights and they never meet. Wrong.

He didn't pause for thought. It was like a litany. Repeatedly told to god knows who, indiscreetly and stupidly if it was true. Stream of Cypriotness. He mentioned EOKA twice in ten seconds. Bring it on mate! All our yesterdays! Warming up the telly for ten minutes to coo at Makarios in his weird drag – get that hat! Grivas's amazing moustache that terrorists with funny names hid in. Bored British tommies getting infected with histoplasmosis from fucking chickens (according to *The Paracelsian*). Cyprus was an exciting part of my childhood.

Chickens came into it again, big time. Vassia's little brother and ward Stav was bullied, beaten about by boy zealots of the ANE (EOKA-Jugend). That was down to his closest schoolfriend being Turkish. One time they left him unconscious in a chicken coop. He choked on shit and dust. When he recovered they went for him again. He was laying flowers on his parents' grave (chicken, botulism). They put him in what, years later, on another continent, was called a Soweto necklace: tyres, petrol . . . But their matches were damp. How much longer would Stav's luck hold? Vassia knew who the tormentors were. He reported them not to the police but to a British intelligence officer whose Frazer Nash he tended like the nurse that believes the child her own. He was recruited as a paid informer. He was the only mechanic in the village of Psevdas. He chatted to everyone. He was all ears. He heard what was going on. He heard too much. He sent men to their death.

Covered in oil, supine beneath a van's gearbox, straining at a spanner, he saw field-booted feet approaching him. A foot kicked the jack supporting the vehicle. It dropped. It pinned him to the garage's concrete floor. He lay squashed for three hours before he was discovered. Broken ribs, damaged liver, ruptured spleen, hopeless shoulder, military hospital, wanted posters showing his face, RAF flight to England, meagre traitor's pension, squalid digs, no sun, no olives, Stav's misery, Stav falling in with the wrong sort, The Doner Squad from Haringey: Roman haircuts, bumfreezers, chisel toes and flick knives, Stav on the run.

Then the unthinkable, the unforeseeable. When Cyprus gained independence fifteen thousand amnestied EOKA fighters were granted asylum in Britain. 20,000 of them in Camden Town. Since that day he had led his life in fear of being recognised by one of them who might take revenge. One was all it'd take. A funny kind of vampire then. Driving the ashtray by night. Living on garage snacks. Sleeping by day in a gas meter bedsit. Waiting to hear from Stav who was ducking in Belgium, diving in Germany. If there was an award for hard luck stories . . . I felt genuinely sorry for the guy, fearing for his life, his fate decided by a rash decision made for what must have seemed the right reasons. Death is egalitarian, treats everyone the same. Until we reach death there is no equality. The meek have been misled. God favours the rich, the pretty, the clever, the big titted, the big cocked.

On a whim I gave him the 500 grams of carlos I had been carrying all day in my satchel. I wanted rid of it. A hex. At first he was reluctant to accept it. Suspicious. Some sort of wind-up? Things like this didn't happen to guys like him. A gift, I explained. No strings. Still suspicious but also amazed. Maybe setting him up for a new life. Getting him back on his feet again. Giving him hope. A humanitarian gesture. A generosity prompted by altruistic duty, the new aristocracy's noblesse oblige, in the new aristocracy's currency. What!

He stared at me with a childlike gratitude. I had to force him to take the meagre fare.

'See you.'

I saluted Davies's milko, grabbed a pint of UHT and a bottle of orange juice from his cute electric cart. Pavilion Road was coming alive. Loyd Parnacott, ten thousand bottles past his prime, squalored out of his nicotine tip, it's even more sordid than he is and he's got a swarm of flies round him like he's a cow's eyes. He pleaded with the milko that he'd pay tomorrow, hawked lavishly. A guy from InterValet was already buffing the Brig's XK 120. The Brig waved. He was wearing a djellaba, saying byebye to last night's popsy – how does he do it? Seventy plus and a beamer . . . he laughs them into the sack, that's how. Mrs G had arranged the balls on the snooker table and got in fresh flowers – bless! Lindy had left a non-urgent to-do list and a must-discuss list: the first essential for a rock legend is a family member who is an eagle-eyed chartered accountant.

I sat at the white piano, transcribed a few bars I had in my head since my bus journey, whenever that had been. I got up to fetch a glass. Vassia was still there outside in a state of wonder. Astonishment had beaten the need to get home before darkness. I called Martine. I left a message telling her to let herself in because I might be kipping.

The few bars would become 'The Temple of Abandon':

Here is the road of rectitude
Here is the righteous lane
I know where these places are
And I'll not come by again

Which is the sea of turpitude
Which are the rivers of shame
Show me where these places are
And I'll not come by again

Where is the shrine to lubricitude
Where is the altar of infame
Tell me where these places are
And I shall come by again

Three chords, the quicker the more memorable: you're out to lure them, hit the bridge, give them the loop but not too much – the earworms that stick are the insinuating ones, you don't know where they've come from, how they gatecrashed the old eustachian.

It took ten, fifteen minutes max. I thought of the most beautiful music in the world, the music of mega-sales, of the muffled clunk of a key locking a safety deposit box. Zurich was always on my mind, so was secrecy, companies within companies within companies, the Isle of Man, the Cayman Islands and Nevis, wherever they are. All totally legit. That is well-paid graft.

It had been a long thirty-six hours – was that right? – it felt like a lifetime. I admired my favourite sight in the magnificent Guarini mirror: I reminded myself to get Bobby With The Habit to refix the fixtures. They were on the wobbly side. I didn't look as wasted as I should have. I crashed on the Madame Recamier daybed wondering, impatiently, when does a Legend become a god? Apotheosis Now! What!

Hh's Crew

When I stride out with my good crew round me I am a bat with leather wings. I am the warrior who renders lucent the night that has befallen our nation. I am the light. I shine the light. I show them the light, my trusty fellows, my black crew. And they gleam in the light, they glisten black, my knights whose honour is loyalty, whose pride is in sacrifice, whose decency and hardness are born of their abjuration of such frailties as:

Sentimentalism, which we demand in our fine womenfolk who are differentiated from us by this trait, admirable in them.

Mercy, a form of self-congratulatory vanity. Among its facets are the English 'fair play' which that imperial people preach but take no further. If practised it acknowledges that our enemy is our peer. No, our enemy is our inferior. It grants him a second chance, the opportunity to fight another day. It is an act of submission. The Jew Jesus turned the other cheek. He was rewarded with nails through his palms. The benefactors of mercy are not those who grant it but those who will continue to infect our blood and infest our soil should we show irresolution.

Alcoholism, a self-inflicted plague of effeminacy and indiscipline. The alcoholic is typically sentimental and merciful. He deludes himself that he loves everyone. He forgives everything, until he becomes indiscriminately violent. He will first berate with foul language then he will set upon his good crew. Most homosexuals are alcoholics. Most alcoholics will kill themselves, for the wrong reasons – self-pity, self-hatred, self-evasion.

The right reasons are:

First, dutiful sacrifice.

Second, the refusal to be taken prisoner, thence to yield to sodium pentothal and betray our secrets, our stratagems, our arcana, our hiding places.

Third, the shame that accrues after such a capture and after such treachery. The treachery may be, so to speak, passive, unwitting. Its effects are nonetheless indistinguishable from those of a turncoat's testimony. To be taken prisoner is, in itself, a traitorous act.

Agnosticism. Flabby thought, dangerously close to the merciful. A superfluity of piety. Guilt-ridden: the agnostic can never be too generous. He is eager to help the weak when the weak are weak because they cannot help themselves. The agnostic cannot make up his mind. He is crippled by indecision. That indecision will cripple others. He is ever anxious to heed others' opinions. He sits on the fence agonising as the world goes by beside him. He allows that everyone is entitled to his particular belief system no matter how profoundly it differs from his own. He appeases because he doesn't know. He is feeble, worthless. He does not act. Doubt is a straitjacket.

Atheism. There is no greater presumption. If we believe that there is no god we cannot become gods ourselves. We limit ourselves. We straiten our aspirations. We accept the mundane. We accede that beyond the probable there is nothing to map, nothing to strive for. What then of the possible? What then of the impossible? We must venture forth as our forebears did from their caves. They looked forward, beyond the sunrise after next. They wore the untreated coats of animals. Then they learnt to treat the pelt. We have progressed. We wear the finest black twill woven in the mills of Chemnitz and Gera. We are cartographers of the unknown. We have denounced the enlightenment, the false light. We shall expunge it from the common memory. Its pernicious suasion has inhibited and diminished us with idle talk of what merely *is*. To linger on the taxonomy of the already existent is an insult to the future. It is also an insult to today. The enlightenment craves a perpetual present, a utopia of the merely likely.

What *could* be: that is the thing! We must overcome the merely likely. We must essay what the fearful tell us is impossible. Heaven on earth is within our grasp. Heaven on earth is heaven. Make no mistake. It is hewn by our rugged hands from the clay which may impede our feet but which inspires our mind. Heaven on earth is the earth rid of its contaminants. Heaven *is* the earth as it would be if cleared of vermin's multifarious forms. Heaven is all around us. Heaven is the ideal earth. Heaven is the earth's potentiality. We can awaken the god within us when we stride across the borders inflicted by mere men, when we cut down the sinks called cities – the basins of atheism and vermin.

Hubris. We must waken the god within us with humility. Rascher was overconfident. He believed he was shielded by Nini's flirtatious wiles. His anxiety to impress turned him into a braggart and a fraud, an antinomian beyond civil and Hippocratic law. His claim that she had given birth three times in her late forties due to treatments that he had devised ought to have been investigated. But his previous exemplary work at Dachau put him above suspicion. No one is above suspicion. This fraudulent fecundity might never have been uncovered had she not been caught attempting to steal a newborn baby from a Wuppertal clinic in order to augment the false family of earlier kidnap victims.

Their deceit and treachery condemned them to become prisoners in Buchenwald and finally back at Dachau. A deserved fate. My order to execute them was among my last, for the time being. Weiss was incredulous. I suspected that he had treated the Raschers with inappropriate leniency. I reminded him that insubordination was as punishable by death as scientific fakery. They will not enjoy the privilege of return.

Indolence. This quality of the obese is endemic to Christianity. At the very heart of it there is feet washing and the eucharist. They did not leave the room as they found it. It was a mess. And someone had to clear it up.

When I stride out with my good crew round me I bare my teeth as a bat does. Remember my smile. Like a bat's . . . It is often noted. Never in my hearing, but I can sense such remarks, I receive them with bat's antennae. My teeth signal our intentions. They are versatile. Teeth are also a gauge, a taxonomic measure. They are perhaps a less certain gauge than occipital length or nose width. The Jew's nose is so sized to give him an olfactory advantage over us, to steal our air, to allow him to sniff out his precious gelt, to allow him to sniff our humanity and exploit it. But make no mistake, teeth are important.[33] I have granted teeth importance. Meatus, nerve, enamel: these severally composed tools bequeathed to us by generation upon generation of good breeding are versatile. They masticate, they charm, they conceal, they threaten, they bite hard and quick so that vermin will have no chance. Teeth, like bone, outlast flesh – which is soft. Teeth live forever. The skeletons of our forebears are blessed with teeth. The teeth of the dead are merciless.

We, the inheritors of the empire of the living dead, are immortal. We wear two faces. The face of our present life, a face with blue eyes, with honourably scarred hardy skin and a nose no more than a centimetre wide. Above our temporal face we wear on our cap the face of our metempsychotic infinity, the face that alludes to our former selves and to the curtailment of each of our cycles when the flesh is stripped to leave clean, well-formed bone. We wear the death's head of the heroes we have been, the heroes whom we have exhumed from tombs in humble Westphalian churches so that they may be reinterred in the cathedrals they are worthy of, the heroes slain by Charlemagne at Verden whom we have commemorated with four and a half thousand granite menhirs that they will recognise because we, their inheritors, recognise them as due acknowledgement of that sacrifice which is ours, which is Germania's.

It is given to us, the indomitable army of the reincarnated, to expand our domain. The pied piper has been grievously misunderstood: he led children to the east to farm fields, render the fields rich for the

---

33 The Director of the Sicherheitsdienst Ernst Kaltenbrunner's teeth were deemed disgusting, stained with the tars of a hundred cigarettes per day. Himmler personally ordered him to have them cleaned.

common good in a way that the ignorant Slav never could. It is given to us, too, to purify our domain with martial endeavours so that when we next return this way we can stride free through our beech woods and birch woods, through oak woods whose leaves are our bond. We shall eradicate the mushrooms and steinpilze which suck at the roots of our trees. Fungi are Jewform plantlife, unworthy of life, they are sylvan pimps parasitical on honest roots, they are gaudy, lubricious, nutritionally void. The parasite believes it is the host. Heaven shall be on earth. My name was not passed down to me by chance. My fate and my duty are written in my name. We are draped in black. We are drenched in blood.

Let me say this: we were correct in our classification of the Jew and the Bolshevik as vermin. When they are collected together, concentrated in the lagers, they behave with the scavenging savagery of beasts. They eat each other. They steal from each other, they prey on each other. They go on all fours. Frail-minded appeasers claim that because Bolsheviks fight so fiercely they cannot be other than human. This is a dangerous conceit. Do we grant humanity to rats because they are efficient vectors of plague!

When ten thousand are processed in a day, an efficient day, none of the vermin cries. When one, *just one*, of us dies we cry. There is the difference. We feel. We mourn. We wonder at the nature of our loss. But they are immune to loss. The very idea of bereavement is alien to them, as it is to rats. When one rat dies the others don't notice. There you have the Jews. They amble about the lagers we have built for them aimlessly, incapable of selflessness. No wonder they never encouraged converts to their 'religion'. No other people could match their carelessness, their lack of consideration, their egocentricity.

This was formerly covert, hidden behind the doors of the shtetl, wrapped around with groaning and wailing. Now we have shown them up for what they are. We have provided the stage on which they reveal their nature for true Germans to see. And we should not despise them but pity them as we hasten their despatch from a world for which they are not fitted. What sort of human after all fights to the death over a rotting turnip? No sort of human, I'd suggest, only the Jew.

Where are your dietary laws now? The abandonment of the kosher order indicates again that these people are only pretending to be religionists. Make no mistake, they are indisputably a *race* as the Führer has identified them.

We have been warning them for more than a generation. We have strongly advised them that they have no place among us.

Fritsch, Chamberlain, Gobineau, von Liebenfels — all of them counselled the Jew and the Jew reacted like the creature he is, insensately unappreciative of our warning to him, ungrateful for the invitation to remove himself before it was too late, greedily eager to pursue his life as usurious parasite and pimp. The fact that these 'people' do not resist, that they are willingly led in packs to their resolution, shows that they are diseased. A German will fight to the last. A Jew meekly accedes. The Jew was too indolent to take up our offer of Madagascar, Isle of Zion. An entire island to themselves. A paradise. But apparently not good enough for these fastidious degenerates.

Our decent comrades in arms must learn to bear the olfactory assault which is regrettable but necessary. I too regret the smell of burning bones and nails and flesh but it must be suffered. It is necessary. And recall that the foul scents are due to the furnaces' fuel being Jewish bodies.

Recall too the proneness of Jews to typhus, to spotted plague unseen in Europe since the Middle Ages and never suffered by anyone but the Jews — and those they passed it on to. There is without doubt a particular gamut of disease that afflicts Jews. They spread those diseases through the lagers, without a care in the world.

My men have to live with the memory of the many thousands of problems they have solved. They are granite, they are steel forged in the Fatherland. The Jew who has been terminally disinfected has no such memory. He is spared that memory. The psychological harm to my men, my warriors, who have never shirked, is far greater than that suffered by the cowardly recipients of their measures. By sheer force they have made machines of themselves, machines of such might that they can erase the swarming bio-hazard of Jewry.

★

We die in the certitude of a new beginning – a funeral is a baptism before entry to New Land and Timelessness. The baptised child does not know where it is going. Nor does the deceased who is aware, nonetheless, that it is going to somewhere for its life is nourished by death. Life does not end with death.

In contrast, we can be sure that when the Jew dies there is no new beginning, just the eternal blankness of the end where there is nothing, an absence that is unthinkable and inescapable and impervious to representation. Neither absolute silence nor white ink on white paper nor the lack of everything can indicate perpetual death's void. Which can be ensured by mutilating the body by fire or force or heaven's breath.

We are not carrying out these special actions for our sake but for the sake of future generations, for the sake of the entire continent, which not only fails to express gratitude but punishes in a spirit of smug hypocrisy. Think of our actions as you might of planting acorns. You will not live in *this* life to see the oaks grown from them but your successors will. We sow in the knowledge of our immortality, of our metempsychotic revenance. We prosecute our special actions in the very same knowledge. Why are these generations so reluctant to celebrate our accomplishments? They should be proud of their forebears' achievements, not ashamed, they should glory in our victory. We did not wage a world war. As the blubbery whale Göring said: It is a racial war. It was us who cleansed Germany, who presented them with an uninfested Germany. The Fourth Reich is there for the making. The greatest hurdle has been leapt. The First Major Task has been accomplished. We built the foundations in the ash of Jews and the sweat of our men. Before our oaks could grow we had to face the challenge of the terrain we had inherited. We sweated blood to purify the soil. We were, so to speak, farmers whose land was polluted by ground elder. It chokes growth. It is difficult to remove. It is a long and wearisome process and the burden of effecting that removal hurts. It takes its toll. You think you are rid of it and still it returns. It has stubbornly criminal roots. Yet we did it! At such cost. It was the most selfless sacrifice we made. Make no mistake, it was not a cheap temporal sacrifice for *our* particular advantage. It was a sacrifice for all time, for a future that we ourselves would not participate in, no. But a future we could assure for our children and our children's children. Those who have cross-pollinated with ground elder sully themselves. What comes of that miscegenation with the ground elder of Zion? What comes of it is a hybrid, a mongrel. Remember 1 per cent impurity is as much an impurity as 99 per cent. The power of adulteration begins with a single seed that contaminates all. Cross an Aryan orchid with the ground elder of Zion and the latter will predominate through slyness, mendacity, usurious double-dealing, disloyalty and the absence of the decency we value. Yet our power will overcome all these fell qualities.

Aryan man is the most successful of species because the most destructive. We vanquish with firm-chinned belligerence. The will to eliminate is manifest in our maxillaries.

The Allies' sophistry was shocking to me. Make no mistake, they knew. Yes. Without any doubt they knew. From as early as the spring of 1942, they wove exculpatory tales, furnished themselves with countless reasons not to take action against the programmes of cleansing being undertaken in accord with the resolutions of Heydrich's little get-together at Am Grossen Wannsee only a few months previously.

They feigned ignorance, claimed that their information derived from unreliable sources, suppressed and destroyed internal documents, blamed the Holy See for providing unverifiable reports which were no more than rumours. Their tergiversation was a source of amusement. Furthermore it allowed us to get on with the job in hand unhindered.

The first night I saw the experimental land colony of Auschwitz from far off it was as though the sun was shining through the night, as though the night had been defeated by our incessant production line, as though we had effected not only a clean land but a clean sky. We created a new kind of new dawn. We have changed the 'natural' order of day and night just as we shall change the climate to create our own National Socialist Weather. Fission will achieve new levels of coldness. We shall replicate the ice age. Auschwitz was chosen as a site of industry and reprocessing because it was celebrated in the

Jewish world. Westphalia for ham, Hamburg for eels, Auschwitz for the carp which were bred and fattened in the hatchery ponds there. The Black Corps added a new significance to the name. It was the pride of the Reich.

Although a god, I consider myself to be the most normal of men even if I can change my appearance at will.

'You look like the booking clerk at Bad Godesberg Kleines Theater . . . You have a twin who mends punctures in the little workshop next to luggage storage at Paderborn Hautbahnhof . . . You remind me of the courteous man behind the desk at the Amber Hotel in Chemnitz where I used to stay when I travelled in shaving soap and allied colognes . . .'

Yes, I probably do resemble these worthy Germans. Why not? Of course I do. They are all fine Germans. My handwriting is jagged as Alpine peaks, fierce, tense with aggression. I am of a German type. I am the one of that type singled out to do for all of us what one man had to do. It is a question of responding to a call for the dutiful, of acknowledging the vocation of putting country before all – that country is the Führer. The flint, Rugen's chalk cliffs, the forests, the lakes, the bolts of German lightning over the Externsteine, our long-houses and autobahnen: they are the Führer.

The objection to shaven heads is incomprehensible. My head has always been shaved at least four centimetres above the top of my ears. But never the crown. Rather, I present to the world as an inverted monk. Hair is for stuffing.

It can be grown on Jews and gypsies. The Aryan does not need hair for it impedes his progress, efficiency and speed. The greater the purity our race achieves the less it will need hair. I repeat. The greater the purity our race achieves the less it will need hair. It is technologically redundant and a threat to hygiene. When, within a few generations, it has vanished our baldness will reveal us. There can be no escape from phrenology. It never lies.

We have freed our people of freedom. Freedom is a burden, inefficient, unwanted, unnecessary. It is a distraction from the pursuit of the goal specified by our Führer. Freedom is an invention of the Catholic church. Free will is no more a fixed tenet of moral behaviour than is the worship of the intellect. Free will is a fashionable illusion. And, anyway, Christian myth is actually based on its very opposite, on pre-destination. Judas's betrayal is predestined and foretold. This most crucial part of the passion is determined according to dogma that the church denies. This is a glaring flaw in the heart of Christian folklore, flagrant hypocrisy.

I warned Pavelić about the danger of too close an alliance – any alliance – between the Ustaše and the Catholic church and the dele-terious effect on the morale of his men. The fool responded by presenting me with a secretaire! As if he thought I might reconsider. He failed to appreciate that I was hewn from tougher rock. Like Dol-fuss he failed to appreciate that thraldom to the Vatican was incompatible with the nationalist ethic. Make no mistake, no man can serve two masters, two ideologies.

What do they mean? What do they mean when they talk of the crimes committed *in the name* of the German people? *In the name of!* The German people take full responsibility for their actions which were not crimes. In a total state with a total morality the actions of the government cannot, by definition, be criminal. The actions that the German government and the German people themselves prose-cuted were our national duty. There was no gulf between government and people. We shared a will. Germany no longer observes Pope Gregory's calendar. The NSDAP does not recognise that measure-ment of time. The Führer does not wear a watch. He creates a time which is his and which he shares with his people.

Nor do we recognise the Jewish science of such obfuscating charla-tans as Einstein. Why should we recognise them when we have our own wise alchemists steeped in the traditions of German science who can make gold from sand and petrol from water? We exploit the soil and all that is buried beneath the soil that will be German soil when we have conquered the Slav Untermenschen who have squatted it and abused it.

'Beyond the limit. Transgressive. A stain on the crew. The apogee of dishonour. The besmirchment of the uniform.' In these terms Sturmbannführer Otto Becker denounced his commanding officer the redoubtable Oberführer Franz Radek. I was not having any of it. The insubordinate Becker objected to Radek's practice of holding his pistol to a woman's head while she fellates him then shooting her through the temple as he achieves orgasm. In her terminal rictus she clamps his member. He did this on a daily basis. He left a trail of blood, brains, bone, pauper's clothes. The experience was fulfilling because it was never the same twice. Interesting, for it suggests every death is a different death.

I issued an order that thanatologists should undertake investigative fieldwork. Becker was promoted to a post in cleansing product procurement.

It cannot be expected that all the volk will initially believe with the intense faith that we require. They will be taught that faith requires no exterior proofs. Faith is its own proof. It is autonomous. There are few things more absurd than the feeble Vatican employing scientists to validate miracles, relics, simony etc. By doing so it is appeasing secularism and undermining its own foundations. My immortality is due to humidity and magic. My past will be there to meet me when I arrive.

We are reasonable men. You can show them the expediency of faith, the necessity, we can instruct that their interest is in the Reich's interest, we can persuade them to try believing and after a time they will realise that the pose they have struck has infected them. They cannot be rid of it.

We did not strip our people of a morality. Far from it. Rather, we provided a new morality. It was the Führer's genius to show the volk that this morality was quintessentially German, not a borrowing from the France of the Enlightenment or the Britain of Empire – the former was godless, the latter a trading arrangement, a form of plunder and piracy beneath a supposedly respectable flag. The British didn't even deign to teach their language to their subjects. They were, however, every bit as hypocritical as the other slaver nations – the French, the Spanish and the Portuguese. These righteous peoples are always prepared to preach a sermon alleging our iniquities while drawing a veil over their commerce in humans and their taste for religious persecution.

In the cause of Christian expansionism and pious land seizure the noble indigenous populations of North and South America were erased – and they weren't even Jews. The expulsion of Jews from the Iberian peninsula was a sorry affair.

The Inquisition was soft-hearted. It may temporarily have quashed Judaism but it did not rid the world of breeding Jews. There is a chasm between the two enterprises. Enforced exile is not elimination. The loophole was gaping. Conversos were able to spread their poison under the sign of the cross. No matter how fulsomely they claim to observe a different god and worship according to a different liturgy they cannot change their genes. Their blood and marrow remain Jewish. We learnt from this weakness.

My black crew is Judenfrei. Not one of them has an ancestor since 1750 contaminated by a single drop of toxic Jewish blood. 1750! Generation upon generation. That is proven purity. No Jew can sneak in, as Jews do, on the sly. That distant date was fixed according to Darré's researches. His knowledge of bloodlines, thoroughbreds and stud books was incomparable.

The bearded Jew in the shtetl who reeks of mutton fat unquestioningly observes the laws of the Talmud or the Torah, laws which he believes to be natural. He is wrong. Tribal law is not natural law. No. Make no mistake, natural law comes to us from god without the intercession of cults. Aryan law is natural law. It is timeless. Natural law is the law of the jungle. A puma steals a baby from outside a shack and makes off with it before anyone can stop it: in the jungle the law of the jungle is plain for all to see.

Where chaos, antagonisms and wars between states which should be allies are to be found there are also to be found the Masters of the Kabbalah who meet on moonless nights, who do not know each other's faces, who converse in ancient Ruthenian, who feast on fillets of Aryan baby, foully supping the poor creature's blood. They are said to resemble weevils. For many centuries they resisted annihilation. As so often, nematodes have come to the rescue. They attack by entering body openings. They release bacteria which cause granular

*

coagulation of the blood. Circulation is gradually impaired as the clots swell. Circulation ceases.

There were rumours of an approximate anthropoid which had been living in the treetops of the Teutoburger Wald, a stage forest whose rock formations were designed by Linsel Murly for *The Enchanted Grave*. It was seen in the ruins of Oradour; like a cackling gargoyle it taunted the ghosts of the victims. It emerged black from abandoned Silesian coal mines. It ploughed through the sump mud of Pomeranian ponds. It sprung through wheat fields on all fours leaving an elaborate trail discernible only from the air. It had long hair, it had no hair, it had a thorny crown en brosse as if suffering an electric shock. It was alarmingly furry . . . a hardly clothed torso . . . its appearance gave it away. Sullen and joyful. It supported itself on a foldable mobility cart 'designed by seniors for seniors'. It had immersed itself in the grass which swayed higher than its leathery head . . . it had taught itself quadrupedalism . . . its top limbs were gnarled . . . crosshatched with grazes and abrasions. The leather was hard as wood.

It enjoyed 'sympathetic resonance' . . . It communed with the other leathery bodies who had slipped their graves in the high peat bogs . . . to dance the dance of death. Some were several millennia old . . . some were not yet born . . . Death and leather are equalisers, they dissolve the fiction of time as surely as acid dissolves bones. It was the bogs which coloured the spring water like whisky, the water of life.

In one subterranean ruin it unwillingly communed too with a creature of which it knew nothing save the letters MP. They were repeatedly inscribed in the rock or written with chalk. They were, presumably, the initials of some creature which had sheltered here previously, hiding its self-loathing. It scraped its own two letters to confirm to its self the very existence which it was frightened to end.

There was no consistency of style or size in its incisions. There were brief phrases . . . My prison is my paradise. There is light in darkness. I am god to those around me. I am god whom I worship, who purges me, who gives me strength . . . but not the strength of obliteration. This creature was weighted by shame, its ghost sought absolution. The caves it inhabited were carceral caverns . . . places of punishment by starvation and darkness and death. They were the tombs of women and children.

Dream spaces . . . waiting rooms where you always wait . . . from which there is no escape from the perpetual present. This is the destination, not an ante-room. Prison is a place where there is no deviation from boredom. Count the shells of Ushant turtles piled high in nacreous cairns . . . count them again and again . . . count the bones of black eagles and aurochs . . . petrified claws of extinct amphibians . . . desiccated hair . . . Some of the caves were as big as cathedrals carpeted with black fungus which clung to feet and devoured them . . . There was water sliding down every wall. Sculpting every wall over aeons . . . pleating rock . . . colouring it and ruching it. The creature drew crude pictures of a long low building with black smoke pouring from its chimneys . . . an experiment devoted to human perfection. Above the gate to the buildings was the cast-iron legend No Regrets. It understood the significance of the uniform worn by the admirably fascist madrassa called Eton College . . . Now it inhabited a world apart . . . it didn't know how long it had been there . . . it feared often that it was followed by a Hidebehind who whenever it turned to confront it would vanish or adapt its camouflage to make itself invisible . . . sometimes it was contemplative and unmoving . . . then it howled to the skies . . . it spent nights quizzing the stars, it spent nights watching badgers bury a cow carcass because the memory of watching came to it unbidden . . . Its actions were determined by hauntings, messages which bypassed all receptors and plunged into the obedient brain . . . the servile brain.

It spent days in the mosses and bogs burrowing with its leathery top limbs . . . its sense of where to exhume its kin was an extra sense. It empowered bodies to exhume themselves, further leather companions. One day there would be a leather army.

It ate birds, bird's eggs, leaves, bark, berries, small rodents, acorns, larch, beechnuts, fungi, roots. It rode a mighty Brandenburger, unsaddled . . . a figure from Goethe. It bathed under cavernous waterfalls . . . it befriended lynxes and fought boars: a wound from a tusk would not heal . . . it was halt . . . it hunted with a bow taller than it was . . . a quiver of long arrows and a retiarius's net . . .

It was sought by police, paramilitary and secret services in several gullible countries which craved a figurehead with genocidal

experience and tyrannical expertise. Egypt, Syria and Iran were at the head of the queue offering lavish blandishments and two-hour loin cloth repairs. But the trappings of worldliness were no inducement. It had its own pit. However much it shared an enemy, it did not want to inhabit a shared pit stinking of garlic and littered with melon seeds. And what were onyx, obsidian and ptarmigan stuffed with dates when it could sleep beneath the stars, force its body to fast and pursue the quarry from which it would fashion the future: feral boys who lived in labyrinthine setts, leaving them only in hours of darkness. It taught them about the great experiment in which it had participated and which it was the boys' duty to repeat. Which they would repeat if they made themselves hard as leather. It told them tales round the campfire while they feasted on berries and leaves and mice. More and more came to it as disciples, acolytes, anchorites, novices of The Sacred Oak Order of The Fourth Manifest. They fashioned esoteric symbols from broken boughs. Its youthful experiments in biological pest control at Kaltenborn had been ridiculed by Jewish scientists. The trampling boot is now on the other foot. The jeering traitors were not forgotten. They have been specially counselled. A new realm is being shaped. It is preparing to be the successor. The true year zero will soon be upon us. It is four beasts whom the children fall down before and worship me that live for ever and ever.

Today all crusaders of The Fourth Manifest know that a weasel will eat rue before it attacks a snake.

Henry Dogg's Tales

Beyond brass monkeys. Way beyond. I was shivering. I was so wrapped up my mum would have been delighted. Apart from her not being my mum that is and dead to boot. I was shivering. I clamped the phone to my jaw and had a go kneading where the sciatic nerve had got right up my right buttock.

'Look at it this way mate,' chirped Shaun Memory. 'Four down, twelve to go. That's right – iznit?'

There are sixteen people called Dogg electorally registered in the UK and so listed in Nametagg.com, the online directory Shaun Memory refers to as 'The Stalker's Chum'. Gleefully refers to. Electoral rolls. Phone directories. Online groups. Social media.

Nametagg knows everything about everyone in the UK and Northern Ireland apart from Wales, where Nametagg.cymru is suspended and facing legal challenges.

Slebs are forced to pay large sums not to be included in *We Know Where You Live*. Demanding money with the menace of disclosure is not just a profitable sideline, it's the mainstay of the business.

I was shivering. It's like that up north. The phone was a leech on my jaw. The sciatica was yelping and pinching the way it does.

'Five down, Shaun. It's five now,' I corrected him.

Two facemasked women were pushing baby-buggies up the black slope into the stinging rain. The pavement glistered slick as pitch. Their soaked clothes were flattened by the wind. They leaned forward with their crow heads down.

I hardly noticed them. I wasn't myself. I was miles away. All the while I had the mobile pressed in my ear my head was pounding. I wasn't listening. I was gazing across the steep street at the gap in the terrace. Stone houses, stained by a hundred years of smoke and what have you, stone houses like bad teeth.

The bad tooth I was after had been pulled. The numbers went 29, 31, 35. Number 33 was a roofless wreck, joists turned to charcoal, nettles, cairns of rubble, sagging buddleia, a mound of sodden underlay, a rust-freckled fridge, the print of a staircase on a party wall, a jagged wall, a history of wallpaper, a keeling lean-to. From the centre of a broken window pane a web of cracks spread like the map of a delta. I took a while to take it all in.

I was well wrapped up – cosy, considering. But I could still feel the cold damp of number 38's wall I was leaning against.

It's penetrative in the coccyx. But it supported me in my shock. I leaned and stared. Far beyond where number 33 had stood there was a dirty brown fellside with a wholly intact terrace in silhouette along its brow. If only that was where they had lived, the people with my name.

Shaun wasn't listening. I had lost count of the times he had said: 'I hear what you're saying.'

There, he said it again. That's Shaun Memory for you.

I wasn't paying attention. I was just gaping at the fellside. It might have been made to measure for me. It fitted my desolation like a glove. Like it was ordained.

This is what I saw. I saw malnourished, shivering horses, all ribs and worn out, waiting for the knacker. Pitiful sad skeletons, abused by humans. I knew how they felt. I shared their surroundings. I could see rolls of barbed wire, hay burst from polythene bale covers, nests of baling twine caught on a nor'easterly, squashed bracken, wetness, collapsed fence posts, thorn clumps, rusting troughs, the black maps of former fires, a future pyre of broken pallets, a dead Christmas tree plantation, a factory chimney's cracked top. We've all been up north.

And, yes, I could see Shaun Memory miles away in the new premises of Someone Else's Baby: The People's Trace Agency. Sitting at his CEO's boast of a desk with his exasperated palms raised to the conference speaker.

Those palms are deterrents telling me: 'Get off of my back. Don't bother me.'

What's he's actually *saying* is: 'I hear you – course I do.'

He believes his gift is to console with such reassurance that I forget everything and am once again persuaded to believe him, to believe that the next one will be the one, to believe that the next Dogg will be the right Dogg, to believe that the breakthrough is close (despite today's disappointment, and yesterday's and the day before's and the month before's).

'Count your blessings you're not called Patel, eh? Serious damage—'

In addition to its online subscription Nametagg.com charges by the hit: that cost, plus Someone Else Baby's (SEB's) operational increment, is borne by the client, as specified in The People's Trace Agency's Terms of Fayre Trade.

'Or Jones. Or White . . . There's more Whites than there is Blacks – not that you'd ever guess it round here.'

'Or here,' I agreed. 'It's all Lals, kebas, and bokos and bollas here. Not over-contributing to the vertical tanning economy.'

I watched the two women's struggle with the weather. Then they stopped – outside number 31. One of them delved into a bag slung from her buggy. I assumed that she was searching for housekeys.

'Shaun. Hang on a second . . . Look, I'll call you right back mate.'

'Look forward to it,' he said, meaning that's a fucking relief.

I forced my numb limbs across the pitted street towards the women. They turned swiftly when they heard my footsteps. (Size 11, F-fit.)

I had whiled away many hours in hotel rooms with half an eye on television programmes like *Show of Hands* and *Talk the Walk* in which Eminent Body Language Professionals compete to interpret the postures and gestures of gameshow contestants, politicians, reality TV slebs, wardrobe malfunction victims, inquiry-helpers with a blanket over their head, sportsmen in defeat, disgraced light entertainers, murder victims' families etc.

I had learnt so much from these highly qualified experts that I was able to detect anxiety in the women's stance.

They stood between me and their children. They were protective, defensive.

'Excuse me. Sorry to . . . I just wondered: you don't happen to know what's happened to the people who lived here? In this one? Where they are now?'

Their anxiety became alarm. They glanced at each other, they didn't realise what power their clothes gave them. They didn't put you at ease. I was uneasy as they were. I had never addressed masked women before.

The tall one of the pair spoke urgently to the other in Urdu. Or Gujarati. Or Punjabi. Or Farsi. Or in a language I had never heard of. Then, without looking at me again, without a further word between themselves, they were gone with the speed of beasts fleeing a raptor, scurrying up the hill, inclined for extra purchase, the open bag flapping, their buggies skidding. They had cast me as the raptor. Not a role to be comfortable in when they might call on a couscous of bruvs to have a quiet word, and instruct me in the degree of respect that the religion of peace's manifestations must always be shown.

What age were they? What ugliness was concealed by their shiny textile disfigurements? What promise? What fear and arrogance? What livid telltales of a good seeing-to by hubbies Osman and Faisal?

I'm an old romantic. I read a bit:

They were unsexed to satisfy possessive misogyny and coarse superstitions.

Religions thrive on corporeal shame like they do on dietary taboos, proselytising, hatred, intolerance, genital mutilation.

I remembered the mohel ritually maiming my little boy's penis, making him shriek and bleed in the name of some ancient tribal baloney. I winced. I was forced into it by my religiously faithful, maritally faithless wife.

What if he decides not to be a Jew? Does he get his foreskin back?

Then I remembered as I had remembered time after time that *my* little boy was the little boy who was someone else's baby, the cuckoo who was now a full-grown stranger, who had cast off his doubly false paternal name.

If only memories were mortal, if only they could be buried forever rather than rise up to invade the moment, marauding like the living dead.

They're deep in a coma for decades, then they are stirred by the illusion that a sensation is a duplicate of something you felt decades ago. That breeze buffing your cheek is the precise weight and heat of that breeze which sauntered between a tawny canvas blind and a window frame while the unseen children splashed and laughed in an inflatable pool.

When a spade scrapes a flint in chalky soil and causes a shiver, the asylum's garden is again being replanted.

This fat hotel room vulva is the very oyster, last of two dozen *creuses*, shared with——on a quay at Noirmoutier where the wind stretched hair and parasols and paper tablecloths: it's the very oyster.

I stepped over the remnant of the house's front wall. My feet crunched damp charcoal. I remembered a lump of halva I had trodden on, oh, fifteen years before, the puttyish compression on the carpet, the tutting march to the kitchen, the ticking off that ended in hugs and laughter. I remembered.

I? As in me.

Remembered?

Whose memories were they? These memories were squatters. I insisted to myself that I harboured the memories of someone else. Of someone, anyway, with a different name. Of someone whose very identity was provisional. Of someone who had believed he was called something other than Dogg, who had yet to learn that he was parentless and childless and historyless.

But not memoryless. Whoever he was, he was spilling over with memories. Yet they were unwanted memories – and if they weren't someone else's they were nonetheless held under false pretences. They conjured up two generations of a family which had evaporated. My family which had not been my family. They were the contaminated exhibits of a life whose foundations had collapsed. Even the best was stained. They were ineradicable like poison in the soil.

I longed to exhume a childhood told between marbled endpapers in frilly-edged monochrome. I longed for summer-coloured snapshots of what never had been and never could be now, of dreamdays and lost content. I longed for a rewrite of long ago, a fresh past, a mint set of yesterdays, brand-new old memories.

Unwanted memories jeopardise reinvention.

Can Jilly fulfil herself as a maquillage consultant when she retains the pre-operative memories of being strapping Jimmy, a hoddie? They're a burden on the brain. His bricks and her blusher don't mix. It's less humiliating to squeeze a callused hand into a cocktail glove than to replay the blokeish larks and catcalls of site life. As they say: vaginoplasty holds out no promises of mnemonic erasure. You can't go the whole hog as a glamourpuss if when it comes round to six o'clock you want to get down the pub for a pint or four.

I anticipated many years hence remembering the masked women. How? I wondered. By their burkas' beaks? By their crabbed flight? Their defiant muteness? And would they remember me?

They, surely, would still be tied to their identity, sexuality problems, servility, age-old superstitions, sleazy faith, and tribal rules about not eating in the street. They would still be themselves, locked into the life sentence they were handed down at birth.

Would I still be Dogg? I was a mutable entity buffeted by circumstances. I was a seeker. When the seeker finds, then the certainties of his role disappear: he ceases to be a seeker. Finding is an end. A finder is a former seeker. Here is a different state of being. And one which I down-in-the-mouthly recognised I was no closer to getting to than I had been when I embarked on the quest which took me to harled bungalows in neap fields, to fuggy rooms matted with cat, to pantries reeking of senility – the way senility really used to reek in the days when senility was stench. All the Doggs listed in Nametagg.com I had so far made contact with inhabited mean dwellings. What I called anthologies of bygone smells. For a Dogg to prosper was rare. A Dogg is handicapped by the very name. He or she is liable to live in a neighbourhood favoured by nonagenarian eastern European war criminals – wizened former sadists with green teeth, a greasy flannel shirt buttoned to the neck and a buried past. The difference was that they knew where it was buried.

I was shaking my head at life's appetite for dealing off the bottom of the pack. I stood in the damp charred former front room. A fly which shouldn't have been out in this weather landed on a brick's honeycomb core. When it inhales it's sort of matt. When it exhales it gleams like mother of pearl. In another state it might have been fishing bait. It has survived to fulfil its cycle. What's become of me? Man envies fly!

I turned away from the house that wasn't a house and walked in the direction where I had parked the hire car (a wrecked dustbin, should be condemned as unfit for human habitation). An ice cream van, as unattuned to the weather as the fly, chimed its grim call based on a song we all once knew, which every child knew, but which has slipped from someone else's memory.

The following Doggs are so far accounted for by me and by SEB's team of crack trace agents, researchers, executive pryers, pro nosey parkers, deceivers and interns: all of them fucking useless so far as I can see.

John Gordon Dogg. 87. Widower suffering from the Niels whose life's acquisitions and mementos were strewn about a Troon bungalow. No siblings. No living cousins on his father's side. Never heard of Vera Sophie Dogg. 'Definitely not – I once did the family tree. Wouldn't know where to find it now. If I do come across it I'll let you know.' Tea with sterilised milk, stale fairy cake, partial view of dunes.

Douglas John Gordon Dogg. 65. Unmarried. Only son of the above. East Kilbride. A recently retired nurse and health professional. Former divisional representative water polo player, still involved in the sport's administration. Chronic eczema from protracted immersion in over-chlorinated pools. 'Dad may look frail but his memory's all there. If he says so it's gospel. I certainly never heard the name.'

'Water polo has been my life. I even had the honour of playing against the legendary Ortéga-Nagy in the Carinthian Tournament. Water polo's history is a history of Scottish endeavour. I made my career in nursing and subsequently in health administration. But my passion, my vocation, my love to the exclusion of cupid has been water polo. Oh there were walk-outs and outings to tournaments with some very comely lady players of our sport but none resulted in tying the knot. The nearest I came to that was with a staunch central defence from Maryhill Mermaids. But like Annie Lawrie it was not to be. I won't mention the lady's name. She emigrated with a flashy winger from Perth Poseidons who joined the Rhodesian Police Force and had an unsavoury reputation as a biter. The best ever team I played on? No question: Bonnyman, Hoof, Vowsden, Mungo, Jack,

Kippax, Egret. Subs: Ollick, Gryst, Magurran, Vaux, McNurdin. Others might have included yours truly!'

(Judith) Harvey Dogg. 30. Logistics manager, Spalding, Lincs. Partner, Graham Ulpha. Named Harvey after the titular rabbit in Mary Chase's play which was adapted as a film vehicle for James Stewart (1950) and after David Harvey, the rabbit-fancying Leeds United goalkeeper (1971–77). 'Judith's a bit ordinary. Harvey's a talking point.' Her late father Edvin bred English Lops as a homage to his adopted country and would rise to the position of Secretary of the Kesteven branch of the British Rabbit Council. Because of persistent teasing at school and workmates barking at him he had changed his name by deed poll from Dog, though he stuck to the same pronunciation. Judith knew of no Vera Sophie Dogg. Nor did her uncle Trevor.

'Trev's still spelling it D-O-G. But he's not what you'd call sensitive. It never got to him. Dad went into this pub once and the name above the door – you know: licensed to sell intoxicating – it was Dogg, two "g"s. He said to the chap my name's Dogg too, two "g"s. And the chap just said: "So what? Bully for you mate." I don't know where it was, the pub. It was a story he used to tell. Sort of family myth. You know?'

Paul Dogg. Old person. Paulo Dogliani and his late brother Sandro migrated to the UK from Bari in 1949. They worked as miners in the north Somerset coalfields at Radstock (owned by the Mogg slaving dynasty). Sandro died in an industrial accident in 1955 leaving a widow and a son. In 1958, shortly after Paulo's naturalisation as a British subject and before his marriage to Barbara Clock, he changed his name. In 1961, with the financial assistance of his father-in-law, he bought a market garden. Later he established a haulage company transporting wholesale fruit and vegetables. To his chagrin both his sons returned to Italy to discover their roots, found them, and retook the name Dogliani. Had never met or even heard of anyone who shared the name he no longer regarded as adoptive.

'You got to understand we got two communities in St Albans. We got the Pugliese and we got the Neapolitans. I am a historic Pugliese. We don't talk to Neapolitans, they're murderous bastards and their cooking's shit. No nuance. All that dough. So I can't help you with them. Tell you what, I'll ask my nephew. I saw him yesterday. We had a little celebration. He only got out last week. It was a matter of honour.'

Melodie Dogg. 'The casting director/producer said I got the lot in spades but I needed more. I told my mum and stepdad that unless they pay for the Botox and body work, breast and buttocks pump-up etc. so I can become a top adult star I'm going to go on the game. Trouble was they're so out of their heads all the time they don't respond to threats because they don't understand them even though I've got leverage. I'm fifth-generation long-term unemployed. Family-wise we don't have a work ethic tradition. We don't have the right temperament. My great-gran had a job as a chamfer machine operator but RSI struck her down sadly. There isn't a week goes by without a team of sociologists or urban theorists or housing gurus or world-class psychologists coming round to inspect us like we're in the zoo. Prod prod. There'd be more but we're on the seventeenth floor and even when the lift's working it's a toilet or New Crew's in there dealing hydrotar. They respect Mum and always let her through. But she doesn't have the shoplifting skills any more down to being out of it and clumsy and likely to steal low-value peff so there's not much to go out for.

'It all came oh so right when I saw this old chap in a wheelchair making a cash withdrawal from a hole in the wall. I checked he was alone then followed him across the wasteground where Tuckers van used to be. My dream of being like posh slag Moira Furnace was within my grasp.

'The Sunday surgeon's hobby was reconditioning hotrods. He botched my face so badly that people laugh at me and point. They're scared of me. The only roles I can get are in the disability genre. So what's not to hate?

'But every cloud . . . Who wants to watch half a dozen pretty-pretty Norma Normals tying themselves in all the knots you seen before on screen when they can get off on a total freak's personal services in person. I can tell you this: at the end of a statesmanlike day, men of power, secretaries of state, important MEPs, vice presidents, chairmen, CEOs, prime ministers, top aristocrats etc. like to unwind with an H-cup, a vigorous arse like two separate medicine balls and a pair of lips from among an abattoir's prime cuts – they shine like plump soft furnishing. And I've got a diary under lock and key.

'I didn't know my dad. He left before I was born. His name was Janek Dogilewski. He changed it to Dogg. I tell you what: I'll bet he'd be proud of what I've achieved.'

Karla Dogg. 38. 'Dad didn't have much luck. He never talked about his first wife. She died of a coronary on a golf course at Polperro a year and a half after they married. She was wearing tartan trousers at the time. He had photos but I never saw him looking at them. He lived alone for thirty years. He grew the business then he sold it so he could devote more time to his mashie niblick.

'I doubt that he ever expected to remarry. He was fifty-nine when I was born. He met Mum when she was temping at the nineteenth hole! A barmaid! You'd never meet anyone who less fitted that description! We were a happy family. He wasn't embarrassed when people thought Mum was his daughter. He was proud. Mum and I did look like sisters after all. I was fourteen when she passed away. She had these headaches. But Doctor Parry-Morgan said it was nothing to worry over and perhaps to cut out the lactic.

'Mrs Kerr called me in just before lunchtime to tell me. She was kindness itself. When you got close you could smell the smoke in her hair. She held me and hugged me. Some buckle or clasp in her clothes scratched me. She did her best but you could tell all she was thinking was getting off the premises so she could have a gasper to make her even hoarser than she was already. It was a Monday. The funeral was the next Monday. I was extra upset because Mum's coffin looked like a chest of drawers. Dad aged years that week. Before no one had believed he was a day over sixty. Now he looked like he was a hundred. It was as though he was grief itself.

'It was the happiest day of my life. It was a lovely sunny day. They all said they'd never seen me look so lovely. The bridesmaids wore peach satin, bias cut. I have to say myself that Celia had put on weight since the fitting but it didn't spoil the day. What is marriage for if not the toleration of love handles? Mum would have been so proud. I felt her looking down on me with her blessing. Dad was proud. He told me so. He told everyone when he made a little speech. He told Ed that he was to take the best ever care of me because he wouldn't be around for much longer, which was sadly true. Ed gripped him on the shoulder and said of course he would. We got back from the honeymoon touring beautiful Scottish scenery in Ed's company car on the Saturday. On the Monday they had to let Ed go. But he's a fighter and now we got a two-car garage and we're trying for a third. All Stephanie's uncles and aunts and cousins are on Ed's side. I'm the last Dogg so to speak.'

Harry Umberson-Dogg. Mark Aarvold's The Faintest of All Human Passions: A Concordance by Araminta Size and Wendy Deflorin.

A gossipy 'who-is-really-who' of the characters in that roman fleuve. Aarvold has seldom denied or confirmed the models for his characters: 'You tell me.' When asked by Someone Else's Baby's senior intern Jemima Fawcett if the late Harry Umberson-Dogg had a kinsperson named Vera Sophie Dogg he replied: 'You tell me.'

Ferdy Hoffman-Moffat is a recurring minor character. According to Size and Deflorin he is almost certainly modelled on Umberson-Dogg, an agriculturalist, fellow traveller of Nazism and *Daily Mail* columnist. Indeed in Aarvold's early sketches he is called Harry Humber. Hoffman-Moffat first appears in *Feet That on Feathers Fly*. At a dinner at Hamish Widdowson's house in Pimlico he refers to Samuel Diamond as 'a little kike with shit under his fingernails and cock cheese behind his ear'. This prompts Lisney Trigg to invite him to join The Greensward Hundreds (itself a defamatory caricature of the Kindred of the Kibbo Kift). Umberson-Dogg was sympathetic to 'green' fascism, a member of The Nordics and, briefly, of the International Fascist League.

Hoffman-Moffat reappears in *Out of the Light They Lie* as Hannah Pulverbatch's lover. He accompanies her to Denby Comper's house in Ronda where he is impressed by a fellow guest, the former SS and current advisor to Gamal Abdel Nasser, Karl Lauterbacher. In *Our Heaving Spleens* he becomes involved in a quixotic but ultimately successful plan of the Exhumations Project to gain reparations for land requisitioned by the War Office and not subsequently yielded to its owners.

Hoffman-Moffat is a southern English landowner. His estate is called Vobster – its whereabouts are not specified: Aarvold's descriptions of its landscapes suggest that it is not the Mendip village of that name. He is an amateur architect and occasional writer of topographical essays. Author of *A Field Guide to the Ruins of Mercia*. Failed parliamentary candidate: he lost his deposit standing for The Oak Leaf League in Chichester in the general elections of 1959 and 1964. The latter was won by Beryl Vowles's stepbrother Seymour Gomme. When Gomme died less than six months later Hoffman-Moffat declined to stand in the by-election.

A number of commentators, most notably the late Hugh Massingberd and Patrick Wright, have proposed that Size and Deflorin's contention that Hoffman-Moffat was inspired solely by Harry Umberson-Dogg is mistaken. They favour Sir Geoffrey Shadoxhurst Bt as at least the partial model. This entrepreneurial landowner, showman, perennial chat show guest, self-parodying aristocrat, collector of historic cars, Nazi paraphernalia and pubic hair was at school with Aarvold. When this was put to Aarvold he replied: 'You tell me.'

Baldwin Dogg. 55. Monk of the Novarus Order. Rumoured to be related to a circus family or perhaps a fishing family. He has lived for over twenty-five years at Trull, that silent order's largest house in the UK, and has duly exercised his right to remain silent on the occasions that he has been charged with sexual offences. Alongside honey, cream, rindwashed cheese, cider and apple brandy he and his fellows have, in god's name, produced many silent pornographic films. These have so often been deemed inoffensive by a variety of courts that even the most stupid police have given up seizing them (for their own consumption) and barging in on their shoots (for their own satisfaction on the off-chance that the participating brothers have wilted and the Ursulines from the neighbouring establishment are still up for it – just one for the road).

All prosecutions have failed. His Honour Judge Richard Griffiths KC remarked that if the Novarus Order's harmless hobbies were curtailed every monastery in Britain would be wound up in what he described as 'a second dissolution'. He did, however, suggest that forcing those who decline to wear white habits with a V for virgin is unnecessarily discriminatory but hardly a matter for a court of law. Baldwin Dogg was obviously unable to say anything about his forebears, relations etc. God stays mum.

Grant Dogg. SEB Section Leader Dave 'Loadshedder' Lawrie notes: The poor old chap's memory is shattered, all he can describe – repetitively – is what must have been his allotment. Regret. But no hope of a coherent reply.

That's where he's digging. He's digging in the ground. You can't see him right because the sun, he's more a silhouette if you get me? He's digging next to where there's that shed made out of broken crates and oh oh oh what d'you – pallets, pallets! Shed made out of crates and pallets, oh and cloches. He's digging and there's Mister Crow sat on a post watching him like he owns the place. All black in the shadow. The sky's well black. There's the trees beside the shed made out of window frames and doors. Not, not what you call healthy trees. They'd be hawking and wheezing if trees could. Then there's the cornfield it's different all in sunlight how they always promise it's going to be. Giant cheeses wrapped up in black plastic that's how . . . how . . . oh . . . oh . . . She, she said how, how they are. Oh, and bales like cotton reels but bigger. She said. He's digging there where no one can see him – he reckons. 'Cept Mister Crow and me. Mister Crow and me.

Denise Dögg. 'It came to a head when I was giving my Rosina in *The Barber of Seville*. It was down to bullying, especially by Justin and Mervyn. They were always giggling like a couple of schoolboys, not like responsible bank employees. They ruined it for me in front of all the younger ones in the chorus. It was the same day that Virotutis – that's Mr Harding from the sixth form college – said in his review in the *Gazette* that I was the finest coloratura the Accademia Gesualdo of Bracknell had ever had in all twelve years of its existence.

'I didn't much like going to the pub after the show but it was all about bonding. I shouldn't have bothered. I could tell they'd been talking about me. So I said to Justin what's all this about and he spluttered on his lager. I could tell he was a bit blotto. All the younger ones were smirking and what have you. Some of them didn't know where to look. They were all making eye contact with each other, deliberately avoiding making eye contact with me, they were sort of conspiring, trying not to laugh.

'"What's so funny?" I asked.

'They all burst out laughing. Well, I didn't know what the joke was but I could see that whatever it was it was on me and that I was being subjected to mental cruelty.

'"It's just a laugh Denny," Justin said.

'"*Denise*," I reminded him.

'"It's down to the way you screw up your face when you're hitting the highest notes."

'"My voice is my instrument," I said.

'"They don't mean it badly."

'"They don't mean what badly?"

'"What they call you."

'"If you please, Justin – what do they call me?"

'"Well, Vinegar Strokes. Everyone knows that. Nothing to get heated about. It's just good-natured banter."

'They were tittering.

'"Calling me *what*? What's vinegar . . . whatsit?"

'"Vinegar Strokes."

'"Vinegar Strokes? What's that when it's at home?"

'"Oh . . . whoops haha hrrm I thought . . . you know – I thought you knew. But Christ it's better than if they called you Moneyshot."

'"What's that?"'

Vibeka Dogg. 'The accident was because my dad was a reckless man, a thoughtless man. Mum was always telling him to slow down. But he never took any notice. He'd sort of grin and glare at her at the same time. It was scary that look. It got worse when mobiles came in and he got a mobile, boasting to his colleagues about how fast he'd got from Meriden to Swadlincote for instance. They were all into cars and boasting. It was black ice and he wasn't making any allowances for it. We went down an embankment. The last thing I saw was his phone bouncing off the steering wheel. It was weeks before they told me I wasn't going to be sighted again. They were kind at the Swindon special school but there was a lot of prayer and I didn't want to spend my life making wicker baskets so with the insurance on Dad's life Mum got me a private tutor and I got into uni to study Studies Studies: Discipline Proliferation in Higher Education 1968–2020. I also got into the amorous life. Better late than never. It was a revelation: I wasn't fussy about looks. Obviously! Some of them must have been really ugly because that's the law of averages. Or worse than ugly – ordinary! I responded to the ones who were sensitive, i.e. not the callow students. They stunk of beer. Always boasting about how many pints they could shift. Funny they never mention the brewer's droop. They're always telling you they got what it takes in the gentleman quarters: I can make up my own mind on that one! The faculty and the tutors were men not boys. It got especially heavy with kinky Cornelius Vander, Reader in Meme Signification Legitimacies. He was always buying me what you might call super-bedroom clothes, though clothes isn't really the word. I thought they felt a bit unusual but I didn't realise how unusual till I made my way to the Union Bar to meet the naughty fellow as per instructed. The place went silent as a tomb. What's fine for the racy parties he took me to looks like attention seeking in the Union Bar. He spent a fortune online at Dream Tupping. PVC skirts and vinyl basques give people the wrong idea, even though as far as Cornelius was concerned it was the right idea. He liked to be taken for my pimp to gain campus cred with the other faculty members. He liked to make them jealous. No one dared take liberties with me. He frightened them. I already frightened them with my vision loss and arrogance. This was the shiny black cherry on top. Fraulein didn't frighten them, she absolutely terrified them. She's a Marcher Hound bitch whose ancestors have feasted on the genitalia of generations of civilly disobedient seditionists and protest kids.

'The unsighted have magical properties. Paradoxically we are seers. We can predict the weather. We hear hidden frequencies. Our sense of smell is so acute that we are suspected of having olfactory hallucinations. I am kind, I am a good listener, I excel at Braille chess, I write poetry, I have turned vision loss to my advantage. I hope to be selected as a parliamentary candidate for the next election. I am shameless about playing the sympathy card.

'I am a competent guitarist, I play piano well, I play the accordion – ironically I always felt deeply for the blind girl with the accordion in the Millais painting which I shall be making a special study of. And yes, as a people person, I enjoy being amorous. But hold the boasting would you guys!

'And wear a nighthood like gallant knights in nights of yore!'

Rodney Dogg. 'I can't remember where we met. It wasn't like she was a stand-out that you noticed. Funnily enough she can't remember either. She was one of the ones round Bev. Bev was out of my league. I knew because Bev told me so and not to bother: we could be friends though. She'd been in beauty contests in places so far distant as Weston-super-Mare and Barry Island. She was runner-up in one at Minehead. She was class and she knew it. Not even Dave the Rave could get a look in with her. Her jumper was fluffy alpaca. You didn't notice the ones round her till they'd all paired off with your mates and only Heather was left. She wasn't bad-looking. Just very ordinary you'd call it. That's why we were suited. We started going together. I often tried to get off with other birds when she wasn't around but they didn't want to know. I dare say she did the same – with blokes, mind! It wasn't to be. So we got married. The boy's forty now. Still living at home in the little house we moved to when he was seven. It does us fine. The neighbourhood has come up a bit. It's no longer the sort of neighbourhood where your neighbours throw dog mess over the fence into your garden. That's neighbours regrettably! Heather has taken early retirement because of her insides and I'm nearing retirement. The Big Question is whether we stay put or move. It's difficult for the boy if we move, with his job and that. Especially with his weight. We have to keep an eye on him. He's got confectionery issues. Not that he's the only one. We heard that Bev got too big even for modelling for XXXL catalogues. She'd been reduced to doing the frumpy ones, the flowery housecoat end of fashion. Type whatsit diabetes. Not so stuck up now I'll bet.'

Dave Dogg. Constable Dave Dogg was dismissed from the Norwich force for fellating a police horse. Claimed he was only doing what every mounted copper does, bonding with his mount – but he was doing it in semi-public. That was his real offence.

Ruben Payton Dogg. 'I was finetuning my tan out on the access deck in the clean bit between Mrs F's cat litter tray, the bins and the needles: what I call my beach. How I know the time is I got my clock out there with me to make sure I get an even overall, no patches like a diseased animal.

'1.50. Linzi the crack kid from two doors away is sitting on the bottom step of the stairwell. It's sticky because of the sun – just the thing for tanning, not so great for surfaces where you got tar.

'2.05 onwards. Every now and again she lets out this moan that she's going to give birth. That's her all over, wanting a starring role when she's got to face it she's one of life's extras. Just because she's about ten months gone looking like some sort of swollen creature of the deep she wants to hog the limelight. She's waiting for Mikey Scratchsore to show up with some gear.

'2.25. I know that because I can hear Blodwyn Mudge yelling down from the third-floor walkway asking where's Mikey the fucker.

'2.55. Linzi screams. So loud it hurts. She goes on screaming get me an ambulance. Me me me. Get me . . . etc. I call for an ambulance.

'3.15. You can hear the ambulance sirens but is it hers? The din is horrible but then it always is. All hard surfaces pinging the noise back and forth to each other.

'3.17. Suddenly there's this even more terrible noise. Blodwyn crashing down the stairs saying stop her stop her stop her stop the little whore. And when she gets to the bottom of the stairwell she hasn't got a wig on. Never saw her like that before. Totally bald. Totally horrifying. Like she'd been skinned. We'd all heard the story. It was a coiffure incident of many years ago when some Crimper of the Valleys lit a gasper too close to her hair all thick with spray for a fuller back comb, we're talking a full ten inches in height so legend has it. The flames hit the ceiling. It was like a forgotten ritual from the distant ages. Her hair never came back. "It was the day my luck ran out, it was a gorgeous blonde mane. I'm a Norse goddess underneath."

'3.19. What she wants is to securitise the £120 she gave Linzi to score with before she is carted off to the hospital to bring a junkie tot into the world. Linzi is writhing moaning but can't writhe that much because of her shape . . .

'3.22. Blodwyn is pushing her out the way rifling through her bag, you might call it a pharmacy. She finds the money. Calls Linzi a slut.

'3.25. Goes back up in a strop.

'3.26. When the ambulance arrives it is too late. Linzi is screaming about her waters. The baby has to be delivered on the spot.

'3.36. This gave Blodwyn time to smear on a nice thick coating of slap, do panda eyes and get into working gear. All leopardskin with purple nylon bob wig.

'3.45. She clickclacks down the stairs again to see if she could perhaps help out the ambulance staff, maybe one of them fancies a quick intimacy special – special discount for public servants. The baby's shouting. Well it would be. It's taken one look at this pisshole and it's wanting to get back inside where it came from. All comforts laid on there – not like in this pisshole.

'3.51. It's going to have to get used to the pisshole. Linzi like a responsible new mum takes a couple of regals, a fat drake and enough zero oblivions to put a herd of elephants to sleep. Then she starts bad-mouthing Mikey Scratchsore.

'The placenta lay on the access deck for days putrefying, a maggots' playground till a hungry fox took it away.'

Immy Dögg. Late twenties? Literary historian who currently has tenure at Archer College, Cambridge. Her essay *The Other Side of the Arras* inspired The Madingley Mummers production of *Hamlet* which rehabilitated Claudius. She regards him as the hero of the play – which was almost certainly, she believes, written by the Duke of Westmoreland. For the sake of Denmark Claudius murdered his brother Hamlet Snr who was even more feckless and irresponsible than the namesake son.

The following declined to impart any information to SEB's research team. Their responses varied between the polite and the surly – who do you think you are prying into my family etc. What we know of them is from Google, Wikipedia, Facebook, Level Best, Open Goals, LinkedIn and Snoopy. Accuracy not guaranteed!

Margaret-Jane Dogg was an evangelical missionary in the Philippines for many years. She is currently Director of Remedial Weaving at Historic England Continued Learning (fka's English Heritage Weekend Breaks).

Gwyneth Dogg took the option of early retirement from her job in human resources at Thamesdown District Council and moved to Bridgwater. She is secretary of the Highbridge Chorale.

Arwen Dogg lives in Far Headingly, Leeds. She is a haematologist whose work on transplant patients' immunosuppression has incurred the wrath and disdain of what she described, in a letter to *The Paracelsian*, as 'the complacent incurious Blood Establishment'. She was on paid leave and had left no clue as to her whereabouts.

A member of the SEB Platinum Community would be able to further instruct. The Team.

Lars Dogg is Reader in Modern Totalitarian and Utopian Behaviours at the University of Mid Lincolnshire Horncastle Campus. He is working on a history of cloud seeding. He said that under other circumstances he'd have been happy to help but he was in Magnitogorsk and his phone was going to run out.

Dagmann Dogg is a licensed cab driver currently on a year's leave due to PTSD. A signalling failure caused the two-carriage 08.25 train from Sea Mills into Bristol Montpelier Station to halt beside One Stump allotments where chef Saqib Mustafi Karim was enjoying penetrative sex with Stephanie, a tethered goat belonging to prize-winning chilli grower Alvin Engineer. The majority of commuters whistled and clapped and volubly encouraged him. 'He speeded up something lovely my baba.' Several filmed him on their phones. One, however, called the Crime and Disorder Reduction Partnership. Dagmann Dogg, tuned in to police frequencies, arrived at the site within three minutes and made a citizen's arrest of Mr Karim before he had an orgasm. As Mr Karim's solicitor pleaded in court: the Ayatollah Khomeini decreed that a man may have sex with an animal but he must kill the animal after he has had his orgasm. He must not sell the meat to the people of his village. A neighbouring village is acceptable, though. Mr Karim had intended to sell the meat to The Star of Bengal in Avonmouth. He was deemed to have acted within the precepts of his faith. Case dismissed. The police were commended for responding within two hours with minimal prior counselling. Dagmann Dogg received a warning not to listen to police communications. He said: 'My thoughts are with Stephanie.'

Sylvia Dogg is currently suspended as deputy manager of Hot Throb, a sex shop in Wallsend, while the police investigate reports of her organising dog fights in a deserted farm building.

'Fat lot of good that was then frankly, Shaun . . . fat lot of fucking good.'

'We're on it, Henry . . . we're moving forward . . . we got a top analyst stepping up to the plate . . . working like an n-word on geographical distributions and relative demographies—'

'Shaun . . . Shaun! How long have we known each other . . . Shall I tell you? Forty years mate, forty years. That's forty years of being continually delighted – no other word for it – continually delighted by your duckin', divin', always survivin' . . . pulling a fast one . . . a scam here . . . an ocean-going yacht there . . . I just don't want to be on the receiving end—'

'Course you don't. I'm waiting for confirmation . . . but just look at the way some of them are spelling Dögg . . . telltale umlaut as our friends the Bosch call them—'

'You're not going to tell me I'm a kraut.'

'I am not. How about Icelandic?'

'Leave it out . . . I don't want to be fucking Icelandic. I'm too old to be fucking Icelandic.'

'They got seniors too. It's not all geysers and raves.'

'What else?'

'The SP is Dogg's a common name up there. Now – let's add that to what a member of my shit-hot staff has come up with. Landry. She's really been painting the runway with a toothbrush . . . she's noticed that we got several cases of Dogg, family name of sorts – they do naming a bit funny in Iceland. They got Dogg family name with a Welsh first name: Emlyn. Arwen. What does that tell you . . . what we looking at? Patterns of migration my son . . . that's what. Names are identity . . . aahh – as, ah, as you well know.'

'So you're saying – hang on, let me get my head round this . . . we got Icelandics in Wales who give their kids Welsh Christian names. Is that right?'

'Could be . . . That's the way it looks. *Given* names by the way. Given names. We're an ecumenical agency. All faiths colours creeds. Assimilation is one of our mottos. Moving on from integration.'

'Yeh yeh and the pope shits in the woods. Wasn't so long ago you was BNP.'

'Henry . . . don't be hurtful . . . I didn't believe a word of it . . . I was only in it for the rough stuff . . . strictly non-ideological . . . maiming for maiming's sake – Shaun and his cleaver . . . yeh, halcyon days eh . . . but mum's the word eh . . . bad for business . . . I got clients who are well ethnic. Not short of a rupee or two.'

I scrolled the phone. I did it again: 'So far as I can see you got Scots, you got Yorkies, you got flatlands blablabla . . . No Wales.'

'Wales is a problem.'

'All the Icelandic illegals in hiding with their lady sheep!' I quipped with a characterful chuckle.

Shaun sighed: 'Wales doesn't subscribe to Nametagg.com. All we get there is civil suits. We got no penetration there.'

'Unlike the Icelandic illegals! Eh?' I quipped again and did my abused sheep impression.

'Privacy issues. Wouldn't know where to start.'

I heard myself say: 'Looks like I'm going to be going on the road again.'

The Chipurnoi Marriages

Elizabeth Rolt Mavroleon and Rudolph Baker Choate Chipurnoi were married at Washington National Cathedral in the early summer of 1961, between Del Shannon's 'Runaway' and the Bay of Pigs. She had given him the mitten (as she put it) when he first proposed. But he persisted. She was impressed that he didn't blow his nose on the sheets like so many members of Skull & Bones. She was touched by the way he knotted his condom after use and disposed of it discreetly rather than dumping it, Bonesman style, in the bedside remains of a takeaway pizza.

I was twelve when she told me that. Even at that age I thought it sounded like an unusual reason to marry someone. On the other hand I can't recall thinking it was a weird thing to tell your prepubescent daughter. She was like that. She got more and more like that, more and more interpersonally challenging.

Their wedding was one of the events of that optimistic year's Georgetown Social Calendar. Betsy and Rudolph were the perfect couple. They were the kind of people who were given houses as wedding presents. They were nicknamed The Blondes. They were destined to go far. That was the *on dit*. The guests were people you know from biographies, memoirs and those endless documentaries: Ich bin ein Berliner, Camelot, the Missile Crisis and – boom! – the Grassy Knoll.

The President himself wasn't there, he had one of his famous headaches, due to be alleviated at 4 p.m. But the First Lady was. Gore Vidal was her walker. This was the occasion when he famously remarked that the holy ghost could not hope to compete with the holy spooks, chief among them Jim Angleton (who had old-boyishly recruited Rudolph in his penultimate year of archaeology and anthropology at Yale: the very word 'spook' is a Skull & Bones coinage). Also present: Cicily Angleton, Henry Fairlie, David and Evangeline Bruce, Buck and Gwennie Vest, Jack and Scottie Lanahan, Peter and Pat Lawford, the Bradlees, the Shrivers and the Meyers whose divorce had not inhibited their bickering and mutual badmouthing. Not the most favourable portent in retrospect or at the time, come to think of it. All these were on the groom's side. The Mavroleon side was less intellectually distinguished, less politically influential but even richer, very rich indeed.

Within months of the wedding Rudolph was posted to the American embassy in London. He was appointed a senior manager of the American Committee for Cultural Freedom (Europe) – a Company post rather than a diplomatic one. As at Langley he was not universally admired. He connected too well. His rarefied social life was despised. His name-dropping was ridiculed. His terminally Scottish tweeds, tattersall shirts and locutions ('What's your toxin?') were subjects of mirth. He knew it. He developed a mockery-resistant hide. He was tirelessly energetic. His private income and *sa jeunesse* were envied. His wife was coveted. The greatest source of resentment was the preferment and protection he enjoyed due to his family's closeness to Angleton.

No HR pro could ever condone such favouritism, especially when so exposed. The demoralising effect on the favourite's co-workers is tangible. The unwarranted boost to the favourite's self-worth is equally evident.[34]

Rudolph, who never mastered casting a dry fly, repaid this compromising debt by buying a house beside the river Test with almost a half mile of double bank riparian rights where Angleton, on his frequent visits to England, could kill brown trout to his black heart's content. The isolated house was built of engineering brick. It was composed of two frighteningly plain octagons. It was anything but homely. It had a utilitarian air. It might have been some sort of martial building, a primitivist chapel or even a penitentiary, a much-inflated local lock-up. Yet it was called Matrimony Farm.

---

34 My sometime colleague, the Hamburg psychologist Gerd Röhrenbeck, has written extensively on the corrosive effects of what he calls *Lieblingssyndrom*.

The name so delighted them that they believed, they *knew*, it must be for them. They were in love. They felt, as people in their state will, that the world favoured them. They would learn that love is a form of psychosis. And it cures itself, along with all the delusions which it incites. Its term is not long.

They thought little about the extent of the house's musty dilapidation even though the earliest photos in the album of its conversion to *une maison des rêves* show piles of plaster on the floor, rotted beams, broken windows, even a bird's nest in the pantry. Progress was slow. Builders came and went, mostly went. They exploited their clients' absence in London.

Oh! the hectic life of gregarious young marrieds. They listened to the MJQ, Bill Evans, Cannonball Adderley, Elmore James, Sonny Terry and Brownie McGhee, Tom Lehrer, 'Mirthful' Paddy Roberts, The Barry Island Five's 'Don't Tell Me to Shush, Mush!'. They entertained frenetically in their mews house off Old Brompton Road. They ate at Nick's Diner, Alexander's, Parkes' and Daquise ('*Daquise to the Highway*'). They slummed it at The Hungry Horse Pie Shop and Dan Farson's Waterman's Arms in the wild east. They danced the twist at The Saddle Room. At The Establishment Club they laughed dutifully even though the sketches' references often escaped them. They drank till the early hours in Le Petit Club Français. Everyone they met became a best friend. They seldom remembered how they got home.

On Friday evenings they would drive down the A30 to scrutinise whatever work had been done on the house. They persistently chivvied the builders, a bunch of amiable C2s with pitch-perfect excuses for tardiness and clumsiness and just-about-plausible reasons for the ever-escalating costs.

Big Bri reckoned it would definitely be way beyond criminal to get tiles before he could pass on the benefit of a deal with a chap in Ludgershall.

Suave Ted (carpenter and cabinet maker) had such worries about his walnut wood supply it brought him out in hives. His handsome powder-white face would be pocked with unsightly red volcanos (he said).

Sparky's van was always breaking down.

'Not on the blink again,' sighed an exasperated Betsy.

'On the what?' asked Sparky, unfamiliar with that American expression.

Rudolph and Betsy faced the exhilaratingly stinging wind on the blackthorn downs. It chased away the smog which, not knowing about the Clean Air Acts, still smothered Londoners in a 15-tog grey-green mantle. Here were the clumps and farms, bartons and barns which would, only a few years later, inspire Toby Trinnick's *Little Gay Tractor* series. (So *childish*, I thought, as a child.) Bobbing scuts scattered to hide in tufts. They rolled like cuddling children down the crisp-leaf slopes of a hill fort gathering twigs and chalk marks. The high beech boughs above them rioted. Crows cawed.

Rudolph spoke doomily: 'They can smell death.'

'No, that's not crows. That's ravens, My Sweet.'

'Satan's air force.'

'Satan doesn't exist.'

'Oh no?' He seemed suddenly surprised that she should think that way.

They shopped arm in arm for antiques in Winchester. They bought furniture at auction in Salisbury. They found a delightful Victorian baroque *canapé* in Lyndhurst. They called Stockbridge 'The Cow Town' and 'Abilene': its one and only street might have been transported from the Wild West. They put up at The Shadoxhurst Arms there and made less of a name for their bickering than they might have done in a hotel unacquainted with the flower of West Point and Colorado Springs seconded to the many nearby bases.

A man with a neck brace and a Manhattan swaying in the snug failed to remember the second line of the only poem by Randall Jarrell that anyone knows. He announced: 'I am US Marines Liaison with NATO Ground Forces in Europe,' fell flat on his face, spilled hardly a drop.

Much of Rudolph's time was spent creating front organisations whose link to the Company was undetectable, meant to be undetectable. Their hierarchy was, in Company jargon: RAF johnnies, beards, double beards, full sets and empty wigs. Bogus foundations and charities organised concerts of unlistenable music, exhibitions of impasto blobs and performances of unwatchable dance. Their purpose was to emphasise the supposedly unconditional freedoms granted to artists in the West. The freedom to be a baby yucking with the contents of its nappy. The freedom to fail. And how!

Legat Totman's oral history *Donkeys of the Avant-Garde* included an interview with the actor Ronnie Fraser conducted shortly before his death in 1997:

'We were having dindins at Kendrick Mews. Somewhat liquid dindins, has to be said. Ruders staggers off to answer the blower. Couple of minutes later he's back, absolutely fucking lachrymose with laughter. Clapping his hands. Whooping. Lurches over to Betsy.

'"We have done it! It is a huge success, my darling. Just about the entire audience walked out after less than twenty minutes. Seems only Stinkovitch and Space Bitch Laika endured to the bitter end. Sounds like job done!"

'It'd have been overstepping it to probe too deeply about these pranks. One imagined they were meant to be hush-hush. Bear baiting it got to be known as. Winding up Eastern bloc embassies all over the world. Pissing off chumski Ivan. Quite how that scuttles the Red Menace . . . only a lackey capitalist running dog like Ruders could explain.

'Something to do with choice I do believe.

'Proclaiming the absence of political censorship . . . In which case how our own dear Lord Chamberlain fitted in is anybody's guess.

'It wasn't actually the chirpy lark Ruders made it out to be. It was deuced serious. Dirty tricks with a veneer of laughter. War by another means. Subtle propaganda. You know I had the uncomfortable suspicion that those earnest clots sloping about the stage going plinky-plonky-plink with farm equipment and toolboxes did not *quite* appreciate their role. It didn't occur to them that they were dear Ruders's puppets. Exploited, one might say . . . But really it was beyond me. Beyond Jimbo too.

'But he did come up with a corking pearl of Jimbo wisdom. Namely: "There are some sorts of tomfoolery that you have to be too clever by half to get the hang of. And being *pleased* to be in a show whose audience take off, take French leave, is one of them. Nail on the head. In my sweet old-fashioned way I reckon it's bums on seats which underwrite artistic freedom. But then what do I know? I'm just a humble thesp."'

The pattern – urban weeks, country weekends – was not long established when it was disrupted by Rudolph's determination to prove himself to the doubters at the embassy. He would eagerly help out. He'd insinuate himself, volunteer for projects outside his remit and, strangely, for routine tasks which would normally be confided to more junior operatives. He was known as The Handyman. A recognisable type, familiar in any organisation. Lone wolf in his own place that he carried with him: think of an invisible camper van or perhaps a tent. Innovative. Not engaging. Brilliant, yes, 'but given to employing any means to achieve self-actualisation. It was widely reckoned his behaviour revealed a profound, enfeebling lack of self-esteem and dissatisfaction at his personal ecology.'

Of course he concealed it socially with charm, bluster and alcohol. His demeanour and secrecy troubled the ambassador, David Bruce. He probably knew the name of no other attaché of Rudolph's rank. It wasn't just that Bruce and Rudolph's father were old friends; the boy was, worryingly, Angleton's creature, his caricature . . . He shared the same 'lucidity in thirst', the same passive recklessness, the same cunning tendency to turn up where least expected. A colleague spoke of 'a life hiding in closets'. He excelled himself in his determination to become the most committed of cold warriors, the spiritual soldier of Our Mores, Our Way, Our Liberty. He wanted to be his patron's heir. The way was eased by the head of the Company's London station being Frank Wisner, a mentally disturbed future suicide over whom Angleton had complete control and who was referred to as The Vegetable.

Rudolph disappeared for weeks at a time to Berlin on Company business. He had been monitoring RIAS (Rundfunken im amerikanischen Sektor), which was widely listened to in the DDR. He sought from Angleton, and was granted, over Bruce's head, permission to take leave in order to amend the broadcaster's diet of theoretical propaganda and boasts that life in the truly democratic West, where human rights were upheld, was an incomparable privilege.

Rudolph considered this way too theoretical. His methods were eye-catchingly coarse. To the fury of the station's managers he heavy-handedly dismissed half a dozen economists, demographers and statisticians and employed in their place 'scriptwriters': gutter journalists, pornographers and admen. Don't tell, show. His simple strategy was to turn much of RIAS's output into soap operas whose characters talked incessantly about the bounty everyone took for granted in the FDR. How the accumulation of possessions was fulfilling. No ideology. But what's ideology when you drive a nice car? Oh the bliss that unlimited choice brought the characters – who are forever shopping. For white goods, brands of beer, foodstuffs, holidays, vacuum cleaners, typewriters, caramel-coloured telephones, slide rules, leather shoes, real coffee, cars, such cars, clothes of countless colours, automatic teamakers, propelling pencils and televisions, televisions! This was the way to coax a Trabi-driving population who drank ersatz coffee to rise up against their cossetted leaders. Incite material resentment. Own a Borgward!

At the city's rainlashed crosspoints, Rudolph, flashing his diplomatic passport, would try to talk to the suspicious, reticent VoPos manning the DDR side. They were nervy, itchy-fingered teenagers, too young for the job. Their fathers would have been more up to it but they were dead turning to leather in the peat of the Don steppe. Their response to Rudolph was to ignore him. He attempted to get close enough to their meagre, *fil-de-rasoir* embellished shelters to listen to *Freundschaft*, *Der Erbe der Hallers* or *Unter Unsand*, to observe how they reacted to the new serials. These improvised field experiments were as unyielding as they were methodically flawed. He liked to offer the boys cigarettes and even give them a pack of Kent, which one or other would swiftly pocket. They tried to hide their gratitude to the caricatural English gentleman with the fedora and vulcanised mac. Their bad diet faces and too large collars were evidence of the DDR's indigence. So probably were the matted coats and low-quality spittle of their *Schaferhunden* pulling at taut plaited sado-leashes. Just their hind legs, all bone and not enough fur, remained on the cracked tarmac. Rudolph had to skip to avoid one which hurled itself and lunged at him. Its restraining handler, like a man winded by a gale, laughed garishly.

'You wouldn't have been so lucky with this fella, Boy,' warned a leathery American dog handler, a top sergeant who had observed Rudolph's escape with amusement. 'This fella' was also a German Shepherd, of sorts. Rudolph peered at it. He had not seen one like it. It was unusually coloured: black body, white head, pink tearful eyes. An albino condor in mourning.

'Bites without mercy. Pitilessly. That's how they were bred. And I tell you, Boy, that breeding stays in the blood. Them VoPo dogs . . . fluffy kittens. Sure they'll take off a baby's face but they're not like ours. Ours are *not* kittens. Nooo . . . Not kittens. They are the heirs, the inheritors from the finest SS dog schools. Mordhunden. Academies where they reprogrammed dogs as weapons . . . This fella here is Heini. He is what they call *sought after*. He and his family. Most sought after. Uncle Adolf had teams of gene marvs building super-animals, crossing wolves with Ridgebacks what have you. New breed reptiles that could survive winter on the steppe. Magnanimous in victory – magnanimous! The land of the free! – we gave these Nazi marvs a second chance . . . found they had no charges to answer . . . built labs for them so that they could continue their work. Grand Junction, Las Cruces, Rapid City, South Dakota. The De-domestication Programme. Turns a gentleman dog into a savage hound. Just like West Point. If you raise your voice to me, Boy, Heini will have your oesophagus. Your intestines will be decorating the sidewalk. Just say hullo to him. Say hullo to Heini – but softly, Boy, softly.'

In several episodes of *Freundschaft* the Alsleben family talk about how ashamed they are to learn that their cousins who live near the Muggelsee (in the East) have acquired a dog whose forebears were in the service of the SS. This crude storyline was not effective or credible in the East for everyone there knew that fascism had been eliminated: ideology, symbols, *Verfahren*, people, laws, *Dekadenz*. All vanished. Especially fascist dogs.

The first time Betsy accompanied Rudolph to Berlin she spent two chilly days wandering through 'a maze made by crippled pyromaniacs' – she repeatedly used that phrase on frilly-edged monochrome postcards.

Germany had gone from defeat to defeat. The second was now more than a decade and a half back in the ever present past. Here and there slumped the half-men, the carcasses. Limbless, legless, eyeless, earless. Prostheses grown into bodies from which they were now inseparable. *Lumpig* tatters glued to pustulating skin. The malodour of their breath. They were revenants from paintings made after the war before last. This generation of ignoble martyrs and maimed heroes would not be painted. The war had turned them into subjects. But paintings no longer had subjects, no longer spoke to anywhere but the eye. Subjects were proscribed by the Company. Street after street of scorched brick and toasted stone that crumbled to the touch: that was the decor. Doorless, windowless apartment blocks were still inhabited. Tarpaulin bivouacs occupied rooms missing walls. Stairwells without stairs. Absences between charred walls stretching to the sky. Street after street was deserted. Yet there were screams from hidden courtyards, entryless alleys. There was chugging machinery, somewhere. There were saws grinding through stone. Cardinal stenches gusted from toothless windows to her nostrils. Every house suffered from *schlechter Mundgeruch*. (Halitosis! – a preoccupation of Germans who had lived through the war when dentists were in short supply. Teeth rotted. Never again.) Chimneys gushed smoke of many colours.

She was orienting her inadequate map to find her way back to the hotel on the second day when snow begins to fall, spinning. She was ill-equipped for such weather. There was no shelter. She was walking in the snow along the deserted streets beneath the high flat facades that succeeded one another, without variation, indefinitely. Beside a crater stood a soldier all but dead: ill-shaven cheeks, a livid scar on the left (windscreen, not duel), visible exhaustion, soiled crumpled army coat, sleeves devoid of stripes. For an instant she wonders what it would be like to hold this vulnerable man in her arms, embrace, *küssen*, feel him – as she has no man since she met Rudolph. That she should wonder such things shocked her. The splinter of a possibility seems to have lodged itself. The snow goes on falling, slow, spinning vertically, uniform; just a few flakes momentarily turn back and clamber upwards. Yellowish snow compacted step by step behind her followed her into the future.

She saw this soldier again two months later.

Rudolph flew early one morning from Berlin to Fulda for a

meeting with representatives of the BND and the BfV about the procurement of attack dogs. He kissed her goodbye. Betsy snuggled up to his T-shirt. It smelled of him and Habit Rouge. When she rewoke she read Shervell Trotman's *Death's Many Uses*. At midday she left the hotel and strolled through the Tiergarten. The zoo pandas were lethargic. The tigers were overweight. The leopards were not notably spotty. The elephants might have been tranquillised. The smell was stinging and sickening. It made her stumble. She held a scarf across her face. She crossed Budapester Strasse near the ruinous church. In the door of a recently built furniture shop on Tauentzien-strasse stood the soldier. Not a soldier, *the* soldier. An incongruous soldier in this part of town. His pressed army coat bore three stripes. He was clean-shaven. He wore a garrison cap and puttees. He now gripped a parcel, a shoe box perhaps, wrapped in greetings paper and ribboned. He was looking round anxiously. She stood watching him. He didn't notice her. His evident anxiety increased his vulnerability. She walked past him towards KaDeWe.

She turned to look at him as soon as she dared. When she did so he had gone.

She didn't know why, but for the next few days until they returned to London, she felt herself compelled to sit for some time round noon at a café near the shop on Tauentzienstrasse. Drifts of dust built up on the terrace. She could not contemplate approaching him even should she see him, which she didn't. She was comforted by the very knowledge of his existence. He had gently punctured the bubble of exclusivity that attached to Rudolph and her. They lived in a world round which they had heedlessly woven a protective skein of tics, private language, endearments.

This soldier had suggested escape. It would have been disrespect-ful to have thought of him as the Unknown Soldier. Yet . . . for her he stood for all men, an idea which was as stubbornly adherent as it was risible. She secretly smiled at her regression. Adolescent crushes, strong profiles: how silly! The sun reflected by a Borgward's bumper sent geometrical creatures dancing up a building's facade, bats in negative. She laughed. This unknown soldier had woken something, legitimised a want, had made her recall what it was to be an animal.

One night of this visit Betsy and Rudolph were walking to dinner through a neon canyon of strip clubs. Impasto local colour and local reeks: stalls selling lascivious bockwurst abounded. Popcorn tips everywhere. There were squads of fubsy underdressed prostitutes and grinning pimps, recipients of generous grants to establish their businesses here rather than in Hamburg or Frankfurt.

'This is what they want and the more we show it them the more they want it.' *They* were the unfortunates on the far side of the Wall.

'We got to make them greedy for our freedoms.'

Betsy thought: what kind of freedom do these dimple-buttocked porkwhores enjoy? She didn't say anything, she squeezed his hand and realised just how predictable he was becoming: in his obstinately straitened view there was nothing that could not be exploited to demonstrate the triumph of the West, there was nothing that did not contain the seed of its own hostile propaganda, there was nothing that could not be turned against itself, there was nothing that resisted his cleverness, his *patriotic* cleverness. He did not differentiate between his *amour propre* and his pride in the Company – which was America. And America was a 400-mile-long seaboard country stretching from Washington DC to Boston.

A local wag had called Matrimony Farm 'The Crystal Palace' – outside the back door was a frozen lava flow of empties. The name stuck. Early evenings, they sat at the scrubbed wood table in Matrimony Farm's bottle-strewn kitchen; when they were alone they neglected the niceties of self-deception, though they were punctilious in their consumption of Buccal Gym mouthwash. Rudolph was absorbed in an article in a month-old edition of *Der Spiegel*. An account of the first investigation of a bog body outside his native Denmark by the archaeologist Peter Glob. A young woman had been buried on Kaltenhofer Moor near Rendsburg between a thousand and fifteen hundred years previously. She had been strangled by a plaited leather rope that reduced the circumference of her neck to that of a bottle neck. The reporter questioned whether she had been an adulteress. Professor Glob, inured to such speculation, said almost certainly yes . . . almost certainly no. Human sacrifice? Again, yes or no. Rudolph looked at the photos of the shiny mahogany tongue whose last act had been to stretch from its mouth as though it might gather breath.

'There's got to be some way . . .'

Betsy looked up to see if he was still talking about exhumation.

'There *will* be a way . . . No one thinks of it like this – but these bog folk have got a big big future.'

He didn't notice Betsy rolling her eyes. He merely stuck out a glass for a refill.

'Doncha think? It's about how we untie them from the past . . . Let them loose on the present . . . Adultery! That's a really rich vein. I mean adultery is adultery whether it's in a what do you call them . . . longhouse, yeah, thatched longhouse hundreds, thousands of years ago or on the back seat of a car last week. Hey, remember that hotel in Garmisch? Thin walls . . . See where I'm heading?'

He didn't bother to interrupt his monologue.

'What I'm saying is that in the DDR . . . it punishes adultery as though it were a criminal offence . . . something from the iron age. Do those poor wretched people realise how backward that is? Here's a way of teaching them. It's graphic . . .'

So began the Mosefolket Project.

It stuttered into half-life. It was soon broadened to include a short film. Rudolph took a risk. He hired a commercials director, Hans H——, who had a reputation as borderline neo-Nazi. The film showed three men, charged as black marketeers, hanged from a gibbet in a forest clearing. The film was convincing but its invented provenance was frail. Supposedly a contrite member of the execution squad had returned to the site to record the victims in their death throes. They were not black marketeers, but robin hoods, distributing stolen food destined for the corrupt rich to the poor. This, it was decided, had been the vocation of many people strangled and dumped in bogs. Professor Glob still neglected to reply.

Less than four weeks after it had begun the project was cancelled. Rudolph blamed its failure on his being prevented from running the operation day to day. He, Rudolph Chipurnoi, would have convinced the people of communist East Berlin and the puritanical, primitive country beyond (Karlmarxstadt, Leipzig) of the cruel fate meted out to adulteresses by a state whose highest officials were depraved orgiasts with boundless sexual appetites. (Ulbricht!)

In fact it was, as Rudolph knew, cancelled by an irate Angleton as soon as he got wind of it in Washington.

More than a decade previously Walter Schellenberg, chief of, successively, Nazi counter-intelligence SD-Ausland and the RSHA, was composing his memoirs in a borrowed villa at Pallanza beside Lake Maggiore. He had made contact with Angleton. The villa's owner, a Milanese notary called Andrea Ventri, knew Junio Borghese, who owed much to Angleton.

A lunch party was breaking up when Angleton arrived early evening in his Jeep. To judge by their scent, their clothes, their cars – a pre-war streamlined RHD Delahaye 165 and a Talbot-Lago 26 – the guests belonged to the pan-European super rich whom he despised and envied, people of flexible morals capable of treating with any regime: among them an aged grande horizontale[35] with a Gainsborough hat and her young, dazzlingly handsome companion. Angleton, educated at Malvern College, could spot an English pervert from a long way off.

Schellenberg belonged to a different caste. He was haggard, unshaven, ill. Wrapped in blankets that smelled of mildew, he was attended by his amanuensis, a former SS sycophant called Ernst, now a doormat stenographer, by his wife Irene ('You're doing it for posterity, *mein liebchen*, for what you believed in . . .') and Irene's white telephone. He must have wondered what he had believed in.

A gardener with the filthiest fingernails – each one a blueblack quarter-moon – served drinks. Schellenberg flattered Angleton. He had heard wonderful things about him! It takes a spy to recognise a spy! The former prowess of OSS! The current prowess of the CIA! He boasted of his own prowess as a spy, of his rise through the ranks of the Black Corps. He was fluent in his curriculum vitae and honours bestowed on him.

Despite suffering what he knew to be terminal cancer he wanted to stage a comeback, an encore. He had just made what he claimed

---

35 James Angleton initially mistook the Vicomtesse Riquetti de Besançon for Coco Chanel, Schellenberg's sometime financial supporter. Chanel was twenty years the Vicomtesse's junior.

he feared might be his last journey, to Madrid to meet Otto Skorzeny whom he neither admired nor trusted. But Skorzeny was known to be tailed by various agencies. Schellenberg reckoned that being seen in the company of such a man might alert the intelligence services of Spain and Italy, maybe France, even the USA and Israel. He was aggrieved that no one considered him dangerous enough to put under surveillance. Surely Angleton could persuade the CIA of how dangerous he was, persuade someone . . . He ranted about the disrespect. He grumbled that the Americans didn't consult him about creating an intelligence service to combat East Germany and Soviet Russia. Angleton lied, he said he'd do whatever he could. Schellenberg knew he was lying and Angleton knew he knew. Nonetheless Schellenberg thanked him, toasted him, clasped his shoulder with a feeble hand as though he believed him man to man, spy to spy, deceiver to deceiver – though there was, actually, no deceit.

Later, looking pointedly at Ernst who had been a gofor on Himmler's staff, he spoke scornfully of Himmler's superstitious gullibility: a mystically besotted filing clerk who'd believe in anything provided it was far-fetched and an insult to reason. He ridiculed the Ahnenerbe's risible preoccupations.

You don't win wars with crazed folklore, astrology and bogus history. Himmler's fixation on bog bodies was a fine example. Following Tacitus's characterisation of them as *corporae infamae* – life unworthy of life, the morally decayed, the ethically corrupt, the sexually deviant, the racially infirm etc. – they were deemed to have deserved strangulation or garrotting followed by undignified burial in a marsh. This was the true German way. Himmler claimed that 'our ancestors only had a few abnormal degenerates. Homosexuals, called Urnings, were drowned in swamps . . . That was not a punishment, but simply the natural termination of an abnormal life. They had to be removed just like when we pull out nettles, stack them and burn them. It was not a question of revenge but simply that they had to be done away with.'

Angleton feared that many East Germans would recall with a shudder the Nazi propaganda uses of bog bodies, 'nature's mummies'. He further considered Rudolph's failure to warn him of the project insubordinate and presumptuous.

Rudolph was surprised by Angleton's terse order to abandon it. But he was undeterred.

His next propaganda exercise resulted from a drunken evening with USAF Brigadier General Tom H. Bavin who in the closing weeks of the Second World War had dropped leaflets on several German cities inciting civilians to insurrection. Between them they decided to drop leaflets on East Berlin advertising the material pleasures of the land of plenty, aka West Berlin. Rudolph wrote a text which boasted of the number of cinemas showing Hollywood films and glorified the food choices that a capitalist economy offered, leather shoes, handmade toys, fine tobacco, fat lava ewers and vases, aviator sunglasses etc. The text was translated by an ever-willing member of the typing pool, Poor Elsa. The leaflets were designed by the art director of *Stars and Stripes'* European edition. They were dropped from a low-flying Cessna 310.

They were met with such incredulity and laughter that for several days they were held up on Rundfunk der DDR's news programmes as examples of the West's slovenly educational standards and near illiteracy. Poor Elsa suffered dyslexia, a condition that did not affect her ability to touch-type, the only task she had previously been asked to perform. Rudolph's failure to have the translation checked was noted.

But no matter. Another opportunity presented itself. A manufacturer of electrical goods in Rostock had recalled a dozen faultily wired toasters. Hans H. was again called in. He filmed nothing. Rather he went through a series of archives including those of insurance companies and sutured together a three-minute collage of fierce house fires. A curt voiceover at the end ascribed the fires to DDR toasters.

Rudolph then began preparing a new eye-catching project. This one about Khrushchev's mistress Yekaterina Furtseva receiving public money. When Langley learnt of it he was ordered to abandon it immediately and to hand over all related documents. Soon after, one of Angleton's lieutenants ordered him to England, immediately.

★

As consolation he bought himself a red convertible Jaguar E-type from a Chiswick showroom scented with Castrol-X. The salesman stroked the paintwork. 'She's a head-turner all right. Oh yes, she's one to catch the ladies' eyes.'

Rudolph feigned puzzlement and affected a Southern accent: 'I have myself a fine lady – as you would be putting it no doubt. I wish for no other.'

And that was true. Despite the many opportunities solitary travel offered he remained faithful to Betsy, as much from a preference for the sodality of hard-drinking males as from the obligations of the marriage contract. He was jokingly addressed as High Fidelity.

He drove the car to the Test Valley. The house was all but finished. The decorators had been quicker than the builders. There was, however, still plenty to do and Betsy did it. Rudolph feigned supervising, waving arty hands. Betsy pored over *nuanciers*. She did much of the painting side by side with Tosh. She grew confident enough to criticise grouting quality. Before Rudolph returned she spent riotous evenings at The Shadoxhurst Arms with the decorating crew and their mates.

The E-type became a familiar sight, envied and admired in South Kensington: oh! the golden couple! It was ogled with wonder in the Test Valley, a token of a life unknowable in tied cottages and toilet-less bucolic slums. It was frequently observed parked briefly outside country phone boxes – on verges, by lychgates, beside signposts at crossroads, beneath muddy oaks, outside the Spar shop near the entrance to the agricultural college. Few houses had a phone. Clover Sevitt's among them. She twice pushed her overladen sit-up-and-beg bike to phone boxes to find them occupied by Rudolph. She noticed that on both occasions – beside a corrugated iron Scout Hut, outside the abandoned ivy-strangled Siloh Independent Chapel 1872 – that he wasn't making a call but noting down the phone's number. And on both occasions he hurried out of the box without acknowledging her as she puffed away to regain her breath.

Xanthe Frame's divorce had brought her a rusting caravan in the thick-aired Sitka-spruce gloom at Pope's Gutter. She snooped on the handsome blond American fellow with her ornithologist's telescope. She was far too distant to hear the phone but Rudolph jumping from the car to answer it made it evident when it rang. He was clumsily urgent. The call, she reflected, must be important. And secret: they've got two sports cars so you can bet that they have a phone in the house. There must be something he doesn't want her, whatever her name is, to know about. Betty . . . Betsy – that's it.

Betsy who's always having to be taken home by one of her fellow boozers at The Shadoxhurst Arms because she's too drunk to drive. Blacks out. Can't hold her liquor. Falls asleep in his car so can't recall Suave Ted singing Timmy-Boy Niel's 'The Heartbreak Shore of Lonesome Lake' or his party-piece story about trying selflessly to save a music hall performer, Daisy of The Fabulous Windermeres, who died when one of a jostling scrum of autograph hunters dropped a cigarette on her stiff beehive and set her on fire.

She can recall Suave Ted advising her not to risk driving: 'You don't want to get your collar felt. New constable fellow's not the easy-going sort, he's like a long lane without a turning. Not like Tone were. Don't worry, I'll get you back.'

She aimed for a double seventeen but got double three. She did a quick calculation. Big Bri screwed up with all three arrers. She aimed for double fourteen and got it. Big Bri bought her another to celebrate her prowess. Not only a girl but an American. Extraordinary. A compatriot (rank – major) with a juicy stye tried to pick her up. 'I knew your sister.'

'Really?'

'Really.'

'She was stillborn,' she said, untruthfully, fatefully. The major felt he was a heel.

She preferred the blokeishness and merry joshing of 'her' workmen.

She can recall a blur of arched trees forming a nave of the road, she can recall cow parsley in the headlights, fleeting animals, stately gate piers briefly lit. She couldn't recall being helped to the front door. She frequently fell asleep on a sofa or daybed and woke in the dark with a mouth like a lorry driver's groin and stiff limbs. She actually enjoyed the walk to fetch her car at sleepless first light. She followed the same path beside a branch of the Test where little bridges gave access to cottages with laundry billowing and jigging.

★

A couple of months later in the throes of what everyone assured her was the worst winter since the war, though it seemed no worse than upstate New York any winter, Betsy, fairly sober, had been obliged to leave the TR2 at the end of the metalled track lest kingsize drifts and compacted ice prevented her getting out the next day. She took a swig of Buccal Gym then trudged through the snow at dusk with her bottles of shopping. Rudolph, car-proud and not taking any chances, had left the E-type in London and would arrive soon in whatever taxi at the station could be persuaded to venture into the deepest sticks.

Neither lock resisted her key. That puzzled her. She was mildly surprised that Rudolph had arrived so early. She closed the door behind her and called his name. No reply. She was more bemused than scared.

'Rudolph!'

'I'm in the sitting room, my dear,' came a stage whisper which was not Rudolph's. It was, unmistakably, Angleton's voice.

He was reading by candlelight. He didn't look up when she entered the room but murmured: 'How are you?'

'How . . . what are you doing here, Jim? How did you get in? How did you get into *my house*?'

He made a squeaky noise, a suppressed giggle. He shook his head as though it were the most ridiculous question imaginable. He had been chewing caraway seeds.

'Help yourself.' He indicated the Moka percolator on the low table.

She stared at him; she thought as she had thought before that he might be a dead child exhumed and crudely made up for the role of a corpse in a school play. His skin was skintight. His white fingers were gothic.

She went to the kitchen to chop onions as small as they would get.

When Rudolph arrived in a scented cloud of Buccal Gym she told him loudly in the flagged hall: 'Guess what . . . Your sugar daddy's here, darling – he broke in.'

Rudolph pecked her on the cheek and said, softly: 'Company Wife – I love you.' That mode of address amused him more than her. He shut the sitting room door behind him. She waited a moment, swung it open so the door frame creaked and followed him into the room.

Angleton said: 'You want me deep-frozen. Alone at the blizzard's mercy . . . Oh you're a mighty hard-hearted woman . . . I tell you, Betsy, it ain't a fit night out for man nor beast.'

She laughed despite herself. Logs crackled on the fire. Gamboge velvet curtains wrapped up the room snugly. She curled up on a daybed with a car rug over her reading *Encounter*, 'our tame rag' Angleton called it. She read a poem by McHarg Bultitude who sometimes delighted her, more often infuriated her.

> *Between dog and wolf two shadows steal,*
> *As shadows do, up high apartment walls,*
> *Spread themselves across the parquet*
> *Not revealing what gives them shape –*
> *You are dog? Am I wolf? We animals cast the*
> *Camel's shadow from five till seven.*
> *Hours of dispensation that shield*
> *Traitors in street-lit rooms, hours when*
> *We play an ancient game of clandestine rites:*
> *Never folding a garment, never having to relearn*
> *Each other, clasping a body with deft fluency.*
> *Our whispers assure us – though no one can hear –*

Unless, thought Betsy, Jim had bugged this house. Was this house bugged? She wouldn't put it past him . . .

> *That we're on the sly, en catimini. Secret minutes*
> *When we're sated in dusk's muddle, virtuosos of the hidden,*
> *Like every couple coupling in this street of deceit.*

She didn't listen to their conversation, but was surprised by Angleton's unusual urgency. His intensity was that of a man who trusted no one to pass on his message. Hence his pathological inability to delegate. She picked up broken sentences, names, Rudolph's sycophantic affirmations: would he never learn to disagree with his puppet-master?

Never trust a telephone . . . bar . . . hotels . . . Annapolis say . . . joints I'd never go . . . yeh, ethnic-heavy right? . . . Silver Spring gas station in Silver Spring . . . tooled up of course (laughter) . . . Capitol

View . . . places rather where no one I know would ever go without protective clothing . . . course the phones may not have withstood . . . a field . . . not ideal but just remember . . . Crozier . . . Rudolph, have you not capiche . . . they're porous, they're sieves . . . sieves! . . . Langley too . . . never the same never . . . novel not to be trusted . . . silly – of course . . . ah! shovel . . . either end . . . this is the only way . . . time . . . place . . . each communication is by unique means . . . that's brilliant . . . alacrity . . . raincoats . . . don't look at Cigar Man . . . the elder son . . . look around him . . . Leave the Gills and the McGaheys and the Sogats to our English brothers . . . Clyde . . . Not even nearly men – but fine fine distractions . . . it'll keep them occupied.

Later they lay in bed together. Betsy asked Rudolph: 'What are you cooking up?'

'Just a little experiment.'

'Does Bruce know?'

'He doesn't need to.'

'Caution, my darling . . . Jim is untouchable. You are not. For a lot of people you are a way of getting at him.'

'I know, I know. Don't worry. It's just elementary intelligence gathering. Harmless exercise. Hardly requires advanced tradecraft. Kindergarten stuff.'

'I'm pregnant.'

Pause.

'Preg . . . as in going to have a baby?'

'That's the kind of pregnant. Yes.'

'Yippee!' Rudolph leapt up from the bed to perform an unprecedented dance. Then he hugged her and stroked her and held her face in his cupped hands and smiled at her with unqualified admiration.

'You genius,' he cried, 'you adorable genius. I love you beyond love.'

He arrived on the island by boat. Angleton had stipulated no helicopter, no light aircraft, no private boat. Too noticeable. Out of season only one hotel and one guest house were open. The hotel was fully booked. The Dynnergh Guest House was a reflection of its characterful owners, a cartoon ex-RAF officer and his overfriendly, over-fed wife. They were insatiable collectors of model lighthouses, model vessels of every shape and class, low-relief maps of the islands, china mermaids and sea horses, lifebuoys, garish paintings of wrecks.

'Ooh a bookwriter eh! Don't get many of you lot round here.'

'What about Jack Tyrell?' suggested Group Captain Leonard Cardy.

'When did we last see him? He's never here any more. Do you know Jack Tyrell?' asked Meg Cardy.

Rudolph shook his head. 'Don't think I do.'

'You'd like him. Very suspenseful – aren't they, Love?'

'Bit on the risqué side – but I'm sure you're a broadminded sort of chap.'

'I must give him a try . . . Now, if you'll forgive me . . .' Rudolph picked up his canvas grip and slung it over his shoulder.

'Off to seek inspiration eh?'

'That's it,' he replied, 'while we've still got the light.'

He opened the front door, was slapped in the face by a frontal gust. He pushed against the wind till he found a sheltered doorway. There was a phone box across the road. The streetfinder map blew and flapped this way and that. He wanted to keep clear of the more populous roads. He chose to continue along Porthcress Road, then turned into Buzza Road. There was a phone box near the corner. He climbed up towards the Buzza Tower on the sandy footpath that led through gorse and heather to the hospital.

A dog walker with a horizontal red scarf saluted him. The sea below shone. Like the sea in the tropics, he decided. Blindingly turquoise. Behind the hospital he took a narrower path, initially a board walk, between the back gardens of mostly shut-up bungalows. The path gave on to Church Road at the junction with Silvesters Lane. The target was in front of him. It was unrendered and so austere that it appeared unfinished, a solid shed.

This rudimentary bungalow was surrounded by a low drystone wall in whose interstices grew toadflax, aubretia, stonecrop. Drifts of sand formed dunes against it. This was his destination. He had arrived. He felt uncomfortable. He was convinced he stood out. Too blond. Too tall. So too memorable. The inbred island people were small and dark, wiry scurriers. He was not the right man for the job.

He wondered if this was the right place. He had no corroboration of Angleton's intelligence, no back-up gen. He crossed the road and walked up Silvesters Lane. The name on the gate, Lowenva, was the one he'd been given. He made a tentative half circuit of the building's exterior, taking care not to venture into the parts of its garden which were overlooked by two neighbouring bungalows, already lit for the evening.

What was French about 'French' windows? he wondered while he was picking the lock. The bungalow was hardly furnished. The living room had a woodblock floor. He crawled over every inch of it trying it for loose-fitting blocks. Nothing. He pulled the drawers from a tatty early Victorian davenport, the single piece of furniture which didn't belong in a holiday home. His hands blindly explored the drawers' spaces.

He pulled a stiff lever. He realised how heavily he was sweating. Out of the top of the desk rose, sluggishly, a shelf of pigeonholes separated by Doric columns. All empty. He turned over mattresses. He wriggled under beds, struggled with deckchairs and a clothes airer whose plastic was peeling to reveal crumbly rust. He stood on shaky folding chairs to reach the dusty top of wardrobes. He wondered about the significance of an empty box of Cuban cigars. He photographed it with his Company issue camera – 'fits in a spectacle case'. He pulled the handful of LPs from their covers – Gilbert and Sullivan, Chris Barber and Ottilie Patterson, Gershwin, brass bands, Holst, Delius. He crushed inner sleeves when ham-fistedly replacing them. The small fridge was disconnected. On top of it was a box of Christmas decorations.

The kitchen cupboard was empty save for tins of mustard powder, salt and instant coffee. A drawer otherwise occupied by cheap picnic cutlery contained a sheaf of household bills, exclusively household bills. He didn't know what he was looking for. Whatever it was he couldn't find it. Several shelves held nothing but green Penguins. He squeezed past an immersion heater into a cupboard. It was like being asphyxiated by an obese dance partner.

The light was going fast. He looked at his watch. He had been in the bungalow for nearly an hour. He held out hopes for the loft (those perilous chairs again). It was empty. He was despairing of places to search when he began to scrutinise a pile of magazines and newspapers: old copies of *Time and Tide*, *The Spectator*, *The Observer* – not promising. But further down the pile he found *Reynolds News*, *Tribune*, *The Daily Worker*, *New Left Review*, *Soviet Weekly*. 'Hah, just the ticket,' he said to himself, aloud.

And as he flicked through the pages of *Soviet Weekly* a sheet of lined paper fell from it. It had been torn from an exercise book. On it were four columns of numbers all in the same hand, mostly in pencil, the tops of them marked D, R, M, G. The bottom few numbers of each column were in ballpoint. In the same hand, also in ballpoint, in the right margin was written, 'Z M J N – A A !!' He put the sheet of paper in his grip. It felt important. A key.

He left by the way he had entered. So far as he could see in the lampless evening there were no scratches around the lock.

The footpaths he had followed to the bungalow were not lit; he thought it less risky to return down Church Road which was orangely lit. The malicious wind picked up and rubbed sand in his eyes. An intermittent flickering came towards him up the hill, bicycle lights whose dynamos were generating insufficient power to achieve a constant beam. The first cyclist was a rodent of a man so short he could not exert pressure on the pedals. His companion was a mass of fat and asthma, wheezing as he zigzagged up the hurtful slope. Neither of the strugglers took much notice of Rudolph.

Mrs Cardy had told him: 'I'm afraid we don't do cuisine out of season. We usually like to recommend our guests go to The Association or The——' Blank. He realised he had forgotten the name of the other pub. The town – really a village – seemed as shut up as the bungalow. The first pub he saw served stale beer. The second's landlord was deep in conversation with a friend and waved a petulant hand when Rudolph ventured a far from aggressive 'Excuse me'. The third was The Association. He ate a pasty with mashed swede, a packet of crisps which belied their name. He drank a bottle of Guinness. Angleton was expecting his call at 3.30 p.m. EST. He had half an hour to kill. He drank two large whiskies. At 8.20 p.m. BST he strolled back along the front to the phone box on the corner of Buzza Road. The brisk air stung therapeutically. The whisky warmed him. He felt happy about his work. A job well done. He withdrew a coarse paper packet of coins from the grip. He prefixed the number Angleton had given him with the eight digits used by phone engineers working on the yet to be implemented transatlantic service – digits which changed monthly to prevent this very abuse. The handpiece was picked up on the first ring. Rudolph reported that there was little to report save for the paper bearing the columns of figures and the letters.

'What are the figures?'

He read them out, painstakingly, one by one, column by column. Angleton repeated them one by one.

Angleton was talking to himself. 'Each one increases. The further down the page the greater the sum . . .'

'Yes, that's right,' said Rudolph, looking at the page in the low-quality light, 'well, like I say apart from the end where amounts are subtracted from three of the columns.'

There was a pause.

'Apart from the winner's,' chirped Angleton.

'The what?'

'The winner's. And these letters. Seven of them no doubt. Look like the name of some fellow who distills potatoes in the Subcarpathian boondocks.'

'No, no – there are six, with a dash before the last two and two exclamation marks.'

'Hmm . . . Ah. OK . . . Yes. I've got it. You hang onto that piece of paper now. Yes?'

'Of course.'

'Thank you, Rudolph. Good work.'

He rang off.

When he got back to the Dynnergh Guest House with its homely smells of cat litter and baking Mrs Cardy popped her fubsy face round the door of the sitting room: 'All right are we? Had a nice tea?'

'Delicious.'

'That's the way. Your friends called round. Said not to worry they'd catch you in the morning.'

'Friends?'

'Yes. Sorry they were to miss you.'

He was shaken: 'Ah . . . yes. Which friends? Did they say who . . . ?'

'Didn't leave their names. I assumed, you know, that you'd know . . . You weren't expecting them then?'

'No. No, I wasn't expecting them.' His hands gripped each other. He bit his bottom lip so that it was tooth-marked. 'Wasn't expecting anyone. Did they say anything? What did they look like?'

'Ooh – chalk and cheese. Little chap – so titchy Len said that he wouldn't have been able to get into the forces. And the big chap. Very big. Well, I'm a one to talk but he was what they call obese. Big o'girth, short o'breath – as they say. Very polite the pair of them. Superior types. They bookwriters too?'

The Fat Wheezer and The Short Rodent. No more than he was.

'Yes.'

'Well I never. Three in one day.'

'I must settle up – I've got to get the early boat.'

He creaked up the stairs to his room, wedged a chair beneath the door handle as potential quarry does in films though it's no deterrent to a beef-shouldered brute, hardly slept, tensed at the slightest sound, got up at 5.45, closed and locked the front door, put the key through the letter box as instructed, wished he had an extra pullover, hurried through the empty streets to the harbour glancing behind him every few yards. He sat in the corner of the Atlantic Café (Formica and surplus MoD furniture) with a pot of tea and a greasy bacon sandwich. Sailors, stevedores and seadogs ragged each other, laughed ribald and long, deflated boasts of sexual conquests on the mainland where 'they're all goers, just beggin''.

The café door opened. An acrid saline wind barged in followed by a lanky duffel coat with a surprisingly patrician accent: 'Anyone here for *Gondolier*? Five minutes.'

Rudolph checked his watch.

'Well, well, well – just in time, eh?' said The Fat Wheezer, wheezing as he entrusted his bulk to a plywood and rust chair on the other side of Rudolph's table. The Short Rodent stood behind him smiling. (He looks like a village idiot, thought Rudolph, a village idiot trying to find a village so shameless it would have him.)

'Early bird aren't we, eh? Gets the worm, what . . . you've got something of ours. Ha, yes, you might say the worm. The worm is ours. You following me?'

The Short Rodent said: 'We don't want to get you into trouble . . . Can you imagine how much red tape that would involve *us* in?'

'Not to mention chokey for you, old bean . . . what are your feelings about anal rape? Hammer and tongs they go at it in some of Her Majesty's guest houses I hear. They like fresh meat. Pretty blond lad like you would have no shortage of admirers.'

'I'm an American diplomat.' Rudolph was as steely as he could muster.

'That might take a bit of verifying – during which time you'd be prey, old bean.'

'I am an American diplomat.'

The Short Rodent laughed: 'Pull the other one. You're a common or garden burglar, sweetie pie. A thief in the night.'

'Dusk, surely.' The Fat Wheezer sounded pleased with himself.

'Why don't you be a good boy and show us what's in that very smart bag of yours.'

Rudolph had had his wits about him all morning.

He didn't say: 'I didn't find anything. Apart from a sheet of paper with a few figures.'

He did say: 'There's nothing in there. See for yourselves. Go ahead.'

They began to rifle through the grip. The sailors and dock workers watched, briefly puzzled, then returned to their chaffing.

A change of shirt and underclothes, a wash bag, the camera, a Fontana paperback of Hampden Mort's *Life's Last Lap* – though sometimes when he told the story it was Mort's *The Truth About Jessica Holland*.

The Short Rodent pocketed the camera with a smirk to which Rudolph didn't respond. He held the now empty grip up to the light and peered into it: 'What have we here?' He pushed two fingers into a gap where the fabric lining had become detached from the canvas. 'What have we here? Don't they teach you anything at wherever it is?'

'Langley,' prompted The Fat Wheezer.

'Langley . . .' The Short Rodent clasped the folded paper with slender fingertips, withdrew it from the grip, opened it, glanced at it with a smirk and said triumphantly: 'Your chums in the service are' – hammy American accent – 'sure going to be mighty proud of your tradecraft. Oh yeah.'

The Fat Wheezer said: 'You've got a boat to catch. We'll see you aboard. Make sure you get to it safe and sound, old bean.'

As they approached the jetty The Fat Wheezer pinned Rudolph against a granite wall. He had never been frisked before. It was an assault, near enough. Which, reflected Rudolph, is what was intended. It was exacerbated by the man's foul breath, a hint of zoo, a stench of silt. Rudolph winced. He turned round as ordered. Close up the stone might have been blue cheese. The Fat Wheezer took evident pleasure in rubbing Rudolph's balls from this side too.

'Socks, shoes.'

He removed them. Double ply socks. Unmalleable veldtschoen. Empty.

'You'd better get your boat ... Nice meeting you – Mr Chipurnoi.'

They grinned at him as he hastily buttoned his clothes, fought to get his shoes on. He ran raggedly to the jetty waving to attract the boatman's attention.

What had taken Angleton a matter of seconds to figure out took MI6's cryptanalysts several weeks. They worked round the clock on the columns of figures on the sheet of folded paper. Once the digits were separated from the paper they took on lives of their own. Sums of money? Dates? Codes? Codes for what? For who? The figures were fed into computers the size of a lorry to no effect. Logarithms and exponentiation revealed nothing. How did the figures relate to the letters?

After five weeks all attempts to decode it had come to an impasse. It was then that an office junior Antonia Neck (the future Secretary of State for Military Procurement, Heritage and Human Rights) delivered a file to the 'legendary' codebreaker Reggie Polidor. While he signed for it she looked through the smoke of his Burma cheroot at a gestetnered copy of the original piece of paper on his desk and said: 'Jazzman! Heavens! Isn't that peachy! Looks like someone got all their letters out on a triple word score. Was that you, Sir?'

Polidor's head jerked forward. He gaped at the paper. Then he turned to her and said: 'Oysters at Overton's, thirteen hundred sharp, my girl.' He stroked her bottom. She giggled.

That's how MI6 realised that they were scrutinising the scores of a Scrabble game whose participants had been the Labour Party's new leader Harold Wilson, his wife Mary, their sons Giles and Robin (the elder, who had won the game in question and scored it). The six letters and one blank were also in his hand, already familiar to MI6's crack team of graphologists (said to be Hounslow gypsies and Antoine Argoud, a member of the OAS then awaiting trial for two assassination attempts on la Grande Zohra).

Try as it might counter-intelligence could conjure nothing to link Wilson to Soviet Intelligence or to the freakish death of his predecessor Hugh Gaitskell. No problem. MI6, like Angleton, would have to be creative. Meanwhile, it was smarting from its humiliation. It had been duped. Someone had to pay for this deception. That someone was Rudolph, the common or garden burglar who had unwittingly sold them a pup.

David Bruce, willing for once to submit to pressure from British security services, took pleasure in relieving him of his post in London. This was not a decision Angleton considered worth fighting. He cast aside, absenting himself in the Lebanon where his friend Kim Philby had disappeared. Should have cursed him but remained in thrall, making excuses for his behaviour. Idolatry and dependence were deep rooted. His stubbornness infuriated Betsy.

I was born in Georgetown University Hospital, 1.50 p.m. EST, 22 November 1963. Twenty minutes previously Jack Kennedy had been murdered. I weighed a little over seven pounds. The news was coming through. The entire hospital was sibilant with Chinese whispers of shooters in Dallas. Rumour spread from bed to bed. Incredulity mounted. It simply couldn't be. A shocking mistake of communication somewhere in Texas. I had a full head of black hair. Confirmation was scarce. Betsy, now a mother, saw a doctor talking to an elegantly dressed woman. It took her some seconds to realise that the woman was her mother, my new-minted maternal grandmother whose face was so contorted in psychic pain that it was unrecognisable. Betsy was confused, she was at a loss to understand why the midwife was in tears. She feared it was because I had a gross birth defect. Betsy clung to me. She didn't want to look at me, to find out what affliction I had harboured within her. She needed Rudolph to be beside her.

He was away on business – destination vague or undisclosed, which had become increasingly usual since their return to America.

By the time I graduated more than four hundred people, all but two of them men, mostly American, had died leaving a confession that they had been Kennedy's killer or one of the conspirators.

Betsy missed England more than she could possibly have anticipated. She pined for her adopted country, not then peopled by psychopaths and collectively self-harming. She felt that she had found herself there. She hung out in smoky pubs. She twice absent-mindedly left me in my Moses basket when she moved on to the next boozer. What parenting! But I was still there when she came frantically back to fetch me. No one wants to steal a baby with a spit of black hair heading towards the bridge of her nose, a Cossack in diapers.

She loved London's quaintness, its relentless suburbs, tattiness and cheery mediocrity, the crumbling stucco and kooky clothes. The sense of sooty failure, the dented pre-war cars, the burgeoning craze for Victoriana were in such contrast to Washington. The first garment of hers I can remember came from London, a pale grey trouser suit from Foale and Tuffin. It was of course dated by the time I came to appreciate it, but elegance is forever. She bought it the week of Harold Wilson's election victory in October 1964. That was on her first trip back after my father's expulsion, or whatever it was called. She had wanted me to be born there. I wasn't. It rankled. She blamed my father and his murky mission (whatever it was), MI6's vindictiveness (or was it MI5's?), David Bruce's disloyalty and, above all, 'Uncle Jimmy' Angleton. Do you know: a less avuncular man never crept this earth. Oh, he was, indisputably, astonishingly clever. Clever, no compass. And a total absence of the uncle-gene. He was a spectral presence in my childhood. Appearing from nowhere and disappearing as though touched with the power of invisibility. He could be such fun of course. The summer before my ninth birthday he taught me how to make a dry Martini and not to bother with nonsense about the yardarm. We were at The Hut on Tilghman Island.

The Hut was not a hut; the name was inversely snobbish. It was a sprawling white clinker-built farmhouse. It was old, just pre-Revolution. Old was important on the island. Our yacht was old though not that old but older than most. It was the most beautiful two-mast schooner, built in France, at Fécamp, in the early Thirties. Oak, teak, streamlined sensuality. It was a precious object moored beside the jetty. Granpa Chipurnoi's work boat (bibulous fishing, invading neighbours' bayside lawns on the hour at Negroni o'clock) was moored on the other side of the jetty. The sound beyond shimmered. The water lapped the shore. A graceful skipjack slid across the bay. Dinghies caught the breeze. Plain one, purl one: a seadog in a row boat cried a greeting.

Uncle Jimmy, as he was then, carried a basket from the house to a table beneath the pines where we sometimes ate crab lunches. He was, as usual, dressed like an undertaker. (His Mercedes ashtray was also a hearse.) Granpa carried a second basket. He was wearing khakis and a sailor-boy top. They giggled like naughty pranksters.

Here were all the ingredients, all the implements: English gin, dry vermouth, green olives, angostura bitters, lemons, an ice bucket with glasses submerged in it, swizzle sticks, a shaker, a much-sharpened knife with a bone handle. These were all lined up in a single rank, with precision. The ritual was excruciating. Granpa put his arm round my shoulder. Uncle Jimmy gripped the knife lightly with those skeletal fingers, cut the lemon's zest in one gesture, in a single spiral. Lemon juice was squeezed into the glasses then thrown from them with a violent jerk of the wrist onto the brittle, sandy grass and pine needles. Angosturas suffered the same fate. So too did vermouth. The shaker was overlooked. The glasses were now ready for cold gin. Would I like to pour it? I held the bottle with both hands. I went about the task gingerly. 'Just to the brim my girl!' ordered Uncle Jimmy.

My mouth stung. My nose felt as though it were being scraped. My eyes watered. I gagged. How Granpa laughed! He didn't notice that Uncle Jimmy was watching me as though I was a laboratory animal: I caught his dead person's stare. That was the first and last time in my life that I tasted alcohol. I am not cursed with Betsy's dedication to intoxicants: I'd like to put that down to willpower but it's more to do with the memory of the foul flavour and of the pathetic rituals built around it. She joined us, rolling her eyes in mock disapproval. Oh I so wanted to look like her. Despite chain smoking and chain drinking she exuded health. Her eyes sparkled. Her tan was deep. Her hair was sun-streaked every shade of blonde. You know, I was jealous. My hair was blueblack as a grackle and my skin was white as gypsum.

It had taken her a long time to get over the premature stillbirth of my sister Daphne. I was five, too young to get a grasp on what was happening, let alone why a dead person who hadn't lived had a name. I didn't know why Betsy sobbed instead of sleeping. Rudolph was my rock during those long long nights. A handsome presence beside my bed weaving stories with happy endings. When I look back I realise that it was the only time then, as parent and child, that we were close, that we had the opportunity to get close. I suspect that despite his protests he was relieved when she said that she needed to be in England for a few weeks. She was not using her loss, their loss, as an excuse to return. In England she felt less diminished by shame. Less abject about her failure to carry the baby to term. In England no one knew she had been pregnant. She could, she said repeatedly, be herself again. The few weeks turned into months. In the country she spent evening upon evening getting tight at The Shadoxhurst Arms with the same old crew who were welded to the flagged floors. In London she led a vigorous, carefree, drunken life in the company of people whom she regarded as politically naive and barmily irresponsible but harmless. Frivolous people whose salon leftism was merely posturing, a trite fashion rather than the threat to the state that it was in America. People who had only the vaguest idea of what Rudolph's peripatetic job was. For that matter Betsy was never quite sure about it either.

As for me – I just had a whale of a time being spoiled, learning to sing for my supper, making lots of friends, running rings round baby-sitters and dressing up as Betsy's cute accessory. Oh, we made such a pair together. My education was a low priority. Provided the fees were paid, the school was quite indifferent to my attendance. Now and again one of her friends would selfishly die (drugs, fast cars) but life had to carry on.

Eventually we returned to Washington; I'd guess there had been pressure from Rudolph. Not that he was always around. Sometimes he would grow his hair, not shave, dress in market-stall denim (ugh!) and disappear for a few weeks. I went to school diligently. I became a bookish American. I read poetry. Donna Mollo, Emily Dickinson, Augusta Dolf. Betsy disapproved of all of them; her taste was for weirdos like Minoushka Wort. Because Rudolph was a temporary attaché at the Tokyo embassy for its duration we visited Expo 70 at Osaka. It was thrilling, a comic book come to life. I struggled with Lafcadio Hearn to start with but grew to love his versions of ghost sickness and doubles. It was not till sometime later that I realised how psychologically astute Japanese folk myth was.

For several years, we were in England only for the summer holidays and for Christmases when the farm would be full of people and laughter and good cheer and too much of everything and dyspepsia pudding and Silent Night and Alka-Seltzer and shiny baubles and bickering and a tree which moulted in the heat.

On Christmas Eve 1974 Uncle Jimmy called Matrimony Farm early evening. The first time he had ever called the house. All his regular communications with my father had previously been from pay phones around Washington to pay phones in western Hampshire and west London. Betsy, who wasn't meant to know about it, mocked it as a Boy Scout system which demanded the Five Prees: preplanning, preparedness, precaution, precision, preposterousness.

I answered. He sounded lightheaded – a new sort of drunkenness maybe. When he wished me a happy Christmas he might have been a robot. He and Rudolph spoke for twenty minutes. In the gloriously yummy-scented kitchen we were all dressed up. They were (and I wasn't) drinking champagne and champagne cocktails, chopping and mixing the stuffing of stale bread soaked in Marsala, broken-up Italian sausages and speck from Leo Giordani, green bacon, prunes in brandy and spinach for the three creamy geese which lay in the middle of the table. Betsy fretted over whether they would be sufficient for fourteen tomorrow given how little meat there is on a goose. Then there was the pork and veal stuffing for the crinkly cabbages that were blanching on top of the Aga. I was peeling potatoes – at least trying to! We were looking busy: me, Betsy and her friends, some of whom were staying, some of whom had weekend boltholes nearby and would be with us tomorrow, to Rudolph's dismay.

Maynard Zeronian and Gaby From The Sixties (to distinguish her from the totally terrifying Gaby Lapsang-Do-You-Hear), Slutty Cornelia, Cornelia's latest beau Sneery Steve (though he was borderline civilised when not boasting that his band's new album *Till That Eagle Grins* was number one in the Spanish and Dutch charts), Cressida from The Alibi who never had time to have hangovers because she was always plegic, Popsy Pfister and his oh so cutesy Schnauzers Freddie and Rolfe, and last and absolutely, totally, least of least, two boring overweight female Chipurnoi cousins 'doing Europe' who put the lard into dullard and had more or less invited themselves and their eating disorders to spend the season of goodwill with us. (Gate-crashing ran in the blood.)

Suave Ted and Big Bri from The Shadoxhurst Arms had dropped in just a few minutes earlier. Terribly *ouvrier*, and Bri was on the *ostrogot* side, but such fun. They were delivering a gift from mine host Colin, a celebratory crate of Hopback India Pale for his thirstiest customer.

The kitchen door opened. Rudolph looked bewildered. He stood in the doorway clinging to it as if he was going to collapse or cry or both.

He said to no one in particular: 'Jim's been fired. That bastard Colby. The finest most loyal . . . he made the Company. Jim made it . . . now—'

He almost screamed: 'Now this fucking betrayal! Not just a bastard, a *cowardly* bastard. The fucker – Colby, Jesus!'

The kitchen was swept by silence. He'd never sworn in front of me before. We all strove not to catch each other's eye. This vacuum seemed to last minutes. It was probably seconds. He looked at us all as though he had not seen us, as though he had not realised he had an audience. It obviously occurred to him now how strange, how brutal his outburst must have seemed. He held up his open palms: 'I do, I do apologise . . . I . . . it's something of a shock. I'm so sorry . . . What's happened . . . I value – ridiculous, old-fashioned – I value loyalty. Colby . . .'

No one spoke till Big Bri said: 'That's awright mate. You tell it 'ow it is! If you can't sound off in your own 'ouse you can't sound off nowhere, it's totally mental. We're with you on this one mate . . . What you need is a nice big snorter.'

His mind in some other place, he smiled shyly at Big Bri: 'Yep, yep, that's an eminently practical proposal, Brian.'

'Bri.'

'Yes, of course.'

Betsy put an arm round his waist. He kissed her forehead. He sunk into a ragged old armchair that had been banished from the sitting room to a kitchen corner alcove. He looked deflated.

Big Bri brought him a large whisky. 'May this Colby fella slip on sty shit and be eaten by the porkers!'

Rudolph tried to balance it on the chair's sweat-shined arm then thought the better of it. Gradually conversation began again. I struggled with a potato peeler. Suave Ted observed my problem, fetched another peeler, pulled up a chair beside me, showed me how to get the rotating blade under the gritty skin. I watched him concentrate. He worked with speed, absorption, deftness. And, hurrah, within minutes I had the knack.

'Nothing I don't know about spud bashing. What they made us do for jankers – better, mind you, than flattening corrugated iron with a cricket roller.'

'What's jankers?'

'Squaddy lingo idn't it. When you been a bad lad you get jankers. Punishment.'

'Were you a bad lad then?' It felt so daring to ask.

'Ooh! That would be telling wouldn't it.'

He deftly dug an eye out of a potato. He left a perfect miniature cone on the table. I reached into the earthy coarse paper bag for another potato. Something made me raise my eyes. You know how you know you're being looked at even when you don't know who is looking at you or where from? That extra sense we developed when we were animals. Rudolph was gaping at me. Like his outburst of swearing, his expression was something I'd never witnessed before. Astonished? Yes. But not good-astonished. More deeply-puzzled-astonished. You might say shocked-astonished. Working-out-the-incomprehensible-astonished. He was staring so intently that he didn't realise I was seeing him, seeing his eyes shift their gaze just slightly from me to Suave Ted then back again. He looked like he had seen a ghost – if that's what people who have seen a ghost really look like. They take on the ghost's properties. They become momentary ghosts themselves. They move onto a different plane. His nails scratched the stained chair arm. Did you hear them rasp? Did you wonder how, in a blink of the eye, a man's face can turn kabuki pale, white beyond recognition, a visitor from another state where complexions are forbidden to display colour?

Having sat and passed their entrance examinations I had expected to go to Waindell, where Betsy had attended, or Benton. Neither would accept me before my twelfth birthday. The Fairlamb School, hardly a byword for *cachet* or *élan*, was unfussed that I was two months short of that birthday. The uniform was inoffensive: red and brown plaid kilt, brown pullover. Betsy was anxious that I should not wait. Or, as likely, that she could not wait to get me off her hands in order to devote more time to writing which meant writing till she had drunk too much to remain coherent and the lines began to stagger across the page. Whereupon she would disappear for hours. Rudolph increasingly disappeared for months, often to Tel Aviv. I knew that from the newspapers he bundled into plastic bags and binned (only for me to open, like a spy). We no longer travelled with him.

The autumn day when I enrolled at Fairlamb I hadn't seen or heard from him for more than six months, since the trip to Langley after we had returned to Washington from that strange Christmas at Matrimony Farm which I thought of as The Ghost Christmas. Betsy didn't mention his absence. I feigned not to notice that many of his possessions were no longer in the house: Russell and Remington paintings, the Staffordshire dogs, shelves of books, filing cabinets, a rolltop desk with hidden compartments.

It was on my first day at Fairlamb that I quit not noticing, that I took on board what I had known . . . I can't be certain that *known* is *le mot juste*. But I had, determinedly, kept it – whatever it was – from me. I wouldn't admit it to myself. Denial. Suppression. They are reckoned unhealthy. But I was moderately happy. That happiness was contingent on my wilful ignorance. Or pretence of ignorance. On partitioning one's head. But it's only so long that we can contain it. The truth forces its way out. Knowledge is a physical burden. It can't be supported indefinitely.

My silent mother drove me there. The distant mountains lived up to their name. Blue. They really were blue, dusty blue in the haze, yearningly achingly blue. The main building was in a heavy, threatening French style. I remembered Rudolph calling some similar houses near Parc Monceau 'pompier'; what it had to do with firemen I didn't learn for years, not that it was on my list of must-find-outs. There were several porters dressed like they were from another century in green tails and top hat. One of them smilingly took my trunk and several suitcases (I didn't travel light). Betsy went to park the Buick Estate, an unwieldy land-barge, dented every time she parked it. I followed the flunky into the chasmic entrance hall, transformed for the day into an echoing reception area for new students. He indicated which desk I should present myself at. I waited as a girl with the worst ever frizzy hair and her mother with the worst ever frizzy hair were dealt with. Then I was greeted by another smiler who couldn't have smiled more had she tried, this one a late middle-aged woman, a knitwear victim with braces on her teeth and a wig like plaited German striezel-bread. She had a simpering saccharine manner. She introduced herself as Elissa.

Then she asked: 'And what's your name, my dear?'

'Phoebe. Phoebe Chipurnoi. C-H-I-P-U-R-N-O-I.'

'What a lovely unusual name!'

She picked up a clipboard. I looked around. A few of my soon-to-be-classmates were standing awkwardly with their parents wondering what was in store for them in this overwhelming building with its protruding excrescences of wood and plaster. The twin staircases were as grand as it gets. People were dwarfed. The scale was wrong. There was a pile of carpets rolled up like culvert pipes.

'Chip – that would be with a C, yes?'

She guided her pen down a list, then up to the top of the page and down the second.

'Hhrm . . . you know a few years back we had three Leas in the same intake. There was one who was L-E-A, one who was L-E-E and would you believe it an L-E-I-G-H. You can imagine how much fun that was . . . I'll bet someone has written it down wrong. Phoebe . . .'

She repeated her inspection. I could see the pen pointing it at given names.

'It'll be Fay in the Admissions Office. Her spelling! And in a place of exacting educational standards . . . Ah Phoebe! Yes, we've got one Phoebe. But it's the wrong Phoebe. Phoebe Mav . . . Mavroleon. That's a nice name too. Fay! I told you. Little wrist slap I think for naughty Fay . . . But it's not you. Let's see.'

It *was* me. It wasn't anything to do with this offstage character Fay. It all became shockingly clear. It was like my voice, my brain, my being were all seized from me. At last I regained control of them.

I yelled: 'It *is* me!'

My shout alarmed her.

'Mavroleon. That was Betsy's maiden name. Betsy's name – before she was married. It's not my name. But it is me. It must be.'

There was a finality here. I felt a freezing rush. I started to cry. I turned away to hide my tears. Betsy had just entered the hall. She was looking about her, wondering where to go in this blank labyrinth. Then she saw me. She clipclopped hurriedly across the patterned tiles. She hugged me. I pushed her off me.

'What is it?'

'My *name* – they've got my name as—'

'Ah. Don't worry. I'd been meaning to tell you . . .'

I couldn't believe it. Well, I could – but I didn't want to.

'You *what*?' I continued, tears or no tears, in an involuntarily mock baby voice: 'You'd been *meaning* to tell me. Just when were you going to get around to telling me?'

'Darling . . .'

'I've lost my name . . . deprived of *my name* . . . what's going on? Why have I suddenly been turned into . . . someone different? Whose idea was that? Why am I the last to know? My identity. Does my identity not mean a fucking thing to you?'

She stared at the distant ceiling then clenched her jaw. She had it off pat.

'Please don't swear. Your father and I have decided to separate.'

It was years before I discovered that was a lie. A lie. There's no word other than lie. But when your father's a spook and your mother's a drunk lies are everyday currency.

'All sorts of things are going to change. We thought it better that you take my name because you're going to be living with me.'

'Living with you? Living with you means living in whatever school you bury me in. Still . . . maybe, *Mommy*, maybe that's better than living at home . . . nursing a fucking drunk.' I wish I hadn't said that.

She was mortified. But I wasn't going to take it back.

'It's my name. Don't I get a say?'

Calling her a fucking drunk to her face recalibrated our interpersonal equilibrium as they say. Recalibrated it long term.

Elissa was worried: her teeth, her fists, her eyes showed it. She was glancing round for help. An audience of half a dozen snoopers was keeping its distance.

She addressed us with cheery desperation: 'First day syndrome. Nothing to worry about.'

'There is,' I replied, 'plenty to worry about.'

'The occasion can be a little overwhelming.'

'Can it? Can it really? As overwhelming as not having a name and not having a father? Not, frankly, that he means much to me. *Meant* much to me.'

Betsy's hurt was the hurt of the vulnerable. She was the sort of alcoholic who wore a mask of peppermints and Buccal Gym mouthwash, not realising what a giveaway they were. She feared the disgrace of being rumbled, and here she was, being exposed by her own daughter in front of a pitiful wig, the pair with the worst ever frizzy hair and a giraffe person putting her hands over her daughter's ears.

I suddenly shrieked with laughter.

'Mother. Go!'

She was diminished, broken. My doing, I'm afraid. She looked at me with disbelief. I had surprised her. Twisting the knife felt like an achievement.

★

My first friend at Fairlamb was Jill Silver. After a week, Brenda Ulm with the worst ever frizzy hair wanted to gang up with us. We allowed her to do so on condition that I shaved her head so that fresh hair could grow. Jill held her down.

It did grow, abundantly and glossily, and with it her confidence and self-esteem. The *jolie-laide*, *tendance laide*, didn't quite turn into a swan but into a better than average-looking duck. We were not embarrassed to be seen with her. Henceforth, too, Brenda was Brandi. My self-esteem grew with Veet depilatory cream which altered my hairline by getting rid of the widow's peak. It grew even more positive when Rudolph, my handsome hero whom I hadn't seen for months, appeared on CBS news, speaking on behalf of the American embassy in Bonn.

The Company's presence in Germany had increased with the threat to American interests by the Red Army Faction and its derivatives. He was issuing a denial that the murder of the suspected Revolutionäre Zellen activists Lothar Sommer and Agna Seidel had been committed by an assassin 'sponsored by an American agency'.

Two weeks after a Hamburg court had found them not guilty on all counts – kidnapping, conspiring to cause explosions, supplying weapons, possession of forged papers – they had been shot while sitting on a bench in the Botanischer Garten in Bremen. It was deemed a professional hit. The weapon was correctly identified as a Skorpion machine pistol. A man 'of Mediterranean appearance, tall, probably Italian or Greek, maybe Lebanese, could be Israeli, with a pronounced facial scar, black hair "glossy like a raven", sunglasses, wearing a black overcoat, aged between twenty-five and sixty', had been seen walking briskly from the park between fifteen minutes and half an hour before the bodies were discovered. A man matching that description was reported to have been in the Café Paris on the morning of the shooting. He was remembered because after eating one P'tit Clamart, a chocolate and candied blood orange millefeuille, he ordered a second and asked sharply if the radio could be turned down. He found the song 'demeaning':

> *I wore a beard in those days – those days: It's dunce to make*
> *that a measure of time,*
> *A gauge of illusion. I downsized to a moustache.*
> *But there was no mistaking who I was.*

The troglodytes, cousins to naked mole rats,
Were repelled by facial hair as I was by their mortadella skin.
They saw through my disguise. A tomb is the last thing
I shall ever need.
I mean that.

Several passers-by thought the entwined couple were heavy petting and averted their eyes. The deaths were reported to a park warden by Emerson Trinkwon, a crippled circus acrobat and seldom-performed playwright with convictions for gross indecency in four countries. The investigating officer suspected that Trinkwon had exposed himself to the couple, only realising they were dead when they frustratingly failed to react.

Allegations of CIA involvement were made in the German and, subsequently, the domestic American media. Such allegations were, Rudolph claimed, 'idle, speculative . . . a ridiculous calumny'. His observation that certain German newspaper reports which also implicated Mossad were anti-Semitic would cause a diplomatic spat in the days to come.

My self-esteem would have grown even larger had I still shared his name. And if what he was saying was not so patently a painstakingly constructed lie.

This was at the time of the Church Committee, which, to the Executive's dismay, was forcing the Company to reveal deep-bed secrets. Now that Uncle Jim had been fired, it appeared that no one had had the guile or will to bury them. Guilty exhumation was the order of the day. When Jim appeared before the investigating committee he was an exhausted husk, prematurely aged and croaking. It would emerge that there were few heads of state who had not, at one time or another, been considered possible targets. And as for armed dissidents and hairy ideologues . . . the more that could be pointed towards the exit, the better. They would continue to be pointed towards the exit, committee or no committee, Colby or no Colby. The Company ruled. No matter what might come the Company was the overdog.

My fifth term at Fairlamb my head swelled to pumpkin size. There was a real boost to my self-esteem! If only by proxy. Not to mention fame throughout the school, though we were by then well established as the eccentric intellectuals. This was down to all the noise about Betsy's first novel, *The Medlar Tree* (Farrar, Straus and Giroux). Cover seals of approval from Minoushka Wort, Donald Barthelme, John Hawkes and – boom! – Erica Jong, then at the height of her notoriety, some of which rubbed off on Betsy with just a tiny fleck of audacious infamy drifting down to me. Even though our relationship remained cool-going-on-Anchorage I was proud of her. At Waindell no one would have noticed. All the parents wrote highbrow fiction, political analyses and critical essays. Fairlamb parents didn't write. No sir. And they read little other than *Tee & Caddy*, *Field & Stream*, *Horse & Rider*, *Guns & Ammo*. Or did they?

Jill, an incorrigible snoop, saw a memo from Mrs Porelli (Chemistry, Gym and Ethics) to Deputy Principal Waterworth reporting that 'certain parents' had worries about the effect on their daughters of the daughter of a novelist whose work was 'licentious, lewd, indecent and immodest . . . a pornographer with a wiseacre's vocabulary'. Yes, yes. It was all those things. Of course it was. The 'certain parents' had, however, almost certainly not actually read 'the depraved sadomasochistic horror'.

Deputy Principal Waterworth invited me to her wood-panelled study. I was prepared. She offered me a glass of sherry. A bad sign. This, then, was woman to woman. She cleared her throat for an eternity. She smiled weakly. Blinked a lot.

I got it going for her: 'Mrs Waterworth . . . I am proud of Betsy. And of her work. I am proud to be her daughter. The opinions of prurient puritans are derisory. Oscar Wilde was correct. "There is no such thing as a moral or an immoral book. Books are well written, or badly written. That is all."'

This went on for about five minutes.

'I appreciate the staunchness of your filial loyalty . . . Familial bonds . . . Fairlamb's liberal tradition of freethinking Christianity . . . The sensibilities of your fellow students . . . I fear I shall have to ask your parents to withdraw you.'

'Parent. You crass fucking bitch.'

I couldn't have been more gleeful.

★

435

A medlar is a fruit that looks like a hugely swollen rose hip. It only becomes sweet and edible when it is near rotten – the correct word is blet or bletted. The heroine of *The Medlar Tree* is a woman who refuses to subscribe to the received equation of rottenness with moral degradation. She considers such decay to be succulent, heady, exciting: characteristics she aspires to and achieves. She is proud of her 'lavish promiscuity', candid about it, guiltless. And very happy. The more anonymous lovers she has, the more transgressive her behaviour, the more arcane and risky her practices, the more submissive, the more contemptuous of Judaeo-Christian strictures the happier she becomes. She does not get the man. She gets the men. And sometimes the women.

How much was founded in Betsy's own experience? She certainly went out at night a lot.

How much was wishful fantasy? Betsy didn't have a stepfather. So the novel's first sentence was invention, that notorious first sentence:

As he came my stepfather's groan descended through two octaves to become a rough roar which filled my head with deafening love.

Furthermore, the unnamed narrator looks nothing like her. She is prey to multiple obsessions and phobias. She is preoccupied by *bella figura* and so eats frugally. She despises *la cuisine familiale*. She is teetotal. She is Jewish. She speaks fluent, unaccented French, reads Gilles Turpin, Olivier Huguet, Monique Mercier etc. She is childless. She listens to classical music. She teaches Mummy Studies and Experimental Paleoanthropology at an unspecified university. Much of her work is concerned with the preservation of bodies in peat and ice. Every dig becomes an orgy.

I didn't speak to her about the book till several years later. I reread it as a freshman the fall semester I entered Yale. My observations were factual and grammatical. On three occasions she had used a singular verb with a plural subject. Coleherne Road is in London SW 10 not SW 5. The 'very peculiar' director of the Victoria & Albert Museum was called Strong not Strang. John Holmes, spelled thus rather than Homes. The Caracalla Club was not closed by the police, it went bust. Nor was La Vahiné closed by the police, but by the IRS. The author of *L'Image* was the pseudonymous Jean Lozano, not

Jeanne. Barney Greengrass, where the narrator eats a breakfast of kippered salmon with last night's lover whose name she has already forgotten, is not open at 7.00 in the morning. Amsterdam Avenue is a two-way street.

She clapped. She hooted with laughter: 'That's the ginchiest criticism I ever did hear.' She waved at someone across the room. We were at The 21 Club. She relished her particular kind of fame. She had by then written two further books, *The Leopard's Stripes* and *Goats Would Be Prophets*.[36]

'Did it never occur to you that *Medlar* might have been a kind of revenge?'

It hadn't.

'Revenge on who?'

She was drinking Martinis. She knew that I almost unconsciously monitored her drinking. I was, as usual, drinking tonic water.

'Think!'

I guess I must have looked bemused. I shrugged.

'Revenge on Rudolph. On your father. Rather . . . Look, you're going to have to help me out here . . . How can I put it, darling . . . It was revenge on the man *you believed* was your father . . . Whom *I* believed was your father.'

She said this with the nonchalance of someone saying they had forgotten their cigarettes. I peered at her, trying to figure if this was for real. She sipped her drink. She smiled resignedly, conspiratorially, as though we were both in this together.

Which we were now.

The famous ceiling distorted before my eyes. There hung from it boxing gloves, baseball bats and gloves, model ships, model cars, model airplanes, model helicopters, life-size steering wheels, replica (?) machine guns and revolvers, jockstraps (disinfected), Buntline Specials, footballs and football helmets, astronaut helmets, ice hockey

---

36 *Goats Would Be Prophets* proposes that Mary chose to abort Jesus and bury him in an unmarked grave. He was exhumed by the mystics who would become his apostles, given life and fed on blood. He never grew. He remained a foetus until he was crucified as a witch at the age of fifty. The book caused riots in Knoxville, Nashville, Jackson and Montgomery. Copies were burnt in those cities and in Little Rock. A library in Memphis and The Lookout Mountain Bookshop in Chattanooga suffered arson attacks.

helmets, ice hockey sticks, joysticks, police car lights, straw hats, microphones, saxophones. Till a few seconds ago it had been border-line clutter.

Now all these hardware mementos suspended from up there coa-lesced in a spinning, gravity-defying whirl of vortex which tantalisingly wanted to seduce me, pull me in.

Betsy continued in her throwaway tone. Was she so *insouciante*, so hurtful on purpose? Or did she simply not realise?

'It wasn't just me he divorced, darling. It was you too. He divorced you . . . He divorced *us*. That's why there was no custody problem, no attrition, no sudden *coup de main*.' That was the word she actually used. An affectation.[37] At a time like this! Here came another:

'*La guerre de la garde d'enfant n'aura pas lieu.*'

'*N'a pas eu lieu*. Tenses, Mommy Dearest. Tenses. And your accent!' She never sounded more American than when attempting to speak French or Italian.

'You are a creepy know-all sometimes.'

'All times. Can we get back to . . . This means . . . This is incredible . . . Who *is* my father?'

'Shall we order?'

'No. For Christ's sake we shall not. Speak, won't you?'

She gave a foal's snort, then wearily asked: 'Do you remember . . .'

When we arrived back in Washington after The Ghost Christmas, Rudolph, still my father, decided that I, still his daughter, was pos-sibly suffering from anaemia. I suffered no symptoms – I wasn't perpetually tired or lethargic, I slept well. I was puzzled but didn't question his diagnosis.

It was a sham.

Betsy didn't take any persuading that I might be ill. I knew I wasn't. Nonetheless I deferred to him. He drove me to Langley to have blood tests. I would take the opportunity to show that I had no fear of needles. Did I ask why the tests could not be done by our regular physician Doctor Moles?

---

37 She also had a lexicon of British and imperial words that would seldom be heard in America: kerfuffle, stramash, skiv, clobber, tonk, hullabaloo, doolally etc.

Rudolph's hidden purpose was to establish whether my blood group was compatible with his and with Betsy's. It wasn't. I am blood group O. Betsy is AB. As a Company wife there was a record of this. Rudolph is A – so, then, he is not my father. AB and A do not make O.

'Do you remember?'

The blood sample was taken by a medical technician. Not a doctor. And I had no conversation with her. There was no examination. Did I query this? All I could really recall was her sour vegetal smell. Rather I could recall mentioning it in the car on the way home and getting a curt response: 'She was raised as a Christadelphian.'

When he got the test result, of which I was of course ignorant, I was sent, reluctantly, to spend the weekend with my Mavroleon grandparents at their house in Mason Neck: all dauntingly formal, dressing for dinner, perfect manners expected, reedy brackish water everywhere. This, again, was an unusual arrangement but, again, I didn't question it. Didn't recognise the flimsiness of the pretext I had been given.

On the Sunday night when my grandfather dropped me home Rudolph was gone. Betsy had a black eye and a further bruise on her cheek from falling down the stairs. Even though I heard my grandfather cursing Rudolph I swallowed that one too. What was the matter with me? Till that night at The 21 I had considered myself to have been an alert and observant child. But what sort of alert and observant child unquestioningly accepts her father's absence, week after week, year after year?

Who was my father?

Betsy told me it was watching me peeling potatoes beside Suave Ted that caused Rudolph Chipurnoi to believe that this ageing small-town Lothario – OK, small-village Lothario – was my natural father whose blueblack hair, faint widow's peak, sharp cheekbones and etiolated complexion I shared. Apparently I resembled him to such an extent that long before Rudolph's terrible epiphany there was talk in the village, wrong side of the sheet talk, which never reached Matrimony Farm, talk of which Betsy and Rudolph were thus ignorant.

At this juncture Betsy was served another Martini sent over by a set of the most perfect teeth you'll ever see. Waves, air kisses. Time for her to think, to weave some excuse. There was no excuse. She could not remember having fucked Suave Ted and getting with me as a result.

How can you forget something like that? Easily, if you're plegic.

She drank for oblivion, for memory loss that might be willed. Suave Ted had on a number of occasions driven her back from The Shadoxhurst Arms to Matrimony Farm. If they fucked, it was when she was drunk. Consensual? I prayed that it was. Lord I prayed. I told myself that likely as not she came onto him. Alcohol blitzed her inhibitions. (It had the opposite effect on Rudolph. It muted him.)

Betsy shrugged. She couldn't remember. She couldn't remember. She thought Rudolph was my father. It had never occurred to her that he wasn't. Now, here at least is one certainty, she was Betsy. I had sprung from her. She didn't know who she had fucked. Well, we are all prone to forgetfulness.

She did drink 'a bit'. That was all she'd own up to. She was delusional, not the sort of drunk who boasts of her addiction. She enjoyed Suave Ted's company: his humour, his yarns, his gossip, his self-deprecating boastfulness, his generosity, his wartime memories, his childish word play: 'god liver oil' dated from the era of UK government Uncle Jimmy called deep pinko.

So what ought my name to be? Betsy looked exaggeratedly blank. How obtuse can you get?

Did Suave Ted have a surname? No doubt. But he was not the sort of man who issued invoices with a name and address. His most deeply held precepts were word-of-mouth and cash ('foldin money if you would be so kind ta muchly'). She didn't know his surname. He was a carpenter and cabinet maker who had been introduced to her in The Shadoxhurst Arms. It had never occurred to her to ask. Whyever would she need to know it? Besides, she didn't want to know it. Any more than she wanted him to know that she had a child by him. She was at this time unaware of the village rumours about my paternity. She would remain unaware of them till her death.

She never returned to Matrimony Farm. It was, anyway, in Rudolph's name. He sold it a few months after learning the truth.

Everything had changed. He thought it over. He talked it over at lunch at The Army and Navy Club with Uncle Jimmy Angleton who, despite having been fired, still haunted Langley. Angleton had found himself so brutally cut off from the vocation that was his life that he daymared suicide. He was touched that Rudolph considered keeping the farm as a fishing lodge for him. He tactfully claimed that his taste was, anyway, moving away from chalk streams towards the white water and deep pools of his childhood. He advised Rudolph to beware of becoming 'identified' with William Colby who, he correctly surmised, would himself be out within the year. His resigned bitterness was not towards Colby, an over-honourable (i.e. weak) man with little grasp of realpolitik and a catastrophic appetite for 'openness', but towards Colby's puppet-master Henry Kissinger whom he nicknamed Herr Thor.

Angleton's hardly dissembled opposition to detente, a 'cosmic three card trick', and his briefing of Mossad and Shin Bet had infuriated the Secretary of State – who would duly be made to suffer retribution. Angleton was a scholar of Kitson and low-tech retribution, a process whose prosecution should be gradual, cumulative. A poisoning by microscopic doses over a period of months, even years. Brief sensory assaults which the victim is hardly aware of. Regular anonymous phone calls to promote paranoia. Small-scale damage to property which appears to be continuous bad luck. Trapped in an elevator. Honey trapped. Honey trapped in an elevator. Framed for a crime (where would counter-intelligence be without paedophilia?). Dogshit on the stoop. False accusations. Rumours fed to journalists whose very trade is a byword for gullibility: once they have dug dirt they cannot put it back. Every exhumation declares itself.

The best-laid plans . . .

Kissinger outlived Angleton by more than thirty years.

Retribution is toying with the adversary, it is a game which one side does not realise it is participating in.

Revenge, another area of Angleton's expertise, was, on the other hand, frank, direct, explicit. The 'utensils' of revenge are risibly crude. Firearms, iron bars, jacks, speeding automobiles, switchblades, a sword, a cheesewire, a brick, a hammer, an axe, *une poignée americaine* (a term he relished). Then they left The Army and Navy Club. They walked across Farragut Square to a basement bar where

Angleton had once been introduced to Jenner Vavra. Another Martini. He patted Rudolph's sleeve: 'I have an idea. I was going to say, an outlandish idea. But no, my dear Rudolph, maybe it's inlandish . . . Pragmatic, to use Harold Be Thy Name's[38] favourite word.'

Everything about this incident is fogged with rumour, disinformation, piggies (English slang, I have learnt) and the redacted records of an installation access control system.

Greenham Common would become known in the early Eighties for a long-lived protest of 'sisters' – not *my* sisters, absolutely not. Prior to its being an insanitary 'peace camp' and mudbath it was an obscure USAF base. It was whiningly moaned about by the boonies and *ploucs* who lived nearby but otherwise unnoticed. At the start of each holiday at Matrimony Farm we would drive there to stock up at the humungous PX: liquor, of course, slobby snacks, popcorn buckets, chocolate bars, milkshake mixes that tasted yummily of chemicals and TV dinners for Popsy Pfister who fed them to Freddie and Rolfe as weekend treats. There were silos that resembled neatly ordered prehistoric tumuli. They held nuclear missiles. Where there are missiles there are dozens of guards, boneheads brainwashed to expect Dmitri and Yuri to come visiting at any moment. Where there are guards there are guard dogs of varying degrees of ferocity. Bite. Rip flesh. Destroy face. Most ferocious of all are Marcher Hounds with the coloration of a condor – black body of long coarse hair, white head – and singular pedigree. If dogs were classified secrets then this one would be available only to selected senior officers.

It was a Marcher Hound answering this description which attempted to murder Suave Ted when he returned to his caravan early one evening. He was feeling for his keys, awkwardly because he didn't want to put down his toolbox on the muddy path. He heard a shrill peal. Metal on metal? There was a flash of gleaming pink eye as the beast hurled itself through the damp air from – where? Where? From the

---

38 Harold Wilson. An English schoolboy version of The Lord's Prayer. Angleton recalled it from Malvern College. He hoped it would become the Company's nickname for the British prime minister whom he believed to be a Soviet mole. It didn't. He wasn't.

darkening bushes and willow stumps? From the broken hedges? From between the apple trees? He hardly saw it before it was on him, a horde of teeth, pink-grey gums, assault-tongue, claws, menace, hatred, swiftness. He did not know what was happening to him. He felt a stingingly pungent pain hurrying through his left hand and wrist. He smelled blood and so did the dog whose name was Troy the Fourth. He cried for help but there was no one to hear – the caravan was at the end of a narrow strip of gardens between even narrower leets. The nearest houses were 200 yards away. He saw exposed bone. Having ripped into his shoulder and mounted his back the creature made for his face. He ducked. Claws scraped his skull. The noise was a noise from charnel hell. And the foul shambles stench, the long ragged pelt, the fermenting meaty breath. He swung his toolbox and caught it on the shoulder. The creature yelped. And leapt again. A corner of the metal toolbox this time struck an eye. Suave Ted was winning. He brought the toolbox down on the dog's head with the most immense blow he could manage. It whimpered. He struck it again. Then kicked its skull till all trembling ceased. He did not want to touch the foul beast. He kicked at it, kicked at it then pushed the ugly corpse till it was on the leet's bank and delivered it a final kick. Not much of a splash. The water was high and swift. It floated some yards before it began to sink. In some versions of this story he buried it. Or buried it and forgot where. Did he butcher it and use the meat as bait in his eel trap? It depended on his audience. And on how he wished to depict himself. To drown, to bury, to butcher. There are evidently nuances of disposal method whose significance is not immediately clear to the lay public.

Twenty-four hours later Suave Ted was still attached to a morphine drip at the RSH in Southampton. He had received two anti-rabies jabs. He had two fingers of his left hand amputated. The pinkie and the ring finger, the latter a source of ribaldry thereafter: Ted not having a ring finger to remove the ring from when out and about.

Meanwhile: 'There were half a dozen of them. Just over there, see down that lane, there were these fellows, yeh? At least six o' them. They weren't in uniform. But it were obvious they was American services – some sort of. You can tell 'em a mile off. Creeping through the gardens. Some of them was on the path down to Ted's caravan along the leet there. All keeping crouching. They're thinking that makes them invisible. It doesn't. It just makes their backs ache. We got eyes out here in the country. Ears too. We could hear them calling Troy, Troy. Soft. They might have been looking for a lost kiddy. Course, we didn't know then Ted was poorly. Often didn't see him for days on end, nothing to worry about. We hadn't heard about the dog and that. It was the dog they was searching after. It got quite heated. Were it buried? Were it chucked in the water? I heard it got swept into one of them drains that goes under the road. Culverts. Got stuck. It could be right under us now. Skeleton of course after all these years. Then it might got trapped in a sluice, like in the grille, you know – they have the grille to stop weed going through – got its head caught between the bars. Then again there are some that say it weren't killed after all. Just shook itself down then off it goes to lead the feral life over Winterslow way. Still haunting the hedgerows thereabouts . . . Making crop circles as well I shouldn't wonder. A lot of folk claim to have seen it. You do have to wonder about the psychiatric social services. You want something stronger than that?'

'I'm fine. Thank you.'

'Not like your mum then.'

'No . . . Not like her.'

'She loves her bevvy.'

'Not loves, Colin. Loved. Loved? She's dead.'

'Oh . . . Oh my dear, I'm so sorry to hear that. D'you know: I never met a better lady darter in my life.'

'The thing you love always kills you.'

'What? Oh no – not a darts tragedy?'

'No – two bottles of vodka a day tragedy. Two bottles being the basic foundations you might say. Upon which are laid layers of gin Martinis, Cognac, mirabelle, applejack. Anything she could lay her hands on.'

'When did she pass on?'

'Just over three months ago. This is the first opportunity I've had to get down here.'

'I can't get me brain fixed on this one. She was so full of life. So positive. What I'd call a coper. Always on the front foot . . .'

I feared that this might go on and on.

I eventually interrupted him: 'Colin, I'm not here to mourn my drunk of a mother. I want to find my biological father. Where's Suave Ted?'

'I knew you was going to ask that. Hand on heart I cannot tell you. Me, I'd love to know where he was too.'

'I don't even know his real name.'

'Join the club! Bit of a man of mystery Ted. There was a lot he didn't let on. Nearly everything, to tell the truth. Name included. He never said nothing about where he come from . . . where he lived before he lived here. He had a few stories mind. Told 'em over and over. Mostly about the war—'

'He got jankers. Squaddy talk, he called it. That was the first time I'd heard the word . . . I don't believe I've heard it since.'

'You wouldn't. Went with the end of national service. Well, fancy him learning you then. I dunno who you could ask about him. None o' them lads he worked with are around here no more, gone their separate ways. I usually get a Christmas card from Bri. He's down near Plymouth. Sparky's in Spain nowadays, he dropped in about a year back when he come to bury his mum. And poor old Tosh. Coronary playing football. It were a derby vee Atletico Sutton Scotney. Classic libero he used to call himself. Your genuine classic libero doesn't weigh twenty stone. But even Tosh, I don't think even Tosh'd have known Ted's name. Ted didn't want no one to know it. Didn't have a bank account. Cash and no questions asked. There was a rumour like he used to bury his money in plastic bags. Did all his business on the pay phone from here. To his way of thinking the electoral roll was the devil's work. When was it Matrimony Farm was sold?'

'Must be fourteen, fifteen years ago.'

'Fifteen! Blimey! It don't half fly by. That'll be fifteen years ago then that Ted left. That same summer. He sold it for a song Matrimony Farm your da did – oh sorry, do 'pologise.'

'Please. Nothing to worry about. I'm an adult. Where did Ted live?'

'Down in Tosh's van most of the time. What you'd call a trailer. Like in trailer trash – is that right? Down the end of the garden.'

'Can I walk there?'

'Course you can. It's only a couple of hundred yards. It's seen better days. To put it mildly. Not that it was ever The Hall. Justine – Tosh's missus, widow I suppose I should say – Justine's got her salons to run and Derek's always blocked out of his head. Total waste of space. Only time I seen him lift a finger was when he got wind of Ted burying his money. He dug up the whole garden. Long after Ted gone and all . . . I don't know . . .'

I followed his directions. I went down a couple of steps beside the entrance to the tunnel/culvert where the peculiar dog may have ended up. The path ran alongside a fierce narrow stream (leet) between two buildings. On the other side a windowless wall rose sheer from the water. Tawny old bricks, rusty old metal ties, S-shaped. On this side was Tosh's widow's house with ruched curtains.

The path continued between the stream's bank and an untended garden. A molehilled lawn, some sadly neglected flowerbeds, shrubs gone to seed followed by the wreckage of a small market garden: beanpoles collapsed like pick-up-sticks, cabbages lay in mummified rows. Two small creosoted sheds in varying states of disrepair, tilting and sinking into the soggy soil. Around them: an old sink, a rusting jerry can, a tractor's skeleton, a sheet of rusting corrugated iron.

I heard his voice vaulting down the years with a swoosh: *flattening corrugated iron with a cricket roller.* Just beyond them was an orchard of lichenous apple trees. What a fine orchard. I walked through it touching the dusty trunks, the furry lichens, the orange lichens, the seagreen lichens, the hairy lichens. There were wasps drunk on rotting fruit. I thought of Betsy, I thought of *The Medlar Tree.* There were boughs which ought to have been pollarded but which grew crazily twisted and intertwined. The caravan (when in England, yah) was hidden by trunks, leaves, branches, wood, dead wood. Its beige and baby-blue paintwork was bleached, streaked with country filth. Pitted chrome. Perished tarpaulins on its roof. Piles of drenched planks held them down. What excepted it from the normal run of abandoned caravans was the paranoid number of locks on the door and bolts on the engrimed windows. Grass grew high around it. A grass snake slithered from goose grass. The stream gurgled incessantly. I suddenly realised how happy I was.

★

'Hellooo?' The voice was not hostile. Hardly suspicious. Puzzled – why should anyone be trespassing here? Inflection on the last few 'o's to signal the question. Little smile. There was a woman on the far side of the orchard by the huts. Amiable wave.

This was the first time I set eyes on Justine.

I was a highly educated, perhaps overeducated, polyglot academic (Yale, master's from Hamburg, doctorate from Cambridge, teaching at UCL and Columbia, now mainly in Hamburg again, working on *Leather People*). I was known, in New York social pages, as the Marble Column. Cold (which was not cool), offhand, insolent, unimpressed, intellectually and socially snobbish – but still a catch because clever heiresses with three apartments across two continents and a house and yacht at Newport, RI always are, though not such catches as unclever heiresses.

It was, on the face of it, improbable that I should fall in with a provincial hairdresser in what I have seen called Hampshire County, England. The social pages she graced were those of *Hampshire Life*. Tanning bar openings, vintage car shows, Rotary discos. That was her (public) scene. It still puzzles me.

She called Suave Ted 'your bio-dad'. His life had been rigorously compartmentalised. He came and went. He never got close to anyone. So far, then, I was a chip off the old block.

There was a rumour that he had been in prison or a military 'glasshouse'. There was a rumour that he had been married. There was a rumour that he was a bigamist. He was believed to have a daughter, or maybe a son. He claimed to possess expertise as a poacher but no one saw any evidence. He ate frugally and drank moderately. She described him as an obsessive loner. But too well balanced to commit a typical obsessive loner gun crime (infant school or shopping mall). Well, that's a relief. But of course he wasn't an American obsessive loner. He had never made a pass at her. Not that she'd have objected. He was amusing to start with. But it was like a record. The same anecdotes. Over-rehearsed, over-repeated. It soon wore off. 'Did I tell you my story about—' was a signal to remember that you'd left a pan on a hotplate. He was generous, neat, preoccupied by his appearance, never late with his rent. He dyed his hair but denied he did so. Hairdressers know. He looked after himself. Fit as a fiddle. Not a spare ounce on him. Hardy. He used the sheds as workshops but preferred to work outside at his saw bench stripped to the waist. Had to be careful in summer. His very pale skin burnt easily (me too).

We sat in her kitchen. She had taste. Or had learnt taste: there was a signed and numbered print by Karen Cherfas, a typically intriguing composition of electrical diagrams and damaged equipment, potentiometers and the like.

'God knows what Ted thought of Tosh. Tosh was an oaf. Oh a nice oaf. But a downwardly mobile oaf. I thought I loved him. But what do you know at that age? He got me up the duff when I was fourteen. We hid the pregnancy. My mum had to pretend that Derek was hers, that he was my baby brother . . . What a toodoo! Everyone scratching each other's eyes out. And all because I'd been stupid enough to go with an oaf. My excuse was he was a very pretty oaf – in those days. He was a premature ejaculator. Served me right, I told myself for years. I thought I *deserved* to be punished for my . . . curiosity, a moment of madness. And it was a moment. Seconds, it lasted seconds with him. He boasted to all his mates about his virility, riding bare-back and so on. Thankfully by the time he left the Tech he was drinking so much he'd lost interest in pawing me . . . physically incapable. A bladder of lard. His parents owned a garage: his dad was always boasting he was the fifth biggest Ford dealer in Hampshire. Honestly. They were always hinting I was common as muck because I came from Geranium Hill. Of course they never said it out loud. Just little digs here and there . . . It just made me even more determined.'

She gave me a sisterly pat on the shoulder. 'I've got to change. Do you want a lift to the station?'

When she reappeared she was wearing an almost ankle-length coat buttoned to the neck.

She took in my quizzical stare and laughed.

'I'm going to entertain my sugar daddy. I'm dressed up the way he likes me.' She held her hands to the coat: 'This is – well, camouflage . . . I don't want to overexcite the neighbours.' She laughed and made a shush sign.

At the station she said: 'I'd like to see you again.'

Without thinking I agreed. And when I did think about it I realised

I was right to have agreed. That was without any presage of what was to come.

We met a few weeks later at Kümmel, off The Strand. Her choice. In those days still a just fashionable ticket, yet to become all Barnet-and-Bromley. The inadequate lighting was intended to suggest sophistication. The decor was a vague approximation of something. So vague it was hard to guess what that something was. A ratskeller restaurant? A Viennese café? An Alsacien brasserie? An Amsterdam brown bar? Being an adoptive New Yorker – we moved there after the divorce – with an apartment on Harvestehuder Weg in Hamburg, I am used to and enjoy, even adore, cooking from the schnitzel and sauerkraut countries. And Kümmel's was OK. I was pleased to be there. When I arrived Justine was, to my surprise, not alone. She was on a stool at the long bar, expensively suited, talking to a man whose back was to me. There was a certain conspiratorial intimacy between them. I spoke her name loudly and waved before I reached her, to alert her of my presence. We brushed cheeks.

'You're looking very good,' I said.

'Adriano Branchi,' she replied.

'You'd have thought,' said the man, disacknowledging me, 'that with the fucking prices Signor Branchi charges he could supply fucking lapels and a fucking collar.'

Despite the gloom he was wearing aviator dark glasses.

'It's just a style.' Justine spoke mock wearily, rolled her eyes and shook her head, exhaled.

'For sure it's a style. It's a style favoured by mass murderers across the globe. Across the globe. Collarlessness and genocide go together. We are taught that from the cradle more or less. It's a warning sign for us. Bavarians, Austrians obviously, Stalin. Mao. Mao . . . How many millions did that beast dupe with his fucking lack of a collar. How do you do, I'm Luc.'

'Luc Shapitra,' said Justine.

'Phoebe. Good to meet you,' I lied.

I proffered a hand. He hardly touched it with his as though mine was diseased. It struck me that he was the right fit for the place. A close approximation of a human. His blueblack hair was astonishingly shiny like some rare corvid. Black lenses. Peculiar photo-realist skin that was as near a perfect forgery of tanned human skin as alcantara is of suede: it recalled Darmande's description of Saint-Just: 'a breathing exemplar of lifelessness'. Perfect — apart from a two-inch vertical white scar down his left cheek, like a Lal's deliberate imperfection. Gay? Doubtful. Asexual? Maybe. Misogynist? To me, yes. Is there such a word as ahuman? That would be just the ticket for Luc. He held a lit cigarette but didn't smoke it. He was cold, expressionless, unsettling. His voice was bleak, from the crypt. It recalled sandpaper and ancient tortures. I thought later that if the dead could speak they would speak like this. His accent was unidentifiable. No place of origin vouchsafed. Not a native anglophone. His looks: generically southern European, maybe North African. Neither tied with his name. His age: indeterminate. Anywhere between thirty-five and sixty-five. That indeterminate. Voracious teeth. He was unlined. Untouched, though, by any human surgeon's scalpel. He was a convincing imitation of a handsome man, exquisitely dressed in an exquisitely cut suit of black silk corduroy. After about ten minutes I decided that I would plead a migraine and go home.

As though rifling through my thoughts he finished his drink, waved to the barman, gave him a starched note with an open-handed gesture to keep the change, pecked Justine on the cheek, achieved a full simulacrum of a frail smile for me, strolled off along the long sepulchral room gyring a white scarf about his neck. I stared after him. Appalled fascination, I'd guess. I turned to Justine.

She laughed: 'No! Before you ask. He is *not* a lover. He is *not* my sugar daddy.'

I must have looked relieved.

'He's in property. Malls. Arcades. He wants me to have the prestige salon at Langstone Shopping Village off the new bit of the M27 . . . the extension. It'd raise the Justine profile to the sky . . . The sky just above the M27 extension, that is.'

'That sounds good.'

I wondered why Justine should be so favoured. Presumably she was in no position to demand a preferential rent or concessions. She was not Leonard of Mayfair or Paulo & Bob or Keith At Smile or the ChopShop. To mention this would have been to belittle her.

'He phoned me out of the blue about a year ago.'

'Wherever does he come from? That *accent* . . .'

'He's worked all over the place. A bit of a nomad he calls himself. Here, I'll show you. Hang on . . . Aaah—' She couldn't reach her bag without leaning perilously from her stool. A passing waiter steadied her, got the bag, handed it to her. She pulled a magazine from it, *Schleswiger Bauzeitung*. She smiled beguilingly at the waiter. He was smugly satisfied.

'He just gave me this. One of his recent projects. Do you know it? He was what they call lead consultant forward slash vision. It was his vision! Much classier than an Arndale or the one in Basingstoke.'

She leafed through the magazine till she came to the article she wanted. She proudly handed it to me. Its first spread showed a top-heavy building, perversely counterintuitive. It might have been on the Yale campus. It was almost the Junta & Cabal Studies Building's *doppelgänger*, the right word here because this behemoth – brick rather than concrete – was in Hamburg's suburbs, beyond the airport at Norderstedt-Center. Unknown territory to me. Two lumbering office blocks sandwiched an immense shopping gallery, laughably described as poetic. Walter Benjamin was of course referenced. So too were the architects HG+2r, surveyors, contractors and the developers Solmecke Kost Gebel AG. Given how irremediably ugly the buildings were, Luc was lucky to have got away without being name-checked while Detlev Gebel, whose daughter Bärbel had been a student of mine and with whom I was on nodding terms, was unlucky, deservedly unlucky.

'And he's going to do one of these where?'

'When they upgrade the M27 there's going to be this spur off it to Thorney Island.'

The road number and the place meant nothing to me.

'When's it going to happen?'

'They keep on putting it off. Planning and all that. Local objections. They go on and on.'

We had an evening of candour and laughter. It was far outside my normal experience of social competitiveness, caution, point scoring, brittle wit and bitching.

I found myself saying things that I would usually have confined to my journal, which I did in fact write up when I got home.

Things like:

'I enjoy the sex, sure – I just don't want to have to endure dinner with the service provider.

'I don't go out to dinner with the guy who fixes the fridge do I? I might fuck him of course. In theory I mean, only in theory – but then I'd send him on his way . . .

'I have no respect for academe – it's catty and petty precisely because there is so little money at stake, prestige accrues from something immeasurable, something other than commercial success . . . critical acclaim is what happens when you steal someone higher up the foodchain's ideas and pay slavering homage to them without actually plagiarising them – it's a fine balance . . .'

'That's just like Stan Gruber – he wouldn't have a career if he hadn't helped himself to all Daniel Galvin's methods . . . Daniel's a genius colourist . . . he's like a painter – fauvist is it? – or something . . . Geoffrey calls him the Bonnard of the Bonce – and would I purlease stop rabbiting on about him.'

'Bonnard of the what?'

'Bonce. Head. No? Old-fashioned slang.'

'What a lovely word. Who is Geoffrey?'

She laughed: 'He . . . well, he looks after me.'

'Aaah . . . he's the one you call your sugar daddy?'

'That's it. But he's not really a sugar daddy. I mean that's how it started . . . but . . . things evolve. We go out to dinner together. We sometimes even go touring together.'

'Touring? How quaint!'

'He has this amazing collection of cars. Facel Vegas, Lagondas, Bugattis, Bristols . . . We drive through France and Italy and, oh, Belgium in them. People always turn out to look. He's got an amazing Mercedes. But we don't go touring in it because, you never know . . . there might be trouble because it belonged to Hitler.'

'How absolutely delightful.'

'That's what Luc said. I said it's only a car.'

'And Hitler was only a politician.'

'I tell you what Geoffrey says. He says the Führer might have been a bit of a silly sausage to gas all those Jews and what have you, gays and cripples, but he built damned fine motorways and got Germany back on its feet again.'

'That's one way of looking at it. What else does he collect?'

'Pubic hair. It takes quite something for him to get his dander up but a brazilian makes him see red. And as for the total shave . . . a monstrous fashion . . . Pudendal correctness gone mad he calls it. I'm not allowed the tiniest trim of mine. He's always on about the grave impact on dedicated collectors. Some of them hire women to grow hair. You got some who sift through waxers' waste. They even collect the powder from electric razors.'

'Well, at least it's not SS memorabilia. Furniture made of human bones.'

'Now that's strange. Luc asked me about that one time.'

'Not strange. More like logical.'

'Luc's always quizzing me about Geoffrey. He's a bit obsessive. Bit of a nosey parker.'

'He's jealous. It's obvious,' I pronounced, with a confidence that could not have been more misplaced.

The germ of *Leather People* dated from when I was nine. In a box room I discovered Rudolph's books and files on bog bodies, relics of his failed propaganda scheme before I was born. I became hooked on the contorted figures. Serene faces despite horrible deaths. An assurance that there was peace in death, at least in this sort of grave. I kept it secret, I hid the books. I didn't know these preserved people from thousands of years ago would become the nearest thing to a vocation that someone of my temperament might be called to.

Betsy's agent, The Slime, had yawned and rolled his eyes: 'Doctoral dissertations! You might sell three hundred copies. Then again it might go massive – you sell five hundred. It's a niche market and it's an overcrowded market: you know how many books on these dead freaks have been published in the last five years? You need an angle . . . Now, how's your love life . . .'

My first 'angle', which demanded that I jettison much of my dissertation, was to show the impact that chance exhumations and discoveries had on the often superstitious rural societies where they were made. I trawled through journals, travellers' logs, parish records, photos of gargoyles and rainwater heads, accounts of reburials in accord with Christian practice, icons, newspapers, illustrations, paintings (rare), representations in the mass media and in films (mostly cheap crude horror of course). That it was a novel angle was obvious from my having to go to primary sources for everything. No one had previously considered these effects. The peat cutters to whom most discoveries were due and the peat cutters' villages had been treated as more or less passive participants, untouched by the momentous finds and by the eerie presence of the manifest past.

My second 'angle' was ethnomycological. Several leather bodies bore protrusions which resembled supernumerary nipples. It had been proposed that it was their existence which caused those so afflicted to be executed as witches. I consider it more likely that the protrusions were symptoms of ergotism or Saint Anthony's Fire. The victims of this contagion by *Claviceps purpurea*, a fungus parasitic on rye, wheat and barley, were feared. Their corpses were deep buried to deny them the opportunity to contaminate the living: this practice had nothing to do with ritual. They may of course have been witches too.

Three encounters:

I.

I did much of my work at the Museum für Völkerkunde and the Warburg Haus. When I left Warburg Haus in the late afternoon it was my habit to walk a couple of hundred yards in the wrong direction, cross the Goernebrücke bridge to dreamily idle home along Leinpfad's leafy riverside path. This roundabout route both avoided the bad-tempered traffic on Heilwigstrasse and allowed me to gaze across the river and the scudding cox and eight at the intensely green gardens behind the grand houses on that street. Some of park-like splendour, some more intimate, some with jolly painted boathouses and bowers, nearly all with the greenest, plumpest shrubs and to-die-for weeping willows. Green.

One afternoon the bridge was closed after an accident. So for the first time in months I took Heilwigstrasse which, despite being narrow, had become an increasingly used rat run: once one van driver learns to peck through a milk-bottle-top every van driver follows his example.

A large Mercedes, coming out of the drive of a white, pompous, more-or-less Jugendstil house was trying in vain to find a gap in the incessant rush hour traffic. It had halted, blocking the pavement. I stood beside it rather than step into the road to get round it. The driver reversed in order to let me do so. As I was about to step in front of the car a window slid down. A voice called my name. Bärbel Gebel leaned from the front passenger seat. We exchanged greetings. The driver inclined his head to see me. This was her father Detlev. He offered me a lift. He had a Swabian accent. The traffic was even heavier. By the time he had gotten into the lane heading south it was at a standstill. Bärbel, an excellent student though over-reticent in drawing conclusions and yet to trust her instincts, talked enthusiastically about her master's research. Her father interrupted her several times to turn to me in the back and thank me for all my efforts in teaching her. I replied, truthfully, that it had been a pleasure.

Then I remembered that evening some months previously at Kümmel.

'I met a colleague of yours in London.'

'Oh yes? Who was that?'

'Luc – he was lead consultant on the Norderstedt-Center mall.'

'You been to my mall? Open less than a year and already five awards won. Six and a half thousand parking spaces. Biggest ticket-less car park in the world. Five hundred and seventy-five thousand square metres of prime retail caviar. And that brickwork. Wow! You know what it is – homage to Hamburg Expressionism. Nineteen twenties. Who's this consultant fellow?'

'Luc he was called . . . Luc – I think it was Shapitra?'

'Nope. Luc. Never heard of him. Not one of my team. I tell you – I know everyone's name, everyone's. I can always fit a name to a face: you remember the lips, the teeth, the eyes, the smiles, the wrinkles, the whole cabdooble as you say. Means a lot to people the boss greeting them by name. Tells them they're valued. Respected. I must take you for a visit. Backstage! The closed circuit TV control. Just like science fiction. Isn't it, darling!' Bärbel, headphoned, didn't hear him, mouthed on.

As the lift ascended to my apartment I looked at myself in the mirror as though my reflection would tell me how to react. On every floor a different and feeble stratagem visited my mind. What ought I to say to Justine? Ought I to say anything? Could she be in danger? Could she be the target of some kind of scam? More likely Luc had inflated his importance. All over the world, every minute of every day, there are men promoting themselves to women who are often willing to be taken in by the most far-fetched boasts. My suspicion, though, was that Justine was not among the willing. She was trustful, open, pliable. Con men and women can only succeed if the mark fails to recognise their play. Justine had not rumbled Luc. Maybe there was nothing to rumble. Maybe it was me. Maybe I had been taken in by Detlev Gebel's boast that he knew all his employees. Were I to reveal my suspicions to Justine and they be ill-founded I would almost surely lose a friend whom I didn't want to lose. That realisation came as a shock when I reviewed it. It felt like an admission of dependence.

I called Franz-Rifat Levendoglu, MEP, to propose that we go dancing later. The Bobby Fitoussi Band Featuring F. R. David was doing a residency at . . .

'Mimi's? I can't make it before midnight. I have to meet with some very angry pâtissiers.'

I love watching him when he goes on the prowl after a boy.

My cowardly decision had been to say nothing to Justine unless she mentioned Luc. Whereupon I'd repeat what I knew as though it were of no moment. I immediately began rehearsing some throwaway phrases. But she only mentioned Luc once again, and then to say that she had not heard from him after the proposed mall beside the new M27 had been denied planning permission. She had, however, opened a third salon, Justine de Montpellier, this one in Ocean Quay Marina (image attached).

2.

Going on for six months later I was in Chester. Kitschy, bogus old world, harmlessly pretentious, well-heeled, very damp. It amused me to be staying at The Fairlamb Inn By Noble Oak Hotels International while I worked in the County Archives. The room service was efficient and attentive. In the wonky lift was a framed faded newspaper photograph of The Barry Island Five, monoglot Welsh language militants who, over twenty years ago, had been arrested in the hotel where they had allegedly planned to assassinate the government minister Emlyn Prosser.

Lucky Dig. Cut through the peat crust anywhere in the 'mosses' or bogs around this city and you are liable to discover a leather person.

The weather is disgraceful. The long dead's graves are soggy, not that the long dead know, do they. No wonder the living whine like they are doing the long dead's whining for them. Even when they are happy they whine. It's a less than ten-minute walk to the early industrial buildings which house the archives, a wet and shivery walk. Every day, without exception, there was fine rain or cold fog. That is the climatic diet. I was glad to be going home.

The taxi to Manchester airport was slow – fog, of course. I feared I would miss my flight. I should not have worried. The flight was delayed – more fog, of course. The departures hall was seething with the sort of people you only ever see in airports. I elbowed my way through thickets of tracksuits, Ron Hills, shellsuits and bactrian knapsacks to the BA executive lounge, showed my ticket to the smiler.

The suite of rooms was the usual deal. Pale, offensively inoffensive hotel decor. Guzzling business bellies conferring importantly. A few staff in striped black and burgundy waistcoats. A long self-service bar. A table of canapés. An elephantine TV tuned to silent rolling news. A screen showing flight times and delays. Piles of *Cheshire Life* recording the glamorous openings of tanning hubs, *Knutsford Knewsround*, *Marianne*, *Time*, *Newsweek*, *Fabric*, *Hornet*, *The Modernist*, *Stern*, *L'Express* etc. A shelf of abandoned airport novels: *The Four Hundred*, *Monte Carlo*, *The Artisan* etc.

I picked up *The Dark Watergang* by Tamara Coolmans, I had at least heard of her. I recalled a teasing interview about an earlier book, *The Tale of an Illicit Monument*, twisting the obviously besotted male interviewer round her little finger, both denying and admitting its factual basis. I vaguely recalled there was some story attached to it.

According to the publicist's dead hand on the cover of *The Dark*

Watergang she was 'the new queen of Flemish Noir'. (Was there an old queen?)

Two rather crudely portrayed teenage girls – Sapphire, novelett-ishly 'sophisticated', i.e. burdened with expensive brand names, and Gertrude, sweaty, puffing and obese from her chocolate addiction – clumsily attempt to terminate the pregnancy of a third young woman, Cornelia, who bleeds to death. In their panic they fear they will be charged with murder. They conceal the body and her blood-ied clothes in a rusting shipping container on an allotment where Sapphire's despised stepfather Wout van't Hoff, a Vlaams Belang quartermaster, stores posters including several advertising the boxing matches fought by his notorious collaborationist grandfather Bruno Vandendaele, torn De Vlag banners, small arms, grenades, baseball bats, mace, tear gas, placards, pamphlets stating that the Shoah is a Jewish invention and street signs honouring Rexist activists and Flemish 'martyrs' to be erected when Vlaams Belang gains power (Degrellestraat, Paul Colinlei, DeVlagstraat, Ten Hovestraat, Staf de Clercqlei, van de Wieleplaats, Joris Wymeerschphplaats, Filip De Pill-ecyn straat, Legion Flandernlei etc.).

Then they make an anonymous call to the police inculpating van't Hoff. They have no idea that the officer who receives the call is a member of Vlaams Belang . . .

That was as far as I had got when a crisp dorsal twinge told me the armchair was ergonomically disastrous, from the Sciatica range no doubt. With a wince I hauled myself from it to search for a less-damaging perch and found myself face to face with Luc Shapitra, his all blueblack hair and his impenetrable dark glasses. I was taken aback.

'Luc,' I blurted, fazed. 'What a surprise . . . We met – d'you—'

That chilling simulacrum of a smile.

'I know we met. Where we met. Who we met with. *Phoebe*. I can always fit a name to a face: you remember the lips, the teeth, the eyes, the smiles, the lines, the whole cabdooble.'

I gaped at him, stupefied.

'We should establish the squatting right in these places.' He indi-cated a sofa. I sat down; it was better designed. He sat beside me, crossed his legs elegantly. Anthracite slubbed silk suit, two-tone shoes – black leather, taupe suede. Was I seeing things or were the soles polished?

He nodded at the paperback: 'You enjoying that? For sure she can write a sentence clumsy . . . But good plot.'

'You've read it?' I was faintly incredulous.

'Yah. Well. No. Not *read* exactly . . . skimmed . . . professional curiosity . . . *the milieu* . . . she accesses some areas of interest . . . she knows things . . . that box . . . most interesting—'

'Box?'

'The street signs. Where the street signs are kept . . .'

'Ah – it was a container.'

'*Container,*' he condescended. 'Invention? Or *real life*? As we call it.'

'Who knows.'

Then I recalled: 'Bit too much real life in her previous one. Super-injuncted. SLAPPED in the face. It obviously angered someone, embarrassed someone. Someone filthy rich. It's outrageous – a recourse to law exclusive to the filthy rich.'

'Hmmm. That sounds interesting,' he said, savouring it. 'They're amusing to unravel, super-injunctions, the weapon of choice of the guilty coward. What you can be certain of – someone will always talk or tweet.'

'And the tweet will be taken down. The entire print run was pulped. *Denkmal: The Tale of an Illicit Monument.* That's what it was called.'

'Neat title. I like it. *The Tale* – I must read it.'

With a hotel-bedside propelling pencil he wrote the title in a small notebook.

'I doubt you'll find a copy.'

'Oh I wouldn't be too sure—'

A phone rang. He frisked himself then picked up his black grip, reptile skin like geometric eczema. He looked at the name of the caller. Accepted, listened.

'Ouai. Suis à Manchester . . . ffffh . . . J'ai raté la correspondance . . . ay yai yai . . . non, *im-poss-ible.*'

'If you please, Sir.' A passing striped waistcoat cleared his throat and took pleasure in pointing to the Quiet Area sign on the wall beside us. Luc glared at him.

'Attends . . . un tout petit instant,' he spoke into the phone, then addressed me: 'Can you keep your eyes on that bag? Precious bag.' An attempt this time to grin. Attempt failed.

Then, what every business belly who has scrambled high enough up the ladder to gain entry to an executive lounge most fears: a rock band whose members earn as much for a single gig as a middle manager does in a year. A couple of these guys were vaguely familiar. They were in no mood to trash the place. They looked whacked. One of them – an Adonis already carrying the germ of Former Adonis – approached me pointing at the empty part of the sofa.

'Regret – it's already taken – he's just on the phone.'

'Another time. Yeh?' He leered then turned round, stumbled into Luc's bag, some of whose contents tumbled to the floor.

'Oh Christ – I'm so sorry.' He leaned to pick up the things that had spilled.

'It's OK. Leave it to me. Find yourself somewhere to sit. You look whacked.'

'Another time then.'

He fancied himself. He had smiling abilities and the most absurdly tight trousers which were a teaching aid in male anatomy.

I crouched beside the sofa, picked up and replaced in the bag an A5 notebook with a rubberised cover, three further smartphones, opera glasses, a folded programme for a 'Dudu Topaz Celebration' with some numbers scribbled on its margins, a white plastic digital camera, a framed black and white snapshot of an early middle-aged couple sitting at a table with palm trees and the corner of a house behind them, a wallet with a passport sticking out of it. Within the wallet were two further passports. I looked round furtively: Luc was nowhere to be seen.

I opened the passports, leafed through them.

Uruguayan: Luis Caphart, b 28 01 1956, Montevideo.

Lebanese: Saul Triphac, b 28 01 1960, Tyre.

Danish: Paul Straich, b 28 01 1946, Kalundborg.

He was obviously aware of the near-impossibility of guessing his age. He exploited it. No one would challenge any of those birth years.

There was also a receipt for an unspecified patisserie and a coffee from La Griotte in Neauphle-le-Château. An unusually decipherable doctor's prescription for fluindione had been issued in Hammerfest to Luc Shapitra. I noticed that it bore the same date as the restaurant receipt. I found myself checking the distance between the outskirts of Paris and remote northern Norway. I tried too to remember the names of the birthplaces.

When Luc reappeared I pretended to be engrossed in *The Dark Watergang*.

'You could say it's in the genes,' he murmured as he sat down. 'But then that wouldn't be correct, would it? No. In your case it's in the nurture. Don't you agree?'

Creepy is one thing, creepy and cryptic is sadism.

With hardly a pause he asked: 'How well do you know Geoffrey Shadoxhurst?'

'*Geoffrey* Shadoxhurst . . . ? I know The Shadoxhurst *Arms* . . . when I was little . . . ah yes . . . I suppose it's named for local gran-dees. The English way. Feudal. You know, I'd never thought about it . . . estate pub I guess . . . But I don't know any actual person. Should I? Who is he?'

Barely audible: 'Justine? . . . Her . . . benefactor?'

'Oh! Yes . . . of course. *Geoffrey*. Yes. I've never met him. Didn't realise he was called Shadoxhurst—'

'Why are you so friendly with an uneducated hairdresser? You're not *sol y sombra*—'

'I'm not *what*?'

'You don't play for both teams. Her neither.'

'What a thing to say! God – how bloody impertinent! I thought she was a friend of yours.'

'Business. Phoebe. Business.'

Gloves off: 'She said you were jealous of him.'

He made a gurgling croak. His imitation of a laugh, presumably. I thought of the tuggee's hanky.

'Not jealous. Interested. We're just a bit curious about this chappie.'

Wherever did he get that *chappie* from?

'What? Who are *we*?'

'Me. My associates.'

'*Associates?* What sort of associates?'

His head slumped into his hand as if it was the dumbest question he'd ever heard. His expression was incredulous.

'Look,' I said, 'what I know about him is he's absolutely loaded, he's old, he calls heads bonces—'

'What? Calls heads *what*? Bonces? What sort of word is this? Who uses this word?' Curiosity brought him briefly to life.

'It's, ah, affectation, I assume . . . out of date slang – like chappie . . .'

He looked affronted.

'He collects classic cars. He's generous to Justine. That's as much as I know. A lot of her life's been a crock of shit. He makes her happy. So what's wrong with that?'

'Nothing. If that's the whole story. If . . . She's just his private whore. He is very lively in the gentleman quarters as they call them.'

'They do?'

'They do. In fact – she is just *one* of his private whores. What does she know about the other closets of his life?'

'Not as much as you by the sound of it. Incidentally *compartments* is the word you're looking for. And it's *caboodle*. Tell me, Luc, was there ever really going to be a mall – or was that some sort of fantasy?'

He didn't reply.

He suddenly sat still as a statue, frozen, watching an old muttering man hauling an old misshapen brown leather suitcase with old stickers all over it. The old man turned towards us. His face was grey with age, his beard was straggly – but his eyes were the purest blue I had ever seen. He smiled a thin wintry smile. His repetitive utterances became just about coherent: 'Not yet . . . not yet . . . not yet.'

Luc was shaken. He watched him go.

'Are you OK?' I asked.

'Why wouldn't I be?' he responded sharply. 'Where were we?'

'The mall.'

'Ah yes. For every fifty malls who are proposed one is built. Norderstedt-Center by example.'

'That's not an answer.'

'Easy to verify.'

'Detlev Gebel says he's never heard of you.'

'Detlev! Old old friend . . . Detlev, ouff, he's . . . *il est déconneur*. You know . . . not a wit. More a lump of clown. Show-off. Terrible show-off. Bit of a big head . . . big *bonce*! But what a sense of humour. He was so enchanted to meet you by the way.'

This was doing *my* bonce in.

'How do you know?'

'He told me when we chew fat just after he drive you home. I don't recall precise date . . . it's in my diary – if you had time to rummage through it more also you'll have found it . . .'

I must have blushed. I guess that he was pleased to have embarrassed me. But with so much of his face obscured it was impossible to know.

'Ah hah. Gate 15. Advice: never fly with an airline whose pilots believe in the afterlife. Muriel Spark.' He came close to smiling. Then he zipped his bag and said with a ghastly steely chill: 'Not wise to mention this encounter to anyone . . . Capiche?'

He stood up. Clutched his bag. Offered neither hand nor cheek. I stood too. I found the nerve to ask him: 'What do you actually do? If I may ask?'

'*Do?* Hmmm . . .' He leaned so close to me I could see myself reflected in the depths of his glasses. 'Job description. Difficult. I bring people together. Let us just say I carry out the special tasks . . . I take care of the things for people. Consultant in reactivity . . . I'm problem solver. Trouble-shooting from hip. Till we meet again.'

Gate 15 was for the El Al Natbag flight.

I went back to *The Dark Watergang*. Turned page after page, wishing that I could write with such hackneyed negligence and such a canny appeal to the film industry.

'Bumper gee and tee ice and slice twice.'

The soon to be former Adonis stood over me grinning, holding two frosted glasses. He looked less weary. He had presumably refreshed in the restroom. The anatomy lesson was worryingly close.

'That's very thoughtful but I'll pass.'

'Vacant now?'

'Yes.'

He slumped on the sofa beside me, spilling gee and tee, but not on me.

'Small world . . . That guy you were just chatting with . . . he's a friend of a friend of mine . . . friend of one of the guys in the band . . . I'm in a band.'

'I'd never have guessed.'

'The Dandy Wraith Rui I call him . . . you in global volatility too?'

'The Dandy what?'

'The Dandy Wraith Rui.'

'*Rui?*'

'Yeh . . . Rui . . . Rui Päschlat – the guy you were rabbiting with.'

'No, no. It was . . .' I began, then thought, then replied: 'Yes actually, yes. In all probability it was . . . Rui . . . Päschlat? Is that right?'

He was bewildered: 'Yeh . . . Rui.'

'Rui Päschlat. Among others!' I hooted with laughter. 'And no – I'm not in global volatility. Whatever that is . . . And I don't rabbit.'

3.

Have you ever set your alarm for 5 a.m. in the Marriott Hotel, Lincoln, Nebraska, so you can get the 7.30 a.m. flight that allows you to check in at the Marriott Hotel, Tulsa, Oklahoma, before being interviewed on the local TV station Oklahoma's Own NewsOn6 by lunchtime disc jockey Kurt who not only hasn't read the book, he hasn't read the press release?

'Time starvation, darlin'. But I sure did appreciate your mom's books. Feisty lady. And it looks like you's hewn from the same timber. *Leather People*, it's a provocative title sure is. You don't mind me asking: are you into bondage yourself? Or are you more the voyeur type? While you think about it here's a bighearted ballad from the man with the golden thorax, Timmy-Boy Niel in duet with Toni Lo Reno, Cavalier on the Highway of Song.'

Then a signing at the local branch of Barnes and Noble attended by five people, one of whom, a scraggy, greasy-haired woman clutching a bumper pack of cat litter, changed her mind when she got to the front of the queue, followed by a reading in the T-shirt department of the University of Tulsa bookstore; twenty or so people, a triumphant two sales.

Bobby The PR Escort pecked me on the cheek.

'Lucky babe – you've got a lie-in tomorrow. Don't need to be at the airport till quarter to nine.'

Then he left, as usual, to make some new friends.

I had an animal burger with added grease in the hotel's coffee shop.

The Slime was slimily candid about using me as 'leverage', a crude bargaining tool who bore her mother's name. If Benzecry & Mincedorf guaranteed me a book tour of major cities then he'll deliver to them Theodora Benedict (a *reeeally* important author, sells like sun-block in Miami, soon out of contract with her current publisher Gammel, Toft, Hender). Hence my enforced familiarity with such major cities as Bismarck, North Dakota, Billings, Montana, Ogden, Utah, with their hotels and their blood-splattered ER departments which I often had to take Bobby to in the small hours.

It was different at home in New York, and in Washington and New Haven. Friends would come because that's what friends do, holding out a book for you to anoint, feigning interest out of loyalty, a unilateral loyalty which I seldom got round to reciprocating.

My Fairlamb friends Jill Silver and Brandi Ulm both showed up. Separately. They weren't speaking to each other. A dispute over men. I didn't have those. Indeed by the time I lost my virginity Jill had had two abortions, had been threatened by WAAF guerrillas and Brandi had learnt that wearing incredibly tight skirts, incredibly high heels, incredibly mascaraed eyes, incredibly big hair, incredibly scarlet Pantone 485C lipstick, incredibly large splashes of Goutal's Ambre Fétiche could, time and again, buy a plain girl a stevedore's love for as long, perhaps, as an entire night.

Her comprehensively tattooed companion the evening I was reading at The Bowery-Burwood Bookstore was Toto. He wore a wife-beater's singlet and collected snakes. Maybe the most extensive collection in the North Bronx. Would I like to meet them? They'd make a great book. He showed me a photo of himself holding his boa constrictor Kent outside Gaetano's Cucina on Arthur Avenue. Kent had, he assured me, a 'very mature personality and outlook'. He had become a local celebrity.

That 'event' and four of the others in New York were, predictably enough, held downtown where the pious odour of the alternative and countercultural was ever in the air. The sixth was, by chance, right around the corner from where I lived, in Civilisation. East 76th at Lexington. North Lenox Hill is steady, rich, safe, rich, going on boring, rich. It's every bit as edgy as Harvestehude in Hamburg, Paris 7ème, St John's Wood in London. Elderly Jewish ladies in furs with fluffy dogs in plaid winter livery are so reassuring. Nothing exciting ever happens here . . . nothing exciting *had* ever happened here.

The Dutch Farm was a supposedly 'intimate' performance space. That means no one has worked out how to use it. Proscenium arch? Theatre in the round? Leering apron? Half an hour before the audience began to arrive I stood downstage at a metal lectern that might have been a prosthesis from the neighbouring hospital. I asked if the house lights would be switched off during the performance. They could be dimmed. Off? No. Current policy was to dim the house lights. Why? Policy. No exceptions. The typically officious stage manager was adamant.

After a minute or so I couldn't be bothered to argue even though so far as I was concerned the less aware I was of individuals in the audience the better. Talking into the dark is upliftingly impersonal. But in the gloom of dimmed lights, in subfusc halls and theatres, certain individuals inevitably catch your eye. No matter how hard you try your gaze will return to them because they crave it. It will be them that you address, bits of them, head and chest. In this instance a soigné black-suited African-American couple whom I had seen at exhibition openings; a scowling crewcut *gouine* with a rigger's build and work clothes; a vaguely familiar neat greybeard with loud cravat near the back; a toothy grinner (there's always a grinner, usually f. but this one was m.: it's a strange, strange way of attention seeking).

I read part of a chapter about the fear among the otherwise lettered, otherwise rational, otherwise unsuperstitious Ascendancy that the several bodies exhumed from puxy bogs and mosses west of Galway in the 1810s were ghosts of starved illiterate Catholics which had regained a semblance of human form. Had they not been found by peat cutters they would have risen by themselves to take vengeance on their aristocratic tormentors and the middlemen who seized their pitiful parcels of land. Hence the ever-increasing practice of paranoiac

466

landlords absenting themselves in Dublin or London. Hence the birth of an instant Protestant folklore populated by malevolent bog sprites, drizzle-drenched mysticism, trees that turn into witches and ghost stories to chill the readily chilled.

The audience was among the more appreciative of the tour. People who could read and write. And listen. Generous applause. Informed questions. The usual disputatious bore: this one accused me of 'politicising' my scholarship. I made my way to the table in the lobby. The two piles of copies were swiftly demolished. They were replenished by the evening's press people Jerry and Someone tearing tape off carton after carton. My hand began to ache. My signature . . . To Kaaren . . . For Helmut and Daisy . . . No date please to Hannah . . . If you could just say . . . And so on for half an hour.

Then they were gone. Jerry and Someone were re-cartoning the few unsold copies – the *few* unsold copies, what music! A figure stood over the table. He handed me a copy. I caught a faint scent of Buccal Gym.

'Who shall I make it to?' I asked. I looked up at him from my chair. Herringboned greybeard from near the back of the auditorium. I smiled my acknowledgement that I had seen him throughout the reading. I opened the book at the title page. He cleared his throat.

'I used to be your father. Just "to Rudolph Chipurnoi" will do.'

My pen fell from my hand.

'My god.'

This was not a ghost. His neatly bearded face reconfigured itself as the face of almost twenty years previously. I cannot begin to think how I can have appeared to Jerry and Someone who were balletic in mid-hefting yet managed to twist in alarm.

A screwed-up ball of shiny pink paper was propelled across the floor by a draught.

I was speechless.

Without knowing what I was doing I stood and hurled myself at him, hugging him and pummelling him, sobbing with pain and delight and relief, such relief. Something had opened, a faucet of inhibition had opened. I felt I had been delivered a gift, a wonderful gift.

Next thing we were on the street walking north. I took his arm, took it with pride.

'I really loved her. She broke my heart. When I heard she'd died . . .'

'You didn't come to the funeral.'

'There was no . . . no slot for me.'

'Did you remarry?'

'It didn't work out.'

'Couldn't you have just said nothing? We were a happy family. You could have kept it a secret. You could have said I was adopted. Lie! You know how. You're a spook.'

'*Was* . . .'

'Was? Was? I've never forgotten what Jimmy said. *Daddy.* Once . . .'

'Aaah OK . . . I'm also a human. You know what they called me in the Company in those days. High Fidelity. Ha! He keeps it in the family. I was the only guy that didn't play around . . . they called me empty wigs behind my back . . . I was humiliated.' He said this as a matter of record, with no rancour. 'I was so humiliated I was out of my mind. I even got – this was down to Jim – I hired some sky-cops from Greenham to set an attack dog on him. Killer dog. Fangs out. A Selective Task that failed . . . Maybe just as well. But I meant it. I really did. I was consumed . . . You cannot possibly imagine how it feels . . . cuckolded by an illiterate.'

'Illiterate? Come on . . . He may not have read Collingwood—'

'Collingwood . . .' He savoured with pleasure the name of his once favourite writer whom he read over and over when I was a child.

'. . . Your memory! No . . .'

He paused, his expression was one of hopelessness.

'. . . No. I mean *illiterate* . . . literally illiterate. He couldn't read and write. That man had never learnt to read.'

I gasped. The streetlights went out of focus. I stared at a twisted wire which a shred of bunting hung from. I thought of a makeshift cross among farm buildings. This was profoundly shocking. As shocking as learning that Rudolph was not my father.

My bastardy was doubled in that instant. My fear that I was the issue of a rape recurred for the first time in years. I felt the shame of that handicap, my father's handicap. I felt it physically, in my womb, as though it were my handicap too, passed down in thumbprints and scraggy crosses marked 'Ted's mark'.

What backwardness, what atavistic ignorance from deep beneath the earth was I heir to?

Letters: a circle with a thing coming out the bottom. A sort of like pyramid frame with a bar across it. Snail shape with hollows. A circle on top of a rod going off to the left . . . no going off to the right. I thought calling cod liver oil god liver oil was wit to delight me rather than uncorrectable mishearing.

Adult illiterates have always appalled me, scared me like dangerous dumb animals.

'He kept it to himself. Tried to . . . But you could tell from his tools, the way the rulers were notched. And no bank account. What's that about. Evading tax sure – but no paying-in slips, no cheques. Nothing to give him away. No invoices . . . I have to say *you* write very well.' He laughed.

'Do you know his real name? No one else does.'

'He was called Edmund Cecil Dogg. Maybe that should be *is* called? Might still be alive.'

'Dog?'

'Two "g"s.'

I screamed asylum laughter. Dogg. What next?

I took home this childless man who used to be my father. Used to be! He was never my father.

We just about got the front door shut behind us.

'Down't dilloy dalloy.' His cockney accent was as laughably imprecise as it had been when he entertained me with it when I was a child.

'I won't dilly dally.' That had been my habitual response long long ago when I was a child. I was a child again.

As he came my stepfather's groan descended through two octaves to become a rough roar which filled my head with deafening love.

Novels are evidently questionable sources of the actual. Betsy Mavroleon's three novels, *The Medlar Tree*, *The Leopard's Stripes* and *Goats Would Be Prophets* (all Farrar, Straus and Giroux), do, however, contain distinctive incidents which are often transported with little alteration or embellishment from her unpublished journals and diaries. These incidents happened more or less as described in the novels. Of course it is possible that the journals and diaries may themselves be fictive. Certain of these incidents recur in her unfinished memoir *Recall on the Blink*.

Investigative inquiries are equally unreliable sources of the actual. *Angleton in the Field: The Pattern of Deception* by Robert J. Morse (Mudeford & Pope) and *Knight's Move: J. J. Angleton's Necessary Labyrinths* by Xanthe Monk with Damian Llewellyn-Patch (Berserker Books) are invaluable despite their biases, omissions, score settlings, defamations, misattributions, startling lies, fabrications and patently false claims. The same may be said for Legat Totman's oral history of cold war 'cultural' propaganda *Donkeys of the Avant-Garde* (Melmont Wilson).

This account is based in my own memories and in conversations with the late Betsy Mavroleon, the late Micky Mavroleon, Deborah Rolt Mavroleon, Colin Harper, Yonatan Alfasi, Justine Bench and Cornelia Prance, all of whom I am profoundly grateful to. A number of others who have also given generously of their time wish to remain anonymous. My greatest debt by far is to my husband Rudolph Chipurnoi.

Back in Time

'Our permanent sale prices reflect the quality of our fleet.' The man in the caravan's bottom lip had a bobbing roll-up attached. The caravan was so sunken its axles were buried. It stunk of hash, tobacco, whisky. Smells from way back. The only decorations were a pin-up calendar and framed browning article and photo from *Estuary Life* of the man when younger. The cars were ancient smokers. They might never become classics. You may not see their like again. Their destiny was elsewhere. A pyramid of scrap and swarf as high as a house was a clue. The unbroken ones were parked in a plot, in rows, on mud and cinders. You don't come across cinders nowadays. They used to be everywhere. Sprayed by a delinquent's handbrake turn. Getting in a graze to turn it septic. That's what it was like back then.

The plot was fenced by rusty corrugated iron sheets, barbed wire, old doors etc. Why bother? Why bother feeding a Marcher Hound on a string that's more a rope? Who was going to steal this metal or these nearly former vehicles? They belonged to an old country. I paid cash.

'When you off-hire it if I'm not here leave the keys with the hotel. There—' He gestured to an unforgiving red-brick box with malevolent dormers. Not so much Victorian gothic as Victorian Victorian. The Severn Bridge and Railway Hotel. A strangely large hotel for this small port. It stood in the shadow of a fissured silo, beside a dock with a cross-hatched complement of further silos, hoppers, grain mills, cranes, massive locks, bulbous bollards. Apart from a few two-up two-down terraces there were no habitations. It was as if a piece of an industrial city had been removed to a bucolic site.

It stood as a full-scale model of such a city, a sample. There were deafening jackhammers and the painful scrape of steel on steel. Pitiless pop music burnt workers' brains. It was all utilitarian drabness and monochrome squalor. Polythene bottles, matt with age, plastic bags and polystyrene granules floated on the petrol-marbled water. It smelled of grime. The air assaulted nostrils and stung eyes. It was every shade of subfusc.

Yet the other side of the great river was all red sandstone cliffs and tree clumps as far as you could see. On this bank, the left, there were fields stretching across the vale.

'Fancy a swift?' he asked. He shook his pointing finger. 'Furthest inland port in good old Blighty. That's something to be proud of.'

The dozen reeling Baltic sailors in the bar raised glasses to us. That is to me and Andy of Andy's Car Services.

'Once every couple of months they're here. They really know how to get on down themselves. Wait till the girls arrive! Animals! They pre-order them. I came here on a timber ship from Rostock forty years ago. Even before she'd docked I knew I'd found my home.'

Andy leaned over me all ominous: 'I wouldn't start from here if I was you. I wouldn't start now if I was you . . . This is a place you escape to. Not from. This is a place you never ought to leave. It's like it's in a different time. Long ago and far away. Like when you're little and you believe that somewhere there's that perfect place. This is that place – for me. Where you heading to?'

'The past.'

'Like I say mate, you're already there.'

'No. My past. My own.'

'That'll be different then.'

There were always leaves blowing in the flat valley bottoms, the brown leaves and the russet leaves, the leaves with rouge and polish, the desiccated leaves. They took off with the wind behind them, then they blew back carried by a retaliatory wind, which repulsed them in curling kinetic pompadours. For every step forward one back. Destination uncertain till they gathered in fat drifts waiting to dance again. Time is not leaves, it is not Gregorian or Julian – there were no lost days. Nor is it Swiss wishfulness, it is not 180 degrees nor is it 360 – cyclical is as much a lie as linear. It is the defining property of existence. Grasping it is like grasping air. Only tyrants deny that. They bypass the conundrum. In their bloody naivete they start from zero as though time is biddable, controllable. There is no Year Zero.

The mystery of the missing udder child at Over Osmingham has been solved. The cheeky toddler has been rewarded with a visual brilliance facial plus a lifestyle size oriental scalp grift with pink hair and veal mud at Staddle's unmissable one-stop wellness and serenity hub Hi De Hilights, formerly Get Your Locks Off.

There were always streams gurgling in the flat valley bottoms, carried to the sea by imperceptible gradients, breaking over smoothed stones to make white water, dashing through gullies as though on the lam in a yarn, spilling onto rocky banks where birches grew, turning into spume that iced my face when I knelt to drink the clear cold water. You have to put out of mind the dead sheep rotting out of sight upstream.

Cheek Green oldster Tallis Snutch, 98, got a nasty shock when he bit into an egg and treacle sandwich. He found a two-pound coin. Quipped Tallis: 'You could say it's my lucky day but I only got the one good tooth left and I come close to breaking him so I got trauma-related issues.'

For an instant the happy smiling people were frozen in a stance of rapture like saints on a baroque cornice. They waved and smiled as I passed through the villages where they lead happy smiling lives in the knowledge of who they are, who their parents are (even if brown bread as Shaun puts it), who their children are. Were they drawing attention to some fault in the car? No, they were happy smiling people from the fellowship of friendship where all is thatch and hollyhocks, yeomen and forelock, frothing and quaffing – Sir John Barleycorn will be spared. Happy smiling people overjoyed to see me. Cheering me on in my quest. Gesturing 'you do it this time'.

On the run shoplifters Kimella Wince and Jason-Justin Cheddy, once described as the Bonnie and Clyde of the Vale of Houndsbotham, have turned themselves in. According to Clipfield Metropolitan police spokesperson

Donnalynn Kine, they had been lying low in a bungalow beside the A647 but were increasingly worried by the panther in the next-door garden.

A smiling fisherman was spinning for trout from the garden of a riverside villa. On the lawn behind him two ranks of very old men in dark glasses and white smocks stared at the sky from wheelchairs. They were so still, so impassive that they might be dead. A couple of hundred yards away where the stream branched two children were rowing a boat. A third and fourth swam beside it. It reminded me of a holiday I had never had but had imagined from reading about it. In an overgrown orchard of lichenous trees the bees were sozzled from rotting fruit, heavy in their laboured flight. In a field of nettles and remedial docks moss grew abundant on a long-deserted summerhouse whose veranda had turned to feed for wood-beetles for many years to come. How ragged the country was! Thatch turned green. Plants grew from within abandoned cottages pushing through the gaps where the panes they had cracked under vegetable force had once held out against the outside rain and gusts. This was my country as it once had been in the time of Good Queen Bess.

Moist Groin drum hero Stafford Prance is facing an industrial tribunal. Former employee Aphra Busk, 23, a junior commis chef at the sticks hero's Quenchwell mansion, alleges that she was wrongfully dismissed. Aphra suffers from Spackman Brock syndrome. It makes her dribble uncontrollably. The rock legend was said to be concerned about environmental damage and was worried that food contamination could lead to the cancellation of Groin's forthcoming tour of Iceland. A spokesperson claimed that Aphra had been offered alternative employment in the gardens but she had refused it because of feathers.

Tree surgeons belonged to the future. So did weekend cottages and trim verges.

When a factory became redundant it was decreed disposable. 'Retrofitting' had yet to be coined. 'Repaired' did the job. It was not rebuilt. A replacement was rebuilt on a neighbouring plot and when that was redundant another was made – so the history of steel manufacture or dairy production or weaving was told in plant in differing states of dereliction (and current use).

Here was a Jersey cow milked in the meadow by hand by a maid, maybe.

Look! A pair of Suffolk Punches hauling a plough followed by scrapping seagulls – who have yet to learn to thieve ice creams, who have yet to learn to live on landfill.

Here's another pair: shire horses delivering ale barrels in a town of jettied houses, outdoor stairways stretching to the sky, warm tiles and not a straight line in sight.

A single horse draws a low-sided wagon across a bridge where river, canal, road and railway cross each other at different levels. It carries blue gas canisters bearing a code in stencilled military font. They will be delivered to a dentist with a Morningside accent.

A muddy avenue of Lombardy poplars, stiff as yard brooms, led to an ancient half-timbered house partially visible through shrubs. A steep hill rose high behind it. Damson trees blossomed in fluffy white ranks. Happy black sheep wandered between them cropping the grass. I had never been here before. I wished I had. It was a scene from a childhood jigsaw, long long lost.

Two men with dunchers and Denbigh terriers stand staring into a churning mill race, chewing.

They don't notice the couple on a tandem bicycle, both dressed in khaki shorts and olive Aertex. No helmets. It wasn't for nothing that it was known as the golden age of head injuries.

A steam train bellows by, caked with coke, its carriage windows encrusted with the grime of the ages, but you can still spy the excited children on their way to the seaside and sunshine, buckets and shrimping nets ready for the rock pools.

Former Internazionale Alverstoke's central defender Mel Crudge did the honours cutting the ribbon at Lee on the Solent's new 24/7 Minimart which is open 9 till 6 every day apart from Sunday. The Alvers legend, whose four own goals in the derby against Olympic Netley in 1991 remains a club record, was full of praise for the Minimart's range of cleaning products: 'Swarfega's been like a brother to me,' he admitted.

The Lamb and Lag's flaking sign squealed as it swung on its rusty frame.

The Cry For Help's sign has broken free and is propped against a wall. It is painted in the chalky tempera colours of the early New Elizabethan era. Both recall the inns in the Aubrey Quested adventures.

In the car park two boys sat on a Vauxhall's bench seat, eating crisps, drinking dandelion and burdock. One mimes driving.

In the car park a pony tail in her early teens holds a transistor radio to her ear and dances beside a collapsing creosoted fence. She smiles at the jumpsuited woman getting into her van marked Second Sight Corneal Transplant Solutions. The four letters 'o' are diagrammatic eyes. The woman does not smile in return.

A bus conductor's ticket machine clacks like a rattle; she hands a ticket to a boy in a magenta school blazer and matching cap.

Watch that two-tone car (maroon and cream) with white wall tyres and a steering column gearshift driven by a man in two-tone driving gloves (tan leather and cream net). It plashes through a ford.

A former airfield. Runway sprouting grasses that have cracked the aggregate. A hangar whose side is painted with the words POPPY TOURS.

Along comes the Corona lorry driven by Mr Jollity with a sparkly cargo of brightly coloured chemicals and American Cream Soda, colourless.

Hikers in tweed and argyle socks, bearing army kitbags and freshly coppiced green woodsticks, crossed a clapper bridge, a very long crocodile set in stone.

Kiddies at Chalmordistonly's Hassan-i-Sabbah primary school have been forbidden from using pencil sharpeners. In a statement head teacher Gwenny Size stated that 'The act of sharpening a pencil into a sharpener simulates rotational and invasive lower middle body sector activities which are likely to incentivise unhealthy euphemism asterisks.'

A tea shop beckons me with the promise that such places hold. Along with the cream, the jam, the tea, it is, within, always the year of my birth: those curtains, that cutlery and floral china, the table lamp shades in false parchment, the homespun napkins, a woven map of the locality, copies of *Illustrated London News* and *Lilliput*, the spinster proprietors who had knitted each other into existence.

I was overtaken by a sporty chap wearing a leather helmet driving a Morgan three-wheeler. Doubtless thought himself a 'swashbuckler'.

I was overtaken by another member of that species, this one with a flat hat whose peak was a pediment. He was at the wheel of a growling Healey 3000. Bullying man and brutal machine were trapped in a warp of tattersall check and British Racing Green. His passenger's long blonde hair escaping from a scarf was horizontal in the wind. The same persons followed in a Frazer Nash Mille Miglia. The same persons followed in an Allard Palm Beach.

Recidivist Henderson Jug wore gloves when he broke into banker Niven Ninian's Browness-on-Tame mansion — but the 22-year-old from Grindhamworth reckoned without his psoriasis. Detective Sergeant Gadney Smart described the flakes from Jug's human parts as repulsive greasy supermammoth XXXXL. They were liberally deposited about the mansion. They contained the DNA that convicted him. He was sentenced at Nix Monchelsea Magistrates to three weeks societal person monitoring and an assessment rebrand. A warning there for all members of the light-fingered community with dermal malfunctions.

The tractor that held me up was pale grey — so instantly recognisable as a Ferguson and the model for The Little Gay Tractor, victimised hero of a series of silly moralistic books which I used to read to the children, when I had children.

A steam yacht plied across the choppy lake. The smoke from its funnel, the birches and peaks, the heathered hillsides and white foals were captured by Derwent colour pencils.

A hatchet-faced crone sat on a bucket on the tarpaulin-patched roof of a narrowboat smoking a pipe, the model for Mrs Malarky the villainous maker of angels in a comic strip of yesteryear. They were not buried in the churchyard with a gross boled yew.

Cob walls crumbled where their thatch hood was bald.

I listened to the jolly gurgle of a brook, I watched the swirling of a stream about a packhorse bridge's piers.

Vet Telford Pluck from Over Unthank is offering Gloatpack — Botox for dogs. You'll remember that last year Doctor Pluck launched a range of aniseed-scented canine mascaras and poochy gentleman dog fragrances. That resulted in him being investigated by the RSPCA, OFCOM and the Over Unthank branch of PAEDONARK. Now he is facing allegations that he cosmeticised Karlita, an award-winning Bedlington terrier hailing from Upper Mildgusset, with Botox that had been pre-loved . . . Karlita is currently in hiding.

The village idiot threw punches at himself and missed. His tongue protruded tautly – he was giving birth from the mouth. His too close eyes were different colours – you could just about make them out through thick spectacle lenses grubby with fingerprints. His congenitally syphilitic no-nose was brittle red sores. A pet chicken was poking from its breast pocket nest. His teeth were like those houses up north, broken caramels stained with meat, pitted by sugar. His army kitbag had his scrumpy in it. The cheery driver of Bonallack and Hattcook's Austin Devon bakery van handed him his daily doughnut.

Five years ago Nether Crayke human outsourcing engineer Digby Goodswine lost his sense of smell in a tragic leaving party incident. Now Digby, 39, a keen amateur surgeon ever since he saw controversial German painter Georg Grosz's Remember Uncle August, *has operated on himself to instal a device in his nose which has restored his sense of smell. So successful is it that he has applied for a patent and intends to go into production with Third Nostril as he calls it. And what's his favourite smell now that the old olfactory gear is no longer on the blink? He says he'd like to pretend it was the nape of partner Perryetta's neck but if he's telling the whole truth and nothing but it's got to be a sizzling full Spanish with extra hot chorizo.*

The bull saw, on the far bank, the picnic party sitting on its helping-with-enquiries tartan blanket. It had a splendid wicker fothergill, thermos flasks, meat-style paste sandwiches, bridge rolls smothered with sandwich spread. He must have enjoyed their peals of shrieks. He swam the river to greet them. They fled, dropping their picnic kit in panic. The ground was heavy, tufty: liverworts and sphagnums for frightened feet to sink into. They climbed three drystone walls, snagging clothes, grazing shins as they went. The bull climbed three drystone walls in his pursuit of them. They had shown him how to do it. He evolved, he reared on his hind legs like the people he wanted to meet. Once wrapped up in their black pre-war car they giggled with relief at their escape while the bull, having peered in, wandered dejectedly along a boggy path wondering no doubt why he was neglected.

A cow flicked its tail at flies like a dominatrix fatigued at the end of her shift.

A bewildered cow was on its side in birthing position. When the calf emerged it, too, was bewildered, peering through the semi-transparent foetal membrane at the incomprehensible world it would inhabit before vealdom or dairy drudgery beckoned.

Nether Crayke inventor Digby Goodswine is fighting for his life in a Dutch prison hospital. According to partner Perryetta Scratchsore an early evening drink at Rotterdam's Sugar Baby Love Bar turned into a waking nightmare that she has still not awoken from.

The keen amateur surgeon, 39, entered the bar, among the city's top Rubettes themed establishments, wearing his soon to be patented Third Nostril device. According to early reports an off-duty police officer mistook him for a suicide bomber and shot him from less than three metres. Although the bullet struck one of the steel plates that he had inserted in his head and did not enter his brain Digby is in deep coma.

Famished from looking. I stopped at a lo-hygiene Chinese. I sat on a bench with a dedicatory plaque to a Lieutenant Roderick Vanier of the 9th Mobile Bath Unit (1911–40). A path between ironstone walls led to a lychgate. A pillar box and a telephone box, bleached beefeater, stood side by side, waiting for a tosh of scarlet or similar. They were an illustration of an earlier period in our island's communications. Saint George's proud flag on the church tower was whipped by a brisk westerly. It would have been prouder with a wash and brush up.

Great news from Holland's Haageland Prison. Inventor Digby Goodswine, 39, who was shot in the head in a controversial bar shooting when mistaken for a suicide bomber, has regained consciousness and is enjoying a hearty canteen lunch of pork style product in the company of three Liberian government ministers facing cannibalism charges at the International Criminal Court. They are expecting a diplomatic freezer bag packed with the trafficked meat of early adolescents. If it doesn't show up they have threatened that they'll graze on Digby. Let's just hope it's an example of that famous Liberian sense of humour.

I ate with a plastic spoon. Number 9, number 11 and number 37. No Szechuan this or Peking that, foxing us all with authenticity. Where it came from, where anything or anybody came from should by rights have been of interest to me but the place names left me cold. Look at me – there was no chance I was from there! Back then we didn't see that the shapes the rice remnants make across the scraped container's bottom are ideograms transmitting incomprehensible griff. I counted the phone box's panes. None was broken. No vandals to break them then.

It reminded me to call Shaun. I left a message telling him I had a good feeling about this one. He'd heard that before but this time it was different from the other times, though he'd have replied, wearisome, as per usual 'this time . . . this time . . .'

Mature student Lisney Trigg from Snettertoft had recently read Samuel Johnson's advice that we should always give to a beggar because, if we don't, the beggar will lack the wherewithal to continue in his chosen profession – which of course is begging. So when Lisney saw a man in rags sitting on the doorstep of an Ugford-on-Roden shop smoking a dimp and holding a Styrofoam cup he virtuously lobbed a coin into the cup. However, instead of the expected grunt of thanks there was an affronted cry of why did you do that? The man was high fashion retail executive Nattrass Palethorpe. He was dressed in destitution chic and drinking his skinny latte outside because he was a snoutcast. And the coffee had spilt over his preciously shredded threads. Palethorpe went into the shop and returned with a mannequin with which to beat Lisney. He slipped under the mannequin's weight and twisted his knee. Conditional discharge. Says Lisney: 'Samuel Johnson sometimes got things wrong – his observation that "Tristram Shandy did not last", for instance.'

★

I was coming home, I was telling myself. That's what I'd have said to Shaun if he'd answered instead of leering at whoever he was having lunch with. Different from my humble scran. We lived in different worlds now. The gap was unspoken.

The road ahead shimmered. A river rippled. Why are kingfishers only ever in the very corner of your eye? How do they gauge the limits of your peripheral vision? Scarecrows stood among megaliths. I counted magpies. The omens were good. This was the final journey. Failure? No longer allowed. I didn't consider the possibility after these months, these years.

I waved. ''Scuse me. I'm looking,' I leaned from the window and shouted at the probably deaf but nonetheless happy smiling old folk tottering along on the verge none too steady as they went, but pluckily persisting, 'for some people called Dogg. I don't suppose—'

'The big house it is you want long way back, you're going the wrong way . . . you want back there . . . I wouldn't have started from here if I was you. No. You can't miss it.'

The woman beside him with a shopping cart agreed: 'You can't miss it . . . Very historical it is . . . Just look out for the poplars . . . they're trees, poplar trees.' She smiled, nodded in agreement with herself. I stared at her tatty cracked leatherette cart, it summoned up their station in life. I almost forgot to thank them.

When I had continued in the wrong direction, found a place to turn round and driven back past them they stretched their arms in a salute of good cheer. How I warmed to them. How desperately I needed small acts of generosity and acknowledgement.

I almost passed the poplar avenue. Coming the way I was coming now the trees did not present as a continuous wall the way they had earlier but as the back of a stage flat, scenery seen from the wrong side. I turned into the avenue. There was a strip of grass down its middle, mud to either side of it, two soggy verges squashed flat here and there by careless tyres like green roadkill. One side of the avenue was a hopyard. The bines grew on wires supported by flimsy frames in ranks. Happy smiling pickers lugged baskets of hops, unloading them in trailers, repeating the action like the machines they were. The other side was a cider orchard where a further flock of

Shropshire Black Temptations fattened themselves on grass and fallers. My nerves were jangly. This was my final journey. This will make or break my quest. Quest! Sounds grand. I had no plan should it fail like all the rest. I distracted myself by looking at clogged ditches, fleecy barbed wire, galvanised troughs, fallen trees. I called Shaun. No reply. I called the landline. Verity answered.

'He's unavailable.'

'Well . . . tell him this could be the one . . . I've got a good feeling about this one.'

'I have told him that I don't know how many times before, Henry — is that it?' Her voice rose irritatingly at the end.

I knew I was putting off the moment. Tomorrow? I'd passed a B&B. The pubs might have rooms. Nip back and book one? I'd prepared for the moment time after time. I was used to the sympathy, the understanding, the trusting openness of strangers who shared my current name and regretted that they must disappoint me. I sat staring at the buildings a couple of hundred yards in front of me. The existence among the outbuildings of an oast house was a good omen. Like all omens it was without reason. On the way to the seaside when I was a little fellow my father who wasn't my father used to say when we spotted an oast house: 'That's where the devil's potion comes from, Henry.'

They were round with a conical roof in those days. This one was square with a pyramidal roof.

Now the air was thickening with dusk. Now it was darkening, damp, dreich as Douglas John Gordon Dogg would have it. Now the pickers had gone to their flood plain caravans. A bird whistled to warn it was about to sing. The balls of mistletoe hung high as though independent of the trees they parasited. A vehicle came up the lane behind me. It waited then flashed its lights. Then it repeated the action. I had no option but to drive forward. There was no place to turn. Besides, the track was not wide enough to accommodate more than one vehicle. It followed me with a friendly siren shriek of the horn. At the end of the avenue the track widened in a sort of yard: former stables, an illumined workshop and beyond it an immensely long barn. The house stood apart, only one room lit. The driver of the vehicle, an LHD Venom Condor Wolf 4×4 Raptor with bull bars as thick as a body builder's thigh, tractor tyres and a battery of search-lights, sauntered over to me. Stetson, jeans, fancy pearl-buttoned cowboy shirt and boots.

'How you doing?'

'I'm sorry to have held you up there.'

'See the only way to widen would be to chop down the trees and we don't want to be going there. You a hop tourist?'

'No . . . not especially.'

'Saw you looking. We get a lot of them . . . It's no secret – we got an ongoing debate whether we extend the cider and perry informa-tion centre . . . to make space . . . give hops their due you might say. Hops are very now.' He addressed me while speaking to himself.

'Why not?'

'Hmmmh. You'll have to ask Dad about that. He's dead set against it. So's Me Old Gran. My brother's on the fence as usual but me and Mum we're all about moving forward . . . if we don't do it someone else will. Ruralism's a dog-eat-dog business.'

I heard myself speak as though I was under water. Twisted dic-tion. Rumbling. Heart pumping so loud he must have been able to hear. I heard myself ask: 'What's your mother's name?' I did my utmost to make that question sound casual.

He looked mildly surprised: 'Vera – why?'

Iced vertigo swamped my body.

He didn't notice: 'D'you know her then?'

I made my mouth speak like a stroke victim: 'Sort of, yeah.' A sort of lie, unconvincing.

But: 'I never know who she knows. She knows so many folk. Sometimes I think she knows everyone.' He shook his head in amazed admiration for the amplitude of her acquaintanceship.

My body didn't know that among the workaday buildings it was damp, claggy, muggy, warm for whatever this season of this vital year it was. It still froze. It accepted no more messages from my brain, it sent shards up my spine, down my spine.

'Want to come in and say hello?'

I was on the edge of a cauldron cliff looking into the deepest syrup of Bosch where there floated the apparatus of misfortune . . .

'You OK?'

How long had he been waiting to say that?

I must not lose my nerve. This looks like . . . and all I could think of was calling Shaun.

'You all right?'

'Yes yes. Just a bit ah . . . fatigued.'

'Gets us all. Come and have a cuppa – or something stronger.' Wink. He stuck out his hand: 'Spotty Dogg.'

I took his hand.

'Hen—' Before I could give my name his phone rang. He beckoned me towards the house as he listened then spoke, exasperatedly.

'It's not just about appearance tell them . . . albeit no one's going to fancy those bald patches . . . it's a health hazard . . . you know some punter could get . . . that's it – zoonotic . . . Yeh yeh, that's what they always say . . . No two ways about it . . . Culpable – that's what I call them.'

He gestured I should enter. The front door was half open.

The walls of the long hall were partly panelled, partly plaster and ancient splintery beams. The floor was uneven stone flags, a hazard for ankles. It was homely, lived-in or tatty according to taste. Many would call it a bit of a shambles. It smelled of wood fires and baking. It was all distressed splendour or was it shabby chic? You see it in magazines for people with ideas above their station wanting to be negligently upper class who are proud to stink of their dogs and don't know the meaning of repointing or elbow grease. Walking sticks, umbrellas, heavy faded velvet curtains, a big wooden chest. Yes, it was definitely more distressed and shabby than splendid or chic.

There was a portrait of a man in osk beaver furs with a hat too big for his head, a torn knights of old hunting deer with killer dogs, pikes and halberds tapestry and a smaller less frayed pastoral tapestry with ravishing satyrs, glubbing goats, cherubs, shepherds playing pipes among classical ruins – the usual rude crew.

'We got to have him ready for Sunday midday . . . I got Priscilla booked . . . it'll cost if I have to cancel him . . . he's hired cranes jibs god knows what . . . I don't care . . . I don't care . . . he's under guarantee . . . just remind them we got them over a barrel. Speak tomorrow.'

He addressed me: 'The cunting bastards. What can you do . . .'

He kicked the door shut behind him with a violent boot. His amiability had been swallowed by his phone.

He cut a strange figure. Dressed for a rodeo – in deepest midmost England. 'I got to freshen up.'

He walked to the bottom of the wide warped stairs, turned momentarily out of sight. The click of a latch and lever. 'Mum – you got a visitor. Mum! You got a visitor.'

He reappeared, pointed in the direction he had come from and leapt up the stairs two at a time. Not wise in those heels I thought. The possibility that he might stumble was a distraction but also a concern.

I stood at the open door of the yeoman kitchen. Vera Dogg had her back and broad shoulders to me. She was at a butcher style wooden work surface taking a break from slicing unidentified pink meat product to sharpen her knife with rasping steel.

'Shan't be . . . almost there.'

I stood, wondering what to say. Is there an etiquette attached to this moment? I was unprepared. So obviously was she. She put down the knife and turned to me. In a long second her face went from a picture of curiosity to the far side of shock. It was suddenly bleached and papery. She could not believe what she was seeing. Puzzlement and fear struck her simultaneously. No mere revenant could produce such a reaction. She said something in a language I didn't recognise. She leaned back steadying herself against the work bench. She stared with an intensity which might have been intended to make me disappear, as though she had the power of life over me, *still* had that power.

Then to my astonishment she laughed. A girlish light laugh. She put her hand to her mouth, turned back to her pastry. 'I would,' she said, 'know that chin anywhere. I have never forgotten it. I've thought of him every day. You're a replica.' She put down the brush again.

'I knew you'd find me. One day. Must wash my hands – I'm making a poison quiche for an Ultra Desperate. They usually want to gorge on something sweet. This one doesn't.'

She said that matter of factly.

Strange – but what wasn't?

She scrubbed, dried, walked across the room, her flour-smeared apron caught on a straying strand of chair wicker. She approached me, enquired almost flirtatiously with her eyes for my consent and then hugged me, cuddled me, swaddled me, engulfed me with decades of unfulfilled yearning. She was half me, half my marrow, half my blood. But not half my being – that was an apparatus of the long decades since she was forced to abandon me. Or chose to abandon me. The latter is the option I had always kept buried, the one I feared.

She didn't know what to do either. Well, it doesn't happen every day! It is a once in a lifetime experience. Like being born!

I found my mother. I found my home; well, a home, sort of. I found a new life, to an extent. It was like some sort of commune or community. Not that I know anything of either or the difference between them. I found my blood family: my half-brothers, the twins Spotty and Puppy, strangers from the same womb, their partners Spotty's Billie Shelf and Puppy's Clover Chugg, an award-winning junior entrepreneur, and the unwelcome Kirsty MacFeral, his terrifying Glaswegian hoodlum of an ex-wife and her junky boyfriend Derek The Vein. He blamed them for his perpetual pain. Spotty's sometime fiancée Josie was now Joe and working in the sheep arena. He/she was known to The Sergeant and his centenarian-plus bucol quaffers at The Cry For Help as The Transit, as much because that's the make of vehicle he/she drove as because of his/her embrace of non-binary shepherding. The van's interior was caked with sheep droppings.

I found their beliefs, their strange trades, their unusual ways of life, their vocations, their travels, their habits, their differences from me. Did I find myself – as mystical soldiers do in the mist of battle and junior politicians in dungeon depravity?

I might have done, yes there was every chance I would have done, if I had not also found my mother's husband, The Sergeant, and his mother Me Old Mum, an accordionist and soothsayer who was considered a sage.

She was reputed to hold the lore of the ages: 'When the river rises high the meadows turn to lakes . . . The leper can't change his spots . . . Me, what I always ask about borrowed time is who lends it to you in the first place . . . Don't take the gospels as gospel . . . There's not enough about housework, ironing and the like in the Bible . . . they didn't foresee gas and electricity back then . . . Just because it's born in a stable doesn't mean that a foal will become the saviour of mankind . . . So – you've got dates on palms.'

This last seemed to mean: 'What do you expect from palms? . . . Apples?'

I was questing. The grail is not the finding, it is the searching: that's what they don't tell you. It's the dogged chase made over years to here. There's nothing much at the end. No chalice, no myth, no suit of armour. Just mild disappointment, pale anti-climax, dashed hopes, broken dreams. I'd imagined the joyful bright family waving flags in greeting. They'd be holding red, white and blue plastic windmills outside the house when I arrived. I had expected a tidier house. A less worn house. I really had hoped for a nicely ordered house. I'd imagined sunny faces, good teeth. Happy smiling people frozen in gestures of rapturous greeting like baroque saints on a cornice.

Spotty said: 'We always knew you'd come. Mum never hid you from us. She called you My Never Forgotten War Baby . . . The Sergeant hoped you'd never show up. He calls you Ernie. You're his worst nightmare. You're what he feared.'

I took a room for a week in The Cry For Help.

The first thing The Sergeant said to me was: 'That's seven days too many.' The next thing he said was: 'If it wasn't for my love of your mother . . . my respect for her . . . you'd have been dumped down a drain unborn, if you follow me. I did well by you and now you come here rooting in the old gene trough. Tracing your ancestors. But they don't live here. They don't belong here any more than you do. Didn't they ought to be left in peace? It's a mug's game going looking for the past. Put it behind you. Scrub it out before it scrubs you out.'

He never wore anything around the farm other than a pair of army trousers, braces, gaiters, boots. He never went anywhere without carrying something, pushing a cart, hauling a stump, dragging an animal (live or dead). His body was a palimpsest. Many of his tattoos – snakes, a moustachioed boxer which might have been him, a crown, fat lips – were on the sites of former, faded tattoos. Time and era were mocked. Everything was compressed. Everything was on the same plane. It was called chronal constancy. Like painting was before they'd got the hang of perspective.

I enjoyed walking with my mother like a callow teenage boy daring to hold a girl's hand which he fears will be withdrawn. It wasn't. I was relieved. We had some good chats but for the life of me

I can't recall what they were about. What I did realise was that she steered conversation away from personal revelation and personal questions, away from her and me and us. She was practised in evasion. It came easily. Just occasionally she spoke of long ago when she was the only girl who had dared to jump through the flames of Sankt Johanns Feuer at the summer solstice. But most of her rare recollections were generalised. They might have come from anyone's childhood: snow drifts as high as houses, the most modern most beautiful highways in the world, cormorants, catechism, kindness to animals, tinted photographs of Sami herding reindeers, a striped beach chair that was a bather's carapace. It all felt second-hand, borrowed from a collective store of childhood impressions or learnt from books.

More often she talked about the family, impersonally like she was disconnected from it. Perhaps that was in sympathy with me: I was disconnected too. The family did not include me. That was hardly surprising but nonetheless exclusion was not my goal. What was my goal? The satisfaction of primal curiosity which itches like eczema but can be relieved by an answer? A further curiosity about heredity, how noses and voices and gestures may repeat themselves as though they have an autonomy independent of the bearer; they're just garments from the bottom of the family trunk. They may skip a couple of generations, unused, then reappear to insist upon the strength of the blood. My goal was not to become a drug smuggler.

Her pride in The Sergeant was palpable. She was proud as a heron as Me Old Mum would put it. She was proud of her too, and of Spotty's business acumen and of Puppy even though he was on the simple side and couldn't be trusted on Poppy Tours because he forgot to drive on the right and would have spent more than three weeks jailed in Louvain-Central had it not been for the policeman taking his statement accepting most of a bottle of schnapps from Puppy's parka so getting well dredged and forgetting the formalities of time, interview was concluded, signature, hefty rubber stamp.

Not so simple eh! Indeed Poppy Tours had grown out of Puppy's interest in World War II comics, was further stimulated by gung-ho patriotic partworks and attending 'historical' re-enactments. The Sergeant came up with the name, having misheard Puppy talking about his plan to launch Puppy tours to World War II sites. So the project was extended to include the killing fields of The Great War.

The greenness was overpoweringly jungle fresh. The sun shone through plump boughs, turning stones green, dyeing walls green, making sheep fleece green. It was nicknamed Chlorophyl Valley and The Fructuous Abundance. It was a great green gothic nave. We crunched beechnuts up there and acorns down here. Different barks, different branches, different leaves made different lights, all of them green. The hues were nuanced, myriad, dazzling.

We explored the ruins of the great house and experimental farm colony of Malpasfang. Massive red sandstone blocks crumbling, hurrying to dust. Big-busted caryatids, steroid-fed Atalants, cheeky putti. Primitive in its dereliction. It might have belonged to some perverse cult.

Feral beasts, descendants of the original colonists, live in the depth of the greenwood. Everyone knows they have scaley tails and merciless claws. They vault onto horses' necks screeching, tearing at the mane, hooking out the eyes. They attack sleeping foxes. They squat in setts from whose occupants they have driven out. They eat bubbling mud and live forever. Everyone knows someone who has seen them violating dead horses, wounded goats etc. They're practised masturbaters, locally renowned. The males ejaculate into streams and lakes hoping that they will fertilise fish and so produce a genus of amphibian. No luck so far. As teenagers Spotty and Puppy had fished those very streams and lakes with explosives: the dead fish floated to the surface. They still kept their hand in from time to time. Honestly billed as today's fresh catch, they were sold on Sunday mornings from a car boot in the car park of The Axeman Cometh. Mine Host Wally Lobb turned a blind eye in exchange for a weekly tithe.

She told me the names of flowers in English, translated them into her childhood patois, picked campions, stood on a footbridge, gazed at the wooded hill above us, at the brook flowing beneath us. The burble and purl are imparting wisdom – the way sunsets and clouds and mountains are said to do. Wisdom? Or does the eternity of water's flow prompt shame in slight lives?

She said what she knew I was waiting to hear. 'I didn't want to abandon you . . . those were difficult times.'

We didn't hug again. I smiled the best I could. I told her I understood, which I did, maybe, or, maybe, not. I feigned interest in the water. We were near contemporaries. Generation is as defining as skin colour, religion, nationality. Generations cluster together. They shut out their seniors, they shut out their juniors. We might have grown up together. She would have been my big sister. Too late now, too late. Too late too for that mother–son bond based in a genetic essence that overcomes the accumulations of the years, the differences of circumstances, attitudes, tastes. I yearned to find that essence, that core.

But all I found was a woman not that much older than me whose beliefs and morals were stained by an alien culture that was, for me, ungraspable. It might have been grown on a funny farm. Her worldview was not life enhancing. No sir. Just the opposite. It did not coincide with mine – not that I'd ever considered what my worldview might be, not being much of a one for introspection and deep thought about how I relate to the world which long ago cast me aside. I left that to the professionals with their *weltanschauungen* and other manges. She had made up hers, a death dogma that clung to her like an aura. Its professional expressions were Dream Topping™, Smotherland and associated enterprises.

She gave her life to hurrying along the last course for the irreversibly disappointed: baking poison quiches, making hemlock compote, crystalising atropine, advising on hanging drops according to weight, veins, access to high buildings, le Pont des Suicides etc. Her vocation was helping those who were beyond help who had reached a place they knew they would never get back from. She encouraged them, gave them the strength for that last final shove. She was a shoulder for the psychically injured to cry on before she fed them into fate's foetid pit. I didn't qualify. My wounds were too deeply camouflaged. I couldn't find the right moment to ask the question I most needed to ask.

She showed me an ancient stone circle. The stones were roughly egg shaped. That proved they were built by women who practised oomancy. Indisputably, she said. I wondered what sort of women could have lifted the stones. She dismissed my query. She spoke with a tour guide's impersonal certainty. She expressed little interest in my life, which surprised me but didn't sadden me. It was just as well since so much of it had been devoted in recent years to finding her. I was reluctant to admit the dependency-at-a-distance which that implied, content just to be in her presence like one of a group of ruddy-cheeked cider tourists.

It's improbable, mind you, that she would have spoken about my half-brothers to tourists as she did to me.

Spotty had just raced past us. A cyclist picked herself from the hedge along the verge, oathed, gesticulated. His bloated vehicle was towing a box with Hickory Hollow Dude Ranch fancily inscribed beneath an airbrushed near-naked cowgirl astride a fine palomino. Puppy waved from the passenger seat. A puzzled horse, rueing that its fate was not to be a fine palomino, stared from the back.

'I wish he wouldn't drive like that . . . The boys . . . They're as accident prone as the lion tamer. Are you coming to Puppy's party? Did he ask you?'

'He did.'

'This isn't the first time he's got engaged. You can be sure it won't be the last. I just hope if there's accidents at the party they'll only be small ones. And no knives. He's hired security with body armour, that's a nice touch . . . he's a caring boy. It was after the last one when he got engaged to Kirsty that . . . that the unspeakable happening happened . . . if it had been anyone else's son I'd have laughed like the drain . . . but it was not anyone else's . . . it was Puppy . . . my silly silly boy.'

One of Kirsty's and Puppy's recreations comprised Puppy smearing his glans with ouzo or pastis for Kirsty to lick off. Harmless fun and a form of contraception approved by over 90 per cent of top cardinals polled. 'It's the way forward,' the Archbishop of Bampopo instructed his flock. The couple were thus conjoined one afternoon in the MacFeral house. A crash, a howl, the sound of splintering wood and bursting plasterboard . . . Kirsty had forgotten that her mother had just popped out for a tin of luncheon meat for the dog she was dog-sitting. Vernon, the neighbour's Marcher Hound, was a deadly weapon disguised as a pet. A deadly weapon with an acute sense of smell and an insatiable appetite for aniseed. He goes upstairs three at a time and gatecrashes the party at the top. He broke through a flimsy panel, leapt onto the blighted bed, claws forth, and went for it, clumsily mistaking plate for snack. What Kirsty called Puppy's gent-nethers were chewed, bitten, torn. He was as good as circum-cised by a dog that must have told itself it was a mohel. It only drew the line at castration because the returning Mrs MacFeral called out: 'Oo's a famished dogsy wogsy then!' The weapon went hurtling in search of further meat. The love that would never end ended.

They saved him. They saved it. It was touch and go. He will never be without testicular dineage, stabbed vitals and groin maskells – sometimes all at once. They have him doubled up and wincing. His case was reported in an article entitled 'Aniseed Balls' published by an obscure magazine called *The Paracelsian.*

Vernon joined the military police. He serves with distinction.

They might have been my (diluted) blood family but they were stran-gers. Like people you meet on holiday, forced into acquaintance with. I sat on a tree stump watching Spotty and one of his wranglers try out the pair of Canadian canoes he had bought as extra attrac-tions for the ranch, no more than a group of converted farm buildings and stables decorated with Wild West motifs, chuck wagons, a cere-monial entrance made of telegraph poles. A man dressed in brown and gooseshit green greeted me with a hail-fellow-well-met boom: 'You the prodigal son . . . Jai good to meet yuh.'

Then he slapped me on the back as though I was choking.

'Touch of the Hiawathas, eh? Spotty the noble savage, eh? I've got a pow-wow with him in just a moment. I'm Bobsih by the way. Ciao. Be seein' yuh.' That was typical of the level of interest shown in me. I didn't feel sorry for myself, I felt sorry for them . . . for their unen-quiring minds. Life for them was not perpetual learning, perpetual discovery. To make the most of this life which is not a rehearsal we must treat it as if we are at school for ever (without the food, the bully-ing, the compulsory sport, the muddy pitches in freezing weather, the hellish communal showers, the bored teachers, the stupid fellow pupils, the brainwashing).

Puppy showed off his gleaming Poppy Tours coaches patriotically painted with the cap badges of valiant regiments. 'We don't let patriot-ism die at Poppy Tours in any shape or form. Trench foot and gangrene, king and country – we don't discriminate. I mean, we do discriminate against deserters, mutineers and that rabble. The ones that let us down.'

Clover Chugg drove me to a picture postcard thatched cottage with leaded lights, the headquarters and store of her mail order lingerie business Dream Tupping. 'Saves them the embarrassment of being seen shopping . . . we're so proud to be bringing in a special new line from Austria . . . quadruple-stitched . . . really strong like it was arc-welded . . . it's for this lady called Jackie . . . normal products won't stand up to the wear and tear of her romantic encounters.'

I feigned interest in cider production, hop varieties, how to prevent mead from tasting like horse piss, and the tiresome game of spoof. Vera made dill soup with dumplings, bacon with cabbage, potato cakes which reminded me of latkes.

She brusquely reproved me: 'Catholics do not cook Jewish dishes.'

Nor do Catholics assist let alone promote suicide. Judas was not a Catholic. He may not even have been a Christian: was there then such a thing?

I couldn't outlive my welcome for I'd hardly received a welcome. I sat around the house avoiding the ranker sofas and The Sergeant and Me Old Mum. You could hear them coming from afar with their coughs and hawking and heavy feet echoing on the stone-flagged corridors. I valued my brief chinwags with Vera, golden moments of filial devotion. She was always 'up to me neck in it I am, me' she'd say, over her shoulder, busy as a bee, hurrying, hauling stuff like The Sergeant. She wasn't going to allow my presence to impinge on her routine. She'd sit down out of puff and watch an episode of *Work-shopping a Plasma Rich Lifestyle*. She showed me a shelf of *Little Gay Tractor* books: 'That's how I learn the language of Shakespeare. I look at a page and remember every word even if I don't understand the word. It all stays for ever. You give me a telephone book and I look at a page then I can tell you every name on it . . . and address. They used to tell me I have a photographic memory – like a Leica.'

I remembered the days when I read the stories aloud to smiling ears.

She took another book from the bookcase. She sat down beside me. 'We are in here! Us. Our oast.' She flipped through the pages of *A Further Toast to the Oast: Hop Kilns of England West of the Severn* by Sir Geoffrey Shadoxhurst Bt.

'Here we are . . .' She pointed proud as a heron. 'Our oast. Atmosphere. Don't you think. You never see cloud that black in real life . . .

493

Milord Charming . . . he was so charming . . . he had an old-fashioned camera plate camera . . . he had an ancient valet person carrying it . . . very wizened . . . beast of burden . . . poor fellow was sadly crippled . . . he wore a built-up shoe like my sister of long ago . . . oh what became of her what became of her . . . he had leg irons too . . . He said: "Don't see many of those any more . . . do we, Ned! Rather *alter hut* . . ."'

'"*Altmodischen!*" I replied to his gracious surprise.

'Milord loved a rich chuckle . . . His saucy joke was our kind of oast is like a doughty oven for burning certain peoples. He knew The Sergeant's name in connection with burying Reichsführer Himmler – it's in all the books you see . . . fascinated to hear about it but I never like to say too much because The Sergeant prefers to tell it his own way and he'd gone to the Bath and West that day.

'It was ever so touching the way Milord ruffled Ned's hair when he said that. The English not usually like that. Doughty, that was his word . . . The cone-shaped ones in Kent and wherever are not so fit for purpose. He wrote ever such a nice thank you letter . . . embossed paper with a crest and fountain pen – definite class ink. Hoped that he could meet The Sergeant. Said he was not just a witness to historic act but participant in historic act.

'I kept the letter hidden. Milord struck my nerve. As a top land-owner he had an eye for how hops, apples, all the valley bounty turns into profit. Or not. He could literally smell in the red, the whiff of receivership on the wind.'

Spotty also had only himself to blame for his big accident, for the big hole in his life, a hole filled by – shudder of yuck – Billie Shelf, the little trollop.

'Josie was made, just made, to be our daughter-in-law. So giving, so considerate, so hard-working . . .'

If only she had had that appointment a different day. She was waiting her turn at Justine de Montfaucon, award-winning colour-ists, chatting about nothing to another customer, Yu with the bob from Planet Dumpling. They were both turning the pages of glossy magazines. Yu squinted. Then she held a page in front of Josie.

'Doesn't that man look just like Spotty.'

An advertorial photo of a kidney-shaped swimming pool beside a long low white Mediterranean style building. Bougainvillea, albizia, box hedges. A couple in the foreground, grinning, stiffly holding hands as though they had only just met, which they had. In the background was another couple. They were seated beneath a gaudy parasol drinking gaudy drinks gaping lustfully at each other oblivious to the photo-shoot in front of them. She wore a tiny cache-sexe, she overflowed her top. He wore pink and lime paisley trunks. Josie stared at the photo transfixed. Yu thought Josie was amazed to find her fiancé had a double – who'd have believed it? Then Josie changed colour. The penny dropped like injurious masonry. She feared Josie was going to faint.

Josie consoled herself with croaks of fury: 'I bought him those trunks . . . he was going to the Euro Cowboy Fair in Jerez . . . when he came back he said he'd had a miserable time . . . he'd missed me so much . . . he'd been so busy . . . They were the most expensive trunks I'd ever seen.'

She burst into tears.

But she got over it, as persons will, by identifying as Joe, a male shepherd with crook, smock, flock, dog – the lot.

He/she was in full kit at Puppy's engagement party in the ranch's loggy saloon, accompanied by the former Melvin, now Miriam – 'Hebrew to Shebrew' was the valley gag.

On a sort of mezzanine above the Abilene style saloon called The Western Caseretta were The Dread Necks – a country band with a cornpone singer, plangent steel guitar and sub-Nudie suits. They whined familiar tales of trailer park deceit, disloyalty, snuggling up with a gun, grits, disputed paternity, crimes of passion, self-pity, adultery, the boulevard of broken dreams, losers in love, lonesome wanderers, fate dealing off the bottom of the pack, rodeo trauma, the pain of parting, staring at the bottom of a half-empty glass.

'I'm going to catch that horse if I can and when I do I'll give her my brand . . . she'll be just like a wife.' They hymned fine mares (more trustworthy than women: who am I to disagree?).

This was not an environment I was at ease in. No sirree as they say in those songs, probably. Airless, muggy, overheated, over-odoured with perfumes, testosterone, oestrogen, alcohol and the sweat of rutting dancers, most of them immodestly dressed because it was airless, muggy etc. – and the fashion.

I had walked from The Cry For Help, breathing in the fine brisk country air, breathing it out in white cataracts. When I arrived at Hickory Hollow some youths on the veranda that stretched along the entrance front were enjoying 'just a friendly playful scrap', so one of them told me. A man called Tokki (?) was being kicked in the head by his mates. Something to do with drugs. Security animals were frankly amateur-night. Average weight nineteen stone, average collar twenty inches: too much bulk not enough stealth. Once I'd been frisked I stuck to murky cider you couldn't see through because of the soup of rat meat. It's said to overstimulate the amorous instincts.

Despite my bladder also being overstimulated I was emboldened. Standing by the bar, jacket hooked over my shoulder like a crooner of long ago, I smiled a skittish, kittenish smile at a contender in the mutton dressed as lamb category: rough as emery paper, western hat, fringed chamois bustier and skirt, wiggling her flirty butt in time to the music, twirling a glacé cherry in an empty glass as a provocation.

'You OK are you?' she asked in an accent as bogus as the singer's.

'Yes, why?'

'Your face – you look like you might be having a stroke.'

I pulled up a stool, hung my jacket on its back, and closed in on this cowgirl.

'That was just my . . . smile.'

'Smile?'

'My kittenish smile, yes,' I twinkled.

'Really . . . I can't think what sort of kittens you must hang with . . .'

'What are you drinking?'

'80 per cent proof Wild Turkey Rare Breed does me nicely, Mister . . . Hits the spot time time and again . . . Let's call the garcon.'

She pointed with a steady finger at the framed portraits of country musicians hung above the Bourboned shelves: 'Legends – every one of them. They lift the troubles from our shoulders. They are saviours. They are redeemers. They have died for us.'

Timmy-Boy Niel, Sullivanetta Hagen, Penn Hillstoke, Toni Lo

Reno, Lod Fothergill, The Smerdon Sisters wrapped in the confederate flag . . .

'Are you sure they're not all still alive?'

'Technicality . . . You know what I mean . . . You know, I never seen you at the boys' parties before . . . you the new sheriff in town?'

'You could say that.'

'Hi diddly dee, Man of Mystery.'

'I'm Henry.'

'*Ah ha . . . that Henry* . . . truly the Man of Mystery. Out of the swirling mists of the past as they say. Me I'm from the present . . . clear and present danger as I'm often told. Pleasure lovin' . . . that's one of the nicer things they say about me . . . I'm Carla – Clover's trashy big sister gone to the bad. Half-sister in actual fact . . . my pappy Duggie put himself about a bit despite being a real shorty . . . I never know if the twins aint my half-brothers too . . . knowin' the state of beds in the valley Clover may well be marrying her father or son or uncle . . . who knows . . . all part of the rich tapestry.'

'I've got to pee.'

'I'll bet you have. And don't think I wouldn't love to watch but I got to get another drink.'

The toilet was full of Nibelungen industriously smithing lines of cocaine from a compressed block. Hoping there were no dogs around I expressed myself loopingly beside the path to the stables. It had begun to drizzle.

When I got back to the bar there was a line dance in progress – militaristic hokey cokey. And Carla was nowhere to be seen. Nor was my jacket. I panicked. My wallet, my cards, my keys. I asked the garcon, as Carla had called him. No idea, too busy pouring. I pushed through the guests attracting grimaces and malign stares. No one gave a toss. I found Spotty. I explained. He became excited.

'Let's have a butcher's at the CCTV.'

We sat in his cubbyhole of an office.

'This,' said Spotty, 'is the best bit of the evening for me. No doubt . . . Thanks for bringing it me. We got suspects by the score.'

He stroked his toy. He speeded the recording, slowed it, magnified it.

'Here we are.'

The screen showed Carla pushing away a very short very fat man.

Shrugging him off, slapping his face with its dropsical folds like a brahman cow, elbowing him off.

'There's Carla. And yes that's her dad Duggie. Duggie Chugg. Duggie the dip. Light-fingered blighter. Totally predictable. I'll fetch him.'

He returned with the very drunken Duggie wearing my jacket, which came down to his knees and devoured his hands. A comedy turn. The Sergeant was with him.

'What you accusing my mate of?'

He prodded my chest.

'He took my jacket.'

'I weren't thieving. It's tradition . . . the bilking of the mark . . . the fiancée's father's loving cup . . . sign of respect. And I was cold.'

'Tradition! What sort of . . . And cold! You're joking. It's like the Black Hole of Calcutta.'

'Don't be rude you . . . I got Rausmuller Syndrome Type F.'

'He is,' said The Sergeant, 'not a well man and you, you're the bleeding cuckoo upsetting the applecart, you're persecuting him. I don't want to see you round here again. Got that?'

He hadn't taken my wallet and its contents.

I nodded my thanks to Spotty. I rejoined the party. Carla, staggering, supported by the similarly staggering singer, launched herself at me: 'It's your choosy nympho, my honey sugar. You wanna play deep frottage with my cute butt. This here is Glen Clent – Glen's gonna join us, aren't you, Glen.'

Glen replied: 'You know I would, Carla, but the old lady's here . . . I'll pass. She's developed them funny sort of neo-bourgeois morality hang-ups since we got the new house.'

His accent was Birmingham, the English one. A fur piece from Alabama.

I found my mother among the bodies supporting each other in case they fell in an undignified pile. We stood outside on the damp veranda. It reeked of vomit.

An ambulance's light flashed. A stretcher team lugged a wounded guest. A woman in a torn dress pummelled a man kneeling in a puddle. Tears, blood, shrieks, threats, a confederate soldier waved a sword, a policeman handcuffed a groggy security guard, a roaring motorcycle lay on its side, its rear wheel digging, spraying earth pellets, grime, stones.

She put her hand on my shoulder. 'It was never going to work out. I'm sorry. I'm not sure about the wisdom of . . . We left it too long. But no hard feelings, my love. I'll always be here for you. It's just that—'

A foundling needs not merely the past, but the right past, the enviable past, the past to take pride in, the patrimonial past to covet.

I had found the right moment to ask the question I most needed to ask.

'Who was my father?'

Breast Milk Cheese and Placenta Fritters

At god knows what hour the doorbell goes. Morning? It's still dark.

There I was preparing our anniversary dinner à deux. Roquefort biscuits, olives, panisse chips, anchoïade; kippered salmon (which Inigo insisted on calling bradan rost) with minted leaves; twelve-hour lamb shoulder and saffron potato puree; Époisses; chocolate apocalypse with caramel armageddon and Cointreau revelation.

I heard the ringtone: 'Don't Tell Me to Shush, Mush!' – remember The Barry Island Five? I love novelty numbers. 'Empty Wigs' with that squeaky accordion and the moomoomoo chorus. Inigo always says The Barry Island Five sound like shorthand for a gross miscarriage of justice! I thought it was safe to assume it was him to say that he had been delayed.

Well, I suppose in a sense he had been.

Irreversible coma sounded like a delay to me. Pretty permanent. Brain dead sounded sort of temporary, somehow worse than dead full stop. Dead full stop is neater, cleaner. More chic even, you might think. Yes, more chic.

The caller from Poppy Tours had a solicitous manner. Welsh? The Welsh are said to be a warm people despite destroying holiday homes. Probably because of deprivation and hardship. Lungs with pneumoconiosis and emphysema just shouldn't be made to sing like that, bellowing at god like god's got hearing difficulties. How do they know he has? Are they ENT specialists or just showing off?

Even though it wasn't his job to do so he apologised that the Belgian police had taken hours to identify the victims and inform the British embassy. The accident had happened at 9.30 in the morning. There had, he said, been complications.

I looked at the invitations on the mantelpiece. Inigo and Dominic . . .

Inigo and Dominic . . . Inigo and Dominic. I thought about cutting between our names and discarding the Inigo bits. The things that cross one's mind! I looked at my face in the mirror above the mantelpiece. Unchanged from when a few moments ago I still had a lifemate.

'Have you got someone to comfort you at this difficult time?'

'A bottle or two of Lagavulin!' I wasn't joking.

'Would it be a help to speak with Mum?'

'I'm afraid my mother died over ten years ago.'

Was it really that long? I was fretting about the saffron potatoes sticking. Would Inigo approve my wine choices . . . As it happens he wouldn't be approving or disapproving.

'No no. I meant would you like to speak to *my* mum?'

Now, that struck me as strange since I didn't know the lady.

'She's skilled in this department,' he said.

I asked: 'What department . . . I mean . . . sorry, I'm not getting—'

'The easing department,' he replied, 'easing . . . no?'

'I really haven't a clue what you're on about.'

'So sorry – you forget . . . some folks aren't so familiar with what we call our special vocabulary . . . what I'm offering to you and shall be offering to all the loved ones afflicted in such tragic circumstances is a Poppy Tours' partnership service . . . in collaboration with our partners in Dream Topping™ – our bespoke guided counselling,' he explained (or not).

'It so happens that Mum was a Founder of Dream Topping™. She's in semi-retirement now – in the autumn of her years – but she retains the title of Eliminator Emeritus. Just as . . . she retains a strong conviction in her mission. I have a feeling that she could be just the person to steady you at this special hour . . . She knows how to help you through the great barrier of bereavement, through that invisible wall of being . . . to rejoin Inigo . . . on the other side. As well as taking care of your psychic travel we endeavour-trigger the physical – how to circumvent the jeopardy beacons . . . watch out for the scalabilities. The process is painless . . . we supply the required medications. Mortar and pestle for the more traditional adventurer . . . Most folks who aren't in poverty prefer to grind them in the Magimix . . . add sugar and alcohol of choice – I'm guessing Lagavulin for you! – then lie back . . . let yourself be carried downstream to the velvet ocean and then to a far port where Inigo will be sitting on the quay waiting to greet you, a chilled glass of Sancerre in his hand . . . how does Ultimate Hospital sound? Tempted? . . . Shall I email you our terms?' Tympanic rehearsal in my head. My mouth was uncouth. I stretched out for Inigo. Then it slowly resolved itself. Last night. The call. The further calls. Booking myself on a flight to Brussels at – when? I worked out what had happened, where he was or wasn't. I remembered. I burst into tears, again.

The bell didn't let up. I opened the door in my dressing gown. Two uniformed policemen and two police dogs stood there. Another policeman in a cheap leather jacket waved a sheet of paper.

'Mister . . . ?'

'What is this? D'you know what time it is?'

'It's the time when you catch people unawares. You would be?'

'What's going on?'

'I asked you who you are.'

'My name's Dominic Rose.'

'This is a warrant for these premises.'

'What? You must—'

'We are not mistaken. Got that? Thirty-four Blenheim Gardens. Going to have a little shufti us, eh!'

'What . . . what are you looking for?'

'Ooh that would be telling now, wouldn't it . . . And you are the what . . . The owner? The tenant?'

'Co-owner . . . I just heard last night my partner has been severely injured so what are you doing? What are you doing?'

I was tearing up again. Welling.

'That would be Ian Noel Horrocks. The co-owner. Your *partner*. Sounds likely more *ex*-partner eh?'

'This is—'

'I repeat. Ian Noel Horrocks. Your partner . . . ex-partner . . . sex partner . . . ooh you two and your love muscles, Sir . . . if we can marry people of the same sex . . . next thing you know it'll be pigs, dogs, marrying donkeys . . . *Ian Noel Horrocks*. Your partner?'

'Yes . . . I suppose—'

'You sound unsure, Dominic.'

'Inigo. He . . . used the name Inigo. As an historian. Nom de plume.'

'Ooh. Did he indeed? *Inigo*. Very fucking fancy. His *nom de plume* – Mister Parlay Vous is he? *Was* he? Never trust a fairy name changer. One of the fundaments of our trade. As taught at Hendon – of which college I am a fucking proud graduate. Are you going to invite us in . . . or shall we get Captain here to have a word?'

Captain was a Marcher Hound with a particularly gloomy outlook on life. I stood aside.

'Not much moolah in being a historian . . . I've noticed that . . . easy to succumb . . . temptation all around . . . *lured* into crime . . . empty wigs.'

He held his face close to mine. Cigarette breath. He picked up the letters from the console table awaiting Inigo's return, sniffed one with a hairy noxious rozzer's nostril. It was like he was channelling reality TV hardman Vince Yarker from *We Know Where You Live*. He was what Inigo called BP. Beyond Parody. That didn't make him any less scary.

'Year or two back we banged up a very naughty historian . . . had a habit of walking out of Greek churches with icons. Specialist in Ionian something or other . . . Supplementing his research grant he said – not much of a fucking defence is it? He was lucky – he got to pay his debt in an English nick . . . Can you imagine a Greek one? Oooooh! Rampant! Not the sojourn of choice for a big girl's blouse – what would that be then . . . 36 F cup? Let's start at the top, lads.'

'I'm going to call my solicitor.'

'He's not going to thank you for being woken up at this hour.'

'*She* . . . And she won't mind.'

Ayesha said to take photographs of every room in the house to record and discourage the filth's vandalism, also learnt at Hendon – or does it come naturally to these louts? She'd be with me in less than forty minutes.

She hugged me: 'Why didn't you call – you silly thing.'

'I know, I know . . . I just wanted to be alone looking at what I'd cooked. Listening to him commenting on it.' I laughed and cried, laughed when I realised how ridiculous I must sound, cried because the finality of finality was rushing in recurring waves. The Boulevard of Broken Dreams was a cul de sac with an unscalable wall at its end.

They were all gathered in Inigo's study.

When the cheap leather jacketed copper saw Ayesha there was a swift intake of breath.

His face went swiftly from confident bully to cornered bully.

Ayesha smiled at him: 'Detective Sergeant Hubback! Great to see you. Great to see you're not suspended . . . at the moment.'

'Detective Inspector it is.'

'Any hint of irregularity and you'll be back to constable. Understood?'

She turned to me: 'Detective *Inspector* Hubback has a remarkable gift. Whatever he seeks he finds. Where there were no seeds he finds plants. Warrant please.'

The lout extracted the now crumpled paper from his cheap leather jacket. She read it. He fiddled with his cheap leather jacket's buckles.

'You're in shit. Have you looked at this?'

'Course I have. It's well valid. Don't you come the learnt fucking friend with me, *Miss*.'

'This isn't a search warrant. It's an arrest warrant – for Mr Horrocks. Granted in response to an Interpol Red Notice. The subject of the arrest warrant is in a coma . . . as you know very well.

'This warrant has no legitimacy. And you are heading back to constable. And I shall bring a formal complaint against you. And another for damages to reputation – which I appreciate you don't understand because you don't have one worth damaging. Now if you dare call me a Paki bitch, again, I have a witness . . . to whom you have caused psychic harm. Even if this was an arrest warrant it would not sanction the presence, the invasive presence, of these dogs. Out!'

I am grateful to Denzil Groob (fractured wrist, abrasions), Len and Terri Mandy (him: facial bruising, her: broken Travel Scrabble set), Fizz Pinniger ('shaken but not stirred!'), Mitch Cannock (nosebleed, whiplash) and Stan 'The Wheels' Corner (aggrieved) for what follows. Any faults are mine.

The coach had been late leaving Antwerp. Poppy Tours executive Spotty Dogg, wearing his 'signature' Stetson and embroidered, pearl-buttoned rodeo shirt, and snuffly Poppy Tours reception coordinator Billie Shelf were unusually slow at stowing the luggage.

It was as if there wasn't enough room because everyone had added a parcel or two of gifts from Souvenirs van Oorlogsvoering or Boutique of The Bulge: oriflammes, iron crosses, Mausers, Wehrmacht helmets etc.

No. They were just slow.

'They were fussing about like old women. Old women with hangovers . . . that'll be it.'

Stan The Wheels was getting impatient. He offered to help them but they refused. Inigo tapped his wrist impatiently. He was about to pick up his Black Watch tartan case.

'Why don't I just take it inside? There's plenty—'

'Regulations. You know that as well as I do,' said Spotty.

Conditions were not much of an improvement on the previous day when the party had been taken by boat around Walcheren Island at the mouth of the choppy Scheldt. Inigo was relieved it was the end of the tour.

When he phoned that evening he complained about yet more broken dykes, yet more collapsed bunkers, yet more Flemish drizzle, yet another opportunistic museum. 'How many damned curators can one battle sustain?' But it's safe to assume that he wasn't really fed up. I knew that. And he knew I knew. He loved imparting knowledge whether it was to an audience of millions or to thirty old soldiers and war tourists.

It was one of the war tourists whose selfishness and unforgivable irresponsibility was the major cause of the tragedy.

Ernest Bective was a Poppy Tours veteran, a Pewter Nectar member with Special Privileges. He was Inigo's bête noir. He was known to fellow tourists as Nappies. He called himself Ernestine.

'I identify as a WRAC,' he or she insisted. She wore heavy make-up, which failed to mask her outlaw stubble, a variety of WRAC uniforms of the Fifties and Sixties, a variety of wigs. She claimed to have worked in the Military Police and in the Judge Advocate's department. There was no sound she savoured as much as a rusting door shrieking as it scraped a gas chamber's floor. Oradour-sur-Glane and Lidice were her Mecca, her Lourdes. War criminals' graves really gave her a hard-on: she would have liked to exhume them, to put the

Bloody Bosch on trial again and show them her kind of justice: 'I'm ready with my cheesewire . . . always ready with my cheesewire.'

The other regulars greeted her each morning with a weary 'Harwich for the Continent Ernestine' as she strode towards her seat at the back of the coach beside the toilet. Beware anyone challenging her for that position!

Off they went on the road to Dunkirk with Stan The Wheels berating Spotty because he was going to have to make up time. It's safe to assume that Inigo was deep in popular scholarship with the more learned of the group. I can see him. That's how it had been on the couple of trips I had made with him.

There were friendly disputes:

Were the 2nd Malverns ever stationed at Douai? Surely Saint Omer . . . where the boat lift is.

Honest . . . your uncle can't have been at Amiens, it was the Yanks who were there . . . he *was* a Yank . . . I only call him my uncle out of habit . . . I found out he was my biological . . .

My dad got the MC but we never talked about it . . .

My dad got the clap but we never talked about it . . .

Chortlingly chucklesome.

And less friendly disputes:

Loading trucks up the NAAFI HQ wasn't contributing . . .

I lost my leg when Jerry bombed the Cunliffe-Owen plant so don't you dare say I didn't do my bit . . . We made Spitfire components . . .

Don't you bloomin' well pull rank with me, you stuck-up gopwo . . . territorial twat . . .

You transvestite desk jockey . . .

Ernestine won most arguments by shouting loudest.

'In my day you'd have been on jankers in Catterick.'

Or 'In my day you'd have been in the glasshouse at Shepton Mallet and they thrown away the key.'

Twenty minutes after the coach had set out Ernestine got up as usual to go to the toilet. It was locked. She glared at the door. Sitting only a yard away from it she knew no one had entered it. She prodded the lock with tweezers. She banged on the door with her banana fists.

'Spotty, where are you? The khazi's locked.'

Terri and Len saw Spotty exchange a furtive glance with Billie. A worried glance she reckoned. Terri lip-read Billie berating Spotty: 'I fucking told you.'

Terri whispered to Len: 'What's that about when it's at home then?'

Neither Spotty nor Billie did anything. They ignored Ernestine's racket.

She yelled: 'You got osteo-inertia or what? You going to see to it?' When they persisted in ignoring her she frustratedly marched up to the front where Spotty and Billie were seated just behind Stan The Wheels.

She stood over them: 'Denying an irritable bowel a toilet it's like denying a dipso a drink.'

Liable to end in tears and fury. If not nappies. That's where the name came from. Liable to end here in tragedy.

'We got a technical on the toilet . . . soreee . . . we'll stop at the first services . . . we got services coming up soon. Promisss!' said snuffling Billie Shelf.

'I'm a Pewter Nectar . . . you got no respect. No fucking respect. I'll soil the bus.'

'We'll be there in just a minute,' Spotty, emollient.

'You hold on . . . you know you can . . . there's a good girl,' encouraged Billie Shelf.

'It's not a fucking whim, it's my bowel. It's not by choice I'm irritable!'

Inigo mock-beat his forehead. He sighed to Fizz Pinniger and Mitch Cannock: 'I guess I'd better try and calm him.'

'*Her*,' giggled Fizz, so nicknamed because strawberry blondes are vivacious and bubbly.

Inigo undid his seat belt, straightened the Poppy Tours brochure in the seat pocket in front of him, and with a shake of the head moved down the aisle.

Wout van't Hoff happily agreed that he had been on the E17 at the time the coach left the road. That was all. So had many other vehicles been on that road. He had not been involved in a collision. He had overtaken many vehicles that morning. And no he had not exceeded the speed limit. Check cameras. They are more reliable than the opinion of an elderly tourist who doesn't speak Flemish.

How could he be expected to register the movement of the vehicles he had overtaken? He had just joined the motorway, at the junction near Damslootsmeer (layer of mist on the water). Two minutes later he was driving down the middle lane overtaking many vehicles, maybe the coach in question. Drizzle, windscreen wiper on pause.

The police would have noticed that the tattoo on his generous spare tyre of neck suet looked like a label sticking out of a coat's collar. It showed a heraldic lion breathing fire or showing off an exceptionally long tongue. He was driving a Guy G40 lorry belonging to Bouw Team K&N Projects. The nicknames he had given himself, THROBBING LOVE MACHINE and KILLING HATE MACHINE, were displayed on registration plates in the windscreen.

Denzil Groob told me that:

Not wanting to join in the barney Nappies had fuelled up, he was watching out of the spray-glazed window, worrying about the unsecured rolls of roofing felt, tar paper and glass fibre and the big plastic jumbo buckets of sealant and liquid mortar in the lorry's open back. Bouw Team – a name to remember (and to later report to the police). He worried too when Wout van't Hoff put a fresh cigarette in his mouth and struggled to light it from the dimp of the previous cigarette.

Switching focus, blinking, trying between swipes of the wiper to keep one eye on the greasy road which the lorry was swiftly swallowing up and one eye on the small inflammatory source two blurred inches from his face, he misjudged the relative positions of the two cigarettes. The fresh one knocked the glowing dimp into his lap. It's safe to assume he couldn't see where it had fallen. He flapped with his driving hand. Panicky, he tried to locate hot tobacco not yet ash somewhere in his sticky roofing-specialist's groin. He heaved his body from the sweaty seat. He swept blindly beneath him. It's safe to assume that this made him momentarily abandon control of the lorry which veered into the path of the Poppy Tours coach. A second was all it took to turn one state into another, trees into timber, life into death.

★

Stan The Wheels had joined in trying to calm Ernestine. Frankly it hadn't helped calling her Nappies to her face. Wobbly is as wobbly does (Terri's little phrase, that). His concentration was impaired. He hadn't seen Wout van't Hoff's lorry violating lane discipline till it was too late. He braked hard as he could and swung the wheel. He avoided a collision by attempting to steer the coach onto the hard shoulder. It was travelling too fast for such a manoeuvre.

The coach went beyond the hard shoulder. It left this raised section of the E17 above the Gentbrugge allotment gardens, demolished the mauve and tan wave-motif retaining wall, hurried through the railings beyond and plunged down and down and down through shrubs and alders for what must have seemed an eternity but was only a second till it flopped with a grunt obliterating a hut beside the allotments' car park and raised a dome of dry earth that could be seen from far far away. It did not turn over.

Wout van't Hoff saw something, he wasn't sure what, in the nearside rear-view mirror. He succeeded in lighting a new cigarette, inhaled thankfully and continued to the Heilige Mariaschool the other side of Ghent at Nazareth.

Screams. Self-searches for signs of continued existence. Collective bewilderment. Collective jolting and jarring. Most of the windows were broken. Hardly see-through. Stan The Wheels punched the epicentre of the webbed windscreen glass. Shards pelted in. Dust poured in. There were oaths and whimpers. Several passengers were concussed. Bry from Oswestry was bleeding from a head wound. A voice called: 'I need a torch. I got to have a torch.' Row 4 couldn't move. 'I've smelled this before – it's going to go up . . . it's going to go up.' There was terror in the sudden silent stillness. Followed by a rush to get out of the coach.

'Unseemly . . . that's the only word for it . . . elbows!' said Fizz.

The world was at a tilt down there. The world had finished for my darling Inigo. With the exception of Ernestine he was the only person not wearing a seat belt. He was thrown off his feet. Being so tall his head crashed against the pneumatic door closer. He didn't suffer (that was for me, forever). He never regained consciousness.

I was there at Ghent University Hospital to sanction switching off life support – without Dream Topping™ greedily claiming a fee for pulling the plug.

Every cloud. When the coach landed the toilet door sprung open. Ernestine's finely tuned extra sense spotted it immediately. She fought her way towards it. Amidst the screams and moans and oaths and cries and the chaotic race to get out in case of fire Ernestine pushed against the tide of her fellows, barging, footing the length of the vehicle from the very front to the back. While the rest of the passengers were in distress and shock, climbing over seats with old limbs on the blink, flailing and stumbling, struggling to move, Ernestine was savouring a mighty evacuation (hints of dried fruit, and were those notes of Maasdammer cheese coming through?).

Stan The Wheels gave Inigo the kiss of life on a patch of damp grass. In vain, in vain. That loving gesture would not correct the deep fault in my darling's brain. The passengers became refugees in the scrawny drizzle. They wondered where they were. The traffic above roared on oblivious. Its spray rose high. The boughs dripped. There was no one around. The allotments were deserted. A flag on top of a rusty shipping container drooped in the damp. They stared at improvised polythene windbreaks and tidy rows of cabbages converging in the distance. An unmade road of puddles disappeared into a wood. They hugged one another, failed to avoid muddy puddles. They hesitated to shelter in the dank spaces between the piers that supported the motorway – drier but uninviting, all grubby sacks and broken axles.

'It was like being marooned.'

'Yes but only for a few minutes . . . that's not a real castaway.'

Spotty was doing a head count with his clipboard. It looked purposeful. There was a feeling that he didn't know what to do. Like the toilet the luggage compartment had burst open. A few cases and rucksacks were on the damp ground along with intact panes of window glass. The coach was squashed. The tyres had burst. The wheels were retracted and invisible, absorbed by the vehicle, making it immobile, settled. It might have been there for years rather than minutes.

'Where the fuck is Nappies?' Spotty asked no one in particular.

★

Dave Maliphant, on his eighth Poppy Tour, had been last off the bus. He started to try to speak, seized his left shoulder with his right hand, gargled, rattled, jerked, his neck spasmed in time to an infernal rhythm. He folded into the ground. Fizz knew the symptoms. She cradled him as he died.

'He went doing what he loved most.' Spotty patted her on the back and hurried away.

Billie found Ernestine sitting in the coach.

'I done my ankle. I can't move.'

The breast of her WRAC dress uniform was covered in white dust. She asked: 'What is it? It's all over the khazi?'

'Just you sit there, dear,' Billie instructed.

Billie was soon outside again, huddled up with Spotty. They had something on their mind. They were neglecting the passengers who were victims. They were not enhancing Poppy Tours' reputation. She went back into the coach.

'Let's see if I can't brush you down,' she said to Ernestine. She wiped the dust with an antimacassar.

'What is it? I'm getting it all tickling my nose. It feels funny. I'm coming over all funny. I need water. I got this ankle. What *is* it?'

'It's like the powder from the airbag. Very technical and that. Gets everywhere. But it's just talc really.'

Billie helped Ernestine out of the coach. Her injury had been caused when she forced her way to the toilet.

Mitch was puzzled. What was Spotty up to when he leapt up the coach's steps with an urgency previously unseen? He was clutching Dave Maliphant's khaki kitbag and Inigo's distinctive suitcase, both of which must have been ejected from the luggage compartment. (We chose the suitcase together in Archie Povey & Nephew on the Royal Mile. Inigo had been for the Balfour. But he came round when I said it looked more like a Japanese tartan than anything RLS would have recognised.) When Spotty re-emerged from the coach he was still holding the suitcase and the kitbag. He was soaked. He looked as though he had been in a shower.

'Just fixing a cistern problem,' he explained to Mitch who thought it seemed an odd thing to be worrying about. No sense of priorities with the young.

The first emergency vehicles ploughed along the unmade road. Wailing sirens, flashing lights. They had responded to calls from witnesses to the coach leaving the motorway and from the bedraggled passengers standing in the drizzle struggling to give a map reference for this patch of land whose characteristics were described variously as 'ordinary . . . spongey underfoot . . . just like you might find anywhere . . . near a sort of track'. It was noted that neither Spotty nor Billie had known the relevant numbers to ring.

'They had the leadership clout of a gnat. No nous, no gumption. They were there . . . but they weren't there. He kept on going on about how his hat was ruined. I don't know what they were on. When in doubt bury your head in the sand . . . You know where that would have got you in Crossmaglen.'

Terri put her arm round me: 'Inigo would have got it shipshape in minutes . . . that's the tragedy of it.'

'That's a bit of a selfish way of looking at it, love,' Len frowned at her.

'No . . . please. It's all right,' I told him. 'It just shows how much he was appreciated . . .' I kept on tearing up. The loss was everywhere. These people meant so well. Salt of the earth. They didn't see, they couldn't see, that he was in everything in the sitting room we were sitting in, everything. Silly keepsakes mean as much as paintings by name artists.

It was one long yearning for the irreplaceable, for our great past together, all sun-dappled days . . . and for my future alone, all darkness. The house, our house, *my* house had changed purpose. It had gone from home to monument, from shelter to memento mori.

They took him to Ghent University Hospital where two days later . . .

The unmade road was narrow and slippery, unsuitable for large vehicles. Hoofdinspecteur Claes Pauwels of the Lokal Politie did have leadership clout. He commissioned vehicles appropriate to need and the road's dimensions. He offered to arrange social services counselling for anyone who might need it: you may not feel you do now, but later . . . He organised accommodation till a way of getting the Fighting Soldiers (as he called them, jovially, in English) back to their homeland.

He was tireless, cheerfully efficient, all good fellowship. What a contrast to morose Spotty and nervy agitated Billie.

'It was *her*,' Fizz reckoned, 'she was always at him she was . . . What was it – three years ago? When we did the Atlantic Wall tour . . . no problem with Spotty . . . not that anything went pearshaped and tragic that time . . . it was different . . . it was Josie then – she was a love, a real coper type . . . nothing too much trouble . . . with Billie it's all about her isn't it . . . wasn't cut out for it . . . whined when we were told they'd found a barracks for us to rest in . . . like it wasn't good enough for her . . . even though it was just temporary. And it wasn't a barracks any longer anyway.'

'Apart from the kennels.'

'Apart from the kennels,' she echoed with a tut tut tut.

An ambulance carried Dave Maliphant to the University Hospital. Another carried Inigo. A minibus took those with minor injuries. The rest of the passengers were transported to the centre of Ghent, to the Leopoldskazerne, a group of fortified buildings that were boorish and fussy, a dandy sergeant major made brick. A van carried the luggage. They were all shown to Salon Galerij, a café cum common room in a part of the barracks that was now De Lantaren arts workshop, theatre, studios etc. Everyone was solicitous. The actors rehearsing Van Ermengen's *Verdwenen* fetched blankets. Cakes, hot chocolate, coffee with a shot of genever were offered in an access of communality. The chairs and sofas were comfortable if shabby. The colourful daubs and posters were cheering. The three-person trauma team was gentle. It was cosy. A prized quality in Flanders. A young doctor who had been summoned was remarked on for his exquisite manners and beautifully manicured hands.

'Nappies would be appreciative, eh?'

But Ernestine wasn't there. She was being treated in hospital for her injured ankle, a strange fit of vomiting, dizziness and breathlessness.

Getting on for an hour after they had arrived at the former barracks Hoofdinspecteur Pauwels reappeared. His demeanour was much changed. His conviviality had dissipated. He was angry.

'Angry? Well . . . more like he looked determined. Sort of betrayed.

What I'd call indignant . . . with reason, it has to be said . . . with reason.'

He was accompanied by three officers. Two armed with sub-machine guns. FN P90s: someone identified them.

'It was scary . . . after all that happened that morning. Suppose it adds a touch of spice . . . a wee soupcon of South Armagh, you might say.'

The third officer with Aspirant Inspecteur Guus Pronk was a dog handler. His dog Lars was a Moorddadige Hond who would sooner have been rampaging through a maternity ward ripping out the intestines of the newborn and guzzling them than mooching duti-fully beside his master.

Ghent is gaunt, Gaunt, bleak, the Middle Ages with trams. Black cobbles, black canals, black clouds. The decor was just the job. Couldn't have been more fitting. When it wasn't pouring it was driz-zling. One thing I learnt during that first spell in Ghent dealing with the death trade's grey faces is that mulled beer relieves melancholy for an hour or two. And then it's time for another: another beer, another bureaucrat. A second thing I learnt: if you speak French you will be met with incomprehension, feigned or real. Just as likely it'll be undisguised hostility. The city is boastfully monoglot, monoglot in a restricted way: non-francophone. Its populace happily responds with gestures and smiles to Italian, Russian, Urdu and of course Eng-lish. It doesn't regard being addressed in them as a patronising insult.

Interpol's headquarters is in Lyon, not a *nederlandophone* city it's safe to assume. That day's several calls and many emails between Ghent and Lyon were – carelessly? wilfully? – misunderstood at both ends. By the time the warrant was served it had been further amended, in a third language, English. Ayesha called it 'a sheaf of Chinese whispers, unfit for purpose'.

The van which had carried the luggage had parked outside the café. The manager told the driver Pim Kok that he would have to find somewhere different to store the luggage: there wasn't room. She suggested a currently unused quartermaster's depot on the other side of the courtyard. The driver did as she said. He had almost finished unloading the van when Aspirant Inspecteur Guus Pronk walked by en route to preparing Lars the Moorddadige Hond's meaty elevenses at the DACH kennel. Lars became suddenly excited, even elated. He sprung towards the back of the van, barged Pim Kok out of the way, leapt onto a Black Watch tartan suitcase and turned triumphantly to Guus Pronk, looking forward to the reward that came his way when he discovered contraband or similar: normally a couple of lusty bitches on heat.

It's safe to assume that Pauwels had expected some form of resistance when seeking the suitcase's owner. Hence his heavy-handed escort – which wasn't needed. Quite what sort of resistance that might have been is anybody's guess.

'He was all formal. Not like before . . . antagonistic . . . he'd turned off the friendly tap . . . blunt.'

'That's right. Didn't explain. Asked very bluntly.'

'When he asked who owned the dark green plaid case – he said "played" – we all looked at one another . . . What on earth is he asking that for . . .'

The passengers' reply was unanimous, an unpractised chorus.

'That's poor Inigo's . . . it belongs to Inigo . . . it's the tour historian's . . . Inigo – the one who's in the hospital . . .'

'I'd say he was a bit taken aback . . . He was looking forward to wringing the truth out of us by foul means.'

'That building . . . it was full of dungeons . . . chains and what have you . . .'

At 3.25 GMT/16.25 CET Doctor Bart Coolmans was standing beside Inigo's hospital bed hoping that some brain activity, any brain activity, might be indicated on the monitor. Hoping, not expecting. Reading the spectral array displays, brain monitors and electro-encephalographic signals didn't give hope.

He was surprised when an unshaven man in a grubby parka entered the room. He announced himself as Commissioner Huysegems. He held up a folded piece of paper, articulated it like he was bidding at auction. He was followed by a wall-eyed policeman in fatigues grasping a submachine gun.

'They were beyond belief,' Bart told me as we afterglowed in my emperor-size bed at the Legation International Hendrik Hotel. We'd played drop the soap for a good hour! Oh! his skin! Oh! the smell of him. The scent of hygiene. Surgical scrub handwash.

'Total out of order.'

They charged a man in an irreversible coma on four counts with the warning that more might follow. Possession of a Class A drug. Import of a Class A drug. Intent to export a Class A drug. Intent to supply a Class A drug. They read him his rights.

'Understood?'

His statement might be used in court.

'Understood?'

They told him he had the right to remain silent.

Bart proposed that Inigo was incapable of doing anything other than remain silent.

They threatened to arrest Bart for obstruction of the forces of order in prosecution of their duty.

They told Inigo that he could be represented by an attorney. He could contact a relative or friend.

'Got that?'

Inigo, being brain dead, did not respond. The police, being police and even more brain dead, put him under guard. Huysegems left.

The animal in fatigues, Stijn Goor, stood outside the door of the room ordering anyone who passed by to identify themselves.

He told an anaesthetist on the way to theatre that a name-tag holder attached to a lanyard was not enough. Any terrorist could get a lanyard. Any criminal accomplice scheming to spring the detained man could get a lanyard. Exasperated, she explained she was in a hurry. He retaliated by putting his gun to her jaw.

When two nurses approached he assumed a kneeling position and held the gun's stock to his shoulder, aiming at them. They screamed, they found refuge in a cleaner's cupboard.

There was a further instance of threatening behaviour. A black porter pushing a young woman in a mobility chair came down the corridor laughing with his charge. Goor stopped him with his gun. He told him what he had read recently in the *Magazine of the Movement*:

'The black man is seldom content with sexual intercourse with the white woman, but culminates his sexual furore by killing the woman, sometimes taking out her womb and eating it.'

The young woman burst into tears.

Goor stared hard at the man.

'Don't worry. Any problems – I'll sort them out.'

The director of the hospital and another administrator arrived to talk to him. He accused them of plotting to help the arrested man to escape. He retreated into the room and locked the door from inside.

When, eventually, Huysegems was recalled he said of his self-incarcerated prodigy:

'Stijn's a bit like that. And all the better for it. He's doing his job. He'll go far. Don't tell me you want a police force riddled with moral laxity. We don't want to go the way of the Netherlands.'

The director of the hospital rejoined: 'Nor of the Third Reich.'

I reached Ghent via Brussels mid-afternoon the day after the accident. All the Poppy Tourists and staff, with the exceptions of Inigo, Dave Maliphant, Stan The Wheels and Ernestine, were once again en route to Dunkirk. It would be a week before I began to make contact with Denzil, Fizz, Len, Terri etc. I knew little of the circumstances of the accident.

I checked in at my hotel and more or less ran to the hospital.

It was surprising, even shocking, to discover an armed guard sitting outside Inigo's room. Why? He was paralysed and could not move. I had not only lost the man I loved . . . I had, strange as it sounds, to clear his name. He was under arrest. Inigo The Drug Mule . . . The idea made me smile. It would have made him smile too if only he could have smiled. I sat with him, I talked to him, I sang to him – 'The Temple of Abandon' (even though it's one of the shit Ricky's) – I told him about the police visit at home, about how brilliantly Ayesha had handled it.

I didn't tell him that there had been an overzealous policeman guarding him here because I had yet to be acquainted with that particular farce. The guard currently on duty was a rookie auxiliary, a bumfluff snoutcast called Wilmots who kept leaving his post to lean from a window down the corridor in an attempt to evade the hospital's ban on smoking.

The nursing staff reprimanded him, as much as it's wise to reprimand an adolescent with a deadly weapon. He sneered in return. They were caring. They understood my plight, they'd seen it before, it was their vocation. I'd never thought of myself as the stiff upper lip type but I found ancestral resources of the stuff. Cry if you want to, I was told. It's no disgrace.

No pupillary responses. No corneal responses. No motor responses. No idea where he was. No idea that he existed. No hope. Not that anyone was saying that – yet. Inigo was a living corpse. It was like expecting movement from a stone. He had so wanted to die swiftly and painlessly while reading the death notices, smugly congratulating himself on outliving this or that acquaintance and in some instances even rueing their passing, rare instances.

After an hour of gazing at what had been Inigo, my lover who wasn't, my husband in name only, I needed to do something else. Anything else. I was a widow. What a thing to realise. Ernestine was on a high floor in the hospital. Courtesy demanded. Curiosity too.

Sitting up in bed with her leg in a hoist was a girl who needed to shave twice a day, whose make-up was cruder than a pantomime dame's. She was entirely, shiningly bald. A backcombed blonde wig sat on a shelf beside her bed. She wore a stained pink see-through baby-doll. She was as obnoxious and self-pitying as Inigo had often described. (He used to make good-natured strangling gestures . . . maybe not so good-natured! That's the sort of sport he was!) What he hadn't mentioned was that she had rotting breath like a workhouse drain.

I asked her what had happened. She omitted her leading role in the tragedy – not, of course, that I knew it then. At that point I had not heard the other passengers' accounts. She pretended to care that Inigo was brain dead. She complained, however, that he had not really sincerely worried about her 'exceptionality'. He told me that he had uncomplainingly sympathised with news of her bowels on several previous tours because that was the way to keep her calm or calmish.

She claimed to be confused because of going to the coach toilet immediately after the crash and being greeted by a cloud of white dust from the airbag: 'It made me go all jiminy cricket if you catch my drift. Like gas at the dentist's in the old days. It was just talc. I never inhaled talc before . . . I'm crust-lucky I didn't inhale more. It can kill nippers with asthma.'

'Do coaches . . . You have some experience of them . . . I mean, is it normal to have an airbag in a coach toilet?'

'You got me there . . . What I'd say is you wouldn't know unless there's a crash . . . then it'll pop out and hit you in the titties.'

'How do you know it was talc?'

I went down to sit at Inigo's bedside again. It was there that I met Bart. Sage-green scrub trousers partnered with cobalt-blue scrub tunic and a jauntily tied matching neckerchief. He knew immediately. I knew too. I thought yum yum, yes indeedy. I felt a tad guilty. But it's safe to assume that Inigo would have given my lust his blessing – he'd never failed to do so before. We had an open civil partnership which we moved forward into an open marriage. No resentment, no jealousy, no recriminations.

Bart introduced himself and the man he was talking with, Aspirant Inspecteur Cornelis Mols.

Mols fed me an automaton's condolences, then listed 'the complexities'.

The arrest warrant could not be withdrawn until a full investigation had been carried out. The regrettable mistakes caused by francophone Interpol officials and the issue of an incorrect warrant did not invalidate the original warrant for the arrest of Ian Noel Horrocks whose suitcase contained a yet to be established quantity of heroin of a yet to be established strength.

Any attempt to reach 'a decisive conclusion' would be regarded as an attempt by third parties to interfere with the conduct of the case and influence the suspect (who was also a witness). Besides which no 'decisive conclusion' could be made without the permission of an examining magistrate.

Bart shook his head, astonished. That is incorrect. It was a medical not a legal judgement that had to be made. Mols ignored him. He stated that the job of the law is to protect and honour the sanctity of life.

The suspect is alive. He indicated the suspect – not a persuasive way of making his point.

The subject was in custody. It was premature – perhaps indecent – to even think about obsequies in the near future. These things take time. An application for bail could be made. These things take time.

The commissariat appreciated the unusual situation. If the bail application was successful the suspect would no longer require a guard. He again indicated the suspect. The suspect would, however, in all instances, require an attorney.

I laughed the laugh of the incredulous: 'He can't instruct an attorney.'

'I regret. For sure there is no provision for these circumstances. I regret . . . So the normal rules must apply. Let me be informed when you have found an attorney . . . I'll tell you, informally, whether you make a good choice . . . is suitable . . . and wise.'

'That is for *the suspect* to decide – isn't it? Not the police, not this ludicrous fucking prosecution.'

Bart put his hand gently on my forearm. He could see where this might go. That was the first time he touched me.

'It is an offence to—'

'Hey hey hey . . . this gentleman is on big stress . . . shall we leave it for now.'

Stress doesn't stop with loss. You realise this absence is permanent. I am in one state. He is in another. The status quo has changed. It's irreversible. The shift is immeasurable. It is also banal. Happens every day. Get over it or sink. My heart hurts, my head hurts. And my hand hurts from signing over and over again.

Inigo developed his 'one slash dash' for book signings. His telly tie-ins brought them out in hordes. My *500 Throws Every Home Needs* didn't. They queued round the block for *Ballad of a Legend* but because every word was supposed to be Ricky van Brabant's were I to so much as show up in the crowd at one of The Great Narcissist's 'events' I'd be in breach of contract. At least I was spared writer's cramp.

Now my hand ached from signing contracts, legitimisations,

permissions, certificates, documents and more documents. My arse hurt from sitting and waiting, sitting and waiting. Death is made for bureaucrats. They were out to make it hard for me. Once it was established that I was next of kin they were relentlessly (but slyly) homophobic. In revenge I signed away – donated! – Inigo's organs to be transplanted in the hope that his whisky-marinaded liver would go to some bastard clerk, infecting him with an addiction to alcohol.

'Or,' said Tamara, 'to a Vlaams Berlang.'

'Whisky,' replied Bart, 'is Scottish or Irish, Kentucky . . . Wherever it's from it's foreign. Very. Probably unacceptable to them. It has to be a genever – liver drenched in genever.'

We laughed over pizza and red wine in Trattoria Renucci on Vridagmarkt.

'But the botanicals in gin, genever . . . aren't they intruders . . . immigrant spices from . . . where are the Spice Islands?' I asked

'Malacca?' suggested Bart. 'Where's that . . . Malaysia?'

'No. Maluku – Indonesia,' grinned Tamara. She ruffled Bart's hair. 'There is nothing my brilliant niece does not know.'

'If only . . .' She held my wrist. '. . . You know, I'd have loved to have met Inigo. Now there was someone who really did know everything . . . the sheer learning! The Darnley and Bothwell book was great, disputed paternity, hint of incest . . . always does it for me . . . and the Show Trials one . . . but *Breast Milk Cheese* . . . *fan*tastic . . . totally inspired. I mean . . . That house . . . oh . . . and Eden – *hullo*! And the quack – Glyde, I didn't know that word crocus. And . . . *sooterkins*! Sooterkins . . . I wrote a story about a woman who has a one-night stand with a stranger then discovers she is pregnant with sooterkins . . . and the stranger may never have existed . . . Till I read *Breast Milk Cheese* I thought I was the only person who knew about them. Wow!'

I was going to tell her that as you get older lots of knowledge you feel is exclusively yours is shared with unknown enthusiasts. The internet tells you you're never alone, there's always someone else who shares your interest in protective-camouflage cushions or collecting *objets de vertu* dated according to the French revolutionary calendar. I didn't say it. I didn't want to patronise this astonishingly clever young woman.

Anyway it's safe to assume she knew it already. She was not yet twenty-five years old, had just published her third Pandora Galland-ers thriller – which was actually her fourth. But *The Exhumation Project* had been withdrawn and was unlikely to be published. It was the subject of an ongoing super-injunction. She was reluctant to talk about it. All she'd say was that it was about politically and ideologic-ally driven militia (or was it militants) brutally attempting to restore the reputation of its former leader who was tarnished by victor's justice. It was based on fact – past fact and future fact.

She was heralded as the New Queen of Flemish Noir.

'As hard and dazzling as an Antwerp diamond,' Roger Baum-johann, author of *Timofei Lopatin: A Grave Robber's Handbook* and *The Lives Beneath Us*.

'*The Dark Watergang* rewrites all the rules of the murky political thriller . . . an unputdownable read. As if Quita Nibb had danced with Larry Cravat to the sound of Iced Unicorn,' Joanne Detasham in *The Times* (London).

'Not quite as ineffable as might be expected from a young untutored woman,' David Starkey in *The Critic*.

Tamara wrote in English and translated herself into Flemish and French. Daunting? 'I'll say! Not 'arf!' To quote Fluff. She even made me wish for a moment that I was one of those rare creatures who was straight! She read my mind: 'I'm seeing someone . . . I'm planning a book about a suicide cult. The guy I'm seeing has experience of one.'

'So you're seeing a corpse,' I said.

'Good try. Not quite – but he is moving in that direction . . . he's twice my age and *totally* unsuitable and I'm exploiting him . . . *totally* shamelessly. He knows even more than I do about poisonous plants . . . and as for the rate of decay in bog bodies . . .'

So I found myself slyly wondering if there was a totally unsuitable Old Queen of Flemish Noir. And if so where do I find him?

'What happened to the rest of the trilogy? How far did he get with it?'

I sighed. I shook my head – in regret, not ignorance.

'It was always mentioned . . . being announced – Amazon, catalogues . . .'

'Erm . . . that's more to do with hope than . . . they're the lies writers and publishers tell themselves . . . tell each other. Some writers anyway. And it wasn't really a trilogy . . . It's complicated. There was a prequel if you like. It had a title. A provisional title – *Life After Afterlife*. There was part of a first draft . . . there were notes, a lot of them, pretty disorganised.'

'So what happened?'

'He burma'd it.'

'He *what'd* it?'

'Burma'd it. Put it aside . . . private joke, sorry. He intended to go back to it. But *Breast Milk Cheese* . . . What went into the book was . . . It was just the tip. There was pretty much an entire iceberg waiting to be explored . . .'

He'd turned up a lot of stuff.

It wasn't just peripheral material that didn't make the cut . . . there was material that was absolutely fascinating . . . he couldn't use it because of the risk of defamation . . . That's why there's a sort of void at the centre.

The material would make a great book. But a suit is a racing certainty. And without risking a suit . . . there's no way it would make a book. He said he might get a magazine piece out of it. Much as he wished otherwise . . . He was quite straight with himself.

The major problem there was Geoffrey Shadoxhurst, Sir Geoffrey . . . Not any old sir . . . a Baronet type Sir no less . . . and a major pain in the arse. He'd been writing some sort of family memoir since the beginning of time, a non-fiction novel he called it – remember them? Inigo called it *Omission*. He had Shadoxhurst down as a world-class name dropper with an haut en bas prose style, aspirantly patrician. Typical of what he called the terminal English tradition of allegiance to the Trinity: Rome, desert warriors with falcons, Debo.

More celebrated exemplars than Shadoxhurst – James Lees-Milne whom Inigo knew and had fucked and Patrick Leigh Fermor whom he didn't and hadn't.

Did I want to go into this? What turned out to be the last two years of Inigo's life were clouded by *Breast Milk Cheese*, by Shadoxhurst's lawyers, by his agent La Négligence, by his publisher Edmund, by Edmund's editors and their pious sensitivity prefects, page upon page of them. Inigo said they must have been recruited from the ranks of creative writing bigots.

Shadoxhurst was a vexatious piece of shit. The descendant of one of the protagonists of *Breast Milk Cheese*. He stole Inigo's research. At the same time he was accusing him of intrusion . . . defamation. He didn't have a legal leg to stand on. Inigo kept reminding him that the dead can't sue. Their descendants can't be summoned to the grave and be instructed by dead bones to sue on their behalf. Shadoxhurst was all bullying threats . . . casual menace. So far right he was outside the frame. A family tradition you might call it . . . going back to Houston Stewart Chamberlain, Mosley, the Harmsworths, Rolf Gardiner, Pitt Rivers of course.

He had a team of security primates . . . a private militia, tawdry no-necks. That was what he relied on. Their presence was enough. They never laid a finger on Inigo. It would have been a different story if he had got wind of Inigo's research methods. The word is imaginative. Inigo could certainly have been prosecuted for theft if nothing else. It was all a bit tit for tat . . . and cat and mouse.

If this wasn't enough there were gormless reviewers who held Inigo culpable of the excesses he was describing. He would say he wished he had never written it. It wouldn't leave him alone. It had a life and reputation independent of him even before it was published. Far more people had *read about it* than had read it.

I must have gone into a trance of remembrance, weighing the pain, listening to some crooner like Nico Fidenco or Mario Uliana half-singing, half-talking, a looming swirling organ: lost love and an empty house deprived of purpose, a house that's no longer a home. A song for me.

'Hey, you OK?'

'What . . . yeh yeh.' The din. Plates clattering, cutlery rattling, glasses' peal, waiters shrieking, punters rumbling. Vivacity – and I had been with the dead.

'You were miles away,' Bart smiled winningly.

'I'm sorry . . . where were we?'

'The sequel that never was . . . it'd be *really* fascinating just to know what happened to those people. I'm not trying to . . . I'm not going to waterboard you, darling,' said Tamara.

'It's OK — let's have some more Primitivo . . . The sequel that never was. That's not the way to describe it. *Life After Afterlife* is a sort of prequel *and* sequel. The successor to *Breast Milk Cheese*. And predecessor. It's notes . . . the stuff he came across . . . the people he came across . . . successor or sequel aren't right. They explicitly pronounce chronology. It connects . . . but it's off in all sorts of directions. There's nothing of what Inigo's telly producer The Oaf called *the journey*. God what a dolt *he* is.'

I was familiar with some of Inigo's ideas. We'd always talk over his projects: I'd get him up to speed with a swift hand.

But there was much more I was unfamiliar with.

Nevertheless I could recall a fair amount of detail.

I must have gone on for — well, I don't know how long. A long time. Mine host Roberto Renucci was delighted by our consumption of wine, Averna, Ramazzotti, grappa, vin santo etc. Oh and those tooth-hazard biscuits. He was so delighted he gave us a bottle of his home-crafted limoncello on the house.

I set to, writing it up. At the very least it kept self-pity at bay. I made what follows from Inigo's first draft and his notes. Liberties have been taken.

What Inigo called the germ of *Breast Milk Cheese* occurred miles away from the once notorious mansion and years away from its once notorious inhabitants.

One of my jobs around the house was to scour travel page ads and internet offers. They bombarded me: Dear Dominic, Hullo Dominic, How you doing, Dominic . . . Made me feel wanted when Inigo was in one of his evil-tempered strops. He was obsessed by bargains. He took 'cheapjack' as a compliment. Destination didn't matter so long as there was a significant reduction. Trains to Chemnitz and Budapest, flights to Cork and Riga. He wasn't fussy. All tax deductible. Claimed as research for a forthcoming TV series. So it was to an extent. We mostly culture toured. You get to some places no one would think of getting to if fares weren't discounted. Some nice surprises: Clermont-Ferrand cathedral is built out of Black Jacks — is that why they dance the tango on its steps? Bari; Uppsala. All very satisfactory.

On the other hand – Myrtle Beach, South Carolina. Cancún. New Jersey. What can you say? And as for Fuengirola!

It was one of those weeks – special offers thin on the ground. When I suggested Fuengirola I thought he'd say why don't we stay home and send out for some overpriced tapas and 300 per cent mark-up Rioja. (He had a taste for masked delivery drivers who kept their helmet on.) I was surprised he was keen. He'd often talked about making a film on the legacy of Ramalama, Arab-Andalus music, the conversos, the Jewish exodus from Spain etc.

About one in ten of his telly projects ever got made. This could be the one: the more semi-familiar a topic the more the executives liked it and there could be cooking in it, they always went for cooking and a journey to find a rare spice (that was actually available in Lidl). Also, he hadn't been to southern Spain since way back. Before my time. He said we could use it as a base to visit Jaén, Granada, Córdoba. He had no idea of distance. He couldn't get the scale of maps. He thought they were just down the road. We wouldn't be able to do those places without overnighting, which defeated the purpose of the Every Day Is Funday In Fuengirola deal.

The Hotel Verdant Spa Collection by Tiger & Luis. That was its name. Everything about it was dreadful. Naff. Seedy. Useless aircon. Hadn't ever been updated. The decoration was offensive: all burnt umber, marmalade, gamboge. Food cartons in the corridors. Uncollected trays. They must have laid off the cleaners years ago. Grouting escaping from between bathroom tiles like pus on the run. Stained porcelain.

Crotch goblins shrieked by the pool. Obese Britz snacked non-stop like they were getting in shape for a so-obese-they-can't-even-waddle competition. All you can eat buffet of grease with grease as a side. Avoid avoid avoid. Proof that you don't have to go on a cruise to contract leptospirosis, legionnaires' disease, norovirus etc.

The first night we went down to the pool late. There were still mounds of humping elephants slapping their flesh against each other, groaning with pleasure and hurt. No way.

I decided to give it a go first thing in the morning even though the sky was milky white with streaks of used bandage. It was so dull that the cluster of palms didn't cast shadows. It was a dead place. All blinds were still drawn against the apology for a day. The leathery pool guy was the one thin, painfully thin, person in this wobbling world of spare tyres and exhibitionistic cellulite. He wore a barbed wire tiara, which was unusual. Thank god I hadn't gone for a dip in the dark. He was using a telescopic skimmer to hoick out the bottles, cans, condoms, bras, bones, plastic sombreros, punctured no longer inflatable dolphins, twisted sun loungers, tampons, water wings, leaves, floater turds etc. No wonder he muttered to himself non-stop. I decided to just say no to Weil's disease. He gestured me to move back from the edge so he could stretch for a pitta bread on the point of disintegrating into an archipelago of bad baking and penicillin.

He flipped it onto the end of the skimmer, nice and neat, one strong sinewy arm only. Like it was a party trick. I smiled to acknowledge it.

He smiled too, with the twinkly charm of the psycho.

'You can't beat an AcquaNet Poseidon. Wuggedly wobust. Puts the Twiton and the Aphwodite to shame. Ugh look at that—' He pointed to a ripped latex harness bobbing, catching the breeze. 'They was bickerwin something terwible. I just told 'em to spank and make up.'

He spoke English with an accent that wasn't quite London. Cockneyish twang with a hint of the bucolix. Clacton? Sheppey?

'Evewy day a miwacle . . . Mark my words: it's goin' to turn out a special super-saturated sunsoaked day today.'

It didn't look it. 'Doesn't look it — unless there's divine intervention.'

'Can be awanged.'

'Let's hope so.'

He glared. 'On me muvver's gwave. It can. Oh yerss.'

He held up his arms, and the dripping skimmer, to the jism white heavens. A sodden nappy detached itself from the skimmer and dropped like a shot gull onto the patterned tiles with a squelch. He looked at it and shook his head.

'Me muvver. She were a one. The lucky lady fwom Loweto. You go' kidz?'

'I haven't. Not so blessed.'

'Blessed! Blessed? Ha! They'd only disappoint yer, not live up to the old man's exactin' standards. My kids 'ave bin a disappointment. Like they set out to 'umiliate me wiv their uselessness. None o'them come to nuffink. Not chips off the old block. No miwacles, no mowality, no anger, no push, no go, no gwand destiny – but that's not surpwising is it. We can't all be the lamb o'god. They should 'ave bin aborted. The lot of them. See, I look for perfection. Like I've often said – be ye perfect even as your farver which is in 'eaven is perfect.'

Inigo appeared with a tray. Churros and cups of thick chocolate.

'Thought I'd find you here. Sweet.'

The pool guy said: 'I wouldn' eat them if I was you. You aven't sin the kitchen – know wha' I min. I was just about to tell your fwiend here that me, I'm Jesus Chwist. I got me barbed wire crown to pwove it. Thorn shortage. It's not a tiawa – I know what you're thinkin', oh yes. It makes the old scalp itch, that's why I only wear it on duty. It's oxidisin' after all these years. Day goin' all wight for you so far? You the 'usband or the wife? The poker or the pokee? No no – let me guess.'

Inigo was so astonished he was quite polite: 'Do you know what time it is to be asking such questions? Christ almighty.'

'Pwecisely, Old Cock, pwecisely . . . Chwist. Moi. Nah don't be alarmed. Stwictly non-judgemental stwictly non-judgemental. Just curewiyus. Only arskin'. I always like to know what bwand of lub-wicant I'm chattin' wiv. Lookin' for the pawable that matches. I would never 'old it against anyone who was usin' udder cweam. Out of fashion wight now but I can wecall when it was all the wage, six hundwed years ago, seems just like yesterday. And mark my words it'll be back. Just like me.'

Inigo caught my eye with an expression saying 'we've got a right one here'.

'I saw tha'. Yerss. I saw tha'. I see what uvvers don' see. I've seen evewything. But I'm lucky. It was touch and go. You might have 'eard this one. Gweat favewit wiv audiences all over the worl'.'

He held his skimmer like it was a prop from ancient games. He recited:

Maywee, eatin' soup for lunch, was still a virgin – just.
Gabwiel, an angel, 'urled by god, like a bolt, bwoke
thwough the casement: these are the words he spoke
to 'er. 'You're up the duff. In the club. You weally must
Believe me. I'm here on god's say so. He's the dad.
Ave Mawia!' It was the first time she heard that song.
'Get on. I'm not some scwubber. I never touched a dong.'
'Love – you're chosen. This is just the start, the launch pad
To planetawy acclaim. It was at pentecost. The old sod
Was disguised – as a dove. Wecall the bird who nestled in your
Lap? 'E's cwafty. 'e knew how to get to your womb door.'
'The swine! You just see! I shall abort the son of god.'

'Luckily for the worl' I've lit with me light these many years, I was unabor'able. Oh they could wipe me from the womb yerss yerss. But I lived on, flew on. I was the son of god. No matter how they twied.'

He took a swig from the tramp flask he kept in the back pocket of his shorts. Fundador? Veterano Osborne? Carlos? I had a yearning for a corrected coffee but it was a bit early for me. Drinking before nine in the morning shows a lack of grit.

'If I'm not mistaken,' said Inigo, sternly, 'that was the Magda Vies adaptation of Belli? Two centuries ago blasphemy was a serious matter. Not a joke without consequences.'

He shrugged: 'Centuwies schmentuwies. Tha's your time – not my time. My time is the Almighty's time, me Farver's time. 'E's enjoyin' a well earned wetirememt now. Of course 'e could do the lot in six days. Course 'e could. And I'll tell you how. One of 'is days is a billion billion years in youah time. There's the pwoblem. Cosmic misunderstandin'. Cwonometwy. That's what you anti-cweationists don't get. Your time comes fwom the tywanny of Swiss 'owologists and Popes. That Gwegowy geezer. Know what I call Popes? Gwoup-ies. Suckers-Up. Bwown-Noses. Lickspittles. Messengers wantin' to take cwedit for the message. Vicar of Chwist! On me muvver's cervix! By whose say-so says I. Puh! Pull the uver one.'

'Where do you come from?'

'When the Wichard Montgomewy went down I twied to swim ashore to Sheerness. You was wight – Sheppey. Spot on, my fwiend.

I knew what you was thinkin'. That's one o' me gifts. Bwain delvin'. All knowin'. I dwowned between ship and shore in the marshes. Full favom five. Lungs full o' water glug glug full o' filfy water. Salt o' the earth they are them Sheppey folk. Just too many of 'em I'd say. It's owerpoplation that dwives them to thievin' – what they call their entwepwenewial bent. Too many mouths to feed. As I lay gaspin' me last they stwipped me of all me worldlies, all me worldlies. I stayed on for years wecovewing them. By force when it were the needful. Like the good Dean said: "There is nuffin inconsistent with Chwistianity imposin' as well as endurwin' personal sacwifice where the 'ighest welfare of the community is at stake." Got that?

'They loved me miracles. Called 'em twicks. Loved me tales of the places I bin. Sad to see me go. But you gotta move on so 'ere I am. You can't keep a good man dahn. I like to piss in a pool, nice barley sugar stweam gives 'em a taste of the weal thing. I got an affinity wiv water. I don't have to put Alka-Seltzer in it to make it bubble like some so-called saviours I could name. Famous for my 'ydrophilia, me. 'Ence me cuwent pwofession. I los' count o' the number o' times I dwowned. I dwowned more often than I got hit by a bus cos back then there wern't no buses and before there weren't no buses there weren't no coaches. But I didn't dwown so often as I got eaten. Sometimes them bastards didn't twouble to lapidate me first.

'It's when I'm beefy they wants to eat me. So I selfshape scwawny. And keep away fwom Cafolics. And I don't go lettin' on who I am. I tell you there are some vewy unimaginative folks out there. Specially wiv the euchawist. That didn' work aht. Sanctioned cannibalism they fink it is. They're too fuckin' litwal minded. Slittin' me veins, suckin' me blood. Butcherwin' choice cuts off of me. Bwingin' along a pedal gwindstone for extwa sharpness. See the sparks. Smell the blade. That dungeon reek of 'ot metaw. They wanna feast on me. Evewy day a diff'rent Golgofa. The more meat they shove dahn their cake'oles the closer to the god'ead they weckon they are. Like I says – litwal.

'I 'ave to go on the lam. Temple to temple, 'ayloft to 'ayloft, 'edge to fuckin' 'edge. Loitewin' under dank bwidges with bad leaves. Disguisin' misself as a bint. Make-up becomes me so they say. They gets a shock when they clock me gentleman quarters. Goin' to the mattwesses in some motel. I tell yer the Bible Belt is 'ell. And twaditional countwy inns – dwop-in centres for evwy midge in Marshwood.

'Likewise Cartaphilus or wha'ewer he's callin' 'iself this centuwee. That didn' work aht neiver. Bad plannin'. The geezer don't want to be weleased fwom eternal wanderwin'. Not stickin' to the storweeline. Extemporatising. Not clever.

'I've returned I 'ave many many times. Everything has been. Everything will come by again. My dilemma. I 'ave a dilemma. Mine and mine alone. Unique to me. If I don't let on who I am I don't get the perks that go wiv bein' the top figure in my field. It's a knotty one. If I do it's like I say: the mob. The 'ungwy mob. 'Oo was it said: "All mobs are descendants of the mob that voted to fwee Bawabbas"? 'Ooever it was got it well wight. I gotta be on my way my childwen. I got burdens to bear, cantless burdens. And wemember this. When you're alive you're just a corpse in waitin'. Ciao.'

Inigo nodded: 'Nice to have met you.'

'Be seein' you,' I said.

'No you won't,' he replied, 'not in your lifetime you won't.'

'It could,' said Inigo, 'do with—'

'—a spot of repointing,' I rejoined.

This was one of our little jokes. We had heard a Manc tourist on the Rialto Bridge pronounce, without irony, on the stones of Venice.

We were lolling under an umbrella pine. The earth was comfortingly hot. Lizards slipped across the ruins. They darted into crevices. The walls clambered up the hill. You might call them deciduous, shed stones lay beside them. It was more like a quarry than a castle.

Inigo was dreaming.

'How many, Dom, do you think there are?'

'How many what?'

'Delusionists, delusionists who believe they're Jesus.'

'Hundreds, thousands. I dare say Rampton would tell you. Is there a name . . . is it an acknowledged syndrome?'

'I think I might put the Arab-Andalus on The Back Burma—' Another little joke, this time from a toffee-nosed rookie editor showing off her trade jargon.

'I'm wondering if there isn't something in Semi Detached Messiahs . . . Saviour Spotted In Reichenfels . . . The Miracle of The Allotments.'

'Healer Crucified On Portsdown Hill,' I suggested.

'That's the spirit. You know those . . . *Honor Oak* allotments – ah, what are they called?'

'I'd have thought that there are more headcases who think they're god. As Our Friend says it's a risky business – owning up to it if you're Jesus. God's a better bet.'

'One Tree Hill, that's it. Sounds like a gibbet. Make a great Calvary – Carel Weightish.'

The next morning we again went down to the pool early. Our Loquacious Friend wasn't there. Inigo was annoyed. He'd been talking late into the night about patterns of delusion, myth systems that provoke identification with idols, the feebleness of faith, the false comfort of conviction. The pool was a liquid landfill. It stank. We had coffee inside.

As we were leaving to drive to Ronda Inigo asked Dermot the receptionist with the identifying lanyard and the identifying lapel badge where Our Friend the pool guy was.

'Him. He gone. Existential crisis he say. Too many stress incrementations.'

'Where does he live?'

'He don't live nowhere permanent. He got his camper van. He likes mountains. He likes to talk to the animals. He likes deserts. He likes to share his life experience narrative at persons in bars. Just him and his guitar. He likes car parks with nice clean toilets.'

'So where would I find him?'

'Prrrr . . . Could be anywhere. They seek him here . . . they seek him there. Man of Mystery. He'll be back but you never know when. He is Man of Mystery and no mistaking. There's only one Christian.'

Inigo read voraciously, followed leads, bounded with coltish enthusiasm into what turned out to be cul de sacs, browsed by night, swore at websites, got so frustrated at his lack of progress that I'd find him half asleep, slobberingly pissed, watching nicely toned boyboys fisting and fucking. It's safe to assume there was an oversupply of seething swollen ruddy monster cocks like Hall Dunnerdale's hawking the gobs of white venom that are the cause of the world's ills. At the same time there was a global shortage of delusionists, something of a Jesus drought and a god famine.

Which is not to say that Christian from Fuengirola was alone in the world. There are always, always have been, always will be pretenders to the Crown of barbed wire. There just weren't as many as there once had been. Back when society was more devout Jesus and god were figures to emulate. Is it a measure of decadence that given the choice of who to model ourselves on and who to emulate/imitate we choose the likes of Ricky van Brabant, Estelle Destiny, Tantric Jones, the Trans Mermaid Sven/Svenette, troubled Emerson Trinkwon (formerly Flash of Flash and The Plastic Hardware and a circus performer), Luigi Bench and Flintie J. Bival from *Celebrity Kidnap* etc.? On the other hand maybe it's a sign that we are less gullible. They may be self-important twats but at least they're real. Sort of.

Not that Inigo saw it that way. He respected the scores of patients (or prisoners) crammed into les Établissements Speciaux like Charenton and Saint Lazare in Marseille who believed they were Napoleon. He was also fascinated by what the Inspector of Psychiatric Hospitals in Brittany, Jacques-Fructidor Pellet, called Acquired Insanity Syndrome, where the nurse or carer takes on the properties of the patient, shares the same delusions.

For example, a sister of the order of Sainte Marie de l'Assomption in Roanne, Elise A. (b. 1868 Le Puy-en-Velay) came to believe that, like the disturbed and illiterate Natalie G. (b. 1856 Basset) who had experienced a vision in a cave – it's always a cave – she was a reincarnation of Sainte Marie Madeleine.

She left the Asile to set herself up in Lyon as a prostitute (*une fille de joie*). She always dressed, outwardly, as a sister of charity, dark blue veil, white coif, black habit. She attracted priests who granted each other absolution and compared their experiences with her. She prospered. When she hung up her whips and clasps she bought a bouchon and became a Mère, celebrated for her way with testicles, rognons blancs, so provoking the jocular euphemism *les joyeuses*. She married a former pimp, an Apache whose hair was stiffened and set with nun blubber, the rendered fat of Ursulines.

Inigo's problem was that her case and many like it were already familiar down to the historiographic craze for constructing narratives from hospital archives, court reports, wills, assorted muniments. A deprecatory obitchery by Anonymous Bastard said: 'At Oxford Horrocks had attended Richard Cobb's Guinness-fuelled lectures. He would never slough the great man's impact on his thought and taste. His bias towards the strangeness and minutiae of everyday lives was the affectation of an imitator rather than the lesson learnt by a disciple.' True of course, but not while the body's still warm.

Among the subjects of his investigations were:

A sprawling former collective farm on the steppe northwest of Volgograd beside the Don. It was the home of Prokhany Veterok, The Roaring Breeze, a cult of immaculacy. Its members all lacked navels. They claimed to be direct descendants of a god whose name they had for so long been forbidden to speak that they had forgotten it, as was god's will. They were rebaptised in the river every day. Some members of the group had belonged to The Children of the Living Dead, an informal network of discriminate grave robbers who hoped to be infected with the heroic qualities of the exhumed but had abandoned the project when two of its number had been infected instead with heroic tetanus.

Inigo was in Volgograd for a conference, *The Tectonic Contamination of Memory*. He was driven to the farm by Natalia Egorov and Daniil Vastutin who had done much of the translation of documents for the Russian chapters of *Proven: A Universal History of Show Trials*. Fieldwork wasn't their thing. They had heard about this commune from an anthropologist friend. The trip was not a success. The deserted road was flanked for miles by invasive robinias and blocked by two police cars. The armed policemen demanded money to let them pass. A police motorcyclist tailed them to their destination. The road was now flanked by brightly painted beehives, limbless robots come to die in the swaying grass. They heard distant explosions. Natalia pointed to a group of fifteen or so very fat men digging in a field.

'They are kastratsiya, chemical kastratsiya — they are working on the Exhumations project.' A bored guard with a submachine gun watched over them. They looked unlikely to get far if they absconded.

'What is the Exhumations project?'

'Not a good idea to ask. So I don't ask. People talk about it . . . but they don't really know. It's just a name.'

Jaakkina Järvinen, the Finnish woman who appeared to be the Leader of the Cult, wore several layers of clothes with an aperture to show the lack of navel. Her tummy was blue from the wind's sting. She told them that no one would answer questions unless they were baptised, which they agreed to. They were immersed in the green autumnal Don. They were told that they were the only people in a world of many millions who were being baptised at this place, at this moment. Inigo thought he might drown. They were then ordered to purge themselves in a pigless pigpen where a rusting feed hopper groaned in the relentless easterly. They took a herbal infusion that caused both diarrhoea and vomiting. Their shit was inspected by Fazan Statistician, a wax-moustached hunchback who had lost his job in the Department of Martyrology and Sacrifice at Magnitogorsk State University when it merged with Magnitogorsk Technical University. He quoted *The Protocols of The Elders of Zion*, demanded to see if Inigo and Daniil were circumcised and told them that Christ was an Aryan. When Inigo remarked that this was a blasphemous claim made by anti-Semites down the ages and loudly propagated by the SS's ancestral research department, the hunchback (who, it is safe to assume, would have been sent on the longest holiday by that murderous corps because of his infirmity) replied that he admired the uniform.

He showed them rows of withered cabbages and an orchard struck with apple canker because some newcomers to the commune had prayed to god to grant them an abundant harvest. They should have known that god abhors prayer. It is an insult for it presumes that his mind can be changed, that human intercession can determine his actions, that he is biddable. Statistician was adamant that only humans can perform miracles. Jesus adopted human form at will. He rose from the dead for no reason other than to avenge his murder: he extended invitations to come quietly to Pilate, many Roman soldiers, Judas's family and the mob who fled to every corner of the earth to escape his wrath. They did not escape. Jesus was a well-travelled man and as merciless as his father. The Jews who refused to acknowledge their king in a show of the utmost presumption were subjected to definitive ordinance. It was a task that would take centuries.

It would require him to conduct pogroms. In the guise of Heydrich, Himmler and Hitler it was Jesus himself who would prosecute the Shoah.

That, according to Statistician, was 'a minor misfortune' which Jews had exploited without scruple. Anne Frank's family . . . their self-pity . . . their invented memories . . . their appeal to journalists and film makers . . . their importunacy, begging for sympathy.

A couple of days later he sent me this email.

> Still chilled from that wretched dip in the Don. Still chilled by those people.
> Last night's dinner was just as weird as it sounds.
> File under: Ivan's English. Better than Inigo's Russian.
> 'Salmon salty, salad of cancer necks, stuff of meat, mystery fiel, calf fist, for two prepared, octopus comb, foetus mousse at equilibrium, snails over cap, serpent in assorted, cutting from chesse, advantages, mush potato under scabs, pig with weed at garden, intestines filled, complications behind walnut, pike perch at the natural plate, udder from a fire, gated canute by oesophogal treacle, the most glue salt, to the broiler crispy, cake of mother, a bap of another.'
> I sat next to Lou Bellocchio. He's got even vaster. He says he deliberately overeats so that there won't be any food left for the rich. As usual he reminded me that as an IMG militant, as an audacious fellow traveller of the Red Brigades and the Red Army Faction, he despised whores who do capitalist telly. As usual I reminded him that if he didn't rub everyone up the wrong way by being so fucking condescending he would right now be whoring in another series of Tchin! Ciao! Lou! I told him the audiences, the British, love him. Blighty's ideal of an Italian: 100 per cent durum wheat pasta smothered in flirtatious

tomato sauce. He looked delighted. I told him the only people who can't stand him are those who have met him. He looked even more delighted.

Remember that he's Torinese and the rights of man don't extend to anyone from further south than Genoa. They're all maroccini, apparently that's not racism – it's tradition so that's all right then . . .

Still, he had a neat co(s)mic gag even though I'd heard it before. It's the way he tells them . . . When you wake a Sicilian in the grave where he has lain for 2000 years he'll stir and say, 'What you doing? Why you bothering me? Leave me alone. Vaffanculo. I'm still planning my revenge!'

Volgograd Oblast Psychiatric Hospital and Sanatorium is fogged by pink and peppermint and orange and baby-blue candyfloss clouds of effluent from the red and white factory chimneys beside the river. It is in an avenue off V. I. Lenin Prospect. All the trees' trunks are painted white up to a metre from the ground. The hospital has black railings so low a child could climb over them.

Inigo had met the Sanatorium Superintendent Gleb Orlov on a conference tour of the soaring *Motherland Calls* statue commemorating the sacrifices of Soviet soldiers in The Great Patriotic War. It looms over the city. Like many Russians Orlov was impressed that *Proven* argued that rigged trials were, in different eras, commonplace in different countries – France, Argentina, Spain, England, USA etc. Russia was not alone in its ignominy. He was interested, so he said, in Inigo's inchoate new project and had invited him to visit.

They sat in an office, files heaped to the ceiling; a tall partially blackened onion-domed doll's house obscured the toxically grimed window. 'It come from a child's grave. Timofei Lopatin . . . Ha! real badhat with obesity issue selling vintage. We fix him gastric band in exchange. Live in non-extraditable territory now.' A bob-haired secretary served them glasses of black tea and liquid jam. Doctor Orlov stroked her arse with his party hands. She giggled and wiggled. He growlingly described her, man to man, as 'lively, big big energy resource, hyperactive, jig jig cutie . . . lovely cattle to have around the joint'.

He told Inigo: 'Guests. We call them guests. That's for their self-esteem – we don't say loony no more . . . enlightened . . . right this moment in time . . . we got a Genghis Kahn – we always got a Genghis Kahn, they always wants a jumbo suite . . . demand a bed . . . we got a Rasputin, we got a Lev Yashin, he's injured, adductor how you say?'

'Adductor . . . groin. Yes, groin.'

'Groin – you right. Hey hey, you know Moist Groin? Amazing band. Saw them in Milwaukee. Top. Totally aura. Pethidine and applejack. Hey where . . . yeh we got a Mercader – that's a first, we only got the one Jesus this moment in time. Mitka . . . He's – how you say it? He's all lower case and doesn't have a spellcheck . . . That's the expression no?'

'If you say so.'

'American vernacular usage – a big big hobby with me. Bipolar bear jokes. Love them, just love them! Don't you just love them! I spend two years at Madison, Wisconsin. Lovely hospital. They sterilise the needles. They sharpen scalpels. I gotta tell you Mitka is – you know football yeh? OK he's playing with a nine-man team. And he ain't never going to get back those two players who splash the bath early, he ain't never going to get them back. So we try to get nine men processing the work of the whole eleven team. We eliminate negativity of negatives. We make handshake with positivity saying shut the door to jerk-off mentationalities. We reprogramme nine men. Build them into supermen, they'll beat eleven men over ninety minutes plus extra time and nailbite penalties . . . Sporting metaphor also is another big big hobby with me.

'I tell you when we got rival Jesus's they all squabble with each other, they all got miracles coming out their ass, they all claim to be the authentic one . . . like Moist Groin since they split. Which is the real one? Ricky van Brabant *is* Moist Groin obvious, but you go telling that to The Groin With Stafford Prance, Moist Groin Part Two, Humid Groin, Groin Fungus, you got legal processes.'

Mitka was thorn-crowned. He was robed in a greasy grey brocade curtain. He was proud of his long narrow cell which he called his garden. The plastic flowers were faded. He wore an ill-fitting false beard. He whispered from a centimetre distant into Inigo's ear: 'Yashin *says* he saves. I *do* save. He's fraud. Too short to save.'

The coarse beard scraped Inigo's face, reminded him of his bad wool childhood. He had to get him to repeat it audibly for the translators Natalia and Daniil.

'Yashin cannot administer extreme unction. I can. Always on call. But no suicides. Despair . . . maybe. If it was despair, me, I'd bend the rules: I make the rules so I can bend them. But it's presumption. Sin of presumption. Much much worse. Know why? Removing fate from the Almighty's hands. Encroaching on his territory. It's a prima facie demarcation issue. Usurping him.'

Natalia and Daniil gaped and gaped. They shook their head as one. They rolled four eyes, an ocular choreographer's marionettes. They wondered what might come next. In fact, next was nothing more than a display of stigmata, as commonplace as tattoos. Mitka moved across the cell. He took off the curtain, stood naked. Then, the sun shone through the slit of window, the ray from the maelstrom in Crivelli's annunciation but thicker, so thick it's a golden log. He leaned against a wall of the cell, arms horizontal, whimpering in pain, his erection quivering. Inigo scrutinised it appreciatively; he was known as a size queen, which was of course beneficial to my reputation in the community. Mitka ejaculated, a projectile missile seeking its target, the far wall. The annunciation is a literal representation of god shooting his load (and giving proof that he is either male or an abnormally appointed gifted woman). His palms bled because he willed them to bleed, rapt in ecstasy and pain. Natalia and Daniil gasped and gasped.

Inigo wondered if Jesus had been a member of the Magic Circle. He wanted to lick the blood to check it was the real thing. The risk of HoTLoVe was too great back in those days of venomous jism.

Doctor Orlov explained the case:

Out in the wetlands far far from the city – 'far far' might, given the people involved and their frail comprehension of clock time and distance, mean 20 kilometres or 200 kilometres or 2,000 kilometres – there lived in a one-room wooden shack a woman called Masha and her son Mitka who was conceived during a heady fifteen-minute romance with the love of her life, a man who introduced himself as Sepp, a wanderer whose summer trade was to strip silver birch of its bark. He sold it and the insects beneath it to herbalists: every time he stole a tree's bark an invisible wood-woman died with a shriek. In winter he indulged his passion for making false teeth. Masha hoped he might return soon. But the trees were slow to grow back their bark so there was no need for him to pass that way again for many a year.

The child wore rabbit furs and beaver skins, talked to the animals he would eat, reassuring them that the dung he would make of their meat would allow their successors to flourish. He conversed with cranes and clouds, with the bodies preserved in peat mosses and turbid meres. He tamed ravens and midges. They assured him of his unique destiny. He and his mother lived on rabbit flesh, freshwater fish, beaver meat, fledglings trapped in nets, waterfowl, grasses. When Mitka was aged ten, though it may have been fifteen, Sepp returned hauling the tools of his trade, breathing breath flavoured with pine tar alcohol, screaming and crying, whining and bellowing, raging, raging that he had been cuckolded by the Almighty, that Mitka was not his child, that Masha must be punished for the infidelity of which she had no knowledge. He attacked her with an adze. Mitka found unprecedented strength in his twelve-year-old limbs, struggled with Sepp, held him down while his mother stabbed him in the throat and chest. They threw his body into a stagnant pond where wild ponies drank.

That night they fled the house to seek their fortune gathering and selling fungi beside a forest track. Mitka sacralised his mother, he fucked Masha, virginated her, reaching deep into the womb that had borne him, excising the stain of Sepp, re-immaculating her and rendering himself the Father as well as the Son, a divine retro-fit. They were arrested when two hikers died having eaten false morels without boiling them for several hours before they were cooked. A hiker who had not shared the fatal meal led four police to the forest. Mitka protested that the officers had no authority over Jesus Christ and the virgin Mary. He cried when they laughed at him. He ran like a sprite to the bank of a rocky forest river. He stared fixatedly at the ever renewing, roaring, tumbling beast of water.

When they caught up with him they taunted him. Mocked him because he couldn't walk on water.

'Go ahead, go on!' they encouraged him. 'Or isn't it the right kind of water?'

He smiled. He stretched his arms wide as they would stretch.

'I do not do many mighty works here because of your unbelief.' He was contemptuous. He allowed his arms to fall, to fall to his sides.

They restrained him. They wrapped him in rusty chains. They dragged him through the forest so that his body was scratched and cut and bruised by the earth and the binding metal.

Doctor Orlov drew specious comparisons with Lot and his daughters and with Jocasta.

Masha was held in a secure unit at Rostov-on-Don. So secure that she was able to affect her assumption by throwing herself from a high window in the direction of earth rather than heaven. Her long dress billowed. She was said to have dropped slowly, floating like a single sheet of paper. She was said to have cried 'Sepp', stretching the vowel so that it lasted throughout the long time without time of her descent into otherness.

'An altogether avoidable incident that is reflecting bad on the staff at Rostov, real bad, Zelenkov gonna be shitting himself real bad,' smiled Doctor Orlov, rubbing his palms.

Mitka shrugged when he was informed. He said: 'Presumption. I warn against it. Taking law into her own hands. Overstepping the mark. Mortal sin. Fifth commandment.'

Monotheistic mumbo-jumbo originated in the Middle East: Judaism, Christianity, Ramalama. We all know that. The eternal struggle between these three forms of superstition was, Inigo believed, really about what he called the God Franchise. Which one owned it? Which had the surest claim on it? (He'd forgotten or hoped that I'd forgotten that *The God Franchise* was the title of a book by Father Murray McMurray SJ.)

Look, I was writing a very important piece on the folk culture reaction against modernism: Tapiovaara's furniture, former futurists going woodsy, fairground horses, diagrammatic flower wallpaper, nineteenth-century typographical fonts, cottagey nostalgia, naive puppets, The Bride of Denmark. Like I say, it was a very important piece but Inigo kept interrupting me like I was a tame sounding board.

He kept on going on: If that's where mumbo-jumbo comes from why do all the fake messiahs and bogus saviours come from Austria or the Quantocks or the arrière-pays of Nice? Fairly temperate, scarce drought, crops don't fail, peace-loving animals, earthquakes a rarity. Suffering exceptional rather than normal etc.

He insisted how affinitied our subjects were. A 'traditional' chair or fabric design belongs to a particular place and a particular era. The copy or 'reworking' of the chair and the fabric doesn't belong to a place or era in the same way. Folk revival is just another style choice. The brown bars in Amsterdam are peculiar to Amsterdam, they're Amsterdam folk architecture, vernacular. They can, of course, be recreated anywhere. In Cardiff, say, or Adelaide, where the circumstances, customs and practices that originally gave rise to this sort of bar don't exist. You just get the tip of the iceberg without the social and demographic causes, you get the physical expression of a complex tranche of habits, law and commerce. You feel bogusness even if every detail of decor and odour is spot on.

Fake messiahs – is there a messiah who isn't fake? – don't need meteorological extremes to get themselves up and at it, miracle working and spouting proverbs.

They have the example of the persons they appropriate, the models whose spirits they feed on, who have done the job for them, who have been inspired to whirl, to live on top of columns in touching distance of heaven, shrieking, embracing the eternal resurrection, speaking the word because they have been driven sheer loco by the red heat, the tsunamis, the slithering tufa, the swarming locusts. The dancing twisters and tornados have elephantine trunks that mutate into probosces and snakes. It is this weather which created the Bible Belt. All the torments that befall West Goff, Oklahoma and Seward, Kansas are foretold in The Good Book.

At those places trees are sucked from the earth. Farms and factories are hurled into the boiling air with cartwheeling trucks and corrugated iron roofs and picket fences and whipcracking guy wires. They all spin dizzily, a murmuration devised by the almighty, that lunatic mechanic on the lam.

★

Groups of Hassidic men wearing beautiful black shiny silk frockcoats and beautiful black shiny broadbrimmed hats strolled in intense conversation across Clapton Common in off-the-map north-east London. It was a parade of sober exoticism among autumn's drifts. Living faith and whatnot. The usual endogamy. Hard to despise the beliefs of such sartorially sharp persons.

But, said Inigo, 'Despise them we must – they brainwash their kids. Yeshivas.'

That Saturday I had driven him to the former Agapemonite Ark of the Covenant in a broad leafy street off the common. The church, according to Inigo's notes, was built in the late 1880s to the designs of a member of that cult, Joseph Morris. It was frightening. The front was decorated – a modest word in the circumstances – with gross statuary representing the beasts in Revelation: a lion, a calf, a man, an eagle. And the four beasts had each of them six wings about him . . . those beasts give glory and honour and thanks to him that sat on the throne, who liveth for ever and ever.

The Rev. J. H. Smyth-Pigott mistook himself for him that sat on the throne. On Sunday, 7 September 1902, he declared himself Christ reborn to an audience of fifty. On Sunday, 14 September 1902, when The Clapton Messiah arrived to conduct the morning service, a crowd of several thousand doubters pelted him with rotten vegetables, bricks, a broken ladder, wheelbarrows, plasterers' tools, umbrellas.

He moved to Spaxton on the eastern side of the Quantocks where, according to Lord Arthur Hervey, the Bishop of Bath and Wells, he lived a life of 'immorality, uncleanness and wickedness'. Just the sort of life the bishop himself would have liked to live had he had the nerve and not hidden behind paltry proscriptions of polygamy.

Although immortal, Smyth-Pigott died in 1927 at the Abode of Love, as he called the Spaxton house and its small estate. He was denied burial in consecrated earth so a grave was dug in a lawn. The number of Soul Brides and Daughters of Judah soon diminished from almost a hundred to fewer than a dozen.

The problem Inigo faced was that there were already several books devoted to Smyth-Pigott. The surviving great-grandchildren of the brides and daughters had already had every fogged memory wrung from them. Indeed there appeared to be no bogus messiah or millenarian crank whose mores and delusions had not attracted historians or psychologists or sensationalist hacks. It was almost a genre. Why?

'Because it's the most fascinating subject. Always with us . . . always . . .'

I knew what was coming next.

He repeated for the umpteenth time: 'Theolatry is superstition. Theology is scholarship.'

He was proud of that maxim. I'm not sure it was his, though.

The neo-Buchanites worship a woman clothed with the sun, and the moon under her feet, who died in 1791 in Galloway. They are led by His Divinity Timothy Rebecca, Burnley's award-winning heating engineer who has installed a sauna in his garage because Jesus is just the type of big lad who'll be wanting to sweat out the imperfections through his super-large pores when he shows up. Which will be soon. He will be borne from heaven at a thousand miles per hour on a sled hauled by prancing, rearing super-stags.

The Greatest Wrath Doris Cake believed her back garden in Accrington was the Garden of Eden. Her biographer took her at her word. Every night she received a message from god. Again, her biographer was her hagiographer. The Greatest Wrath, too, was immortal yet she died, in 1957.

Her few followers live in expectation of The Fourth Coming. (The first three comings were The Great Wrath's late husbands who had died in domestic accidents and were buried beneath the lawn of the greenest green that was ever seen.) The disciples made salubrious interventions. In expectation of The Fourth Coming needing a nice hot scrub-up a new shower was installed. But not by Mr Rebecca despite his workshop being only a few miles distant: irreconcilable liturgical and sacramental differences. Chocolate is not sanctioned in The Great Wrath's eucharist. Chocolate is blasphemous. Mr Rebecca, a two-bars-of-Lindt-Excellence-Noir-75%-per-day man, disagrees.

The Welsh Marches. In those valleys and on those hills there is no meteorological cause of insane religiosity – is there any religiosity which is not insane? We are not awestruck by these pleasant scapes.

The chequerboard fields and heathery heaths are pretty, sometimes verdantly beautiful, but they are not agents of sublimity. The weather is Anglican going on chapel – temperate, mild, sometimes rainy, seldom exaggerated. It is not a *passionate* climate, not operatic, not symphonic. Apt then that this should be where Inigo found his ideal subject.

Actually it was found for him, sort of, by McHarg Bultitude, though Inigo forgot to acknowledge it.

It's in that choleric poet's account of his walk round England's coasts and borders, *A Blister in My Head*. The walk – keeping on the move – was taken in the hope of avoiding arrest for having enjoyed sexual relations with a schoolgirl of indeterminate age at a remote residential learning centre.

The Marcher Hound. The pub sign was a jigsawed silhouette of one of those weapons-grade animals. It creaked in the drizzle. Mine hosts: 'gluten intolerant Terry, guest ales specialist Siobhan, award winning pie-meister Josh. Our dedicated team is dedicated to helping you relax and unwind, fireside, in our traditional cottage style pub and restaurant . . .' The Poet Bultitude, shaky hand hovering like a helicopter in a gale over his notebook, was belching at the bar with a guest ale, a chaser or two, pork scratchings, fucking *artisan* pork scratchings no less. Every time he was about to put pen to paper he was importuned into conversation by gluten intolerant Terry. He wanted to scream at the fussy tosser. He wanted to sit and think and write about the disparity in the palette of Wenlock Edge (chlorophyll rich) and the Long Mynd (bleached, near monochrome). Gluten intolerant Terry was obviously wetting himself at having a writer he thought Siobhan who likes a 'good read' might have heard of staying at the inn with origins as far back as the seventeenth century. Yoy'll be into history being a writer, so he had drooled on about a local simpleton belief that Jesus accompanied by Joseph of Arimathea had visited the Tree of Tyre on several occasions. The last couple of centuries Joseph had been too weak. Jesus had come alone in mufti, to avoid being eaten by his disciples or turned into artisan scratchings.

Know about it?

No. The Poet Bultitude sprayed him with scratchings shards while making it pretty damned clear that no he did not know and what's more he did not want to know thank you very much so why not piss off back into the gluten-scope cellar with your crock of folkloric baloney. But he wasn't to be deterred.

The Tree of Tyre is on the Malpasfang Lodge estate. A place no one goes near to. Horrible, overgrown, all in ruins. Doesn't need to be rewilded because Sister Nature's done it. Meaning re-ratted and god knows what else lives there besides. Bad vibrations. Haunted. Spooky-wooky. Not that anyone ever tries to get in after all that went on there, terrible goings on. The number of myths . . . it's myth rich no mistake. We've been here eight years and we never been up there to see the mansion. I've got some old postcards, I'll just fetch them.

The Poet Bultitude glared. The autochrome process was attractive. The subject wasn't. Clodhopping provincial gothic on a mammoth scale. He groaned audibly. He reckoned it was time for supper. The special of the day was Poole Pie: coney rabbit cushion-smothered for a painless passing and oven-baked in nasturtium crust; hand-harvested bracken ferns; fair trade clackmans; whipped melon. He groaned in despair.

Bultitude habitually went off-piste. This time he didn't. His atypical lack of interest in exploring the Malpasfang estate and finding the Tree of Tyre was, it's safe to assume, down to his eagerness the next morning to get away as early as possible and as far as possible from The Marcher Hound and its chatty owners.

He devoted a mere brief paragraph to the 'folkloric baloney'. It was an unwitting invitation to someone else to investigate. That was Inigo's good fortune. When he read that paragraph it was the first time he had ever heard of Malpasfang Lodge. It was like something being unlocked. It was what we called an ulrika moment.

He checked out the Pevsner, which called it 'a typically debased and over-inflated design by Milford Sanders. The ne plus ultra of High Victorian mercantile confidence'. The word 'ruinated' came up twice. Ruinated clockwork carillon by Howard & Dodson of Chester . . . ruinated octagonal tower . . . crumbling . . . misjudged aggregate . . . partially demolished great hall . . . remnants of a hammerbeam roof . . . baroque Perseus and Andromeda in Portland stone by Hermann Rowe . . . also by Rowe a virtuoso Icarus on fire, his wings melted, his hands trying to pull out his burning hair, his face partially destroyed and half a skull exposed. The influence of anatomical models is unmistakable. Home Farm (2 miles north) is unique in size and technological innovation.

Then, would you believe it . . . Out of politeness I'd told Ricky van Brabant's father how interesting his magazine *The Paracelsian* sounded. He generously gave me some back issues which I could hardly refuse. They sat, unread, unloved, unwanted on a pile of proof copies sent to Inigo for his worthless endorsement. He had no sooner checked out where we were to stay on our first visit to the Marches (not, evidently, at The Marcher Hound) than one of those uncanny déjà-vu-ish coincidences occurred. Willed? If so by what agency? Destiny? What does that mean? He had shown no interest in the *Paracelsians* which had been gathering dust for months. As if controlled by an exterior force he picked one up. Extraordinarily, it contained a short article about Malpasfang Lodge. He felt he was being directed. Here was the road he must take.

'Vaut le voyage.'

It was. Destination ever changing. A journey, but not what The Oaf would have acknowledged as such. He liked to know the end point. That was essential for his tidy mind. Inigo had the spirit of the adventurer who has lost his map. No – who has *thrown away* his map.

The book that became *Breast Milk Cheese and Placenta Fritters* began as an investigation into the imitators of Christ, delusionists, off-the-peg messiahs.

It turned out to be all that and much more besides – an account of decadence, all-purpose 1890s grotesquery, fin de siècle febrility, rich prats' pseudo-science, haut arriviste entitlement, OTT eugenicists, euthanasia, endogamy, exhumation, zoophilia, the experimental community (a euphemism for misogynistic exploitation), fascism's endurance and the human appetite for abusing and exploiting other humans whom they regard as sub-humans or treat in such a way that they become sub-humans. The victors are victorious, the vulnerable are vanquished.

★

The bush-telegraph which reached *The Worcester Trumpet*, *The Shrewsbury Sentinel*, *The Radnorshire Couriant*, *Illais y Wlad* and *Udgorn Rhyddid* remained parish pump till it was picked up by *The Pall Mall Gazette* and duly pursued by *Punch* and *The Review of Reviews*. The tone changed swiftly from jocular bafflement to shock and 'grievous disgust'. Newspaper and magazine accounts denouncing the depraved society of Malpasfang Lodge grew from a trickle to a torrent. This was within months of the sentence passed on Oscar Wilde which had given the moralists of the yellow press licence to pry and decry. They became fearless in their high-minded bigotry. They named the people associated with Malpasfang Lodge.

Soft furnishings are so zeitgeisty, so gestalty. You can read an era's mood in them. A regretful goodbye to greenery-yallery's glamorous artifice. A resentful hullo to gloomy artlessness and all-round brown.

England had ceased to be a land fit for libertines. And libertines knew it. They were hounded.

Among those who decided that their fate lay outside Albion were Father Linsel Murly, Marcus Phimister who had often entertained him at Malpasfang Lodge, and Jezzard Dogg who had taught him to ride a camel there. They had been building the foundations of a better world, 'a world purged by a demographic enema'.

That phrase recurs in Inigo's many fragments of *Life After Afterlife*. Fragments, frankly, are all that remain of it, all that will ever exist. Unfinished. A ruin before it was even the shell of a building. However, most of the fragments, apart from cryptic aide-memoires, are clear enough in themselves. How they relate to each other is less clear. Whatever Inigo intended to write died with Ian on the death certificate. Be that as it may, a bodge was on the cards – with misgivings.

He had a worrying habit of failing to record the source of the quotes, phrases, aphorisms and whole paras he recorded. He would write down things *he wished he had thought of himself*.

Then, without realising, he'd convince himself that he had thought of them. This left him open to accusations of plagiarism by default or negligence. A hostile reviewer wrote: 'There's a whiff of borrowing from a source that's on the tip of one's tongue, just beyond the limit of memory, ungraspable; borrowing and not returning.' Very likely Inigo had himself forgotten the source, even forgotten whether it was his creation or someone else's.

For instance, is this Inigo or is it Anon? 'We are all provided at birth with a set of grievances which we can subsequently exploit.'

It sounds just like him. But knowing his light-fingered ways I wouldn't count on it. It is, though, particularly appropriate to some of the people who would have graced – or more likely disgraced – his text.

Life After Afterlife

Inigo called them the immortals as an expression of contempt. These Christs without end. These Old English Fascists. These deathless death executives from Sobibor and Treblinka. He derided their hubris. They believed that if only they had the recipe life could be extended, if not indefinitely then to the point where the age of two hundred years would become normal. Of course the recipe would be no protection, went the joke, against the firing squad or the noose, cancer or diabetes. Or would it?

After his death in captivity at Second British Army HQ in Luneburg Heinrich Himmler was found to be carrying over two hundred pills, incuriously presumed to be medication for his constant intestinal pain. This was a strange load to carry for a man who intended to commit suicide if captured: information on that load was never meant to have crept out. (It was of no advantage to any camp: Himmler had been well and truly had by the doctors and researchers under his command.)

The orthodox position held by apologists for Nazism and believers in its second coming is that Himmler did not commit suicide, that the cyanide phial in a hollow tooth was invention. A tall story! Secret passages in the mouth! Boy's Own dentistry!

The truth, they contend, is that he was murdered on orders 'from the very top', beaten to a pulp and buried with his pills on the vast desolate heath in a hidden grave, a grown-over unmarked grave. So long as his body was unfound it could never then disclose the absolute absence of cyanide.

Why such subterfuge?

British high command feared that were he to take the stand at a war crimes trial – Nuremberg had not yet been designated – he'd have attempted to exonerate himself by revealing that he had treated, albeit unsuccessfully, with Britain, which, reliably perfidious, had gone behind the backs of both the USA and the USSR: the already fragile alliance would be further jeopardised.

According to Second British Army HQ the reason for this disposal of the body was to avoid the grave becoming a place of homage and pilgrimage.

There is an undisputed belief that odessa was an acronym for Organisation der ehemaligen SS-Angehörigen (Organisation of former SS members). This was a result of black propaganda deftly rumour-seeded by a team led by first Walter Schellenberg as early as December 1943, then, after the war, while he was in prison, by his future amanuensis Ernst Stech-Pelz. The purpose was to trick Allied forces into wasting resources and years tracking down non-existent escape routes and false trails in the chaos of Europe's wreckage. There were countless ways war criminals got out of Germany but there was no machine coordinating them. Many escapes were improvisations, opportunities seized.

Odessa was a rejuvenatory fix, a super-zingy placebo. It would make men messiahs. Its effectiveness was down to individual gullibility, individual delusion. It was claimed to have been successfully synthesised by SS chemists during the late autumn of 1944. The name was the birthplace of the senior chemist on the project Angel Klimov. He had escaped from the USSR to Germany fearing arrest by the NKVD for disputing Lysenko's concept of vernalisation. He revealed copious intelligence about the USSR's chemical warfare capability, much of it invented or plausibly exaggerated.

His name changed to Hans Klemm, he spent three years in Detmold at Temmler Werke GmbH working on ever stronger forms of Pervitin in order to satisfy the Nazi appetite for amphetamines in the field and in the air. He claimed that a soldier could hyper-function for ten days on nothing bur Pervitin and water. He was subsequently posted to the laboratories of Achermann Steidl Pharma in Fulda. His remit was to develop a drug which would amend the internal biological clock of high echelon Nazis so that they might live far beyond their span. They would have the capability of creating a Fourth Reich when the moment presented itself, when the will of the people, sickened by democracy's deceits, decreed it.

Large birds attain great ages; centenarian geese and bustards are commonplace. One cause of their longevity is their ability to excrete food almost immediately after it has been ingested. Much of his work was consequently based on bowel detoxication. This was designed to gain the approval of Hitler and Himmler, both of whom suffered intestinal problems. Himmler was also gulled by cures derived from 'nature'. Klemm knew that such a drug was a fantasy. But he kept it to himself: progress was slow, he reported, but it was coming along . . . Lies mingled with delusion.

Doubters in his research team were sent to dose themselves with zoonotic viruses in far distant Experimental Agrarian Colonies. As well as developing a placebo he relaxed by studying the belligerent uses of fungi, insects and snake venom. He was smuggled out of Germany to Italy in USAF fatigues and then to the USA by the CIA officer James Angleton who, lacking even the most elementary pharmaceutical nous, had unshakable faith in his research.

Odessa was subsequently manufactured under licence by Barmettler Jäggi in Basel. It was made plausible by the admission that it was a work in progress which carried side-effects. It was a medication that had to be taken every five days, a life sentence of intravenous injections or pills and abstention from an extensive gamut of other drugs and foods. It was repeatedly emphasised that it might adversely affect lungs, limbs, blood density, motor skills, peripheral vision – motes will swarm. There were risks attached. It was a long-term investment in men and the cause. And of course its benefits might not be felt for many years, no one knew how many years.

Restricted production of odessa and a protected formula ensured that only a select group of SS would be dosed, an elite in waiting, most of whom had disappeared after the debacle at Reichenfels. For an indefinite period they hid in full view, ghosts in mufti . . . They led comfortable lives (judiciary, medicine) under the regimes of

Adenauer, Kiesinger, Schmidt etc. They would re-emerge as a crack stormforce of messiahs in wheelchairs, prophets clutching Zimmer frames, vicious apostles with incontinence pads and fond memories of Einsatzgruppen duties: oh those golden days. They are biding their time: whatever else is there to bide? Time is the only judge. When one of their sort passes into Walhalla it is claimed to be the exception, not the rule, even though the mortality rate of these guinea pigs is unusually high.

They shall effect the Third Reich's revival at a future date to be confirmed. How will it be signalled? A hooked-cross cloud formation? Would The Strong Man come again? Were they to wait sleeplessly for the returning Christ, all Aryan wrath and curdling stigmata, out to annihilate the Jews who had scorned him, who had failed to respect the etiquette INRI? If so, how long must they wait? When will they conspire to overturn orders and take matters into their own bony hands without a celestial sanction? What age are they when they first decide? The elite will be hyper-gerontocratic, porous two-hundred-year-old brains in bodies no more convincing than had they been shot up with appetite suppressants and liposuctioned (the drained fat sold to fire pottery kilns). The *Todbetrügen* look quite like life-size models of thirty-year-olds or fifty-year-olds, simulacra of themselves, pituitaries on hold so long as they keep up their medication. That anyway is what they believe. They believe in odessa because they want to believe in the utopia within them which they will lead from deep visualisation to actuality. They don't realise that they are ageing – and if they don't realise it, they aren't ageing, they can't be. They've been had. Maybe they wanted to be had. The evidence in the mirror is ignored. The symptoms are ignored – unoiled limbs, bunions, the ineradicable knowledge of the body closing down, gradual stalling of thought, aphasia's many flavours, rheumatic fingers that put on hold a senior officer's ability to grope. They are not ascribed to ageing. Immortals do not suffer from incontinence. Odessa blunts receptors. Many mechanisms in the frantic workshop beneath the skin are stalled and the workers are on strike.

How would the elite achieve their goal, re-equip the Reich? Breeding like Lebensborn? Propaganda? Boasts of racial superiority?

They are leaderless. They have no one to direct them. They prolong life for the want of anything better. The causeless fears and the fears of the void that multiply with age are not eliminated but are ignored in an access of brainwashed meliorism. The fears actually accumulate for there are more years in which to be afflicted by them. Hold the hemlock, they have odessa.

So did Adolf Hitler. His physician Theodor Morell commandeered a sample and added it to the eighteen drugs he was already pumping into the Führer every day: uterine blood plasma, Testoviron, Orchikrin derived from bull's testicles, vitamultin etc. They brought colour to the bunker. Had it had the results claimed for it, odessa would have frozen Hitler as he was in those final months – a broken man, a screeching tyrant lambasting the volk who have let him down, who never deserved him. He is fifty-six years old with the mien of a very old man, a very sick man. Does he really want to be like that forever, a trembling junkie wearing the cap of a station master on an obscure line beside a Danube tributary? Surely better to put a bullet through the temple, shut down first life and be honoured as a fulminating flame of fire, the master of trance infecting the Black Corps with the will to die for him, the beast whose name is The Word of god who rose from the lake of brimstone – and will again.

Odessa, the miracle rejuvenator, was as bogus as odessa the escape route. A *Mannschaft* of optimistic users might be taken for a stout of papery-skinned elderly lesbians. Be that as it may, when, over twenty years later, the Bee Gees released an album called *Odessa* with a scratchy static flock cover, James Angleton had half a dozen interns, graduates of Paranoia 3, decrypting the lyrics for covert propaganda, high-pitched exhortations to civil disobedience, even insurrection. They played the record backwards in search of secret messages but found only meaningless squeaks. What does 'no way José' mean?

Must messiahs be drugged to believe their own schtick? Or is belief itself the drug? A drug they feed themselves, which seeps from within them. Are messiahs' followers capable of rapture without psychotropic guidance, whirling, fasting? Or is belief enough for them too? Belief is the acceptance of dogma, rites, creeds, mumbo-jumbo and supernatural miracles with no empirical evidence. No shred of proof needed. It's safe to assume that, for those who have it, belief is a gift but it's a gift which belittles, which depends on suppressing reason, a willingness to shut down part of the brain.

Linsel Murly had from a young age studied the means by which martyrs have been put to death. He made fine detailed drawings of lapidations, beheadings by sword and by axe, of bodies burnt, of bodies broken on racks, of bodies fed to scaley pond monsters who reject all flesh but that of the apostate, of bodies buried deep in silt.

He was only the third ordinand since its inception to be expelled from Saint Barnabas Theological College, North Adelaide. Unspecified unnatural unforgivable acts. Near blind from masturbation. Dangerously Anglo-Catholic tendencies. Mariolatrous urges. A hardly dissembled papism. A Roman in all but name. No matter that his work on biblical presages of the eternal return was exemplary. His body, his hands, his face were often bleeding from his self-scourging. He had grasped the potential of Billbob Steels, a form of fencing material manufactured in Broken Arrow, Oklahoma, and not yet known as barbed wire. It was his enthusiastic exhibition of his penis's chastising lacerations to fellow ordinands which eventually prompted the college authorities to act.

His shamed Anglican missionary parents, low church and frugal, had disowned him. They intended to disinherit him. They had not got round to altering their wills when they were murdered in a eucalyptus grove in the Northern Territory. Their mission wagon had been looted and burnt. Their horses had disappeared. The Native Police arrested three Tiwi blackfellas, Wabvrai and the Anbarra cousins, 'rowdy hooligan no-good drunks': they were, as is often the case, shot while trying to escape.

Murly had read about Malpasfang Lodge in the art quarterly *Froth and Bubble*: 'an unprecedented experiment which might truly be described as New Walden'.

He had long yearned to be there. When probate was granted and the tiny family house sold he left Australia for ever.

Father Linsel Murly sailed from Brisbane to London. He spent his first night in The Gallions near Royal Albert Dock. The prostitutes' youth pleased him. Their accent's proximity to the one he'd struggled to shed didn't. He struck a bargain with a child. If the girl sucked him off he'd give her something more valuable than money. He'd give her the secret of eternal life. The girl insisted she wanted money. She wasn't interested in eternal life because she longed to die. She fetched her protector to threaten Murly for her pittance. He put up no fight. He breathed in the stevedore odour of his aggressor, all paraffin, meat, coal and billiard chalk. The secret, he shrieked down the wide, flickeringly lit staircase, clutching his broken glasses and pressing a cold flannel to his bruised eye, *the secret is not to die, not to die.*

Like many young men he 'believed' in art, in gouache, multiple glazes, lacquer work, carving as fine as that of the netsuke masters, Joseph Southall's tempera, Walter Crane's sgraffito, Atkinson Grimshaw's nocturnes and the golden hour according to Maxfield Parrish. He 'believed' in what he – and no one else, disciples apart – called faith-craft, best practised by the exceptionally myopic who can weave intricate patterns without a jeweller's glass.

He 'believed' in those artists' work. To 'believe' in this instance means nothing less than to worship . . . to admire fellow men to idol-atry's far side, wishing to 'be' them, to emulate them. He wore a broad-brimmed black hat which, according to who he was address-ing, he referred to as a priest's camauro or a fedora in homage to the venerable Pissarro of Strang's portrait. He was amusingly derided as 'Corvo in Ned Kelly's armour'.

He believed from observing aboriginals that the darker the skin the more impermeable it is. Black people don't feel the rain. To prove it the *Titania*'s lascar crew stood smoking, stung by horizontal Indian Ocean squalls. They mutely revered him as they might a god. He was very tall and very blond. He breathed in the tobacco. For hours he gazed at the sea's blurred churn, the inviting sea – it beckoned, it tantalised him. He tried to calculate whether, were he to throw himself into it, he would have time during his leap to repine. Time's infinite flexibility might be unforgiving, years, centuries, might elapse between his scaling the rail and the water consuming him.

The boat's throbbing entered him. Even when it put into port the infernal rhythm persisted. He stared at the rust-pocked ceiling of his cabin which was a coffin. The bed was a narrow litter but not so narrow as the one to which his father had tied his wrists every night to prevent him masturbating.

Murly believed that the eucharist should be celebrated with lamb and sweet pastry because Jesus is the *sweet* lamb of god . . . and the whole land thereof is brimstone, and *salt*, and burning. Also it tasted good.

He believed in the literality of miracles. He believed too that they existed independent of doctrine or dogma. And, obviously, that they pre-dated Christ. Orthodox Christian teachings took little account of the actuality of human behaviour and the human realm. They were at best an irrelevant sideshow, more often a schoolteacher's dreary rulebook. To adhere to them was to deny humanity's marvellous essence. Jesus practised supernatural acts but he preached self-subjugation, he fetishised restraint and curtailment. Christian joy is not joy.

He believed that death is nothing more than long-term anaesthesia during which we dream recurrently, timelessly, that the anaesthetist has anaesthetised himself from shame at his having administered us an excessive dose (small print, decimal point) so cannot give us an antidote to waken us.

He believed like the Roman that he was human so nothing human could be *strange* to him. It was human to sate every appetite, to feed every caprice no matter what the cost to other humans whose destiny it was to be devoured – uncomfortable perhaps, but not *strange*.

He believed too that childhood was a chimerical state of being, a collective delusion available only in the Judaeo-Christian societies which had dreamed it, propagated it. The boundary between pre-sexual and sexual stages of development was artificial. According to Father Murly the acts of mutually appreciative friction which bourgeois Europeans (and Australians) called paedophilia were not crimes but, as that word makes explicit, expressions of fondness. Moreover, bestiality is sanctioned by both the Bible and the Ramalamaleth.

What Father Linsel Murly believed, the Idyllic Brotherhood duly believed with him. They were his disciples. He talked of Trinity Extra, he talked of his liturgy-in-progress called Sacreed. He boasted of the messiah yet to be revealed. Disciples are a client species. They depend on a messiah to give them purpose just as the messiah depends on them to confirm his status. There were seldom more than six brothers and two sisters. Their practice was distantly based on Creuse masons who from spring to autumn wander France seeking work and building to the highest standard, stone cut to the millimetre, made pliable like clay.

The Idyllic Brotherhood moved from one country to another creating beautiful works. They committed abominable acts: possibly murder, probably rape, certainly kidnap and sequestration.

By day they begged in parks and squares. They blessed the alms givers. Those who failed in their duty of charity were struck with stout sacral sticks – a single blow condemns a street miser to hell.

By night they robbed churches whose heathen congregations they considered incapable of appreciating plate, censers, fonts, paintings, woodwormed baldacchinos and stained glass. They exhumed bodies, cracked long-dead fingers to remove rings, drank a two-century-old methuselah of rum which had improved with keeping, plucked rotting violas which hadn't, posed for photos in clouded pince-nez and lace gnawed by the rodents of the ages. Then they'd be on their way, on the road again.

Father Linsel Murly's 'gift to an ingrate England' which he also described as his 'Britannic legacy' included three works made when he was attempting to become a 'society' portraitist, a lost, allegedly pornographic painting called *Youth*.

His account of his ordination at Saint Patrick's Cathedral, Parramatta, was crisply detailed, unvarying. He spoke of it with such radiant joy that he received a number of commissions from the Roman Catholic diocese of Portsmouth: a finely detailed cloisonné lectern for the church of Saint Blaise, Havant, a partially executed stained-glass window at Saint Boudewijn of All Mercies in Highcliffe and a similarly unfinished mural in the same church. The last was achieved by taking photos at Friar's Cliff of boys wrestling on the sharp-grassed dunes, girls splashing in the lagoons. The photos were then projected onto the roughcast walls of the church, a guide for the painter whose work was persistently interrupted by the epidiascope overheating. The children were naked. They made no attempt to cover their modesty. A euphemism Inigo relished.

What he didn't relish was the mob's ignorant confusion of paedophilia with acts of fond vigour between adults. A confusion aggravated by men like Murly.

He would soon fetch up in Dieppe.

He officiated at mass as he would in other churches in other lands down the years. He had the griff. He knew the score. His lack of the local language was no bar. Walter Sickert described him as 'a needful dog who may turn on its owner without warning'. He rented a studio in a damp villa formerly occupied by Guillaume Desdemaines-Hugon, who had left for the painters' colony at Worpswede, and one of his mistresses, who hadn't – the buxom fourteen-year-old Polish model Maria Zamoyska. She was even taller than Murly and blonder too.

She made violent carmine portraits with her fingers. The paint stood in irregular low relief an inch proud of the boards she used instead of canvas. She collected shells and driftwood. She was puzzled by Murly's feigned lack of interest in her. Such indifference was an unwonted insult. She was offended by his importuning, in the name of Christ, children who were her juniors with whom he swam and splashed and lifted onto his shoulders like Saint Christopher while releasing his seed to the grateful sea to make hybrids of the deep.

It's safe to assume that if Murly and Maria were lovers it was only briefly. Their relationship was otherwise. They left for Nantes where he was beaten up by a gang of check-trousered stevedores who bilked him, refusing to pay the price he had demanded for her. They sailed from Saint Nazaire to Panama.

There are years when nothing is known of them.

Dogg family folklore was patchy. That was one of Inigo's sources. Predominantly oral: 'We're not much of a family for writing and that . . . We do know that Greatgreatgramps was a bit of a one for prayer and animals.' The most fruitful source was the papers (letters, diaries, photo albums, wills etc.) of the Phimister and Shadoxhurst families. It was these that would cause Inigo to put aside messiahs in favour of *Breast Milk Cheese*. The second subject in a few months to have hit The Back Burma.

The earliest print reference to the Idyllic Brotherhood Inigo found was in the San Francisco review *The Call*, vol. 86, no. 78, October 1908. It states that Father Linsel Murly is the guide and beacon of 'a band of devout fraternal guildsmen of the brush and the chisel who roam wherever their spirit takes them, currently to our Golden State's southern hills and mountains'.

Among the brothers was 'mastercraftsman Jezzard Dogg, a distinguished English copper hammerer'. Where he had appeared from is not known. Where he had learnt that craft is not known. Sister Maria of the Ursuline Order is described as 'a Rodin in the making'.

Despite Murly's petitioning and self-advertisement the Brotherhood's only architectural commission was a garden studio for Dudley Genge's farmhouse in the hardly populated hills inland from Malibu. Otherwise their work was ornamenting the interiors of houses designed by Elisa Chinn. After Julia Morgan she was the most prolific Californian woman architect of that era. Much of the work they did for Chinn and for Wilson Carillo has been destroyed: paintings of women in togas with their hair on fire; pink putti with rubies stopping their anus; a mural showing rows of seated old men staring at the sun; a frieze of horned apes with scaley bodies frozen in repetitive sodomy. Murly's mission was as much artistic as spiritual.

The people who commissioned the houses or the houses' subsequent owners feared being polluted by the daily presence of work created by Satan's sgraffitists. The Shaun Hare House, the Mazel Cronk House, the Beausoleil House were stripped of all evidence of the Idyllic Brotherhood's participation and former presence which, supposedly, lived on in the cherrywood, pewter, marquetry, glass and plaster it had wrought.

Inigo was always scornful about the idea – bonehead's sentimentality, he called it – that stones have memories. But if they had . . .

Murly, Maria, whom he called The Infanta, Dogg, a Chicagoan weaver turned grifter Hinton Trunck, a fugitive yeggman Goffard Corner and the engraver Wanda Tiscenko (provenance undisclosed) were enthusiastic participants in Baron Duke's 'Japanese' parties at

Topanga and in similar diversions at the Elysian League (motto: 'All You Can Eat') and the Rollo Hauser Belvedere. The name Prophets of Perversity was a jest that stuck. It would be used against them.

Wherever Linsel Murly fled, Maria fled with him. She wanted to be ligatured to him. She wanted to exist in his skin. She wanted to escape him, to go far far from him. She knew her dependence was excessive. He was everything to her: father, lover, brother, teacher, pimp, bully, comforter. She beat him till he bled and begged her for more, till his skin was cross-hatched, till it was shredded, till it was Golgotha tartare. He wanted to die.

He didn't want to die. If he died he risked the same chastisement being unavailable in the other kingdom where, furthermore, his body might have adopted a form impervious to multiple blades and emery paper towels.

Goffard Corner had turned grass in exchange for charges against him being dropped. They were sought for questioning in three counties of California. Murly grew a beard. He didn't wear his glasses; so benches, walls, door jambs and café chairs attacked him. Maria coloured her hair. Dogg shaved his head.

They headed to the blinding white of Veracruz where they whiled away anxious days in arcade cafés where shark survivors displayed their stumps. Murly considered them cowards for having blasphemed, for having denied god's will by not having submitted to their attackers. The devout would have yielded. They would have understood that god had arranged this ocean rendezvous.

They prayed that a ship to Europe would arrive tomorrow or the day after, by god's mercy. Navigation was unreliable. The city was under military occupation. The American boy soldiers were flush and gullible, readily exploitable Hoosiers. Dogg grinned the wild grin of the con who has found a limitless trove of marks.

Maria complained of the pressure she was under and the indignities she suffered. The boy soldiers stank: semen, shit, smegma, smoke, sweat. Their mouths were halitotic censers. Murly told her it was god's will that she should yield to them. He told her to bathe and pray more often. He promised her only a very few further . . . then the ship will arrive. This was little more than a variation on the lie he always told.

A gentleman called Walter always raised his tricorn hat to her in the Gran Café del Portal. One morning he proffered a pair of goggles. She was thrilled to be driven in his dashing Oakland car to his villa by the sea. In its park of screaming polychromatic birds and fruiting cacti stood a row of heads three or four times the height of a human. He showed her the monstrous steam-driven Bucyrus-Erie excavator and Fairbairn crane that had been used to transport them here from their centuries-deep burial. He boasted that with such tools he could exhume the entire population of the Panteón Jardín Veracruzano. He had got his start in life breaking into mausolea and tombs.

Though they exhibited minor variations of detail the thick-lipped punch-drunk heads were as standardised as icons of the virgin. She was enchanted – she remembered the old times when she had sculpted all day, she longed for the joy that work had brought her.

Olmec civilisation, he told her, and asked if she would stay, indicating the house, the extent of the estate and the auto-destructive waves. She was tempted.

Father Murly, accompanied by a pick-up commando of boy soldiers, arrived after hours of searching to deliver her from temptation. He shook hands with Walter, one grave robber saluting another. He instructed the boy soldiers to punish Maria. When they had finished punishing her, he comforted her.

They disembarked in Algiers.

He had the photographs, 'my precious memento of California'. Precious indeed. He had blackmailed several senior priests and lay officers of the diocese of Monterey and Los Angeles into providing him with introductions to important ecclesiastical figures in Algiers' sacred archdiocesan underworld.

Questions were asked in high places – never answered, always ducked – about this priest from nowhere, about the 'monstrously top' fees he was paid for designing and making stained glass and plate for the new churches programme initiated by Archbishop Combes and expanded by Archbishop Leynaud: la Voile de Sainte Véronique, le Chapelet des Larmes de la Madeleine, Sacré-Coeur d'Alger and Notre-Dame de Toutes Aides at Bône. In the hardly accessible heights of towers and domes the Brotherhood painted scenes of abandon like the devils Beardsley, Bosch and Bouts. Oh the ease with which he could have flung himself through the cat's cradle of wooden scaffolding to the welcoming stacks of ashlared stone hundreds of feet below. Their exteriors resembled tabers. They were exercises in architectural ecumenicism and proselytising. Invitations to convert. Invitations ignored.

A little more than a year after his arrival he bought a house among orchards in a suburb of Algiers. He sacralised it with holy gewgaws, pointed arches, tiles copied from a book of hours, tortuous columns, a stained font, statues of the virgin, censers, candles, bones including the maxilla of a Roman soldier punished for daring to bow to the Saviour nailed to the cross, the desiccated kidney of an unknown apostle, bloodstained scraps of hallowed fabric, relics. It was described as 'fairground gothic' and 'gimcrack dark ages'.

Murly's reputations spread. An inventive, deft craftsman whose originality was often someone else's. But that's the invariable way of craft. His messianic delusions were risible. He wished to be feared, not laughed at. He usually wore a white djellaba with an appliquéd cross.

He could feel that the house was haunted by the ghosts of people not yet born who would one day live in it, pass through it, die in it. In half-light he could see an adolescent boy whose bile-black hair gleamed. He held a bloodstained bronze statuette. A raggedly dressed girl stared at him incredulously.

Gossip whispered Murly was a disgraced ordinand, had never been consecrated, was not a suitable employer of destitute boys and runaways whom he referred to as 'my orphans' and 'les petits frères de mon idylle'. They followed him in prayer. They were told that they could share his visions: they spent hours locked in a blacked-out room summoning them to no avail but not daring to admit their failure in case he buried them alive. They did most of the building. They wore habits fashioned from blankets, swept, slept in outhouses, ran errands, went begging in bands, picked fruit as they had learnt to at the Sainte Dorothée de Césarée orphanage, the tyrannically nun-run market garden from which several had absconded. The favoured, spared manual labour, assisted Murly. He taught them the techniques of scagliola, sgraffito, Amarah silversmithing, enamelling, lithography, etching, photography.

They posed for his cameras. He rubbed his hands in satisfaction at their lack of inhibition. Whatever abuses they endured these children who had never seen snow were determined not to be shipped to icy rude barracks in Savoie and high on the Aubrac. Murly often jested: 'Who'd ever vote for chilblains when he could be spreading the Lord's seed instead?' And he'd laugh exultantly.

Swift spite rather than blunt bludgeon was his arm as a cruel blond bully. It's safe to assume then that the other side of the same tarnished coin was complementary sentimentality. When he read *La Vigie's* account of Charles de Foucauld's murder he wept. Dogg made him tea. He clutched Maria and told her how much that hermit's austere and frugal example meant to him.

She was astonished. His version of himself did not accord with hers. De Foucauld was a holy man, she told him. Holy! You are not.

He wiped (his genuine) tears. He conceded that he was a pimp, a plagiarist, a grave robber, a blackmailer, a rapist . . . But he was a priestly pimp, a priestly plagiarist, a priestly robber etc. And he would be a priestly martyr.

God had endowed him with an apostle's dozen of qualities on condition that he would one day atone.

Or he would be persuasively atoned in a god-sanctioned Health Amendment.

Either way it was god who would choose the path taken.

'God's grace has peaced my soul. He shall continue to peace my soul until in his mercy he wills that I should be pointed towards the final door where putti with wings of gold await to carry me on soothing zephyrs to the kingdom.'

At the same time he would imagine himself being identified in a morgue, soft-focus figures around him brushing away the flies attracted by the putrefaction of the defunct industrial plant beneath his skin. The bloodied pits where the eyes had been don't tell where they had gone.

It was a matter of faith, of reason quashed, of following god's will which was within him. Father Murly did not know why he was drawn to the distant mountains where Father de Foucauld had fulfilled his destiny as a martyr for France and Christianity. He had lived as though every day he might die a martyr. He was impatient for martyrdom. Death had invited him to come visit for once and ever. In death he was the imitation of Christ, although shot in the head: Christ has died in many ways, many times.

Father Murly was jolted on unsprung seats. No soft fat cushion. Lack of shock absorbers is when soft furnishings really come into their own with something to say. He fell in and out of sleep. He wore a white robe with a red appliqué cross, a thick cord around his waist, sandals: de Foucauld's invariable garb. He wondered if he was unworthy to be anything more than an imitation of an imitation.

The plump smoke from the locomotive hauling the train from Algiers to the end of the line garrison town of Colomb-Béchar deposited a heavy mantle of soot, everywhere. The quick-change from white to black pleased Murly. Flocks of frightened sheep fled the train, herding for their lives, a seething mass of inflated maggots. Disgruntled shepherds with bad teeth spat at the train, shook their crooks. The train laid a constant shadow bouncing and skipping over rocks and shrubs. Maria pulled down the blinds so that they would be spared the sight of skeletal children fighting off pi-dogs to gnaw at animal carcasses and the less fortunate crawling towards the train with their begging hands extended, their tongues lolling, their ribs posed to burst through skin. Murly said: 'I bring them a greater sustenance.'

Dogg assured him: 'You do, Father, you do.' He was fiddling with the key to his blue and gold carpet bag.

All the world knows Colomb-Béchar is bright and hard.

Dogg hired a dragoman. Then he hired another. He haggled for six camels for the price of three. He settled on six for the price of four. Camels know the way even if they have not trodden the route: it is within them, inherited like the family face. Zouaves' eyes feasted on Maria. This strange trio was, out of his curiosity, entertained by the colonel of the 4th cavalry regiment Jean De Berg in the quarters where he lived like a prince of the desert. Sartorially he had, apart from an incongruous Sam Browne, gone end-of-pier native: multi-coloured babouches, a tasselled fez, blue striped facial make-up, Berber jewellery jangling, flouncy burnoose. His souvenirs of Guyane where he had policed the gold rush were ingots and an ocelot. He enjoyed the privileges of rank and polygyny: camel races, opium and several women, all of them tattooed, painted, ornamentally scarred. They had gold stubs in lieu of teeth.

The daughter of one of them cooked barley couscous which reminded Maria of kasha in Danzig before it all went wrong and she was sold to a pigtailed sailor from Rostock. Only a few days later in a bar whose ceiling was hung with models of clipper ships he had offered her to a Lübeck lard-purifier in exchange for a gambling debt.

The colonel was worried that Dogg should have employed both Lal and Berber guides. The only circumstances under which they will acknowledge each other is when they are plotting against you. Watch out.

Murly murmured: 'Whoever follows me will walk into darkness.'

He assumed that the Brotherhood would die with him, that its remaining members would join him.

The Brotherhood had other ideas.

The colonel probably cleared his throat or gurned his astonishment.

He quoted Aloïs Vernet's *The Enchantments of Purgatory*: 'Those who die in a foreign language will hear only that language in their next stage of existence. They will, then, understand little of that existence. And not understanding it they will not be able to escape it.'

It sounded like a warning. A ten to fifteen days' warning, a seven-hundred-mile warning; that was the distance from Colomb-Béchar to the Hoggar.

Birds observed their caravan. Supposedly extinct lizards proved not to be. Hyenas' eyes were dressed with kohl. Dunes grew overnight. The sand was black. The sand was red. The sand sparkled in the moonlight. Animals changed colour and form. They could self-amputate, turn themselves inside out. Cats with horns, snakes with horns, gazelles with horns, ibexes with horns watched for signs of fatigue and weakness: a two legs faint from sunblast, a four legs reduced to two legs, animosity's gestures slowed by the heat. Stone had been gnawed by the wind to mimic organ pipes, lacey spires and domes long before god created them. Holy acacias grew in wadis below basalt cliffs. Sites of cosmic lapidation from a long while back were now moraines. Violently twisted rocks are petrified devils, garrotted and left standing to increase the chastisement. Earth pyramids line up in ranks as fortifications. Scarp formations are the ruins of forgotten civilisations that came and went in the blink of god's eye.

The pillars' virile characteristics – Christians and Lals, avert your prudish gaze – delight the greedy Amasag eye. For them all that is visible is holy. God's face is everywhere. And god's limbs. His out-stretched arm is made of wood, it is made of stone, it is made of sand. Everything has instructive qualities. To claim otherwise is blasphemous, a slight to the multiple gods around us.

De Foucauld was murdered by a band of Amasags. Striped boulder blocks had told them to punish him for his abhorrence of slavery. And for the way he expressed his abhorrence – calm, serene, reasonable. He was not man enough to throw down the gauntlet. They considered a white man who opposed slavery a traitor to his kind. They had never encountered such a man. White men were their clients. Slavery was sanctioned by all that the Amasag worshipped: sheep tracks, random hamadas, clouds, gothic bark, sunsets, rocks' folds and abrasions. Saint Augustine of Hippo had noted their worship of rocks. Slavery was sanctioned too by the French army and by the warrior Prynne of whom legend was made. De Foucauld was also not quite the ticket as a messiah: he did not lead them, he did not read their future in patterns of pebbles, he did not eat meat nor let it be eaten in his presence, so he lacked soothsaying entrails to divine.

Murly foresaw his future. A fine sense of fate had allowed him to escape the judges who would judge him for his crimes and trespasses in this kingdom. Here, he had resolved, he would find the other kingdom, in a foreign language, in a foreign sandscape of nicotine teeth bluffs and the decor devised by a billion years of wind.

Above a group of adobe huts, sheepskin tents and rush shelters the Amasag had paid tribute to their victim by copying the sole item of decoration and veneration in his hermitage. Using military supply distemper from the magasin de vivres at Tamanrasset they had tried to reproduce on the surface of a cliff a devotional postcard showing the virgin with her breast rent to reveal the immaculate heart. They had no idea who the card represented, had never heard of the virgin Mary, but were besotted by her appearance.

The postcard was massively magnified, three metres plus from the virgin's Habsburg jaw to the crown of her vivacious blonde hair. Her halo (an unsanctioned sable) was a Hassidic planet, her eyes too large for her face. There was no sense of scale. It's safe to assume the size was inspired by the advertisements that had recently been painted on blind walls in Tamanrasset: Bouillon Kub, Suze, Les Bons Biscuits Pernot etc. All faded now.

It's safe to assume also that the Amasag didn't really get the hang of perspective. And even if they had they'd have reckoned it was a trick. They'd have been right. Their eyes hadn't been conditioned to see that way. The world they saw was not the world their colonial masters saw. The vanishing point is a device of European supremacy. It signals the end of the earth, the end of civilisation.

It wasn't art to the colonial masters' eyes – that would come, soon, that penitence by aestheticism, that self-scourging elevation of barbarian daubs and tribal splodges to the level of, say, Caspar David Friedrich and Jacques-Louis David. Their art, which was hardly art, was single plane, flat. No illusionism. No depth. Be that as it may, it was representational enough for them to make a link between the coloured shapes they themselves had daubed on the cliff with black lines round them and Maria Zamoyska, a three-dimensional blonde virgin Mary given to them to wonder at in collective delirium, to worship, to anoint as the messiah promised in tales within tales within tales stretching back to far distant aeons when the sun was many colours and the Amasag's predator was not Christians, not Lals but glistening black crocodiles from the Cretaceous who had missed time's bus when the rivers dried. They adapted to a spelaean existence beside gueltas, leaving their caves only to seek quarry: thirsty animals come to drink or attack passing caravans. They'd greedily gorge on everything. Saddles, blankets, baskets, camels, people. Survivors of the attacks were revered. Their stumps, tattooed with crude, just decipherable reptiles and birds, were venerated, badges of honour.

The Amasag were scarlet-swathed Berbers who took nothing on trust from the bellicose Christian French or the bellicose Sartans. They resisted both. They were animists who ridiculed the worship of a god they could not see, hear, feel, smell – a god which evidently didn't exist. They dismissed this pitiful notion as a sign of monotheism's mental incapacity and incuriosity about the actual. They mocked its flight into the fantasy of a blindly invented single god when the multiple gods were everywhere, in wind, in rain fallen to earth because too heavy to remain in the clouds, in love's eyes, petrified trees, cactus spines. They were moved to random acts of worship. Prostrate, kneeling, bowing, hands pressed firm together, forefingers pointed to the ground then the earth where everything comes from, not to the sky where the feeble fantasy is said to live in the clouds but never shows, never falls. Supplication is ecumenical. Prayer's bodily positions transcend beliefs and ape basic sexual arrangements. All gods are sex gods urging pleasure as well as procreation, keeping the cup full.

In the centre of the village the women wreathed Maria in garlands of acacia plaited so its malevolent spikes would pierce the skin of supplicants. She was seated on an overwrought Second Empire chair. They circled her eyes with kohl. They intricately patterned her hands and feet with henna as though to imitate lace. They braided her hair and bejewelled it but did not colour it because it was its very blondeness that lent her unique power. Her face emerged from a deep chainmail collar around her neck. They blackened her nipples with charcoal. They anointed her with musk and incense. They approached her one by one in Indian file chanting. The men, greased hair like multiple antlers, faces striped vermilion, did the same, each firing a single shot into the sky before hurling themselves on her so the acacia spikes might wound them. The oldest man excised a sand viper's venom sacs, poured their contents into a Roman lachrymatory, handed her the snake which she held without fear. The oldest woman indicated that she should insert it in her vagina and compress it till it died.

Murly, agitated, protesting, was restrained by two red-toothed smilers. Maria tranced, she worked her pelvic muscles with determination and craft. When she slid the dead serpent from within her drums were pounded. And she was queen, sorcerer, fount of magic. Her gaze was ardent. Her body gleamed. Her skin was burnished. Any man who penetrates her knows that he is forsaking his life. But she may not deny him. That's the compact. That's the way it is with tribes.

It's safe to assume, as Inigo did, that Murly was sulking. Sand blew into his eyes. He wasn't used to ceding his place centre stage. They had got the wrong messiah. Maria had no prophetic powers, no line to the other kingdom. But he realised that the Amasag had visions of a woman, perhaps any women, in whom they could discern messianic properties; they were not spared delusions of their own. They had known she would be brought to them. Murly's job was done. He had delivered most of what they had longed for: be that as it may, they resented that the messenger had not also brought them *things*: baubles, glittery cutlery, medals and ribbons, cut glass vases, brass goggles, porcelain cats, thaumatropes, slide rules, music boxes, mincers, delivery forceps, ear trumpets, spinning tops, whistles, harmonicas. Things to revere. They harangued him for his meanness. They showed no gratitude. His ultimate mission linked him in failure to his parents whom he despised but could never escape. The Amasag offered oblations to Maria: honey cakes, camel milk cheese, barbary figs, a newborn baby. When she resisted they cajoled the food into her mouth. Guilty goats, tried and sentenced the previous day for destroying an ancient and precious teipara tree, were roasted over a fire on a device adapted from theodolites, bounty from a legendary ambush no one but the very elderly could recall.

The Amasag improvise ceremony, make ritual on the hoof. Formal worship is as alien to them as the invisible god. They know no more about it than they know about the sea. The air was dense with kif, woodsmoke and the fumes of alcohol distilled from dates. Fruit bats, who eat their own body weight in vegetable matter every day, tumbled lumbering, wheeled, spun through the smoke. Drums thudded, dog-whistles and pipes shrilled. A man with no feet pranced on his leathery stumps, cartwheeling and spiralling, bullying and teasing, and prodding and threatening with burning boughs. He moved clockwise, dartingly. The majority of straw hats and bandanas didn't. Only the men danced and cantered. Every one was fleetingly lit. They went in and out of darkness, disappearing. Bad teeth accounted for so many covered faces. Jigging and swaying. Ribbons, bells and trinkets hung from sleeves. Quivering in grand mal's throes. Braying like a long-haired donkey. Dancing with mincing steps, flapping hands and limp wrists – ooh! an XXXL girl's blouse as Detective Inspector Hubback might have said. He recalled the morris dancing he'd seen at Malpasfang Lodge and would never see again.

Night wore on. Murly's legs buckled beneath kif. Dogg couldn't whirl any more. They were helped to an ill-lit adobe chamber. Dogg lay with his lumpy blue and gold carpet bag as a pillow. They did not realise in the dark that apart from two small round apertures it was windowless. It was not airless: there were also vents in the low ceiling which allowed odours (sweat, terminal fear) to escape. When the door was bolted without they did not hear the hollow slap; muffled by the frenetic music. They didn't hear the brusque hushed voices; conspiracy sounds the same in every language. Had they heard them they'd have known.

This, then, was it.

No rehearsal. No tuition. No preparation. Martyrdom is a once in a lifetime opportunity. But the martyrdom you dreamed of, the martyrdom you longed for, is not the martyrdom you get. God's tricky that way. Pain goes with the role which is no role, this isn't a game – the pain proves that. You enter a compact with your torturers. To them you are a lab specimen, to be tested and toyed with. Count their ways, their many ways.

There is, however, only one acceptable outcome. All paths lead to the same grove: the rain has stopped, it still drips green off the trees; the sun is baking the earth so hard it splits like an artery map; the fog hides the crazed trunks; the melting snow weighs down the leaves. It never varies, it's always the same place, the final place.

Through the night he listened: hammering, grunting, cursing – the sour music of enforced labour regally decreed.

He peers out of the mud building's wall holes, hardly portholes.

They have raised a scaffold which they call a Prynne. Did they? Was his hearing right? He couldn't sleep for more than a few seconds at a time. Parts of words were familiar from some life or other. They echoed in his brain's chambers. Is that the scent of bedsheets scalded by an iron? He dreamed of a boy in Brisbane. He fretfully tries to recall his name. One time he woke from tremors, he sat up, he said to Dogg: 'I can hear De Berg . . . remember De Berg . . . Those who die in a foreign language will hear only that language in their next stage of existence. Remember?'

There was no reply. Dogg was not there. There was no one beside him on the hard palliasse. Man and carpet bag had gone.

They came for him at dawn. The night's curtains slid back to reveal the stage of day. At the centre the Prynne scaffold. They were his accomplices. They didn't know it. They didn't know they were party to his destiny. They expected Murly to resist. They were going to haul him to the Prynne scaffold. They had measured the drop – approximately. He went willingly. Were those eyes peeping from a carmine cheich in the throng Dogg's? Betrayal only increased his sense of glorious victimhood. The sharp stones grazing his feet pre-occupied him. Just scrapes and sticky bleeding but they displaced mortal anxiety. He bent to remove a bismuth chip from between the little and fourth toe of his right foot. A toothless man pulled on the leash. Another knew where to find a nerve in his spine. He lurched forward holding to his face the chip whose colours were all the colours of the world. Maria – who was no longer Maria, but Maria's body regally inhabited – gestured to the men beside the scaffold, a fatal twist of her left hand. She smiled courteously at Murly, without animosity, as at a stranger who once violated her and is now being repented by a force greater than spite, juster than her vengeance – by The Law. The sentence is carried out, maladroitly. His Christ-like projection of despair of humankind is the fifth eschatological tribu-lation, expressed in glistening gobs.

When he was cut down he was not yet a martyr. He screamed till his chords were blasted. They eviscerated him. His organs were thrown on the pyres in front of him. He may have lived long enough, have retained consciousness, to watch his liver crisping and spitting. That squeal you hear is air escaping flaming lungs. That hearthside crackle is exploding intestines spraying shit on an audience of puzzled sheep.

They daubed him with ochre, buried him in the foetal position, pasted him with feathers. His broken neck was packed with ostrich eggs and jewels. His incisors were knocked out with a hammer so that he could not rise to bite the living. The great black birds were alert. They hung on thermals waiting, crying, stuttering, trilling, exhaling vulture breath. Soon they were descending upon him, a congregation of flapping funereal black feathers competing in mourning as they feasted. His eyes were the first to go, bloodied dark pits they were, portals to the final place Father Linsel Murly was bound for.

When we next catch up with Jezzard Dogg he too is in his grave, in a small Welsh village, three thousand miles from Tamanrasset and eighty from Malpasfang. He lived into his nineties despite a daily regime of forty Seniors and a bottle of Gordon's. He suffered Root's Canker, which he passed on to his offspring and they to their offspring and so on. It's safe to assume they were infected because animals don't usually practise safe sex, and nor did Jezzard Dogg. Early onset arthritis, bursting sores, myopia and seepage – like 'the syphilitic prick of the British grenadier', as the old ditty has it.

Mind: it isn't all one way. The crossbreed mothers 'inherit' horizontally from the children/cubs/pups/kids/kittens they are carrying. They are retrofitted by foetal cells which sneak into their bloodstream and bring a different DNA to the next pregnancy: the second offspring will exhibit traits of the first as well as of the parents. What a labyrinth he erected. His gravestone is inscribed: 'He loved all creatures.'

There came a time when Inigo could exhume no more information on the messiah of the Hoggar, the unacknowledged martyr. Despite his intolerance of physical discomfort he had been keen to go to Tamanrasset to do some digging and to see the place he had been writing about without any first-hand knowledge. Get the feel of it. Whatever that means. He was eventually dissuaded by government warnings to tourists of piratical activities in the western Sahara.

Anti-post-colonial-revanchists is a bit of a mouthful. The most notorious group was the Dib family whose sacred ideology was to capture Europeans during the festival of falnadath and hold them to ransom. They had recently murdered a party of Finnish ornithologists believing them to be French spies.

It was at this point that he read McHarg Bultitude's *A Blister in My Head*.

Inigo broached what turned out to be the rich seam that was Malpasfang Lodge. It just kept giving, like the sort of coal measure a dynasty is based on. But at that point all he knew of it was that McHarg Bultitude had given it a miss and had despised the folklore attached to it, which Inigo found compelling. 'It stuck to me. It just chose me' was his only explanation for what would become his obsession. 'Oh, and the name Malpasfang – it sent shivers down my spine.'

Bart and Tamara were engrossed by that narrative – what Inigo disparaged as the N-word. I'd worked on *Afterlife* for four weeks. Sorting and junking, cutting and pasting, obviously maintaining Inigo's presence as creator. Their interest surprised me till I sussed I was so familiar with these tales and Inigo's deductions that the strange cruelties were no longer shocking . . . I was inoculated against what I was giving them. It gave me pleasure to give them pleasure. There was pleasure in the telling. It's safe to assume that they weren't flattering me when they praised my efforts.

For them it obviously all came out the blue.

'What are you going to do with it?' asked Tamara.

'Do?'

'It's a terrific story. *Stories*, I mean.'

'It should be published . . . as a tribute to Inigo. Posthumous is box office.' Bart was encouraging. That's love for you.

'It's only a fragment. Unpolished stone. How Inigo got into this world of Malpasfang. Just the start . . . The trigger . . . He'd have gone back to it.'

I knew it was great material. Inigo had congratulated himself on it often enough. No problem with it legally. Nor with the material in *Breast Milk Cheese* . . . They were all dead . . .

Look at it like this.

The messiahs – *Life After Afterlife* – are the first act. Unfinished.

Victorian Malpasfang – *Breast Milk Cheese* – is the second act. Famously done.

The third act is *Venom's Genealogy*, let's call it that. It was one of the titles Inigo had considered. There were mucho notes. Very little finished text. Hardly started really. Malpasfang today . . .

Not the house obviously but the ongoing vibe, the ethic, the aesthetic . . . the inheritors, its tentacles, the far right freakery. It runs in families, 'grand' families, and their weird hangers-on, their endless yes-men. Feudalism lives. Democracy is something alien, something that happens outside the walls of the estate. Be that as it may, hierarchy is hierarchy even if it's dressed up as equality: everyone addressed by their given name, open collars, handshakes all round . . . fake equality. That house has haunted people. Poisonous ideology dwells in the ruins and jungle round it, the specimen trees gone native . . . Yes, *Venom's Genealogy*.

He'd exhumed a can of worms, a wholesale can that was a hot potato.

Oh dear! Beg your pudding! How about a can of potatoes?

La Négligence had told him it was unpublishable. Unfortunately she was right. Meaning her girlfriend Antonia, who she always parroted, was right. Antonia was a shrewish bitch of a publisher.

Inigo called her an ethical derelict: 'She'd have put the Jews on the train.'

She was a serial founder of publishing houses. Her speciality was getting gullible backers to fund new imprints then giving La Négligence's clients absurdly high advances of the backers' money . . . advances which could never be recouped. But so what – La Négligence got her 15 per cent. Sharp practice but no more illegal than her pomposity. It wasn't just La Négligence and Antonia who said the third act wasn't worth even beginning.

Inigo hadn't wanted to believe them. He outlined it to Ayesha who, with regret, agreed. She took us to dinner with her friend Pelly Duncanson KC (£2,000 per hour for civilians). After 'The Sorcery Trial' – Hebdomeros and Gant v Panglobal Medicare Ultra – she was that season's smartest libel brief. She reiterated what Ayesha had said:

the very imputation is libellous, it's defamatory, trouble et cetera. You don't have even to spell it out. Just a coded hint will bring a tonne of bricks down on you.

It was naive to believe that it being 'true' was some sort of defence.

Pelly: 'Such a quaint concept, truth – I'm surprised at you!'

Besides, some of Inigo's 'investigative' methods *were* without question illegal. Paying teenage pick-ups to hack computers was illegal. Obtaining DNA samples without consent was illegal.

Inigo obstinately retaliated: 'I'm not an investigative journalist.'

'That,' said Pelly, 'is all too obvious.'

A resounding collective: 'Don't do it, Inigo . . . You'll be shooting yourself in the foot, in both feet. And what for? Let's go to a club.'

The sand in the gearbox was that several of the persons involved were still alive: David Irving, Geoffrey Shadoxhurst, Robert Faurisson, Ahmed Rami. Even those who by rights ought to have been showing signs of mortality were failing to do so.

Plus, those who weren't bankrupt or banged up weren't short of a bob or two. And the perfidious UK libel laws . . . The rich and powerful make laws that favour the rich and powerful.

'Risk does make cowards of us all, me included.' That was Inigo's coinage, so he claimed.

I knew my limits: Inigo had often reminded me of them.

Let me further remind you of them:

Penning articles on lifestyle-class interiors and totally happening soft furnishings. Soft furnishings are the beacons of your soul. Soft furnishings make a home. As for carpets – my little boast is that I can tell an Esari pardah from a Charshango torba at a hundred metres! Unfortunately *Big Picture Window* hired a new editor who was a sopht phurnishings philistine!!

Penning an autobiography for an arrogant prick of a rock star.

Picture editor of *Bulk Girth*.

Dialogue coach on *Neck Brace*, *Fire Island Fuckfest* and *Fisting The Night Away*.

Compiling *The Wonder Book of One Hit Wonders*. Two of the surviving members of The Karisma Set settled out of court: their definition of a hit was broader than mine.

Compiling a fun book of madcap headlines and standfirsts entitled *Serial Sperm Donor In Legal Clash With Lesbian Grandmother's Cat*. It won the Auld Wee Donnie Trelford Comfi-Wipes For Seniors™ Investigative Loo Book of The Year award. Here are some classix from it:

Drunk tube driver, 36, wore stag mask, not guilty of terrorism.

Nuns' giant candles a threat to forest tribe's lifestyle.

Blazing Bluebottle: Top stylist Bob de Bruges sets light to woman bobby's bob.

BBC anchor dead in solo sex game with pervert avocado and pet jug.

Amputee fire-boss put woman, 24, over metal knee and spanked her.

All the cutlery you need for a trip to the sapphire afterlife.

Team GB dog-sled racer intimate with trans husky allegations.

Supply teacher in infra-traction after clash with salad.

Disabled dog rescues tragic tot buried alive by teen mum's shame.

Wannabee adult star, 14, robbed blind lollipop lady to pay for penis enlargement.

Tango-crazy Schnauzer Mario's owner Ashleigh Dipp, 28, had scorching fling with close pal's world champion Marcher Hound trainer boyfriend.

(Inigo cruelly joked that I could have thought them up: why didn't I get a job on *The Moron*. That hurt. He could be all asperity when he wanted.)

Sourcing a hundred solid-gold chuckleworthy Catholic gags for another award-winning loo book *The Pope's Perk is the Prelate's Perineum*.

Wordsmithing three editions of the *Little Gay Tractor* franchise including the cult *Farmer Geddon* episodes. I introduced substantive major characters. Sulky The Suave Dumpertruck, Victor The Venomous Veal Crate, Bruce The Churn With Hygiene Issues, Sneaky The Organiciser, and Quentin The Trailer who always brings up the rear.

Despite Sulky and Victor being top of the podium-lead-merchandise products my contract was not renewed.

Illustrator bitch Toby 'Bitch' Trinnick thought I was getting too much attention. Bitch!

Proud as I was of my achievements, I wasn't sure that they qualified me to undertake a proper book. Apart from the effort involved it would almost surely end in litigation. I knew my limits.

'How do you know? No one knows their limits, not till they've tried to go beyond them. Qualifications, Dom! Come on!'

Tamara was not having it. No way José.

'When I started *Sleeping Fox*[39] all I'd ever written was angsty adolescent poems . . . I was working in a florist's for Christ's sake . . . I thought of this name Pandora Gallanders . . . More like it just came to me . . . And I followed it . . . there was this oily old smoothie . . . very la-di-da . . . we called him The Gent . . . stinking rich . . . the colour of Oxford marmalade . . . he was banging the hairdresser across the street . . . used to come into the shop just to ogle me . . . it was like he was always on heat . . . had all these fancy old cars, Bugattis . . . Bentleys . . . he'd hand out Balkan Sobranies to the oiky kids who came to look at them . . . used to sit there revving them like he owned the street . . . I was walking past one day . . .

'"Hear that? . . . That raaw of satisfaction . . . Just like a woman . . . How'd you like to come for a jaunt? Vroom vroom . . ." He was coming on all groovesome like he was god's gift not a leathery hundred-year-old lecher . . . hundred-and-fifty-year-old.

'I gave him my supercilious smile. God I wouldn't have got in his car if I was paid . . . And I'm sure he would have paid – classic DOM[40] . . . can't begin to think how old . . . MTF[41] . . .

'But I *imagined* what would happen if Pandora got in his car . . . and got involved with someone like that . . . totally mercenary

---

39 Full title: *Sleeping Fox Attacked By Baby.*
40 Dirty old man.
41 Must touch flesh.

motives . . . five times her age . . . then found out a terrible secret about him . . . that puts her life in danger from him . . .'

Tamara was encouraging, not nagging like some life coaches I could mention. 'Get on with it. Push yourself. Test your determination. Try. It'll be an adventure. What are you going to do when you're through with all of this horror . . . the fucking police and the officialdom . . . *work* your way out of grief . . . even if you have got Bart you're going to find there's a huge gap in your life . . . fill it! And here's an idea. Old as the hills. Change the locations: I mean *Sleeping Fox* was set in England to start with. Change the names of the characters. That's what I do. It's what writers *do*. Since time immemorial . . .'

'Well, maybe I shall . . . yes, I'll have a go.'

There was no one to warn me: 'You'll be fucking up your career.'

That's because I didn't have much of a career to fuck up. (See above.) I had been offered the opportunity to host a monthly cuff-links podcast. After some deep brain mind-wrangling I decided to get in touch with the team at *Serious Eyewear* and turn it down.

'And if it doesn't work out . . .'

'Nothing ventured nothing gained,' said Bart. 'We are learning that saying in first year English age three. For sure it's on the spot. Audax mijn gabber. Audax!'

Venom's Genealogy

I was shocked, truly shocked by how shocked they were when they read what follows, woven together by me from my memory of our conversations and Inigo's notes and verbatim tapes. Scotch tape and Mnemosyne! Only kidding!

Me, no, I was not shocked.

Subjection to brutalisation (even at second hand), to incidents no lapsed Christian househusband should ever hear of, to the behaviour of people who had stepped beyond the far bounds of decency had made me unshockable. My reservoir of condemnation had run dry. Films of starved bodies piled high, millions of pairs of broken spectacles and ripped-open wombs had, to my shame, ceased to touch me. It's strange what shocks and what doesn't.

Here's an instance: Inigo had an obsession with secret messages in *Deutsches Requiem* . . . he claimed it was a work of 'vatic encryption', that Brahms predicted a gullible nation tragically following Wagner's orders to commit monstrous acts, then obediently following orders to join in the collective ignominy, then cravenly following orders to be contrite and, when healed, following orders to rise en masse from the dead. 1 Corinthians 15:52 comes into it somewhere. And when they have risen . . . the whole hideous cycle starts over. Ludicrous presumption . . . typical, I'm afraid, of Inigo's intellectual dishonesty or vanity . . . Brahms and Wagner had a spikey relationship but this was absurd.

Of course it was nothing more than a boast.

But it did shock me. It really did. I was thankful that I wasn't entirely desensitised.

> *It was the hour like no other hour*
> *A White Lady, a Sidecar, a Whisky Sour*
> (McHarg Bultitude)

This was one of our little rituals, often observed. I was mixing Perfects.

'Easy on the Angostura, Captain!'

'Aye aye, Commodore.'

'Your friend Ricky . . . Moist Groin wasn't he?'

He knew very well he was. And he knew too that I hadn't seen him for a while. He enjoyed winding me up by calling him 'my friend' when I had told him time and again that I couldn't take the narcissistic little prick for more than a few minutes at a time. He was also taking a dig at me for being associated with a band with a particularly noisome name. Just how tacky does it get? Memorable though.

As Ricky said: 'A band is a brand. You don't want a *nice* name, you want a catchy name . . . I thought it up . . . and the logotype . . . brand identity . . . you'll never see that font used for anything else . . . I designed it . . . Me . . . I own the copyright.'

Inigo pretended to despise pop music even though there was nothing he enjoyed more than getting blocked out of his head on regals and sharksmarts and getting on down (as he put it) to Gloria Gaynor, Donna Summer, Big Tache, Wild Leather Swordsmen, The Audiocrats, Captain and Tennille etc.

'So you know Stafford Prance then?'

'*Staff!* . . . Why on earth? . . . I met him a couple of times . . . talked to him for the book—'

'And?'

'And what?'

'Tell me about him . . .'

'I thought I had. Not that there's much to tell. File under twenty-something multimillionaires with a massive chip . . . make that the whole chip shop.'

'Remind me, Liebes Herz.'

Real name Stafford Philip Rance.

The others were tacitly resigned to Ricky being the star attraction. Didn't give a heron's molar. They knew it was down to Ricky that they were making more bread than Hovis. The dinari they trousered in a week was more than most people make in several lifetimes.

Staff wasn't resigned tacitly or otherwise. It's safe to assume that he didn't admit to himself that he was only in the band in the first place because he had a direct line to Transits. When they met him his puppy fat was already turning to dog fat. He had a bottle of Light and Bright, bad breath and a drum kit he could barely play. There are literally thousands of adolescents with a drum kit they can't play in their bedroom. Most of them don't have a dad with a commercial vehicles dealership. He got to have his pick of old smokers, the garbage taken in part exchange. Plus there was an unused workshop where they rehearsed.

But . . . short-term gain long-term pain. The snag: they were stuck with him. Long after they'd said byebye to Transits and their preferred form of travel was private jets he was still there . . . Nomen non est omen. Prance? Prance! No way. He was a five-foot-six, eighteen-stone embarrassment on four-inch heels. He lumbered, he sweated, he waddled with his tongue curling down his chin 'like an obscene zoo animal misjudging how to lure a child into its cage'.

He was laughably unself-aware. No idea how lucky he'd been. I remember saying to him: Ricky writes, sings, plays lead, plays piano – various other instruments too – including drums, arranges, produces, even does the album art.

And he replied: 'But I do the interviews.'

For a moment I stupidly thought he was being ironic. No! No sir. Didn't do irony. Swollen ego doesn't begin to get it . . . So pompous it was glorious to behold . . .

And wondrously gullible: Ricky loved winding him up. He told him 'Miss Otis Regrets' was about people stuck in a lift waiting for an engineer. He believed him. No bullshit detector.

He's on the immensely plump side for a rock musician . . . not great for the brand . . . two lunch merchant . . . slobbering glutton . . . even bought shares in Inglescrunch – the all chemical organic lifestyle snack chew. The others were satyromaniacs. According to Ricky, Staff's sex life was sex death . . . troppo saddo. Just voyeurism. He had . . . still has . . . a woman friend. 'Die Zürcherin', she was known as . . . well, that's what Ricky calls her.

Very big-time pharma heiress. Barmettler Jäggi. Ripping off health services the world over: keeping the population in check. Eye-wateringly loaded. Has never been on public transport in her life. Philanthropist of course. You name it she'd save it: old masters, mountains, rare species of vulture, chateaux. She's always commissioning pretentious architects to build houses and galleries . . .

They make a strange couple to say the least. Impossible to tell what age she is. Very tall, towers over him, very thin, very severe hairdo, asymmetric bob, brilliantined maybe – looks like one of the less amiable guards at Treblinka . . . You could say he's the world's shortest toy boy . . . not to mention fattest. The attraction of course is that he's not a gold digger . . . she's archered at least three husbands who were . . .

'Zurich?'

'Yes. Zurich. They used to go to sex clubs . . . maybe still do.'

'Interesting.'

'Watching . . . that's what turned him on. He'd never join in. He had a real hang-up about penetration. Ricky reckoned it was because he suffered premature ejaculation . . . didn't want to show himself up so to speak.

'You could say that and changing his name were the only interesting things about him . . . And they're really not *that* interesting.'

'Depends how you look at it. What clubs did they go to? Where?'

'Paris mostly. More anonymous, so they thought: Zee Baden Bath, Les Chandelles, Aux Shenanigans in Brussels . . . high end – anywhere you'd find No-Man-Died.[42] Why this sudden curiosity?'

'His name's come up a couple of times.'

'Meaning?'

'He's got some unsavoury friends. Questionable taste.'

'Inigo! He's a *rock musician* for god's sake . . .'

'I'm not talking about *that* sort of unsavoury.'

'What sort then? It's not all dealers and groupies. These guys don't lead sheltered lives. They're fully equipped climbers. Ricky knows some very strange people . . . "from the shadows to the limelight" as he says. He's got oligarchs on speed dial. He fucks top Eurotrash . . . royalty from countries you've never heard of . . . He hangs out with shipowners . . . Then there's a guy called Rui he's really thick with who brokers stuff between Saudis, Israel, central Asian tyrannies . . . probably organises hits for Mossad too.'

'*Does* he?'

'Does he what?'

'Organise hits . . .'

'Who knows? That may just be Ricky boasting. The man's a fixer . . . travels on half a dozen passports in different names . . . Odd come to think of it . . . he was sort of being prying round Staff too. But . . . for heaven's sake – last time I looked he'd bought a major stake in Robert J. Carl aka Seven Figure Bobby New York rare book dealer who touches nothing less than first folios and Magna Carta . . . Gutenberg Bibles. Is that Mossad behaviour? But like I say who knows?

------

42 'Il n'y a pas mort d'homme' was Jack Lang's tactless clichéd reaction to his friend Dominique Strauss-Kahn's arrest on a charge of rape at the New York Sofitel 14.05.2011. It means 'it's not *that* serious'. It became our nickname for the probably fitted-up presidential candidate. Ricky van Brabant took a close interest in the affair and wrote what he described as a feminist reggae song, 'Bite My Bite Bitch'.

'Thing about Ricky he's a groupie . . . he has heroes . . . he can walk into any party . . . he likes to go alone so he has the field to play . . . he heads for the biggest name . . . craves excitement . . . loves greasing up to the super rich . . . they treat him as one of theirs . . . because *he* is super rich and he's famous and he's charming – charming to them anyway . . . they stick together . . . tribal . . . way of the world . . . the bears are Catholic and the pope shits in the woods . . .

'That reminds me – Staff's the only goy in the band . . .'

'Aaa . . . haah . . . indeed . . . now that is most fascinating.'

He clapped his hands and rubbed them with pantomime glee.

Faineant Park (pron. Fenant) is a late eighteenth-century house, palatial in scale, designed for the slave and sugar trader Sir Jacob Bouverie Shadoxhurst Bt by Seth Tribbeck whose friend and rival Roland Mundy wrote that 'for raciness, invention, resource and grandeur it beats anything . . . Tribbeck is certainly not a gentleman in his works'. In Gillian Darley's words: 'The disparity between the most achingly romantic exemplar of the Greek Revival and the squalor of the fortune on which it was founded is cruelly emphasised by the fidelity of the house's preservation. The telamons, modelled on near-naked slaves crushed beneath back-breaking loads, have been restored with great and inglorious craft.'

Preserved against all odds, it might be said, by Sir Geoffrey Shadoxhurst Bt (b. 1927) and maintained with the revenues from numerous enterprises, some successful.

Montagu of Beaulieu – cars; Bath of Longleat – lions, apes etc.; Bedford of Woburn – rhinos, giraffes; Lenchwick of Lenchwick – monorail, arboretum. They were the pioneers. One of Geoffrey Shadoxhurst's many maxims, pretty obvious from his commercial behaviour, is 'if a chap's got a park he's got to act like a tart. A house and park must pay their way. And if our Hebrew friend Doktor Pevsner won't contribute to its preservation he can't come in and his common as cruet handbook will have to get by without his barbs about the finest house in the four counties.'

Certain attractions achieved notoriety, as they were intended to. Shadoxhurst revelled in stirring the moralistic disapprobation of

Gleaner, The Mores, The Splash, Our Values, Sentinel etc. There's nothing like a ticking off from the finger-pointing hypocrites of the British press to whet the appetite of the prurient mob, send it corkscrewing and screaming through 5-plus g-forces and skeins of twisted metal.

The amusement park is two miles distant from the house. The rides have included *Odin's Express, Hell Hath Fury, Blood Twister, Apocalypse Free Fall, Niagara, Nagasaki Nightmare*. After the death of fifteen people when *Meet Your Maker* left the track during a 90mph vertical descent the park was closed indefinitely for four well-connected months.

He blamed the slow take-up of the Führer World exhibition in the home farm's former brewhouse on 'the usual forces'. In fact it initially attracted opprobrium because it was tawdry and overpriced rather than because of the subject matter: Hitlerians are as cost-conscious as the next scholarly collector. Its ambition, of course, was to educate, inform and entertain.

It celebrated all that was great in the Third Reich: the upside of twelve years of solid overachievement. Green before 'green' ever was. Organic before 'organic' was. Respectful of animals and plants. Landscaped freeways. Cathedrals of light (miserably represented by domestic bulbs and cardboard). There was a collection of holy relics. A Biedermeier secretaire, mahogany inlaid with brass presented to Himmler by Ante Pavelić. Axonometric illustrations of KdF Prora. Perspectives of Ordensburg Vogelsang and Ordensburg Sonthofen. Two copies of *Der Stürmer*; postcards of the Führer, of Göring, and of hooked-nosed Jews fleeing with their money bags from hooked-cross flags; a pewter eagle; a taxidermised otter claimed to be Henry Williamson's fellow travelling National Socialist Otter Tarka; a metal whistle stamped with a death's head; an Allach porcelain figurine of an SS officer mounted on a white steed; lederhosen; leather coats; threadbare trachtenjanker; insignia; helmets; decommissioned weaponry; a child's SS uniform. And outside the brewhouse two black cars, one of them supposedly Hitler's own Mercedes.

Photo albums:

1) Captain Sir Frederick Shadoxhurst's record of the 1938 Nuremberg rally which he attended in the company of his son Geoffrey, dressed as a Hitler Youth.

2) A 1953 Silver Cities flight by Sir Geoffrey Shadoxhurst from Lympne to Le Touquet and thence by road to a meeting, arranged by his correspondent Jorian Jenks of the Soil Association and internee under regulation 18B, with Richard Walther Darré at Bad Harzburg where tales of a probably Welsh madman dressed in rags and furs who had lived in the woods and had stolen children to mate them with animals or sell them to a circus were, half a century on, still recalled with a shudder.

A jocular note in clogged type stated that 'the genial old idealist of blood and soil enjoyed his himbeergeist while reminiscing about his time as Minister of Agriculture, the worldwide acceptance of his doctrines, Heinrich Himmler's intellectual thefts, the absurdity of the Anglo-American invention of "the Shoah", schooldays in Wimbledon, his fondness for his science teacher, his poor opinion of English food, suburbs, street lighting, bookbinding, discipline, horses, fountain pens, soap, central heating, cars, dentistry, intestinal cleanliness and moral laxity'.

'Führer World is what happens when a sick hobbyist with surprisingly limited resources shows off his dirty secret' was the opinion of the local freesheet *South Ahoy* in its 'What Not To Do This Weekend' feature. That caught the eye of a slow learner who was entertainment editor of *The Moron*. Once he had commissioned and published an article lambasting the sick disgrace, the denial of British values, the insult to the millions put to death and starved, the rest of the yellow press got on the bandwagon and wrote exactly the same. Local TV was followed by national TV. And the exhibition was made.

It expanded. A concrete gun emplacement in the shape of a vizor was built in imitation of those on Guernsey. Then came a watchtower equipped, as it would never have been, with furniture from an Ordinanschule and the themes of Reaching Out To The Reich and Panzers For Peace.

Animals, animals. Farmyard of the Senses prompted untrammelled wrath. It was advertised as The Zoo for the Zoophiliac Community.

The Society for Responsibility in Zoological Welfare, The Zebra Trust, Love Life Love Llamas, Burning Bright, The Marmot Identity

Council, Just Because We're Rodents, Fair Play For Schnauzers, Equine Ethics Watch, The Veal League, The Alpaca Front and We're Not Dumb combined to have it closed down a week after it opened. It was re-opened within three days when the constabulary was threatened with civil action for having exceeded its authority. Faineant Park Estate was breaking no law: the number of animals did not require a licence; the welfare standards were exceptional; the transgenic infections consult-ant Everett Awmack had been readmitted by the Royal College of Veterinary Surgeons. Jerome X, the animal rights activist (or terrorist) who was mauled to death by a lion, had hacked his way into the cage with equipment which 'would have granted him entry to Fort Knox'. There was no indication that security procedures were lax or that pro-tective measures were inadequate. Case dismissed. It was again widely mediated.

Country house entrepreneurs always need something extra. To make the house and park pay their way. And to put one over on the oppos-ition. They may be friends – of a sort – but they're deadly rivals too. They have to go beyond steam trains, traction engine festivals. Look, country crafts: artisan jam doesn't cut the mustard. But what greater more enduring country craft is there than zoophilia? That's when he came up with Farmyard of the Senses: Britain's First Heavy Petting Zoo – playmares rather than playmates.

It's safe to assume that the idea for an interactive zoo was not actu-ally his but came from The Infamous Hanna N, as he called her, specifically from her fantasies about masturbating dogs, bulls, horses and so on . . . about notching up species. Milord Shadox was a special guest, always welcome in Les Chandelles under that name, because a direct link to the inspirational post-war partouzes organised by the legendary Vicomtesse. It was love at first sight: the first time he spot-ted The Infamous Hanna N she was complexly conjoined to five men including Pas Mort D'Homme. Her pimpish whale of a boyfiend ges-ticulated and cajoled. He was not masturbating like the rest of the thirty or so spectators who were awaiting their turn. He smugly seemed to think this lent him a bouquet of élan, that it was a classy touch. Rather, he was self-importantly directing the participants in the creation of a tableau vivant, the ringmaster of a porno film without a fourth wall. They were too preoccupied burrowing to pay him attention.

It is safe to assume too that The Infamous Hanna N is Die Zürcherin – and that the pimpish boyfiend failing to stage the scene is Stafford Prance. Reason is not asleep nor is order: but the bodily conjunctions are immune to them. This was Milord Shadox's introduction to them. There are few other circumstances in which they might have met.

Before they actually spoke Milord had miscalculated and aimed badly: he ruined a six-inch heel.

'I never saw you.' She playfully slapped his face and sipped menthe à l'eau in the bar. Staff joined in the jollity.

A heavily jewelled Russian who had watched her perform offered to take her by private jet to a party on his Adriatic island. He mimed counting off banknotes with his fingers.

'A. I am not a prostitute. I am not cheap. I am free. B. I could buy your shitty little primitive island with spare change. So why not fuck off. Try your luck with those doughy Michelin Milfs.'

She indicated a couple of burlies bursting out of latex, looking for love.

It would be hard to imagine an unholier trinity. Or more improbable allies. They were up to something. Staff couldn't help himself dropping coy hints about 'the project we're getting together'. He was rather hurt when the other guys in the band showed no interest. They hoped that whatever the 'project' was it would get so preoccupying that Staff would leave the band or fail to make rehearsals, enabling them to lose him from the line-up. But so long as he didn't trade on the name they were indifferent. Staff, Milord and Die Zürcherin were conspiring in a scheme that obviously had nothing to do with music and was outside the bounds of exaggerated polyandry.

What they had in common was a complicated portfolio of contradictions. They owned sumptuous unearned wealth. They despised little people who pay taxes. They believed in the universality of nationalism, in the common interests of nationalists in all countries – which sounds not altogether unlike internationalism. They were infected with both alt-right paranoia and right-on, sentimental, pro-Palestinianism. They were far from alt-right in their anti-Zionism and 'polite' anti-Semitism (hold the Zyklon B – for the moment).

Given that particular *olla podrida* of unlovely characteristics why on earth should they be cosying up to a self-promoting Israeli entertainer, Dudu Topaz?

Indeed, not long ago, he had been *the* self-promoting Israeli entertainer, the undisputed king of the Tel Aviv airwaves. Talk show host, actor, comedian, vaudevillian, impressionist, monologist, newspaper columnist . . . An undeniable star, but dimming. Still, however, a star narcissist who hadn't begun to come to terms with life in the descendent. He pretended he wasn't heading for the boulevard of broken dreams. He was kidding himself. He was still congratulating himself on every word, every moue, every sly twist of his once handsome face. His rich seam of gimmicks was now close to worked out. His real name by the way was David Goldenberg.

Dudu's attention-seeking contrarianism had taken various forms down the years. During the 1981 elections speaking on behalf of Labor he denounced Likud as the party of Israel's 'Levantisation', of Sephardim and Mizrahim whom he called *chachchachim*, an insult based on their supposedly sibilant speech. He added that their toilet habits were unhygienic and disgusting. Of course he strengthened the Likud vote. But his intra-Jewish racism got himself noticed.

He wrote and played the title role in a Beatrix Potter adaptation entitled *Peter Rabbi*, an allegory of false friendship, lettuce and treacherous allies of convenience which offended secular Jews, reform Jews, orthodox Jews, all Jews, innumerable goys and, suggested *Haaretz*, foxes and badgers. Some achievement. As ever he was forgiven.

When the Argentinian diva Natalia Oreiro sang on his show he bit her.

In another show he talked about this season's fashions in suicide vests, taunting a man who had lost limbs and family in an attack. When the man tearfully chastised him he was accused of not being able to take a joke. Domestic accident victims, far more numerous than people who get in the way of a bomb, do not whine self-pityingly and special plead. More recently he assaulted a television critic, punching her in the face, breaking her glasses. She had mocked him, wounded his amour propre, described him as an attention-seeking child too ignorant even to realise that he was out of his depth: he should stick to funny voices, gurning and flattering unknown celebrities. The cause was a documentary. He accused the government of abdicating its responsibility to hunt and bring to trial Nazi aggressors because it has been 'infiltrated' by Sephardim and Mizrahim who were largely unaffected by the Shoah. They are indifferent to the suffering of European Jewry. They display no solidarity with survivors. They raise obstructions to revenue being spent on detection, extradition proceedings and what they claim would be show trials. He pursued this baseless campaign obsessively in newspaper articles, radio phone-ins and blogs. He was guyed for wishing to turn Israel into Warsaw-on-Sea. He claims that official estimates of the number of surviving nonagenarian and centenarian veterans of the death's head corps are deliberately underestimated. They dose themselves with eternal life pills called ods. They must be hunted down. The government doesn't even carry out checks on immigrants to Israel – hence one of the gags all his fans appreciated and knew by heart back then till it outstayed its welcome, which he typically failed to acknowledge.

Dudu: 'Where is the best place for a Nazi war criminal to hide?'

Audience: 'In the state of Israel.'

Dudu: 'Yes Yes Yes. They are among us.' (His eyes pan across the audience, playing at seeking.)

If the government neglects its duty then freelance vigilantes and sleuths must step in, led by Dudu Topaz himself, who had abandoned his training at RADA to fly home and do his bit as a proud reservist in the Six-Day War. He played a vital role in the Yom Kippur War. A man who was once hailed as the Voice of Israel. The Voice will silence the pusillanimous government. And Dudu will resurrect his glorious career.

If only . . . if only the pretty boy had not lost his looks, had not lost the plot, had not lost his audience by going too far, too often. His audience had once adored him. It came to regret that he did not reciprocate. The compact was broken. He would do anything to repair it. But it's too late, Dudu, too late. He alone fails to see it. He's old hat. Hence his flailing, self-abasing attempt to reinvent himself by concocting a comeback in association with people who are the enemies of Jewry. Who is playing who?

His big-hearted, dentally formidable, glossily sincere promise to launch a campaign to flush out destroyers who'd make a pyre of the Jewish race would be more credible were it not made in confederation with those very destroyers' fellow travellers. It is a patent career move, a desperate ploy to save himself from an appearance on *Where Are They Now?* presented by a justifiably gloating Esther Gaventa. Details later.

In a BBC2 *Against The Flow* interview about Farmyard of the Senses Sir Geoffrey Shadoxhurst told Joan Bakewell: 'No matter what a phalanx of you bearded lesbians may say, it is an evocation of classical antiquity when our race was constantly strengthened by the blood and genes of other species – we married out as our Jewish friends would say. We ought not to consign the great heroes to mere mythology. That is just schoolmasterly tosh. They existed. Mark my words. They existed and will exist again when we overcome the hangover of Christianity. This is just a first step on the long road back to paganism.'

Contacted later he said: 'I have nothing to apologise for. Don't know the meaning of the word.'

The appeal was limited to specialists. Few visitors to Britain's first Heavy Petting Zoo wished to avail themselves of the facilities and those who might have had the appetite already had private arrangements. The Ectopig scared children and repulsed adults. A few specialists enquired. They were politely directed towards more conventional potential partners: alpacas, ewes, calves.

The Faineant Park Stud is today managed by Luc Jérome, formerly of the Haras National de Pompadour at Arnac in the Corrèze. He is known throughout the bloodstock world for his work 'under light', countering anoestrus with daylight floodlamps and heated paddocks surrounded by indeciduous trees, i.e. camouflaging the seasons in pursuit of perpetual summer. The artificial disruption prolongs a mare's oestrous phase so enabling a stallion to work the year round and not simply when a future dam is 'naturally' receptive. The stud currently standing, Moscatel, has fathered twenty-eight G1 and twelve classics winners, among them Party Hands, Bright Andy, No Sweat, Major Ron, Call That An Alibi, Flaming Hair, Handsome Claude, One For The Road, What A Whopper, Medallion Man, Briarpipe, U Saucy Scamp, Tickertape Lad.

Captain Sir Frederick Shadoxhurst, 10th baronet, a well-known jump jockey, 'the Napoleon of the weighing room', established the stud in 1928. Among his reasons for doing so was his wish to repay friends of a lower social class, who did not enjoy his material advantages, by providing work for them. The arrangement was frictionless till late summer 1938 when the martinet stud-manager Paul Milman sacked the senior strapper Davy Skitch for feigning illness so that he could take his little boy Ned up to town for the day. Strapper! Senior sinecurist if truth be known. They had gone to watch England v Australia at the Kennington Oval. When they got off the train at Waterloo they had no idea that it would prove to be an historic match. They saw Len Hutton in his prime. He would complete the marathon innings which brought him what was then the highest ever score in test cricket: 364 in thirteen hours at the wicket, as every schoolboy used to know.

They were spotted getting on the train home by Wanda Milman.

Some weeks later Sir Frederick came back from *Götterdämmerung*, *Parsifal* and *Tristan und Isolde* at Bayreuth, a visit to an Austria grateful for Anschluss, some fine motoring on green banked autobahnen, and the most magnificent of all Nuremberg rallies. Geoffrey Shadoxhurst, eleven years old, was dressed in SS finery.

After inspecting the estate Sir Frederick remarked to Paul Milman that he hadn't seen Skitch. Milman explained that he was no longer employed. He had had no choice but to dismiss 'the wretched lazybones' for dishonesty.

Sir Frederick was furious. Skitch was a faithful comrade, a loyal batman, who had been at his side in the most trying and dangerous of circumstances. There was a tacit compact – gentleman and villein, nothing on paper – that he was rewarded with a job for life and a tied cottage. Further, Sir Frederick was, so he told his close friend and co-conspirator Roderick Vanier, waiting, desperately waiting, for Ned to reach puberty when he hoped to 'have a crack at the little chap'. The boy's callipers stirred him. Droit du seigneur was on the cards.

Years of deprivation and drudge, breadlessness and whey that generation after generation of his forebears had suffered showed in Davy Skitch's face. He had been born worn out. He had been leader of a group of fellow prisoners in Wormwood Scrubs who had protected Sir Frederick when he was serving two years for 'conspiring to incite male persons to commit acts of gross indecency known as buggery'. Not easy being a toff in chokey. And as for a queer toff . . . Captain Sir needs all the muscle he can get that'll respond to his promises of a better life after tronk. Davy Skitch was precious to Sir Frederick. The offer was open too, *sine die*, to the other lads who'd taken scarring blades, broken bottles and crunching mallets for him. He sacked Milman whose hair en brosse he had never taken to. He retrieved Davy, Dot and Ned from a Grith Fyrd work camp in a wood.

More than seventy years later Inigo traced the aged Paul Milman to the north London suburb of Bounds Green. An airless flat, greasy cushions, all felt particulates, clogged wool and cigarette smoke. The single 'l' made the search easy:

'We didn't anglicise . . . why should we . . . we were going to . . . we fled Ukraine, we fled . . . we fled Prague . . . we fled oh I don't . . . my memory you know . . . we fled Chantilly a good post that . . . but La Cagoule was active there . . . you know their ideas about employment were based on slavers' practices . . . they appealed because the slavers treated their slaves as if they were valuable horses . . . dressage thoroughbreds . . . they are capital . . . feed them . . . don't let them die . . . The one place we didn't flee was Faineant Park – we *were* fled!' A chuckle turned into a violent cough.

The pile of blankets on a collapsible sofa bed stirred. A voice within them said: 'You're too young to remember the evening races at Ally Pally.'

'What?'

'You heard me,' accused the voice.

'No I'm not. Mondays. They were. Monday evenings.'

'You're saying what you think we want to hear. Why do you think we didn't anglicise . . . it would have been cowardice . . . because the

English pogrom . . . it sniffs you out . . . sniff sniff like a Marcher Hound . . . it's quiet, you don't see it . . . it isn't cattle trucks . . . gas chambers, no . . . no . . . no . . . not at all . . . it is polite . . . it destroys the soul not the body . . . our name had one "l" and that's how it stayed. Pride. Captain Sir Frederick . . . he changed when he saw we had just the one "l" . . . he thought it was a spelling mistake on a foal's birth certificate . . . he hadn't realised we were Jews . . . but there you are . . . we didn't realise he was *rosa winkel* till . . . who was it told us? Ach!'

From within the blankets: 'Bert.'

'*Rosa winkel?*'

'Pink triangle . . . Pansy. Lavender. Crackerjack . . . many words for it. Bert the Groper that'll have been. Bert the Toper never said a word. Bert the Groper . . . you couldn't shut him up . . . mister chatterbox we called him . . . it was lucky for him that Captain Sir Frederick was chairman of the bench . . . that's England all over . . . he'd been in jail two years . . . but he's a nob . . . so appointed chairman of the bench soon as he's out . . . Bert the Groper he was up before him regularly . . . never sufficient evidence . . . case dismissed . . . he used to stand in the middle of the road outside the Salamanca Gate . . . the cars had to stop . . . if it was a lady who wound down the window he'd grasp her breast . . . called himself a lady's man . . .

'He claimed that the child Geoffrey couldn't be Captain Sir Frederick's son because the Captain was banged up when the boy was conceived . . . "I'm not one for the arithmetic," he'd say, "but it's easy as scraping the piles out your arse." A rich turn of phrase he had . . .'

That checked all right – unless Viola Shadoxhurst (née Phimister) had an exceptional gestation of eighteen months. This was of course commonplace aristocratic behaviour. There is a long tradition of not knowing who the father is. Indeed in certain milieux it's considered bad form, not to mention thuddingly bourgeois, to have any idea of who sired you – so long as it was a house guest. The higher up the absurd unchanging social hierarchy you go the greater the pride in ignorance.

She didn't go into lag-wife mourning while her husband was away.

Far from it. She made the most of her freedom. Sobriety and sexual restraint would have betrayed the principles of her marriage. She carried on just as normal. There were even more parties than usual, parties lasting days, parties with Fragonard themes, parties with Roman and Neanderthal and Crusader costume, shrill guests, guests she'd never seen, guests who stole, guests who danced the black bottom till they dropped, jazz bands, cocaine, cocktails. Very much *not* to Captain Sir Frederick's taste. Young things but far from bright. The future travel writer and war correspondent Lulu Kraft described them as 'brute cattle . . . the ranks of the conventionally unconventional'.

Viola's father Marcus Phimister was often there. Practically moved in for a time. Until his son-in-law's enforced absence he had not visited Faineant Park since the wedding. It was reliably rumoured that they thoroughly disliked each other, no doubt because they were so obviously cut from the same cloth – itchy, squaddy-issue cloth: contemplative, depressive, socially ill at ease, brusque and shy, happy in the company of vagabond countrymen, happier in the company of horses. Both were blond. Though her father was by then a former blond, white-haired and white-bearded.

'An odd cockle to be sure. Lived in Bern . . .'

'Zurich,' said the blankets.

'We saw him twice . . .'

'Three times!' came the voice . . .

'*Seldom* then. He only visited when the Captain was away.'

Paul Milman shrugged. 'Very learned man so it is said . . . The melancholy Herr Marcus . . . Never recovered from his wife's suicide . . .'

'Did *you*? Did you recover? Did you ever ask why I . . . ?' asked the blankets.

'He blamed himself . . . He was simply enjoying a romantic liaison with a mare who'd caught his eye . . . a fine spotted Knabstrupper, Amalianie . . . a big filly, seventeen hands plus – he had to use a ladder to reach the optimal core penetration . . . if you have spent years working stud farms you become familiar with ladder abuse . . . the relationship seems to have been somewhat one-sided . . . the mare was perhaps growing bored with this courtship and was preparing herself for a more suitable swain. As he invaded her premises she flung back her head with a screeching whinny and slipped awkwardly, a hind hoof kicked out as her flank struck heavily against the side of the stall. The suddenly unsupported ladder teetered. He watched aghast as she fell in stages, all coordination gone, all grace gone, motor skill-less. And then he fell too, as though thrown by the ladder. The smooth stone floor rushed to meet him. He lay concussed, skull fractured, stamped on, bleeding, his jodhpurs round his ankles.

'That's how the steward – Holzmann? Höchheim? – found him. The steward had loathed him from the moment he had arrived at Kaltenborn as a hermit. Höldrich, that's it . . . Sebastian Höldrich. He didn't call for medical assistance. Instead he found Marcus's wife and brought her to the scene. You can perhaps imagine her shame, perhaps not, for this was an unusual betrayal. She was not the sort of wife who was willing to overlook being deceived, she did not want to be made a cuckquean. The only revenge was self-obliteration. She blamed herself for her terrible rashness in allowing fascination with a wild man to overcome her loneliness and bulk. One option was the prospect of a lifetime recalling her revulsion at the squalid sight in that stable and the wedge of chill pale sky above the door beyond the stalls. Another option was a 2.5cl bottle in a desk drawer.

Drowsily, slowly, prickle-eyed, he awoke. He worked out where he was. Who was the stiff black astrakhan-collared overcoat beside the hospital bed? It took him long seconds to piece together the fleshless ivory features of the Dumpbergs' lawyer Herr Röhrenbeck.

His sight seemed impaired, the field of vision limited.

'How is she?' he heard himself say, hoarsely.

'Aah,' breathed Röhrenbeck. 'They haven't told you then . . . I strictly forbade them . . . I must commend them. I feared they might usurp my role.'

'No . . . no . . . no one has told me anything.' He felt heavy, blurred, his limbs were pushing through thick air.

Röhrenbeck made to leave the room.

'How is she?' he insisted.

'Do not move – I shall be back in just a minute.'

'Move! How can I move!' His head bore a turban. One ankle was in plaster.

The man was a fool. He left the room. There was a conversation in the corridor. Three voices. Through the frosted glass he could see the profile of a nun's wimple. He couldn't make out the words but the pre-verbal humours were unmistakable. Accusation, indignation, hardly repressed fury.

Röhrenbeck returned: 'There has been a breakdown in communication.'

'How *is* she?'

A porcine priest shuddered his way into the room

'She is . . . I regret to tell you . . .' Röhrenbeck flicked his hand at the priest who clucked dismissively and didn't move. 'She has . . . she has moved on . . . it was painless . . . save apparently for a second's sore throat . . . It is a painless kind of death . . . very rapid kind of death . . . she is unequivocally dead. Dead without qualification. And while it is not my place to stand in judgement nonetheless I shall.'

'Dead?'

'You are right. It is not your place,' the priest was stentorian.

Röhrenbeck grimaced: 'I believe beyond all reasonable doubt that your actions, your probably criminal actions, your certainly perverted actions were wholly responsible for all that befell my late client.'

'Late client? What are you . . . late client?'

'Your wife is — was — represented by my cabinet.'

'My wife? What's this to do with her? What I want to know is did that worm Höldrich . . . did he get the equine vet . . . the sound one . . . not that pathetic generalist? Well, did he?'

'Your wife took her own life.'

'My wife took . . . what? My wife! My wife! You misunderstand, Sir.'

'The balance of her mind was . . . how to put it . . . its equilibrium was shattered by your behaviour . . . which in all probability she suspected was not a unique aberration but an episode in a habitual pattern of zoophilia. She poisoned herself six hours after she witnessed your ignominy, she poisoned herself. She left no note but she really didn't need to—'

'Oh do stop blathering. I thought you were here to report on Amalianie. How is she? Will you—'

'The mare you assaulted was traumatised . . . She had to be put down.'

'Amalianie . . . no . . . no . . . no . . .'

Here began the infamous legal actions with the Dumpberg cousins that dragged on through Viola's childhood. Marcus declined to have the suits heard in camera: that would have implied that he was ashamed of the transgenic experiments to which he had devoted much of his life. He was proud to have militated for man and pig, dog and otter, woman and stag. He scorned Judaeo-Christian morality. Leviticus was an anti-life manual, a curb on being human, an invitation to parsimony of the spirit and to bodily caution. The little girl was all he had . . . he doted on her . . . she could twist him round her little finger. He loved his child's fortune and the many properties which could never be taken from him as Malpasfang had been.

Sebastian Höldrich had never tried to blackmail Marcus Phimister. Blackmail with no evidence save that of one's eyes is merely threat. But Marcus took no chances. He continued to employ the man as though nothing had happened. He treated him with a respect that was insufficiently exaggerated to be taken for sarcasm.

Höldrich was able, then, to continue stalking der Schlager. He could be seen from the house trotting from one copse to another, dismounting, rifle over his shoulder, leaving his horse tethered while he followed the trail of the stag's fewmets. Day after day he pushed through the humid woods, through the dripping heather, treading soggy cones into the sandy soil and collapsed foxholes. Exposed roots twined with branches felled by the Föhn. Accretions of dead bark, dead leaves, dead mulch, dead humus, dead wanwood, dead snags were alive with microscopic palpitation. Teeming beetles were bloated at a banquet of decomposition.

A black brook trickled. Light was scarce. Höldrich bent to inspect from close a fresh hoof print. The dead boughs in a knitted thicket groaned, gratingly, metal on metal, an unoiled hinge pining for WD40. Höldrich looked up. The eyes that shone were his executioner's. The dead boughs were the magical tines of der Schlager. The beast had the chest of a bull and the breath of an aurochs. Its foetid miasma thickened the atmosphere and poisoned the earth: that was the last sensation he suffered. The prongs that pierced him – surroyal, bez, pearl, beam – made his name his destiny. The great beast was dainty and potent, flying on fly agaric, rearing on hind legs, boxing and dancing with fearless joy, all inhibitions excised, demob happy, taking revenge for all its kind down the aeons.

Grasping his weekly bouquet Röhrenbeck left his office one evening in a violent rain storm. A junior employee looking down from his desk into the black rain-shined street below noted that he inhaled the scent of flowers and smiled with satisfaction. He stumbled as he clambered onto the Ostfriedhof tram and raised his hat in apology to a fellow passenger. He was never seen again.

Frederick Geoffrey Otto Bouverie Shadoxhurst, future 10th baronet, was born on 21 January 1900, seven months after his parents Alexandra and Valentine had returned from Bavaria to Faineant Park. Valentine had just inherited the estate on the death of his father, the 8th baronet.

Alexandra learnt she was pregnant the morning of the funeral, carrying the child of the lascivious donkey Marcus who had betrayed her with a horse. A garrulous family doctor let slip news of her condition. He was thankfully ignorant of the father's identity. She was said to have attended the service at the estate church in the guise of a ghost. Valentine shyly, lightheadedly received congratulations as well as commiserations.

His reproductive prowess came as a surprise to the congregated mourners, among them his four elder sisters and their brutish, bookless, mutually antipathetic husbands who had vied with each other to produce an heir in the hope that chance, accidental deaths and Valentine's predilection would favour them and their dumb-ox offspring. Two of Valentine's nephews and nieces were older than he was, such was the age difference between the four sisters, 'Irish twins', and the benjamin, their 'baby brother' or (spoken with a sneer) 'god's tardy gift' who had confounded them. Most likely they soon agreed, in a rare access of bitchy harmony, this was the deed of Valentine's proxy or Alexandra's German gigolo.

The baby bore a thick coat of blond hair.

'More fleecy lamb than bonny bairn' was Nanny Shadox's opinion and she knew her bairns all right, having started in wet nursing service long ago in the time of good Queen Adelaide. Oh the cheese that might have been made from those dugs once upon a day when they were swollen rather than dry wrinkled hag flasks.

The child was of no interest to Valentine. The heir was. He was delighted to have an heir. That he was not the child's father was a matter of supreme indifference. So was his having been cuckolded by his sometime lover Marcus Phimister whose body was also springily hirsute. He didn't begrudge Marcus his afternoon distractions with Alexandra which he had long suspected, maybe even connived at. She did not reciprocate when Valentine betrayed himself with a badered slip of the tongue. He was dandling the child at breakfast under Nanny Shadox's watchful eye, feeding him porridge, honey and bread soaked in port, and addressing him: 'That'll make yer coat grow into a fine rich *pelzmantel* like Marcus's. All weather cover!'

A spoonful of yolk dribbled from Alexandra's spoon onto the table. Nanny tutted at her frankly parvenu use of a spoon rather than sucking the yolk from the circumcised shell. She gaped at her rapt husband, so engaged with the baby that he did not notice her.

Of course he and Marcus had spent hours together, planning a better world, drinking toasts to a brighter future, talking of super primates and so on. She was disgusted by the thought that Marcus might have come to her sweating from the bed he had just shared with her gynophobic husband, hair shiny with Atkinson's bear grease pomade, smelling of the Schwarzlose Finale they both wore . . . The deceit of it all!

He had not been fencing. They had not been fencing. Was sated Valentine aware of his next port of call? If he knew did he care?

He was, she guessed, relieved that the animal Marcus spared him the distasteful duty of having to quench her sexual appetite and, more importantly, provide an inheritor, the guarantor of continuity, the bearer of the name and the blood (evidently optional). A messy business. Perhaps Valentine had even instigated the arrangement. She could ask no one other than herself if she was passively complicit. Was that the reason she was ashamed that certain of the practices

Marcus demanded of her were not potentially reproductive? They were – she had it by rumour – exclusive to homosexuals.

He laughed and directed her to erotic prints from what he referred to as the libertine epoch.

He quoted John Wilkes:

> *Life can, then, little else supply*
> *But a few good fucks and then you die.*

But, she protested, they were seldom fucks *per se*. She realised that her pregnancy and the repulsive baby end-product were the result of Marcus's grudging atonement for his side-saddle sodomy, for his insistence that she gave him a hundred to eight.

Suicide creates its own symmetries. Freddie was there. He was only six months old. He could not, then, remember it. For ever after he rode the chalky path to the monument, summoning images of that day, inventing that and other pasts which might have come to pass, which he might have lived had things gone differently, had bustling gusts forced her to hold onto her hat and cling to the dogs' leashes like *Diana of the Uplands* even though there were no dogs and she was hatless, ceremonially hatless. That is how he pictured her despite the evidence of photographs. He styled himself 'Captain' even though he had not been commissioned, had not served in the world war: he was not yet nineteen when the vindictive Treaty of Versailles was drawn up as a guarantee of 'a further show', as he would put it. It was the rank he believed he deserved to have attained before he was shot by a sniper who was also his brother.

She made to kiss the soon-to-be-damaged child but desisted. There was no obligation. She could do as she wished at last . . . There was no one to witness her final act of indifference: it was closer to casual neglect than to contempt for the happy gurgling parasite. She was free in the last of life as she would be in death. That act of maternal lack was a sample of the nothingness to come, a preparation for eternity – which may be finite. She left him on the parched grass in the hopsack swaddling pouch that she gathered him in to ride. Cedric her pony grazed unconcernedly. The door to the stairs to the top of the column was oiled and easy. She climbed in the quickly enveloping darkness. The spiral bereaved senses. Bits of her brain struggled with others. She doubted that she was going upwards. She was weightless. She counted the steps till she could count no more. One hundred feet: she was puffed and giddy when she got there. For the first and last time in her life she overcame her fear of heights. Sunlight assaulted her swimmingly. Halos stretched and contracted. Everyone loved the scent of burnt stubble. Everyone loved the sight of the countless acres of green downs, their punctuations of blackthorn bushes and beech clumps, and fifteen miles distant the twinkling sea.

For as far as Alexandra could see the land belonged to her family or Valentine's.

And they belonged to it too, reciprocally. Incredibly, she believed. They felt they were born of the thin topsoil, and the combes, hill forts, barrows, strip lynchets' chiaroscuro, dusty yews. Even the sheep.

Yet it meant nothing to her. It never had, never would, now. She supposed her unwanted child would be madrassa'd into the sentimental error of oneness with the earth. The earth which, unprompted and passive, not knowing what it was doing, came rushing to greet her. Freddie didn't notice a thing, didn't heed the scream which could be heard in three counties, didn't heed the deflationary sigh as breath escaped her. Cedric grazed unconcernedly. Alexandra was linked to nothing, definitively. Probably.

'What these people need . . .' said Inigo, 'is a special needs genealogist . . . some kind of three-dimensional family tree. Molecular structure model . . . Isometric . . . Escher . . . Escher – that's it.'

The motherless Viola grew up at Kaltenborn under her father's stifling protection. The only freedom she had was to ride a motorbike built specially for her: for hours on end she turned parkland turf to mud, skidding and drifting and making the machine rear up roaring like a mechanical horse. Marcus watched her vandalism with pride: she was such an accomplished vandal. He doted on her, his only child, so far as he knew. The fear of kidnap preyed on him. He scrutinised her friends. He scrutinised her friends' parents and their employees. He scrutinised her governesses, tutors and chaperones.

The prying Dumpberg family were, whenever they visited, made to feel ill at ease by ostentatious invigilation. They learnt to expect the chilliest of welcomes. In the end they stopped coming.

Marcus Phimister detected malevolent intentions in farmhands, tranters, mechanics, clerks, stewards. He was the strictest of fathers, paranoiac and suspicious, anxious and ill-tempered.

Astride a bucking rearing grey whose nostrils emitted billows of intestinal steam he raged at a surveyor whom he didn't recognise and threatened him with a sabre, having mistaken the man's theodolite for a prying telescope.

In Munich her security was even more zealously effected. However, Marcus could hardly fail to draw attention to their wealth with his boastful cars – E-M-F, Audi Typ F, Benz Prinz Heinrich – whose grey and French navy liveries were matched by his chauffeurs' uniforms and the rugs under which he and Viola huddled together against the Bavarian winter. In summer she would sit on his lap and pretend to steer. The smell of Castrol excited her.

It was not until their enforced flight to Zurich that she was able to stroll alone with a mere three guards, discreet shadows indistinguishable from the mass of men hurrying – referred to as 'English urgency'. Under orders to abstain from strong liquor on duty the guards followed her on her (now full size) motorbike from one country tavern to the next. She frequented city cafés too: Schober, Haller and especially Roleder with its violent woodcuts, meaningless slogans in gold paint, letters in different fonts and point sizes, porcelain fuses attached to a dog collar, a hurricane lamp with a goldfish swimming in it, guignol masks pierced by nails: she longed for the sophistication to understand these important works of random menace. She acquired a taste for fruit sorbets corrected with the appropriate alcool blanc. The guards watched her with mute resignation, played cards, smoked.

She (and they) spent hours in couturiers' studios and hatters. Doelker was a glimpse of paradise. She wore a bob, a cloche, carried a Chinese parasol, was measured for what she called her lesbian suits by a smooth tailor at PKZ who championed made-to-measure garments because they lessened the possibility of suffering a ready-to-wear death struggling with the wrong size and a weak heart in a cramped fitting booth.

Potential boyfriends: Marcus acted ruthlessly, crudely.

Handholding, a kiss on the cheek, a nervous request to see her again . . . These 'paths of shy friendship that might lead to avenues of intimacy' would be reported to Marcus despite Viola's attempts to silence the guards with bribes.

Without remarking on them Marcus would leave on the breakfast table, beside her almond cake, gingerbread and yogurt, papers from Magnus Hirschfeld's Institut für Sexualwissenschaft with illustrations of venereally infected mouths and genitalia (m & f), a monograph entitled *Entwicklungstorungen*, Profound Development Disorder, and that sexologist's book *Geschlechtiche*, Sexual Abstinence. The staff pretended not to notice. Viola thought the gaudy hand-coloured fleshscapes of suppurations, warts, lesions, cloisonné blotches ought to be on Café Roleder's walls. They were rather beautiful.

Eight hundred miles distant her unknown half-brother Freddie was motherless too, and all but fatherless. From time to time exploring the vast house he bumped into his father (who wasn't his father). He would be in the company of young men who might be salesmen bouncing on a mattress to test it or friends who had dropped by for a shower. Sometimes his father would be having a grown-up rest, face down in a corridor. Sometimes his father recognised Freddie and stopped to talk to him. Tertiary, sarsens, the Library of Human Amelioration, Neolithic, grit, Phimister, pug, paleo . . . in time Freddie hoped to meet the Beaker People. He liked the sound of these words his father spoke. He dropped them into conversation with his long-suffering tutors. His lexicon swelled. Devonian, radical dermatology, the Jew, steppe pastoralists, tumulus, Hirschfeld, strip lynchets, clunch. He read stories. Black people were probably not Beaker People, but they were loyal and noble, if limited. Firm-chinned chaps taught them fair play and civilised cooking. Great men fought loyal and valiant tigers, worthy opponents who had to be defeated. They spanned bottomless chasms with rope bridges. They dug trenches to conquer the foul Boer.

He had two good wars.

When he was just seven years old he conscripted the sons of the estate's dependants to build a concentration camp in imitation of that at Heilbron in the Orange Free State, which he had found an illustration of in a pile of old editions of the *Westminster Gazette*.

Elsie Ladysmith Hopkin, a year Freddie's senior, was appointed matron. She wore an apron and a wimple made of cardboard. She was supplied with a rusty pram. Those selected to be Boers were made to speak accented nonsense, double Dutch, and to run weighted by sacks of cattle feed. They were whipped when they flagged.

Three months after the assassination in Sarajevo, a dozen boys under Freddie's command, the Faineant Park Rifles, dressed in ragged infantry battledress and massively oversized fatigues, dug trenches in Botanical Wood, henceforth Le Bois Botanique. They covered them in webbing from stalls in stables. They surrounded them with lavish coils of barbed wire which Freddie had instructed the land agent's office to supply. Freddie drilled his men. Helmets must be worn at all times. No smoking. The Hun was not a sportsman: he waited for the third light. Some had rifles they had carved themselves. Slackers got jankers. Graver disobedience was punished by being tied to a tree by ever-tightening strands of barbed wire and cut with bayonets. No one dared complain. They were warned that their parents' houses were at stake. They crawled on their stomach from redoubt to salient through leafmeal and sharp roots. They took up sniper positions high in trees. When a plucky tommy collapsed he was made to eat mud. Why, asked a cowman's lad with a papier mâché Maxim gun, had he not seen an angel? Freddie replied that such sightings were restricted to commissioned officers and he would have to await OCTU and promotion. By the end of the war many more trenches had been dug.

Bones, metal shards, fossils and pottery had been eagerly presented to Valentine, whose reactions swung from occasional delight and pride in the boy's interests to more usual fractious fulminations that he was being interrupted in his work. 'Bugger off, you little chit!'

Freddie realised that he might never be introduced to the Beaker People.

★

Armistice came. The boy's own war culminated in Freddie having attained the rank of Captain. He had been awarded the Military Cross and the Victoria Cross.

He enjoyed exercising droit du seigneur over farm lads, fence erectors, hurdle makers, apprentice coppice cutters, poachers – though he'd never dare try it on with Killer Miller, the man with a beheaded stag in a blood-drenched sack.

The court was astonished when he called himself Brevet Captain and mentioned his awards for gallantry. It was baffled when he called his victims as character witnesses who, having obviously been rehearsed, all stumbled through a claim, in the very same words, that he was the finest, most loyal, most generous employer they could hope for and they were only doing their job. What's more if I can speak out of turn he's not a falling-down-barleyed-up gent like the late Sir Valentine, may he rest . . .

Was Freddie sane? He would, now he had inherited the baronetcy and Faineant Park, soon be on the bench himself. Insufficient evidence: clearly not guilty.

Valentine's last words were with a housemaid scrubbing the stone-flagged corridor to the muniment room.

'Is this the way to Damerham?' he asked.

She looked up from her bucket: ''Fraid to say I don't know, me lord.'

He stared at her red peeling hands.

'D'you know, if I had my time again I'd do something about bleach and household soap . . . that's what it's called isn't it. Carbolic.'

'It is, Sir.'

He fumbled in his jacket, found his wallet, handed her £20.

'Oh no, Sir, you shouldn't . . .'

He was gone, blakeys sparking, mumbling.

No one could recall having heard the shot. But shots are common throughout the year. There's always some creature to be hunted down for pleasure or poached for the pot.

The body was found the next day in the Friary Field ha-ha by two ferret-folk. It was found a week later at Hag Hill. It was found at Vetch Weir by Tozer and his son when they arrived with scythes to cut waterweed.

'Well well . . . so he threw a seven at last . . . he had it coming to him,' was Freddie's response when the steward Major Crawley informed him. 'Any other business, Dick?'

London's post-war feverishness achieved a reputation that spread to Zurich. Viola cajoled and begged and nagged and twisted her darling Vati round her little finger till he agreed that they could spend some time there improving her English. He took a three months' let on an apartment in a gaudily terracotta'd block in St James's. They had few acquaintances, most of them his 'old friends . . . haven't seen them for twenty-five years or more – you can't forgive them for leading dull lives that have turned them into dull people, for having changed immeasurably . . . and they can't forgive you for having changed too . . . better discarded . . . start anew.'

One grey drenching afternoon he saw Jervoise Vanier struggling across Waterloo Place, crouching, near cowering, failing to revel in the fat rain gusting horizontal, treating it as an antagonist: a beaten man. Face, clothes, hands tell all. His once closest friend – friend is inadequate – had become the sort of man they had warned themselves against, despised and mocked, a guardian of the status quo, a leader of the lifeless life of the English. He passed by Marcus without noticing him.

Viola's neglect of her English lessons in favour of preparing herself for fashionable clubs jeopardised her acceptance in those clubs (The 43, The KitCat, Cecil's, The Folly), some of whose denizens, bright young xenophobes alert to her accent, cut her or mocked her or deprecated her: Hun, Bosch, Kraut, Gerry.

She wanted to belong, to be a fast flapper caressed by many men with glossy hair and two-tone shoes.

She was hampered by her name. Phimister's infamy did not match that of Wilde or Dilke or Mrs Monk-Mullinger but the name still made the prurient pulse race. It transcended generations, prompted further spiteful taunts: 'Oh no! Surely not *that* Phimister' went the chorus of vindictive libertines. She felt bullied. Her beauty was not thrived on.

She didn't succumb to the temptation of describing herself as an heiress. It's improbable, anyway, that she would have been believed. She ate like a navvy. She copied her father who chomped raw vegetables and still-beating hearts with his hands after living in the wild. He scorned conventional table manners; he derided grace as 'buttering the Bible'. Her unknown mother had believed that cutlery was a Calvinist device to curtail immersive gluttony: this quirk was necessarily transmitted genetically rather than by example.

A man blinded by a member of his own platoon hurling a grenade at him heard her voice, stumbled across the bar in what he misjudged to be Viola's direction and flailingly assaulted her English companion of five minutes with a broken glass. When informed that he had missed his target he hawked at his bleeding victim and called her a traitor. His aim was again poor.

The dripping oyster of mucus struck a pouting transvestite who shrieked: 'I accept nothing but grand cru jism. This is gob plonk, matey.' He struck the blind man's forehead with a heavily ringed fist.

'You killed our men,' a ginny bitch flapper told Viola, 'you killed my brothers, you killed all their friends . . . now you're stealing the ones who survived. Just look at them . . .'

The mute shellshocked excelled at dancing the jitterbug; they were neurally advantaged, trembling with the remembrance of terror. Their limbs talked for them. Their past lay so heavy on them it quashed the possibility of the future whose existence we have, anyway, no proof of. Thick head bandages turned brown from the seepage of reopened wounds. A man with a rusting metal jaw grinned like the devil. An amputee laid the stumps where his arms ended on a girl's chest. He bellowed that he could still feel with his fingers. She kissed him and held a cocktail glass of Black Samarra to his mouth. Lights flickered. Crutches were heaped in a bonfire of survivor guilt and grief. Girls got off with girls for want of men. A rare complete man – no prostheses – remarked that maybe he was unclaimed because that's how they wanted it anyway. They were lesbians at heart just as men were queers at heart if his school and his regiment were anything to go by. He was looking forward to going up to Oxford. The young women only complained of lack of men because that was social obligation, the orthodoxy held to in bad faith. Besides, the ones with 'natural' tastes have all had the clap so often it sounds like applause. The men have war wounds; the women, competing, have peace wounds. Viola didn't know if she was natural or not.

She wanted to belong, to be a fast flapper caressed by many men with glossy hair and two-tone shoes.

Marcus wandered after dusk through canyons of baleful smog the colour of snot, through the charnel gloom of the necropolis without term: the dead were everywhere, in the names of shops and streets, in the worn metal of the banisters of flights of steps, in the sooty bricks and quoins. They were journeys of infinite sleepless weariness. He walked for remorseless hours. High gabled mansions, domes and spires loomed dully. A haggard toothless face streaked with smuts waving a tramp flask in greeting begged alms. The streets are black as sewers, heaven is black. By a black canal he saw the terrible maw and heard the carnivorous belch. Hell's wrought gates glimmered. The glaucous phantoms of former men shrieked. Where is joy, where is relief?

He sidled through mews and stables, glimpsed his familiars in their stalls, breathed in the grating smell of burning hoof. He heard the clipclop of iron feet on cobbles, the music of jingling harnesses, the swish of a whip, of rattling wheels, of prancing horses. He was soothed by the voices of men talking to animals. Every night he felt the dust of death. He was livened by the siren screech of hornets being burnt in their nest by men in skep masks which prompted a memory he could not quite grasp. He saw a great number of carcasses. Sides of slaughtered oxen loitered like Assyrian reliefs. The shambles ran red. The multitude of whoredoms and well-favoured harlots did not appeal to him. Nor did the frotting men at the Turkish baths. He felt apart from the city and pools of sweat.

He ventured into the suburbs which was where the country had been. The bricks had marched. Reservoirs had multiplied. A race of stooped survivors lived in chicken coops they had built amid vegetable patches. He admired the elegant power of the beasts at Kempton and Sandown but regarded owners' colours and jockeys' silks as a humiliation of them. They had been tamed for commerce and spectacle, their liberty was stolen from them.

★

Viola sat daringly alone at the long bar in The Aztec on the first night of Hot Heels Valdez's residency featuring Benita Maroon. She stared into her glass seeking profundity where there was none. A pretty young man, having summoned up courage, smilingly gestured at the stool beside her. He was all the prettier for having a bruised and cut upper lip.

'You're the one,' he blurted, smugly, 'they are all talking about . . .'

'Because of how I am talking . . . they are not talking *to* me.' She mourned and shrugged, resigned.

'D'you know, our people used to know each other . . .'

'People? Domestic staff you mean?'

'Our people. Our parents . . . were friends.'

'Oh. Really? Ees that so?'

'Yup. I'm Freddie Shadoxhurst . . . It's a delight to meet you.'

'Viola Phimister—' She held out a hand, gloved to beyond the elbow.

Anyone who saw them would have thought that they were two children dressed as adults, aping adults' mores.

'I know you are . . . Phimister is one of the first words I learnt . . .'

'For sure? Strange word to learn, no? Do many children learn it? I'm not twigging the English education. Not a jot.'

'No no . . . I learnt it from my papa.'

'Ah! Your *people* . . .'

'Not quite . . . I don't think we'd use it in that context . . .' He sounded like a schoolboy.

'What happened to your face? Did you have a fight?'

'No, just a spill. Nothing serious. My horse threw me . . . Badbury Rings . . . home turf so to speak . . . I should know every inch of it . . . silly me took a jump at . . . wrong point of origin as we say . . . hoist by me own wotsit. D'you ride?'

'Not since I am thirteen years . . . when we move out from the country . . . Kaltenborn . . . we had there many beautiful horses.'

'You should come down to Faineant. Breathe some fine upland air . . . There's only so much of the Great Wen one can take. Don't you agree? The filth, the dregs, the degradation, the lower life forms unworthy of life, the Jews.'

She laughed: 'I'm sure I agree – if I can understand!'

She was terrified of what she wanted: to belong, to be a fast flapper caressed by many lotharios with glossy hair and two-tone shoes. Yet here she was, gauche, drunk, listening to a mere boy, encouraging him, for want of anyone else, to fill her time with his callow boasts – the sheer number of follies on his estates, his record in National Hunt races, the injuries he'd suffered in those races, the regard in which he was held by his employees, the quality of milk, butter and cheese from the estates' farms, the clemency he grants to poachers (whose families might otherwise starve), his plans to one day establish a stud.

Viola told her father they were going to the country.

'We are invited at Faineant Park. By Freddie Shadoxhurst.'

Marcus's immediate reaction was of amused astonishment. Shadoxhurst . . .

'He says you knew his parents.'

'Yes yes . . . Not well. Not well at all. Long ago . . . in Munich . . . I think they never came to Kaltenborn . . . No . . . I'd see them from time to time. So this Freddie . . . he must be Valentine and Alexandra's boy . . .'

'He says Phimister is one of the first words he learnt. His father told it to him . . .'

'Did he indeed? Rum couple. Disappeared without trace . . . heard they'd gone back to England . . . strange not to have made contact . . . that was the last I saw of them . . . that's how it goes . . . people come in and out of your life . . .'

'People. Jah. Vati.'

He uttered his familiar refrain, forced on him by isolation and his social awkwardness: 'Must be twenty years since I saw them . . . no time when you're my age . . . time, the runaway train, always accelerating . . . as they say a year when you're nine is a week when you're ninety . . . we must hope that they have not led dull lives . . . dull lives make for dull people . . . It'll be interesting to meet them after so long . . . interesting . . . We shall need to buy a country wardrobe . . . You know I'm rather looking forward to it . . . to seeing how they've changed . . .'

'Vati. I have to tell you . . . you are going to find them changed . . .'

'Ah hah . . . how so?'

'They are dead.'

'Yes indeed . . . *very* changed.'

'Freddie's parents . . . they committed suicide . . . both . . .'

'Did they by jove. We'll still need the right clothes . . .'

'Like my Mama,' she cried and wiped her eyes.

He had taught her that it's the absence that they should regret . . . not how she made herself absent . . . nor why . . . if that was her selfish choice . . . so be it.

'We don't want to roll up looking like tramps . . . that'd be letting your boyfriend down . . .'

Viola sobbed: 'He's not my boyfriend, Vati – you know I don't have a boyfriend.' She flung her arms around his neck. 'If I have my darling Vati I don't need no boyfriend.' She stroked his hair.

They sat opposite each other. He wore a Bedford cord chevalier coat and a brown bowler; she, astride habits and a trench-warm. They both had shiny, over-new riding boots. The passing landscape recalled his misery on the lightless day he left Malpasfang forever. England's low grey skies and sodden fields. Had they been worth the slaughter? The Pudding's drear acres. Viola was immersed in Löns's *Dahinten in der Haide*. At her age Eden was already the chatelaine of Malpasfang.

He closed his eyes to imagine Eden beside him. His memory of her flesh was so often summoned it was always at the ready to flee. Over quarter of a century it was never more than a memory of loss which he could not resist rehearsing, no matter that it stung. And the more he remembered the more it shifted from the distant actuality of Eden. He opened his eyes to the rain-dashed window, droplets streaking the grime. Beside the track more chicken coops, more shacks, more mud, more desperate optimism (children waving shredded union flags). A wooden scaffold supported a signboard: Welcome To Palestine.

There was a glimmer of sun and a dog cart to greet them. They drank beef tea from a samovar in a tack room perfumed with beeswax. The wooden walls were hung with rosettes and heroic paintings of steeds. A leather-aproned groom poured shots of sherry into their silver mugs. They chose their mounts in a black stable chiaroscuro'd by the light of a clerestory. Marcus admired the Piranesian drama. He declined a saddle: he wanted to be at one with the fine bay mare Freddie proposed, he wanted to feel the rush of stimulation from a different species, a reminder of the mare Amalianie and exogamous bliss.

Flanked by two strapping Marcher Hounds Freddie trotted the way, clearing the clouds before him. He showed them steep dry valleys whose sides were turf cliffs. Hedges were busy with pro-creation. The hounds relished the rabbits, ripping them to bits before applying themselves to a sett, a favoured target. The downs were green bolsters foxed with blackthorn. Chalk pushed through the threadbare carpet of grass. The white horse and rider in the style of Stubbs cut into a hillside had been a rehearsal for the one at Osmington.

They rode through a dark nave of yews in whose gnarled boles were discernible the taunting leers of crones, silently screaming imps, corn gods gone to the bad. Ghost warriors were embedded forever in the trunks beneath the sloughing pages of bark. Roots stretched across the dusty reddish floor, molesters' fingers in wait for children lost in the wood. Potent still, they put out new growths. The underworld and the overworld embraced in a twisted impene-trable knot.

Freddie pointed west. His estates extended beyond the horizon. He pointed south. Marcus watched Viola's wonder at the park and house. When she suggested that they ride up to the distant monu-ment there came a sudden asperity in the air. 'Some other time. Perhaps,' said Freddie, firmly. She hardly noticed his tone, though Marcus did. The place embraced her, surrounded her, cosseted her. She was the most diligent visitor, remarking on mankind's triumph over nature, the palimpsest of field systems, exclaiming her pleasure at the many and atypically English pollards, the dreamy sweep of undulating lawns, the naddered stream, the fine cascade. Steam-powered tractors worked in concert hauling between them a plough to create precise straight furrows. The breeze was crisp, exhilarating, tonic. It brought water to his eyes. He saw through an apricot gauze. He was dizzily happy for her. It was Kaltenborn rediscovered. For a day . . . only a day, just a day?

Is that all? Marcus wondered as he negotiated the seams of mud at the abandoned excavations of Pentridge Cursus hill fort. He realised that he was, without thinking, holding back, a hundred yards behind Viola and Freddie who were walking side by side now. Their peals of laughter were carried on the wind, carefree and gay. Swallows swooped, masked martins danced, a jay plodded through the air seemingly trying to remember flight, not quite getting the hang of it. The sun was fully out as they returned to Faineant Park for lunch. The grass and the crops shone with droplets. The world was a better place than a couple of hours before. He had the muscular memory of the mare between his legs when they sat to eat.

They were watched over by ancestor portraits, the most recent William Orpen's of Valentine with a microscope and a partly reconstructed bowl, and Alexandra, classically diaphanous, unmistakably by Linsel Murley, who rendered her boyish as though she was one of his catamites. Marcus did not mention that in a different life he had known the artist. While Viola and Freddie chattered he played a variation of grandmother's footsteps, turning suddenly to see if her eyes were following him. They weren't, nor were Valentine's. He was glad of that. And again.

They ate very dead salmon en gelée, pheasant baked dry, overcooked woodcock on burnt croutongs smeared with a jam style ointment, pigeon braised to shreds with flaccid pommes paillasson which made father and daughter long for their Zurich cook Magda's rösti. Then a flaming roasted pineapple with so-called hindoo spices and sherbet like bitter aloes, a savoury of unspeakably salt anchovies on toast. Viola and Marcus ate with their hands, which encouraged Freddie to do the same. A footman summoned a junior hallboy to pick up the bones before the dogs choked on them. Freddie merrily announced that Mrs Cheddy would have the fittiest fit when she saw the state of the table!

They retired to Malmsey in a room called the junior library, entirely bookless. On its shelves there stood ranked plunder: hundreds of canopic jars intended to hold the inner organs of the temporarily dead. Their tops took the form of wolves, foxes, owls, jackals, priests, baboons.

'They are good company . . . when one is alone in a house like this one needs . . . sympathetic spirits . . . you know . . . keeping the Red Sea pedestrians at bay . . . Mister Cartaphilus and his incarnations . . . they're always with us . . . god will cleanse their blood – some hope . . . the sooner they're all packed off to Palestine the better . . . hard cheese on Mustapha Mustapha of course . . . Let's go for a jaunt.'

They bumped over plough and lurched across heathland, followed a track up to Hag Hill – a group of hastily assembled barracks, now all rotting wood and pitted corrugated iron. 'I'm hoping for some sort of restitution before the next show starts.' They roared down lanes where a coating of soft mud concealed a coccyx-battering core of hard mud. The engine screamed for help while the wheels dug ever deeper. The staff in the accompanying car had to free the Rolls-Royce with shovels and muscle while its occupants walked to the church, gleaming white stone and oysterish flint, high-spired, proud and solitary within a low wall at the edge of the deer park. It was enthroned on its mound of dais like a dreamed creature from a benevolent bestiary. An arthritic verger was sweeping up rice. He patted Freddie on the back, grunted a dialect greeting 'toffeedatemast' or something similar. The interior was exultantly bright, breathtakingly lovely. Stained glass cast shifting boiled sweets on the undecorated alabaster walls. Sun poured through a rose window. In another window Cain follows his brother into a field. He bludgeons him with a stone that crumbles on the skull. He takes his brother's wife, who is also his sister, to the land of Nod where there is no sleep, where there are no walls. He invents walls. He constructs them with homicidal stones and lays claim to the land within them.

'I love this place . . . who could not love it . . . it's meat for the soul . . . should we have one . . . just shapes and colours . . . that's all . . . shapes and colours . . . but for me it's England . . . essence of . . . distil England and this is what you arrive at . . . of course all the religious stuff . . . gets in the way of contemplation . . . bishop's piffle rank baloney . . . the days of creeds are as dead and done with as the days of the pterodactyls . . . don't believe a word of them . . . but that's outside the trough . . . it's what we *do* . . . church on Sunday . . . social obligation . . . the Fenant Peal it's called . . . called by the bells caught by the balls . . . it's expected of me . . . it's my flock my family . . . Dutt knows that very well . . . and he knows the living is in my gift so he keeps it short . . . not a minute over half an hour thanks be . . . squeaky voice like a hinge that needs oiling . . . puts you on edge . . . misuse of a splendid building . . . it echoes . . . of course it's at its most . . . most majestic when there's no one about . . . the spirit thrives . . .'

Marcus looked up from the family tomb he was reading to see Viola and Freddie standing side by side contemplating the altar.

'His father was a common thief . . . he was conceived by rape when his mother was menstruating . . . he was not nailed to a cross . . . he was not hung from a tree but from a cabbage stalk . . . Yet the most rapturous buildings in the world have been devoted to him. If I had the courage I'd raze this to the ground. But moral duty would be aesthetic offence.'

They passed a pooled cricket pitch, a wet dog of a thatched pavilion and a crenelated folly which concealed a squash court.

They parked by a doorway in a squat buttressed wall.

'This owns me. I am its keeper for my stay on earth. All of this . . . I must answer to it.'

A walled garden, the warmth of immemorial red brick, trees so intricately espaliered that their inter-relationship was a puzzle against nature – a bough's beginning was its end and the end its beginning, an intimation of eternal recurrence. A great greenhouse of curved panes and filigree ironwork dominated one corner. It was heady with the ripeness of forced fruit carried on steam. A chimney behind it outside the walls puffed crematorium smoke signals. They stroked unripe peaches' adolescent bloom.

'What do you say to the idea of a dip?'

The cars struggled up a hill.

'Slope Hide – heaven knows where it got that name from!'

Viola gazed at the crown of the monument above them through trees. So tall now that they were close to it. But still without her curiosity's grasp.

They descended to the valley where the Allen River stalled according to the whim of Freddie's grandfather. Sixty years previously he had embanked it, built sluices, dredged the floated meadows, dug fishing ponds, dammed the pool above Vetch Weir and built primitivist huts with colonnades of green-painted pine trunks, walls of twisted roots and bark ripped in ribbons from a tree struck by lightning from heaven. What had been derided as 'a suburban park' was now, in its unkempt desuetude, the apogee of picturesque artifice. Freddie stripped and plunged into the deep green water. Marcus followed his example. Viola stared rapt at their densely hirsute matching torsos. Then she took off her clothes, tried the water with a toe. The servants in the supporting car looked on wilfully expressionless. Freddie propelled himself from the depths – a leaping, bucking salmon.

There was more to it than the pelt. Marcus realised that the body's very form was imitative of his. He had found himself sympathetically in tune with Freddie's gestural lexicon. The baritone register. Marcus was patiently admitting to himself that the young man was his son. He had suffered intimations all day. They larked, shouted and splashed and ducked each other. They trembled collectively, all shrivelled balls and gooseflesh breasts. The servants brought rugs and towels. They'd seen a thing or two in their time and they'd see more. They were inured to landed mores. This didn't register at the time. Later they considered it a presage unread.

Viola lay in a bath breathing brandy fumes. Freddie invited Marcus to shower with him in the terracotta-tiled cube where his father had often entertained. Hot water jets stung them from all directions. Freddie enjoyed Marcus's insufficiently dissembled shuftis at him through the steam and spray but affected not to notice them. He was impressed by Marcus's sumptuous coat, even denser than his own. Bristly hair spread from his belly button to his pubis, filings subjected to a magnet.

They both will have thought about it for some time before Marcus moved to stroke his son and future son-in-law's irresistible cock, a quivering thick gothic member, its shaft tapering from bottle-width to brutally bloated purple-domed glans, a swelling he mafekinged with relish.

The wedding was at Faineant. Dutt kept the god-bothering to a minimum. A day of joy and bulk air, billowing white clouds, billowing white organza, maidens' faces unveiled by the douce wind. Possibilities were big as the sky. The proud parent beamed with delight. It amused him that, as a champion of exogamy, he had preached and practised unions which were explicitly opposed to that of this bride and this groom, these siblings, his children. He recalled Shaw: 'The only fundamental and possible socialism is the socialisation of the selective breeding of man.'

His hail-fellow-well-met jocularity, adopted for the day, concealed the secret that tickled him no end. He yearned for a grandchild, the result of his sly experiment, a superchild, *übermenschlich*, due to its double helping of Phimister. That name, that name. A resentful squad of elderly, embittered, shabbily kempt Shadoxhursts who rued primogeniture and Freddie's gender advantage stared at the monster Marcus with the jealousy of the indigent, acknowledged him with February smiles, spread sotto gossip about his successfully getting his cock in a Bavarian till, his strange experiments at Malpasfang when young, his curious relationship with the bride, the heiress who was so drunk that she had to be steadied to cut the metre-tall croquembouche on a dais in the great rococo room. More chaperone than father it was decided, no normal father would pay such attention to the minutiae of his daughter's life, would devote weeks to the mise-en-scène of a country wedding to which many of the invited did not reply either because of that name's tarnished cachet or because they did not associate it with the strangely accented young woman who was so eager to be liked it hurt. On the other hand no normal father would recklessly condone his daughter's union with a pansy who was sure to follow *his* father down the primrose path: 'father' is, evidently, an approximation.

They honeymooned on Nepenthe. Every day Freddie made friends with tawny-skinned, black-eyed urchins and cherubic ragamuffins.

He spent hours with them splashing about in the sea, playing hide and seek on the rocks.

They had a separate suite for their clothes and luggage. Viola would try on several outfits before choosing what to wear. She thought it appropriate to dress democratically, like a fisherwoman would had the fisherwoman had the nous to patronise Schiaparelli rather than a sail-maker. She walked along clifftops, explored coves, took delight in contorted stone pines and gazed for hours at rock pools. She was dazzled by blossoms, blooms, broom, bougainvillea. She inhaled eucalypti and thyme. She limped back one afternoon having twisted her foot in rope-soled shoes. She spent a couple of days on a terrace with an ice compress renewed every hour. So long as she had a companionable drink to sip she hardly noticed Freddie's absences, though she did notice the staff's glances to each other when he brought three of his young chums for pastries and sorbets. Towels were found to protect their modesty. She noticed too the once gauntly handsome man with lank white nicotine-stained hair, a pee-stained white suit, food-stained white shirt, sweat-stained tortoiseshell spectacles. He was often at the incongruous Vitrolite bar. She was surprised one afternoon to see Freddie in fractious conversation with him in the hotel's near vertical garden. She hobbled painfully down a flight of rock stairs only for Freddie to dismiss her testily, with a shake of his head and fluttering fingers. This was men's talk. She resignedly sat on a bench of concrete logs. She could catch only so much of what was said between them.

'There's no cause to be . . . proprietorial . . . there are plenty enough to go round . . . enough meat for a feast . . .'

'Passing thrrough dear boy is differrent . . . therre is no time to establish trrust . . . so our young frriends become *mistrrustful* . . . which queerrs the pitch . . . if I may say so . . . for those of us confined to this gilded Alcatrraz . . . the damage that's done by brribing them with trreats . . . it makes them feel they are commodities . . . by jove they *are* commodities . . . unloved and for sale . . . that is no way to trreat fellow humans . . . no . . . no . . . no. Sir.'

And with a gently warning finger he stalked off. Viola dared not ask Freddie who the man was nor to explain what was already explained were she to admit it to herself rather than bury it with a proscription on exhumation, an untenable proscription (and she knew it). She loved this man, this boy, who was meant to share her life and she his. Monogamy with a person of a different sex was something that he had not learnt and he needed to learn it because it was evidently for him unnatural, it did not come unbidden, it was not a programmed stage of life and state of development. It was to be striven for. Even daily acquaintance with another person, sex immaterial, was an unconcealed trial for him. He was preoccupied by the need for an heir just as her mother had been, just as her late father-in-law Valentine had been. The Shadoxhurst kinsmen and women were vultures, readers of small print, covetous of land and houses.

Freddie's ideal of marriage was securing the legacy with a breeder. Viola was that broodmare. Marriage also demanded the fulfilment, as a couple (a word he abhorred), of a modicum of social obligations and acts of noblesse oblige which his father, preoccupied with arrow-heads and bodies preserved in peat, had neglected to the cost of the estate's morale and salubrity. Beyond the dutiful facade the state of marriage was wrestling, riding, steeplechasing, mortification of the body, hard cottaging for quick love in the dark (on the common, at the railway station: the price of a platform ticket bought bliss with a clerk).

They made their way home – home! – to Faineant by way of Naples (where Freddie was again injured, this time falling down some steps). They admired the squads of muscular blackshirts on bicycles keeping order in small towns in the Abruzzi and robustly managing disputatious smallholders at L'Aquila. They stayed with the Vair-Vairs (aka Mungosons) at Villa Jana (aka Vairseilles) at Livorno (aka Leghorn). At Rapallo they were lavishly entertained at the de Bergs' Villa Bleu where the servants were Zouaves and Freddie caused a scene. They moved on to her childhood friend Maria and her husband Maxi's crenelated, turreted, drawbridged 'toy' schloss above the Danube, far too pokey and small to have been requisitioned, as Kaltenborn had been. It was almost ten years since her home had been lost to her. Despite Marcus's expensive lawyers' efforts in Munich and Berlin the house was still occupied. With difficulty she resisted its pull: it was only a hundred kilometres distant. She longed to see it, ached for it, yet knew that the limpid domain in her memory could never be matched. And though it was more potent than any actuality, she feared that crystalline memory might be contaminated by revisiting its subject, the estate as it stood today. It was a risk to avoid.

The British Consul in Munich had to intervene after Freddie had got into a spot of bother with some members of a Freikorps in a Regensburg café who misunderstood his interest in their leather uniform of bibs and shorts. 'Nothing to worry about . . . mountain out of a molehill . . . sound chaps . . . me not having German . . . them not having English . . . only a few grazes . . .' he reassured her through two black eyes and a stitched lip.

She was proud to show him the Zurich house. It was, he sniffed, insufficiently worn for his taste. Her presence caused Marcus to realise the extent of his loss. He had only returned to the house a week previously having stayed on in London after the wedding. It was a lonely billet.

He skulked, he pleaded with Viola not to leave him. He warned her against her husband's predilections with an obliquity that passed over details. He hinted at nothing which she had not already surmised and which was further confirmed when Freddie, in a fit of grappa-fired morality, claimed to be disgusted and stalked out of an energetic tableau vivant which Alain de Berg had arranged for the young marrieds' entertainment. 'Too many bloody German whores, not enough cocks, simply not enough cocks!' he complained as he collapsed onto a canapé waving his glass for it to be refilled. Everyone laughed. Viola joined in, suppressing her embarrassment. She knew that, drunk or not, he was in earnest. Jeanne de Berg stroked her thigh, whispering: 'What sort of man turns away from German whores? German whores are the finest this side of Shanghai, the most deft . . . pliable. We ordered these in from Bremen and Hamburg . . . My darling . . . It was to be your treat . . . *both* of you . . . What sort of man have you married?'

The sort of man who had not yet proved himself anything but timidly, flaccidly, dribblingly impotent with the wife he adored as much as he could adore any person whose sad fate was to be a she and not a he.

The sort of man who less than three months after his wedding

(*Tatler*, *Illustrated London News*) is arrested at an 'unnatural gathering' at Rolfe's Private Hotel in Marylebone. The charges included gross indecency with four boy gunners from St John's Wood barracks, buying one of them a Bagendozer racing bicycle in return for 'special services', paying a bootblack to lick malt extract from his penis (*Daily Mail*, *The Whirlwind* et al.).

He incriminated himself when he went outside to look for the exceptionally gifted magician and contortionist Mary-Ann whom they were expecting. They assumed that he couldn't find his way to Rolfe's concealed back doorway and the notorious playground beyond it. In the ill-lit drizzly brick alley Freddie heard hue and cry and discovered a young man who was breathless, looking this way and that, probably scratching his head, clasping a thick fascinum that Freddie assumed was a prop if he even thought about it.

The young man was surprised to find Freddie beside him.

'Here we are. I'll take you in, I'm so looking forward to this,' said Freddie.

The young man was puzzled: 'What d'you mean, Sir?'

'Ooh . . . so coy! Don't be such a shy little lamb.' Freddie put his arm round him and took him by the hand. He nuzzled his smooth face: 'Mmmm . . . I can't wait to see you turn yourself inside out.'

The young man looked at Freddie in horror. He bolted. At the end of the alley he turned, looked back, remembered to hold high the fascinum. Freddie should have been alarmed but wasn't. He shook his head in incomprehension, re-entered The Cities of the Plain.

Within an hour a furore of peelers led by the young man, a sprog rozzer, had arrived, waving batons.

To a manboy every one of Freddie's friends turned king's evidence.

Freddie had twice been public schools bantamweight champion. He was fit. It's safe to assume he believed he could take care of himself. He was wrong. Queensberry Rules were scorned in Wormwood Scrubs. Tronk was piss and slopping out, strops and being held down by Lag A so that Lags B, C, D – all careless hygienists and bad washers – could travel the Bovril Turnpike and never pay the toll.

Exercise was the infliction of pain. He bled through his coarse striped uniform – 'He's got the rags out – the little diddy sweetheart!'

Freddie shuffled his shackled ankles wondering how it had come to this. Round and round the courtyard, round and round. Screws and cons alike leered at him, they licked their lips, they mimed masturbation, they made fists of bone and sinew. Round and round, day after day. At least it wasn't the cell. And the shackles were the germ of his life-long taste for licking leg irons and crude prostheses to get a rush of ferrous effervescence.

A man hobbling beside him gripped his sleeve, amiably – which was unprecedented.

'You don't know me . . . but you saved my bacon. Captain Sir. Can't tell you how grateful I am, Captain Sir, to you. It was you what waylaid that rozzer.'

Freddie shook his head, not getting.

Davy Skitch explained how on the tenth of March he had been forcing entry through a barred first floor window at 29 Millard Street Marylebone when a rookie copper in the adjacent alley spotted him. He jumped from the window reveal. His fall was broken by a pyramid of mungo in a yard the other side of the alley. He hid there, burying himself. 'Diabolical itchy like chats all over you it were. Worse than these patches.' It was at this point that he heard 'the voice of the quality' chatting up the rozzer, distracting him, eventually alarming him so he skedaddled. Davy Skitch waited a few minutes till he was certain it was safe to come out of hiding then scaled the wall and sauntered away. Within hours, all the talk from Lisson Grove to Tyburnia was about the raid on Cities of The Plain at 31 Millard Street and the buggering baronet with his kecks round his ankles.

A few days later Davy Skitch was arrested leaving The Clee Hound where he had tried to sell jewellery stolen during a break-in at St Edmund Terrace.

'You might,' he told bemused Freddie, 'say it was fate itself what brought us together here . . . Well . . . fate and me nose for a mutually beneficial commercial affair.' He tapped his nose for emphasis.

'These glocks . . . they's a bunch of yegs . . . but they ain't goin' to let up . . . they got your scent . . . you a 'untin' man . . . so you understand . . . they's softenin' you . . . afore they goes for the kill . . .

I seen it before . . . now what I propose, Captain Sir, is to 'ave you properly looked after . . . appropriate for your status indoors and outdoors all weather . . . benefittin' your stretch . . . benefitt . . . *befittin*' a Captain Baron . . . extendin' your 'ealth prospects . . . it can be terrible for the 'ealth . . . b'leave me I'm not comin' the old ackamarackus . . . we'll 'ave a learned friend put it all on legit terms . . . 'ow say you, Captain Sir?'

'Put *what* on legal terms . . . what are you—'

'You got the moola, I got the muscle . . . If you trust us all we need is a gentlemen's agreement. Leave your bloodsucking briefs out of it.'

He nodded towards a group of watching prisoners whose walk had clanked to a halt. 'Think o' them as the makins of your loyal regiment. They'll see you through no matter what they reckon to your funnyboy crimes . . . They don't sit in judgement . . . you'll find some of them idn't above hawkin' their brawn when needs must – profit rather than pleasure . . . that's the difference.'

Freddie tried to laugh. 'My . . . What a jolly jackanapes you are . . . Mister . . . ?'

'Skitch. Davy Skitch. Mister, plain Mister. And please don' call me a jackanapes . . . I been cruelly ribbed all me life about me simian demeanour they always call it.'

'Extortion. Is that what you're at? It sure as damn it sounds it.'

'Not to my way of thinkin' it don't . . . it's just an insurance what you'll be investin' in . . . but no one's twistin' your arm . . . why don't you sleep on it . . .'

'Sleep!'

He seldom slept. It's not a fucktoy's lot to sleep. He didn't sleep till the last halitotic visitor had left his mark and it was time to wipe up, then shit rectal porridge, clotted blood and digested gruel into the slops bucket in the corner while his cellmate Liffey Jim grinds his teeth in the night. Thank god for his alcoholic impotence.

'You know well as I do that no one here has any money. Against regs.'

'If I may say so, Captain Sir, you're green as a leaf . . . No no no . . . it's not dinari my crew wants . . . it's a livin' . . . a place to live . . . roof over our 'eads . . . three acres and a cow . . . nature's bounty all around . . . trees and bean stalks . . . we's reckonin' you with your jewelled acres . . . you might have a plot or two to spare . . . Hag Hill Camp by way of example.'

Freddie cried with laughter for the first time since the judge had ordered that he be taken down. He felt a wave of astonished gratitude at the very mention of somewhere so familiar that it momentarily transported him even though it sullied those jewelled acres, his jewelled acres.

'Hag Hill,' he murmured dreamily, 'Mister Skitch – you have such audacity.'

'Like I say . . . it's me nose for cooperation and compromise . . . and me diligent study of *Country Life* magazine . . . the gonif's catechism . . . where to find rich pickins . . . not to mention accounts of places where the fuckin' War Office besmirched our green and pleasant and the nobs – that's you – you're all up in 'igh dudgeon and seethin' with umbrage wantin' their land back . . . even though the land's no use, it's wasteland, Captain Sir . . . you 'eard about this new-fangled Distributism I'm sure . . .'

Even with remission for good behaviour he had more than a year to endure. He would accept anything, anything, to avoid the pain, humiliation and violence, to alleviate the fear that shadows him, no matter that the deal eventually struck was weighted against him. He exchanged part of his birthright for a prospect of temporary safety. Gentlemen's agreement.

This was the beginning of the transformation of the Faineant Park Rifles into the notorious Faineant Militia. He didn't yet understand the profound desperation of damaged men whose youth had disappeared at Spion Kop, whose middle years were clagged in Flemish mud watching their chums being struck by snipers, gassed and pleading to be put out of their misery. King and country cast them off in penury and red tape. They longed for revenge against the generals and the sleek International Financiers whom everyone knew to be the true victors. They stole for want of jobs and alms, for shelter greater than a tarpaulin can provide, greater than 'homes fit for heroes' – a slogan doesn't keep out the wind and the rain.

'There's thousands of us, tens of thousands, what are needful . . . we're an embarrassment to the nation . . . the brass would sooner we'd

all been dead . . . they sent us to die . . . we're not askin' for much . . .
we're 'onourable . . . if I say so meself we're 'onourable. Nature's
gents. Like yourself, Captain Sir, it's in the blood. You keep a bargain
we keep it too . . . and if you don't we'll be on you like a whirlwind . . .
like in the song – talons rippin' out your inner organs . . . for hospital
teachin' purposes only of course . . . but it's not goin' to come to that.
Is it? Captain Sir?' Gentlemen's agreement.

Because of their criminal records Bert, Bert, Dimps, Crimper,
Tug and Dogg had all been dismissed by agents of the Land Settlement Scheme as undeserving of grants. The families of those that
had families subsisted in noxious slums (Irishtown, Fegg Hayes,
Angel Meadow, Jacob's Island) or in workhouses. Looking after Captain Sir was a route to the qualified paradise of self-determination
and fresh veg. It meant taking punishment from lifer lags who had
nothing to lose by adding to their tally of murders. No one ever
swung for showing a fellow lifer lag the way to the Last Cul De Sac.
Freddie was proud of his men. He was excited to see the grave
wounds he inflicted on his former tormentors. He determined to
provide a healthy and fruitful future for them.

Bert Lugsden and Dimps Tozer were released before Freddie.
They were made unwelcome by the estate agent and steward Major
Dick Crawley. He disapproved of didicoys, he disapproved of Freddie's bountiful scheme, he disapproved of Freddie, half his age,
styling himself Captain: an officer who has not attained field rank
(i.e. Major) is forbidden to retain that rank once demobbed. This
vexed him.

Viola thought she ought to 'do something' about Crawley's obstructive officiousness. She went on thinking what something might be but
didn't do it whatever it was. On one of her prison visits she complained about Crawley to Freddie who remained mute while he stared
at her. Her pregnancy was unmistakable. He wordlessly acknowledged the site of incubation. He echoed his father precisely. The
child was of no interest to Freddie. The heir was. He was delighted
to have an heir.

'Well, that's taken care of then,' was all he said.

That he was not the child's father was a matter of supreme indifference. Its a clever Belgian that knows it's children's fathers. Why

restrict it to Belgians? It didn't occur to him to ask who the progenitor was. It would have been bad form and the name would, anyway, mean nothing to him – or so he thought.

It had gradually been rumoured that the friendless girl with the strange accent ('ees only liddle piece Gairman') was a multimillionaire with several estates and a nine-bob-note husband. As knowledge about her expanded so did her popularity. Her drunken excesses were a hoot. She ingratiated herself by making an exhibition of herself. New friends were easy to come by. She knew the names of some of them. She had filled the house with them to make up for Freddie's absence. He left a void. She told him about them with giggly excitement. The more she spoke the more he felt they were vacuous, careless people, vain vamps, self-proclaimed wits, greedy creepy spongers, afternoon men, silly girls, indistinguishable one from the next.

Viola stroked the creature within, felt for it.

'Vati ees so proud,' she told Freddie, 'real top dollar proud.'

Marcus took the opportunity afforded by Freddie's enforced absence to visit her regularly. He was often there for weeks at a time. 'Surveying . . . casting an eye over these pretty bipeds – in the paddock, so to speak.'

During the long parties he was a watcher rather than a participant, an anomaly due to his age and his shyness. His inability to gush small talk was taken as mean-spirited, for meaningless drool and effortful punning were the very cement of Viola's new milieu. He would breakfast wearing a djellaba seated in a highbacked Stuart chair, drinking coffee from a bowl, ripping hunks of bread and smearing them with potted meat and calf's foot jelly. He seldom acknowledged his fellow guests. Occasionally he would astonish one with virulent complaints about the lack of effective heating or the sharpness of the pickles.

Whenever Viola mentioned Marcus, Freddie replied with an unenthusiastic 'Jolly good' or a bored 'Really?' He effected a distance and maintained it. It's safe to assume that Marcus and Freddie never met after the latter's honeymoon visit to Zurich.

'He looks just like his dad. A ringer he is of you, Captain Zir!' said Bert.

'That should squash them rumours. Well and true. Oh yezz that'll zee them off.'

Freddie smiled calmly. He knew Bert meant well. The blond furry-pelted baby Geoffrey perched at the front of the tooled tandem saddle and gurgled. Ribera whinnied and snorted. Homely Mrs Twibill at the kitchen window scooted out of the home that had been a barracks with a shot of syrupy damson liquor for the Captain. 'Ooh Oi'll say sew . . . he's got yurr wicked twinkle if thou don't moind me saying sew. Does 'e like that honey?' she asked as she always asked.

'He loves it . . .' he replied as he always replied. 'Can't get enough of it. Hag Hill Honey. You spoil him.'

'He's got your sweet tooth if thou don't moind my saying sew.'

Brightly painted hives dotted the slopes among the seedling apple trees. Freddie took pride in his men's enterprises and his men's women's elbow grease, pickles and chutneys. Viola considered malt vinegar to be barbarous. Indeed she loathed the leaden coarseness of English cooking: poufdies, mincepies ('ees for *eating*?'), sausages, sponge cake ('so vell named'), greasy batter, parkin. 'Ees zere no one in zis contry who can bake?' Jars of marmalade were delivered to the kitchen like tithes, filling cupboard after cupboard.

Chefs were imported from Zurich, from Besançon, from Strasbourg so that the cooking might ascend.

Mrs Cheddy, Major Crawley and various senior members of the household staff – Staines, Bould, Mrs Pitman, 'Boy' Bourne, Mrs Rutherford – made their life hell. Drove them out. They crept home cowered by the English way of welcome. Viola's attempts to wrest control of the kitchen were thwarted by Freddie's reluctance to take her part. She was exasperated by his distaste for confrontation, his failure to dismiss any member of this hereditary parasitical tribe who lived a life of sated leisure and cushy sloth. They despised him (he knew, he knew).

He ignored them. Viola pitied what she regarded as an infirmity. She mocked him: 'Vot sort of man ees frighten of his servants? Leedle mouse of a man!'

He ignored her.

He was at his happiest galloping over the downs with the rush of wind on his limbs, in his liquid eyes and stinging ears.

He was at his happiest wandering with Davy Skitch and a gun. It's safe to assume that he believed, correctly, that he was indebted to Skitch, that he owed his life to the rascal. Rascal, scoundrel, blackguard . . . these are colourful, mitigating euphemisms with which Freddie deluded himself to the point that they were the truth. He didn't allow himself to acknowledge that Skitch was a common criminal, had possibly killed a shepherd, was certainly an arsonist, a thief and a cattle rustler. When Freddie spoke of the world being sullied by putrid loose-ness and perfumed by decay Skitch agreed with every word.

More oftentimes they walked in silence broken only by the testy rasp of corncrakes, by twigs underfoot, by groaning boughs, by a shot at a barely perceived movement in a covert. They always stopped for a smoke in the dark sunken lane that led eventually to the down above Catherine Barn and Little Silver. Towards the end of the lane Davy Skitch always announced: 'Light at the end of the tunnel, Captain Sir.'

He was at his happiest planning and establishing the Faineant Stud, which still exists in a much-altered form, and the Faineant Fasces Press, which doesn't. It closed for many years before it was revived as Steep Combe Editions.

He was at his happiest planning and effecting the transformation of the kindergarten Faineant Park Rifles into the grown-up Faineant Militia composed of estate workers and those of his former prison guardians who had accepted invitations to a new life at Faineant. The Militia duplicates the Rifles.

Helmets must be worn at all times. No smoking. Slackers got jankers. They crawled on their stomach from redoubt to salient through slithey wanwood and sharp roots. They took up sniper positions high in trees. When a plucky tommy collapsed he was made to eat mud. Why, asked a cowman with a functioning Maxim gun, had he not seen an angel? Freddie replied that such sightings were restricted to commissioned officers and privileged NCOs (Sergeant-Major Skitch and Bombardier Twibill) and he would have to await promotion. Promotion was of course in Freddie's gift alone. He designed the uniform, planned field days, drilled the troops, taught them horsemanship.

To the concern of the rest of the bench Freddie, in his capacity as chairman of the magistrates, granted the entire troop firearms certificates, criminal record or not. To the bemusement of their inhabitants Freddie marched the fully armed Militia through nearby villages. He rode at their head. Everything shone: his mount, his crop, the men's gaiters, rifle stocks, helmets, the bugle, the drum. Urchins gaped in awe at the force. Their parents stood respectfully at attention outside their tied cottages. The precision and order were martial; this was not akin to the troops of recent memory slouching unwillingly to war and death singing songs of hatred for the braided generals. Outside The Shadoxhurst Arms two smocked apprentices raised their tankards, not obviously in jest but Freddie couldn't be sure. His was a serious enterprise. It was not to be mocked.

He instructed his men that:

'The enemy today is no longer the Hun. The enemy today is the Jew. There can be no doubt whatsoever that it was the Jew who started the war. There can equally be no doubt that it was the Jew who won the war with not a drop of blood spilled.

'The Hun was a blameless warrior duped by the real enemy. The Jew. I repeat: the Jew started the war and won the war without spilling a drop of his blood . . . No Jewblood was spilled. The Jew sits on the sidelines, in a grandstand seat, watching, relishing, stroking his sheeny beard, accumulating profit while kinsman kills kinsman. With every valiant Tommy who fell the Jew's gelt grew, with every loyal Hun who fell the Jew's gelt grew.'

Viola paid little attention to Freddie's activities. While she was an attentive bigot and generally sympathetic to her husband's preoccupations, she lacked his ardour. Her tastes did not stretch to the essays, rants and pamphlets he wrote, or co-wrote with Roddie. They were published by The Faineant Fasces Press in conjunction with The Sir Frederick Shadoxhurst Bt Mission For Armed Peace: *The Yeoman Reacts*; *The Kosher Fascist Oswald Mosley*; *Madagascar: The Promised Land*; *Under the Jewish Jackboot*; *The Suppression of Social Disorder in Utero*; *The Diary of a Gombeen Man*; *Respiratory Diseases in Tigers*. They bored her.

She did read *Some Mercian Pub Signs* and *Chalk, Flint, Thatch and Pug*. They were mostly composed of captioned photographs and included some of Geoffrey's accomplished school-of-Tunnicliffe woodcuts. She was proud of his astonishing maturity as an artist and, even more, as a human body – he was a man by the age of eleven, abundantly hirsute with a five o'clock shadow and a suave baritone.

Motor racing got her. Speed was like alcohol, it dissolved the present. At many meetings (Donington, Crystal Palace, Castle Combe) she was the only female competitor. Her best result was coming seventh in a race won by Prince Bira at Montlhéry. The sport's links to fascism and National Socialism commended it to Freddie as an activity of the strong. Man and machine in all-conquering harmony. Viola was an honorary man in his view. A man built for breeding.

She rode a Brough Superior and raced ever more powerful cars. After a series of accidents and scrapes, Davy Skitch dictated to Dot a letter for Freddie: 'We don't know how to tell 'er ladyship she's a liability to 'er good self . . . she's going to do 'erself a mischief . . . drivin' at one 'undred an' thirty miles an hour . . . I'm 'fraid to say young Sir Geoffrey . . . he just eggs 'er on . . . they bin racin' each other . . . road racin' . . . out by King's Stag . . . I 'ate to say it but they's like tearaways together . . . she's bought that silver strimlin she calls it from young Nangle's widow . . . there weren't enough of him left to warrant a coffin they says . . . he'd have fitted in a tea caddy . . . every time she looked at the car she wept an ocean 'cause it was 'is true love . . . the only one in existence she says . . .'

The day after the declaration of war, Monday, 4 September 1939, Freddie made an appointment with his tailor. Eight weeks later when two service dress uniforms and a mess dress uniform were delivered (double quick time, chop chop) he was still having a spot of bother finding a regiment. He told Geoffrey:

'Age is against me of course. Dogmeat made that clear. He eased the way for Roddie of course . . . but a couple of years make all the difference . . . I had great hopes of serving under him. High degree of respect for the fella. Couldn't offer me anything himself . . . very decently put in a word here there and everywhere – to no avail. I had great hopes too of Tom Mungoson's ancient papa . . . he was vair vair sympathetic but as he put it "a darby and joan general with a hip full of shrapnel and gut full of whisky has no clout whatsoever". Jye nice chap – almost coherent if you catch him before nine thirty in the morning . . . So it looks like it's The Hoggs or nothing . . . and nothing means getting called up when things are desperate and a baronetcy will get you nowhere and I'll be the oldest second-lieutenant in living memory . . . I've always considered myself a captain . . . I am a captain!'

There was more against him than age.

His publications; his championship of Norah Elam – a pudding-faced fascist and anti-vivisectionist; the school harvest camps and sleep-under-the-stars child 'pioneer' camps he established on the Faineant estate which were described in *The News Chronicle* as 'boot camps for the bootless' and 'Nazi madrassas'; his insistence that the soya beans which formed the staple diet of those camps be renamed Nazi beans; the Rural Regeneration League's sword dances; his affiliation to the Northern Federation; his provision of shelter and hospitality to Hitler Youth cycling tours (which were daylight reconnaissance exercises); his intercepted correspondence with Arjan van Beek and Rost van Tonningen, then editor of *Het Nationale Dagblad* and subsequently Dutch Commissioner of Liquidation; his patronage of the Britannia Youth Movement and the Square Shoulders Band.

On the morning of 24 May 1940 Sir Frederick Shadoxhurst Bt, a civilian auxiliary attached to The Royal Hampshire Regiment, dressed in a captain's uniform to which he was not entitled, was supervising the installation of Spigot mortars, Bren and Lewis guns at an emplacement on the Weston shore in Southampton's suburbs. The troops were used to him ranting that he was the servant of king and country not of Warmonger Churchill who had in plain daylight effected a coup d'état. Why could no one but him and a few kindred seers understand that we were being hauled to the edge of the abyss to satisfy a dotard's belligerence?

At 11.30 Police Constables Natrass and Budd arrived to detain him under Regulation 18B as 'a person whom the Home Secretary believed to be of hostile associations'. He was driven to Alma Barracks in Winchester. He was spared the humiliation of handcuffs.

The arresting officers reported that he seemed 'bewildered'. He claimed that there had been a mistake, that he had been confused with someone else.

He repeatedly demanded to see the commanding officer: 'He shoots on my land for heaven's sake . . . he shoots as my guest.'

He repeatedly advised: 'It's my wife you want . . . she's the German. I'm an English patriot . . . serving my country. She's the German.'

He spent five days in a wing of Brixton Prison allotted to bickering, affronted detainees, among them the Rev. Kenneth Haworth, William Farquharson, his son Henry Farquharson, Harry Umberson-Dogg, Jorian Jenks, Admiral Barry Domville, Archibald Ramsay MP, Robert 'Crookback' Thompson, Sir Oswald Mosley, Sir Arnold Leese, the Arabists Captain Robert Gordon-Canning and St John Philby, the woodcut artist Christian Gravesen who had been heard speaking Danish which was assumed to be German: the man to whom he had been talking escaped by putting on his hat and mac and sauntering out of the café where Gravesen continued drawing in a notebook. He was still doing so when the police arrived. He was shyly delighted when Freddie told him of Geoffrey's admiration for his work. With the exception of Gravesen, who sobbed uncontrollably and was bereft of opinions, these men were united in high dudgeon, in contempt for the sheerly wanton provocation of the British Expeditionary Force, in disdain for the narcissistic Warmonger Churchill having seized power. They smilingly loathed each other. They mocked each other's policies, biases, visions and manifestos. They were united by being believers, proud of their wretched convictions.

Crookback Thompson believed that lest his brain should become befuddled no common man should read more than three books in his life and two of those books should be *The Art of War* and *Mein Kampf*. Henry Farquharson held that in powerful societies people must swarm like locusts and eat each other when food sources are exhausted. Mosley was already worried about how far the Führer's programme of persecution of deserving Jews would go, prompting Ramsay to denounce him as a traitor to the fascist cause. Jenks insisted that defeat of communism was conditional on the adoption of biological pest control. Leese disputed the Rev. Kenneth Haworth's claim to have seen the Führer's stigmata. Freddie repeatedly asserted that fascism was 'augmented patriotism'. Gravesen sobbed uncontrollably.

When the wing was full beyond capacity they were moved to an improvised internment camp at Tangley Beech Clump on the eastern edge of Salisbury Plain, the winter quarters of Dogg Brothers' Circus and still occupied by performers who were unable to work.

In a healthy society Freddie opined — and his fellow detainees agreed unanimously — such persons would be offered the humane choice of lethal injection or cyanide vial. They included: Georgie Porgie, a mute clown with sciatica; Maxi, a far from mute alcoholic dwarf tumbler; a quadriplegic acrobat; Freya Leo, an amputee lion tamer: the same industrial accident had befallen her father whose gleaming prosthesis, 'leather and silver, a vampiric tentacle', she had inherited. It didn't fit. Achilles The Third, a lion in retirement, slouched about a rusting cage on wheels. When he roared the thin metal panels of the detainees' caravans rattled. The caravans were cramped. Decades of fried food had left a layer of grease everywhere and had been absorbed by the yucky soft furnishings. It's safe to assume that the curtains, chairs and beds were insanitary. The guards were class warriors hand-picked for their willingness to taunt their traitorous betters and for their olfactory incapacity. The stench of the place grated the mucous membranes of those that had them.

They were instructed one afternoon to be ready to travel at 6 p.m. They were driven to a station whose identifying signs had been removed. For twelve hours they travelled on a train whose windows had been hurriedly distempered to prevent them seeing the anyway unseeable country they passed through, stopping often. Even when the rain struck the windows and the paint was streaked there was, as one of the guards joked with a friendly prod of a rifle butt: 'Not much to report back to Berlin, eh?'

Soon after glaucous dawn Leese, face pressed to the window, growled:

'Transporter bridge . . . My grandson made it in Meccano. That's Runcorn down there. Fine organiser we have there, Harry Osmundson — if he hasn't been nabbed of course. I know this line. Known it all my life. In about ten minutes there's a haunted bridge . . . a deaf-mute girl threw herself from it . . . said to have spoken for the only time in her life as she jumped . . . countless sightings . . . she's always in the same place on the bridge's parapet but always dressed differently . . . to my way of thinking fascism is founded in collective metempsychosis . . . the fascist will always return when the world needs cleansing . . . in a fresh guise of course . . . but the same soul of iron.'

He was right. He was wrong a few minutes later when he supposed that they must be bound for Canada. They were marched from Oriel Road station to Bootle docks where the *Lady of Mann* was berthed. They were allowed to stop at a hole in a wall where a smiling Chinese woman sold a mess of noodles and an approximation of meat from a saucepan the shape of an inverted coolie hat. Most of it was projectile-vomited into the choppy Irish Sea an hour later. The ship bounced up and down on the blowsy churning briny. Beyond the black smoke from its funnel Douglas tilted like a see-saw as the vessel approached its harbour.

My Dearest Darling Viola

I have no idea how much of this will get past the censors. I am restricted in the number of 'communications' I am permitted to send. How I miss you my love and the jollity that surrounds you.

What can one say about the Isle of Man? It is hideous. Boarding houses and barbed wire. Quite quite hideous. Terrace after terrace of vulgar Victorian jerry building. Tawdry theatres.

On the plus side. The triskelion, the Manx flag, is a cousin to the hooked cross. A welcome sight. It flies everywhere. Taut as a sail. The wind never lets up. The landscape – what you can see of it beyond the hideous buildings – is doomladen and dramatic. Purple hills, bracken, gorse, ling and fuchsia.

Security is agreeably lax. There isn't the manpower for containment.

You can pop out for an Eyetie ice cream whenever you like. Just slip the guard a florin to turn a blind eye. There's a jazz style café plus handcarts with awnings. Top notch hokey pokey flavour – do you remember the drunk in the teddy bear coat who told us about the hokey pokey men who made their ice cream in unwashed chamber pots? The Eyeties haven't been interred, they're naturalised. Peddling their wares for half a century. An amiable enough bunch. They've acquired horrible mongrel Manx accents, however. I can't imagine they'll escape Il Duce's wrath when the invasion happens. The Manx themselves are a primitive people. Northern but not Nordic. Celtic, that's to say self-pitying, sly and so gullible that a talking mongoose is widely worshipped.

I have a room to myself. I had absolutely no compunction about pulling rank. No shame attached. I was damned if I was going to share with a yid. That's the negative side. The governor – previous experience keeping down the natives in Bongo Bongo – doesn't have the wit to segregate the various factions. The yids are everywhere. 'Refugees' so called.

Their calumnies about the Führer are grotesque, totally unbeliev-able. They will reap what they have sown, make no mistake. Swine with a yellow streak who despise the saviour of their country. They made impossible demands of the kitchen. Is blaeberry jam permitted, that sort of thing. Go and ask the rabbi. They now have their own kosher dining hut. They have to be forcibly restrained from nabbing all the smoked fish, which, can you believe, they steep in hot water rather than grill: if ever there was proof of their being a lower life form that is it. They have such an appetite for it they call themselves the Yom Kippur from Bagel Alley! That must be the celebrated Jew humour. Where is Bagel Alley I wonder? As well as eating Jew food they play Jew music on the gramophone: Mendelssohn, Mahler and more Mendelssohn. Farqu-harson Senior across the landing from me counters with thunderous Wagner.

Many of the chosen are 'intellectuals'. I'm not one for god-bothering. As you know I'm all for free speech, in its place. But there are limits. Their disrespect for the Christian faith is iniqui-tous. I attended a lecture where a 'distinguished scholar' mocked Jesus's birth story and the virgin birth. Jesus's father was a cashiered soldier called Pantera. Jesus was conceived by rape. Jesus's mother was menstruating at the time of conception. And so on. Gratuit-ous, snide, unnecessary.

After the lecture I remarked to one of them that in my family experience intellectuals kill themselves. I wouldn't say I was actively inviting the blighter to throw himself under a tram. Just hinting! Another of them had the temerity to criticise the cut of my uniform. Is Savile Row in Krakow? Quite!

Don't drive too fast. Don't let Geoffrey drive too fast.

Ich vermisse dich, alles Liebe

Freddie

Dear dear Freddieschnucki

I am so so so glad the island I find on map is just top dollar barrack. I love the islands.

Papa took me at Rugen. The sea is so so blue. It is beautiful you want to wrap up in it. It want to embrace all of you. Hug you like lover! The magic woods. Great German painter Caspar David Friedrich been there. You find magic woods at Man I am really hoping. Really hoping. Papa cannot escape Zurich.

I have the fantastic new car I buy from Margot now that bastard husband is blown up and not beating at her but she loves him still so so sad. Hushhush but I got petrol 'source'. Nothing money can't buy. Especially in war. Swiney very good in this trading arena.

Vroom vroom liebling. When war finish soon I will race at Nürburgring. I will win at Nürburgring. Presented at by the Führer. Proud day of my life.

Davy and Dot they telling me every day you must not to drive fast. I tell them without drive fast I do not learn to drive faster. They good people. Mean so so well. They worry about you.

Hushhush. Geoffrey say Poor Ned is going to be 'taken to vet' when Waffen SS arrive.

I say we hide Poor Ned in haystack! Geoffrey he just tell me Mama you so so so softheart. Anyway they find him with their pitchfork spiking through the hay. Pity is weakness. He tell me what is going to happen to Poor Ned in the life to come? What can he do? What job can he ever follow? He is born cripple parasite. Geoffrey only laugh when I speak of the compassion. He say the compassion is cowardice.

He say tell me about meek – how are meek inheriting the earth, Mama? And when? Tell me, darling Mama. Explain.

Tick tock. It is Martini o'clock here! I have date with an olive. Is often Martini o'clock! How lucky is that! Vroom vroom.

Big hugs and big big loves to my brave soldier boy.

Viola

In his diary Freddie listed details of everyday routine, exceptions to that routine, conversations, acquaintances, sundry incidents:

A football match after luncheon. Proud English Yeoman Patriots versus rodent yiddy 'refugees'. No wonder these people are loathed and despised wherever they go. No sporting instinct whatsoever. Strangers to fair play. Their centre half or whatever he was broke young Henry Farquharson's leg. Deliberately. No two ways about it. The boy was on the ground. The hulking lout brought all his weight down on him. You could hear the bone snap. You could hear the hush around the pitch. The Proud English were so shaken they didn't retaliate. I think that says something about the frailty of their pride. Our pride. It's wilting. The Redcap who was hauled in to referee said it was an accident: the wretched fellow was shit scared of the yids. The culprit had been in Dachau camp, which apparently gave him some sort of special status. It certainly hadn't knocked decent good manners into him.

Wish I could feel there was a will for recriminations welling up. But there's a snag. Mosley. He considers himself our leader – though for how much longer? He has a problem with yids in person so to speak. He's too much of a gentleman, a man of his word. He treats them face to face with the courtesy that he'd extend to any other inferior life form. He's incapable of hating the individual. He's sound on the generality, the faceless masses that stink of the shtetl and lamb fat and carry Asia in their beards. They incur his wrath. Of course in his pomp he left the corrective measures to the likes of Roddie, the biff boys and the noble stevedores.

On many pages of his diaries he drew figures with Murillo urchin faces wearing cracked-lens spectacles, callipers and prostheses.

Evening cloud is described as 'a ploughed field of red Devon earth suspended above the Irish Sea'.

He was pleased with that figure of speech. He employed it in several letters almost as often as he complained that 'if I had my own brigade . . .'

'Today is Roddie's birthday. Today would have been Roddie's birthday.'

He observes in the library that the books most read by 'refugees' are by Marx, Husserl, Benjamin, Bloch, Roth, Musil, Trotsky, Werfel etc.:

Those preferences tell their own story. Patriots prefer philosophical texts. Hitler, Rosenberg, Gobineau, Darré, Houston Stewart Chamberlain, Karl May. The physical educationist Hans Surén's *Mensch und Sonne* is one of several commendable and very popular works which celebrates the powerful oiled body rather than the weak diseased communist brain.

Private Pugh Pugh, a guard of severely limited literacy, asked him to help write a 'billydouche' to his 'best girl' who was not aware of his disability. Freddie was willing. But when he wrote the conventional greeting N.O.R.W.I.C.H. on the back of the envelope the guard became agitated. He was convinced that Freddie was trying to reveal his secret:

'What are you up to? What I know is what I know and I know that knickers is a trick . . . it begin with the K letter, I been taught that so it's got to be K.O.R.W.I.C.H.'

It's safe to assume that Freddie started to explain but, sensing a lost cause, shrugged and obliged.

Some weeks later he recorded that Private Pugh Pugh was on duty. He tearfully regretted that his 'best girl' was no longer his best girl. She had sent him a Dear John: 'There'll be no more L.O.W.E.S.T.O.F.T. for you. I'm in the family way. It was going with a chap I met at the NAAFI. He's a bookreader. He's good at it. I shouldn't say but he didn't half laugh when I told him about K.O.R.W.I.C.H. We're getting married. Sorry.'

★

A letter from of all people Gerda Brechenmacher! Our splendid Faineant cook. Rounded up and held in the Women's Camp at Port Erin.

Some yids pretend they are Lutherans. They don't pull the wool over my eyes. No. They take us for dupes. Heine tried that one: the NSDAP has got his measure all right. Where they burn books, they will ultimately burn people. Quite right too. Worthless books, worthless people.

Do they really believe that converting [to] a different faith means they're not yids any more? They'll still have their gigantic noses so they can snaffle more than their fair share of our air. They plunder our Aryan oxygen. They have special suction devices implanted at birth!!

The idea that respiratory capability supported his 'scientific' racist fantasy pleased him so much he uses it with variations in several letters: to Viola, Geoffrey, Davy Skitch, and Tom Mungoson whom he also apprised of 'one of the clippies on the tram that stops on the Promenade near My Gilded Cage might be up your street. A luscious little McFeral of indeterminate sex. Girlish boy? Boyish girl? Difficult to see because when the tram gets close enough for precise triage it is the other side of the rolls of barbed wire. Can't be a day over fifteen.'

What excitement! Three Belgian chaps managed to steal a boat and head for Ayr or Barrow or somewhere. A boxer, a chap from the Belgian Boxing Federation and *Volk En Staat*'s boxing correspondent I'd chewed the fat with a week or so back. Spoke excellent English. Fascinated by drystone walls: he said we don't get those at home. A bit browned off to say the least by the Warmonger dispensing with habeas corpus and, ignorant pig that he is, trampling on seven hundred years of English history. Further put out by the failure of the British authorities to make the yids wear a yellow star.

Had seen the boxer Vandendaele training. Punishing his superb body. Superb! Muscles like tanned downland just bulging with vitamin goodness and the strength of righteousness. They were arrested because they belonged to Vlaaamsch Nationaal Verbond. It goes without saying that, like all of us, they were not charged. In this particularly disgusting instance it was on the say-so of the Belgian embassy, a veritable kennel of French poodles.

Who's got the griff? Gen hard to come by. Seems that their best laid plans didn't work out smoothly. Actually didn't work out at all. The boat ran out of fuel leaving them floundering in the Irish Sea. Not a fate to be recommended. Rescued by a trawler. Hypothermia. Gangrene. Amputation. Solitary. The *Volk En Staat* reporter lost three toes and his balance.

Ice cream and ersatz coffee with Gerda at Toto's. She was full of gossip and news. Civilised under the circs. Almost like the old days before we were invited to lay down our lives for Poland. She brought me a delicious marzipan cake. Explained what bagels are: don't like the sound of them. She always has an inch of ash precipitously balanced on the end of her cigarette. One just gapes at it.

She hoped I might be able to help her appeal. Me! Poor girl. She'd picked the wrong chap. I obviously said I'd do what I could. But in the current climate? Well – what can one say.

She had been detained because her work permit had lapsed. Not Lady Shadoxhurst's fault. She insisted. It was clear as daylight to me that Lady Shadoxhurst had taken her eye off the ball. What to expect with a twenty-four-hour-a-day cocktail hour!! What to expect from a negligent alcoholic but negligence? Crawley was different. He was treacherous. Gerda is sure that he 'grassed' her. He has a neurotic hatred of garlic.

The WO has started what it threatened. It's vandalising the estate with Nissen huts. If this one is like the first show they'll be left there to rot when it's over unless the Reich triumphs (fingers crossed) when they will acknowledge the sullying stain these built-to-rust horrors inflict on great landscape. Thankfully so far only on the further reaches, several miles from The Park have been affected. The REME Pongo In Chief sounds like an officious ranker. He won't deal with Viola. Hardly surprising I suppose. Insists on talking to Crawley as my 'authorised representative'.

Gerda says when she was detained Davy was still keeping the

Drove below Vetch Weir flooded. He shuts the sluices at night. Valiant effort. So there's no access to Furlong Hundreds and Burnt Tree: REME shall not pass. Not that way.

But all it takes is for Crawley to work out [what] Davy is up to and let the Pongo In Chief know. That man and his precious 'duty'. Even if there was a way to shunt him, now is not the time. He knows he is indispensable. He's got me over a barrel. They'll drain the Drove.

Result: the 'finest late eighteenth-century parkland south of the Thames' will be turned into a short cut for tracked vehicles. Does Lady S fucking well care?

'And two hundred years steady growth has been ended in less than two hours.' Hardy was always on the button. Sacrificed for this criminal war. Unwinnable war. The best that can be said for it is it's a leveller. I doubt that I've ever spoken to Gerda before for as long as I did today.

Certainly never as painfully.

Gerda repeated: 'Not to blame. So much on her mind. So much to prepare for. She miss you. She miss her Papa. Now she miss my cooking. Geoffrey looks after her. He's such a big boy now. Film star handsome young man. Extra big.'

The guard I had tipped to accompany me to the café was even more dull and backward than Pugh Pugh with a half-inch forehead and a widow's peak that peeped out of his beret to join a single fat moustache where a more evolved primitive might have two eyebrows. He tapped his wrist as though he had a watch and knew how to tell the time.

We walked to the tram halt. A trim greensward sloped gently to a beach being raked by bored refugees. A pitiless wind blew black clouds from the north. The old tune 'The Silver Lining Is Nickel Brass' came into my head. (Stella Rich? Ruth Etting?)

Her mood changed suddenly. 'Strange times. You proud? I bet you are. Geoffrey so so proud. Pretend not to be but no fooling Gerda!'

I was more than a jot discombob. My principled stance on this war apart, what was I being asked to be proud about?

She held my arm. 'Don't be . . . oh, word word, ech bashful? Ja bashful. Very English word. Very English sentiment. Like people saying to you "Get Knitting". Or saying to eat eel in time of short-age: Ned has his own eel trap now. I hope she OK – I rally round I rally round like everyone say to do. But not Major Crawley no. He suspect something Geoffrey says. And Mrs Cheddy, real nosey barker. Always sniffing about, that why she has dog face. Lovely names they choose. Valentina Frederika Bouverie . . . Bouverie. Lovely.'

I was lost. I heard myself shouting: 'They? They! Who are they? Who is this, this Valentina?' I felt I was going round the bend.

Gerda babbled: 'When Lady talks to her she calls her Little Beel-zebub Dancing Inside. Mein Kleiner Teufel. She knows for certain Beelzebub is a her. Ickle little Miss Beelzebubby she say. So sweet. Due soon. She say she may have to hide her away – hide her from prime eyes, not to tell, shush, because big trouble for her, big trouble for Geoffrey.'

The next thing I recall I was supine staring at the bad sky with a throb in my head where it had hit the metal bench outside the tram halt. The roof's overhang made perspective wrong from this angle. I didn't know which way up I was. Private Pugh Pugh too was pan-icky. Hissing at me to get up get up get up. Looking round to check if he'd been seen. He feared he would be on a charge. Gerda was bending over me. Patriot warriors never flinch but I didn't want that crescent of cigarette ash to fall on my face. Please not.

That's the summum of this day of malice. I had never fainted before.

This room is profoundly ingrained with the fluids of the years. Sweat, spittle, blood, jism. One can feel them, smell them, sense the former presence of bodies that they seeped out of. The room shrinks. The walls compress. Time stains. Sit on the side of the bed. The mat-tress has had all the life knocked out of it by holiday romances. Stare at the face in the foxed mirror. Marzipan cake crumbs in my fingers. Lick them.

I fight myself not to, but I fail – I am compelled, I just have to run my fingers through my hair, feeling for what I know must be there on my scalp. Feeling the future is happening. The future where horns bud bright. They will mushroom from my crown. Look! They will grow in the future I reject: the Cornish future, the twin tines future.

I'll take another westerly future. The intellectual path.

My Viola, my careless wife,

Do you remember the Haras at Arnac-Pompadour? You said the chateau was like a fairy tale, that the horses might start speaking. You even charmed Jo Darnand. Do you remember the tomb he took us to see? Do you remember? I shall remind you.

> Here lies the son, here lies the mother,
> Here lies the daughter with the father,
> Here lies the sister, here lies the brother,
> Here lies the wife, here lies the husband,
> Here lies the grandmother,
> Here lies the grandchild too.
> There are only four bodies here.

Ring a bell?

What versatility some have in swapping family roles! What a variety of roles one person can play! What a web of deceptions they weave! What lives of lies they lead! I don't know you. I don't know myself. I don't know my father, your father. Our father?

We have overstepped the mark. We have gone beyond responsible adultery. We have created ourselves as creatures of tortuous myth far beyond Phèdre and Hippolyte. Our blood is contaminated by assonance (if that makes sense). Two bolts no nut. Two nuts no bolt. Magnets that are meant to repulse each other – but don't. We carry the same venom of Malpasfang in our cells and plasma.

I am absurd. I've tried to draw a genealogical tree. On the wall – for want of a canvas the size of *The Temptation of the Mother*. Do you remember me saying that if there was a Liborum Prohibitorum for paintings it'd be on it? Recall? That village, forget its name – the pope who was born there built a palace. That was a fine day. You ate fonduta, I ate coffee ice cream and mulberry sorbet! A squadra of fascisti honoured us with a salute.

It's chaos. Marcus has made it chaos. It's fitting, one tree will not suffice. The lines meld where they should diverge. Strange how a squiggle should be so spot-on accurate of the whole sickening mess. It's a trap we can't escape. You can't escape. Finding a maker of angels is doubtless beyond you.

This is for you to read in your shame and your squalor.

Our shame, our squalor. Our curse. Our? Our? I'm being generous. I'm being forgiving. I am merely a bystander to your crimes, witness and victim, negligently complicit. Virtuoso of the blind eye. Cuckolded by my father, cuckolded by my son. If only I'd been a man . . .

That is the last entry in Freddie Shadoxhurst's irregular diary.

Before Inigo opened the envelope that had, decades previously, been addressed to Viola, the diary had never been read. Viola feared the contents. She had no intention of confirming her fear. She put it in a 'concealed' drawer of her elaborate Biedermeier secretaire and forgot about it.

Geoffrey does not know of its existence. And even if he did he'd expect it to be in Zurich rather than in one of the teetering, ceiling high piles of papers, dossiers and ring binders in the dust tip grandly called the muniments room (such filthy windows). He conceives of it as a cache of leases, covenants, dull family lore, coy 'secrets', picayune skeletons on paper and photographic plates. The triple deathmask he took of his mother cum half-sister cum lover within minutes of her last breath he keeps about his person, dirtier than dirty postcards in a drawer.

Freddie didn't date entries. It's safe to assume that it was written either the day his life ended or the evening before.

He threw himself from a cliff.

He walked into the sea after consuming two bottles of gin and an outsize dose of aspirins, followed by second helpings, his pockets weighted by shingle.

He collapsed on a beach after consuming two bottles of gin and an outsize helping of aspirins and was swept away by maddened white steeds to join his suicidal parents. And Roddie, his beloved. And angels with callipers and shining prosthetic wings.

They exhumed him from the deep. A fish larger than any fish that inhabits the deep Irish Sea. A raggedly clothed fish. A surprise in fishnets which for all the thickness of their twine were sexy as those I used to wear with tranny heels when I danced for my swiftly bulging bigboy Inigo. (We nances are turned on by the same gear as straights.) The fleshier areas of his body had been eaten by killer lobsters which continued to feast even after they had been hauled from the water with him. Greedy pigs!

What remained of the skin was dappled as a leper's, bark like and rough, brined by the coarsening salt. The sleetwinds shaped the sea, drove it horizontally, wrinkled it.

Trawlermen are supposed to be hardened. The men of the Millom fleet were no exceptions. The everyday dangers of their job caused them to face their own unknowable mortality. The posthumous pathos of this ill-fortuned creature they could see and smell angered them. This had been a man like them. Now it – not he – was an anonymous big catch, dissolved, swollen, partial yet recognisable, reeking of decay. It was their ill-fortune to have caught it. It prompted revulsion rather than sympathy. This could be their fate too. It was craned off the deck splattered with the crew's vomit from their deepest collective jejunum.

The Millom Monster was not identified for several weeks. Viola, who didn't see the remnants, was proud of that nickname. 'Gothic beast from deep at last,' she is said to have said, giggling. Marcus, now a two-walking-sticks gimp, arrived for the funeral and stayed on. He expressed his pride to Geoffrey: 'We are an experimental family. There is much to be said for keeping it close.'

It would become yet more experimental with the birth of Valentina and, as day follows night, her pregnancy at the age of thirteen.

Bart and Tamara: 'Impossible to tell which is Inigo and which is you. He's impersonating you from the other dimension! Chapeau!'

Tamara: 'I love it. These people are like the bad-hats in the Bible . . . And as accident prone as the Kennedys. It'd scramble your brain trying to make a family tree. A truthful family tree I mean . . . what did they realise about themselves . . . their . . . their essence . . . their core? Did they know they were denials of themselves . . . crammed full of snobbish genes that wouldn't mix . . . shy genes too timid to cross the room and ask for a whirl?'

According to Vera

So this, then, is my story.

When I was a little girl my name was Vera Zofia Klockowska. It could be frightening going out alone, the Soviet army camp was not even five kilometres away. They treated us to rides in tanks. They let us play with rocket launchers. It was said they stole children. For sure, one child, little Lech Haas, never returned. He had been a good crow-scarer. The soldier who had taken him was brave. He judged himself. He found himself guilty. He drank battery acid. I loved to pick mushrooms beneath the birch trees and berries from the hedges. The lakes were the most beautiful place on earth. A girl might fish in peace seated on a willow stump with a stout wicker basket beside her. One time I caught a pike.

We were a happy family even though my little brother Jedrzej was born dead: my mother was in tears, I thought he looked beautiful and peaceful. He had gone straight to heaven without having to live life. I wished I could go with him. My older sister had to have a built-up shoe. People used to come to the house to admire the difference in the length of her legs. They believed she was blessed. The soldiers would pay her to try and run. The drunk ones kissed her: I was not to tell my mother.

The house was painted pretty blue. My father didn't beat me. When he thought we weren't hearing he was spiteful to my mother about whether he was my real father but he never laid a finger on her. I wasn't meant to know about all that. (Vadim was his former friend in the webbing and springs department, he was blond like me.)

I worked in our strip plots after school before my father cycled back from the furniture factory. We grew cucumbers, beans, marrows, sorrel, dill etc. It was my job to keep the rows weed free, clean the cloches, tidy the hay bales who looked like little people. I shredded the cabbages for salting. I grated potato for pancakes. I helped Mother with pierogi dough, we baked pike and kibinai. We simmered flaki and served it with kasha – my father's favourite, he ate it with the cider he made from our little renety orchard.

The Soviets fled. The Germans had a dragon machine that breathed fire and burnt down our village. That was the day I stopped believing in god. If he had seen my father after the Germans had shot his face off when he had stabbed one of them with a pitchfork he would have stopped believing in himself. My father died in my arms even if he wasn't my father. Was the blood that soaked me the blood that made me? I never saw my mother and sister again. The village was like charcoal. There were burnt bodies. Some were posed like athletes. I ran into the woods where I was going to make a hidden foxhole or a penpit big enough for me as I grew up and got taller. The Germans were there, in the woods, searching for Soviets. Jedrzej had been lucky.

The train was a normal passenger train. It wasn't a cattle train. It was crowded with children and babies. The windows and doors were locked. The older children tried to care for the babies. We were to learn later that the ones in our carriage were considered 'racially valuable' because we had blonde hair. But obviously not all that valuable because we had little food and drink, no air worth the name. It's wrong to complain. Most of us survived. We weren't headed for one of the camps we had heard whispers about: KZ this, KZ that. The roster of infamous names the whole world knows now were known by few people then. News travels slower than armies when you live in a village a day's ride from Druskininkai. For instance: the three cars that we used sometimes to see nearby had all gone. Where? There was nowhere to flee too.

There were whole days, whole nights, the train spent not moving. We were low priority freight. We stalled in sidings. We watched the operations clanking in marshalling yards. For sure we didn't know these were Eichmann's convoys to the camps: we had never heard of that obedient servant. I believe, though, that we suspected something terrible. They drew alongside us. We saw through the slats in the wagons. We saw the faces. Jewish children, Jewish mothers. Few men. I realised the death they were going to was not the death they wanted. They knew it too. They felt the horrors of anticipation. They feared. Whatever else they did, they feared. They lacked what it takes to get rid of their fear. They could not cheat the SS by killing themselves: the SS would never have allowed that for how then would they get their murderous satisfaction? They would deny the most human thing a human could do to its self because of their greed.

To kill yourself takes not just courage. It takes tools, resources and opportunity. The suicide needs an accomplice. Suicide is collaborative. That is what those numberless days taught me.

All along that journey Germans with clipboards and ledger books would get on the train and go from carriage to carriage calling names then carrying out brief inspections. They measured our heads and shone lights in our eyes. They ordered: open wide and cough. They held stethoscopes to famished chests. They did not tell us where we were or where we were going. No one dared ask. There were never explanations with Germans. They kept you in the dark. The reason for any act was never disclosed. Knowledge was power. Lack of knowledge was weakness that could not be corrected. Children disembarked. We could see them revived by air. Then the train would be off again. By the time my turn came there were only twenty of us left in our carriage. I was so weak I could walk only a few paces. My back and legs were pierced by waves of pain. I was dragged off the train at a station beside a sluggish river. A dark hill of conifers rose from its far bank. Dense fumes blew along the valley and stung. We were scrutinised by an SS officer and a female nurse who divided us into two groups. He touched the shoulder of his selected.

The others were formed into ranks and marched away. Six of us waited beside a pyramid of coal as tall as a house. The doleful SS guard Serge was not German. He was ugly and dark, a boy scared because far far from home. Some of the other children agreed that you could tell from his accent he was French. You could tell from his eyes that he was vicious. He looked at me in a way that I didn't understand then but that I was soon used to. He put his hand under my coat and touched my chest. He said something with a brown-toothed smile that smelled like a lavatory. One of the girls translated. He says you're ripening nicely like a fruit. He said something more. I caught the words *puff haus*. He repeated them with greedy relish. He says he regrets you aren't going to the House of Dolls because he'd have liked to come to see you there. I had never heard of a House of Dolls.

That was where the others had been taken to, in this town which was a barracks. When it was explained to me I was so relieved I sobbed. My relief was short lived. My destination was Lebensborn-Heim-Kaltenborn: officers only, selected officers only. Serge will have to become a blond officer, joked the nurse.

It was a lonely old house in a park, a palace even, turned into a sanatorium whose visitors were invited guests. It was inhabited by nurses, always smiling doctors and blonde girls: we were not yet young women. We were instructed that when we were young women we would become mothers for the Reich. We were vessels in waiting. We tried to hide our 'ripening' by suppressing puberty, signs of menstruation, telltale body hair. We were fighting hormonal inevitability, programmed pituitaries, swelling, the production of mucus. This was difficult because our bodies were not our own to manage and respond to as we willed. They were objects owned by the Reich or the SS or the Reichsführer Heinrich Himmler. By men, anyway, not good men. It was risky disguising our maturity. Every train back to the east was a threat. They inspected us as though we were machines. We were machines.

My name was now Vera Sophia Klock. I had my first child when I was still twelve years old. I don't know who the father was. I lost count of the violators: I was going to say *my* violators but they were not mine, they were nothing to me. That was what I told myself. I often shut my eyes so I could not see their faces. Then they would order me to watch as their faces twisted and knotted in their small triumph.

I think the child was a girl. I feel that . . . I cannot be certain. I was pregnant again six weeks after giving birth. I was used. We all were used. But we were not so used as the women in the House of Dolls who were abased dozens of times each day, raped and humiliated and beaten in the name of the fatherland, to give pleasure to the fatherland's proud warriors.

Pleasure! Was that what these foul-smelling savages sought? They queued at the door for their fifteen minutes conquering the weakest, brutalising the vulnerable, despising fellow human beings. They waged war inside women's bodies. They watched without curiosity when a woman broke through the shutters of a dormer window to fling herself six storeys to the pavement beside the queue where she lay in a blood pond that was an inconvenience. Part of the House of Dolls had been a synagogue. Its current use was intended to add insult to injury. Not that there were any Jews left to insult but German hatred was obsessively symbolic.

Unlike those poor women we might go a few days without another visitor, another blond SS officer who believed himself a god from Hyperborea. Their pleasure was selflessly suspended. The discharge of strong Aryan seed was duty. If it was enjoyed so much the better. The Reichsführer took a men-will-be-men attitude to his stallions' behaviour and rape in general. Procreation might be recreation for them. If the procreative act occurred at night in a cemetery on the moonlit tomb of a dead warrior then the child would inherit the powers of that warrior as well as the genetic gift of the parents; indeed, the child would have three parents. One of them, me, would also have lacerations and bruises. *Das Schwarze Korps* published lists of sex cemeteries.

The second pregnancy resulted in a stillborn boy. I was ashamed that I felt nothing. An interior cyst was removed. That's all. It was – *it*, not he – merely random tissue and bone to feed to the Mordhunden handlers. The vicious dogs, wearing winter coats of fur and human hair, patrolled the sanatorium grounds and maimed anyone who was not of the Elected Elite. They enjoyed fine cuts of meat. The Mordhunden handlers, lithe young black men and brown men, had been born in this very sanatorium to women, a few willingly seduced, many more assaulted and raped, by occupying French and American troops after the previous war, the war to end all wars: they got that wrong. Although they had been trained at the Oranienburg Experimental Establishment they did not know what country they belonged to. One of them had an American name, Buster, and a phrase of American: 'I may be Jim Crow but I'll still take a bullet for Uncle Sam.' He often said that as we took the air, avoiding him. We were forbidden to 'fraternise' with them in case the sins of their mothers be repeated. That was an offence which could mean being sent to the

House of Dolls. I was warned that if I had another stillbirth I would be sent there too. I prayed that my third pregnancy would be 'successful'. I thank that child wherever she is now. What country might she be in?

I always wore my crucifix and locket with a picture of the virgin. Having been raped by god she knew what I was going through. We knew little of the war's progress. We were non-people who would never be informed. There was no need to tell us. We were locked away. We lost track of time. The state of pregnancy was our clock. Officers might use us, for instance, for four days or perhaps seven in succession, even when we were pregnant, which was supposed to be forbidden, but the law was not applied. Post-partum misery was forbidden as weak bordering on treachery. The law was applied. Reimpregnation is a laughable fantasy which did not benefit the fatherland. But because some preferred us in that state officers would remind doctors with objections who was senior. Then we might not see them again for weeks. Or was it months?

Routine dissolves the calendar. Porridge for breakfast because, according to the scholars of the Ahnenerbe, the English upper classes ate porridge and stayed slim. Pregnancy, birth, snow, buds, pregnancy, showers, birth, porridge, mushrooms, beautifully sprung prams bearing the hooked cross, flowers, pregnancy, porridge, sauntering, pregnancy. Kidnap. Babies whisked away in the middle of the night. Ripped from the breast. The wet nurses were only a slightly superior form of life to us. Babies were the product. When the product is made it leaves the factory farm.

We might never see them again, these death's head husbands six or seven of whom we would marry on a bad day. They might have been posted to 'the east' or to 'Africa': not actual places, but ideas that terrified them, tomorrow's graveyards, better not spoken about because every place on the map was a future cemetery. They might be dead, unmourned by us. We'd be laughing and spitting on their unmarked graves. They would never know whatever it was they bequeathed us. Their work was impersonal. They were as much machines as we were.

They did not speak about the annihilation their diseased nation was attempting. It could hardly lose. It was one-sided. All the dice were loaded in its favour. The more they boasted of 'triumphs in the field' the more they were deluding themselves. The war waged with Panzers and Nebelwerfers was a cover for the secret war of Zyklon B and experiments on civilians. We didn't know that then. If they knew, they did not speak about it. But there were telltale signs that talk of triumphs was just that. Talk. The lack of vehicles, lack of food, water to be fetched from the lake – that was what told the story. One of the starving wild horses that roamed the park was shot and butchered, a Knabstrupper, a big filly, seventeen hands plus. Some women made one pot meals from plants and leaves, hoping they were abortifacients. They never are, not when you want. Because guards were sleeping on duty a woman from Poznan was able to eat a handful of yew berries. They didn't kill her.

The bad days grew fewer. Staff left the sanatorium without warning. The contents of the pharmacy disappeared, pillaged. I had my own supply of Methergine to stem post-partum bleeding. There were no delivery forceps on the premises and only two nurses to attend a birth. Piles of dossiers and papers were burnt. A tattooist had abandoned her equipment. It hurt. The supply of Heidelberg-scarred sires was drying up. They were younger and younger. Uniformed but hardly soldiers. They were more forthcoming. Their confidence in the destiny promised by the Führer waned. Their confidence in the Reich was gone. They were making plans for their survival, not the Reich's. Sometimes they would share schnapps from a flask after the transaction taking care to wipe it after you had drunk from it. Making sure you saw they were wiping it. Sometimes they would tell you their given name.

Hauptsturmführer Stech-Pelz was different. A fine physical specimen, just what the Reich ordered: blond, lavish facial scar, powerfully muscled with a high forehead indicating a big brain. He covered seven women in two days. I was the eighth. He told me he'd seen me and was saving me: leave the best till last. I was flattered not to be subjected to the usual abuse. He was, he told me, a male of exceptional potency. After the first transaction we remained in the ward, which he considered an inappropriate place for conversation.

We sat in the 'day room', once a ballroom, all crumbling plaster and ghosts of cupids. This was where the former owner of the house had poisoned herself many years before. So it was said. Some said it was in one of the thirty bedrooms. Did it matter which? She had made a courageous choice because of . . . Did it matter what? The act itself is the thing. An act of the most extreme privacy. You turn in on yourself. It has similarities to masturbation. Her husband had betrayed her with cattle and horses. That was the legend. Rumour lived in the bricks and mortar.

There were torn dust covers over the furniture, marks on the walls where paintings had been removed and the striped flock paper was as bright as the day it was hung, back in the old days. From the centre of a broken window pane spread a web of cracks like the lines on a centenarian's face. He told me his full name. Hauptsturmführer Ernst Friedrich Stech-Pelz. He was surprised that I did not recognise it for his late father Lothar Friedrich Stech-Pelz had once been a celebrated composer, though his work was seldom performed during the NSDAP imperium because Himmler had detected the influence on his three symphonies of the Jew Mendelssohn and had instructed the Reichsmusikkammer to proscribe all but a few lieder. Ernst was proud to have agreed with the Reichsführer's musicologically wise decision.

He asked me what my name was. He was the first officer to have done that. He told me how important he was to the war effort. He was planning the Reich after the war.

The children born from his seed were destined to be vanguards of the shining future. He was the youngest soldier of his rank in the SS. He was the youngest member of the Reichsführer's private staff. His honour was his loyalty. His loyalty was to the Reichsführer SS Heinrich Himmler rather than to the Führer himself, a stale man whose day had passed. Ernst was almost certainly the future Protector of Czechoslovakia, a position that has been inadequately filled since Heydrich's death. He would bring Slavs to their knees. He would destroy their language. And should he be appointed to rule the Baltic states he would take as a foundation the admirable if murky sylvan paganism that infected them, and bring the lightness of the dark corps to our forests. He would make them German.

He went out to his car in the ruins of the stables. There were fascinating tight masks over the headlights cut with lightning symbols. I watched. I liked his failure to strut. He almost fell over in the slippery slush. He turned, sensing that I was watching (that animal instinct humans retain). He smiled. I laughed for the first time in four years. He returned with a canteen of bottles: Killepitsch, himbeergeist, Finnish Terva schnapps and Schwartzhog. No food.

'When my mother saw me in my uniform she called me Schwartzhog. She clucked, she went back to reading a woman's frothy book. No respect for the uniform means no respect for the Führer. If I had been a better son I would have had her arrested . . . I showed weakness.' I didn't believe him. He boasted to make up for not being naturally threatening. He was the first man I slept with meaning spent the night with. Transactions usually lasted between two and ten minutes. Twenty was exceptional, thankfully. I felt nourished by him, secure in his arms. He was just a blond boy dressed up. He was anxious to get north to Flensburg where a provisional government had been established. He insisted that he was needed. Hours on faulty phones told him that. But his car had no fuel. The vast house was empty of all but a dozen women, five uncollected babies shrilling, a cook who had no food to cook, two blond Hitler Youth who, having completed their transactions, chopped up furnitures as firewood. I wandered the endless long lugubrious corridors listening to the echoes of the ages.

Rumours multiplied. Buster and the other dog handlers had fled through the snow with their dogs to protect them because they had heard that a company of hungry Vlasovsty – Red Army turncoat bastard traitors become Wehrmacht's honourable auxiliaries – was wandering nearby, looting, violating, raping as they attempted to reach Allied lines where they could surrender in the hope they would not be returned to the country they had first betrayed. In a room with broken windows a recently 'recruited' woman wrapped in a tarpaulin told me she had heard there had been an order to evacuate. What exactly was an evacuation? How was it going to be carried out? How was it different from just leaving? Where had the message come from? She couldn't say. What would we encounter outside this backwater? War seemed distant. Ernst tried every phone number he knew. Many lines were down. At last he had a sort of success. Determination and persistence brought luck. He held a finger to his lips. He listened to the sound of a vehicle approaching. It was the early morning after the second night I had slept with him. An ambulance arrived. He had the sort of initiative that was so lacking in the NSDAP. The curse of hierarchy I have heard it called. Always looking for an order from higher up before you can make a move. He instructed the two Hitler Youth to push his frozen car through the snow and ice to a position beside the ambulance. He instructed them to siphon that vehicle's petrol. It was more difficult than it is supposed to be. He saluted them. I loaded my few possessions, stole whatever I could carry including some good clothes and a green enamel wine jug, got my file from the Intendant's empty office, filled the boot, stood rubbing my hands and shivering in the light snow. The ambulance orderly ran from the house shouting when he saw what was happening. He remonstrated, he begged, there were babies to deliver to the orphanage hospital at Nordlingen. Ernst, my Ernst, smiled at him. He told him it was, regrettably, out of his hands, that he was ordered to the new seat of government, that he was on the Reichsführer's private staff, that his task took precedence, that he had a duty to fulfil. The orderly was flustered, incredulous. He muttered that he was not merely saving lives, he was working to build the Reich's future. This is theft, he said, this is theft. You are a thief. You are a disgrace to your uniform. You insult your uniform.

Hauptsturmführer Stech-Pelz responded by firing a warning shot into his forehead. He looked affronted, puzzled. Then he slumped like an uncomplaining animal. My Ernst shrugged as though to ask what choice had he had?

He ordered the Hitler Youth to bury the insubordinate's body without honours. He told them they were soldiers of promise and that he would recommend they be promoted. I began to believe in god again, for a while.

That was the last I saw of Kaltenborn, where five children had been germinated in me. They were not my children. Each had a regiment for a father. The broken palace dissolved in snow flurries as the car bumped down the pitted avenue away from it and the shame it spelled. Mordhunden raced beside us, hurled themselves repeatedly at the doors, not letting themselves be rebuffed. I stayed calm. Frozen snow slipped from black branches. I had, I discovered later, lived there for four years, a womb slave. Now I was free. A chapter was closed. Soon there would be buds. Spring was around the corner. There was a new life ahead of me. My blond saviour was at the wheel. The far north beckoned us. I wondered if I was in love.

During those four years I had not once left Kaltenborn. Strange to say but I had been protected. Outside that great park snow gave way to sleet. Germany was fatally wounded. It was many kinds of casualty. There were dead bodies beside the roads piled high in monumental pyramids. There were still living bodies, less healthy, hundreds of them, the living dead in pyjamas driven in convoys by mounted SS who saluted us. They earned my Ernst's approval by wielding their whips to force their prisoners to the ground where they could shoot them. Mud absorbed blood. We were fortunate to have fuel. Drivers of broken-down trucks sat grumpily on their running boards. Queues awaited food and clean water. Queues to obtain clothes, queues to donate clothes to new recruits, most younger than I was. The Führer was everywhere on banners and posters instructing his people that it was their duty to fight to the end. They were admissions that Germany was already defeated. The wounded lurked on corners in rubble towns wrapped in greatcoats and rugs. Beside a crater stood a soldier all but dead: ill-shaven cheeks, a livid scar on the left (windscreen, not duel), visible exhaustion, soiled crumpled army coat, sleeves devoid of stripes. Amputees showed off their cauterisations. Abbreviated limbs are better for begging. And always beg from the poor who stay poor because they give to such people. All of Germany looked like my village after the Germans had burnt it. The justice of the poets. Everywhere was scraps, bits, unrecognisable stuff, breakages. Facades stood like scenery with nothing to support them when the winds came, so they crumpled into a thousand pieces. Like a giant had stamped on his model town. We drove for what seemed hours behind tank transporters and lorries carrying amphibious vehicles. We slept a few hours in the car. On a plain of mud and high grass the men of a vanguard retreating from the east met the men of a vanguard retreating from the west.

At a broken-down tavern surrounded by swaying steppe grass and painted with runes they drank awaiting an order that didn't come. Which direction to take next? Those coming from the west advised us that many dikes along already swollen rivers and canals were broken, that roads were impassable. Drenched earth policy. Those coming from the east warned against everything. They addressed Ernst. They had found the bodies of SS captured and garrotted. They hoped to see out the war here, in a bar, with friendly Yankees. They meant it. All incentive to fight was gone. They feared both capture by the Red Army and summary justice as deserters.

Soon after we left the tavern, Ernst drove the car into a deserted farmyard. He unscrewed the registration plate. He changed into civilian clothes. What he called that 'old chap Oxford look': he had fond memories of the great seat of learning which he had visited on a Hitler Youth bicycling tour to England's historic houses and cathedrals. He folded his uniform carefully and packed it beneath the back seat. He put a straw bale on the seat. He took some ods pills.

Regrets began near Verden. We spent what would be our last hours together at Sachsenhain. Our last hours. I sensed our idyll might soon be over. Our last hours . . . We walked through the groves of stones that remember the five thousand Saxon victims of Charlemagne The Slaughterer. A beautiful memorial conceived by the Reichsführer's historians and constructed in His name. Ernst believed it was a holy place. He welcomed its spirit into his soul. He was like a blond god among the stones. Handsome and powerful.

There were animal footprints in the snow. Happy creatures ignorant of war and its victims. We didn't know it was our last hours together but there was an unspoken sadness between us because we suspected. There was also gaiety between us. An unspoken understanding of the joy we brought each other, a joy that would be cruelly quashed.

'What the fuck's this then for a game of soldiers?'

That was the first time I heard The Sergeant's voice. It was raspy and harsh like it came out of cracked leather. He was an ugly bugger all right, squashed face, crooked nose, scar tissue. Like he was carved from potato by a bad carver. Despite the freezing weather all he was wearing was khaki trousers held up by khaki webbing braces over his bare wiry tattooed torso: a pin-up with a cheeky bottom and a peek-a-boo; a walrus-moustached face; hearts; a wreath of roses; boxing gloves; a swooping eagle. Very he-man he was. He was holding a submachine gun, prodding its muzzle at the front of the car. The rookie soldier with him walked round the car randomly banging it.

We hadn't seen the checkpoint coming. It looked like a few vehicles in the distance, scattered anyhow. No different from the dozens of others ruined and abandoned on the outskirts of ruined and abandoned towns. That's what it looked like . . . When we realised what it was my Ernst breathed with relief: 'Thank god they're British.'

'Out!'

The rookie held his weapon to the window. Then Ernst stood beside the car. He held his hands on his head without being told to.

The rookie searched Ernst. When he found Ernst's pistol he waved it, high in the air like a celebration trophy. He fired two rounds.

One of the three soldiers slumped on a sofa on the slushy pavement held up a warning hand: 'No accidents now, Nobby. Take it easy.'

'Open wide. Now!' Nobby explored Ernst's mouth with an unhygienic hand.

Then he did the same to me.

'I hope you're not dreaming of topping yourself today, Love.' He gripped my jaw like a cruel dentist, felt my teeth, stooped to inspect the upper case. I can't remember how many SS had proudly shown me the sealed zyankali capsule they carried in a hollow tooth. It was as if it was more intimate than their Schwarze Korps fertility organ.

I looked over his shoulder. The shell of a little house, a garden with a rotting wicket fence, a brightly decorated wheelbarrow full of broken glass cloches. I thought how sad, remembering how much they cost in the old days. I thought how sad war is for gardens that have been their cultivators' pride.

'They're clean, Sarge.'

Then he began to feel parts of my body. Tommy Atkins was no better than Hans Wurst. Tommy Atkins was as clumsy and coarse: 'What you got hidden up your gash, Love? Don't mind if I do a recce do you? How'd you like to feel the sticky end of my fuck-gun?'

I kicked him.

'Fucking bitch.' He spat at me.

'Come on, Nobby son . . . easy does it. Where's your decorum?'

He looked resentfully at The Sergeant.

Then he reached into the back of the car, hauled out the bale, huffing and straining. I could tell Ernst was alarmed.

The Sergeant said: 'Someone's pulled the funnies with the registration number. Would that someone be you? Does someone not want to be recognised? Eh?'

Ernst shrugged: 'The jalopy's requisitioned.' That's the English word he used.

'The jalopy, eh? Hmmm . . . Papers if you please.'

'What we got here then?' said rookie Nobby. He was holding Ernst's SS uniform tunic.

'I'd say that makes the papers a bit of a formality, wouldn't you? Your war just went fubar mate.' The Sergeant grinned. An alarming sight. His teeth were stumps, black, brown, mustard-yellowish. A ruined and abandoned town in miniature.

Ernst was rightly indignant: 'You do not address an officer as Mate.'

'I address an officer with the respect due to his rank. I address you how I fucking well like. Murdering scum . . .

'Nobby – you take Scum here up to Jake With The Neck Brace. You tell him to fix transport up to interrogation at 73rd Anti-Tank. They want as many of these scum as they can get. Alive, sorry to say.'

That was the last time I saw my Ernst. I watched him shuffling away from me along a street all mud and walls collapsed into brick piles. Shuffling, not striding with an officer's dignity and purpose. All his pride drained from him like wax out a syringed ear. Shuffling to a different tune, a different future. Our paths had crossed. Now they must cross no more. Life is cruel and love is crueller. Nobby kept on pushing him and hurrying him with his submachine gun. He never turned his head to look back at me. The trees were skeletons. Too proud to reveal himself as a defeated warrior. I wondered where I was. I cried out of pity for myself. The one soldier on the sofa who wasn't asleep was leaning forward boiling water on a spirit stove.

'What you needs is a nice strong cup of cha and a wad.'

I couldn't take my eyes off the body of a German soldier. Part of his head was wrapped in bloody bandages caked with brain tissue. Two famine dogs were eating brain from the battledress. The remnants of his face were blue. His wire spectacles were twisted, a lens stuck to his nose. He lay on a haycart. The horse that had pulled the cart was also dead, propped between the shafts. Its eyes and gums were a banquet for crows.

The squaddie making cha said: 'We thought it might be Himmler in civvies hiding under those bandages and all. They were saying he was escaping down this way. When we told him to take off his bandages he said he'd die if he did. Well . . . you got to say he was on the money with that one. His brain fell out his nut.'

'Right then,' said The Sergeant, 'what we going to do with you then? I think we can say for certain that you're *not* Himmler in civvies. That's very much in your favour. Let's have a butcher's at your papers.'

Was I Vera Sophia Klock? That was my German name. That was the only name I had. Those were the only papers I had. But I had not been German, just a German prisoner. A prisoner of love – love! – so we were called. Now, that is funny. That made him laugh. More teeth. That Germany – the Germany that issued the papers and changed my name – was down the khazi he said. It hardly existed. It was almost over. It was just rubble and guilt and mass suicide for the lucky ones avoiding retribution by the hordes from the steppes. Thank god they're British.

Was I Vera Zofia Klockowska? That was my baptismal name. What had the trinity ever done for me? No one comes back from the dead. Mary was a cow, hypocritical cow. They're fair-weather friends the trinity. I was fearing that I might have to return to where I came from even though my family was dead or missing and I had already been a slave for four years. I had a bad feeling of what would be waiting for me there, damned as a collaborator in the Reich's population-replenishing whether I liked it or not. Victims get no sympathy. Victims bring it on themselves. Victims deserve to be victims. I was told this by men, always men, just now and again a steel-faced woman, a traitor to her sex. I was treated as a collaborator because I had been detained in the company of the war criminal Hauptsturmführer Ernst Stech-Pelz (identifying sign: no ear lobes) and had no way of proving I was Vera Zofia Klockowska.

How many brown committees and boards and panels did I plead before? Always the same tired men, they all look the same (khaki uniform, khaki moustache), they all smell the same (pipe tobacco, beer), always the same barracks with the Nazi insignia smashed, always the same pink eyes, always the same red-nosed Padre who wants you for god, the same mugs of tea, the same cannot-concentrate because the subalterns come in every minute to call someone away. They are bored. Classifying us day after day. Picking out the danger-ous ones, the impenitent ones, the ones who won't accept defeat, the ones who want to start it all over again. Oh please not.

At last. My 'saviour' was different from all the rest. Dressed differ-ent but it was more than the clothes. Appearance not English. Smarter. Clean shaven. No moustache. No pipe. Pack of Luckies: he didn't smoke them but pointed with them. He wore combat clothes like they were fashion items, ironed crisp. Tar black hair. Not an English accent so far as I could tell. But not American either. Voice like a recording of a recording. Immediate but distant.

'What,' he asked, 'do you know about O-D-S?'

I didn't know what he was talking about. I shook my head. 'What is this?'

'Thats what I'm asking you.'

'I never heard of O-D-S.'

'How about odessa?'

'What about Od . . . Big port. Famous city. I never went there. I never go anywhere past my village till they kidnap me. A thousand kilometres my village to Odessa.'

'You know very well that's not what Pat's after,' said one of the pipe and moustaches like it was a threat.

I was threatened. I think quickly and say: 'If O-D-S is not O-D-S . . . if it's ods, all joined up, it's a drug, booster drug the SS take.'

That shocked them.

'And Hermann Göring is a ballerina.'

'I see them take it. I promise. What they say it's Pervitin for the elite.'

'Of course it is!' He rolled his eyes, and his pipe rolled with them. Funny major.

They talked among themselves.

Then: After all that she's been through. Yes yes yes – give the girl a chit. Chit! The magic word. The open sesame. That made me a Displaced Person who will, *for the immediate future*, remain in the western zone. I waited to learn what camp I would be taken to. Sitting around: that's what global conflict means. I had been beaming my gratitude to everyone who came through the draughty hall where I twiddled. Some of the men who had questioned me walked past. The black-haired officer in smart combats noticed me: 'Good luck. You'll be OK . . . See you at a wake someday.'

A what?

But he had gone, striding to catch up with his colleagues.

Soon I would be in a former KZ lager, where the smell of burnt flesh is what I would wake to every day, where some of the guards had changed uniform, but hadn't changed jobs – I am convinced. Why did they guard us? There was nothing to escape to. Nowhere to go. Not such a hell as the sanatorium but a hell all the same. I am thankful to chance that it didn't last.

The second camp I was sent to was at the outskirts of Hamburg. There were not so many guards. That *for the immediate future* followed me around. When did the immediate future come to an end? How immediate was immediate?

I had a head cold. All stuffed up and aching. Lucky it wasn't more. The camp hygiene was bad. I was scavenging in Blankenese high above the shining Elbe. The rain was biting rain. It was my strategy to scavenge in the ruins of the rich. The pickings might be rich too. There were rats everywhere. They profit from war. They had the same idea as me! I was rummaging in what had been the garden of a lovely villa with balconies supreming the trees. A Jeep going this way and that way all widdershins because of the potholes full of rusty water drove past me. Then it stopped and reversed. I was fearful. What infringement this time? I wondered.

'I'd know that pretty face anywhere.' It was The Sergeant. That was a twinkle in his bruised eyes. He greeted me to that same exhibition of teeth and, this time, black gums and tongue like a creepy cave at a funfair. Still not wearing a shirt or battledress. All torso like twisted hawsers.

The back of the Jeep was loaded with loot from looting. He proudly showed off bath taps, gold and black clocks with myth statues, paintings in fancy frames of German villages before they were rubble, a harp, a microscope, rolled-up carpets, a doll's house, a soaked Red Indian headdress, a marquetry table, a magnificent portrait of a man in osk beaver furs with a hat too big for his head, a desk with bulgy strong men pretending to hold it up, a jewel box, little naked babies supporting a blue globe, a fruit bowl with silver butterflies, swords, several cameras, chandeliers hanging over the side, a stack of metal chairs, naval binoculars, carved mugs with hinged tops etc.

Quite a healthy haul! And I could do with those furs coming to life to wrap around me!

'A squirrel that forgets to hoard is heading for famine,' he said. 'I tell you – this little haul makes up for some of the truly horrible tasks that have come my way lately.'

He shook his head all puzzled and distracted: 'Just touching him . . . The poison under the skin . . . I feel dirtied. After all I've seen. I been showering whenever I can. Wash away the stain.'

I knew a thing or two about being sullied but it wasn't a competition so mum's the word.

He offered me a cigarette: that's what he thought I had been scavenging for. A dimp, he called it. That was one of the first English words I knew. It was the first cigarette I smoked in my life. He laughed when I told him I didn't know what I was looking for – buried treasure maybe!

'That'll sort your cold out. Clear out the old bronchioles . . . the dog with one nostril only gets half the prize.' He laughed, and how he laughed at my beginner-smoker's choking cough and dizziness and lightheadedness. He'd never seen anything like it. God spare him. He laughed like the drain.

That's how I made him fall for me. Laughter. It's how to say hullo, it breaks down the ice like an icebreaker. It's the glue between folk, it's the great way to go when your time comes, relishing a chuckle and a naughty giggle with your loved ones at the bedside while the cosseting liquid from the drip takes you warm and smooth to your specified destination. Yes, laughter overcomes colours and faiths. It links them. Unless it's laughing at different coloured folk because of their filthy toilet habits and stupid faiths that only the uneducated and superstitious like I once was can give the time of day to. Everyone enjoys mirth-rich classics like *Sawing off the Branch, Careful With the Liquid Propellant, Trev and Nev's Gag Emporium* and *Bob Dobney: Store Detective* (though that wasn't actually meant to be funny I don't think). Banana skins are an international language like Volapük.

It was laughter that bonded us two together as one from the moment he lit my second cigarette from his, a sure sign of developing intimacy. That's why it's called a Dutch fuck. He rescued me without realising I made him rescue me. Frankly he wasn't top catch. Not like pike. More like roach or perch if you follow. He was almost three times my age. But what does age matter when you're in love or desperate not to get sent back to the east?

I'd have preferred an officer with officer class status, a Sam Browne and money and better teeth. But he was my one-way ticket from Hell to Tomorrow even if he was likely to go into a sort of trance with no notice. It just happened. He went funny. So funny I was alarmed. Mumbling and shouting, screaming, banging his forehead with his fists. Truth be told he didn't know when he had been like it. He'd come out of it as quick as he had gone in. I put it down to PTSD, which hadn't been invented then. Quivering and going on about being sullied by touching the sweaty scaley skin he was a reptile a human reptile.

What it was that had driven him all doolally was burying Himmler.

Simple as that. More than twenty-four hours after the most wanted man in Europe had made what was jokingly called 'his concluding statement' they were all a tizz. They left his body on the floor of the room where 'he had abruptly curtailed his interrogation by biting an annealed phial of potassium cyanide concealed in a hollow tooth'.

The phial should have been found. The doctor who had inspected him had been too gentle, too 'Hippocratic' it was said. He shouldn't have been gentle with a man like that, a monster disguised as the booking clerk at Bad Godesberg station. Confusion stalled Ülzenerstrasse 31a in Luneburg. No one knew what to do with the body. No one wanted to take responsibility for the loss of the greatest catch. The reaction of the senior officers ('public school pansies') whose inexperience and negligence had allowed their prisoner to resolve his own fate was to drain the cellar of the red-brick house that had been requisitioned a few days previously. They drunkenly blamed the doctor, who responded that he was not qualified to do body searches, had indeed never done one. Lacking orders from above, someone decided that the body should be disposed of as quickly as possible.

It was sod's law. The Sergeant had the bad luck to be the senior NCO on the premises. Burial was unquestionably an other rank's task. So he was volunteered (as he said) to organise a troop of gravediggers. Even that long after the death the body smelled of almonds. They wrapped the body in camouflage netting and a rubber groundsheet, tied with telephone cable. The only car available was a right-hand-drive Daimler, cobalt blue and fawn, abandoned at Dunkirk five years previously. They drove to Luneburg Heath. This normally deserted area was unusually populated by refugees, broken soldiers and stalled vehicles blocking the roads. A group of escaped deserters was trying to cook an entire pig on a failing fire of damp branches. They drove for hours. Straw hives, black-roofed longhouses, black-faced sheep, dead black-faced sheep, victims of packs of feral starving Mordhunds. Much of the ground was frozen. Melting snow formed pools on lush moss pierced by stalks and sundew. The ground around the ponds and sinkholes was diggable. At last they found a place which was hidden, far from trails and paths. The grave they dug was deep. They laid him to writhe in hell, in dark peat, east by north-east of Bispingen, probably.

I seized the day even though it was spitting cats and dogs, stinging. Typical Elbe day I'd say. Sneeze snuffle sneeze. I was muddy and my dress was torn. I've got a smoker's cough to this day but it was worth it. I seized it.

'You're quite a guttersnipe,' The Sergeant told me. It was many years since anyone had spoken to me fondly.

I almost forgot about Ernst, in jail awaiting trial on several counts of crimes against humanity. He hadn't told me he was rated among his fellows for forcing prisoners to dig their own graves with their hands: no half measures then. Only a coward refuses to dig his own grave: that was the SS's maxim. I tried to wash him out of my mind with a cleansing enema but I never forgot him totally.

The Sergeant took me dancing. You should have seen him go! He put a lot of effort into it and he didn't mind the laughter. He taught me the jitterbug and the lindy hop. We kissed in the moonlit ruins of the Reich. He had the hot blood of his distant Italian heritage. But was shy with it. A gentleman. As he explained: no bottom pinching where he came from. He also had a posting back to Blighty Island in two weeks. Why didn't I come with him? Why? Because I was a DP with unresolved nationality. I couldn't go anywhere. I didn't even have a name. He looked into my eyes. No more twinkling, they were imploring. He asked me to marry him.

Like I say, no great catch what with his beaten-up face from when he was a boxer at the fairgrounds in The Depression and terrible mouth (ditto) and his coughing and hawking up shiny green lungslime and his low priority personal hygiene apart from his hands (see below) and being so old he'd been in the trenches last time round. But it was as much as I could hope for. I told him yes and that I loved him.

The burial damned him. It damaged him. It haunted him. Himmler was always with him. He's there to this day. All along his long life. Dead eyes staring, veiled, matt. He dreams he is in a cell where the walls are the eyes of a murderer who murmurs untruths, who perverts words: purify, soap production, customer connectivity, cleanse, increase aggregates, maximal performance. I could have told him about what I had felt and seen and endured. I skipped the details, the small print of my years of humiliation. I didn't want to compete. I was free, comparatively. I had not known so much freedom since I was a child, long long ago. Liberty is relative. He couldn't escape. A few hours of the past captured him. He wanted to hurt Himmler brutally on behalf of the millions. Although he abided by the fair play he longed to torture him, but how do you torture the dead? They are beyond the crudest lowest kind of punishment. And torture harms the torturer (so it is said, but the kind of people who torture don't have fine feelings to damage, that is why they are torturers). After everything that had happened to me I was full of joy at my new life. I got used to him washing his hands several times per day so he was washday red to the elbows like Mrs Mop The Queen Mother. I got used to the cruel spite carried on the breeze, whispered through the curtains: 'Damaged goods.' It was as it had been for the past four years. I was still a machine. *Goods . . .*

A simple ceremony. He requisitioned a lovely house near where he had found me scavenging. He put on a shirt and jacket for the occasion. A few of his best mates. Nobby was under orders not to leer at me. I became Vera Zofia Dogg. I buried Sophia Klock, that was the bad past, I put it behind me even though I had no papers, no proof that I once had been Vera Zofia Klockowska before I was Klock The Slave. I didn't want reminding. Klock The Slave was dead. Now I was a joyous teenage war bride. One of the earliest war brides. Celebrating with victor's champagne, victor's brandy, victor's matjes, victor's hummersuppe, victor's rinderrouladen, victor's roast swan and ginger sauce but not victor's leberwurst because that had grown green fur.

Our troth was a symbol of reconciliation of our two nations, said the army padre. He did not understand that I was not German. He was the first not to understand that I was ethnic Polish from Lithuania Western Vilnius Zone – again Soviet controlled, collaborators being sourced for reprocessing. I was not German. Most British people don't understand. Most have never heard of other places. If they've heard of them they don't know where they are. They don't care. Foreigners are foreign. Wogs begin at Calais. Some even begin the other side of the Severn. And taking the Aust ferry means going to fraternise with the enemy etc. etc. I like to think I have helped many British, especially superstitious Welsh, western fringe folk, escape this life in shackles for the broad horizons of a sunlit yonder place.

The dates didn't add up. I first knew you were inside me when we were on the SS *Forde* from Bremerhaven to Harwich. I thought it was sea sickness. I'd never seen the sea before, never been on a ship. Then I realised. I could tell. I had experience, hadn't I. I wished I hadn't. I wondered whether to throw myself into the German Ocean, chopped by a whirring propellor, claimed by the mighty deep, making food for seafoods, herrings and hakes etc. But I never counsel striving for Dreamopolis or Smotherland because of grudge, because of revenge.

The Sergeant had such a hatred for Germans in his bile, in his entrails that for his lovely young bride to be bearing a German war criminal's child was the other side of shame. I didn't want to give up my new life – my sentimental bouquet, my liberated ring, liberated necklace, liberated furs, liberated wedding gifts all captured on a liberated Leica including us beside the liberated Opel which we had driven to the reception.

I feared getting sent back. Why would he want me in the state I was in? I revealed nothing. I concealed my nausea. I vomited in private. This was my only chance of future happiness. He was my ticket. He was the key to future happiness – how I deserved it! You were an inconvenience. A barrier to future happiness. He could lock the door to future happiness if he wanted.

Not to mention throwing away the key. I was almost there. Only hours till we arrived in the land of freedom. The ship was a pirate ship. It was filled with stolen souvenirs. All the cars on board were war spoils. The Sergeant had requisitioned a Borgward staff car. 'She's laden,' he said many times, 'she's laden.' She was 'n' all. (My very words. My English was coming along nicely.)

So laden that soon after we left Harwich we had to stop to move the load around the car to prevent the back bumper scraping and grating like bad torture noises. My first experience of my new island home was of daybreak on a strange land – or was it strange water or strange both at the same time? It was mystifying. Land and water at the same level. Liquid land, solid water. It was playing tricks with my eyes. I was feeling bad. I didn't want to be lifting furniture. We were being watched by strange mournful rust colour animals which couldn't do the mobility. Their legs had been amputated, perhaps for the war effort. No wonder they looked so sad. So they had to push themselves across the mud on their stomachs. Bad for digestion. No wonder they looked so sad. They got the short straw all right.

Gifts. To the Customs officers at Harwich. To Scuffer Warren of the motor pool at Woolwich Garrison. To Nifty Kenny with the lock-ups on Shoot Up Hill. To Brigadier Hugh Gammeltoft whose life Sergeant Dogg had saved in 1917, carrying him on his back for two miles just about. The Brigadier had 'looked after' The Sergeant ever since.

First home. We began married life in a flat above the sergeants' mess at Woolwich. It would be our home for the six months till The Sergeant was discharged. He had few duties. For peace of mind The Young Bride wandered about the windy common, screaming.

Dressed in furs I looked rich. People were scared of me. I felt mad. You were present in me. I found the garrison hospital without difficulty. It might have been a prison. The corridors were glossy cream and green. There were out of focus people beyond frosted glass. Whoever I asked to direct me to a doctor stared at me blankly like I was asking for something you don't expect to find in a hospital, amputee animals for instance. I walked for hours in those corridors crying. I saw a human foetus in a kidney bowl on a trolley: it was covered in black blood like deep-bed offal. I might have been invisible. No one saw me. There was damp sacking round leaking pipes. Sometimes there were sprays of steam from them. Everywhere reeked of bleach. Everywhere reeked of coal.

I took candles from a chapel. The nuns in the convent near my lost village of my childhood used candles to self-abort sooner than give birth and face the punishment of the Cardinal who was usually the father. They hurt. No result.

One day when I got back with my shopping (turnips, curry powder, tripe) The Sergeant was drinking beer, reading *Reveille*.

He didn't look up. He said: 'I been in touch with an adoption society. It's all arranged. Fixed.'

I froze. He stood right up beside me. Then he tweaked my ear lobe sharply, pinched. It hurt. He meant it to hurt.

'Don't go trying to keep things from me, Gel – it's not worth it . . . you'll get found out . . . I got eyes and ears and extra senses. And you'll be glad you will – we don't want to go backstreet do we. That can be very messy so I hear. Very messy.'

He put down his magazine. 'Now why don't you give me a nice friendly hundred to eight. Least said soonest mended – and in the circumstances you can't say nothing. Ha! Eh?'

You were born. You were taken away. I kept my eyes shut so I couldn't see you. The midwife was talkative: they always are. I knew you were a boy. I called you Heini. It was written in the waters that you became Henry. I hoped you'd never order anyone to dig their own grave with their hands.

It's not much to ask.

★

We settled down nicely enough on the fruitholding in the green Vale with The Sergeant's mother Me Old Mum who was immortal. She alarmed me the first time I met her. She opened the door to The Sergeant, gave him a kiss, looked me up and down and told me: 'I'm waiting to die . . . You're a pretty one. He's done all right for himself. You done all right for yourself I say.'

No day went by without her saying she was expecting to die. She wanted to die but she was immortal. She was a spritely old soul but the pain she had to bear wore her down. Arthritis crippled her joints and there were days when she had to be fed because she couldn't pick up a cup or fork. On the Life/Quality graph she was down in the deep negatives. But she didn't complain. She was thankful for the help we gave. Gracious in her helplessness. We did all we could for her. When the twins were born she was a granny in a million even though she dropped Puppy on his head because her arms couldn't clasp. The doctor whispered that her cuddles should be supervised. But they gave her such joy it would have been cruel to deprive her. They fought for my milk. Spotty was stronger. He'd usually have won if I hadn't intervened. Me Old Mum was a golden granny. She looked after them the way she looked after me. I was a hurt person. A damage site. I made a life out of what I'd been through. Finding a purpose there was no definition for. I created it myself.

When we went down The Pike and Duckling near the weir I pushed the twins in the pram – they were local stars! The Sergeant would push Me Old Mum in her smooth-running chair she called The Throne. She loved it. It wasn't even half a mile from Orchard End to The Pike and Duckling but it'd take an age to get there because Me Old Mum wanted to chatter with everyone en route whether she knew them or not showing off the twins while The Sergeant was always sizing up what our neighbours (and rivals) were growing. He scrutinised the boxes of fruit and veg outside the shacks all along the road. He had an entrepreneurial eye. He darted round behind them like the nosey barber he was. He was getting interested in spicy pickles, chutneys and what the trade called 'queer gear'. Produce like courgette, fennel, lettuces with fancy names, breeds of cabbage. They fetched top sterling. Me Old Mum thought they were a lot of nonsense.

'Once upon a time they said that about asparagus,' The Sergeant replied. Wise words indeed. The pub was on one side of the dusty road, the river was on the other. There was no fence or barrier.

She gave it very deepest deep thought. She always looked to where the road disappeared from view climbing away from the river. She looked at it with a sort of longing.

Then she said as she always said: 'It's an illegal act . . . Over that hill there . . . not far beyond . . . that's where Charlie The Witch was murdered . . . *they say murdered* . . . decapitated with his scythe, carved up with his own billhook . . . that's a way to go . . . but murder . . . no no . . . willing sacrifice . . . cooperative suicide. If they want to cut a cross into my flesh when I'm gone I'd tell them yes . . . that's their business but it doesn't do to go releasing psychic powers you don't understand. They'd hurtle out my body like a whirlwind.'

She said: 'I could just roll down that bank there – then I'd be gone. Of course if I rolled down that bank I wouldn't be gone – know why . . . a bunch of beer garden heroes . . . they'd run across the road and jump in to rescue me because they wanted their photos in *The Vale Advertiser* . . . That's the risk . . . It's the public . . . they wanting you to share their optimistic morality.'

Death's presence was everyday rabbit. I was the daughter she never had. We talked about girl things like thwarted suicides. Her suspicion of beer garden heroes came from the old days when she was walking down from the old times gateway in the abbey gardens.

An expensively suited man with a raven's blueblack hair was standing on the river bank. Not the sort that you saw round here every day of the week. He was talking to himself. That was more common round here. Jabbering folk are two a penny. His voice was getting louder and louder. He was agitated like there was electricity going through him. The shakes, the jumping judders. Then he leapt into the deep water. He didn't resurface. Three youths who had been larking about spoke urgently to each other. Hardly divested they dived in after him, denying him the right to drown. They ought to have desisted. They ought to have gone on larking rather than show off their life-saving drill. Me Old Mum ran down the slope waving, telling the youths to leave him be, leave him be, let him get on with it. The small crowd that had gathered turned into a mob with one mind, one voice. It screamed at her, told her she was a killer, told her she wasn't fit to walk the same earth as the valiant boys whom the suicide was fighting off by ducking himself and choking himself on the petrol veiled waters of the historic river. The valiant boys might perish. They were joined by more valiant boys who had been in a pedalo race. Eventually he relented.

So he lived to die another day. Is that right? Did he?

He stumbled away, soaked to the skin, hissed by the mob. He nodded his thanks to Me Old Mum for her efforts, shook her hand: 'I'm Chris Lapatu . . . how do you do . . . I'm grateful . . . it's painful knowing there's no end . . . no escape . . . knowing that I'm here forever . . . I can't *hate* them for their good intentions . . . they're doing god's will . . . but you know their god may not be my god . . . their god is different from mine . . . they think he exists whether they know it or not . . . they are his creatures whether they know it or not . . . it's tribal . . . the god of wrath and punishment . . . the sacred infects the temporal . . . god owns Caesar's things . . . Jesus was lying . . . Jesus! . . . I swear I never met a more vindictive bastard . . . ever in my life. Be seeing you.'

'Go and get yourself dry . . .'

'I know . . . Else I'll catch a death of cold . . . If only . . . if only I could . . .'

He smiled the saddest smile Me Old Mum had seen. There was so much grief, so much helplessness, so much futility written in his strange ageless features. He hurried away along the path beside the river. How old was he? Me Old Mum wondered. He didn't look quite human. Like someone posing as a human.

It echoed: 'It's painful knowing there's no end . . . no escape . . . knowing that I'm here forever.'

Do not try to talk down the woman on the parapet. She has a right to do with her life as she pleases. Just walk by. Don't get involved. MYOB (that's one I use a lot). It's her choice to write the Full Stop. There'll always be a pride of opportunists coming to the rescue. Obstruct them. They are not 'helpers'. They are the opposite. They hinder. They seek congratulation for edging along the crumbly stone showing all who can see that their life is imperilled too. What big hearts they boast of. What sick intentions they reveal. Their officious piety denies their fellow humans free will. Should you see someone attempting to gain access to Mordberg walk on, do not waste the emergency services' time, ignore the situation. A blind eye does not spy the wasp in the pear.

Here's a web of sadness and misunderstandings that touched me. Good intentions again. Yet again. When will they learn? Me Old Mum knew all about it. It happened nearby in the vale:

Saul Tarr had had enough. He questioned the purpose of purpose. He loathed the wallpaper but couldn't change it because it was what his late wife Una (née Torpy) had chosen just before she got ill. He was trapped, surrounded by this design over and over again, this design of a lurid thatched cottage, a fluorescent country garden, a pair of gaudy birds, a bubbling stream that went uphill and the pack-horse bridge over it, every stone picked out. There was no escape. Every Saturday morning, carrying his washing kit in an old canvas bag, he bought a return ticket, took a bus (upstairs, front seat, left side) to the cemetery. He put flowers on Una's grave, polished the black headstone and cleaned the green glass chippings, all the while lying to her about how much he liked the wallpaper and how work challenges were going really well. He had been let go (with, of course, great regret) over a year ago.

After he said 'Till next week then my love' he would sit on a memorial bench beyond the chapel eating a carrot or an apple. One day in autumn as the drifts of leaves picked up speed between the angels and crosses he took from his canvas bag a litre of superior NAAFI brand gin and a bottle of one hundred Secobarbital capsules. He numbed his mouth with gin. The barbs were astonishingly easy to swallow because he had the will. He waited for the great shift to the country beyond where there are no fluorescent gardens to attack the eyes, just a gently welcoming softness and a ubiquitous unprecedented presence that resists vision, scent, touch. He coasted towards dissolution of earthly sensibilities. The heaviness of hyper-relaxed limbs was lifted. He soared without moving. The wind that hit his face was effervescent. His muscles decontracted, freed from material duty. He didn't know if he could say his name. His tongue was not responding and he didn't know he didn't care.

Then: 'Oh dear oh dear what are you doin'?'

A blurred figure, angular and bony, different, in quality and kind, from the cossetting immaterial balm of just a second or an hour before, grabbed him by the shoulders, shook him, shook him.

'It was going so well, just let me go . . .' murmured Saul Tarr. Could this beanpole porlock make out the words? It didn't matter. He had his duty to do. He'd spotted the empty pill bottle, the empty gin bottle.

Welcome to Ludovic Scales, on the way back from his monthly ancestor worship. He too was a Life Saver. A stringy gawky busy-body. A coarse interrupter. A cultist. He had to keep the man awake. He was all duty. He was invested with the strength of the valiant. He carried and hauled and dragged the dying Saul to the chapel where mourners were congregating for the 11.45. Two young women burst into tears. An ambulance was called. A sour-faced priest whispered to the funeral director. A man in a muffler shouted at Ludovic Scales and at Saul, now supine and asleep on a greasy car rug on the chapel steps: 'What gives you two the right to ruin our big day?'

'He's losing consciousness. He's going into a coma.'

'Coma! You selfish bastard. You fuck off out of here with your comas so we can give my blessed nan her sacred due.'

The ambulance driver held his hand on the horn to get the hearse to move. The 11.15 had overrun. 'Too much speechifying.'

Tyres failing to get a grip smeared damp lawns with brown mud.

'You his carer?' asked one of the ambulance crew.

'Never saw him before in my life . . . I was sent.'

'Sent? We're going to have to report this to the constabulary. They'll need a witness statement.'

'He's got a lot to thank you for,' said the officer who came to Ludovic Scales's airless little flat to take the statement. 'Now . . . You say you were sent . . .'

'I was.'

'Right you are, Sir. Who would that be then . . . Sending you . . . Who sent you?'

'Some might call it god, some might call it Destiny . . . It was the Lord's wish that I should save him.'

'I see. You didn't know him previously.'

'No.'

'So you happened to be there like a good Samaritan.'

'Fated to be there . . . That'd be one way of putting it.'

'What I'm wondering . . . what we have to ask in these cases . . . is . . . was there a degree of complicity . . . it's sensitive . . . but are we looking at a pact that went wrong?'

'Pact?'

'Pact. What they sometimes call seeing him through. Helping hand.'

'Certainly not.'

'You're sure of that.'

They sat in heavy silence. Ludovic Scales's long limbs took up most of the room.

'I wouldn't have thought he'll get more than a verbal, mind. Punishment enough having gastric lavage. So not to worry.'

'I'm in two minds about that,' replied Ludovic Scales. 'It's against nature, it's against holy writ . . . I'm in training for the episcopate. I'm a bishop in the making. Limbering up.'

'In my experience it's better to ignore them . . . let them get on with it. Don't burden yourself being your brother's keeper.'

'Let me give you these.' Ludovic Scales handed him a thick wodge of bumf.

He wrote 'Fruitcake wants mitre' on the dossier. He'd tell the sergeant it was a crossword clue.

Versions vary here. Was it a few days or a few weeks or maybe several months later that Saul Tarr was disturbed by a knock on his front door as he was sawing. He didn't recognise the tall awkward man who stood there, smiling abundantly, holding a manila envelope.

'How are we getting on? Back on the path? Are we?'

Saul stared open mouthed. 'Sorry . . . I'm . . . who are you from? Are you the special needs – I called in to cancel . . .'

The man noticed the jaggedtooth-saw which Saul was gripping. He attempted joviality: 'Nothing to be scared of . . . you don't need small arms where I'm concerned.'

He stuck out a hand. 'Ludovic Scales.'

It didn't rise to the surface immediately. He looked questioningly

Saul hid beneath a table, sometimes sleeping there. The virtually unread religious pamphlets, manifestos and boastful inventories of charitable missions in unknown South American countries piled up. When they were no longer delivered (on the doorstep, seldom through the letter box) Saul found himself mildly affronted, vaguely neglected. When deliveries recommenced he was relieved.

At dawn he began his tramp from one market garden to another picking vegetables, gathering fruit, getting sacked for flagging and not meeting quotas. It was work he was physically unfit for, which he had despised when he had a desk job. He'd try anything. His back gave him gip. Ludovic Scales would trail him, intercept him when he least expected it. Seldom speaking, they played hide and seek in cabbage fields, behind the brick bothies where pickers would shelter and sing songs of the old country, in the caravan parks where seasonals subsisted in metal carapaces, in the gypsy encampments on the old droves, in the orchards where hedgehogs were turned on spits over dead wood fires, on the cinder paths beside the railway through the vale, on the destitution roads and the coffin roads.

This was Ludovic Scales's territory. He moved through it like an animated scarecrow. When he was out he had worked here on and off since he was a lad. Markers told him where he was. The configuration of a water butt and a skein of barbed wire was to his eye unique, nothing like the configuration of those two objects several miles distant and within earshot of the glossy roaring weir. He sought his faithless, graceless quarry, teasing him by popping out from behind a midden with a big twinkling grin: 'I can tell you're coming round to the true way.'

One dusk Saul trudged hopelessly to the road past a meagrely lit brick box of a house. He was clutching two apples given him out of pity. Ludovic Scales called his name. He looked around. He saw no one.

Ludovic Scales spoke as to a baby: 'Guess who's closer to heaven!'

Saul shook his head at Ludovic Scales's game seeing the ladder propped against a barren old pear tree. On its top rung were Ludovic Scales's boots, the rest of Ludovic Scales was cross-hatched with boughs, an unseen figure from a tree tale with a bad end. Saul acted in Ludovic Scales's larky spirit. He pulled the ladder in jest, just a joke, admittedly giving it more of a heave than he had intended, quite an almighty heave. To his astonishment Ludovic Scales hurtled down waving his limbs in crazy semaphore. His head sought the edge of a rusted harrow. Helpless, Saul's eyes filled with tears. The harrow had pierced the skull of the only human with whom he had any contact. It was not Ludovic Scales who was meant to rendezvous with nothingness.

On his knees Saul ricked in spasms. He succumbed to prayer. The Angelus rang from the backplaces of memory. Ave Maria, gratia plena, Dominus tecum. Benedicta tu in mulieribus, et benedictus fructus ventris tui, Iesus. He lived. He hauled Ludovic Scales to the brick box. There were no phones back then. A drunk man with no love for fellow humans got his tractor going. They took the body into town. A medical orderly remarked on the carelessness of workers in the fields. Leaving their tools like that. He had a feeling he'd seen Saul before. Probably at the culmination of another life.

Saul, the sole mourner, watched as one half (which?) of this pantomime horse of a friendship was laid to rest beside his ancestors. Who would visit them now?

Out of dutiful curiosity he looked at the pamphlets his only friend had left over several months. He read the chummy incitements and suave encouragements. He wondered if the Radiant Redeemer emerging from what might be a bowl of fruit was painted by the same hand as the wallpaper. On several manifestos there was a blank box with a legend smearily rubber stamped in it: The Church of Damnation Postponed, 70 Miserwitch Street, Bengeworth, Worcs. He went to a dentist who couldn't help but laugh when he said he wanted a sunshine smile and asked if he had been reading *National Geographic*. The scrape was uncomfortable but not wholly unsuccessful. He felt ready.

Walking home from a field of swaying asparagus he diverted to Miserwitch Street. Number 70 was a recently built three-storey block of flats, brick and concrete. It didn't look like a church. Saint Edmund's at the end of the road did – spire, gothic windows, yew tree, graves. Number 70 lacked all those. There were six bells. Two had a name attached. Not knowing which bell to press he walked down an alley between the block and the end of a terrace. In a grubby puddled yard in front of a row of lock-ups a squat man in overalls was hosing down a psychotic Marcher Hound. The dog eyed Saul, licking its lips waiting for the command to go for the throat. The man straightened up.

'Good evening . . . I'm looking for the church.'

'Church? The church is down the road. Can't miss it . . . it . . . it looks like a church.'

'70 Miserwitch Street. The Church of Damnation Postponed.'

'The what?'

'That's the address I've got.'

'I think you've been misled.' He gurned we got a right one here. 'Tell you what . . . if I find a church lurking I'll let you know.' The dog smiled.

Saul pulled a pamphlet from his canvas bag, proffered it with a stretch that kept him distant, by his approximate estimate, from the dog. The man took spectacles from his overalls, read the indicated part of the brochure, removed his spectacles.

'Aaah . . . right you are then mate, this'll be Vic. God bless him . . . dear Vic . . . But we're better off without him . . . Not a well man . . . sick in the head . . . They should have kept him in Powick. Mistake to release him I'd say . . . He used to buttonhole people and tell them he was a bishop . . . But he wasn't . . . he hadn't qualified . . . he hadn't finished his course . . . ten easy steps to being a bishop . . . it was a life-ark in Indiana I think it was that was teaching him . . . Illinois maybe it was . . . I can't recall.

'He'd have been better off over there . . . Evangelising. Preaching the way of the Lord. The Church of Damnation Postponed . . . The Yanks they go for that in a big way . . .

'His passing . . . it's been a relief to one and all – especially Marge. Salt of the earth she is – did everything she could for him . . . got treated like a doormat . . . she was so rapturous – that was one of his words – she was so rapturous she didn't go to the funeral . . . we had a celebration brasier barbecue instead . . . the whole street came . . . he had all this stuff squirrelled away in the freezer at Bonsey's abattoir – hares, rabbits, bits of pony, couple of otters, a badger, a deer, a fox or two . . . we drank a toast . . . all gratitude to whatever it was that made him fall out that tree.

'Could have been the bustards they're raising on the hill . . . Or ravens . . . going for his eyes the way they do with lambs . . . Rotten branch?

'It's what you want . . . it's the proper way to go: short and sharp, no pain, full on death in a split second, never knowing what happened because you ain't got the whatsit . . . the ability to know. Knowing is for when you're alive. Right. If you ask me death is the point of life's little joke.

'But who am I to say . . . I'm not a religious man . . . I prefer my dog, don't I, Hermann pet – ooose a little princey wincey then, ooose a little princey wincey! His mum and dad worked at Treblinka. Didn't they, pet . . . That's what I call pedigree.'

There are many versions of this tale. Date, time, place, names: all fluid. Me Old Mum told it to me, told it a different way every time she told it. When I was told about that dog I made a big mental note never to go near Miserwitch Street, not that you'd want to anyway I hear. Even Ludovic Scales's ghost doesn't go there. He's voted no to it in death. There's a wraith they say has been seen before dusk on the causeway across the bleak fields. A gangly thin silhouette carrying a rifle or a stick: you can't get close enough to tell. It revisits the fatal tree. It steals through the miles of greenhouses, glass cities crimson with sunset: crimson is the only colour in this otherwise subfusc tale. It shuffles between teetering towers of pallets. It creeps past middens of snugly mulching dung, rotting veg, uprooted stumps. It dissolves where corrugated iron hovels are supported by old tyres, tied with baling twine.

Saul Tarr made a second attempt to deliver himself to the kingdom. It would be a final attempt. If he failed he would punish himself by living. He shunned a home-based gala because of the presence of Una's replacenta: she had returned from the hospital to die at home so that it would be in Saul's presence. His new approach also did without gin and barbiturates. Even were he to administer himself the deadly combination at night, in a remote wood, in an electric storm, the chances were, given his luck, he would be found. (A poacher. A hardy courting couple.) Besides he might need the six pounds fourteen shillings and eight pence should he be punished and remain in Caesar's world.

His plan was simple. He walked into the lofty saloon bar of The Hop Market Hotel. Polished marble, bevelled glass. He had never dared enter it before. He tried to play the old habitué.

The Sergeant and his Cousin Enzo Smart, his soon-to-be partner in the pickle business, were in convivial mood chatting with the barman. The Sergeant acknowledged Saul with a head-jerk of fellowship while not knowing quite who he was. He ordered an Apollinaris water. The Sergeant hawked a mustard-coloured oyster onto the lavishly tiled floor. He remarked to the barman: 'You know, I miss the spittoons, Jumbo.'

Jumbo replied: 'But you always did.'

The porkpink terracotta babies clutching the ceiling leered at Saul. The sculpted heads in cowls between the booths were stern. He could discern mocking faces in the stilton-veined marble panels. The tiled yeomen pushing out from the vast baroque fireplace swinging trugs of enamel hops were lusty lovers of life. He feared they all had his number.

He walked from the bar into the reception hall of the residential part of the hotel. A gentleman in a tailcoat almost bowed. His resolve was not undone. He had never ridden in an ascending room. He greeted the uniformed attendant, a shaver of perhaps sixteen years. 'To the cupola if you will.' He was astonished that the youth ceded. 'Sir'll be wanting to survey the view.'

'That's it . . . the peerless view.'

The shaver smiled.

How kind these people were. How unwittingly complicit. The room's trembling alarmed him.

'Nothing to worry about, Sir.'

He had chosen the second tallest building. Only the cathedral was taller. But messing with god's house was messing with god's honour. God craves respect. It would have been asking for it – whatever *it* was – when an equally topping spot presented itself.

Beneath the scrolly capitals and columns and open pediments of the oxidised cupola was a circular room with a writing desk, a telescope and a single chair. Its long windows gave onto a balustraded observation platform.

'What,' wondered Cousin Enzo, 'was that?'

He was looking over The Sergeant's shoulder. He looked at The Sergeant to see if he'd seen but he was facing the wrong way. There was a distinct gap between something he saw flash past the upper clear glass and lower opaque panes of a window and a dull muffled thud. There was another gap before the scream of a car's engine, an out-of-control roaring, grating metal on grinding metal whose heat was smelled before it was smelled, sound anticipated olfactory certainty. Then – screeching humans and shrieking animals, a deeper growl of further blows, for every instrument gets its turn.

Cousin Enzo tried to jump to see through the clear part of the nearest window which was not the one momentarily darkened by the plummeting object. He hadn't enough spring in his spatted boots. He and The Sergeant hurried into the street along with the rest of the bar's patrons. A dazed-looking Saul Tarr was attempting to stand on the soft top of the Alvis that he had squashed when he landed on it head-first. He kept on losing his balance. Every time he slipped a desperate breathy squeak came from beneath the canvas and bent metal – bars and hinges and wingnuts – of the top. The driver had been thrust forward onto the steering wheel. He had lost control. His passenger tore her coat manoeuvring awkwardly to reach him. Steam was rising from the car's radiator. It had collided with a stationary pick-up transporting two Old Spot pigs. The driver of the pick-up ran from a tobacconist's shop. A vegetarian schoolboy recognised that the vehicle belonged to Lugg's Farm. The driver of the Alvis called for help. He bled from his forehead. The breathy squeaking from somewhere between the soft top and the car's rear seat stopped. Saul sat on the pavement with his head in his hands. The passenger asked him what had happened, where had he fallen from.

Saul replied: 'God intervened. He intervened again. He doesn't want me to. I've got a life sentence. I've been sentenced to life.'

The passenger shook her head in incomprehension: 'Where's Bostin?' she asked. 'Where's Bostin?' She grappled with the obstinate canvas.

The vegetarian schoolboy shouted: 'They're from the devil's sty.' He believed (may even have invented) the rumours that Lugg's Farm bred pigs for an experimental NHS scheme to supply spare parts for humans – the Kidneys On Ice project. Saul sat on the pavement with his head in his hands. The bleeding trapped Alvis driver moaned. The passenger cradled dead Bostin (a vicious Marcher Hound who had it coming to him). She rocked back and forth beside his wicker basket on the back seat. A policeman, Wally The Off Spinner, entered the scene. Witnesses agreed that there had been something falling from the hotel. It might have been that dog, helped one. You'll find it's definitely a discovered adultery on the third floor with a lady throwing her husband's clothes out the window because she caught him with a popsy. The hotel has that ill-reputation. Nonsense! It was that chappie on the pavement. The back of the pick-up was rudimentarily secured. Its driver was remonstrating with the other driver who was now crying for a sedative. The passenger was keening for Bostin. The policeman was out of his depth. Traffic was backing up in both directions. The vegetarian schoolboy slipped the catch and lever. The pigs gracefully raised themselves, went in search of liberty and scran, trotted down Temegate with a demob-happy swagger. They bit a toddler who offered them candyfloss. The policeman said: 'Hold on a mo . . . what they up to?' They barged a mirror in a jeweller's door-way. The policeman ran into the street and into a cyclist taking advantage of stalled vehicles. The cyclist went over his handlebars, all his books were flung from his basket. He shook himself down, turned indignantly to accuse the man who had stepped in front of him but found himself staring at a flattened dog who was as threatening in death as he had been in life. Saul sat on the pavement with his head in his hands. The jeweller's mirror slid like an icefall into a thousand dagger shards. An ambulance team was trying to clumsy the driver from the Alvis. The pigs found a pork butcher Ray & Nephew of Heaven's Pasture Farm. Not being fussy they helped themselves in a cannibalistic gaudy but drew a line at cold crust pastry. There was no one qualified to administer morphia to the impaled driver. It had to be aspirins.

'Well?' said Wally The Inspector.

'Bad day in Gadara I'd call it, Chief,' said Wally The Off Spinner.

'You what?'

'The good book, Wally,' said The Sergeant.

'Ah . . . not my area of expertise . . . But then hunting down pigs and sorting out this right biriani isn't neither.'

'Criminal masterminds is more up your street eh, Wal,' said Cousin Enzo.

'You are so right . . . When the cavalry's arrived it'll be time for a teabreak I'd say. Meanwhile let's get this shower sorted out.'

Saul was charged with criminal damage and taken into custody. There was insufficient proof to charge him with attempted suicide, still a crime in those dark days. The lift operator was witness to his polite cheerfulness.

The Sergeant's opinion was that if our Icarus Wings operatives had been helping him, creating a strategy, judging the timing, he could have got a clear dive at the street when there was a gap in the late afternoon traffic. Just watch the traffic lights. It makes sense. Furthermore Saturday was a busy shopping day: the missus takes home the shopping and the nippers while the lads go to the pubs at six. No suicide in their right mind would choose late Saturday afternoon. The chances of collateralising a pedestrian were higher than on a Monday (slow trade) or Wednesday (half day closing). The Alvis was hardly moving when he assaulted it headfirst, killed Bostin, hospitalised the driver Nicholas Gregory who limped thereafter and provoked Rosamund Gregory to suffer a lifetime's nightmares. The bitten toddler was given a rabies injection. The cyclist suffered blackouts and numbness in his gear-changing hand.

The pigs swam the river. They answered the call of the wild in high hills and deep forests. They interbred with feral boars and with stub-legged swine alleged to be the heirs of hybrids raised many years ago on the experimental farm at Malpasfang Lodge. They gorged on acorns and beechnuts. They depleted hopyards. They marauded in orchards. They were hunted down. Most escaped. A few that didn't threw themselves when cornered from a cliff at Gullet quarry, showing Saul how it should be done. They were an example to us all. They have so much more deathgriff than atheists burdened with Christian ethics which they are incapable of shedding. The teachings of Christianity are in deliberate and direct conflict with human reality and human experience. Free thinkers aren't free.

Several Years Later

The vegetarian schoolboy – known to fellow animal rightists by the nom de guerre Jerome – would, at the age of twenty-one, die a martyr to the wilding cause when attacked by a lion whom he was trying to release from the heavy petting zoo Farmyard of the Senses at Faineant Park. The lion didn't want a liberator, let alone a liberator so piously well intentioned as this one who in his death throes absolved the lion of all blame saying he shared his frustration and anger. The lion wanted fun. He was a goodtime lion. After he had torn out Jerome's heart and lungs he continued to sloth about his cage as he had before he was interrupted. He looked forward to his next gargantuan meal.

A spokesvegan said: 'We are all proud of our loss.'

I spoke ex cathedra as Dream Topping™'s Founding Harbinger and Lifeskipper. I was sceptical: 'There was little to be proud of. It was an accidental elimination . . . The sort of incident lay-people might consider "suicide" but which is not, underline not, real suicide, true suicide without the quotes, proper suicide. "Suicide" is reckless, irresponsible, unthinking. Above all it is silly.'

There were so many botchjobs which came to our notice. We felt so sad for the ones who had undeservedly been failures not through lack of nerve but because they hadn't the right team alongside them – or any team come to that! It was our duty to assist. A vocation is not a matter of choice. It seizes you. There was a need which only we could answer. We were spurred into action in a very strange strange way. It was lunchtime. A Monday lunchtime. I knew that because it was shepherd's pie though no shepherd ever made a pie as creamy and all round lovely as I did – the secret was to put potato purée *beneath* the meat as well as all around it, that's the way to stop it drying. Don't mince the meat too fine. Braise it in beer. Make the onions nice and soft in beef dripping whatever meat you're using. There was a knock at the front door. The Sergeant was scoffing. The twins were inquisitive. They didn't wait to be told they could get down. Off they went.

When they came back they said in unison: 'There's a man who wants to know if we want to buy a helicopter.'

'Get on,' said The Sergeant. 'You haven't even made that Airfix one.'

'Snot Airfix, it's Revel.'

'You tell him to come back when you've finished making it. Then we'll see.'

They scampered away. Then: 'It's a real helicopter. It's a real one. Please . . . please. Condition as new he says.'

'Does he now,' said The Sergeant, 'did he mention the one careful lady pilot?'

'No.'

I was on my way.

We had such a lovely old farmhouse. Rickety mind, in need of repair. Dry rot here, wet rot there. It had been in Me Old Mum's family since Boney stalked the earth. It came down to her because all her brothers and sisters died young. She believed that they clubbed together to give her all the years they didn't live. We had a nice garden laid to mud mostly. Nice flowerbeds. Nice poplar avenue, to remind me of my village that wasn't any more. Muddy in winter. Outbuildings. There wasn't another house for miles. Everything we could see was ours. We owned till the horizons. All around were vegetable fields and fruit orchards. It was comfy and we loved it. But it wasn't the house of the helicopter-owning class.

Try telling that to Sam as he was called. Frankly Sam I came to call him. What a smile! What conviction!

'You need one. You are frankly just the kind of family which needs one. A Sikorsky H-18. Not just a means of transport – more like being put on a surgical drip of self-worth. Fun. The boys'll love it. Practical. Frankly so long as you watch out for pylons and the like it's a doddle . . . a pedalo in the sky . . . I've got a V-bomber if you fancy one but they're no use to man or beast frankly. A Sikorsky H-18 on the other hand . . . Now you're talking grace and elegance. And you got an ideal landing site. Impress your friends . . . But be quick, I got clients queuing for test rides . . . It is frankly the offer of a lifetime . . . I can see you're dubious . . . You are right . . . I would be too frankly . . . put my hand on my heart: I'd think what is this chappie up to . . . what's his trick then . . . I tell you . . . his trick is there's no trick . . . which in this day and age must be unique . . .'

And so he went on for a good half hour.

Several Years Later

The Sergeant, Me Old Mum and me. That was us, 'the irrepressible visionary trio' that established The Dream Topping™ Foundation. Frankly Sam was our first employee. He had gone house to house with his helicopter so why not our programme's Guided Counselling For Change, Conclusive Lustratio: A User's Guide and Absolute Purification. He was resourceful. He'd get lists of cancer patients from hospitals, of the terminally ill in hospices, of the poor folk suffering in care homes, of the poor folk soiling themselves in the family home making everything smelly and disgusting for their beloveds. He sold our service with a generous smile that opened many a door. A few crafty quid will buy a vintage Amstrad full of confidential medical dossiers from an ill-paid middle manager at the NHS. When personal computers came in they brought a free market for all the info you'd ever need in a pocket or handbag. Think of us like blind dogs for the blind he'd tell them. We are guides. But we do not lead. We do not propose which road to take. We guide our needy clients where they themselves have decided they want to go, if they are in a condition to decide of course. If they change their mind at the last they are entitled to a refund of 15 per cent of their fee not negotiable.

It was no cakewalk. Natural Law is outside 'the law'. 'The law' is unnatural. It is stupid, harsh. No empathy. No sympathy. Based on the terrorist god who has an opinion about everything. Why can't he sit on the fence for once . . . We worked hard to devise top fondness strategies and best-loved programmes, among them: The Helping Hand, Smotherland, Cushioned Ending, Lungbuster, Happiest Finish, Mastering Oblivion, Fear Not My Angel Delight, Fall On Your Sword, Instant Sunshine, A Song In A Heart That Beats No Longer, Twilight Turns To Night, Easy As You Go There Now, The Roman Road, Hume's Way. We advertised discreetly. But word of mouth was the most powerful messenger.

Me Old Mum was our Philosopher till she ran out of philosophy, suffering philosopher's block. Professor Darren Clent became our philosophy counsellor. The Sergeant had read excerpts from Darren's books *Buried Under an Allotment* and *The Vegetarian Charnel House*. He thought Darren would be the right fit for Team Dream Topping™ when he was released.

We contacted him when our ideas were beginning to bloom.

Our first mission was modest. It was an unusual one. We had been recommended to the septuagenarian (looked nonagenarian) Big Brian Bunstone, a recovering alcoholic who would never recover. He was on the road to recovery but that's where he would stay, on the road, shuffling along, never reaching recovery altar itself. It was as obstinately far away as it had ever been. The further along that endless road he trekked the more he needed alcohol to sustain him. His meagre pension was not enough to pay for his habit, to feed himself and Raymond, his constantly hungry Marcher Hound. He had remortgaged his little bungalow and signed a pledge to himself never to drink anything other than bottom of the range own-brand spirits at knockdown prices. Team Dream Topping™'s advice to Brian was to pursue a physical rather than a chemical solution. We supplied stout nylon rope and a stepladder whose review in *Choice*™ concluded promisingly: 'Better suited to the circus ring than the home, this slapstick product should be immediately recalled before it causes further domestic tragedies.'

'Just the ticket,' said The Sergeant. He delivered the kit to Brian, knotted the rope, powerdrilled a stout hook into the ceiling, received the fee (cash terms only), wished him good luck and came home. That was on a Saturday afternoon. The last thing Brian wanted to do before he moved on to The Special Place was check the football results against his pools entry to prove to himself that god did not favour him. He was right. God didn't. He was confirmed as a loser: there was no reprieve. The stepladder collapsed as it was meant to, the ceiling just held, the two-metre drop was sufficient, Raymond ate his master. Undisturbed, the dog zealously stripped every shred of flesh off the vast carcass and devoured all the organs before howling for counselling several days later.

Taking care that there's no future is often excused by coroners. 'While the balance of mind is disturbed' is the formula. It is well meant. It is even more well meant for the coroner to bring in a verdict of misadventure – which is kind to the family especially if insurance policies will be invalidated. But it's dishonest. And not only dishonest, it refuses to acknowledge the key assistance provided by Dream Topping™.

These following histories demonstrate the value of Dream Topping™ to those on Desperation Boulevard.

Landry Nordtveit

I've asked myself over and over why, why, why did it happen? Why choose me? Why him? Why it? It.

It wasn't as if there was that airport novel magnetic moment of irresistibility which I've never experienced. I'm not sure if it really exists. People kid themselves. It's expected of them. Love! Coup de foudre! A couple of nights together and then it's off to SCP to choose homeware. Cosy.

Get real, people! We're animals. Sometimes we're on heat and up for it, more often not.

His facial skin was tight as a stocking mask. It looked as if it might have been retouched. It had certainly been blasted by the elements. Maybe I put it down to the lighting in Den Danske Frugthave. Tenebrous: that's the poet word. We talked very easily, unforcedly. I failed to place his accent, hindered by his actorish sandpaper voice. Gravelly: that's the word. Like he was playing a role in a foreign tongue.

He was interested in my doctoral thesis which I was turning into a certain-to-be-a-bestseller! *Herring and Schnapps: The Lived Actualities of Scandinavian Fairy Tales and Hanseatic Marine Folkmyths*. It's not exactly a popular topic but he was clued up in a pub-quiz way. He knew Hamburg and Lübeck, Tallinn and Tartu.

'Café Paris in Bremen . . . long-term favourite. Wow. Those Jugendstil toilets!'

'I thought it burnt down . . . wasn't that the Café Paris . . . the hairdresser next door set fire to one of her customers . . . must have been . . . well, it was some years ago.'

'Really? Seems only yesterday I was eating a P'tit Clamart . . . delicious confection – chocolate and candied blood orange . . .'

'How come you know these places?' I asked.

'I travel . . . I have an interest in the Exhumations Project . . . it's my vocation . . .' he growled as though there could be no other reply, 'from long way back . . . the wind in the poop . . . yah?'

That'll be the cause of the facial texture.

'You know the Exhumations Project?'

'Sure . . .' I said, '. . . but I don't know how they happen.'

'Of course not . . . no.'

We agreed jocularly that a Danish bar was a strange choice for me given that country's belligerence towards the Hansa. When he said he was going I found myself asking him: 'Shall I come with you?' I thought to myself: Landry, did you hear what you just said? (That's what I always asked myself.) He seemed surprised.

I've replayed this. It doesn't add up. We took a cab. We kissed. It was more about erotic efficiency than passion.

Maida Vale is all canyons between red-brick cliffs relieved here and there by grey quoins and yellow terracotta. He paid the driver. We walked up the broad steps to the front door. We walked up the broad steps . . . I can't get those steps out of my mind.

At their bottom the pavement was spray painted with electricians' codes. The top was patterned with a stylised flower. He pressed the key code. Try again. He tried again. 'Can't keep numbers in my head. So many to remember.' He composed a third combination without success. He pulled a thin green notebook from a jacket pocket. He turned its pages squinting. 'Got it.' He took my hand and we sprung up the two flights of stairs. Another pause while he found the keys to the apartment. He must have tried six or seven on three key rings – which ought to have made me suspicious. It didn't. He fumbled for the light switch, bumping into things, knocking over things in the dark and cursing under his breath. The same happened in the bedroom. We tripped, falling onto the unlit bed together. That was a comical icebreaker.

It was memorable. Undeniably memorable. He was tender and clean smelling: Bois du Portugal I'm pretty sure. He knew how to touch a woman. He seemed to weigh nothing. So light. Like he wasn't there. He went from gentle to probingly potent.

But . . . it felt like it was sex by numbers – learnt, studied: *Aspire!*

Love to Love Loving or *Release Your Inner Eros*. It was textbook stuff. It even crossed my mind that he might have been a virgin. I tried to encourage him, told him he fucked like a black man which is what every white male longs to hear. Well, every white male apart from this one who replied, hoarse: 'Let's lose the myth of the schwartzer's dick. It's just black power trouser division. Shall we have some bubbles?'

We lay on the bed drinking Taittinger's *Collabo Inconnu* and talking small talk about where his vocation would take him next till it was time for more. Each quaking snore was suffixed by a shrill wolf whistle. I fell into deep, sated sleep. I dreamed of a gnarled leathery pool cleaner with a skimmer chasing two aquatically acrobatic rodents, turning from time to time to harangue people watching from the precarious balconies of the unfinished high buildings around the pool. It became a vertigo dream. I woke.

Quiet as a rodent I went to the toilet. 'Ouch,' I cried when boiling water came out of the bathroom basin. The immersion heater burped and belched like aldermen at a function. I had not, unsurprisingly, realised how unlived-in the apartment was. The fridge contained only wine and mineral water. The living area was a dead area – no books, art, DVDs, magazines. It was an even less convincing token of a home than a property developer's show flat. I douched, showered, dressed. I don't like to use a stranger's toothbrush: he was a stranger. I thought that a smooth exit without embarrassment on either side was appropriate.

I took a swig from a bottle of Vichy Célestins then checked I had everything. The room was light now. How lovely it must be to be able to write an aubade for parting lovers who'll never meet again. I picked up my Longchamp bag, bent over him, kissed him with a fleeting kiss light as a butterfly landing on his lips.

His lips were cold. I started. An involuntary body wince. I must be kissing wrong! I raised my head to look. I wouldn't call them blue, blueish maybe, sort of blue grey – that's more like it. It was incredible. Different metabolism I told myself, that must be it. Or was this some sort of lark? Surely? His face was even more retouched than it had been before midnight. I wasn't sure if I trusted my reactions. I held where I believed the pulse to be. Unpractised I'd call myself.

Not an RSN. I passed on Civics And First Aid In The Case Of Nuclear Catastrophe and took the Zurbarán And Joints With Gay Miguel The Art Teacher option. Thank god. But now I unthanked him.

I'd heard of pulse points at the wrists and behind the ears but human wrists don't come with arrows, dotted lines, diagrams and instructions where to press. I tore into my Longchamp like I was a vulture snaffling its carrion. Even in these unprecedented circumstances I found myself checking my lippy before I put the mirror to his mouth to watch it cloud with breath's bloom. Which it didn't. Keep focused. I touched his eyes. That's another thing you do. Don't panic, Landry! Don't panic and don't get hung on accusing your parents of having given you a gender-neutral name because it was so *amusing*. It makes it hard on phone calls.

'There's a bloke called Landry on the dog,' you'd hear them say. 'Sounds like a girl.'

Now no one could say that because there was no phone. Mine was out of battery. I found his on a bedside table. It was locked. So were two others in a drawer of a marble-topped Louis Le Bidon commode. I tried the pockets of the single suit hanging in a cramped walk-in dressing room, a cupboard really. In the sock drawer and underwear drawers there were only socks and underwear. There was no landline. I was in electronic solitude.

I ran out of the apartment tripping painfully on a broken umbrella. Down the stairs two at a time to the street door – where I realised that I had no key to the apartment so hurried back up the stairs but not before the front door's door-closer had closed the door with a hydraulic piston's faint hiss of satisfaction at closing it on me. I ran back down. I stood at the street door, keeping it open with my foot while I pressed the intercom for all six apartments accessed by this entry. No reply, followed by no reply, followed by consecutive voids. I persisted long enough to stir last night's drunks from their muffled slumber, long enough to prompt daybreak rage, long enough to realise that the block was deserted (country weekends), long enough to assume it was inhabited by the profoundly deaf or profoundly slothful. My foot was hurting from the weight of the door and from the broken umbrella. My black silk scarf – I had left it. My lucky scarf.

The street was empty. How do you call an ambulance without a phone? The answer of course is that you find a phone. I can't get misty eyed about the age-old public phone boxes, destroyed by urine and progress. I picked up my bag and walked. These was no sun to give me a compass, the sky was milky drab, the colour of whites in a laundrette. Every street was its neighbour and every neighbour was the double of the turning off it. The eternity of red brick, stone quoins. At last – a car drove towards me, I waved it down. The driver played a tune on the horn and continued. I sat on a bench. Sometime later a man in running clothes trotted past.

'Excuse me,' I said. He looked at me as though I had sworn at him, picked up his pace and was gone.

A woman in a dressing gown hurried from the extremity of my peripheral vision to a car she didn't even get into to sort through its glove box.

I had hardly opened my mouth when she spat: 'I'm not falling for that one. Bit early in the day for your squalid little scam isn't it?'

'Whoa whoa . . . Don't,' warned the mounted policeman, 'alarm him.' I was running down the centre of the avenue towards them.

The mounted policewoman explained: 'Graham's gone temperamental. Too many yobs with firecrackers . . . he's retraining . . . starting in the quiet . . . re-establishing inner serenity.'

'How can we help?'

'It's an ambulance I need.'

'Have you called one?'

'I don't have a phone . . . I mean I do have a phone but the battery's gone.'

'What's the patient's problem?'

'I think he might be dead.'

'Not sure an ambulance is what's required in that case . . . Still, where do we want it sent?'

'Er . . . well . . . near here. Just a few streets . . . ah that way. I don't know the address.'

They looked at each other.

'We got someone who might be dead at an unknown location.'

'I know it sounds . . .'

'It does, doesn't it.'

'I don't know how to describe it . . . by the entrance there were those fluorescent sort of shorthand marks . . . for electrical work . . . the steps had a sort of fleur-de-lys motif . . .'

'A what?' he asked.

'It's heraldry isn't it,' the policewoman said.

'So what are we asking the ambulance to look for?'

I walked beside the policewoman's horse Douglas. I kept as far as possible from Graham. I explained as vaguely as I could what had happened. They tactfully kept their judgemental opinions to themselves. I skipped up steps of building after building. I lost count. I could tell they were going to give up on me when I saw marks along the pavement, purple, orange, red. I followed the trail and they followed me.

'It's all Linear B to me,' I joked. It fell on deaf uncomprehending ears. I stood radiating my pride that I had refound the entrance to a building called Reichenfels Court.

The policeman took a tool from his pocket and probed the locks. The policewoman was on the phone giving the address and emphasising the urgency.

We went up the stairs.

'No point in knocking, eh? Ah . . . this'll be a cinch. Doesn't deserve to be called a lock. Fools the public every time – if it looks clunky it must be the deal . . . Not so – there we go.'

I led the way. The apartment was as dark as it had been – no natural light. The broken umbrella that I had tripped over when I had gone for help still obstructed the corridor: 'Watch out, I did my foot on it.' I opened the door to the bedroom.

Everything was the same, just as it had been however long ago it was when I left it. His peculiarly neat, not scrambled-out-of clothes including trousers that might have stood up by themselves, might have been a photorealist sculpture of a pile of clothes, a sculpture too perfect to trick the eye. The empty Taittinger bottle and two flutes, one with a lipstick segment, stood on a bedside table. There is the half-empty bottle of Célestins I had left on the fancy Louis commode when I was searching for a phone, my black silk scarf is on the floor at the foot of the bed.

Everything was the same, save the body. There was no body. The body was absent. No show. Gone. That's not what bodies do. Bodies are done to. They don't do.

The policeman stared at the bed. He felt the sheets with the back of his hand: 'In my opinion – and there's nothing controversial about my opinion – in my opinion you're either dead or alive. There's not degrees of deadness. You don't get comparatively dead or fairly dead . . . Not in the real world.'

I almost yawned at his quaint binarism.

I repeated I repeated I repeated. My accounts of the night, the morning, the lack of phones, my desperation – I sensed they were becoming rehearsed, learnt. We walked from bedroom to kitchen/living room and back again. I pointed to the scarf that was mine. If he cared to look he would see that a couple of tassels were torn: only I could know that. The dead personage had been removed, naked. His clothes from last night were proof. Only his phones were missing.

'He must have been moved . . . don't you see . . . his clothes are on that chair . . . where he put them.'

'What if he was one of those strange folks that changes their clothes?'

I walked confidently to the walk-in dressing room. The suit was still there. I gestured to the emptiness, satisfied I'd made my point. I hadn't.

'How can you be sure he didn't have other clothes . . . Can you describe him?'

Caucasian, dark hair, probably not a native English speaker, hint of accent, difficult to place. Persian?

'Assuming there were these phones. Three? That's unusual. But it's all unusual, wouldn't you say . . . Everything's unusual. This dead chappie, dark-haired foreigner, gone on the lam . . . Unusual . . . No name . . . You didn't think to ask . . . So you could murmur it – nice to have someone nuzzle in your ear isn't it if you'll forgive me . . . What we have to consider . . . Was he ever here . . . Or – and we have to ask – were you for that matter?'

'My scarf . . .' I said indignantly.

'Your scarf . . . Yes . . . We have had a creeping suspicion WPC Wigglesworth and me that you're wasting police time.'

'Creeping suspicion . . . ?'

'Just these last few minutes . . . Mutual intuition . . . nothing spoken . . . it's what being a mounted bobby is all about.'

'She's outside with the horses . . . How can you—'

'Like I said – nothing spoken.'

'Please believe me—'

'Look love, I don't know what your problem is . . . but you have got one . . . I'm not going to charge you . . . I probably should but I shan't . . . but what about counselling? Think about it . . . That ambulance could be saving a life in a tragic RTA instead of going on a wild goose chase . . . Now you get in touch if there's ongoing developments . . . Do you know how many people go missing every year?'

He ushered me out of the apartment. I preceded him down the exterior steps willing the electricians' pavement code to be an answer to a question not yet asked.

'Dead is not the same as missing.'

'Like I say you just tell us if the dead personage shows up. As he no doubt will' – misogyny wrapped in mateyness – 'who'd be able to resist the temptation of a lovely lady like you? Then we can put Graham and Douglas on the case. What say you?'

I say you patronising shit. Off they cantered. I found a chic café with couples both of whom had survived the night. I ate toasted brioche, to-die-for super buttery croissants with apricot jam and a café crème. Then ordered a large Kümmel: it came in a balloon glass I wanted to lose my head in. I had seldom drunk it previously, most memorably in Deventer when studying sailors' fanciful carvings of sea monsters in De Waag Museum. I expected it to soothe. The rush of the burn was electrifying. The smiling barista called a cab for me. I slept for hours. I felt clammy and sick. I managed to read one unseasonal poem from Erskine Garn's new collection.

> *Summer stifles. It's a British Warm.*
> *Plump and stuffy, heat that's dull,*
> *Snug, muggy, muffling.*
>
> *Summer cuddles. All wool blankets.*
> *Dense and swaddling. Heavy*
> *As a heater's hefty lagging.*

Summer muffles. It's muddy sludge
To wade through weighed down
In a lard barded sweat stew.

Who was he? Who was he? Who moved him? Was I mistaken? Hallucinating? I hadn't dropped acid for years, not since the days of Gay Miguel. Could he have been cold and greyish blue and suffering rigor mortis yet still alive? Exhibiting the symptoms of death but not dead? The two words rigor and mortis suggest not. Did he rise from the dead and walk naked from the apartment? No. No, people didn't do that any more. Words like resurrection, transportation and transmigration had been phased out. They had been coined for superstitious phenomena reason had quashed, only recently and far from wholly. The history of the world is many millennia of sick men's dreams followed by a few centuries of doubt. I knew what The Living Dead looked like – panda eyes, filed teeth, holed skin stretched by the skull. He wasn't one of them.

I spent hours with my hands clasped round my knees rocking gently. Mollo mollo. I started to phone the boss of the trace agency where I used to work some vacations. He had a superhuman gift for finding people. But I didn't press the call key because he'd be all over me with the tentacles and suckers of a needy octopus, he'd plead then get baby truculent when I didn't respond. He nicknamed me Chastity. Then he'd try shameless self-pity, for instance:

'I was getting a nice massage. Phuket. Lovely piece of arse—'

'Shaun . . . must you?'

'Magic hands . . . makes you feel all tingly . . . well toned. She says, "You want masturbate?" I say you bet . . . then she gives me this cheeky grin and says, "I go find you dirty magazine then." . . . I mean . . . the humiliation.'

'You really are incorrigible.'

Just thinking about Shaun cheered me. Oh to live a life as breezily uncomplicated as his, with so few complexes! Keeping his wife and family in the dark took priority of course, followed by money (cash says so much more about you), sex, mates, drink, cars.

★

Mine had never been uncomplicated. Now it never would be. My mind was racing. I was wondering, fretting, questioning myself. I revisited Den Danske Frugthave every night. The staff were all casuals who didn't recognise me from one night to the next let alone three, four, five nights ago. I described my lover – what an absurd word! My efforts prompted sympathetic shrugs. I doubted my perceptions and memory. I came to doubt my existence, my being, my actuality.

Reichenfels Court was managed for Misselbrook Projects by the agents Drawbridge on behalf of the London (England) property portfolio of Dudley Rogg Warner, a wholly owned subsidiary of Deuteron & Don Investments which is itself . . . A brick wall within a brick wall within a brick wall . . . Charming brick walls of course, Los Angeles teeth and Dedalo Pirlo suits. I called the surviving A&Es and several undertakers. I went shopping. I bought a pretty black Clark Beesley dress after a fitting room struggle. 'They do come up small . . . you'll often need a size up from your normal size.' Something to cheer: card not cancelled.

I dragged myself to the Institute. As soon as I was at my desk-share I forgot how I'd got there. I gave a small group lecture which included references to Pontus Tinnerholm's groundbreaking research at Malmö proving that seventeenth-century Baltic pirates, distant successors to the Victual Brothers, were early slavers. Towards the end of the lecture I noticed that my hands were stained purple. I must somewhere have eaten some raspberries. I don't like raspberries.

One of the students approached me after. She tried but couldn't take her eyes off my hands. She seemed appalled, like she was looking at a strangler's weapons. She nervously recalled that she had heard me deliver a version of the lecture some months previously. On that occasion I had insisted that Professor Tinnerholm's research had been widely questioned, not least by me. She showed me her laptop with a list of English words which, I had noted, derived from Low Dutch rather than plattdeutsch as Professor Tinnerholm had wrongly claimed: jeer, dredge, beaker, poppycock, quack etc.

I had argued that his inaccuracies had led to false conclusions. I had argued . . .

Had I? I had no memory of doing so. I laughed it off. 'Fallible . . . I'm not the Pope. Yet!'

She was fazed by my flippancy, alarmed by my hands. As she left the little theatre she glanced over her shoulder, worried that this confused woman, only a few years her senior, might, in the not too distant future, be her supervisor. I wondered, as I often did, if I were dead.

I somehow bought more raspberries, ate them in the cab home and was just settling down to fret about everything when I realised there was no drink in the flat so I'd have to fret sober. No way. I trudged round the corner to Mr Haral's for ouzo, Metaxa and unresinated white wine. I impulse bought green tomatoes, black olives, halloumi, smoked roe, pitta bread. I put it on the slate. Mr Haral winced.

Sweet little Helios offered to carry it for me but I was in no mood to have him hang about discussing his doubtless commendable discoveries in Eng. Lit. so declined and hauled the lot myself. By the time I'd dumped it in the kitchen I'd forgotten what I was going to do with the tomatoes etc. The ingredients should have been a clue but I couldn't be bothered to eat. I merely wanted ouzo-engineered oblivion. Not even fretting. I was forgetting what it was like to be unforgetful.

Some hours later I was stung back into wakefulness by Chummy, a bad foe but a worse friend who delivered belly cramp like it was a rebuke.

Our bodies are programmed. 'Our' is the wrong possessive. It's presumptuous to claim ownership of kit which happens to be attached to 'us' but which skives, which fails to respond to the will, which opposes the will, which is an independent automaton.

It is not *me* that might suffer cancer, it is some part of the attached works, the obligatory mechanism, over which I have only marginal control. The belly cramp disappeared without my intercession. It asserted its intestinal autarky. Ten days later it reasserted it, reversed it. I was bent double in pain.

Uchenna Jonathan is as much a friend as a doctor. She would never ask how much I drank or how much I failed to eat. She knew. We giggled girlishly about the euphemism 'seeing' people: how alarming it would have been to the generation which supposedly kept the lights off and conjoined pleasurelessly in the dark. No I was not 'seeing' anyone. Just a male creature missing presumed dead or body-snatched. I saw, once. I was not seeing. She shocked me by suggesting I take a pregnancy test although she knew that I took Loestrin 20 every day. She shocked me further by telling me it was 'positive'. I knew she wasn't joking. Was there no end to this humiliation? I was a puppet, strings pulled by unseen forces of malice – most likely male malice, were a gender to be attached.

It is not *me* that is assaulted by pregnancy, it is the generative apparatus within the machine, an apparatus I never asked for, never wanted. Find out where it came from so it can be sent back! The last thing I need, after *my* childhood, is a child. A bewildered burden clinging to a porter of resentment, gurgling. I was sixteen when I first told my parents that I wanted my womb removed.

It is my work that is my life. It would be imprecise to claim that it has been purposely conceived (bad word, bad) as an avoidance of dia-pered domesticity. Rather, I discerned my behavioural patterns, turned them into the template of my existence. I followed myself. I followed, still follow, my free will which would not be denied me by WAAF's murderous ideologues.

Uchenna rubbed sticky gel on my belly. She ran an ultrasound transducer over me so that I could see the micro-invader on a screen little more decipherable than a snowstorm television from way back. I cursed the creature. Did I see its face? Or were its spiteful scrambled features my visualisation, my wishful loathing: eyes, teeth, tongue, noseholes – but not in the right order. And that was definitely a tail I saw.

'What's that . . . *tail* thing?' I pointed at it.

Uchenna shook her head without looking: 'Some foetuses have a pseudo tail. It disappears in a few weeks.'

'That's not what I'm seeing. It's twice the length of the monster . . . Look at it, Chenna . . . it's more like a rodent tail . . . and what the fuck are those teeth?'

It had protruding teeth of different shapes and sizes that made it look like a vicious bumpkin. Eyes randomly disposed. Skin like ploughed mucous membrane. None of the items in the right place. This was a freak show within me. A blind man's collage. It was a sod to read.

at the stranger, then: 'Aaaah. Right. Ludovic Scales. Yes. Yes of course . . . You're the chap, yes—'

'Who saved your life with his quick thinking.' The smile stretched to show auxiliary laughing teeth.

'So . . . I was just passing and I thought let's see how Saul's getting along.'

'Well . . . let's just say . . .'

'You've seen the error of your ways. And felt the hand of god. He didn't want you to despair . . . despair is a sin against hope . . . He sacrificed his only son so that we should have hope . . . He didn't want you to die. It's an insult to the Light of the World frankly. Presumption is a lesser sin but it's still a sin . . . It's cutting him out. He can get very tetchy. But let me tell you – he's on your side.'

'Is that so?'

'It is.'

'Then why did he let me spend six pounds, fourteen and eight on gin and barbiturates . . . *waste* six pounds, fourteen and eight . . . I'm sorry but I got to go.'

'Of course you have, yes . . . I must be on me way too . . . my ministry beckons . . . so that's it then. No . . . er, little token of thanks then . . . I don't mean a physical . . . statuette or whatever . . . I'm not one for medals and goblets . . . just a little word of gratitude. Perhaps. Purrrhaps.'

Saul shut the door. The next time he opened it he found an envelope with glossy evangelical leaflets selling The Open Road To A Place At The Lord's Side – there are no toll charges as in some so-called denominations and the cars are two-tone with fins and the family shines with health and normal normality. Hear Beatific Revelations In A Laurel Bower . . . Find Peace In The Divine Hammock . . . Fear Not The Giant With Six Fingers On Each Hand He Shall Be Slaughtered In The Canyon Of Righteous Boulders.

Saul's teeth were a showcase of neglect – bad vitamin vegan diet that had killed his Una. His gums seeped. He loathed them. He resented gleaming enamel intruding into his life.

Ludovic Scales took to dropping by. He never got across the grimy mosaic of the front doorstep. When there was no answer to his knocking he'd peep through the shredded curtains while the tormented

'Let's take a shufti like this.'

She magnified the image. She rolled the transducer at different angles, peering and squinting. 'How many weeks did you say?'

'Six . . . and three days.'

'Sure?'

'Yep.'

'We've got to get you to a specialist. This is . . . this is unusual . . . I mean it's outside my . . . I've known about this . . . *The Paracelsian*[43] . . . but you don't' – vast intake of breath – 'you don't expect to actually see it.' She sounded apologetic.

'More. I'm not squeamish, darling . . . so far as I'm concerned it's a trespasser to be shooed off my land with a twelve bore.'

'It may not be that straightforward. It's too big for six weeks . . . I mean it's enormous . . . more like six months . . .'

In my head I heard:

> *huge great teeth, like to a tusked Bore;*
> *for he liv'd all on ravin and on rape*
> *of men and beasts; and fed on fleshly gore.*

Is that what I was giving shelter and succour to?

Only hags of horrendous disposition and chancre-faced witches with organs in dripping decay cede themselves to monsters' germination. It's letting yourself go in a big way. Lie . . . pretend it's happening to someone else . . . I wondered, as I often did, if I were dead.

Host to a teratoma is not an enviable sobriquet any more than it's an enviable state to be in. It's not to be advertised. I was up to my neck in foulness's rising tide.

In my head I heard: 'El sueño de la razón . . .' Yes, he was right. But Goya was a man. And it doesn't happen to men. Not inside them anyway. All pregnancies are without-by-your-leave intrusions even when they aren't rapes. Agreement to succumb to intrusion is not

---

43 *The Paracelsian* developed from a cyclostyled medical student jape into an early success of desktop publishing. Then, funded by the vast estate of a rock star who probably died crushed when a baroque mirror fell on him, it became a notoriously perverse 'shock-glossy', described as 'uniquely and utterly foul . . . the nadir of Hippocratic pornography'.

permission to dump sick genes in a nameless uterus then throw a seven. Not that WAAF would understand.

Mr Kyle Bogue's office was dominated by a framed photo of him with a four-metre-long great white sturgeon. Mr Kyle Bogue looked proud. The great white sturgeon looked surprised.

He looked over the top of his spectacles, the gesture of pompous authority figures since spectacles were invented to provide them with a prop.

'Landry Nordtveit . . . I wasn't sure whether to expect a lady or a gentleman – we're seeing a lot more gentlemen nowadays. Gynaecology isn't as exclusive as it was . . . but then what is . . . Now I can see that you're not a Dutch pirate – far from it, far too alluring if I may say so – but you have an internal *incident* whose only precedents are . . . how shall we put it . . . mythical . . . fictional . . . sci-fi legends and widescreen weirdness – or were the only precedents till I saw this . . . this is real – as you well know . . .'

'And it validates my work . . .'

'It does?' He was incredulous.

'Old salts' yarns.'

I explained my doctorate to him. And my deduction that the barrier around what we guilelessly call 'reality' had been breached. Reality had been infected by activity in my brain. A fissure had opened up, deep seepage had occurred. It was akin to a predictive dream. I had it worked out.

My body had succumbed to my mind. It had proved the truth of the fairy tales I studied, analysed and – against all expectation – had come to believe in. They were founded in actuality, albeit contorted actuality, rather than in the pure inventions of sailors designed to scare and delight landlubbers, in the inventions of fishwives boasting of their menfolk's courage, in the competitive yarns of children showing pride in their fathers facing ocean adversity: waves high as frothing cathedrals; immense beasts barrelling through the briny depths rising to the churning surface to swallow ships and their crews whole in a single ravening gulp. All these things were the routine stuff of maritime life and death.

I repeat: my body had succumbed to my mind. It had experienced the untransformed subject matter, the raw material of fairy tales, it had *felt* their truth, the physicality of pescophilia: the left-handed tales of the Fisherman's Friend; the love of a skate's vulva-aping apertures; the litters of sooterkins yarned in quayside taverns; clingy amorous dolphins; rough sex with pilot whales; romantic fish swam in nets, unknowing captives who'll sate lusty bosuns before they get gutted; soft cuddles with lumbering manatees, the sort of creature that looks like an adult who lives at home with its parents.

At some point Mr Kyle Bogue glazed over. He reminded me that there was a parasitical teratoma in me. I hardly needed to be reminded. He insultingly rejected the connection between my 'condition' and my years of research.

'Fascinating as your theories are . . . love the skate stories . . . who was that Belgian fellow . . . sooterkins . . . sooterkins . . . damned fine word . . . there was more of that malarky in the old days . . . periwigs sedan chairs what have you. Back from the past . . . like him.' He pointed to the photo of the sturgeon. 'One hundred and fifty years old if it was a day . . . never been tagged . . . Fraser River . . . people who lived on its banks all their lives had given up on ever seeing such a beauty . . . I brought them hope . . . the magic gift of the Bogues – whether with rod and line or delivery forceps – that's what I've got to bring you, Young Lady . . .'

I winced at the style of address.

'You are commendably *robust* about your condition.'

I wanted a solution not patronisation. I told him: 'Nothing that's human is strange to me.'

'Yes . . . but . . . the question is: is this human?'

'What is human *fluctuates*,' I asserted. I spoke as an inadvertent lab rat jabbing aggression.

'That's certainly true in this case . . . but medical science doesn't fluctuate – at least not quickly enough . . . we're always trying to keep up . . . Eradicate a disease and it crops up in another guise . . . take kuru . . . quick-change artist . . . You are presenting with a condition for which there is no known treatment . . . This is not a conventional ectopic situation . . .'

'Aah . . . Now there's a name for it – Ectopig!' I was delirious, overjoyed at that coinage.

'As I say. This is not a conventional extra-uterine pregnancy . . . both mother and . . . ah . . .'

'Ectopig.'

'If you must . . .'

'I must . . . Freak conceives Ectopig . . . And Freak wants rid of Ectopig.'

'You must realise that the parasite is feeding on your reproductive system. It is eating you. Think of it as cancerous. It has already inflicted considerable damage. It's greedy . . . indiscriminate. It treats you as an all-you-can-eat buffet. A termination will be difficult.'

'Don't tell me you're scared of WAAF,' I laughed. It hurt when I laughed. It stung.

He didn't find it funny. He replied: 'No . . . not scared. Contemptuous. They drenched a colleague's small daughter with blood they stole from a black pudding factory . . . And we've been having to send clients to Ireland . . . You must understand that after the procedure there will be no chance of conceiving in the future.'

'At last – the silver lining.' I perked up no end. Music to my ears. 'In that case,' I told Mr Kyle Bogue, 'let's go for it. Rip the invader from my body.'

'Don't be hasty . . . But . . . the longer we postpone the intervention the greater the danger to you . . . I cannot emphasise that strongly enough . . . It's my job neither to persuade you nor dissuade you.'

I could hear him saying that every day of his life-taking life. Well-practised abstention.

The longer we leave it . . . the longer we leave it . . . 'I do not need persuading.'

'We will, then, operate this week . . . I'll talk to Bream . . . check his availability.'

'Bream?'

'Vigo Bream . . . doesn't ring a bell? No? Really? Vet. *The* vet. The future of veterinary science and art.'

I read up about this radical zoophiliac. He asks what do pigeons make of humans. Answer: we are there to feed them. We serve them. We also provide architecture – eaves, ledges – which they can exploit as their own homes. The dairy industry is a machine for the propagation of cattle. We are food for bears, sharks, wolves. Household pets are despots. They bully their owners – who are owned. Much of his writing is a paean to transgenic mongrelism. New species excite him tremendously. He champions métissages. He creates life forms without precedent. He rewilds with abandon.

The operating room was all wires and monitor screens, blinding lights and stirrups. Drips everywhere. Bulbous bags of dense clear liquid. It was fit for torture.

On a sticky July morning Ectopig was removed from within me by Caesarean section while I floated in the blackness of temporary death administered by a mask.

When I came round from the anaesthetic a man with a bushy moustache was clutching a distended sack of slime to a shoulder of his scrubs.

Vigo Bream introduced himself: 'You are a procreative marvel. Congratulations. I salute you. You've provided us with a pretty quandary here, quite a novelty, an authentic novelty. Aborted is not the word. The word is liberated. Our friend here is very much alive – and so, by the look of it, are you.'

Really? I had progressed from inadvertent lab rat to abattoir victim. Blood, bruises, seepage, stiches, gauze dressings, modular bandages in case of haemorrhage. I wondered, as I often did, if I were dead – how do you tell?

I dreaded it. I disgusted myself. I had an unquenchable longing to see what I knew would most appal me.

Sure enough Ectopig was the most hideous thing I had ever set eyes on. It possessed, according to Vigo Bream, both male and female genitalia. 'It' is the appropriate pronoun: the formula 'he/she' is inadequate.

Ectopig was also the most lovable thing I had ever set eyes on. It changed my idea of beauty from something to be viewed objectively, disinterestedly, close to prettiness to something that touched me deeply with its irreversible pathos and grotesque grandeur. I was proud.

My anthropomorphism is shameless: transgenic conjunction is the greatest leveller. It makes animals of humans, it makes humans of animals. The two meet in equality and equilibrium, unrecognisable to their kin on either side of the divide for whom they are mistakes to be shunned and mocked. We've been here before: Romeo was a bull, Juliet was a mare.

The features I had seen on Uchenna's screen in monochrome were now in full gaudy colour: caramel-brown beak, nails, two tufts of rusty hair otherwise hairless, violet mucous membrane, patent leather liver, half a coxcomb, contorted tongue, a wing whose raven feathers were clagged with mucus, a diseased green trotter, several bulging eyes of different colours, ridged teeth, teeth like needles, rodent teeth, knotted intestines sprouting filaments of mycelium, a black webbed claw, a bullwhip-thick tail protruding from a ragged aperture and meandering over the transparent plastic tub where it lay. It was all mine.

It was gloriously asymmetric, an aggressively impure assault on the senses. It was unvaryingly noisy. Each quaking snore was suffixed by a shrill wolf whistle. Gingerly I touched it. If there was breath it was undetectable. It felt gelatinous but firm, spongey yet resistant. I couldn't put my finger on what it felt like – but you know the stiff jelly in really top pork pies and charcuteries like hure and tête gourmand . . .

For hours or days or longer I wandered in and out of sleep. Vigo Bream was ever present when I woke. He talked of something known as the Malpasfang experiments. He was astonished that I had never heard of them. His descriptions were so vivid that he might have been there. It was his ambition to emulate them.

He observed, measured and fed. Ectopig was constantly hungry. Its diet was anything resembling my profoundest inner organs which had sustained it before liberation: worms, insects, raw offal, raw meat (not red), raw fish and raw cephalopod (which must, if it had sentience as well as appetite, have seemed like cannibalism). It rejected processed meat and fish – cooked, salted, smoked, pickled. So no ham, no blindman's mortadella, no readyflesh. It ate when it was not overlooked. Eat is approximate. It wriggled across the many kilos of nutrition provided in its expanding pens, absorbing them or sucking them in by processes Vigo Bream was working to understand.

He was foxed. Its inability or unwillingness to excrete also preoccupied him. He was worried that he was thinking along such lines endowing it with a form of consciousness. He puzzled over its means of internal composting. There was no waste to expel. It processed everything it took in as fuel for a machine whose purpose was to expand rapidly. It grew irregularly in several directions, budding a paw with eight toes, causing skin to foam and shine, producing ligament clusters. It distended from within itself. Some unprecedented analogue of the pituitary gland worked without cease. Every day, every hour it required a bigger billet.

Kyle Bogue soon considered it:

Primo: an inconvenience occupying a private ward in the clinic which might be more profitably used by Our NHS. When discussing it he looked at me accusingly.

Secundo: an inconvenience which might attract WAAF terrorists, the fishwifely reporters of *The Gusset* and the rest of the yellow press.

Tertio: an inconvenience for which a home had to be found.

This last was the most taxing problem, for Vigo Bream's observations had led to the conclusion that Ectopig was, despite its abundance of animal features, not an animal. It mimicked some generic animal. It could adapt its coloration. His initial analyses were mistaken: it did not, for instance, possess double genitalia. And, further, its expansion might, probably would, continue for ever. There were no evident impediments on growth. Hence the problem of its future habitation: it required a space without limits. A yard. Then a garden. Then a field. Then the entire farm . . .

'Farm, Vigo . . . that's the answer.'

Foraging, hunting, feasting on carrion, rooting, animals of all species seek nutrition and having found it eat it.

Ectopig was not an animal. It was a fungus which mutated according to what nourishment was available. It was knotted to what it consumed. If nourishment was unavailable it would consume itself.

'If it was starved it would pass on,' suggested Kyle Bogue.

'Starving it . . . that'd be murder. Infanticide,' I protested.

'What do you think this clinic's for?' He grinned like it was his catchphrase.

'I wouldn't be too sure that *fungi* are murderable,' replied Vigo Bream. (He used that word – 'murderable'.) 'That's not how fungi work. Fungi are immortal.'

'I shall remind the next mushroom I eat of that.'

'If Landry agrees . . .'

The number of times I'd heard the two men say that . . . They paid me scantest attention. It was lip service, nothing more. They pretended in a courteous pavane of the mind. Why bother? They knew that I knew that Ectopig's future was out of my hands. These few weeks and the incidents they contained would be erased. Life would be reprised as normal. I would return to the Institute after an undefined health scare which was now behind me, which I didn't want to talk about, which I brushed off with classic modesty, which had no long-term consequence – thanks for asking, thanks for all the expressions of get-well-soon. That, I regret, was wishfulness.

'If Landry agrees . . . then Farmyard of the Senses is the obvious fit.'

'What? *What* of the senses?'

'If a chap's got a park he's got to act like a tart!' the two men spoke in adolescent unison.

I had never heard of Farmyard of the Senses nor of Fenant Park nor of its proprietor Geoffrey someone – 'the chap with the park'. A Heavy Petting Zoo meant nothing to me. It claimed to be 'an evocation of classical antiquity when our race was constantly strengthened by the blood and genes of other species'. It was advertised as The Mecca for the Zoophiliac Community. The startling thing about Farmyard of the Senses was the fierce criticism it received.

Action groups and special pleaders attempted to have it closed within days of its opening. Its fate hung in the balance. But it was deemed to be breaking no law. The welfare standards were exceptional; the briefly suspended transgenic infections consultant Everett Awmack was readmitted by the Royal College of Veterinary Surgeons. When a Panthers Are People Too activist was mauled to death by a drugged leopard sex worker whom he was trying to rescue but who didn't want to be rescued the inquest ruled that there was no indication that security procedures were lax or that protective measures were inadequate. Death by misadventure. The nickname Bestiality Towers was undeserved. However, the local freesheet *The Clarion* reported:

Animals at an animal sanctuary are behaving like real animals according to Central Mercia's Lead Bestiality Monitor Doug

Garment. Doug has proposed a controversial scheme to chemically castrate repeat offender sanctuary animals who prey on the tots who come to see them. They expose themselves shamelessly to kiddies as young as five. In Doug's opinion it's the llamas who are the worst. As he says, llamas are literally nothing but wolves in sheep's clothing.

It would be a happy home for Ectopig. It was arranged that I could visit whenever I wished. My wounds healed. Physical pain gradually abated. I was proud that it was mine. The visitors' faces were full of joy. I watched alongside them, not revealing my relationship to the unique attraction whose fame grew with its dimensions. I was stoic. I kept my tears in a drawer at home. Sir Geoffrey Shadoxhurst Bt roamed about, a glad-handing nabob enjoying the congratulations of the people on his remarkable discovery. I was one of the people. That's the way I wanted it, anonymous, unidentified. I could feel their fascinated repulsion. A horror movie without a fourth wall.

Ecto was variously described: 'a naked mole rat with the dimensions of a beaver', 'a clavier on the point of eruption', 'a worrying lump of mould', 'a sea cow mangled by a propellor', 'the mutilated marvel', 'even uglier than Melodie Dogg', 'a dauntingly clever hydrophilic maybe mammal', 'forget the face, Ecto is charm itself', 'Amanita phalloides going undercover', 'a melting electric board', 'a failed animal', 'the tragic mongrel that forgot its mask', 'a cry for reconstructive help'.

Deformity is akin to sublimity. Ectopig belonged to tomorrow's mythology. Our own myths are forming silently within us as a collective web which is passed down generation upon generation. The myths that have infected us on the sly don't reveal themselves till we are in the final avenue.

Only a month after its arrival at the Farmyard it had to be provided with a new spacious dell, 'The Glen', from which it would disappear for days: its way of telling both management and punters that it was not simply an exploitable exhibit, that it had a fake-life of its own wandering, splashing, morphing and contaminating the atmosphere with ergot spores which produced hallucinations. The mayhem caused by that state was alarming. Women wailed, men scratched the earth, they broke their teeth on roots and flints. They saw god. Not a pretty sight. They saw Christ mocked and handing down his most terrible sentence. Ectopig released poison that incapacitated motor functions. It could disguise itself as a bole, sloughed bark, humus, leafmeal, sheered boughs, a carpet of pine needles, yew berries. It was an ill-conceived electric octopus, it was a fluorescent weapon, rolling, knotting itself, devising a cat's cradle of seething green strands. It changed shape, it split into numberless fragments, following itself, swooping and morphing like shining starlings drilled by Busby Berkeley. It grew wings black as umbrella bats and wide as a condor. It hid for many days then reappeared to eat the unwanted newborns thrown to it by reluctant parents, plump pink scran unaborted because of the WAAF terror.

There was only so much I could take. There existed no lachrymatory so large it could contain the overflowing ducts of my hurt.

I would leave Farmyard of the Senses and explore the sprawling estate. Chimpanzees spoke and signed. A horse did sums. In the slinky swaying long grass women were copulating with goats and sucking off donkeys. Men were riding white swans which they held by the neck. Some were buggering placid sows. Those who did not dare to make new acquaintances watched with dread. They hated themselves for their pudeur. Their tongues quivered, jealous, envious.

Führer World was in a better state than its dedicatee. I detoured far from it. The white rock concerts attracted unattractive audiences and horrible 'musicians'.[44] The very existence of these tattooed bands and their foul, beserker-faced, shaven, hawking, jeering, stamping, cleaver-wielding disciples whose air I was obliged to share sickened me. And they were so ugly.

One late afternoon I spent a few foul minutes with the sinister kitsch in the gift shop: Allach pottery figures of SS men, ceremonial

---

44 They include Avalon, Battlezone, Brutal Attack, Bulldog Breed, Celtic Connection, Celtic Warrior, Chingford Attack, English Rose, Enoch Enoch, Eye Of Odin, Hobnail, The Late Ian Stuart, Ken McLellan, Legion of St Lionheart, Luft Wallah (India's foremost neo-Nazi band, a tribute to Chandra Boas), Nigger's Slum, No Fear No Justice, No Quarter No Remorse, Ovaltinees, Paul Burnley & The Fourth Reich, Pavement Rape, Rage 'N' Fury, Raven's Wing, Razor's Edge, Retaliator, Sink The Windrush, Skrewdriver, Skullhead, Spearhead, Stab A Paki, Steelcap Strength, Stormbringer Squadron, Stigger, Test Site Mutants, The Theydon Boys, The Klansmen, Violent Storm, White Law, White Lightning.

bayonets, posters, medals, all manner of eagles, pennants, flags, shields. Is there nothing that cannot be embossed with a swastika? I needed to cleanse. I wandered down a track to where nature, in the form of thorns, nettles, buddleia and ivy, was reclaiming a group of long wooden hutments. Former barracks no doubt. An elderly man wearing the most built-up surgical boot I'd ever seen emerged from what appeared to be the only inhabited building waving his loose hands to shoo me away as though I were a stray from Farmyard of the Senses.

'No visitors allowed up Hag Hill. Out of bounds. You be off if you please.'

He dragged one leg behind him, stumbling to dead head a plant in the seedy remnants of a garden. I mooched off. I sensed I was being watched. I turned. There was a face at a streaked window beside the front door. It was passive, so flat and static I first thought it was a life-size photo stuck to a pane. It had faded to wan. Indeterminate age and sex. It peered. I peered back. Somewhere a child cried, and the face was gone.

As I idled back for what I knew would be my last glimpse of Ecto-pig two riders and two pony-size Marcher Hounds approached at terrifying speed on the stud farm's post-and-railed gallops. Sir Geof-frey Shadoxhurst Bt and a woman bound in the tightest riding tailoring imaginable whose hair was sweeping horizontal in the taut breeze. They didn't acknowledge me. They hammered the earth. Given my chosen anonymity I ought not to have felt slighted. I had done my bit. That's when I decided.

I have a clean works, the pills, the artisan gin from Alsop's Botanicals (I'll bet that's a first: a couple of litres of Gordon's is the time-honoured mixer with *felo de se*).

My thanks are due to everyone in the Icarus Wings team at Dream Topping™, its Partnerships and Associates. A special Level Handshake for The Sergeant, the Dream Topping™ Leadership Leader Emeritus, proving that age is no impediment to great Leadership. His advocacy on the part of The Far Carnival has been persuasive. My every best wish for The Heath Project.

Dogs!

Daph and Rhys Kenfig made their annual trip to the theatre. The play was the former circus performer Emerson 'Flash' Trinkwon's *I Put My Head In The Oven But I'd Run Out Of Coins For The Meter*. 'Ten out of Ten on the Chortleometer' was *The Chronicle Incorporating The Courant*'s verdict. The rest of the audience lapped it up. It only strengthened Mr and Mrs Kenfig's determination to shun a world contaminated by playwrights with convictions for sexual offences, bad puns, vulgar innuendo, lavatory gags, knotted penis gags, double D cup gags, priest and choirboy gags and, especially, people who enjoyed gags.

They cleared up their affairs in an orderly manner. They made wills in favour of their two Airedale terriers, Micky and Griff. Dream Topping™ prescribed a classic Instant Sunshine: tequila, aspirins, orange, LSD with a sambuca and cyanide topping. Everything was done to perfection. The six-hour delay between ingestion of LSD and cyanide was observed to the minute. They died tripping through pulsating wisteria and ruins reddened by the last ever sunset . . . sitting still while hurtling into an unknown of swarming horse-brasses, throbbing samplers . . . their skin wobbled.

They talked of their courting days . . . remember the slag heaps, the shale . . . remember those vicious shards . . . spewed up from the pits . . . it was a better world . . . remember the smell of the smoke . . . oh and those bubbling puddles . . . yellow sulphur . . . the burning stacks below the surface.

They were so far in the past they didn't realise when they crept into Afterplace One.

They forgot the dogs. By the time a worried neighbour pried about then called the police the dogs were as dead as their owners, described in the paper as 'callously, unthinkingly selfish'. We knew that was incorrect.

A Contract Carpet Dynasty

Here's a warm feelgood pat on the back for Dream Topping™. It foregrounds our discretion and loyalty to those who put their trust in us.

When Howard Janka made contact with us he was in a desperate state. A failure, in his own eyes, in his chosen vocation of contract carpet provision. He was chronically ill. His intestines were enraged. He was heavily indebted. He struggled to repay loans and mortgages. His suppliers pursued him. He gambled on anything: horses, football, the royal baby's name, the date and time of the apocalypse, the national lottery, the lifespan of this or that zoo animal, the subject of the prime minister's next lie . . . His son and employee Gerard, a once persuasive salesman, resented being treated like a minion. He wanted to be a partner. Name on letterhead. His father refused to grant him that status. So he used the business as a cash cow. He skimmed money to subsidise his dissolution, his drugs, his drink, his doxies. He was confident that his father didn't notice.

When Howard was diagnosed with inoperable cancer of the colon and given less than two months to live he decided to have his revenge on Gerard whom he didn't tell about the cancer. After consulting Frankly Sam he called Gerard into his office and told him that he was making him a partner. Ten days later he died with a Senior Eliminator by his side to guide and cheer and clear up after The Event. Gerard inherited the business. Within a matter of days he learnt that he had also inherited debts of half a million pounds which, as the sole surviving partner, he was responsible for.

Here comes the heartwarming part. Sifting through his father's effects Gerard found a multi-draw national lottery ticket. He checked three weeks ago's numbers online. He was a winner. The debts turned to chicken feed. He sold the business and moved to Estepona. Everyone was a winner: Gerard financially, Howard emotionally, dying happy in the sure knowledge that he had ruined his son.

A Cry For Help

This was a tough one which demanded that Dream Topping™ had to overlook its own best practice. We had to legislate for the situation. Pragmatic morality is the only morality worth the name.

Nietzsche: 'All idealism is mendacity in the face of what is necessary.'

From the age of fifteen Cressie Bole demanded that her multiply-alimonied, multiply-Botoxed mother pay for her lip flip together with a cheek filler and breast implants. 'Just like you – Mommy Dearest.'

She was repeatedly told she must wait till she was eighteen.

'But I'll be so old when I'm eighteen. If you don't buy me what I want I'm going to top myself.'

Dream Topping™ supplied a precise prescription of barbiturates and emetics. Never can a cry for help have been more effective. Within a week of having gastric irrigation she was on the operating table at NeueVisage. And only a month later was she uberflaunting, an eye-poppingly sizzling display in *The Grime* promoting I-Spy-Eyewear and being linked with top deposed dictator Varas Zagadov's son Axel.

We were tickled pink by her little subterfuge!

Freya's Way

This is a tale of nice people, gentle people, decent people – people like we'd all like to be – trapped in a maelstrom of their own devising, hurled hither and thither not to mention yon by gusts of raw emotion. I wouldn't call it a failure on our part here at Dream Topping™. It was more a tragic tragedy worthy of Greeks and Romans whose lesson was that for full satisfaction it's essential to follow to the letter the instructions provided in the *Easy As You Go There Now* step by step user's manual. Don't deviate. There was crucial neglect in that area. Deviations galore.

Chute Ducis is a large village or small town with a full complement of necessities, among them: Tam Ogden's sustainable bentwood showcase; Lucas and Teeth award-winning gentlemen thatchers; Wellness Ultra; Leon's Wellness; The Wellnecessary Barn; an award-winning two-person architectural practice with a particular expertise in buildings roofed in Netherlandish pantiles shipped to the former ports of Bridgwater and Topsham; Golden Posture Pilates; Matt's Matwork Pilates; the award-winning Balsam and Applepip hammock weavers; an ecologically responsible trout farm; the award-winning La Rascasse restaurant with rooms; three artisan bed and breakfasts; The Shadoxhurst Tap and Craft Brewery; four gastropubs; an award-winning smokery; Vinyasa Lunchtime Yoga; Maxim Cool-mans's award-winning artisan bakery; a studio designed by Linsel Murly for Calloway Owens and built by the Idyllic Brotherhood, now occupied by an internationally renowned harpsichord maker; Naomi's Shop specialising in advanced soft toys made from recycled, leprosy-free rags sourced by authenticated Bangladeshi orphans; a Disciples of Oblivion self-harm eisteddfod; The Art Of Living In France Boutique Property Consultancy; Tom Jason's award-winning organic wines; bark and lichen foraging life encounters with Denise Tiplady; the Pierrepoint biodiversity narrative hub; the Masters Of Life-Writing Bivouac; Kate Niven-Burt treehouse designer and builder; three residential creative writing hubs; Jerry's earthworks fibrillation workshop; Martin and Anna's rare breeds farm; Tibby Bexley's Creativity Blanket Community for Pre-Literates; La Charogne locally grown charcuterie; Liv and Mia interspecies healers; Thursday transphobia cliché elimination clinic and binary negative soft fruit trample; a bardic poetry polygender moot on turf; Red Mist Anger Management Control; themed open garden days; an award-winning enforcement grade nuclear butter churner; an Alexander Technique loft; a bookshop serving award-winning free range doughnuts and clotted molasses stobbies; a buskins array (scorned in private by the professional actors who live in the village); Marchbank's Botanical Gin Distillery; a biodynamic treacle well; Come Again Drycleaners; six art galleries and the Curtis Adrian sculpture park which shows work by Sokari Douglas Camp, Duggie Fields, Gus Cummins, Valerio Adami, Mick Rooney, Anselm Kiefer, Emily Meyer; the Byre spa hub and hotel converted from a Victorian model farm designed by Milford Sanders and described by Gavin Stamp as 'unmistakably a dress rehearsal for his extravagant horror show at Malpasfang Lodge'; a transcultural handshake shed; Foot Club With Lindy Bristle Podologist; a jeopardy beacon platform (currently closed); Sabrina Jacka's rubber lifestyle atelier; an understanding coprophagia therapy lodge; two craft potteries; an award-winning creative pathfinder; a gym cluster; the Spinney Recording Studio used by bands like Radiohead, The Cactus Plovers and Moist Groin; two hair studios, the No Pun and Justine de Montfaucon.

Freya and Imo could have met at any of the above. It's the kind of place where people acknowledge people they know by sight with a restrained smile. They will likely have known of each other as Scatty Freya and Mutton Dressed As Imogen. They had not exchanged a word till they found themselves in the same group after they were rescheduled by apologetic Pilates teacher Matt (sick child). At the end of the session one or other suggested a cup of tea: a sign of an invitation to acquaintance which might develop into friendship. An invitation to which the response is 'how silly it is we haven't met before . . . don't you know Larry and Simon/Dave and Andrea/the Holkingskips?'

'Doesn't old Ethel Littlewort do for you?' asked Imo.

'She did. She did do . . . but with her back and Walter's oesophagus . . . she doesn't do any more. Did she do for you?'

'Yes she did do . . . I miss her,' said Imo. 'Nightmarish cleaner of course . . . endless breakages . . . lays on polish so thick . . . turns a parquet floor into a skid pan in seconds . . . but it was such a joy to hear her talk . . . the sound of real people makes you just jump for joy . . . those accents are disappearing . . . she's a genuine link with the past . . . the heritage . . . the old bucolic ways . . .'

'I thought she came from Smethwick . . .' Freya said.

'Oh . . . I didn't know . . . she's been here since the beginning of time . . .'

'Indeed . . . she's been married to Walter for getting on sixty years. Can you imagine.'

'Heavens . . . I've barely managed six so far.'

They were drinking fair trade and eating nettle cake.

'This is so absolutely horrid it must be good for you.'

'Which? The tea or the—'

'Both!'

They laughingly agreed that they preferred coffee and what Imo called 'wicked' patisserie. They were a bit coy about it. They walked down the street to Le Sorbier, treated themselves to a Paris-Brest and a lemon tart. They mock reproached themselves and each other for their gourmandise. They pretended to feel guilty.

'I,' said Freya, 'must go and shower.'

'And I,' said Imo, 'must go and fling myself in the river.'

'Really?'

'It's delicious. Tones the soul.'

'I thought that was what we've just been doing.'

'You should try it . . .'

'Hmmm . . .'

'Come on. It's only five minutes the place I go to. Very few turds.'

'I haven't got a cozzie.'

'Neither have I . . . Don't worry – there's never anyone around . . . besides you've got nothing to hide. It's what Pilates is for . . . Come on.'

And off she led Freya, taking her arm. They walked down a track that Freya had never noticed.

They bathed late afternoon in a pool of the soft clear green chalk-stream unconcerned about possible effluents from upstream. Lush tufty meadows and water crowfoots on the right bank, a thick jungly decor of sallows and willows on the left. They were overlooked by nothing other than an elegant heron on a stump. It was a kind of bliss – and so close to home!

'I did fear it was going to be like one of those, you know, Lord Leightonish . . . nymphs in a pond spied on by the satyrs.'

'Bring 'em on, darling. If you can find them . . . I'd say that Ducis is suffering from satyr famine.'

They lay baking themselves dry on the meadow grass.

'Snifter?' Imo proposed as they reached the High Street.

'I'd love to but I've got to get back . . . order I need to have ready for collection tomorrow . . . But I tell you what – why not come over on Friday for supper. Roger and I have got some friends coming. Nothing formal. It'd be lovely to see you. Today's been a real treat. Bring your other half of course.'

'Ah . . . Teensy problem there . . . Imogen Skye doesn't actually have one of those. She currently has what you might call two quarters . . . but they don't add up to a half. Solo OK?'

'Of course . . . Yes, yes, absolutely.'

'And I'll be able to see your work!'

Freya watched her sashay away, light along the pavement in pedal pushers and ballet pumps.

★

Imo had showed up late. Show is the word. She made an entry: vertigo heels, moulded Azzedine Alaïa LBD (described in *W* as 'liquid engineering') and short black jacket, 5 denier sheer black nylons, big hair. It was like she was dressed for clubbing with a toy boy or one of those elusive satyrs, rather than a bobo supper (never dinner) in a sprawling house of old beams and old carpets, of furniture and prints by modern master splodgers and not least an industrial kitchen bearing a chef's name.

'Oh it's exquisite. Robust yet so delicate.'

'Fifteen-year project. We found it when we were doing our doctorates. Derelict all but. A very failed brewery.'

'Gosh you must be proud . . . it just exudes inspiration, such tee-ell-cee.' She was slightly drunk, probably ought not to have driven, heavily scented (to mask the drink?), heavily made up with cracks showing in the stucco, smiley in a wildly grimacing way, thirsty, good company till she became exhausting name-dropping company. Name hurling is more like it. Who were these people? Why did so many of them have the names of terriers: Norfolk, Fox, Bull, Kerry, Cairn? Who was Gemma Bedlington of whom she said 'one does not ask an actor of *her* stature to *read* for a vaginal deodorant podcast'. No doubt reputed in acting and freshness circles but lacking recognition without. The list was apparently endless. Needless to say, she couldn't remember from one minute to the next the names of her fellow guests.

Luke, Megan, Jill, Lindy and Silent Jerry were mildly astounded when she compared 'the stern challenges' of her voice-role as Sulky The Suave Dumpertruck in *The Little Gay Tractor* to those of playing Olivia in *Twelfth Night*.

Roger thought it was a hoot. He egged her on: 'Have you met Lennie The Lion . . . how did you get on with Emu?' By that time she was so pissed she didn't notice his teasing malice, taking it as an invitation to lob more names of the largely unknown.

She did, however, notice Silent Jerry's party hand in its usual quest beneath the table: 'Darling – if you're going to grope a girl do please familiarise yourself with female anatomy first . . . Freya, you must show me your work before I succumb to Young Lochinvar here.'

They walked across the yard to the studio. Former stables with original style stable doors. Worn cobbles. Imo clung to Freya. She valued her legs.

'Actually nothing shocks me . . . just about the first thing you learn as a soubrette is that many actors have a certain predilection for exploration . . . quite a few are into self-exposure. Not all but a healthy minority. Sympathetic laughter and a concerned "is that all . . . is that *it* then" generally does the job.'

'Oh these are so so elegant. Such serenity. I love the plainness . . . Protestant austerity, no decoration, they remind me of those marvellous cool paintings of Dutch churches.'

'They're waiting to be decorated.'

'Oooh. Whoops . . . are they . . . You didn't tell me you were a sculptor too.'

'Sorry?'

'This . . . it's so energetic . . . so daring . . . such movement . . . real oomph.'

'It's Mrs L's breakages bodged together, refired in fury . . . I'm delighted you approve.'

'Oh I am putting my foot in it . . .'

'Not at all – great things come out of accidents . . . I'll think of it differently. It's good to have a fresh eye.'

'What this divine space tells me is that the thing about ceramics is the same as the thing about painting, isn't it – you can do it by yourself. In your own time. To your own schedule. Marvellous . . . I'm so envious . . . The less than brill thing about being a mere interpretative artist is that you can't really do it alone . . . it isn't the real thing . . . so between jobs – I refuse to use the R word, it's just so self-deluding – one's vocation is on hold. A pianist or a snooker player can practise . . . but an actor's instrument is her body . . . it's different . . . It's not something you just pick up and strum . . . the instrument has to bend to the inner demand of the will . . . it's Frankenstein and Monster . . .

'D'you know what I think . . . why so many of us are doing these great one woman shows in manky village halls and pub theatres . . . it's not me me me, not therapy. No non nein no . . . It's all about keeping the instrument in tune, responsive . . . it's keeping fit . . . it's down to monologues being the only things actors can workshop alone . . . getting into yourself, deep down . . . who was it said deep feeling doesn't make for good poetry? Oh fuck who was it? Deep feeling doesn't . . . Thom Gunn! What a fuckbutt! It's the opposite – it's all about feeling. Thom with that silly H. A way with language would be a bit of a help. A bit of a help . . . How wrong can you get. It's a giant splash of feeling that's a help . . . just to the brim.

'I'm giving my Gertrude in Southampton next month . . . I'd say Willie S was much much more about feeling than a way with language – if, that is, it was Willie S: the Earl of Westmoreland is a more plausible candidate . . . or is it Cumberland . . . anyway a man of breeding . . . Rehearsals begin Tuesday . . . I'm word perfect. Imogen Skye will of course be told to unlearn the role by the twelve-year-old director . . . and he will of course cut some of her lines. Seems only yesterday that I played Ophelia in the very same theatre. Super dressing rooms. The last time I was there there was a murder in the hotel I was in . . . not to mention some sort of gay Nazi disco . . . A travelling player sure sees life . . . First stop on a three-month tour . . . Madingley Mummers. Claudius vindicated. The twelve-year-old has plagiarised Immy Dögg – well, I don't know if it's plagiarism but he's got all his ideas from her . . . I suppose he hopes no one has read her . . . she is on the obscure side. In her essay Claudius is the hero. Claudius murders Hamlet Senior for the sake of Denmark . . . it's political assassination. He was even more feckless and useless than the namesake son. Total loose cannon. Such a brave interpretation . . .'

Jill and Lindy drove her home.

Freya slumped. She kicked off her shoes. She said to Roger: 'Darling, I'm sorry I asked her . . . d'you know what she said just now . . . she dresses like that because *it's expected of her* . . . it's how she was in *The Gent.*'

'God . . . *The Gent* . . . wasn't that the one with the moustache who was done for cottaging . . . I sort of knew it was there . . . can't remember if I actually ever saw it . . .'

'She was going on about how many fans go to *Gent* Conventions.'

'They must be a truly fascinating bunch . . . Can you imagine . . .'

'Anyway I shan't ask her again.'

'No . . . Do. I loved her shoes . . . very Weimar. She's fun . . . just not with The Pullovers.'

'I wish you wouldn't call them that – you'll forget . . . you'll say it in front of them.'

'Prancing stags hauling sledges . . . what age are they? And they *always* wear them.'

'Well, I'm sure we all have our little foibles. It's just that Imo seems to have slept with hers.'

'She's an actress for god's sake . . . isn't that what actresses are for?'

'You sexist beast. And you know very well it's not actress – it's ac*tor*.'

Imo was back early afternoon the next day to fetch her car which she had parked in a gravelled space between two of the several unmatching buildings which comprised the former brewery. She was in rehearsal mode. She had no idea which building last night's hosts might be in. She heard a voice in the studio.

Freya was saying: 'I've been trying to get the feel of those seventeenth-century Dutch church interiors. Somewhat icy. Very still. Saenredam.' Imo put her head round the door, smiled collusively and waved her car keys merrily. Freya was wearing artfully stained overalls that shouted 'working artist'. She was addressing twenty craft tourists. She did not want to be interrupted. She acknowledged Imo with a cursory wince. She mouthed: 'Roger's in his office.'

Imo backed off disgruntled. She walked into the house and called his name. Then she recalled that Freya had pointed out his office last night. The pyramid-roofed malthouse with an outside staircase at the end of the yard. No apparent door. She walked round it. A glass wall faced a lawn and a cedar of Lebanon. There he was. Head down at a long table.

Roger was preoccupied. He was gazing at a computer screen from a few inches, swearing at the proofs of his new revision of *A Grave Robber's Handbook* and listening to *Death and the Maiden*. He didn't hear Imo's tap on the window. She banged again, grinning a generous smile. He looked up from his computer and squinted distractedly to the point where his eyes were horizontal apertures. Then he turned away apparently searching for something on the paper-strewn table. How sweetly vulnerable he was.

He didn't recognise the figure in a shapeless smock top, hair scraped back, a no-slap look achieved with abundant No-Slap, leggings, ankle boots. He peered. He had asked Freya countless times to put up signs on these open days to prevent gawpers. He held up his right hand, pointing with a jabbing finger, indicating, he intended, that this errant craft tourist should go round the malthouse to the yard. He even managed a wince of goodwill. He returned to a sentence mangled by a half-witted editorial apprentice who seemed to think a frenchie was a toasted sandwich or a soldier.

Imo, infuriated, turned on her heels. She released the clutch with such ire that her Mini Cooper made gravel a weapon, spraying some of the house's windows, a gesture that went unheeded because the room in question was currently empty.

'Oh dear . . . the sisterhood isn't showing much solidarity . . . this is splendid: "the fiasco is further exacerbated by Imogen Skye's Gertrude, apparently a former nightclub hostess or, more appropriately, a largely forgotten television starlet whose ever-diminishing wardrobe will please a constituency seldom noted for its interest in rogue readings of the canon" . . . What on earth am I going to say the next time I see her?'

'Don't mention it . . . If you don't she won't.'

Roger was right. Imo had other things on her mind.

She was ambling in Ducis High Street. Sartorially she was in a Luberon village. The Art of Living in France demanded a floaty Provençal print dress (sun-bleached mauve, crimson chevrons), roman sandals, a straw hat, a straw basket with shiny aubergines and peppers. Freya, stained and streaked overalls, walked out of the bakery as Imo walked in.

'Imo! We didn't know you were back – you should have let us know.'

'Should I? Should I really . . . after your double snub.'

'My . . . my what?'

Imo raised her eyebrows and tightened her glabella in incredulous reproach. She shook her head. 'Come off it . . . you know bloody well what I'm talking about . . . you shooed me out of your studio . . . remember – when I came to fetch my car. You were embarrassed by me . . . God knows why . . . You were surrounded by what do you call them . . . shabby bunch of . . . pottery grockles I suppose.'

'Oh *then* . . . I was giving a talk . . . my clients are not shabby . . . I didn't shoo you, I was just trying to show you how to . . . where you'd find Roger. I was in the middle of a talk . . . I wouldn't interrupt you, I wouldn't try to butt in when you were on stage.'

'Oh don't be absurd . . . there's no comparison . . . an informal chat is not a structured performance . . .'

'I was preoccupied – I'm sorry if you thought I was discourteous . . . I do find talking like that stressful. I am not an ac*tress*.'

'And do you know when I found Roger he glared at me . . . like I was some trespasser . . . he waved me away.' She imitated his hand movements with such assurance that she might have been rehearsing them. 'Family trait!'

'He didn't mention having seen you – so far as I remember.'

'He told me to bugger off.'

'I'm sure he didn't. He probably couldn't see who you were . . . he's incredibly short-sighted. And besides he'd have been slaving away.'

'Do not use that word casually. It demeans enslaved people.'

'Imo, I must be going. Can I tell you something . . . You said it's not all me me me. I'm sorry . . . it is. You're behaving – if you really want to know – like you're a skin short of the whole Rizla pack—'

To which Imo responded by slapping Freya's face. It rang out crisp and sharp. The High Street halted in open-mouthed shock. Passers-by, couples arm in arm, a man with a buggy full of beer bottles, two elderly real people, a falling tray of yellow emulsion, a van driver and a cyclist looking over her shoulder held their position as if the frame was frozen.

Freya, without touching her stinging cheek, broke the silence with an unwounded smile '. . . as we used to say'.

And life went on. Imo stomped off but with measured aggression – roman sandals have no shock absorbers.

One of the real people whom Freya knew only as Biddy told her: 'You spoke right and prompt, my baba.'

'Thank you . . . Thank you, Mrs . . . ?'

'It's all right, just call me Biddy, my baba. Everyone else does.'

Imo was on tour again: Kettering, Lincoln, Scarborough, Wrexham etc. When she arrived back in Ducis it was to the sound of trumpets that she alone could hear:

'Not quite as bad as it was made out to be.' Star columnist Stephie Gilbert in *Kettering, Wellingborough and Rushden Live*.

'Interesting . . . Ms Skye has not lost her eagerness to get her kit off so long as it's valid within the context of the script.' Andy Boyle, *Plays and Players*.

'Not Shakespeare "As We Like Him" despite the production being ornamented by the evergreen Imogen Skye.' *Scarborough Advertiser*.

'Crewe is famous as a place where touring theatrical troupes would meet en route to destinations far and wide. It was never meant to be a place where they could squat for two weeks. There are numerous other destinations Madingley Mummers might profitably inflict themselves on. They are, however, welcome to leave behind veteran dolly bird Imogen Skye, unwithered by age, though no one could accuse her of infinite variety!' *Cheshire Life*.

Freya was teaching a residential summer school at the Mercian University of Crafts.

Roger was working haltingly on a chapter of *A Grave Robber's Handbook* entitled 'Cloudesley Shovell's' Emerald and watching racing on TV.

'The lady that slapped the pottery lady came in . . . bought a lovely big bouquet of tulips, one of the biggest this year to give to the pottery lady . . . to make up . . . ever such a nice gesture . . . it's what flowers are for . . . life's too short, isn't it.'

Roger walked to the front door when he heard the bell. He opened it with the germ of a greeting on his tongue. When he realised that the caller was not who he expected he hurriedly and awkwardly removed his glasses, pocketed them, flustered.

'Oh hulloo . . . I thought it was . . . how are you. Nice to . . . Trevo's meant to be coming . . . service one of the kilns.'

She was wearing a biker jacket, ripped jeans, cowboy boots. She hid coquettishly behind her swollen bouquet.

'Beyond my capabilities – kilns. I brought these for Freya . . . olive branch . . . kiss and make up.'

'That's so sweet of you . . . she's not here at the moment . . . she's doing her annual penance . . . teaching beardies at Warwick . . . press ganged into it . . . would you like a cup of tea or something?'

'I'd love to but I've an awful lot of sorting to get through. I've only been back since yesterday . . . so liberating to be in one's own nest . . . little things . . . not having to think where the light switches are . . . eating alone . . . being able to make yourself a proper jambon beurre . . . now look, make sure they get plenty of water . . . won't you . . . promise . . . By the way when will Freya be home?'

'She only went yesterday. She'll be back Wednesday lunchtime.'

'Plenty of time then . . . Super . . .'

Roger held the flowers in front of him while he admired his blurred self in the hall mirror, thrust his head forward so his nose was almost touching the foxed glass. He winked.

He was halfway along the stone-flagged corridor that led from the pantry to the conservatory where misshapen vases and imperfect jardinieres were stored when the bell sounded again. He trudged back to the front door, wondering what she might have forgotten. He checked himself in the mirror again.

'Who was that then,' asked Trevo, 'spot of extra-curricular?'

'Haha . . . No . . .' He laughed. Then he heard himself say: 'Not yet.'

Trevo leered: 'Very tasty.'

'Imogen Skye.'

'Ah yeah . . . yeah, thought she looked familiar. Heard she lives round here . . . If I'm not much mistaken I used to wank on photos of her when I was a kid. 'Alcyon days. Sweet memories.'

'You should share them with her.'

'You were right, I was being all me me me . . . me me me. What I call my me me meme . . . Me culpa. All Imogen and no Imo. You've been so gracious . . . stoic. Forgiving . . . it makes me want to tear up . . .'

'Big Girls Don't Cry.'

'Oh – I was the love interest . . .'

'Sorry?'

'In *Jersey Boys* . . . Four Seasons . . . it was one of their big . . . oh here I am me me meing again.'

'The flowers were fabulous . . . tonic . . . four days' teaching . . . feels like forty.'

'I think of white tulips as sort of personifying me . . . I really identify with them.'

They were sitting on opposite sides of the great farmhouse table in the copious living space – arty, tasteful, strictly no gaudy. Warm exposed bricks, beams, muted greyish green paint, abstract prints, a pub settle, a fireplace where two sculpted busts faced each other and an outsize failed cylinder of an earthenware vase held the white bouquet which had touched Freya with its goodwill.

'I'll turn the light on so we can see the tulips . . . get the best of them while they last.' Freya started to stand, pushing back the bench, intending to walk round the table.

Imo said: 'It's all right . . . I'll get it.' She skipped the pace from her chair to the cavernous fireplace, casually, unthinkingly, and smoothly led by manual memory, reached into it and with a single gesture of self-betrayal found the occluded switch, illumined the vase and busts and turned – palm outstretched presenting the flowers, tiddly om pom pom – to see Freya's face blood-drained white with the shock of recognition, the hatred of realisation, the shame of adulterous humiliation.

Imo muttered 'whoops' under her breath. She knew she had been rumbled, fingers in the till, flagrante delicto. She nonetheless feigned puzzlement, pointlessly, she knew they both knew, wishing all the while she could undo the last few days – then reconsidering, assailed by flashes of slapping flesh, full fulfilment, gouts of sweat, appreciative laughter and saying 'Oh poor Trevo having to make do with mere photos when you get the real thing'.

What is 'the form' when this happens? Me Old Mum and The Sergeant couldn't agree. It's an everyday occurrence, all over the world. Reaction varies culture to culture. England is one big mystery. Example: No proper patriotic nationalistic national poet, not like our Adam Mickiewicz and Kristijonas Donelaitis. No proper constitution so it relies on gristle-stew of custom, practice, tradition. They add up to 'the form', so far as I can see. Behaviour is dictated according to which is your rung on the ladder of destiny.

Maybe Freya muttered back: 'Whore.' Stretch that vowel. Or maybe she hissed: 'Bitchhh.' Maybe she looked daggers at Imo, venomous daggers, strutted from the room without a word, for words would make a link, no matter how hostile, between the two of them. Maybe she flung a glass at Imo, it smashed against the black iron spit: the shards reform, she holds the glass steady as a statue of contempt. Maybe she sat, glaring. Maybe she went to his office to scream at Roger who was yet unaware of what had happened during a matter of seconds, yet to learn that the world had tilted and he was one of the three who had slid off the edge into a state of imbalance.

Even though he had built most of it himself he did not hesitate to walk out of his home. It shifted in his conception from being a life's work to a former life's work.

Freya – hair ever wilder, ever more matted, dull as curry powder – expressed her fury by printing and magnifying Imo's unfavourable reviews and pasting them on walls throughout Chute Ducis. She encouraged anyone whom she met to join her in abusing Imo – stuck up, wanton, can't act, man-thief, false friend, a skin short of a Rizla pack. In magazines like *Nova*, *Deluxe*, *Boulevard* and *Troubadour* she found old interviews with titles such as 'My Tragic Taste In Men', 'Skye's The Limit', 'Bachelor Girl With No Regrets', 'I Wish I'd Kept My Baby'. Freya gleefully paid over the odds for brittle old copies of *Lui*, *QT*, *Knave*, *Okay*, *Ciao*, *Candid*, *Peep-Peep*, *Classy Keen* and *Caper* for which Imo had posed like a WAAC showing she'd be pleased to meet you, as The Sergeant put it. The town was plastered with the evidence of Freya's fishwifery. Imo seldom ventured out of her ouvrier cottage to hear the snides whispering while the small boys compared gynaecological notes. When she did, her garb – oriental low pay chic including coolie hat or fake leopard coat and hat – proved an ineffective disguise. She would have liked to venture more but she was terrified of Freya who – I have forgotten to mention this – was six inches taller with muscles developed by her craft, by archaeological digs. She was especially terrified of encountering Freya at night. There was no mistaking Freya's mood. Her work had turned from the serene to the farouche. Volcanic glazes and angry crater glazes, monochrome, roughly shaped, primitivist. Neo-Expressionist, it was suggested. Neo-Pissed-Off-With-That-Treacherous-Cowist, she corrected.

Imo wanted to escape from the house. It would have been escape from Roger. Implanted. Embedded. Uninvited. Unwelcome. The man who came to stay. The man she hadn't the heart to expel because she was the very cause of an unprecedented rupture. She didn't suspect how greedily delighted he was to have chanced on a way out of a dull stagnant marriage, out of a house whose creation had for years fulfilled his need for a project outside academe and writing popular history: planning, process and teaching himself several skills had been all. Once finished, however, it was evidently not finished. It perpetually demanded attention, repair, upkeep. A complex house is an exacting taskmaster, a machine to be serviced daily. He had thought on and off of writing a book about the arts and crafts with an emphasis on the crafts: brick bonds, joints, glass blowing, pargeting. But it would be a burden, it would be no more than a proxy for his spadework.

He was surprised how comfortable he felt in Imo's artless shrine to herself, to a life largely unedited. Theatrical posters, film posters – among them Georges Franju's *Chantage*, the title in ransom-note typography. Her sole scene had, to the director's fury, been cut by the producer – it impeded the narrative.[45] There were lobby cards, photos, favourable reviews, not entirely hostile reviews, magazine advertisements (Gee Whizz, Rolls Razor washing machines, Cyril Lawn) were everywhere displayed in peeling baroque gold leaf frames beside masks, break-a-leg/Scottish-play telegrams and letters pinned to a corkboard. It was a *Who's Who In The Theatre* biography in an extra dimension of dust, foxing, dampstains, sunbleaching, tears. An Eric Paice Award statuette for Best Supporting Comedy Role (Mouthy Denise in *It's Alright For Some*) was used as a doorstop to demonstrate that such trifles were to be treated with ostentatious disdain. A twice life-size cut-out of Imo dominated the staircase. An

---

45 'I despise narrative.' Franju to Jacques Doniol-Valcroze: *Bulletin de l'IDHEC*, Septembre 1957.

entire room was devoted to her wardrobe. Fifteen shelves were devoted to shoes. The walls of the main bedroom were covered by photos that were sensual or pornographic according to the size of the mind whose eyes beheld them. He took smug pride in having both the mere photos and the real thing. He toyed with the idea that the photos *were* the real thing, a stimulus for callers whose cynosure was the distant Imo of decades long past when the world's palette shifted from monochrome's hard-edge eroticism to the cosiness of pink, pastels, Kodachrome, Agfa and, where the emulsion contracts leaving white patches on flesh, the appearance of vitiligo.

Imo was chucking frenziedly. She arrived home after two days in London. Roger, driven by sloth, sat quietly as she hurled books, china, a table lamp and a stool. Chairs collided with walls and doors. She screamed repetitively: 'You do not ask – ask! command! – you do not order an actor of Imogen Skye's stature to read for Girl Friday in some manky *Robinson Crusoe* in some manky theatre in some manky dump like Loughborough. It makes Imogen Skye want to fucking kill herself.'

'Don't be silly, you're only saying that—'

'As a matter of fact Roger I'm not . . . *only saying that* . . . I'm not . . . What makes you think I'm not in fucking earnest . . . Jack . . . poor Jack Lavery topped himself . . .'

Roger shrugged. Yet another name world famous in his own kitchen – with a gas oven, no doubt.

'I'm fucking sick of . . . they got me there on entirely false pretences . . . Loughborough . . . I'm going to strangle that arsehole George . . . calls himself an agent!'

This wasn't how she presented her dilemma to Dream Topping™. If you are not in the 'profession' it's hard to understand the levels of humiliation (intended or not), the covert insults, the bias against age, the misogyny, the impudence of young men reinventing the wheel.

Of course she talked reluctantly about having once had a choice between Girl Friday at Loughborough and Maid Marion at Redcar when all she was good for, due to the deficiencies of a rival provider, was Long John Silver at Hornchurch. It was, she cried choking and tearful, all she'd ever be good for . . .

Beyond these causes, however, she cited 'private reasons': inability to stop snoring like a Marcher Hound and making the house shake; failed marriages (quantity undisclosed); failed relationships with lovers of both sexes (ditto); unwillingness to repent for breaking up friends' marriages (ditto); resentment that a 'boy I taught everything to *absolutely everything* has become Israeli TV's top star but refuses to put me on his show . . . won't even acknowledge my existence: without me he'd still be plain David Goldenberg'; exacerbating the guilt about the psychic harm inflicted on her former friend Freya by deriving so little satisfaction from her affair with the former friend's husband. Was it worth it? No. But having instigated it she felt trapped in a way that she never had before. She could not reconcile herself to her gaucheness and naivete. Her behaviour was at odds with her conception of herself. She was not who she wanted to be. She could no longer bend herself to be that person. She took a short cut to redemption.

It's bad form (that again) to slag so-called rivals but You Own Yourself's negligence and interpersonal recklessness beggars belief. They are a disgrace to the vocation. If there was a responsible professional body like the British Meat Processors Association or the Chartered Institute of Phrenologists they would be struck off but there isn't because we operate in an area as grey and greasy as crematorium ash gleaming with petrol and so they won't be. Their solace-time preparations are prescribed according to body weight. This is normal practice, scientific as well as extra-ethical. Like many vain persons, mainly but not exclusively ladies, Imo had lied about her weight, subtracting several kilos then subtracting more. It was one of the many fibs that came automatically to her. You Own Yourself did not, as they ought to have, question the information she disclosed. Consequently she was provided with kit for a woman about two-thirds of her size.

She did not die. Roger was in the Isles of Scilly for research. She wished she cared for him as much as he seemed to care for her. It wasn't enough. Day after day she tried to accept that she would soon, very soon, be too old for anything but character roles which meant dissembling her looks and plumping up or minx-of-a-certain-age roles which meant reshaping her looks to compete in the Botox stakes with a face that resembled a thousand others.

She did it pat. Her will was strong. There was no agitation, no catatonia, just a void which may be black, a noise in one ear ... a book's pages being flicked over rapidly by a machine without end? A stick dragged along a clinker-built fence? Then she was in another stage of existence or non-existence which was a white room.

She had collapsed in a coma. Circulation to her right foot was cut off. Several days had passed before she was found by Trevo, booked in to fix a shuddering pipe. No reply the first time he visited. No reply when he phoned. When he dropped by again he noticed that lights were on in the bright afternoon. His bucolic extra alert senses alerted him. He clambered over the wall at the end of the garden. He stumbled in shrubs. He crushed a ceanothus, he broke a pot, he banged on the back door as he had on the front. He forced it. His eye was caught by her monuments to herself. She lay on a recamier behind a scrapscreen of her ingenue self and Trevo's 'alcyon days. Such sweet memories. A broken-spined copy of Roger's *French Ways: The Life and Cadettes of Mrs Baxter Monk-Mullinger* was propped against one of the bed's legs. She was still breathing, a faint rasp. She hadn't eaten for days. She was dehydrated. It was almost too late. He had a pretty good idea what a foot which might have been smeared with damp charcoal meant. He called an ambulance. While waiting for it to come he tried mouth to mouth resuscitation with tongues. Because she was annoyingly unresponsive he went wandering, rummaging. He found a chest of drawers dedicated to lingerie. Esprit d'Endoume stockings, Dream Tupping suspender belts, Hector Beausoleil strings. He pocketed as much as his pockets and eager toolbox would decently allow.

'That foot ... black as a fuckstar of colour's dong ... ooohf weren't 'alf whiffy.' Trevo was wearing his fun T-shirt printed with the head of a rooster and the legend *Have You Seen My Cock? ? !!* He was down The Tap with his fellow campanologists Dobbo and Kevo. He continued: 'On the other 'and – what's that smell of sweet perfume, lads ... I got you a souvenir thong each ... plus a special one for Mitcho when he shows up. He's an open crotch man ... common as empty wigs.'

Gangrene had set in. Post-coma and floatingly sedated she laughed when she was advised that the only solution was amputation. Thereafter all the length of her days she repeated to herself and anyone who'd listen the litany 'Death goes dogging everywhere'. She lumbered clumsily with a clumpy crutch from a props store. Hence the not invariably friendly remarks that she was made for the role of Long John Silver, a natural. A shoo-in, it was said down The Tap where a pun earns you another sleever of Craft. Her days were swifter than a post; they flee away.

'She looked so amazing in shoes . . . It's such a terrible pity. Shoes really were her thing. She had over fifty pairs of heels,' said Roger.

Some months later she was determined not to fail. She had buried the external reasons why she had yearned to take the path to Dreamopolis. Now, taking the path was itself the reason. She needed to take the path to prove that she could do it, to prove she had the courage to move from 'she' and 'her' to 'it' and 'its', from something to the possibility of nothing, someone to no one.

She wisely changed provider to Dream Topping™ Proudly Partnering Venture Doseology™. 100 per cent accurate. This time there was no mistake. Not anyway until the inquest, which returned an open verdict – a deliberate insult to Imo's wilful determination and, equally, to Dream Topping™. Taps For Ever is not a crime yet here was some pipsqueak coroner demanding a criminal standard of proof be applied rather than the balance of probabilities. Taps For Ever is not a crime but it is still called self-murder, a term which is meaningless and moralistic. Self? Maybe. Murder? No, totally not. As my life journey demonstrates there are many selves, selves within selves which succeed each other, but do not obliterate each other, piling up. We grow many fluctuating selves, they share space. Murder demands a cast of at least two: the unwilling victim and the other(s), the perpetrator(s). Separate entities. Nothing could be further from the monolithic indivisibility of the being and the being's putting the end to its being. They are in perfect concord. The shot/the strike/the stroke is the player. The final breath is the summation of all previous breaths – it is caused by the breath's owner and Dream Topping™ working on behalf of the owner. It differs only from its millions of

733

predecessor breaths in its finality. Who knows whether it has successors in the empire of the lungless.

'She brought it on herself.'

It was meant as a put-down. But just ignore the gossips' venom. It is bang on accurate reflecting well on both Imo and her travel beacons here at Dream Topping™. There was no 'character development' as they call it. That's a delusion learnt from duff stories. She went from one Imo to the next Imo in a blink.

The funeral (humanist, in rainy woodland: readings from Liz Loodmer, Jenner Vavra and Erskine Garn by Erskine himself) was not that badly attended. It wasn't the weather for a fun funeral. The train service is a disgrace. They never clean the windows. Once off the motorway the roads are slow. Many of her friends were in rehab. A dozen patients at Clinic Nilsson-Gothenburg hired a Dream Topping™ partnered Poppy Tours minibus with driver, Stan The Wheels. Sad to say, because they were ahead of schedule and didn't want to arrive early, they stopped at a pub to kill time. They were still there at closing time. They didn't make it to the ceremony.

I led the mourners. Funerals are for relatives and friends. Barrows, graves and whatsits lend the gravity, solemnity. Funeral is second baptism. The baptised baby doesn't know what's going on. Nor does the deceased probably. I met some of the good folk of Ducis. Including a nearby aristo! What a gent! He just reeked of money and privilege. Very la-di-da. He had fond memories of Imo. The legendary Belgian baker of daytime TV fame Maxim Coolmans seemed genuinely upset by Imo's moving along but managed to joke that her brioche will never fail to rise again. The reception was in his café. His daughter Tabitha of thriller-writing fame apparently, though she looked too young, was a hoity toity haughty miss no mistake and her detective's buddy apparently was a sociopath Marcher Hound. She was a questing busybody prying into the Dream Topping™ Philosophy. And talk about an acid tongue! She called Milord the aristo an 'oily old facho', 'a grubby old lecher', his skin was 'the colour of Oxford marmalade', she remembered him from way back when he was her hairdresser's lover. The hairdresser chargrilled one of her clients' hair with straightening irons and hairspray – I think I've got that right. Tabitha was very smart in a purple suit with orange cuffs and lapels.

She had followed the request not to dress gloomy. The mourners had too, with one exception, a man dressed for a funeral in a white shirt, black suit and tie with the most profoundly shimmering black hair, black as black gold. He was deep in conversation with Tabitha for some while. I got a teensy feeling they were talking about the aristo. It was like a business meeting. The funeral was a rendezvous for them . . . Could that be? I felt I had seen him before. I couldn't place him. Suddenly he was beside me.

'Have we met . . . I'm trying to place you . . . Where? I'm—'

'Vera . . . We encountered each other . . . many years ago . . . it seems only yesterday . . . we talked about O-D-S – you got it right – ods. Clever call.'

A bolt of chill targeted my spine. He realised. He shook his head with a slightly proprietorial smile.

'Keine sorge . . . We should talk about it some more sometime.'

'Should we—?'

'I'll be in touch. A pleasure . . . to have met you . . . again . . . a real pleasure . . . I told you it'd be at a wake . . .'

'You are who?'

But he had dematerialised, leaving just the negative of his strange humanish face and the echo of his strange dry voice and the puzzle of him looking exactly the same as he had many years before save for the hair – just as profoundly black but slightly longer. I returned to my social duties, unsettled.

Roger was awkward playing the part of Imo's last love. He didn't know 'the form'. He was confused. When Imo's niece Eunice Pethica hugged him he asked her why she was doing so.

'Sympathy,' she said. 'Solidarity.'

'Oh *that*!'

He wanted to be elsewhere. That was obvious. Kept taking off and putting on his glasses. Some deep neurosis there. Couldn't string three words together. Shock. Moved among the guests like a stumbling helpless ghost. Distracted. We get used to these behaviours. He's a bookwriter; there's no need in that line for small talk. You don't need to be a people person to sit alone filling a blank page/screen with nasty fantasies all day long.

A trampwoman, all dishevelled and gone to grime, was watching from under her dripping hood under a dripping tree on the river bank down from the bridge. She was swigging from a trampflask, clearly in need of a healing leader with a blanket to assist reprocessing and sensitisation. Failing that, Dream Topping™ is always available. Be clear – we do not advertise. We work by word of mouth beneath the radar, door to door for that personal touch as pioneered by Frankly Sam offering the key to the Palace of Nembutal or a one-way ticket to the Distillery of Discovery.

Roger didn't see her. Or he saw her and made no sign of recognition let alone greeting. This was the woman who phoned him constantly. He didn't pick up. She sent notes and emails. She banged on the door. She broke windows with stones. Did Roger's brain process what his eyes saw? He didn't acknowledge that this was the woman he had been married to for twenty years. She might have been an anonymous vagrant. To him she *was* an anonymous vagrant. We all know that we do not recognise vagrants as anything other than vagrants – a type, not individuals, non-people with an outstretched hand, vicious low-quality mongrel bitches with future killers at the teat, a tale of multiple misfortunes and uncontrollable events. All tramps look the same. All tramps have the same sleeping bag, the same sore, the same flea, the same itch, the same pitch beside hot air extractors.

'Bad place to be in this weather,' was all he remarked.

'That's Roger's wife,' Pilates Matt said, 'she's absconded to Golden Posture . . . Know why? . . . it was my place where she met Imo – absurd . . . she really wants Roger back . . . but . . .'

But Roger preferred to live with Imo's ghost, to commune with her. 'He's got taste,' said Leonie Vane, one of the few co-stars to attend. 'Imo dead is more vibrant than most people alive . . . living *creatures* . . . she was fun fun fun.'

Every morning he laid out clothes and shoes for her after discussing what she wanted to do that day, the weather forecast, her mood. Sometimes he added a wig. He made lapsang tea, served her low-fat yogurt which he told her was not past its use-by, said he must get on with his work. At lunchtime he cleared away her breakfast, putting aside the yogurt for the next day. He told her how many words he had written. He sometimes read to her, laptop beside his ham sand-wich or sardines straight from the can or cheese and crackers, spraying crumbs when he laughed at what he had written and apologising to her. For supper he decreed that they should seldom eat meat. Life could not have been less demanding or more productive. He could picture her with a literality and detail that almost scared him. He could feel her swaying, hear her singing 'Love Letters' into a cocktail glass held like a microphone. They walked along the path beside the river. He carried a torch so that she could avoid puddles and roots. He had never felt so loved. He had never felt such love for another person.

Imo, against our advice, never found time to draw up a will. She voyaged intestate. Her niece Eunice Pethica inherited the little house and a burdensome tax bill. The house would have to be sold. She anticipated problems with Roger. There were none. He told her that he would take Imo with him wherever he might go. Some years later we heard that Freya had married again. Neither his agent nor his publisher would disclose Roger's address. Someone said that after several years moving between cheap rentals and no-star hotels in northern Europe he had settled close to the Belgian border with the Netherlands. He had bought a bungalow among dunes, lagoons and marram grass. He spent many hours with binoculars clutched to his face watching seals and container vessels trafficking drugs and chil-dren. He rejoiced in the limitless greyness of the German Ocean.

DREAM TOPPING™: MISSION REFLECTIONS ON PHILOSOPHY AND PRACTICES BY VERA DOGG WITH DR DARREN CLENT

Death is a human invention. Other species have little conception of it. Death doesn't happen to them. They know nothing of nitrous oxide. They may suffer a changed state of being but they don't live a life in the knowledge of what's coming to them. They don't live in fearful anticipation of it. They live exclusively in the present. The idea of tenses – has been, was, is, will be – is unknown to them. The very idea of an idea is unknown to them. In a sunset home the sun never sets, but nor does it rise. The demented are fed atropine and stramonium which annul senility, the point of view from which the past looks like the past. Both point of view and object viewed are annulled. The past is the greatest source of regrets. The drugs impair motor skills. Control over lachrymatory glands and the bowels is lost. The sufferer doesn't realise that coordination becomes frail. Falls are frequent, their cause a mystery. Amnesia is aggravated rather than enhanced. Unable to recall who they are, where they are, they invent ever succeeding presents in a parody of life.

It is humans' burden that they are aware of the past, of their own past, of the future which may be measured in decades or seconds. Their own past and the weight of the present may presage a future they wish to negotiate in a fresh form. As autonomous creatures they may elect to discover that form. It is not only the terminally ill – in unbearable pain, feeling they've overstayed their welcome, aware of their infantile dependence and mutation into a dysfunctional machine – who should copy the Ammassalik and paddle their kayak into the midnight sun. We have free will. If the future looks like a daunting slag heap that will slide and bury us, why not make a dash for it. Olivier Sadirac's *L'esprit du Terril* is an anthem to the relief that escape from the environs of the slag heap can bring. It is a literal manifestation of the darkness which subsumes those who fail to find the courage to sign off.

Bespoke and Creative. These are two of our watchwords. Here they are cleaving together, in action, a multifaceted alloy of imagination, audacity and chainmailed fist clasping chainmailed fist to forge into strength greater than the sum of its parts. If you're old enough to vote, to marry, to hold a driving licence you're old enough to choose your own mysterious destination. Which is your personal destination. No two Recipients share the same experience: we'll meet again? Who can tell. Post-Stage-One state of being is no more uniform than Stage-One state of being. We have reason to believe that the next stop is as rich and vibrantly diverse as The Place You're Leaving – but happier, much happier. Think dappled glades, gently murmuring streams and dulcet songbirds. But don't think too literally. And evacuate before prosecution of The Shift: it's a kindness to the pathologist whom you'll never meet, probably, unless the screen between states is frail due to meteorological exceptionalities.

Let us present a truly iconic relocation. The long-practised means of making The Shift are indeed to be honoured, respected, revered: they would not be long-practised were they anything other than fit for purpose. They are invested with multiple purposes. They are, however, not the only ways. To certain clients they may present as being 'off the peg', 'one size fits all', even 'old hat'. Why do so many vegans choose Dream Topping™? As vegans they have experienced discrimination, mockery, name calling . . . the entire gamut of dietist prejudice. They are often loath to adopt Ausgang Stratagen favoured by carnivores simply because it is favoured by carnivores.

Leaf Coneybear and Shaun Hare were vegan hog rights activists who had twice attempted arson at laboratories where vivisections were performed. They had twice been arrested: security at such installations is everywhere, and effective. Both had served jail sentences.

At Wormwood Hill, an ethically squalid, physically squalid factory farm close by a motorway service station, pigs are bred to provide spare parts for humans.

Piglets are separated from their mother a few days after they are born. The sow is then impregnated again. This cycle may continue for up to five years. It goes without saying that we have every sympathy for these poor sows. I have no difficulty in identifying with them. Leaf and Shaun felt waves of cosmic guilt and shame at man's and woman's cruelty towards pigs, lovely intelligent beasts capable of learning to play shove ha'penny, switch on the telly, root for truffles, help about the house and go walkies like in Rops's painting of a naked woman in a blindfold being led to orgiastic adventure or zoophiliac party by a faithful Middle White.

Compared with a laboratory a factory farm is a soft target. The softest of all was one of Wormwood Hill's fields which could be seen from the motorway. It was a deceptive advertisement suggesting that the farm's pigs were treated humanely. The majority of the farm's stock, over a thousand pigs, was hidden away, imprisoned in sheds, subsisting in tiny crates which allow no movement, while forty or fifty show pigs, Large Blacks, gambolled in the tufty field. They wallowed in the churned mud. It dried on them. Then they were two-tone pigs, black and rich reddish. They were a high-spirited team grunting and running as if they were enjoying a game of tag. They did not spare themselves, the boars charged each other head on with ill-willed violence and tusker's viciousness. They mounted sows who shrugged unimpressed. They ate their young and mangelwurzels. They chewed metal troughs and water butts. They played to their audience of nose to tail tailbacks and drivetime favourite snarlups in the contraflow without end: they saved their best for 16.00–17.50 on Fridays. Their inner clocks told them when to take to the stage. This was the time that Leaf and Shaun chose for their sacrifice. Dream Topping™ prepped them in a copse on the other side of the motorway. There was a time lag on the temporary traffic lights to allow for stragglers. A minute or more with an infinite tailback in one direction and no traffic in the other.

We dosed them with N-Joy and Carfentanil. The former a synapse busting hallucinogen that plays fast and loose with neurotransmitters and invites a zoo into your head, the latter a painkiller capable of making the entire zoo go sleepybyes but more frequently prescribed by doctors to render old folk insensible to cold in winter: they may suffer hypothermia but they don't feel it, not even when their extremities are bruise-blue and their nails are falling out.

Leaf and Shaun took off their clothes: we were to donate them to Simians Feel The Cold Too. They kissed us, hugged us. They clambered over the metal barrier, walked across the hard shoulder and skipped hand in hand over the empty nearside carriageway then weaved their way between the stalled vehicles heading south to the sounds of parping horns and a wag's 'Get them on!' And then they were away, turning to wave goodbye, jumping over a ditch, running up the slope to meet the pigs to whom they would feed themselves in a passionately planned Dream Topping™ act of expiation that was recorded on scores of mobile phones and caused further traffic chaos not to mention great publicity. The CMPG arrived in a flurry of sirens, lights, hi-vis vests and self-importance. Whatever offence had been committed was not on the motorway so it was outside their jurisdiction. Besides, by then, the pigs were enjoying a festive frenzy. The damage done to their kin was being bloodily absolved, according to The Sergeant and his dashing captain's telescope (a souvenir of Hamburg when our love was young). He kept up a commemorative commentary which celebrated Leaf and Shaun even as they were still being speed-gnawed and taking the righteous road into the Fields of Justice. Bless them!

To die for Ramalama. Within Dream Topping™ we have discussed long and hard the Separate Airlines For Lals. No one wants to be part of their selfish suicide, no one wants to be collateral. Your own end in your own time – that's the Dream Topping™ way.

Aspirant suicide bombers must be counselled. For their own sake they must be reminded that glory is a once in a life/once in a death occasion. Even with Ramalama's blessing and bung they cannot, however much they might wish it, become Repeat Offender suicide bombers. They can become role models for future suicide bombers. We produce pro-quality videos in finest HD. Hair and make-up. A product your loved ones will cherish. Technical and presentational training. It is a matter of regret that at the BBC's Annual Martyrdom awards the winner cannot be present to collect the prize – an installation of body parts, ball bearings, ripped texts, nails.

If 'life' is inadequate, turning on you spitefully, failing to fulfil expectations and furnish essential needs then why not pack up your troubles in your old kitbag and take that path over the hills and far away to a place where you can validify a new approach to personally bespoke healthcaring: your choice of site and of the wellwishers to bid you bon voyage is of utmost importance.

A familiar mentholated environment with plumped pillows steeped in jasmine or basil oil is an ever popular choice. But so too is the Backwoodsman Trekahoy where the seeker, eating nothing and hungered, often suffering dementia, is released in her/his final days into Mother Nature's capricious clasp, there to meet such companions as the devil, bears, rewilded venomous snakes, wolves, bearded AK47 hickfolks with fishing grenades, prisoners on the run and the challenges of falling timber, poisonous fungi, thirst, blinding sandstorms, mantraps, floods. (Certain of these unavailable in UK.) The client is invited to select psychotropics which are a channel to past positives, should there have been any (which is, ipso facto, unlikely) or opioids which enhance anticipation by aggravating amnesia, inducing aphasia, impairing motor skills and prompting slapstick coordination – again, the client is unaware of the Trekahoy *present* as anything more than a notion. Hallucinations of animals, for instance, may be indistinguishable from 'actual' animals, especially those which have been genetically amended or gaudily dyed before rewilding. There are no such states as primary reality, secondary, tertiary – they all belong to the same spatial and achronical plane, like a painting before perspective misled us into the fictions of foreground, middle ground, background, disappearing points and so on. It taught us to see wrongly.

For those who sense that The Own Goal is not definitive (the linesman or VAR may rule it out!) cremation is not advised. It can impair trips down The Hippocampus. It doesn't help with revisits, taunting and haunting and the pleasurable task of bringing terror to those who have driven you to opt out of this 'life'. A couple of kilos of ashes is an ineffective weapon compared with a grave-fresh skeleton ornamented with strands of rodent-gnawed flesh, rotten organ meat, funeral-best togs all shreds and mildew.

A dog buries its bones then it exhumes them. We too can be buried then dug up with the help of Man's Best Friend sniffing and burrowing. A burial is not forever. It is provisional. Flexibility is the key here.

When the body has been cremated the border between Livion and Oblivion is strict, tangible and visible. When the body has been buried that border is disputed. It is not rigorously defined. It shifts. We come and go from one state to the other.

Time capsules and exhumation reveal the past's secrets. Lack of burial is posthumous indignity. Burial is not permanent.

Christ was not buried in order that he might return from time to time to see how things were going. Obviously he has to return. It's his self-imposed duty. Maybe god-imposed. And when he does return it's *en catimini*, in the guise of someone ordinary and not liable to be noticed. Man, woman, child. He shifts between genders. There are only two – got that? And between colours, many of them – and welcome to you all. That way he won't be mobbed and dished up as body and blood. So he may have been back often, incognito, playing darts, riding in the pampas, working as a stage hand or short order cook . . . We don't know. Very likely never shall. He has the good sense not to boast about his special status.

The history of Dream Topping Healthcaring™ is not all peaks. There was a big trough, they dig it so big it might be a grave that an Einsatzgruppen made prisoners dig for themselves before they were shot in the back of the head and pushed in by the ones that hadn't been shot in the back of the head yet. So big this trough, it could have diverted us from our mission. Almost did.

The Reverend Ursula Bonbernard was the cause. A wicked woman – it goes with the job. You could see it in her flour-white face. Drapes of hanging fat yet all sharp angles, the devil in a wood-cut from out of the old days. Her evil hair stood a foot high, a wire mitre covered in moss. Children ran away when they saw her. She attracted fanatic disciples: Osmund Kenthwaite, Daniele Cup, Yunus Bungay, Barbara Gammack were the most notorious among Ursula Bonbernard's Terrorists in WAAF (War Against Abortion & Foeticide). Its propaganda was full of photographs of World War II women's auxiliary air crew cuddling bonny babes begat by valiant pilots between missions to firebomb. They were the most pious self-publicists. Cause-whores I call them. There is no other word for them – well, apart from terrorists, killers, self-righteous hypocrites. Deaf to argument, to the needs of others. They were above all laws but god's laws which they made up in his name.

There was no abortion clinic in the land they had not molotoved, defaced with red paint, called the emergency services to on false pretences in order to attack them as accomplices. WAAF carbombed and firebombed. It had murdered doctors, the children of doctors, the friends of children of doctors, the neighbours of nurses, persons whose name was the same as that of a 'culpable' receptionist or laundry worker or delivery driver (wrong place, wrong time). Its inability to get house numbers and registration plates correct indicates its stupidity. It was approved by the cretinous scion of slavers and mine owners Mogg ap Mogg. 'Not even when they've been raped' was his chivalrous catchphrase. He inadvertently demonstrated the favour done to cretins if they are aborted, as he should have been, in order not to beget further cretinism, as he has.

Ursula Bonbernard's vigilantes were called The Life-Squads. Murder, maiming, arson, GBH, threats . . . they all failed to cancel the female determination to control her own body, a right that has existed for many millennia and is not to be relinquished to Christian thuggery and sanctimony, priests, 'believers'. Because they are victims of Ursula Bonbernard's ideology (as false as every other ideology), the vigilantes do not realise that the body is a machine, no more or less, nor that the impingement of religion is insolent, presumptuous bad manners. Whatever has it got to do with god? Especially when the virgin they never stop going on about lived in a state of shame. She had been raped by the Almighty disguised as a dove. She aborted the son of god.

That's what they don't tell you.

The long-haired messiah and miracle worker was a team of impostors, each with a speciality: crucifixion, mass catering, raising the dead, cures, ascension, fasts etc. All learnt in marketplace circuses and carnivals, as touring mountebanks, saltimbanques, tricksters.

They say The Life-Squads reported to Ursula Bonbernard that there existed in clinics' operation wastebins living abortions. Survivors. They were ready for incineration unmurdered by Apollyon's white-coats, held up as proof that life begins immediately the roughrider splits or the train hurtles on through Fratton. The squads were instructed to gather the tiny embryos, feed them in vitro, prescribe a holistic diet, build them up with lacto-amniosis. This gave them the chance they had never had.

They live with recovery animals. Cradles, hypodermic syringes, high chairs, teddy bears and light arms are scaled appropriately. They are taught about the natural wonders of the natural world with an emphasis on childbirth. Ursula Bonbernard's Multi Ecumenical Madrassa brainwashes them. It teaches them to kill like midget stormtroops, to sacrifice themselves as micro suicide bombers. They were trained as mini-warriors to attack the clinics where their mothers had denied their existence.

Brought back to blood life they were given a cause to die for. Here they come, creatures from the Palaeozoic haunting en masse, swaying as one like starlings of the sea, crawling and slipping, gelatinous and slimy, slithering muscleless like hunter-lampreys, voracious for a host to attach to and leech the life from. They're swarming seething all across the park at Hemlock Lawns, croaking faintly. The potential victims, the clinic's staff, cannot understand what they are seeing. They can't figure what this army crawling on its belly is. Killer tapioca tooled up hungry for revenge, set on destruction. It was personal. Couldn't be more personal. A commune of the aborted, all of them disabled, all of them fanaticised and ready to die because they knew nothing beyond the subsistence as Glass Foundlings.

This was Ursula Bonbernard's dream fulfilled. How can it have been made up? Everyone knows that her next obsessional campaign would have destroyed Dream Topping™. She planned to kidnap clients seeking The Hidden Doorway in order to keep them alive and to 're-educate' them, denying them the death they crave no matter what psychic pain they're in, no matter what cancer they might be suffering, no matter what twisted thread in the head implores them to murder: it is for the sake of their fellows and family that they want to find the Doorway.

Humans, uniquely, have the ability to Live Death To The Full, to wittingly Exchange Breath For Death. Embrace a vibrant death, an almost still beating death (but not quite, no). Enjoy an iconically iconic passing.

But do not expect too much. We can't all be top of the bill. Each has his or her place. Sometimes that place is at home in the bosom of the family. Take the Fifth Horseman of the Apocalypse: he didn't want to come out that day, he preferred to stay at home and enjoy some quality time with the wife and kids, maybe do a few odd jobs around the house.

Just because you're born in a stable you aren't going to become the saviour of mankind. But you are in with a very slight chance of winning the Derby and a better chance of being placed in a field of three in the 3.30 at Market Rasen.

It's possible that's what relocation to Dreamopolis is like. Not the groaning hurdy-gurdy and hurtling roller-coaster that exposure to daily psychotropics has promised but something quieter, more serene. Dreamopolis is not rowdy but dignified – Breughel's tower. A gentle place with murmuring fruit and the scents of that kingdom, not this. Elect Dreamopolis or Smotherland or The Last Pillow Talk. A Cushioned Ending, maybe? Last Bites (unfragranced 'like spring water'). Last Rights (the call to self-determination). Happy Finish. New Life. Change Without End. Total Option. The Choice Is Yours. Resolution. It's not the end, but a new beginning. Long anaesthesia – as if the anaesthetist has gone on holiday forgetting to check the patient in the theatre.

Shopping at the historic listed cast-iron masterpiece covered market (stained glass by the Idyllic Brotherhood). I was with Me Old Mum. She was stocking up on butter and honey. Me: it was meat balls and faggots from the Heaven's Pasture Farms stall. Try as I may I can't make them as good.

'What's the secret?' I always ask and Nephew would always reply with a finger to his nose and 'If you could make 'em so tasty as us do, you wouldn't have no reason to come and see us . . . we'd miss that.' Then he'd add a couple extra or a nice thick slice of haslet and I'd blow him a kiss and be on my way.

On my way straight into the path of the man with black as black gold hair from Imo's funeral . . . the man from my distant past I owed a great debt of gratitude to . . . who claimed he knew we'd meet at a wake . . . he was dressed as he had been at the funeral, white shirt, black suit and tie . . . like he was prepared for another death, another mourning.

He nodded as though he had arranged to meet me. Then he screwed up his face: 'Pork. You're carrying pork.' He made it sound like a criminal act. Charming, I thought.

Then there was a tiny hint of humanity about him and he said with a malicious smile: 'King rabbit.'

He was a strange presence. But not strange in an obviously threatening way. More a cosmically puzzling way, otherworldly, like he was an imposter, one of those full-scale dummies you used to see in men's outfitters' windows come to life, more or less.

'I would like to ask you a professional favour. This is my card. Please call me.'

And he was gone as quick as magic, waving his right arm high as a goodbye sign he smoothed away, not looking back, rudely.

'That,' said Me Old Mum hobbling towards me, 'that . . . I'm all but certain . . . that was the one that went for Davy Jones's Locker Option . . . but total amateur . . . no no not in a river that's only ten foot deep . . . Abbey Gardens . . . Remember . . . Rescued by meddling kids . . . Oh what was his name . . . Chris . . . Chris . . . Chris Lapatu . . . that was it.'

'He gave me his card.' I got it out of my purse. 'Chris . . . No . . . no, he's called Patric Laush. If that's how you pronounce it? Lorsh? Lowsh?'

I handed the card to her.

'Well, I'd swear on the fountain at Thanatos Strand he said his name was Chris Lapatu. Made me think of the old Eskimo. Snacking on living seals as he paddles his last kayak towards the curvature of the earth.'

Patric Laush was in an ordinary place, colourless and fairly silent, typical weather, not worth a second glance.

He said: 'Bad days, bad years . . . I am curious to understand what it is to be like every other person . . . I wish to shed a load of lexicon from my brain . . . the tics which weigh down my skull . . . words not to utter . . . thoughts that must remain unthought . . . the measures of time: never, forever, without end, perpetual etc.

'Also dump these: prison, straitjacket, irreversible, weary, cyclical, nothing new under the sun, already seen, already heard, already smelled, already tasted, foreseen so foretold. And eternal return. Especially that.

'But it is not even within the bounds of hope. It's my fate to be unwilling to accept my fate. I turn away, which is cowardly. It is an admission that I cannot contend with reality. This is common enough I know . . . So I repeat to myself that there is no reality. When of course there is *my* reality – and on the other hand everyone else's reality, that is everyone, without exception. My condition was caused by a fleeting encounter long long ago, in different days, different times. It makes me unique – that's a truth, not a boast. For everyone else death is not postponable no matter how much they might desire a reprieve.'

Patric Laush spoke in riddles.

Dream Topping™ cannot reverse the inevitable. He didn't realise that the illusion of immortality is with us till the point where it isn't. Was I mistaken to tell him that? It puzzled him. He was incredulous. He had invested too much hope in our cures.

I speak the truth.

Wreaths with Feeling: Celia's Fortune

It was all so long ago. We didn't live in hiding then. You couldn't foresee what was going to happen . . . nobody could have . . . it was like a total freak occurrence . . . occurrences. Old proverb (on T-shirt): you can't legislate for tsunamis . . .

It was all so unfair. Mrs Kerr called me in . . . end of the day after afternoon lessons just as I was about to leave . . . as per usual she was holding her glasses like she was trying to hide them up her sleeve . . . she was so so vain . . . she hated being seen in them . . . she was so short-sighted she had to squint to see me across her desk . . .

She told me it was me, that I was going to be in charge of the Field Study group . . . I was all skewbalded . . . I reminded her I was a probationary . . . Whatever she said I did tell her, I *did* – she lied through her feet about that. I *did* tell her. I swear!

Not that she was taking any notice . . . you could tell the importance she was attaching to this – not! . . . You could tell all she was thinking was getting off the premises so she could have a gasper to make her even hoarser than she was already . . . even though it wasn't raining she already had her oh so chic belted black mac with purple piping on all belted up . . . then she was daubing on slap and lipstick . . . she daubed it on the bags under her eyes . . . they might be Hermès bags was the joke in the staff room but they're still bags . . . off to one of her socials again . . . head teacher dressed as lamb IMHO . . . lamb with panda eyes! Then she was taking her mobile apart as per usual . . . tut-tutting all exasperated . . . peering . . . peering. My little joke was it was because she was so tall that she could never get a signal . . . because of having her own stratosphere! Seriously all it was was the battery wouldn't take a charge . . . I don't know why she didn't get a new one. It was so old it ought to have been in sheltered accommodation! She scowled whenever I made my little joke.

I said Group Leadership . . . Group Leadership was way beyond my learnt competencies . . . I didn't have the training in Group Leadership. My entry-level option was Emergency Midwifery . . . I hadn't got to the Group Leadership module . . . the way I'd structured it – with her support! – was I'd do it second year after Special Needs. I'd never been on a Field Studies Residential Course so called . . . not even at school or college . . . let alone led one.

It was like she just laughed . . . you know waved it away with that infectious throaty steeped-in-tar voice of hers saying it was sort of irreverent . . . sort of a formality like. She was all flirty and smiley . . . though that didn't make her any less commanding . . . she used her height as a weapon . . . no wonder Mr Kerr walked out . . . he ditched her for a Burmese midget kickboxer . . . or was she Sri Lankan? She's going 'don't worry it's easy peasy'. Nothing to it . . . matter of common sense for an achiever like me . . . and anyway basically the girls are big enough to look after themselves . . . and there are only ten of them . . . she put on her glasses for a moment looking at a sheet of paper . . . thirteen of them . . . and like it's only two days . . . and frankly there's no one else available . . . what with Janine awaiting a kidney after her sister in Toronto decided when she got to the airport not to donate after all because it was too much hassle and anyway she didn't like Janine anyway despite Janine paying for the ticket and Mitch being suspended on bail before her trial for multiple historic inappropriates with Year 10s in her school before last and the other Celia's morning sickness and obviously Old Monsieur Calafato not being allowed because of gender issues because it was a girls only group even though he's gay as a tractor. At least she didn't throw the phone across the room . . . I'd seen her do it on other occasions then tick herself off. She rolled her lips against each other to get the lipstick spread for all evening permanent blood-red.

It wasn't two days it was three days when you count in the travel, like getting on five hours each way to Brodrick Hall in the drizzle . . . having to listen to driver Local Lothario Stan The Van's choice of very loud music . . . Moist Groin, The Bobby Fitoussi Band, Handsome

Albino, Hungry As A Fox and The Darkness!!! (Two of them hail ironically from East Anglia though Stan is a Totton chap with the greying Down-May-Hee-Co-Way droopo badman moustache and greying bumper burns and cowboy hat to prove it.) When we were stalled in a snarl-up I did go and have a word with him . . . he said when he was top contract driver for Poppy Tours it was part of the deal he had to play Vera Lynn, the Andrews Sisters, Run Rabbit Run, etc. etc. etc. . . .

'You get well sick of it . . . How many effin' times can you listen to a bunch of effin' geriatrics forgettin' the words to "It's A Long Way To Tipperary" . . . does your 'ead in . . . Ten days of what I call kitbag songs . . . talk about empty wigs . . . ten days . . . you ever been to effin' Armentières . . . total empty wigs . . . for me heavier sounds are more my foal . . . they express the real me . . . here tell you what – them fellas that own Poppy Tours . . . they's called Dogg too . . . two "g"s . . . relatives?'

'Might be . . . don't know . . . my dad's family's bit of a closed book . . . I got an aunt and her . . . my cousin and that's about it . . .'

'That's all right then . . . Me and the Doggs we had our differences . . . put it this way they's lowlifes . . . no badges of honour, them – if you know what I mean.'

I didn't want to stand there awkward next to the dashboard juddering on two levels . . . him sniding some namesake of mine . . . relatives? Him not taking a blind bit of notice of what I'd requested . . . his x-ray eyes drilling into my generous bosom assessing my cup size . . . I went back to my seat a couple of rows back . . . out of range unless he had x-ray eyes in the back of his head!

I was flattered that ever so nice Bethany had come and sat in the seat next to me . . . I didn't teach her but we was on noddings sharing a hullo and weather comment every so often . . . nice lass with an open smile . . . of course I knew all about her from hearsay . . . Mrs Kerr had told me it hadn't half been a job and a half persuading her parents to let her come on the trip. Who would take care of her . . . like chaperone her etc. etc.?

That's what I'm for I said to Mr and Mrs Sluytwn when they come into school with their happy smiling red apple faces – they look like a healthy diet advert . . . it's not rouge because make-up is forbidden – for ladies too!! I was secretly proud Bethany respected me by wanting to sit next to me . . . I thought of myself as being like I'm her big sister not that I'd ever let on . . . just a fantasy. She's a bit of a loner . . . not a troubled loner rampaging through school with automatic weapons bringing death to the playground type loner . . . but a friendly, thoughtful introvert . . . the other kids keep their distance . . . they whisper about her . . . all very hush hush.

That's down to her upbringing in The Charismatic Brethren of the Great Tribulation . . . famous for having the highest proportion of functioning centenarians of any congregation in Britain . . . they complain that longevity without end isn't the way to wheedle your way into the DSS's good books . . . they all got distinctive red apple complexions on their merry faces . . . you can always spot them in the crowd holding banners and screaming to heaven when there's a riot outside a newly discovered abortion clinic . . . red as red can be . . . throwing missiles at doctors' cars . . . Mrs Sluytwn and Old Mrs Sluytwn her nan and even Older Mrs Sluytwn her nan's nan always wearing celluloid things on their heads like half a nun's wimple thing and half a tea room waitress in period drama from the days of seed cake and cake stands when people had manners almost as strict as her dad . . . if anything his ruddy face is ruddier than hers . . . is it the diet? He won't have a television in the house . . . saying grace before meals in funny dialect . . . Old Brabancon whatever that is when it's at home . . . no chocolates can you believe . . . When he came into school that day he kept looking away when I talked . . . excuse me – when I *tried* to talk to him . . . as though it's sinful to look at women because we're unclean or something . . . no one ever gets invited to their house . . . if you can call it a house . . . I mean it is a house, obviously . . . but is it a home, a true home?

They're hutments so called . . . like wooden barracks patched up with tarpaulin . . . they were where the travelling folk with their scrap metal and dogs in defiance of the Dangerous Dogs Act were decanted at when they were rounded up from Lockerley Common and Foyers Inclosure and all over the forest because of sanitation or lack of it more like . . . Mum says it was known as the 'concentration camp' . . . but it was originally an old DP camp . . . for those ravaged by the scourges of World War I, the Spanish flu which struck . . . it didn't suit the travelling folk with their carefree romantic way of life under threat with the dogs being prosecuted regularly for babies' faces offences and the scrap . . . the travelling folk got picky notwithstanding the elevation in their accommodation level . . . they moved on leaving their bad reputation behind not to mention rusting fridges in the hedgerows, wheelbarrows, tractor parts, what have you. They left the name too. Gyppo Brook . . . Gyppo Brook isn't the official name . . . it wouldn't be would it!? The actual brook's not much more than a ditch . . . rank in summer, all flooded in winter.

You get some wrong people living there . . . it was a readymade sink estate . . . the council dump for the prob-fams . . . the underachievers . . . the workshies. The respectable ones like Bethany's and the decent hardworking boat people with their lovely fragrant pho soups got tarred with the same brush.

Bethany's exceptionally mature for a fifteen-year-old, not a silly frivolous flibbertigibbet . . . like totally serious about her studies . . . she has what teaching professionals praise as avid knowledge-thirst . . . the names of flowers and birds for instance . . . 'The lord god made them all,' she half sang, smiling . . . she had the gumption to ask Local Lothario Stan The Van to turn down the vol switch which he did but then he turned it up again after the toilet and crisps break at what ought to be known as Keele Insanitary Services & Toilet Seat Diseases hoping we wouldn't notice.

Brodrick Hall was old . . . but not quaint old, more barracks style old, dead grimy like a maze of old backstairs corridors, all extensions from when it had been a mental sanatorium once, then it homed behavioural kids. It still looked it . . . flaking cream paint . . . all the furniture was scuffed. Personally I found the whole experience a bit naff . . . I might even have had the experience down as a bit boring if it hadn't been for the antics of Twinkly Bobby (as I called him because of his twinkly smile and all round twinkly enthusiasm). He really was the life and soul – among other things, AITO.[46]

The other school group at the Hall was mixed . . . and noisier.

---

46 As it turned out.

Ooh, the din! You forget how immature boys are . . . all those zits! And as for personal hygiene! They didn't have so far to come . . . they came from Stamford. Twinkly Bobby and Sullen Megan were in charge of them. Megan was a right cow . . . she couldn't believe that I hadn't heard of Stamford . . . like it was the centre of the universe! Twinkly Bobby had to fetch a road atlas to show me where it was.

He was really passionate about his geology . . . with one flick of a movement he drew a sort of back to front S on the road atlas's page-indicator to show that the stone Stamford is built from is out of the same 'belt' of stone as our part of the country is built out of . . . he quipped that we are geologically related by oolite (a new word) . . . he drew with a nonchalant dash . . . like an artist and with one arm round my shoulder! I thought he was a bit fresh but didn't mind because he smelled so nice and his voice was just velvet! His wickedly risqué catchphrase was 'Butter my nipples'! That was one I hadn't heard before!

The resident geologist was wheezy old Mr Bultitude. Talk about whiffy! Some might say he'd never heard of soap . . . positively reeked . . . people reeled away from him at first sniff . . . rumour: he was once famous in wordsmith circles as the author of *With a Blister on My Heel* and as a leading 'nature poet', WTM.[47] You don't even want to imagine what nature festers down in his codpiece dominions! You can tell as much about a man from his groin hygiene as from the way he sneezes . . . and he was a sneezer . . . 'archer cherokee' he went . . . his reputation pear-shaped when he penned a disgusting sounding book *The Riddle of the Sphincter* about this chap that gets the sack from his manager's job in a linoleum factory . . . he takes revenge by breaking in at night to do big ones on his former bosses' desks . . . not to mention a stranger to shampoo like his rat tail hair had Trex on it . . . no stranger though to thinks-no-one-notices nips from his tramp's flask hidden in his seen-better-days overcoat . . . talk about letting himself go! He made generously voluptuous sensuously curved comfortably rounded me feel good . . . like I'd been on the fashionable-among-A-listers Ravensbruck Diet™. He didn't take to Twinkly

---

47 Whatever that means.

Bobby's effervescence . . . it didn't half piss him off Twinkly Bobby being cocky and vivacious not to mention a show-off . . . always picking up Mr Bultitude when Mr Bultitude's identification capabilities went on the blink and he confused his jurassics and triassics with his liassics (also new words). He was so all over the shop I couldn't help wondering if he wasn't in dementia's cruel grip.

And did he wheeze! Ooh that cough hurt just to listen to . . . he spread his germs generously . . . he had issues from sixty cigarettes a day . . . didn't help with him getting up some of those steep paths . . . puffing away even though it was a distinctly chilly day . . . I wondered if he was going to make it without a myocardial infarction . . . luckily my health and safety skills including improvising a splint from green twigs were not required but it was touch and go . . . not applicable . . . I'd done Emergency Midwifery as an option because you never know when it might come in handy . . . delivering a new life into this world . . . welcoming the cute gurgling bundle of joy . . . not that that was applicable with Mr Bultitude!

Students' behaviour diagnostic was satisfactory even though a couple of the Stamford lads should have been cautioned for imitating Mr Bultitude's cough but Twinkly Bobby took their side . . . he wasn't so laid back about some lads showing more interest in the USAF air disaster remnants from long ago when they should have been absorbing his fossil wisdom . . . a number of girls benefitted from deep immersion field practice, notably Bethany and Sandrine who dug deep into geological strata like experienced treasure hunters searching for pirate's treasure earning Twinkly Bobby's smiley congratulations and generous hugs.

I don't think anyone was surprised when Mr Bultitude didn't show up for dinner or The Welcome Disco after . . . not that he missed much, at all actually. The dinner was so-called mixed grill . . . all day breakfast with kidneys, bacon, beans and sausages. The kidneys made me think of poor Janine waiting for hers from an anonymous donor . . . just as anonymous as the sheep, whose were delicious. The fried bread was 150 per cent grease though and there was no proper pudding just fruit . . . thankfully I'd had the foresight to pack some chocolate bars . . .

The disco was so boring . . . no line dancing. Twinkly Bobby only stayed a couple of minutes because of having preparation to do for tomorrow. So I was left watching Local Lothario Stan The Van's frankly pathetic efforts at DJ-ing and playing his awful naff sounds (again) . . . when he wasn't making an arse of himself DJ-ing he was all over Megan who looked a real slag squeezed into a mini-dress that must have come from a pound shop that was ever so crackly with static . . . a really disgraceful role model for the Stamford girls who were all plastered in make-up . . . not that the boys were interested, they were too shy apart from Lairy Midget Casanova Andy . . . it was a real effort to stay up till Hall Rector Mr Whiteside said time's up. I was out on my feet frankly.

The next night was The Farewell Disco.

You can imagine my shock when six of my girls all showed up at dinner in pelmets and stilettos . . . it was like there had been an accident in a mascara factory. Apparently after we got back from Kinder Scout they persuaded Local Lothario Stan The Van to drive them into Glossop – that well-known fashion hub! They all bought cheap and nasty tarty outfits à la Megan . . . Bethany, Teagan and Charlene with the spina bifida had the good sense not to get swept along on the tide of wanton tartiness.

I told Ashleigh in no uncertain terms to change out of the tat she had bought because she looked like an escort.

She goes: 'An escort can make as much money in a night as a schoolteacher makes in a month, Miss . . . but you can't be an escort unless you're toney and buff and not a KFC jumbo bucket.'

Quick as a flash I went: 'That's your Prostitute Work Ethic then is it.' She didn't get my subtle reference . . . she just made a face . . . I knew better than to hit the little whore . . . in my prayers I asked for a sexually transmitted infection to be transmitted to her – not HIV but one of the good old-fashioned ones like syphilis or gonorrhoea and chlamydia.

That night there was a DJ from the local village. Mr Bultitude was courteous in a shy gentleman way sparing time for the more studious students such as Bethany and Charlene with the spina bifida (and not long to live) . . . he absented every few minutes for a shivering fag break very much the dedicated snoutcast.

Twinkly Bobby was the star turn . . . he was in his element . . . dashing . . . that would be the word for it. He was such a vigorous dancer with his air guitar and his Ricky van Brabant impressions . . . he just loved being the centre of attention . . . but I have to say he went a bit far with the suggestive wiggling and pumping and tirelessly stroking his crotch . . . and when dancing up close he had those wandering party hands . . . not very becoming in a man of his age the wrong side of forty.

I had my doubts when he kept purring: 'Get on down . . . butter my nipples.'

He kept on like leering making chauvinist purrs and growls and muttering things like 'Cor what little stunners' when Amber and Courtney were being wantonly provocative . . . anyone else I'd have told him to shut it but he looked so dashing with his cartoon superhero novelty socks, characterful blazer (baby blue and wickedly dark chocolate stripes) with matching bow tie.

And he was so attentive towards me between his dance turns replenishing my glass flirtatiously . . . I began to wonder if he had dishonourable intentions!! I secretly hoped he was the sort of real man that prefers the fuller figure and a cup size from the middle of the alphabet.

So far only Barry had and he turned out to be commitment-phobic.

I think of myself as pretty but a teensy bit podgy – emphasis on the pretty. I'm a spritzer sort of gal . . . I wasn't used to the red wine Twinkly Bobby had brought with him – heady's the word . . . and moreish . . . it made me doze off on the settee. I woke up with my mouth like the proverbial . . . the party had almost broken up . . . the music had stopped . . . Twinkly Bobby was nowhere to be seen . . . Lairy Midget Casanova Andy, Amalinder and Kryss were 'dancing' together . . . i.e. blatantly rubbing themselves against each other. I gave them such a look but all Kryss did was twerk her booty (the little slut's word for it). She grinned all snidey . . . superior like *aren't you jealous of me having a guy when you haven't got one* . . . if I'd risen to the bait I'd have told her what she had was actually 50 per cent of a stuck-up tosser. But I didn't . . . I turned the other cheek – and my inner GPS went on the blink.

I found myself not knowing which way I should go along a stuffy corridor with pipes lagged with sacking . . . it dawned on me how tiddly I was . . . I must have taken the wrong door . . . easily done . . . there were cleaning rosters pinned on a baize notice board . . . I thought to myself *that's rich, the place doesn't look like it's been cleaned in months!* Even the drawing pins pinning the rosters were rusty . . . at one end of the corridor was a wicker laundry basket on wheels overflowing with soiled sheets . . . it was all a tad grubby but without my glasses from a distance it might have been a giant meringue topping. Yum! I squeezed past it.

Round a corner there was a door with one of those automatic closing things that makes them close slowly . . . then there was a service staircase . . . dimly lit, darker the further up you went, it smelled of fungus . . . obviously wasn't used much if at all, there was dust and cobwebs everywhere – creepeee! At the top of it was a door with two glass panes in it . . . through them you could see a very long wider corridor brightly lit going off into the distance.

This was 'upstairs', so to speak, this was a corridor for the 'quality', the miladies and honourables what have you, not the skivvies and underlings . . . the door was jammed . . . that'll have been down to the lack of use. I was looking to see how the handle worked when there was the grating squeak of another door being opened far off down the corridor . . . it opened slowly . . . to reveal a ruffled head. I didn't immediately recognise it . . . time stood still or went backwards while my brain unravelled that it was Twinkly Bobby's head . . . I did one of those can't believe it at first glance so look again stares they used to do in the golden age of Hollywood which I'd never done myself in real life till I caught myself doing it without knowing it. He peeped out from the room . . . looked left, he looked right . . . he didn't see me in the shadows behind the unpolished panes of glass keeping still and silent as the night. He slipped out into the corridor.

That's when I saw what he was 'wearing'. Nothing. As Dad used to say: stark b*ll*ck naked, all but. He was in his birthday suit! The altogether! And nothing else apart from his cartoon hero novelty socks and his bow tie tied informally round his gent's endowment that was bobbling up and down like a puce novelty nose attached to the wrong bit of his body. He was clutching a bottle of champagne style wine . . . he skipped merrily towards where I was, lightly, he was on tiptoe like . . . but thankfully not as far as me . . . just to the next door but two or three to the one he'd come from . . . he knocked gently on it . . . another glance around making sure he was not observed. I could tell from his expression he was making one of his purring noises. More a big cat than a domestic moggy like my lovely tabby Oats . . . then he waited till the door was opened – by an unseen hand! He went in.

I'd never felt so embarrassed in all my life . . . what I saw in those few short sickening seconds sickened me . . . like profoundly sickened . . . I was gobsmacked . . . shocked and, well, amazed . . . I thought about what I *hadn't* seen – thank god . . . what a grossout . . . if the wind had changed I'd have been lumbered with an open mouth for ever.

At breakfast I avoided eye contact with him . . . not that he noticed . . . he was that busy laughing and joking with his audience of easily impressed teenies still dressed in their hussy gear from last night . . . he was so full of himself laughing at one of his own jokes his mouth sprayed the table with Grape-Nuts cereal . . . it was like all juvenile cheers when it was actually disgusting . . . not to mention totally unhygienic . . . but kids don't see that side of things.

Local Lothario Stan The Van and Sullen Megan crept in when everyone had just about finished . . . no mistaking what they'd been up to . . . isn't 'sleeping together' just the most inaccurate description!? They hadn't had forty winks between them . . . my core concern was whether he was up to a four-hour forty-five-minute drive but he told me he was fresh as a daisy . . . no worries my baba . . . he looked ashen as an ashtray though.

The last morning was given over to two sessions.

First. Attitudinal assessment with extrinsic motivation criteria: like how much do previous learning and the students' foreknowledge of the subject impact their experiential gain from intense fieldwork.

Second. After a tea and fruitful ideas-mart morning break, it was on to rubric management and the neural forest in which there are neural forest rangers hunting down the tree of knowledge – it might be a sapling, it might be a full-grown beech, it might even be a toppled trunk that has lost its bark.

It's fair to say that not either school covered itself in knowledge-rich glory. Ashleigh proudly displayed her bigotry saying how sick she was of the 'Hollow Course' which is 'just so yesterday . . . who cares . . . and it's only in black and white'.

No absentees: I counted that as one small triumph for me and my clipboard . . . the byebyes took an age . . . I thought we'd never get going . . . swapping addresses . . . hugging . . . a bit of surreptitious necking more like slobbering – ugh! With Mr Bultitude it was what I call correct . . . he coughed his way through friendly smiles . . . polite handshakes . . . what have you. With Twinkly Bobby it was tactile time stroking everyone on the back yours truly included like he was thanking us for coming to his show . . . I gave him what I like to call my best 'winter smile' . . . icy as an ice lolly . . . he pretended not to notice.

Bethany was ever so chatty on the way back . . . girly . . . almost mouthy you might say . . . it was great seeing her so relaxed . . . not so serious as usual . . . but not silly like so many of them . . . carefree, showing the benefit of escaping being downtrodden by her parents for once . . . it was like a weight lifted from her shoulders . . . not that she said so in so many words . . . she wasn't disloyal . . . she's not that sort . . . But just from some of the things she said without realising what she was saying really you realise that she thinks they're as weird as everyone else does. (Everyone else mind who isn't part of their faith group . . . you can't call it a church because their 'church' is that rusty what used to be the Scout Hut set back from the Fair Oak Road.)

I did feel sorry for her not having telly or radio at home . . . she didn't know the songs to join in with on the singalongs, which made some of the other girls snigger.

What a wonderful relief it was to be back home-ee-o to moggy Oats and a piping hot Fray Bentos Classic Steak and Kidney Pie followed by a Fray Bentos Just Chicken Pie with artisan-crafted oven chips and a scrumptious also piping hot Lardy Cake from Warner's . . . their 'secret' is to steep the raisins in rum (!) till they plump up . . . all rounded off with a hearty tub of Ash Vale cheddar-style spread.

It was afternoon on a sports Thursday . . . one of those lovely drying days . . . on the clothes lines in the back gardens on the other side of the path that goes alongside the playing field all the sheets were like billowing galleon style and the pyjams were dancing . . . it was a lovely old-fashioned sight transporting me back to the good old days before we all had dryers when people were kind to each other . . . also reminding me of an illustration in a book I had when I was a kid. I was just putting the wickets, pads etc. back in the sports hut prior to locking up when a Year 7, a freckly little chap, runs up all panting for puff . . . so he had to wait to get his breath back before he can tell me breathlessly that I was required immediately by Mrs Kerr.

Why did she send this poor nipper when she could of phoned . . . but of course yes her phone'll have been out of juice again . . . and all imperial like she can just get a slave instead.

So there went my post-sports cuppa! But I felt chuffed because I had a hunch I was going to get a pat on my back recognising my contribution to the Sports-Wellness-Synergy programme.

I'd usually have ridden round the long way because of the horrible pink-eyed albino dog . . . but I went along the cinder path . . . they were dragging their feet on the way back to the changing rooms . . . when I cycled past them there was all jovial type banter . . . clapping and jeers . . . good naturedly trying to push me off my bike into the stingers.

Knock knock. I considerately waited a mo before entering so she could take off her glasses . . . she really deluded herself about not needing them . . . I entered with a beaming smile. A weensy bit on the smug side I shouldn't wonder!

But then . . .

Her face! She was standing behind her desk six foot two and imperious with her face like her insides were boiling up inside her . . . Like she was telling me something bad was happening.

There was this time stood still moment (or minute) before I twigged. It was me. I was the something bad . . . She didn't even say hello, it was just all seething and staring me down with her squint like I was something the cat dragged in . . . you got the feeling that she delegated her charm to persons unknown and unseen . . . how long can you go staring someone down like that . . . telling them with your eyes and your lip curls that they are what the cat dragged in. If you're Mrs Kerr about five minutes at least it seemed without actually precisely timing it of course (again). There are some things you just know interpersonally without having to learn them . . . I felt my smile vanish and take its leave . . . it was replaced by inner turmoil.

'Do you,' she sneered – but it wasn't really a sneer because it had more hatred than a sneer has . . . it was a twenty a day growl, 'do you know the meaning of in loco parentis?'

I had to confess I didn't . . . I do now all right. She glared . . . like the effort of glaring that hard took all the colour out of her . . . where does the blood go?

'You were in charge of the Year Twelves at Roderick's Hall. You were, then, in loco parentis. Yes?'

'It was *Brodrick* Hall.'

That was a mistake correcting her, I knew instantly I heard myself say it.

If looks could . . .

'Those girls, those *children*, were your responsibility.'

'Yes Mrs Kerr.'

'Which means that it was your job to supervise them. To watch over them. Watch out for them. You understand the concept of pastoral care I take it.'

'Yes Mrs Kerr.'

'Are you, then,' she mocked, 'also familiar with the dereliction of pastoral care and – perhaps – with the concept of *pregnancy*?'

I was bewildered, getting on all-a-frazzle. Was she having some sort of a turn connected to the oncoming approach of the menopause which she must be due for soon which will be why her office was always so stuffy with her wearing extra layers because of feeling cold after the hot flushes came over her.

'Of course I do,' I said. I'd say my emotional state was puzzled, hesitant and fragile.

'It may interest you to learn, then, that two of the girls you were in loco parentis for are pregnant.'

There was a screechy lorry making revving noises in the street like its engine was in pain.

'Pregnant? No. That can't be right . . .'

'Can't it indeed? Amber Germy and Courtney Jump . . . They returned from . . . *the Hall* with child – as they used to say . . . Even though they are hardly more than children themselves.'

She spat these words like they were venom-laced.

'What on earth were you thinking of?'

I pictured Twinkly Bobby skipping down that corridor . . .

Keep mum, I told myself.

'I supervised them all I could . . .'

I didn't mention the clothes buying trip into Glossop.

'I stayed up till way after they'd all gone to bed . . .'

'As they obviously did. With each other. It sounds as though there was an orgy going on . . . and you had no idea!'

She said orgy with a 'hard g' . . . I knew that was wrong.

She was scaring me. There was a chill down my spine . . . I was panicking, I could feel my inner turmoil was going to bring on an asthma attack even though I'd been a regular at The Allergen Workshop.

'They admit to having multiple partners. I can't say I'm surprised by Amber . . . with that background . . . the family . . . Stonehouse Waters Estate, well . . . But Courtney . . . of all people . . . she is Worthy Fruit.'

'She's *what*?' I asked.

'Worthy Fruit. The term we use in Modern Moral Methodism – the code I live by. Worthy Fruit. The children of parents who are not married but cohabit nonetheless in a secure and loving Christian environment. I can't believe you don't know how vulnerable these children are.'

'But they're like sixteen, Mrs Kerr . . . If you'll forgive . . . they're over the age of consent. They could be married.'

She hadn't thought of that . . . She stood up. D'you know I

thought she was going to strike me for thinking out of turn. I felt so tense yet wobbly at the same time . . . I was angry . . . I could see where this was going . . . I was thinking I wish I had the nerve to say your opinions aren't worth the spittle that comes out your mouth when you say them. But I hadn't.

'Didn't you have any inkling . . . the threat posed by Robin . . . what's the man's name' – she consulted a piece of paper on her desk holding it about an inch from her face – 'Robert Tedcastle. No suspicions?'

That was Twinkly Bobby.

He was only Twinkly Bobby to me . . . even he didn't know he was Twinkly Bobby. He was Twinkly Bobby till he betrayed my affection which might have been true love . . . I found out too from looking at a special geological map that what's more he betrayed me geologically as well . . . we weren't 'linked by oolite'. There's no oolite stone hereabouts or for miles around . . . it was just a pound shop chat-up line . . . or would be if you could get a man-of-knowledge chat-up line for 99p.

'No. No suspicions,' I lied.

She raised her eyebrows, am-dram style.

'Really?' She blew out to show how exasperated she was.

'I'm in communication with South Kesteven – the people at the education authority for Stamford . . . So we have this teacher . . . this predator . . . And then we have this student whose name . . . all we have is a given name – Andy. Andy – ring a bell?'

She looked inquisitive in a threatening inquisitive way.

'I think there was an Andy . . . No . . . or was he an Anthony? There was one who danced with some of the girls . . . nothing untoward . . . I'd say very proper in fact.'

I could feel my fibbing competencies coming along all in a rush.

They weren't enough to save me alas.

There was paperwork . . . official records . . . certificates (lack of . . . ironically!) to prove that I didn't ever ought to have been appointed in charge of that party albeit they were all above the age of consent or more.

But it reached the *Metro*'s ears, the so-called prestigious Eastleigh,

Romsey and Andover freesheet. A leak most likely . . . they treated it like it was a scandal . . . what they say about scandals is there is always a villain. That was me – I was the one portrayed as the villain. More like a victim I'd say.

Blame is like stinky manure . . . it sticks . . . and it was all getting heaped on me. Me! I was the one getting scapegoated . . . leaving me stinky as one of the silos at Fair Oak.

It should have been heaped on those animals . . . those primitive animals with sex incontinence issues that did the deeds. But Twinkly Bobby had not committed an offence because he was not in charge of Amber and Courtney . . . as for Andy – nothing doing there either with him and both girls being the age they were.

It should have been heaped on Mrs Kerr . . . putting me in charge knowing full well I was not authorised in such duties . . . I was a trainee teacher not a condom.

I didn't know I was meant to keep a log of the rooms who slept where and the rest . . . I didn't go into teaching so that I'd become a warder!

Mrs Kerr's job was on the line . . . even with having powerful friends among the school governors and the trust committee – especially Len Cardy the local building supplies magnate with whom it was rumoured . . . She told lie after lie . . . oh ever so charming and simpering . . . plausible . . . making out how much she felt let down by my so-called derelictions because she had put so much trust in me . . . she said she couldn't recall but to her recollection it was not mentioned my being unqualified, after all it was over two months ago at a very busy time in the school calendar.

She said it was irrelevant anyway what with all members of the group being over the age of consent – we know where she got that one from don't we!?

She said that if it was mentioned – if! – it was just my way of trying to get out of onerous duties which anyone else would have happily undertaken because hard as it was for her to say it I was the sort that never pulled her weight much to her regret. Also a little bird tells me she made a cruel jibe about my generous curvaceousness . . . resulting in the consequent related low energy levels blabla that I won't repeat.

I prayed to Our Lord that He would punish her by her coming to grief in an accident at the notorious blind corner accident black spot just down the road from where she lived.

Not fatal, mind, just comfily quadriplegic.

The governors were hostile . . . Mrs Kerr had bitch-mouthed me to them that I had a criminal conviction I had not admitted when I was accepted as a probationary. I didn't have a criminal conviction . . . I told them that I had told her even though I wasn't obliged to tell her that I had been given an unconditional discharge for 'shoplifting' six bars of 75 per cent Cocoa Lindt Lemon Excellence all down to mis-understanding the confusing Buy Two Get One Free offer often the fate of an unpopular range that won't get off the shelf . . . The magistrates bench actually ticked off Densmores for the offer being confusing. The magistrates bench even made them pay costs because of the 'frivolous, vindictive, frankly petty-minded manner' they had persecuted me in.

Typical, the school governors totally ignored the facts . . . when I challenged Mrs Kerr's lies the chair of the governors told me I was disrespectful . . . they didn't even try to check out the facts even though it was all on record . . . they took Mrs Kerr at her word. Of course they did – she was one of their kind . . . she said I was living on borrowed time . . . *borrowed from who* I asked wittily knowing there was nothing to lose any more not giving a stuffed membrane.

Sure enough at the end of the governors' meeting I was summoned back to be informed what I knew was going to happen . . . the long and the short of it was that with great regret they were having to let me go and thanking me for all the hard work I'd put in and wishing me all the very best in the future.

Future! What a joke! What future? I wished boats-made-of-blood on them!

When I went for a drink at Nonchalant & Debonair with my ex, Commitment-phobic Barry, he was his usual sympathetic self, reminding me of the words of that C&W song we used to sing along to in the good old times dancing the night away with slide guitars and deep emotion:

You're on the highway to oblivion,
To a trailer park named Hate,
Loserville's your destination,
Zilchtown's your likely fate.

After two bottles of wine – of which yours truly got about one glass – he persuaded me, just for good old times' sake he said, to Do Disgusting again.

Oh where oh where is my strength of will? And where oh where was his wallet . . . I paid, as so often . . .

Still I'm not sorry I gave in to his ever such animal appetites even if his latest low calibre management company car was a manual with an inconveniently positioned gearstick . . . a romantic deluxe suite at The Ritz it was not . . . nut butter-wise it can't be said that he produces the hot thick cream of legend, more like thin curdling milk that stains . . . but to be frank I didn't mind those ninety thrusty seconds that much even if it was in the lane leading down to The Berm where the fly-tipping has polluted the orangey so-called 'river' River Mank (!) due to the geology and there's a joke sign on a gate Beware of the Dogger – so sordido.

Not so long after, I was hinting to Mum about possibly perhaps having to move back in just temporary so as not to set off alarm bells in her because since Dad passed on she has enjoyed what they call the 'luxury lifestyle of the silver solitary – alone but not lonely' . . . She was visibly wincing at the thought when my phone goes. It was Barry calling to say that was a fabulous evening he was so sorry he had forgotten his wallet and *tell you what* – his sister Pauline is looking for someone responsible to manage Bloomin' Marvellous for the foreseeable because she was expecting again and the doctors were advising her she might lose the kiddy if she kept up her punishing schedule. Little Bruce is a high-spirited toddler now . . . three and a half! How time flies! Big Bruce works all hours to grow his online sales. The part-time assistant Part-Time Tabitha is not ready yet to step up to the challenge of running a (soon to be hopefully award-winning) cutting-edge florist because of her studies and at-risk domestic problems (her mum Juno's abusive boyfriend Psycho Carl The Sociopath). She's a bit of a know-all encyclopaedia swot. Just the sort you don't want in your class as a probationary but in a florist context a versatile lieutenant.

So how about it? Wolf from the door, after all.

It was just my second day managing Bloomin' Marvellous when I had what can only be described as my road to Damascus moment at 2.15. I wasn't on the highway to nowhere!

I was hurrying back to the shop after getting an organic egg with free trade avocado on wholewheat and responsible root crisps which I couldn't have got earlier even though I was famished because Part-Time Tabitha (what had her mutually incompatible parents been thinking of . . . sweetest girl, well-meaning, a true friend from the moment we instantly bonded, a touch leap-before-you-look with dippy intellectual tendencies claiming she can see into the future and multilingual capabilities down to her gone-a-wandering dad being a Belgian master baker, not that there's much call for Belgian speaking cakes hereabouts!) didn't arrive till 2.07 which was thirty-seven minutes late, not that she noticed. Waiting to cross the street I looked across at the shop on the other side with its flowery fascia the letters spelling out *Bloomin' Marvellous* all entwined with lovingly caressing creepers like those naughty figures on Indian temples . . . its windows rich in cut flowers and little shrubs . . . pastel colour buckets . . . baked earth planters and tiddler bonsais . . . plants of every refrain . . . living things in all god's glory – even if some are poisonous and others make you come out in raw red rashes . . . they are still god's. It was at 2.15 when I realised that the florist's calling was mine.

No, that's wrong . . . I didn't *realise*, I was *told* . . . vocations don't get chosen . . . they smother you with sweet warm hugs, another area Barry's not up to scratch in. At least mine did – smother me I mean. It was like a warm blanket voice but also challenging going *this is what you're going to do . . . this is going to be Your Life* . . . but the voice couldn't actually be heard so to speak . . . it was my voice but not my voice . . . it was not under my control like it was sort of a rebel with a voice of its own which was just like mine.

For me it was like Saul of Tarsus who becomes Saint Paul in the original scenario being told by god 'forget all that about being an apostle or whatever spreading the word – you're going to be a florist'.

I felt to myself this is my real home at last . . . my sanctuary of sheltering and faith. My church . . .

Not My Lord I beg you . . . it was never going to replace Saint Jerome's but down on a deeply needed personal level . . . like a different menu of spiritual superfood . . . especially with the Rev. Root's rasping noise when she is always scratching her lady parts throughout services through her lace trim surplice-thing like she's itching with lice or a nasty case of the crabs . . . not realising the overhead mic can pick it up amplifying it up in the chancel, nave etc. very like the noise when there's an avalanche on its way . . . maybe an earthquake . . . dry rumbling anyway . . . embarrassing to all the congregation . . . no one dares say anything because The Parish of Saint Jerome being pledged onto the anti-sexism and gender agendas . . . ironically what with the actual Saint Jerome being a world-class misogynist and sadistic criminal chauvinist wife beater . . . it is said. Flowers aren't like that . . . whoever heard of domestics in a flower-strewn home?

They honestly bring goodness into this world like milk and honey but with stamens (new word) and petals some of them nutritious like milk and honey for example nasturtiums being all peppery – delish!

I got the Botanica Britannia app . . . what riches . . . showcasing them . . . wondrous variety of nature, the colours and shapes, the remedials and the lotions . . . not to mention the bad side, all those venoms that paralyse you . . . the hallucinogenic chappies which drive you so loufouky you're seeing hippos coming out the tap . . . potions that make you die in agony with your blackened intestines in no end of a twist. Tell you what . . . Mother Nature can be a right old hag as in the Scottish Play as we were told to call it at The Mummers Soc because of single magpies or something. Its pages were falling out from Pauline bettering her knowledge-thirst reading it so much showing how well loved it is . . . such a heavy book you have to read it at a table but the touchability of paper beats apps hands down . . . memorising what floristry professionals call the common names, what they call the genera and the species. I cut stems at acute angles . . . I dyed carnations by capillary action . . . easy peasy when you know how . . . I followed arrangements Pauline had made giving me the confidence that I then ventured into the unknown world making my own arrangements . . . not so classic as Pauline perhaps but reflecting my natural vivacity and bubbliness . . . for instance the RTA special . . . my colourful roadside bouquet for laying with respect on the verge where the fatality occurred reflected on the full life lived . . . not on the life lost because of a few too many for the road in the snug down at The Hanging Judge and black ice. I even bespoked a more lavish one for the tragic victims of a helicopter crash . . . like a big insect that forgets to check for the wires between pylons. I wouldn't have done that again if I had known, but I'm not an oracle.

I discovered parts of me I never knew existed . . . I had never dreamed I was an artist . . . or a manager – a team leader . . . the team was Part-Time Tabitha with her 'ginchy urchin cut . . . do it myself with nail scissors' wrapped up in her mum Juno's vintage chinchilla coat which was a bit mangey bald on the right shoulder where her mum Juno's boyfriend Psycho Carl The Sociopath had attacked her with a blow-torch in a fit of depressive jealousy. We made a good team with her docile temperament and gift-wrapping competencies complementing my more fiery artistic temperament branching out into decadent scented candles, succulents, cacti and gifty treats such as irresistible wicked dark sophisticated chocolates with such flavours as candy apricot, chilli, salt caramel, toasted sesame, pistachio, and caraway . . . I furthered my creative skills creating a fun poster above the chocolate zone *Carried Away By Caraway*, all the letters being in different styles I made up myself . . . Part-Time Tabitha couldn't believe I hadn't been to art school – yeh mucho meano! . . . As she would say. We had a great banting thing going e.g. our morning greeting was Dildos To You Dykey! Always said with a generous brightside grin.

Whenever Pauline looked in she was totally smiles congrats on the profits high fives all around . . . pay-rises for me and Part-Time Tabitha pro-rata of course albeit mini-incremental in proportion to the upsurge in the takings down to my pro-active window dressing . . . yes, that's another talent I discovered within me just lurking in the shadows . . . sort of hibernating.

Life was rosy, all *hi-tiddly-hi-ti* . . . Mum's joke was that's how you greet a drunk Italian airline pilot!!

And then . . .

★

770

And then. It wasn't half pissing down. No one outdoors if they could help it for sure. We were perilous . . . on the edge of Storm Gavin with flood red-alerts. A month's rain in sixteen hours. Cats and dogs. The cats were bigger cats than moggy Oats . . . they were big cats like for example roaring tigers and the dogs were – well, big dogs, the vicious ones like Marcher Hounds you find in scuzzy barbed wire farmyards! Not a classic shopping day you might say. The lights were on at half past two in the afternoon but it was still dark. Like in that painting *Unpolished Pewter* by whatsisface. We were cheering ourselves up with the news on Vespasian FM. Stolen car runs out of fuel near Hedge End . . . Rownhams mum inconsolable after prize-winning treacle tart falls off table at fete . . . teenager assaulted with a comb and brush set outside pub at Chandlers Ford . . . allegedly genocidal dictator of the Democratic Republic of Kananga-Ilebo President Narcisse-Achille Helpful and his interior minister Doctor Matriculation Bones gunned down as they leave a Paris arms and ammunition exhibition – man with 'unusually glistening' black hair is being actively sought . . .

We were getting ever such a nice fug up. Cozeee!

You couldn't hardly see out the window because of trickles sliding like lab sperms through the microscope with fat heads and waggly tails turning into soft drops over and over, waiting to give new life . . . you were getting the feeling of being in a submarine submerged in water but you could see enough to see that there was someone staring through into the shop from the pavement not having the sense to shelter.

All bedraggled. A piece of face, just eyes and nose peeping out of a rain hood. Like a tragic foundling pressed against the glass longingly from the outside as in one of those ever so heartbreaking films I can really identify with where the richly wicked ganaches and yumsome truffles are unreachable . . . The face was sort of familiar. It took a few seconds for the penny to drop, for the face shape to turn into a face I knew. I realised that the drowned rat was Bethany!

Bethany! Whatever was she up to?

I hurried out the door and putting my arm around her I hurried her back inside. *Bethany!*

What was she thinking of? She was soaked to the skin, poor mite, all a-tremble including shivery spasms. Chattering teeth.

'There there.'

Her hippy-folk-bag of many colours was sodden. I helped her off with her jerkin. It wasn't drizzle-proof even. Nowhere near the right thing to be wearing when what you want is a heavy waxed barber and wellies and one of them oiled pullovers with prancing stags pulling a sledge. If you have to go out! Stick inside in the warm is my advice. Snuggle up nice and cosy with a nice mug of cocoa, a chocolate bar and a calming smooth shove ha'penny board. The down on the comfy chair with a travel rug round her, touch on the manky side but never mind. She might of been a tsunami victim in the jungle with all the new range exotic shrubs all surrounding her with the display of succulent care manuals. Her old-fashioned ankle-length skirt was soaked. (The Charismatic Brethren of the Great Tribulation don't allow even knee-length skirts. Trousers and jeans are heretics.)

Part-Time Tabitha fetched Bethany some kitchen roll. She put the kettle on without being told. That's teamwork in action like a well-oiled machine.

'There's that leak again Celia,' she said all exasperated.

Did I catch a touch of *you're to blame*?

I lit jasmine and frangipani joss sticks from the Soothing Serenity Selection.

Bethany hunched down into the depths of her tea. Lost in it. Cupped the cup like it was the last heat on earth.

'It *is* ever so nice to see you love . . . Not much of a day to go a-calling though!' I quipped with my toff voice, ringing the changes like a heroine in a costume drama of yore with a bonnet.

Sadly lost on her because she was gaping into that tea like it held strangely powerful secrets, maybe even The Answer.

Bethany raised her face up at me. So plaintive. D'you know, moving things don't happen to the likes of me. We don't have that kind of life normally. But this was not normal. I could see that it weren't rain on her face but a Storm Gavin floodgate of tears.

'What's the matter Bethany?'

'I just . . . I just well . . . I don't know who to turn to you know it's . . . it's delicate . . .'

On a technical point I'd say that down to her evident distress there was deep emotionalism or something going on . . . her vowels were on the blink. It was a strange way she was speaking. Like asthmatic short of breath, wheezy you might say, croaky. Angry fat rain hurled itself at the window.

'I didn't know where else to go. I couldn't go to Mrs Kerr . . . she's been kind in the past. But I heard how horrible she was to you. Everyone heard. You got everyone's sympathy. I couldn't talk to her not after what she done to you. And Miss Vodden – well . . .'

Vodden?

'The supply – they got her in after they let you go. She's not—'

'Let go? Ha! . . . Sacked! I was sacked. Sacked. I wasn't let go. I was sacked! Let go!'

There, I'd said it. I heard myself say it. I spoke very deliberate.

That was the moment I came to terms with 'the hand destiny dealt me/off the bottom of the deck'. That was the first time I had said *sacked* to myself let alone anyone else. I was very proud at my courage. Chuffed with self.

Oh, Bethany was like a little sister to me. She brought out the best in me. She said: 'I didn't like to – you know, to use the S word.'

She sobbed. Her compassion for my plight was so so touching. But it wasn't needed.

'I tell you what. It really hurt, really really really. But that witch bag did me a favour. Every cloud and that . . . it's true. If she hadn't lied like a tapeworm saving her precious skin . . . I wouldn't have found my vocation. What I never realised – teaching was just a job. I got a vocation now. Oh it's so lovely to see you Bethany.'

I gave her a big hug there and then. I was so carefree I took no notice of all the soggy kitchen roll stuck to her that then stuck to me like one of those hilarious comedy moments in a sitcom. You could almost hear the audience roaring with infectious laughter. You could definitely hear the rain roaring!

'Miss Vodden she's ever so nice but sort of vague? Bit all over the place? – not quite there . . . Might be down to her being short-sighted . . . which is why I've come to see you, Miss.'

'Celia. You call me Celia now.'

'May I?' She sounded so grateful it was embarrassing. But she was yearning to share my pain.

Part-Time Tabitha was out back in what Pauline calls 'the

greenhouse' (an extension bodged up by Barry when job-seeking). She was teetering on a chair balanced on the table stretching up to push a tea towel into a gap where the ceiling windows were letting in water. Guess whose caulking to blame! Plop plop plop.

'I'm pregnant,' said Bethany.

The rain went silent. Not a difficult two/three-word sentence but it took a while to sink in. When it did sink in I felt a goose glide over my grave . . . I was that surprised you could have knocked me down with a feather . . . well I never . . . had I heard right? I had. I looked at her wondering if it were a wind-up . . . a tasteless joke . . . I sort of snort-laughed — and wondered why. I suddenly felt betrayed . . . betrayed by Bethany . . . betrayed by Twinkly Bobby . . . even betrayed by yours truly — I should have pledged my troth to him when I had the chance then he wouldn't have come on all knight-errant in his birthday suit. My word for him is cur . . . treacherous cur . . . just like Kerr! . . . prancing, preening . . . predator! That's it . . . the dorm stalker with an attachment. We'll soon learn what *that* was all about. Ooh, now my eyes have the scales taken off of them like in the song . . . I see the twinkle was so false . . . think a sparkly wrapped Xmas box that turns out to have low cocoa content and claggy soft centres not to mention the ones you break your crown on.

'Brodrick Hall?'

She nodded a curt nod confirming. She was close to weeping.

'Did you consent? Actually consent to him . . . *doing* . . . ?' I asked, on the vindictive trail I have to admit, scenting revenge, a-naming and a-shaming, relishing the custodial sentence waiting just around the corner for our Twinkly Friend.

'How much consent was there?'

Bethany looked genuinely puzzled. Unlike her to be slow on the uptake. Was I speaking a different language to her?

'How much what?'

'Consent. On a scale of one to five where five is total willing to go all the way, gagging for it, you're making the running . . .'

'It's not a game.' She sounded hurt.

'It is not, *absolutely*, I'm with you there, pet. 110 per cent.'

'I don't know what to do.'

'What was it? Four – pleased to pleasure you but not making it too obvious. Three – sort of grudging agreement. One – rape, no question, minimum ten years' hard labour.'

'What are you on about, Miss . . . Celia? Look if there was any consenting to do it was him. If you follow me. Him doing the consenting. Me doing the whatever . . . Funny as it might . . . I fancied him.'

Her voice was shaded with shades of bitter bravado.

'And I hadn't had a carnal for two weeks.'

'You what . . . ?' My head was spinning like a thing. I focused on a jardiniere. Ivy and nasturtiums. It wasn't that I was admiring my own work. It was more like a calming cuppa while I awaited the next shock.

Here it came: 'It's always older men I fancy. Boys are so into themselves . . . not you. Older men are just as gropey aren't they . . . but they know what they're groping for. Boys haven't a clue. No sense of direction.'

I was about to quip: But the child groper is father to the man groper!

But she went on: 'Men make me feel whole.'

Where did she get *that* line from? I wondered.

'It's the weight that's . . . a mature body. Crushing me. Hefty . . . Squeezing all the breath out of me.'

She'd chosen right there then. Twinkly Bobby was also Bulky Bobby. Hulky-Bastard-Traitor-Suet-Fat Bobby. This was a Bethany I'd never seen, couldn't have ever dreamed of.

Part-Time Tabitha stormed through, fuming like I'd never seen her. This wasn't half an afternoon for surprises. 'I'm calling Barry. Get him back. Never seen work like it. Talk about bodging. Him an' his Birmingham fuckin' screwdriver. Never heard of rawlplugs!'

Bethany pleaded: 'What am I going to do? Celia . . . I can't . . . the procedure, you know . . . the AB word, I can't have it done, not without my parents' permission . . . not till I'm sixteen . . . And my birthday's not till . . . I'll be seven months gone. I can't tell them . . . Father Sluytwn would be furious . . .'

'I can imagine.'

What a quaint thing to call your dad: Father! That was what children called their dads in black and white . . . in the classics . . . the
Contessa Pavesi – all back along then.

'I'm scared, honest . . . honest*ly* – if he finds out . . . if he gets to
know I've been doing it with other people . . .'

'What are you on about? Other people . . .'

'Other people apart from him. He thinks I'm a virgin. It would
break Father Sluytwn's heart . . .'

She read my expression which said *whatever-is-this-I'm-being-let-
in-on?* She understood.

'I've carnaled with Father Sluytwn since . . . I'm his special jewel,
the precious diamond in the crown he calls me.'

I stared at this sweet girl with more and more astonishment. She
looked so innocent yet . . .

'What . . . do you . . . he thinks you're a *virgin* – how can he?'

How's your father indeedy!

'Virginity was consecrated by paradise. So long as I don't go with
no one else I am a virgin . . . That's what we believe – it's a buttress
tenet of the faith.'

She was most matter of fact. *Buttress tenet!* Fancy!

'You believe that?'

'Of course I do.' She might have added what she meant: Silly
Celia!

'I have sinned – that doesn't mean I've abandoned my faith.' She
sounded like she was reading from a script, a bit prissy, a bit righteous, considering. 'I just don't want him to find out. He'd put two
and two together. He'd know it wasn't him. Round the time we went
up to Brodrick Hall we weren't doing it because of him having a little
sniffle . . . he got the drips off Damaris.'

'Drips? Is that what I think it is . . . Ugh! This is . . .'

Offloading her nightmare on me. That's what she was doing.
Making me an accomplice. What world, what mad, mad world was I
being made part of? Was I an accessory now? How many crimes . . .
I was forced to peer into a dark place . . . abyss sort of place . . . I was
getting grim sordid glimpses. It wasn't hints. Not hints at all. It was
the plain facts.

'Damaris. Who's Damaris?'

'She's my sister. My big sister.'

Hang about, I thought . . . 'So she also . . . she and your father . . . ah, they . . .' I wiggled my hands.

She nodded.

'She's not his special jewel not like me . . . She's fast and loose . . . She surrendered her virginity . . . Father Sluytwn gives her the bull-whip lash. She begat his child, Little Zacharias. Mother Sluytwn was hopping mad. She still hasn't got over it. So he lives in the shed except when it gets really cold. We call him Zac.'

I held my hands over my eyes the way you do in a film when you want to look but can't bear to look. Peeking.

'I never knew most girls don't go with their fathers till Ginny said when I said something to her not meaning to . . . Year Eight that was . . . She called me a freak . . . an abnormal freak . . . she squitted to the class. I thought it was normal because it was normal for me. See? . . . It wasn't whether I liked it or hated it . . . it just was . . . It's what you do. And it's what you find in the Bible. We got a Bible family tree sampler on the family room wall: begat, begat, begat, begat, begat, begat . . . Do you know how many begats there are in the Bible . . . almost one hundred and fifty . . . It was normal for everyone back then, in Bible days. For us, Bible days aren't far away . . . they're still with us . . . every day's a Bible day. Every day the Lamb of God is within us and all about us. His wrath and his afflatus.'

That script again. It told her she sounded like those shiny-teeth evangelists . . . The Fresh Anointing Calvary Church of God in Christ . . . that was it . . . won't let you shut the door on them . . . steel toecaps . . . Holy Robots I call them.

She said: 'Yes they are very strange people, very strange customs they have.'

Muffled thunder growled in the distance. I suddenly felt exhausted, weary as a drudge. All my emotions had been siphoned off into the reservoir of lamentation – that's the only Holy Robot expression I can recall.

I looked her in the eye: 'Have you told him? How did he take it? You have been in touch?'

'I'm not following.'

'Twinkly Bobby. Does he know? Have you tol—'

'Twinkly Bobby? . . . Who—'

'Oh sorry love – that's my little . . . Mr Tedcastle.'

'What – Mr Tedcastle from *Stamford*?? What's he . . . I don't get. Why should I get in touch with . . . ?'

Courtesy . . . alms . . . maintenance . . . DNA test . . . blackmail . . . blackmail.

'I'm still not with you . . .'

Then the penny dropped making her gape so wide I could have seen her tonsils (if I'd been a nosey parker).

'Oh luvaduck Miss, you don't think it was *him*. No. Not in a million years . . . I never seen such a tiny baton of righteousness. It was a real tiddler . . . the size of someone's thumb . . . why go for a minnow when you can find a trout. I just told him run along find someone who wasn't so fussy . . . So he went and carnaled with Amber. Honest it was so small you'd think it was harmless . . . not much cop for begetting!'

Surely then not shy Mr Whiteside? Lairy Midget Casanova Andy? Some other Stamford blackhead? Whiffy old Bultitude?

'*It was*. It was Mr Bultitude, Celia . . . got me this way . . . Mr Bultitude.'

When you think things have got as bad as they can get . . . Along comes the devil's mechanic turning the screw making it worse.

'Bethany! How could you?'

'He was just reading me some poems and it happened . . . In a way I made it happen. His poems filled me with such joy—'

'He stank,' my plain speaking got the better of me. 'Bethany . . . He stank like a landfill.' Oh those foul gulls flocking over split black bags, guzzling rancid surgical waste matter.

'I wouldn't know,' she said, hoity toity, 'I've got no sense of smell. Runs in the family. Passed from generation to generation . . . congenital anosmia . . . Father Sluytwn and Mother Sluytwn are the same. And their father is too . . .'

Hang on a mo, I thought, hang on: *their* father, their *father*. No s. No plural. I didn't want to ask, I really didn't.

But, in spite of myself: '*Their* . . . Just one . . . one father?'

Bethany shrugged: 'They're sort of cousins, Father Sluytwn and Mother Sluytwn.'

'What sort of cousins?'

'Brother and sister sort,' she confirmed, defiantly. 'That's why I've got to get rid of this . . . this thing . . . intruder . . . I don't want to be giving birth to bad genes . . . you know, passing on genes from outside our pool, it's contamination . . . not the right blood.'

'Even though his poems *fill you with joy*!?' Yes, I can be satirical when it's called for.

'We brethren do not marry out . . .'

You can say that again. She was in the family way all right I witticised to myself.

Then another slogan: 'Inclusivity is profoundly within our DNA.'

And what DNA that must be! Extra Strong is what I'd call it . . . undiluted . . . That's what recessive means – 100 per cent proof. Still if it's good enough for the royals it's good enough for the Brethren.

I was aching for a solution to help Bethany with. Waiting for inspiration's arrow to strike I cheered her up with a couple of Hermann's Armagnac ganaches, the ones in a barrel-shaped coating recalling the old days of smugglers . . . milady's lace and brandy . . . wicked wreckers on distant clifftops. Not always the nicest of folks . . . but larger-than-life personalities . . . oh so manly . . . their personal hygiene might have been wobbly, mind you. It'll have been Mr Bultitude that made me think of that.

'Oh flippin Nora!' I said out loud. 'What next?'

Now there was a leak coming through onto *Botanica Britannica* left by Part-Time Tabitha carelessly lying on an artistic trough with droplets bouncing off the cover thankfully not the pages. I grabbed up the hefty tome and moved it to a chair while I fetched a bucket to catch the droplets. As I positioned the bucket I caught the book out of the corner of my eye—

And that was my eureka moment!!!

It called to me . . . the book called to me . . . honest to goodness it called to me . . . I looked at it on the chair . . . it was saying to me: What is a florist if she is not a magician with plants?

That was inspiration . . . which literally means breathing in . . . I breathed in the shop's pollens, the spores, the fragrant molecules . . . I breathed in my future competencies as a magician of plants . . . they were revealed to me by breath. It was like when I had my vocation revealed to me . . . just shown me on a plate. My talents as a magi of plants and flowers, pods and blossoms were imparted to me. They were gifts I hadn't put on my wishlist. I was chosen . . . I was chosen to receive them, to use them wisely and well.

'I've got an idea,' I announced formally with quiet authority that made Bethany and Part-Time Tabitha stand up and listen though Bethany was already standing up. 'To tell you the truth – it's more than an idea . . . it's more like a vision like. As soon as it clears up . . .' But it didn't clear up. And every minute counted.

The Berm . . . that's the nearest countryside to the shop . . . sort of countryside . . . not real full-on countryside . . . not the countryside where you'd go for a picnic and a cuddle . . . you wouldn't want to chill an ice cold bottle of Chablis in the waters there because of the high toxicity not to mention the sewage turds the floating filth . . . it curves across the old water meadows . . . they're all out of shape . . . broken sluices and blocked up channels . . . it's a raised causeway but it's never called that it's always The Berm. At the end are the pill boxes built in the defence of our island nation against the all-conquering jackboot in 1940 or thereabouts. There's only so much of it you can drive along . . . after that it's shanks's pony . . . it's single lane with the tarmac crumbling away down both sides . . . because it's six foot higher than the meadows you get a view across but you wouldn't call it a beauty spot . . . No way José! It's more a dumping spot for foam spilling out of those leatherette sofas, soggy mattresses, cooking oil cannisters, split open black bags, rusty cement mixers and stolen vehicles . . . they joyride them then push them off of The Berm . . . they get trapped in the mud . . . then the tractors that come to winch them out get trapped too . . . then the bulldozers that come to winch out the tractors . . . It's a bit like life itself . . . Also it's a sordid tipping area frankly . . . then there's the lovers lane aspect . . . the dogging spot which isn't for the timid despite my name! Till not so long ago it was the area's most prestigious dogging rendezvous with five stars on TripAdvisor . . . that was before the oinkies began to take an interest . . . if they didn't get first dibs with the ladies they noted down registration numbers . . . threatened to arrest all and sundry . . . Charley's Chow Cabin stopped showing up . . . no one was going to hang around for a whopping restore-your-strength Super Special Post-Coital Burger with Justin or was it Jason leering as he suggestively smothered the condemned meat in mustard and ketchup! And he calls himself a poet!

On the other side of the river, marmalade colour because of geology, up the slope, there are the backs of semis . . . long gardens sloping down to river level with rotting huts falling in. They were boathouses once. Not that the river's a natural river but diverted according to local history buff Barry's dad in the nineteenth century or maybe it was the eighteenth, even the fifteenth . . . anyway way back whenever it was the mill was built . . . The Berm's a flood defence. Now the mill's a chichi hotel hidden behind willow trees . . . visitors are spared seeing the despoilation of nature by trashing. No such luck for the houses . . .

Swings and roundabouts though . . . in the back bedrooms they all have telephoto lens cameras on tripods and binoculars for the dogging . . . some with infra-red night vision it is said . . . you can bet some nosey parkers and peeping toms were watching us. What would they make of us?

It was like a school nature trail adventure ramble but you don't ramble at dusk . . . I led looking left . . . Bethany was behind me looking right . . . A few years later we'd have been able to misidentify the plants with a programme like *Whadyoucallit*. As it was, Part-Time Tabitha came last hefting *Botanica Britannica* . . . it wasn't designed for carrying 'in the field' not just on account of the weight but the shape. It dwarfed her like it was a piece of furniture. But you have to say '*her burden she gamely bore* . . .' Where does that line come from? Not applicable to Bethany though! Her observational powers weren't focused. Anything but. They were impacted by her being *embaras*. That's Catalan for pregnant . . . the mot juste couldn't be juster! I learnt it on my Emergency Midwifery. There was this girl from near Barcelona. Estel . . . such a cute voice she had.

Concentrate! I felt like telling Bethany out loud but I'm too tender-hearted for my own good. We're out here with lashings of weather because of you Bethany . . . because of you falling into temptation which is a weird thing to think of Mr Bultitude as and not taking precautions. I felt like saying that too. Out here without wellies – which are precautions for our feet! Or would be if we had them! She couldn't keep her mind on the task. The rain pummelled us . . . the wind was a stinging wet towel . . . if you could detain weather it would be up on a charge of assault and battery not to mention grievous floral harm! Not that I was joking like that in the eye of the storm. *Hail rapes the vine* . . . It was getting on that way not that there was actually any hail as such. There were just bedraggled sheep and their dignified security alpaca. There were unloved sad horses without horse-blankets . . . not much to be joyful about living in those fields . . . troughs with holes, apathetic defeatist attitudes . . . then there's the damp from being flooded so often they'll get the hoof-fungus from . . . there was only so far you could go . . . beyond the pill boxes was where some of the travelling folk park up there from time to time with their vicious Marcher Hounds not to mention still a bad reputation in the locality.

My plan for Bethany? It was intimate with my Emergency Midwifery gleanings . . . I never thought they would come in handy in a practical sense. It was *Botanica Britannica* there brought it all back . . . we were given a list . . . what the pregnant lady needs to avoid during pregnancy . . . meaning if complications are arising the midwife can check out which dangerous toxins the patient has been in contact with . . . has she eaten shellfish or rubbed against venomous bark of the quauitl tree aka the soap apple . . . has she ingested poisonous herbs/berries/leaves?

Tarum tarum taree!!!

Instead of avoiding the items on the list . . . embrace them!!

Make them your friend . . . make them the foetus's enemy!

Flush out the intruder . . . poisonous herbs . . . I said it over and over . . . it was music to my ears . . . ought to have been to Bethany's too . . . though she was only half listening when I told her I had the solution to her predicament if only we could find it. Oh I laughed with joy . . . simple and complicated all at once!

Let's just find those plants, gals! As team leader I set out in front of the team facing up to the clouds . . . all a-swirling all a-gurning they were.

Parsley, pennyroyal, mugwort, ergot, stramonium, fairywort,

rue . . . known as herb of grace such a lovely name it brings serenity to the AB word . . . I remembered the names . . . all the names . . . it was the answer to a question we were told often came up in the final exam . . . I mugged up on them . . . sure enough it did come up . . . sure enough I came out top of the class . . . near enough anyway . . .

I silently saluted myself for remembering . . . but . . . but . . . the problem was that's all I remembered – the names. Knowing what these names looked like . . . fitting visuals to the words . . . matching this name to that leaf . . . that was a different skill set . . . I mean imagine just imagine getting it wrong . . . giving Bethany some brew that's totally harmless . . . does nothing . . . won't pull the rabbit out the hat so to speak . . . that's not the ticket is it, no way . . .

Here's where Part-Time Tabitha came in . . . her plant knowledge was profound in one so young . . . she knew all the Belgian names and the French ones too . . . she was into botany in general . . . she was often cheerily joking on about knowing the plants to poison Psycho Carl The Sociopath . . .

She'd say: 'I love my mum so much . . . but she goes and shares her bed with a beast . . . she can't see he's a beast even when he's beating her.' Isn't that super-loyal!

Me I was the flowers and ornamental one . . . herbalism wasn't my foal . . . not yet anyway . . . she trudged . . . such determination . . . checking every suspect leaf against the photos in the book . . . no luck . . . we were a team of novices . . . we'd only just started, there was little time to spare but when the lights in the houses started to go on and Part-Time Tabitha was having to use her phone as a torch I led the troops back to HQ!

There was a way to go before anyone called me 'slaghag' let alone 'witch' . . . my explanation . . . my defence if you want was that I was lending a helping hand . . . in an hour of real need . . . I had nothing to be ashamed of . . . Also I was saying up yours chum to the patriarchy that controls our bodies in its own interests . . . my lode-star was the Comparative Religions and Conflicting Belief Systems module with feisty Mrs Browning . . . Roman morality and pagan morality . . . they were there before there was Christian morality which is all don't don't don't don't . . . Who is to say which is right?

It's all made up by this tribe or the next tribe . . . I learnt pagan means *from the country* . . . something like that anyway . . . close in touch with nature . . . and nature doesn't do judgemental about the AB word . . . caribous, orca whales, gelada primates, osk beavers . . . they aren't sentimental about the unwanted *embaras* . . . it's men . . . their bit is done and dusted in a few mins . . . ninety seconds if you're Barry . . . compare that to nine months with an uninvited gatecrasher parasite swimming around inside . . .

Next day lunchtime I closed the shop for an hour . . . Part-Time Tabitha and me were out there on The Berm . . . eyes peeled . . . there's a horrible image when you come to think about it, how much do you peel? . . . doesn't bear thinking about . . . our luck was out again . . . That flower there . . . that hairy stem . . . that red stem . . . what's this pod . . . is that ergot . . . it says here vermin eat rue before they attack snakes . . . putting down the book on the wet grass made it wet and mucky . . . *grasses*, we were learning how many thousands there are just in one small area . . . like round the stile which isn't half an obstacle for the fuller figure . . .

Some of what we identified was burdock, ragwort, giant hogweed (keep your distance!), henbit, hare bells . . . it's different with goose grass, thistles, nettles and dock leaves – you know them anyway . . . none of them was going to do the trick. Bethany was at school . . . she called to say I had given her a great idea . . . this was the last of her credit . . . she'd be round later to explain . . . she sounded ever so bouncy I could hardly believe it was her, not to mention the morning sickness. Her pay-as-you-go is an immoral secret hidden from her phonephobic parents . . . *parents* – I can hardly bring myself to call them that though they are . . . they are . . . she keeps it in her school locker . . . it's always getting stolen or the money used up by slimebag thieving fellow pupils . . . what a relief it is not having to face up to the scum every day any more!

When you're just aching for a chocolate mousse or some scrummy ganache fillings to zhuzh up teatime . . . maybe a sneaky-in-between-meals-forbidden-bingette . . . you don't go and have to climb up a cacao tree to get the pods . . . possibly injuring yourself in the process . . . you go to the supermarket or when it's a rare-spoil-yourself-with-a-wicked-treat-why-not-occasion to Choc-A-Doodle-Do . . . Netta always slips an extra something in the bag. She's a great advert for her artisan yumminess. Her sister's the volleyball international . . . not so big-boned as Netta.

Bethany's great idea was *my idea* as she admitted . . . the same idea but different . . . just tweaked a bit . . .

The Team's third reconnaissance sortie later that day delivered another empty basket again . . . We were cheering ourselves with deluxe cocoa and doughnuts when Bethany arrived. Without further ado she says: 'It's plain obvious . . . it's staring us in the face . . . Just look . . .' Me and Part-Time Tabitha exchanged those glances where you pull down your mouth and go vertical-faced . . . you don't need to be a face-language pro to know that means *what the juggling otter is she on about?*

'There!' She pointed at the window display . . . symphony in carmine I thought of it as . . . there was a lady on the pavement looking through the window at it . . . to buy or not to buy! Buy! Not . . . she didn't . . . as soon as she saw us looking at her she moved off.

'Can't you see?'

I looked at the display . . . I looked through the window . . . traffic was tailing back from the junction . . . it often does that time of day . . . some of the vehicles had their lights on some didn't . . . it was that time of day . . . what was she getting at? I shrugged. It was like I was in some silly game which I hadn't been told the rules of as a wind-up . . . she was shaking her head in that can't-believe-you-don't-get-it way . . .

'Across the road!'

'What . . . the hairdressers?'

Across the road was Justine de Montparnasse: Coiffure Supreme . . . at those prices it bloomin' well should be supreme! Justine got the premises at bargain basement price after The Hair That I Breathe went into receivership . . . sued by a customer whose ironic beehive they set light to causing second degree burns and reconstructive surgery including multiple grafts. She is a stuck-up piece of work to my way of thinking, airs and graces . . . whored her way up so far she can't help looking down at you . . . she has this snotty American BFF who was like born to paaaaatronise . . . she's got a gent caller of a certain age . . . he certainly hasn't come for a bob and rinse . . . you might even say he's from a different age . . . genetically posh . . . remember Loyd Parnacott as St John de Vere Babbington Matravers in *The Gent* on Sunday afternoons all those years ago. He's along those lines . . . distinguished . . . cravat and buttonhole . . . thinks nothing of double parking . . . couldn't be more inconsiderate if he tried . . . don't know how many classic cars he's got . . . must have a hangar to house them . . . pops in now and again to buy lavish-but-elegant all-one-species all-one-colour bouquets . . . drawls to me gaping over my shoulder flagrantly mentally undressing Part-Time Tabitha who isn't mature enough to appreciate that she is being taken for a piece of meat.

'No! Next door . . . the health food shop . . . there . . . in front of you. Opposite.'

Oh . . . the health food shop . . . it was not strictly opposite . . . more at an angle on the other side of the road . . . I saw it every day but I never saw it . . . I'd never been inside . . . it's not that I'm against fellowship among us in the retail community . . . no I just hadn't got round to poking my head round the door to say how-de-dooo . . . introduced myself . . . perhaps swank a little about my takings compared with theirs! . . . I mean I've never seen anyone in there . . .

'They've got it all in pill form . . . they stock everything I need . . . well everything you said . . . everything that'll send it packing . . . Satan within . . .'

My idea . . . *my* idea . . . repackaged. But this was no time to be starting a barney about copyright! Satan . . . to my way of thinking calling it Satan was her way of impersonalising it. She was calling it unworthy of life . . . it was kinder to deny it life than send it out into a life for which it would be unfit . . . life was a challenge which it couldn't meet due to tainted blood . . . life would be hell for it . . . she had to hunt it down . . . so she could send it to hospice-heaven where Jesus personally oversees disciples who dripfeed it honey . . . not to mention opiates unavailable without prescription on this side . . .

Once the pills were finished the Naturopathway labels could be soaked off the little plastic bottles . . . you never know when they might come in handy . . . the name Naturopathway made me suddenly picture psychopath nudists peeping out from behind trees . . . stalking us decent ordinary folk . . . the ones they sneer down as 'textiles' just out for a stroll along sandy pathways through the woods. Bethany was obedient, an ideal patient . . . or should I say guinea pig. That afternoon was the first experiment . . . not surprising the health food shop's always empty . . . daylight robbery! As the only fully waged one on the team I felt the hurt . . . but we're all in this together . . . I'm the one she confided in . . . you can be sure some of them are quack remedies . . . but nothing ventured . . . Part-Time Tabitha dodged through the traffic . . . she fetched a nice array of leaves for infusions and a 'cocktail of pills' . . . like the bitter nibbles suicides gorge themselves on along with a pint of gin and a slit wrist in the newspaper coroner report . . . always a sad read.

Three hours later Bethany was frisky as a puppy dog, regrettably . . . no stomach pains regrettably . . . no nothing regrettably . . . no symptoms of what they call 'evacuation' regrettably . . . it was time for her to go home . . . it hadn't been much of a start . . . we decided to try the next day though Bethany would be late down to remedial psychogeography being outside normal hours . . . she couldn't risk missing it . . . she didn't want anyone getting suspicious . . . the whole school was already suspicious of each other.

A pattern emerged. We'd sit around in the shop from about five o'clock with Bethany popping pills by the handful . . . I'd have the kidney-bowl, gloves, sterile-kit and what have you all ready for the moment . . . please don't get the idea we were doing invasive, we weren't . . . just following shaman recipes from long ago and far away . . . that was us . . . sometimes it was just the two of us when Part-Time Tabitha was doing one of her other part-time jobs waitressing at The Neon Castanet or Nonchalant & Debonair or helping out over at Mac's Half Way Lazaret . . . no matter how many of us there were – two or the entire team – we kept it festive with music and dancing to overcome the pain and potential remorse and emptiness not to mention savoury snacks inc. artisan crisps and chocolates . . . I had a nifty bottle of Cointreau . . . snuggy and warming, you don't want ice in it. Bethany was immune to everything I began to think . . . to everything . . . nothing had any effect . . . I have to say it was lovely being with her circumstances or no circumstances . . . she chatted all sorts . . . her religion's beliefs about cattle . . . her 'tryst' with Mr Bultitude for instance . . . he referred several times to an actress and a bishop . . . weird-ola! . . . she hadn't said it to him but he reminded her of Bishop Timmy of The Charismatic Brethren of the Great Tribulation . . . the one who went missing because of offences . . . not to get him mixed up with the one on *The Big Story*'s front page . . . the Metropolitan Apostolic Bishop of the Global Light Revival . . . he went missing after (among other naughties) he ticked off a Croydon Facelift for her repeated fornications by cutting off her pony tail when she was performing a Redemptive Sex Act (RSA) on him . . . two of god's representatives on earth . . . two international arrest warrants . . . blimey what's it all coming to! Bethany couldn't have agreed more profoundly. Her moods swung like a swing.

The more days that passed . . . the more painful the process . . . there are times when even the crispiest crisp churros live from the microwave wouldn't make the sun shine in her heart . . . I tried not to say the AB word . . . she would keep bringing it up though . . . oh all the worries she had . . . she was one of the ones gifted with knowledge-thirst and sensitivity . . . it makes life that much more difficult . . . she fretted about the psychological after-effects . . . about how one day she'd be looking back to now and now would be the past but still with her . . . about making sure no one knew . . . she wanted to marry a man from her faith . . . it was her desire and her duty . . . but if it was known that . . .

Sunday . . . day broke brightish and so-so . . . byebye totally gloomy grey sky all overcast and drizzly and making me miz . . . a big hullo to a lovely less grey sky not exactly cloudless . . . certainly not a hardly a cloud in the sky day . . . but all made up for by one of those kindly breezes that kisses you like a prince . . . albeit a minor prince . . . you feel soothed by a minor prince's blue blood electricity . . . there was no hint that it was going to be the worst day of my life . . . in fact at that moment it was 7/10 for happiness harbingering.

Bethany was at the shop when I arrived. I hadn't expected her before afternoon. She'd told her parents she was sick with food poisoning so couldn't go with them to first chapel. She had said she would go later . . . they said if she didn't she would end in hell – again . . . how many deaths can they heartlessly wish on her? After chapel they were taking a train to a protest at the Terminus Radical Thanatology Clinic in Thames Ditton . . . they had their slingshots . . . they were hoping to lapidate the doctors of evil . . . they shout through megaphones . . . screaming at the patients inside . . . telling them that the aborted hunt their parents and haunt them forever.

'Well I am sick aren't I? Sick! I defiled my garments.' She burst into floodgates of tears . . . it was like an eye enema . . . the reservoir burst . . . I hugged her there-there there in the doorway . . . then I found my keys and we went inside for a good old heart to heart which basically came down to her getting all het up going 'They're all quack remedies . . . it's all a fraud Naturopathway . . .' Well, I didn't want to remind her it was her idea . . . my idea was nature's remedies not pasteurised not homogenised not pills not capsules not packaged with all the harmful goodness processed out of them . . . we had to listen to Mother Nature herself I said and she agreed . . . cut out the middlemen from Naturopathway Inc . . . parasites! We agreed we had to hunt harder. Part-Time Tabitha arrived with the hangover from hell plus a bright suggestion straight from the classroom . . . 'Dildos To You Dykey . . . a different environment . . . that's where we need to go looking in . . . an ecological paradise . . . somewhere totally different flora from yon Berm . . .' The weather was infectious see. Her motion was unanimously approved. She glugged a couple of gallons of water . . . not strictly Adam's ale down to the amount of chlorine.

'Where?' wondered Bethany, mirroring my thought. 'Where do you expect to find it . . . ecological paradise?'

'Yaffle Moor.'

'Yaffle Moor. Isn't that the one they call date rape glen . . . it's miles away. It's haunted.'

'No, that's Tolly Dene . . . date rape *dell* . . .'

'Whatever. Used to be haunted . . . well it was thought spiritual,' I said. 'That was before it was taken over by the dogging community I heard.'

Part-Time Tabitha grinned at us . . . she shook a bunch of keys like a castanet. Ole!

'I know where the bastard Psycho Carl hides them . . . With his VHS porn from the old days when they weren't shaven . . . he keeps them out of sentimental attachment . . . I've liberated his pick-up . . . They've gone to Alicante for a week . . . this month's fresh start . . . It'll drive itself there . . . it knows the way . . . it's one of his dogging places . . .'

I so admired her daring. I told her so. She was in such a skittish playful mood despite the seriousness of our task . . . she said that if Psycho Carl The Sociopath found out she'd taken the pick-up and came on uber-psycho she'd grass him up to the oinkies . . . she had the proof.

'Proof of what?' I didn't like to pry . . . but . . .

'I'll think of something.'

Not so much skittish, more like determined. I never dreamed she meant it.

When Bethany went to the senoritas behind a shrub Part-Time Tabitha was different . . . she whispered in earnest: 'We got to get it done soon Celia, first trimester . . . I've been reading this book called *You Missed The Bus Luv* . . . about leaving it too late . . . bit like a how-to book for butchering . . .'

She waved the keys again. She opened the door . . . a rude gust gatecrashed in . . . silhouetted against the bright day . . . she flung her olive paisley scarf around her neck and over her shoulder . . . she flung her blueblack scarf around her neck and over her shoulder . . . again again again . . . it was sent looping by the burly wind . . . it disobeyed her. She tucked her down like rugby and pushed into the wind.

'I'll go and fetch the hearse round . . .' I heard her say . . . but it wasn't her . . . she was out in the noisy street . . . too far away for me to hear anything she said . . . it echoed . . . Had I heard it before . . . *hearse* . . .

It was a whooshy spine-creepy repetition of . . . something . . . where . . . where . . . when . . . I was trying to grab it . . . nail it down . . . it was slipping away . . . where was it from . . . when was it from . . . that silhouette . . . just exactly . . . the scarf getting there at fourth attempt . . . Part-Time Tabitha silhouetted.

★

'You sure about Yaffle Moor?'

'Don't worry . . . done my research. Scholastic, moi! Mucho meano! I got that app and . . . get this . . . I even downloaded the *Latchmore and Bartley Botanical Society Proceedings* no less . . . and *Glyde's Remedialis, Herbal Palliative and Botanical Reformer* . . . I think I got that right . . . anyway the one I was saying about . . . known as Satan's Sanative Speedwell . . . lewd wicked witchcraft . . .'

It's all deep in the earth . . . where the roots live . . . it's all down to geology's time scale . . .

I hadn't been out this way for quite some time. You forget that there's loveliness within your grasp just a twenty-minute drive . . . if you've got a pick-up . . . even if the pick-up cab is playing sardines with not enough on the space/comfort ratio to score more than a measly 3/10 . . . talk about tightfit . . . if the weather wasn't the full mank someone could have volunteered to ride in the back on the 'bed' bit with all the rolls of roofing felt, tar paper and glass fibre, big plastic jumbo buckets of sealant and liquid mortar . . . but at least the cab was all shipshape and bristol fashion with Psycho Carl's crisp overalls hung from a hook and smelling lavender fresh which you don't expect a Psycho's overalls to smell. And what about this! A fun plastic tissue dispenser which played 'Ave Maria' with each tissue pulled out . . . a deluxe DVD player . . . lots of big emotion trailer park favourites from lesser-known Nashville artistes Murray Collins, Campbell Allanson and Timmy-Boy 'Mr Velvet Baritone' Niel on DVD . . . a red and white hand vacu like an invasion from Saturn ray gun with its own holster . . . an unopened pack of Nebraska Minted Menthol . . . an unopened pack of surgical gloves . . . an unopened three pack of man knickers (black) . . . an unopened three pack of T-shirts (black) . . . an unopened pack of Markwick's Tablet . . . an unopened pack of Bombay Mix . . . unopened was a bit of a theme . . . till you got to the charcoal biscuits in the depths of the glove compartment . . . they were nibbled . . . we all know what they're for! But what was the novelty joke fun-fur lumberjack cap for? Ear flaps down the sides . . . C-A-R-L in big letters on the front . . . big soft floppy antlers on top . . . ready for a party . . . what a hoot Cap'n Moose . . . I tried it on for a laugh . . . get this – when you pulled the strings on the ear flaps the antlers stood up like a jack in the box . . .

'Not just a Psycho – I told you he was a prat,' said Part-Time Tabitha.

It was nice and cuddly but what the mirror said was 'not the most flattering fascinator ever!'

Cattle grids are an invitation to expectation! The countryside doesn't have to be sad mank like The Berm. It can be happy with rhododendrons and giant pine trees. It can be joyful with smiling ponies and bracken (or ferns) even when it's gloomy. It can be awesome . . . Yaffle Moor is ever so epic . . . heathery purple stretching off to distant far away with glints of bronzey orange . . . dabs of blue sky where water has pooled and hasn't sunk in . . . is there anything that lifts your heart more than ponies grazing between silver birches on tight cropped grass . . . lawns but not garden lawns . . . natural lawns . . . then there's the 'moss' . . . the bog where a garrotted turned-to-leather girl they called 'The Little Mystery from Dark Prehistory' gave the peat cutter that found her such a turn . . . poor bloke never hoisted a tarasgeir (posh word for sort of spade of the trade) again . . . went and sought employment in the transport sector at Redbridge . . . heaven is the gently bubbling trout rich stream . . . heaven is the mist floating ghostly across god's bracken (or ferns) acres . . .

There's nothing like nicely manicured gravel. The Yaffle Moor (North) car park wasn't very full at all – too early. So this important (to me) feature was visible. The low stripped log fences were spruce as a hospital corner. The bin bags clipped to metal frames were empty. Lovely! Gloria in excelsis . . . The sights . . . the light . . . the air you can't see but feel soothing like a considerate lover crept to your room at night . . . the sound of bird song tweetering cooing . . .

But then the smell hit . . . it hit just seconds after when we got out the pick-up when the wind gusted . . . talk about rank . . . talk about Dien Bien Pue as old Monsieur Calafato used to joke but it wasn't much of a joke because he always had to remind most of the class what it was a joke about and even then the dull and backwards didn't get! You couldn't see where it came from straight off . . . but I knew that smell . . . strange . . . it was a totally familiar smell . . . it was like I had smelled that smell before . . . that exact same smell . . . and then there it was . . . more or less hidden the other side of a couple of motorhomes (No Overnight Parking Clamping Possible After 11pm) was Charley's Chow Cabin . . . it had been resprayed canary yellow . . . there was new red lettering on the side saying 'Where The Meat Is' . . . the hydrogenated whatsit and the mechanically recovered unspeakables were committing an environmental crime, terrorising ordinary folks' nostrils with nasal GBH . . . natch Bethany didn't get why we were screwing up our faces . . . Jason or was it Justin? . . . came round the side of the van zipping up from going to nature's gents . . . he gave a friendly salute.

Now wash your hands before handling food you insanitary so-called poet!

No *Botanica Britannica* that day. Part-Time Tabitha had got herself Pod@Snap© – plant visualisation software with rich image recognition capacity . . . out damned smell! . . . we beat a hasty into the wilderness to get away from it . . . we ventured into the wildwood! Part-Time Tabitha to the fore with her multi-pocket multi-buckle multi-Velcro backpack on her back . . . a special compartment for every foreseeable need.

There were permanent puddles . . . unofficial pools . . . there were nasty busy bristly blow flies . . . nasty but lovely iridescence . . . dung beetles . . . plucky little chaps . . . if only they weren't saddled with that name they'd have so much going for them in terms of industriousness and ingenuity. We skirted along a babbling brook . . . there were horse hoof imprints in the sandy mud . . . a suddenly big sky where the brook broke free of the tunnel of trees it had flowed through . . . its bed was suddenly revealed . . . all smoothed gingery to brown pebbles . . . the water was so clear the tiny fishes could see their way . . . but unless they grow up quick they'll become starter portions for the pikes of death that dwell in the weeds downstream where the brook widens into a river . . . we were taking note of the flora . . . the plants were so different . . .

Part-Time Tabitha was keeping up a running commentary . . . it was a lesson without slides with the real things instead of slides . . . this wort that wort . . . judith bells . . . robin bells . . .

brettleberries . . . hederalia . . . dominicus shrub . . . greenstem . . . giant candles . . . Tasmanian lady ferns . . . dwarf tree ferns . . . dwarf birches . . . altogether more dwarfs than Snow White! It was heavy going . . . quite a plod . . . more for your nothing-but-skin-and-bone charity-advert compassion-fatigue-style marathon champ than the sprint fraternity . . . I had to have a sit-down whenever a suitable log hoved into view even if it was a damp earwig hostel and more a rotten stump than a log. I sat. Solid shafts of sunbeam invasive through the boughs . . . ironically with the motes and what have you particules they looked frozen . . . it's a revelation of what you're breathing in. Part-Time Tabitha focused solemnly . . . checking petals and stamens against her iPhone images . . . the forest was her laboratory . . . Bethany stalked restless . . . pulled at leaves . . . peeled bark from twigs . . . she was rubbing elasticky tufty grass between her fingers when she cried shrill as shrill could be:

'Oh my god look! Isn't that what you call it? What d'you call it?' And it was . . . Raven's Bane.

'It *is* Raven's Bane, it really is! Good spot!' said Part-Time Tabitha giving Bethany a hug . . . she was trying to clap . . . but holding onto her iPhone was the better part of valour.

We took a collective breath before Part-Time Tabitha summarised her screen read: 'Flowers for less than forty-eight hours . . . raised crest . . . often mistaken for Ebony Can . . . ah, sorry – Ebony Candytuft . . . unlike Ebony Candytuft, Raven's Bane stalks emit black liquid when squeezed or cut . . . blabla . . . oooh yummeee . . . get this – narcotic, hallucinogenic, poisonous . . . extremely dangerous to pregnant women . . . notorious in Sicily and Calabria . . . administered by witches . . . s . . . t . . . r . . . e . . . *streghe* . . . how d'you say it?'

'When shall we three meet again?' I quipped. I must admit I'd been rehearsing that one . . . looking for a window to slip it in with a certain je ne sais quoi.

'What do I do?' asked poor suddenly-vulnerable Bethany now facing the coal face of decision . . . not to mention destiny . . . this wasn't low energy pills from Naturopathway . . . not such a great idea that hadn't been . . . an age seemed to pass . . . the trees floaty-swayed just like those mime artistes you get in shopping malls pretending to be trees . . . she was 9/10 for prevarication . . . or is it procrastination . . . anyway taking the plunge wasn't coming easy . . . Part-Time Tabitha was sawing away at the tough stem with her Tundra Survival knife . . . the blade was black with sap or whatever . . . not the yummiest looking plant . . . but needs must . . .

We showed solidarity me and Part-Time Tabitha . . . we took a few leaves . . . swallowed them . . . bitter but interesting . . . suddenly Bethany impetuously – most unlike her – grabbed a handful of leaves and a flower . . . she forced them into her mouth so much her cheeks swelled . . . her eyes almost popped out of her head . . . what a giggle . . . a hilarious comedy moment . . . you could almost hear the audience roaring with infectious laughter . . . but she couldn't see the funny side obviously . . . she looked indignant at being laughed at . . . that didn't help her swallow. I thought she was going to choke but she got it all down . . . she turned away hurt . . . Part-Time Tabitha gave her water from her knapsack . . . it's vital to keep hydrated . . . before you knew it she had plucked another handful of the plant and swallowed that too.

We sat side by side on a trunk for minutes or hours . . . a mighty oak felled by Storm Deidre or Storm Desmond . . . Bethany sat in the middle and we watched her . . . exchanging glances when she was staring in front of her . . . getting up now and again for a stretch . . . really to check on how dilated her eyes were getting . . .

'What's that?' shrieked Bethany.

She stood up with an electric jolt . . . she's seeing things I thought . . . so did Part-Time Tabitha think . . . so did a bird hurrying away from where it had been hiding close by disguised as lichen.

Then it was my turn to jump . . . there was what I'd call a shape moving among the trees . . . a luminous yellow shape . . . when it came out of its bush it was just a welcome stout yellow lady in a rain cloak . . . cinched with a belt . . . matching yellow and black fun wellies perhaps unsuitable for muddy underfoot . . . that was a relief . . . nothing to worry about . . . she had an important lanyard round her neck, a clipboard and a moustache . . . she introduced herself, Heath Management Volunteer Force . . . her voice was a comforting chocolate brown . . . she sat down with us . . . she'd like to ask our opinion on the Yaffle Moor Experience . . . I love a box to tick . . .

Accessibility 7/10. Signage 8/10. Maintenance (state of) 9/10. Emotional Impact 9/10 (a difficult one to judge). Visual Impact 9/10. Disabled Provisions 10/10. Floral Diversity 10/10 (if we could have given it 11/10 we would have).

We couldn't come up with specialist extras which would add value to the experience.

'I'll leave that blank then . . . the purpose of your visit?' she asked.

'Botanical research,' I said.

Bethany said louder over the top of me: 'Abortion . . . my abortion.'

The stout yellow lady stood . . . she grew stouter and stouter till she was super-stout . . . she nodded . . . she put down her clipboard and pen . . . her moustache bristled with thought.

'We get more and more of those . . . it's the future oh yes . . . the old ways are the new ways . . . do as you will little sister . . . never listen to god . . . she craves lives so that she may visit upon them plagues, frogs, sores, boils the size of a crown green jack, pussy abscesses . . . Remember Herod's cleansing ways . . .' She waved at the sky with a clench fist.

'Remember – once upon a time he was called Hero no "d" . . . Cleanse yourself, little sister . . . cleanse yourself oh yes.'

And she was gone. Striding away getting larger and larger the further away she was . . . that wasn't right.

Later the sun was moving about jerkily . . . making our shadows shift around us and shorten because we didn't seem to want to move and so we sat still and stayed put . . .

Two riders, m & f, riding at a frisky trot bowed to us as they rode past . . . bowed with twirly hands and frilly cuffs like they were in a play with ruffs wigs beauty spots (faces, not quaint villages). They were dressed to the nines . . . daringly tight leather breeches, gorgeous his 'n' hers hunting pink sage green jackets, black top hats with his 'n' hers blond hair and auburn hair cascading . . . quite the everyday rural picture – I don't think! Her rain-shined horse reared . . . it danced . . . it was a horse not a pony, you could tell from the size of the nostrils each one like a cave entrance to the unknown . . . she brought it under control . . . spurred it to a canter along a grassy avenue . . . birds hurled themselves into the air . . . isn't it funny the way jays are so clumsy at flying for birds . . . like they have some hard evolving to do . . .

I don't know how long we'd been there wrapped in nature's embrace when all of a sudden Bethany leaned forward from our seat . . . she vomited projectilely . . . what strength! . . . black black bile . . . it was as if there was something inside her forcing it out . . . hurling her stomach belongings . . . a water cannon . . .

Bethany held our hands. 'It's beginning,' she said.

We were walking silently . . . seeking the sun . . . it had gone before it should have . . . we were walking where there was no path, crispy leaves underfoot and grey bark beech trees with their arms in the air like they were being held up in a stick-up . . . mossy banks and frightening mushrooms . . . knotted mazes of roots of trees blown down by Deidre or Desmond . . . I thought to myself this must be what 'nature' poets get up to writing about but I kept mum because of Bethany . . . not knowing one minute to the next how sensitive she was about *the father* . . . for instance she said: 'I don't know so long as I live if I'll ever want to carnal again.' Then I caught her looking so intently at a leaf . . . if she'd been a light source she'd have set it on fire . . . the leaf was more real than real to her . . . she was seeing things in a way that I couldn't not having had so much Raven's Bane . . . not to mention a top-up of Heath Speedwell . . . Part-Time Tabitha swooped on them like the wolf on the Assyrian . . . Bethany came on Boudicca-like . . . she grabbed the plant . . . munched the flowers . . . pale mauve and white striped like shirts that oily baddies wear in big business dramas . . . have you ever watched some tiddly blottissimo draining every last drop of every last bottle at the end of the party when the party's over and he/she doesn't think anyone's watching? Well that was like Bethany . . . she was going 'More, more, more' . . . her mouth was bleeding from the nasty hairy stems . . . she was bending double in agony or pain or whatever it was . . . all loufouky . . .

Then screeching pained animal style when she saw the naked people come gliding out of the undergrowth . . . bold as brass . . . might as well be descending from heaven . . . you'd never have thought naked was camouflage but one minute there was just green growth the next there was The Shepherds of the Empyrean Light

Reborn sometimes almost clapping their hands almost but not quite so no noise made in time to god the Conductor's rhythms they felt by way of their Enchanted Culvert . . . mouthing words but not saying them . . . sometimes walking tall like evolved gods . . . sometimes walking crouched like monkeys with evolving to do . . . scratching themselves . . . scratching the one in front picking nits and clinkers from cavities . . . they move primate-fashion grubbing in the muddy leaves and rooty undergrowth . . . his followers follow him . . . Indian file like pine processionaries as decreed by their leader at their head . . . The Man of the Cloth Ear . . . rangy as a lion . . . years ago he lost his hearing playing in a world-famous uber-hyper-savage-metal rock band it is said . . . before my time . . . I never knowingly heard them . . . Strapadiktome . . .

That's when The Man of the Cloth Ear began to hear god the Conductor within him . . . telling himself to lead people through sunlit meadows, dark woods, maze woods, dappled woods . . . loving the trees . . . the women make so-called fascina . . . ultimately they take their satisfactions from branches by friction . . . the men track down the holes where knots in the wood were . . . they meet with them . . . no law against it . . . they all live in a cul de sac of condemned houses near the refinery . . . unlike most captains of religion The Man of the Cloth Ear has committed no known offences . . . I've done research . . . I've checked it out that two prosecutions under Section 5 of the Public Order Act 1986 were thrown out of court . . . both times the oinkies ordered to pay costs . . .

The Man of the Cloth Ear walks puff-chested like he is about to spread his arms to fill the world with spirit power and the pulse of eternity . . . bellowing proclaiming his ecstatic light . . . what an ethereal sight . . . hair flowing like a marmalade mane (not natural eco-marmalade I don't think) . . . he's like god in one of those powerful musicals with a sumptuous strings finale . . . epic glissando . . . clashing drum rolls . . . bolts of lightning . . . he can bleed at will. Bethany put her hands over her ears: 'Why have they got drums and those . . . those cymbal things why are they beating drums and cymbals? Why so loud . . .' There was not a drum or cymbal to be seen . . . no not a drum or cymbal to be seen anywhere . . .

She was hearing what was being sent from The Man of the Cloth

Ear . . . noises that existed in his head . . . then in her head . . . noises no one else can hear them . . . she was trying to shut out the noises . . . they were hurting so much she scowled in pain . . . it must have been thunderous . . . he howled to the skies . . . blood seeped from his ears . . . red drizzle clouded on the wind . . . then The Shepherds of the Empyrean Light Reborn were vanished . . . now you see them now you don't . . . they were gone in the twinkle of an eye . . . if you didn't know you'd say they were just ordinary naturists with strange movement who had ever so many grazes and scratches itchy weal things . . . that's what communing with deer-frayed bark brambles holly etc. brings to the party . . . you end up like you are cross-hatched as they say in valuable teaching aid *Make Friends With a Pencil*.

Bethany moaned rocking back and forward to and fro holding her stomach . . . for about the umpteenth time she said 'it' was beginning . . . but I ask how many beginnings can you have . . . not that I said anything . . . I don't have the impatience DNA . . . poor thing, she had enough on her plate . . . she had even more when Part-Time Tabitha gave her more Heath Speedwell . . . she munched it in a daze . . . was she forgetting why she was here? Her all-weather jacket was stained in black black bile . . . lucky it was wipe-down non-stain so the stains wouldn't show . . . it was only drizzle on and off but her hair was stuck flat to her scalp . . . her ankle-length skirt was soaked to the knees . . . she was scratching . . . more tearing at the flesh.

The wet trees screwed up their boughs . . . they were fed up to the teeth with being trees don't you think . . . when the wind blew they shivered . . . every jewelled drop of water on a leaf seemed to contain everything . . . fish scale bark shone 3-D . . . poor Bethany was sobbing and gasping in an un-Bethany way . . . attention seeking I'd call it . . . saying it was all black when it was obviously not all black but darker green because of the sun having a rest from rollin' around heaven all day . . . I love that song . . . we should be grateful to the sun . . . understanding when it takes time out for a well-deserved snack break . . . I said so to Bethany . . . she wailed out-of-control . . . she shocked the piggies on acorn hunt . . . she was crawling . . . she clung to my arm . . . 'There's those cymbals again . . . oh won't they please please stop . . . Celia make them stop!' I thought that maybe

she was having a low blood sugar moment . . . I offered her a generous square of Rosenthal 80 per cent cocoa decadence with candied
lemon . . . she waved it away and lowed like a sick cow.

Then I realised . . . I could hear them too. Or something like
cymbals . . . banging in time . . . from far off close by . . . the next
moment we were there . . . the next hour we were there . . . time
goes in reverse . . . in a far off part of the far off . . . in the forest's
hidden heart which is a dark decayed heart . . . nick nack paddy
wack . . . spreading tomorrow's sweet poison through the forest's
body today . . . where a path through last season's bracken track
petered out in a dell which it turned out was a magnificent sacred
grove one day a week for a dozen not quite naked men with blood all
over their limbs and two Marcher Hounds . . . the men were so hairy
their backs were fur coats muddied from wrestling in the mud . . .
they had nose rings . . . those things they wore Part-Time Tabitha
said were cock rings (I had heard of them before but hadn't seen one
not to mention a dozen) . . . tell you what, Barry could benefit. They
make the package look super potent but − and this isn't part of the
plannification I'll bet − they aren't half vulnerable to sharps . . . fingernails . . . those filed teeth I keep hearing about . . . amazing!
cocorico! . . . not to mention multiple tattoos and leather leather leather . . . whole herds had been abattoirised to give these men clothes
that can't have kept them warm . . . just all straps and buckles and
thongs and caps and masks . . . these men were knotted together in a
circle of hell . . . they were drumming on jerry cans . . . hitting a
wrecked arsoned car's bits and doors with metal bars . . . some of
them just watched the others roughpawing each other shamelessly . . . animals regressing the beasts of the forest . . . singing nick
nack paddy wack . . . some with their stiff tongues lapping into the
split body of a stag with a crossbow bolt through its head . . . communion . . . novelty eucharisting . . . blood all around . . . their
bodies were covered in it . . . it was drying brown all caked . . . the
dogs were joining in the fun there too ripping at the stag's liver . . .
bits of lung . . . give a dog a bone . . . wheresoever the body is, thither
will the eagles be gathered together . . . that's not literal eagles
understand.

'They're the Smiths and Tinkers of The Shining Beztine,'

whispered Part-Time Tabitha, 'they got a special dispensation from The Moot to slaughter stags. Not in summer though.'

This old man he played three . . . it was a sight from one of those religious paintings way back in history warning about hell . . . scary . . . but tell you what hell looks like more fun than heaven if you're the sort that goes for that sort of carnage malarkey with a group of likeminded gent chums and a couple of dangerous dogs . . . if you're one of those gents with their ringed cocks trembling and swollen like an RIB bouncing on choppy water . . . seeking random throats and no.2 holes . . . give the dog a bone give the dog a bone . . . they yelled in chorus – all those without mouths that weren't full up . . . not everyone's cup of pee!! – lovely to see people enjoying themselves in such a boistering (if messy) way.

We did not put them off their carousel . . . they didn't mind at all . . . they do their thing we do ours . . . toleration is where it's at . . . 8/10 for making their own fun the good old-fashioned way . . . and not sitting in front of a screen watching someone else's bits . . . they hardly took no notice of us . . . not even when Bethany crawled between hairy limbs getting hot and friendly with each other . . . she wanted the companionship . . . I kept seeing muscles exploding out of the stretched skin keeping them in – just . . . all that pumping adds muscle like it's been smuggled in from outside . . . then Bethany was scratching and scratching saying she had ants all over her crying and crying trying to sweep them off her . . . but we couldn't see them . . . she claimed they were red ants from an anthill high as a tree but we couldn't see them . . . we couldn't see the anthill . . . we were seeing different things . . . we were seeing things . . . what Bethany said was the anthill was actually a bush winking at Part-Time Tabitha . . . it was the sun on the droplets silly . . . for me it was actually shadows jumping mad as a broom like long ago in grandma days . . . stiff petticoats, coshes and sideburns Saint Vitus jitterbugging . . . that is if I was looking at the same thing they were which was hard to say . . . impossible to get a comprehensive overview now . . . you see everything back to front when you're seeing things . . . same in dreams . . . it's like those photos in *Telly Tasties* where they used to get full colour Dish of the Month the wrong way round . . . The Gent's breast pocket handkerchief was on the right side of his jacket on my bedroom wall for yonks before I realised . . . I found myself up a tree . . . high up . . . not knowing how I got there . . . nick nack paddy wack soared to the sky . . . I was looking down on the games the games – that was it – the games like in ancient times but without the nets and forks and lions . . . mind you Marcher Hounds are top stand-ins . . . bird's eye view . . . from up here you could see where one of the men who used to be a unicorn had had his unicorn severed off the top of his head leaving scars and bleeding sores . . . bomb damage . . . you could see Bethany laid out relaxing on a bed of pine cones . . . when you see them super close what a wonderful sculptor Mother Nature is . . . there was a chap beside her smoking a cigar size joint . . . how did I know the unicorn had been forcibly cut off . . .

Suddenly a whistle sounded . . . like a football ref . . . they're all fascists Barry says refs are . . . suddenly I was on the ground again at the bottom of the tree . . . wind whooshed through the sacred grove . . . the man with the whistle had smart uniform overalls . . . obvious from his body language he was an authority figure . . . all the leathermen ceased doing the disgusting . . . they didn't complain . . . along with his air of quiet authority the whistle man had very white skin needing to get out more . . . he had a group of other men in the same uniform alongside him also needing to get out more . . .

He called loud: 'Time's up lads . . . back on the bus now lads.'

The man with the cigar size joint's leather apron brushed against me. I started. He put out two say-sorry palms.

'Don't worry luv I'm on Omaxapron.'

Whatever that is when it's at home.

He poked a finger towards where Bethany was: 'Your mate's gone to sleep . . . hope she's all right . . . fancy a toke?'

There was blood on the mouth end of the joint . . . I shook my head.

'I'll put it behind my ear for later then . . . Right! Back to Alcatraz it is . . . nice seeing you luv – and you look after her eh.'

The leathermen followed the uniforms obediently . . . four of them carried the stag on their shoulders like a coffin . . . even the Marcher Hounds were obedient . . . knew the drill . . . they fell in almost military on parade . . . all their fierceness had vanished . . . they were a zoo troop . . . where did that meekness come from?

Some were bleeding from their no.2 holes . . . who were they? I went and sat myself near where Bethany was having her forty winks. The stage was deserted . . . all that was left was the burnt broken abandoned car . . . poor car . . . someone must have cared for it once . . . washed it of a Sunday with the kids splashing in the hose water . . . it was all eerie empty . . . like it had never happened . . . like those energetic folk had never existed . . . as if a battle that had been fought here had been fought long ago by ghosts . . .

I was hoarse as dobbin . . . Part-Time Tabitha found me some water from her knapsack. 'What's happening?' I asked. 'What's going on . . . who are they . . . where do they come from? They were like ghosts.'

She laughed: 'Oh they're from Landford . . . the Open Prison . . . they're allowed out on day release for worship purposes . . . they got this ruling . . . high court ruling . . . that The Shining Beztine is a religion not a cult . . . then end of day . . . warders come and fetch them . . . like the mummies and daddies in "Teddy Bears' Picnic" I always think . . .'

That song always gave me the creeps. It got worse.

Part-Time Tabitha added: 'Most of them are murderers . . .'

She saw my face.

'Don't you worry Celia . . . they're non-violent murderers.'

I hadn't heard of that kind of murderer before.

'The others have been chemically castrated with Lupron – the really bad ones. That's what makes them religious . . .'

Would they ever make their way back into the society of the fully balled? I wondered.

A cloud dropped down . . . a black tent of weather . . . showing just how mood swings come from the weather with us both thinking at the very same moment that we were neglecting Bethany . . . it was her big day after all.

Part-Time Tabitha hurried across the glade between the oil drums, chains, rotting batteries with greenish bits, wires every which way. Mindful of tinea pedis I tried to squeeze some of the water out of my trainers . . . I hadn't come out that morning got up for a jaunt in the country! I was still struggling to put on the left one when Part-Time Tabitha shrieked my name . . . she shrieked it again . . . I hastened best I could . . . she was kneeling bending over Bethany with a twig the shape of a tuning fork stuck to her shoulder . . . funny how you remember the little things like that . . .

She looked up at me . . . that moment will stay with me for so long as I live . . . she didn't need to speak . . . I froze literally . . . cold as a corpse on a hook in a freezer . . .

Your mate's gone to sleep . . . your mate's gone to sleep . . . your mate's gone to sleep.

I gaped . . . frozen and still.

Part-Time Tabitha was what I'd call turned to stone . . . statuary like . . . Bethany looked beautiful . . . serene at peace.

She was . . . I didn't know how to think it . . . how to say it to myself . . . she was dead . . . past all help or need of it . . . yet where were the traces of her cares . . . her sufferings . . . she seemed a creature fresh from the hand of god . . . waiting for the breath of life, not one who had lived and suffered death.

'Oh fuck . . . fuck!' Part-Time Tabitha at last moved. She pointed at Bethany's soaked skirt . . . it was darker than just water would make it . . . She hanked up the skirt . . . there was a tiny dark shrivelly bloodclot thing caught in the fabric folds. She stared at me . . . she was sobbing.

'She gave birth. She gave birth – here . . .'

The thing wasn't like the rodent type evil sooterkins in Part-Time Tabitha's creepy Belgian folk tales. It wasn't any bigger than a chocolate-coated raisin. That's how I like to remember it. Not as the AB word . . . not as a lump bred in darkness . . . not that I want to remember it . . . let's sweep it under the carpet gal . . . let's try and forget that day . . . which wasn't over yet . . . the darkness was all around but you knew it was meant to be light . . . the weather was disobeying the clock . . . despite me sobbing too . . . as team leader I felt I had to give a lead . . .

'What are we going to do?' I asked Part-Time Tabitha.

Her head was in her hands. She looked pleading at me, helpless as Bethany, though alive: 'What have we done?'

'We're going to keep calm . . . I tell you what we're *not* going to do . . . we're not going to call an ambulance . . . if we call an ambulance that means the oinkies get informed . . .' I couldn't go on . . .

I thought: She lay her down to die on a bed of acorns . . .

I thought: Awake thou that sleepest and arise from the dead, and Christ shall give the light.

But that's not how things happen . . . when was the last time one of my prayers was answered . . .

Part-Time Tabitha hugged me wanting succour and comfort.

She asked: 'What are we? Accomplices? Manslaughter? . . . Accessories to murder . . . Accessories before the fact . . .'

It was what you read happening in problem zones Stonehouse Waters Estate etc.

I was thinking of those facilitators for Dream Topping™ that were sent to prison . . . the headlines like 'Murderers In All But Name'.

'Accident . . . tragic accident,' I said. I was in shock. They got three years . . . three years. The forest seemed as empty as my heart . . . cold and unforgiving . . . the trees were hostile . . . darkly shaped witnesses ranked against us.

I stood up to them. 'We have done nothing wrong . . . it was Bethany's choice . . . it went wrong . . .'

'Sure. *We* know that . . . how do we prove it . . . how do we prove it was her choice? We *supplied* her . . .' Part-Time Tabitha couldn't believe this place we were in . . . I couldn't either.

I heard myself say: 'If we're murderers we're non-violent murderers . . . but we're not murderers . . . not not not . . .' I didn't panic any more than anyone would looking down the barrel of a custodial sentence with bulldyke warders with moustaches . . . not to mention prison food . . .

Part-Time Tabitha looked so pained: 'We can't leave her here . . . I mean – disrespect . . . honour your dead and that . . . if you disrespect you get haunted . . .'

Not to mention the number of people who had seen us together . . . it was fate – going to the forest and finding it full of people . . . not reliable witnesses maybe . . . but so many of them . . . and let's not forget the foraging pigs . . . their right of mast guzzling all before them not just those acorns and beechnuts but anything that can't defend itself . . . we couldn't leave her as a snack for them . . .

'We got to get her to . . .' Where? I wondered. Get her to where? And while we're at it:

'Where are we . . . I lost my bearings . . .'

'I'll find them . . . don't worry.' She used the Up Sh★t C★eek app on her iPhone . . . she closed her eyes . . . clutching forehead . . . deep thought immersion . . .

'We need to get her back . . . less than six hundred metres as the crow flies . . . it's not that far . . .'

Oh no?

Have you ever dragged a body through a dark wet wood with the wind whistling the chant of death?

'Like wading through soggy blotch' as Vivian The Rotovator says in *The Little Gay Tractor*. What looks like level ground isn't level never . . . fallen trees . . . thick-knotted undergrowth . . . invisible things . . . those that have dragged bodies through dark wet woods will sympathise . . . they alone will appreciate the difficulties needing to be overcome . . . ditches . . . thorns . . . skiddy ground . . . obstacles your flying crow isn't having to put up with . . . by the time we arrived back at the car park we might have been in the trenches . . . sweat and muck . . . and a few cheerful kitbag songs to keep the spirits up . . . other than that we hardly spoke but to cuss and swear under our breath . . . poor Bethany deader than ever even though there wasn't rigor mortis yet . . . she was cold but not blue . . . quite bendy still . . . that was a useful blessing . . . I secretly thanked her . . .

There was more strange light now. Like it had been photoshopped for dramatic effects. Was it really hours we had been in the forest? It seemed like a lifetime ago we had set out . . . maybe it was only minutes . . . when we set out we were a team of three . . . there was no tragic event being anticipated . . . because of that, Part-Time Tabitha hadn't paid attention to where she parked up in the case of the unforeseen.

It was the dogging hour . . . the car park was packed . . . no way could we get Bethany to the pick-up – the hearse! – without these heaving grunting ferals seeing us . . . and if they saw us they might want Bethany to join in . . . the hearse was parked the far side of the car park . . . we'd have had to push through them – ugh! . . . little groups between vehicles . . . stretched out on bonnets which could cause nasty burns unless sufficient time were allowed for the engine to cool – do they consider that? Tarty lingerie and tattooed donkeys . . . you could see they were on the lookout for newcomers . . . sharp eyes glancing here there and everywhere . . . on the lookout for oinkies too I'll bet . . . no you couldn't carry a body across the car park . . . it would be obvious to everyone even if they were wrapped up in their hobby . . .

We watched from a cluster of birches . . . nice to see Jason The Poet or was it Justin doing a roaring trade . . . helping out keen like a Boy Scout taking phone photos for souvenirs for those who want more than a selfie with a stranger adjusting his or her dress. What a day for flesh on display! Sickening, yes . . . yet scintillating, yes.

'You stick here,' said Part-Time Tabitha, 'I'll go and fetch the hearse round.'

What did she say? Did she say what I heard?

Before I could get my head half working round the internal resonances the heavens opened. Again. I half picked up and half dragged Bethany . . . got her to under a shrub . . . the chocolate-covered raisin plus bloodclot still stuck to her skirt . . . my protectiveness might be considered a bit girly in practical terms since keeping dry wasn't important to Bethany in her condition . . . it must have been down to my instinctive respect for life coming through . . . not to mention making sure she didn't get humped by a roaming roger . . . those people don't stand still . . . they're always hungry for a new link-up, live or otherwise.

How long did it take Part-Time Tabitha? So long that I was going hot from nerves and fruzz from rain . . . disloyal me even wondered if she had got herself caught up in the activities . . . there were vehicles parked any which way . . . signalling with their headlights some of them . . . others with their windscreen wipers slow slow quick etc. – or were they just shooing off the rain . . . not paying attention to the highway code anyway or to me . . . oh it was such a relief when I saw the pick-up weaving its way even though she was getting some hostile looks from persons that had to move out the way . . . my big realise was hostile looks from exhibitioners with their trousers round their ankles aren't as hostile as they would be if the trousers were normally conducted and less vulnerable.

She parked up . . . the passenger door flush tight to the low stripped log fence where the grass is one side and the gravel is the other side apart from where gravel bits are pushed onto the grass because of being pushed by tyres . . . they shoal up like sand does with tides . . . not very environmental . . .

She slid across the front seat to open the passenger door as far as it would go which wasn't that far because it got obstructed by the low stripped log fence. She had to twist herself to get out. I gave her a hug out of small happiness . . . it was a day to seize at anything which wasn't totally mank to be grateful for . . . my brain was twisting with conflicting emotions . . . without thinking I squeezed to reach into the cab to grab Psycho Carl's antler cap.

I plonked it on my head.

Was I identifying with that poor dead stag?

Was I just bringing vivacious bubbliness and good cheer to the task? Was I keeping my wet head from getting wetter and my hair going all frizz?

Was a little bit of me inside wishing to be someone who wasn't me?

I tied the strings under my chin so the antlers stood up, not that I could see. It was snuggy comforting.

The pick-up was parked up *here*. Poor Tragic Bethany was laid down *there*. About ten metres away . . . have ten metres ever been so long? . . . the rain made ten metres more like fifteen metres . . . not to mention the circs adding on some more.

I bustled back towards the shrub where she was with the rain blasting me . . . Part-Time Tabitha followed . . . I took command: 'No! Keep the engine running . . . get back in the cab!'

I could literally *feel* her resentful respect for my order even though she was behind me. I was thinking of a quick getaway in case of worst possible scenario . . . namely we are seen to be dragging a body.

Seen to be dragging a body . . . seen to be dragging a body . . . it won't sound too good in court . . . I was walking backwards . . . step by ploddy step . . . it was like taking Our Lord Jesus down from the cross . . . me looking over my shoulder with each pace . . . dragging the totally drenched body of my friend and former pupil . . . former pupil – how's that going to sound . . . my hands gripped into her armpits which wasn't top ceremony and elegance but needs must . . . it was like drowning in a car wash . . . these ten metres were so much harder than the previous 600 metres . . . psychologically that is . . . because of the proximity of other people . . . especially other people grunting their animal grunts and lowing like cows and screams . . . they don't know how threatening they are . . . talk about a free-range zoo!

I was altering my hand positions so as to be able to lift her into the pick-up when I hear:

'Carl! Where've you been hiding . . . ooh you're a naughty stag,' then all singsong – 'I'm–coming–to–get–you . . .'

I gaped through the rain at a looming figure towering towards me from the dripping trees. I knew that steeped-in-nicotine voice . . . where? whose?

'Are you coming to play Carl . . . Are you coming to play with queen pussy . . . queen pussy's very wet Carl . . . sticky wet Carl . . . shall I make you hard as rock Carl . . . shall I milk the stag milk the king stag . . .'

She was opening a black mac to reveal . . . a not-really-there pound shop thong . . . slutty bottom of the range Dream Tupping Dungeon of Desire wetlook basque and stockings . . . and the shoes . . . total aggression heightwise with those heels even though they were sinking into the grass . . . she must have been most of the way to seven foot tall . . . 10/10 for obviousness!

I'd like to give her the benefit and say she looked like a scarlet lady of the night but truth must out . . . she looked more like a gent in drag playing a scarlet lady of the night in a controversial production at The Mummers Soc . . . actually let's tell it how it is . . . she looked like she was a gent in drag auditioning to play a scarlet lady of the night and wasn't going to get the part because she was really scary going on superhuman like she was from a spinechilling film . . .

That's when I realised . . . that's when I put all the parts together to make a familiar whole . . .

You know how it is when you see people out of context . . . out of uniform so to speak . . . the plumber who's usually in overalls dressed up in a tuxedo for the Soil Pipe Oscars . . . in a place where

you'd never expect to see them . . . living a life you'd never have
dreamed of . . . knowing friends you never knew they knew . . . they
are not the same person . . . life is all roles . . .

OMG it's Mrs Kerr . . . What is she doing here? The answer to
that one was obvious . . . I couldn't believe it.

Panic. I recognised her before she recognised me . . . but I had
nowhere to run to nowhere to hide . . .

No wonder she thought I was Carl . . . what with his unique
antlers . . . her challenged sight . . . her no glasses vanity . . . the driving rain . . . the murky dusk . . .

She was only a couple of metres from me when she saw her mistake. Saw that I wasn't Carl . . . there was a gap before she realised
who I was . . . it all went slomo. She recoiled – that's the word. Her
face went total disbelief as she solved the puzzle of Carl's hat . . . it
went wincey with embarrassment . . . she was scrambling with her
flapping mac to close it in the rain . . . to shut out the shame . . .
where is Carl she must have been wondering . . . it went horror
when she saw very dead Poor Tragic Bethany . . . she put her hand
to her mouth . . . then her face was a taut knot of accusation and
twistedness . . . judgemental . . . vindictive (it came easy). The
Modern Moral Methodist twisted her body wanting to make herself
invisible. She said nothing . . . she didn't need to say anything . . .
she turned on her sinking heels awkward as a giraffe on blancmange . . . she loomed away frisking her pockets and finding her
phone.

This was all over in a matter of seconds that were hours . . . she
had had a long enough look at Bethany . . . she can't have had any
doubt . . . it was all so quick that Part-Time Tabitha didn't know
what was going down till I had hauled Poor Tragic Bethany into the
cab hardly able to talk from lack of puff and mental friction and
nerve asthma rattling in my chest.

'We got to get out of here.'

Gravel flew like grapeshot. There were oi-watchit yells from angry
dodging doggers!

Calm Celia calm . . . I explained as best I could the situation. She
drove too fast through the car park . . . more cries and shrieks . . .
other times I'd have had a giggle at naked people jumping out the

way giving us the finger (!) . . . all bossy hand waving . . . you'd think they were rozzers . . . maybe they were . . . I peeped looking out for Mrs Kerr . . . nowhere to be seen . . . with our luck her phone would actually be working and she'd already be snitching us up. Poor Tragic Bethany kept bumping against me . . . I had to make sure she didn't impede Part-Time Tabitha at the wheel. She drove responsibly apart from when I had to light her joints for her. I'd call it an unusual situation.

'She won't grass,' said Part-Time Tabitha overconfidential, 'she wouldn't dare. How does she explain what she was doing there?'

'Sex with yucky strangers isn't a crime. Murder is—'

'Her rep-u-ta-tion . . . anyway I've put a hex on her . . .'

She could be so immature.

'What if she buys a pay-as-you-go . . . anonymous letter . . . words cut out the newspaper.'

'Where's the proof? Where's the body?' She giggled. A tad callous I thought.

'Come to think of it,' she said, 'we ought to put her in the back . . .' And all of a jolt she swerved off the road into an abandoned petrol station . . . all wrecked with big brawny weeds pushing through the concrete forecourt . . . rusty frames with jagged glass – the pump attendant's booth was beyond repair. She drove round behind the wreck what must have been the shop/office where we couldn't be seen from the road . . . more jagged glass . . . totally sordid not to mention tetanus risk for kids who love playing in this sort of environment . . . decaying pipes . . . broken holes down to where the tanks had been . . . bins and filth . . . like nature was fighting back led by warrior rats . . . every available hole or dent in the mud was an overflowing puddle bubbling.

We got Poor Tragic Bethany out of the cab. I held her till Part-Time Tabitha climbed onto the back . . . the angles were hostile . . . we hauled her up. It wasn't exactly dignified . . . it was steep. Up onto the back she went then . . . her clothes were all awry . . . there was still a glimmer of light in her eyes . . . it made me choke with tears . . . I climbed up too . . . putting my foot on a tyre and heaving myself . . . climbing is not really my thing . . . I grazed my wrist . . . all puffed I was . . . we were stood on rolls of tar paper and roofing felt that we both struggled with to make a hidey hole among . . . they were hefty batons . . . so heavy that lifting them could be an Olympic sport . . . how strange it was to be there doing what I'd never done in my life before . . . a few hours before I couldn't have dreamed of being party to manslaughter or worse and having to dispose of a body and feeling peckish beyond belief . . . we got her tucked safe and snug under the level of the pick-up's sides . . . I needed post-exertion pick-me-up chocolate to rid me of this nightmare but I knew it wouldn't, a whole bowl of mousse for eight which I could get my head into.

'We got all week to think about it . . . well six days . . . before they're back,' she replied when I asked her where we were going to put Poor Tragic Bethany to rest . . . too casual by half her attitude was I thought but then I'm a worrier . . . it was a human body though . . . and we were Up Sh★t C★eek – the place not the app . . . murderers in all but name . . . it echoed over and over.

'We'll figure it out don't worry.'

I held out long as I could after we'd got back on the road: 'I got to have some chocolate.'

She gave me such a look . . . me who'd been lighting her joints for her.

'No way . . . we got to get back and get parked up in the garage. Safe and sound.'

'Meanie . . .'

'Don't be soft Celia it's only ten minutes . . . quarter an hour outside.'

We didn't pass any shops anyway.

We were almost back at Part-Time Tabitha's . . . there were comforting streetlights now . . . we came round the corner near The Baulks Historic Field System where you got some spectacular examples of ridge and furrow . . . Year 8 it's foal, they're full of interest . . . by the time they're Year 9 it's total mungo and they're getting off with each other . . . rain was bouncing up off the road . . . there was a BMW police car parked across the road flashing danger lights . . . hi-vis jackets lemon and lime . . . crime scene tape everywhere. I immediately got butterflies, big butterflies, those evil ones with skeleton patterns or are they moths? We'd been caught . . . driven straight into their trap. A rozzer waved us down to arrest us . . . as soon as I saw his eyes I thought of Mrs Kerr in a public phone box sniffing the heady sweet urinal bouquet phoning 999 in a funny voice . . . smiling as she did her citizen's duty . . . awarding herself 10/10 for civics . . . I thought of cells with dried blood on the tiles . . . I thought of boredom stretching away to the infinite place . . . I thought of sapphic sisters . . . I thought of counting away the days till I was dried as a prune . . . I thought of bringing disgrace to the family name (frankly irrelevant that one) . . . I thought of ways to put an end to it all . . .

But the rozzer was busy with coping with his squawky . . . didn't give the back of the pick-up a glance . . . all he did was he pointed to the holloway that leads up past the posh riding stables . . . water sloshing down it like it wanted to be a river . . . he bellowed 'affirmative'.

Cool as you like Part-Time Tabitha opens her window with such a sickly butter-wouldn't-melt voice.

'Good afternoon Officer . . . Is there a . . . problem?'

Ooh the greasy little creep I thought. Then I thought thank you god for making her a greasy little creep . . . I realised I was still wearing Carl's antler hat but the rozzer didn't even see it though he looked straight at it . . . he had his mind on the job.

'You going to have to take the road up there luv . . . we got an incident . . . three-car head-on on-going . . . straight into town's closed for the foreseeable. All right then? On your way. Drive careful now.' I took the hat off . . . peered inquisitively into the dusk . . . some might say ghoulishly . . . disappointingly I couldn't see anything apart from another rozzer erecting a folding sign directing traffic up the damp sunken lane where we were going already. They give me the creeps these sorts of lanes with their lurking sex attackers . . . I'd always steered clear of this one as much as I could . . . my advice is grip a bunch of keys so they are sticking out between the fingers and go for the eyes . . . almost a tunnel the way the trees on either side knit together over the top . . . slip one, purl one . . . it's always dark and haunted . . . good place to bury a body . . . but with our luck some hoity toity brat out cantering on her birthday present would find it. Last light was coming through that overhead web . . . I'm as certain as could be that I could make out a living breathing

Poor Tragic Bethany swaying serene and soaked floating in the boughs . . . the spirit watching the body it had discarded . . . and which we us, us had wrapped in damp roofing felt without proper dignity or ceremony.

'We're in this together don't forget.' I don't think she meant to but it came out like a threat. Maybe she did mean to. It was like she was taking command.

'Don't you worry,' she repeated over and over like a chant. 'Don't you worry.' Like I was just a classroom assistant or something . . . having to be comforted . . . but so was she . . . we were both in a vulnerable hub . . . I was more mature at assessing the risks we faced . . . we didn't have that much to be confident about was my assessment.

Whenever she said we got six days it panicked me . . . no plan . . . I basically couldn't get my head round . . . it was like there were so many issues . . . we got six days to dispose of Poor Tragic Bethany . . . or dump her . . . leave her somewhere so it's like she just died naturally – as she would have wanted.

'Would she?' Soothsayer Part-Time Tabitha laughed scornfully. 'Does it matter what she'd have wanted . . . You got to think positive Celia. We got to dig deep to get ourselves out of this. Get ourselves so we are not connected no way. I'll see you tomorrow afternoon. Best if I drop you here. I'll pull in at the bus stop.'

'What? You just . . . Here?' We weren't that far from my flat but that wasn't the point.

'Look I got a date – I need to get back. Got to have a bath—'

'A date? . . . It's Sunday . . . Tonight . . . you . . . I mean—'

'She's not going anywhere,' she almost snapped. 'I'll pop her in the garage for safe keeping. That OK with you?'

'Well I guess—'

'Good. I got extra French in the afternoon . . . Might not be able to make it. Dildos To You Dykey Luv.'

Let down again! I stood there soaking. There was water dripping through the zigzag crack in the bus shelter's roof. There were what you might call vertical puddles on the furniture store windows. Watching the pick-up's blurry tail lights speed away, treacherously. What a night for a date. I stocked up at the Mini-Market. Dejan was looking at me in a funny way . . . was he reading something in my face . . . he kept glancing up at me between swiping each item . . . his eyes were plunging deep into my mind . . . extracting guilty secrets, sensing unusual mental circuits.

I sat at home with darling Oats . . . what if she got preggers . . . would I have the nerve to intrude on her right to kittens and a lifestyle-size litter tray . . . I wanted to cry . . . I was frozen with fear . . . I could only pick at my chocolate mousse, my box of dates, my artisan shortbread, my bottle of maraschino cherries, my tiramisu (too cold, straight from the fridge). I couldn't get it out of my mind . . . it just would not budge . . . so Oats and me did nick nack paddy wack which lifted us spirits no end . . . but then it was lights out . . . I said my prayers imploring not to get found out by divine grace . . . hoping He would understand that it was an accident . . . hinting gently that perhaps some other party should get the blame when the body is discovered . . . some other party who has been truly evil . . . deserving of the most condign punishment . . . I even wondered if it was just possible as a special favour, please, that Poor Tragic Bethany could be brought back to life though I knew that was a big big ask but nothing ventured . . . they still came sliding out the wardrobe . . . tormenting spectres . . . from behind the curtains too . . . leaping up . . . crawling across the ceiling hissing insinuations . . . whispering the names of notorious child killers . . . the gallery of infamy . . . Elizabeth Báthory, Mother Root, Rhonda Telford, Robson Davidson, Alexa Leclerc . . . telling me I was like them . . . telling me I was going to suffer like them . . . in solitary forever . . . I trembled under the bedclothes but they got in despite tight hospital corners . . . I escaped . . . switched on all the lights . . . went to the kitchen for the night so when dawn came I hadn't had any sleep but had treated myself to toasted Dundee cake with peanut butter and yummy dulce de leche . . . that was Sunday then . . . not a good day . . . now here was Monday waiting in store to greet me with sky the colour of the soil blocking a soil pipe.

Monday

A mature florist will never ask who the flowers and bouquets and wreaths are destined for. Only give advice when asked. Only express congratulations when invited to . . . ditto condolences. It's a people business . . . don't go treading on sensitivities . . . don't go presuming . . . don't wink saucily when you suspect that the stems are not for the gentleman's wife . . . flowers are a language the lay person doesn't speak fluently . . . we don't want to rub it in to them that they're ignorant . . . don't correct them . . . ascertain from their description what it is they want . . . let them think it's them making the choice.

Mondays can be slow. My head hurt . . . I promised myself – no more natural highs Celia!

No way . . . no more being helpful to those in distress . . . I fretted . . . it was that bad . . . I thought about taking up smoking for the first time in my life . . . was Part-Time Tabitha a responsible co-killer – that word just came to me . . . you want your co-killer to be cautious not a hothead . . . a calculating virtuoso of murder (I must have read that off the back of a book).

'Er, hullo there,' went a voice, 'if you're not—'

'Ooh . . . soreee!'

I'd wandered off into a dark trancette of the spirit . . . hadn't noticed the first customer of the day had crept in . . . senior, gnarled, tattooed, well weathered . . . all sinews and outdoors labour . . . bit of a rough bundle in earlier days I shouldn't wonder . . . can look after himself as they say . . . touch of the tarbrush maybe . . . bit of a gyppo no mistaking . . . but you know it was nice to have company even if he was wearing oily dungarees with no shirt . . . just muscles under the shoulder straps and bib thing.

'Flowers for a tribute . . . for a special lady.'

That's what he said he wanted.

'That would be . . . ?'

'Eh?'

'What . . . well, what sort of special lady?'

'Friend sort.'

'Right you are . . . let's talk colours . . . like are we looking at the whole . . . whole spectrum from unbridled love to amiable affection?'

He looked at me like I was round the twist. He might have been right!!

'Colours . . . what colours does she like?'

'Puh . . . more a question ain't it . . . what she *did* like . . . that I have to say.' And his fairly noble face cracked. He came close as could be to sobbing. I so felt for him. He had one of those lovely accents you don't hear no more . . . accents that smell of hayricks and traction engines.

'So she has . . . ah . . . moved on . . . onto a different . . . stage?' I suggested.

He held a well oily hanky to his face. Could be a fairground worker I said to myself.

'Black and purple . . . those were her colours . . . that's what I want to remember her with . . .'

'That would be purple calla lily . . . black with purple trim so to speak.'

I held a stem in front of him . . . he scrutinised suspiciously . . .

'Black roses of course . . . always a favourite . . . team them with lisianthus . . . dark purple . . . then there's ranunculus — I'll show you . . .'

I hurried over to the shelf.

'Don't you bother. Bunch of these'll . . . oh dear I . . .'

His face all contorted up with grief.

He spoke to himself: 'Brace up mate . . . 'tten-shun . . . yup these'll do the needful . . . mustn't let it get to me now . . . comes to all of us in the end . . . doesn't it? But you don't want to go in a pile-up . . .'

'Oh that's so sad . . . why didn't you say . . . I do an RTA special . . . for laying with respect on the verge where the fatality occurred . . . it's vibrantly multicoloured to reflect the variety of the life lived . . . not the life lost.'

'Black and purple . . . they'll do fine.'

He had paid . . . he was about to leave with his bouquet when the door opens (I kept telling myself to get that bell fixed, not to mention the blistered paint). In came a little leprechaun of a fellow . . . so weatherbeaten he was, he might have been up the chimney at The Boar & Robin getting smoked like a ham.

'Badger!' he greeted my first of the day gent.

'Skipper! Ye old reprobate . . .'

They man-hugged . . . friendship . . . fondness sustains us all through thick and thin . . . they both shook their heads.

'Don't need to ask why you're here . . .'

'It's a sorry . . . oh why *her* of all people . . . it's a waste and no gainsaying—' He was tearing up again.

'Fate and telecommunications . . .'

Gainsaying . . . fate . . . telecommunications . . . where were they when they were at home . . . what chapter of what cult did these two belong to?

'You got the right colours there to be sure . . .'

'It's what she would have wanted . . .'

Borr-ring . . . if I had a pound every time I'd heard 'it's what she would have wanted' I'd . . .

'I'll have the same then if you please . . . with that black bow like that, that's a class touch—'

'Class touch for a class lady.'

A popular lady too . . . very popular . . . there were three other gentlemen customers after bouquets that morning. Two – hurrah! – went for my RTA Commemorative Bespoke Lifetime Shrine . . . *Life*time . . . you never want to say the D word especially when you got Poor Tragic Bethany on your conscience . . . off stage at the minute . . . but for how long?

Not long at all . . . for in sweeps Part-Time Tabitha all smiley jolly as a jackanapes . . . despite a walloping swelled up shiner round her left eye . . . blue and burnt orange like a mutant oyster . . .

'What you . . . I thought you said you got remedial—'

'I have . . . I just popped in 'cause I didn't want to phone (touches her nose conspirator style) . . . we got developments Celia . . . we got onward movement.'

My body came over all hot and frozen . . . tingly trembly . . . I worried about my blood pressure . . . I'm a big boned gal.

'What does that mean . . . onward movement . . . what's onward movement . . . onward movement!'

It meant this:

Part-Time Tabitha's date turned out to be 1.5/10. Breath like a whiff of those silos out on the Fair Oak Road. Soggy pizza. House wine only. Leathery wart on his groping finger. She fled when he went to the caballeros.

When she got home she thought the house had been targeted for a rave . . . all the lights were on . . . the sounds were deafening . . . when she peeked through the window it was Mum Juno and Psycho Carl slumped in a bottle bank . . . they were home six days early . . . their flight had been delayed several times then cancelled . . . they got blind drunk drinking hospitality tequilas . . . they got in a fight with two hospitality personnels . . . they were arrested but released without charge because more than twenty passengers on the same flight got arrested as well . . . so there wasn't enough cell space without having a Black Hole of Calcutta frenzy . . . eventually FlugWings paid for an airport hotel and they slept it off before coming back.

I kept on interrupting her: 'And where's you know who in all this . . . what's happening . . . what are you doing with her . . . what are we doing with her . . . we've got to get her moved . . . we can't just leave her in the pick-up.'

She stared me down: 'Yes we can. We are going to leave her right where she is.'

'You out your mind!?'

'It has come to us on a plate. The good lord has delivered Plan B.'

'We never had a Plan A . . . we was just helping her get nature's T word.'

'Whever. Thought it was the A word . . . Any which way . . . We have a plan . . .'

Part-Time Tabitha had turned down the music . . . she pulled the curtains . . . Psycho Carl was all falling about the room picking up bottles . . . turning them upside-down for dregs to drip down his throat . . . in case there was anything left in them . . . Mum Juno was moaning about feeling sick . . . Psycho Carl told her to button it . . . Part-Time Tabitha was trying to clear up . . . she was picking up bottles off the floor and wherever . . . Psycho Carl made a grab for one that was empty but he thought wasn't . . . she sort of moved back out his way with her arms full of bottles . . . then he laid one on her . . . punched her . . . that's where the shiner came from . . . called her a cow . . . stomped out the room.

'You got to bring an assault charge . . . you'll need to go to A&E.'

'No way! That'd total The Plan!'

The Plan had come to her in that instant . . . in a flash of hatred . . . even more hatred at him than she had before . . . he was due to be away for a week . . . he had no work arranged for that week . . . she knew that from hearing when Mum Juno was planning the trip . . .

So *theoretically* the pick-up would be in the garage all week . . . he never used it apart from work and working late . . . so-called working late was dogging . . . that was what he said he was doing when he was dogging . . . *theoretically* he'd be using his Cordoba Vitesse all week . . . posher wheels than the pick-up . . . they don't look down their noses at a Cordoba Vitesse at the South Dun Valley Golf and Country Club where he smarmed for work . . . it was all so *theoretically* . . .

Theoretically meant nothing but *with a bit of luck* . . . with a bit of luck the pick-up will remain undisturbed in the garage while Psycho Carl drives about in his Cordoba Vitesse or slumps in front of the snooker/golf/tennis/football on telly belching a hop yard. The longer, she reckoned, the body goes undiscovered the deeper, the further Up Sh★t C★eek Psycho Carl is going to find himself. What sort of alibi is belching a hop yard . . . no one to corroborate . . . day after day after unaccountable day . . .

I listened . . . I struggled internally to make contact with my forensic side . . . thinking straight didn't come easy . . .

'It won't work . . . don't you see it won't work . . . people have seen us in the pick-up . . . they've seen us with her . . . not just seen . . . identified . . . put the finger . . . frankly I'm shit scared . . . just waiting . . . Constable Rozzer . . . he could come through that door at any moment . . . arrest me on suspicion . . . we . . . well . . . I . . . me me actually yes? . . . me I can be identified by Mrs Kerr . . .'

Part-Time Tabitha giggled . . . the words trilled out of her: 'No you can't . . . d'you know I forgot to say – special treat, I was saving it up for you – Mrs Kerr is dead.'

'What . . . don't mess with my brain . . . you can be so effing—'

'Dead. Dead. Dead. Mrs Kerr's dead . . . that accident last night. That was her . . . I told you I put a hex on her . . . wooooooo . . .'

She shook her hands like she was an epileptic on the electroconvulsive . . . she flobbled her mouth and cheeks . . . laughed like a cacklewitch.

'Why didn't you tell me?'

'I've told you now . . . one down . . . more to go.'

A film of life's patterns unrolled in front of me . . . the black and purple . . . the stems . . . the cheap sex-ware . . . all the gents paying tribute in roadside commemoration . . . they were from the dogging community . . . which she was an active and popular member of . . . life's patterns . . . life's fates . . . the cracks in the paint on the ceiling spoke to me . . . if only I knew what they were saying.

'She was on the phone . . . that's what they reckon . . . and overtaking . . . it was on Vespasian FM . . . I call that a result . . .' Part-Time Tabitha was in excelsis.

Who says there's no god . . . that he/she/it doesn't listen? But what I prayed for was nothing more than quadriplegia . . . I got the D word . . . Maybe I wasn't greedy enough . . . I got more than I asked for . . . that's not usual for the likes of us . . . I mean in his firmament he gets home delivery of whatever he wants . . . I felt well awed . . . one of those times when you just know there's something bigger than us . . . benevolent forces working for us through the spheres . . .

My reverie of gratitude was interrupted by my grasp on the cold grip of reality: 'What happens if he does use the pick-up?'

'Celia I really got to run,' she false apologised, quick kiss, 'see you Wednesday. Dildos To You Dykey.'

Another kiss blown from the door . . . and then I was alone . . . marooned on my own shore . . . with no one to share my life crisis with . . . was it an existential crisis . . . crises so often are!

'Tributes have been paid,' goes the voice of Mike Catch, the Voice of Vespasian FM, 'to popular Misselbrook West Heuristic head teacher Jackie Kerr who sadly died in a tragic traffic accident on Sunday night.'

Popular! Who's kidding who?

'The popular teacher is thought to have been returning home from a social engagement when she was involved in a head-on collision with an articulated lorry at the approach to The Baulks Gyratory. She was killed instantly. The driver of the lorry, who has not been named, is receiving Trauma Maintenance at Saint Kieran's Hospital. Vespasian FM understands that no charges will be brought. Tragically it appears from unconfirmed eye witness reports that Jackie was speaking on her phone when the accident occurred.'

'Tributes have been paid,' goes the voice of Mike Catch on the hour every hour . . . d'you know it became quite comforting . . . a wee dram of solace as they say . . . knowing that she is definitively passed on to whatever hell it is where them who tell whoppers to save their own skin are condemned to for all eternity – with luck . . .

I went home . . . I found myself sobbing as I tucked into a Middle Eastern array of falnadath festival specials – halva and baklava with just-believe-you're-in-a-romantic-souk sweet mint tea like sweet boiling toothpaste . . . usually reliable pick-me-ups but not on this occasion . . . sometimes my life is a river of regret . . . then the river turns into a torrent and I am hurled about on the rocks of angst.

Tuesday

On the hour every hour.

But today it was different: 'Sources close to the enquiry into popular Misselbrook West Heuristic head teacher Jackie Kerr's fatal accident at The Baulks on Sunday have revealed that in the sixteen minutes before the fatal accident the popular Misselbrook West Heuristic head teacher had tried to call the police three times but had each time been cut off when her signal failed.'

It froze down my back . . . I got such a shock from that . . . it was like they were closing in . . . not accepting it was a regular RTA . . . fret fret fret . . . I wish I could be like Part-Time Tabitha . . . not worry . . . buried in her book of creepy Flemish folk tales *not in translation* . . . but they were investigating . . . what had she said before those calls got cut off?

Mid-afternoon 4 p.m. bulletin. It got worse. It got worse than worse. It got so terrible my face rictused up . . . like paralysis . . . or lockjaw which I've feared all my life.

'Concerns are being raised about the whereabouts of missing teen Bethany Sluytwn, ironically a Year Twelve pupil at Misselbrook West Heuristic whose popular head teacher Jackie Kerr died tragically in a traffic accident on Sunday night. Let's go over to Liz Gripp who's at the gates of Misselbrook West Heuristic. Liz—'

'Yes Mike. Here at Misselbrook West Heuristic concerns are being raised about the whereabouts of missing teen Bethany Sluytwn, a Year Twelve student. Bethany is noted for her sense of responsibility, her compassion towards her fellow students, her readiness to help out, her academic excellence, her deeply held faith, her promise as a Team Leader in field sports with an emphasis on the javelin. Bethany was last seen by her parents early on Sunday morning. She failed to return home that night and has not been seen since. The police have appealed to anyone having—'

I switched it off as a burly built young chap came into the shop . . . a heftily built young rozzer? . . . no taking chances me . . . I didn't want him casting his expert eye on me listening to the radio and recognising guilt in my facial frozenness . . . I shouldn't have worried . . .

'It's for my aunty she's . . .' Ooh he drooled and drooled about her abscesses suppurating and the brilliant care she was receiving and how grateful he was . . .

'Carers care for chocs,' I alliterated with a sparkly grin insofar as I could grin.

Well that was a prime sale I said to myself . . . the said chocolates . . . what I call an obese glutton size box . . . four separate CEO status bouquets and a Scent-Of-A-Country-Garden posy.

It took my mind off the pressing matter . . . until the next suspicious customer came in . . . they were all suspicious of me . . . smiling unnecessarily trying to put me at ease so I'll slip up . . .

Wednesday slunk into Thursday

Daily Echo. Bethany: first story you come to online. Her photo was on the front page of the paper version. Circulation 102,821 daily (total combined), 21,185 daily (print), 81,636 daily (online). That's a lot of people keeping an eye out for her. It only needs one eye . . . or pair of eyes . . .

'Precisely, you got it . . .'
'Tension doesn't suit me . . .'
'Just sit tight Celia . . . calm calm Celia.'

'Sometimes I'm thinking just go in the police station and confess . . .'

'Yellow strip down your spine! Don't even think about it Dykcy. I've been reading about post-mortems . . . how accurately a pathologist can pinpoint when the deceased became the deceased.'

I was proud that Part-Time Tabitha had the same knowledge-thirst as Poor Tragic Bethany had . . . and a cunning that our victim didn't have . . . because—

Friday

She was meant to be in for mid to late afternoon . . . the busy pre-weekend redemption moment when traditionally gents make up for the week's neglect of the wife. But remember:

> *The uxoricide is a gallant of smiling charm and dash;*
> *fleeting, as he presents his troth, sharp gold canines flash.*

Lovely lines (by Liz Loodmer) and so true, so true . . . as any florist knows deep down when she looks at men, those animals called men.

She eventually turned up at 5.30 would you believe . . . I was literally struggling with a cactus with the properties of a prickly snake. There was a queue testifying to the popularity of Bloomin' Marvellous and the job I had done growing the business.

I looked daggers at her . . . but we didn't have a private moment for me to bo★★ock her till about 7.00. By which time I was too exhausted. I slump down and she holds up an old-fashioned mobile in front of me . . . like it's saying something . . . all I thought was how day-before-yesterday it looked.

'I got it at John Davey Plaza.'

'Whyever d'you go *there*?'

Scuzzy mall featuring doner stench . . . unemptied bins . . . desperate bin-divers . . . abandoned prams . . . homeless street bundles and that.

'Their CCTV was on the blink . . . security couldn't manage . . .

they've had all these opportunistics . . . kids nicking clothes . . . some bloke even took a widescreen just walked out the shop.'

'Oh my god you haven't been thieving . . .' I looked at her pleading her to say no. Larceny added to all the rest . . .

She rolled her eyes.

'Untraceable purchase . . . *for the time, Celiaaaa, is nigh!*' She put on that ghouls-rising-from-the-crypt-covered-in-cobwebs voice . . .

Saturday

Oh get out of my head . . . this wasn't an earworm . . . it was swollen and burly thick . . . an ear eel! Out damned eel out damned . . . but it wouldn't budge . . .

Hell is: 'Fears fears missing growing fellow students Heuristic responsibility Bethany Sluytwn field sports chapel last seen Misselbrook attend fears fears fears growing feeling unwell teen fears growing missing sense of compassion towards the javelin fellow students her her her promise teen fears chapel West deeply held faith last seen are growing unwell missing teen feeling readiness to help out emphasis on academic excellence unwell for missing teen did not attend javelin compassion Bethany Sluytwn Team Leader Heuristic Heuristic chapel . . . Parents' lengthy interviews . . . parents' further lengthy interviews . . . parents' unorthodox beliefs . . . parents parents parents.'

Well, even if it knew the squalid unnatural truth Vespasian FM wasn't going to call them incestuous funny farmers was it?

'Do you,' I tensely quizzed Part-Time Tabitha over a cooling craft beer ('power hops, the essence of the Lugg valley') in a private corner in The Boar & Robin after a day when we admitted to each other that perhaps we should not be ashamed to be greedy capitalist bastards after all, 'think they're going to arrest Mr and Mrs Sluytwn – you know . . . like out of desperation?'

'Faute de mieux you mean?'

'Do I?' I asked.

'You do . . . and I really fucking hope not – that is *not* part of the plan . . . I heard him tell Mum there was a funny smell in the garage when he was getting the lawnmower.'

The more I quaffed the more I gave up on asking what the plan was. I achieved getting home.

Sunday

The anniversary of Poor Tragic Bethany's death. One long week ago. To mark the occasion I stayed in bed. I kept my head under the heavy 16.5 tog duvet . . . in the dark . . . fighting off the fearsomes . . . I couldn't escape them . . . the quilt wasn't much of a solace because it rhymes with guilt . . . uncanny . . . like they are made for each other . . . they tormented me . . . the stubborn images . . . the shame . . . the quills pricking through the lifeless fabric . . .

The funny smell in the garage . . . I couldn't really imagine what Poor Tragic Bethany could be smelling like . . . oh I forced myself to try to imagine the whiffiness . . . Kit-e-Kat perhaps . . . but I'm not one of those folk that have what's called a 'library of scents' in my head . . . so not a great idea . . . as for trying to picture her ugh!! and she wasn't a her any more . . . she was an it . . . all gases and maggots . . . that's what it comes to . . . her poor delicate intestines rotting red . . . swelling till they burst . . . the tropical style humidity that week was like the starter for your home-made yogurt . . . accelerates decomposition . . . turning a lovely vital youngster into mulch for the garden . . . phosphates to make the blooms ready for Bloomin' Marvellous . . . ooh I so hated myself for thinking that but bad actions don't half make for bad thoughts as well as the other way round.

Take your mind off your destiny I said to myself . . . cheering myself with a jaunt down Memory Lane . . . recreating Sunday afternoons of long ago back before I was even born so not real memory then (more Mum's) . . . watching several episodes of the legendary fourth series of *The Gent* with Loyd Parnacott as St John de Vere Babbington Matravers, Imogen Skye as Fizz Breeze his ebullient Girl Friday and Pete Chisel as Nipper . . . I've got the box set . . . classic fayre . . . the fourth series is the one which ends with criminal masterminds Billy Girth and Lennie Crust falling to their death in St John de Vere Babbington Matravers's conversation pit . . . it's always voted the *The Gent* of *The Gents* at *The Gent* Conventions . . . Some of the ephemera and memorabilia stands are all tat but they're sort of fun – Gent snuff boxes (!), ashtrays and cigarette holders, lighters, braces, malted milk drink, socks, bow ties, fanzines, Bourbon whiskey.

Imogen Skye always looks amazing, she's ever so generous with her autograph. But they can be a bit sad when Loyd Parnacott himself turns up. He's dead seedy, all rats tails, threadbare, embittered, sponging drinks, groping blindly, getting abusive, putting avocado and prawn sandwiches in his pockets 'for later' . . . It's all down to his follow-up vehicle *Bob Dobney: Store Detective* getting cancelled halfway through the first series by what he called 'industry pygmies' . . . he hired a crippled former stuntman to assault two of the pygmies . . . they ended up in hospital . . . the stuntman said he didn't know his own strength . . . he got a suspended . . . Loyd Parnacott got a stiff custodial . . . not so stiff mind it didn't stop a copycat . . . that famous Israeli entertainer with the silly name which no one can remember who no one outside Israel had heard of till he became an internationally celebrated criminally inclined has-been who'd had his producer or someone beaten up . . . frankly I'm surprised it doesn't happen more often what with all the Jews in showbiz at each other's throats.

No wonder the roles are not coming Loyd's way the next century and a half . . . the reservoir of goodwill his big-hearted loyal fans had to him even after the custodial dried up when he was always getting arrested for drunk and disorderly back in the nick . . . drink driving . . . back in the nick . . . falling off his chair on chat shows . . . lost his looks and didn't know where to find them . . . lost his licence and didn't know where to find it . . . he'd already lost an 'l' from his name and didn't know where to find that either . . . people joked he couldn't spell his own name . . . remembered for being forgotten . . . record number of appearances on Where-Are-They-Now shows and in Whatever-Happened-To articles . . . it's a cruel world . . . my prospects were as bottom of the bucket as his . . . but better a has-been than a never-was . . . me I'd never had the chance to squander a fortune on Bourbon, frilly shirts and six foot plus chorus girls . . . well I wouldn't have. I was never worshipped. No matter what depths he plumbed Loyd Parnacott was a god to many.

Me I wept for all that might have been . . . and all that was . . . if it was a fair play custodial it wouldn't be so bad . . . I could always move away after . . . fresh start in a distant land . . . a character cottage with a stream cascading beside it . . . a new identity . . . a new past . . . a new name . . . I might go for Phoebe . . .

Q. How many more days like this was it going to go on for?

A. Four getting on five.

The day of the toad. The day of the albino sea viper. The day of the dromedary louse. The day of the Marcher Hound. The day of the hairless lab rat. The day of the reeking Oskudi Boar . . . I'm an animal person as well as a people person but I do draw a line . . . these were not good days.

Part-Time Tabitha was unusually quiet . . . for once! . . . buried in one book after another revising moving her head gently to her head-phones apart from when she took them off to listen to the news. Poor Tragic Bethany was old news . . . no longer merited a mention . . . isn't that another of life being all random cruelties . . . one day you are news values the next day you are just another victim of short-termism . . . we had been a team, now it was just Part-Time Tabitha and me . . . me and my BFF . . . but was I hers?

I'll never forget the moment.

She was making me test her on a list: 'False French Friends' e.g. décevoir does not mean deceive, hurluberlu does not mean hurly-burly, I can't frankly remember the others.

Her iPhone went (stupid ringsound). She screen-checked the caller. Her face just swooned with warmth.

'Mum!!' Oh that greeting like a sumptuous rich soft centre saying welcome me in.

She listened for a while then she's like: 'Whaaat?'

Listens a bit more: 'Whyyy?'

Then: 'Oh nooooo!'

Then: 'How come?'

Then: 'Oh there's got to be some mistake.'

Then: 'This is terrible . . . total unbelievable.'

Then: 'I'm on my way.'

Her voice was total astonishment. Concern. Sympathy.

And total fake . . . her body language was totally out of kilter with her language language . . . her face was saying something so different . . . it was saying the opposite – her face was grinning crazily . . . the drunk that got the moonshine.

She terminated the call. She turned to me . . . she punched the air . . . beyond bruiserish . . . triumphant . . . brutal . . . a she-warrior that's slaughtered the evil prince . . . she was a different person from what I knew. She did a little jump onto a chair like only the naturally lithe can do . . . boasting with her arms.

'They've got him!' Clenched fists. 'They've arrested him!'

'Who?' I wasn't following.

'The fucking Psycho . . . Carl's in custody . . . the fucker's banged up.'

'How come?'

She looked at me like I was simple. Exhaled her exasperation.

'Well . . . how about a little birdy had a word in plod's ear . . . hee heee hee . . .' she squealed like a wounded concertina . . . rubbed her hands . . . evil glee rays beamed out from her . . . victorious malice rays . . . The penny dropped like it was a feather . . . very very slowly . . . reluctant . . .

It was all falling into place . . . coming to greet me . . . oh god . . . shame's got its own colour – dirty brown rat fur grey . . . it wraps you up tight . . . you are bound up in a hot dirty brown rat fur grey prickly thick blanket . . . it's stifling . . . lung squashing . . . all the breath is asphyxiated out of you . . . bringing the self-hatred to the surface . . . you suddenly find yourself down a tunnel without end . . . no light . . . a sense of death lying in wait . . . you can't feel or see or taste . . . just a smell of scorched . . . scorched what? . . . scorched conscience? . . . the stench of being implicated in a 'profounder stratum of tort' (Erskine Garn – who she was always quoting).

She was dancing round the shop mad as a madthing. There went a bucket of irises. She must have sensed my concerns for her mental health . . . not to mention my concerns for me for my state of existence . . . even keel: 1/10 . . . she grabbed me by the shoulders.

'Don't worry I got rid of the phone . . . chucked it in the river won't be able to trace it . . . it's all mud . . . I stamped on it first.'

She did a funny peculiar little mime to show me what stamped meant . . . then she did it again . . . it stopped being funny peculiar . . . it went 150 per cent funny farm.

I couldn't move.

Due to the gravity severity cruelty enormity of the offence . . . Carl Roland Trench I hereby . . . it was chilling . . . thank god it wasn't me . . .

D'you know even though I'd heard about him so often from Part-Time Tabitha I'd never met him. Not even seen him in the flesh . . . still haven't really . . . newspaper online photos but not recent . . . ordinary looking lank hair and vacant expression . . . at one of the hearings he had a tartan blanket over his head with a rozzer pushing his head down to get in the van/car . . . rozzers always do that to The Accused . . . do they get special training in pushing heads down . . . the rug was that lovely Bolitho tartan . . . tan and French navy . . . draped over hunched shoulders and eyes that want to hide from the world . . . pretend the world doesn't exist . . . I'll bet you pretend you don't exist . . . that there's nothing outside the rug's darkness . . . you don't want to see The Guillotine Community who've all come to see you they have . . . screaming their hatred . . . braying for blood outside of the assizes . . . hammering on the police van . . . howling . . . holding placards Justice For Bethany . . . taking photos through the windows though all they're going to get are blurry ones with the cameras reflected . . . why bother?

If I'd squitted on Part-Time Tabitha I'd have been opening the pro-verbial can of worms . . . yucky maggots seething in claggy orange stuff like tinned spaghetti I imagine the proverbial can as . . . basically I'd have been shopping myself . . . why would I do that . . . anyway who would have believed me what with Psycho Carl's psycho past . . . assaults affrays GBH ABH aggravated burglary . . . with the best will in the world what would be the point . . . I was sympathetic . . . not to mention my profound sense of the injustice that was coming Psycho Carl's way . . . I just had to remind myself that life isn't fair . . . especially not for the Psycho Carls of this world with their unmanaged anger . . . that's a lesson you learn from weeping to trailer park favourites in the wee small hours . . .

You know those disturbed sads craving attention claiming they perpetrated foul kiddy murders when they were a hundred miles away at the time . . . wobbly sort of masochism that is IMHO . . . I wasn't going to barge to the front of the queue to admit my guilt . . .

I decided to make it up to him . . . I baked him a chocolate fondant cake . . . I sent it anonymously to HM Prison Hog Hatch where he was on remand. It was all I could do. I don't know if chocolate fondant cake was his favourite but put me in his shoes and I couldn't have wished for anything more – apart from justice and freedom.

What would be the point in me fessing up to my part in the tragic turn of events . . . events that resulted in the passing of a life . . . two lives if you're a pro-lifer . . . Poor Tragic Bethany and her unnamed foetus . . . let's call it Lindsay . . . nice and gender neutral . . . I couldn't fess up because no one would believe me . . . that's tough for Psycho Carl I know . . . but that's the way it goes. Sorry.

In years to come I would find love with Myles Deuteron.

We hit it off from the start when he sauntered into the shop to order a bespoke bouquet for Mother's Day. As he proffered his Double Platinum card he nodded at the mute telly screen and said:

'That's *The Gent* isn't it. The vat of taramasalata episode . . .'

'Are you a fan?' I asked.

'Am I a fan . . . my bedroom was a shrine to Imogen Skye . . . so sad I couldn't believe it when I heard . . .'

Almost instinctively we stood in contemplative silence, bound as one by profound remembering.

'If you fast forward to where he rescues Tamara you'll see the life guard he pushes out the way is the young Lionel Knave before he transed into Leonie Vane! Uncredited.'

I made a good impression on Mrs Deuteron when we met a few weeks later . . . she welcomed me into the family bosom which consisted of Myles, his dad Geoff In The Incapacity Mobility from an industrial injury and his sister Clover. Myles was still a policeman then . . . but you could tell he was going to go places with his no-nonsense, no-second-chance attitude to criminals and benefit-scrounging immigrants who don't embrace our way of life and Jews who just pretend to . . . fancy – me and a rozzer!! An unusual one mind: bespoke puppytooth suits with a flap over the breast pocket (very Gent!) warfaring international corporate fraud and laundryism having been a Graduate Entry . . . he not only has a degree in Slavic Studies but a doctorate, thesis title: *Incubating Ideological Pragmatisms: Taking the Construction of Neo-Realpolitik to Term.* He had heard of the Bethany Sluytwn case because of it being his home town . . . he didn't know that much about it because he had always worked in London, Switzerland, Frankfurt, Toronto etc. . . . frankly he wasn't that curious . . . it was just a tad too 'local interest' for him . . . he visions pan-globally . . . so I thought it wiser and more mature not to trouble him with 'insider knowledge', so I said no more than only I had known her slightly when I was a probationary teacher at Misselbrook West Heuristic . . . all relationships need their little secrets . . . like those hidden compartments in secretaires and davenports . . . for instance when I heard best man Graduate Entry Inspector Ivor Hinde was secretly hiring a Randy Fireman for my hen night. I secretly reciprocated with maid of honour Janine – newly kidney-rich (that's what fatal accidents are for, giving) – hiring a Stripping WPC for his stag night.

That's the thing about us – we both enjoy a good laugh. For instance, on our first date he wooed me with flattery: 'D'you know Celia, if you lost about four stone you'd look like a Playboy Centre-fold.' Perhaps that's not such a good example after all.

He left the force to take a big step up into a prestigious post in the private security consultancy sector . . . that's not a thick neck with a lanyard and a Marcher Hound – that's tradesman's entrance Senti-nelitude Praetorian Group-style tasking not to mention fighting off yucky smalltimer Sentinelitude Praetorian Chairperson Shaun's caving fingers.

No . . . Myles's world – our world! – developed into a high-flying world of leverage, brokerage, advising international business leaders, managing some of the greatest fortunes on the planet (and off it: outer space is the new Virgin Islands), fine dining in hushed cathe-drals with carpets, strategic meetings in distant cities, cupping your hand so you can't be lip-read, lavishly sponsored conferences of life-decision gurus, foreign languages (I discovered I had a gift for them – 'facciamo shopping!'), four or five mobiles about the person, our own helicopter, oil pipeline strategies, checking rooms for bugs, cash payments, private jets, loitering munition 'kamikaze' drones with 25kg warheads, missiles with 400kg warheads, ethical mentoring, early hours phone calls e.g. 'you be sweetie pie tell him there's hive problem in Druskininkai – he'll understand', strange rumours, coups, prison visiting, the Caymans . . . not to mention hair extensions, ladybird oil, ayurvedic spa camps, Christian Louboutin, Jimmy Choo, Coco de Mer, Azzedine Alaïa, Versace, Antony Price etc. and, to squeeze into them, medically overseen fast-and-starve regimes for yours truly with her jaw wired shut attacking layers of unsightly subcutaneous suet squatting there like a tide of illegal immigrants . . . an expression I'm not allowed to use. There's nothing I don't know about the Ravensbruck Diet™ not to mention gastric bands and chocolate addiction workshops.

All very distant from Bloomin' Marvellous where Part-Time Tabitha stepped up to the plate and became Full-Time Tabitha. Due to poor sales, whiffy flower water because of lack of attention to freshness management, slovenly accounting, too much looking into the future and not enough paying attention to the present, too much book reading, reading everything she could get her hands on about grave robbers and bodysnatchers, not just from wayback but quite contemporary too. Who'd have thought it! In this day and age! Then she was always writing poems, not to mention 1/10 for customer relations going 'Hang on would you I just need to finish this line.' She couldn't grasp the concept of in-shop hospitality even though she'd been excellently taught by moi. Pauline had regrettably to let her go . . . No-Time Tabitha is my little joke. She could only foresee what was going to happen in the future because she was going to make it happen. That included getting fired.

We didn't keep in touch . . . funny that when you've been so close . . . forced into intimacy sort of . . . last I heard she was living on the Belgian Coast, in Belgium.

After he was denied a second appeal Carl Roland Trench sadly hanged himself in his cell at HM Prison Waterlooville . . . there was a story going round that a prison visitor claiming to be his cousin was actually an Emissary Eliminator from Dream Topping™ . . .

maybe . . . maybe not . . . either way hanging is typical psychopathic attention-seeking overreaction . . . he used his elite roofer skills to rig up a gibbet . . . I never actually met him . . . like I said I only knew him by his reputation . . . by what No-Time Tabitha portrayed him as . . . he was a face online . . . a head under a tartan blanket . . . I would be hypocritical pretending I felt anything . . . I'm over it . . . it was just one of those things wasn't it . . . life goes on.

Ah the impetuousness of youth! It was so yesterday . . . all so long ago . . . so long ago . . . I've put it behind me . . . that chapter of my life is closed. No return. I've locked the door on it and thrown away the key in a swamp full of reptiles.

Janine said I reminded her of that poem we did in the Representations of Exploitation module, 'The Spoiled Maid' . . . I reminded her it was 'The Ruined Maid' . . . and I said she'd done well for herself with her gay bracelets and bright feathers . . . like I had . . . so I suppose yes there was a similarity . . . and exploitation doesn't come into it.

Money has brought us great happiness and interesting friends, grudgingly a few token Jews and token blacks of colour among them for appearance's sake.

We have a town house a few minutes from Marble Arch for when we have to stay over. The only people who opposed excavating three basement levels for sauna, pool, gym, five-a-side pitch and tennis court were twisted and jealous. They overlooked that we were creating jobs and wealth for more than a hundred skilled workmen from Volgograd including craftsmen who had been castrated chemically, *kastratsiya* – lovely chaps who didn't seem to regret their loss. When human bones were found deep down it was first presumed that they were from criminals hanged at Tyburn. This was challenged by a snooty Heritage Professional, an archaeological consultant with a funny accent and a drunken husband old enough to be her father. Work was delayed for ten months. But was the wait worth it! Twenty lengths every morning. It's an essential part of my beauty routine. We also have a modest manoir chateau near Saumur – no make-up for a natural look in keeping with the country. We have our eyes on an island for extra privacy and exclusive entertaining.

Our latest first home is a lovely older style home featuring a minstrel gallery, tile hanging and so-called decorative gallets in the mortar in the Surrey Hills with top-of-the-range bespoke security including infrared sensors . . . chemosensory antennae that 'smell' strangers . . . tomographic motion detectors . . . automatically activated drones . . .

We have a lovely large thirty-acres . . . what ordinary people spend on a house we spend on a Murano bidet.

We have a lovely son Bradley Myles Oleg Deuteron. He's four and a half now, a real little terror and a football fanatic – not only two dozen replica shirts but Pavel Smolov's own shirt, signed and personally presented by the oft red-carded midfield legend in mineral-rich Rostov-on-Don! And he's so excited to have a lovely little brother on the way! Unfortunately we are obliged to live in hiding for the moment protected 24/7 by a team of top detention creatives passionate about their vocation.

K. Winston Dogg

I never really knew my dad till his last few years really and since he passed on (after, frankly, overstaying his welcome) I don't know hardly anyone who knew him to talk to about him, to ask what he was like before the dementia.

What I know is from hearsay and old photos mainly. As a young man he wore a neat collar and tie but everyone did back then. He was a powerfully built sort of fellow, broad shouldered, tall and barrel chested. But lean. A handsome devil. Not a scrap, not an ounce of spare tyre. He was like a rugby player who has worked out in the gym. But I don't know if he played the game as there's so much I don't know about him or if they had proper gyms in those days. He was very dark haired, a bit wavy with a pronounced widow's peak just like me, it's in the genes. He had a clipped moustache. I never had one. A moustache isn't in the genes. It's a voluntary appendage. He looks dark skinned but it's difficult to tell from just the few old black and white photos mostly with frilly edges which I've got instead of memories. When he was old he was yellowish but that's not to say he was yellow when he was a young buck.

He was a cabinet maker not that you'd have known it from those four good fingers, sausage fingers. On the stubby side for that trade in my opinion, unusually stubby. A handicap he overcame to become a master cabinet maker and, surprisingly, an accomplished weaver. Fingerwise I'm more like Mum thankfully. He might have been Welsh but that's a guess because of the swarthiness and the rugby of course. But I never heard he was musical as the Welsh are supposed to be like Alun Wynford Wynford or Gwylim Bench or Pandora Preece or those rousing miners' choirs but then no one spoke about him. Gordon says that Ricky van Brabant's dad – he's got a pop-up sputum analysis tent at festivals. Just cashing in on his son's fate. The Legend in The Perpetual Coma frankly – Gordon says that he says lungs with pneumoconiosis and emphysema just shouldn't be made to sing like that, bellowing at god like god's got hearing difficulties. How do they know he has? Or are they just showing off?

Sometimes it was as though he had never existed. I think Mum forced herself to forget him. Eventually she did forget him just about, she tried so hard she almost succeeded. She wished him out of her memory. She wanted to wish him out of mine too. But there was the problem as she saw it of my genes, me reminding her of him. Little tics and gestures, and my voice, things like that which I had no control over and nor did she. She couldn't forgive me for resembling him. It was in our common genes, my dad's and me, to live long lives. He outlived Mum by quarter of a century. When he died he hadn't seen her for getting on sixty years. It was almost as long as he hadn't seen me for, for that matter. After she died I had been going to take the plunge and get in touch with him but you know how these things are. Gordon was against it initially so it wasn't till very late in his life that we were reunited, if that's the word, by Mr Gough who had power of attorney down to Dad's dementia. There were times when he was lucid, sewing away at one of his samplers (always a house with flowers round it), there were times when he didn't know who he was talking to. You wouldn't call him great company the way he swore and spat. But he wasn't a bad man. It was just petulance mainly so far as I can gather but you know how petulance can turn. With Dad it did turn. Petulance plus upper body strength equals trouble. He had this surefire knack of picking on the wrong people.

He sometimes thought I was Shirelle. I never found out who Shirelle was. He sometimes mistook me for a certain Bet whoever she was. He liked to sniff my neck and pinch my ear lobes which was funny peculiar when you're seventy and he's almost a hundred. Maybe he'd got the idea from one of those parenting articles that it was how fathers behaved.

I thought I was getting to the bottom of it all. Then only nine days before he was due to get his telegram from The Palace – do they still send them? – the call came from nice caring Mrs Brockdorff at Copse

Garth (the insensitive taxi drivers at Pokesdown Station think they're comedians, they call it Corpse Garth).

It must have come as a relief to her. I mean all his humorous pranks such as putting his used incontinence pads in cushion covers and down the backs of sofas . . . the legacy of his profession you might say. He was embarrassing the way he was always showing off his amputation stub. And he had incurable Spackman-Brock syndrome with the projectile vomiting, it was getting out of hand, it was like liquid pebbledash. In summer he'd go out in the garden with his food and bury it, plate and all, in the flowerbeds – 'for later' he said. Like a dog. And sure enough it was the local strays that dug it up later. There's no knowing what they thought of the Porkcullis brand sausages: Gordon won't have them in the house.

Then – and there's no way to put this delicately – he had masturbation issues. It's what did for him in the end. His heart just wasn't built for such vigorous activity. You might call it manic. I suppose you could say he went the way he wanted to go, doing the thing he loved. He did it using his good hand, the one with the full set of fingers, grinning at the nurses and the kitchen staff. They very sensibly didn't bother with taking any notice of him, wheezing away like the effort might kill him which of course it did. It was different with visitors to the other old folk, some of them were just kiddies come to see their gran. They were downright shocked. The way he ground his teeth when he was at it – they sort of shrilled like metal on metal! When the staff tried to move him to get him out of the room he'd put on the wheelchair's brake and they'd have to struggle to make him let go of it. He verbally abused visitors coming back from the toilet. He would be asking them if they'd done a number one or a number two. Sometimes he'd shock them in the crudest way: 'Been choking a darky have we? Did we wash our hands? Did we?' The hairdressers who came round from Hair In The Community refused to cut his hair because he was always like: 'Do you have a brazilian do you? Or do you entertain the lads fully shaven? I'm not fussy – I'll lap 'em both up!' So his hair was down to his shoulders.

Also, you know what, I could have got along without him introducing me as 'my lad the Screaming Pansy' and 'Pierrepoint's popsy' and calling Gordon 'the husband' or 'Hilda Handcuffs' – Gordon was only in the Prison Service for less than four years. He was not some common or garden screw let alone a hangman – a bit late for that! He was an executive library officer/decontaminations. Not that the other old folk seemed to take much notice of what Dad said. He could have told them I was an Eliminator from Dream Topping™ or The Instant Whip Iceman[48] come to give them their Neutraliser, they'd still have nodded smiling soppily and making what Gordon – trust him! – calls 'gloopygloopgloop noises from the drowned crypt'. It's all about their sticky, pus-rich gums plus the sordid ruins of their teeth. Such was their way. It was a bit puzzling that they and the staff all called Dad 'Arthur'. I called him Dad because you do. Where that nickname came from is anybody's guess. One of the staff said she thought it was because he looked like Arthur the next-door neighbour in *Pull The Other One*. Perhaps it was only used at Copse Garth.

When we cleansed his flatlet – real whiffo landfill it was – all the letters Gordon and I found were, sure enough, addressed to Edmund or Edmond Dogg. Most of them unopened. It was funny how his signature was so different from one official document to the next. In the papers in Mr Gough the solicitor's keeping he was 'Edmund Cecil Dogg' or 'Edmond Cecil Dogg'. That's what he was to the social services, NHS and HMP. The Revenue hadn't heard of him so far as we could tell. HSBC hadn't either! With him it was cash and barter. We found just over £1,000 in the wardrobe which was a nice reward for such a noisome experience. We took up the floorboards and the skirting, disabled the plumbing to search the pipes and cisterns, slit the mattress (not a pretty sight!), pulled out the oven. There was nothing more. No hidden fortune.

Let's be frank. To start with, it wasn't much of a funeral. A lovely day, mind, which made up for it a tad. Nice fluffy clouds shaped like piglets, Gordon remarked. Shrubs in vibrant bloom. The coffin looked like a chest of drawers. I left it to the vicar, the Rev. Eileen Shorto, to choose the hymns and what have you, when to stand and

---

48 Several smaller agencies were also represented on site at Copse Garth: Smotherland, Last Bites, Cushioned Ending, Happy Finish, Long Nap, Forty Winks Extra.

all that. I have to say that her boast that the vitality Crematorium 'puts the Fun in Funeral' was a tad wide of the mark. Still, good as her word she was when I asked her to keep it brief because you got some tenth decade bladders in the audience. 'Congregation,' she corrected me.

She said not to worry. She gave me an unvicarlike wink.

Then I stood there in the Crem cloister with a few tired floral tributes scattered about while a dozen people, mostly strangers, lined up to shake hands after the service. There was oh so caring Mrs Brockdorff with her sympathetic tribal touch: you'd never guess from looking at her that she was of African origin. She was accompanied by her talented nephew (or was it grandson) plus Copse Garth staff and some of the fitter 'inmates' – there goes Gordon again! The last in the queue was a smartly turned-out lady who knew how to dress for a funeral, black suit, hair up beneath a wide brimmed black hat. I thought she must be Copse Garth's unseen owner the mysterious Mrs Brady. She wasn't.

She offered her hand and said: 'I'm Phoebe . . . Phoebe Chipurnoi? . . .' She looked questioning at me to see if her name rang a bell. It didn't.

'Phoebe Chipurnoi?'

Funny name. How you spelling it? It still didn't mean anything. A tad rum, I thought, her insistent tone. 'Well,' I shook my head, 'well . . . how d'you do then. Good to meet you. Uh . . . nice of you to come.'

Imagine then my astonishment, there is no other word, my sheer astonishment when this Phoebe Chipurnoi clasped my hand with her other hand too and announced:

'I'm your half-sister.'

I wondered if I was hearing right. You could have knocked me down with a feather.

All of a sudden I felt like I was a different man. A man I didn't recognise. A man with a life he didn't know about that had not been revealed to him. Where had it been buried? I was at a loss for words. It was all slow motion. It was all rushing. In extreme peripheral vision (right) I could see Gordon glance away from Mr Gough and the vicar who he was talking to. He was puzzled. Worried for me.

He registered me being totally gob-smacked. It's a tad coarse that expression. But as he said later he'd never seen anyone so open-mouthed. Gaping at this stranger like the proverbial village idiot.

'Oh dear, I didn't mean to shock you.'

'Cor . . . Let me . . . I don't know what . . . well, what *do* you say? You, well, you're not having me on? I'm sorry to ask . . . But it's not the right occasion to go playing japes. I mean there couldn't be some mistake? Are you sure?'

I wondered if she might be one of those ghoul people of the night you read about that feast on the distress of others. Whether it be car crashes or it be horses put down at the Grand National (a shocking eight last year) or socialites on fire because of the tragic consequence of a wrongly adjusted lighter and too much inflammable hairspray or letting skeletons out of the cupboard. Wrenching them out might be more like it.

'I *am* sure. Yes. Of course I appreciate how troubling . . . I *am* your father's daughter – by Betsy Mavroleon. *Our* father's . . .'

She bit her lip and winced. She had the strangest accent.

Hang on, I thought to myself: who's Betsy Mavroleon when she's at home?

Phoebe Chipurnoi told me: 'I've been rather fearing this . . . ever since I saw the death announcement . . . I've been wondering what this moment would be like? I only saw it by chance. Last week was the first time I'd been here since I was a child. I didn't know he lived here. I didn't know where he lived. There were a couple of times when I thought of trying to find him . . . I didn't even know he was still alive . . . If you see what I mean. I was just glancing through . . . *The Echo*, isn't it? *The Echo*. In the back of a taxi. I have a *tendresse particulière* for small town papers.'

Did I detect any emotion? I don't believe I did. She talked about herself like she was talking about someone else. Calm. Upbeat. What's that called? Displacement?

'One asks oneself how many people can there be called Edmund Cecil Dogg – it is the most . . .'

(She was going to say *ridiculous*, I could tell.)

'. . . it's an *unusual* name . . . obviously it had to be him.'

There wasn't a formal gathering as such. We retired to The

Halyard, a comfy lounge bar across the road from the Cake Artistry Centre. Me and my new half-sister, Gordon, Mr Gough, the vicar, Mrs Brockdorff and her nephew (or was it grandson) Jason, a 'poet' apparently. He couldn't stay for more than five minutes 'because of minding the ice cream van', which seemed at odds with a poet's vocation.

There was no getting away from it. Phoebe Chipurnoi was haughty, very aloof. You might say severe. Not a people person was the verdict I returned pdq. Unforthcoming to say the least. And secretive: we know where she gets that from! After getting on for an hour in her company I knew nothing about her:

Gay or straight? Married? Divorced? Children? Where did that accent come from? Profession? Last week she'd been down here to give a lecture. We're a conference town. You can often tell them, they have their look. But her . . . Business Consultant? Motivational Guru? Urban Regenerator/Property Developer? High End Real Estate?

And where did she live?

She had that knack of putting you off asking anything directly. And anything indirect she brushed aside.

We all had a snorter or two apart from her. Lemon tea was her tipple. When she stood up to go I had a feeling I'd never had before, for obvious reasons – sibling solidarity. A new sort of affection. So I showed her a token of my affection. I made her what I considered was a most generous offer.

'Do you want to split the ashes? Share them? We could go fifty fifty – I'll send them on to you if you tell me where—'

She was quite taken aback by my generosity.

She looked at me somewhat astonished. And slightly down her nose you might say. Like I wasn't sixteen annas to the rupee: 'It's . . . uh . . . very thoughtful of you . . . But to be honest I don't think I've got anywhere to display them . . . as they deserve to be displayed. No, nowhere. I've got to run.'

And that was the last I saw or heard of her till the whole thing blew up many moons later.

Rui Päschlat

My ears are syringed to perfection. My hearing is as acute as a Marcher Hound's. (The German Mordhund is more evocative.) My peripheral vision has been intensely trained. I am all eyes, no face despite the four-centimetre vertical white scar it bears. I see 180 degrees and more. I see. I am not seen. I am a revenant unrecognised where I once was greeted. I am a ghost in daylight on a crowded street. Eye to brain beyond the speed of light. Keeping an eye on things, many things. That's my job, my will, my vocation. There are persons of interest who must be watched: they are not necessarily centre stage. Hence my sensory superpowers. I am alert to the slightest sign.

It's every Jew's duty to be forever on the qui vive, it's a duty to every other Jew. 'Social' anti-Semitism is anti-Semitism, full stop. It exists. It is not imagined. It is quite contrary to 'Ramalamaphobia', an invention of Ramalama, which claims to be persecuted, whose bleating pleading is listened to, whose victimisation goes unchallenged even as its bombs tear apart the bodies of mushes and goras who pathetically bend over backwards to appease it, giving in to its demands to lead a life of elective apartheid, barbaric punishments, brainwashing and hatred for the host country whose shores they have washed up on.

We are well informed. In the cause of the greater good we rob suspects and potential enemies of their privacy without their knowledge. Our methods are not crude like those of the Stasi, which was staffed by Gestapo graduates. We have superior technology available and we have superior minds – we are, after all, Jews, even if we never set foot in a synagogue, even if we habitually eat treyf, even if we regard Leviticus as the work of a comedian obsessed by cattle and cleaning products.

It was study of the 'literature' disseminated by The Stout As Oak Moot (a heretical secession from The Sacred Oak Order of The Fourth Manifest) that revealed its pedantic insistence on 'Clean English', uncontaminated by American (i.e. supposedly Jewish) usages. This dialectic underpinning was as telling as their 'Earth Reckonings' – acts of violence towards tree surgeons, road builders, hedge trimmers, agriculturalists and shepherds shooting packs of rewilded wolves and happy bears. They have shipped polecats into territories where those vermin have never lived. They attempt to create brand new old watercourses with meanders and ox-bows while obliterating the culverts and navigations created in the eighteenth and nineteenth centuries. They use a modern armoury of belligerence to achieve environmental backwardness. Who funds them?

Ludicrous name, ludicrous congregation. The Unspire Maniple comprises malign self-proclaimed 'yeomen of yore'. It holds that the true English church has a tower with crockets, finials and pinnacles. The bells peal. The flag bulges in the breeze. There's a promise of ancient fertility. No spire. A spire is an immigrant form. A spire is a vagrant from Lal Sicily by way of Normandy. A spire reaches for heaven. A tower, however, is grounded, squat in yeoman earth, rich in the potassium of yeoman forebears it grows from the earth which is god's earth, his domain where life begins and returns to. Again, who funds them?

These freakish fringe groupuscules concern us: the microscopic germ may swell into the poison plant. They attract each other, fellow outsiders and outriders with nothing in common but their cosy alienation; their beliefs and practices may be contrary but they have a common cause, a common enemy – they want to quash liberty of expression, tolerant decency, the freedom to challenge their demagoguery. They cannot accept opposition. They are *au fond* unimaginative, incurious, strangers to empathy and doubt, so trapped in their own delusion that they insist the world should think as they think, behave as they behave, chastise as they chastise – woundingly, murderously. They are passionate, intense. They are believers, infected by faith.

The divisions that existed between groups before they formed alliances are to be exhumed and exploited. In the Middle East, for instance, advantage must be taken of their being burdened by incompatible ideologies. The task is to dissolve the amalgam by emphasising the insurmountable differences in the Lal world. Wedges of mistrust must be driven between Charies and Mufts, between Turk and Egyptian, between Yemeni and Omani. Let us remind them of ancient tribalism. Let us set neighbour against neighbour even though they are all riddled with the same fervour of falnadath. Let us foment hatred and encourage persecution of minorities, the scapegoats unfortunate enough to find themselves on the wrong side of the border speaking the wrong language, writing the wrong script.

It is by the rigorous application of these stratagems that peace is maintained and the equilibrium achieved. And exploiting opportunities such as this:

At a London underground station, Westminster, a posthumous work of Piranesi, I heard an overalled technician bellowing into his phone.

'No CCTV on District westbound . . . is that what you're saying no CCTV on . . . at most ten minutes . . . OK . . . copy that.'

I required no further invitation. Calmly, not ostentatiously, not attracting attention, I hurried unhurriedly to that platform through a metal maze of escalators and swooping drops wrapping a scarf around my face as though cold-ridden. I ignored my duty to buskers and beggars. The next train, to Edgware Road, was in four minutes, the one following, to Richmond, was in fourteen. So I had four minutes to find my target. I needed less than four seconds. The platform was sparsely inhabited. There he was: beard no moustache; crocheted kufi; calf-length smock (qamis?); indecently hirsute legs; trainers. He stood at the very end of the platform close by the entrance to the tunnel the train would emerge from. He was holding a fat briefcase, smiling smugly to himself, evidently plotting an outrage.

The only other people towards that end of the platform were a group of preoccupied adolescent schoolchildren staring at each other's phones, grabbing each other's phones, holding each other's phones high so the owner could not reach it. When I was their age I was past horsing about, I was settling scores, fighting for my people, bringing justice, speaking for the righteous. Since an intemporal blue night in

Parc Guerland I had not ceased to obliterate the worthless and the wrong. There is no comparison with the genocide. My people were murdered by the trainload because of who we are, not what we do.

He was unaware of my proximity. His body didn't have time to tense in resistance. My playful shove was not quite as cleanly decisive as I'd have wished but the timing was impeccable. It did the trick. He looked up from the track where he sprawled. He was surprised. He didn't have time for fear. He had a moment to adjust matters with his god before he was struck and his head exploded. It quit being a head. The train was driven by Frank Buttifant, 41, of Palmers Green N13. He was treated for shock at Saint Thomas's Hospital. 'It's every driver's nightmare. My thoughts are with his family.'

I was already past the noisy adolescents on my way to the exit before they realised what had happened. I walked the length of the platform as the screams of the living were drowned in the din of alarms and of an unbloodied train arriving from the other direction.

Myles Deuteron. I read the name then I heard it again only a matter of days later. A coincidence may be no more than just that. But it may be a warning, a presage. A suggestion that god is to be found in aleatory things. It was not to be ignored. Seize the chance for it may not be chance. It's an unusual name, memorable, perhaps too memorable for his own welfare.

Out of some sort of courtesy I had accepted an invitation to the Royal Opera House. My antipathy is to be found in the first two parts of its name. And then there is Wagner – not just a venomous anti-Semite but a dire composer, and a difficult one to sleep through. The racket was deafening. To take my mind off it I read a PR brochure listing the theatre's 'philanthropists', 'patrons' and so on. A commando of social alpinists with a taste for tax breaks and dressing up. A couple called Myles and Celia Deuteron had thrown £260,000 p.a. into the kitty. Snobbery comes at a price.

Lambert Roy was doing some digging for me in Zurich. He was a low-grade indic I called on from time to time. What I paid him boosted his stipend: his field of research at CHU Strasbourg was parasites' parasites' parasites, the chain of dependence that is a metaphor for life itself. He was meant to be fetching the griff on the orgiastic heiress Hanna N. Who she connected with, what organisations and agencies her foundation supported. He called to report a total lack of progress. I was finishing a P'tit Clamart at a café in a courtyard off rue Cognacq-Jay, a Paris street Judex had never previously returned to. Retrospective pride in a crisply timed elimination is a satisfying sensation.

After I'd painstakingly wiped the crumbs from my mouth and ordered a second coffee I told Roy that I was weary of his imaginatively impressive suit of excuses. Then he added – no doubt to justify his existence and reingratiate himself – that he had undertaken an investigation which he knew would interest me. He had by chance spotted something that was entirely unconnected to his enquiries.

The catalogue of the day's lots was displayed outside Steppler Auktionen on Untere Zäune. The main sale was advertised as being part of the estate of the scion of a landowning family in the Valais.

In addition there were some miscellaneous items. Lot 88 was a Biedermeier secretaire, mahogany with metal inlays. 88! He was familiar with the coded use of 88 but had not seen it used so blatantly or in such a supposedly respectable milieu. He was impressionable. He didn't realise that auctioneers the world over are moral derelicts in bespoke tailoring: they'll sell anything. He wandered into the halls. The secretaire was scuffed, tarnished, veneerless in part. It was incongruous in a sale of otherwise handsome and well-maintained pieces. When the lot was called bidding was initially slow. It became clear, however, once the reserve had been exceeded that there were only two interested parties. One was linked to a phone clasped by a Steppler employee. The other was a squat myope whose fury at being progressively outbid caused his pocked face to ruddy and sweat, his spectacles steamed up 'like condensation' said Roy. Eventually he reached his limit. He threw his catalogue to the floor and stamped from the rooms.

'Eight eight you say.'

'Eight eight . . . Why else a price like that – twelve thousand Swiss francs – that's down to where it comes from.'

'Eight eight.'

'I hung around till the halls were closing . . . I tipped the porter . . . have to tip him again . . . money-lust sort of guy. It's not *the* normal eight eight . . . We all know eight eight what it means . . . This one isn't. Same letters. Same number down alphabet . . . Yeh? HH . . . I tell you – Heinrich Himmler. The furniture . . . it belonged to this old woman . . . she'd been his mistress . . . She lived in Baden-Baden . . . she was looked after by Aribert Heim the monster of Mauthausen the doctor from hell . . . he eventually had to escape . . . Spain . . . Chile . . . he died a few years back the porter says . . . It'd be illegal to sell it in Germany that's why . . . The man that buys . . . name is Osman Osmanović . . . bidding from London the porter says. This information . . . not so cheap to come by . . . and by the way I put a tracking device in the desk.'

'You did?'

'I can follow it on my phone . . . I thought you'd be interested.'

'I am impressed. Jolly good show! As they say.'

'Yeh, they have secret compartments . . . my great-gran had one . . . just have to feel about . . . for the spring.'

'Where is it now – the secretaire?'

'Still at Stepplers . . . waiting to be collected.'

Buying a desk for ten times the price it would normally command is the act of an obsessive, a completist, a hobbyist whose collecting invests objects with the qualities of those who used them. The object is not neutral. It is charged.

It is the desk of a woman who bore two children to a mass murderer. He destroyed children in their millions, their parents, their grandparents – and the children they might have had. The only reason for acquiring such an object can be as a celebration of genocide. Celebration leads to emulation.

It is diplomatically unwise to employ such ethically compromised organisations as Memory@Mnemonic™, a division of Sentinelitude Praetorian. But if bloodyminded UK agencies refuse to share information with us (as they are obliged to do under the terms of the Aachen Agreements) then there is little option but to resort to a knowledge bank which has acquired much of its knowledge by theft, hacking, bribery etc. No questions asked.

Quasi Hubback was back to me within an hour. He can sully you by phone. Just wash your ears.

'Your man Osman's a fucking free range war criminal . . . miraculously unconvicted . . . fucking Bosniak . . . you familiar—'

'I am.'

'Torture, rape, murder . . . typical fucking keba footsoldier . . . if I'm not mistaken the courts found all Serbs guilty and Lals innocent . . . if fucking Ramalama says it's OK then cutting off some poor sod's cock and shoving it in his mouth is OK because it's decreed by your fucking faith.'

'You're not mistaken. The Ramalamaleth sanctions it. What's our friend up to now?'

'He's been under the radar for a while . . . but . . . as luck would have it . . . he was involved in an RTA a month ago. Nothing serious but Five picked up on it because he was driving a fucking oligarch . . . he's a chauffeur . . . sounds more like a fucking gofor . . . he's versatile . . . also works as a gardener . . . and he's a guinea pig for pharma trials of shit that might kill you . . . stuff they're scared to test elsewhere . . . Now . . . you'll never get this . . . This oligarch . . . wait for it . . . he's fucking English . . . You ever hear of an English oligarch?'

I was not prepared to admit that I hadn't. My reputation for omniscience must be preserved.

'He's called Myles Deuteron—'

'Deuteron!' He didn't need to know that I had recently encountered that name (and so would, inevitably, be bound to re-encounter it).

'Hiding in plain fucking sight . . . this guy . . . apart from a sod-you yacht, a sod-you fucking chateau, a sod-you island in the Blackwater estuary, a sod-you helicopter, a sod-you townhouse on Hamilton fucking Terrace and a sod-you Botox doll he's totally low profile . . . I mean that . . . no one's put two and two together . . . publicity shy . . . you got to ask why does this party have a friend like Terrorist Osman running his fucking errands for him . . . potential fucking liability I'd say . . . but then who am I to ask . . . not having a sod-you yacht and a sod-you fleet of fucking classic cars . . . makes you wonder what sort of errands – but then I got a suspicious mind.'

'No other mind worth having, Quasi.'

★

It angered me that this man had escaped my attention. Myles Deuteron was, henceforth, a person of interest. His slide upwards was hardly visible. He was drawn to concealment. He covered his tracks There was little to read. I fed off scraps in newsletters, industry subscription bulletins, oblique paragraphs, the ill-informed claims of think tanks, the ill-informed claims of financial and business pages in the laughably named 'serious' press. His name was known to certain agencies. But beyond the name and recycled epithets ('reclusive', 'mysterious', 'enigmatic') there was nothing. There was, for instance, no publicly available photograph. There was no gossip, professional or private. He was cagey. He avoided routine like a man with a price on his head. He also avoided offices, met in hotel bars and lobbies, coffee shops, often used public phones, wrote down as little as possible, left no trace, remembered everything.

He employed short contract staff whose knowledge was limited to what he told them. He had no advisors. He was appointed Chairman of TEK Strelka and its wholly owned subsidiaries VABST, Gorsk Intergas and BIT-2. It has raised oil prices to countries reliant on it by between approx. 30 per cent and 45 per cent. Because TEK controls Pipeline Marevna, Israel, which produces less than 1 per cent of its oil needs, is over a barrel — or quarter of a million barrels per day, as Dudu Topaz regularly reminds us. He doesn't let up. It's almost a catchphrase.

Even though he was discreet going on invisible Deuteron has the usual oligarch infection. Greed. A disease manifest in Veblen goods, multiple properties and, most likely, skin tone: oh that infuriating lack of photo. He became competitively acquisitive. Keeping up with the Popovs drove him on. He compounded his infractions. Through companies called Arms For Reconciliation[49] and The League of Mutual Understanding he brokered risky deals to Iran and Palestine and, on a parochial scale, to expatriate Turkish groups in France.

Risk 1): The Russian Federation outlawed such sales in exchange for Israel agreeing not to supply Ukraine and Georgia. There are factions within government and the security services which profit by

---

49 Myles Deuteron was known to his former colleagues in the Secret Service as 'Arms For Oblivion'.

turning a blind eye. There are equally factions that cannot be relied on no matter how generous the birthday gifts they receive every day of the year. Jealousy and rivalry between the FSB and the SVR exacerbates the problems faced by sales teams.

Risk 2): The anti-Semitism that once pervaded the highest level of Russian political life has evaporated. Spud[50] surrounds himself with Jews whom he considers Russians, as they consider themselves. He is indifferent to their religion and ethnicity.

Risk 3): This was the greatest punt Deuteron took. The one most likely to cost him. The gamble he carelessly failed to recognise as a gamble.

We are all knowing. Yahweh's justice is merciless, harsh, final. It is a fearful thing to fall into the hands of the living god.

Our enemies are pursued to the ends of the earth. And when they get there they fall off the edge. Or are pushed by the likes of former Detective Inspector Desmond 'Quasimodo' Hubback.

This was a man with no saving graces. He was easily impressed. Famous faces aroused him. He was flattered to be invited to meet at Koritsas. 'Well above my pay grade. Heard about it course but never manufactured a reason to bust it. More's the fucking pity. All this fucking unearned wealth sickens me.' He jabbed an unseen target with his clenched fist.

'Quasimodo! Tush, please, tush.'

I grabbed the wrist of Evangelos Manikas who was snorting back from the restroom.

'Van – I want you to meet Desmond Hubback – just about the smartest—'

'All security needs catered,' grinned Quasi.

Van rolled his eyes: 'Sounds exciting – now if you'll excuse me.'

I told him: 'His father was a blacksmith . . . Unearned?'

'I could arrest him for . . . Christ he's got a half fucking strap of carlos in his tache.'

---

50 UK's Moscow Embassy's jocular usage coined by the ebullient sometime military attaché Colonel Mike Mungoson. Fried Spud signifies anger, Boiled Spud intransigence, Creamed Spud emollience (rare). *Sentinel*, vol. 90, no. 7, 06.09.2016.

'You could not arrest him . . . you are former, Desmond, former, remember . . . very former . . . early retirement . . . interesting euphemism that . . . I have to say the Met is extremely generous to its miscreants. And I am too, you are useful, Desmond . . . if I had friends – normal human behaviour I choose not to subscribe to – it is unlikely that you would be among them . . . which is not to say that you are unappreciated . . . I admire your moral vacuity . . . your empty wigs . . .'

'This is a well tasty drop.' He stretched his neck to read the bottle.

'Pinot nero . . .' I spared his eyes . . . 'pauper's Burgundy – Alto Aldige . . . Italy where they speak German . . .'

'I'm going there next week.'

'*Alto Aldige?*'

'No. Germany. I'm chaperoning one of Shaun's mates, top fucking client. Weirdo . . . ex-undertaker . . . been looking for his birth parents since the beginning of time . . . found his mother – I think we can say that proved a disappointment on both sides . . . too old to need his hand holding but can't speak a word . . . me, I sprachen sort of . . . whatever happened to that idea . . . post-war . . . remember . . . eliminate the German language make them speak English . . . still, nice earner . . . I already told him I says keep your head down Henry . . . do not reveal your admiration for the late Mister Hitler or, come to that, get nostalgic about the DDR.'

'You would – correct me if I'm wrong – you'd have been as happy working for the BND as for the Stasi.'

'Silly question, course I would . . . You said it . . . I got moral vacuity.'

'And low cunning.'

'The lower the cunning the higher the fee . . . my motto . . . I've had some tidy dinari from you lot.'

'*You lot?* Who are this *you lot*?'

'Yids. Four by twos. Oven dodgers. Four wheel—'

'I don't care what you call me, Quasi . . . and you sound like you've swallowed Green's dictionary . . . I belong to no lot . . . Sole trader as they say . . . always have been . . . always will be . . . Sanctioned by a higher power.' I flashed a smile.

He gaped at me not knowing whether or not to believe me. I gave him no clue.

'Now – business.'

This is what I told Quasi.

The secretaire was collected mid-morning Friday. Roy followed its progress for less than twenty minutes. Then the position from which the signal was being transmitted ceased to move.

Do you know Zurich's northern outskirts? Its insipid villas and capacious parking lots, its abundant garden centres, its celebrated turning points for buses on routes 17 and 26, its neat allotments, its commanding views of its neighbouring suburbs, its laybys fully equipped with shivering prostitutes. Roy considered treating himself. He stopped his Vespa to look at another poor wretch from a country without vowels, he reconsidered.

Half-timbered Weiningen. Picture postcard village. The signal came from a wide service road behind shops. There were overflowing bins and rusted skips. The semi-trailer of an artic had been converted into an ad-hoc brothel, apertures had been hacked in its side as crude windows. An underage girl stared helplessly through one of them. As he tried to locate its position two guest-worker pimps, graduates of Tirana's Academy of Advanced Proxenetism, watched him. They sat on the steps of a restaurant kitchen beside drums of cheap cooking oil. They smoked, they eyed him warily. From inside came the shrieks and howls of underlings, the chef's bellows, the plongeur's Wagnerian cacophony. He parked the Vespa. Next door there was a workshop that comprised a wooden lean-to supported by a lean-to supported by a lean-to. Parasites' parasites' . . . he thought. Pleased with the thought he looked for an entrance. There were wood shavings underfoot and sawdust for the lungs. The two doors he found were padlocked. A polished panel was attached to one of them: incised, gold-painted gothic lettering *Antikschreinerei Reus*. The windows were barred. He jumped with a spring in order to peer through them. The grime was thick.

As he began a second tour of the premises a beefy moustached peasant grandmother emerged from the kitchen bearing a miller's cleaver. She moved with surprising elegance between the guest workers.

'You prying boy?'

'No – I'm . . .' At a loss for words.

'I call it prying boy . . .' She reached into the pocket of her blood-caked murderer's apron.

'This what you're looking for?' She held up the tracker, a tiny trophy, dropped it and with her stout army boots ground it into the metalled surface of the road.

'Ahmet and Idris here are going to have a little word in your ear.' She fondly ruffled the curly hair of one of the guest-worker pimps then disappeared into the kitchen.

He ran for his Vespa, tripping, spraining, stubbing, trying to start it before they knocked him off it. They too wore heavy boots.

He called me from hospital. Ahmet and Idris had run away. They had been interrupted by Brown Owl and her pack of blue-shirted, black-woggled guides of iron. If not for them he said, if not for them . . .

A swollen lip twisted his speech. He was to be detained overnight in case he was concussed, in case a scan should reveal anything more than bruising to his ribs and adductors, in case he suffered internal bleeding.

'If that's your plan for me,' wondered Quasi, 'I got pressing engagements for the foreseeable. Land of the Hun as I said.'

'I want more, much more, on Deuteron. That was a provoked attack. Read it as such. It didn't just happen. Why did it happen? Target Osmanović.'

'Black and Decker?'

'If necessary . . . Good . . . ah . . . what do you call it?'

'Good old-fashioned British coppering.'

'That's the one . . . yes. Let's eat.'

Veal and oyster tartare. Grilled red mullet. Leg of lamb stuffed with cèpe duxelles. Blette gratin. Truffled moliterno. Millefeuille.

'A: There's a photo of Ante Pavelić, whose ear lobes hung like cuts of meat, presenting Himmler with a mahogany Biedermeier secretaire . . . a sort of fawning tribute. A pompous little ceremony . . .

'B: The world is full of Biedermeier secretaires but few of them are mahogany . . . an expensive wood for the bourgeoisie . . . Few of them have been owned by mass murderers. This is a relic. It's infused with the squalor they believe sacred . . . Evil exists . . . not just as an idea of repugnance but as an absolute . . . it is tangible . . . it is tangible in a piece of furniture . . . this is steeped in evil . . . marinated . . . by breath, by hands, by the presences about it . . . And for them it's doubly holy . . . from one genocide to another. When it's found it'll be destroyed . . . without ceremony.'

The target of a low intensity operation is unaware that it is a target. And when his brain explodes he is equally unaware.

The target of a high intensity operation is aware he is a target because he's chained to a chair which he soils with shit, urine, blood, fear. He is subjected to puny electrodes – oh oh oh ou sont ces gégènes d'antan . . . ces fidèles gégènes . . . les outils pédagogiques de là-bas? Since a distant night in Parc Guerland I had not ceased to erase the worthless and to become the man I am. The perfume of scorched skin never leaves your olfactory memory. Now it's toasted, now it's burnt. Always delicious. A dislocation's groan is different from that splintering cry which announces a urethral intrusion with a sharp instrument. Screams and pleas and squeals of pain form the sound-track of winning. Winning is a pleasure. Icy water, boiling water, a cricket bat – I have never understood the game, but this is a less vulgar instrument than a baseball bat.

The scene of course unfolds in an abandoned repair shop for heavy machinery. Oil slicks, chipped brick, splintered pallets, dead rats, petrol puddles, chains, winches, pin-ups, a drift of swarf, old tabloids. Let's add treadless tyres, there are always treadless tyres, they're mandatory decor. Light is losing its fight against turbid gloom. A balaclava'd Quasi Hubback swigs from a bottle of Lidl own-brand seeking the maddening energy for another session which he hopes will be the last. His amour propre is damaged. By now he should have answers. This is when he resorts to a hammer drill, a Black and Decker C12OBC Impact Driver bought specially for this operation. 'It's a trusty friend about the home.' Cordless: the electricity here was cut off years ago.

Hubback concluded that Osman Osmanović was telling the truth, he didn't know whom the secretaire was intended for because the bleeding injured man was eventually willing to disclose much else. Had he spoken sooner he might still be able to speak. He wouldn't be in such a condition without reprieve. Hubback told himself that his obstinate silence was responsible for his injuries. He had only himself to blame. He had made Hubback go too far, not for the first time. Hubback idly wondered whether Osmanović would ever breathe again. He didn't care: that's what made him a valuable employee.

Osmanović declared himself illiterate. He unquestionably possessed a memory typical of the illiterate: retentive and precise, but incoherent, random. Every image was independent, an orphan. Sounds did not incite the recall of other sounds. Movements from different quartets. Snapshots from unrelated albums. His memory was a collage: fragments that don't add up, without purpose, without end. He had not known what he was bidding for . . . Mr Deuteron had instructed him to buy at all costs. He had not imposed a 'ceiling'. He did not know how to contact Mr Deuteron: he always waited for his call. He would often not hear from him for weeks on end. It was only in Britain that he worked for Mr Deuteron. Travel outside the country that had foolhardily, softly, granted him asylum was a risk. He was uncertain of his safety and his status in legislatures less tolerant of Ramalama's crack commandos and égorgers. Mr Deuteron has other people to assist him in other countries.

Hubback drove to a road of bungalows west of Heathrow. He dumped Osmanović among bushes at the bottom of the retaining slope of a reservoir. Not dog-walking territory but not to worry: 'Ramalama'll fucking find you.'

Hubback's intelligence about Deuteron:

'In brief. The guy's a gamekeeper turned total fucking poacher.

'Former police seconded to the Security Services. No one he worked with knew much about him. Never one to disguise his contempt for the common plod. Can't be said to have been popular. But then fast track graduate entries never are.

'Traced frauds and laundry reckoned to fund terrorism. We're talking eight figure sums.

'Investigated charities, human rights organisations and NGOs – fucking fronts for terrorists/militias.

'Expert in detecting and putting the spanner in the works of cosmic scams.

'Not a friend of Israel. Enemy of Israel I'd say – but does it go beyond thought crimes?'

I told him: 'A thought crime is a crime tout court when the thought is genocide, "clearance and cleansing", hecatombs. Heine (a poet, Quasi – one of my people) wrote: Thought precedes action as lightning precedes thunder.'

'Point taken. Where was I? . . . Advised Saudi on security of container vessels.

'Spoke at SHADE – Shared Awareness and Deconfliction – conferences on combatting piracy.

'Knows his way round international law. Knows his way round maritime law. Auto fucking didact of major fraud practices. Then he got his big break. Oleg Sidorov spotted his potential. Recruited him. Purpose: to oil the wheels with Saudi re relieving embargos. That's when he crossed. That's when he was bought. He had his head so fucking turned it's gone through three sixty degrees time after fucking time. He saw big rock candy mountain come in to view.

'He's now got fucking fingers in dozens of fucking pies but the fucking gravy never seems to stick.

'He's thick with the P L fucking O. Transferred loyalty to the Hams and Hezzies. Or whatever the fuckers are called this week. Frequent contact with Fashed Faisal – who's got some sort of fucking fellowship at Oxford when he's not out bombing or raping or lecturing on peace. Saint Hereward's College. Aka Ramalama Central. Where old spooks go to write their memoirs of Glubb . . . wishing they was Lawrence of Fucking Arabia.

'He's got police contacts working for him in every fucking country you can think of. All over. If he's got a weak link it's his only real pal anyone knows about is Ivor Hinde. Remember? The guy who forged evidence in the Loomis Nikolić case . . . Cosmo slimeball . . . of course he got away with it. But it's not a good one to have against your name.

'What else we got . . . He's got a fantastic memory. Legendary. And he speaks about half a dozen languages.

'Dutiful son. Visits parents every month. Old chap's in a wheelchair. He built them a handicap bungalow. Spare fucking change. Hard to believe but he blames "the Jews" – not specific about which ones – for his dad not getting proper compensation for an industrial injury. That's where his anti-Semitism comes from. A tad OTT as reactions go I'd say.

'Problem with Friend Osman. He doesn't know where he takes Deuteron. He gets given GPS coordinates and that's it. No place names just turn right turn left etc. Destination is always always different.

'He doesn't know what our man gets up to when he gets out of the fucking car. Sits waiting for him for hours. Doesn't know what he gets up to when he's not in fucking Blighty. He doesn't know what anything means. Ideal employee I'd say.

'There was this thing he heard him talking about . . . Denkmal . . . wouldn't let up . . . on and on, sometimes he'd make four or five successive calls about Denkmal . . . Is the injunction going to hold . . . Our Osman heard it so . . . often he learnt by heart – fucking over and over again but he didn't know who or what Denkmal was. Someone who'd let him down? Who was going to pay . . . He heard Deuteron swearing about him for weeks on end and getting well fucking worked up saying like how could I have been so stupid to trust the bastard . . . what kind of fuckwit . . . is it effective against social media . . . these injunctions . . . what was I fucking thinking of . . . then he'd be pleading . . . going it wasn't down to me . . . blame——(name unintelligible) . . . some quality self-loathing . . . some quality buck passing . . . not all of it in English . . . that's the long and the fucking short of it.'

Denkmal simply means monument. Germany is riddled with them. Why such a commonplace object should have tried Deuteron's temper to such an extent was not vouchsafed. And what had a monument to do with an injunction? Then a bell rang distantly across fields of time. Something was almost visible out of my exaggerated eyeline. A gap between a door and a jamb revealed for a fraction of a second a view. Then it was no longer there and I was mining within myself to no avail. Denkmal. Injunction. How did they entwine? It teased me, exposed my mnemonic decline. I closed my eyes. Twenty men sat in wheelchairs. They wore respirator masks like muzzles. They wore a uniform of white bedshirts and dark glasses. They stared blankly at the glistening sea and the sky. This was something I was going to dream. I was here many millennia in the future.

It all comes round, again and again. That's what you realise when, with the subtlest shift, you divest yourself of belief in the clock and the calendar and the dull plod of narrative, when you are freed from linearity, when effect is no such thing but random incident, random sensation, a foundling with no causal parent owning up to having put it in a baby hatch. The past awaits us, the future has come and gone.

Every few weeks Former Detective Inspector Desmond Hubback – 'Don't call me Quasi' – delivered more information. He has a wild imagination with no checks for plausibility. This was all legit, as he would say. It was too banal to be his invention.

Deuteron's social ambitions proved to be utterly conventional. Witness the following:

Chair of Imperial Orthodox Society of Gethsemane and Gadara; President of the D. D. Denisov Society; Patron of the Anglo-Azeri Weal of Recognition and Friendship; Chair of the United Charities Stepping Stones Unit; Patron of the Arabian Cousinage Fellowship; Founder of the Tarbert Deer Stalking Society; Founder of the Ellesmere Wildfowl Trust; President of the English Speaking Union of Gaza; Order of Saint Yuri (3rd class) Belarus; Chevalier of the Royal Order of the Crocodile of Uganda (Grand Cross). Clubs: Garrick, Travellers.

This is a man who enjoys nothing more than bowing to royalty and 'leaders'. As Hubback has it: 'He gives great curtsey.'

There was nothing visible that might link him to the sorts of activity that concerned me. The longer groupuscules remain invisible the more worryingly potent and organised they are when they do show themselves.

Something clicked. The motion of the train. The speed agitates the brain. *Denkmal: The Tale of an Illicit Monument!* I'm there. It reappears as if it had never been absent. Airport lounge. Manchester. I was on a train from Paris to Metz. That woman. Justine's improbable friend. Her name . . . Phoebe . . . of course Phoebe . . . I started to write it down . . . the jobsworth in a waistcoat . . . why do they always wear waistcoats? A blind boy wearing a neck brace and waving galloped a white stallion through the swaying Lorraine steppe grass beside the train . . . She had scrutinised the contents of my grip. Phoebe Chipurnoi in the airport. I could hardly suppress my laughter. She had mentioned, indignantly, that the author of *The Dark*

Watergang Tamara Coolmans had also written something called *Denkmal: The Tale of an Illicit Monument* which according to rumour – correct information that will be denied – was the subject of an iniquitous English super-injunction, an atrocious legal weapon available only to the very rich. An evidently effective super-injunction for there was no mention of it on the net. But there wouldn't be. The injunction's very existence is not acknowledged. No doubt any reference would be strangled at birth.

After two dark days in the dark city of Metz, where it always rains and the black cathedral looms in mist and men shave their fingernails with knives that cut throats, I received a brusque email from Tamara Coolmans.

'How did you get my private email? Now I may have to change it again. I have received serious threats. How do I know not to fear a complete stranger? I have realised that writing as I do releases evil by naming it and naming them that carry it within them. Why are you interested in a book which will never be published?'

I replied that I wished her no ill, that I had enjoyed *The Dark Watergang*. (No mention of ragged prose: but who wants writing in a thriller, besides there was an image I admired although I had a feeling I had encountered it before or would encounter it again, 'from the centre of a broken window pane spread a web of cracks like creases on an old poet's scrotum.') I took a chance on flattering frankness. I said that it had been useful in learning to monitor Vlaams Belang. The suppression of *Denkmal: The Tale of an Illicit Monument* made me wonder if it too had upset sensibilities and exposed corruption in the state of Belgium. I added that I was particularly fascinated by the title.

'I am under surveillance. Not all the time. But enough. The police deny it – of course because it's the police themselves going freelance . . . on the black . . . they're the culprits. They're as bent as a nine-bob note as Carl used to say. They listen in, reading my mails. They'll be reading this. Won't you, boys!!! They even keep tabs on my friends.

'What do they think I'm going to do? That's not the point of course. It's just to irritate. No. It's more. It's to frighten me because I'm a soft target. I live alone.

'*The Dark Watergang* hit a nerve, dead on target – il a fait mouche!'

That expression sent me spinning back to a seawater swimming pool and watching a game of water polo and lazing on the rocks.

After a gap of several weeks she wrote: 'If I publish details of the unnameable in a private email – *a private email!* – I'll be in contempt of court. It's an admission they're monitoring me.'

Negotiations were trying and slow. Her mistrust was close to paranoia. She agreed eventually to meet. She then changed the date, the time, the venue (twice).

We eventually settled on a tea room in Lille where she was talking at the annual *Polémiques Sur Les Polars* about her '*reinterpretation*' of the death of Anke Postma, a policewoman living under an assumed identity in a witness protection programme which had failed to protect her: she had ended up in the Gota Canal.

Méert is a marvel of mid-nineteenth-century aggressive fussiness. The decor is as richly coloured as the patisseries. (The P'tit Clamart was leaden, I hardly touched it.) I sat on a tortuously wrought metal chair so she could take the banquette: that way I could look at myself in the mirror behind her and escape through it should she bore me. I could just disappear. She made for me without scrutinising the room. She was taller than I expected. She was intense, loquacious, older than her years, slightly touched. She wore the lustre of early success. Her appearance was loud understatement. Blonde streaked chestnut urchin cut (beyond the budget of an authentic urchin). Black peplum jacket, black leggings, black suede ankle boots, black polo neck, black shades, black obsidian necklace, big black bag. Snap, I thought. My sartorial double. I stood, greeted her. Snap, she thought, she told me later.

Tamara Coolmans

I'll tell you why this is a good place to meet. The surfaces are hard. Yeh? Non-absorbent. You can't be overheard. Noise bounces. Like a squash court, indecipherable. It's seeing life through factory noises. Lives, rather, emitting auditory blur.

D'you know how many people this morning asked me about the book whose name I'm not allowed to say? I lost count. They all ask the same question. Chorus of dummies. They know I'm not allowed to say anything, not allowed even to admit it exists or that the injunction exists. I wonder if some of them aren't agents provocateurs. I walked off the stage. I could do with a drink.

I hate readers. But not so much as I hate writers who care about their readers. I don't want to interact . . . they buy a book . . . then they think they own you. When they buy a bowl do they think oh I've got a right to trespass on the potter's psyche? No. They do not. Or only in artsy fartsy places like Ducis.

Order me a large Manhattan would you.

Oh god here comes another.

A very old male. Gnarled, gnomeish, knapsack, Nikon. Colour blind, so his clothes told. I had noticed that while he was retrieving a vulgar 'fun' umbrella from a hatstand he was tilting his head and squinting, scrutinising us. He shuffled across the tiled floor towards us. And he ignored me. I was surprised to feel unwanted.

He said to Rui: 'Pardon me for . . . I could swear you were my father's friend . . . Ralph Scutia. His school mate . . . you kept up with down the years. Oh excuse me but I liked you so much, such a generous man, so kind. Helped Papa out of scrapes . . . Fancy finding you here of all places. I used to join you on your walks up to Forte Sperone. But you can't be him . . . can you? My father died eighty-three years ago . . . we buried him in the Staglieno do you recall . . . I never saw you again . . . not till now . . . I heard you had passed on soon after . . . you haven't aged . . . you must be a hundred and fifty . . . That can't be right . . . No no . . . What am I thinking of . . . But . . . you still smoke Royale Gout Maryland! (Points to pack.) Ah everything has been, everything will come by again . . . You look just as you did . . . You always wore black always in black . . . You must be blessed by magic.'

Rui's face was blank, icy, inhuman. He was a ghost in daylight in that crowded café. He was blocking out what the man was saying. He knew the man was well meaning – they're always the worst, the harbingers of cheer. He was struggling to contain himself. He stared over my shoulder into the foxed mirror. Then he looked up at the old man and shook his head. 'Go. Please. Capiche.' Deadly whisper. Nonetheless other customers were watching. The old man burst into tears. Leaving his patisserie barely touched, Rui grabbed my arm, strode to the till, paid cash and dragged me out into cobbles and driz-zle. He clutched my shoulders and smiled a private smile that was to be read by no one. As if he had enjoyed a magnificent aperçu never to be shared. I never asked him what that might be. I never again men-tioned that strange encounter any more than I asked about his scar.

By the time I realised what that smile meant it was too late and, besides, I wouldn't have wanted it any other way.

We walked, at ease with each other, through that unresolved city of shaped gables and crooked Flemish lanes, of pompier blocks and boulevards of the French imperium.

'The heavy hand of Haussmann's epigone,' he smiled, pleased with his epithet which I taught him years later as we went. We walked round the Citadelle and along quays of pigeon-breasted canals.

I told him: 'You're difficult to check out. A contact at the Office of Documentation in Prague did several searches. She told me she had no idea who you are though it was obvious she did. Two days later she got back to me. All clear. She explained: "I used my Scrabble app."'

I told him: 'I foresee incidents. Gestures . . . It happens. It's not sooth-saying swank. It just is . . . in *The Dark Watergang* I seem to – no, not seem to – I did predict events that were . . . well, they hadn't occurred.'

And *Denkmal*?

'What? Prediction? Ha! Not so far. Decidedly not. If only I had seen what was coming . . . No no – it was luck and research. Bad luck. *That's the killer. It's beyond our control.* The story was actual. Camou-flaged actuality. Less invention than in the others. I was a bit running out of ideas but when you've got contracts like a golden ball and chain you don't take liberties. I wanted to touch ground with reality.'

I saw your expression when I said that! I could tell you were work-ing out a way to excuse me for having said it. And a way to excuse yourself for saying nothing.

We walked for hours past fragments of lives we would never see again: a happy gurgling baby in a buggy, a forlorn group of ten-year-old footballers gaping at their flooded pitch, an enraged woman in tram conductor's uniform banging a door with a knocker in the form of a bull's head.

I told him: 'All I know about "investigative" journalism was from a conversation at a party with a lisping man in lingerie named Molly.

He boasted of having the full set. Interviews with terrorists and drug barons on the lam. Tracking down shooters gone to the mattresses. Hanging out with fugitive white collars in the Philippines. All you need, he advised, was brass neck, being swift across the carpet and doubting every single thing anyone tells you. I mean, you wouldn't be investigating them unless they had something to hide. I doubted every single thing he told me.'

I told Rui: 'I'd been reading about endgame 1945. You can't go wrong with one of those covers with a gold swastika, a stocking top, red nails et cetera, perhaps a low relief Luger, plus a couple of embossed bullet holes revealing a pre-title page. All I needed was a story to go with the cliché.

'Schellenberg's *Memoirs*. Do you know them? Clever kind of whitewash. Total self-exculpation. He never mentions the crimes so he doesn't have to play down his part in them. Crimes? What crimes? The Shoah might as well have not happened. So he doesn't have to deny the camps' existence. Gross. A massive sin of omission. I read the English edition. Alan Bullock, Louis Hagen.

'Then I came across the German text in a second-hand bookshop in Emden. Revised edition. Published by Bremmer Verlag. Maybe pirated. A different book anyhow. The afterword was by Schellenberg's secretary who called himself an amanuensis. It was astonishing.

'Self-serving to say the least. More or less credits himself with having written the book. Ernst Stech-Pelz, former Hauptsturmführer. His master's voice. Good fido. He had never heard of Treblinka till he saw a staged American film about a place that never existed or if it had existed had failed to meet its processing targets – if it had existed. And so on. He was defiant. Not just the feigned ignorance . . . feigned for so long it baked on hard. Fully ingrained ignorance. A sort of soupy nostalgia for the Reich. Encouraging it to rise up again.

'It was dotty. It was dangerously deranged. Really loopy. There's something in the tone that makes you realise the guy's in absolute earnest. He had this plan of mustering all the SS escapees in Argentina and Spain and Syria, Egypt, god knows where, Paraguay, and staging a putsch.'

I told him: 'That's not all. It gets seriously psychotic. The dead heroes of the Reich were to be dug up from their graves to lead the

Mannschaft into battle. Skeletons. The dance of death. Dead horses. Scythes. There is a ready-made plot here.'

Restricted production of odessa and a protected formula ensured that only a select group of SS would be dosed, an elite in waiting. For an indefinite period they had slipped into mufti and hid in full view. They led comfortable lives (judiciary, medicine) under the regimes of Adenauer, Kiesinger, Schmidt etc.

He didn't seem to realise that what he was proposing was the re-emergence of a crack stormforce of messiahs in wheelchairs, Zimmer frame prophets, vicious apostles with incontinence pads and fond memories of Einsatzgruppen duties: oh those golden days.

Rui agreed. I wondered if he wasn't a tad jealous that I had such volatile gen.

'You're right. There is for sure quite a plot.'

Isn't it just every girl's dream to meet centenarians who wore the death's head badge? No, perhaps not. Me, I'd never met a war criminal. If he was a war criminal rather than a mere dutiful dogsbody. Could be both. Dogsbodies doubled up as desk murderers.

He said: 'While the crimes may be as interesting as they are foul, the criminals themselves are . . . I was going to say nobodies, zilches . . . but of course that's not correct. The banality of evil is a misleading cliché. These people were not banal. Their crimes were not banal. They were anything but banal. They were extraordinary. Extraordinarily, uniquely atrocious. Criminals are defined by their crimes. It's their crimes that give them distinction in their eyes, in the eyes of their companions and disciples.'

Not finding this man was frustrating. Bremmer Verlag had been out of business for years. He might be dead. There are numerous archives – archives of infamy. You evidently know them. The Documentation Centre in Prague, the Interagency Working Group, the Bundesarchiv, the Wiener Library, the Arolsen Archives, the Heine Institute . . . none of them had a record of the name Stech-Pelz or his whereabouts after his early release. He vanished.

Rui said: 'No surprise – maybe there were crimes he hadn't been charged with . . . evidence might be uncovered. The SS went on destroying files well into the Fifties. They knew they would be judged as criminals. They knew their moral posture was provisional.

They knew it would be overturned. They had seen the victor's just-ice meted out to the higher echelons. So they obliterated themselves. Made themselves scarce. They no longer existed. No trace. Tens of thousands of Germans and collaborators vanished in the years after the war. Fled Europe, changed their name, changed their uniform. The golden age of identity switch, the golden age of primitive plastic surgery. It was sixteen years after the end of the war that we cap-tured Eichmann. Sixteen years . . . There were still others left to bring to justice . . . Allofs for instance . . . We were close and he knew it. The Old Men of Denya had hired Spanish fishermen to get him to Morocco . . . put him on a freighter to Brazil. It appears the fisher-men turned up a day early. Allofs thought they were the commando that had been tracking him and bit on his cyanide capsule.'

Murphy's law. To your advantage.

'No . . . no, we wanted to put him on trial. It was frustrating.'

A lift bridge. A cox and eight scudded across the water. All around us were the familiar components of 'cultural' regeneration: bicycles, dance studios, bollards and chains employed as large ornaments, post-production facilities and galleries for a better world – plus many cafés beside the one we were sitting outside, all raw brick and girders. A boy, cross-legged and growing his first moustache, was strumming and singing:

> *You are the man we met a longtime ago, in the future,*
> *When red sandstone was not yet quarried out.*
> *I laughed when subtitled 'linear narrator'*
> *I picked the words from the bumbling aston.*
> *I dashed them on pantiles that had yet to be fired.*
> *A tomb is the last thing I shall ever need.*
> *I mean that.*

Rui stood over him and handed him a 20 note.

'That's to ask you to make your music elsewhere . . . Otherwise I break your guitar over your bonce.'

The boy, alarmed as I was, muttered puzzled thanks and sloped off.

★

After I kicked out my unsuitable boyfriend I decided to get the apartment redecorated . . . the alcohol seeped out of his pores. It got everywhere. I was translating *The House in Laburnum Terrace* . . . I called it *Accident aan de Houba de Strooperlaan*.

'I read it. I am proud to meet the author. I am proud to sit with her beside that monument.' He indicated a sculpture of three diagrammatic anthropoids.

'It reminds us of their sacrifice . . . thousands like them. But that is not all. It reminds us that the perpetrators and the sons of perpetrators lived free lives . . . still live free lives unburdened by conscience . . . forgetful lives . . . And the future generations – they must be punished. An eye for an eye. It defies natural justice that a creature like Stech-Pelz should live.'

I'd forgotten about him. No. Not exactly forgot. I'd put him behind my ear for later, put it on The Back Burma – that's my uncle's boyfriend's joke.

The day I finished the translation I was dancing round the apartment for joy. It was so clean and light and fresh and I had a brainwave. Das Telefonbuch.com . . . ridiculous – I can't get my head round why I hadn't tried it before.

I guess I hadn't thought Stech-Pelz could possibly be listed. Would he be advertising his existence? It's an unusual name. It took hours rather than weeks to find him. There he was, bold as brass, living in Lübeck. I wrote to him. Not really expecting a reply. I got one within days.

He enjoyed, he said, talking to historians (!) and scholars (!). He claimed to be something of a scholar himself. But I had to come to him.

He didn't travel much nowadays. His eyesight was going. It had robbed him of his beloved car. He disliked the smell of people who use public transport. With a few exceptions, whom he knew by name, taxi drivers tried to take advantage of him. Some have even tried to charge for his walking frame which was a stumbling frame, a waddling frame.

I was greeted by a leering old man squinting at me from the grubby tiled threshold of a decrepit villa which didn't fit him. Its rooms were capacious but not capacious enough. He was the lard side of obese.

He got jammed in doorways. He got jammed between pieces of furniture. He tripped and blundered, clumsy and near blind, bumping into accumulated objects.

The house was an atrocity. Every surface was occupied by Third Reich horror kitsch. Busts of the Führer. Portraits. Allach pottery. Dozens of framed photographs. Oriflammes, flags, pennants. How many other terrible houses like it are there? You felt soiled. It reminded me of the stash of VHS porn my mother's thankfully late boyfriend kept. The place was a shrine. The object of devotion was not Hitler, not Schellenberg, but Heinrich Himmler, the clerk whose glasses shone like the eyes of an immane god.

I recalled the bitter gag: Wenn Sie als Hühnerbauer versagen, warum nicht Massenmörder werden?[51] It was beyond creepy. This temple of malicious junk seemed at odds with him. The jovial garrulous creator. Curator, everyone's a curator now. He was uninhibited like a drunk, shorn of reserve. Happily not speedy enough to grope successfully. He stroked a desk, a davenport, with lubricious hairy fingers. It had belonged to the mother of Himmler's children. It was a gift from his 'fond fellow adventurer Myles Deuteron'. Is Myles with a 'y' higher caste than with an 'i'? Or lower? Or couldn't the parents spell?

He offered me an ods everlasting-life pill. I could have an injection if I preferred. Either way everlasting life would probably be mine if I kept up the course. I'd not, however, realise how effective ods is till I had outlived all my contemporaries. I took the pill. The needle was in a rusty kidney bowl that had been peed in. A less appealing placebo. Most of the soft furnishings were malodorous and damp.

He boasted about his lifelong virility. As a young man he had impregnated many *mädchen* as part of his duty to the race. The children they bore in Lebensborn clinics were not his. They were the Führer's children – as were all the German people. The Führer was married to Germany and the German people. Too busy to breed. He denied himself. It was only when the people abandoned him, that terrible betrayal after all that he had done for them, it was only then

---

51 If you don't succeed as a chicken farmer, why not become a mass murderer?

that he was free to descend from on high, to relinquish divinity, enter the human realm, forge a union with Eva Braun.

Every Sunday a young operative from Hansa Hostessenagentur, Tina, came to have lunch with Stech-Pelz. After lunch she masturbates him while they watch football on television. He looked at me with relish. I told him I was a phallophobic lesbian. He took it in his stride, didn't attempt to convert me.

An emaciated housekeeper, worn to the bone by everlasting life, entered the room where we sat to announce lunch. From the centre of a broken window spread a web of cracks like marbling in a steak. He slobbered, sprayed and spat with abandon as though he had little control over his mouth. He ate and drank greedily like a starved animal. He fed the distinctly unstarved Mordhund whose table manners were superior to his. He waved his hand to encourage me to follow him. Eat with your hands how man did before he was infected by cutlery.

I have little appetite for fat pork with added fat and some sort of sweet sour chutney (damson?).

'Ah the exuberance of youth!' he wheezed when I reminded him I had come to talk about the gerontocratic Fourth Reich.

'That was many years ago. My plans were ardent then. They became more modest – but they were still too ambitious for the young people . . . their enthusiasm waned . . . they were impatient . . . to me young people is anyone under the age of eighty-five . . . they let me down . . . all I am left with is what you see around you.

'The Reichsführer's funeral would have been peerlessly magnificent. Quedlinburg Cathedral. A lavish night-time ceremony, flaming torches, Wagner, martial drums, men wearing antlers, horses in heraldic chanfrons and cruppers.'

His memorial would have exceeded any in the world. He entertained a scheme to build a 150-metre-tall memorial to the Reichsführer. The vicious hag Mother Russia would be dwarfed. He had folders full of perspective drawings and plans. He had various sites in mind.

Like the Befreiungshalle and the Valhalla – both above the Danube – it had to stand on a hilltop. It had to dominate the surrounding country and its inhabitants, to proclaim the Fourth Reich's omnipotent potency. It was a weapon of intimidation.

He had a fondness for an eternal flame. A hooked cross that could never be extinguished.

He had spent many years attempting to raise funds to accomplish this sacred mission. It was the ambition that made his life worth living.

He led me into what he called the 'command room'.

One wall was given to a grubby tatty large-scale map of Luneburg Heath. Its edges were rough frayed fringes. It was pocked with stuck-on-peeling-off red circles. There were more old photos. Wobbly and off-horizontal. Age had not treated him kindly. He identified a handsome young man with a Mordhund on a leash and wearing the murderer's black uniform as his former self. A pretty young woman in a related black uniform stood beside him.

'We were in love . . . she was known as the Death Child . . . a title she relished . . . she was an organisational genius . . . expert in transport planning . . . she had a photographic memory like a Leica I used to tell her . . . she really could look at a page and remember every word . . . much commended . . . she constantly delivered up to 20 or even 30 per cent excess product to the experimental research colonies . . . a true servant of the Reich . . . a born eliminator . . . we were captured and separated . . . I never saw her again . . . I don't know if she lived or died. My one true love . . . we were victims of societal imperfection . . .'

Through contacts in The Freed From Freedom Network Stech-Pelz had found donors, 'passionate investors in conviction', who recognised his project's vital importance to the continent's mental and political health. They stood *foursquare* behind him. He had been proud of the conviction they showed in him and he was proud of them. They belonged to a generation of Europeans which was able to look at the Third Reich objectively, 'to contrast its magnificence with the shabbiness of failing democracies'.

'They had shed the bias against our paradise of green verged autobahnen and god-given cleanliness. They had seen through the lies and calumnies.'

He nattered about the investors fulsomely and indiscreetly. He had no compunction about disclosing details of their lives. That's what spelled trouble for me.

He regretted that none of his backers had been German. He claimed that Germans of several generations 'had been brainwashed into an abject posture of penitence and shame for the crimes – crimes? what crimes? – of their fathers, grandfathers and so on'.

My take is: those who implemented Nazi rule and those who accepted it were equally brainwashed. That's what it means to be a German. You create the zeitgeist then succumb to it. You share in collective delusion. You follow fashion, as instructed, because you think it's your will. You're instructed to listen to krautrock, to goose-step, to spy on neighbours, to eat paprika-flavoured crisps . . .

I treated my characters like that . . . like they were Germans. Obedient. They respond to a slap. After all they were my personae, my chessmen . . . suggested by 'real' people of whom I knew very little. I was quite fascinated by the actuality of these people's lives. But the actuality is full of pratfalls. I couldn't make them behave how I needed them to if they were already burdened with identities and quirks and defining characteristics. You can't turn the king's bishop's pawn into the queen's rook.

Despite what I said about touching ground with reality I had to allow myself space to invent, to manipulate them. I gave them different backgrounds, different lives. I believed I'd made the characters unrecognisable. And even where I had included details raw, without mediation, they were unlikely to be the sort of thing anyone would complain about.

I couldn't have composed a book with characters from The Freed From Freedom Network's rank and file because the rank and file are the rank and file because they're poor. They can't afford to underwrite the fantasies of a megalomaniac whose maxims, heard at his trial, include 'Only a coward refuses to dig his own grave'. Nor could they have afforded to sue. The book would only be plausible if these people were loaded, as they are. Loaded enough to injunct with their spare change and so thin-skinned it's a miracle that their blood doesn't leak out.

The brief who legalled it for Gospatrick Darmady didn't consider that there was the slightest risk of a suit for defamation or libel let alone a super-injunction – and nor did I. All clear. Green light. How wrong can you get . . . Tim at Van der Werf didn't even bother to show it to a lawyer. But then Belgium is another country. That's why I live here.

Stech-Pelz's litigious donors were an odd bunch of applicant stormtroopers, informally linked to The Freed From Freedom Network and its online site Liberty's A Liability. They included:

Myles Deuteron of course. There's a limited pool of British oligarchs. A pool of one. So he became Linus, and Swedish. (It was sod's law that I should dress Linus in puppytooth suits with cuffs and breast pocket flaps – which Deuteron apparently called his 'style signature'. I must have picked it up from the title character in *The Gent*, a hammy old TV series on a tiresome loop in the florist's shop where I once worked.)

Hanna Nowak, a pharma heiress and celebrated libertine aka Die Zürcherin also became Swedish. Among her company's products are medications that promise to extend average lifespan (of those who can afford it) to well beyond 140 years: the very old are the very rich, endlessly rebuilt like a 'mediaeval' cathedral which is actually Victorian. To place her far from Cap Ferrat, Zurich and Paris I gave her an Östermalm mansion, a riad in Fez and a Baltic island summer house I found in a magazine: 'Agricultural precedents are reworked in both the form and materiality of the architecture.'

Her sometime lover Sir Geoffrey Shadoxhurst Bt, an ancient English aristo, a friend of Stech-Pelz from way back, addicted to ods, said to have attended Nuremberg rallies as a child. The founder of Führer World.

The Fawzy brothers, Egyptian construction magnates, whose father had been in the Handschar Division of the SS. Notorious for their lighthearted Nazi dress parties where drinks and canapés are served by emaciated children in the striped uniform of the camps.

Aatamprakash Prasanna, 'born an untouchable, he stripped the west's assets'.

The French industrialist Claudie Desmarais, supposedly the last word in green effluent treatment, an admirer of Himmler's homeopathic pest control.

Spencer Prestige, founder of The Wall of the Newly Immaculate, a chain of revirgining clinics, an anti-Semite of convenience – his clients are mostly Middle Eastern.

Obviously I knew who <u>Gérald Tol</u> was. Negationist publisher and promoter of bands: Endstufe, Die Lunikoff Verschwörung, The Wrath and proprietor of the Sachsenhain Hotel in Brighton, UK.

The polemicist <u>William Toothgold</u>, 'a conviction anti-Semite', had changed his surname from Sproston in an act of reverse nominal determinism. Author of a eulogistic biography of Massimo Morsello, singer and co-founder of Forza Nuova and of *The Master Builders from Brooklyn*, an incitement to Palestinians 'to cleanse their territory of settlements and settlers: they're easy to spot'.

The dotty former starlet <u>Frida Fings</u> – you know the one, marmots are cleverer than people, the United Species of Animals (USA) should rule the world. Amazed she was still alive. She concurred with Himmler's conviction that all animals were a higher life form than Jews. The lambs on her Marie-Antoinetteish farm wore bells in the hope that they would not be trodden on at night. Unhappily they alerted wolves, beneficiaries of her rewilding programme.

I provided aliases, names and bogus social circumstances for this undeserving crew.

Certain names – and there were many others – meant nothing. This wasn't my world. Not even at fourth hand through gossip magazines like *Not From Far Ma'am, In The Know, Indiscretion, Trousseau*.

It was evident, however, that no matter how vocal some of these people were in their authoritarian righteousness, their castigation of moral infirmity and their disgust at street bundles they did not want to be observed conniving with a former SS who had narrowly avoided the gallows. That association took them into an altogether different territory, a boundary was broken.

I didn't give Stech-Pelz a nom de guerre because he, or his name, was there, on the unerasable record, from the Wilhelmstrasse trials: he was sentenced to four years' imprisonment. A predictably lenient sentence handed down by a National Socialist in mufti, a member of the caste that ruled West Germany during the years of the economic miracle and well into the Seventies. He served only eighteen months in Oldenburg prison. Health problems (chest cold and ever such a nasty cough). He was teased for having carved his own facial scar.

The increasingly fractious investors began to talk of a bottomless pit. There was no progress in the search for a suitable location. They bickered by phone, by email, by Zoom and conference call. Sir Geoffrey Shadoxhurst and Hanna Nowak increasingly distanced themselves from the others whom they regarded as vulgar parvenus.

The vulgar parvenus were in turn affronted by Shadoxhurst's oh-so-British affect of social superiority – he was attached to his title. Nowak's Switzer secrecy was irritating. What were these two dilettantes up to? And where had the considerable sums remitted to Stech-Pelz gone? Had they been used to bribe local government officials and planners as he claimed? Stech-Pelz's indignation that he might have misappropriated donations made him turn colour. That didn't mean that he had not misappropriated them. It was noted that Shadoxhurst and Nowak took Stech-Pelz's side unconditionally. Stech-Pelz was crawlingly grateful.

The Fawzy brothers were unimpressed by the plans presented to them. They insisted that Thiery Azodi must design it, whatever it turned out to be. Azodi was 'the architectural virtuoso and sculptural master who brought classic European classical gold leaf high-end elegance to Azerbaijan'. If some other architect was chosen the Fawzy brothers would withdraw their funding. They, together with Spencer Prestige, conceived of the monument as a wake-up call to the Ramalaman world, an exhortation to a pan-European intifada and an incitement to continue the sun god Himmler's sacred task.

Stech-Pelz's preference was for a vast cyclopean structure which would take its inspiration though not its form from Sachsenhain, a place that Stech-Pelz had told me he considered 'holy'. More than four and a half thousand stones each commemorated the Saxon pagans, proto-Nazis, massacred there by Charlemagne in 782. It's a bogus henge or grove built by slave labour in 1935: the 'credit' for its conception was the subject of a dispute between Himmler and Rosenberg.

Stech-Pelz owned a sentimental attachment to it: 'That's where I was in love. She was wonderful. A trained psychiatric nurse and midwife – such a repertoire of treatments. And brave – she cut the throats of disabled babies in the name of the Reich . . . If they lived they would become burdens on the Reich. Her knife was so sharp they felt nothing. Her duty overcame her personal qualms, any selfish qualms.'

★

There was no consensus about the Heinrich Himmler Denkmal. How was a single structure to reflect his polymathic diversity, his refulgence, the sun that shone like jet from his eyes, his intellectual curiosity about runes, Atlantis, anthropometrics, archaeology, ice theory? Each investor had her or his own Himmler. What a protean slaughterer he was. A murderer of many masks.

Ought it to be figurative? Volkisch? Columnar? As vast as Speer's regrettably unrealised Ruhmeshalle? As terrifying as the Dolmen di Sa Coveccada?

After two years of argument and accusations of bad faith the investors withdrew one by one. They blamed each other, selectively. They were unanimous in berating Stech-Pelz whose self-pity was immense. They had come to be worried by his lax book-keeping and his gossipy name dropping. Omertà had been breached. He was worryingly literal in his conviction that a secret is to be shared. Reputations would not be enhanced by association with a project that was both morally toxic and preposterous. Myles Deuteron was advised that the garrulous Toothgold had been talking about him admiringly in The Travellers Club: 'Sound as a cow . . . he's one of ours.'

Deuteron's enthusiasm dissipated. Grudges festered. Rancour swelled. The second Reichenfels Symposium was postponed *sine die*. Stech-Pelz retreated into his house of memories rueing what might have been, wondering what might be. You never know.

I started writing the book that first evening in my hotel in Lübeck. The end of a bizarre day. I talked to him over the next two days as well. 'Interview' suggests an equable balance. It didn't exist. He wouldn't listen. He rambled and digressed and digressed from digressions, created non-sequiturs with abandon, began sentences whose end, by the time he reached it, he had forgotten.

He was intermittently droll: 'You wait thousands of years for a world war then two come along within a couple of decades of each other.' He was pleased with this well-rehearsed epigram. He repeated it several times. He knew Pascal: all the ills of man come from a single source, the inability to repose alone in a room. He considered then that he suffered no ills save pain, the price of achieving old age.

When I arrived home – change at Hanover for Belsen: every

German railway station is an unwitting memorial – I had written eight thousand words, a chapter that drew heavily (as they say) on *The Master Builders from Brooklyn*, or those parts of it where Toothgold's rants and crude propaganda for John Bull's Bully Boys gave way to historiographic probity. It was a matter to which I gave greater prominence than it merited because of the personal and collective conflict of shame and patriotism many Israelis experienced as witnesses to a religious landgrab by immigrants to an originally secular state. They claimed, absurdly, to be acting in the tradition of frontiersmen. They might be total bastards who spoke Hebrew with a Midwood accent but they were our total bastards and had to be protected, however reluctantly. It did not escape Palestinian eyes that many of the settlements resembled the Tegart fortresses built during the loathed British Mandate.

I finished the book three months later. It was nothing like my others. I found myself laughing out loud at what I wrote. High comedy? No thank you Sir! Low, very low, is, I think, more like it. Docu-farce, my agent called it.

Denkmal: The Tale of an Illicit Monument . . . The monument that never was. The book that never was. The SLAPP, the super-injunction that was, is and ever shall be.

It was granted without warning six weeks before publication. I'd already started on the round of interviews. Svelte and self-deprecating – c'est moi. Review copies had gone out. A couple of reviews had even appeared – a publisher's embargo, a gentleman's agreement, doesn't have quite the force of a super-injunction imposed by a judge doing a favour to the plaintiff, a fellow member of The Garrick – an altogether different kind of gentleman's agreement. The pernicious kind.

The first I heard of this legal hammer was when Stech-Pelz telephoned late one night. He was hardly coherent. I had spoken to him only twice since 'the interview'. The questions I had asked him were hardly sly, just elucidations of things he himself had mentioned. He knew very well what I was writing.

He was drunk, tearful, screaming, in a hole, scary, viciously rude. Most of all he was volcanically angry. I had betrayed his trust. Falstaff's balls! All I had betrayed was his boastfulness.

His investors had turned on him. They threatened him. Had he no idea of the damage he had done to The Cause? Did he not understand trust? He might be an old fool but he was, still, an inexcusable fool. A traitor to The Freed From Freedom Network's higher echelons.

It will, Stech-Pelz told me, be you that pays the price for your prying indiscretion. I took your word that you were a historian not an affiliate of the gutter press. You have cost me the friendship of valued colleagues. Retribution is more than likely.

Somehow – we don't know how – a copy had got into the hands of one or other of the investors.

William Cattle KC and his junior Selina Trunk, punningly known as The Slapper due to her judge-pleasing clothes, represented GHJ (the initials are code to bolster anonymity, they are not those of a petitioner). Like most of his profession Cattle was an ethical dwarf who would defend the most abject psychopath. He confidently listed twenty-four instances of Higher Recognition Plateau, as the relevant part of the 1999 legislation is commonly known: positions held, public statements, works of art owned, estates owned, films starred in, alleged lovers, policies pursued, protracted negligence actions defended, places they lived, magazine articles ghostwritten in their name, ecological boasts, good works, charities supported, honorifics.

Selina Trunk: 'The properties granted to the characters in the book happened, My Lord, just happened' – leaden one-of-the-boys irony – 'to belong to the plaintiff and his associates. The author has breached the privacy of real people. She has broken into their minds in an act of what must be described as psychological trespass. She has wantonly infringed their human rights for commercial gain. She has, by her own admission, treated her characters like chess pieces – inanimate pieces of mineral if I may remind My Lord. She has linked public figures and figures less public to a regime of evil unalloyed, perhaps the most barbaric in history. I repeat: for commercial gain. Besmirchment in not a facet of free speech.

'The weight of coincidence is heavy. Of course a work of so-called fiction might include characters with two legs, brown hair, a particular idiolect, a taste for bacon and eggs. These are common-place. The reader sees herself or himself in these characters because she or he shares their qualities, their likes and dislikes.

'There are, however, properties ascribed to this book's characters which are far from commonplace. Ill-gotten wealth and all that it affords. A life of undeserved ease. Acts of alleged illegality. A form of implied gangsterism. Political extremism. Association with con-victed war criminals. These do not invite "identification".'

William Cattle KC: 'Even the most incurious reader is liable to wonder – who are the characters behind the characters? There can be little doubt that the "mindless din and babble" of social media will provide answers – to the cost of blameless people's reputa-tion. Answers which may very likely be rumours. But the public makes no distinction between what is rumoured and what is indis-putable fact.

'This is prying gutter journalism in disguise. The disclaimer "None of the characters in this book is based on a living person" is risible, an outright lie. What we see before us is a work of systematic defamation. My Lord will recall a more courteous and civilised era when the author of words which are knowingly spiteful, malicious and mendacious might find himself – or herself! – incarcerated . . . Many greater writers than Miss Coolmans have suffered such a fate. She is fortunate to live and write (sneer) in an age of shameless laxity where the burning of a meretricious book does not lead to the burn-ing of people – much, My Lord, as they might, in certain eyes, deserve to be burnt.'

Myles Deuteron's violent death was a question of when not if. When you swim with sharks . . .

It unlocked certain information – embarrassing to the British, Turkish and Saudi governments – that had been legally suppressed by amiable judges often sitting in camera. The *Denkmal* injunction was one of more than a dozen orders he had been granted in UK courts. Much remained suppressed under Official Secrets legislation.

Not, however, his association, reported in detail in *De Morgen*, with Vlaams Belang, one of several quasi fascist groupuscules (among them Hamas and Hezbollah) which had been supplied with weaponry of an extent and potency out of proportion to its size and ambition. It was an incitement to increase that ambition. This was not commerce, it was ideology.

The surprise, the sheer astonishment for me was that Deuteron's widow Celia was a woman who had employed me, in another life, as an assistant in a florist shop she managed. I was dumbfounded. In newspaper photographs she was all but unrecognisable: had it not been for the caption beneath them I'd never have put the two together. I hadn't thought of her in years – during which she had evolved from provincial dumpling to high maintenance cosmopolitan arm-candy with a cosmetic surgeon in her LV luggage.

At a slickly PR'd press conference after the inquest she, her two lawyers, her advisor, her PA and the helicopter pilot's son disputed the coroner's verdict of accidental death. The pilot Daley Sinkgraven had made the flight from London Docklands Airport many times since the Deuterons had bought Soaked Island. He was reliable: he wouldn't have been on the payroll if he hadn't been. He was a friend as much as an employee. He diligently checked the helicopter, a recently bought Wolferstan Thor Miranda H702, before every flight.

The Air Accidents Investigation Branch's scrutiny of the wreckage was claimed to be perfunctory: it was cold and dark, the tide was coming in, consuming the evidence. None of the seals that frequented the glistening mud shoals was injured. Several witnesses, including 'a courting couple with a groundsheet', claim to have heard an explosion *before* the craft 'belly-flopped out of the sky'. They were told that they were mistaken: they were three-quarters of a mile away across the estuary on the mainland between Gates Farm and Andrews Causeway.

Myles Deuteron was described as a billionaire philanthropist and businessman whose close relations with Russia, Saudi Arabia, Uzbekistan and Turkey had caused questions to be asked in the UK parliament. He paid to keep his name off rich lists. He had received death threats. It was claimed that the police had been indifferent to the dangers he faced, or imagined. They dismissed them as expressions of self-aggrandising victimhood. He had increased security. His chauffeur had been tortured and murdered: the coroner considered this irrelevant to the current inquest given that Mr Osmanović, perpetually fighting extradition, was wanted in several jurisdictions whose agents 'perhaps lacked the British virtue of patience and had regrettably chosen to act outside the law'.

Myles Deuteron had recently told his close friend Ivor Hinde, who sat at Celia's right hand throughout the conference, that any accident he might meet would not be an accident. The coroner, acquainted with Hinde's reputation, had treated his evidence with courteous disdain.

Deuteron had been 'desperately worried' about her and the boys' safety. *Pause. Tears wiped.* He rued the collapse of a project he had been involved in. The court order intended to keep the project out of the public domain had had the very opposite effect. Celia was loath to talk about it. She said: 'It's hardly worth going into. You lot know everything there is to know about it. It's all been leaked – along with a gallimaufry of spiteful lies and deliberate misunderstandings. Myles had been let down, abandoned by his fairweather partners.'

Above all she blamed a prying writer who had no respect for privacy, who could not appreciate family life because she was deprived of it, who was consequently embittered towards those who knew its joys, who was jealous of the Deuterons' wealth and referred to the departed as 'Myles Offshore'. Gnomically she warned the press that information was a valuable weapon which she could deploy. She declined to elaborate. She said she was determined to forge ahead with a scheme that had been dear to Myles's heart. She would pursue it as his solid legacy: the Myles Deuteron Foundation For Geopolitical Guidance.

A journalist stuck out her microphone: 'Will it be tax deductible?'

She withered the poor woman.

At the end of the press conference she thanked those who had attended, paused for so long that no one was sure what was going on, then said, without a smile: 'Dildos To The Dykes.'

The journalists and TV crews looked at each other foxed and incredulous, wondering what they were hearing. They pulled faces, uncertain whether it was appropriate to laugh.

★

I alone knew who that message was for. I alone knew that it was a threat: the omertà of the years was wearing thin.

Another message. A postcard from Tallinn. An old black and white photograph of contorted metal wreckage on rough terrain. It might have been anything had it not been for an undamaged tail rotor.

On the verso in an italic trained hand: Judex.

Luneburg

This is the story of Heini Stech-Pelz who came, one fine May morning, to be digging with his spade on Luneburg Heath, digging among
oak leaves and silver rolls of sloughed birch bark, digging through
strata of leafmeal the colour of cooked blood and of sphagnum moss
and of cakey rich peat, digging with the practised rhythm of his
trade, digging for the mortal remains of Heinrich Himmler. Although
its end is exhumation it evidently demands the same repetitive digging as when the end is inhumation. A coffin is little different from
swaddling garments. It is simply encountered at a different stage of
existence.

The grass withereth, and the flower thereof falleth away.

And this is how his father Ernst Stech-Pelz, near blind, 20 per cent
hearing and, thus, 80 per cent shouting, long since a centenarian,
archaeologist, sometime member of the Artamanen Bund and the
Ahnenerbe, came to be there too, dressed in his gay collarless tra-
chten jacket with green embroidery and horn buttons, dressed for
winter because he's always cold, exhorting Heini Stech-Pelz to dig.
He jerkily mimes the motions, lifts his fleecy-booted foot to force an
imagined spade into the ground, mumbles his memories of their
quarry. They are memories which Heini Stech-Pelz is so well
acquainted with that they might be his own.

He feels he knows Reichsführer Heinrich Himmler as an old
friend, as one of the crew round the campfire, the boy who told them
which bird's egg was mottled and which was glacier blue, the boy
who tramped and sang the songs of the land and the winding track
and who shared his bread and cheese with Ernst. He feels he knows
the long dead engineer of death so well that when his spade (a Men-
necke, bought during a thunderstorm the previous afternoon in a

suburb of Hamelin) strikes the wire and bone, and he genuflects in awe and he terriers the earth with his hands, and he comes face to face with the skull he will abandon all punctilios, all notions of rank and respect, and whisper with impudent affection the echoic diminutive 'Heini'.

And if Ernst berates him for so recklessly overfamiliar a slight he will amend the form of address to 'Uncle Heini'. Which is how he would have addressed him had the devil not brokered an alliance of cynical convenience between International Capital, International Usury and International Bolshevism to overcome a nation that dared to live out a dream.

It's how he would have addressed him had Uncle Heini chosen to evade the outlaw victors, had he fled his own land to the continent of the Aztecs, in simulacra of whose ceremonial he had participated as a black god. He had dazzled the infinite ranks of martial votaries with his spectacles. Those were not chance reflections, those were cryptic heliograms, for he spoke through the sun, he was its medium, he was its agent of cleansing light. He absorbed that light, too, in the swart rep of his priestly uniform. He led his Black Corps and all Germanic people in unshackling themselves from the covert Judaism called Christianity and in their rediscovery of the True Way from which they had been diverted by Charlemagne, the concupiscent tyrants of Rome, the agitator Luther, the perverters of the solstices, the libertines of the lie that was the Enlightenment, the urban nomads who made nothing yet profited from everything like protean fungi.

There was nothing Heini Stech-Pelz had not learnt from Ernst Stech-Pelz about the man he dug for. He had learnt, for instance, of the value he set on the very act of digging, on subterranean enquiry, on the revelation of a nation's skull beneath its skin of stone and clay, on the physicality of historic research, on the necessary fitness and athleticism of archaeologists, on the centrality of speleology to the re-creation of an ancestral heritage. As he digs and sweats Heini Stech-Pelz momentarily longs for the cool of a cave, longs to brush his brow against a shiny stalactite, longs for an ice lolly to hold there till his frontal sinuses thud and he desists.

But the tidy wooden cabin selling drinks-on-sticks and drinks-in-cans and paprika-flavoured crisps was now wayback, hidden in the open labyrinth of broom, sand, stagnant shallow water, brown moss hummocks. It was somewhere on the tourist route between the museum of thatched longhouses with runic fetishes in their gables and the grave of this great grim heath's encomiast, the green warrior Hermann Löns, who had died in 1914 at Loivre near Reims. His body had been exhumed and brought home to the heath.

> *There is no infinity more infinite than yours*
> *Save that of the heavens which you are measured by.*

The rebuilt huts at the site of Bergen-Belsen were nearby.

Ernst Stech-Pelz is sanguine about them: 'They are monuments to an endeavour. Why deny it?'

He quotes Thomas Merton: 'Even Christians can shake off their sentimental prejudices about charity and become sane like Eichmann.' Heini Stech-Pelz didn't like to suggest that maybe it was perhaps not meant to be taken literally but was infected by the weapon of the impotent, irony. The more impotent the more bitter the irony.

He vilifies the anachronisms and tectonic anomalies of the rebuilt lagers and rebuilt longhouses. They are 'lazy copies of themselves, imprecise copies'. The thatch is blatantly incorrect. Heather was evidently abundant and widely used in the epoch of the original construction. The replicas are long straw that was then seldom harvested and was not anyway employed for roof covering. It is gathered in faggots of a gross, mechanical smoothness that was unknown in Schleswig Holstein and Lower Saxony until the effeminate un-Germanic aristocracy of the late eighteenth century commissioned effeminate French architects such as Jacques-Claude Lillie to effect a thatch revival.

As for Hermann Löns, he deserved the burial he received amidst great pageant (armoured knights on armoured horses), in the presence of Darré and Rosenberg, in Year Two (1934). No doubt he warranted two memorials, a monument (*Denkmal*) and a birch grove a few kilometres distant.

Yet he was only a precursor, a tributary's tributary, a believer *avant la lettre*, a dreamer not a doer. If Hermann Löns is thus honoured why should Heinrich Himmler, who *acted* to make our dreams come true, be wrapped in camouflage netting and wire, and hidden as though he had never existed, hidden for all eternity?

Or for short eternity!

Ernst Stech-Pelz is pleased with his notion of eternity as manipulable. Like such inconstants as the human form or the weather. The weather! They had the will to determine the weather. There is no doubt that the means was just around the corner. Will breeds resolution.

Heini Stech-Pelz would not have had to labour in today's weather. His sweat is abundant. The colour of his clothes measures the temperature. The liquid salts' share of his shirt expands until it has darkened the entire garment. Heini Stech-Pelz digs on, undeterred, digging robotically as though every cell of him has been designed for this day, this dig, this purpose, this quest. The old man admires his vigour and sinews. He watches Heini Stech-Pelz. He recalls reverently how he too once dug for Heinrich Himmler, and for Germany's future whose key was occluded, buried in its deepest pasts and in its soil enriched with generation upon generation's phosphate, marrow and spirit.

Here was that process being repeated. Here was the cycle being renewed. Heini Stech-Pelz was digging through more than half a century's alien accretion, through the humus and mulch that had accumulated during the years of victor's justice, occupation, division, communism, federalism, internationalism, years when one Germany was the USA's ape and the other the USSR's, years when Germany did not exist. Years when Germany suffered the alien contaminations of white goods and ideological lies. Years when Germany was nothing more than a cloven entity confined to a plane of reality defined by contrary economic programmes and contrary idioms of pragmatic secularity – a low plane of reality. Ernst Stech-Pelz's Germany, the Germany he had dug for and in whose service he had applied his scholarship, was neither a mere suture of federal convenience where individuals prospered nor a potholed dictatorship where shoes were made of cardboard.

His Germany was an integrated organism. It was a force of nature. It was an idea. It was an idea composed of hundreds of thousands of congruent ideas. It was a totality of ideas each of which was a model of the whole, each of which carried the whole in it – the gulf between macrocosm and microcosm was closed, a process that was to have been ocularly abetted by supplying every German family with a tele scope so it might become as well acquainted with German stars as it was with German soil. This Germany had been thwarted because it had, uniquely, conflated the ideal and the actual.

It had achieved a higher reality by rupturing the membrane that in all other societies, all other states, makes the ideal and the actual mutually exclusive. This Germany had proved that men might be mythic creatures, that gods might be made of blood and tissue and that every cell, every gesture, every word and every deed might be a symbol of its purposeful unity. It said the same thing by manifold means. It dispensed with the narcissistic indulgences of individualism – no wonder it had so infuriated the English who had used the annexation of Poland as an excuse for their hypocritical belligerence.

Ernst Stech-Pelz knew the English. He had spent two summers, 1912 and 1913, with his father's cousin's family in the West Riding of Yorkshire, in the Bradford suburb of Manningtree. The Bluncks still bore a German name (they would change it to Block in 1916) but like many of their German neighbours in the wool trade they were Anglicised, embourgeoised, private, obsessed by hobbies which they pursued in solitude.

They were indifferent to the ruination of the fells by mills and mean houses. Their religious observance was a social rather than a spiritual rite. They were vigorous only in the accumulation of wealth and in their appreciation of smutty allusions to bodily functions (the body's meridional parts) and of the painted grotesques who took the stage at the decoratively frivolous Alhambra, to which Ernst declined invitations his second summer.

His slightly older contemporaries, Richard and Martin, spoke a German which was strangely accented, littered with anachronistic slang and vulgarities, grammatically imprecise. And when he begged to correct them they stared at him with an hauteur which was indefinably yet unmistakably English. They fought, they swore, they were routinely disobedient (a trait to which their parents were inured and which went uncorrected). They mocked Ernst for his lobeless ears. They were disrespectful to girls and wanton in their aspirations.

The family ate disgusting unseasoned English food. The first time Ernst Stech-Pelz was offered Yorkshire pudding he assumed that it was the cooked by-product of a wool mill, shoddy perhaps, or something akin.

All his life, whenever he's been in the tub or shower, he has grasped his sponge as though it were a mnemonic intended to remind him of the all-too-aptly named sponge cake that he ate in Manningtree Lane when he was thirteen and fourteen. He knows the English. He despises their readiness – which is merely a form of apathy – to accommodate and thus to pervert Germans. He despises their immunity to anything which challenges the quotidian and their unconscionable capacity to make a virtue out of common sense – which is common only in the sense of base, pragmatic, uninspirational. He despises grim little lives unenhanced by transcendental hope.

What kind of nation uses locutions such as 'down to earth' and 'feet on the ground' in an approbatory way? A nation which lives in fear of the possible, which acknowledges the limits of the possible, which perennially shies away from risking it all. A nation whose artists are revered for their very treachery unto the nation, for their parasitism upon the dregs (Dickens, Gissing, Douglas, Swift). A nation which is proud to be the oxymoron 'a good loser' and believes in 'fair play'. A nation of such inertia it built armies from conscripts, from unwilling fellows who couldn't march in time, who'd shirk, who'd shoot their own officers.

Ernst Stech-Pelz has no idea of how much he idealises England.

He looks at Heini Stech-Pelz leaning against a nude birch with his shirt gone from royal to navy, his mouth a mere conduit for Güstrower water and his muscles shiny and his veins protrusive. Even in this moment of relaxation he realises that he is reclaiming Heini for Germany as a tardy compensation for his cousin Richard Block who died at Sedan in the summer of 1918 in the colours of the York and Lancaster Regiment. Richard Block died as a traitor to Germany and to his forebears. In his mitigation it can be said that the Germany he mortally opposed was not the sacred ideal that it was to become, even though its seed already existed. Hermann Löns, who had died in the first month of the war, had written: 'Germans may pretend to be Christian but we are not Christian and we never can be Christian.

Christianity and race consciousness are incompatible. They can no more exist together than Socialism and culture can.' Much of Ernst Stech-Pelz's life had been devoted to the acquisition and creation of proofs of that dictum (which was hardly exclusive to Löns).

Now Heini Stech-Pelz digs in Ernst's name, digs as an extension of him, digs for the irrefutable symbol of his race's antipathy to Christianity, for a symbol even more potent than the hooked cross which while it mocked the Christian cross also included it, acknowledged it in a gesture of placatory compromise akin to the declaration that Christ was not a Jew but an Aryan. Christianity could be tolerated so long as its adherents understood the race of its earthly idol. Tolerated – but no more than tolerated. And not indefinitely. Ernst Stech-Pelz considered the Catholic revival of the post-war decade to have been occasioned by collective spiritual cowardice, by what the French were beginning to routinely characterise as bad faith. He regarded it as a rebuttal of the living gods who had led Germany for twelve glorious years.

That those gods were no longer subject to primary life and had moved on through their own volition or through victor's justice did not mean that they were *dead*.

The conceit that when the pulse stops death occurs belongs to the most banal school of materialism. Famous men and heroes and those who bestride the earth in order to make it theirs do not die. Their example, their spirit, their feats live on. They inhabit future generations (the children and grandchildren of those Catholic cowards). If they *are* dead why are they so feared when their breath has left them? Why are they burnt? Why are they hidden? Why was poor Heinrich wrapped in camouflage netting and barbed wire and driven, thirty-three hours after he bit on the capsule and turned a delicate cyanotic blue like bone china, from Luneburg to the heath and buried in this lonely place if not because in all but corporeal functions he was still living? Why?

Men do not die unless those who succeed them let them die. They may die through the future's forgetfulness or neglect but not through mere lack of oxygen. It is those who still breathe, who read, who remember, who look at films and photographs of the fine times when the world was new who grant afterlife. Afterlife is the gift of the quick to the notionally dead. They can be made to live forever.

It is The Word that is the foundation of immortality, not potions and yogurt, The Word passed from one generation to the next. Of course our science would, one day, have discovered a means to a literal immortality just as it would have discovered a means to bring us our own controlled weather. Christ's afterlife was ensured not by the borrowed miracle of rising from the dead (standard practice in all myth systems) but by his posthumous proselytisers, his grieving laureates who compensated for their loss and justified their thraldom by exaggerating their idol's feats. It was The Word that created Christ for all time and made him immortal. Immortality begins with obituaries and biographical remembrances. The Reich which Ernst Stech-Pelz served and which he believed in as he believed in nothing before or since may have, in its first manifestation, fallen short of its god-allotted millennium by nine hundred and eighty-seven years and eight months but it is indubitably immortal.

By the time Ernst Stech-Pelz and Heini Stech-Pelz had decided where, this particular day, to dig for Heinrich Himmler's grave the Third Reich had engendered sixty thousand books – one book for every two hours of its gubernatorial existence. That these books are seldom approbatory is, he considers, an impertinence. It's neither here nor there. It's The Word, the sheer volume of words – conflicting words, disputative words, plagiarised words, repeated words – which has lifted the Third Reich into immortality, which granted it the eternal life that Bolshevism will never achieve.

Who were Bolshevism's gods? It owned no gods, just men of clay whose life after life was taxidermal fabrication. This post-breath imitation of life dies, swiftly, because it is a counterfeit extension of that life. It is the victim of its very literalness. It refuses to acknowledge death's mystery, the shift from one mode into another which is thus far unknown but which we would have made knowable.

Bolshevik death is stuck with terrestrial representation. It demands the banalities of realism. The glories of the twelve year and four month Reich demand a different sort of valediction, a valediction which denies itself, which emphasises transcendence, which shows that it was a Germanic, racial and above all a religious state of ecstasy that we created. It was only political insofar as politics had allowed us to arrive at the point of creation. Political systems come and go. They are the caterpillar, the crude form before the beauty of a winged faith. Political systems are responsive, reactive.

Great religions are rocks of certainty, bastions of the absolute. They are founded on repositories of superstition, upon depths of imaginative irreason. Such properties are conditions of a religion's longevity. Without superhumanness a religion is not a religion. A religion's success is in direct proportion to the volume of its breaches of naturalism – the more winged gods, the more bleeding statuary, the more miracles, the more magical mutations, the more paranormalcy, the more extravagant its creationist myth, the more dependent it is on aberrant feats and facts and fasts, the more insouciant its denials of science, the greater the number of adherents that it will gather to it.

There is, however, a paradox of faith: because the credulous do not consider themselves credulous they demand physical 'proofs' to sustain their credulity. Hence relics. Hence scraps of material, bone shards, stained vessels, dust that once was hair, lumps of wood – all of them inevitably found wanting by carbon date tests, which the credulous disregard because, for them, scientism is merely a hostile *faith*. Relics are synonymous with fakery.

Ernst Stech-Pelz craves, before he dies his first death, to bequeath to the pan-Germanic people a relic of unimpeachable provenance, of such tonic probity and enchantment that it will effect the rebirth of that people.

It will unite them in contempt of half a century's betrayal.

It will unite them against the continuing dilution of the blood.

It will enjoin them to wrestle serpents, vault across clouds.

They will create a fresh world from ice and struggle.

They will copulate in military cemeteries so that the children conceived therein will inherit the warrior spirit of the fallen heroes who are thus reborn in those children. This is immortality for the unfamous, their names may not live forevermore but their life-spirit, a sort of baton passed down through the ages at the moment when the *apfelmus* meets the hungry egg, is perpetuated by the generative inevitabilities of the barrow, of the tumulus, of the burial cave, of the cold lichenous slab beneath a winged helmet frozen in stone.

Relics have such power. Even the most blatant counterfeits have power because they are endowed (unless they are the fraudulent creations of International Capitalism) with honourable intention: they are substitutes, replicas of the real, replicas which are standing in, understudies.

Sincerely made replicas are better than no relics at all. They serve the cause. Ernst Stech-Pelz served the cause by devotedly applying archaeological scholarship to the invention of bogus archaeological artefacts whose use was merely temporary and would be curtailed when the real was revealed. He worked at that, too, though he came to fear that there is no need to distinguish between the two for the faithful showed their faith by accepting anything that was offered them. And then the faithful disappeared: they lost their faith.

The opportunism of the vanquished made them lose it or, different, deny it in deference to the certitudes of victor's justice. Ernst Stech-Pelz is convinced of a relic's capacity to revive in others the dormant faith which he has never lost. He believes that a relic, the right relic, *this* relic above all relics will be a trigger. Christians crave the grail, whose glamour is nomenclatural – 'the legend of the holy plate or sacred chalice' has less of a ring to it. And what is a plate, a mere receptacle, beside the bones of the man who was to Hitler what Saint John the Baptist was to the Aryan Jesus Christ?

Lunchbreak: they eat potato and pickled cucumber salad whose *remouladensauce* has separated because the clear plastic tubs were left above the car's dashboard in the sun. They wonder what has happened to the earth mover that was meant to have been delivered no later than 11.30: they had enjoyed a lively discussion about the comparative qualities of Terex and Berkow machines but settled for Wacker Neuson because the agent claimed it could be delivered days before either of the others. It was a day for kit. Heini's muscle and minder Desmond Hubback will arrive soon with a ground penetrating radar system (GPR) which cost Hanna Nowak €230,000.

As the worn map in his office indicated, Ernst Stech-Pelz's great powers of divination did not invariably direct him accurately. Each sticker on the map signified a place where, during more than half a century since his release, he had, most weekends till increasing darkness filled his eyes, dug for Himmler's grave with spades, forks and trowels using a tripod and a timer.

Digging was an addiction. Until recently when he was reunited with his son, he had always dug alone. He compared himself to a truffle hunter. The prize was not to be shared. He did not want to reveal his positions so had not hired helpers until he was unable to do without them. The positions were gifted to him by divination, a practice which he had learnt serving in the Ahnenerbe, an organisation whose practices 'on the far side of reason' incurred the disdain of the spy Schellenberg: he called them 'witchcraft', tending to patronisingly tweak his amanuensis's ear when he did so.

But what did he know! Himmler, contemptuous of reason ('a discredited thought system'), wisely put rats on trial in the hope that if found guilty they would be susceptible to rehabilitation and change their ways – so proving their superiority to the Jew.

A combination of lumbago, immobility, impaired vision and gout at last prevented him digging.

The chances of finding any grave – let alone the *right grave*, a grave zealously concealed many decades past – were slight. The area of Luneburg Heath exceeds 100,000 hectares. At any given time there will be at least three squads digging for a body, someone or other: eight out of ten murderers from as far away as Neubrandenburg and Münster prefer to bury their victims here. The diggers tend to be competitive. They argue about whose patch is whose. They sabotage each other's digs. Hundreds of 'amateurs' walk unsystematically across the great heather-purple heath prodding the sandy ground with sturdy sticks. They are the bane of Naturwachter Hans Lautermilch's life.

Watch him warn a group of Turkish workers hired by Ernst Stech-Pelz and paid by Hanna Nowak. They are infringing a Protected Area Ordinance. They claimed to be digging on behalf of a friend of the prophet, which of course they were. When they continued to dig he rang for the BPOL, one of whom was a woman officer. Due to her presence the Turks refused to recognise the police's authority. More police were called.

The Turks accused the police of racial harassment. Ernst Stech-Pelz will in future employ only workers of 100 per cent German stock. He will tell Hanna that while Turks are tireless and cheap their

lunches have proved problematic. 100 per cent German stock workers demand higher wages but eat anything so long as it's pork and
comply with the German way of life.

He is irritated by Herr Lautermilch's favouritism towards the production crew and cast of *Der kleine schwule Traktor rettet den Fuchs vor
der Jagd*. 'His brush with fame,' says Heini but Ernst doesn't get.

Ernst Stech-Pelz contrasts the cleansing of Europe with the genocidal programmes prosecuted in Argentina and the United States
against the *native* population by incomers: that, he insists, is the difference. The British, fully cognisant of the Reich's covert war and of
the sites of the plant (he means Treblinka, Auschwitz-Birkenau),
could have bombed them. But they didn't – and here he leans forward in his folding chair kneading the air – because even the hack
journalist Churchill (the Führer's description) respected our right to
have our land to ourselves. Yes, he was with us because he was a
Zionist. He too wanted these wretched people, these pimps and parasites, to be settled by themselves, in their own land which they had
deserted to wander the world like cuckoos with lisps and crinkly
hair, leeching on us, pretending to be us, perverting our blood and
our language. Yiddish is bad German, Heini, bad but dependent.

We gave them every opportunity to leave and some of them did
leave. But then they started to come back. They could not take a
hint. Thick-skinned? I'd say so.

You know of Heinrich Himmler's weakness towards the end. He
tried to appease a man whom the traitorous spy Schellenberg had
spirited in, a man from the World Jewish Congress (the very name
gives their game away):

It's time that we Germans and you Jews buried the hatchet. Heinrich said that to Izzy Cohen (*Norbert Masur*, in fact). Oh, why did he
do that? He was a man of such purpose, such resolve. And, you know,
that very expression, bury the hatchet – it makes me think of tomahawks. The tomahawks which the Sioux used to scalp the Protestant
incomers were forged in the city of Birmingham, the manufactory
of the British Empire, your Essen. You see whose side the British
were on then. They knew the difference. They understood the iniquity, the tort. Fair play old chap. Support those whose land it is,

who are bound to the earth by virtue of having for generations entered into a mutual contract of succour and dependence with it . . .

And let's keep the earth you've dug, Heini, let's put it in sacks – for that's the earth which has been strengthened by his phosphates, that earth is as sacred as my dear old friend himself.

Heini Stech-Pelz, leaning against the side of the car, inspects a burgeoning blister, takes up his spade and prepares to dig again through the newly sacred earth.

Of course god exists. Man has created him and refined him – so he exists. But so too do other fabrications of man: elves, Valkyries, giants with hands the size of a mountain and eyes which can see forever, and cows who talk riddles and ghosts made of leather and beneficent men who carry children on their shoulders across swollen rivers.

Whatever man wants to exist does exist. Man has an idea – an idea begins as a fiction, which is a blueprint of tomorrow. Then we make it physical. We had an idea of a Germany we might make. It was an invention . . . A dream is drawn by the man that the dream came to – then it is realised in the form of a religion or a building or a book. These are mere triggers, catalysts until dimensions are added. The Reichsführer's bones and teeth are the springboard to a dream. When those bones and teeth are found we shall move swiftly from larva to imago. The death's head hawkmoth is our familiar.

He had planned tracking down the families of all the British tommies who had callously consigned Himmler to an unmarked grave, track them down and go to whatever lengths were needed to get them to yield up the resting place where no man let alone a great man should rest. They would not be spared.

Myles Deuteron had been persuaded to depute Osman Osmanović to question the tommies' descendants. This was not an advisable move. Osman eventually found a Phyllis Sanger, whom he believed to be the granddaughter of one of them. Osman went about his task with enthusiasm. He was arrested for threatening behaviour at the Swindon hospital where this surgeon worked. She was a namesake of his quarry and twenty years younger. The Thamesdown magistrate who heard the case regretted that the lout (her word) could not be deported at the end of his short sentence.

The Judiciary Judicially Judged Panel reprimanded her for xenophobic insensitivity. Nonetheless Deuteron, fearing exposure, was relieved to cancel the plan (and so obliterate Stech-Pelz's dream). It had been so close he might have grasped it, made it actuality. Now it dissolved, inked letters sliding down a poster in the rain.

When those bones and teeth remain unfound even Ernst Stech-Pelz's modest, pared-down Trust of Homage is floundering.

But for once in his life of abject self-pity and delusions of hurt, fate favours him.

Joy! A man claiming to be his natural son – the biological, facial link to stalled love and torn happiness he wants to believe in – had made contact. His motives were impenetrable. His companion/gofor/muscle was not to be toyed with. He'd kick an old man when he's down.

The son Henry, soon to be Heini, had a despised nominal 'step-father', The Sergeant, who had led the commando that buried Germania's thwarted saviour. The biological father did not know that The Sergeant was the man who arrested him in April 1945. The Sergeant did not, however, share that ignorance. The woman they have loved – Stech-Pelz for weeks, The Sergeant for decades – was apprised of their connection.

She has a good reason to want it kept unspoken. Stay schtum, Ernst my love, stay schtum, speak only of my tribulations and pain as a breeder of the Führer's children.

Stech-Pelz, lifted and aspiring, requested and received the financial backing of his old friend Sir Geoffrey Shadoxhurst Bt and his some-time lover Hanna Nowak, both former 'passionate investors in conviction', both seeking the greatest of the Third Reich's prizes.

Both apostates to The Freed From Freedom Network, both were contemptuous of Myles Deuteron's fear that his social alpinism might be compromised by his associates. They were appalled by the Fawzy brothers' vulgarity. They were smirkingly amused by Spencer Prestige's 'not getting it quite right' – his bogus British tweeds, cravats and brogues (too polished by far).

Several Days Later

Where the coney-cropped, interior-sprung lawn stopped, the bog began. Land and liquid coalesced. What was fluid? Which was solid? The watery light was the light of water colour. Desmond Hubback had a screen strapped to him like a cigarette girl's tray. 'Makes me fuckin' feel like some fuckin' perv in fuckin' drag. LBG . . . how does it go.' It received information from a septuaped SVJ Zone Warrior 600 drone, a malevolent metal insect which also transmitted to Ernst's benefactors, to The Sergeant, to their lawyers. The bog stretched to the horizon. The peat was old and so deep a house could be hidden in it. Could once have been hidden . . . Now nothing was foreign to this machine whose forebears had visited distant planets.

The breadline labour force Ernst employed was, as he told himself repeatedly, 100 per cent German stock. Just by looking at them he could discern the absence of mongrelism and contamination by Jew genes. They might have been heroic blond hay-balers in the glorious summer of Year Two when a refulgent future was to be had. If only.

They moved along the imaginary line stretching from the now single watchtower. The other had been struck by lightning on, it was said, the very day the Führer sacrificed his life for Germany, the elemental act which enjoined his Honourable Disciples to preach Dream Topping™.

Its disappearance exacerbated the task. They uncovered animal bones, a horse's skeleton, part of an aircraft's fuselage, countless sheep skulls, several bicycles, spectacles, a cache of rusty small arms, a bubble car, a baby's body in a plastic bag. With every trove Ernst made himself busy giggling: 'We're getting warmer . . . we're getting warmer.'

They were not told what they were looking for whenever Hubback responded to the screen and ordered them to excavate. Chop chop. But they were, Ernst told himself, surely looking in their young life for a strong man to lead them. A figurehead that is more than a figurehead.

My Personal Eucharist: Shirelle

So he is mini-bar abuser! Dogg (Holistic Thanatological Guru) is mini-bar abuser!

Even without valuable Mandatory Recognition Criteria Training (special discount GBP 11.50 for Absolute Discretion Assured kittens) I so have known. Any kitten so have known. Is plain obvious. He is written all over. I can tell straight off right from moment he is opening door.

And me I am seeing more than few. Colleague on The QT, on The Fast and The Loose, The Wife hundreds of mile down a road. He stocking up on The Old Dutch Courage to make phone prayer for Quality Intimacy Companion. He is taking time to come to door because he is disorientated and nor too steady on The Feet. Might even forget I am coming.

I reword.

Do you know – I can tell even *before* he is opening door Dogg (Holistic Thanatological Guru) is mini-bar abuser! He takes *that* long to open. He could be a tough sandwich for eating from this evening. But he is Shaun Memory friend. Shaun is regular clientele, big payer. He personally recommend me as Little Hotsy Wotsy!

So I do not count how long. You do not. Kitten is busy doing unobtrusive. Like she is not there? Like if you are there you are all busy validating why you are hanging in corridor and not being in room right?

Maybe have just had Lover Tiff.

Maybe have lost keycard and you are waiting for new one to deliver.

Maybe your partner is in shower toning and soaping and does not hear knockknock not estimating you to arrive back early from sustainable abundance meeting.

Carrying of briefcase or workbag is counselled at all times.

Absolute Discretion Assured is gift-generous to all concierge and head porter. But some of him still are not letting up gropy pestering for walk-in-cupboard preferential such as Durkan at Trafalgar Century Elite★★★★ notwithstand he shows off snapz of his little nipper (10) in football strip.

Does not mean they can always turn blind eye if they get loitering complaint whatever favours they have been pleasured (they are often being buying big drinks plus lip service). They have livelihoods to consider about gaining wherewithal to provide for their love ones in our jungle-style world of ours.

I do not begrudge. I have learnt positive alpha value life lessons from hotel hospitality professionals because kittens are in same enterprise arena basically.

For instance lesson from crafty ginger Len Sleath at Purity By Spencer Prestige International Health Hydros. Len Sleath advice: get money up front if suspecting gonk might be contemplate putting end it all suiciding himself off from high window. Telltales: checks in alone, withdrawn, far away eyelook, lavishing chateaubottle and foie gras self-indulge on theirselves way beyond what expenses will allow chased by vintage koňacs. Even more telltale: not used to asking maitre'd if he can supply sophisticate deluxe companionship. Nervy. If electronic transaction is not processed by time of death (to minute precise) hotel is going to oblige to claim against deceased estate taking long months probating before what is due is remitting.

So personally speaking I am not having heart to go troubling grieving widow in her loss for GBP469.50 if her old man bilks me for my sensual attentions during his final tragic hours by going out on balcony and jump.

What is money, even GBP469.50, when life lays shattered on executive limousine roof on forecourt in wee small hours – waiting to be valet-parked walnut-interior top-range Jaguar by example (dented).

What is card in just-dead man's wallet without PIN? Just plastic. Only good for no contact low level purchase. Dead as man.

Let me share you corridor secrets.

Remain confident at all times. An extra strong mint help to calm yourself.

Remember *Pressed For Agenda*? Dorleac Vinte is just punching PIN codes into ATM machine? Till she finds The Right One without initiating suspicion at passbyers because she knows Mambas Agents are there? And she does not know which one are them? Yeh?

How many times can you do pretend routine searching in clutch-bag nonchalant all casual for keycard? Doing that tipping out bag bits and species then pretending to toothcomb what is on floor. Problem is it gets unwanted white knights. Funny isn't it way men become gentlemen with me when they not with My Mother?

They just being wearing gallantry thinking cap in Lovelog Area!

As luck ironically two coming out room next door are roger-rogers. It is upper lip that is giveaway – searching prey for devouring. They do not hardly notice me because I am woman and they have only eyes for each other and other men who are not as other men. They do not half drive me in XXXL shock. I am pretending to search in clutchbag and looking with exasperated-style smile showing what I am doing.

Christ On Crack! I am almost jumping Out The Skin.

So they only dress clothes like Nazis.

English sense humour! You never get used to him. Saying he is Just A Laugh. Saying where is your sense humour? You got no sense humour! Your sense humour left behind on ringroad? Etc.

If *their* village is burning down.

If *their* Grandmother being only one to escape genocide massacre because she is little child been seeking in wood for fungus mush-room (boil four hour with different waters for toxic) to make special family secret recipe at time they come with tanks and flame-thrower. She hiding in ditch. She watch SS officer shoot brother in eye. SS officer, he is leading strange dog – a Mordhund, Alsatian shape (German Shepherd for American gonks), 100 per cent black body, 100 per cent white head, pigment deficiency defect pinky eyes reminds of giant vulture condor. SS officer, he has no ear lobe. So she is staying two days in ditch. All her life My Grandmother is nightmaring about that dog and ears with no ear lobe and brother's headback falling off head in red spray like rock falling off cliff at angry ocean storm.

And there they go party party wearing black uniforms with death-head skeleton skulls on cap, dazzle swastika bling, beware high voltage overhead on collar, armbands, jackboots shine like liquid vinyl etc. etc.

Creepy or what? Just like real thing they were apart from holding hands and whiff of popper I got off of them. Blond devils from next room but also from Hell even though they wasn't goosestepping and exterminating. Just casual and that more terrifying for it. It must have been this month's LöngNifeNite at d:Generator — top reputation neozyklon club on coast, in basement at Sachsenhain Hotel. They belong to The Stout As Oak Moot. They come from all over mostly rogerrogers and burglars and highwaymen but some electro-diesels also. It is not just nitrate they are doing but peroxiding up litres Lite'n'Brite. Some say they are always with us The Nazis. I am agreeing, specially where there is bleach there is evil.

Check out ambient logistics of . . .

Floor-services room. Locked. Stop guests light-fingering towelling gown, actual towel, high-tog quilt, silky rock spa, individual cedar or option lemon balm soap, teabag, vanilla aerosol, sugar sachet, nature-bath-scrub, verbena fragranced deodoriser, toilet cleaner with swan neck for directional.

Hotel make thief of all of us.

Authoritative CEO so tell me.

Hotel are catalyst trigger to low level criminal opportunism. They breed culture tolerating sociopathic. Everyone on-take. Staffs and guest. That is why walls paintings is never real. Just clever-clever fake with oil paint bobble uber-faux texturing. They will even liberate janitorial trolley comprehensive kentucky mop and wringer, 5 litre bottle Janitol Ultra Sanitiser, neutralPH heavy duty hand cleaner. All manner serviette, cutlery, showerhead. Baby changing unit going The Walkie if and when they is not screw to surface.

So nowhere to slip into there then.

I knock again at Dogg (Holistic Thanatological Guru) door. Wait. When nothing happen there is tension. Scratchy. Personal speaking I am worrying at scalp scratching. If life gets stress I will be bald as a thing.

One room along there is tray slovenly on carpet.

Ought to be collected hours backs.

Full congealed English. All butts in streaky yolk, rinds, crusts, ugh, ash, yuckymucky tissues smeared like they miss their mouths with ketchup and have to wipe down like Desna when she was only tot (2) but it was forgivable then.

Newspaper folded any old how they have not got origami gene!

Front page: mercy killing or murder?

As per usual.

Photo of scrummy but so slightly sinister Burmese Doctor it say underneath:

EUTHAN**ASIAN**.

Who does 'Doctor' Dedge think he is?

God?

Let's hear from our caring readers.

If YOU think he deserves a taste of his own medicine

Call 0800 666 789

Calls charged at £10.20 a minute

It is going on weeks. What *I* am thinking is apart Doctor Bhanubandh Dedge himself only Tragic Cancerpensioner Tillie Gandey (86) know deep truth about her empowering him to release her into Yon Cypress Dusk©. And she is passed on.

Tragic Cancerpensioner Tillie would have being gone beyond anyway in fortnight, no one disputing. Is it circumstantial they ask about all The Literature from Dream Topping™? Wardens say they found The Literature in her sheltered accommodation pod.

A real-life (and death!) mystery. To be cont'd.

Is it same with assisted suicide as real suicide?

Watch out! My Mother is telling me it is against Religion because real suicide missing out special highspeed treat having Your Whole Life flashing before their very eye. The god punish real suicide. The god has behaviour issue. Sacred text say so. He is behaving like jealous psychopath. He is not attending anger management workshop. He is leaving largactyl in halfway house. His wrath! He is preventing Your Whole Life flashing before their very eye because they is taking law in their own hand. Because they is cutting him out The Loop of Destiny.

I am not clue why My Mother is considering it being treat! There is all sorts which I am ever so grateful thank you very much when my time come if they are left buried in cutting room vault! The Whole Life! No thank you Mister God! I mean . . . some gonks! Even regulars.

Such as:

<u>Mr Denny Vivary</u>
Kitten Embers saying Mr Denny is reputation having biggest prick in his special professional field hydrographic data processing. Me I saying he is reputation to *being* biggest prick in special professional field hydrographic data processing! He is typical no accounting taste gonk special in clothes front. He is sort of gonk secretly seeking The Mum always denied by cruel destiny twist of domestic accident when him impressionist child. Cannot be too estimating of dangers lurking in home. Suchlike stepladders slaughter more than terrorists, thick polish layers are turning floor as skidpan deathtrap. Or like Tragic Mum he hardly know knitting machine who is wiring on blink.

Each week with Mr Denny I reacting scenario Your Home Is A Killer. Sometimes I wearing Mum clobber my eye weep at lifetime mothball. His eye weep at poignant. Mum no accounting taste neither. She is built for HGV purpose so her clothes hanging every which way but flattery. Mr Denny is throwing The Wobbly if everything not just so. For instance example: this game underfoot soap in shower is driver of sustainable brain injury. I am pretending that I fall myself against clinical tiles. So he is getting in sulky pet because I do not fall myself hard enough. He is wanting me to risk injury even coma blackout. Every week he is demanding for more danger option.

I tell him: Absolute Discretion Assured is Award Winning Quality Intimacy Companionship Boutique not somersort stunt artisans!

Barry 'The' Rug

I did not ought to complain. Taxi Tuesdays at his secluded distinctive older style property benefitting mature gardens of rhododendron accents and water feature. Lounge space is so culture. There paintings, fine art enamels, special feature authentic Roman potteries display flasks and plates some dug at local neighbourhood fields by Barry himself departed dog Kym.

£250: I sit at concert grand piano I am pretending to play legendary virtuosi pianist Russ Conway repertoire and miming Toni Lo Reno's greatest hits. Barry bringing himself off in corner behind valuable antique armchair with other hand trying to stop that woolly hairpiece slipping over his eyes. He can't stick it down because of scalp eczema condition skin.

It is poor fellow's face I do not want flashing before my eyes.

Sorry! But he is all shiny Plado like Desna (3) is playing with when nipper. Victimed by tragic salon fire in own salon suffering top percentage burn accident from bursting aerosols. All plastic reconstructed surgeries people look like same person. They lose out on individual features and join wannabe young tribe like they are trying to fetch back past but past is on shore and they are on speedboat racing away from shore. No chance.

Barry 'The' Rug is considered by strangers for Gallant Few Guinea Pig.

It started with them when Guinea Pigs are given new face so they can meet girls they defended Our Blighty Shore for in summer sky and it ends with Beatle Paul turning into tragic old lesbo-face. Barry is cursing his clumsy hands with missing fingers and just stubs. He is unable to engineer new technology of remote track skipping in digital remastery of *Pixilated Penguin*.

Sir Geoffrey Shadoxhurst Bt

It is said as bart. My little joke – they are saving on ink because of ink shortage in olden days.

Routine go: meets me at ferry terminal only five minutes away from here ironically in special vintage left hand drive 'charabanc' car from his personal worldclass collection of suchsame with important history associations. I am wearing raunchy jaunty beret, stretch Breton stripey top, hobble skirt, carrying string of onions as specified. Drinkdrives to woodland service station talking at himself in French, playing Edith Piaf type witch rolling her 'r's on CD deck and accordion music. I am wondering what kind of silly billy has no regret. Parks at end away from petrol pumps beside handwash facility. Then has me paradise myself. With him hand-foaming up car from outside using creamy thick Delicate Lustrewash all over black enamel bodywork and windows. I can't see out from soapy coffin. He can not see in. He is imagining. He is coming in his nappy. Me I am saying I am coming even if I am not which I am not. Never deals finger on me not even to touch how wet. Honour on trust. Gentleman's behaviour. I am lady so I am not counting money when he remits me. He holds one end of quality paper envelope I take other end. Then we go to deluxe luxury home of his. A palace. Pioneer heavy petting zoo. Mature trees. Flagpole. Carved gables. We eat foie gras and drink sweet wine in sophistica-tion of dining room. The walls are original bird paintings of world famous artist Orbison. He so learned knows the name of every bird. This is the life.

It is all lovely until that dog – not for petting. Back of historic vin-tage car Panhard 1936. Tell truth it is not so much dog itself being problem. Big big dog . . . But he is wearing dog muzzle. Like mask at fencing gymnasium.

Problem is dog breed. Chance is having his limelight. Dog is like dog in tragic Grandmother memory. This is breed with shape of Alsatian (German Shepherd for American gonks), 100 per cent black body, 100 per cent white head, pigment deficient defective pinky eyes but different name Mordhund. He is only time I ever see same dog My Grandmother is nightmaring of and speaking of in valley of fear. Till that time I admit I wonder like a traitor not believing My Grandmother there is such a dog in existence.

I say I am hoping he is understanding. I can read reservoir of deep-down disappointment in Sir Geoffrey's eyes, but also respect for me as person. Which I cannot say dog has. Dog has no respect for me as person. Dog's pigment deficient defective pinky eyes are sex crime eyes.

Sir Geoffrey does not throw regret wobbly but it is long time before I get call from him after that. There is fourteen months shortfall of not being valued regular client.

When he call again no worry there is no longer dog. He sound on rack of melancholy. Dog was dognapped. Dog thieving professionals at work. Elite dog worth tens of thousands. Unique pedigree dog. Most sought after special breed dog from ancestors at SS Hundeschule. His great great great great great grandparents worked on Auschwitz ramp. That figure with dog My Grandmother have seen. Sir Geoffrey heartbroken to tears when he find bones and sticks thieved dog has buried.

We sit on mellow brick terrace at his lovely home looking at flowers and massaged lawns and worldclass cedars reflecting life tragedy quaffing vintage.

He hold up his glass. 'Motacilla cinerea.' He murmur elixir words to me.

I tell him how much I am getting plum notes taste. His eyebrows are puzzled.

'Of wagtail?'

'Wagtail?' I ask.

He point: 'Grey wagtail – over there near the lavender.'

Mandatory Recognition Criteria Training warning. Kitten never wear spectacles at work arena. If short-sighted squint. I squint. I can't see no dog. Maybe because grey it blends in. What about we go inside because of nippy chill air I propose. I don't want dog nearby frotting at leg even cuddly dinky rogerroger dog.

Larky joshy pisstakey voices round corner.

He is funny, little stick man on fire escape sign running like getaway thief because he has already lost feet and hands like Barry 'The' Rug in heat of unforgiving salon furnace inferno. Melts eyeballs.

I opened fire escape retardant door. I pushed hard against the springhinge to shut it. Voices closed in. Then they stop. Leaning to look down concrete stairwell.

It's like picture puzzle. After few secs: is it up you are looking? Or is it down you are looking?

But picture puzzles are not whiffyish. Not stinky stale of piss and rust. Not creepy, not silent with strange dangers. Then distant footsteps echoing many levels down – or up. Plastic on banister all patchworn like poochy pelt diseased with the Niels. Every made-for-teev ever has chase down a stairwell. Race against elevator. Metal blakeys on shoes for added clickclack. Her, she take off her heels but clutch hold of them because she need them for steamy sunset beach semi-adult when they are about to live happy ever with surf and credits rolling over.

You can move anything up and down this stairwell with no one seeing.

(Same as The Secret Smuggler Passages in Olden Days. Brandy barrels and romantic lace for milady.) Shooters, air to grounds, underage illegals, sacks of toot and carlos, bulgy luggage with millions in banknotes, bludgeoned body wrap in moist carpet like Swiss roll with nasty surprise filling. No one police stairwells.

I touchtone number Dogg (Holistic Thanatological Guru) has sluffed. Busy. Which might mean anything frankly. I spy through wiretoughened panel to see voices are not still in corridor which they are not and walk back out stairwell with relief. I said to myself take deep breaths for calm procedure Shirelle, give it two more minutes this time counting secs if necessary.

Did not half lay into Dogg (Holistic Thanatological Guru) door. Soldier quality joinery. Better than average hotel door. Normally they are using C grade ply – that is C for cheap! And they are making drumming noises so to speak. Always risk tactic because attracting neighbouring attention.

These particular gonks, they are backbone of our calling. Give us this day our daily bread (and lo-fat spread! I like to joke). And give thanks this day for early caller, happy hour gonk they are known as. They got wherewithal to pay price but they are not looking for night shift.

But this one!

This Dogg (Holistic Thanatological Guru), he is different.

When the door open (at last!) you can see he is above and beyond.

Tongue is purple, all bruised looking, lolling out down chin. His lips are stained like he has been at the raspberry lolly. Which he has not. I can tell he is trying to smile. He is stood still but he trips over. He looks like he has been in a fight with worst enemy – and worst enemy is himself! He bangs into door. He stares at keycard slot like he is wondering how come door is opening without keycard in it forgetting he is opening it just a second ago himself from inside.

He is shrugging, puzzled-style.

He: 'Eltham.'

'What?' I ask.

'Eltham!'

It is like he is full mouth of pillow chomper. Not mentioning to my hearing never being more than 75 per cent on account of That Abscess I am pained with when I am tot.

Then penny is falling that his meaning is 'welcome' but it comes out 'Eltham'.

I cannot say I am not spooked because I am.

Eltham is the place I go with My Mother all those years ago as soon as we arrive to Our Blighty Shore which is soon after I have That Abscess ironically. We are looking for My Father because that is place The Letter comes from. I long to see his craggy film star features including big smile with gleaming incisor teeth and hug him daughter-style all laughter and cuddles.

There are poplar trees. There is chippie by roundabout.

Nice and sunny but batter is soggy.

We do not find him. At the little house with broken hedge mended by soggy hardboard man wearing yukky vest is new here he does not know My Father's name. My Mother knocks on every door in street. She points at little house with broken hedge. The neighbours do not know. They have not known My Father's mother Shirley. They are suspecting people looking round the edge of door.

We get on train. Into carriage with man holds pliers there's sticky plaster on his throat.

My Mother is holding her head and cries tears for lost love and father of child.

My Father is important electrical engineer consultant foreman. With special responsibility at new power station of sixth fourth year in Our Country working on contract. He loves My Mother. She is young. She is so respecting education she is bookreading. One day she will be Teacher of Model Citizens of Tomorrow. They walk hand in hand. Spring blossom days in orchards in Our Country. Later orchard trees will be bearing fruit. They stare in blue waters of our famous lakes. They lie together in clearing of our scented pinewoods. He earths dangerous electrical timber-saw in yard of My Grand-mother. It is potentially lifesaving repair. Then his contract is finished and he must attend in Good Old Blighty promising to return but all that comes is The Letter. He is never seeing his daughter Shirley so named because that is name of Mother of My Father.

Man with pliers is tearing off sticky plaster to show me his crusty throat wound bleeding.

That is all way way back. Long ago before I take fulltime option for sake of Desna (7 months).

I never take her to look for *Her* Father.

Her Father is just passing gonk. Faceless trade. Wheezy creepy. With bottle-thick glasses, milky white glasses frames so you hardly see his eyes are tiny dots like they are dipped in milk and it leaves coating. He is short of breath so I even think he is going to die on me squashing all breath out of me. It does happen, yes it does happen. That is all I am remembering. I am almost sure he is The One.

It does not make me love her less.

I admit it hands up. I am working even before I have her little mouth to feed. But only as casual, mind, freelance, as common as pudding Shirley, not luxury brand Shirelle. It is for My Mother's I work in those days. With her industrial restricting her work oppor-tunities, frankly her being into worklessness. Her domestic economy contributions are shortfalled. But it is temporary basis only.

There is long time to go between then and hospital diagnosis My Mother sick with Happy Larry. Untreatable Happy Larry.

'In the matrilineal tradition, following the fate you were apparently born to . . . The endemic criminality of the Demerara Park area is a stain on the city, a social plague which must be eradicated . . . I've no doubt your father is ashamed of you both . . .'

That is what foul cow is saying to me. Her real words. They are paste in book of My Mother. Cutout souvenirs to remember past with. Straight out court record as reported.

What is Posh Old Beak Milady Vanier JP knowing concerning My Father?

What is she knowing concerning how he turns back on us? How he disappears.

Cow. Posh Vanier Cow better-than-you cow. C-word Bitch-style cunt. Presuming this, presuming that, telling me I have no moral compass. Is that crime? Have you seen price of compass at local branch North Face?

Milady Vanier JP remembers My Mother is up before her – Cow – in past because of name and address as luck would.

It is not like I am butterface munter all sub-zero blue veins shivering. It is not like I am shame minger built for comfort not for speed so can't even get checkout job because of institutionalised obesity prejudice.

It is not like I am apprehended in sad kerbies backstreet under flickery light in shadows.

Who does she think I am? Ten quid trick?

Did anyone ever want hot surging love with *her*? No sir! She got old non-gloss spiral-wire hair.

150 per cent gods' truth is I was only up before Milady Vanier JP Beak Cow because of so freak fatality incident.

I am not even working am I! Yeh? I am not working in escort culture that night. Not looking to doing intimacy. It is off-duty bus-driver romance we are talking.

Fate or what?

Me I am bringing luck for people see? I am bringing luck for distinguished visitor to Our Blighty Shore.

Steel grey at temples, sleek presentation with hefty watch valid to 1,000 metres scuba depths and not comedy cufflinks as favoured by middle ranking UK middle managers. No sir, white-gold debonair clusters of priceless popcorn. Big man. Exceptional big man. Big as two men. Inform estimate: 160kg = 25 stone. Swell belly travels before him as warning of him arriving. So he is rich rich. A Lord.

I first see him as he is sitting all across two chairs at roulette at exclusive Casino Club Tivoli (Restricted – Members Only). Tower of chips stacked up high. I wonder mischievous if he is making subtle mission statement about his geronimo potential as well as showing he is rich. I am not targeting but I cannot pretend there is not fleeting murmur of glances, little electric bonsoir of optical acknowledging we are two people astride the same planet world. He stacks chips higher.

Time passes. About half an hour?

When I go by the table again the tower of chips is no more but just a stub like it has been demolished in controlled explosion set off by heartrending brave cancerkiddy as treat before they die. When they show on local news I weep.

He was drained off of colour. And sweat running down his distinguished features is bad sweat, worry sweat. Not good sweat nor workout sweat. I am telling from its dribbling thin. Not good sweat with thick syrup stickiness. When he sees me there is this expression. He pushes chips across table towards me not looking where they are going fixing me with expression that is pleading with me pleading bless choice of numbers and colours saying it is now or never do or die with big expression underwater eyes of his. Pisces or what?

He is making me responsible for him dicing with chance.

The wheel spins.

Whirring ahead his fate at its mercy.

Ominous revolving. He is transfixed. Whirring stops and ball clickclacks towards date with destiny. I cannot see exactly what square his chips are down on because of myopia from The Measles (5) makes it blurry.

But I can see from reading his face he wins. He is looking like his man in shock. Good shock, bad shock, it is different from sweat, it is all shock – the way you do not believe it is happening to you. Just gaping not believing. Then he is raising his eyes to me and they speak maximum volumes to say I am accomplice to him from that moment on. Two of us together. In it.

Do you ever see man on winning streak? Empowered. Win win win. The croupier is all worry – tower of chips is growing into sky-scrapers. Each time he wins he looks at me. There is uncooked energy conducting from him. He is Lord. Then he stops. Has he intimated run of luck ending? Does he believe inevitable is about to stop occurring?

He stands and gathers his chips.

We walk out together without saying word to each other – romantic as lush strings stopping only to cash his chips. GBP 4,200 in crispy notes. I will never forget that night.

He is Timofei.

He quip: 'Where I come from there is vowel famine. According to Government there is problem of vowel distribution!'

Bell is ringing for Sir Geoffrey. I am saying little joke again how a bart is writing as bt because of saving ink tradition of aristocracy top people.

Timofei coincidencing. He has been negotiating with a bart/bt since being on Our Blighty Shore. Important leverage interfaces. Confidential. Hushhush. Where Timofei come from is special place Crimea which is beautiful place with troubled history and special scuba activities I must go there.

He is top man international consultant in his field of applied galvanology and corrosion limitation with application to new container technology.

I tell him I am in The International Communications executivising between option weighing. Impressed, he longs for seduction candlelight and heady exoticism. He has never before luxuriated in anywhere like Horeb El Isha Bar & Diner, its deep sumptuous cushions, its traditional Berber tent accommodation, its ambience of The Aromas of The Souk, its taste of The Mysterious Tuareg, its authentic accents of The Maghreb, its colourful recollection of The Desert and Nomad Appeal, its four hour long Happy Hour – but that is over before we get there.

That night I learn life lesson: you can still be happy when happy hour has passed. You can be happy till hour when dawn relights world bright anew. You can be more than happy. You can be seethed with light of love. If only for hour or two.

That was all we have together Timofei and me. We recline on deep sumptuous cushions. He has healthy healthy appetite eating plate of little pies and carrot salad and mechoui, then big sugar pastry pie of pigeon meat I quip it's seagull who knows, then luxury perfume duck and pear tajine, then couscous with braised lamb, grilled lamb, grilled lamb kofta and grilled lamb merguez that are colouring his face orange. He tell me Vegetarian cannot enter Kingdom of Heaven: research in Russian region Crimea prove that. I stir hot sauce in broth for him because this is new for him. Then he eats honey cakes, then more almond paste cakes, pistachio pastry, rosewater jelly. When he go burpy burpy burp burp I laugh, not ticking him off!

At his recently moved into fully appointed service apartment still awaiting phone connection and curtains we dyson carlos then we make rapture love like a body symphony of senses starting at French kissing moving to French without any light but moonlight because of curtains not delivered and being overlooked by adjoining.

Tree boughs swishing romantic seasonal soundtrack empowered by whispering breezes.

He is powerful lover hulk. He is directing extra-heavyweight capacity so I feel full torque and gigadrive of his geronimo.

Then he is unburdening his lovelog.

I feel his Formerly Soviet Loveload flowing within me like famous quiet river The Don. I lie still side by side in bath of warm satisfaction coatings.

I think at Desna fingers crossed she will be all right with My Mother knowing to make herself jumbo milkshake breakfast.

We dyson more carlos. He has handsome supply. We quaff class scotchwhisky and Timofei joke he is only Russian in whole Russia who drink scotchwhisky poison of choice instead of traditional vodka because it helps chronic indigestion resulting in chest pain!

We are soulmates with so many interests shared such as knowledge-thirst and curiosity and interest in world. We could exchange chat all night long. But he is having afterglow and early morning rendezvousing with colleagues of much respected Sevastopol business fraternity from homeland Crimea too! I watch deep sleep sweep over him wishing him sweet dreams. First he is making snores shuddering like big lorry with braking defect. Then he is making snores who are pleadings and cries of whimpery little tot followed by sound of two-stroke spluttering into distance when torturer leave for work in bakery.

I am not rifling furtive through cash-rich wallet and possessions even though he does not know my identity because this is start of something many splendoured, seachanging of life itself hopefully so best behaviour.

When I wake up it is such new day. It is our first morning. Grey sky. I walk through service apartment with unpacked luggage, boxes, crates, trunks and benefits big possibilities of full aspiration into luxury. I step out on little balcony and breath air, all clean from abundance leaves and chlorophyll environment. Birds singing in trees I do not know which sort not being expert but they are lovely trilly chirpy songbirds. And lovely trees also as full of leaves like full head of nurture hair.

Perfect green striped lawn. It is having cosseted grooming at a upscale salon stretching to the next block. Only downside to little slice of paradise is ginger-biscuit rust flakes on my hands from balcony rail. Opportunity for refurbish. Also opportunity for refurbish — tarnished gold tap in bathroom. I wash my hands with powerful musky masculine soap — so very Timofei!

Soap squeak from my lathering. My Mother saying squeaks soap makes they are yelps of ghosts of aborted children they manufacture soap from. They are buying little mite-kiddies wholesale from clinics backdoors under cover of night. That is why I keep Desna in my wound till she is ready as lovely gurgle baby. I do not want to find myself thinking I am applying her as face-cleanser albeit non-animal tested.

What fantastic home this would make for me and Desna I dream to myself weighing up step-parenting potentialities of Timofei incisively. I am ticking boxes.

Kind ✓.

Money ✓.

Prospects (professional) ✓.

Travel (longhaul plus Frequent Flyer upgrades) ✓.

Second language for Desna assist at career future ✓.

Etc ✓.

I step into kitchenette to make my new love cup of coffée ready to prepare him for important meeting and take it to him wifestyle. Dainty. But there is no coffée or tea and kettle is filled by dusty fungus smelling dead. Obvious he pursues Crimea custom of eating out always even breakfast. I can get into that, I can get my head round that. No pain. I have glass of tap water and look at pictures in illustrated auction catalogues of worldclass auction of Christies, Drouot, Sotheby – names I hear from Sir Geoffrey Shadoxhurst Bt. There are so many beautiful things in Our Worldclass World. Timofei is writing notes in margins. Little writing with turquoise pen.

I go and get back in the bed ready for second helpings.

My Mother has saying of Our Country: Sleep is Swaddling Fleece of Night. I must shave fleece from Timofei like he is ram-sheep. He is so gentle considerate loving lover but not Wideawake Club member number one. My dozy Lovelord. He loves carlos for breakfast: Full Crimean he quips. He is gradual surging. Going through gears like slow powerful artic that carries extra wide cargo. Then there is this happening. Powerful artic is stopping being slow. Is just stopping. Like hill is too steep for engine. Timofei is making so funny noises. Castanets noises from Spain. Rattling.

'Flamenco and fan for senorita please!' I joke at him.

He is just weight on top of me. More heavy ever than was. Sacks and sacks style total weight like ocean. He is pinning me on bed. This is Russian sense of humour joke so I interject playful tease tickle on rubbery thick cloud of fat hanging off of him over side of me all way to bedsheet. Same cloud on other side of me also. I am filling in pie! I am looking over bulk shoulder of Timofei to sky through window. Strange bird black as crow but not crow flutters past window like she is learning to fly paddling in air. She is kind of transparency but not see-through transparency. Like she is made of negligee netting.

I say: 'Timofei my honeybabe you squashing me.'

They are denouncing I am vampire.

Men are hooked on vampire. Newspaper says top soapstar divorces vampire movies actress Vadi Sadgrove because she refuse to wear false vampire teeth when she do loveplay gobbling.

Not true I am vampire. That is not nice to say. Vampire is drinking from blood of still living. I am not fulfilling strange vice habit. For thirty minutes poor Timofei does not move. Nor I cannot move. Nor I cannot move him. This is beyond joke.

So I can tell straight off he is dead. My love is dead. The dove of life is flown dressed as crow. Then he is cold. Colder than ambient which is frankly muggy for time of year. No joke at all.

Absolute Discretion Assured is overlooking what kitten must do in total irreversible fatality circumstance.

His lips are blue like same blue as blue bits of blue cheese. Yeh? Drinking from blood of dead is not vampire. It is sacrament drinking. I make bond with my dead Lovelord. But not till I am wriggling out from under him inciting bruising to ribs and breasts which is professional no-no albeit not vocation threat.

Why?

I am asking why does he die.

I am not referring The Mycardial Infection.

It is fate question I demand answer to.

When I am having good luck why must bad luck be following straightaway like woodjaw after good old knees up night on town?

There is family jigsaw puzzle when I am living in Our Country. Difficult difficult puzzle because so much so white and I am child. Many months to complete.

When pieces are joined picture is showing faithful dog guarding body of Master perished in snow blizzard. Scene is so sad so many pathos. Beard of Master has icicles in him and eyebrows also. There is loyal tear in eyes of dog. There is same tear in my eyes too. There is blood on dogteeth of dog, blood on snow. Dog is hungry. He drinks Master to survive himself. It is not same as me.

I am personal eucharisting in tradition of Our Country where we are religious, just like Pope. It makes My Departed Love holy like Blessed Jesus lamb of god. I drink Jesus lamb of god every week. I drink so much him there should be nothing left! But Jesus not running dry like pub nor popular bar in happy hour. He is special case, Jesus.

Hunters from Grandmother village hunting The Savage Elk With Crown of Infinity Tines find man living in rock cave inside Hooknose

Mountain of famous mists legend in Our Country. Mists are pale ghost wreaths dancing slowly.

Man is very old and very young. He is eating red white spot fungus mushrooms. He is saying I Am Blessed Jesus lamb of god. He is saying Saviour is returned to earth. In order to do Saving. Starting with hunters who are finding him. He makes miracles with tree resin and moss. With clouds and ice. He has hand palm marks. Strange strange voice. Sweet sweet breath. He knows to mend engine of tractor. Distributor head who is at fault.

He sits with hunters in tractor trailer. They forget The Savage Elk With Crown of Infinity Tines. Blessed Jesus lamb of god shivers at mountain descent where forest begin to grow so all is dusk in road between dark high trees. But he brings light with his eyes and being. He shivers because he is victim thin from diet of fungus mushrooms and pine needle and lichen.

The hunters chain him to floor at old pig sty house. They fit for right size barbed wire crown.

They feed him *milla* grain, orchard fruits apple greengage pear plum, root of swede, duck eggs, hen eggs, goose eggs, potato pie, *bruss*, ass's curd, onion broth, fresh cheese, barley bread soup they make with woman breast milk for honoured guest.

Month after month Blessed Jesus lamb of god grow fat fat.

When he is fat enough so fat he cannot move they pull him from pig sty house. So fat they have to break pig sty house walls so they can move him on trolley.

They try crucify him on hill but he cannot climb hill.

They build new cross near river. But wood of cross snap break because Blessed Jesus lamb of god is obesity heavy like My Beloved Timofei.

So instead they are silently cutting his throat at altar in historical monument church of Santa Hessel.

They eat him because that is way to honour communion oneness with him in Ultimate Eucharist in remembrance of him.

He is so fat there is goodmouth morsel for everyone of Grandmother village.

They drink honey beer they sing they are joyous shouting dancing they free-feast him every bit. Warm blood, strip flesh bones, colon, intestines coil (which are being wash and brushed up because Blessed Jesus lamb of god is constipated by eggs), kidneys, white kidneys, brain, liver.

My Mother is just tiny nipper when she partake Ultimate Eucharist.

She make joke when she come to Our Blighty Shore about god liver oil that Welfare government tells she must feed me for my crumbly bones! Frequent guest calls government deep pinko.

See! It is not because of body thirst I am drinking Timofei. It is spirit thirst. It is souvenir snorter of remembrance. Memory is rust taste of elite blood. I am never forgetting My Timofei because of that taste.

Other souvenir is cash he is winning. GBP 4,200. He cannot take them with him is he? I believe myself full entitlement.

Credit/debit cards: Elysium Diamond, Odysseus, Lagoon, Orchid, Nimrod, Otter, Plantagenet, Aristocard, Pegasus, Zephyr, Ambrosia.

I am not stealing thief. They are all signed with Timofei's manful signature, dead manful signature.

I leave also passports. He has three passports from different countries – he is international consultant. No use for me: face is not fitting!

Bonus souvenir is in wardrobe where I look because Timofei passing on orbits me in deepvein shock. There are boxes and many suitcases. There is strange strange smell. Not bad smell but smell like forest in autumn time, brown smell not box and suitcase smell. I am wondering. I open.

I never see so much toys. So much old toys from far-off time. Such beautiful toys. Owl with turning head is money box. Tin horses pulling carriage with driver and milady in high wig inside. Wooden theatre stage with curtains and rows of pirates and sailors and rigging ships and town tavern on olden days quay and cloud with lightning. Dogs. Wigwams. Kaleidoscopes. There are many many. Country farm with barn, cows, hayricks, milkmaids, nosering bull, gates who open, churns, farmer, cart, pig sty . . . Is so like real farm because so dirty. All beautiful old toys are so dirty. Why does no one look after them? It is like lovely ruined buildings. Why I ask myself. Why does everything have to be like us human folks and die? Many toys are rusty. I am thinking Timofei has not done corrosion limitation! I do not know if Desna (9) will like them because they are old and dirty. I take two suitcases of toys. So heavy I can hardly walk. I call taxi control. No available vehicular solution they say. I have to wait till one come along.

I mourn for Timofei.

World is sad. Sun is hiding now. Sky needs wash and brush up. There is grime type dirt on rhododendrons. There is plastic bag litter tidemarking round roots. Pavement is dog toilet even in quality leaf suburb.

The taxi driver make improper suggestion. He is old, he is ugly. I repartee him he has to be joking matey.

I am wondering now: is it him grassing me up because I am scorning?

Next Saturday bright and early boys in blue come calling. They are not vice boys in blue. I gratify mutual benefit aplenty in working relationship with vice boys in blue.

No. Boys in blue who come calling are The Revenue. They are going rattattattatt on front door. Rattattattatt go their pick axes. They do that because they are wanting neighbours to hear for humiliating purpose at breakfast. They are asking question about Timofei. They are rough men and bad voices.

Where are toys in suitcases? They are cruel joking me that I manslaughter Timofei with energy sex. Where are toys in suitcases? They threaten. How do I like sound of prison? Where are toys in suitcases? How do I like sound of lesbo-butch electrodiesel screws rupturing me with strapadictomy in piss stink cell? I am weeping. Where are toys in suitcases? My Mother is trying to enter room for comforting. They are saying she is obstructing in execution of duty. They are saying she is old whore. They are laughing saying she is worse: she is old whore trying to make comeback. My Timofei is fat thieving vat-dodging bastard crim fraud. Why was he not connecting his landline? Where is his mobile? Where are toys in suitcases? I am heartless bitch. Do I know where toys in suitcases come from?

They come from graves of children.

In olden days there is more illness epidemic issues to name scarlet fever, yellow fever, mauve fever, grey fever, mallowrash, the Wailes, diphtheria, witherhives, Quartermaine's, typhus, the Niels, Spackman-Brock syndrome. In olden days children die often. In France, Germany and others they are burying precious sentiment toys with tragic tot.

They are saying My Timofei with accomplice unknown possibly Swiss featuring eastern Mediterranean origins male (35) and accomplice unknown probably Turkish speaker German at Bavarian accent bald male (45–50) – do I know them? – are pretending to be cemetery workers so they are digging up kiddy graves for looting toys from coffin sometimes under cover of night at many far-off cemeteries such as Mulhouse, Metz, Sedan (France), Braunschweig, Verden, Regensburg (Germany) plus other places many more. They say me I am accomplice too of evil desecration trade. Me.

Upstairs I show them toys I give to Desna (9). I am innocent. If I am knowing do I give them to Desna? No – because of tetanus disease risk. My way of thinking is tragic tots are not playing with dirty rusty toys in heaven. Now they are angels with angel toys. No sharp edges and do not put bag over head.

The Revenue are labelling toys each one to sterilise container. It is slow work. They are yearning in their eyes to spit on me when they go but they do not. Instead they are promising they are going to throw books at me.

There is no proof I am witting receiving stolen property. So they measure me. I am charged with Soliciting in Casino Club Tivoli (Restricted Members Only). Duty Manager Baudoin says that he is wanting to help but he has livelihood to consider about gaining wherewithal to provide for his love ones in our jungle-style world of ours.

What is good in nick is . . .

I reword.

What is bad in nick is everything and then some, plus.

Smell.

Mingers that live all life there.

Strapadictomy community have metal lovelogs bigger hurtier than real lovelog.

Nick sniffers they come 'prison-visiting' for no-payment suck and fuck because they know we sick of self-paradising. Dog-Food Freud he was always on the pounce. He bring Armagnac. I never see that famous from long ago Daffy Loopy Longford that had eyes for Evil Incarnation Myra only.

Desna is Taken Into Care but she is brought back.

The Sosh never think it right she is Taken Into Care, it is Beak Cow Vanier ignoring their considered recommendations.

She will go to college studying to be eminent lawyer like Mr Anwar Yunus. He is man with good heart in right place showing wandering hands and good heart are going together so I am not saying nothing nor backchatting.

He has fine business brain. It is found in family gene.

His cousin Mr Tariq Yunus is international businessman with business interests in property, investment, leisure, residential-care and hospitality sectors. They will look after her.

Mr Tariq's most proudest achievement as CEO Absolute Discretion Assured is he is introducing Mandatory Recognition Criteria Training. It is necessary for kittens without much on first floor. But they are silly cows who are complaining what he is docking for training. They are not appreciating it is safety and wellbeing. Ironically ones without much on first floor are from Uni. They have hair and grace style behaviour system.

Mr Anwar and Mr Tariq share my dream of better life for Desna (9): she already has head start because I fill her father name in birth certificate with aristocratic Arnaud von Arnaud so she is Desna von Arnaud.

Like me, Mr Anwar and Mr Tariq do not want her turning tricks before she is out of school. They do not want her truanting to bread-win at tender age, apprenticing as kitten before GCSE, learning how to strategise likes of Dogg (Holistic Thanatological Guru).

They are all same frankly. They are flapping hands all nervy anxiety to get you in room but ironically they are not sure they really want you in room. They are gesturalising inner conflict.

It is conscience who is struggling in wrestler match against desire. You are thinking desire is always going to be winning but official statistic is different – between 50 and 60 per cent. It is when

920

conscience is winning wrestler you are asking for trouble because gonk is going to deflect mechanism guilt, deflect mechanism shame. You are advised watch out because you may be focus for his anger issue.

He is not going to direct self-hatred at himself is he? What you have to consider is namely till he opens door you are just fantasy. Even if you are matching his fantasy he may be consuming overwhelming self-disgust for infidelity.

What I am weighing is: is GBP 587.50 (inc. VAT, less 20% commission = GBP 469.50 gross but there might be gratuity tip on top) and candlelight dinner worth taking risk? What is chance of him being welcher or abusive hitter?

I have mere seconds for making mature decision. Also hotels turn blind eye because concierge is always on backhander but that doesn't mean they don't get up hump if there is trade transaction going on in corridors, haggling and that.

Is this Dogg (Holistic Thanatological Guru) reliable punter?

Recognition Criteria/Client Profile:

Age: Near-average Businessman age.

Social Status: The Jubilee Blue Riband is International Executive Hotel★★★★★.

Hair: Medium-short tidy groomed blond. Suspicion that out of bottle assist.

Face: Regular features. Clean shaving. Expression is younger than he, puzzled, hurt. He is wearing that lost look of youth. He is abundance tanned from considered tanning.

Dress: Smart casual, krisp-prest, comes to door jacket buttoned.

Other: Apart he is smelling mini-bar breath he is smelling fresh. He is lavishly splashing on fragrance in lively Mediterranean accents. Lemon notes with followthru pine. That is good sign like he launder clothes. Fragrance and grooming signify sure sign of pride and confidence.

All kittens will tell you it is stinky gonks with crusty smeg of low self-esteem and body hygiene telltale are ones that turn.

Them and mini-bar abusers.

Even when they are steadying across carpet they are risk. Nor can Dogg (Holistic Thanatological Guru) stand hardly. He is tasking to remember where he is. Just because he is legless as legend air-ace does not prove he cannot hit. He may have latent violence agendas who are remaining unaddressed. When they are like this they can kill and forget what they have done.

The other thing they forget is whereabouts of wallet.

Blimey that smile!

Is he learning his smiling skills from bookreading and is not learning well?

It is how my My Grandmother is after osteoarthrosis gimp her hands – she is still knitting. She drops needles like pick-sticks. It is touching. I am being sincere sorry for her even if my devil side as I call it drivers me so I am laughing to myself. Shhshh!

That is how I am considering about Dogg (Holistic Thanatological Guru), it is like with clowns taking tumbles. But I do not let my feminine sympathy get in way of rational overview and mature judgement.

There were no hatreds in his eyes, not left eye not right eye. They are pleading windows to vulnerable soul. Drunk and sober some gonks show wrong courtesy. He holds out both hands to shake. Big so big like goalkeeper gloves of legend goalkeeper Miodrag Galca. But soft. His hands are soft. Hitter's hands? There are no hatreds in them neither.

It is all humiliation visiting into A&E at RSH with another package of shiners for poor paid nurses to snigger. Shiners are not career enhancers, short-term or long-term. My looks are my life till I am stashing up enough to move on upskilling in new vocation rectangle.

Dogg (Holistic Thanatological Guru) has mystified expression about me standing there. He looks like cutesy puppydog on birthday card. Begging.

Never let on your doubt. It fires the resentment. Which also leads to anger. Lesson hard learnt. I take chance. I am raising my eyebrows how they do in old films, haughty and knowing, letting on that I know what he has been up to, kidding ticking him off for being such naughty one making free with miniatures and quarter-bottles. He plays along making face like little boy caught out bang to right behind shed.

I consider we are digging deep foundations of mutual respect.

★

Interpersonal compact must extend beyond provider and client if The Transaction is to be successfully expedited.

I am proceeding by single step into room mental mindful to remain on corridor side of him. I am leaning towards right to lean against him. Making him feel you are together in stadium of friendship. Greeting him with hug who implies friendly mate intimacy nor just promise of service.

It is also way with gonk in jacket to sussing if he is carrying wallet. He is. It is in his puppytooth jacket inside pocket. I feel big bulge in his ribcage. I train bosom to learn wallet detecting!

That settles him.

Game on!

I guide him past open bathroom door. Vanitory top is clustering colognes, moisturisers, shampoos, conditioners etc. etc. More bottles than I ever know man travel with, more than women travel with even frankly.

The room is same like every executive hotel room I ever work in.

I am world expert about them, I could attend big money quiz, my special subject is hotel room. I study them off by my heart. They are nice and tasteful with varnish and baby blues and beiges and taupes and pretty stencilling patterns and every so comfy chairs and glaze cotton curtains always match something else, they have those tasselly ropes for client wanting bondage (extra: negotiable tariff). Always framed olden-time scenes of foreign cities with empty wigs and bridges, special leather binder for literature relating abundant museums of steam heritage on This Shore and country parks such as Führer World, light switches who cannot ever work out how they lower to romantic ambience grade, desks, fancy wastebins match curtains, extra cushions, adult pay channel option TV I am welcoming because it is assist who hurry along experience, clean carpet not forgetting mini-bar, not forgetting bed, not forgetting tissue wipes in box who is matching curtains also. You get pissed gonks wiping lovelog on curtains – they are getting grief grazes when they forget new style boutique hotels have metal venetian blinds!

I know this room back to hand but that is not saying I like them.

If you gent is operating fork-lift in warehouse do you like fork-lift? Nor warehouse?

For me hotel room is just workplace with all everyday workplace stress issue. Acting moaning plus pleasure murmurful noises. Ecstasy excitement theatre. Telling same old love lies. Not showing I am bored from my skull. Praying all while to egress in one piece back home with Desna.

Because I am here so many times so to speak I do not make many observations immediate on entering to tell truth. He is moving paper bundle for me to sit making myself every so comfy before I take it all in. The room in itself is no different per se. They always have the telly on sound switched down like he is lonely with it lighting up room if no lighting.

What is different is mess who feature total total clutter.

There is so many stuffs all over room. Not usually how one night stopover is. It is not like even he is Privileged Traveller on Epée four-night conference package inclusive Fidelity Full English. Conference package gonks are Wed and Thurs business usually – days when they find nerve to register for quality companion. On Tues such as this is it is usually slow due to colleagues become interpersonal dialoguing each other loosening tie over bottle bonding from Conference.

There is not anywhere where there is not something. They all have phone/camera/laptop/DVD/pen-drive/external hard drive etc. etc. Dogg (Holistic Thanatological Guru) even has so day before yester-day floppy-discs. He has boxes including them on desk scattered around plus box-files, pens, notepads, post-its, staplers whathaveyous. Not mentioning papers, folders stretched with papers. Readdressed envelopes who are never being open. Telephone directories, towers of telephone directories – telltale he is not subscribing to online 118. Naturally going without saying empty miniatures lined up on teev. Also wine empties like he is into room-service abuse as extra.

I never see that many things in hotel room. There is just so much piling up any old how. Broken suitcases, grips, shirt in packets back from dryclean, jackets sleeves out of wardrobe, big black shoes, orange cartons, carrier bags.

It is making me think at filthy street-subs. Yucky clothes all piss drip stained, no hair care, face wound, operative scar, scabby sore, all their life possession in rust supermarket trolley. But Dogg (Holistic

Thanatological Guru) is not street-sub. I bet you long odd he never has pavement pitch who he swaps for executive hotel room even if he is drinking short! He has self-respect because he is clean with hairdye and his fragrance.

What else is on the desk? Weird. There is two snapz feature teenage kids. Pretty boy coming on sourpuss. Girl doing pouty real little miss. What is weird is they both have faces all scratched across. They are torn, scribbled-up, stabbed. They are subjected to frenzied attack. Then put back in frame behind glass. Weird or what?

He is so stumbly I go fetch him water in toothglass from mixer-tap set in class marble vanitory. It takes while before it comes cold. I observe he is not pampering with gratuity products. Shampoo sachets and luxuriating body foamscrub are not opened.

When I come back he is sitting on edge of bed. Feet dangle like they say depressed suicide sits on parapet of tall building about to precipitate himself into void of oblivion but no danger here it is different because of carpet being so close.

He is jerking remote control at telly with wrong end pointing like special-needs.

I turn it round for him so he surf till his heart content. He would not be first who makes me sit there during vital European clash and him swearing. If I have GBP1 for every gonk who is losing urge because of watching his Blighty Nation team losing to amateurs with hard-to-say names from mighty footballing Malta or Faroes I would so been running my own vocation nail clinic by now not this.

He had button punching gene. It is man thing. Women do not have it in us to be impatient hardly waiting to see What The Digital Treasure Chest In Your Living Room Holds albeit hotel room then going on to next channel choice. He was not into football. Both games were team in red and white v. teams in all blue ironically not same blue but spooky or what?

The adult is not his cup of tea neither. Bull Hose and Amethyst de Kala co-starring Kennydé Skill introducing Hall Dunnerdale in *Tradesmans Entrance* with triple as come-on but it does not do anything for him watching just free preview up to invite to subscribe with no volume then shifting through music channels muttering it is all programmes for brats he call them.

He burrows in pile of newspapers like dog digging for bone throwing them about not caring where they go. He finds bulk channel guide book leafing through it. He select on screen selection for Stadium Gold Privilege menu. He swears. He finds volume switches right up full toot.

I so observe definite psychological mood swing.

Dogg (Holistic Thanatological Guru) is deep concentration hunched studying in manner of speaking. You cannot mistake he is looking for something. Stadium Gold Privilege is all niche sports. He clicks slowly waterski, hang-gliding, curly, all weather hockey, bowls on tempting velvety lawn you just long to stretch out to relax awhile and caress yourself on. He tunes to racing yachts leaning over water one way with all crewmen leaning out other side, on-board cameras capture high drama of man pitting with ocean. It is not ocean because in distant shore background chimneys and picksticks puzzle of pipe flames industrial-might canisters are Petrol Refinery definitely.

To make The Repartee I tell him it has been called wryly hilarious scary incident of life-threatening life-experience in exclusive marina down there near Petrol Refinery:

This uppity gonk owns de-luxe motor-cruiser wants to do lick-off for GBP 100 extra. He smears jar of runny honey with crunchy comb inclusive over my box on deck. Then he forgets. He must go inside to fetch cooling sangrilla jug. He is having to crawl because folk on boat in next marina berth are not seeing he wears nor birthday suit, not only but with a lifestyle-size geronimo on him because of prelude menu!

I am lying there, cheap-at-price lunchmeat slab on deck, honey dripping on towel and just my shades pleasuring myself as he request and hating myself as I tell Dogg (Holistic Thanatological Guru) in my confidence.

Gonk is just crawling back out from cabin – when all these wasps, cloud of them like starlings in top-grossing eco-menace *Viral The Prequel 2*. Because they smell honey I am attacked by wasps honey is attracting them to.

Gonk screams and drops jug. There is sangrilla flood everywhere. And he is totally panic and shuts cabin door to keep wasp cloud out.

They are all over my box like wildlife. I am staring so much death in face so to speak. Wasps have wasplike instinct.

I do not lose cool it is sense it is happening to someone person different place and time. I act purposeful. I leap myself over boat rail in water so I am not becoming freak fatality statistic twisting my ankle. Bugger it what folk in next berth are thinking. Wasps drown.

So this is what honey-smother with crunchy comb leads to on boat. Down marina way anyway. Because there are wasps every whichway there because of orchards, glasshouses My Mother is calling fruitholdings which is funny word she is learning from friend but not so funny thank you when they are trying to sting you for death in hunting pack. Plus splintery needles of sangrilla jug up ball of foot.

It does not break ice with Dogg (Holistic Thanatological Guru).

He does not hear a word I am saying.

He is all self wrapped in looking at his watch then telly then channel guide then his watch again not listening or even forgetting I am there with his back to me.

Frankly it was more interesting looking out crimson window.

Far-off treetops up over Tolly Dene. Strange how they are romance from distance, trees up Tolly Dene are fat green clouds. But full mank when you get up there among them which I do not because of my total self respect not to mention litter, kerbies, flashers, date rapers.

Other way there, down the port, colourful containers stretch for ever like little toy building blocks all ready to have a magic castle built out of them. I think at poor Timofei.

There are traffic jams of cruiseliners clogging the estuary. They are big as sink estates which no one gets off because norovirus. They have to wait till vomiting has stopped. Some kittens hire little boats out to them. They are being winched up to service hungry logs. Fatwad GBP but the dangers of the winching! Unnecessary risk! They might fall. They might get norovirus sexually transmitted. On dry land there's patient snakes of cars and coaches queuing for ferry with traffic officers directing in their hi-visibility luminous protective clothes – there used to be more luminous tangerine now they nearly all favour luminous lemon with some into luminous lime. You can almost hear their walky-squawkies as I call them.

Alongside docks giant cranes silhouetting sunset to-die-for, deep pink and baby-blue stripes, sort of giant babygro. Very dusk, very poetic, with nursery feel to him. It is one of perks, relaxed contemplation of awesome sunset from high-up quality places.

Other perks include sophisticated conversation with fine minds with so many letters after their names it's like Scrabble™ I tell them. Never forget even intelligentsia living life of mind have their sexual needs and unnatural (!) urges, especially gents in advertising and corporate marketing sectors who are often bookwriters of important books about insourcing resolve and curating feasibility of alternative productivity assumptions. They have language command I frankly envy and do not mind telling them because flattery will get you everywhere including a generous tip on most occasions because they are lavish perk culture.

The worst fortnight of year regrettably is arts festival because operatives in arts sector are low waged and would sooner go without nor than treat themselves. Not forgetting they also get so-called blacklegs and scabsluts who will do him for nothing silly cows but amateur fashion so as not to guarantee satisfaction. Mr Tariq Yunus he is right to say you do not visit amateur solicitor or amateur dentist would you? If you got obtrusive lodging in anus you visit professional to remove him. It takes skilled professional in any field to get job done properly guaranteeing satisfaction.

That is why professionals are not coming on The Cheap. Albeit if you are professional you got obligation to client, you got responsibility to more than just profit maximising. In right circumstances you are prepared to offer loss leader, like legal aid or two fillings for price of one style deal. Absolute Discretion Assured tasks us to strategising long term. To adopting a mature interface which is a driver of goodwill, generating future custom through ethical brand recognition.

Here's for-instance:

Last time I am tendering in The Jubilee Blue Riband gentleman is elderly gentleman. Real old sweetheart gonk, Teddy. Lovely courtesy of yore with maroon beret, and row of ribbons, and medals pinned to blazer all gleaming from elbow grease because he is bespoke coach tour D-Day veterans. Pilgrimming Normandy memorial revisiting beaches where more than hundred years ago they fight for our precious freedoms and graves of fallen comrades. Their Name Shall Live For Evermore.

I give him freebie gobble because I am so into patriotism knowing Mr Tariq would understand.

Then would you believe after about twenty minutes he says he is up for another.

And so he is – standing to attention, liver spots on shaft notwithstanding, perky as teenage loofah.

Commerce get better of conscience. I am obliged to charge him. How cheap would I feel if I do not? But brightside he receive full Absolute Discretion Assured's Sunset Concessions Tariff so Teddy does not have valid complaint. It gives him something to boast to old contemptibles about when they are back from pill box visit with Local British Legion hosting.

We are good long chatting. About this and that. His wife is sadly passing on soon. No lane discipline any more. Shopping mall lack respect for them who served their country. Breakdown of the nuclear courtesy. Gobbing everywhere – if folk had a handkerchief up sleeve they are not littering mucous wetwipes on shopping mall bench. The way folk thrusts their allergy up nose expecting pity. Teddy is saying about pizza-face bespoke coach driver Spotty (!). Albeit it is not his fault, but he has The Psoriasis, Spotty has – he is leaving trail of skin flakes behind him like old-fashioned paperchase Teddy enjoyed running on gorse heath salad day.

And when anyone notice trail Spotty is joking: 'Only blossom in spring.'

He is hoping for sympathy for being disgusting. All greasy and stinky skin flakes.

Do you know, I am predicting whenever from today on I look at patient snake of coaches with ruby lights heading to The Faraway I am always remembering Gentleman Teddy, putting old stallion through paces.

★

Signs of life from Dogg (Holistic Thanatological Guru). He was getting all impatient. Doing fidgets like an itchy aspergers.

He so has that executive predator inner concentration that sets them apart up their corporate jungle world of theirs. He is staring like tiger. Stroking himself obsessive compulsive style. Rubbing at wrist hair like he's never seen it before, like he got a sore he can feel but no one can see like when rash is on its way but it does not show? When bloke realises he is a werewolf within himself?

Smiles at me what I call pathetical. His get-up-and-go got up and gone. He is staring at carpet-mysteries in world of flooring. Is he believing stainmaster polytufts send message for him, code message?

Then I consider. His face down so far he is searching.

'You losing something?'

I am big sympathy at contact lens problems with my sight not to mention hearing. I am identifying there.

'Lost something? Lost . . . ? Aah . . . hahhahhah. Aaah. That's good . . . Lost something!'

He is so strange laugh. Animal in trap with pain issue, that sort of laugh.

Then every so silent. Wraps arms around knees. Rocking backwards and forwards on carpet. He is protecting himself. From something. From himself? Voice is quiet in that hoarse way. Murmuring quiet, is deep felt, sugar-coat with sincerity but sort of mockery at himself.

'Yeh, I've lost something. Mislaid it in perpetuity.'

Rocking movements getting agitational fanatical, he is embarking into self-induced trance at this rate. Tantric is on the increase in the business community.

This is driven by the creative subornment of eastern disciplines by eminent enabler gurus in the stadia of positive zoning and differentiation analysis.

Then he stops.

He cannot not find whatever he is looking for.

So I am deep breathing and asking: 'And, so . . . Erm—?'

Just his puzzled smile again, this time more grin really.

He does not get I am trying to invite him tell his name.

It is not area to venture at too direct, name. You have to strike up balance – pretence at being interested in how he is called but not coming on prying. In my experience all executives are fearing black-mail or kiss-and-tell. Not that anyone give The Toss in executive kiss-and-tell but that is their corporate vanity on parade. You are not wanting them turning on defensive because that drives hostility. Give them time for initiating alias. Alias helps them in escaping themselves. They are more relax if they are believing you are believing they are someone else.

Then I think: mind you, name like Dogg (Holistic Thanatological Guru) is alias right off from start. Sicko alias.

Like he is after ladydog bitch to rough up.

Like Dogg (Holistic Thanatological Guru) goes dogging in car park and beauty spot with lo-hygiene amateurs with full mank rusty hatchback and is not ashamed to let on.

Like Dogg (Holistic Thanatological Guru) is letting on he is into doggy-fashion with side-order reach-around or anal.

Anal instigates fresh tariff. Danger money: helminth burrowing like POW in escape movie. Body can be bacteria bomb. If my body is bacteria bomb I am not fit for the purpose.

'Caressed with care'. 'Safe sex is happy sex'. 'Strong and rugged yet sensitive too – like you'. I use proper protection. Unless gonk is paying jumbo surcharge.

Back off kitten! I am self advising re Dogg (Holistic Thanatological Guru).

But my cavalry side is winning and I am introducing: 'I am Shirelle. I am pleased to meet you.' I am inviting his alias first name. A kitten addresses her client by name as often as possible which cement an intimacy bond. Just like tosser cold calls to sell insulation programme.

'Don't feel like eating yet, dinner. Not hungry. Didn't have much of a day. Life! Tell you what' – Dogg (Holistic Thanatological Guru) is chirping between knees, all very in command again – 'why don't I ring down for . . . What'd you like? Kümmel? Bottle of Kümmel in an ice bucket . . . But if you want something else . . . Liberty Hall here, Shirelle.'

He is remembering my name. Dogg (Holistic Thanatological Guru) so sweet, so courtesy! True gentleman!

Kümmel for post-coital in my experience, sipped on rocks in longlasting afterglow moment. I make top flight Chablis choice.

'Jerome!' He is greeting roomservice as friend man to man. He does not shoo me off in the bathroom which is another sign of gentleman. He is not ashamed he is entertaining me. Jerome ties towel round bottleneck pulling it tight so it is like a mannequin in old style magazines in The Age of Elegance. Or a cocky squash player! He sniffs cork, sophisticatedly. Dogg (Holistic Thanatological Guru) josh rough-house with him which is big-tipper way of slipping him tenner for his trouble always a good sign.

I raise honeyed glass.

'Cheers – er?' I quaffed. 'Er . . . ?' Leaving so to speak dotted line for him to fill in name on.

'It sounds funny but I just got you down as Dogg – with career vocations in brackets so to speak.' I am rash but I cannot help it.

'Two gees I hope: dee-oh-double-gee. Not ruf ruff rarff,' he barks with smile – that smile again. He is not taking hint about alias first name.

'So what business you here on then?' I try him on that.

They can be shy about repartee. Often best to get them started with something not too personal. Give them the space to talk their spreadsheets.

'You wouldn't believe me if I told you.'

There is definite regret in his voice. He means it. It is not like he is telling me MYOB or nothing.

'Try me then,' I say.

'I'm . . . I'm looking for something.'

I can identify with that.

'Aren't we all? Anything in particular?' I licks my lips intimating subtly, nothing too forward. I pop pistachio between them. May contain nuts or traces of nuts!!!

He leans his head back on bed edge and looks at ceiling: 'How about everything?'

'What's your name?' I whisper.

'It's . . .'

He is going to tell to me I swear. But he sort of jumps like he thinks of something scary. You can tell he is hurting.

He murmurs sad as can be: 'Sometimes I forget that I don't know who I am.'

He has that imploring look.

He is asking with his eyes: Do I understand him? Do I believe him?

There is no understanding what he is getting at.

But the way he looks at you you cannot help believe him.

Is he one of those tragic human interests that took blow to head and finds themselves in strange place not knowing who they are, where they come from?

'You been injured?' I ask.

Dogg (Holistic Thanatological Guru) laughs.

I moved to nearer beside him, kneel medium close.

He is a fascinating enigma for man of mystery. Maybe he forgets why I am there. He is not like any other gonk I ever met. I feel that feeling that we have known each other in almost another life, there is that spontaneous feeling of special bond between us – totally mutual especially from my way of looking. There are immense surging droves of cosmic pulses flocking like we are birds just taken on wave of flight helpless to help ourselves in our destiny.

I am putting my hand in his lap and mouth-grazing his ear. The way my heart beats tells me something really deep. Don't ask what!

He responds. There is evidence of a geronimo in making. I am experiencing so professional pleasure at his pleasure.

He may have forgotten who he is but he knows way down The Dark Highway of Love. He clasps my throat with big soft goalkeeper legend hands. They are strong and gentle as scented wipes. Power in his thumbs is awesome.

He is full of regret in advance for his actions. This is person to person profession. I cannot outsource my role.

Everyone loves pink sky reflecting on walls. Very very dusk. Like crimson blood turning to night. It is colour of going to sleep when you are mite-tot put to bed early and wondering how can you be sure you will ever wake up.

You cannot ever be sure sure, can you?

We are people grade level higher above Demerera Park. The street called Demerera Park.

We are living in area, not street.

My Mother would not be extra tertiary if doctors were not snobs about home area, mistaking street and area.

Reap as you are sowing is doctor diagnosis verdict looking down their noses talking with big potato in mouth.

Risk is name of game. I always knew it was. You would be shelf-stacking if you were not turned on by risk. With bravado that you are undertaking risk feasibility assessment.

An arrest is imminent. A head will be pushed down firm to get it in pig's squad car.

There are poplar trees in Eltham.

Desna's eyes are disappearing behind glasses thick as bottle bottoms.

Light is going.

There is pounding in my head. Apache hooves are thundering through rocky canyon.

The Force is behind thick black curtains. Compression is agonising and every so sweet. I am special in his life, I have special role in Dogg (Holistic Thanatological Guru)'s life.

I never have a role like this in anyone else's life. It is once in a lifetime role opportunity. I have never felt this way before in my life. I will never feel this way again. Breath is so precious gift. Never take breath for granted, taste each breath giving you life, savour each breath as though it is your last.

Now Known as Sacha Lipurt

We watched. We listened. We always had.

Speedwell and Meadway were our telephone exchanges, our peo-ple's telephone exchanges, the give-aways, the out-in-the-open code as sure as calling The Suburb 'The Suburb' and a wally 'a wally'. For me these ostentatious hooks of belonging were embarrassingly col-lective but Dudu binged on badges of identity because, he said, they made the wallet beat faster.

A dozen members of a Hasidic family, age range four to forty, processed past us. I watched Dudu watching. He was ill at ease, lost in doubt, gently shaking his head.

'Remember Imogen Skye?'

'How could I forget?'

'It all began with her here. That's why I like coming . . . For the guilt. I treated her like shit but there you are . . . The penitent didn't tend the foal.'

(There were other reasons too: it was a showcase of English bour-geois mediocrity, where you'd never see anyone you knew apart from your aunt, who'd approve of your staid site of recreation.)

Near the café garden where we were watching and listening there was a relic from the days when this part of London was not yet London. An unmade road of disparate, once prosperous village houses, many yet to be re-prospered, some with seldom tended front gardens, some with walls and hostile foliage (negligence rather than privacy), some which composed a Georgian terrace, whose front doors, on the contrary, opened onto the unpavemented road. From the centre of a broken window pane spread a web of cracks like the glyphs of a forgotten tribe. David, not yet Dudu, recently released from national service, was staying with his aunt and great-aunt. He was looking in vain for the greatest city on earth. His aunt oppressed him. His great-aunt slipped him money, encouraged his adventures, i.e. hanging about outside nightclubs failing to summon the courage to enter and be humiliated. He wanted to be those people with back-combed hair and intricate dance steps. Instead he was a friendless young man fighting boredom.

One sticky afternoon the week before he was to return home with tales of conquests and contacts, he walked along that unmade road. An adolescent boy sat on a folding chair outside one of the Georgian houses. He was frustratedly practising lighting a Zippo with one hand. There were strange noises in the air. Yodelling (yes, really), thumping, creaking thuds coming from the open windows.

And then, after a silence, the venom of whisper from somewhere higher in the house, the hiss of hatred and curdled words which chilled him deep.

'You fucking yid whore . . . you piece of kike shiit.' Deep south accent. Corncob plus.

David looked at the boy with the Zippo. He remained blank and set on his task.

David howled like the wind up the stairs there from the front door three at a time. A youth was flipping a deck of cards. A girl in a leo-tard beside him was trying to belch. He danced through the open door of a room where a paunchy middle-aged man in a linen jacket was strangling a woman in shorts and a vest. His squashed straw hat was on the floor.

'You four by two bitch . . . Fucking Red Sea pedestrian.'

David flung himself to the rescue, grabbing the man who recoiled, then lost his balance. David held him down. Punched his face. The woman picked herself up from the floor. She struck kneeling David's head and face with a book, and again. He clasped his cheek. His lower lip was cut.

'What on earth do you think you're doing?' asked the sprawled man, no longer speaking corncob but fruity as a pudding in velvet.

'Is this one of Keith's little pranks, the turd,' she said.

'Who's Keith . . . No . . . What am I doing . . . what d'you think I'm doing?' asked David. 'Did you hear what he was calling you . . . you some sort of masochist? I thought he was going to kill you.'

'Proves, darling,' she addressed the man, grinning, 'how very convincing we are.'

To David: 'We are a*ctors* my love. We live in a state of make believe. We aspire to the highest naturalism. Acting which is not acting. Poor boy . . .' She stroked David. 'So very very valiant. Riding to the rescue. Young Lochinvar. You'll get your reward in Imo.'

'Errhmm, lucky cunty aren't we,' oohed the man. He would get a two-paragraph obituary in *The Stage*.

The play they were rehearsing was Montgomery Palm's *Klan Bake*. The yodelling grew louder.

A head looked into the room. 'Is this . . . no . . . no this isn't advanced somersaulting is it . . . Sorry.'

'It was duty to go to Imo's aid. Unthinking duty. You don't stop to consider. I thought she was Jewish I mean if I'd known she was just acting . . . But I thought she was Jewish . . . Look I'd do it for them. If one of the children was spat on . . . the way kids are.'

He indicated the Hasidic family.

'Duty. It's in the blood.'

'Depends . . .'

'No not depends . . . Not contingent . . . Despite those shtreimel . . . that's it . . . I loathe those hats though I wouldn't mind one . . . they look great . . . but it's what they stand for . . . empty wigs . . . I despise their silly hair . . . their mumbo-jumbo . . . I despise their you-know . . . obstinacy . . . hanging onto the old ways not assimilating . . . their look-at-me-I'm-different . . . they're fucking our state our secularism . . . they're agents provocateurs baiting the Hals . . . their superiority . . . they're landgrabbers . . . it's the Wild West out there . . . oh their women are hideous . . . But I still have to fight for them. They are our people. They are total bastards but they are our total bastards! I've met a few times with Ahmad Tibi[52] . . . he understands our quandary . . . It's not a question of Babtous against Hals . . . it's a question of ancient dogmas and superstitions versus no dogma, no supernatural consolations.'

The café where we sat, that early summer evening, was in a north

---

52 Arab-Israeli gynaecologist, political advisor and member of the Knesset.

London park. It was here that the late Imogen Skye had encouraged her boy lover David with the national service body to become an actor and had decided that he should be Dudu Topaz, a pillow name out of nowhere which she assured him, oddly, rang of entertainment for all the family and seaside postcards. At RADA his alternation between Dudu Topaz and David Goldenberg was hardly remarked upon since most of his contemporaries were also trying out new names: Alan became Leigh, Harold became Hessel, Linda became Treacy, Pitman became Bourne.

Pergolas, hedges, wicket fences, plump adolescent girls exposing fubsiness to the tepid sun in hope, their little brothers holding cricket bats, bee hum, leaden cakes, tea stinking of metal polish, looking like mud, tasting of tannic mouth scrape. If it's good after stewing for an hour it'll be twice as good after two hours.

Here was the essence of English backwardness, of poetry about uncomplaining acceptance of mediocrity. Even the celebration of mediocrity. When he watched and listened it was as though he was at the circus, laughing and giggling and prodding me pitilessly pointing to a nasty case of sunburn or a subcutaneous cyst the size of a golf ball or a mewling child bullied by loutish crows: scare them off or they'll take out the eyes. They were all putting on a performance for him. He enjoyed social sadism. He called himself a 'thought crim-inal'. He had the ear of an accomplished mimic. It was part of his job – he'd call his job his art.

His devotees, acolytes and fans might agree. Anything is art if the artist, the perpetrator, says it is. Assassination, thaneting, torture, sequestration . . . they're all art. So are menace and body disposal. It takes a good lot of chopping to achieve atomisation and identifica-tion loss. One seldom talks of such matters.

'My associates,' I told him, 'want that map . . . that document. They have to have it.'

'Sure they do . . . Your *associates*. They've got to realise that they get it on my terms.'

'You don't know what you're messing with.'

He laughed: 'My guess is I'm messing with chachchahim who've learnt to tie a tie. Low level bureaucrats. Officious little people. That's who I'm messing with. You know . . . Mizrahi infiltrators wearing a suit over their djellaba. De . . . ceiv . . . ers! You can't live two thousand years among bleds and not become bled. And their hair—'

'You're going in out of your depth . . . And don't forget where I come from.'

'*Came* . . . long ago. *Came* . . . long long ago. You, my friend, are not two thousand years behind us.'

'I wouldn't be too sure about that.'

He was momentarily fazed: 'You Sephardim are not Mizrahim. Don't come on all compassionate. Solidarity with primitive inferiors is not your style. I've never noticed that real people were your style either. When Dudu Topaz made that announcement . . . historic announcement . . . saying there were going to be aliens on the show . . . which half of Israel do you think it was tuned in? 51 per cent of all homes. *More* than half the homes in the country. It was the chachchahim . . . all they can do is breed. Seven children per family *average*. They speak with Crown Heights accents. They can't read Hebrew . . . can't even say their prayers. Hey, breed read. There's a rhyme for your buddy Ricky . . . He could sing it on the show. That's the magic of Dudu Topaz. King of the Ratings. Monarch of the Masses. Prince of Populism. Sees opportunity everywhere. The man that takes the temperature of a gullible nation . . . So says *Haaretz*.'

'Aliens was . . . a jest . . . a prank. This is serious.'

'Ooh I know. And the deal is serious, meyn lib. Not negotiable. His continued presence in our midst . . . who knew . . . it's an absolute secret till he's a guest on my show . . . forty-minute chat . . . after that you can have him. Do what you like with him.'

'And Shadoxhurst? And Nowak?'

'What about them? They're there to be used. He-and-she patsies. As they'll discover. They trust me, poor chumps. I'll miss them. I like them. But they're marks, baby, marks. This is going to be one of the greatest of all coups de théâtre . . . no no . . . it's going to be *the* greatest, yeah, no question. The master entertainer makes chat show history . . . *television* history. The master entertainer transforms himself. It's got everything.'

'Including an interviewee who is, let us say, mute.'

'*Guest*. Guest. OK?'

'OK. If you will . . . guest.'

'First catch the guest. No problem. Not with the kit we've got . . . some of this tech is hyper-detector . . . conjunct it with cadaver dogs and . . . wow! there is no place on earth left where you can hide . . . It doesn't come cheap . . . The price is frightening . . . But . . . Hanna . . . woman of superlatives . . . one of the deepest pockets in the world. It won't be a problem – but you, dear heart, are not going to get a look-in till our boy is under contract to Dudu's Prime of Entertainment.

'His first public appearance in decades . . . is on my show. That's the deal. Interview him . . . remind the audience who he is . . . life story . . . what's he's known for . . . the ups and downs of his career . . . some of the fabulous people he's worked with . . . where he's going on holiday . . . then questions from the floor . . . let the little people have their moment . . . it's a talk show after all . . . the audience isn't going to know what's hit them . . . it's going to make headlines all over the world . . . and the whole world gets to hear about Führer World. Do ut des . . . This is a one-off unrepeatable event . . . even if he gets an agent and goes on tour it's always going to be remembered as Dudu Topaz's triumph . . . got him first . . . he's going to be Dudu Topaz's guest.'

By my leave. More strictly by my leave and that of persons (faceless, nameless) whom he describes in italics as my *associates*. Much as I loved Dudu – OK, liked, all right, tolerated – I intended to thwart his plan. We, my associates and I, had strategies of our own which would be undermined by his frivolous idiocies: we are serious people, we did not wish our duty towards our race to be compromised by a morally infirm circus act.

We didn't know how it would end. We could not have predicted how it would end. Who could have foreseen Dudu's foolhardy rashness and extravagant behaviour? His proxy violence? Who could have predicted that he would be so maddened that he would do everything possible to substantiate Erskine Garn's dictum that 'life is mere tragic slapstick' then follow it with incontrovertible proof that it is tragic, full stop. Hold the slapstick.

This is third hand. My information is from Dudu who wasn't even in the country. His information was from Hanna Nowak. Mendacity amalgamated with fantasy, then.

The knowledge was, emphatically, The Sergeant's and no one else's. He was in no doubt about it. He could name his price, he believed.

He tapped his crown: 'It's all in here. Nowhere else. Fort Knox. You're getting a gift no one else could give you.' He was in earnest. He meant it when he held the elaborate map and sheath of papers in one hand and waved a lighter in the other.

Eunice Pethica, Hanna's crisp lawyer (and convenor of the John Amery Society), looked alarmed. Not for the first time. The decrepit state of the house and farm did not conform to her Gray's Inn idea of bucolic cheer. Every ornament was chipped, every drift of dust was feeding an insect, every chair was splintered, every sofa was collapsing, every pot plant was ill, every cushion was greasy, every plug was a future fire, every plate was an ashtray and every ashtray was like those in a pub you'd never dream of frequenting. There were mouse droppings. The air was thick with dog hairs. Anti-macassars were steeped in the macassar of a different age. And as for The Sergeant's solicitor, the purple-faced, profusely sweating Mr Norman Bullwinkle . . . a disgrace to the profession. Did he have to scratch his fat arse so raspingly and persistently?

'It's you,' The Sergeant said to Hanna Nowak, 'who should have me over a barrel – but it isn't, is it . . .'

A coarse negotiating tactic appealing to a billionairess's altruism: 'You know what all this means to me . . . I built it . . . built it with my own hands . . . You could beat me down . . .'

'I wouldn't dream of it. The farm is your life. We give you a loan *sine die* . . . a gift in all but name . . . the Pharma Princess is the tax efficient princess.'

Poor people cannot begin to conceive of the electronic fastness I control. It makes the moderately well-off such as Mr Norman Bullwinkle feel poor . . .

'And you,' said Shadoxhurst, less spendthrift, suspicious of The Sergeant, dismissive of the map's accuracy, jokily threatening but threatening nonetheless, 'will admit us into the secret labyrinth of your bonce. Righty oh?'

'When the transfer is through,' The Sergeant smiled, '. . . when it's cleared . . . when Mr Bullwinkle here gets the call. 'Nother cuppa?'

When Mr Bullwinkle received confirmation that the first instalment had been paid into his practice's clients' account they celebrated with cider and poppyseed cake. Then they got down to business. They sat around a table encrusted with food which turned the BKG map into a relief map with little mountains. The Sergeant was proud of the exercise book he called the log and of his map from memory. He outlined as many details as he could, qualifying them 'with the passing of years – who knows'. He repeated this litany many times.

His map was fanciful and crude, *carte brute* (Shadoxhurst's coinage), an all but useless crayoned composition of diagrammatic trees, roads, paths, ponds without context. There were purposeless arrows and dotted routes. Hanna told Dudu it was 'nothing but a begging bowl'.

Hours after death the body still smelled of almonds. They wrapped it in tent canvas and baling twine. The only available vehicle was a right-hand-drive two-tone Daimler abandoned by a British brigadier five years earlier at Dunkirk and well treated by SS Standartenführer Wilhelm Mohnke who had requisitioned it and had the carriagework repainted black and red. He had in turn abandoned it as he fled retribution – which was never meted.

They drove south from Luneburg. This normally deserted area was unusually populated by refugees, broken soldiers and stalled vehicles blocking the roads as they escaped south in the hope of avoiding capture, rape and death by the Red Army. A group of skeletal people wearing the ragged striped pyjamas of the camps was trying to cook part of a human torso, pouring petrol on a failing fire of damp branches. It was an anatomy lesson gone to the bad. They drove for hours, were held up for hours. There were straw hives, children hauling horse carts, longhouses whose thatch was rotting, black-faced sheep, dead black-faced sheep, victims of packs of feral starving Mordhunds which leapt up at the car's windows with savage intent. They smelled the almond-scented corpse in the boot. They scraped the paint with killer claws. Bodies lay prone and bloating in the straight leets of floated meadows, spoiling the symmetry. A horse whose legs had been blown off tried in vain to stand on the stumps it was left with. A violated woman bleeding from her vagina howled begging mercy from an unseen rapist already on his way to his next appointment.

Near Bad Bevensen The Sergeant instructed the driver to turn west. As they approached the first bridge across the Elbe Seitenkanal, they were stopped by a patrol of the South Staffordshires.

A corporal recognised The Sergeant: 'You're what's 'is face ain't you . . . from where is it . . . which mob were it?'

'That's it, son. On the button.'

'We just got word that Himmler's gone missing . . . could be he just walked out of where they was holding him . . . some of the lads heard he'd been sprung by werewolves in Yank uniforms . . .'

'Well well.'

'Unbelievable idn't it . . . Now, don't take this bridge. Not your finest jerry engineering . . . could go any moment.'

There were points where The Sergeant's map from memory did not accord with the BKG's.

New roads, new forests, new theme parks, new year-round lidos, new buildings obscured his authoritative certainties which he had now to admit seemed speculative. 'With the passing of years – who knows.'

The folly at Bispingen, an industrialist's fin de siècle joke, took on a gravity never previously ascribed to it. They had never seen it. They were not so absorbed in their task that they didn't stop to marvel for a minute at the mad crenelated towers, the walls of giant's pebbles, the gardens fenced by logs cast in concrete, the crude sculpted volcanic eruption. Then on they drove. An hour after they had stopped to look at the Bispingen folly they found themselves driving past it again, in the opposite direction.

The Sergeant's meteorological memory was frail. There was thick mist over the heath, dirty as turned milk. There was drizzle over the heath. There was fat rain that the single windscreen wiper fought with and lost. There were charcoal clouds. Snow was melting. Snow was massing in malignant banks. The tracks were all mud to skid in. The tracks were all mud turned to rutted rock. The Sergeant offered a rich menu of weathers.

Much of the ground was frozen. The Sergeant was sweating. He recalled coming over the brow of a low wold. In front of them was a sand pit, 'a quarry as big as a stadium': not good burying ground, too susceptible to the weather. A waterlogged lorry abandoned at the bottom of it was partially buried. Beyond the pit was a further wooded hill of scrubby pines.

A watchtower rose above the trees. They drove downhill, skirting the sand pit. The track round it was partly buried by a gale's new dunes. They arrived at a deserted saw mill 'somewhere in the ambit of Uelzen'. A long rudimentary building entirely open at either end. Poles were piled high and orderly. Planks were stacked. Sawdust turned to porridge. Sawdust blew in waves. Cranes and conveyor belts had been sabotaged by sledgehammers. Petrol fuelled saws and generators had been burnt. Cylindrical reservoirs had been colandered. The scent was sappy fresh, clean at last. The wooden barracks showed no signs of life. The French slaves of the Service du Travail Obligatoire had fled.

A few private possessions were left on the splintered bunks and rough tables. French comics, a torn copy of *Les Nouveaux Temps*, a single empty beer bottle, worn stained clothes and blood-crusted bandages. The drawings on the walls made up in longing for what they lacked in art. To The Sergeant's self-proclaimed expert eye it was clear that this was a site producing the carpentered and shaped components of prefabrication, many of them marked for their destinations which had that week just begun their move from rumour to infamy: Bergen-Belsen, Sachsenhausen etc. This was where watchtowers were hewn from the heath's pines, measured and planed ready for assembly at the end of a rail line through the festering dark of a German wood, a line that speaks of immane horror.

It was secret work even though two fully built towers stood side by side, experimental essays of different design, trials that were of necessity tall and thus above the trees, inadvertently advertising the mill's existence. They were beacons of death. The heath's shepherds were discouraged from bringing their flocks close by.

Hanna Nowak was, she insisted, sweetly patient. 'I'm a devil with a saintly side. Big generous part of me.'

Uelzen – she tapped the BKG large-scale map – is, was, south of Schneverdingen. Look.

Buchholz was north. Look.

The Sergeant was affronted. He blamed cartographers, a tricky bunch at the best of times, more interested in inventing false features to trap copyright infringers than in depicting the lie of the land. Hanna was determined that he should not relax till every last detail of the burial was dragged out of him. If he wanted to save his farm . . .

'Watchtower or watch*towers*?' asked Shadoxhurst impatiently. 'You said there were two watchtowers. Your map shows one.'

'That's right. Two. Yes. That was when we were down in the saw mill.'

At last they had found a place which was hidden, far from trails and paths.

Thus it was by chance that the Reichsführer SS was buried close by a rural factory which had assisted in making his dream an actuality.

Melting snow formed pools on lush moss which stalks and sundew protruded through. The ground around the ponds and sinkholes was firm but diggable. There were ranks of peat rectangles left to dry. The narrow ditches they had been dug from were waterlogged. The grave they dug was a deep grave. The digging was hard. Slave labour, the men complained. The Sergeant didn't spare himself, his sinews bulged like rope beneath the skin. He was confident that from the place where the grave was dug the watchtower was visible. He repeated that when he wiped his sweating brow and looked up to see 'how we was doing for light' the watchtower was visible even though dusk was creeping up on us. It was silhouetted against the layered western sky. Pink and grey and turquoise.

'Like a . . .' He walked to the door and yelled: 'Vera, Vera . . . what d'you call that striped ice cream thing old Capaldi makes?'

Distant, accented voice: 'Cassata.'

'That's it – cassata. Sky like a cassata.'

Heavenly cassata. Hellish hole. They hoped. As night closed in our crack scratch squad of gravedigging conscripts laid Heinrich Himmler, once the Reichsführer, now the equal of all corpses, to writhe restless forevermore in dark peat, north by north-east of Schneverdingen, probably. On the road to Buchholz, probably.

The Sergeant was looking mighty pleased with himself, Hanna told Dudu: smug as a priest who'd got away with it.

'There is, if I might say so,' said Shadoxhurst – *of course* he might – 'a disparity here . . . When you came upon the sand pit you saw, on its far side, the hillock above the saw mill . . .' here he drew a circle on the BKG map indicating where the car must have been when they saw the hillock, '. . . though you hadn't yet reached the saw mill evidently . . . indeed had no idea it was there . . . it was beneath the far slope of the hillock. Your first intimation of the saw mill was the tower . . . but when you reached the mill . . . the tower had pupped . . . begat another tower . . . as they do . . . yet by some towering miracle once you began digging the grave of this unjustly judged statesman . . . by some towering miracle the towers were once more diminished . . . there was just a single tower . . . how do you account for that? . . .'

He considered The Sergeant to be either stupid or obstructive. With no concession to French pronunciation he drawled: 'Un train peut en cacher un autre – as they say.'

'They do?' wondered The Sergeant, mystified at aristocratic ways.

'No? No capiche? I'll tell you how *I* account for it . . . From where you first saw the single tower across the sand pit and from where you saw the single tower when you were digging what happened was that the tower nearer you obliterated the other tower. The two appeared as one. They were in line. In between those vantage points – that is, when you were at the saw mill – you saw the two towers. Now, we need to pinpoint the place from where the two towers amalgamate . . . so to speak . . . from where they appear as one. Obviously not from the sand pit side . . . no . . . from wherever you dug *after* you had found the saw mill . . . There can't be that many such places . . . And they will be in a line – that's certain.'

'I get the feeling' – Shadoxhurst looked hard at The Sergeant – 'I've got a suspicion we're doing your work for you.'

He told Hanna that he felt like Erskine Garn's sleuth the Hon. Denise Tiplady at the dénouement of the parodic murder mystery *Sensible Shoes* where the characters have to have information dragged out of them 'like a stillborn child from its dead mother'.

That was later. Now Hanna was on her phone to one of her assistants: 'Give me the saw mills on Luneburger Heide from 1933 onwards. Sites of all saw mills. Now, darling!' she whispered. She was a powerful woman. She didn't have to bellow. She had exhausted the BKG maps and aerial views on her hypertablet. They disclosed a lack of saw mills.

While she waited for her assistants to reply she quizzed The Sergeant on the distance between the saw mill and the grave.

'With the passing of the years – who knows.' Perhaps he had failed to pay attention. It could be that he had forgotten. He may have had a poor sense of distance. His unit of measurement was the football pitch.

'Definitely wasn't more than a couple of pitches distant . . . definitely wasn't no more than . . . suppose it could be three . . . yes, come to think of it maybe four at a push . . . it was a job we wanted to do and quick . . . no slacking . . . I mean it's only with hindsight that you realise you should have been jotting down the detail for posterity.'

'What's this?' She was scrutinising The Sergeant's map. She suspected they were being sold a pup.

'What's what?'

'I wouldn't be asking if I knew what it was . . . looks like a sketch of a bookshelf.'

'Bookshelf!' The Sergeant was affronted. He shook his head. 'That's not a bookshelf . . . it's a railway line. There was this narrow-gauge railway from the saw mill . . . that's the rails, those are the sleepers . . . it didn't go nowhere just stopped . . . like they'd put down the sleepers then stopped laying the rails. There was a handcar . . . manually powered . . . all rusted over . . . non-runner.'

Hanna, wearily: 'How are you getting on, darling . . . now we're looking for a saw mill which had a narrow-gauge railway . . . just a few rails laid . . . there might be plans somewhere . . . Organisation Todt archives? Are they digitised? And a handcar . . .'

She addressed The Sergeant again: 'What else? . . . Distinguishing features for god's sake. Landmarks. How long was this track?'

'You're getting me going on distances again . . . it's not me strong point.'

'How many football pitches long was it?'

'Oh that's easy. Not even one . . . It was just from here to there . . . I tell you something . . . there was all sorts of metal they took to use for armaments . . .'

'I know.'

Her phone rang. Her 'aaah' of satisfaction was quasi-sexual. She nodded bobbingly at Shadoxhurst.

A decree of August 1939 stated inter alia that 'cartographic works shall contain no information whose publication might jeopardise the common good'.

The Sergeant had been right: 'cartographers . . . a tricky bunch at the best of times.' A saw mill's presence on a map could, then, be construed as jeopardising the common good.

In Zurich the methodical assistant Gaetan had noted that the 1941 amendments to that part of the Deutsche Grundkarte for north-western Luneburg Heath had omitted a group of buildings east of Handeloh and a railway that linked them to an extension of Handeloh station. Both railway and buildings were shown in the 1936 edition. Its gauge was not indicated. He observed that the narrow gauge – 900mm – of the Mollibahn between Bad Doberan and Kühlungsborn was not indicated as differing from other lines and so concluded that given the rarity of such a gauge there was no special cartographic convention that had been created to represent it. He noted too a disparity between the hachures describing the terrain in the 1936 version and the 1941: sandhills change height and shape.

'Handeloh is getting on for fifty kilometres from Luneburg.' Shadoxhurst arched his thumb and first finger to make an approximate measurement. 'Nonetheless this is the only feasible site we have . . . now – we aren't in the business of being led up the garden path . . . did you really drive that far . . . did you have the fuel?'

'Suppose we must have done . . . like I said, we got well lost . . . went round and round in circles.'

Hanna phoned Ernst. She read out to him the fourteen-figure coordinates. The old man was fractious and defensive. He dismissed the place they signalled. He insisted that it did not belong to the heath, whose boundaries he defended with proprietorial indignation.

'Doesn't,' Eunice Pethica spat, 'the old fool realise that our friend The Sergeant here may not have known the precise boundaries? Do you know when you drive from one postcode into another? No.'

'Good point well made, Eugenia,' oiled The Sergeant. Maybe he feared his grip on his fee was being loosened.

Hanna was stern: 'Size constancy, Hauptsturmführer . . . It's sympathetic to the human need for comprehension . . . so it reorders rogue information . . . makes it palatable. It tells a lie . . . do not believe that lie, Hauptsturmführer. Remember . . . the watchtowers . . . if they're still standing . . . they'll trick your eye. You may be close by them, you may be far from them . . . the line extending from their amalgamation – from the apparent single tower – that line is the key.'

'Of course they'll bloody trick my eye . . . I'm almost blind.'

'It's retina versus brain and brain wins. Your distance from the towers may deceive you.'

Ernst laughed mockingly: 'You believe they'll still be there. I'd say not . . . all the towers from back then have gone. I know the heath . . . no one knows it better . . . it's my soil . . . let me tell you the fire towers have gone . . . rotted away . . . the ones they built since are squatted mostly . . . Slavs and blacks . . .'

Gaetan again: according to the most recent survey by Naturschutzgebeit in cooperation with Staatsforst eight watchtowers built according to the original NSG design from the Twenties remain intact. Their locations are not disclosed.

Hanna had turned on an amplifier. Ernst groaned: 'Wrong wrong wrong. Only a fool is guided by the hand of ignorance . . . look at my homeland since our Führer was betrayed by his people and his Dauphin ignominiously buried. Democracy is hypocrisy. This exhumation will reawaken our nation.'

I watched. I listened.

I got mud on my shoes and chided myself. The drone gave their location away. It was longer, wider and more complicated than the hobbyists' machines which are as abundant as kites once were. They reliably fall from the sky. I ate a chocolate and candied orange millefeuille. I planned an ambush. Why here. Why now. I have been asking myself those questions forever. Without rancour I idly analysed the web of circumstances that had brought me here, to this heath on this day. Randomness, chance, accident. This was the fate I was born to, once, long ago. Strange-pipped dice my hand has thrown me. And an embarrassing hire car. When I booked a vehicle that I stipulated should be unnoticeable, I hadn't realised that in the world of grease monkeys the word was a synonym for a mechanically defective pollutant.

They moved slowly: Hubback strapped and laden, Ernst Stech-Pelz stumbling with his stick, Heini Stech-Pelz, disengaged, wondering at the money and effort poured into this project and shooed away from the drone by Hubback lest his hands, bulky hazchem gloves in my magnification, should clumsily blink it.

For two days I watched from the car, secluded and high on a pinous dune. All the colours of mauve, purple, lavender, mallow stretched to the sky, to white clouds as fluffy as the heath's sheep. I quashed boredom with Moist Groin, Mahler's Kindertotenlieder and Ein Deutsches Requiem. I love 'selig sind die Toten', it proved to be the prophetic justification for Germany's next century. I failed to quash boredom with the oeuvre of Hermann Löns:[53] a Nazi *avant la lettre*, all noble peasants and hearthside nationalism. Here was a cheering hoopoe, here was a jay, struggling through air thick with sticky insects it couldn't catch: it had yet to get the hang of flight.

My fieldcraft instincts taught me this: observe from that hide there. A rickety shack elevated a metre on rusty metal pylons, well occluded by broom, juniper, spruce, alder. A couple of rats in a corner glanced at me then fearlessly continued to feast on a used condom. A sac of seed loutishly fly-tipped by a fornicator. Leave them be. Let them crossbreed. Rats, clever maligned creatures, were equated by Sahh al-Bukari and the NSDAP, specifically by *Der Stürmer*, with Jews. Rats should then be honoured. And we Jews should find the good in them. Rats are a life form far higher than Julius Streicher. When they ran out of my people to burn they murdered rats.

These twins are powerful – 37×120. Every few minutes I raise them to my eyes. They allow me to see stillicides of sweat like glycerine drops sliding down the labourers' sun-coshed faces. Five or six of them, each of them sworn to secrecy. Each of them garrulous on Saturday night when their first week's pay had been converted into alcohol. A predictable eventuality which neither Stech-Pelz had

---

53 *Blut und Boden* – blood and soil – was among his coinages. Before the NSDAP's *Machtergreifung* it was commonly regarded as risible and mocked as '*blubo*'.

predicted. They were not yet apprised of it. And Hubback had not considered the probability because he was not paid to consider. Demarcation. Unknown to Ernst, Heini, Shadoxhurst and Hanna, he was, however, paid to report to me. A mistake. He was not a man to be trusted. Treachery (with or without a smile) was his norm. It came to him as easily as breathing. Paying him for information was throwing away money. I had of course not told him that I would be following their every movement. He believed, because I had told him, that I was 'on a project' in Hamburg and might, just might, summon him to a meeting far from the Gasthof Geiger where the diviners and the workers were put up.

He claimed that they had so far found nothing worth finding. That appeared to be true. I confirmed it in conversation with a callow boy still sweaty and mealy odoured from the week's frustrating spade-work. Like most of the troop he was a member of Querdenken.

'You were a duellist?' he asked me, in awe. 'Tübingen? Heidelberg?'

I didn't reply. I didn't want to lie to him nor did I want to invite ridicule. He longed to touch the scar. I was happy to let him. I led him from the gasthof's bar into a crepuscular garden where a pergola was decorated with hop bines. His soft hand was blistered, unused to labouring. He stroked the deathly white cicatrix on my left cheek.

'It doesn't feel how I thought it would feel.'

'Really? You had expectations? Now: do ut des. I would be most appreciative were you to let me know the progress of this venture.' I gave him a card with a number on it.

'I don't . . . don't know about that. No I'm not sure . . . We've been told . . .'

'Let me help you make up your mind.'

He was a frail little thing. His body was a filly's. With a deft movement learnt a lifetime ago I locked his arm and threw him to the ground. He looked up at me from the paving where he had landed. He looked up at me bewildered. I gave him a hand. He dusted himself down, cowering.

Little Teddy Benzer made all the difference. He amplified Hubback's frugal messages.

The routine of the diggers became settled. Their progress was slow and weary. Some days they covered only a few metres. They followed the course of a series of ponds in a line from where the two towers were estimated to have been one. Every couple of hours they stopped to swig from water bottles, at lunchtime sandwiches, crisps and oranges were fetched from a minibus and distributed. Those were atypical moments in what looked like the drudge of forced labour. The drone demanded constant attention. The adolescents proved to be technologically capable. Their fear of Hubback was an incitement to apply themselves to constant adjustments and repairs.

Work stopped at 17.00. On Thursday 16th it didn't stop. The drone was grounded. Hubback was treading delicately on ground where brown water pooled, drifts of scum on the surface. Silver birch bark was pinkened by the early evening sky. He was gazing at the GPR's screen. Then he was gazing at that sky. After an evidently intense conversation two of the diggers began to penetrate the bog at the place Hubback specified. They had evidently been instructed to work cautiously. They looked towards him for his nodded approval.

When I spoke to Hubback he lied. He's a contra-indication. The discovery they had made was, in his opinion, nugatory. That was a sure clue that it was important. 'I'd like to be delivering top griff, Skipper, but, you know, fucking zilch is fucking zilch. It's just a fucking groundsheet . . . leather the one side perished rubber the other . . . perished . . . not even officer's groundsheet . . . hurhurhur. They're treating it like it's some fucking stash from a bullion job.'

'They think,' Teddy Benzer gushed after I'd plied him with a child's measure of schnapps, 'they've made a significant find but they don't want to dig with lights because of the attention lights attract. Not just criminally inclined humans but animals too . . . animals can be as much a problem as criminally inclined vagrants and opportunistic wanderers. We – that is to say my *Mannschaft* that is to say Querdenken that is to say Germany's future – believe they should be euthanised – but not in a cruel way like the Nazis did, no. That's the old hat. We're looking today at a cosy embarkation, a comforting shoulder, amiability, at a better state of life-leaving. In nice clinics. Nice white coats, crisply laundered. Impeccable stand- ard of cleanliness. A temple of hygiene. With the bonus of spare parts for the physically infirm but morally deserving. Dedicated needles: reuse forbidden. We build on the example of Dream

Topping™ but with extra friendly persuasion. You could say Querdenken doesn't offer choice. We go further. We offer more than choice. We offer a better place which no one can resist. No one has ever turned down the opportunity to take the Querdenken Pathway.'

Later I returned to the heath. The minibus had moved close as terrain would allow to where four of the diggers remained, slouching on guard. Not knowing what they were guarding, not knowing where the criminally inclined vagrants and animals they were guarding against might appear from. Two of them were armed. These night twins are 20×60 allies, they magnified the stinging mauve and the orange in torches' swerving rainbow trails.

They magnified the illumined faces of two somnolent guards on night watch.

They took turns to sleep and to spray the body every hour, as Frau Doctor Chipurnoi had proposed.

The next morning I watched, again from the rat hide. Cadaver dogs, lean and vicious Mordhunds, were led on leashes to the site where the boy soldiers were pitched.

I had long ago learnt lip reading at Ephesus while observing a group of persons of interest pretending to be Pauline-trail tourists.

There was a dispute about payment with the dogs' handler-in-chief. The lower grade handlers looked ready to let their charges go marauding. Ernst Stech-Pelz was at a loss. Heini had only sign language. Hubback did the talking for him. Quasi had never smiled and patted fucking backs and clasped fucking shoulders with such fucking manly conviction. I warmed to him as you always do to a rogue – provided he's on your side. Now that was a mistake. For which I deserved whipping.

A stray child, or something, was found for the dogs' scran.

Hubback reappeared walking beside a cute tracked crawler 1.5 tonne excavator and earth mover. Almost a toy. Its driver was explaining its mechanisms. Its turquoise paintwork was incongruous. Hubback repeatedly said move only gingerly. The driver didn't understand that. And Hubback didn't understand how to keep control of the machine. They achieved a concord with Hubback sitting behind the garrulous driver (whose name was Bernd. Hobbies: fun parties and girls.).

Delicate. Take it fucking easy. She sounds fucking lovely mate just what the fucking doctor ordered mate please fucking concentrate watch out for god's sake ... couple of centimetres at a fucking time ... we got as long as it fucking takes.

It was early afternoon when the left eye of the exhausted child soldier Uwe Teller, prone, marvelling at the texture of the damp moss which god had provided for him to stroke during his post-lunchbreak five-minute free time, caught a glint in the dun where the sun struck something. He raised his head. It had gone. He resumed his former position. The sharply reflective surface had disappeared like a kingfisher that's no more than a brilliant streak for as long as it takes to register. He had a decision to make: he could rupture the epicurean serenity of the three minutes remaining by satisfying his curiosity or he could stay captivated by the purplish chestnut sphagnum leaves which, if he suppressed all sense of scale and stared hard at their still reflection, appeared like a clump of trees. His curiosity triumphed. He trod with careful urgency realising that he didn't know how far whatever it was was from where he had lain.

The subsequent scene is one of elation cut with paranoid confusion. Uwe Teller has alerted Ernst Stech-Pelz. The old man uses a spade as a walking stick. His ill-shaped body contorts, bone against bone, all cartilage worn. He kneels with difficulty and picks up what appears to be an intact pair of wire-rimmed spectacles. One lens clouded, the other clear. The earth mover is repositioned. The drone is employed to warn against the proximity of curious hikers and joggers. The Mordhunds stand as sentries, gatekeepers to hell's pit where Ernst must still squat, now obscured by a shelter in the form of a sort of yurt or geodesic dome lugged from the minibus and erected by the youths. It was taking on the appearance of a full-scale archaeological dig. The degree of preparation surprised me. Hubback wouldn't answer his phone.

I watched mouths. I read expressions. I listened with my eyes. I employed senses you don't know of.

With the exception of Hubback and Stech-Pelz father and son the actors didn't appreciate the immensity of the moment, the unprecedented strangeness of their destiny even as supports without a credit.

'You'll never forget it,' I anticipated telling Teddy Benzer, ruffling his cute blond martial brushcut, 'you'll be able to tell your grandchildren you were there.' (This conversation did not take place.)

Teddy was there. He was part of a chain passing buckets of pond water to the dig site.

I read his sweet lips as he addressed one of his fellows, a cigarette smoker, who was struggling to grow an early adolescent moustache.

'It's like it's been roasted . . . I mean so dark it's over-roasted like when my sister leaves it in too long because she's upstairs with her boyfriend before my parents get back from golf and she doesn't turn it down and it gets all blackened but sort of marmalade colour as well . . . We thought it was a suitcase . . . an old-fashioned suitcase.'

Activity. Movement. New people arrived. The excavator was being used as a crane. It was carrying a bath, a domestic bath, rich lilac, a fashionable colour in those days. It was bereft of taps and full of water. Heini was directing it with practised gestures, agitated fingers and still palms. I couldn't figure it. What was the bath for? Whatever it was for was hidden. A Mordhund savaged a small visiting dog. It had the genes and appetite of its ancestors who worked in the camps. After twenty-seven minutes the bath came back into view as it was loaded onto the excavator. It contained something, its sides were too high to see what. Then it disappeared once more in the direction of the minibus which had been joined by several other vehicles, not legible from here.

There was no effort to repair the site, to disguise what had happened. Indeed – what had happened? I was baffled. Not least by the bath which water lapped from. The entire squad from bounding Mordhund to crippled Ernst exited stage right towards the vehicles. They were in a hurry. They left copious piles of muddy sand and earth, topsoil and gouged heaps of deep damp peat: strata of every hue from chestnut to spraints, from Sam Browne to brown sauce, a layer cake of age-old leguminous deposits chewed by the voracity of a modern maw. Hubback's phone was off. So too was the prepaid I had given little Teddy as an appreciative godfather would.

He was not at the Gasthof Geiger. The receptionist leeringly told me that 'You're out of luck, your little friend has gone . . . all the little boys have gone. Such a shame . . . But we have our own little boys from the seminary for those who appreciate the spiritual side of Uranus.'

I ignored the creep: 'And Herr Stech-Pelz?'

'All gone . . . the coach was ready.'

I hadn't seen a coach: 'What coach? Where have they gone?'

'Poppy Tours . . . they often stay . . . you've got Monty . . . the surrender on the heath in forty-five . . . the Hoch Haus . . . that's their itinerary . . . then on to Prora . . .'

'They were going to *Prora*?'

'No no no, they were going back to England.'

'*England?* With that bath? With a corpse in it?'

'Ingerlandlandland they call it.'

'They do?'

'The football ones do.'

I was already on speed dial. I didn't care if this aspirant pimp heard. I had to speak to my associates, instigate a selective stoppage, DQT.

'Which port?'

He shrugged: 'Emden . . . Travemunde . . . I don't know.'

'Think hard.'

'I can't, I don't know, I really don't know,' he pleaded, pitifully.

He'll regain its use, in time.

They left it late. The coach was pulled over only five minutes from the Wilhelmshaven ferry terminal by my uniformed associates on the elevated carriageway above the allotments of Kleingartnerverein Heppens. It was a dangerous manoeuvre. My people cut up the coach like a knife through lung. They blocked it, forcing it onto the hard shoulder. It might have demolished the mauve and tan wave-motif retaining wall, hurried through the railings beyond and plunged down and down and down through shrubs and alders for what would have seemed an eternity but was only a second till it flopped with a grunt obliterating a hut beside the allotments' car park, raising a dome of dry earth that could be seen from far far way. No, it was not like that.

It was an expertly executed action, hardly noticed by the passing traffic. No one was injured. Associate B took the coach's keys and hurled them far across the fast lane to the edge of the central reservation among the plastic bottles, cellophane wrappings, grimed cartons and strips of tyre rubber. The other contraband was heroin, buried in boxes of Milbenkäse and Alter Hirte, olfactory assaults that are reputed to cause permanent damage to the septum. They deter even the most dutiful Mordhund. The heroin was left untouched. Ernst Stech-Pelz's dream was ripped from him. Hubback, Heini and Spotty Dogg, the driver, were forced at Uzi point to shoulder the dripping bath and carry it to my associates' 6×6 Tank SUV, an iguana of a vehicle, the professionals' choice.

We must leave them now beside the hurtling cars and articulated lorries of Autobahn 29, seeking a gap in the traffic so they might recover the keys. They didn't know how lucky they were. My associates would have been persuasive if necessary.

I did, however, phone my commiserations to Hubback.

He replied, with mondaine resignation: 'Well fucking rumbled Skipper! Nice play. But as they say – win some lose some – see you around. Some place or other. Some time or other.'

'I doubt it—' I heard myself utter. It felt like a curt prophecy. It felt as though someone was speaking through me, briefly inhabiting me.

The Man In The Lilac Bath passed, then, into my stewardship. I didn't consider it theft. I wasn't receiving stolen property, I wasn't fencing it. I had arrested him in the name of the government I represented. This was a special case. Not since Eichmann . . .

For two days we kept him at the Altenwerder terminal in one of many thousand containers beside the Elbe. We dressed as workmen. Phoebe Chipurnoi was the only person in Hamburg whom I could turn to for advice on preservation, temperature, humidity etc. She was overdressed for a container terminal. Elegant and expensive rather than the usual trashy, cheap tragics moonlighting from Saint Pauli. Our acquaintance, such as it is, has always been rebarbative. One problem is that she attracted attention. A second was that she had brought along her grey-bearded, flat-capped, Donegal-clad husband. He looked old enough to be her father. Indeed he had been her father till DNA tests said otherwise. He had to be cared for while she delivered her opinions. He was instructed to see nothing, hear nothing. To which he replied, testily: 'How do you think I got on in the Company if I didn't keep my mouth shut about . . .' And here he blabbed about twenty or so Cold War 'secret' missions, mostly still classified, that he had undertaken on behalf of J. J. Angleton, himself an infamous loudmouth (and no friend of my people). Seventeen of those missions had been failures. I know my stuff.

My Associate C took him to a workman's snack-hut where he corrected his brandy with coffee. They returned with that morning's *MoPo*. A brief news item:

Luneburg Heath park managers believe that unsanctioned excavations in the vicinity of Handeloh point to an exhumation in the vicinity of Handeloh contrary to by-laws. Unconfirmed rumours among heath folk spread like wildfire that the body exhumed in the vicinity of Handeloh was the body of notorious Nazi leader Heinrich Himmler. Popular Community Police spokesvanguard Toni Ullrich called a press conference at which he spoke one sentence: 'Wenn Schweine fliegen.' Nonetheless the force is investigating in cooperation with the State Criminal Police.

I had him. I had him. He was my captive. In my wet grasp there was not just the monster of the Third Reich but his predecessors and his successors in Judenhass: the kings of Spain, Little Hugh of Lincoln, Poles, la Grande Zohra, Bavarians, the mob of Ambrosian Christians who will forever exact retribution for the death of Jesus even though it was the Romans who killed him, Esterhazy of Harpenden, Ramalama in its many hateful forms, pogrom upon pogrom – the inventory of obloquy is long and grim.

He was my captive. And I wanted rid of him. I felt contaminated. I was, equally, gleeful. The Reichsführer would not be displayed at Führer World.[54] Hanna Nowak, Geoffrey Shadoxhurst, Staff, Celia Deuteron and Ernst Stech-Pelz were thwarted by an operation that

---

54 The exhibit at Führer World is a fake or 'replica'. It replaces an earlier 'replica' so poorly modelled that officers of the Sacred Oak Order of Heinrich Himmler accused Saxonhurst [*sic*] of 'iconic apostasy'.

would be commended as top value for money. Dudu was thwarted too. His support by far right fantasists and self-proclaiming anti-Semites was to say the least unorthodox. It would cause at least minor damage to his aspirations once it became widely known.

The comparison with the kidnapping of Adolf Eichmann was unexceptionable, save that it wasn't like with like. I modestly refuted it, pointing out that Eichmann had been alive when arrested. When there are no live Nazis left to hunt we have to hunt dead Nazis . . . A transformation from live to dead – a mere change of chemistry – neither lessens the crime nor excuses it. But finding the criminal is arguably more difficult.

'This is a one-off unrepeatable event . . . it's always going to be remembered as Dudu Topaz's triumph . . . got him first . . . he's going to be Dudu Topaz's guest. Dudu's pet genocide!'

By my leave. More strictly by my leave and that of persons (face-less, nameless) whom he describes in italics as my *associates*. Much as I loved Dudu – OK, liked, all right, tolerated in small doses – I intended to thwart his plan too.

What are friends for if not to cross, to turn into former friends. It was me, plus my associates, who were in possession of the prize. I wanted to be a good servant, loyal to our secular state, its constitu-tion, its polity and, where applicable, its laws – though these should of course not be considered absolute. Judex is the agent of natural justice which transcends the laws of state.

It's always going to be remembered as Dudu Topaz's triumph . . . Really?

He repeated that it was the commando that took Eichmann who became national heroes then international heroes. It wasn't the ranks of lawyers, the judges, the famous writer whose famous dictum is wrong. It was the commando. The men on the ground: Litan, Malkin, Aharoni, courageous men, Jews of steely righteousness. He knew their names by heart. The men who captured Himmler will be granted the same honour, the same respect.

I often heard this from Dudu. So often that it had the force of a litany, beyond sense. Now, the former Himmler was in my maroon container (stencilled RF071000). Dudu was 3,000 kilometres distant. It was evident that he was not the man who had captured the mass murderer. It wasn't him. It was me. It broke on me. I realised it with bemusement and delight. It was me. I was that man. And my commando. What court would challenge our detention of the Monster? He would no longer be offered as an exhibit, a base entertainment in a theme park devoted to the propagation of National Socialism. Dudu obviously intended that I would do his fetching and carrying. His concord with Shadoxhurst and with that malevolent baronet's diverse group of neo-fascists was genuine. They supported him. They were not his patsies as he pretended. They were in it together whatever it was. From the night at Koritsas when I saw him deep in conspiracy with that indecently hyper-net-worth pharma-whore and the squalid ancient whose dreams are the nightmares of my people, he had tried to play me as a god does his devotees. All we know of god is that he overreaches. Hubris goes with the job. No longer.

Life After Afterlife

I am invisible. I am not there. They don't see me. It's not that they don't acknowledge me . . . they don't even realise there's someone to acknowledge. I tell you what . . . I think they think it's like being in a photo booth – you don't say good evening to the automatic camera you don't say have a nice day to the automatic camera so they don't say good morning have a nice day to me because they think of me like I'm an automatic camera . . . a machine.

That was Sacha's 'obs' as he called it. He was leaning against the wall of my atelier oh so languid and cooled out while I was repairing Dudu's face with Celestial, the special emphasis vegetal mousse not tested on most animals, covering the sagging which he pretended he didn't notice. But the cameras don't go along with pretending. They would mercilessly pick out any imperfection so it was my vocation . . . mine, ironically enough . . . my vocation and vision to correct what he had been handed . . . which was due for a major overhaul . . . god's gift is for more than Christmas but it's not forever . . . just because it's god's gift doesn't mean to say that it doesn't have built in obsolescence like a long-life battery or fancy chronometer. Perpetual is just a name. The job was to spread enough serum to hide all those lifestyle lines from his late night after-show winding down with Bourbon and slit-skirt slappers he didn't respect as people. No way did he respect me as people neither but different from those mouthy little misses.

I snipped at his hair to layer it so it bounced with body and vitality and didn't lie flat like a raven's corpse on the crown. Face it! He was thinning. Every somebody becomes a nobody when that bald patch goes public.

That's my opinion in my role as 'the doormat who clips his syrup'. I heard a floor manager call me that: these trailers' metal walls aren't sound insulated. I put a malediction on the bitch hoping her hair would go up in flames from too much spray too close to the lights. It did.

That evening he'd been talking to Sacha about Dudu Topaz's direction meaning what direction the *Dudu Topaz First In Entertainment* show should go for. He called himself Dudu Topaz like he was still David Goldenberg and Dudu Topaz was the character he played. It wasn't as simple as that. The two were knotted together like wool in a knitting basket which has also got glue stuck in it.

Sacha was unique. He was the only one who didn't flatter him. This wasn't the first time he told him he'd be crazy if the show went more political: it was about the twentieth time. You'll lose half your audience . . .

Stick to after-dinner balladeers with chest wigs like Toni Lo Reno, the sometime acrobat Emerson Trinkwon (if out on bail), novelty dance ensembles, faded variety turns like The Barry Island Five, talking dogs and your sketches, the sketches we all love, everyone loves and knows the words of: the village idiot, the cook that destroys the kitchen, the Japanese businessman, the family on a day out in the country. Dudu was contemptuous about the channel, about the board, the CEO, a former Mitz Paz fizzy drinks marketing manager who's frightened of the board, the vice presidents who are frightened of the CEO, the middle managers who are frightened of the vice presidents . . . Right down to the bean counters who are frightened of everyone. They all live in fear, looking over their shoulder.

The kitchens make a special fuss over him, they make a special falafel, a special extra spicy houmous for him. They fawn on him. The canteen staff dote on him. He is one of theirs. He isn't – and they know it and he knows it – but he pretends to be and they love him for it. He buys gifts for their children's birthdays.

Dudu Topaz is the channel's prized possession. The golden goose is a spoiled child. They know it – but what can they do. He is the ratings king of our country's television. They are used to putting up with his demands and moods and hissy fits and me-me-me and vanity . . . It's the vanity that Sacha picked up on that evening. Although he had seen it often he had not thought about exploiting it – that is, exploiting his friend. What struck him was that Dudu was badmouthing

Mordechai Banin, Alon Atar and Ora Winterberg as though there was no one to hear him. In other words he ignored me. I didn't count. He was looking at himself, loving himself, getting pudgy – not that he could see what I could see. Like I say, I was invisible.

Dudu goes for a sound check.

Sacha asks me – casually, he is working hard at being casual, like he has just thought of it – he asks me if Dudu is getting more beyond self-control in the make-up atelier and if he is why don't I keep Sacha 'in the loop'.

I told him there and then: 'This idea of a political show . . . it's not what you think . . . it's not *about* politics. It's . . . he wants to use the show to launch himself . . . as a politician . . . he's got this phrase "turn ratings into votes" – lost count of how many times I've heard him say it.'

Sacha looked at me with those liquid zircon eyes of his. What were they thinking? The one thing they aren't thinking of is mentally undressing me. He has a chilly hard centre.

I went to myself: he's jealous that I'm more in the loop than he is. He and his associates are interested in what Dudu is up to . . . he's been seen in London with some people they are also interested in. Well, I wasn't one to pry but like I say while Dudu is admiring his looks and forgetting to thank yours truly for supplying them he is dimming and brightening the lights around the mirror while chatterboxing or boasting or slagging or moaning or screaming. He moues, pouts, rehearses his full smile range from shy and modest through to full ale-house bibber with a foaming tankard in a days of yore film (B&W).

And he is saying nasty poison venom things about people: 'slimy creep, unfuckable pudding, deserves live wires attached to his balls, should be hanged, sculpted out of cellulite, face like operation waste, syphilitic goat fucker, if that's what her mouth looks like just picture her cunt, smells like a lymphatic drainage bag, mouth like anyone else's anus, dry as Ursula Bonbernard's minge . . .' and so on. He might be saying this to Sacha over his shoulder not looking nowhere but at himself. One day he's going to forget Sacha's in the room when he starts slagging Sacha for his cult of mystery and solitude and secrecy and disappearing.

More often he is saying it into the phone tirading to his agent Reuven Vered telling him he's empty wigs, telling him he's going to find a proper agent. Then he's coming on cuddly with his tame journalists who fight his battles for him.

The story that Tamis Afek is a paedo beast was planted by Dudu. He made it up. He spread a rumour that Afek had paid to have his name removed from the register of offenders against children. Afek is a funny one all right – strange taste in blusher . . . suffering inner torment about the length of his sideburns. I ask you! But paedo? No way. Dudu made it up because he heard that Afek is earning big, not so big as Dudu, but more in a week than I get in my long lifetime . . . oh so long. And Afek was the voice of Mikey The Baler-Wrapper Combination in the *Little Gay Tractor* franchise, which gave him real leverage among the just-learning-to-reads. That really hurt Dudu who just couldn't get into that market. He ruined Afek because he could. It doesn't matter that it was proved to be total fabrication . . . those stories stick . . . And there isn't even a register of offenders. It doesn't exist.

What I told Sacha was that Dudu's got statesman ambitions . . . prime minister maybe . . . he's got a presidential complex. He thinks he is the people. He thinks he is the state.

Sacha couldn't believe it . . . He couldn't stop laughing. A presidential . . . His laughter was incredulous . . . Mocking. They were friends but this was a step too far . . . It could upset the applecart . . . Sacha's vocation is not to let it get upset. Nothing, he said, brings people together like a common enemy. And once they're together they immediately start working on becoming enemies of each other . . .

Is that philosophy or a fortune cookie?

I tell him 66 per cent of the electorate wants Dudu to be prime minister. I repeated 66 per cent.

He laughed till he coughed. 66 per cent of the electorate might come to its senses when it casts its vote, he said. What polls have you been looking at? Do they have polls in *Pnai Plus*?[55] I never

---

55 A magazine largely devoted to quiz show contestants, hostesses in bikinis and 'reality' TV participants. Its readership is discounted as *ars* and *arsits*.

looked at *Pnai Plus*. But that's what they had me down as – a *Pnai Plus* reader.

Sacha was scornful of Dudu. He was also jealous: he tries not to let on. What he resents is Dudu has a chance of being chosen as The Chosen of The Chosen. Sacha has no chance. A man in the shadows has no chance. Until he comes out of the shadows, into the full glare, modestly letting on that he was – for instance – the anonymous planner of Selective Sharon, the executant of Flexible Oblivion, chief of the Alder Commando, the author of the Bonfadini Trap and the reckoning in Bremen Botanischer Garten . . . Until he shows that he has placed himself above the law in the service of our country, in the service of natural justice, his aspirations don't get any further than just that, aspirations.

Dudu is canny: for such a loudmouth he is clever at keeping it to himself (apart from myself). He retains a gift for shyly receiving endearments with what appears sincere modesty – until you have seen it a hundred times over.

He has no wish to make himself look a fool. He is planning a coup de théâtre as a prelude to a mightier action. Like any coup it depends on surprise. There is no possibility of a rehearsal (so he claimed). No possibility of a repeat. It's a unique event.

'It's Eichmann for an attention deficit generation,' Dudu says slyly, smiling smugly, brimming with self-love.

'This is going to be one of the greatest of all coups de théâtre . . . no no . . . it's going to be *the* greatest, yeah, no question. The master entertainer makes chat show history . . . *television* history. The master entertainer transforms himself. It's got everything.'

I didn't know what he meant by that. I do know now. I think everyone knows. Back then he didn't explain. I didn't want to ask. I had a grandstand seat at the ringside. I saw what was going down. I may not have understood it but I saw it. It was true theatre. There were all the signs beforehand, not that I recognised them . . . not that anyone did. Remember the show when he bit Natalia Oreiro . . . you don't bite child stars . . . not on prime time anyway . . . it was going too far . . . not just a little bit too far . . . she was swooning and swanning all over the stage . . . he was looking embarrassed doing pathetic dad-dancing trying to get the audience on side and failing . . . he was being upstaged . . . that's why he bit her . . . resentment and revenge . . .

He adored the audience so long as it adored him . . . he was a hero to the mob . . . he liked being moved along by the people trying to touch him . . . the seething crush and the body sweat and the hot garlic breath and lamb fat breath drove him . . . he needed that closeness and that's when it started to go . . . with Natalia Oreiro . . . almost half the nation saw him . . . they didn't like what they saw . . . we all knew he was out of control but he had kept it hidden till then.

Well, *we* had kept it hidden for him . . . made excuses . . . covered up his errant ways . . . in everyday language errant ways means groping at the very least . . . soubrettes ingenues chorus girls . . . what they'll put up with from young men . . . what they may even pretend to welcome . . .

Well, that doesn't go for older men – to their regret . . . the way of the world . . . he never admitted to himself that he'd lost his looks . . . and his charm . . . that went too. He slipped from gaudy to grey. The colour drained out of him . . . and the bitterness seeped in.

Then there were the coypus . . . live coypus in 'the dock, on trial' . . . swamp rats splashing about the studio after escaping the glass tank that formed 'the dock' . . .

This was Sacha's doing. He had planted the idea . . . He drew Dudu's attention to trials of animals . . . pigs, donkeys . . . the Middle Ages . . . He was adamant . . . rats get more respect than Jews have done down the centuries . . . rats at least got a trial . . . He never let up from that refrain.

Dudu was enthused. He really went for it. It was a strange way to introduce the audience to his so-called serious side, to show he was a man of weight . . . a man with bottom – that was an expression he'd picked up in London. I wondered.

The set was corny. No one believed in it. No one believed in the sketch – which took up half the show. He talked about it being a breakthrough. The new Dudu. No one would challenge him to his face. The newspapers were different. The critics had their day. One snide cheapjoked that he should get a pair of glasses to signal his new intellectualism. Another called the coypus 'comedy otters'. Dudu belongs to an age long gone . . . Why does the channel inflict this drivel on its audience? Call this entertainment!?

He pleaded for the defence (long-established species, can no longer be considered invasive; the raw material of charcuterie and fur).

As the prosecution Dudu was fiery, angry, righteous. He demanded the death penalty (destroyers of river banks and dykes, vectors of diseases).

He was the judge summing up. On the one hand . . . at the same time . . .

The audience was the jury. They were bewildered. It was obvious he'd lost it. Everyone knew it apart from him.

After that show he was going: 'That's nothing . . . just you wait . . .'

His agent Reuven Vered was muttering to himself, shaking his head. Especially about the coypu that was electrocuted. He was furious. Not as furious as he'd be two weeks later. Nowhere near as furious.

That was when 'the creaking edifice collapsed' – Sacha's way of putting it. It has to be said that Sacha was more than an onlooker, he gave the edifice an almighty shove, more or less singlehandedly helped it on its way. He knew what he was doing. He was preparing to present himself as a contender for The Chosen of The Chosen.

Two Weeks Later

11.45

The first of four shows entitled *You're Going To Love This* staged in the Roman amphitheatre at Caesarea: Dudu Live At Caesarea's Palace. He dreamed of playing Vegas. Dream on.

We were like a gypsies' encampment: the trailers and their thin walls, the Winnebagos (Dudu's was the largest, he actually checked it out with a measuring tape), the twelve-wheeled outside-broadcast artic trucks with satellite dishes and vertical antennae, the food trucks, the shower and toilet trucks, the crew minibuses etc.

★

Dudu is trying to beat down Jerry Basis, his dealer who has raised his prices for the second time in a month. Dudu is unshaven, tidemarks on his Dudu Loves Ya! T-shirt, grubby tennis shoes. He looks like a derelict. There was an incident that had to be hushed up when a security guard wouldn't let him into the VIP corral and Dudu goes ballistic, goes into hospitalising mood. 'I am the V in VIP. Prick.'

As usual he stumbles into my humble atelier – you might call it a cupboard. He's clutching a flaking Supersol plastic shopping bag full of burner phones. He makes and receives calls here because he suspects that his Winnebago, which is about ten times the size, is bugged. He is probably right. It may even have been bugged by Sacha's associates. (That is not mentioned.) He tells Jerry that he is a greedy criminal but he won't grass him up if he comes over straightaway.

13.20

Jerry is sitting at my 'throne', a little school-style desk with green legs. He is cutting lines of Prince with a bank card. He didn't acknowledge me when he arrived. But then he never does. I'm just furniture like my little school-style desk with green legs. He doesn't offer me any but even if he did I wouldn't take it – I've seen what it's done to Dudu. He is learning a script that includes a tired old gag which he doesn't need to learn. He calls it a trusty faithful. Time was, no matter how many times they heard it Dudu's people lapped it up . . . That was then, this is now . . . It doesn't cut the mustard any more.

'How many apes did it take to write this script . . . this treyf . . . Oh whoops! Would you know it . . . it took just this one ape and his one typewriter.' False modesty doesn't come much falser than that. He's developed the habit of laughing before he speaks, to signal what he's going to say is funny in case no one realises. He used to be way better than that. Now he's at a stage of his career where just about getting away with it is the best he can hope for. Of course he doesn't admit that to himself either. The Prince won't let him. It tells him he is Moshe Dayan or Alexander the Great or Orde Wingate or Phil Silvers. It never tells him he is Mike and Bernie Winters.

★

On recording days I have a routine. I like to get out for a light lunch by myself – but enough to see me through till late because you never know. Chickpea salad, flatbread, lamb bourekas, cheese bourekas, skewers of ecumenical king rabbit from Gadara, veggie bourekas, pide, baba ganoush, halloumi from the food trucks each with its specialities. That's my usual. My colleagues don't like to remark on my lordly appetite as I call it. If their gossip word for me is fatso glutton, well, amen to that. I eat among the ruins that transport me back in time to when handsome centurions fought wild animals and the mob was behind the animals: nothing can be done about that, it's the way of the world: hierarchy.

Then I amble for forty minutes, perhaps having a shady relax amid the boundless aroma of the eucalypti. For dessert I have a violet booza – sort of ice cream with stretchy elastane and Lebanese heritage. I'm a good time keeper and time maker but there's nothing to be gained from getting back so early you have to wait around in a state of sun deprivation. So sometimes I go down to the sea. Despite the size abuse from mooning yoks louting about on the beach the sight of the breakers glinting releases powerful emotions in me, not to mention a fond longing for waves as high as mountains destroying cities and obliterating life.

When I got back to the gypsies' encampment it was unlike I'd ever seen it before. The audience queue doesn't usually build up till about an hour before the show goes on air. This was unprecedented. It was twice as long as even the queues for classic Dudu summer extravaganzas like *West Bank Wet T-Shirt* and *Miss Jerusalem Thong* or *Dudu Asks The Questions*, e.g. What is god's day job? 1) Midwife 2) Funeral Director 3) Cosmetic Surgeon.

There were three hours to go still and the queue was already stretching down the road and out of sight getting drifts of sand blown at them. Security Consultant Ofer and Security Consultant Shuli were doing crowd control: they loved it, bellowing into their squawkies and making important traffic cop gestures.

It wasn't expected. No way. After the Aliens fiasco – the Aliens didn't show up – half a cheated nation that had stayed in to watch them join Dudu jammed the switchboard for days on end.

No one in their right mind believed that another outrageous

promise would have any effect. But . . . gullibility feeds on itself . . . That's the only conclusion you can come to . . . Mugs never learn. Correction: they don't want to learn. The previous week Dudu signed off yet another really limp show with that humble sincere voice of his. To me it oozed the bad faith of a bad actor. If only they knew! He spoke of his word of honour. They took him at his word of honour. He pledged that his next show would be a 'sea change', that its very special guest was the Jewish people's greatest ever enemy and this Specialmost Guest appearance would be the first time he or (coyly) she had been seen in three-quarters of a century. He, Dudu, was going to ask the big question 'Why?'

He had left the set with actorish humility. (There's no such thing.)

The newspapers' memories are so short they might be suffering dementia. They had forgotten the 'comedy otters'. They had forgotten that Dudu belongs to an age long gone . . . They had forgotten they asked in big letters WHY DOES THE CHANNEL INFLICT THIS TRASH ON ITS AUDIENCE? They were obsessed by Dudu's announcement. Drooling over him. They were doing his publicity for him. Making it a 'news event'. It wasn't. It was a staged stunt.

They were waving competitive bundles of cash at stage hands and script consultants to disclose the identity of the most special of special guests. They didn't get anywhere because no one knew. He or she would arrive at the amphitheatre in an armoured truck just before the start of the show. Or delivered by helicopter maybe. He or she was already in hiding in the luxury trailer.

Security Shuli gave me his friendly salute combined with a whatever-next, hunch-shouldered, racial-stereotype shrug towards the excitable throng who gave up their individuality to become a brown uniform mass. Why do all those colours add up to brown like dirty painting water? Dissolution of Person syndrome. What it means is that everyone accepts familiar mob thought, mob adoration, mob chatter, mob hate, mob laughter, mob melancholy, mob giggling etc. No one knows who's instigating and who's copying.

Like I was practising breast stroke I had to double elbow my way through the invitation-only area, a strange open-sided tent that had been attacked for resembling the 1972 Olympic stadium. There were people I'd never seen before. Who was this dance troupe in leotards? They were shamelessly showing off their malnutrition. Word of mouth is a strange conundrum isn't it. Sacha calls it the Arab telephone. A bottle blonde bob with roots negligence impeded me. She told me I didn't have an identity photo on a lanyard. Where is it? I told her I worked here. I was a long-term employee with my own atelier. She was an intruder. Who did she think she was?

I was planning to kick her to the ground, sit on her and squash the life out of her when Sacha appeared and spoke to her in a language I don't know. Ooh if the wind changes while she's scowling like that . . . These then were Sacha's associates. Despite her, mostly men. You wouldn't call them amiable.

But put it this way: they were people you'd rather have on your side than not. A group was wearing Haganah vintage combat kit. Three men dressed like Sacha – dark suits, white shirts – were deep in conversation. There was excited anticipation in the air. Excited anticipation smells like sour sweat. As the afternoon wore on little groups of people showed up who were not Dudu fans. They were given a clear pass through security. Some poked their head round my door, didn't disguise their sniffiness. They were politicians, important business figures, television industry big cheeses, newspaper editors, young comers from the channel all milling around gladhanding and hugging exclusive hugs, not for the likes of me. They all knew each other. Dudu was their chouchou. No . . . he *had* been their chouchou. They wished Dudu well. No . . . to tell the truth they wished him ill. Their public proclamations of support were bogus. They were no longer prepared to indulge him. They didn't know how to effect the break. Week after week they hoped that Dudu would give them a reason to push him sideways. An early morning slot would be found for him. They searched for an excuse. They needed to take the little people with them, his fanbase, the 66 per cent had to be won round. No one will ever know how complicit Sacha and his associates were.

I greyed Dudu's hair, brushed in just a few streaks of face powder, talc, fixative. There was so much Prince around I could have used that! I did warn him of the old saying 'premature greyness is the sign of the charlatan'. He was untroubled – but that's the way the Prince takes you. He believed himself impregnable. Sacha wasn't around to dissuade him from a double barrel blast just before he went on. That was unusual, that absence. If Sacha was in town he was always there with Dudu just before the start of the show, ribbing him about his chant of orchestra and beginners which he had learnt at RADA.

Dudu said: 'I'm going to need god on my side for this one.'

'I'll see what I can do!' I said with a wink which he didn't see because he was lost in self-admiration.

I guessed Sacha was busy with important people. Earlier he had mentioned in his insinuating way that 'he had heard' that Caesarea was the codename of a 'fate-determining corps which does not exist'. I didn't read anything into it. Maybe I should have. Anyway, what could I have done?

A floor manager, ever more invisible than me, herded in the malnourished dancers. There was no end of them. Abel Perez, the new producer who'd been employed 'to shake things up', had told her to tell me to make them up to look 'ghostly, dead or diseased'.

A few minutes later Abel himself flustered in, a whirl of chaos and panic.

'Let yourself go!' he instructed me.

'Dead isn't the same as diseased,' I told him.

'In Dudu world it is.'

Shtik drek!

I did an OTT job. I exaggerated Annemarie Busschers's paintings in *De Perfectie van Imperfectie*. They were exquisite and delicate. I was way cruder. Blancoed faces, then some impressionistic rashes, blisters, gross poxes, sores, scabs, juicy buboes, rosaceas, melanomas. They said they were looking forward to what they called regimented writhing. It might be a big break for some of them. They didn't know what their place was in the entertainment.

The gallery truck was unrecognisable. I'd never seen it with anyone but the staff in it. Now the mixers, synchronisers and technicians were having to move visitors so they didn't get in the way: not the easiest task when you have a job to do and a self-important member of the Knesset is preventing you doing it because he's taken your chair and his wife is toying with your controls.

The signature tune sounded. A Dudu creation. It did its job. It said

'Dudu' catchily enough but Cole Porter he wasn't. Its existence was down to his bullying. If he didn't get his way there were tantrums.

The stage was obscured by moonless nightfall and sea mist. There was silence broken only by the amplified roar of waves battering the stony shore and the croaks of ravens hunting bats in aerial combat. There was nothing to see. It seemed interminable. The audience became restless. Some of the VIPs who hadn't consented to move on from the gallery truck demanded to know what was happening. They were told to keep quiet. It was a sensory deprivation exercise. It was more comfortable than what followed.

Eardrum damaging rude brutal music.

Collaged, frantic, quick-cut film, spoiled film, out of focus film, magnified film of: an Arbeit Macht Frei sign, firing squads, Einsatzgruppen Mordhunds, forced marches, piles of bodies, barbed wire, desperate faces, more bodies, the tramp of boots, Kristallnacht, explosions, gunfire, books burning, anti-Jewish signs, Nuremberg rallies etc.

It was repetitive, agonising. These were our people reduced to non-people and Ben-Gurion's horrible verdict: 'Everything they had endured purged their souls of all good.'

Nothing that had not been seen before, nothing that the audience can have been unfamiliar with, nothing though that failed still to shock after all these years of exposure. Familiarity doesn't lessen the horror. Quite the opposite. Yet . . . this was a Dudu Topaz show: where was the laughter and fun, the spills and the pranks, the comedy otters . . .

And here was Dudu Topaz himself, a long-faced Dudu all in white − not flattering to the fuller figure! − with atrocity footage projected onto him while the malnourished dancers, dressed in the striped uniform of the camps, writhed and whined in a pile like an obscene multi-limbed, multi-headed animal. It recalled Jerry Coe's famous painting of the shipwreck. The audience recoiled as one. It had recongregated as the mob it had been while it queued in antici-pation. Anticipation that turned to restless embarrassed silence as Dudu spoke, preached. All white didn't suit him.

'Why did we allow ourselves to become the victims of the greatest atrocity? How did we allow it? Did we allow it because we were too trusting, too optimistic about the motives of mankind? Did we allow ourselves to believe that the unbelievable could never happen even though the unbelievable – annihilation, extermination – was a publicly proclaimed project . . . of a faction that was so readily despised, so palpably absurd, so funny, yes funny (weedy book-keepers dressed for combat), that it could not be taken seriously? We allowed ourselves to ignore what we knew, that a germ grows into a plant, that a ditch becomes a brook, a stream, a river whose tidal bore drowns us. We allowed ourselves to forget history, *our* history of persecution, our history of providing a ready target, of being brought into this world branded with a star announcing our culpability – for anything. We are not Jews, we are not a religion, we are not a race, we are not a people . . . we are scapegoats.

'Why us? Why do we possess the gift of being hated? That is our precious gift, the gift which defines us – wrongly. Why us? Why us still? Blood libels . . . Jesus's death . . . they were a long long time ago but they are here today . . . they're ever present. We must not allow ourselves to be thought of as victims, as passive patients when the aggressive agents tread the world with heavy hate. It is their wickedness, not ours.

'These are some of the questions I'm going to put to my special guest tonight. But first – I want to show you how much I care about the past and correcting the past and tracking down our enemies who as we all know go into hiding like the cowards they are: Syria, Spain, Egypt, even Israel, the last place anyone looks.'

Film of sometime Nazis in Aleppo, Alexandria, playing tennis in Istanbul, Gulf States, drinking in Murcia, chatting over churros in Recoleta . . .

Rousing chorus: Horst Wessel Lied.

'My special guest was different: he's been in hiding underground . . .

'We've given him a grooming, a wash and brush-up. We don't want a scruffy goy making television history, do we Pals? We want our special guest looking dapper and clean . . . and murderous. Remember those folk who got a hard-on from looking at Eichmann in uniform . . . let's have no gender inequality, we all know shiksas who drowned in their own liquid excitement . . . Genitalia can betray our country and our race as much as foul thoughts do. Don't let's go there.'

Loud chorale singing Deutschland über Alles. Six dancers in black basques and thigh-high boots exaggeratedly goosestep onto the set, stiff arm salutes.

(They'd done their own hooker make-up – straight out of the Otto Dix maquillage guide.)

They are followed by six actors dressed in black SS uniforms and wearing Halloween skull-face masks. They strode onto the set pushing an expressly built wooden gurney decorated with runes, swastikas, eagles, the black sun, flags and oak leaf emblems. Behind them upstage a troop of ten-year-old Stormtoddlers in scale-model uniforms marched on the spot.

Dudu was at his smilingest: 'OK, here we go, this is the one you've been waiting for – Let's hear it now for Dudu's special guest . . . Former Reichsführer SS, Heinrich Himmler.'

The black uniforms tilted the gurney so that its passenger gradually became visible to the cameras, to the audience, which drew horrified breath as one, a programmed machine. It was repulsed, it gasped. Then it was silent, shock made it mute.

The man . . . the creature . . . the thing in the gurney was in the twisted position in which it had been captured. An anaerobic contortionist fixed in uterine limbo and turned to leather by acidic turbary. He didn't have the knack of escaping from the rusted barbed wire and bedraggled webbing which he was wrapped in. His skin and hair intact and tanned the colour of whisky and peat, I think I'd call it high-gloss treacly caramel-black obsidian . . . like a nasty accident in a tanning parlour . . . so cooked it was as if he had changed race and – here's a terrible fate for a racist – had joined the enemy, had become a member of some dark-skinned people of such inferiority he couldn't shake his own hand. He'd be hating himself if he could.

Himmler looked too like reused kit from the corner of a wax-scented tack room, several highly polished dressage saddles tortured into an approximation of human form by a disabled groom resentful of undamaged bodies. The leather kneaded by a callipered leg.

There was commotion in the gallery. 'For fuck's sake what's going on, what's that thing . . . what's this Himmler business . . . what's he doing . . .'

Followed by: 'That *is* Himmler. That thing is Himmler . . . that thing . . . That's what happens when they're buried in peat . . . I can tell you're not a Holsteiner . . . that's what oxygen starvation does . . .'

'You can be sure his bones and teeth and skull will have dissolved . . .'

'It's a negative image of a usual buried body where the skin and soft tissue get all rotted and holed and putrid by exposure to oxygen and the bacteria.'

'This is a body without rot. It doesn't have an armature so to speak. There is nothing to rot. Virtually boneless.'

Dudu was in joyful mood. The cries and barracking and curses bounced off him.

Tell us, Heini – you're OK with me calling you Heini, aren't you Heini – you've worked with some of the biggest names in the geno-cide game . . . world-class mass murderers. How do you rate yourself alongside say Lavrenti Beria?

No reply.

What . . . just an apparatchik . . . is that what you're thinking?

No reply.

Would you describe yourself as a committee man of state terror?

No reply.

What's your verdict on Elizabeth Báthory?

No reply.

Genghis Khan . . . now there was a real killer . . . Leopold II . . . Gilles de Rais . . . Come on man, let's hear from you! Let's have it. Don't mumble. Mao . . . does he make you feel you underachieved . . . I'll bet he does . . . Do you resent his popular-ity with the kids?

No reply.

When you're at the hairdresser do you find his idle boring chitchat enough to send him to Dachau?

No reply.

Where are you going on holiday this year???

No reply.

Tell us about some of those fabulous ladies you met . . . what about Marlene Dietrich?

No reply.

How did you get on with Marianne Hoppe? She liked a Nazi . . . or two . . .

No reply.

I'll bet you had some fun with the girls at Babelsberg Studios you dashing old rogue. Don't be shy.

No reply.

Music . . . Tell us about your taste in music.

No reply.

Silence . . . total silence eh? Never had you down as being into the old avant-garde . . . totally out of fashion now you know.

Das Ledern Himmler might have been playing Grandma's Footsteps. It might move at any moment.

Dudu turned to the audience with a shoulder-juddering laugh.

A man rose from the front row of the frozen speechless auditorium. A spotlight picked him out. For a moment I thought it was Sacha. He was draped in a loose lawyer's gown. He wore starched white neck bands.

Dudu greeted him with a mockingly facetious fop's bow and multiple curlicues of the wrist. He presented him to the bewildered audience: 'Maître Paul Christea . . . avocat au barreau de Paris.'[56]

His features were so like Sacha's. But his aura, tics, bodily presence and motor movements were not. The shadow he cast wasn't Sacha's . . . Nor did he possess Sacha's suggestive tone of voice . . . Maybe Paul Christea was the not quite double of Sacha Lipurt.

'My client,' said the lawyer, striving to become the second most unpopular man in Tel Aviv, 'reserves the right to remain silent.' The audience hissed.

'Of course he does – but let him answer this—'

'The citizen has a right to a defence, which includes, as I say, the right to remain silent.'

More hissing, heckling, boos.

Maître Paul Christea: 'No matter how grave the crime, the accused must be dealt justice and not the law of the lynch mob, which is no law but the vengeance of animals. Animals. I am not defending my client's crimes – which in accord with the ethical programme of the NSDAP he did not believe to be crimes. That moral system privileged darkness over light, death over life. Pollarding trees rather than

---

56 There is no record of a member of the Paris bar named Paul Christea.

letting them grow at the expense of the shrubs whose water they appropriate. No, I am defending *him*, the actor rather than the action – I am defending the man no matter how monstrous his crimes. The accused must be fairly tried, for otherwise the democracy that the court represents descends to the level of the criminal state he was largely responsible for. There is of course no society without crime. But there are many just societies which do not sanction state crimes, which do not normalise them and so betray their citizens rather than protect them.

'A man shows what he is made of when destiny is not on his side, when it cheats him, grinds him down – as it has ground down my client. Fate weighs heavy on him. Fate is another name for victor's justice.'

Dudu strode about the stage: 'Heinrich Himmler. You are charged with crimes against humanity—'

Maître Christea: 'Humanity? My client, as I have suggested, does not recognise the subjects of his clearances as belonging to humanity. Humanity is relative—'

Dudu: 'Heinrich Himmler. You are charged with crimes against humanity . . . murder, extermination, enslavement, massacre, rape, deportation, disfranchisement, torture, abduction of minors for prostitution, starvation.'

A man with glossy seniority smeared all over him stood beside me in the gallery. The way he rubbed proprietorially against me. I had him down as a senior executive with frotting rights. He said to no one in particular: 'This is not what we pay this jumped-up comedian for. Who the fuck does he think he is?'

'He's making television history,' I ventured timidly.

'History my arse, he's making us look fools. Not just us . . . He's turning the nation into a joke. Why d'you let him do it?'

'He's got free will, hasn't he? . . . I'm just his make-up artiste,' I lied. 'It's a satire . . . it's teaching us . . . I assure you . . .'

'You must be joking. Dancing girls and chorus boys . . . It's more like some homage . . . a tribute to a monster. He's turning the Shoah into a sick gag. The Shoah . . . Our people died in their millions and this schlump . . .'

Countless iterations of that sentiment spread across the gallery, a

wave working up to a roar. Someone spat: 'Nuremberg choreographed by Tami Lenzini.'[57]

Phoning, pissed off to get no response from yours truly, he pushed
through the screen gapers shoving each other for a better view of
history in the making. He had a point – drawn from a limited understanding and first impressions.

One of the actors dressed as an SS belched. Ravens croaked their
mimic's response. It grumbled out of the helpless mouth. The audience's spine froze. They believed the noise in three movements had
come from Himmler.

Dudu: 'How do you plead?'

No reply.

Dudu to audience: 'You lovely people . . . you lovely people . . .
you are Dudu's friends . . . you are the friends of Dudu, my devoted
audience . . . my faithful disciples . . . Now . . . are you going to help
me out here . . . help me out . . . and ask the war criminal's war criminal some probing questions . . . where is my family for instance . . .
where are their ashes . . . what did you do to my twins . . . when you
tread on a pile of foetid reeking emaciated bodies do you recognise
them as fellow humans?'

Maître Christea: 'Objection, my client—'

'How did you feel when a Jew's blown-out brain disfigured your
uniform . . . splashed on your face like a money shot—'

The silence was sharp. Antagonism is crisp and cold. Dudu misread the audience's mood. The audience realised. It read itself right.
It was appalled. There were cries of 'no no no'. Fury sped through
the throng.

Maître Christea: 'Because he cannot escape being the leather
Himmler, who shines like the stout veldtschoen of the Wandervögel
and the Boers – further victims of British imperialism – he is unable
himself to address this kangaroo court of people who have no right
to try him. Only Apollyon and Adolf Hitler may try him . . .'

The clouds parted to reveal Baal on high in his majesty, fire
burning before his throne, a tithe-child's blood and marrow

---

57 Solange 'Tami' Lenzini (1912–45) was a ballerina, actor, choreographer and enthusiastic
collaborator during the German occupation of Paris.

dripping from his avaricious face. Without warning came jagged bolts of lightning in the form of the SS rune. They lit the sky. They made the glass sea shiver. Horned beasts rose from it, put the birds to flight. Thunder screeched its killing symphony. Clattering batteries and crazed tympany scraped shrieking heaven. They drummed the name of blasphemy. Women gorged on the seed of serpents.

People tell how winged beasts with the bodies of bulls and the manes of lions and the skin of ancient reptiles raised from its cradle the ghost of the Reichsführer SS. They raised it in raiments of high ceremony, its boots and buckles and death's head gleamed. A sword swung in its scabbard. The creature was as much a priest in prayer as a degorger of children. It sprung from its cradle and looked about itself, listened with ears of a jackal. It sprung from its cradle as from the longest sleep. It saluted the celestial runes, in awe and wonder and swollen pride. Its eyes were holes into black eternity.

Then it was no longer there. It melted into dissolution. Anthems greeted it. No one knew till then that Ein Deutsches Requiem had been composed for this moment. It strode into the night. Its tail was tautly erect. Its body was vertically exaggerated as if by El Greco. The chorus was still audible when it was no longer to be seen. It had been there.

People tell about that night . . . Me, I had witnessed those few seconds which were stretched beyond measure. Me, I had seen the most terrifying revenant. Had I seen it? Had we all? Remember the rumour that Napoleon was a creation of French collective wishfulness. The audience gasped and yelled and sought breath and succour and suffered mass hysteria. Some fainted. They all tried to scatter, all impeded each other. They were felled and trampled. Broken teeth and broken glasses, limbs splintered, marrow leaking, organs crushed. Blood, fright, indignity. Ripped clothes, empty wigs. It was a peacetime simulacrum of bodies piled high in the camps. Peacetime? So long as that ghost treads the earth there will be no peace. I can't be held responsible.

Where did it go? Did it haunt the cliffs? Did it hide in caves when it felt a black storm screaming towards the shore? Did it conform to space and time's bogus programme? All evidence points elsewhere. It was simultaneously spotted round a campfire with boy disciples in the Harz, picking ticks from a gorilla's fur in the last treehouse guinguette at Plessis-Robinson and counting the number of skulls in the evil walls of Wallenstein Gardens a few kilometres from where the potential usurper Heydrich was assassinated, not a moment too soon.

It hoped it looked like god – some hope! It was wrathful despite its dreary mien: it might be taken for a junior member of the sub-committee on death and terror. Its glasses which occluded the eyes transmitted heliographic maxims. Warrants for its arrest were issued by:

The state of Israel

The German government

The federal state of Lower Saxony

The international war crimes tribunal at The Hague

The Polish government

The Czech and Slovakian governments

The governments of the Russian Federation, Hungary, Greece and Italy

The United Kingdom government

The French government.

The consequences of that unique show, of Dudu's ill-founded attempt to present himself as a political figure, have often been recounted. Sometimes with sadness, sometimes with gleeful relish. Always with a fearful distaste for his careless release of powers from another realm. He allowed hallucinatory squalor to impair the certainties of our everyday normality. He called those certainties into question. He showed up their fragility.

He paid the price. *Dudu Topaz First In Entertainment* was cancelled. The channel didn't wait for the persuasion of the communications ministry. It had made up its mind even before the indignant clamour in the Knesset which united the routinely antagonistic. What else could have caused Itzik Sinai and Motti Harari to stand shoulder to shoulder! The Minister of Communications Nina Bar addressed the nation through her tangled web of hair. (Conditioner please!) She spoke of 'a night of shame, a night of obloquy . . . an irresponsible act of immeasurable self-importance . . . which insulted the nation . . . made a joke of suffering . . . opened wounds for the sake of low-level so-called entertainment . . . which tarnished our international prestige. The next time Mr Topaz attempts self-harm he should do what the name says . . . self . . . Yes? He should not harm his compatriots too.'

She wouldn't for a moment recognise what was obvious – that we had witnessed an act beyond the boundaries of understanding. No one in the arena, perhaps no one in the world had previous experience of a gratuitous act like that. It happened causelessly. Was it *un tour de passepasse* or prestidigitation or a third party's intervention? All conjuring, all sleight of hand. I believe that god is a magician. It's obvious isn't it. Bad Baal too.

There was a global banterstorm. Racially harmonious sociopaths of all creeds, colours, cults, hates etc. united to condemn Israel for demanding sympathy when it was a hypocrite that exploited the masochism it was steeped in. A hypocrite that cultivated an exceptionalism based in victimhood and self-pity. A hypocrite whose only purpose was to exact Yahweh's revanchism to drive from their land poor Palestinians. They, in their turn, were learning victimhood and self-pity.

Dudu had given his antagonists further fuel for his pyre. Dudu's comeback vehicle as an actor, *Bubot*, had already been cancelled. *First In Entertainment* was cancelled. *Everything Moves With Dudu Topaz* was cancelled. Dudu's 'serious' column in *Haaretz* was cancelled. *Dudu Meets With*[58] was cancelled. Dudu himself was cancelled.

His fall was deep and long – the well was deep. His friends deserted him. That's what friends are for: even I know that. They are not around when needed.

Maddened, all he could think of was revenge. Hot revenge, coarse revenge, wild, ill-considered revenge. The Dudu Topaz he believed

---

58 *Dudu Meets With* was disparagingly known as *Dudu Meets With Sad Fucks So Desperate To Revive Their Career They Are Willing To Meet With Dudu*. E.g. *Dudu Meets With* Snork Bagdossarian/ Dickinson Vlasto/Priscilla Mister/Anthea Stevenette/Maria Hufnangel/Fleur Brebner/Ledesma Defty/Lebo Lala/Danielle Méla/Toni Lo Reno/Avram Benayoun/Loyd Parnacott et al.

himself to be did not accord with the Dudu Topaz his dwindling number of fans idolised but with the Dudu reflected in the mirror. When I crouched beside him so our heads were level the reflected man he admired was not the man I saw.

The desire to break lives as he believed his had been broken ate him to the exclusion of all else.

The first contract he took out was on his disloyal, treacherous, self-seeking, two-timing, gossiping agent Reuven Vered. He employed Security Ape Motti and Security Ape Nabil. Because of Dudu's scribble they mistook Vered's address. They attacked a teenage girl on her way to school rather than a middle-aged man. The girl fled into a laundry. Motive: possible sexual assault. No suspects, no arrests. No one to put it to rights.

They were more successful in beating up the television executives Mordechai Banin and Eli Klinger as they waited for their car beneath Eyal At The Golden Calf's porte-cochère. Baseball bats, knuckle-dusters. Security Ape Motti was recognised by the parking valet who delivered the car just as the first blow was struck. Eli Klinger's skull was fractured and his jaw broken. Motti was arrested two days later. Security Ape Nabil is believed to have fled to Fez.

Dudu was undeterred. He recruited a cashiered soldier recommended by his dealer Jerry Basis as a 'man who gets things tidy'. Ronen Shum had just been released from Prison Four's Company Gimel. He was grateful for any job let alone the opportunity to work for a big name. His attack on the Director of Future Creative Creation (Factual) Eliot Atar was ill-considered. Atar was a former stunt performer and professional boxer. Having lost two teeth Shum ran away. Less than a week later the casting director Naomi Ginsburg temporarily blinded Shum with a pepper spray in the Cremieux Street car park where he had ambushed her. Unable to see he stumbled in front of a van that had just been stolen by two joyriders. Punctured lung. The joyriders were trapped in the van, bleeding heavily. Because they were minors they were referred to as Y and H. All three malefactors were detained at the scene.

'No sane woman even enters an underground car park without a pepper or mace spray,' Naomi Ginsburg told a reporter from i24 News.

The doubly unfortunate Shum did a trade with the police. Dudu was arrested. He made his first suicide attempt after only ten days in prison. He wrote that he had failed because of 'lack of math' rather than lack of will: he underestimated the dose of insulin required to kill him. A fellow prisoner gave him a copy of the Dream Topping™ publication *Small Space Solutions & Improvisational Challenges*. He suspected that the flimsy shower towels would not bear his weight. He succeeded with the cord of an electric kettle attached to a stout window hook. His very first attempt to kick away the chair he stood on sent him soaring to a palace of gurgling fountains and shady arbours where ocelots basked and dancing houris, attentive to a handsome man, proffered sweetmeats and opium and their mishmish. Really? Sorry. But next time, Dudu, next time, maybe.

The hooked cross on the dunes was made of rusted reinforcing rods and a beached boat's timbers bleached like bones. The wiry, half-naked old panhandler with a ragged beard wears glasses matt with salt. His barbed wire crown is rusty and flaking. Metal is a defence against resurrection. Oxygen will destroy leather.

The man claimed he was Jesus Christ, an Aryan prophet. I can validate that claim. He sat with his tin mug for alms beside his handiwork. He wore shredded overalls, he smiled with pride and benevolence.

He nodded and said: 'The sentence is ended. That was your lives. Redemption? Or is it expiation . . . How should I know – you don't ask a horse to explain an accumulator.'

Luc takes Tamara by the hand: 'Now I can die.'

Stinging sand is whipped up by the wind. Land and sea are indivisible.

They stumble towards the pounding shore.

In a moment, in a twinkling of an eye . . .

She feels for what is not there.

Years later she remembered . . . the black-suited magician calling himself Luc Shapitra wandered beside her on the dunes. He whispered: 'Judex.' Doves flew from his extravagant cuffs. Become starlings, they swirled alone then gathered together in a choreographed troupe to murmurate axels and pikes in the sky. They transformed themselves into ravens whose razor beaks were the last thing they saw. Mistaking their eyes for jewels the greedy birds plucked them out. They clutched each other in the darkness and fell from the illusion of life into the insensate abyss where organs of sight and taste and sound and memory are not known. It's different here.

Unbound is the world's first crowdfunding publisher, established in 2011.

We believe that wonderful things can happen when you clear a path for people who share a passion. That's why we've built a platform that brings together readers and authors to crowdfund books they believe in – and give fresh ideas that don't fit the traditional mould the chance they deserve.

This book is in your hands because readers made it possible. Everyone who pledged their support is listed below. Join them by visiting unbound.com and supporting a book today.

Adam Alcock
Ashley Allen
Benjamin Anderson
Keith Anderson
Nathaniel C R Anderson
Kirk Annett
Gregory Arrowsmith
Christine Asbury
Adrian Atterbury
Thomas Austin
James Aylett
Ed Baines
Lori Baluta
Robert "Bobby" Banks
Mark Barnett

Jack Barrie
Jason Barrow
John Bateson
Kevin Batt
Raymond Francis Beard
Phil Beddow
Thomas W Beeson
Andy Bell
Ian Bentley
Sean Berry
Stuart Betts
Beyond The Zero Podcast
Matthew Blake
Peter Bonnalie
David Book

Jon Bounds
Alexander Bourne
Bruce Bowie
Roger Bowles
David Bowman
Liam Boyce
Chris Brace
Harriet Bramley
Phil Bramley
Richard W H Bray
Mick Bridgman
Tim Bromfield
Jonathan Brooker
Anthony Brown
John Brown
Brian Browne
Emily Bryce-Perkins
Karen Bulmer
Neil Burgess
Richard Burgess
Michael and Lindy Burleigh
Mike Burn
Nigel Burwood
Richard Butchins
Samuel Caddick
Ian Callaway
Alisdair Cameron
Peter Campbell
Stuart Canning
Darren Richard Carlaw
Erin Carrington
Charlie Cassarino
Rodney Challis
Robert Chilton
Simon Christie
Richard Clack
Derek Calado Clark

John Clark
Ross Clark
Keith Javier Claxton
James Clive-Matthews
Andrew Clubb
Gary Coates
James Coen
Edward Collier
Michael Connors
Bailey Cooper
Daniel Copley
Andrew Copson
Joseph Cotter
Geoff Coupe
Tom Crane
John Crawford
Malcolm Crosby
N. Crotty
Stephen Crowe
Paul Cuff
Matt Curran
Andrew Curtis
Kae Dale
Nick Davey
Adam Davies
Gareth Davies
Marquis de Chard
Martin de Cogan
Philip de Jersey
Henry de Vroome
Christian DeFeo
Callum Delhoy
Paul Dembina
Neil Denny
Ben Diamond
Les Dodd
Peter Dodge

Michael Dombrowski
Kevin Donnellon
Martin Donnelly
J Doran
Andrew Duke
Robbie Duncan
Jane Dunster
Stephen and Karen Durrant
Bilge Ebiri
Max Patzak Edwards
Michael Edwards
John Eley
Louis Emmett
JM Esq
John W. Fail
Simon Faircliff
Mauro Falcone
Steven Fennell
George Ferguson
Paul Finch
Steven Finch
William Firebrace
Mark Fleming
Claudine Ford
N W Ford
Timothy Fortescue
Anthony Forth
Daniel Frankenburg
Jonathan Fraser
Justin Freeman
Peter Frost
Adrian Fry
James Fry
Richard Furniss
Mark Gamble
Alexander Gann
Andrea Gates

Amro Gebreel
Julie Giles
Richard Gladman
John Goddard
Charlie Goodier
Giles Goodland
Tim Grainger
Colin Greenwood
David Guest
Gary Hall
Rick Halsall
Henrik Hamelius
Nathan Hamer
Francis Hanly
J Hanson
Robin Hardie
Mark Harding
David Hare
Matthew Harle
James Hartley
Jonathan Hartwright
Guy Haslam
Barry Hasler
Eivind Hasvik
Amanda Hay
Paul Hayes
Jonathan Haynes
Anthony Heath
Simon and Diana Heffer
Peter Hemington
Susan Henesy
Nicholas C. Henry
Deborah Herron
Jeremy Hill
Steve Hill
Joeri Hilte
Duncan Hiscock

Christopher James Hodges

Mike Hodges

John Hodgkinson

Andy Holbrook

Finn Holding

Chris Hough

David Housham

Paul Howard

Danny Howell

Matt Huggins

Matthew J. Hughes

Patrick Hughes

Richard Hughes

Pierpaolo Inga

Fred Ingrams

Intrigued

Ian Irvine

David Isaak

David Jackson

Oliver Jackson

Louis Jagger

Lucy Jago

Ian Jamison

Graeme Jarvie

Zak Jeffcoat

Mark Jeffery

Toby Jeffries

Dan Jenkins

Ric Jerrom

Mark Jewell

Jacob Johannsen

Rebecca John

Jeremy Langford Johnson

Ian Johnston

Denis Jones

Ieuan Jones

Nick Jones

Peter Jones

Kyle Jorvina-Rudden

Andres Kabel

John Kane

Coleman Kendall

Christopher Kennard

Seán Kenny

Rolfe Kentish

Peter Kettle

Inara Khan & Otis Doyle

George Brown Kinghorn

Brian Kirkbride

Joyce Kittenplan

Cate Kneale

Grégoire Kretz

Robert and Patrick Lagneau

Mit Lahiri

Ray Lakeman

Sam Lamplugh

Conrad Landin

Andriejus Lasys

Dafydd Launder

Jeremy Lee

Simon Lee

Tobias Lee

Mark Leggott

Rowley Leigh

Ruth Leonard

Geoff Levett

Geoffrey Levett

Paul Levy

Jerry Lewington

Simon Lewis

Jonathan Light

Ben Lindner

Robert Lipfriend

Anthony John Loftus

Paul Love
Philip Lovell
Pat Lowe
Brian Lunn
Nick Lupton
Rodin Lyasoff
Mike Lynd
Ava M
D.W. M.
Chris Macdonald
Colin Macfarlane
Ross MacFarlane
Seonaid Mackenzie
Simon Mackley
Carl Major
Elliott Mannis
Colin Mason
Sara Masson
A Mathers
Rob McBride
Douglas McCabe
Bryan McConachie
Ian McGowan
Martin McMahon
Jim McNally
Christopher McWilliam
Riaz Meer
Catherine Mellor
Rebecca Clare Mellor
Molly Millar
Ben Miller
Alastair Mitchell
Anno Mitchell
Steve Mitchell
John Mitchinson
Gordon Moar
Linda Monckton

Ian Mond
Simon Monkman
Diego Montoyer
Jack Moore
Denese Morden
James Morgan
Stephen Morris
Jonathan Morrow
Michael Mosbacher
Bernard Moxham
Andrew Moxon
Andy Muggleton
Robin Mulvihill
John Murphy
Jonathan Murphy
Stephen Musgrave
Kathy Nagle
Supporter Names
Neville Nancliff
Carlo Navato
Joachim New
Miles Newlyn
Daniel Newman
Melanie Nicholls
Maria Nightingale
Markku Nivalainen
Andrew Nixon
Rodney O'Connor
John O'Dea
Rory O'Gara
Mark O'Neill
Jerome O'Gorman
Alfredo Orrego
Kassia Oset
Stuart & Lesley Oxbrow-Trim
Neil Pace
Marc Pacitti

Jack Page
Michael Paley
Matthew Parden
Steph Parker
Matthew Parry
Timothy Patrick and Lewis
  Fortescue
Geoff Patterson
Mark Peachey
Bianca Pellet
Ian Perry
Mark Phillips
Kenny Pieper
Caroline Ross Pirie
Stephen Pochin
Shae Poffley
John Porter
Mark Porter
Thomas Powell
Stephen Press
Donald Proud
Jonathan Pugh
Mark Pugh
Caroline Pulver
Nicky Quint
JS Rafaeli
Duncan Raggett
William Rankin
Dean Rawding
Jonny Rawlings
Nicholas Redding
Dean Redfearn
Bambi Redux
Mark Reed
Hugh Rees
Cornelia Rémi
Mark Revelle

Hugh D. Reynolds
Ben Richardson
David Richardson
Philip Richardson
Stuart Riddle
Thomas Ridgway
David Roche
Frank Rooney
Mick Rooney
Tom Roper
Anthony Michael Rowland
Michael Rozyla
Piers Russell-Cobb
S.C. Rutherford
SC Rutherford
Ian Sandall
Mark Sanderson
Jerry Sargent
Ari Sarkar
Alex Sarll
Andrew Seaman
Rupert Sexton
Andrew Shearer
Ian Shipley
Paul Sills
Nathan Silver and Roxy
  Beaujolais
Ian Simmons
Iain Sinclair
Joe Skade
Paul Skinner
Gary Slater
Greg Sloman
Ross Smail
Gavin Smith
Ian Smith
Iain Smith

Nigel Smith
Paul C Smith
Simon Smith
Richard Smyth
Nikolaos Sotiriadis
Richard Soundy
Russell Southwood
Caroline Sproule
Julian F Squire
Owen Stagg
Neil Stanley
Christopher Stanwell
Ian Stewart
Philip Stout
Reuben Straker
William Streek
Roderick Stuart
Andrew Stubbs
Ben Sulaiman
David John Sutherst Bruce
James Suttie
Christopher Sykes
Carl Taylor
Colin Taylor
Frances Tew
Mike Thirlwell
John Thompson
Rupert Thomson
Sara Tilley
Joanna Tindall
Robert Tinker
James Tobin
Giles Todd
Rob Tolfts
John Tozer
Alex Twiggs
Ben Tye

Paul Tyrrell
Wilko Ufert
John Underkoffler
Andrei V.
Wouter Van Gysel
Mark Vent
Gary Vernon
Tom Viney
Ian Boyd Walker
Steve Walker
James Wallin
Jeremy Walsh
Martin Walsh
Digby Warde-Aldam
Andy Way
Edward JD Webb
John Welsh
Mark West
Peter Whiley
Donald Whitaker
Nicky Whitaker
Antony Whitehead
Tim Whitehouse
Ed Whitfield
Daniel Whitford
Michael Whitworth
Jennifer Wigzell
Patrick Wildgust
Will Wiles
Tom Wilkinson
Peter Willatts
Ian Willetts
Paul Willetts
Gary Williams
Dennis Williamson
David Willis
Clarke Wilson

Thom Winterburn
Stephen Wise
Jodi Red Wolf
Johanna Wolf
Andy Wood
Ruth E Wood
Tom Woodhead

Steve Woodward
Stuart Wright
Duncan Wu
David Yarrow
Jeff Young
Richard Young
Sam Young

A Note on the Author

Jonathan Meades is a writer, journalist, essayist and film-maker. His books include three works of fiction – *Filthy English, Pompey* and *The Fowler Family Business* – and several collections including *Museum Without Walls*, which received thirteen nominations as a book of the year in 2012. *An Encyclopaedia of Myself* was longlisted for the Samuel Johnson Prize in 2014 and shortlisted for the PEN Ackerley Prize in 2015. His first and only cookbook, *The Plagiarist in the Kitchen*, was published in 2017. *Pedro and Ricky Come Again* (2021) was the sequel to *Peter Knows What Dick Likes* (1989).

Meades has written and performed in more than sixty highly acclaimed television films on predominantly topographical subjects such as shacks, garden cities, post Vatican II churches, French nationalism, megastructures, herrings and schnapps, the Hebridean scrap cult, buildings associated with vertigo, beer, pigs, lower division Scottish football grounds and the architecture of Hitler, Stalin, Mussolini and Franco. Most are at Meadesshrine.blogspot

He also creates *artknacks* and *treyfs*. *Treyf* means impure, not kosher: it defines his approach to all writing, film and art.

A Note on the Type

The text of this book is set in Bembo. Created by Monotype in 1928–1929, Bembo is a member of the old style of serif fonts that date back to 1465. Its regular, roman style is based on a design cut around 1495 by Francesco Griffo for Venetian printer Aldus Manutius, sometimes generically called the "Aldine roman". Bembo is named for Manutius's first publication with it, a small 1496 book by the poet and cleric Pietro Bembo. The italic is based on work by Giovanni Antonio Tagliente, a calligrapher who worked as a printer in the 1520s, after the time of Manutius and Griffo.

Monotype created Bembo during a period of renewed interest in the printing of the Italian Renaissance. It continues to enjoy popularity as an attractive, legible book typeface.